Sticky Stick

MW00997527

90 Erotic Lesbian Stories from 20 Books (FF, FFF)

By Alana Meehan, Alannah Kieran, Emilia Russell, Jennifer G. Steen, L. J. Orellana, Sandra R. Galaz, Sarah Rodgers and Sophie Poulin

TABLE OF CONTENT

All Rights Reserved. No part of this publication may be reproduced in any form or by any means, including scanning, photocopying, or otherwise without prior written permission of the copyright holder. Copyright © 2023

This book is entirely a work of fiction. The names, characters and incidents portrayed in it are the work of the author's imagination. Any resemblance to actual persons, living or dead, events or localities is entirely coincidental.

Super Erotic Lesbian Encounters

12 Hot Short Sexy Stories for Women (FF, FFF)

Alana Meehan

All Rights Reserved. No part of this publication may be reproduced in any form or by any means, including scanning, photocopying, or otherwise without prior written permission of the copyright holder. Copyright © 2020

This book is entirely a work of fiction. The names, characters and incidents portrayed in it are the work of the author's imagination. Any resemblance to actual persons, living or dead, events or localities is entirely coincidental.

Story 01

Ok. It's ringing... once... twice... three times. Is she ever going to answer? Oh, wait, she's picking it up now. Why is my heart pounding like this? "Jenny? Hi love, it's me. Are you still coming over tonight? Good! I'll be here waiting for you. See you soon honey."

I can't believe it's really going to happen. Don't know if I'll be able to control myself. This young woman excites me so. Hope my need for her doesn't scare her off. Seems like it's taking forever for her to get here. But I have waited this long, guess I can wait a little longer. Is that her in the driveway now? Ooohhh, it is! Got to pull myself together, look like I'm cool. Wonder if she is half as nervous as I am? She's at the door, got to go open it. God, she's so pretty and young and she turns me on so much, be cool, be cool...

Good, she's smiling standing there in the doorway. Hope she doesn't notice how my hands are trembling as I unhook the screen. Should I hug her? Of course I should. What else is there to do? She feels so good in my arms, just like I knew she would. Look at those lips. Just got to get a little kiss. Just a little one, just a quick soft pressure on her lips. She must have been thinking the same thing, she's kissing me back. And neither one of us seems to be letting go. I can't help it, my mouth is opening and I am kissing her harder, pulling her closer. Her mouth is open too and my tongue is sliding slowly inside, running along the edges of her teeth and finally meeting her own soft tongue. If I don't break away now, we will be naked on the floor in minutes.

"Jenny, it is so good to see you, to finally have you here with me. Would you like something to drink? Some wine or some beer? Sit down, make yourself comfortable while I get it. We have so many things to talk about, but I need to relax a little first. Hope you don't mind."

I can't keep my eyes off this girl. Probably won't be able to keep my hands off of her much longer. I am already tingling just from the touch of her fingers when she took the glass from my hand. This conversation is killing me. I want to know all about her, everything there is. But it is all I can do to just sit here on the couch next to her. I am as close as I can be without looking like I am going to jump on her. She keeps leaning towards me, and I lean towards her. It seems that we are sitting much closer than we were just a few minutes ago. Maybe it is the wine that is making me feel so warm. She's looking a little flushed too. Did she notice the way my hand brushed her thigh? Maybe she thought it was an accident. Or maybe she knows...

This is making me crazy. I have to do something or I am going to be all over her. Turn on some music, maybe that will help. "Would you dance with me Jenny? I know it isn't like being out in a club, but then again, it could be nicer." Ummm... she seems to like this too. She moves so gracefully. Wonder if she will move as well when our naked bodies are melting together under my mirror? Uh oh, getting ahead of myself again. Here comes a slow record. Take her in your arms, easy now, easy, just dance with her. Just feel those flat nipples getting harder as they rub against yours. I think she likes it too. Let your hands slide down from her waist to gently cup her rounded behind. I think she likes it too. Her neck looks so soft and smooth. Feels good giving her neck little kisses, running the tip of my tongue all the way up to her ear lobe, all around the rim, licking the inside. Our bellies seem to fit naturally, shifting back and forth as we dance. She is getting me so hot, playing with my hair. Is she really pulling my face to her for another kiss? Her kiss is making me dizzy, her mouth so open and accepting. This kiss is getting hotter and hotter and I am getting wetter and wetter. Is she feeling the same? If I slide my hand between the thighs that are pressing mine, will it come away slippery? Will she let me?

She seems to be relaxing. And she hasn't complained yet. As a matter of fact, she is holding me pretty tight. Did I hear a soft moan when my hand slipped under the waistband of her skirt? Her skin is so soft. If I pull a little, it might just pop open... there it goes... is she glancing towards the bed?... is it time?

Well it didn't take us long to get naked. She was so sexy taking her clothes off. That skirt slid down her thighs real slow and easy. What a turn on watching her strip. Seems like it took forever for her panties to come off exposing that hairless mound. I bet I'll go crazy kissing it, going lower and lower, discovering her wet secrets. I didn't expect her boldness, reaching to remove my blouse and then my bra. Look at how big her eyes are! Guess she didn't think my tits would be so big. Ummm.. her hands and her mouth feel so good on them. Maybe later she will bite them. Or maybe she will let me rub them between her legs. It must feel different than the little nipples that have rubbed my clit in the past. Bet hers will feel just as nice. Can't believe how flat she is, but god, those nipples. Am I falling in love with this woman's body or what? Is that why I am so attracted to her? Because she reminds me of a girl with those flat nipples and all that skin where her pussy hair should be? I knew that I loved her before, but now I am totally lost. Am I going to be able to let her go? I already want to keep her around me as much as possible.

I thought it would be hard to get her in my bed, but it wasn't. It was almost too easy. But that first moment of full body contact! Nearly came right then. If just hugging and kissing her like this has me so excited, what will it be like later when our desire is satisfied? The bliss will be total. Have to get control of my hands. They are running wildly all over her body. We look so good together in the mirror above us. And her hands are making me wilder, rolling my nipples between her fingers, getting them harder than I have ever seen before. Let me run my finger gently up and down her slit. It is so wet my finger is sliding inside, stroking her clit. It won't be hard for her to find mine, it is sticking out already, like a little penis. She likes that, jumps a little every time I brush her clit. But she keeps moving back to my finger. Does she taste good? Yes!...going to lick all of her juice from my finger... no... wait... she wants one too. This is such a turn-on. One finger in my own mouth while she sucks the others. Wait till I get to suck on her, she will find out what it is like to be sucked and licked and nursed. I plan to make it better than she has ever known. I don't want this one to get away.

This is a good song on the radio, that guy that used to sing with Shalimar. It's good that he's making it on his own. Good lyrics...

What we share is very special...

It's mystical...

Your love to me is very serious...

I won't play games with your tender heart...

And when I look into your eyes and say I love you girl...

That's what I feel. I'm for real. And I am for real with this sweet woman. I didn't think it would be *this good. Her nipples seem to keep getting bigger and bigger in my mouth. Love the way she pushes them up to me. There is already a wet spot underneath her. The way she is wriggling and squirming thrills me. She'll be screaming by the time my mouth gets down there where my fingers are now. Ummmm...got to hurry up and get there... but not too soon. I want this to be good for her. Just going to take my time, lick her all the way down, trace a wet trail from the bottom of her breasts to her navel. Liked that soft giggle when my tongue tickled her navel for a second. Kiss her stomach, give her more of the butterflies she says are there. This is so good. And her pussy is so smooth. I could lick and kiss it all night. But I know better things are waiting. And her hands are pushing my head lower and lower. Guess that means she likes it and wants more. I'll give it to her... in just a few seconds. But first... let me kiss her squarely on her swollen lips, suck one of them between my lips. Oooooooo... she's so wet, so sweet. And she is making me so hot. Open the lips a little, look for that hot button. There it is. Just going to blow on it for a second... yes... she likes that. But she is moving her hips to get closer to my mouth. Should I take her now? I know she wants it as much as I want her. I'll stick my tongue out now, tease her a little bit. The smell of her is in my nose, better than any perfume. Can't wait anymore. Got to take her clit in my mouth, suck on it like a little piece of candy. Move back to lick it from the base to the tip. Oh yes, she wants it. Her legs are on my shoulders now. The come is leaking out of her. Maybe I can stop the flow with my tongue. Slide it deep in her, yes...just like that. She is so open, grinding her cunt in my face. Licking and sucking on her clit as hard as I can, probing her open pussy with 2 fingers, sliding them in and out of her. Is she loving this as much as me? Her moans are getting louder, the movements of her hips getting faster and wilder. Her head is thrashing back and forth on the pillow, her eyes squeezed closed, not even looking in the mirror anymore. What is she saying? Don't stop, don't stop... was that it? No way am I going to stop now. The come is running out of her so fast she must be almost ready. I'm ready, mouth open at the fountain of her love while my fingers vibrate on her clit. Oh yes, oh yes, here she comes, flooding my mouth with her come. I knew she would scream, I knew it. Her thighs locked around my neck, clit throbbing under my fingers. Just gonna close her lips over her clit and press it until she stops coming, until she relaxes her grip on me. And then I'll lay next to her, take her in my arms and hug her and squeeze her and tell her how much I love her and how good she was. And then....

Story 02

While I was putting the final touches on my packing for the dream vacation of a lifetime, the telephone shrilled. My fiance, who was to accompany me, called to say he had a business emergency and would have to fly to New York tonight. He urged me to begin the trip alone saying that he would join me in four days. I didn't particularly care to travel solo, but we had been planning for six months. The travel agency had our semi-luxury accomodations booked for two glorious weeks.

The plane landed on time and I was whisked off in a hotel limousine. After generously tipping the bell boy, I gently closed the door, dying for a shower. Showers in paradise are just as good as those at home, but with an added element. There were all kinds of exotic oils and soaps in the shower of which I made full use.

Smelling like flowers and wrapped in the soft terry cloth robe provided by the hotel, I stepped out onto the terrace. The beach and ocean nearly hypnotized me with their simple beauty. Looking at the terrace next to me, I saw a lovely, full head of silver hair being brushed by a young, blonde woman. They must have felt me staring as they both turned to look at me.

"Hello, ladies," I called, caught. "Beautiful day isn't it?"

"Hello," they responded in unison. "Quite," said the older.

The face that went with the silver hair was lovely and unlined. The body was slim and shapely in a two piece bathing suit. The lady was probably only twice as old as my own 22 years.

"How long is your vacation,' I asked, prolonging the scene.

"Helga and I--Helga is my social secretary/companion--are here for two weeks," she answered with a smile. "I'm Jessica."

"I'm Anabel. And so am I. My fiance is joining me in four days," I

volunteered. "Well, I'll let you get back to what you were doing. Nice meeting you. I'm sure we'll see each other around."

I saw them that night in the hotel's casino. Holding a drink, I wandered around the huge room taking in all the sights, including them. Jessica was seated at a dollar slot machine with Helga standing behind her, hands on her shoulders. Over and over Jessica inserted coins and pulled the handle. When the machine finally paid off, they were ecstatic as they hugged. Helga kissed her full on the lips as she caressed her back. Were these two lovers I wondered. Just the thought that they could be making love to each other right next door to me excited me. They are both very beautiful women and I could easily see why each would want the other.

I lay in bed that night thinking about them. Were they doing it now? Was one of them sucking the other's pussy? Were they doing it at the same time? Were breasts being sucked or pussies melded together straining toward orgasm? I fingered myself to orgasm imagining myself holding a silver head between my thighs and having a tall blonde sucking at my breasts.

At breakfast, I saw Helga at a table alone and decided to approach her. "Hi, Helga. May I join you?" I asked.

"Of course, Anabel," she said smiling up at me. "Say, one of the maids told me about a real nude beach on another island. Would you like to go with me?"

"Sure,"I said perking up. "I'd love to have an even tan for my fiance. Is Jessica joining us?"

"No. She's conducting business by telephone this morning."

On the ferry ride over, Helga told me more about herself and her relationship with Jessica. "She and her husband vacationed in Sweden several years ago," Helga began. "I had a summer job as a chambermaid. Jessica and her husband, Harlan, took a special interest in me. They told me all about America and made sure that I didn't have to work too hard for them. At the end of three weeks, they asked if I would like to go back to America with them as a member of their staff. Well, I was 18 already and jumped on the idea. In gratitude, I let Harlan and Jessica touch me a bit more than they had before. Separately, of course. By the time we flew to the United States, I had fully fucked both of them several times. My position was to be a social secretary/personal companion. Harlan and Jessica discovered the truth about each other where I was concerned. Being their social secretary, I simply set up a schedule for when each one could fuck me."

"Wow, Helga. Did you enjoy them or merely endure them because they helped you?"

"Anabel, I truly loved it. We were devastated when Harlan died in an airplane crash two years ago. Jessica and I got even closer. Actually, we love each other."

We arrived at the beach. There was nudity everywhere. Helga and I shucked our clothes and spread out on beach towels. I couldn't help but admire Helga's lush body. She is about 5'11" and stacked-- long, shapely legs, full high breasts, big blue eyes and long, blond straight hair. I'm not quite as tall as her, but my breasts are as big. My black hair is a thick shoulder length and lightly curly. I have been told that my violet eyes resemble Elizabeth Taylor's. I suppose Helga and I made striking opposites by the way people were watching us.

We continued our conversation as we sunned. "Helga," I inquired, "do you think Jessica would object to us being like this?"

"I love her dearly, Anabel, but I don't tell her everything. For example, I didn't tell her about the cute little teenage redhead and her boyfriend that I picked up in the movies three days ago. I sat between them and let them feel me up. Their hands were practically fighting for my pussy. We went back to her parent's apartment and fucked our brains out. The guy was much shorter than me, but made up for the lack with one of the biggest dicks I've even seen on a boy. He really knew what to do with it. Besides, I suspect Jessica is fucking her accountant on the side. No harm done."

The couple next to us began to get quite amorous. Before long he was stoking his dick deep into her pussy. The were oblivious to us and everyone else as they fucked loudly. "This is making me really hot," Helga said squirming. "Anabel, may I touch you. I've wanted to since I first met you."

"Ok, Helga, but I've never done anything with a woman before--I've only imagined."

"Let me show you," she said before she took one of my breasts in her mouth. "It is so, so good with a woman," she mumbled as she stroked my slit. "It is wonderful, isn't it? I can make you come so easily," she crooned as she finger fucked me to orgasm. "Feel this, Anabel," she almost shouted as she climbed on me, melded her large pussy to mine and rode me hard. We came together at the same time as the couple beside us, then ran to the ocean to cool off.

Waves crashed around us at the water's edge as, entwined, we kissed and screwed hungrily. When Helga kept telling me how beautiful I was, I moved up on the sand and let her eat my pussy. She said she would just perish if she couldn't put her tongue inside my dark pussy. She brought me over the edge again and again. The ferry took us, exhausted and fucked-up to the eyeballs, back to the other island in the afternoon.

We said goodbye at my door. I watched Helga as she went in to her lover. She said that she and Jessica had not made love this morning. "Jessica will be very horny," she said smiling at me.

Again I imagined them fucking. I could see in my mind Helga screwing Jessica's pussy like she did mine on the beach. I showered and lay down to take a nap. I awoke at 5pm to a ringing telephone. It was Jessica inviting me to dine with them at 8.

We had a six course dinner at an elegant restaurant in the city. Wine and conversation flowed. Facts about my life spilled forth as I played footsie with Helga under the table. Jessica seemed fascinated with me. We arrived back at our hotel a little giddy from the wines. When I could't find my key card easily, Jessica took my arm. "Come, darling. You can sleep with us tonight."

In their bedroom, we undressed to our birthday suits and fell into bed still giggling. Jessica said goodnight and kissed me deeply. The kiss traveled south to my pussy as I moaned in her mouth.

"My turn," said Helga, who followed suit, but covered my pussy with her hand. Then the two of them reached over me and kissed each other. We all fell asleep.

Some time later, I felt a warm tongue licking my pussy. I opened my eyes to see Jessica's silver hair between my legs. She tongue-fucked me hard to a shattering orgasm. I rewarded her with a mouthful of my nectar. Jeff was not even in the same league as these women in pussy-eating skills. "I knew you would taste wonderful, darling," she said as she licked away the remaining juice. Helga was watching us from across the room. Her hair was in wild disarray, her eyes shining and she beautiful as she approached us. A seven inch dick protruded from her pelvis.

"Come, Jessica, darling" she said, spreading her legs. "I need you now."

I settled back to watch as Helga dipped the dick into Jessica's dripping pussy. Jessica moaned deeply as Helga took her powerfully. Helga then pulled her wet dick out and aimed it at her lover's asshole.

"Please, Helga. Please, do it hard, just like I love it," Jessica begged. She was turned on to the hilt.

Helga slid the dick into Jessica's asshole in one fell swoop. Jessica bucked as Helga fucked her asshole hard and furious, pulling out and ramming in repeatedly. I could hear flesh on flesh as as their wet skin slapped together.

Helga was in seventh heaven as she fucked. Her lithe body gyrated as she thrust in and out. A myriad of emotions crossed her beautiful, flushed face as she came in Jessica's ass, screaming in lust. I kissed them both lightly and dressed to leave them alone. The night of love was surely not over for them. Helga was still in Jessica, kissing her and screwing lightly. I left quietly.

My fiance arrived two days earlier than expected and was in our room when I walked next door. With a wet, open pussy, sensitive breasts, swollen lips and in a turned-on state of mind, I fucked him better than I had done in the whole of our relationship. The fucking that I knew was happening next door was still high in my mind.

Jeff was still dead to the world when I slipped out of the room the next morning. I left a note explaining that I had gone jogging. Instead I knocked at Jessica's. I wanted to thank them for last night. Jessica answered, pulling me in. "Helga's swimming at the beach. Let's go on the terrace."

"Thanks for last night," I said. "It is fortunate I went to my room. My fiance, Jeff, had arrived."

"I'm glad for you, darling. Now take off those clothes and let me fuck you outside."

I was nervous, even a little frightened. Jeff could walk out and see us. The fear of discovery also turned me on. Jessica expertly ate my pussy at a very leisurely pace. Threading my fingers through her silver hair, I pushed my pussy up allowing her full access to it. Jessica let me cum twice before she laid down on the other chaise. She asked me to lay on her, pussy to pussy. The position that I was in allowed me to screw her and watch my terrace. Fucking the silver-haired Jessica was what I needed to do from the first time I laid eyes on her. I was so caught up in the lustful act, I would not have stopped even if Jeff appeared. I would not stop moving on this exquisite pussy with the short silver hairs that tickled me slightly as I screwed--not until I had my fill. When Jessica rubbed a wet finger over my asshole, I sawed our mingled pussies to another sweet orgasm.

Sliding from Jessica to the floor, still high from our loving, I kneeled between her legs. Jessica was wet and open from her last cum. I rubbed my entire face--cheeks, nose, forehead in the sweet warmth of her. Her smell intoxicated me. And then, at long last, I tasted the first pussy of my life. I proceeded to do to her what she and Helga had done to me. I feasted. I touched. I sucked. I licked. I tasted. I plunged. She came. She came. I came. I gloried in the flesh of this woman.

With one and a half weeks left on our vacations, I saw the women as often as I could when Jeff was not around. Helga and I slipped back to the nude beach for a leisurely fucking and put on quite a show in front of the other bathers. Jessica and I fucked when Jeff swam or slept. We became intense quickie experts, but the cumming was just as sweet.

Never again will I look at two beautiful women together and not wonder if they have tasted each other.

Story 03

Right after my honeymoon, I left Frank to visit with my family who had missed our impulsive Las Vegas wedding. I boarded a plane in Denver to fly to Dallas where they'd meet me. I expected everyone to be at the airport, their usual habit. Mom, Dad, Grandma, Grandpa, Uncle Charles, two brothers and two sisters. I hadn't seen them in over a year since going off to college.

The flight was uneventful except for a brat, two rows ahead and across on the left of the aisle, that kept trying to look up my short dress. My dress was super shear and light, but I had a slip, panties, and bra on, so there wasn't much to see. Finally, in frustration, I lifted the hem of my dress and said, "There, are you satisfied, now?"

The woman sitting beside me said, "I've always wanted to do that."

"Do you want to change seats? He's still looking."

"I don't mean I want to; I mean I wish I had the courage."

"I wish I had the courage to go in the rest room and take these panties off. I'd fog his glasses for him."

"I dare you."

"You dare me?"

"I double dare you."

"Nobody double dares Lucy Stevens, I mean Evers. I just got married. I should try to keep my panties on now that I'm a wife; besides, my husband shaved me on our honeymoon. I shaved it again right before we left for the airport. If I shot a beaver now, I might do the kid brain damage."

"You've been double dared."

"Are you serious?"

"Marge Weaver never double dares unless she is dead serious."

"Save my seat."

The woman who double dared me had plopped down beside me shortly after take off. She was traveling alone and wanted company. I was a bit miffed by her intrusion, because I had a whole row of seats to myself on the near empty plane. I like the window seat and only moved to the aisle to make the job of feeding us our in- flight snack easier on the flight attendants. I intended to scoot back. I didn't want to seem like a dumb country girl, all excited by a plane ride, so I stayed put on the aisle. Marge seemed so worldly and mature, though she wasn't much older than my nineteen years. She may have been twenty-two or three.

I flashed the boy to impress her with my boldness. Actually, the boldest thing I ever did was to shave my pussy at my husband's request. I was a virgin on my wedding night, three weeks prior. Just admitting to Marge that I was shaved was a huge step for me.

When I stripped off my panties in the bathroom, I got a terrific rush from my daring act. Marge's obvious surprise and approval upon hearing my secret news had my heart fluttering. I assumed she'd never heard of such an outrageous act. Flashing my shaved and naked vagina took all the courage I could muster, but I was determined to shock and impress Marge further.

I returned two minutes later and plopped down. The kid immediately turned to gawk. Marge sat forward and stared expectantly to my lap. I gave her a curious look, then said, "I'm supposed to flash him, not you."

"I'm the one that double dared you. How will I know you took your panties off or have a shaved beaver if I don't look?"

"Good point." I started to lift, but her hand blocked me. I said, "What?"

"Before you do this, we need to go over the terms of the dare."

"There's rules to this?"

"It's my double dare."

"All right. What are the rules?"

"First, slump down in your seat. More. A little more. Put your butt on the edge."

I felt ridiculous, slumped so low that the seat back bent my head forward. The boy was all eyes, expecting another flash of panties. I said, "You've more than piqued his interest already."

"Now, when you lift your skirt, lift it past your hip bones, past here." Marge placed both hands firmly on my hip bones, then drew a line across my belly with her right hand. I eyed her suspiciously when she touched me that way, then more so when she didn't let go. When the hand that drew the line rested flat on my pubic mound, I knew I had a lesbian in the seat beside me. Having never met a real lesbian, I was stunned to find my first one looking so normal, so feminine.

The woman said, "Now, there's a time condition. You must maintain your pose until someone comes along. Since the plane is almost empty, and they already served us, that might be a while. You might ride like this all the way to Dallas."

I felt the pressure increase over my mound and said, "Or until Junior says, 'Mommy, Mommy, look what that lady's doing.'"

"He won't say anything. He wants a show; besides, I can see her from here. She's asleep."

She was right; Junior wanted to see my pussy. The thought of actually riding two more hours with my naked vagina between a horny kid and a lesbian was simply too exciting to pass up, though I figured we may get five minutes at most. Flight attendants don't stay put, even in near-empty planes. I said, "All right. Is there anything else?"

"Yes, you must spread your legs as wide as possible, and you can't touch your skirt or close your legs even one inch until the pose is legally broken, no matter what."

That crafty lezzie knew exactly what to say. "No matter what," I may be a country hick, but I knew what that meant. I said with a smile, "If you're going to pull out a contract, I'd like to run it by my lawyer."

"I'm queen of the double dares, what can I say? Are you chicken?"

"No, I'm not chicken."

"All right, then do it."

I took a gander up and down the aisle, looked to the boy, then pulled my skirt up past the line by two inches. I fanned my legs out to their maximum, which placed my knees three feet apart. The boy's mouth dropped. So did the lesbian's. I watched her hand travel up my right inner thigh to close on my pussy. I said, as fingers slid into my wet slit, "I thought the idea was to show him my vagina. All he can see is the back of your hand."

"He's going to see your pussy. I'll see to that, but he'll see it wet and juicy as a pussy should be."

The lesbian's two middle fingers on her right hand entered my hole and massaged me internally by rubbing against the underside of my pubic bone, massaging my 'G' spot, I suppose. The first two fingers of her left hand rubbed rapidly in short flurries on my clit, just the way I like it. I said, "I thought my pussy was wet and juicy in the rest room."

"Bone dry. You ain't seen wet and juicy yet."

"I take it you've done this before, getting a pussy wet and juicy, I mean."

"A few times. Oh, yeah, baby, you're flowing now. You are one hot little bitch, aren't you?"

"Yes, and if you keep that up, I'm going to be a hot little pissing bitch. Oh, god damn! Oh, you fucking dyke."

I couldn't believe I said that; but then, she called me a bitch first. She went on, "Come on, Juicy Lucy. Let go. Cum for me, sugar. Yeah, baby. Come on. Give it up, you juicy little whore."

"Ugggh! Ohhhhh! Oh Fuck! Oh lord. Oh Jesus. Mother fucker. Damn! Damn! Damn! Damn! Damn! God Damnnnnnnnnnnnnnnn!"

I never came so hard, or yelled so loudly in whispers. I slumped lower in my seat, trying to catch my breath. Marge said, "Now let's show the boy some juicy pussy." She pulled my cunt lips wide for the boy while blowing cool air across the wet membranes of my pussy innards. We were startled by a stewardess kneeling by my aisle seat.

The stewardess softly said, "Hey, look, I'm one of the sisterhood, but you guys need to get a room."

Marge did not pause in her activities, and I made no attempt to cover myself. The stewardess stared longingly at my open spread as Marge said, "This chick is straight. I put in some hard work getting her like this. This is the room."

"You have an audience, you know."

"I know. He's been watching from the start. He won't tell. It was his staring up her dress that got her all hot and bothered. We're a team."

"Well, I guess you're pretty safe, come to think of it. Most everyone's asleep, and the crew is cool."

"Great."

I was stunned when the stewardess said, "You know, he'd probably like to see her tits. Let's take the dress off."

"I like your style. I'm Marge; I can see you're Pam." Marge offered Pam her sopping wet right hand, and the two lesbians shook hands over my face. After the hand shake, both licked their hands. I couldn't help but wonder if I had witnessed the secret handshake of the Sisterhood of Muff. Marge said, "Lift up, sugar puss."

I lifted my ass to allow Marge to push my dress and slip to my middle. When I sat, Marge pulled me forward and Pam unzipped the dress. Together, they removed the dress and slip. Pam removed my bra. Except for my shoes, I was naked on an airplane.

The stewardess laid all my clothing on the empty seat by the window, then pulled a blanket from the overhead compartment. She laid the blanket over the clothes and said, "If anyone does come, you can cover her with this. I'll stay here and serve as a lookout; if that's all right with you?"

Marge said, "Join in; the more the merrier."

"Thanks, I was hoping you'd share her. I go positively ga ga over straight chicks, and this one is gorgeous." Pam picked up my left hand, saying, "And she's married, too. That's even better."

I loved the way they talked around me and not to me as though I were in the grips of some lesbian trance. With all pretense of the game disposed, Marge got down on the floor and placed my legs over the arm rests, as Pam laid my seat back and knelt by my tits. As Marge went down on my pussy, Pam took my left tit and offered the squeezed mound to the boy's hungry eyes, saying, "He likes these titties. You like these don't you, kid?"

The grinning boy nodded hard. Pam pinched the nipple to distention and flicked the tip with her tongue. "I'll bet you'd like to do this to them...[flick, flick]...and this...[flutter, flutter, flick, flick, nibble]."

She sucked most of my tit in her mouth and sucked hard while softly chewing. Marge's talented mouth quickly had me grinding my loins, and Pam's efforts had me arching my back. They quickly brought me to a state of delirium, then Pam stood and pulled her skirt up from the center of the hem, exposing her bare pussy through pantyhose that had no crotch panel.

I stared at the pussy framed by nylon. She had a soft, pretty pussy free of all hair, and a gold ring in her clit. She thrust her mound forward toward my face in blatant offering, saying, "Eat me, bitch!"

In my lesbian-induced trance, I dove at the pussy with a flailing tongue and incurred more slanderous invectives, such as: "Suck my cunt, you little whore!" and "Lick my pussy, slut!"

I screamed out a muff-muffled climax, then sucked a climax out of Pam. I remained glued to the cunt to slurp the product of that climax, as Pam held her cunt lips open and instructed me to clean her pussy good. I pulled my face in tightly by gripping Pam's firm ass. As the job neared completion, Pam said, "I've got to bring Sherry in on this. She'd kill me if I had a straight chick and didn't bring her in on it. Do you mind?"

Marge lifted up with a totally wet face and said, "Like I said, the more the merrier."

Pam adjusted her skirt and headed up the aisle, pausing to ruffle the boy's hair in passing. He watched her ass shimmy down the aisle in her tight-assed skirt. She returned minutes later with a short smiling blond wearing a pixie hair cut. Both rubbed the boy's head. When the blond stood over me and gazed on my body, she said, "Oh, god, she's a doll."

Her slender fingers went into my crotch as Marge made room. Her free hand massaged my tit flesh. Sherry brought pussy-wet fingers to her lips and sucked, making a face like a kid sucking chocolate. She cleaned her fingers then raised her skirt as Pam had, showing another shaved, ringed pussy framed by nylon. Hers also had a rose tattoo on the left cunt lip with the stem disappearing in her pussy. I licked the rose, then licked the pot. I came while licking the pot. Ten minutes later, the pot came, and I came again under Pam's talented tongue.

For two hundred and eighty miles, the three lesbians took turns trading places. Had it not been for the mother waking up and dragging the boy away, we might have gone three-twenty. As it was, I had just enough time to get back in my clothes and freshen-up, but Marge would not give me anything but the dress. Lesbians turn into bitches if you refuse to go home with them to join the Sister's of Muff and learn the secret handshake. When I persisted, she ripped up my bra, panties, and my slip. I had no carry-on luggage. The dress was all I had; everything else was in the baggage compartment.

I stood before the mirror of that bathroom and stared at the sight my family would see. Though the dress had a flowery print, everything showed through; my tits, my nipples, my denuded pussy crack, even my ass crack showed. I was as good as naked in pumps, and I saw no alternative but to exit the plane that way. I scrubbed my face and gargled with hand soap. My family is big on hugs and kisses.

I stayed in the bathroom until Pam called everyone to return to their seats. Marge was gone when I got there, but the boy and his mother weren't. He looked for more beaver as she fought to wrest him into his seat facing forward, looking back occasionally to me and firing me a look that said, "You are the most disgusting person I've ever seen."

I was the last person to exit the plane and had to pass Pam and Sherry on the way out. Pam said, "Hope you had a nice flight." Sherry said, "Come again." As I passed by, two pairs of slimy wet hands covered my face, mouth, and neck. Those bitches slimed me. I struggled free of those laughing bitches, reeking of the Sisterhood's revenge.

I walked off that plane on shaky legs, smelling like low tide, terrified of meeting my family. I paused in the rampway to decide how to act. I could think of no story that would explain my loss of under clothes that wasn't worse than letting them think I dress this way. I had told them that I'd undergone many changes. With no other choice, I squared my shoulders and entered the boarding area. Nine jaws dropped in unison. Mom said, "Lucy."

The name fell from her lips like a wet turd. I moved bravely forward and said, "Hi everybody. I'm home." You should have seen their faces after hugs and kisses. After wiping her lips on the back of her hand, Mom said, "Lucy, you've got some splainin' to do."

Like I said, other than that, the flight was uneventful.

Story 04

It happened 2 years ago, I never planned it, it just happened. I'm a woman 40yrs old now and married since I've been 18. I've never had an extra marital affair, not that I didn't think about it, I just never strayed. I consider myself a great wife, mother and an excellent consultant. Sometimes on my job I travel and my travels some times take me to remote areas of the country. This was such a trip, it was in Hurricane Mills Tn. Not much there except for a motel, a gas station and resturant/truck stop and a few odd factories. It was 7 oclock in the evening after a long day of travel and meeting with my client when I finally checked into the motel and I thought I'd take advantage of my free drink cupon at the small bar they had. Needless to say the bar was empty except for myself, another woman who was a guest and the bartender. After a few minutes at the bar, the other woman struck up a conversation and we exchanged small talk. She was in the area on business as well and she travel extensivley on her job. Her name was Julie and she was a very pleasant and well spoken woman. She was 42 yrs old and she kept herself very well. We chated til around 9 or so and we said our good nights and I retired to my room.

It was the next evening that changed my life. Again I arrived back at the motel around 7pm and thought I'd stop by the bar and have a drink before going for diner. Julie was there when I arrived and of course I sat at her table, we ordered wine and began to chat. We decided to have diner together since she had not gone yet herself. It was nice, not to have diner alone for a change. We ordered wine with our diner and we got along great, we chatted about our husbands, kids, work ect. it was incredible just how well we got along. It was like we had been friends for years. I'm somewhat outgoing but Julie had a way of making you feel comfortable. We just seemed to click. After diner we walked back to the motel and discovered that the bar was closed, thinking it odd since it was only 10pm. She suggested that we go to her room and finish the 2 bottles of wine that she had from the airlines flight. Since it was only 10pm, I thought it was a good idea for half an hour or so. We joked about how some guys can be such pigs and we giggled and chatted all the way to her room. Once in her room, I sat on the chair beside a small work desk and she busied herself opening the wine. Julie poured the wine brought mine to me and we took a sip, I kicked my heels off, "they were killing me" I said as I kicked them off and she said "if you don't mind, I'm going to get out of these things I've been bound up in these clothes since 7am. I didn't give it a second thought since I myself was in the same situation not having the chance to change. Julie was wearing a dark blue skirt and jacket suit with a plain white blouse. She wore her skirt above the knees more on the short side, almost tight but not quite, it looked great on her. As she was changing, we were discussing diets and our weights and I noticed that after she removed her jacket, skirt and blouse that Julie was quite shaply for her age. Little if any sags. I said to her that she looked great for her age and that I wish I could look half as good. She turned to me from the other side of the room as she put on her bathrobe and commented that she thought I looked pretty for having 3 kids as well and that she thought I was very pretty. Maybe it was the wine that we were plowing back during diner but with that comment, I felt myself go blush...we were friends i guess but I still thought it rather odd that she would just go ahead and change like that I don't know if she noticed or not but up untill then, I had never given a second thought about perhaps a woman comming on to me. Oh sure I've fantized on many occasions that I was being eaten out by a woman while making love to my husband, no one in particular just a female. She said "that you look good in your clothes and most woman would envy me". I felt a little strange, almost flirty if I could describe it. My mind began to wonder what it might be like to carress another woman, What it might be like to kiss Julie. Crazy thoughts I was having and I attributed them to the wine.

Julie walked over to me and sat at the edge of the bed starring at me. I smiled nervously at her and said "what?" she commented on how nice my perfume was..."was it Claibourne?" she asked I said "yes do you like it?" she leaned over closer to get a better smell and I noticed her bare breasts exposed within her bath robe. She must have slipped her bra off after putting on her bathrobe. I was flushed and she explained that she had enjoyed our diner and that she never felt so comfortable with another person after such a short period of time and I told her I felt the same way. She leaned over again and gave me a hug, my heart was throbing and I felt flushed. A sisterly type hug I summmized but then her lips touched my neck as she commented on my perfume again. Still with her arms around my shoulders Julie faced me and asked me if she could kiss me. By now I had been wondering about my feelings towards her and although I tried to say yes, I don't think any words actually came out. She gently kissed me full on the lips and I was in a daze. I stood up and embraced her as if in a trance and we kissed and held each other tightly for a few moments.

By now I was beside myself. Reluctant at first but I was enjoying this forbidden encounter. Julie broke the kiss off and said "I've wanted to find a woman that I could feel comfortable with so that I could fulfill my curiousity." She had never done this before" she explained "and if I've offended you please forgive me". I said "no not at all and that I feel flattered" Julie placed her hand on my breast and we kissed, a deep pasionate kiss as I moved my arms her waist. Our kiss lingered and then she began to undress me, slowly at first then I helped her. She removed her robe and we lay on the bed totally naked side by side trying to make contact with every part of our bodies. Julie was a gentle aggressor as she moved her hand down to my now soaking wet vagina and began rubbing my clit with her fingers. She said that "I was really wet down there" and I took that as an invitation for me to feel hers. I glided my fingers to her cunt as we lay side by side facing each other smiling and we began to mutually masterbate each other. I came first and I never come that fast in my life! I was surprised at the intensity of my orgasim. I rarely have them! Julie came right after me and as she came, I sucked on her breasts feeling rather smug with myself.

We carressed and held each other for what seemed to be an eternity and she asked me if my husband ever goes down on me I replied "yes but not as often as I'd like him to" with that Julie began to kiss my breasts and stomach and lick my navel. She placed her mouth on my vagina and began to lick me there. It was nothing like how my husband ever did it! It felt like I was being eaten for the first time! my mind was reeling the pictures in my mind of my years of fantasy and now it was really happening. I came again and again with such intensity that I felt almost faint. It was amazing. I eventually ate her but at first she said that I didn't have to do it if I didn't want to, "I wanted to" I said. We spent that night eating, holding, kissing and carressing each other till early dawn. Fortunatly the next day was a travel day for both of us and I slept on the plane. We have phoned each other several times since then but we have never gotten together. I haven't persued other woman, I'm afraid of the rejection I guess but it has spruced up my sex life with my husband. Of course he doesn't know about this. I was curious if there are any other woman who have had a bi experience that they would like to share.

Story 05

Metropolitan Museum of Art on Fifth Avenue, when something happened that has changed my life.

There was a woman sitting a few steps up from me...about 15 feet away She was so pretty, in fact, beautiful. I couldn't take my eyes from her. I leaned back against the wall and sat sideways while I ate my lunch of a sandwich and soft drink and kept glancing at her. I'm youngish...23, and pretty, but this woman was like a model of perfection...long legs in nylons, a very expensive taupe colored tropical wool skirt, and a white rayon blouse. She had on only a little gold jewelry, but need nothing to accent her looks. She was very special. Her hair fell in pale thick waves of light gold, almost to her waist.

After a moment she pivoted her bottom on the steps so that she was facing more directly toward me. She had a magazine on the step next to her, and seemed to be reading it. It was later in the day than the normal lunch hour and although there were more than 50 people on the massive expanse of steps, it was as though no one else was there, certainly no one that could see her from my vantage point.

Then she dropped the bomb. She kept reading, and dropped one leg down straight along the steps, opening herself up to me. I could see everything under her skirt clearly, vividly. She had no panties on at all, and wore only garters, and nylons. With her long legs apart like that I could see the pale insides of her thighs, as white as fresh cream, and her cunt. She was shaved almost totally bare...there was only a little triangle of blonde hair above the open lips of her slit. I was completely mesmerized. I didn't think she knew I was watching, so I just stared. I looked aroud once or twice, but the world was oblivious to us.

At one point she lifted her leg again into the normal position, and putting her knees together spread her high heeled feet about twelve inches apart so that I was still afforded that view. Then she rested her hands under her skirt... her palms on her thighs just above her ass cheeks, and softly rubbed them up and down on her naked skin. My cunt was dripping like a faucet. My panties were soaked.

She then placed her hands so close to her cunt that her fingernails, beautifully manicured, were almost meeting at the "vee" of her lips. Pulling her thighs gently open, using her finger tips, she spread her cunt lips apart and started rubbing the tip of one finger across her lips, and almost imperceptibly began flicking the little pink head of her clitoris. Oh god....I was almost going out of my mind. I've never seen another woman do that....and such a beautiful one...wow!

She startled me by looking down towards me and smiling. She had a beautiful smile. God she was flawless, but she continued to touch herself while looking at me. I wanted to faint.

Well... to get to the point she approached me, took my hand, (surprised the hell out of me) and said "c'mon... come walk with me...I want to show you something nice." I didn't hesitate to follow. I'm twenty three...and here I was being held by the hand...and led along like a school girl.

We didn't talk...not a word. She led me only a little over a city block, to the entrance of a Fifth Avenue apartment building. Two doormen. Tres chic. She led me in, the doormen just nodding to her as we passed, holding the doors open, and we went into the elevator. Still not one word more from her. I just stared at her as we went up nine floors. She turned once and smiled. She also leaned over and kissed me once...softly...on my mouth...Oh god. It was as though I was in a movie...or a dream.

Her apartment was like something from an interior design magazine. Unbelievable. Windows overlooking the park and museum. It must have cost millons. She wasted no time. Not one second. She led me over to the window...to a black leather couch knd of thing...but with no back..a kind of single bed sized seat. The floors were black and white marble squares. She sat me down and told me to stay there...and left the room.

In a moment she returned...with a bottle of Louis Roederer "Cristal" Champagne, and two glasses. Still no words other than little short statements. Little nothings. She poured two glasses of the champagne and set the bottle on the marble floor.

Then she said something I thought very odd. She said "Don't spill one drop..not one drop...ok?... You'll drink it all won't you?... Promise me!"

I said "Yes..." thinking she meant the champagne, and took a sip. It was so good.

Then she lifted her skirt up..to her waist, and coming right up to me as I sat there, shaking a bit, put one heeled foot on the leather of the day couch, at my side, and spread open just in front of my face. I was flabbergasted, and excited. I could smell her perfume...and the fragrance of her cunt. I began to quiver all over.

She then said, "Now you can touch what you've been looking at for the past twenty minutes." She just stood there, naked to me, and sipped her champagne. I leaned forward to touch her. As soon as my hand slipped under her, to cup her cunt and fondle it, she put her hands on the back of my head and pulled it into her thighs. I resisted...just a little... and she gently pulled my face so that the lips of my mouth met the lips of her cunt. She was warm, smooth as a baby, and slippery wet in between her lips. I kissed her there. She smelled like expensive french perfume...she tasted like honey and baby powder. I put my tongue out, in between her lips, and sucked the inner ones into my mouth. She was a goddess, and I'd never been with a woman.

She began unbuttoning her blouse, unwrapped her skirt and tossed it aside, and began to pull my clothes off. First my top...over my head...then my bra... Then she lifted me by the hand.

Kneeling at "MY" feet, she removed my skirt and panties. She looked up at me and sucked the wet crotch of my nylon panties into her mouth...she sucked all of the wetness from the crotch, looking up at my eyes and fingering her cunt.

She lay me down on the cool black leather and pushed my legs wide open...I'm blond too, and have my pussy trimmed for my personal feeling of sexiness. But I look about seventeen, and have little fur there. My cunt was drenched.

She pulled me halfway off the end of the low leather seat, so my head and shoulders were on the marble. Then she straddled my face and wasted no time in burying her mouth down between my legs. Her mouth on my wetness was unbelievable. She did things with her lips and tongue that I could never imagine. I tried to do the same kind of things to her. If you have never sucked on a woman's cunt when she was wet...you have no idea how erotic it is...how soft..the lips...the inside, when you push your tongue in. I had never done it before but I felt like a baby drinking mothers milk...moaning and sucking. Licking her insides and sucking on her little pink hard clit.

The she held my face between her thighs as she closed them on me....and... she began to pee. At first I just thought she was gettting wetter. It just was a little. Then it spurted out into my mouth and caught me by surprise. I didn't know what to do. I tried to struggle free but she held my head in between the soft skin above her nylons.

She then said...kind of sternly..."You promised not to waste a drop,"..."If you do I make you lick it up!" I was afraid, but very excited...I closed my mouth over her cunt hole..completely covering it and gulped as fast as I could as she pissed nto my mouth. It was hot. Hotter than I expected...but tasted so sexy. Raunchy. I was captivated, and kept swallowing.

I drank, swallowing furiously until she finished, and stayed there licking up everything from her lips, from her thighs and nylons. Then she relaxed her legs and let them spread open again, releasing my face. But I wanted to stay there...looking up into her beauty.

Then she asked me to pee for HER....

At first it was hard to do...I couldn't relax enough...

...then it began to come. She held me in such a way that my piss squirted straight up..like a drinking fountain. And she drank it. She let it splash over her lips and mouth for a minute...maybe not on purpose...and then clamped her mouth on my cunt.

I could actually hear her gulping it as she swallowed it all. She swallowed every bit. Then she used her mouth to suck me to an orgasm like I've never had before.

When I had finished shaking from the orgasm, she leaned over and kissed my mouth. She tasted like my pee, and her mouth was slippery from my cum. I licked her mouth and tasted it all. It was sooo hot.

It was all over very quickly, an hour at most. She directed me to the bath and told me I could shower if I wanted, but I didn't. I washed my face, and dressed, and walked back out into the salon.

She kissed me. Holding my hand, slipped a little gold ring on my finger. Like a wedding band, but thin... Only now do I believe there was a significance to this gift. A fine, delicate bit of gold. She then took me to the door, kissed me once more and slid her hand under my skirt to touch my cunt again. I had left the wet panties in her bathroom on purpose, and she was surprised to feel me completely exposed, naked to her caress, but she didn't say anything to me. Just "goodbye".

I've never done this again. But I fantasize about it all of the time. and masturbate thinking of it more often than you can imagine.

When I pee now, on the toilet, I put my fingers into the hot stream and taste them. It still makes me excited. I love to look at pee pictures now...and stories about women who drink pee. Karina, of course is not my real name, but it's very close. I've never wated to share this with men...The thought is not the same for me, it's a woman that I desire now. The softness, the lips opening, the stream...

I'm 23 years old, blond, hazel green eyes 5'4" tall and my measurements are 34c-22-34. That's it. You would never imagine me to be caught in this web of fantasy if you were to see me. But if you were a beautiful woman, My mind would be on your thighs, the soft mound of your cunt sheathed in the wisp of your nylon panties, on the taste of you...hot, streaming, pale yellow champagne. Oh goddd!

Watch for me. Let your legs part and tease me...

Story 06

I went into the shop on my way home from work on a whim. I was going to suprise my husband with some new lingerie. My husband usually bought my lingerie, I don't see the point to it, no sooner have I put in on when he immediately begins to remove it again. It was a small shop, narrow but it stretched back along way from the doorway. I was the only customer in the place, it was getting close to closing time. I was only still in the downtown area as I had been kept late at work because of a meeting. I don't even know why I had been told to attend the meeting it had nothing to do with my department. Most of the stuff I found very boring. My mind was constantly wandering. Maybe that was why I had decided to buy some lingerie on the way home. I had been doing a lot of thinking about my husband. I loved the feel of his hands on my body, caressing my breasts, sliding down between my legs. I loved the feel as his tongue gently flicked across my clit. I didn't like him sticking his tongue inside me. So when he went down on me he would usually trace his tongue lightly around my labia occasionally brushing my clit. Then he would begin to focus more on my clit, flitting his tongue across it. Teasing me. As I begin to moan in pleasure he increases the pressure. I need more, I press his head down into my crotch. He spreads my legs with his powerful hands, holding me open to his tongue. As he increases the pressure on my clit I feel the wave of my orgasm building. Sliding his hands under my buttocks he pulls me up against his tongue. The extra pressure sends me over the edge, I moan loudly. I feel the pressure of my husband's tongue let up, but he licks faster prolonging my orgasm.

With thoughts like these it you can see why it had been hard to concentrate during the meeting. At one point in the meeting I pulled my chair in closer to the table. This was so I could slip my hand down to my crotch without anybody noticing. My skirt, cut just a little above the knee, had a slit at the front which made my job easier. I traced my finger lightly over my silk underwear up and down my pussy lips. My panties are wet. I push the silk material down into my cleft as I increase the pressure on my clit. I want to get off, but I don't think I could do it quietly. I will myself to stop. It's difficult. I find my mind and hands keep drifting back to my crotch throughout the meeting.

The sales assistant appears from behind a curtain at the back of the shop and walks up to the small display counter with the cash register on top. "Hi, I'm Nicky, is there anything I can help you with?". She's cute, mid-twenties, with short bobbed blonde hair. I walk up to the counter. It has a glass see through top, the lower shelves are mirrors with silk panties displayed on them. "I just came in to browse" I say. I look down into the display case, there is a bright red pair of panties, my husband likes me to wear red. I notice that I can look up under Nicky's short cotton dress because of the mirrored shelf. She is wearing a red pair of panties, only they look skimpier that the ones in the display case. There is a small triangle of red silk fabric stretched tightly over her pussy. I bend over to get a closer look, "I like the red ones, are they pure silk?".

"One hundred percent. Don't you love the feel of pure silk against your skin? Would you like to try them on?".

"I'll just browse for a few minutes" I say. I'm still bent over looking up Nicky's dress. She can't be sure where I'm looking, but she knows that what she is showing. I pretend to look at the other things in the display case by moving my head, but my eyes remain fixed on the tight triangle of red. Nicky shifts around behind the counter. She turns and I can see a thin red thong running up between her rounded buttocks. Her skin is wonderfully smooth, her ass looks firm. She bends down slightly, pushing her buttocks towards me. Nicky's putting on a show.

"I have to go and rearrange some of the displays. When you would like to try something, let me know." With that Nicky walks from behind the counter into the main body of the store. The show's over. On the left wall there are a series of shelves with half mannequins on the very top. These are the ones Nicky decides to rearrange. Using a small ladder she climbs up to redress one of the mannequins. As she climbs I get and even better view of her firm ass. I walk over to where she is working. Nicky's putting on a display I don't want to miss. I want to get a closer look at her gorgeous ass, I try not to be too obvious but she knows what I came over to look at. I'm standing at the foot of the ladder pretending to look at items on the shelf. Nicky's buttocks are about eighteen inches diagonally up to my left. Her legs are just as firm as her buttocks, both of which are lightly tanned, no lines.

"While you're there do you mind passing me those white lace panties from the shelf right in front of you?" She's looking down at me, she can see where I've been looking. A little flustered I reach for the panties. They're very soft, flimsy. As I pass them up to her. my eyes follow her legs up under her dress. Nicky's turned slightly towards me, I catch a glimpse of the small red triangle covering her pussy. As I look up Nicky is smiling down at me. "Nice aren't they? The red ones, I mean" "Very attractive" I say. My pussy is getting wet again. I want to reach down and rub it as I did in the meeting. Nicky turns back to finish her work on the mannequin. With one last glance up her skirt I wander off to look for a pair of panties like the ones Nicky has on. If they have this effect on me they will work wonders for my husband.

As I walk to the wall opposite Nicky I slip my hand in through the slit in my skirt and give my pussy a rub. I'm dying to get off. The wet silk clings to my slit. I give my clit a few gentle strokes. I glance over my shoulder, Nicky is still working up on the ladder. Although now I'm too far away to get a good look up her skirt. I turn back to the display case in front of me My clit wants to be stroked again. I can't do it here. My hand goes down, I press my skirt up against my crotch. The pressure feels good against my pussy.

"Would you like to try these on" says Nicky. I hadn't noticed her come over. As I turn to her I see she is holding out a pair of red thong panties like the ones she is wearing. Automatically I reach for them. I hadn't told her I wanted to try them on. My hand feels the soft silk of the panties, they're warm, there's no tag on them. I hold the silk up my cheek it's soft, smooth. The panties still smell warm, they smell of Nicky.

"Shall we see if they fit?" I nod. Nicky takes the panties from my hand, kneels in front of me. Her hands reach up under my skirt and begin to pull my panties down.

"No, what if someone comes in."

"The doors locked and I've closed the shutters" Nicky says as she smiles up at me. "I thought you might need a little more personal attention in picking something out. I thought it best if we weren't interrupted. Its pretty much closing time anyway."

Nicky pulls my panties down. As I step out of them Nicky lifts them up to her face. She rubs them against her face. "These are good quality" she says. "They smell good too." I'm sure she noticed the wet patch, but she made no comment.

"Why don't we take your skirt off, that way we'll be able to see how these panties really fit you." With that Nicky unfastens my business skirt and lets it fall to the floor. Except for my shoes I'm naked from the waist down, with a cute blond kneeling at my feet, my wet panties in her hand. I'm glad I decided to buy something for my husband.

Nicky holds out the red panties for me to step into. She slides them slowly up my legs. She's caressing my legs. Although they aren't as firm as hers I'm in pretty good shape. She pulls the waist band up over my hips. The thong settles in the cleft between my buttocks. A few of my pubic hairs are sticking out even though I keep my bush neatly trimmed. Nicky's fingers reach behind the silk touching my bush as she spreads the fabric. My hairs disappear. Then she pushes the fabric against me smoothing it out. She slides her hands between my legs pulling the thong up between my buttocks. Her hands sliding over the silk feels wonderful.

"How do those feel?" she says as she gets to her feet.

"Sexy" I say.

Nicky reaches down with her hand smoothing out the panties. She uses slightly more pressure this time. One of her fingers pushes the material into my cleft, brushing my clit. I'm wetting these panties too.

"That does feel sexy doesn't it." She says. "Go see how they look in that mirror while I go and get a few more things for you to try on." I turn to the mirror. The panties look pretty good on me. As I said before I'm in good shape. I look a little silly though, standing in my shoes, red thong panties and my business shirt. I slip my shoes off and begin to undo my shirt. By the time Nicky gets back I only have a bra and panties on. I look pretty good in the mirror. My breasts are firm and don't need a lot of support. The lacy bra I'm wearing is all I need. Lace makes me feel sexy. Occasionally I'll undo an extra button while I'm at work. I like to tease some of the men who come to my office with an eyeful of my firm breasts nestled in flimsy lace. It's fun to see them maneuver around as they try to get a second look.

Nicky is standing behind me looking in the mirror. "You look great. Try this bra on, I think it's the right size." The bra she's holding is white lace, underwired, there's also less fabric than the one I'm already wearing. "This will make you even more eye catching" she says. She places the clothes she's brought on the chair next to the mirror. Sliding her arms around me from behind she releases my breasts from the "front loader" as my husband likes bras with a clasp at the front. "You're firm" Nicky says as she cradles by breasts. My nipples begin to harden. I can feel Nicky's breasts pressing against my back. Her soft hands feel totally different than my husbands rough hands. Warm, caressing my breasts, brushing my nipples lightly. Different is good.

"Why don't I try that bra on a little later. I'd like to feel something a little softer." I like my breasts being free. Nicky slides her hands down over my stomach, pressing her breasts harder against my back. She's looking into my eyes in the mirror as her hands smooth out my panties again. First she spreads the fabric out the fabric over my pussy. Then she reaches her right hand down between my legs, slowly bringing it back up, one finger applying more pressure between my lips, tracing upwards over my clit. I close my eyes and let out a slight moan. Nicky presses down between my legs again, harder this time, than lightly brings her finger back up. Her left hand reaches up to cradle my right breast, pulling my body back against her breasts. I reach back, slide my hands up her legs, going up under her dress until I have her firm round buttocks in my hands. I pull her crotch tight up against my bare buttocks. I open my eyes, Nicky is smiling at me in the mirror.

Nicky releases me and takes a soft cotton night shirt she had brought over off the chair. She spreads it on the ground at her feet. Next she pulls her cotton dress off over her head and spreads this on the floor. She has no bra on. She doesn't need one. Her breasts are smaller than mine and firmer, pert. On top of the clothes on the floor, Nicky spreads a couple of silk camisoles. Taking my hand she draws me down to the floor. I lie back on the silk. Nicky leans over me lowering her mouth to my right nipple, the more sensitive one. She flicks it lightly with her tongue. Her left hand traces it way down my abdomen. She slides it under the panties. I'm very wet. Her finger slides easily into my slit. Down it slides between my legs. I spread my legs and push up against her hand. Her finger slick from my juices comes to rest against my puckered asshole. My husband's never done this. It feels good, Nicky just applies gentle pressure, then her hand moves back up between my lips. As it grazes my clit I let out another moan of pleasure, louder this time.

Nicky's head moves from my breast. I can feel her warm breath moving down my belly. Pulling the panty fabric to one side her hands are caressing my pussy. Pushing her fingers down into my cleft. Teasing my clit. She doesn't try to penetrate me, I'm glad, that would be a distraction. She spreads my legs further, her tongue brushes my clit. A jolt passes through me. Again her tongue passes over my clit, down between my legs. As she brings her head back up she covers my clit with her mouth, lightly sucking on it. After only a few seconds I come. I've needed that all afternoon. Nicky lies down next to me her head resting on my leg. She smiles up at me then begins to lightly run her fingers over my pussy lips, occasionally brushing my clit. I'm very sensitive down there, even the lightest touch sends shivers through me. Turning on my side towards her I rest my head on her leg. I can see moisture on her blond pussy hairs. Her clit is moist and protruding. I spread her pussy lips revealing her tantalizing moist coral colored inner flesh. I lick my finger and run it up her slit, teasing. She spreads her legs wider. I move my head towards her pussy. My tongue flits rapidly, yet lightly across her clit. Nicky moans loudly. Her fingers press between my legs. She's close to coming. I lighten the pressure on her clit, teasing her. Her hand moves to the back of my head, she wants more pressure. I resist, teasing her lightly. Her moaning gets louder. She is about to go over the edge. I can feel her tongue on my clit again, pressing, insistent. My mouth engulfs her clit. I increase the pressure. Her hand presses me on. Her pussy presses against my face. I feel her body shudder as she comes. As I feel the pressure on the back of my head lessen, Nicky moves her hands to my bottom pulling my pussy tightly against her mouth. I come again.

Needless to say I bought the red panties. My husband was very pleased with them. He was surprised that I had bought them. "Not like you" he said. I told him not to be surprised if I bought some more.

I live in a lakeside town on the coast of Michigan. It's small and pretty, often filled with visitors passing through or vacation- ing--both winter and summer. One of the most interesting places to meet people is at Willhouse Inn, a bed-and-breakfast-like hotel with a great restaurant and large, active lounge.

Just this past summer I stopped there one evening after work. It was warm enough to get the urges flowing, but not so hot to be oppressive. After I'd sat down and my eyes had a chance to adjust to the light, I noticed an attractive, nicely dressed blonde sitting by herself near the window. She was very inviting as she stared dreamily at the lake and the gulls.

I got up and moved close enough to her that we could talk without seeming as if I was pushing myself on her. After the usual ice-breaking comments about the weather, the season and our surroundings, she gradually opened up to conversation. When we got around to introductions, she told me her name was Connie.

"Pleased to meet you, Connie, I'm Samantha," I said with a smile while extending my hand.

As she reached out to me, I admired the outline of her braless breasts showing through her thin blouse. My boobs are pretty well developed, but she had the best set of tits I've ever seen! Their shape and the high, proud way they hung excited me. Her nipples were erect, but I couldn't tell if she was chilled by the air conditioning or if she had something else going on to stimulate her. Our conversation perhaps? Me?

I mentally compared our builds and idly wondered how well her 5"1' 105-pound frame might fit with my own. I'm almost 5'6" and weight 110 pounds, but I sure didn't see a problem! Her cobalt blue eyes danced with a certain fire when she talked. I responded by concentrating intently on her. Her glance repeatedly returned to my eyes and I could tell she was fascinated by the color, which, though normally grey, were purple this night thanks to my contact lenses.

As we sipped our drinks and talked, we talked about being relaxed and feeling kind of sexy. I probed a little and learned that she wasn't into girl-girl stuff. Damn! She was so inviting, too! Instead, I suggested we find a couple of guys to fulfill our NEEDS. She liked that.

The only problem was there was only one single guy around. He was pretty good looking, too. I really wanted her, not him, but if that's the way it was to be, I told her to go after him. Since she was afraid her husband would find out, I offered her the use of my place. She thought about that, looked at the guy and said, "Well, thanks. I'll do it!" I drew her a map to my place on a napkin. She put it in her purse and winked at me.

She moved close to the guy, and soon they were talking. I struck up a side conversation with the bartender but kept an eye on Connie. She was blocking his view so he didn't even see me.

In about a half-hour they got up to leave. I dashed out a side door, and took a short-cut to my place so it looked as if I'd been there for hours when they arrived. I said I was Connie's roommate. I got Connie alone in the kitchen for a few minutes and told her where the bedroom was. I volunteered to stay in the kitchen until she and Steve (that was his name) dropped out of sight.

They had some preliminaries on the couch before finally going into the bedroom, and I stayed out of sight. I went back into the living room, acutely aware of what was happening on the other side of the door. I couldn't be anything BUT aware because they couldn't have disguised THOSE noises if they had tried: she was a screamer!

I finally drifted off to sleep on the couch, which is very comfortable and not punishment of any kind. I've slept on it many times and done lots of colorful things on it too!

Awakening around 3:30 in the morning after dreaming about Connie and Steve in the bedroom, I was horny and ready. I got up and fumbled around in my dildo collection, selected one and took it back to the couch with me. The dream had made me wet, and the dildo slid in up to the hilt with no trouble at all. I gave it to myself long and slow.

About 4 a.m., Steve slipped quietly out of the bedroom. It looked as if he was going to take off without even a good-bye. When he passed me, I reached out and grabbed his sleeve. He was startled and kind of jerked at my touch. By some accident the covers just happened to fall off me! There I was, his sleeve in one hand, and a dildo in the other. He gracefully picked up the blanket.

He wasn't fully dressed and I pulled off his underwear. Then we re-did the scene in the bedroom, only I got to scream. He was nice, but not repeatable. He seemed more interested in hustling his buns out instead of moving them for me! He said he had to catch a plane so he dressed, kissed me lightly and left.

Still not satisfied despite the fucking I'd just had, I locked the door after Steve and debated about what to do next. I went back to my "toy" drawer, took out a strap-on dildo and put it on. (This one is special to me because I had fastened a small strip with tiny rubber fingers on it. Certain kinds of action with it can produce the most exquisite orgasms!) With my "equipment" in place, I walked into the bedroom.

Connie was awake, but the dim light just faintly exposed my lower body. All Connie could see was my "hard-on." Suddenly she started to purr.

"Who is it?" she cooed.

Wordlessly, I slipped into bed and started feeling all over her body. I kept her at arm's length so she couldn't detect my curves. Certainly HER curves were turning me on! I knelt between her legs and slowly slid my tongue between her secret lips. (Below the panty line, I later discovered, she was a redhead!!)

My hot oral work on her soon had her panting. She loved it and moved her hips in rhythm with my tongue motions. She took my head in her hands to guide me where she wanted me. My hair is kind of short so in the dark she couldn't tell that she was caressing a woman.

"Oh, I have to have more," she whispered. "Slide your cock into me. Plunge it in deep!"

I got up on my knees, positioned myself at her opening, and mounted her. I guided my "cock" where my mouth had been seconds before. She moaned with delight and reached up to rub my chest. Then she felt my tits and screamed.

I was going crazy trying to calm her down. I kept the fake prick in her as I soothed her, but it seemed to be doing more harm than good. I finally pulled it out and took it off, talking quietly to her as I did. About 15 minutes later she had calmed down but was still pretty well freaked. She said she just wanted to go home, and I felt like shit.

That made me decide to lay low the following night, even though the experience with Connie left me longing for pussy. (I love guys and I need them, but I love women, too. Sometimes I need only what a woman has to offer.) I had just finished dinner and was watching TV when the doorbell rang.

I couldn't believe my eyes when I opened the door and there stood Connie, fetchingly dressed in shorts and a halter top! She didn't leave much to the imagination, and I know my eyes must have opened wide as I stared at her bare, well-shaped legs in full light.

She smiled sweetly but stammered when she spoke. "You've been on my mind lately, and I wanted to come back and apologize for running out the way I did last night."

I was delighted and invited her in. She brushed close when she stepped inside, and desire laced through me. I opened a bottle of wine and we both sat down--chatting as we sipped. She told me that she and her husband had been having problems and that she hadn't been fucked very well in a long time, even by Steve the night before.

"When I left here early this morning," Connie said, "I had the most peculiar feeling. It wasn't bad, in fact it was good, but it sure was strange. All day I thought about what happened with you, and I repeatedly got hot. When dusk arrived, the urge overpowered me and I had to come back to see you. I want to try it again, only this time I want to participate!"

My mind raced, and I could feel a delicious warmth erupt and gradually spread through me. I told her how beautiful she was and how much I wanted her. Our talk became hot and explicit. When I suggested we slowly undress each other, Connie immediately got up.

"How about coming over here so I can get at you," she said.

I stood and walked to her. All I had on was a man's dress shirt that hung to the middle of my thighs. She immediately began opening the shirt one button at a time. Slowly, almost hypnotically, she slid it off, exposing myself to her. I loved the hungry look this produced, and I seductively shifted my weight from one foot to the other. Still trance-like with her eyes half-closed, Connie caressed me, stopping to focus on my nipples. She still seemed shy and didn't let her hands drift below my waist.

Shaking myself back to reality, I said, "Connie, your touch is exciting, and you're really getting to me, but how about letting me return the favor?"

She smiled and slightly pushed out her inviting chest. I melted and kissed her lightly on the mouth. When she didn't recoil from it, I kissed her again--only deeper, longer, invading her soul. I massaged her breasts as we hugged.

We both gasped when I finally broke loose and groped for her halter. I slyly tugged out the bottom edge. Holding it out from her body, my fingers slid underneath and danced across the nipples. Wanting more, I continued to move the halter upward.

"Raise your arms above your head for me, OK?" I coaxed.

She did and I popped the sliver of material over her head. Those gorgeous, now-liberated tits begged for attention, standing out with both nipples puckered and firm. I had to have them and immediately took one in my mouth to gently squeeze and suck. I centered my attention on the nipple. Connie held the breast in her hand, steering it to where she wanted it most--first over my tongue, then against the roof of my mouth, occasionally raking it lightly against my teeth.

I reached down and felt her crotch. She was still wearing her shorts, and I slithered my hand up underneath. She had obviously prepared to visit me because she was wearing no underpants. I probed my fingers into her bush and found she was dripping hot liquid.

Pulling myself off her breast, I paused to open her shorts and lower them. She deftly stepped out of them and stood before me, naked, beautiful, and ready. Her eyes smouldered, and she held one breast up to her mouth and licked it all over. As she offered me this little show, she gradually spread her legs further and further apart. Her free hand disappeared into the wet down between her legs.

I wanted to be part of this so I gently replaced her hand with my own. She was drenched, and I wanted to suck her. And she wanted me to!

"Please lick me, Samantha," she pleaded. "My cunt is ready for you. Is yours ready for me?"

"See for yourself," I offered, standing and moving her hand to my own wet pussy.

Presenting myself to her searching hand, I maneuvered my fingers past her swollen doors and into her love tunnel. Fastened together that way, we approached each other and kissed again with growing passion. Our mouths opened wide while our hands feverishly massaged each other's mounds. I sucked on her tongue as it glided far into the back of my mouth. Then we reversed and I "fucked" her mouth with my tongue.

Finally I stepped back, moved her to the couch, and had her sit down on the back with her feet on the cushions. She leaned against the wall and spread her legs. I knelt on the cushions and faced her gaping snatch. I was so hot I trembled at the sight.

I kissed her cunt in the same open-mouthed way I had just kissed her face. My lips created a seal around her pussy lips so that I could suck at the same time I tongued the sweetness overflowing from inside her. The sensation made her jerk. I liked having her twitch that way so I rolled her clit lewdly between my lips. She raised her hips to meet and then grind against me.

As I ate her, I took her nipples in my hands and pinched them. The nipples swelled even more. I rolled them so that they were covered by the other flesh of her breasts, and then I squeezed them inside the "pocket" that this created. She groaned in response.

Finally she retreated slightly and said, "Please, Samantha, I think I want to try it, too. Let's go into the bedroom so we can really get to each other. But please be patient with me since I'm a little unsure of myself."

We uncoupled and went into the other room. As she bent over to pull down the bedspread, I leaned down, spread her cheeks from behind and stabbed my tongue into her puckered anus. She loved it, but begged me to stop so she could get some too. When I did, she turned around, put her arms around me and pulled me down to the bed on top of her. Still holding on, she rolled over so she was on top.

She was completely engrossed now. She ran her fingers through my hair and held my head in place as she repeatedly sucked my mouth and gave me her tongue in return. Our pelvises rubbed together, and I could occasionally feel her clit against my own. We were locked in a deep, abandoned embrace.

Connie's intensity was startling and incredibly arousing. I kept reaching higher plateaus of desire for her. She shifted slightly, and her left leg came to rest on my mound. Her own love spot pressed against my thigh. I desperately wanted friction and moved my clit against her. The fucking motion translated to her, and she humped my leg. Her arms surrounded my head and her eager fingers laced through my hair. Breathing heavily, her kiss was ablaze. It may have been a new experience, but the sexual longing overcame her and she surrendered completely. Our arms and legs became so intertwined that we were like one body. I had to have her. Now!

I repeated her earlier movement and rolled over so that she was now beneath me. Disentangling our arms, I ran my hands up and down the insides of her thighs, pressing outward as I did so her legs would be wide apart when I arrived at her "V." Connie needed little convincing. She kept spreading her legs farther and farther until they formed a straight line broken only by the dip into her bush. She was lithe and supple, her body well conditioned and rippling slightly with muscle.

Moving down and kneeling before her, I teased, "Tell me what you want, Connie. Tell me and I'll do it." My breath was close enough to her most sensitive spots that she trembled when it struck her.

"Please suck me like you did last night. Let me feel your soft, warm mouth on me. And while you do it, let me worship you. Give me your wetness. I can't wait any longer."

I swung around and positioned my legs on either side of her head. I wanted first to overcome any lingering reservations she might have. I rested my elbows on the bed below her legs, gently rolled back the hood of her clit and exposed its erect head, red, hard and glistening with moisture.

I shaped my mouth into an erotic oval, darted my tongue several times against her clit, and then ringed it with a moist suction. She writhed and wrapped her arms around my legs, pulling slightly at my own clit-hood so I would be as exposed to her as she was to me. I lowered my wet down close to her face.

Connie sucked on either side of my bush, mouthing my groin muscles. I liked it a lot. She repeatedly worked back and forth, occasionally grazing my lips with her tongue. My action was having a delirious effect, and her hips developed a circular, rolling movement. In that moment, her mouth came to rest against my opening. She licked tentatively, not entirely sure how to proceed.

I demonstrated on her, rhythmically tonguing her button. Taking the cue, she slipped her tongue between my pussy lips. Her hip movements stopped abruptly and she moved her hands in place around my opening, spreading my lips far apart. I loved the feeling of having the INSIDE of my cunt exposed to her.

She extended her tongue farther and farther, then stopped and held like that for a long moment, savoring the sensation. Her tongue started moving in and out of me, and I moved my hips in a classic fucking motion. A cat-like growl came from Connie as she unexpectedly found my clit and focused on it. In that instant she lost her "virginity" to a woman, sucking me off and being sucked in return.

Our act was complete. Our drenched mouths and wet cunts were the perfect complement. We fused together in this mouth-to-cunt/ cunt-to-mouth embrace, rolling together on the bed. As we exchanged positions that way, our mouths never lost their fusion. First Connie was on top, fucking and eating me at the same time. Then I replaced her in the top position to bury my face in her snatch while receiving her.

I gave her face a fast, hard fucking and fastened on her clit. It was bulging and erect, almost like a two-inch penis. I didn't know a clit could be this long and I rapidly moved my head up and down, sucking her the way I'd blown guys.

I paused for an instant and whispered, "Now, Connie, let's cum NOWWW!!"

Connie cried out and madly humped my face. I held her down with my hands and fucked her as hard as she fucked me. My insides rolled and a shot of the most delicious heat tore through me.

Connie's cunt suddenly opened wide on its own. I sank my lips and tongue, even my nose, inside her gushing gash. I was rewarded by a series of strong contractions, and Connie bucked out of control. She jerked over and over. The repeated tightening of her sexual muscles catapulted me into orbit. I let my orgasm go, sitting slightly on Connie's face so she could thrust her tongue inside me.

"Oh, fuck me, Connie, fuck me with your tongue," I exclaimed into her cumming cunt. I drank deeply as she spun off into repeated orgasms.

When the intensity of our climaxes subsided a little, I started playing with her ass. It startled her and she said, "Oh, Samantha, not there. Oh, please not there. Ohhhh, please, oh, oh, unhhhh!!"

It seemed that the words didn't match the emotion behind them. She didn't really want me to stop at all; in this case "stop" meant "go a little faster"! I ignored her pleas and continued working on her ass. I rubbed and massaged it, which was easy to do with all the moisture that had leaked out.

It apparently intrigued her enough that she pulled my lower body down on her in such a way that she could reach my anus. Her hot breath made me contract slightly, and I jerked when her tongue struck my sphincter. She spread my ass checks and slowly worked her tongue into me. There we lay, our tongues implanted, paying anal homage to each other.

I had an idea, a way to make Connie's "deflowering" nearly complete. I slowly separated from her and said, "Roll over on your stomach and crouch down with your ass in the air. Then spread your legs."

She obediently did as I asked, displaying her lovely legs and well-shaped ass. I savored the view of her anus and the downy patch that began there and stretched down to her mound. I put my hands on her cheeks and, with my thumbs, spread them to expose the small pucker that I was about to assault. I blew my breath against it and enjoyed seeing her quiver in response.

Bracing my elbows on her thighs, I leaned down and slowly licked her anus. Her sounds were gibberish, but I knew what pleasure she was taking. I reached between her legs, felt around to relocate her clit, and snapped it back in forth.

I needed more, and stopped briefly to move her right foot slightly. I settled on it so that my own clit could rub against her heel and began humping. I resumed my wanton tongue-rape of her ass. I soon found a rhythm and synchronized my tongue and my hand with the rubbing I was getting from her foot. She wiggled it, adding to my gratification.

I couldn't stand the intensity and lost myself to the building orgasm. I jerked her clit with one hand while tweaking and rubbing one of her nipples with the other. She groaned, long and deep. I sucked her ass with my open mouth, occasionally shooting my tongue in. Connie unexpectedly shoved her ass even farther into me and I realized I was about to lose it.

I paused long enough in my frenzy to whisper anxiously, "You're so gorgeous, Connie. I'm going to cum because of you. Let's cum together--you with your ass full of my woman's tongue and my clit being rubbed by your foot."

The shriek that followed was so loud I thought the entire city would hear her! The abrasion against my clit finally did it and I spilled over the edge, feeling my orgasm burst onto her foot. Her anus constricted around my tongue.. We hung for a long moment before we were overwhelmed.

The scene that followed was blissfully out of control. We both thrashed and moaned. With the orgasm pounding through me, I unsteadily backed off, rolled Connie over and spread her legs. I jammed my clit against hers and scissor-fucked her hard. She held her legs wide apart in complete surrender to our organs' mutual stimulation. My fucking motions were nearly involuntary as we wrung the last spasms from each other.

The slow descent from that pinnacle left us both trembling and spent. A warm glow washed over us, and we gradually relaxed. I got some warm wash cloths from the bathroom and bathed us both. When I was finished, I got back into bed with her.

We softly, affectionately kissed and fondled each other. Soon we were asleep in each other's arms. It had been a night to remember--for both of us.

Story 08

I looked up as the tall, cool blonde stepped through the door of my exclusive lingerie shop in an upscale mall up north. She was a sight to behold, I thought, and instinctively began to juice as I imagined touching her, making her hot for me. I cater to a rich clientele and my reputation for product, foresight, service and discretion has spread by word of mouth. I hoped to be of royal service to this beauty today.

"May I help you?" I asked as the game began.

"Of course you may," she responded haughtily. "I'd like to see some silk panties, if you will--for my trousseau."

I lead her to the racks containing my most expensive stock. This woman deserves my best, I thought, as she fingered through the apparel and chose a few. I have a great love for good lingerie, but I love even more the flesh it encases.

"I'd like to try these on and I'll need your help." I looked around the shop. Only one other customer was browsing and my sales clerk was at the register.

"Yes, ma'am." I replied subserviently. "You may go in the second dressing room." My dressing rooms are richly appointed with all of the comforts of home.

I followed her in and watched as she removed and handed me her clothing. She revealed porcelain skin as she stripped slowly. Holding her clothes to my chest, my eyes were fascinated at each part that she revealed. She looked ultimately fuckable.

"Do you like what you see, dear? My body is beautiful, isn't it?" she said as turned in the mirrors.

"Yes, you are very beautiful," I said as I hung her things. She was naked except for the brief silk panties that barely covered her ass but highlighted her mound.

She cupped her pussy, then slowly began to rub. "I love the way silk feels against my pussy." I noticed a wet spot appear as she pleasured herself. She seemed to have forgotten that I was there.

"Ma'am, you'll have to be dry to try on the merchandise," I said.

"Of course, I must. Come and help me with these."

I put my hands in the waistband. She sighed and trembled as my hands touched her flesh. Suddenly, she put her hands on my shoulders and pushed me down, my face in her crotch.

"Lick me through my panties. I do have the sweetest pussy," she mumbled as she licked the hand that had caressed her pussy.

Smiling to myself, I snaked my tongue out and licked tentatively at her covered mound.

"I know you can do better that. I've heard you're an expert with a pussy. I want your very best." she whispered.

She grabbed my head and pushed her pussy in my face. "Oh, oh, oh," she chanted as I licked harder. I got bolder and sucked her pussy hard through the soft, wet fabric as she pressed herself forward. Then the desire to see hot pussy on a cool blonde overtook me. I slowly began to peel the panties away as I looked into her triumphant, eager eyes. I only got them to her knees before I began to feast at her alter.

I licked her slowly, up and down and up and down. I tongued the moisture that dripped from her. When I finally drove my tongue into her, her knees weakened as she came on it.

"I need to lie on the chaise for a moment," she said breathing erratically. She stepped completely out of the panties. I grabbed the wet silk and brought it to my nose. She smiled knowingly as she watched me sniff and taste them.

"Join me, now. I want you to screw the perfect pussy. Mine. Leave your panties on. I want to feel the silk I know you're wearing."

I removed my top, bra and slacks. Straddling the lounge, I brought my clothed pussy to meet perfection. I lightly screwed my pussy onto and into hers. She moaned quietly, looking into the mirrors, as my silk-clad ass rotated above her. Sliding my pussy back and forth on hers, she screwed her pretty ass on the lounge, straining up to me. The soft hands inside my panties alternately caressed my ass cheeks and the puckered hole between them.

"Fuck me harder! Harder! Yes, that's it. Make me cum hard! Please! Yes! Yes! Mmmm!"

I lifted then jammed my pussy into hers as hard as I could, repeatedly. I heard a muffled choke as she came gushing onto my own silk panties. I leaned to suckle her breasts, but she took my head and allowed me her tongue instead. I came again as I ravished her luscious mouth.

"I'll take a dozen pair of the silks," she mumbled past my thick tongue, "and keep two for yourself. I seem to have destroyed yours."

I bit and sucked a long, erect nipple as I adjusted myself to give her more of what she came here for. I moved down, slipped my hands beneath her ass, pulled her up to my mouth and ate her until she begged me to stop. She came over and over muffling her screams.

I sell these rich ladies my expensive lingerie, but the side-pussy many of them crave is a gratuity. They are mere mannequins for their successful husbands or lovers, but they come alive beneath me. Rich people love getting things for free. In my shop, dispensing good pussy to deserving women is my ultimate gratuity.

If you do anything worthwhile today, "do it" with a woman.

Story 09

My workout at the club was wonderful this morning. But more importantly was my session with the new masseuse. As the young woman rubbed me down, nearing my pussy, I became highly excited. I knew I'd have a vibrator moment when I got home. Strange, I've never been turned on by a woman before.

On the drive home, I remembered that my daughter wanted me to stop at a shop in the mall and pick up a gift for a friend's birthday party. People were crowded very thickly at my entrance awaiting some sort of demonstration. As I couldn't move very far, I settled in to wait it out.

Standing directly in front of me was a young woman about my height. Her jet black hair was cut short and becomingly in back. I tapped her shoulder. "Excuse me, miss. Do you know what the demonstration is about?"

"They're advertising jewelry. There will be a free drawing when it ends," she said excitedly.

I was suddenly enthralled by the beautiful ruby-red lips speaking to me. Her bangs moved slightly as she breathed, breasts heaving. "I've never been to one of these things. There are so many people here," I said.

"I know and I love it. My kids are with their grandmother and I have a free day at the mall. I'm taking advantage of everything. By the way, I'm Brianna."

"Nice to meet you, Brianna. I'm Taylor. How old are your children? And how old are you? You look so young to have two children."

"Thank you. The boy is three, the girl is five and I'm 26."

I wanted to keep her talking just to look at her. She was so cute and perky. She smiled almost seductively at me and told me that she admired the way I look. I am 37, tall, with dark brown hair brushing my shoulders and green eyes. My body is lean and athletic from years of tennis at our country club.

"Let me return the compliment, Brianna. You're a beautiful young mother." I smiled back at her. God, those lips are lush. I could look at this woman all day and not get tired of the sight of her. Could she tell I was ogling her?

I turned from her as the lights dimmed and demonstration began. Suddenly the crowd surged forward. Her hands went to my shoulders as my ass was caught in her pelvis. I moaned as I pushed it further back into her instinctively, slightly rotating it. Damn, I thought, as a sweet shiver went through my pussy, this woman is exciting me.

The demonstration droned on. Just the thought of my ass in her pussy, let alone the feel of it, was making me dizzy. I was hot and I needed more. Suddenly, she inched closer as if she read my thoughts. She reached for my breasts and rotated her pussy on my ass as she felt me up. She sighed as she ran her tongue lightly over my ears. The crowd was so thickly packed, I was sure no one noticed her taking me. Not a word was spoken as she touched me.

She drug her hands from my breasts and caught them in the waistband of my slacks. She unbelted and unzipped me slowly as I looked around the crowd. No one seem to notice as she put her hands inside my pants. She was met with brief silk bikinis already soaked. She messaged my pussy thought the panties as she screwed my ass.

My silk panties were a barrier to the flesh she wanted to touch. As she slipped one hand inside, she grabbed my pussy, found my clit and went to work on it. My head fell back as she furiously hand-fucked me. God, it was so good! I knew we didn't have much time left, but she had me cumming in three minutes flat. Next she slipped two fingers inside my pussy and finger- fucked me while rubbing my clit. The sweet little thing put me in heaven as I came yet again.

I whimpered as she removed her hands from my warmth and re-did my slacks. The crowd began to disperse. I turned to thank her for knowing what I needed and giving it to me so beautifully. She had slipped away. I stood there a minute still feeling her hands and imagining those lush ruby lips traveling slowly toward my pussy.

Story 10

I lay in my hotel room fantasizing about a hard cock pumping inside me. My need for human contact overwhelms me. It has been four weeks since my married lover has come near my pussy claiming his wife is suspicious. On top of that, my office sent me to this meaningless conference in Chicago and I haven't made a single friend here. Real boredom has set in.

Luckily, I packed a few toys with which to amuse myself. I pull a 10-inch rubber cock from my stash and proceeded to have some fun.

Now this particular dick is a favorite of mine. It has a base that adheres to almost any surface. I put it in various places in the hotel room and slide my pussy onto it, cumming around the room.I had my little friend on the coffee table taking my pussy down on it when the door suddenly opened. The maid had knocked, but I didn't hear her as I was moaning loudly as I took the vibrating cock into me. I am cumming as I look into her face. She seemed fascinated as I fucked the table, so to speak.

"I'm sorry, ma'am, but I did knock," she said nervously.

"That's all right. As you can see, I was preoccupied."

"I'll get on with my work, if that's ok?" she questioned.

I watch her as she goes around straightening the room. I reluctantly rise from my friend and don a thin see-through robe. She sneaks glances at me as she cleans. I trail her to the bathroom as she comes across my stash. A two-headed dildo is hanging from the bag. I look at her name tag. "Lakecia," I said boldly, "have you ever been fucked by a woman with a strap on dildo?"

"No I haven't. she said "I've never been with a woman, but it might be fun though." That's the right answer honey.

"Lakecia, would you let me to fuck you with this right now?" I am dangling the dildo in one hand. Please say yes, darling.

"Ok," Lakecia said. She was remembering the sight of this woman sensuously fucking the coffee table. She was hot. Letting her fuck me would certainly break up an otherwise dull morning, she thought.

"Go into the bedroom and take off your clothes." She looks to be 23 or 24, probably working her way through college. She certainly is a beautiful black girl. I excitedly remove my robe and strap on the toy.

Fully erect, nipples and cock, I walk into the bedroom armed and ready for her pussy. Seven inches of dick is lodged firmly in my own pussy. She is standing in the middle of the room, nude and waiting for me to fuck her. I walk over to her, take head between my hands, and jam my tongue in her mouth.

"Mmmm," she mummers. I dip to let the dick slide below her pussy. She instinctively moves back and forth on it as I squeeze her ass cheeks. We were heating up nicely as she gyrates and sucks on my tongue.

"Do you think you can take all of me, Lakecia?" I finger her and push two fingers in her wet pussy.

She lustily looks me in the eye. "Try me, please."

I push her back onto the bed, then move her to the center. Her legs spread to reveal her dark pink treasures already moist for me. I would drink her nectar much, much later. I poise above her. "Are you ready to be dicked, sweetheart? I'll make it real good for you. I'll make you cum over and over."

She had caught the fire. "Oh, please, yes, please," she moaned.

I dive into her pussy in one fell swoop. The sudden contact lifts her ass from the bed up to me. "Oh, baby, baby, fuck it, baby," I scream as I take her to the hilt, our pussies touching. I fuck her sweet pussy in and out and in and out endlessly. We are both sweating and moaning as we strain toward climax.

"Mmmm, so good, so gooood, so good," she chants. She has me on fire as I drive my dick harder and harder into her. I lean into her to suck her tongue and rub her clit and I fuck her hard and close. Her motions push my half of the tool deeper into my pussy. I feel her tense beneath me.

"I'm cumming, I'm cumming," she screams. I take my dick even deeper as she pushes up to me. She digs her nails into my ass as she pushes up and screws me. I lose it then. I cum on her sweet meat violently as she spasms endlessly on my dick.

After a while, we came back to the planet. "I'm not finished with you yet, Lakecia," I said, my dick still pressing into in her. I licked her face like a puppy, then kissed her deeply.

"Okay," she breathes excitedly.

I slide from her warmth to position her for her next dicking session. "Get on your hands and knees at the end of the bed, Lakecia." I stand behind her. "Have you ever had it in the ass, darling?"

"No, but I'm so hot now, I'll try anything." Right answer again!

I part her coffee with cream-colored cheeks and lean down to run my tongue over her tight little asshole. She squirms beneath my mouth. I wet her good, then dip my dick in her still wet pussy to lube it.. I proceed to take the ass offered up to me as I slide into Lakecia slowly. Virgin ass! I was getting some virgin ass. I shudder as I gently push home, initiating her.

I drive my dick in and out of that tight ass as she moves back to capture more. Her rotating ass pushes her dick deep into my pussy. This sweet virgin ass is fucking me so well. I watch myself in the mirror as I gloriously fuck her just like a man.

After a while, "Miss, I must be getting back to my post." she said nervously, but still pumping me.

Alarmed, I immediately pick up the phone and dial the desk, still pumping as madly into her as she is in me. There was no way--no way I could pull out now and let her go. I was consumed with the girl on the end of my dick whose virgin ass was fucking me so well.

"Hi. This is room 707. Your maid,(pump, pump)Lakecia, is cleaning my room, but I need her(pump, pump) a little longer(pump, pump, pump) to help me. Is that ok? Thanks." I am still pumping her ass as I let the phone fall from my hand.

"It's taken care of, darling. They let me have you." She just pushes back on me hard and screws her little ass into me in thanks. I jam her ass once again to the very hilt, then reach under to rub her clit. I am locked in her ass and locked onto her back. I am rubbing and humping, rubbing and humping until we both scream out our climaxes.

She is laying flat, face down on the bed, unable to sustain the all-fours position after cumming. I am sprawled across her back sucking her shoulders and fondling her breasts. I let Lakecia slowly come down from her orgasms by softly talking to her, screwing her gently before I pull out. She dresses quickly and heads for the door.

"Wait," I said. I walk to her in the thin robe with my dick peeking through. Fifty dollars for tips is in the stand beside the door. I ease the money in her pocket. I grab her ass and drive her clothed crotch onto my protruding dick. I whisper in her mouth, "You are the best fuck I've ever had, man or woman. Come back when your shift ends. I'll be waiting for you, just like this."

"God, yes," she said slipping out the door.

I turn dreamily and think of Lakecia's sweet young pussy in my mouth, her juices on my tongue. I missed her already. In the meantime, I unstap and dislodge my dick. The coffee table looms in front of me. I ease my pussy down slowly and take up where I left off before I dicked Lakecia.

Story 11

My only daughter was getting married in just three hours. My husband and I are delighted that she chose to marry at home in a small but dignified ceremony. My bath behind me, my husband and daughter sneaking naps, I came downstairs in only a dressing gown to survey the completed preparations. Everything looked beautiful and in order.

I thought I heard a sound in our walk-in pantry just off the kitchen and went to investigate.

The young caterer that we hired was putting away a few of the supplies she would need later when serving. When I say young, I mean 27 years old and running her own business. I'm a firm believer of supporting small businesses operated by women. I,myself, was one of them. This young woman, on top of being well-spoken of by clients, was stunningly beautiful. She had milk white skin, thick, curly red-orange curls to her shoulders, and naturally full red lips. She was wearing the uniform of her staff-black tuxedo pants with suspenders, and snow white long-sleeved shirt. In that man's attire, it was still easy to make out her womanly curves.

"I heard a noise," I said as I approached her.

"I'm sorry, Mrs. St. John. I thought you went upstairs." She smiled.

"I'm just down for a last look around before I start dressing. Everything is beautiful, by the way.

"I'm all done for the moment, ma'am. Are you okay? You look a little tense. I give great messages. Sit down here," she said pulling out a chair.

"Well...

"It's okay, Mrs. St. John. I'm very good at this. I'll have you purring in no time," she said easing me down.

She stood behind rubbing the tension from my shoulders and neck. It felt wonderful. My head dropped back touching her belt. She kept rubbing until I realized her hands had slipped into my robe and were messaging my breasts.

"Shhh," she said quietly. "I'm very good at this, too. By the way, I saw your daughter this morning. She is gorgeous. She is so much like you, the two of you could be sisters," she crooned as she rubbed my globes and squeezed my nipples.

My pussy was beginning to get a little juicy as I realized what this could lead to. Did I really want it?

"How are you feeling, Mrs. St. John? Better? Are you becoming excited? Do you like what I'm doing? I can do much more. Would you like me to?

"Well, Laurel, I am a little turned on, but I've never...you know. And time is important here. You'll have to be good and quick."

She walked from the back of my chair and got down on her knees before me. Taking my head and pulling it forward to her, she kissed me like I had never been kissed in my entire life. There was erect tongue everywhere, filling my mouth, pushing for more space, lips pulling and releasing lips, teeth bumping, saliva dripping. She pulled the sash and parted my gown. She sucked each of my breasts as she spread my legs. I was wet, hot and ready when her lips found me.

Laurel sucked on my clit until I released. She was definitely good at this. She then expertly fucked my pussy with her tongue. I muffled a scream with one fist while holding on to her hair with the other. My tension was further relieved with the two orgasms.

The wedding ceremony went off beautifully. My pussy tingled as I watched Laurel as she served and I mingled among my guests. I was chatting with my brother and his wife when she came up behind me and whispered in my ear.

"I need you in the pantry ma'am. Now, please. " I excused my self and followed her to see what the problem was.

She eased the door shut, put her hand under my dress, inside my pantyhose and cupped my pussy. I was on fire with her touch.

"You are so beautiful out there. I'm so hungry again, Mrs. St. John," she said directly into my eyes. "I need your pussy in my mouth right now."

I wanted it as much as she did. I pulled my dress up as she lowered my pantyhose. The doorknob pressed in my back as Laurel took my pussy again. I simply loved the sight of that red hair between my legs. Cumming again was very easy and very exquisite. Laurel sucked me until she was sated, cleaning the juice from me.

She eased by hose back up, kissing on the journey up. I straightened my dress as I watched her shake out her curls and lick her lips. Not wanting to disturb the lipstick of the mother of the bride, Laurel pulled the top of my dress to one side, took a breast from by push-up bra and feasted on it.

I went back to our guests with a well-eaten pussy, a throbbing breast and a great big smile. I will definitely use this girl for my next social function.

"If you want do anything worthwhile today, 'do it' with a woman."

Story 12

Jenny decided to go hiking through a mountain about half an hour from her house. Jenny was walking through along a mountain trail, wearing a white t-shirt over a bikini top and a pair of daisy dukes over a bikini bottom. Jenny is a 40D-30-34, beautiful face surrounded by long blonde hair.

Jenny was getting urges to starting taking off clothes, and that is what she did. She started with her t-shirt, then her shorts...dropped them off in a ditch and buried them with sticks and leave so she would be able to find them later... by this point, she could hardly stop herself from stripping... her pussy was getting wet, her nipples hardened... she wanted to wait until she reached the riverbank before she finished taking off her clothes, so she slid her hand into her bikini bottom in order to tease her clit and sooth her urges to finger herself.

She heard voices in the distance, and she thought that she would give them a treat by walking by in her bikini. She had never been so underdressed in such a secluded area... fear began to run through her head, she started to step back to go the opposite direction when two men walked out from behind the trees... One man in a blue t-shirt, the other in a black t-shirt. They were just as surprised to see a woman in a bikini and she was to see them.

Jenny was frozen by the men's staring eyes... the man in the blue shirt commented on the size of her breasts to the man in the black shirt, then the man in the black shirt said, "She's a slut dressed like that out here." to the man in the blue shirt.

They both started to walk toward Jenny, she turned around and ran. The two men made no attempt to run after her, but she didn't realize it.

She continued to run through some trees, her large breasts bouncing, her bikini top becoming loose until it fell off of her.

By the time she managed to glance back and notice that there was no one chasing her, she had totally lost her breath, and dropped to the ground in exhaustion. She had hoped to meet some women to treat... she feared men.

After about five minutes of rest, she heard other voices, and was sure that they were female voices, so she slid off her bikini bottom, threw it aside, out of her sight. She placed one hand upon her breasts and the other between her thighs, and pretended to be sleeping, waiting for the women to arrive. The conversation between the women got louder, and Jenny knew that the women were getting closer, her pussy was getting wetter, she had to force herself to stay out of her clit in order to continue to pretend to be asleep.

Two women appeared, and Jenny opened her eyes just to take a peek at them, without them knowing. One girl was taller and thinner, a 36C or so, red hair, she was wearing hiking shorts and a button down shirt. The other women was slightly shorter and a little heavier, her breasts were much larger, probably 44DD.

Jenny continued to pretend to sleep, the two women were commenting on her, but Jenny couldn't make out their conversation until she heard, "I want that pussy... if she is sleeping naked here, she wants me to take it" in a few seconds Jenny felt hands on her thighs, opening her legs, a tongue soon met her clit.

Jenny made no reaction except her moans of pleasure, she was trying to give the girls total control. One of the women grabs Jenny's tits with both hands, fondling them roughly... Jenny could hear clothing sliding off their bodies and hitting the ground, she realized that they were both naked when one woman sat on her face, expecting Jenny to eat her... that's is what she did... The three women continued, eating each other, touching each other, until it became dark and cold, the two women got up and got dressed, and left, Jenny never spoke a word to them, and she hardly even saw the two women she had just had sex with, and that is the way she wanted it... Jenny laid there naked for a while, until she fingered herself roughly, remembering the experience she had just had.

All Rights Reserved. No part of this publication may be reproduced in any form or by any means, including scanning, photocopying, or otherwise without prior written permission of the copyright holder. Copyright © 2020

This book is entirely a work of fiction. The names, characters and incidents portrayed in it are the work of the author's imagination. Any resemblance to actual persons, living or dead, events or localities is entirely coincidental.

Story 01

Megan sat across from her sister, seething with anger but controlling her emotions to not add to the crying hysterics. "Oh Megan! How could he? I thought he loved me!" Crystal sobbed. "I know it took a while for us to have a baby. But now that I am pregnant he decides to fool around?! What am I going to do?"

"Okay calm down Sis. You know that's not good for the baby. First of all, are you sure that Jared is cheating on you?" Megan asked. "It may just be the hormones brought on by your pregnancy."

"At first I thought it was just my over active imagination but when I started seeing how he would act whenever he would get texts or calls from her I knew for sure. I mean if you were not hiding anything you wouldn't be acting antsy."

"Alright. Do we know who she is? Where does she work or live?"

"All I got was a name when I took a peek at his cellphone when he was asleep. Her name is Valerie Summers. Wait... What are we planning to do? I see that glint in your eye and that means you have something planned."

"We are not doing anything. You will just be calm and just enjoy your being pregnant. You will act normal with your husband and be the loving wife that you are. Just leave everything to me."

"Aren't you even going to tell me what it is you plan to do?"

"Well it's as simple as finding her, meeting her, wooing her then bedding her to slap Jared's face with it."

"What?! How do you even know she will fall for you?" Her sister asked.

"I have my ways. I'm not called 'The Heartbreaker' for nothing. Now I have to go. See you soon Sis." Kissing her on the forehead as she went.

Megan was still furious hours after leaving her sister's house as she was on her way to meet her friends at the local bar they frequented every weekend. 'Ugh! So like a man to promise you the moon and the stars and when they have you they throw you away like an old shirt.' She thought angrily. 'And what about the bitch? Doesn't she know she is destroying a family?' She pressed on the gas pedal as she increased her speed, channeling her fury to the car.

"Hey Megan! Over here!" Beth waved her over to the corner of the room. "Wow! Do you look gorgeous and dangerous tonight girlfriend! What's gotten your goat?"

"I'm so pissed that I am planning retribution!" she answered as she sat and flipped her auburn hair.

"Ooh! And to whom are we exacting revenge on?"

"What I am about to tell you is strictly confidential and does not leave the two of us. Got It! I don't want the others knowing or too much cooks will spoil the broth."

"Hey! I'm your wingman.... Wingwoman.... Or is it wingperson?"

"Whatever! Anyway, my sister believes that her husband is cheating on her. She doesn't have any other information about the other woman but her name. I will find this Valerie Summers meet her, get to know her, woo her, then bed her and slap it on my brother-in-law's face to show him what a two bit whore she really is."

"Hokee! Remind me never to get on your bad side. I'd hate to be on the receiving end of your wrath. So how do we go about locating this Valerie Summers bitch?"

"I don't know yet. Will think about it first thing tomorrow morning." She said as they saw their friends, Tina, Rachel, and Naomi by the doorway and waved them to their table.

"I'm glad you were able to get us a table or we would end up just standing around." Tina shouted over the booming music. "Oh! By the way, I brought with me a new friend from work. This is Valerie Summers. Valerie, meet Beth and Megan."

As Megan turned towards the woman standing beside Tina, she was simply struck by the beauty standing before her. The woman was about the same height her with shoulder-length curly dark hair and mesmerizing brown eyes. It had to take Beth to nudge her for her to respond to the introduction. "Oh! Ummm....Hi Valerie! I'm Megan. Nice to meet you." And before Valerie could respond, Beth stands up from her chair and offers it to her to sit beside Megan. "Here. You could take my seat. I have to talk to Tina about our barbeque for next weekend."

"I'm glad to finally meet you Megan. Tina has been talking about you guys that I feel that I already know you."

"Well I hope that what you have heard are all good things about us?"

"Tina told me all of your antics since when you guys were in college until now. I can't believe that you guys are still close even after all this time." Valerie smiled, flashing her dimples.

'Oh my God! It's no wonder Jared fell for her. She is so beautiful.' Megan thought as she looked at the deep blue of her eyes and the curly brunette hair. 'I just want to make her look at me like that.' She then angrily scolded herself to stick to the plan.

"Well it is rare to find people who are loyal these days." Megan said somewhat sarcastically, which made the brunette give her a concerned look.

"Are you okay? You sounded a little angry there for a moment." Valerie asked Megan, amazed at just how gorgeous this dark-haired woman was. Everything about Valerie seemed so perfect from her long black wavy hair to her emerald green eyes.

"Umm... Yes I am. Sorry just had a bad memory come back to haunt me." Smiling sheepishly. "So how long have you been working with Tina?"

"I just started two months ago when I moved here with my son from Chicago." The brunette said sadly.

"Hey! You okay there? You looked like a bad memory came back to haunt you." Megan touched her hand softly, rubbing her fingers on top of it. Two things happened when she did this. Valerie gave a slight shudder, and Megan felt a slight jolt to her loins. 'Oh great! If touching her hand gives me this feeling what happens when I get to touch her whole body?!' She asked herself.

Valerie visibly shakes her head. "I'm okay. Just have both good and bad memories. Let's not talk about that. Let's just have fun tonight." She can't believe she reacted that way from a simple touch.

"So you have a son. Are you married?" She asked the brunette.

"Umm...No I'm a single mother. My son is 2 years old. He could be trying at times but he's my life."

The girls had fun that night talking, drinking, and dancing. Valerie had to leave around ten p.m. since she still had to relieve the babysitter. They invited her to their barbecue next weekend and any other outing the group may have. This suited Megan perfectly since it will give her all the time to pursue her plans. But she started asking herself if she was pursuing her plans or Chloe herself.

"Well aren't you the cat that ate the canary!" Beth elbowed Megan as she watched Valerie leave the bar. While Tina, Rachel, and Naomi were dancing with some guys.

"What do you mean?" Megan growled, rubbing the spot where Beth elbowed her.

"Well, the Gods must be smiling down at you cuz we were just talking about you know who and voila she is brought to you literally on a platter. Although, I must say she doesn't look to me like the mistress type. She seems to be pretty down to earth and nice."

"We can't decide with just one night of meeting her if she is really nice and not the vamp. With that face and body?"

"I don't know Megan, you seem to be pretty taken with her. I hope you don't fall on your face with this one. I got really good vibes with Valerie." She warned.

"We'll see..." With all her bravado, Megan can't help but feel warring emotions about Valerie.

Megan taps her fingers on the table as she waits for Tina to pick up her direct line at the office.

"Tina Sanders speaking. How may I help you?"

"Hey T! It's Megan. I was wondering if I could get from you Valerie's number?"

"Hey Meg! Ooh! I knew there was something brewing between the two of you last weekend! You do know that she was asking about you after that night." Tina said gleefully.

"Huh? What do you mean asking about me? Like what kind of questions?" She asked warily.

"Oh you know....things like.... If you were single, if you were into guys, girls or both, what is your type....those kinds of questions." She giggled.

"Uh huh.... And what did you say?"

"Well, I said that yes you were single & into girls totally. And as for your type I really wouldn't know since you date various types of the female species."

"Wait.... So you're telling me she is into me? Doesn't she have a son? So that makes her bi?"

"Okay Megan, promise me you will not breathe a word of this to anyone alright?"

"Alright I promise. What is it?"

"Valerie told me in confidence that she was raped three years ago." Megan gasped out loud. "She doesn't want her son to know that he was a product of such violence. She told him his father died in a car accident."

"Oh my God!" Megan closed her eyes, rubbing her forehead. Somehow thinking that she can't push thru with what she planned. 'I don't think I'm that heartless.' She thought to herself. 'Maybe if I just befriend her and then try to talk to her about Jared. Who am I kidding? I want to be more than just her friend.' Thoughts were swirling in her head.

"With regards to her orientation, I wouldn't know but she seemed pretty interested in you. So that says something right? Megan just..."

"What?" Still deciding a better way of approaching Valerie.

"Just be gentle with her she seems fragile... to me that is." Tina gently advised her friend. "So you still want her number?"

"Yes please."

Megan was staring at nothing in particular as she waited for the phone to be picked up.

"This is Valerie Summers. How may I help you?"

"Umm... Hi Valerie. This Megan... friend of Tina.... We met last weekend. Remember me?"

"Oh hi Megan! Of course I remember you. What's up? You looking for Tina?"

"No... I mean... No I'm not looking for Tina. I called to ask if maybe you are okay to have dinner with me."

"I would love to have dinner with you. When?"

"Oh...Ummm... When would be a good day for you?"

"Well... let's see...are you okay coming over to my place tomorrow night for dinner with my son Jacob? I am making his favorite Lasagna. I guarantee it will make you forget your name." She teased.

"I'm cool with that....What time should I come over? Oh! And what do you want me to bring?" Liking the sound of the happy voice of the brunette over the phone.

"How about red wine? Jacob has dinner early so you could come over around six."

"Red wine it is. See you tomorrow at six then."

"Can't wait. Bye Megan."

"Me too. Bye Valerie." She can't seem to stop smiling long after the phone conversation ended. "Maybe Beth is right I might just end up falling on my face here." She muttered to herself.

At ten to six, Megan was standing in front of the door of Valerie's house. She was checking herself to see if her outfit, which consisted of dark bootleg jeans, low heeled shoes, and an emerald green buttoned downblouse, was fine. 'Why do I feel so nervous like it's my first date ever.' She asked herself. Visibly shaking her head, she took a deep breath and rang the bell.

"Mommy! Mommy! Open door!" Megan heard an exuberant child's voice from inside.

The door opens to Valerie, looking back at her son, talking to him. "Alright sport! Take it easy or you might just scare the guest away with your enthusiasm." She turns to Megan, and they both gave a slight gasp at seeing each other. Valerie was wearing a summer dress that clung in all the right places.

"Umm... Hi... Uh ... you look great!" Megan complimented, passing the bottle of red wine to her host.

"You too! I love the way the blouse brings out the color of your eyes." Valerie shyly said. "Please come in to our humble abode."

as Megan enters, she sees a small boy standing by the sofa's side looking at her curiously. "Oh! And this dashing young man is my son Jacob. Could you say 'Hi' to our guest, Jacob?" Valerie asked the boy as he slowly approaches and stands in front of Megan.

"Hello there Jacob. My name is Megan." She kneels to keep at eye level with the child.

Jacob reaches out to touch Megan in the face. "Pwetty Megan!" Giving her a big dimpled smile so much like his mom that she fell in love with the boy.

"Yes she is pretty." the voice behind her whispers.

"So who wants Lasagna?" Valrie asked, hoping Megan did not hear her whispered words.

"Me! Me! Mon pwetty Megan! Eat!" Her hand grabbed and tugged towards the small round dining table. Jacob was sitting in between the two adults smiling at his excitement then at each other as they ate their dinner.

After dinner, Valerie took the boy to his room to prepare him for bed while Megan sat on the sofa, drinking the wine. "He asleep?" she asked as Valerie sat beside her taking her drink from the table then faced her with her right arm on top of the back of the sofa.

"Yes he had a full day." she said as she took a sip from her drink, looking at her guest from the rim of her glass.

"You have an adorable son. He looks so much like you."

"Why thank you. I'll take that both as a compliment."

"You know you're right you do make a mean Lasagna. I'm glad that you invited me over for dinner." putting the side of her head at the back of the sofa, making a strand of hair fall forward.

"Well I'm glad you called me to have dinner." Valerie reached over and moved the fallen strand of hair behind Megan's ear, making her slightly gasp. Then as if realizing what she just did, she pulls back her hand.

"Umm....I don't know how to go about this... but you do know that I'm totally into girls right?" She asked Valerie directly.

"Uh yeah.... I asked Tina about you after last weekend. I hope you don't mind?"

"No I don't mind. I just... What about you? Are you into girls as well or are you bi since you have a child?"

"I've never been bi...I'm totally into girls as well. As for Jacob, I don't really announce this but I was raped three years ago..." She halted tears forming in her eyes, recalling the horrific event.

Seeing this, Megan pulls her in for a hug hoping to alleviate the pain seen in the brunette's eyes. "Hey c'mere! It's okay. I'm sorry that had to happen to you." Rubbing Valerie's back with her right hand while cradling her head with her left. Megan, while holding the brunette close, decides she simply could not go thru with her original plan and inflict any more pain to the person she was slowly falling for.

After a few minutes, Valerie reluctantly pulls away, not wanting to lose the feeling of those arms around her. "I'm sorry about that. I thought I was over it." She wipes at her eyes.

"It's okay. It gave me the excuse to hold you in my arms." She teased as she wipes the wetness from Valerie's cheeks. She was drowning in those soulful brown eyes.

"It's getting late. I think I should go." Megan said as she slowly stands up. Valerie stands as well and walks her to the door. As they neared the door, Megan turns and asks. " Ummm.... Since you fed me dinner tonight would it be alright if I bring over dinner here on Friday same time? If you don't have any other plans that is."

"Yes.... I mean.... Yes it would be alright." She says with a big smile on her face.

"It's a date then!" Megan beamed as she turns around and heads toward her car.

Over the next two months, they fell into a comfortable pattern of having family dinner at Valerie's house two to three times a week and picnics on the weekends. Jacob adored Megan and relished the attention he was getting from both women. If Megan were not around, he would always look for her, and when she is, he would always make sure to be near both women. It was a Saturday late afternoon, and Tina came over with her son Matthew to pick up Jacob to go to the zoo and sleepover their house. Valerie and Megan were sitting on the couch when Jacob launched in between them, hugging them both before he left.

"Bye Mommy! See you tomowow." As he kissed Valerie on the lips. "Bye Baby! Be good for Auntie Tina."

Turning to Megan and kissing her on the lips as well. "Bye Mommy Megan! See you tomowow." All three adults gasped. "Umm... Bye Sport! Missing you already." Megan softly responded, not knowing how Valerie will take what her son just said.

"Well as they say out of the mouth of babes. At least he knows what he wants and says so. Which is more than I can say for some people I know." Tina was addressing the two women on the couch. "Well c'mon kiddos let's hit the road!" As she and the two boys left.

"Umm... I'm sorry about that... Will talk to Jacob tomorrow when he gets back." Valerie said, looking anywhere, but Megan.

Grabbing hold of Valerie's hand and waiting for her to look at her. "Hey! It's okay really.... Unless you are not comfortable with it I completely understand."

Looking down at their hands. "It's not that.... It's just that..."

"What? What is it?" Tightening her hold on the brunette's hand.

Lifting her eyes. "What is happening to us?..... I mean.... What are we?"

"What do you want us to be?" Megan asked to hope that Valerie wants the same thing she does.

Linking their fingers together, she continues to look at Megan and taking a deep breath. "I want for us to be more. I want so much for us to be a couple." Hoping she is not setting herself up for heartache if the dark-haired girl does not want the same thing. She holds her breath while waiting for a response.

Megan lifts her hand and gently rubs the back of it on Valerie's face. "I want that too. I've been wanting it since the time you asked me to have dinner here and I held you for the first time." She huskily said as she pulled the brunette towards her for a hug. Burying her face in her neck, lips slightly touching the skin, breathing her in. "You smell so good."

"You feel so good. I don't think I want to let go." She sighed, closing her eyes.

After a few minutes, Megan pulls her face from Valerie's neck and kisses her forehead. "Do you want to go out for dinner and a movie?"

"No. I'd rather have we have dinner and watch a DVD here. Is that okay?"

"More than okay." She smiled.

After a simple dinner, they went back to the living room. Megan was lying on her side facing the tv while Valerie was setting up the DVD player. As the movie started, Valerie walked to the couch, and Megan was lifting herself to make room when the brunette stops her. "No don't please stay where you are."

"What about you? Where will you be?" And as soon as she asked, Valerie lies down in the couch, pushing Megan to the back, grabbing her right arm and pulling it down across her torso to rest just below her breast with her hand on top of the dark-haired girl.

"Here with you of course. Where else will I be?" She teased, giving that dimpled smile.

"I wouldn't have it any other way." Megan softly said as she pulled her closer, kissing her at the back of her neck, feeling Valerie shudder.

The last thing Megan remembers is putting her head in between the shoulders of Valerie while they watched the movie as she fell asleep. She slowly opens her eyes, sees Valerie facing her, and watches her with the most loving and serene look that her breath hitches.

"Hey." She whispered.

"Hey back." Whispered Valerie tracing Megan's face with her fingers.

"Sorry I fell asleep on you. What time is it?" Loving the feel of the brunette's fingers on her face.

"Just a little after ten."

"It's getting late I think I should go." She said reluctantly, not wanting to leave.

"Did you... Umm... Do you want to stay the night?" Valerie hesitantly asked.

"I would love to. But are you sure? You once said that you haven't had anyone touch you that way since you know..."

"I'm sure. I... I want you to be my first.... To take away the ugliness and give me back that loving feeling." She said, emotionally tears glistening in her eyes.

Megan brings her head closer as she tentatively kisses the brunette tracing her lips with the tip of her tongue. Their kisses became more passionate with tounges dueling like they couldn't get enough of each other. Megan breaks off the kiss breathing deeply.

"What's wrong?" Valerie asked worriedly.

"nothing's wrong honey. I just want to take this to the bedroom and do it right for your first time. C'mon." she stands up, holding out her hand for Valerie to take and lead her to the bedroom.

They stood at the side of the bed, slowly removing their clothes, and as they both looked at their nakedness, Megan was the first to say it. "You are so beautiful." She said adoringly. "So do you." Valerie responded shyly. They moved to the center of the bed with Megan on top, positioning herself in between Valerie's legs. They both sighed as their naked bodies touched for the first time aligned from breast to their cunts. Megan slowly rubs her cunt to Valerie's loving the abrasive feel of their pubic hairs together as she kisses her from the lips, neck, and to her full breasts. She takes one breast, thoroughly sucking it in her mouth as her tongue rolls around the turgid nipple and does the same thing to the other. Valerie lifts her chest towards her mouth, groaning.

"Oh God! That feels so good baby!" Megan releases the breast and tenderly kisses her way down to her stomach, licking the navel then lower as she spreads Valerie's legs and gazes for the first time at her lover's cunt. "My God Valerie! You are so so beautiful." She reverently touches the folds as she looks up to the brunette, who bucks upward at the touch. As their eyes meet, she slowly, without breaking eye contact, goes down, makes love with Valerie's pussy, licks and sucking her folds and clit.

"Oh!...God!..... Uugghh..... That's it right there baby! Don't.... Don't stop!" Grabbing Megan's head, pushing it into her cunt as she humped on her face. Megan pushes her tongue into Valerie, making it go around and licking the warm wet walls. "Yes! Yes! Oh God! I'm cumming! Aaauugghh!" Her whole body lay spent and slightly twitching from the aftermath of her orgasm.

Megan pushes her way back up to Valerie, kissing her, making her taste her juice from her lips. "Are you okay baby?" She asked the brunette as she lovingly brushes her hair away from her face and neck. Words could not describe what Chloe was feeling, so she decided to show her lover how okay she was. She pushed her back to the bed and moved on top of her as she made the sweetest love to Megan, making her moan and, at one point, scream. They continued well into the night ending with both of them facing each other on their sides hands inside the other's cunts, making themselves cum together. They fell asleep, spooning each other with Megan behind Valerie, her face buried in her curly hair.

Waking up slowly, Megan stretches feeling for Valerie's body, but she's not there. She opens her eyes to look around the room, and that's when she heard voices coming from the living room. Wondering who the visitor was, she stood up to put on her clothes last night and ventures out. As she enters the living room, she sees Jared, Crystal, and Valerie, and picking up on the tension in the room, somehow knew that something was wrong.

"My God Megan! You really did it?!? You couldn't even talk to me first before doing anything so stupid?! Valerie is my half sister! We have the same father! She only found out about me after her mom died and she got in contact with me four months ago. I asked her to come over here so that we could get to know each other since we are the only ones left in our family! Then I find out from Crystal what she thought and what you planned to do! Are you both crazy?!?" Jared snarled.

"Megan I'm so sorry...I..." Crystal started with tears rolling down her face.

But Megan wasn't hearing or seeing her sister and brother-in-law. All she could see was Valerie looking at her with so much pain and hurt in her beautiful face. "You thought that of me?" There wasn't even a thread of anger in her voice just hurt so much hurt. "You thought I was some... Some whore you had to teach a lesson so you could throw it at your brother-in-law's face?" Her pale face arms wrapped around her middle to somehow ward off any more pain.

"Wait! Let me explain Valerie. Please!" Fear and panic in her voice as she approaches Valerie.

Jared grabs Crystal's hand as they head off towards the door. "Look, it's best if we leave you two alone to talk things out. Crystal and I need to do the same thing."

As Megan tries to reach out to touch Valerie, she takes a step back. Megan closes her eyes at the pain of rejection. 'How could everything so right go so wrong so fast? I should have just talked to Valerie before all this.' She thought to herself.

Valerie's head was bent down, her eyes staring blankly at the floor. "Three years ago I was raped by someone I thought was my friend. He admitted to liking me and wanting more but I told him I was into girls. Guess he didn't like that cuz he decided to teach me a lesson and did what he did. His parting shot as he left me was that I should thank him for teaching me how it is to be with a man." her voice devoid of any emotion. "Then you come along thinking I'm some home wrecker bitch that needs to be taught a lesson. God! What is it with me?"

"Valerie please... Let's talk about this." Megan begged.

"What for? You got what you set out to do. You taught me a lesson not to trust anyone." Valerie walks to her door and opens it. "Please leave Megan. I have nothing else to say to you." Still not looking at Megan.

Fighting back the tears, Megan walks out the clicking of the door behind her, a finality. As she got in her car, she let out a broken sob and cried her heart out on the steering wheel.

It's been more than a month, and things have not worked out with Megan and Valerie. Not for lack of trying on her part, she had tried calling and leaving messages but to no avail. She was happy though that her sister and brother-in-law have worked things out with their relationship, especially with the birth of her nephew, but can't help but feel a little jealous that she can't live with her and Valerie. The phone rings, bringing her out from her musings.

"Hello."

"Hey sis! Could I ask you a huge favor?"

"What is it Crystal?"

"Could I borrow your griller for tonight? We're having barbecue at our place and your welcome to join us. Jared's monstrosity of a griller is not working and we already have the food set up."

"Alright be there in a few minutes." she sighs, deciding to stop her pity party and enjoy a night with the family.

"Great! Thanks! Will tell Jared to set up another plate. See you in a few."

As Megan parks across her sister's house, she gasps as she sees the car of Valerie parked in front. 'I'm going to kill Crystal!' She thought as she realizes what her sister is trying to do. She shakes her head and takes a deep breath. 'Okay Megan, just go ring the doorbell give the griller and just go back home.' Telling herself as she got out of the car.

"Jared honey could you get the door?" Crystal shouts from inside the house as Megan rang the doorbell.

"Hey Megan! So sorry about the last minute borrowing. Come on in. Crystal is out in the backyard. Here let me help you with that." Jared relieves Megan of the griller.

"Umm... No Jared...I'm sorry but I won't be joining you and I think you know why. Just tell Crystal to give back the griller whenever. I don't really get to use it."

"Megan, please don't be mad at your sister. She feels that she is to be blamed with what happened to you and Valerie. She just wants to fix it."

"Crystal wants to fix things but Valerie doesn't. That was made very clear to me with all my unanswered phone calls and messages for the past month. Let's just leave it at that, Jared." Tears were forming in her eyes. "Look I have to go. Give Crystal and my God child a kiss for me will you."

"Alright Megan," Sighed Jared.

As Megan crosses the street to her car, she hears Jacob's excited voice calling out. "Mommy Megan! Mommy Megan!" Jacob shouted out.

"Jacob! No!" Jared screams. Megan turning around, sees Jacob running towards her and a car coming from the right going fast on a curve. Instinctively she runs towards the boy and pushes him out of the way of the oncoming vehicle, and then total blackness envelops her.

Megan wakes up in a hospital bed with Crystal holding her uninjured hand while crying and Jared standing by the window. "What... What happened?" She asked hoarsely.

"Jared! She's awake!" Crystal calls out to her husband. "Oh honey! You had us so scared!" Softly brushing back her sister's hair, careful not to touch the bruise on her temple.

"Hi Megan. You got hit by the car when you pushed Jacob out of the way. I swear I thought I was gonna have a heart attack when I saw it happen." Jared still visibly shaken. "The doctor said you were very lucky. You only suffered a broken arm and leg. It could have been worse given the impact."

"What about Jacob? How is he?" Megan asked.

"He is another room being tended to for the bruising he got on his forehead. Doctor says he'll be fine." Crystal responded.

Jared gently touches Megan's shoulder. "Look Megan, I know we haven't really talked about this you and I.... But I wanted to say that I'm really sorry for what happened between you and my sister. Yes, in the beginning I was angry at you for hurting her but seeing the way you have been these past month makes me realize that your hurting as well. I wish I could make things right for both of you since it is so obvious that you love each other."

Tears fall from Megan's eyes. "Oh Jared! I love her so much! It may have started as a stupid plan, but from the very first time I met her and held her in my arms I had already decided I wasn't gonna push thru with it.... I just couldn't do it. God! I am so stupid and it's no ones fault but my own.... I met the most beautiful person and I lost her!" She sobbed loudly.

"Hey! Hey! C'mon now sis." Crystal wiping at the tears on Megan's face. "You rest now alright.. Doctor says you could go home tomorrow. So we'll pick you up, bring you home, and I will take care of you while you get better. Obviously you won't be able to with both your arm and leg in a cast." Both Jared and Crystal were kissing her on the forehead goodbye. No one notices the door to the room that was slightly open, closed softly. When Jared and Crystal stepped out of the room, they were surprised to find Valerie standing by the door, tears running down her face.

"I need to talk to both of you. I need your help." Valerie said with determination on her face.

It was late in the afternoon when they arrived in her place from the hospital. Crystal helped her to bed and told her to get some sleep while running a few errands and coming back to prepare dinner for her.

"So anything special you want for dinner?" Crystal asked.

"I'm craving for lasagna." Megan responded with a small smile.

"Alright then! Lasagna it is! Now get some rest!" Crystal waves off.

When Megan awoke, her room was dark except for the light coming from her window. As she looked towards her door, she sees Jacob standing just outside, looking at her quietly.

"Mommy Megan you wake?" Jacob softly asked.

"Hey sport. Yes I am. Are you okay?" Megan asked as the boy came towards her bed, leaning his body on the mattress.

"Am okay. Am sowy I hoit you." The boy's chin trembled as tears started in his eyes.

And with Megan's good arm, lifted the boy to her and hugged him as they lay down on the bed. "Oh baby no! You didnt hurt me... Ssshhh... It's okay... I'm okay." She sniffed, loving the feel of the boy's warm body close to her as she rubbed his back, comforting him.

"Baby, I told you not to bother Mommy Megan she needs her rest." Valerie admonished the boy as she went to bed and sat on the side of it.

"Didnt wake her Mommy. She was wake. Wight Mommy Megan?" The boy asked, still hugging her tightly.

Still quite stunned with Valerie being there and calling her 'Mommy Megan' made her heart run wild. "Umm.. No he didn't wake me up. I was already awake when he came in." Trying to see Valerie's face in the semi-darkened room.

"Oh! Well am glad then cuz I wanted you to be resting before dinner. I made for us Lasagna. It will be ready in a few minutes or so."

"Umm...Valerie I dont know why you are here but I just want to let you know that..." Stopping in mid-sentence as Valerie places her finger on Megan's lips.

"You don't have to explain... I heard what you said to both Jared and Crystal at the hospital. Did you mean everything you said?" Valerie asked, hopefully, with eyes glistening with tears.

"Every single damn word! And I swear it on everything I hold dear!" Megan said with the conviction of tears in her eyes as well.

"God! I so want to hug you right now but I'm afraid I'll hurt you." Frustration in Valerie's voice.

"I'd rather feel the physical pain than the pain of not feeling you in my arms." Megan responded in equal frustration.

"Spoon Mommy! Like we do in my bed! Spoon Mommy Megan!" Jacob piped in. Both adults forgot the presence of the child for a moment.

"Out of the mouth of babes!" They both said in unison and laughed. Valerie joined them in the bed, spooning Megan from behind, holding her tight and buried her face in her neck. Megan gave a loud sigh as she shuddered to love the feel of Valerie's body behind her.

"God! I missed you so much Valerie! I love you with all my heart!" Megan cried out.

"I love you too Megan!"

"Me too! Me too! Wove my mommies!" Jacob sat up, looking at both women giving them his famous dimpled smile. Both women laughed out loud. "Mommy, I want baby boy!" The boy demanded.

"Ask Mommy Megan for your baby brother." Valerie told the child, surprising Megan.

"Are you serious?" Turning her head to look at the brunette as she asked.

"Do you want to?" the brunette asked, gently rubbing Megan's stomach.

"I would love to but only if you're with me." She responded.

"I wouldn't have it any other way." Valerie lovingly whispered as she brought her head closer and kissed Megan with all the love that she felt.

Story 02

Rachel stood outside the door of the apartment. Her right hand moved up and down the side of her jeans, wiping off her palm's wetness. Coming here, deciding to be with her would end up hurting another. 'But it's how I feel... What I want!' She thought to herself. Taking a deep breath and exhaling loudly, Rachel lifted her hand, unlocking the door to enter. A door that slowly opened to her new life.

A year ago.

'head hurts.... What are those noises?' Rachel's head felt like someone had poked a hot iron into her skull, making it hurt to open her eyes. She could hear sounds like a machine humming and a beeping noise that was close to her side. She tried to move her arm, but the searing pain brought on by her movement made her gasp out loud.

"Oh my God! She's awake! Call the Doctor!" A female voice shouted. Then she felt a hand brushing back her hair tenderly. "Rachel? Can you hear me? Can you open your eyes?" The same voice asked her.

As she slowly opened her eyes, Rachel saw an Asian woman in her 60's standing beside her bed. "Oh thank God! Taylor! She's awake! She's awake!" The woman started to cry. "We thought we'd lost you!"

Rachel tried to say something to console the woman but had difficulty finding her voice. As she cleared her throat, she saw another woman hesitantly approach the bed from the same side. This one was younger, probably in her mid 30's with brown curly hair, round brown eyes, and creamy white skin.

Clearing her throat again, Rachel tried to speak. "Who are you?" She asked both women who looked shocked at her question. "You called me Rachel. Is that my name? What happened to me?" She asked the older woman.

Before either woman could respond, the Doctor came in with a nurse in tow. "Well now! I see our patient has finally decided to join us! You gave your mom and your partner quite a scare there." He said, smiling at the women then asked Rachel: "How are you feeling?"

"Ummm... I don't remember anything. Who am I? Why am I here? Who are they?" She answered. "I'm sorry." She apologized as she saw the two women wince at her, not being able to recognize them.

"OK let me see if I can fill in the blanks: you are Rachel Reyes. You are here because you were a victim of an attempted robbery of a grocery store across the street from where you live. You were shot, but luckily for you, the bullet grazed your head -- the furrow was pretty deep, but no actual brain tissue was injured by the bullet. However, due to the impact, you had massive swelling in your brain. Initially, we could not be certain if there was a bleed in your brain, so for your own safety we induced a coma as you weren't responding to the usual meds. You have been in a coma for just over a month. It seems you have amnesia and we won't know if it is temporary or permanent until we complete a battery of tests." The Doctor responded in a kind voice. "Also because of the coma, you will most definitely need physical therapy before you walk again as your muscles have atrophied. However, with therapy and your determination we will have you mobile in no time. As for these two beautiful ladies, this is your Mom, Agnes and this is your partner, Taylor. Now that the introductions have been done, I will leave you ladies alone so you can talk." With that, the Doctor left the room.

Rachel looked at the two ladies again. Her mom was on the left side of the bed. "So... you're my mom?" Rachel asked, and her mom nodded. "I'm so sorry I don't remember you." Agnes just tenderly brushed back the hair from Rachel's face and said with a quivering voice: "It's alright. The important thing is that you are back with us and we will have you better in no time."

Looking at Taylor beside her mom, she asked, "So...you're my partner? How long have we been together?"

The other woman looked like she was in pain when the question was asked. Clearing her throat, Taylor responded: "Ummm... Close to ten years." Her eyes teared up as she said this.

"Hey...are you OK?" Rachel asked worriedly, seeing the expression on Taylor's face.

Agnes looked from her daughter to Taylor, smiled, and grabbed hold of each of their hands, bringing them together. The moment her hand touched that of Taylor's, Rachel felt an electric current go up to her arm and flood through her body. "She's OK. Aren't you, Taylor?" Agnes said, looking at Taylor and giving her a wink. "She was just really worried about you, dear." She let go of both their hands, leaving them still linked together.

Rachel, loving the feel of the skin on skin contact with Taylor, continued to hold on. She slowly started to rub her thumb across her partner's skin, feeling her shiver just a bit. "I'm so sorry I worried you."

Taylor half-smiled, her body was reacting to the touch of Rachel. 'God! It has really been a while since we've had any type of contact like this! I never thought I could actually miss such a simple touch.' She thought to herself. Realizing that she had yet to respond to Rachel's apology, she squeezed her hand to reassure her.

"It's alright...you couldn't have known what was to happen. Just don't do anymore ice-cream runs late at night." Taylor replied, trying to lighten the mood.

"Well, I most definitely won't be doing that considering I can't use my legs." Rachel replied with a smirk. 'It's funny that even though I don't remember these two women I feel a certain kinship to them.' She thought to herself.

"Now don't you be saying that! You have to be positive!" Agnes inserts. "The doctor said that with a little therapy and a whole lot of determination from you we can get you mobile!"

"We? Don't you mean me?" She asked.

"No. I mean exactly what I said and I did say we. As in, you, me and Taylor. Isn't that right, Taylor?" She turned to Taylor as she asked the question.

"Yes. Yes of course. I will be bringing you over to your sessions in the morning and if I have to go in for work then Mom here could take my place."

"Well that settles it then. We will do this!" Agnes stated emphatically, her face beaming, making her look younger than her years.

A week later.

Rachel was riding beside Taylor on their way home after being discharged from the hospital. Taylor's face was serious as she maneuvered the small red car along the busy highway. Her left hand was on the steering wheel, and her right hand was on top of the stick shift. Her thumb lightly tapped on the wheel as the sound of 'Freshly Ground's -- I'd like' played softly in the background.

For lack of anything to do, Rachel was looking at the dashboard of the vehicle. Inspecting all the dials and buttons, she was suddenly struck by the funny thought that the emergency light button looked like something you would see on an espresso-maker.

'Either I'm that bored or I'm losing it.' She thought wryly. As she looked down to her left, she saw Taylor's right hand holding on to the stick shift and began admiring the soft white skin and long fingers of her partner. It looked smooth, delicate, and beautiful. She suddenly had a vision so clear in her head of two hands - brown one atop the white one with fingers intertwined as they held on to a stick shift. Before she could stop herself, her left hand lifted from her lap and moved on top of Taylor's hand, startling her.

"Oh!" She jumped a little as she said this.

"I'm sorry. I didn't mean to startle you." Rachel quickly took her hand away.

"It's alright. I was just so concentrated on the traffic. What's wrong?" She asked. But he was deep in thought and so very nervous about being bringing Rachel home. 'What if she starts to wonder and ask about us? What if she starts to remember little things about how we really were as a couple?'

"Nothing's wrong. I... I just saw your hand and...ummm....wanted to touch and hold it as you drove. Stupid huh?" She said sheepishly, looking down.

"No. It's not stupid. When we drove, you would put your hand on top of mine and intertwine our fingers as I hold on to the gear shift." Rachel noticed the slight blush on Taylor's face as she said this.

"I did? I do? I just saw that vision in my head right before I placed my hand atop yours. So I do that huh?"

"Yes you do." Taylor answered, but her thoughts were saying a different thing. 'You used to do that and other things. You used to not be able to touch me... my hand... my arm... my curls... God! I really missed that! I missed you!' She wanted to say her thoughts out loud, but could not. Not now.

"So... Could I... I mean... Could I touch and hold you as you drive?" Rachel asked.

"You want to?"

"Ummm... Yes I do... Unless it messes with your driving, then it's alright."

"No... No... It doesn't bother my driving... Please do." Taylor said with a slight pleading note in her voice. She craved Rachel's touch.

With that said, Rachel lifted her hand again and gently placed it on top of Taylor's. The moment their hands touched, they both felt the slight current of electricity that went through them. Taylor turned to look at Rachel and saw her watching their hands intently.

"What is it?" She asked.

"Is it just me? Or does that look good to you too?"

"What does? Our hands?"

"Yes our hands...but also the colour of our hands...brown and white...together like that." Rachel whispered. Looking up, Rachel suddenly noticed the traffic flow around them.

"Taylor, the right lane is faster."

"Yes I noticed that."

"Don't you want to change lanes and go there?"

"Not really."

"No?"

"Uh-uh."

"Why?"

"I find that I like...no...let me correct myself...I love driving leisurely with your hand on mine." Both women looked at each other and gave each other a shy smile as they drove home.

As Taylor opened the door to the apartment, Rachel's mouth was open in awe at what she was seeing. "Is this ours? Is this our home?" She asked while wheeling herself in. "How big is it? How many rooms are there? How do we keep it clean? How can we afford this? What the heck do we both do for a living?" She fired off so many questions while wheeling around in circles.

"Whoa! That's a whole lot of questions there!" Taylor laughed, "Let me see if I can answer all of them." She stood up, holding on to Rachel's wheelchair from behind. "Yes it's ours. We bought it in the fourth year that we were together. It's 2,690 square feet. It has four bedrooms consisting of the master bedroom, one guest bedroom and the other two bedrooms we converted into a gym and office for both of us. We generally keep it clean with a house help that comes in everyday except weekends from 8 in the morning till 5 in the afternoon. We could afford this because we both have good, high paying jobs. You are a part owner of a successful company that does mergers and acquisitions. I'm a Senior Editor for a known publishing house and I dabble in writing now and again. In fact, I have sold 5 books in the almost ten years that we've been together. Now - have I answered all of your questions?" Taylor took a deep breath as she finished. She then saw that Rachel was just staring at her wide-eyed, with her mouth wide open.

She approached Rachel and kneeling in front of her, touched her arm gently. "Hey...hey my angel baby...are you alright?" She whispered worriedly. "I'm sorry if I gave you too much information there. I forgot that you're still trying to remember things. That all of this is like new to you."

Rachel's body shivered a bit when Taylor called her 'my angel baby.' She had a vision of two naked bodies moving together...a sheen of sweat on both their bodies, making them glisten as they aligned themselves, a voice whispering "my angel baby."

"Could you say that again?" Rachel asked the woman kneeling before her.

"What? Everything I've just said?" Taylor's fingers gently glided against Rachel's arm.

"No. When you called me 'my angel baby.' I liked that. Could you call me that again?"

"My angel baby." Taylor whispered with a teary smile on her face. "You always did love it when I call you that. Would you like to freshen up before having something to eat?" She added as she stood.

"Yes please?!" Rachel responded excitedly.

"Alright. Come on, follow me. I've had Lourdes - she's the house help - prepare the bath before she left a few minutes ago." Taylor led the way to their bedroom.

As they entered the en-suite bathroom, Taylor positioned the wheelchair close to the bathtub and checked to feel the water temperature. As she bent down to do this, her curls fell to cover the side of her face, and Rachel felt such a longing to reach out and tuck it behind those cute delicate ears.

"Oh good! Just right!" Taylor turned to Rachel. "Do you want me to help you take off your clothes?"

"Ummm...OK." Rachel shyly responded.

Taylor once again knelt in front of Rachel and slowly started to take off her clothes. She noticed that Rachel's breathing started to become ragged, and she seemed to be feeling shy about her nakedness. She made herself remember that to Rachel, and she was to all intents and purposes, virtually a stranger. She cupped and lifted Rachel's face in her hand. "Hey, I know that to you I'm a stranger seeing your nakedness for the first time. But I want you to know that for me I have known you in every sense of the word for almost ten years. You have and always will be beautiful to me." She lovingly whispered. Rachel took a calming breath and smiled.

"OK?" Taylor asked.

"Yes, OK." Rachel affirmed.

After hearing this, she stood up to take her clothes off, leaving on her bright turquoise bra and pair of blue and red 'days of the week' underwear. Rachel just sat with a wide-eyed look at the sight before her.

As Taylor looked down at Rachel and saw her expression, she realizes what she had done. "Oh my God! I'm so sorry! I didn't mean to make you uncomfortable! It's just that with my helping you with the bath I didn't want to end up getting my clothes wet. I'll just put them back on!" Bending down, she began to gather her clothes but was halted by Rachel's hand, grabbing her arm.

"No please don't! I'm not uncomfortable with what you did. I was....I was just surprised at your very colourful and cute ensemble there." She said blushing.

"Are you sure?"

"Yes I'm sure. I hope I don't make you uncomfortable in saying that the turquoise bra and those panties really look good on your white, creamy skin." Rachel blushed more furiously.

"Oh! You are still so adorable even with amnesia you know that?" Taylor laughed as she started to help Rachel with her bath.

As soon as she had Rachel in the tub, she knelt beside it and began to rub her body with a soapy sponge. 'God! I haven't done this in a really long time! Don't let me lose it now!' Taylor silently prayed to be able to keep it together.

She started with Rachel's neck, going slowly down towards her shoulders, then her arms, softly stroking the top of her chest. She circled the sponge on each breast, making Rachel's nipples darken and become taut. Both women started to breathe hard, and as Taylor looked at Rachel's face, she saw that her eyes were closed and she was biting her lip.

"OK now! I think you're all nice and clean in front how about bending forward a bit so I could wash your back there?" Taylor said a bit loudly, making Rachel open her eyes and do just that. As she leaned back again after having her back washed, Taylor gave her the sponge to wash.

"I...uh...think it would be better if you were to take over from here." Taylor stammered.

"Ummm...OK." Rachel took the sponge and did so. Once done, she handed it back to Taylor and watched as the soapy water drained out the tub, and she was thoroughly rinsed, dried, and brought back to the wheelchair for her to be dressed in her nightclothes.

"Ready for dinner?" Taylor asked Rachel as she put on her robe.

"Yes I am!" Rachel responded with a smile as they both headed off towards the kitchen.

"Is it OK to ask you some questions?" Rachel asked as they were having their dinner.

"Of course. What is it?" Taylor put down her fork as she gave her attention to the woman across from her.

"What do I call you?"

"Ummm... What do you mean?"

"Well you call me 'my angel baby.' I have to assume that I have an endearment for you as well. Unless I'm one of those boring types that just calls their partner by their name? Now that's sad."

"I actually have many endearments for you and you for me. But you almost always call me 'my baybee.' Which I find totally adorable." Taylor smiled while saying this.

Closing her eyes, Rachel had a vision of her running towards Taylor, toppling her down on the bed as she called out to her excitedly 'Baybee! My beautiful, beautiful baybee!' kissing her all over her face with Taylor laughing out loud.

"Having another vision there?" Taylor asked, beginning to recognize when her partner was having one.

Opening her eyes and looking at Taylor. "Yes." She smiled.

"Care to share?"

"It was me running towards you, toppling you down on the bed saying 'Baybee! My beautiful, beautiful baybee!' rather excitedly and I was kissing you all over your face while you were laughing out loud." Rachel shared.

Taylor's eyes started to tear, and she smiled wistfully. "Yes. That was when you surprised me with this place. You came home all excited about the fact that you had signed and sealed the deal."

"How did we meet? With our professional backgrounds it was highly unlikely that we ran in the same circles."

"Well, it was at a dinner party that was hosted by a common friend of your business partner and a good client of mine."

"Ooh! Was it love at first sight?" Rachel asked excitedly.

"Eh? Hardly! I could definitely say it was a total embarrassment on my part!"

"Huh? What do you mean?"

"I was with a group of people discussing the latest mergers and acquisitions of a certain young and aggressive company. I started to spout off some not so kind words regarding the matter and this small woman with long silky dark hair wearing a sexy red dress and high heeled shoes started to defend said company. When I asked her what would she know about these things she said that she was one of the owners. I just wanted to shrink and have the floor swallow me whole. I was never so embarrassed in my whole life."

"You mean that was how we met?"

"Uh-huh! And when I excused myself to go out into the garden, said sexy small woman apparently followed me and I thought she was going to let me have it. She completely took me by surprise and asked me to have dinner with her the next day saying we needed to discuss the matter further! And we never looked back." Taylor said with a grin.

"Wow! Are you sure we're talking about me here?"

"Oh hell, yeah! You were so sure and confident about yourself in a quiet way that it made you hella sexy! For me that is." Taylor admitted, blushing.

"Wow! I don't know what to say." Rachel shook her head as she said this.

"Well I do. Seeing how late it is and with you starting your therapy session early tomorrow morning it's time for you to go to bed."

"Alright. I am feeling a bit bushed." Rachel admitted with a slight yawn.

As both women were sleeping side by side, Rachel's body began to twitch, dreaming about that horrific night she got shot. In her dream, she entered the grocery store with her head down, taking out the amount of money needed for her ice-cream. As she entered, she lifted her head and saw the barrel of a gun pointed at her. Before she could even react, the sound of a loud bang reverberated in her ears, and she felt the searing pain on her head as she fell backward.

"No! No! No!" Rachel yelled as she sat up from the bed, her body shaking, and a sheen of the sweat of developing over her skin. She buried her face in her hands, sobbing. She felt Taylor gather her in her arms and gently rock her.

"Shhh.... It's OK... It was just a dream... It's over..." Taylor kept saying.

"I saw it! I saw what happened to me! It was so awful!" Rachel cried out.

"I'm here my angel baby. It's over. No one's going to hurt you." She whispered as she kissed the top of Rachel's head.

After a few minutes of gentle rocking, Taylor could feel Rachel's body slowly relaxing. "Want to try sleep again?" She asked her distraught partner and felt her head nod in assent.

Taylor slowly lowered her body to the bed, taking Rachel along with her. The dark-haired woman buried her face in Taylor's neck and held on to her tightly. "Please hold me? Don't let me go!" Rachel pleaded.

"Sleep now. I'll be here holding you in my arms as you sleep." She whispered, rubbing her back to soothe her.

It wasn't long before Taylor felt Rachel's body relax in sleep. Pressing her lips to the smaller woman's forehead, she closed her eyes and relished Rachel's body against hers. 'I miss this. I miss cradling my angel baby in my arms as we sleep.' It was the last thought in her mind before she fell asleep as well.

Waking up on her side, Taylor opened her eyes and saw Rachel lying beside her, looking at her. "Good morning." The dark-haired girl whispered.

"Hey there. How's my angel this morning?" She asked worriedly.

"I'm better. Slept soundly with your arms around me. No nightmares." Rachel smiled as she responded.

"Oh good. I'm glad then." Taylor smiled back.

"I could get used to that you know?"

"Get used to what?"

"Sleeping with your arms around me and my face buried in your neck breathing in your scent."

"I would love that."

"You would?"

"Yes I would." The alarm sounded shrilly, startling them both. "OK that's our cue to get a move on for your invigorating session." Taylor moved off from the bed to help Rachel get up and get ready.

"Awww... Do I have to?" Rachel pouted, dreading having to face the strain and pain she knew was coming.

Putting her hands on her hips, Taylor mock-glared at her: "Yes you have to! I mean WE have to! You don't want Mom to be on our backs hounding us, do you?" Taylor asked.

"How long do I have to do this?"

"Now that would totally depend on how determined you are to walk without assistance again! Now let's get moving or we'll be late!"

As Rachel wheeled herself to the bathroom, she stopped and turned around.

"Taylor?"

"Yes?"

"Thank you."

"For what, my angel?"

"For you... For being who you are... For being my baybee." With a big smile, she turned back around and headed for the bathroom.

Taylor was closing her eyes and putting her right hand on her chest where her heart is. 'God! Please let me still be that ... Be your baby when you get to remember everything.'

It was close to four months before Rachel was able to walk without assistance and no longer needed therapy, but her memory still drew a blank. She would have visions now and then but not enough to bring it back. Despite not having recovered her memory fully, her relationship with Taylor blossomed. It was like getting to know each other all over again.

Although they would sleep in the same bed every night with their arms wrapped around each other, they had yet to make love. It's not that they didn't want to because every time the two of them were in the same room, the sexual tension was palpable. It was as if they had a silent understanding of not wanting it to be just about sex but that it was special for them.

Most of their time was spent with each other unless Taylor went to her office to meet a client. They would go out in the mornings to walk and have brunch at one of the restaurants around their area.

It was hard to imagine that before the accident, Rachel almost always had to be out dining and dancing. Now they would always stay in at night having a quiet dinner and drinking a glass of wine or coffee in front of their fireplace before heading off to sleep.

It was in one of the window-shopping days that they passed by a pet store, and they're displayed in the window was a golden brown Labrador retriever. "Awww... Look at the cute puppy! C'mon! Let's go inside and check it out!' Rachel excitedly said as she entered the store, not seeing the surprised look on her partner's face.

Once inside, she headed straight for the puppy that was displayed in the window. She picked the dog up and cradled it in her arms. "Hey there little fella!" The puppy proceeded to lick every inch of her face making Rachel laugh out loud. She looked at Taylor and saw the expression on her face. "Oh! I didn't even bother to ask. You don't like dogs do you?"

Shaking her head while trying to find her voice, Taylor quietly said: "Uh mean I love dogs and cats. But...ummm...you don't." Taylor clarified. "You said that the apartment is too small for pets to be in and that they would make a mess."

"Why didn't we get a bigger place? Or a house or a farm?" Rachel asked.

"I wanted us to buy my Aunt's farm up north three years ago. Well, it's not really a farm farm. Just a big property with a homey cabin but you said that it was too hick and too far a commute for you to go to and from work."

Rachel's face turned serious as she digested this information. Then she smiled as she looked at Taylor then back at the puppy in her arms. "What's not to love about this cute creature? You're certainly lovable aren't you, Bossworth?" She said to the puppy.

"Ummm...Bossworth? You're naming a puppy that's not even ours?" Taylor asked her, a smile in her voice.

"Well, that's why I'm naming him...because he will be ours."

"He will?! Are you serious?! You're not teasing me are you? What about the apartment being too small and getting messy?" Taylor didn't want to get her hopes up, but the look of longing on her face gave her away. She desperately wanted the puppy as well.

"As serious as I was with my therapy sessions." Rachel quipped then turned serious again. "C'mon! Let's do the necessary paperwork so we can have this little guy with us ASAP!" The two of them headed towards the man at the counter.

And with very little fuss, they were able to buy Bosworth and arranged to have him delivered to their place the next day. As they got out of the store, Rachel grabbed hold of Taylor's hand. Taylor looked down at their joined hands with a look of surprise and wonder.

"What? Is something wrong?" Rachel asked, seeing the expression on the taller woman's face.

Shaking her head and smiling, Taylor replied: "No..nothing's wrong...it's just that.."

"It's just what? You have a problem with public displays of affection?"

"Oh I don't...but you do." Taylor clarified.

"But...I held your hand while you were driving. You said so yourself that I would do that all the time."

"Yes. But it was inside the car. You don't have a problem touching me whenever it's just the two of us but the moment we are in public anywhere it's a 'no touchy' zone."

Rachel stopped walking and faced Taylor. "You know what?" She asks.

"What?"

Rachel lifted Taylor's hand to her lips and kissed it tenderly as she looked into her eyes. "That was the 'stoopid' me. This is the new 'dopey' me. OK?" She said with a big smile on her face.

Taylor threw her head back and laughed. "You are just so adorable you know that? Now come on and let's grab dessert and coffee!" Pulling Rachel by the hand, she led her to their favorite coffee shop.

A month later, as Rachel was sitting on the couch reading with Bosworth sleeping at her feet, she was told by Taylor that Shannen, her college friend, and business partner, had called to say that the people at the office were throwing her a party. Rachel was very adamant about not going as she didn't remember anyone who would be there. The last thing she wanted was to be pitied - or worse, be looked at like a freak. Instead of voicing her fears when Taylor asked why she didn't want to go, she lashed out at Taylor, saying that she was not going and walked off to go to their room.

Rachel sat on top of their balcony ledge, gazing up at the stars, her thoughts in turmoil. She was feeling bad about being abrupt with Taylor, but she just couldn't face attending the party and not knowing anyone. Lost in her thoughts, she didn't see Taylor walk up to her and insert herself in between her legs as she wrapped her arms around Rachel's waist. Since Taylor was taller, this made her mound rest up against Rachel's stomach. The contact made them both shiver.

"Hey there." Taylor whispered.

"Hey." Rachel said with her head down, not able to look at Taylor.

"You OK?"

"I'm sorry I snapped at you back there. I didn't mean to." She apologized.

"It's OK, my angel." She cupped the smaller woman's face so she could look at her. "But you haven't answered my question. Are you OK?"

"I'm just so scared of going to that party. I don't remember anyone and I'm afraid that I'll make a complete fool of myself!" Her eyes teared up as she said this.

Gathering Rachel in her arms, Taylor rubbed her back to soothe her and whispered in her ear. "It's going to be alright, my angel baby. I'll be with you the whole time." She kissed Rachel's forehead, then the side of her face, and before both of them realized it, their lips touched. Both women moaned at the same time. For Taylor, it was feeling Rachel's full lips against hers after such a long time. For Rachel, it was feeling Taylor's lips as if for the very first time.

It started as an exploratory kiss, but as it progressed, it became heated. Taylor traced Rachel's lips with the tip of her tongue before pushing it inside her mouth to mate with hers. The kiss went on for a while until both felt the need to breathe and pulled apart, taking deep breaths.

Taylor placed her forehead on Rachel's. Her right hand was on the smaller woman's chest, her fingers gliding up and down. Lowering her head, she kissed the part where her hand was. She slowly moved to the side and kissed Rachel's breast on her right with the shirt in-between. Rachel whimpered as she pushed her chest forward, her hard nipple pushing through the shirt. Seeing this, Taylor simply couldn't resist any longer. She opened her mouth and sucked on Rachel's breast through her shirt, flicking the tip of her tongue on her hardening nipple.

"God! Baby!" Rachel gasped as she felt the sensation rocket from her nipple down to her clit. Before her whole body could comprehend what was happening, Taylor moved to her other breast, giving it the same attention. She lowered her head close to Taylor's ear. "That feels so good. Please don't stop."

Taylor lifted her head. "We need to take this inside so we can do this properly." She pulled the smaller woman to her. "Wrap your legs around my waist and hold on." She ordered.

"Wait! I'm too heavy. Let me down so I can walk." Rachel shyly said.

"Ummm...let me remind you that I am taller than you aannd that I have upper body strength to spare." She smirked. "Besides which, I have done this before...carried you like this to either our bed or sofa when the...mmm...mood hit us."

"You have? We have? Have I tried carrying you?" Rachel asked.

"Uh...yes you have tried...and no, you couldn't carry me." The taller woman responded with a smile. Then with a serious face, she said softly: "Now listen, I will be carrying you to our bed and I don't want to hear another word about it. OK?" And she proceeded to do just that, kissing Rachel on the lips as they went.

Sitting on the side of the bed with Rachel straddling her lap, she lifted the shirt from the smaller woman and threw it to the side. Holding both breasts with each hand, she started to fondle and caress them gently. "Oh my angel. You are so beautiful." She lovingly whispered as she lowered her head and softly licked first one nipple then the other, making them wet and glistening. Seeing both nipples get hard, pebbled, and dark, she moaned as she brought her mouth down to suckle on each breast. Pulling Rachel tightly towards her, she lowered herself to the bed, moving them both to the center. They both started to take off their clothes, turning each other on with every bit of their body they exposed. Taylor turned them around, making the smaller woman lie on her back while she continued to suckle. Rachel's hands held on to Taylor's head, her fingers buried in her curls, her body arching upwards, pushing her breast even further inside her lover's mouth.

Taylor released Rachel's breast and began her descent kissing, suckling, nibbling, and licking every inch of skin she encountered. As she approached her mound, she looked down at it and touched it reverently, making Rachel lift her lower body and whimper from being touched.

Rachel looked down to see Taylor staring at her mound and caressing it with her hand, gliding her fingers up and down. Lowering her hand, she put it on top of Taylor's hand, which was still touching her mound, making Taylor look up at her with a sheen of tears in her eyes. Taking a deep breath, she huskily whispered: "I...I haven't seen or touched you like this in a long time. I've missed you so much I ache."

Cupping Taylor's face with her other hand, Rachel whispered: "I ache with wanting you." She guided Taylor's hand on her mound to touch her some more. Both of them could feel the warmth and the wetness seeping from the smaller woman.

"God baby! I've forgotten how beautiful you look with your dark and plump pussy lips glistening wet with your arousal!" Taylor moaned as she lowered her head to taste her lover after such a long time. It tasted the same as it always had, with a hint of both tanginess and freshness. She started kissing her all over her mound, then with her tongue, she licked her from the bottom of her slit, going up towards her clit, gathering her wetness as she ascended. Once she made it to the top, she pressed her tongue and the wetness she had gathered onto the clit, making Rachel gasp and moan. She started to twirl her tongue around Rachel's clit, making it engorged and peek out of its hood so she could suckle on it softly and then go harder and faster.

Rachel grabbed hold of the sheets with one hand while the other found its way to Taylor's head, pulling her into her mound. "Unggh! God! My baybee! Make me yours!" She pleaded with her lover.

Hearing these words while still suckling on the smaller woman's clit, Taylor moved her right hand down and pushed her middle finger inside her hot core. "Please! Some more! Put in some more!" Rachel begged.

Taylor did just that. She pushed in two fingers and felt the muscles inside her lover clutching at her fingers as she pumped into her. She also felt the heat and tightness within making her want and urge for more. Her suckling and pumping became harder and faster.

"Oh God! Oh God! I'm gonna come! Make me come! Please...please..." Rachel gasped.

While still pumping her fingers in and out of her lover, Taylor started to feel her lover's contractions. She instantly stopped suckling on her clit and pulled on it with her lips, pushing Rachel over the edge.

"Unnggghhhh!!" Rachel's body arched like a bow as she came. She lowered her whole body to the bed as she slowly allowed her breathing to go back to normal. "Wow!" It was all she could say.

"I most definitely second that emotion!" Taylor whispered, her head resting on Rachel's stomach.

"Come up here, woman!" Rachel softly commanded.

"Ooh! OK!" Taylor responded and started to make her way up the smaller woman's body. She laid her body atop Rachel's, her arms on either side of her lover's head as they kissed, tasting Rachel's wetness from each other's mouth. The kiss went on as Taylor was kneading and cupping Rachel's breasts. 'I missed this! Missed the kissing and cuddling after we've made love!' Taylor voiced in her head.

Before she could even think about going down to kiss and suckle once again on her lover's burgeoning breasts, she feels her whole world spin. She found herself on her back with Rachel on top.

"My turn!" Rachel said with a big smile and a wink.

Cupping the smaller woman's face, Taylor looked deeply into her eyes. "You don't have to, my angel baby. I know that for you this will be like the first time. I'm just so happy that I was able to love your body all over again."

"But that's what I want. For you to be my first." Rachel huskily whispered, lowering her head to kiss Taylor. Her hands rested upon her lover's breasts to cup, knead, and massage. As she moved her lips downwards, she inserted her thigh, in-between the taller woman's legs and brought it higher, feeling the wetness of Rachel's pussy lips against her skin.

"God my baybee! I want to expose as much of you as I can." Rachel whispered lovingly.

"Yes my baby." Taylor opened her arms, laying them on either side of her head. "Use your lips and tongue to expose as much of me as you want, my angel. I'm all yours." Taylor posed seductively.

Rachel's eyes turned into slits from looking at the vision of Taylor in front of her. She licked her full lips and lowered her head to kiss Taylor's chest above her heart. As she headed towards one breast, she could feel the heat and smell the scent of arousal emanating from the taller woman.

She lingered first on one breast, licking, kissing, sucking, then suckling as she flicked the tip of her tongue on the top of Taylor's dusky pink nipple. She did the same to the other breast, not wanting it to feel neglected. She lowered herself some more and swirled her tongue inside Taylor's cute belly button. Going further down, she pressed her lips on her lower stomach. Then, just at the top of her lover's mound, she stopped and started to nuzzle and caress it with her cheek, tongue, and lips.

"Oh god! That feels so good, my angel baby." Taylor exclaimed.

Encouraged, Rachel lowered her head further, holding her face just a few inches away from Taylor's hot, wet, pulsing and throbbing mound. She looked at it in awe of the beauty in front of her. "Please... Please my angel." Taylor begged.

Rachel moved her face closer, pushing her tongue out and licking along Taylor's slit. Gathering the wetness on her tongue, she copied what her lover had done to her. As she reached the top of Taylor's slit, she pulled her clit in her mouth together with the wetness and started to suck slowly, gradually picking up the pace as she felt the reaction she was getting from her lover.

When she felt her start to come, she let go of her clit and blew on it while her hands glided on Taylor's thighs, calming her down from her high. She looked up to see Taylor's chest heaving, her eyes in slits looking at Rachel as if she couldn't believe that she'd just stop. She looked back at her clit, seeing it all red, throbbing, peeking out, begging to be licked and sucked. Rachel moved up Taylor's body, and right before she lowered herself, she moved her hand to her mound and separated her lips, making her wet clit peek out. She brought it down to mate with Taylor's, and she started to slowly hump her mound, her dark, plump pussy lips contracting and expanding as she moved sensually on top of Taylor.

She grabbed both of Taylor's hands and put them on either side of her head, their fingers intertwined. She started to pick up her humping pace, her breasts hanging down and moving just above her lover's face. "God my baby! You're gonna make me come!" Taylor gasped as she grabbed Rachel's nipple with her mouth, holding and sucking on her while the smaller woman humped her clit, their wetness mixing. The sounds of their wet lips rubbing together filled the room. The smell of their arousals permeating around them, taking them further, making them harder and faster.

"Auugggghhh!!!" The sound of both women coming together.

Lifting herself off Taylor, Rachel turned on her side as her lover cuddled her from behind. Taylor's right hand gently caressed her stomach, her left hand cupping her breasts, and her right leg hooked over her hip.

"I love you with all my heart, Taylor my baybee." Rachel whispered.

"And I love you with all my heart, Rachel my angel." Taylor responded.

After a few minutes, both fell into a deep sleep.

Rachel was so excited as she opened the door of the apartment. Bosworth ran and jumped as if seeing her after a long time when it had only been for a few hours. "Hey there! How's my boy?" She asked as he wagged his tail and barked in excitement at picking up on her emotions.

Lourdes, their house help, came out of the kitchen. "Oh! Ms. Rachel! Where have you been? I was so worried when you just left without telling me where you were going!" Lourdes exclaimed, her hand on her heart.

"I'm so sorry, Lourdes. I just needed to get out and do some stuff. I promise to tell you where I'm going next time I decide to just up and go, OK?" She explained, hoping that her face wouldn't give her secret away.

"OK. OK. But when Ms. Taylor called a while ago asking for you and I couldn't tell her where you went she got a bit upset. She cut short her trip and is on her way home tonight instead of tomorrow morning." Lourdes grumbled as she walked back into the kitchen to finish the dinner she was preparing.

"Uh Oh! Gotta hide my surprise!" Rachel mumbled to herself before she ran towards their room, Bosworth following close behind.

Trying to find the best place to hide the brown envelope with the important documents enclosed, she decided to hide it in Taylor's unused drawers. As she opened one of the drawers, she saw a bundle of small purple envelopes. She took them out and started to read one of the letters, which was both love and the sexual letter addressed to Taylor. "I must be one romantic dopey girlfriend." She smiled to herself. Closing the letter, she was about to read the others when she heard the doorbell and Lourdes calling out her name. She stuffed the letters back into the drawer together with the brown envelope and walked out.

As she exited the room, she met Lourdes by the hallway. "Ah! There you are, Ms. Rachel. You have a visitor."

"Who is it, Lourdes?" She asked, not particularly happy about meeting someone without Taylor to help her.

"It's Shannen your business partner." Lourdes replied, pointing her towards where the guest was waiting.

Upon entering the room, Rachel spotted the woman standing by the window, looking down at the scenery below. She was tall with wavy reddish-brown hair.

"Shannen?" She called out.

Turning around from the window, the woman said: "Hey there my friend!" Shannen gave her a quick hug. "I'm sorry that I have only visited you now but I was told that you needed the space and time to heal." She walked towards the couch where her bag was. "Oh before I forget. I have something for you." She opened her bag, took out a medium-sized box, and handed it to Rachel.

"Look, I won't stay long. But I just really wanted to see how you are because I've missed you and I wanted to ask you to please come to the party that the office is preparing for you. A lot of people are worried and just want to see you. Please think about it?" She hugged her quickly one more time before taking her to leave.

Rachel looked down at the box on her lap and began to open it. As she pulled the top off, she saw a Blackberry phone and an envelope lying underneath it. She picked up the cellphone, then the envelope and read the note inside. 'Heard that your cellphone was stolen on the night of the accident. Here's another one. Hurry back and don't be a stranger! -- Shannen.' Rachel smiled, but that didn't last long as she began to realize something. She stood up from the couch and headed back to their room. She opened the drawer and read all of the letters in each of the purple envelopes. The same type of envelope that she had just received from her college friend and business partner.

It was dark when Taylor entered the apartment, dropping her overnight bag next to the front door. Bosworth came running out to greet her. "Hey there, Bossy! Where's your other Momma?" She asked as she rubbed his coat.

She began to look for Rachel. "Rachel? Baby? Where are you?" She switched on a light in passing and found her lover sitting on the couch, staring at the fire. "Here you are! Why didn't you answer me? And where did you go when you left this afternoon you had me and...." Before she could finish, Rachel lifted her hand, holding the bundle of purple envelopes addressed to Taylor.

"It happened before my accident?" She angrily asked.

Seeing what was in Rachel's hand and hearing her question. "Oh God! Oh God!" She frantically whispered. "Baby I..." Once again, she was interrupted by an angry Rachel.

Standing up from the couch, Rachel rounded on her, her face furious. "You and Shannen?! Before my accident?!" She shouted angrily, standing in front of the taller woman.

"Once! It just happened once then never again!" She frantically explained. "She kept trying and trying but I told her off! It was different then! We were different then!"

"I don't even remember how we were then, Taylor!" Rachel threw the envelopes at Taylor and started to walk towards the apartment's door, just wanting to get out of there before she did or said anything that she might regret.

Opening the door, she was halted by Taylor's quivering voice. "Rachel! Please! We didn't have a good relationship for the past three years but we're better now! Please don't walk away! Not like this! Not now!" She begged as tears ran down her face.

"I need to get out." It was all that Rachel could say, not able to look at Taylor as she walked out and closed the door of their apartment.

Taylor's knees buckled, and she fell to the floor, sobbing her heart out. Bosworth approached her, putting his face on her leg and whined as he watched her cry.

Agnes opened her door to see her distressed daughter standing outside. She ushered her in and hugged her tight without uttering a word. Rachel collapsed on her mom and began to cry out her anger and pain.

She was lying on the couch, exhausted after telling Agnes everything that happened. "Do you know what you're going to do?" Her mom asked.

Rachel shook her head. "No. No I don't. All I know is that I'm hurt and angry."

"Honey, I don't profess to know everything about life because I really don't. But please try to look beyond your hurt and pain and see what you have. What's in front of you right now."

"What do you mean?" She asked her mom.

"Well, I've seen you and Taylor together for the past ten years. I've seen how you were when things were getting rough before and believe me when I say that you are not totally faultless. It does take two you know. Then, I see how you are after your accident with you getting to know each other all over again." Standing up, she looked down at her daughter. "I won't tell you what to do but I will ask you to take a long hard look at your life. Realize what you want and how you're going to get it. They do say that the best things in life don't come without a price." She kissed Rachel on her head and walked away.

It took a long while before Rachel realized what she was going to do. She eventually fell asleep for the first time in months without the arms of Taylor around her.

Morning came too soon for Rachel as she got her plan into action. She spoke to her mom about what she was going to do before leaving. Agnes had a big smile on her face as she saw her daughter drive off.

She entered the building with determination written all over her face. People would stop and greet her as they recognized her. Upon reaching Shannen's door, she didn't bother knocking and just entered. She saw Shannen and a petite blond woman going over some papers.

"Rachel, I'm in a meeting right now." Said Shannen, visibly uncomfortable with Rachel there.

"I need to talk with you privately and this won't take long."

"Ummm...alright...Hannah, could you please excuse us? I'll talk to you later." Shannen addressed the smaller woman.

As the woman named Hannah passed Rachel, she gave her a teary and longing look that Rachel found to be disturbing. "I'm glad that you're well. I...we missed you." She whispered before leaving the room.

"Look Rachel about me and Taylor..." Taylor had told Shannen that she already knew about them.

"I don't want to discuss it. It's over and done with. I'm here to tell you that I will be selling my share of the business. I want out."

"What? Are you sure about this? You love this business! If it's about what happened with me and Taylor..."

Rachel put up her hand to stop Shannen. "I already said I don't want to talk about it. As for the business, I used to love it then. Not now. I'm a different person now." Having said her piece, she turned around and walked towards the door to leave.

"What about us? Our friendship?" Can you ever forgive me?" Shannen asked.

Stopping at the door to look back at Shannen, Rachel paused. "You used to be my friend. Forgive you? I've already forgotten you." She said without emotion as she stepped out.

Walking out of Shannen's office, she asked the nearest person where her office was. There she was met by her secretary who introduced herself as Rose. She requested that Rose bring her a box, and she proceeded to pack all of her personal effects into the container. When she picked up the framed photo of her and Taylor in their younger days, she smiled through the sudden welling of tears in her eyes. As she finished packing, the door to her office opened, and Hannah came in.

"Can I help you?" Rachel asked.

"You don't remember me at all do you?" Hannah's eyes began to tear as she asked the question.

"I'm sorry, but no I don't."

Hannah took a deep breath. "Three years ago we started an affair and last year you told me you were going to leave her for me. I guess that's not going to happen now, right?" Tears slowly fell down her cheeks.

Rachel felt her head bowing under the weight of this new information. She closed her eyes. 'God! What kind of a woman was I before the accident?' She asked herself. Lifting her head, she looked at Hannah. "Please believe me when I say that I am so, so sorry. I never meant to hurt you or anyone. I don't remember you and even with the visions or flashbacks that I have had, it was never of you."

Hannah wiped her tears away. "It's all right. I knew you were still so in love with her. I just hoped that you would get to love me the same way. I wish you well, Rachel." And with that said, the petite blond woman quietly left her office.

Taking the small box with her belongings, Rachel left the office for good.

Present time.

Rachel stood outside the door of the apartment. Her right hand moved up and down the side of her jeans, wiping off her palm's wetness. Coming here, deciding to be with her would end up hurting another. 'But it's how I feel... What I want!' She thought to herself. Taking a deep breath and exhaling loudly, Rachel lifted her hand, unlocking the door to enter the apartment.

As she entered, she heard sounds coming from their bedroom. The door was open, and Taylor was packing her things inside a suitcase while sniffling now and then. Bosworth was lying beside her feet, sleeping. Rachel felt her heart slam in her chest as she realized that Taylor would be leaving her.

She cleared her throat. "Ummm...hi." She greeted Taylor. Both Taylor and Bosworth jumped at hearing her voice. The dog barked excitedly and ran over to greet her. Taylor stayed where she was and just looked at her with trepidation.

"Hi...I didn't hear you come in." Taylor noticed Rachel staring at her suitcase. "I'm just taking my things out of this room and transferring them to the guest bedroom. I hope you don't mind, but I'll have to stay there for a short while until I can finalise my living arrangements." She explained, trying hard not to cry in front of Rachel.

Not knowing what to say to get things back the way they were, Rachel walked over to the drawer where she hid the brown envelope, hoping it was still there.

"Ummm... I cleared my things from the cabinets and drawers. You don't have to check."

Opening the drawer, Rachel retrieved the brown envelope and walked back to where Taylor was standing and handed it over to her.

"Open it. Please?" She whispered.

Not knowing where this was going, Taylor opened the envelope and took out the document showing that the farm her Aunt used to own was now their farm. She looked at her name next to Rachel's name on the deed of sale and gasped out loud as she looked at the smaller woman.

"What does this mean?"

"Please don't leave me, Taylor. If that's what you want then I'll respect your wishes, but it's not what I want." She pleaded with tears in her eyes.

"Oh God! My angel!" Taylor launched herself against the smaller woman and hugged her tight, not wanting to let go. "I thought that you didn't want me anymore! That you hate me because of what I've done! Please! Please forgive me!"

Holding Taylor tight to her and burying her face in her neck to breathe in her scent, Rachel said: "Please forgive me as well for all the things I've done to us, my baybee. I want us to have a new life together. And I want us to start by living in a new place. That's why I bought the farm for us. I knew that's what you've been wanting for such a long time now."

"But what about your work and the rest?"

"Maybe I used to like them but I'm a different person now. I'm selling my shares of the company and will just be a consultant since I should be getting a tidy sum from the sale. I have my savings as well so that should tide us over for a long time." She explained.

"Whatever you want, my angel. So long as you're happy then I'm happy."

Holding Taylor's face with both her hands, Rachel looked deep into her eyes. "I want you and only you. You make me happy."

Laughing with tears in her eyes, Taylor said softly: "I most definitely second that emotion." She smiled at Rachel as they kissed.

After a few minutes of kissing, Taylor felt herself being lifted. She moved her head and looked down at Rachel. "Ummm...what are you doing?"

"What does it look like I'm doing?"

"I appreciate the effort, my angel, but you can't carry me."

"My baybee?"

"Yes, my angel?"

"Borrowing a phrase from someone I know...now listen, I'm going to be carrying you to our bed and I don't want to hear another word, alright!" Rachel said as she winked at the taller woman.

Throwing her head back to laugh, Taylor gave in. "God! You are just so adorable! Alright! Take me I'm yours!" She said as she wrapped her legs around Rachel's waist.

"Oh! I most definitely will my Baybee!" Rachel said as she carried her slowly but surely to their bed to start their new life.

Marie Garcia was finishing her report as she glanced up at her window to take a break, looking at the setting sun. She leaned back in her chair, her elbow on the armrest, her forefinger tracing her lips as she thought again of how she came to be there. Looking at Marie, you could see from her long dark brown hair, almond eyes, and brown skin that she was most definitely not an American. Still, some mistook her for being Spanish or Mexican and was always surprised when she was told she was Asian.

It had been a year since she left her country to move to Denver, U.S.A. Growing up, she never imagined she could do such a thing, considering she was born and raised in a very strict and conservative society - a culture where the women only got to leave the house when they were married off and not before then.

Her reason for leaving was to be with the woman she loved. A woman she thought felt the same way about her. Her move to Denver was supposed to have been a pleasant surprise for Jasmine, but Marie ended up being surprised, no, make that shocked & devastated. Her heart twinged at the thought of Jasmine, Jasmine Ward. Even after things went wrong, Marie decided to forge ahead and accept the overseas job. It would give her a chance to live a life of independence away from her restrictive family and upbringing and, most of all, herself, a woman attracted to other women. Although there were women like her in her country, it was most definitely not accepted and frowned upon.

It all started with the two women meeting online in a chat room. Marie was hesitant to connect at first since she had never done anything remotely like it before. For reasons she could not for the life of her explain, she took to Jasmine right away. All she knew was that she felt very calm and comfortable with her. They were both career women - Marie was a loan officer at a local bank in her country while Jasmine, although British by birth, worked as a doctor in Denver. She had studied in the US and decided to stay and work there, electing not to return to London.

They chatted innocently at first, but as the weeks went by, they realized that they had a lot in common. Both women were single, and they had both had their share of boyfriends. Although they had been attracted to women in the past, neither had done anything about it. Each had an experience where they had a female friend come on to them but were afraid to pursue it despite their attraction for fear of how their personal and professional lives would be affected. Although Marie had dated men in the past, she had never felt so attracted to anyone that she wanted to share everything with them. She was still a virgin and, at some point, had begun to believe that she must be as frigid as past dates had described her. That thought was blown apart when she met Jasmine in cyberspace.

When they moved from the chat room to e-mail, Marie was the first to send her picture then Jasmine followed after a while. Both liked what they saw, and slowly their conversations turned flirty, then seductive, then sexual. As the months went by, they progressed to other means of communicating, moving from e-mail to text messages and voice calls to video calls. Their messages or calls started with the two women sharing their thoughts and visions of how they wanted to be with each other and ended with them coming together. They had explosive phone sex, which left them both satisfied but wanting so much more.

They had been corresponding for close a year when Marie thought of applying for a job in Denver to be together finally. To be each other's first time with another woman, to finally do to each other what they had imagined so often. She didn't tell Jasmine her plans since she wanted to surprise her, so when her application was approved, she couldn't wait to tell her the news when they had their next scheduled video call.

The moment the call started, Marie felt that something was off with Jasmine - her attitude and demeanor spoke volumes even if she said nothing. Finally, Marie could no longer handle the tension and asked her point-blank what was wrong. Jasmine couldn't even look her in the eyes as she said, "Baby, I don't want to say this...this is so hard for me...but it would never work with us. What we have is a long-distance virtual relationship. I think we should both move on and be with someone that we can actually be with...I mean physically." Marie could feel her heart thumping so hard and fast. It clenched so tight and hurt so much she thought it would break into pieces. With an effort, she kept calm, looking at Jasmine and, in a soft voice, asked, "Why don't you just tell me what's really going on? You and I have discussed visiting each other so that's not the problem. At least give me that."

"Ummm...Tracy is back here in Denver, and I...ummm...want to see if...." Jasmine said hesitantly. Marie closed her eyes from the intense pain she felt with those words and hearing that name. Tracy was the friend who had come onto Jasmine a long time before, but she hadn't done anything to pursue it despite her attraction, fearing her family and friends' reaction. "You want to see if things could finally work out between you." She finished for Jasmine.

"Baby, I'm...." Before Jasmine could say anything more, Marie lifted her palm to the screen to stop her. "Please...please don't call me that...you don't have the right to call me that anymore. I'm no longer your baby...I don't think I ever was." Taking a deep calming breath, she prayed to all that's holy that she wouldn't break before she finished. "I... I really wish you all the best. Goodbye, Jasmine." She ended the call as tears started to run down her face.

Marie's thoughts were broken by knocking on her office door. Coming back to the present, she was surprised to find wetness on her cheeks. She quickly wiped the tears away as she answered, "Yes? Come in." She turned towards the door which opened to reveal her boss, Toni Stevens.

"Hey Marie! It's quitting time. You about ready to join me in our other job? Liz is waiting for us...says it's a slow night at the bar and with our combined beauties it might encourage both the women and men to enter the place!" Toni said with a smile. "Hey, you alright?" she asked, noticing the telltale redness of Marie's eyes.

"Oh! I'm fine...thanks for asking. Well, we can't have Liz waiting now especially with her being pregnant and all. Just let me shut off my computer and get my things." Marie stood up from her chair and packed up. "What about Laurel? Will she be joining us? With her around we would be like the femme fatale trio!" Marie said, with a big smile on her face.

"You know Marie you're very pretty but when you smile it makes you beautiful. Just keep smiling and be happy alright?" Toni encouraged Marie. "As for Laurel, my beautiful baby, she'll join us as soon as she's done with her client. Now let's haul ass shall we?"

It was a slow Tuesday morning at work as Marie looked at the e-mail message sent to her by Jasmine just a few minutes before. It wasn't the first time that Jasmine had sent her an e-mail. In the previous six months, she had sent numerous messages asking how she was and if they could talk. Marie ignored everyone, wondering what on earth they possibly had to talk about. And if Jasmine wanted to be friends, well tough cookie! Marie couldn't think of them being 'just friends' after everything they had shared over the one year they were corresponding. How could she go from explicit talks of caressing, touching, kissing, and making each other come to "how's the weather" and "how's your day coming along?"

The e-mail was simple: "Hey there...I know we didn't end things right and it was all my fault...You could probably just ignore this message along with the others I've sent you these past months...But if you could please, please talk to me...It wouldn't take that long I promise you...And you don't have to say anything...I would just like to say what I have to say and that would be it if you prefer. Jasmine."

Marie took a deep breath, and without really understanding why, she replied to Jasmine's e-mail. "I'm OK to talk now." It wasn't even ten minutes later when an alert popped up for a new mail. "Hey! Hi! Do you still use the same user name?" Jasmine replied. "Yes." was all that Marie could write, already half regretting her actions.

Marie felt like she was going to have an asthma attack. She couldn't properly breathe while waiting for Jasmine to go online. Her whole body felt like it was shaking. She started taking deep calming breaths as Jasmine did just that and started the video call. Their breaths hitched at the same time when they saw each other on the screen for the first time. "Ummm... Hi... Thank you for allowing me this.... You look great... Your hair is longer ... It...ummm... It suits you." Jasmine stumbled on her words as she was rendered breathless by the sight of Marie on the screen. 'God! She looks so gorgeous with her long dark hair falling just below her grogeous breasts. Her full lips still look like a perfect bow,' she thought to herself.

"You don't look so bad yourself." Marie replied. 'Dammit! You haven't seen or spoken to her in a year and that's all you have to say?!' She scolded herself. 'God! Her curly hair surrounding her face is so beautiful! She's still so beautiful!' She thought.

"I called your office once a few months back and they told me you had quit and didn't know where you went... Don't worry though I said I was a client." Jasmine quickly said, seeing the panic in Marie's eyes, but misreading the cause. "You moved to a different bank? Sorry...You don't have to answer that... I've no right to ask." Jasmine apologized.

"Ummm... you're right I don't have to...." before Marie could finish her sentence, the door to her office burst open, and Toni announced in a loud, jovial voice, "Hey Marie! My sister just called to say that she just came from the Denver Health Hospital and has some good news! So you, me and Laurel are invited for dinner at her house tonight! Oh! She also said not to take Arapahoe Road since there's construction going on and to take County Line Road instead." With that, she grinned and swept out again. As the door closed, both women sat, frozen, one feeling dread, the other feeling disbelief at what she had heard.

"Dammit!" Marie whispered and closed her eyes, rubbing her forehead, trying to erase the headache that was beginning to develop. She hoped against hope that Jasmine hadn't heard Toni.

"Where are you exactly, Marie? And please don't tell me you're somewhere in your country because so far as I know there is only one Denver Health Hospital and that's where I work. And if I'm not mistaken," she said a little drily, "Arapahoe and County Line road are also in Denver!" Jasmine's voice raised just a bit brought on by both excitement and disbelief that Marie could be in the same country, not to mention the same city as her.

Seeing no other way out, Marie opened her eyes and looked at Jasmine. "As you've clearly heard and figured out, I'm in Denver just like you, Jasmine." Marie sighed.

"Oh my God! Oh God! How? When?" Jasmine spouted off. "Please... Please Marie... I know I don't have any right to ask... but could we please see each other?" She pleaded.

Marie shook her head. "You're forgetting something... or should I say someone?"

"What? Who am I forgetting here?" Jasmine asked.

"Tracy. Your girlfriend? I don't want you to do to her what you did to me." Marie replied, somewhat angrily.

"Wait... Hold on... Tracy and I aren't together... look it's something I would rather talk to you about face to face, OK? Even if it's just for coffee... In fact if you want, it will give you the chance to throw the coffee in my face." Jasmine told Marie not caring how stupid her idea sounded.

After a few seconds of hesitation, Marie agreed but refused to make it easy for Jasmine. "Alright. Fine. Coffee it is. Meet me at Stella's Coffee House in thirty minutes. It's across from where I work."

"OK. Stella's Coffee House. Thirty minutes." Jasmine repeated before they both ended the call.

'Oh God! Oh God!' Jasmine repeatedly said in her head as she sat cradling her coffee in her hands, hoping the heat from the mug would warm up her cold and numb hands. She chose a table that had privacy yet could be seen upon entering the coffee shop.

'Oh God! Oh God!' Marie was saying over and over in her head as she stood just outside the coffee shop. Both arms were wrapped around her stomach, trying to control the butterflies running amock inside. 'It's now or never! Probably good to have closure. It will help me to move on.' Marie thought to herself, trying to give herself the courage to enter the coffee shop. Her breath hitched as she saw Jasmine sitting at the corner table. She would always recognize those curls. She had always imagined her fingers buried inside those curls, holding her head as they kissed.

Jasmine, engrossed in her thoughts, was looking down at her coffee cup. She was too involved in her head to realize that Marie was already standing beside the table. "Ummm... Is this seat taken?" Marie asked, making Jasmine jump up a bit from her voice right next to her.

Jasmine raised her eyes to look at Marie for the first time in person finally, and she felt as if she was in Heaven, seeing her sweet angel's face. She had many endearments for Marie when they were still together, but the one that she had always called her was 'sweet angel.' She had dreamt of so many nights, and now that moment finally arrived. She couldn't even for the life of her say anything. She shook her head sharply to try and clear the fog. "Uh... Yes... I mean.... No... It's for you." She stuttered as she held onto her coffee mug for dear life.

Sitting down across from Jasmine, she clasped her hands together on the table to stop them from shaking. Marie again took deep, calming breaths. Seeing Jasmine's face for the first time had made her knees all weak and trembling. It was either sit down or fall flat on her feet in front of the woman. The pictures and videos didn't do her justice.

"So... ummm... God! Now that you're in front of me I don't even know what to say!" Jasmine confessed.

"Let's start with Tracy." Marie supplied.

"OK...First of all, Tracy is not my girlfriend... She never was... I...We...tried but I should have remembered how she was...she was chaotic...over-dramatic...too negative...And before we even got started we were done." Jasmine explained. "Look...Ba...Marie...I'm really, really sorry...I never meant to hurt you...I made a mistake...Please...please forgive me? If you want you could still throw this coffee in my face...I deserve it." She pushed her coffee towards Marie as she said this.

Bringing her gaze from the cup to Jasmine's face, Marie pushed the coffee back towards her saying, "You forget I'm not built that way. I've already forgiven you but I'm not likely to forget. "

"I don't expect you to...I just hope that in time you will be able to." Jasmine said softly. "Could I... Could I ask how long you've been in Denver? She asked Marie.

"I've been living and working here for a year now. I arrived May of last year." She replied, looking at Jasmine to see if she would realize what the time-frame meant.

"May?... A year? How long before you knew you were going to be living here?" Jasmine asked, dreading the answer.

"I knew the day we had our last video call. I was going to surprise you with the news and I ended up being the one surprised...and not in a good way..." Marie's eyes teared up as she said this.

"Oh God! You must really hate me and I don't blame you at all." Jasmine whispered, her eyes welling up as well.

"I don't. Not anymore. You wanted someone else and you were honest about it. I can give you that." Marie said as she made a show of looking at her watch to signal that she needed to be going. "I'm actually glad we did this... I was really hesitant at first but now I feel like a weight has been lifted from me. I have to get back to the office." Standing up from the table, she looked at Jasmine. "I wish you all the best, Jasmine." When Jasmine called out to her, she stopped and turned around.

"Wait... Marie... Can't we at least be friends?" Jasmine asked. 'Dammit! That was definitely not what I wanted to ask!' Jasmine thought, wanting to kick herself. She wanted so much to give them another try, especially now that they were both in the same city.

Marie closed her eyes for a few seconds before looking at Jasmine and asking, "Do you actually believe that after what we had we could just be friends, Jasmine?" Shaking her head, she continued, "Let's just leave it like this. It's better this way." She turned and left the coffee shop before changing her mind and ended up losing her heart again.

Marie was back at her office but didn't know how she could get through the day. It felt like she was running on auto-pilot, finishing all the paperwork for the clients whose loans would be released for the month. Her mind was still replaying the scene in the coffee shop like a movie in her head.

'Friends? She wants us to be FRIENDS?!' She thought angrily. 'If she had asked if we could give it another try I might have given in! Friends?!' Her fingers flew fast and hard on the keyboard as her thoughts swirled around her head. She didn't notice her office door had opened and that Toni was standing by the entrance looking at her.

"Hey you! What did that keyboard ever do to you?" Toni asked, trying to lighten the mood of the smaller woman.

"Good Lord! You startled me!" Marie exclaimed with a hand on her heart. "I'm sorry I didn't hear you knock. Is there something you needed, Toni?" She asked her boss.

Toni sat on the chair in front of Marie's desk and looked at her, contemplating what she was going to say without being too intrusive. She could feel and see that something was affecting the woman who was not only her loans officer but someone she considered a friend.

When she first met Marie, there was a certain sadness about her that made her appear aloof and detached from others. She was a good and hard worker but didn't seem to have anything outside of work. It took several invites from Toni to go to the bar she and her sister Liz owned before Marie finally agreed. Thankfully with her sister's persistence and no-nonsense attitude, they were eventually able to break down the wall that the smaller woman had encased herself in.

"Marie, I know that you and I have been working together for a year now. In that time I have come to think of you not only as someone working for me, but also as a friend...A good friend. If there is something or someone bothering or upsetting you I just wanted you to know that I am here for you, alright?" She said softly but firmly.

Marie just broke down with those words and told Toni everything that happened to her before she came over to Denver, to her having coffee with the woman who had broken her heart a year before. When she was done telling her story, both women had tears in their eyes.

"I'm so sorry, Marie. But you still pushed through with coming over here despite what happened?" Toni asked incredulously.

"I know it sounds stupid but I was already accepted for the job. Didn't want to lose out on the opportunity. Besides I figured that Denver was a big place that there wasn't much chance that we would bump into each other." The smaller woman replied, slightly shaking her head.

Trying to lighten the mood a bit, Toni teased Marie ruefully. "Well... That'll teach me not to just barge in your office and announce things loudly! Sheesh!" The two women laughed at that.

"Ah well... Guess it was meant to happen that way so we could finally have closure of some sort." Marie sighed.

"Hope you don't mind my asking, but if she had asked you if you would try again, would you have agreed?" Toni asked.

"No... Yes... I mean I don't know! But geez! Friends?! I really don't think so! Again... I know it sounds stupid but after what I more or less shared with this woman for a year, being 'just friends' just won't do! It was a relationship for me... She was my girlfriend."

"Do you still have feelings for her? You seem to be still affected by her."

"I could just deny it but it's pretty obvious that I still do... God! To finally see and hear her live... To see her eyes... Lips... Chin... Curls in her hair... And damn that British accent! Do you know how many nights I dreamt of seeing her in the flesh? I had to get out of the coffee shop fast or risk making a complete fool of myself!"

"Hmmm... What's with the chin?"

"She used to ask me the same question every time I would focus on that... Wanting to nibble on it... Kiss it." Marie reminisced. "I really can't explain."

"Okaaay...we seem to have a chin fetish going on with you." Toni teased.

"Only with her apparently." Marie whispered.

Toni looked at Marie thoughtfully. "Marie, I really appreciate you sharing this with me. And I promise you that I will keep this confidential. If you ever ever need someone to talk to or need a shoulder to cry on, I'm here for you."

"Thank you, Toni. That really means a lot to me." Marie said with wet eyes.

"Phew! Now that that's settled how's about we go head off to my sister's find out what her good news is and enjoy her scrumptious home-cooked meal! Laurel will be meeting us there." Toni said, standing up from the chair.

"I'm all for that! Let's go." Marie said.

"I see Laurel is already here." Toni pointed at her lover's car parked at the front of the house as they walked up to the front door.

"Whose car is that in front of Lauren's? Could that be the good news Liz is talking about?" Marie noticed the brand new red Fiat 500 with no plates. "Kinda small for her family, don't you think?"

"Let's go ask my sibling then! Cute car though." Toni said as she rang the doorbell.

"Hold your horses!" Liz hollered as she opened the door to the two women. "Well! If it isn't my late sister and sort of adopted sister. It's about time you guys got here. We're starving!"

"Hey sis! Is the new red car in front your good news?" Toni asks. "I agree with Marie - it's a bit small for your growing family."

"I wish! But no, my sisters. That's my doctor's new baby." Liz replies. "Hope you don't mind my asking her to join us? Seeing as she was the one who gave me the good news I figured why not have her celebrate with us." Walking in front of the two women, she led them to the dining area.

"Alright! The cavalry is here so if we could all have a seat, I can share my announcement and finally get to eat this scrumptious meal I slaved away at!" Liz excitedly said as she headed to the front of the table. "Sis you sit beside Laurel on this side. And sorta adopted sis you sit on this side beside...." And before she could finish, both her guest and Marie whispered each other's name.

"Jasmine."

"Marie."

The three other women in the room had different reactions to what had happened between the doctor and their friend. The two women looked at each other while the rest looked from one to the other, trying to figure out the situation.

"Hey!" Liz shouted.

"Uh oh!" Toni said softly. Suddenly realizing that this was the 'doctor' that Marie had been telling her about.

"Oh!" Laurel whispered.

Liz leaned closer to Toni. "Uh oh? What do you mean by 'Uh oh?' Is there something I should know?" She asked, still looking at the two other women.

"Just try to act normal and get this show on the road and I will tell you when we go to the kitchen to get the dessert later." Toni whispered as she gave Laurel a wink, telling her silently that she would explain later. Lauren smiled back at her.

"Right! Well... alright then... Ummm... Where was I?...." Liz fumbled as she attempted normalcy.

"Seating arrangements, honey." Ed said, speaking out for the first time and patting his wife's hand, helping her out.

"Oh right! Right! Marie please sit on this side beside Jasmine. She's my doctor...if I haven't already said that." Liz says.

"Hi." Both women whispered to each other as Marie took her seat beside Jasmine.

"So... now that everyone is seated and hopefully comfortable... I would just like to announce my good news!" Liz shouted, getting all excited again. "You guys know I'm pregnant but apparently I'm not carrying just one but TWO!"

Everyone broke out with excitement over the news and congratulated the couple. It helped ease the slight tension in the room and made dinner light and enjoyable affair. As dinner was over and dessert was to be served, Liz stood up and called on Toni to help her in the kitchen leaving behind her husband and Laurel with Jasmine and Marie.

"Alright! I've been patient enough... Spill!" Liz demanded as she and Toni entered her kitchen.

"You don't waste time do you?" Toni laughed. "OK... Remember when you first met Marie you said that there was something there? That you felt that the reason she was the way she was because someone had hurt her?"

"Yes... I remember... I'm pregnant not old, Sister." Liz reminded Toni.

"Well... I was able to make Marie open up to me before coming here. And you're right - she did get hurt by someone. A doctor... apparently your doctor from what transpired back there with your guest and our friend." Toni explained.

"Oh! Uh oh!" Liz reacted.

"I know, right? We have a situation... well... they have a situation. I can definitely see that Marie still has feelings for Jasmine but just can't seem to move forward and give it another try for fear of... Something I don't know." Toni said.

"So what do we do?" Liz asked. "It's pretty obvious with what happened early this evening that whatever it is with the two of them is very much alive."

"What do you mean by what do we do?" Toni asked. "Sister! You let them handle this for themselves." She warned her sister, knowing the gleam in her eyes all too well.

"What? What? If I remember correctly had I not 'handled' YOUR situation with Lauren the two of you would not be here now. Hmmm?" Liz reminded her sister.

"OK... OK... Doesn't matter what I say... You'd just do what you want to do." Toni sighed.

"Exactly!" Liz said, giving her imitation of a Cheshire grin. "Now let's go serve dessert!"

An hour had passed since dinner had finished, and Jasmine had already left, leaving behind the four women sitting in the family room. All three pairs of eyes directed at Marie as she told her history with their dinner guest.

".... So there." Marie finished as she sighed deeply.

"What do you mean by so there? Are you not going to do anything? It will just end with Jasmine leaving here after dinner?" Liz asked incredulously.

"Sis..." Toni tried to warn her sister.

"Don't sis me!" Liz gave Toni a look that said she meant business. She then continued with Marie. "And you Marie, you can't just sit there and tell me that you no longer have feelings whatsoever for Jasmine because it's clear to anyone with eyes that you do!"

"But...I think it's better this way. We've already spoken and I believe we had our closure. Besides, I don't think we could ever have again what we had." Marie reasoned.

"Exactly what did you have? You had two people who met and corresponded on the net, with the plus of getting each other off with flashes of skin and talks of sex. I understand now why you don't want to go further in the real world. You never really cared for each other. It was all an excuse to make what you were doing acceptable." Liz taunted the smaller woman, not liking herself for doing so but wanting to push Marie's buttons to get her to see the truth.

"Stop! Stop that! Don't say it like that!" Marie raised her voice, shocking all three women.

"Marie, I don't think..." Toni tried to soothe her.

"No! It wasn't like that! It wasn't just about the sexual part it was everything! The way we would share everything about each other's lives... The good and the bad... It meant something to me! She means something to me! I love her! I love her with all of my heart! I just don't want to have to lose her all over again, because this time I know it would totally devastate me, especially since it would be for real now!" Marie started to cry as she dropped her head to her hands, sobbing.

Toni tried to stand up from the couch to try to get to the smaller woman, but Liz stopped her and instead wrapped her arms around her adopted sister rocking her.

"I'm sorry kiddo. I'm sorry." She said, kissing the top of her head. "Knowing what I know about you it was most definitely not what I said it was. And seeing the way Jasmine was looking at you tonight I'd bet my life she feels the exact same way you do. I was just saying that to jolt you into accepting what you really feel for her. Forgive me?" Marie couldn't speak, so she just nodded her head in answer to Liz's question.

"Marie, may I say something here?" Laurel asked as the smaller woman nodded again. "I agree with Liz when she says that both you and Jasmine still have strong feelings for each other. Deny it all you want but it was very palpable to all of us. I can't speak for Jasmine but I do know how it feels to hurt when you've hurt the one you love and want to fix things and have the person back into your life." She grabbed hold of Toni's hand as she said this. "I know how it is to want to say and do the right things but end up fumbling it. I'm just very thankful I got to have another chance with Toni." Lauren finished as Toni kissed her and put her head on her shoulder.

"You've already lost a whole year. Do you really want to lose another year without her in your life? I won't give you any guarantees that you won't get hurt along the way but heck no relationship is perfect. You'd both have to work at it." Toni spoke out finally.

"No I don't want to lose another moment without her in my life. You guys are right. I still do have feelings for Jasmine and I want so much for us to be able to work things out." Marie replied. "But how do I go about doing that? Where do I start?" She asked.

"She reached out to you this morning and asked to meet with you to talk things out. Why not do the same? Only this time don't let your hurt and pride get in the way. Take the plunge." Liz said.

"Yeah I agree with Liz. But do it differently. Go to her and talk things out. Tell her how you really feel." Toni added.

"OK... OK I will!" Marie said with a bit of a smile.

It was mid-morning Saturday, and Marie was sitting at her bay window drinking coffee, staring at nothing in particular outside. She knew that she would have to talk things out with Jasmine if she ever wanted them to make a go of things, but had no idea how to go about it. She didn't know her home address, and no way was she going over to her work. Her phone alerted her to a new message, and upon opening it, she saw that Liz had forwarded Jasmine's cell number.

Shaking her head in wonder and saying out loud, "Geez, Liz! It's like you have eyes all over!" she took a deep breath and sent a text message to Jasmine. 'Hi, Jasmine. If you're not busy, could we talk? Marie." Putting down her phone, she waited anxiously for the response. After less than a minute, she received a text from Jasmine. 'Hey! Yes, I am OK to talk. Skype?' Smiling at the positive response, she agreed and booted up her laptop.

As she waited for Jasmine to go online, Marie checked herself in the small mirror on the table, beating hard and fast. 'What if she doesn't want to work things out? Especially after what I said at the coffee shop when she asked if we could be friends! What if she only wants to be friends?' With her thoughts running wildly around her head, she jumped as her laptop alerted her to Jasmine ringing for a video call. Exhaling slowly, she answered the call.

Both women's breaths hitched at seeing each other on the screen. It never failed to surprise them how in that entire year that they were corresponding, every time they got to talk on the phone or do video calls, the sight and sound of each other gave them that hot, tingly, breathless, flustered, 'goosebumps on your goosebumps' feeling. This time was no exception.

"Hi." Marie greeted Jasmine waving her hand on the screen.

"Hi back." Jasmine greeted her the same way.

"Ummm... Thank you for responding right away." Marie smiled.

"No... I should thank you for wanting to talk to me." The taller woman smiled back. "Is everything alright? Are you OK?" She asked worriedly.

"Yes. Yes I'm fine. I just..." Marie stopped mid-sentence, not knowing what to say.

"Hey, I just want to tell you that I didn't know Liz is your friend. I was as surprised as you were that night. Don't worry though I won't say anything." Jasmine explained.

"Ummm.... No it's alright... They know about us. What happened and everything." Marie said. "I had to tell them because they more or less figured it out when both our actions that night spoke louder than words ever could, apparently."

"Oh dear! I'm guessing Liz will be wanting a different doctor, huh?"

"No, of course not! Believe it or not all three women, who I consider more like sisters than friends, were not taking any sides. In fact, it was because of them I'm reaching out to you now. I would like to say that they showed me the light but they more or less bopped me on the head with it... figuratively speaking." Marie explained.

"They did? Ummm.... May I ask what they said?"

"In a nutshell, they said that yes, shit happens... people get hurt... but if you really... ummm... care and have strong feelings for the person you would work things out."

"Do you?"

"Do I what?"

"Do you... care and have strong feelings for me?"

Marie paused for just a second, then responded right away. "Yes. Yes I do. I never stopped. Do you know that even now I still sleep with the shirt you gave me for my birthday two years ago?"

"You do? God! We are such a pair! Do you know that to this very day I still sleep with the shirt you gave me?"

"Did you really just want us to be friends?" Marie asked, cutting to the chase.

"No. I was just all flustered seeing you standing there in front of me for the very first time that I ended up saying the wrong words. I meant to ask if we could work things out. Be friends and lovers again." Jasmine's voice broke a little at saying this.

Marie's eyes started to tear as she smiled what she always called her 'big stupid smile,' which Jasmine always loved. "Oh good! I'm really... really... did I mention REALLY glad you said that. I would most definitely want us to be friends and lovers again."

"Oh god! Do you really mean that? I hope I'm not dreaming all of this." Jasmine said softly, closing her eyes her one hand on her heart, trying to calm the hard beating going on there.

"Jasmine?" Marie called out.

"Yes." Jasmine opened her eyes as she answered.

"Tell me where you live and how to get there. I will show you that this time it's for real." Marie's face beamed with longing and confidence.

As they entered the room, Marie walked on ahead, stopping just at the foot of the big bed, staring down at it. Her arms were wrapped around her middle, trying to ward off the chill going through her while Jasmine looked at her as she closed the door. Jasmine could feel and see that the smaller woman was both nervous and shy.

'God! What if I disappoint her? What if I don't satisfy her? What if? What if?' Marie's thoughts roiled in turmoil.

'Oh God! What if I don't do a thing for her? What if seeing my naked body will have her running out of here? What if? What if?' Jasmine thought she tried to calm herself, taking a deep breath and walking towards Marie.

Stopping just a few inches from the smaller woman, she leaned forward and whispered in her ear: "Hey...we don't have to do anything, you know." This had been the agreement between the two of them since they first started talking – that either of them could back out any time. She didn't touch Marie, knowing that if this was to happen, it had to be Marie who made the first move.

The smaller woman turned around to face Jasmine. "I know... I just..." She faltered, biting her lower lip.

"What? You just what? Talk to me, Marie." Jasmine pleaded.

"I just...don't know where to start....or what to do...or if I'd be doing it right." Marie shrugged.

"I feel the same way too, you know. What if when you see me naked you run in the opposite direction?" Jasmine asked.

"You forget I've seen you already - well parts of you, anyway – you know, when we were corresponding and believe me, with what I've seen you'll have me running towards you and not away." Marie shyly said.

"Yes... but we are talking about seeing me live... where you can see every nook and cranny."

"It doesn't matter to me... It's still you." Marie simply stated.

"OK... OK... Hey, remember what we once agreed to do when we get to see each other live?" Jasmine asked.

"Of course I do. We said no expectations but that we would give each other a hug." Marie smiled at her, remembering.

Opening her arms wide, Jasmine looked longingly at Marie. "Well...here I am...waiting for my hug." Her voice broke a little bit.

Marie, with the same emotion on her face, closed the distance between them. She hugged Jasmine and did what she had been writing in their e-mails and texts since the very beginning - she buried her head in the neck of the taller woman and breathed in her scent. Both women held their breath as their bodies touched for the first time.

"God! You don't how long I've been dreaming of this." Jasmine whispered as her left hand cradled Marie's head while her right hand slipped to her back. Her body shuddered as she felt the tip of the smaller woman's tongue on her neck, and she smiled as she asked. "Did you just do what I think you did?"

Marie giggled softly. "I did promise that when we eventually got to hug that I would sneak a lick of your neck." She lifted her head and looked at Jasmine. "Thank you."

"For what?" Jasmine asked.

"For reminding me... for making it OK." Marie replied, smiling.

"My pleasure." Jasmine smiled back. She brushed back the smaller woman's hair, and brought her hand down, tracing her full lips with her thumb. "Your lips have always reminded me of a perfect bow." She then lowered her head and kissed Marie for the very first time.

The smaller woman pulled Jasmine tighter to her body, arching her neck upwards as she pushed her tongue in, deepening the kiss. Neither woman knew how they got there, but they found themselves standing at the foot of the bed, still kissing. They moved on their knees, face to face in the middle of the bed, taking each other's clothes off piece by piece. When they were both finally naked, Jasmine slowly lay Marie down on her back while she lay on her side, staring at the woman beside her, not making any attempt to touch, and before the smaller woman could make any movements, she halted her.

"What is it?" Marie asked, wondering why they were stopping.

"Wait...give it a moment." Jasmine whispered in awe at the sight of the naked woman in bed with her.

"You finally get me naked in bed and you want to wait?" Marie asked incredulously.

"I just...I just want to relish this moment...have the vision of you naked here with me etched in my memory forever." Jasmine explained.

"Do you know how beautiful you are?" Both women said at the same time. They looked at each other and laughed.

"We are such a pair!" Jasmine said, shaking her head.

"That we are." Marie agreed, smiling.

Jasmine tentatively touched the breast of the smaller woman. "I didn't think I would get to see let alone touch my babies." She whispered as Marie smiled, remembering the pet name Jasmine had for her breasts. "I know that there are seven wonders of the world... but my babies? They're the two wonders of my world." She smilingly said.

"Oh my God! Did you just say that?" Marie asked, laughing.

"Hey! What do you want from me, woman? I'm only human and besides they're just... THERE!" Jasmine said sheepishly.

As their eyes met, their faces showed the passion and yearning they felt for each other. Jasmine moved closer to Marie, taking both her hands and placed them either side of her head, entwining their fingers as she moved on top of her. Aligning their bodies, she slowly lowered herself onto the smaller woman. Their eyes never leaving the other's face, one woman hissed while the other moaned at the intense sensation of feeling flesh against flesh. "You make me feel so many things I can't even begin to describe it." Marie whispered.

"It's the same for me." Jasmine said, she slowly brought her head down towards the smaller woman to give her the most loving and sweetest kiss she had ever experienced, evoking such an intense response that Marie thought she could almost come. As if sensing this, Jasmine pulled back, looking at Marie intensely and said, "No, baby...not yet...we have all night." She spread her fingers in Marie's hair and pulling it back she started to kiss her from her neck down to her breasts, just going around the soft mounds before sucking the pebbled nipple into her mouth.

Marie's body lifted from the bed as she clutched Jasmine's head to her as her lips performed the same magic on her other breast then continued down her stomach, teasing her thighs then to her mound. She didn't kiss or tongue it right away - she nuzzled her face into Marie's soft pussy, enjoying the feel of it on her face. Bringing her head up slightly, she whispered, "Look at me. Watch me love you." Marie looked down, her eyes glazed with passion as Jasmine flicked out her tongue, tasting Marie's cunt and kissing her gently.

Marie felt herself building with Jasmine's tongue on her, her lips and tongue licking, sucking, and kissing her throbbing pussy. Marie was humping her mound on Jasmine's face as she began to shudder. The taller woman slowly moved back up Marie's body, rubbing her slit with her long fingers, and with her other hand, she held the back of Marie's neck, looking at her with fierce, loving eyes. Her voice husky, Jasmine said, "Look at me...stay with me...please." Marie looked up as Jasmine slowly and gently slid a finger inside her. Watching Marie's face for any signs of pain, she reached a barrier inside the smaller woman's body and felt her jolt as she started to cry a little.

Seeing this, Jasmine felt her tears well up as she lovingly said, "Oh Marie! I'm so sorry. If I could take away the pain for you I would." Marie started taking calming breaths. "It's OK. It's OK. Make me yours. I want to be yours." Pushing her hips up against Jasmine's hand, Marie urged her on, and she felt the moment intensely as Jasmine broke through her barrier with all her love and tears shining on her face. Jasmine softly stroked her through the pain until she could feel Marie moving against her again. She intensified her movements, adding friction onto Marie's clit until she felt the smaller woman clench against her and gasp as she came. They both came down from such intense loving with Jasmine still on top of Marie, her face buried in the crook of her neck, softly kissing it now and then while gently massaging and squeezing her breasts.

"Are you OK?" She asked softly.

Marie was still a little breathless when she responded, "You once said that you wanted to make it so good for me that I wouldn't want any other woman after you. Well congratulations. I don't want anyone else."

Jasmine lifted her head and gave her a big goofy grin. "Oh really? You want to go for seconds?" she asked, bringing her hand down on Marie's mound and sliding her long fingers up and down her slit. The smaller woman's body lifted, and her breath hitched as she reacted to the caress, groaning. Marie brought her hand down to Jasmine's as she lifted and held it to her chest and looked at her with so much passion, desire, and love in her dark eyes that the taller woman gasped. "Jasmine...could you...ummm...could you take me with your strap-on now?"

"Are you sure? We don't have to do it, you know...that was just one of my fantasies and this moment is all about you - not me." Jasmine whispered as her other hand, lovingly brushed the hair from Marie's face.

Marie gently cupped Jasmine's face and said, "No...this is ours. It's about both of us. Please... I want you to...make me totally yours."

Jasmine got up from the bed as Marie reluctantly let her go. She took the strap-on from her drawer and slipped it on before climbing back on the bed and slowly lowering her body onto Marie. "Hey," Jasmine said as she looked into Marie's eyes as she aligned her body on top of Marie.

"I missed you." Marie whispered as Jasmine gave her a gentle kiss, then turned into an intensely devouring kiss. Jasmine held Marie's head, burying her fingers in her long silky hair, and as she broke the kiss, a thin thread of saliva still clung to their lips, somehow connecting them. The taller woman licked her lips, breaking the connection.

Breathing hard, Jasmine brought one hand to Marie's breasts, rubbing them. "God! They feel so soft and silky." She lowered her head, licking the space between her breasts, then kissing it as both her hands palmed a breast each, massaging, rubbing, pinching, and cupping them. The smaller woman's chest pushed forward, wanting more and moaning out loud..."Please! Please! God Jasmine! Please suck them... I want your mouth on them."

Jasmine moved her head to first one breast, licking the nipple in short slow flicks, then laving it longer as the nipple became hard, pebbled, and crinkled. She then literally swallowed the breast into her mouth and started to suck on it gently, then harder and licking the nipple creating a sensation of pleasure and pain. She gave the same attention to the other breast as she brought her hand to Marie's mound, drawing out the pleasure even more. With her fingers, she felt if the smaller woman was wet enough and ready to take her. She felt Marie's juices slick on her fingers and knew she was ready, so she let go of her breast and slid slowly up Marie's body. The smaller woman groaned in a complaint, clutching at her. "No! Don't leave me!" Marie cried out.

"'Shhh...it's OK...I'm here." Jasmine whispered as she held on to the rubber penis positioned between her legs, rubbing Marie's wetness. She placed it at Marie's entrance and looked at her, asking, "Are you sure about this?"

Marie placed her hand on top of Jasmine's. "I'm sure. I want this more than you'll ever know. Please Jasmine?" Tears glistened in both their eyes as Jasmine slowly inserted the head into the hot, wet core of the smaller woman. Jasmine could feel the resistance even though the rubber toy. "God Marie! You are so tight!" Jasmine said out loud as she steadily pushed the length into the woman below her, making Marie completely hers. Marie felt an intense sensation of being filled and felt like every nerve ending in her pussy had been lit up at the same time and then blackness.

Marie woke up to the feeling of her chest being rubbed and Jasmine's panicky voice calling out. "Baby, please wake up... Please?"

"What happened?" She asked the distraught Jasmine.

"You blacked out and you scared me. Are you OK, my baby?" Jasmine asked.

"I'm alright. It was just.... Just so intense and so good..." Marie replied, smiling.

"It was? Wait...wait for it...I feel a tingling in my tail-feathers...hmmm...F-LUFF!" Jasmine smirked, and they both laughed.

"God!" Marie exclaimed.

"What? What is it? Are you in pain?" Jasmine asked worriedly.

"You called me 'my baby.' I thought that I would never get to hear you call me that again and I've been wanting you to. So much." Marie admitted.

"My baby. My beautiful, beautiful baby." Jasmine whispered as she cupped Marie's face.

"And you're mine." Marie whispered back, kissing Jasmine tenderly on the lips then deepening it.

Jasmine lifted her head and asked, "Do you want to have something to eat first?" clearly still a bit worried about her lover. Marie looked at Jasmine with a slightly raised eyebrow and said: "I would really want to eat you first before anything else."

"I think I've just created a sex monster." Jasmine teased, rolling her eyes.

"That you have." Marie replied as she pushed Jasmine onto her back on the bed reversing their positions. She straddled the taller woman gazing lovingly at her breasts, then tentatively touching them and lowering her head to kiss the skin between. Jasmine grabbed Marie's head, cradling it to her chest and moaned.

"You OK, baby?" Marie asked.

Taking a deep breath, Jasmine replied, "Yes & no...I'm nervous & excited."

Marie started with one breast, then the other; kissing, licking, sucking, and biting to give her lover the same feeling of intense pleasure and pain that was given to her. Jasmine's body lifted from the bed as Marie started to move down, kissing her on her stomach, licking her navel, kissing her thighs, her inner thighs as she slowly approached her slightly dripping pussy. She saw the wetness and licked it, making the taller woman jerk at the contact and groan out loud. Jasmine grabbed the smaller woman's head with one hand while the other clutched the sheet. Marie held on to Jasmine's thighs and mouthed her mound, sucking her engorged clit into her mouth as she pushed her finger into the squirming woman. She was pumping into her slowly, then starting to pick up the rhythm and not easing up until Jasmine lifted her body from the bed and screamed.

Marie's head lay on her lover's shoulder as her fingers gently glided on Jasmine's stomach, calming her down. "Is it my turn to F-LUFF my tail-feathers?" She teasingly asked.

"God yes! F-LUFF to your heart's content! You deserve it!" Jasmine said, still trying to catch her breath. "I never came that hard and strong! I'm so wet that if I was to walk right now I'd be squelching!"

"Ummm...could you say that word again?" Marie asked.

"What word, my baby?"

"Ummm...'squelch'" Marie said shyly.

"Squelch." Jasmine repeated the word. "Oh my God! Baby! I'd forgotten how you used to ask me to say certain words cos' it gets you turned on!"

"Well now that you remember, could you now say the following words to me to me now that we're finally 'live'? 'Swollen', 'succulent' AND 'suppository!'" Marie pleaded.

"You're crazy, you know that woman?" Jasmine started laughing.

"Yes... I am crazy... Crazy about you, my baby." Marie whispered with love glowing on her face.

"Yes, my sweet angel...your baby." Jasmine affirmed, her face alight with the same glow, holding Marie's body tightly to her, never wanting to let her go.

Lesbian Threeway
Three HOT, Erotic, Sexy & Short Stories for Adults
Alana Meehan

All Rights Reserved. No part of this publication may be reproduced in any form or by any means, including scanning, photocopying, or otherwise without prior written permission of the copyright holder. Copyright © 2021

This book is entirely a work of fiction. The names, characters and incidents portrayed in it are the work of the author's imagination. Any resemblance to actual persons, living or dead, events or localities is entirely coincidental.

Story 01

Lucy and her husband, Bruce, were enjoying dinner at a fine restaurant in New York City. The 22yr-old couple drove up here from their home in rural Virginia. The blond 5'2" blue-eyed beauty was fascinated with the big city; it was a far cry from her farm in Va. The couple loved their farm, but it was good to get away for a week. The farm provided ample income, and they thought it would be a good time to get away before they had any children. They both wanted kids but planned to wait for about another year; they had been married only eight months.

Lucy noticed an exotic beauty standing at the bar. The woman stood out from the crowd; she was tall, over 6'. Her skin was dark, and she had long black hair past her shoulders, and halfway down her back, her eyes sparkled, and her 42DD breast pointed upward. Lucy was mesmerized by the captivating creature, as was everyone in the room.

Lucy excused herself and went to the ladies' room; when she exited the stall, Lucy was startled to see the sensual beauty looking in the mirror and admiring herself. "Hi!" Lucy said while washing her hands after she dried them, the woman placed her hands on the young blond's shoulders and spun her around and kissed her full on the lips, whirling her tongue in the frightened young wife's mouth.

Lucy felt tingles down her spine, and she felt the dampness form in her panties. She was on fire and couldn't understand it. She had never been with a female before, not even another man, only her husband. The dominating dark-haired beauty squeezed Lucy's 34C cup breast and ushered the blond wife by the arm inside the end stall. With her other hand, she slid her fingers up Lucy's leg and inside her panties.

While squeezing her breast, she inserted two fingers in Lucy's pussy, and finger fucked her obscenely. Lucy was gasping for breath and moaning. The fingers became a blur as they fucked her sopping cunt feverishly. Lucy was fucking back as her body shook, and she reached a powerful orgasm. "What is your name?"

"My..my.. name is Lucy." the aroused blond answered.

"I'll just call you Juicy Lucy, you are so fucking wet. Here, smell and suck my wet fingers, taste yourself."

Lucy was in a daze, she felt compelled to obey this gorgeous woman, and she could not understand why. She wondered what was wrong with her as she sucked her pussy juice from the authoritative woman's fingers.

With a firm hand, she was pushed to sit on the toilet seat. The voluptuous beauty lifted her dress and displayed her hairy cunt just inches from Lucy's pretty face. On the other hand, she guided that pretty face to her waiting cunt. The scent that was omitted from the aroused cunt was overpowering and intoxicating. Lucy kissed and licked the pussy without ever being told! The woman roughly held her face to the sopping cunt. Lucy ate the pussy like it was the best meal she ever had. Her face glistened with pussy juice as she was pushed away from the delicious cunt. "Enough for now, little one. Is that your husband at the table?"

"Yes." It is all that the bewildered blond could reply.

"Clean yourself up, you are a mess, I will meet you at the table!"

Lucy looked her in the eyes and was lost in the deep black sea; it was as if her eyes were an ocean, and it was pulling her in. She was mesmerized and had no will of her own, she wondered how this could happen to her, but Lucy knew that she would do anything this woman told her to do! As she looked in the mirror, Lucy saw that she was indeed a mess, the pretty face was glowing with pussy juice, the hair was all messed up, and her dress was twisted. The young blond did her best to make herself presentable and endeavored to return to the table.

Bruce was standing and conversing with the exotic sex goddess. He looked so handsome in his blue suit; it matched his blue eyes, his brown hair looked lighter next to her black hair. Bruce was 6" tall and had to look up to her, she was about 6"3', but she did wear high-heels.

"Isis tells me you two met in the ladies room and hit it off right away."

"Yes, you could say that." Lucy blushed as she recalled what happened in the ladies' room. The waitress brought us a round of drinks and could not keep her eyes off the buxom beauty; neither could Bruce.

"Lucy is such a nice person, a giving person, wouldn't you say."

"Yes she is, I'm amazed that you got to know her so well in such a short time." Bruce answered.

"Indeed, we have become very close, she is very special, it was destiny that we met." Then Isis placed her hand on the young woman's thigh.

"Where are you from?" Bruce inquired.

"I live right here in New York, but my family is from Egypt, I still have relatives in Cairo. Where are you from?"

"We have a farm in Virginia and we love it but it's good to get away for a vacation, Lucy and I will be here for about a week, this is our first night in town."

" I own a club and tomorrow night I insist that you two visit my place for dinner, a show and drinks, it will be on the house of course."

"Oh, how nice of you, but you don't have to do that for us." Lucy said.

"I know that I don't have to, but I want to give you a nice welcome to the city, I am very fond of you." Isis's hand moved to lightly brush Lucy's pussy. The young wife was embarrassed and hoped her husband could not tell what was going on.

"Where are you two staying?"

"We think we are staying next door but our reservations got lost and they are trying to help us." Bruce answered.

"Nonsense, you will stay with me, my husband and I have a large home and it would be my pleasure to have you as guest; my husband will be back tomorrow. He is in the import-export business and comes and goes quite a bit, it would please me to have you stay with us."

"No, we could not impose on you like that," Lucy was going to say more, but a finger slipped in her pussy, and she was afraid to say anything else.

Isis placed her arm around the younger woman's shoulders and said, "Come on, you know that you want to stay with me and I would love the company."

"Well I...I.. guess so!" Lucy mumbled, not wanting to reveal her arousal as the 31yr-old woman moved her finger inside Lucy's now wet cunt.

"Let's go home and relax, where is your luggage?"

"It's in our car."

Isis called her driver, and he came to the table and got the keys to drive the couple's car. Lucy and Bruce walked with Isis to her Rolls outside the front door. All passers-by stared at Isis; her presence commanded attention.

After a half-hour drive, the Rolls parked in front of a large apartment building with a doorman. The elevator took them to the top floor, and they entered the room and were stunned by the size and beauty of the place. Isis gave them a tour and directed her driver to their room with the luggage.

Isis turned on some music and led them to the balcony, where they sipped champagne and enjoyed the breathtaking view of the city.

"Your place is fantastic, I love it!" exclaimed Lucy.

"I'm so glad you like it, little girl." She kissed Lucy full on the mouth.

Bruce stared at the sight of his young wife being held and kissed by this exotic beauty.

Isis pulled him to them and kissed him passionately. She felt his cock stiffen and press against her; she held their hands and led them to the master bedroom.

Isis glided the zipper down and let her dress fall to the floor; she stepped out of it and stood before the young couple naked except for her high heels and stockings. Her brown skin glowed, long legs led to her hair-covered love pot, her big brown aureoles circled her huge breast, and her long nipples pointed straight out invitingly. Lust filled her beautiful eyes, and she commanded them to disrobe.

Bewitched, they both took their clothes off and stood before the sex goddess nude. She pulled them to her and fed the couple each a nipple to suck on. "That's good, suck them, don't be afraid, bite my nipples, yes, like that!"

"You are so sexy." Bruce moaned.

"These are the most beautiful tits I have ever seen." Lucy cooed.

"Now both of you, get on your knees and kiss my legs, thighs, pussy and ass, kiss and lick all over, don't miss an inch!" The married couple complied and worshiped the sex goddess with their mouths and tongues.

Once again, Lucy found herself eating her smoldering pussy as Bruce kissed her ass. "Eat that cunt bitch, put your whole face in there, put your tongue up my ass hole, fuck me with your tongue, yes." Isis hissed. She trembled and quivered to a rousing orgasm.

The exotic beauty pulled the couple to their feet and stuck two fingers in Lucy's cunt and stroked Bruce's stiff cock."I want you in me now, I want you to fuck me." as she shoved Bruce on the bed, "Lucy! I want you to stand there and play with yourself and watch me fuck your husband!"

Lucy just stood there and watched as this dominating woman straddled her man's 7" cock and fucked furiously. They both groaned and yelled out in wild lust. The little wife was fucking her self with her fingers and hating herself for being aroused while watching another woman fuck her husband.

Isis moaned in orgasm, and Bruce followed by shooting a load up her hot cunt. She rolled off her lover and said."Get up here and lick him clean." Lucy climbed on the bed and was once more on her knees as she licked Bruce's cock clean of his cum and Isis's pussy juice.

Isis ordered, "Now crawl over to my cunt and lick it all up, Yes that's it, don't forget my ass, its dripping down there, get every drop, good girl; I know you enjoy the taste of my juice mixed with your husband's cum."

The sexy woman gathered her clothes and bid them goodnight saying."Get plenty of sleep my little pets and we will have a busy day tomorrow,see you in the morning."

Lucy was crying, "What's wrong?" Bruce asked.

"What's wrong!. how could you ask me that? We have become her sex slaves, how could we let this happen?"

"Now, now, it's not that bad, she has a power over people that can't be resisted, at least we did it together and I still love you, with her it is just fabulous sex; let's enjoy it together and then go back to our farm and our life as a loving married couple."

"She does have a presence that demands attention, I can't be angry with you when I can't resist her myself. I never dreamed that I would be doing that with anyone but you, let alone a woman!"

"Like I said, let's just enjoy it together, she is truly amazing, as long as you still love me, nothing else matters."

"I do, I love you with all my heart, but this is so strange." They drifted off to sleep.

The young couple woke up and enjoyed their bathroom as they dressed for the day, Lucy wore a pink sundress, and Bruce had on a pair of shorts and a polo shirt.

They joined Isis at the kitchen table for coffee. The shower was running, "Who's that," Lucy inquired.

"Kek, my husband."

"Oh, does he know about last night?"

"Of course he does, we keep no secrets from each other, I hope that you don't either."

"No, you are the only person other than my husband that I have ever had sex with!"

"How about you, Bruce?"

"NO, no secrets, I love my wife too much to ever cheat on her, I never want to hurt her. You are the only one I've been with since my marriage."

"Good I admire that." Isis said as she sipped her coffee.

Kek entered the room wearing only boxer shorts.

And a tank-top. Lucy blushed as she gazed at the outline of his huge cock. He caught her gaze, and she quickly looked away.

Isis grabbed the young housewife by the wrist and placed her hand on the huge cock. "Oh my," the startled blond gasped.

"Feel his big cock, make it grow, show him how much you like it and give Bruce and I a show." Isis got up from her chair and pulled her husband's shorts down, revealing a long, thick, uncircumcised semi-hard cock. Then Isis moved Lucy's chair out from the table so that it was facing Kek.

The dominating woman was no longer holding her hand to the big cock, but Lucy did not move her hand away. She was squeezing it lovingly; the young housewife had never seen an uncircumcised cock before; she was a virgin when she married, but she did play with a couple of cocks and even sucked one before she got married, but nothing like this monster!

She moved her small hand up and down the shaft as she cupped his ball-sack with her other hand. The big cock stiffened and grew to a fully erect 11 thick inches. Lucy could not fit her hand around his cock; the wedding ring was obscenely on display as the young wife stroked this man's fat cock. Her eyes never left the huge cock; she was fascinated with his big hunk of meat.

"Kek, rub it on her face, then I want you to suck his big cock, bitch! My hand is on your husband's cock and you are turning us on," ordered the authoritative siren.

He rubbed his cock all over her pretty face and then placed the bulbous prick head to her lips. Her sweet red lips kissed the brown invader with loving adoration. The big cock entered her mouth, and you could see the indentations on her cheeks as the large tool probed her mouth. He was fucking her face hard and jamming his cock down her throat.

Lucy took as much of the big fat cock in her sweet little mouth as she could; she was gasping and choking, saliva was dripping down her chin. Lucy was moaning with pleasure.

Isis got up from her chair and grabbed a fistful of blond hair and pulled her from the big cock, and pushed her head down on the table, bending her over, saying, "Pull her panties down and fuck her. I want to see this little bitch get fucked royally."

Kek stuffed his cock in her pussy and began fucking her from behind.

"Oh. it's so biggg, oh, I can feel my pussy stretching wide open, Oh Godddd, uhhh... ummmnnn, oh shittt..."

Kek was now fucking her furiously; you could hear a clapping sound as his balls hit her ass. He was pumping hard and fast; they were both moaning in lust.

Clutching the blond hair, Isis lifted her head from the table and said, "Look in Bruce's eyes and tell him how much you like my husband's big cock up your snatch. I want you to look at Bruce when you cum! Let him see what a little fuck-slut you really are!"

Kek was grunting, and Lucy was groaning, the young wife tried not to show the pleasure she was feeling, but her body was betraying her. Lucy felt her orgasm mount and could no longer control herself; her whole body was tingling, goosebumps appeared all over her arms; she was fucking back at the pleasure pole in her hungry cunt!

"Look in his eyes, tell your husband how much you like the big cock!"

"Oh, oh yessss, it feels soooo goodd, his big fat cock is making meee cummmm.. oh, oh god, fuck me, fuck meeee, yessss!!!" Isis pushed the young wife to the floor and commanded, "Get on your knees and lick him clean, Bruce get over here and cum in her mouth, not in your hand!!"

She licked the big cock clean and then took her husband's cock in her mouth and sucked with passionately; it did not take long before he was shooting his load in her hot little mouth.

"Swallow it all, swallow every single drop of his hot cum, then I will allow you to eat my cunt, I'm so fucking hot!"

The demanding beauty straddled her face and pushed that pretty face into her cunt; the young wife licked and sucked until they were both spent, and her face was glistening with pussy juice.

"What a good little pussy licker you are, just think, in two days you have become a total fuck slut." Lucy felt so humiliated, so degraded. She looked up at her husband and said, "I'm sorry, I couldn't help it, I love you so much."

"I love you Lucy, more than I can say."

"Good, you love each other, Kek and I are in love as well, We are all just very good fucking friends,

The young couple was washing up and changing, and Lucy said, "You know, she's right, I am a fuck-slut! How can you ever feel the same way about me after my slutty actions?"

"Things are not the same, they are better, you have experienced a sexual awakening, hell, we both have. Don't feel bad about it, go with it, enjoy yourself. As long as we do everything together and you don't cheat on me and deceive me, look at it as a wild adventure."

"You liked watching me fuck him and licking her pussy? I felt so guilty looking in your eyes while I was cumming on his big fat cock! It felt so good, I just couldn't help it."

"Yes I did, as long as you still love me, don't confuse love and sex."

"As much as I loved the feelings his big cock gave me, I don't have any feelings for him at-all. I just love only you."

"Good, She is a sexy woman and fucking her was great but I love you not her. Let's enjoy our vacation and have no regrets; when we grow old and grey, we won't have to worry about the things that we didn't do." They hugged and kissed passionately.

The young couple joined Isis and Kek on the balcony and marveled again at the city's view. "New York looks so beautiful from up here!" Lucy exclaimed.

"Yes it does, it's a nice day to go shopping, come with me Lucy and I will buy you some sexy clothes for tonight."

"I have clothes with me."

"I know but a girl can always use more, there is no such thing as having enough, that goes for clothes as well as sex; it will be fun, shopping is one of my favorite pastimes."

"Ok, but what about the boys, what will they do?"

"I am going to take Bruce to the race track, my horse is running in the 7th race at the big"A" today."

"Sounds great, a day at the races, the sport of kings." Bruce said.

The new clothes were placed in the car trunk, and the girls entered a tavern to have lunch. As they sipped their drinks, Lucy wondered. "How come you never eat me, why am I always the one to go down on you?" Lucy was embarrassed to notice that the buxom redhead young waitress had returned to the table with another round and had overheard her question. The lovely young thing placed the drinks on the table and told them that they were compliments of the house, pointing to the sexy barmaid and smiling at them.

Isis answered the question, telling the redhead to remain and listen, "I don't eat pussy, you do, and you lick my cunt so good, I know that you love it. Here is a fact for you; I can get any man or woman that I want, to eat my delicious pussy, to do what ever I want them to do. Everyone desire's me and you know it."

Looking the waitress straight in the eye, she asked, "Wouldn't you like to put your sexy lips on my luscious cunt?"

"I...I guess so, you are very sexy and I must admit that I feel a very strong attraction to you. I get an hour break in ten minutes and there's a storeroom we could go to."

The 21yr.old girl led them behind the bar and thru a door to the storeroom; the barmaid also joined them, saying that she was on break also and wanted to join the fun.

The storeroom was full of bar and restaurant supplies, with boxes piled high. The 27yr-old barmaid brushed back her long brown hair and stated to Isis, "There is something about you that draws me to you. I just can't resist you." as she got to her knees and kissed up the exotic beauty's leg, Isis took off her skirt and Instructed the woman to eat her cunt.

Observing the name tag on the waitress, Isis commanded, "Lucy, while Maggie is waiting to service me, lick her cunt, show her what you can do."

Maggie disrobed and leaned back against the boxes next to Isis and spread her legs invitingly. Lucy was soon lapping the succulent, sparsely red-haired pussy. The aroused redhead put her hand on Isis's breast and pleaded, "Can I suck your tits while Kim eats your cunt?"

"Yes baby, do it, suck my big tits!" Maggie vigorously sucked both nipples, pressing the huge globes together and sucking both nipples at the same time. Lucy reached up and massaged Maggie's firm tits as she licked her sopping pussy.

"Oh yeah, eat me, suck that pussy!" Maggie cried out as she reached orgasm.

Isis told Maggie to replace Kim at her cunt and told Kim to worship her ass. "Lucy! Fuck Kim from behind, fuck her pussy and ass with your talented little tongue; repay her for the tongue fucking she gave me."

"Oh goddd, work those tongues, suck my cunt, stick your tongue up my ass hole. Oh shittt.. I'mmm...Cummingggg. Ohhh...yesssss...sooo good!"

They all kissed, and Isis and Lucy went back to their table and finished lunch."How does your lunch taste mixed with pussy juice?"

"Not bad, I like it."

"I noticed you gobble that red-haired pussy up, I almost got jealous."

"She was hot, I would like her to eat my pussy too, or maybe share her with our husbands, they would love to fuck that hot little bitch."

"My, my, you are becoming such a sexual animal, I can't imagine you talking like that a couple of days ago, how you have changed in such a short time."

"It's your fault, you have changed me; you have opened me up sexually."

"You haven't even washed the pussy juice off of your face, you wear it like a badge of honor! At the club tonight you will receive your reward; I have two young Egyptian belly-dancers working for me, they will eat your cunt so good that you will cum better than you ever have in your whole life, they are experts and your pussy will finally have a woman's tongue in it. That is your desire, is it not?"

"Yes it is, I wanted you to eat me, but it sounds great. I'm looking forward to tonight.

They were in the living room, getting ready to go to the club, and Lucy was wearing a sexy outfit that Isis had purchased for her. "I feel like a slut in this short red dress, it's so tight, it barely covers my ass and my nipples are on full display!"

"What do you mean, you feel like a slut? You are a slut," Isis offered

"You look sexy baby, you look so fuckable." Kek said as he lifted her dress to confirm the fact that she wore no underwear.

"Oh, Lucy, with that short red dress, the black stockings, and black high-heels, I'm getting hot just looking at you, just knowing that there is nothing else covering your sweet pussy is getting me hard!" Her husband stated.

They were seated in a cozy booth near the stage and enjoyed a gourmet dinner. While sipping their drinks, they talked about the last few days and told the men about how Isis had seduced the waitress and how the four women had sex in the storeroom. The band played Mideastern music, and the belly dancers displayed their exotic wares.

A new dancer was on the stage, moving her slim dark body in a sensual manner that caught the crowd's attention. "Layla is one of the favorite dancers at the club. Do you like her Lucy?"

"Yes I do, she can really dance and she is so lovely and sexy."

"Good dear, after she is finished her show we will go back to her dressing room and she will eat your pussy and you can cum all over her sexy face!"

"Uhmmm, sounds so erotic, I can hardly wait."

"Lucy has been complaining that she is always eating pussy and want's a woman to eat her cunt for a change."

Both men said that they would gladly eat her pussy. The dancer finished, and Isis took Lucy's hand and said, "Excuse us, gentlemen, we will see you in a little while, it's time for Lucy's treat.

The woman entered the door to the dressing room and disappeared. Bruce said, "I would like to see that."

"Good, follow me, it's Showtime!"

Kek led the way to a door behind a curtain that brought them to another showroom; they were seated and served drinks. "What's this!" Bruce inquired with a look of puzzlement on his face.

"This is the private showroom, where only special guest may come and cum. Get ready for a show that you will never forget."

Inside the small dressing room, two dancers were changing from their costumes. Isis poured a green-colored liquid in a shot glass and told Lucy to drink it. The young wife did and asked what it was. "It's just something to turn you on and relax you."

"Is this the young lady you told us about? The sweet little housewife that wants us to eat her pussy."

"Yes, this is Lucy, meet Femi and Layla, two hot Egyptian women that will rock your world."

The two exotic females were naked. Both were 5'10" tall, slender, and had small breasts. They moved toward the blond wife, their dark skin contrasted with her white skin, her dress was lifted, and the top of her red dress was lowered, exposing her pussy and breast. Lips sucked her tits, and three fingers were stuffed in her hot cunt.

"Wow! This cunt is soaked, what a slut!

"That is why I call her Juicy-Lucy. She is always ready."

The two dancers took her hands and told her that they were taking her to a larger room. They opened a door and guided her to the center of a stage. Her dress was once again lifted to her waist and rolled up so that it looked like a large red belt.

One woman was kissing her on the lips, and the other was kissing her neck; they traveled down her body until they reached her pussy and ass. Lucy squealed with delight as her pussy and ass were being tongued by the sexy women. Lucy felt dizzy and aroused more than she had ever been before. The young wife wondered what the bright lights were, and she thought she heard voices. This is a funny room; she reasoned.

Isis joined the men at the table and sat in the center, placing a hand on each cock she said, "Let's watch our little slut in action, I gave her something to dull her mind and heighten her sexual feelings, this should be a performance to remember, you guys are getting hard already!"

"What did you give her? Not drugs I hope, I don't want any harm to come to her!" Bruce worriedly asked.

"No, No drugs, just ancient herb, it will not harm her, just relax her and stimulate her pussy, now let's watch," she said as she squeezed both cocks.

Lucy was moaning and hissing, "Oh, oh, yes, please don't stop, it feels so good!" as both tongues brought her to orgasm. She was trembling, and goosebumps appeared all over her body. She could hardly stand; her legs were wobbly. Lucy was startled to see a dwarf run on stage. (to her dulled mind, enter the room.) The small man circled her as the two women held her to keep from falling. He wore just a pair of slacks and slippers; the dwarf stood between her legs and started licking. He didn't even have to kneel. Her eyes were wide, and her mouth hung open as she gave way to the pleasure he was giving her.

The women guided her to the floor, and the dwarf dropped his pants and revealed a stiff cock that looked so much bigger than it's seven thick inches. He straddled her face and placed his cock on her sweet red lips and slowly entered her mouth. The young housewife willingly accepted his hunk of meat and feverishly sucked as saliva oozed from her sweet mouth.

Isis was jerking two cocks off, and both men were sucking her tits and finger fucking her as they all watched the action on stage. The club's patrons were engaged in various sexual acts, masturbation, oral, fucking, groups, man & man, woman &woman, and every combination one could imagine!

Isis got up and walked to a nearby table and came back with a man, his wife, and her sister; the sisters were in their early 20's with light brown hair, brown eyes, petite bodies, and pretty faces. The man was extremely handsome, with piercing blue eyes and long blond hair. Isis ordered the women to suck cock, and the blond husband to eat her cunt.

Back on stage, the dwarf withdrew his cock from her hungry mouth with a plop sound. Lucy looked so disappointed. She wanted his cock in her mouth so bad. The little man straddled her and teased the young wife by moving his cock over her pussy. He rubbed it all over her pussy lips. He lingered at her clit and slowly rubbed it with his throbbing cock. Then he taunted her, saying, "Tell me you want me to fuck you, tell me how much you want my cock."

"Yes fuck me, I want your cock in me."

"Not good enough bitch, beg for it, Tell me how much you want me to fuck your slutty cunt." He chided the extremely aroused blonde.

"Oh, yes, please fuck me. please put your cock in my nasty cunt. I want it in my pussy so bad, please!"

He smiled and said, "That's much better slut, I'm going to fuck the shit out of your stinking cunt, you will do anything I say!" He plowed his cock in her eager cunt.

"Oh, so good, thank you, don't stop, I love it, fuck me.!" He pulled his cock out of her. "What's wrong? Please put it back in me, fuck me."

"Get on your knees bitch! I want to fuck you from behind, fuck you like a dog, make you squeal like the pig that you are."

The blond housewife quickly got on her knees and stuck her ass and pussy obscenely in the air to give him easy access to her hungry cunt. "There, just as you want, now please fuck me some more!"

"Look bitch, move your shitty ass and slut cunt back to me, rub my cock with your sex and beg me to fuck you."

She pushed back until her cunt and ass made contact with his stiff cock; she wiggled her ass lewdly in the air and implored him," Please fuck me, stick it in my pussy, please."

The dwarf put his cock in her pussy and said, "Yeah, that's it, fuck back at my cock, good girl, I can feel your hungry cunt tighten on my prick, you like it don't you slut?"

"Oh yes, it feels so good, ohhh, I'm cumminggg...,fuck meeee,ohhhh yessss,don't stop pleaseeesss...!" as she reached several orgasms. He kept fucking her feverishly. She came again.

The dwarf pulled his still stiff throbbing cock out of her sopping cunt; his dick was covered with her juices, her cunt was dripping wet. He shoved his cock in her tight little ass hole.

"NO, not in my ass, it hurts, don't do this to me, please stop, noooo.."

He fucked her ass hard; his cock was all the way up her ass, the slapping sound of his balls hitting her ass was loud as he pumped her ass with passion.

The pain gave way to pleasure; she was now fucking back with fervor, crying out loud, "Oh god, yesss. fuck my ass, yes!"

"You like my big old dick stuffed up your smelly little ass hole, You fucking slut, beg some more, tell me that you want it!" As he grabbed a fist full of blond hair and pulled her head back.

"I want it, I want it all the way up my tight ass, it feels good, please don't stop, yes, fuck my slut ass."

"That's it, fuck back with all you got, give it to me, your ass is mine, I'm going to shoot you full of slime!"

"Oh god, yes, shoot your cum up my ass, I'm cumming again, ohh...yessss...ughhhh mmnnn, shitttt...!!"

"Here it cums slut, I'm filling your ass with my cum, take it, take it all, yes, ohhhhh..yeahhhh...!!"

She fell to the floor in an exhausted clump; he turned her over and made the sweet little wife lick him clean. She lovingly devoured every drop of juice and cum from his semi-hard prick.

The two dancers were extremely aroused and forced Lucy to eat their cunt's and lick ass before they escorted the completely disoriented young wife to Isis's table. The applause from the crowd only made her more confused.

She sat next to Isis and rested her head on the dark beauty's shoulder and fell asleep.

They decided to leave the orgy and go home.

The drive home was filled with a chat about the night. They had all cum many times and were tired.

"Your wife was the star of the show, if she ever want's a job, let me know. I would hire her in a New York minute. She would be the star attraction, the club would be full all of the time, the crowd loved her and the dwarf want's to work with her again!" Isis laughed.

"I bet he does, but he will have to abuse someone else, we are going back to the farm. Oh, Kek, I now see what you meant about the secret club when you said they come to cum!"

The men carried Lucy to bed; she was still out cold. They all slept late the next morning.

Lucy and Bruce helped themselves to coffee and relaxed at the kitchen table. Isis came in and got some more coffee for Kek and herself and was surprised to see them. "Good morning sleepy heads, about time you got up. Bring your coffee with you and join us in the game room."

"We thought you were still asleep!" Lucy exclaimed.

"Care to challenge us to a game of pool." Isis asked.

"Wow, what a room you have here, a jukebox, hockey game, darts, a beautiful pool table and pinball machines, awesome, I love it." Lucy excitedly exclaimed.

"I play some pool but Lucy don't play at all, but what the hell, let's give it a shot." Bruce answered.

After hours of playing games, they had lunch and beer on the balcony. "You don't have to go home now, you can earn lots of money at my club."

"Thanks, but we are looking forward to going back to the quiet life, but I must confess, it's been exciting and I will never forget this week. I will never forget you, but Isis, anyone that gets the pleasure of knowing you will always remember, you are truly unforgettable."

"You are so sweet, we will miss you more than you will ever know, I've become so fond of both of you. When will you be leaving us?"

"Tomorrow afternoon before the rush hour traffic starts, we were going to leave early in the morning but none of us are used to getting up early and we do want to see you before we go." Bruce announced.

"Please, can we stay home and just hang out together on our last night with you, after last night I could use a break from the night life, Bruce and I want to be with just you two!"

"We will stay home tonight and I have a special evening planned for us, it's my going away gift to my juicy-Lucy." Lucy had a concerned look on her face, wondering what her special evening would consist of.

After dinner, they just sat around and enjoyed each other's company. Isis said, "Time to get ready for the big night." She led Lucy to the master bedroom by the hand.

"Try them on." as she handed the blond a big box from her closet. Lucy excitedly opened the box, and her face showed her delight as she held a satin robe in her hands."Get your clothes off, I want to see you in everything."

Lucy quickly disrobed and modeled everything; there were several sets of lingerie and five silk and satin robes, shoes, slippers, and stockings. "Oh, they are all so beautiful, thank you, I love you!" Lucy said as tears of joy filled her big blue eyes.

"I love you too, you will always be special to me, I will never forget you, let me help you select a sexy outfit for our last night together." The blond wife beamed as she gazed in the mirror wearing a baby blue brassiere, matching thong and silk robe that barely covered her buttocks, set off with black stockings and garter and black high-heels.

Isis exclaimed, "Oh my god, you are a vision of beauty, you look good enough to eat. The baby blue makes your eyes sparkle and stand out .So sexy, now let me slip into something and we will join the boys." Isis wore the same thing except it was all black. "One more thing, we can't spoil your surprise," a black blindfold was placed around her eyes, and she was led to the living room.

Lucy heard the sound of cheering, but there were too many voices, more women voices than there should be. She had been spun around and told to kiss whomever she stopped in front of. The blond wife felt soft lips kiss her lips, and it was not Isis, but she was sure that it was a woman's lips. Who could this be, she wondered?

The blindfold was removed, and Lucy was shocked to see Maggie standing in front of her. Kim was there as well."What a total surprise, this is super! Thank you everybody."

Isis commanded, "Ok, now all of you grab a seat and play with each other and watch the show; jucy-Lucy and I are going to entertain you and you will see me do something that I have never done before!"

The amazonian sex goddess kissed the petite blond wife full on the lips and inserted her long tongue in the submissive little mouth; she broke the kiss and unstrapped her bra and instructed the young wife to suck her tits. Lucy adoringly nursed the ample breast and cooed with ecstasy as she sucked the pointy nipples. The authoritative beauty pushed the blond to her knees and commanded, "Eat my cunt, lap it up, suck on my pussy lips, yes, give me that sweet tongue, oh hell yeah!"

The little wife licked and slurped with fervor. She just could not get enough of her succulent cunt; you taste so good she moaned, I love your delicious pussy, I will miss you."

After her quaking orgasm, she lifted the young woman to her feet and kissed her and said, "Mmnnn, I do taste good don't I! Now let me taste you!" as she knelt before the startled young wife.

Two firm hands dragged the thong down her shaky legs, and sensual lips kissed up her legs, lingering at her thighs, over her waiting for pussy to her stomach and tenderly licked and kissed back to her eager pussy. Lucy moaned as the long tongue flicked in and out of her tingling tunnel of love.

Isis buried her face deep into the hungry pussy and kissed, licked, and sucked furiously. She did not relent; she gobbled the sweet pussy up and brought the young wife to a rousing orgasm. Lucy fell to the floor, totally spent, and satisfied.

As she composed herself, Lucy exclaimed, " I thought you never ate pussy, you sure are great at it!"

"Outside of my husband I have never felt so strong toward another person, I wanted to express my feelings for you, to let you know just how much that I care for you. You're just too good to be true,. as the song goes, it was my first time and if I did it good, it's because I did it with love; I'm so happy that you enjoyed it."

With her hand, Isis beckoned the others to Lucy and said that this night was all about pleasing the pretty little wife who pleased others so much. Kek inserted his big cock in her as Bruce placed his in her mouth; the women all kissed her breast and any other space on her body that they could find room. Lucy passed out from pure pleasure, and Bruce carried her to their room, all the while, she had a great big smile on her pretty face.

The next day as they departed, the women had tears in their eyes as they kissed goodbye. Isis said, "You will have to come back soon or I will come to the farm and visit you. So long and remember we love you!"

Story 02

It had been a long hard year at work. Krissy's business was going great guns, and she decided she needed a break. She decided to ask Julia to accompany her, knowing fine well that her young girlfriend would accept and provide suitable 'entertainment' to satisfy Krissy's developing sexual tastes.

A couple of weeks later, they found themselves poolside at the fabulous old school Bangkok Oriental Hotel, undoubtedly one of the best hotels in the Far East. They had got over the jetlag in the first day or two and taken in a few sights with the aid of a very pretty local guide, a student who worked as a tour guide to fund her studies.

The guide was confused as to Krissy and Julia's relationship, close and touchy like sisters, but physically obviously not. They must be friends, but the way they were with each other was not like the other tourists she met. Typically, Thai, she was far too polite to ask. Krissy enjoyed teasing her and making her blush and wondered what it would be like to corrupt this innocent young girl with the small boyish frame. She and Julia made love that night after speculating about the guide's tiny tits and whether or not she would have a shaved pussy or a soft black bush.

Day three and the girls decided to chill out by the pool and enjoy the hazy sunshine. The pool was a standard 1920's type, long and rectangular, rather than the resort-type, which curves and is laid out to provide privacy to sunbathers. Here you sat out on the bed and could see everyone else lying facing the pool. Hidden behind sunglasses, Krissy was able to watch the wealthy patrons of the Oriental enjoying the fruits of their labors. Mostly it was couples or wives on their own, but fortunately, no kids – it just wasn't that kind of hotel, thank God.

One couple confused Krissy. In fact, they didn't look like a couple at all, mother and daughter, perhaps? One was a slim brunette, about 19 years old, beautifully tanned, and resplendent in a small bright red bikini. It wasn't just her imagination that the girl was capturing the attention of most of the men around the pool, but also her lover, Julia.

The girl was holidaying with an older woman, early forties, but well kept. She was still toned, though curvaceous with it, her tits at least a D cup and her ass well rounded, but not flabby. The thing that struck Krissy was that the older woman showed no signs of previous pregnancy, any stretch marks or scars, and there was just a little similarity between her and the younger one. Their relationship was not like Krissy's own with her young partner. She vowed to find out.

It wasn't hard to do. After lunch, she waited to see where the couple set themselves down to catch the afternoon sun. Krissy positioned Julia and herself on the bed next to them. There would be no objection from Julia, who was captivated by the slim brunette. When the young girl headed for the pool, Krissy suggested with a knowing look that Julia might like a swim too.

Even in this, Krissy had been naughty, getting Julia to wear a white bikini that, when wet, showed her fantastic nipples in all their glory, the dark circles visible through the wet material and Julia's erect nipples utterly obvious against the material. Once in the pool, it didn't take Julia long to strike up a conversation with the girl. Stood against the wall in the shallow end, Julia's breasts were just above the waterline, and Krissy could see that the brunette was having difficulty in not ogling them.

Both devoid of their young accomplices, it was an easy matter for Krissy to strike up a conversation with the older woman. Soon she learned that her name was Maggie and the girl, her niece, was Sara. Maggie was a wealthy single woman who had never married and had no family of her own, so she had offered to take her sister's daughter Sara away during her university holidays in England. Her parents were delighted that Maggie would be there to show Sara a bit of the world. She would look after her.

'Is she a bit of a handful' enquired Krissy.

'Not really, but she is a bit more mature than I give her credit for in some ways,' replied Maggie. 'I see the way she turns the guys' heads here – oh how I wish I could still do that so easily...' she joked.

'I am sure they are looking when you walk past as well' complimented Krissy. 'You have nothing to be ashamed of!' Krissy wondered if the inference had been understood, but despite Maggie's blushes, she thought not.

At that moment, they were interrupted by the two younger girls returning and toweling themselves down. Did Krissy just clock Maggie taking in Julia's fabulous tits? After brief introductions, Sara spoke.

'Maggie, Julia is going to show me the suite that she is staying in – it sounds awesome. We'll probably be down for a drink soon. See ya!'

Krissy looked at Julia and smiled – she knew what was happening. 'Have a great time the two of you and if there is anything you want, just charge it to the room. I'll send out the search parties if you aren't back by supper time'. Laughing and chatting, they headed off, leaving Krissy and Maggie to talk.

Krissy suggested that they might enjoy a cocktail or two while they chatted, and sure enough, this seemed to relax Maggie, the conversation flowing ever easier. Krissy pulled their beds closer together. From behind her sunnies, she was able to fully appreciate her new friend's physical charms. Maggie's tits were huge, a fabulous cleavage encased in a pale blue bikini. The fact that she could easily get away with this style showed that time and nature had been kind to her.

Maggie had long brown hair, which she repeatedly brushed over her head in an incredibly unconscious but sexy way. Her full lips looked good enough to eat, and it was all Krissy could do not to kiss her there and then. This was truly the first time that Krissy had looked at an older woman in this way.

A couple of hours had passed, and there was no sign of Julia and Sara, not that they were missed. Krissy thought that Julia would probably be getting to know Sara very well by now.

Inevitably the conversation came round to relationships. Krissy asked why Maggie was not married and got the straightforward response of career had come first, and it was all probably a bit late to worry about now. Maggie was bursting to ask the same question back, but could not have banked on the answer she would receive.

'Never quite met the right chap – anyway I'm now having far too much fun as a single girl. I get to play with who I want when I want...' Krissy left the last comment hanging.

Maggie fell into the trap laid. 'So who is Julia then? Is she your niece or something?'

'Er no, nothing like that...' smiled Krissy as she prepared to drop the bombshell '...she is my lover. I have been fucking her for a few months now – amongst others, men and girls'.

Maggie's face was a picture. 'You mean you actually sleep together,' she said rhetorically. Krissy nodded. Maggie was struggling to regain her composure and stammered a couple of comments along the lines of her not looking like a lesbian. Eventually, a mix of the cocktails and curiosity took over. 'So why, how, what do you do?'

Krissy began gently with a straightforward admission that making love to a woman was pretty straightforward and utterly pleasurable before letting Maggie know that she could tell her some more extreme stories if she wished.

'I'm not sure Krissy – I've never really thought about this before...' However, curiosity was getting the better of her. 'I suppose it would be interesting to know though...' she said, blushing at her forwardness, then again not thinking for a second that Krissy would be as graphic as she was.

Krissy told her almost everything. She continued as she could see that Maggie was riveted to her every word, hands, and fingers idly touching her body. Though never overtly sexually, Krissy knew that the conversation was turning her new friend on.

Suddenly it was dawning on Maggie that her niece was upstairs with a girl who liked to sleep with girls. 'Oh my god, will they being doing those things?' she spluttered. Krissy took her hand and said to follow.

Up in the suite, Krissy opened one door that leads through into what was a lounge area. Her suite had two bedrooms, but one of them was obviously in use from the moans and purring that were emanating from it. Krissy raised her finger to Maggie's lips, warning her to be quiet. As instructed, Julia had left the door open a little – Krissy had wanted at least a glimpse of that fabulous slim brunette body, her tiny tits a perfect opposite to Julia's.

And what a view it was. Sara was flat on her back; eyes screwed closed, crying out obscenities and instructions to Julia, who, in turn, was diving into Sara's trimmed bush with all of her newly gained skills. It was quite likely that a finger was rammed up inside Sara's ass, judging from their positions and the appreciative noises coming from her lover.

Maggie was transfixed – she was watching a fabulous young woman feasting on her niece, who herself was undeniably beautiful. Faced with her niece's nakedness, Maggie was forced to admit to herself that she had always somewhat more than admired the young relative's body, but never had she dreamt she would see it in action this way.

After watching spellbound for a few minutes, Krissy eased Maggie away from the door. She led her out of the suite by the hand. 'Let's go to your room and talk about this eh?' said Krissy with a smile on her face. Talking was the last thing she had on her mind.

Once inside the room, Krissy began her seduction proper without delay. She could tell how turned on Maggie was and knew she would take very little persuading. 'Pretty horny sight wasn't it?' she inquired rhetorically. She reached out and stroking Maggie's face.

'I...I...never thought...god, I can't believe I was watching all that,' she stammered, looking at Krissy in a way that demanded acceptance that this was okay to feel.

Krissy came in for the kill - 'Of course watching is rarely as much fun as doing' at which point she eased forward and kissed Maggie full on the lips for a few moments longer than polite. 'Nobody need ever know if you are worried, but I suggest you take the holiday spirit and just go with it. It looks like Sara won't be missing you for a while yet'.

The mere mention of Sara's name inflamed both of their passions, Krissy, just the pure lust for a fit young woman; Maggie's an altogether deeper stimulus. They kissed again, and Krissy pushed Maggie towards the bed. Before they tumbled backward, Krissy flicked open the catch on the older woman's bikini top. A small step back and a gaze at the breasts she had been dying to see revealed something different to the other girls Krissy had fucked. Maggie's tits were big and round, the nipples just starting to point slightly downwards, already semi-erect despite the warmth. Krissy's hands could do nothing but brush across them from bottom to top, tracing the lines and shape of them as she resumed her passionate kissing.

Maggie was a passenger now, her head a swirl of images of her gasping niece, Julia's anus and pussy so rudely displayed, and her own body being taken by this gorgeous slim blonde. She had never really thought of women so sexually before, and yet here she was with her mind full of pussy and breasts, assholes, and smooth, soft skin. She realized how much she wanted to be taken, no more than that, be fucked remorselessly, abandoning all previous notions of what was right and wrong.

She reached behind Krissy and undid her top. 'Let me see you naked,' she whispered to her lover. Krissy smiled a knowing smile, and dropped her top, stood up to let Maggie see her tiny A-cup chest, certain that the contrast with Maggie's large soft breasts would turn Maggie on. Sure enough, the gasp and the tentative outreaching hand confirmed her idea.

Not wishing to lose momentum and hugely turned on herself, she quickly removed her G-string bottoms to reveal her tiny tuft of blonde pubic hair above an otherwise baby smooth pussy. 'And you' Krissy whispered as she reached over and slid down Maggie's bottoms. Delightfully she was well-groomed but had a full pussy, and an aroused one at that, judging from the aroma that told the blonde that her partner was ready.

Not wishing to tempt embarrassment at their nakedness, Krissy tumbled them to the bed. Kissing was quickly followed by hands squeezing and stroking breasts, bums, legs, stomachs, and hair as both women found their way around each other. Eventually, Krissy decided to get serious with their loving and slid a finger right through the middle of Maggie's pussy, causing her partner to nearly explode there and then.

She pushed on relentlessly, soon two, then three fingers twisting in and out of the soaking slit, thumb brushing clit, mouth ducking to breasts and neck. Maggie was powerless to resist as Krissy slid down the bed to the holy grail of concession from Maggie. As if to confirm what she was about to do, Krissy offered a couple of fingers, freshly covered her lovers' juices, to Maggie, who, in turn, eagerly tasted herself on them.

For Maggie, this was all a blur. Her mind was unable to keep up with the pace of the events unfolding with her body and mind, these gorgeous strangers who seemed to be uncovering a side to her personality that even she didn't know existed. Of course, she had tasted herself before, but always on her own fingers or the cock of some man friend pushing himself into her mouth after sex. She now knew that she did enjoy cleaning all those cocks that had cum inside her.

Krissy knew that the older woman was hers. Maggie eagerly sucked her fingers clean, a confirmation in Krissy's mind that she was ready to be taken in mind as well as the body. Positioned between her new friend's beautiful thighs, Krissy allowed herself rye and knowing smile before gently descending toward the dark, lush haired pussy in front of her. Maggie bit her bottom lip, held her breath and the back of Krissy's head, and awaited Krissy's experienced touch to continue. It came first with little kisses to the deep inner thighs, held and gently sucking, teasing ever closer to the soaking slit. Then it came, the long, firm rasping tongue plowing from the hole to the clit, the back again and again.

Maggie's back arched, her eyes screwed closed at the incredible sensations. Krissy brought a finger into the equation and gently pressed it against Maggie's back passage. So wet was the opening that the tip of the finger made easy progress. This was a virgin orifice for the businesswoman, but this interference felt so right, gentle, and caring.

Krissy was desperately turned on herself. She dry-humped the bed slowly, trying to give herself some relief though with little success. Her attention would have to be concentrated on Maggie for now, and so it was. The groan and whimpers from above her told Krissy that this first orgasm would not take long to arrive. She began to speed up the licks, apply just that little more pressure for a minute or two, than slow again, and lighten the touch. The finger at the anus delved slightly deeper, then her other hand reached up and began to stroke and squeezed her lover's large breasts. Krissy delighted in their feel, something new a different to Julia's biggish breasts, which were younger and firmer.

Maggie was almost at the point of no return and gave in willingly, loudly, and certainly, forcing Krissy's face hard into her cunt. Krissy felt the liquid cum running from the dark pussy and lifted her face back to stare at her handiwork. Maggie was slumped back into the bed; her legs lewdly spread, the dark pubic hair matted with copious juice and saliva. Krissy couldn't resist pushing a couple of fingers slowly into Maggie, then added another and yet another with ease.

A wicked thought entered her mind - could Maggie take a fist? She certainly wouldn't expect it, but Krissy had the evil thought now and decided to try. 'Maggie, you enjoyed that didn't you?' she probed rhetorically, 'Now lie back and trust me to take you even higher...'

A thumb now began to slide in alongside the palm. Gently twisting her hand, Krissy was easing Maggie's cunt, opening wider and wider. The low guttural moans told Krissy that permission was granted to continue with what she was doing, and so she pressed on, firmly forcing her hand into Maggie's opening.

'Don't you look and feel like such a horny slut now?' Krissy goaded, adding, 'You see these pleasures are not just to be enjoyed by gorgeous young women like Sara.' It seemed that the mention of Sara electrified Maggie, Krissy sensing that a picture in Maggie's mind may well have featured her niece.

In turn, Maggie's hand seemed to slide down to her clit involuntarily, teasing it and adding to the pleasures she was taking. The other hand-kneaded and squeezed her breast, pulling hard at the nipple and making it swell and harden with the blood rushing to it.

There was no way she would avoid another orgasm now, fuller than she had ever been before. Sure enough, her head was thrown back, her legs wide apart, both mind and body gave over totally to her surprising new lover. Maggie's cum was huge; her whole body convulsed on the bed, her cries desperate and breathless, her slit now rudely stretched but sopping wet with her juices.

'God Krissy, I never... that was... I can't believe I just came so hard. That was... unbelievable.' She stammered her appreciation of Krissy's technique. Thanks were all well and good, but now Krissy needed relief, and she was going to extract it from Maggie this very minute.

She slid up the bed and once again thrust her fingers into Maggie's mouth, forcing her to clean them off before descending onto her with a passionate and exploring kiss. Maggie could taste herself on Krissy and shivered as she pictured again the blonde licking her pussy.

The kiss lasted but a minute or two before Krissy suddenly knelt up on the bed and straddled Maggie's face. For a moment, Maggie's courage of the last couple of hours deserted her - 'I don't know if I can Krissy, I've never...' – she was cut off in mid-sentence by Krissy forcing herself on her.

Instinctively Maggie just did what she wanted to be done to her. Her reluctance was the last vestige of her old sexual being, and it evaporated instantly. Here she was, a successful businesswoman, mature and sexually experienced, flat on her back drinking and licking at the sodden pussy of a near stranger, her pussy gaping wide from the fucking it had just endured, and she loved it. Fingers joined tongue exploring her partner, opening the pussy lips, seeking out Krissy's now enormously swollen clit and at one point even tentatively introducing a fingertip to Krissy's lubricated ass.

Krissy was getting close to her own cum, and began to drive down harder while making small rubbing motions up and down Maggie's face. The thrusting soon brought its desired result, and she cried out loudly as she came, urging the older woman to continue her onslaught until she was totally spent.

Collapsing back down, the two women held each other, this time more passionate and soft, kisses and caresses bringing them both security and affirmation. Then from the door of the room came a voice.

'Aunt Maggie and Krissy, that was amazing to see – we clearly have made a discovery today!' There at the door were Julia and Sara. Julia was smiling, seeing that her plan had come to a perfect conclusion, Sara gazing in awe at the scene before her.

Krissy was the first to speak. 'Sara, we saw you and Julia too – that looked equally as hot. Why don't you show your Aunt your own technique as I think she is about ready to try again?'

Sara looked at her Aunt's dark pussy, so different from her own and that of Julia, herself now urging Sara forward. Krissy stood and faced Sara. She wasn't going to pass up the chance to at least hold this exquisite brunette. She held Sara's face and kissed her full on, hands roaming across her body and a finger inserting itself into a soaking and readily open hole. Julia starred at the scene, her lover kissing her latest conquest, the older woman fixated on the kiss lying on the bed, beginning to finger her gaping hole, trying to regain some feeling in it.

Sara then showed her confident side. 'Aunt, it looks like you like to be dominated and to be honest, I like the thought of fucking an older woman like you who will do whatever I demand.' And with that, she descended on Maggie's pussy. She had seen the fisting take place and was intrigued to see the result close up. 'I'm going to call you Maggie from now on, not Aunt, and I'm going to take a share of that soaking pussy in front of me.' With that, she began to force her fingers into Maggie and rasp her tongue across the clit above.

Krissy and Julia kissed as lovers and slid down to join in. It would be some night that followed. Maggie was fucked and sucked, made to bring each of them to orgasm after orgasm and used in every conceivable way by the three younger women, who in turn enjoyed each other as well.

The combinations were endless, the sex fabulous -what a holiday it was for all of them.

Story 03

Ada heaved a huge sigh and tugged again at the bodice of her hideous, pink, fluffy bridesmaid's dress. The damn thing was so tight her generous C-cup tits were bulging out of the top. She was terrified that, at any moment, they'd lose the battle to stay safely tucked away and just pop out in front of everyone. If she didn't love her best friend Rhea as much as she did, there was no way in hell she'd put up with this torture. Who the hell designed such awful creations for bridesmaid's dresses anyway?

Attempting to smooth the seemingly hundreds of yards of fluff in her skirt, she wondered again how the hell she was supposed to take a leak. Cussing quietly and quite creatively, she glanced around the fancy house's third-floor hallway where her best friend was getting married to make sure no one could see or hear her. Spying no one, Ada was relieved and stomped towards the only unoccupied bathroom in the whole place.

Shaking her honey brown, meticulously curled hair, she grimaced as she felt yet another pin slip loosen. With a growl at having to fix it once again, she grasped the cool, antique door handle and stopped suddenly, having heard a giggle from inside. Dammit! I gotta pee! Ada thought frantically.

"God you're wet, you naughty, naughty girl." The man's voice, rough with lust, was familiar enough to ring all kinds of alarm bells in Ada's head.

Another giggle, followed by a quick gasp and moan, had Ada frozen with her hand on the doorknob. "Oh fuck, Todd, you're the naughty one. What would Rhea say if she knew where your fingers were right now?" The feminine voice was high pitched and childlike, instantly grating on Ada's already frazzled nerves.

A cold shiver iced its way down Ada's spine. Todd? The Todd that her best friend Rhea was supposed to be marrying today? The sounds inside the room became more obvious as the seconds went by. There was no mistaking the moans and groans and wet smacking sounds.

"I'm gonna be stuck with that bitch for years so I'm getting it good while I can. Now come on baby, turn around, bend over and let me see that beautiful ass."

Ada's mouth dropped open in shock, and her blue eyes went wide. Stuck with that bitch? Oh no, he did not just say that. It was obvious at this point, but Ada wanted the proof. Fishing around under her left boob in her too-tight bodice, she pulled out her cell phone and quickly opened up the camera app. Very carefully and quietly, praying with all her might that the door didn't squeak, she turned the knob and slipped just her phone through the smallest crack she could manage.

There, on the screen, was all the evidence she needed. Taking a quick snap, Ada realized that she could probably make all the noise she wanted. The high pitched squeals coming from Rhea's cousin, Heather, would drown out a herd of elephants stomping down the hall. With a shrug, she pushed open the door a little wider and took a good look.

Todd stood behind Heather, dressed in his wedding tux but with his pants bogged down around his hips. He was seriously dog fucking the cute, fluffy blond, spread wide and leaning over the sink until her face was nearly pressed into the mirror above it. Her bright blue sundress was tossed up over her back, panties down around one ankle, and somehow her golden hair was still perfectly curled and in place. Ada sneered and touched her own carefully styled up-do. If she were in the bitch's place, any hairstyle she had would be in tatters. God, she hated girls like Heather.

A twinge in her bladder reminded her why she was spying on this nasty little scene. Carefully closing the door, she tucked her phone back away and hurried to find another bathroom and get back to Rhea. What the hell was she supposed to say to her star-struck best friend anyway?

Ada lost several more precious minutes finding a bathroom and managing to get the poof of her skirt under control long enough to relieve her aching bladder. Hurrying down the hall toward the bridal suite, she saw Todd disappearing into another room. Well, that was quick; she sneered to herself.

She knocked the secret bridesmaid knock and entered the room, her steps faltering and her breath leaving in a rush. There stood Rhea in her wedding dress, looking more beautiful than she'd ever been. Layers and layers of lush tulle sparkled with thousands of tiny beads, her auburn hair covered by a wispy, sparkling veil. Rhea looked every inch the princess bride she had wanted to be.

Taking a deep breath, Ada went over to the other bridesmaid, Talia, who was taking a quick picture with her cell phone. "I have a picture for you," Ada said as she pulled out her phone and quickly showed Talia the picture of Todd and Heather.

"Fucking hell, that total fucking bastard!" Talia exclaimed as her face contorted with fury.

Rhea stopped fussing in the mirror and turned with an amused smile. "What the hell?"

Immediately, tears filled Talia's dark brown eyes. "Oh Rhea, I'm so sorry."

Frowning, Rhea asked, "For what? I've heard you cuss worse than that." She then looked to Ada, tilted her head, and smirked. "Ada dear you're about to pop out of your dress. That would certainly make my wedding interesting but I'd prefer eyes on me and not your boobs."

Talia looked to Ada. "Show her. She has to know."

With another heavy sigh, Ada turned her phone toward Rhea. "I'm sorry Rhea. I went to the third floor to pee in peace and found this instead. I'm really so, so sorry."

Rhea's face went deathly pale as she reached for Ada's phone with shaking fingers. While Rhea's pain-filled green eyes stared at the tiny screen, the girls stared at Rhea. After a minute and after allowing herself only a small tremble of her full lower lip, Rhea calmly said, "Well, we're not actually married yet."

Rage filled Ada. "What? You can't just let this pass. Girl, he called you a bitch and said he'd be stuck with you. This is your fucking wedding day!!!"

Rhea handed Ada back her phone. "You're my two very best friends in the whole world right?"

Both girls nodded emphatically.

"Well, apparently, it's NOT my wedding day. I need a minute to put my thoughts together."

Ada and Talia exchanged a glance. "Not your wedding day?" Ada asked.

With a sad smile, Rhea shook her head. "No. There's no way I can marry Todd after this. I never could stand Heather, but the point is, if he'll do this now, today, then he'll do this whenever and where ever and with whomever. But just calling things off isn't enough. No, I need something that will make an impression on him."

Ada attempted to tuck her phone back in her bodice when it finally happened. Down slid her bodice and out popped her tits, lightly bouncing as they were finally free of her dress's tight confines. Talia's giggles and Ada's curses mixed together as she began to try to pull the damn thing back in place.

Rhea walked over to her and very lightly brushed her fingertips over Ada's full breast. With a twinkle in her eye and a wicked smile, she met Ada's startled gaze. "Up for a little show?" she asked.

"Huh?"

Looking from Ada to Talia, Rhea smiled. "Lets show him what he's missing out on. A little girl on girl action. And then when his balls are about to explode, leave him hanging."

Talia grinned. Ada knew that Talia was firmly bi sexual and fully up to the challenge. She'd never mess with her best friends without an invitation, and here was her invitation. She imagined that Talia's pussy would already be buzzing with excitement.

Ada was a different story. "Ah, um, Rhea, sweetie, you know I love you with all my heart but, uh, I really don't swing that way and honest to god, I didn't know you did." Ada went back to frantically trying to stuff her breasts back into her dress.

Rhea threw back her head and laughed. "I don't dear, trust me. This is all for show, although Talia might get some fun out of it."

Ada glanced at Talia and then gave a second look. The dark, exotic beauty was nearly drooling. Never before had she felt threatened by her other best friend, but the lustful look in Talia's eye made her pause and drew back a little. Looking back at Rhea and seeing the humor there, Ada decided she trusted her friends, and no one would make her do something she wasn't comfortable doing.

Finally, giving up on her boobs and letting them bounce free, she smiled. "I'm only touching boobs and kissing."

"Me too," Rhea exclaimed.

The light dimmed in Talia's eyes. "But I love you guys and you're so fucking sexy. I don't know if I can stick to that."

Rhea put her arm around Ada and pulled her close, "If you're okay with us doing only what we're comfortable doing, I'm okay with letting you do whatever you want. Ada?"

With a shrug, Ada agreed. "Sure, what the hell."

"But we gotta plan this out. We need a reason to get Todd here." Rhea was staring at Ada's boobs again as she spoke.

Talia was in heaven. "Let me handle that." And out the door, she went.

"You're staring."

"Mmhmm. Never noticed how pretty your tits are."

"You've never seen my naked tits before."

"Good point." Rhea smiled and gently touched Ada's bright pink nipple.

"Of course, if you had picked out a dress for me that actually fit, you wouldn't be seeing them now." Ada was mildly surprised to find she liked Rhea's touch. It was cool and gentle and SO different from a man's heavy hand.

"Those really are hideous dresses, aren't they?" Rhea asked with a giggle.

Drawing back a little, Ada glared at her friend. "Then why the hell am I wearing it?"

"So you didn't look better than the bride, silly!"

As Ada was cussing and laughing at Rhea, Talia bounded back into the room. "Okay girls, gotta make this quick. Ceremony starts in 15 minutes, we're cutting it close."

"But I'm not getting married." Rhea was confused.

"That's right! But you're going to leave Todd standing at the altar with little Megan waiting to give him the message to come here to talk to you."

"Megan, as in Heather's little sister?" Ada asked.

"Yup. She has no clue what's going on, I just gave her twenty bucks to wait until everyone starts squirming, 'cuz you're not walking down the aisle to go up to Todd and tell him to come here."

Rhea smiled. "You're evil."

"Yes, I know. Now, my turn with those lovely boobies." Talia turned to Ada with an eager look.

With a laugh, Rhea grabbed Talia and pulled her away. "Over here, you freaky woman." She moved across the room to a chaise lounge sat with her legs straddled across the seat. "Talia, in the middle. Ada, beside her. That way the bi lady can reach both the straight ladies." Rhea's wedding dress was seriously puffed up and seemed to be everywhere at once, but Ada had to admit it looked damn sexy, seeing her sitting like that with Talia's darker skin and black hair leaning in close.

Sitting down next to Talia, Ada's puffy skirt joined in the others. Talia had leaned over and was lightly kissing Rhea, her hands gently cupping her friend's face. As she sat there wondering what to do, she watched as Rhea reached out and pulled down the bodice of Talia's dress so that her small breasts sprang free. While Rhea cupped one of Talia's breasts and teased the dark brown nipple, Ada cupped the other.

Ada had touched her breasts plenty, but never another woman. It was weird, but she was surprised to find that it was quite erotic as well. Talia's breast was small and fit perfectly in her hand. It was super soft, almost velvety to the touch, but firm, and the tiny nipple was a hard little bud.

As she started to finger the dark nipple, Talia moved, turning from Rhea to her. She cupped Ada's face in her gentle hands and softly kissed her lips. Oh god, so soft, was all Ada could think as the warm lips moved over hers. No scratchy facial hair, no rough, male lips. These were incredibly soft and warm, and a liquid buzzing slid slowly down her body to settle in her pussy.

Leaning in, Ada pressed her large breasts to Talia's smaller ones. More tingles raced through her at the new and unfamiliar contact. She felt hands massaging her breasts, pressing them against Talia's, and realized that they had to be Rhea's hands. Reaching around Talia, Ada felt for Rhea and pulled her closer so that the three of them were all pressed together.

Finally, breaking off the kiss, Talia looked into Ada's blue eyes. "Damn girl, you can kiss!"

With a giggle, Ada tugged on Rhea's bodice. "Come on, show us yours."

As Rhea's dress had tiny straps, she had to wiggle and squirm a little before getting free. Her breasts were nicely rounded, the nipples larger with a more peachy color to go with her auburn hair. Talia gently cupped a breast and brought it up, lowering her mouth to pull one of those nipples into her mouth.

Rhea's eyes grew huge as they met Ada's, and she mouthed an amazed "fuck" before letting her head drop back and pressing her breast more fully into Talia's mouth. Ada played gently with Talia's nipples and breasts, trying not to interfere. She couldn't believe or understand how turned on she was getting by all this. Never in her wildest dreams had she ever considered getting it on with another woman.

Eventually, Talia lifted her head and gave Rhea and smile before turning back to Ada. "Now, let me have those pretty beauties of yours." Dipping her head, she latched onto one of Ada's nipples. The warm, wet heat of Talia's mouth gently pulling on her went straight to her gut. Soft hands caressed her as the heat rose through her body.

Rhea stood, working her way through the many layers of her dress and managed to get her panties off, artfully draping them over the back of a nearby chair. Bundling up the huge skirt, she straddled the lounge again but this time, had the fluffy tulle bunched up around her waist, her rosy pussy shaved clean glistening with moisture.

Ada had the insane urge to touch that tender valley. Her own was nearly dripping at this point after Talia worked on her nipples and breasts. Finally, Talia's dark head lifted, and Ada caught her lips in another gentle kiss before letting her go.

When Talia turned to see the sight of Rhea's pussy on display, she gave a little gasp and looked into Rhea's eyes, seeming to ask for permission. Rhea gave a little nod and bit her lip in anticipation. Talia leaned down but couldn't reach Rhea for Ada sitting behind her. Realizing the problem, Ada popped up and moved to the side, dropping to her knees beside Rhea.

Talia gave her a grateful look before scooting back and leaning down. She trailed kisses over Rhea's thigh, heading for the sweet wetness. She gently kissed her way around the outer lips before carefully sipping from the creamy middle.

"Oh, fuck," Rhea moaned. She reached up and tangled her fingers in Ada's honey-brown hair, pulling her down for a kiss. The two kissed deeply, hands caressing breasts as Talia began to eat her friend's pussy. When Ada felt Rhea's fingers reaching under her dress, she helped pull it up out of the way. Soon Rhea was gently stroking Ada's sopping, wet pussy as Ada sucked her nipples into her mouth.

The three were moaning and moving in a sinuous collection of female bodies, totally forgetting that it was all for show. They never heard the quick knock on the door or the sharp gasp that came after. Rhea grabbed for Ada in a long hot kiss as Talia took her over the edge in the best orgasm she'd ever had.

"Holy fucking hell, Rhea!" the male barked, jerking them out of their sexual haze.

Turning as one, they all looked over at Todd, who stood just inside the door with an obvious bulge in his pants. Talia deliberately lifted her hand and started to wipe her mouth. Ada gave a quick squeak and grabbed her hand, leaning over Rhea to kiss and lick her best friend's pussy juices from her face.

There was another quiet "fuck" from near the door, but the women ignored it. Once Ada felt she had cleaned Talia enough, she leaned back, her plump breasts nearly in Rhea's face. Rhea causally gave her nipple a little soft tweak before rising from the lounge.

Striding over to Todd, her perky breasts bare and free, she noted he couldn't take his eyes off of them. "So, how was fucking Heather? Was it worth it?" Ada and Talia, also leaving their breasts free, went to Rhea and put their arms around her, supporting her.

Todd stared at the beauty before him, mouth gaping like a fish before he managed to find his voice. "What? Rhea, what the fuck? I never knew you were into girls."

"There's a lot you're never going to find out about me, Todd. Now answer the question, was fucking Heather worth losing this?" Both Ada and Talia each cupped one of Rhea's breasts, gently squeezing and each giving her a quick kiss.

"What do you mean fucking Heather? I don't know what you're talking about." Todd was looking slightly desperate.

Ada said nothing and only held up her phone with the picture of Todd and Heather in the bathroom.

"Baby, no that's not what it looks like," Todd started.

"Shut up Todd." Rhea trailed her fingers over the dick, straining against his pants. "The Heather's of this world are all you're going to have. This good stuff here, you'll never know and you'll never touch."

"Baby, please. I can explain." It appeared that Todd could tell what was coming his way, and the fingers gently caressing him were causing a sweet pain that was actually really starting to hurt.

Turning, Rhea kissed each of her friends, long and sweetly. Caressing breasts, rubbing them together, putting on quite the show, wanting to draw it out knowing Todd was watching everything. "Get out, Todd, and go tell your mother just WHY we're not getting married today." Looking him straight in the eye, she continued, "Go tell my father who just paid for all of this why I will never speak to you again."

At those words, she saw the fear come into Todd's eyes. She gave him a light shove back out the door. "Now excuse us, please. There's something we'd like to finish." And she shut the door in his stunned face.

Turning to her best friends, they all squealed and grabbed for hugs. They chattered about the look on his face and just what repercussions Rhea's father would have for the cheating bridegroom. In their excitement, they forgot the exposed breasts and the lingering scent of sex in the air.

Finally, Talia looked to Rhea, "Did you mean it?"

Confused, she asked, "Mean what?"

With a slight blush on her dusky skin, Talia answered, "Something to finish."

The warmth immediately returned to Ada's pussy. She looked to Rhea, who shrugged and said, "Well, I got mine and let me tell you, it was the best I have ever, EVER had."

Rhea reached out and tugged Ada's hair. "I can recommend giving it a try. But I do actually need to go down and face the crowd that's waiting on a wedding that's not gonna happen." She kissed her friends lightly and, with their help, quickly changed out of her wedding dress and into the outfit she'd planned to wear to her honeymoon. After a quick discussion on the three of them turning the honeymoon trip into a girl's getaway, Rhea kissed them both, gave Ada an encouraging nudge, and left the room.

Ada bit her lip. Looking at Talia's eager face, she said, "I'm good with you... you know... to me, but I honestly can't say if I can do it to you."

Talia frantically shook her head, black curls flying. "No, no, no. I would never ask you. Honestly, I love to give pleasure and if needed, I can take care of my own."

"Well, that's not fair," Ada complained, but looking into Talia's pleading, brown eyes, there was no resisting that. Nodding, she smiled and said, "Lets do this."

In unspoken agreement, Talia locked the door as Ada unzipped the too-tight dress and happily let it fall to the floor in a pile of pink fluff. Standing in only a pair of silky red panties, she turned and took a deep breath. She idly wondered what she was doing and why, but watching Talia step out of her dress and seeing that long, lean body, the buzz in her pussy spoke a little louder.

Shaking her head and totally mystified at her body's reaction to another woman (something that had never happened before), Ada reached out to Talia and took her hand. They kissed long and slow, the gentleness taking Ada's breath away. Naked bodies pressed lightly together, one slim and dark, and the other paler and lush with curves.

Talia gently pushed Ada's panties over her hips and let them fall to the floor before pulling Ada down onto the lounge, pushing her back. Ada let her legs fall to either side, leaving her wide open and slick with honey juices. Talia took her time, kissing her way over Ada's plump ripe breasts, sucking softly at the hard berry nipples, her hands smoothing over satiny skin.

Moving farther down Ada's body, she paused and played lightly with the little tuft of brown hair at the top of her pussy. Never had Ada felt such an amazing heat and yearning from someone just playing with her pussy hair. She squirmed and reached up to squeeze her breasts, her hips arching up, seeking Talia's mouth.

Finally, Talia moved down, raining tiny kisses over Ada's inner thighs, taking deep breaths of the sweet musky scent. When her warm, wet tongue finally touched Ada's soaking and steaming pussy, Ada had to bit her lip to hold back the scream. Once again, she marveled over the softness of Talia's lips.

God, this was incredible, she thought. Never ever, in her whole life, had she considered doing something like this and now couldn't understand why. The difference between the soft face of a woman from a man's rough whiskered face was beyond comparison. Talia's tongue was magic, sliding over her wet valley, dipping into her tight tunnel and gently sucking out the juices, Ada felt loved and cherished and wanted.

Ada couldn't hold back the moan when two gentle fingers began to press into her pussy. Talia moved so slowly, so gently, her mouth sucking on Ada's clit as her fingers worked their way inside. Ada squeezed her breasts harder, her breath coming in fast gasps as those fingers began to move, stroking her pussy, curling up deep inside her.

The combination of the mouth persistently working her clit and the fingers slowly fucking her had her orgasm building fast. With her fingers pulling frantically at her nipples, her hips were arching, fucking them back, and the hot mouth and tongue working on her clit, she was lost in a sea of sensation. Talia suddenly pulled sharply on her aching clit, and she rubbed her fingertips on that spot inside her. Ada erupted in orgasm.

Talia continued to lick and suck Ada's sweet juices even as she writhed and squirmed on the lounge. As the waves crashed through Ada, she decided that she agreed with Rhea that this was the best she'd ever had. When she finally felt the last of the spasms slowly easing away, she collapsed on the lounge and took a deep breath, trying to still her racing heart.

She felt Talia kissing her way back up her body but was too lethargic to move. When she reached her breasts, Talia gently sucked the slightly sore nipples. Ada moaned again at the soothing caress and wrapped her arms around her best friend, holding her close.

They shared a long, slow kiss, Ada's frazzled brain slowly coming back to reality. Finally, the slow movements of Talia's hips against her made her realize that Talia had one hand in her pussy, stroking herself. Frowning, Ada met those soft brown eyes. "Tell me how help you."

Talia smiled and simply took Ada's hand in her free one and slid it down her body to her dripping pussy. With her hands guiding Ada's, she slid her fingers over her clit in a gentle rhythm. "Just like you do to yourself."

Ada felt her friend's hot wet pussy juice squishing through her fingers. The incredible softness of another woman's pussy just amazed her. She grew bolder, pushing Talia's fingers out of the way as she explored this new territory.

Talia kissed her more passionately, her hips twitching faster into Ada's hand. Experimenting a little, Ada carefully slipped a finger into Talia's hot pussy and heard her moan and push harder against her. The realization that her friend's orgasm was literally in her hands made Ada's head swim with the knowledge and the power.

"More," Talia whispered.

Ada carefully and gently started to push in a second finger. Talia moaned and pushed her hips against Ada's fingers, seeming to try to get her to hurry. Tossing aside the caution and hoping like hell that she wouldn't hurt her friend with her inexperience, she pushed in deeper with the two fingers.

Talia gasped and arched against her. Ada began to fuck her pussy with her fingers, the palm of her hand rubbing against Talia's clit. She was so wet, there was pussy juice squishing out everywhere, and Ada began to feel her pussy buzzing again.

This was so fucking hot. Her arms were full of a naked woman and her fingers buried in pussy. She was kissing her best friend and so turned on she wondered if she'd orgasm again just from their bodies friction rubbing together.

Talia suddenly reached down and shoved two fingers of her own inside herself, along with the two of Ada's. With another gasp and jerk of her hips, Ada could feel the inside walls of Talia's pussy contracting as her orgasm rolled through her. Those pussy walls clamped down so tightly on her fingers she couldn't move them for a few seconds until Talia released her again.

Awe over what she had just done had Ada grinning like mad at her friend. Talia gave a breathless giggle as she slowly relaxed into Ada's arms. "Damn woman you'd make a hell of a bi if you're interested."

Ada laughed and thought about the upcoming impromptu honeymoon trip. "You never know what could happen."

They shared another sweet kiss before rousing to dress and go find Rhea.

All Rights Reserved. No part of this publication may be reproduced in any form or by any means, including scanning, photocopying, or otherwise without prior written permission of the copyright holder. Copyright © 2020

This book is entirely a work of fiction. The names, characters and incidents portrayed in it are the work of the author's imagination. Any resemblance to actual persons, living or dead, events or localities is entirely coincidental.

Story 01

Chapter 01

In my last year of college, I had once kissed a few of my girlfriends during a late-night truth-or-dare session. Nothing more than a few quick pecks on the lips. It had never happened again, probably a result of promising myself never again to get quite that drunk. In 10 years, those kisses had been the entirety of my experience in a same-sex relationship, until tonight.

Five minutes into warming up my Thursday night Zumba class, the door at the back of the workout room opened. A woman I'd never seen before entered and closed the door behind her. She carried a towel in one hand and a blue index card in the other. Without intending or realizing it, I stopped moving and stared, causing most of the women in the class, all of whom had been focused on my leading, to turn around to see for themselves what had distracted me.

Zumba combines spicy Latin music and sensual moves into an intense workout. The exhilarating routine feels more like vigorous dancing at a great night club than exercise, and most Zumba students experience incredible changes to their bodies, all the while claiming to be having the most fun in their lives. Many of the women in my Zumba classes are attractive, and even more, are in fantastic shape. And every single one of them, myself included, was immediately jealous of the woman with the blue index card.

The warmup routine came almost to a complete standstill as she made her way toward me at the front of the class. Her body was stunning, emphasized with obvious intent by a black Lycra workout bikini trimmed in hot pink borders. Outrageous Zumba outfits were commonplace, but bikinis were rare if not unheard of. Even women in fantastic shape usually had something they wanted or needed to hide. If they didn't, wearing a bikini to an aerobics workout was something like wearing an elegant cocktail dress to McDonald's: wholly unnecessary, but you could be sure everyone would be looking and looking, we were. I guessed her to be about my age, somewhere in her late twenties or early thirties, and about five foot nine or ten inches tall. Her body proportions were perfect, her muscles firm and defined while still feminine, and her skin almost glowed with a smooth, natural tan. She had straight, sandy brown hair pulled back into a ponytail, and a gorgeous, compelling face. While watching her approach, sudden strange feelings swept through me that I'd only felt a few times, and never when looking at a woman. I wanted to touch her, run my hands over the graceful curves and toned muscles of her body, play with her long soft hair, and brush my fingers across her face and lips. And then, out of nowhere, I wondered it would be like to kiss her.

Surprise yanked me from my thoughts. Where had that came from! I had little time to consider it, because she'd arrived where I was standing and was extending her arm, offering me the blue index card. I took it and examined it. She was joining just the Thursday night Zumba class, and her name was Megan.

New students were a regular occurrence. They often showed up just before a class, and sometimes, like Megan, they would show up during the warmup. In both cases, either before class when few other women were present, or during the warmup when the class was already moving and working, only a handful of women would learn or hear the name of the new student, who on her first night would then would blend into the class. Some of those new students would become regulars, and some of those would make a large circle of friends, while others would remain relatively quiet and obscure. It was clear that Megan would neither blend nor remain obscure. The room was near still as I greeted her. The warmup music was low enough for the front half of the class to have no problem hearing me. Though I doubted anyone would approach her, women generally are as intimidated by a more beautiful woman as men are by a larger and more muscular man. There was no question that by the end of class, every woman in the room would know her name.

"Hello, Megan. My name is Lisa." I started to reach out and shake her hand, then held back, ironically, because I wanted to touch her. I felt that if I took her hand, somehow she'd know I wanted to touch her, that she would perceive in the grasp more than just a welcome. Then I thought I was ridiculous. My thoughts bounced back and forth like this for a moment, until I finally managed a feeble "welcome to class" while keeping my hands to myself. She smiled and found an open spot at the back of the group and to my right. My eyes, and many others, followed her all the way.

For the next hour, I found it tough to keep my eyes off her. I'd never before looked at a woman with any feeling I could describe as desire, but her sports bikini covered her body in a way that made me want to see more of her. It exposed neither too little nor too much, covering everything that a sensible woman would cover at a public pool or beach, but nothing more—a fraction more material to the outfit. I doubt I would have been drawn back to watching her, while a fraction less material would have been considered indecent by the more conservative women in the class. My mind wandered, wondering if the hidden parts were as perfect as the rest, and I found myself drawn to watching her dance. I was surprised by the intensity of my desire to catch even a glimpse of what was under the outfit, hoping the animated Zumba routines would pull the bikini back even the smallest bit. It never happened, but this only distracted me more. The level of arousal I began experiencing shocked me, and by the end of class, I was in a state of real sexual frustration. While I found this disturbing, it also motivated a quick trip home. I skipped the usual routines of showering, changing clothes, and socializing. A record thirty minutes after class ended, I walked into my house and found Adam in the living room watching television.

By the time he turned to look at me, my shoes and shirt were already on the floor, and my pants were on their way to joining them. I saw his eyebrows raise. As married couples go, I would describe our sex life as above average, occasionally great, but it was rare for me to be the aggressor. With Adam watching, undoubtedly curious about where my unusual behavior was heading, I continued undressing, removing my leggings and then my panties. Naked except for my sports bra, I walked over and straddled him on the couch, my knees resting on the cushions on either side of him. With my right hand, I reached behind his head and pulled his lips to mine in a lustful kiss, and with my left hand, I grabbed his right hand and brought it up between my open legs. The instant he touched me, intense sensations of pleasure coursed through my body. Using both hands, I pulled him into the kiss with complete abandon as his hand and fingers explored and caressed my most sensitive parts. But he was too gentle, too slow. I reached down and grasped his middle and index fingers, squeezing them together, and then forced them inside me. He stopped kissing me, and in the flickering light of the television, his eyes registered surprise.

I grabbed his hand lower, pushing his fingers up inside me as far as they would go and ground my body downward. "Finger fuck me. Hard."

My behavior and words were a long way from anything Adam likely ever expected, but they had the desired effect. His mouth opened in disbelief, but I watched the look in his eyes change from amazement to lust. I pressed my mouth back to his, and now he kissed back with a desire of his own. He spread his legs apart several inches, forcing my legs further open, and gave me the finger fucking of my life. With each thrust, he drove his fingers deeper and deeper into me, increasing the pace. Sometimes he jammed them into me so hard it hurt, but that only made me wetter, even though I knew I'd probably be sore tomorrow.

I had to stop kissing him because I needed to breathe. I locked my fingers behind his neck, arched my body backward, and began forcing my pussy forward and down onto his hand with each thrust. Soon I was fucking his hand as much as his hand was fucking me. At some point, I began moaning, beginning to lose myself in the growing sensations. And then, during one of the thrusts, Adam's thumb touched my clit. The contact was light, I wasn't even sure at first if it was intentional, but I gasped and arched forward, bringing my head down between my arms. Within seconds I knew it wasn't an accident; my clit was touched with every stroke now, and although his fingers penetrated me hard, the sensations on my clit remained light. A slight shudder passed through me each time I was touched, and the teasing drove me to the point of complete wanton desire. I pulled in close to him, laying my head on his shoulder, and driving myself down onto his hand now with all my strength. Every exhale was an uncontrolled moan, I squeezed my arms and pulled in tighter, I even bit his shoulder, but the torment did not relent. And then, as I reached the point where I didn't think I could bear it any longer, he buried his fingers deep inside me and began massaging my clit hard with his thumb. The orgasm exploded through me in neverending waves, my body shaking uncontrollably with each peak as my muscles tensed and then relaxed. I know I screamed, how many times and how loudly I'm not sure, but Adam kept fucking me until I managed a few weak gasps telling him to stop.

For a few minutes, I could only continue holding him, my head lying on his shoulder, catching my breath. When I finally looked up, I could see the question on his face, and his mouth started to move to give it voice, but before he could speak, I pulled him tight into another deep, passionate kiss. I had intended just to lie back now and let Adam fuck me, but as we kissed, I felt myself growing wet again and wanting more. I started moaning softly and running my hands over his back and shoulders. He ran his own hands on my arms, over my shoulders, and down my back. Then, very lightly, across my ass and down my legs. When he ran his fingers up the inside of my thighs but stopped short of touching me where I wanted to be touched again, I decided to take control.

I climbed off the couch and Adam's lap. He was wearing his usual lounging-around-the-house clothes: boxer shorts and a t-shirt. Even though the only light in the room was from the television, the erection under the shorts was unmistakable. I pushed him back against the couch and then pulled off the boxers. His face was twisted into an odd expression as if he didn't know what to expect next, and it made me smile. I leaned in and kissed him once on the mouth, then turned and straddled his legs again, this time with my back towards him. And then I sat on his lap, guiding him inside me as I lowered my body onto his.

His muscles tensed and then relaxed, followed by a long low moan as he grabbed my hips, trying to move me up and down. Adam and I had used this position only a few times in our six years of marriage, but I remembered how much control it gave me. I moved up and down on him with slow, small motions. His moaning and attempts to fuck me harder only made me wetter and him more frustrated. Slowly I increased the stroke and the speed, beginning to lose control again when he unhooked my sports bra and yanked it off me. He reached around and cupped my breasts, massaging them gently at first, then grabbing both erect nipples and pinching them hard. I groaned and surrendered my body to his then, fucking his cock as hard and fast as possible, timing my motions with his upward thrusts. His breathing deepened, and his moans of pleasure grew louder, and I could sense he was close. I reached down between my legs and began massaging my clit with hard, rough strokes. He came first, but I followed only a second or two behind. I could feel Adam's body pulsing beneath me, and it made my orgasm more intense. With each wave, my body tensed, the contractions so powerful to be almost painful, and I screamed each time. I'm not sure how long it lasted, the two of us bound together in a rhythm of pleasure, but when it was over, I could only slump backward against his chest, exhausted.

As we rested, Adam kissed my cheek and neck while he continued caressing my breasts and now sensitive nipples in soft and gentle circles. I closed my eyes and let my body relax to the sensual fondling. Adam was still inside me, and over several minutes as we just sat, quiet and peaceful, he went limp and slipped out with a teasing, excruciating slowness. When that happened, he pushed me off his lap and walked off toward the bedroom, and I stretched out on the couch on my stomach and laid my head on one of the pillows. I don't know how long I laid there, but I think I was close to falling asleep when I felt Adam's hand on my shoulder. He dressed in his boxers again, standing in front of me, holding out a washcloth. I reached up and took it and found it warm, almost hot. I flipped over on my back and wiped down my entire body. I was amazed at how wet I still was. Adam stood watching, waiting to take the washcloth back from me, I guessed, but it turned out there was more.

He did take the washcloth, but instead of walking away, he continued watching me. The continuing gaze started to make me feel odd and overly self-aware. I grabbed another pillow and pulled it to my chest while turning slightly on my side and pulling up my knees.

"What?"

He took a deep breath, then let it out slowly. It became clear that he wanted to ask me something, and there could be no doubt what it was.

"What?" I continued playing dumb.

"I want to ask you something." He paused, and then, "What got into you?"

"What do you mean?" I'd never been an excellent liar. I didn't sound convincing even to myself.

"What do I mean?" He smiled. "We've been married almost six years, and that is by far the strongest you've ever come on to me. Including even before we were married!"

"So?"

"So? So I want to know what set it off. Don't get me wrong, I liked it. A lot. But I want to know what did it."

"Nothing." I relaxed and tried to act like I was blowing it off. "I was just horny."

He smiled. "You're a terrible liar you know."

"Adam, there was nothing, really." It wasn't intentional, but I pulled the pillow tighter into my chest and curled toward a fetal position.

Adam laughed. "Yeah, your body language says truth all over it. Give me that."

He yanked the pillow away from me, pushed me back over onto my back, and pushed my knees to straighten my legs.

"Hey!" I chased after the pillow, but he was too fast and already had it out of my reach. I tried to sit up, but Adam pushed me back down.

"Shhh! Close your eyes." He held me in place, not letting me up.

"What? Why?"

"Lay back and close your eyes. Just do it."

And I did. I rested my head on the pillow and closed my eyes, lying stretched out, flat on my back. Adam saw me naked all the time but lying here like this with him looking made me feel odd and tingly.

"Today," he said, "you saw something or heard something or maybe even did something that really worked you up."

I opened my eyes and looked over at him, starting to get up again. "Adam, there really---"

"Lay down." He pushed me back down again. "Whatever it was, picture it."

"There wasn't anything, I'm telling you." Even as I spoke the words, an image of Megan began to form.

"Just picture it, remember it, look at it again, or hear it or do it in your head again, whatever it is."

"This is stupid." My protest was considerably weaker. I had a clear mental image of Megan now, her perfect body dancing around in that damned bikini. All the feelings I'd had in the class started returning. For maybe thirty seconds, Adam said or did nothing. As I tried to see behind that bikini in my mind, my body reacted in several subtle ways that I wasn't paying attention to, but Adam was. My breathing deepened, my legs parted slightly, I put my hands on my stomach near my waist. Then something touched my hand and made me jump. I opened my eyes, and Adam had grabbed my right hand.

"Close your eyes. Go back there. Go."

I closed my eyes again. Adam lifted my hand and then placed it right between my legs. The instant explosion of nerves throughout my body was intense. I almost came from that single touch. Using my fingers, he began stroking me and then pulled his hand away. I almost stopped, too embarrassed to continue, but Megan danced in front of me, and desire was powerful. I rubbed harder as Megan in my mind began undressing, pulling down the bikini top to reveal perfect, perky breasts and tiny erect nipples. With her back to me, the bikini bottoms came down, and her gorgeous little ass swayed to my mind's music. I had never masturbated in front of Adam before, but I was doing it now with complete abandon. As Megan in my head began to turn around and finally reveal that perfect, naked form, I was close to my third climax. A few more seconds were all I needed.

Adam grabbed my hand and pulled it away. I opened my eyes, and they pleaded with his own to let go, but as much as I struggled, he was more powerful.

"What are you looking at?" One corner of his mouth turned up in a slight, wry smile.

"nothing. let me go!"

"No way, not until you tell me." As if to make his point, he sat across my legs, stretched my hands out above my head over the arm of the couch, and leaned in close, looking in my eyes straight. The sly smile grew bigger. "Come on, give it up."

I twisted and turned, struggling for some freedom, but he had me pinned. "Come on Adam, let me go. There's nothing. I was just giving you a show."

He laughed at that. "Do people on the stand lie as badly as you do? You're not getting your hands back until you tell me. What did this to you?"

I gave up then, relaxing and letting out a long sigh. I could have made something up, but he was right, I was a lousy liar, and what does it matter if he knew? I made a show of wrenching my face into a look of pouty defiance, and then gave him the answer that, while true, would be the last thing he would imagine.

"A girl."

Chapter 02

Five weeks had passed since the night I first saw Megan, and telling Adam had made things worse. His disbelief passed faster than I would have thought, and then he began pushing me on the idea of pursuing her! A few nights after that first one, he described what it would be like to have another girl go down on me, how another girl would be able to do things only another girl would know-how. It had made me so wet that I came the instant his tongue touched me for a demonstration, but the whole episode only spun me deeper into a web of tangled emotions. At first, his behavior shocked me, but a couple of male acquaintances in college had told me there isn't a man alive who's not turned on by the idea of two girls together, so maybe Adam had his motives. For a couple of weeks, he bugged me about it almost continually. The feelings had me confused and conflicted, though, and I didn't want to discuss it with him any further. To get him to leave it alone, I managed, to my amazement, to pull off a rather big lie. The small part of the lie was that I'd told him that Megan had left the class after two weeks and that I knew nothing about her other than her name, so whatever it had been, it was over. The major part of the lie was that it wasn't over, that the feelings in me were complicated but intense, and I had to hide them from Adam while my feelings were growing intense. I found Megan creeping into my thoughts with increasing frequency. She'd become a mental tool for my imagination to explore how a relationship with a girl might feel, both physically and emotionally. Those musings had become quite powerful now, having developed into a full-on fantasy that I both desired and feared—a fantasy with Megan at its center.

Tonight she was late to class, and it distracted me. Most nights, just waiting for her to walk in the door was enough to create a warm tingling between my legs, not arousal, but something close to it. I found myself anticipating her presence every Thursday night, excited by the thought of her dancing around the floor next to nothing. It was the first time she'd ever been late, however, and the first thought that screamed across my mind was a mixture of fear and relief. What if she weren't coming back? My stomach churned and twisted in knots until, about five minutes in the main workout, the door at the back of the room opened and in walked Megan, followed by a tall, attractive blond I'd never seen before. They were dressed in identical sweatsuits sporting a logo I couldn't entirely read from across the room. Simultaneously, as if the motions had been practiced, Megan and the blond girl removed their sweatshirts over their heads, their movements more sensual than necessary, and they seemed to be staring right at me as they tossed the shirts to the floor. Underneath, they were wearing the sexiest tight black sports bras I'd ever seen. Before I'd finished looking them over, they took down their pants. This time there was no question they were casting intentional looks straight at me. If their sports bras were skimpy, the boyshorts they wore could be described as next to nonexistent. I watched them walk out onto the exercise floor, causing a few other women to stop and turn to look behind them. I saw several eyes rolling as they turned back around and returned to the routine.

For the next forty-five minutes, Megan and the blond put on a show. There's no other way to describe it. And it was a show that appeared to be for my benefit; I had the only clear view of the two of them. Many of the motions in Zumba are already quite sensual; tonight, Megan and her friend made them overtly sexual. They left no doubt that I was the target audience, and the idea that it was intentional to get my attention sent small shivers through my midsection. I enjoyed watching it. It didn't affect me until we came to a point where the hands are clapped together down low the body, kept together as the arms are raised. Then the arms swung apart in big arcs as if the dancer is trying to swim upwards through the air. The blond girl, for the most part, started performing the moves just like everyone else. Megan, however, instead of clapping her hands together, placed them between her legs. She caressed her abdomen's muscles up to her breasts, which she would squeeze each time and finally up through hair. After the third or fourth pass, I could see her nipples began poking rock hard through the thin sports bra. The blond girl watched Megan for a moment and then began an identical routine. What finally got me was when Megan performed the motion. She pulled her shorts tighter and tighter into herself until the material was being pulled up taught between her labia, forming a crease that made it clear she had no underwear. When she began dragging her fingers through that crease, I lost control. Watching them made me wet, stirring a deep, almost primal sexual feeling that I didn't know I had. I wanted to join them to stimulate my own body the way they were stimulating theirs. So strong was the feeling, I almost did. Horrified that I was on the verge of masturbating in front of a room full of other women, I collected my thoughts and focused on the routine, thankful that the exertion masked my arousal. I repositioned myself a bit, and for the remaining ten minutes of the class tried not to look in their direction. I looked anyway, unable to help myself, but though they both continued to keep their eyes on me, they had decided to end the show.

After class, they were the last to emerge from the locker room, and other than the three of us, the room was empty now. Showered and dressed again in their light sweatsuits, they approached me. Megan introduced the blond girl, Kim, a college friend she hadn't seen for a couple of years, and they invited me out for drinks. My heart raced. Given the performance they'd put on in class, drinks couldn't possibly be all they had in mind, and it caught me off guard, both thrilling me and scaring me all at once. I was sure I was blushing deep red, and I caught Megan and Kim exchanging sly glances. After some scattered thoughts that I couldn't quite collect and coaxing from both Megan and Kim, I accepted. I wanted a shower first, but they convinced me I was fine the way I was. I called Adam and told him I was going out for a while with a couple of the girls from class. Several of my friends were in my classes, and after-class outings were not unusual, but had he known I was heading out for drinks with Megan and Megan's new friend, he would have been far more inquisitive. In my car, I followed Megan and Kim in Megan's beautiful Saturn Aura to the Chili's on Shoreline Drive. One hour and two daiquiris later, I'd learned a lot about them. They had both grown up in Connecticut, had met at UConn, and now they were both teachers. Megan was starting a new job in the fall at Prisk Elementary in Long Beach and moved here six weeks ago. Kim lived in Boston and was visiting for about a month. Our casual conversation continued until I took the final sip of my second daiquiri, and I thought it was time to exit. Megan must have noticed me glancing at my watch.

"How did you like the show tonight?" Megan's question blew the rest of the night's conversation to pieces. I hadn't been sure what form it was going to take, but I'd known it was coming. My heart jumped at the question, and I fumbled for words to voice an answer.

"Why don't you come back to Megan's place with us and we'll finish the show?" Kim asked the question in a soft disarming voice. I hadn't even managed a reply to Megan's question when Kim's new one sent my head spinning. Inside I was a mess. A mixture of excitement and apprehension had my stomach in knots.

The question hung in the air. I wanted to go with them and ideas about what might happen, running through my imagination, but I felt unprepared and unsure. An uncomfortable silence screamed at me for an answer, pressuring me to speak even though I didn't know what to say. "I'm sorry, I can't," I said, surprising myself that the words escaped my lips. Disappointment registered on their faces, but having spoken the words, I stuck by them, and a few minutes later, after an awkward goodbye, I was in my car heading for home, my thoughts spinning in every direction. By the time I reached my driveway, I had regretted my choice. I almost kept driving. I could turn around and go back. But, they were sure to be gone, and I didn't know where Megan lived. If I had, I would have driven straight there. I began considering ways I might find her address, but then I felt silly. I pulled the car into the drive, turned off the engine, and sat for several minutes, collecting myself and putting the events out of my mind.

Instead, for the next week, I could think of nothing else. I managed to keep it hidden from Adam--- he didn't ask questions at least---but regret and anticipation tore at me the entire week. When Thursday night arrived, I bounced back and forth between being fearful that Megan and Kim wouldn't show, and fearful that they would.

They arrived on time, taking positions near the back of the class, but there was no show tonight. They spent a lot of time looking in my direction, dancing in sync with the class, but giving their routines none of the outright sexuality they'd added the week before. It turned out this was worse for me than if they'd performed it all for me again. Because they didn't, I wanted them to. I wanted to see them running their hands over their bodies, touching themselves, making their nipples hard, outlining their most sensitive parts with the fabric of their shorts. The same primal sexual feelings I'd experienced a week ago surged through me again. Two-thirds through the class, I had to excuse myself; the class would keep going; they knew the routine. I needed several handfuls of tissue in the bathroom to dry the wetness that had formed between my legs. Before returning to the class, I sat, trying to focus my mind on anything but Megan and Kim. Fortunately, the time remaining was short, and when class ended, Megan and Kim came straight to the front of the room.

"Hey Lisa, we're going back to my place to get cleaned up. You want to join us?" Megan asked.

The loaded question started me tingling all over again. I nodded. "Sure." As I spoke the word, an odd sensation came over me. At first, I thought it might be guilt, but it was more like naughtiness. Like I was ten years old again and about to steal from the cookie jar---knowing it was wrong, but unable to deny the pleasure that waited. The other women leaving the class seemed to be taking no notice of the three of us.

"Are you okay leaving your car here?" Megan asked. "Parking at my place is kind of limited."

I nodded, and thirty minutes later, I knew why. Megan lived in a beachfront townhouse on Ocean Boulevard. "This is amazing! How do you afford it?"

"On a teacher's salary, you mean?" Megan smiled. "Divorce was good to me." For a moment, a huge grin filled her face.

Megan unlocked the door, and Kim disappeared inside. I followed her up the steps but hesitated before entering. Stepping inside was like some sort of final commitment, a point of no return. Megan stood just inside, waiting. I looked at her, and her beautiful gray-blue eyes stared back. She was gorgeous. Light brown hair fell across her shoulders down to the middle of her breasts. Smooth, soft skin covered high cheekbones that accented perfect lips. She raised her eyebrows and tossed her head toward the room behind her to signal me inside. I took a few steps, entering just far enough for Megan to close the door. I turned and watched as she bolted the lock. As the click echoed across my senses, Megan embraced me. She placed her hands behind my head and pulled my face close to hers. When her lips touched mine, I dropped my gym bag to the floor, returning the embrace, and for the first time in my life, all reservation fading away to nothing, I kissed---really kissed---a girl.

It was different than kissing Adam. Not better, not worse, just different. The lips were softer, and the kiss itself was gentler but more sensual. I ran my fingers through what turned out to be hair as soft as silk and pulled her in tighter as I returned the kiss. Parted lips gave way to full open mouths. Megan backed me up against the door, her gentleness becoming a deeper hunger growing in both of us. At some point, she pulled back from the kiss, then ran her tongue lightly across my lips. My legs went weak at the sensation, and I chased her tongue with my mouth, kissing and sucking it as she teased me with it. I grabbed her head hard and pulled her mouth back to mine, our tongues now meeting in the kiss.

Before I was ready to stop, she pulled away again. I pulled her head back toward me, chasing her lips with my own, but she pushed my head to the side with one hand and began kissing my cheek and earlobes, and then down into the small of my neck. Chills spread across my entire body. As she focused her mouth on my neck's sides, her hands began exploring the rest of me, caressing my stomach, then up between my breasts, and then down my back. As her hands traveled downward, I anticipated the feeling of her fingers passing below my waist and caressing me through the fabric of the exercise tights, but when she reached the top of the tights, she stopped and reversed direction. On the way back up, she ran her hands up my sides and across the outside of my breasts. When she reached my neck, she pulled me back into a kiss. It was my turn to explore. Between her head and waist, I ran my hands over everything, through her sweatshirt finding her incredibly hard nipples and even the firm but feminine lines of her stomach muscles.

Then she stopped again---I'd lost all track of time---and took me by the hand, leading me to a large room on the other side of the house. It was a living room of sorts. A large, floor-to-ceiling sliding glass window opened onto a deck overlooking the beach. She pulled me onto a couch, laid down next to me, and brought her lips back to mine. The sound of waves crashing against the beach floated through the open door, filling the room with its sensual music. I closed my eyes, pulled her close, lost myself in the touch of her lips, and roamed her hands. I'm not sure how much time had passed when someone clearing their throat startled me, sending a quick shiver of surprise through my body. I'd forgotten all about Kim. Standing in a doorway that led down a hall was Kim, wet hair falling across her shoulders, her body wrapped in a large yellow and white striped towel.

Megan kissed me, stood, and excused herself so she can take a shower. Kim walked over and sat next to me on the couch. One side of her towel fell away, exposing the left side of her slender body high enough to make out the feminine curves of a smooth waistline. She didn't have the carved abdominals I'd felt through Megan's sweatshirt, but what I could see of her stomach was flat and fit. The tip of a tattoo, a vine or ivy, trailed away from her leg toward her left thigh.

"Would you like to see more?" Kim asked.

I'd been staring. I looked up, blushing deep red. I opened my mouth to speak, but Kim leaned in, placed a short, soft kiss on my parted lips, then pulled back, looked into my eyes, and waited for my response. The scent of a floral shampoo lingered in the air, combining with the crashing ocean and the teasing beauty of her partially exposed body into an intoxicating assault on my senses. I leaned into her and embraced her neck. The cold strands of her damp hair brushed across my skin, sending erotic chills up my arms and back. Our lips touched in a long, soft kiss. Just as kissing Megan was different from kissing Adam, kissing Kim was different from kissing Megan. Kim's kiss was less aggressive and more sensual. Something hinted of strawberries, and I savored the taste of her lips. As we kissed, her hands began to explore my body, caressing first my back and arms with slow, soft strokes, then moving to my sides and stomach.

When she finally touched my breasts, my nipples were rock hard, and the light brushing of her hands across the tight fabric of my workout top sent me tingling from the inside out. I began roaming my hands around her body and running my fingers through her damp hair, and caressing the exposed skin of her shoulders, upper back, and chest. Suddenly she pinched and held both my nipples, not hard, but enough to evoke an involuntary moan. She continued to hold them, applying more pressure. The sensation brought that primal sexual urge inside me to the surface. I grabbed her head, kissed her hard, and slid my hands between the towel folds. When my hand touched something hard and cold on her stomach, I pulled back, surprised.

Kim smiled, then stood, pulling the towel open to reveal a belly button piercing, a small metal bar with diamonds on both ends. It wasn't her belly button that drew my attention, though. She wasn't merely shaved, she was baby smooth, and there was only the faintest hint of tan lines. The tattoo inside her left thigh was a vine with four little flowers blooming from it, maybe four to five inches long overall. With me watching, she pulled the towel entirely off and dropped it to the floor. I throbbed deep inside. I would never have believed that I could approach an orgasm at the mere sight of a nude body, especially a woman's, but if I touched myself right then, I was sure I would explode. The emotions I was experiencing were the same as those the night I'd first seen Megan and had gone home and fucked Adam like I never had before; I was swept up in deep, pure lust.

"Can I see you?" As she asked the question, she began caressing her stomach and breasts with the same light, gentle motions she'd been exploring me with just moments before.

My heart pounded. Desire and fear were at odds within me. Desire had long since won the fight, but an overwhelming fear of the unknown and doubts about whether I should be here were still lingering in the background, sending my pulse racing and tying my stomach in one huge knot. I took a long, slow breath and then pulled my top off my head in a single motion. The knot in my stomach tightened. My nipples stood out more than I knew they could, so hard they hurt. Kim smiled, her eyes roaming my body. She nodded at my tights, and I took another deep breath and pulled them down. But I was nervous, and the tights were awkward to remove, and I fell backward onto the couch struggling to remove them.

Kim laughed, then knelt on the floor and helped me finish the task, hooking her fingers inside my underwear and tights at the same time, and removing them both in one smooth motion. When she finished, she kneeled in front of me, positioned between my legs as I sat on the edge of the couch. Kim pulled me close and kissed me, but this time the kissing didn't linger long on my lips. She kissed her way down my neck, sending shivers through my body and then my chest. She continued down between my breasts and down my abdomen. I grew wetter in anticipation, but she stopped at my belly button, then ran her tongue from my belly button up under my chin. Another unexpected moan escaped my lips. Kim looked me in the eyes, then kissed me full on the mouth, hard this time. She pinched my nipples again and gave my lower lip a soft, playful bite before placing a trail of kisses down my neck and chest. This time she didn't ignore my breasts. She kissed and licked them all over, but she ignored my nipples, standing erect and screaming for attention for a while.

When her tongue finally touched one, I let out a small scream and grabbed her head, pushing it hard into my breast. She bit my nipple then. Quick but hard, and the surprise and shock of the sensation made me jump. Then she spent the next thirty seconds licking and kissing it as if to say she was sorry. She moved to another breast, and it received the same treatment—a quick, hard bite, followed by soft, warm attention from her tongue. I was in ecstasy beyond imagining, and whether from the physical sensations, the emotional ones, or both, I can't say, but I was shocked to feel a tear streak from the corner of one eye and then the other. Kim noticed, smiled, and kissed them away.

She pushed me back on the couch, pushed my legs apart with her hands, and then caressed my nipples lightly with her palms, made a trail of soft wet kisses from just above my breasts straight down the front of my body. I'd never been so close to orgasm without having even been touched yet. The line of kisses stopped just as I thought the next one would land directly on my clit. It was swollen and ready, and my lips were parted and wet. The whole area ached and throbbed in a pre-orgasmic state; a single touch would probably send me over the edge. But she teased me. She caressed and licked everywhere to within a millimeter of the truly delicate parts. The sensations of her fingers and tongue on my smooth, shaved skin was almost enough. At one point, she pressed down hard at the base of my pubic bone, and I honestly thought I would come. I didn't, but more uncontrolled tears flowed down my cheeks as I became lost in the physical and emotional pleasure.

And then she did it. She ran her tongue straight up the middle of me, a deep stroke that touched everything that had been aching for attention, stopping on my clit, and staying there. It took only seconds when a powerful orgasm pulsed through me, waves of pleasure that started at the end of Kim's tongue and exploded outward through my every extremity. Somehow, Kim kept it going a long, long time. Her tongue knew just the right spots at just the right time. When I finally opened my eyes, Megan was standing naked in the doorway that led down the hall, caressing her breasts with one hand and masturbating gently with the other. I felt suddenly embarrassed and awkward.

I don't know if my posture changed, but Megan walked over, embraced me, and gave me a long, tender kiss, then told me to turn over. I must have looked confused. "What?" was all I could manage.

"Turn over." She patted the top edge of the couch. "Rest your head and arms here, and put your knees up on the couch."

Despite the intense orgasm I'd just experienced, the knot in my stomach began to work it's way back. It's part excitement, part apprehension, just as before, but more apprehension this time. Why that was, I didn't know, but when I didn't move, Kim grabbed my hand and pulled me up from where I'd been leaning against the couch. "Come on, we'll make it worth your while, promise." She pulled harder on my hand.

So, without thinking about it any further, I did it. It was an impulse behavior. I think that somewhere deep inside, something told me that maybe I shouldn't be here, but I didn't want to hear it right now. Kim helped me up, turned and faced the couch, and then kneeled on it, knees together.

"Oh cute butterfly." Kim had noticed my tattoo.

"I've always wondered what the rest of that thing looked like," added Megan.

I leaned forward, resting my head and arms on the back of the couch and closing my eyes, finding the position more comfortable than I'd anticipated. Even with my legs still tight together, though, I also felt vulnerable and exposed.

A hand stroked the back of my leg, upward from just above the knee, then on my exposed ass. The hand was Megan's. Kim's hands were warm now, and she had long fingernails. Her hand was crisp to the touch and had short, smooth nails. Over the next few minutes, her hands warmed as she caressed and massaged my legs and ass. I started to relax, and then a sudden smack across my rear jolted me.

"Ow!" The exclamation was more from surprise than anything else. The blow had been hard but not overly painful.

My ass was spanked again on the other side, just as hard. Then again. And again. Megan was giving me a real spanking! The realization of it made me immediately wet again, and without realizing it, I parted my legs a bit. The blows came faster, some of them very hard now, and I could feel my bottom warming up. As it progressed, though, pain disappeared, and pleasure took its place. Each blow sent erotic sensations throughout my body, and the spanking became entirely sexual.

I felt the couch move a bit on my right, and I opened my eyes for a moment. Kim had taken a sitting position next to me. She smiled, and I closed my eyes again, lost in the sensuality of the spanking. At some point, I wasn't sure when I'd moved my legs further apart, and I was entirely open and exposed. Raw sexual feelings were stirring again.

When fingers suddenly entered me, forceful yet pleasant, I jumped and then moaned. The intensity of the spanking increased again. I leaned further forward on the couch and spread my legs wide now, pushing my ass upward. I didn't know which one of them was fucking me with her fingers, and I didn't care. I guessed it was Kim since Megan was busy spanking me, but whoever it was, the feelings were so erotic it went beyond mere physical pleasure. At times I almost felt like I needed to pee. When that sensation overwhelmed me, and I thought I actually would, it changed to a warm glowing sensation that wasn't orgasm but gave tremendous pleasure both physically and emotionally.

The spanking suddenly stopped, but the finger fucking didn't, and I realized I was moaning, almost crying. Embarrassed, I tried to stop.

"It's okay. Let it out. Let it go." Megan spoke the words from somewhere behind me.

For another moment, I held it in, then lost all control when another new sensation assaulted me. My ass was spread wide, and something warm and slippery, a lubricated finger, began massaging its opening. The sensations were exquisite, sending new waves of pleasure through me. Then the fucking I was getting grew more intense, adding fingers and spending more time on my clit now. My second orgasm in ten minutes was building fast. And then the finger massaging my ass began pushing its way past the opening. I froze and clenched involuntarily. For a moment, the spell was broken, but Megan and Kim knew what they were doing, and I was soon lost again under their skilled hands. The finger teasing my ass began again, pushing its way inside me.

"No." I squeaked out the word as I froze again.

There was a pause, then. It lasted maybe two seconds but seemed like two hours. "Okay. I'm sorry," said Megan from behind me.

But this time, the spell did break. A weird feeling formed in the pit of my stomach, and all of a sudden, everything felt disconnected and wrong. I felt like the victim of a terrible practical joke that a million eyes were watching and laughing at me, alone and exposed. I raised myself to a kneeling position and reached down and stopped Kim's hand. With her other hand, she stroked my hair and then leaned in and kissed my cheek, whispering to me that it was okay to relax and let myself go. She ran her hand back up the inside of my now closed legs, but I stopped her again.

"I'm sorry," I said. I stood and grabbed my clothes, and then almost ran from the room through the doorway that led to a bathroom somewhere. I found it and closed the door. My body was shaking, so I sat for a few minutes and calmed down. My mind spun everywhere, my thoughts a jumbled mess, and I decided I needed just to leave and do some thinking.

When I came out, Megan and Kim had put on shorts and t-shirts. They were both quiet as I walked through the room to the front of the house. Megan followed me. "Please stay."

Part of me wanted to, but part of me wasn't ready for this. Right now, what I wanted was Adam. To just curl up in his arms and go to sleep. "I really need to go, I'm sorry."

She offered to drive me home, but I wanted to take the bus. I wanted the time to think, to gather my thoughts.

An hour later, after two short walks and a bus ride, my thoughts were anything but gathered. It was after 10:30, and Adam was already in bed, but I couldn't have talked to him anyway. I poured a glass of wine, grabbed my laptop, turned off all the lights, and made myself comfortable on the living room couch. Maybe I could distract myself and just let it all go for a while. I opened the laptop, sipping the wine while I waited for it to boot. The wine tasted and felt great; by the time my email was finally open, I'd finished the entire glass, and I felt calmer, soothed by its warming glow.

I had only two new messages, and one of them was from Megan. She must have copied my email address off the bulletin board at the gym. I wanted to ignore it and read it later when it might not bother me as much, but curiosity overcame me, and I opened it. The message was short and not what I expected. "Lisa, we know you want this. The confusion will pass. Here's a short video that we think can help. Just be careful with it. We wouldn't want the wrong people to see it. Love, Megan and Kim." Just below the text was a link, and that was the entire message.

I rolled my eyes, imagining possible scenarios for the video they thought could "help" me, all of them seem ridiculous. The link indicated it was sixty-three seconds. I almost deleted the email without clicking the link, but curiosity compelled me to click it. It should be amusing at least, and a one-minute video wasn't going to change anything anyway.

It turned out I was wrong. For the next sixty-three seconds, I didn't breathe.

The video was six ten-second scenes. As each one appeared, my jaw dropped further, and my mind scrambled for explanations. In the first scene, I stood in the entryway of Megan's house, backed against the door, the two of us kissing and groping. In the second one, Megan and I were making out on her couch. In the third one, I was taking off my clothes while an already naked Kim watched. In the fourth one, I was lying back on the couch, moaning in pleasure with Kim's blond head between my legs. In the fifth one, I was kneeling on the couch, Kim watching and Megan spanking me; a few seconds into it, I watched myself spread my knees wide apart push my ass up into the air. The camera had excellent resolution; it exposed me with shocking clarity. In the final segment, Kim was sitting on the couch next to me, fucking me with her hand, while Megan fingered the opening of my ass.

When it stopped, I was in shock. I played it again, and then one final time. It seemed surreal, and only after playing it the third time did I begin to accept what I was seeing.

And then I reread the text of the message. This time, the final sentence filled me with horror.

"Oh my god."

Story 02

Chapter 01

My name is Zoey, and I want to share my story with you.

About me? Well, I think I'm relatively average: slim, 5' 5", smallish boobs (perky C's), quite fit and athletic.

That's about it. Oh, and I'm a nerdy, geeky scientist too (yeah, white coat and all!)

The other thing you need to be clear about is that I'm 100% straight! Not even a tiny bit curious.

It was a Friday night, and I was reluctantly going out with a bunch of friends for a girl's birthday. We often went out together, and the nights always end up the same, meet at a bar, have some food, get drunk and go dancing, then end up picking up some guy and having disappointing drunken sex. The last bit was the reluctance that I felt that evening. I was just a bit fed up with it.

That evening, we were going to meet up with some other girls that I didn't know. I'm not so good at these situations, and I tend to go a bit quiet. My friends and I were at the bar, chatting and laughing when the other five girls joined us. They all looked dressed to kill, and I learned that two worked in the fashion industry (whatever that meant). Across the table from me was the most interesting girl named Fiona. She had striking deep eyes, was quiet, but soon enough, we started to chat. I was drawn in, and the chitter-chatter of the other girls receding into the background. We talked about all sorts, the topics just flowing from one thing to another. I couldn't remember ever having had a conversation like that, or one as natural. I liked her a lot and hoped she felt the same. I remember thinking that we could be good friends.

After we had eaten, everyone was well oiled and ready to go to a club on the pull. I was thinking about ducking out, saying I didn't feel so good. Fiona felt much the same and suggested we stayed and let the others go on.

We were there until the bar closed and the time flew by. It was one of my most enjoyable Friday nights ever. We shared a taxi even though she lived miles away from me, and it was nice to have some company. We made rough plans to meet up for lunch on Sunday. Great!

I spent Saturday with the worst hangover in history, so it was a bit of a washout. I'm never drinking again (until Friday)!

As lunchtime on Sunday rolled around, I felt nervous. What if we got on because we were just drunk or had nothing left to talk about?

Of course, I shouldn't have been stressed out about this sort of thing; we met, had lunch, chatted regularly, and sat in Christchurch meadow. It was great. I had made a new friend, and we were getting on well. Perfect.

Things continued like this for a while; we got to know each other better and had a lot of fun. One day I was at her stunning house for lunch, and she was rather quiet (very unusual for her), with a careful look on her face. She told me that she was gay and that she should have told me earlier and was sorry to keep it. She also hoped that it wouldn't affect our friendship.

I told her that I already knew as one of her friends had told me on that first night when we met and stayed behind together. Why should it matter? Things quickly went back to normal, except we saw more of each other and called in the evenings.

One night, sitting in bed, I had spoken to her on the phone. It was a random conversation, but I went to sleep very happy only to be woken up a few hours later from the most erotic dream I have ever had. It was about Fiona and me. It felt so authentic, and I think I woke because I was having an orgasm! My knickers were super wet and sticky, and I had to change them, but I was floating on cloud nine in post-orgasmic bliss. I wanted to masturbate, but it felt weird after my dream, and I didn't want to betray her in that way. It felt wrong somehow.

This dream-scene repeatedly replayed for the next few days, and I often found myself with a small damp patch afterward.

I tried masturbating in the evenings, telling myself that it was because I hadn't had sex for quite a while. No unsatisfactory one-night stands, and indeed no relationships. I hadn't met a relationship type of guy in absolute ages as most of the guys seemed to be total wankers!

Anyway, needs must, and so I masturbated but couldn't help but think of Fiona just as I was on the verge of cumming. Wow, explosive would be an understatement. I had never cum so hard by myself, and indeed, no man had ever done that to me.

I felt guilty, but not enough to stop. If thinking about a girl (it only really worked with Fiona) was going to give me massive orgasms, I was going to keep doing it, and how! It became my nighty ritual; we usually called before bed, just for a chat, to see how our day had gone. I was always looking forward to some pussy action after her call. Jesus, what was happening to me? I didn't fancy her or anything; she was just good fantasy material. I started masturbating during one of these calls but had to stop as it nearly made me cum instantly. This was getting out of control.

A few weeks went by. I was taking more risks with fantasies of sex and Fiona. I had gone out with the usual friends and picked up a guy I knew (he liked to call us fuck-buddies even though we weren't!) to see if it took my mind off Fiona. It didn't work. All I could think about while fucking, was her. It was not a good sign. I'm straight. I don't want a hot lesbian relationship with my best friend (although it didn't sound all that bad). Maybe, just maybe, had I become slightly curious?

The answer came a week later. We went out together for expensive dinner and drinks, getting somewhat drunk on champagne, excellent wine, and a couple of cocktails. I stayed over at her house, which had become usual as I lived miles away (I had my room with an en suite and even some of my clothes). We got back to her place and had another drink. While she was making it, I got close to her and kissed her! She kissed me back but then froze.

"What are you doing?" she gasped.

"Make love to me Fiona, I want you ..." I moaned in reply.

Fiona looked at me; lust filled her eyes, and she said, "Not when you're like this; ask me again when you're sober. Think it all through first. I don't want to take advantage of you and ruin our valued friendship. We are friends first."

So I kissed her, and that's the last I remembered of that evening.

I was woken up in the morning by the sunlight streaming through the window because of the open curtains, burning my retinas right through my eyelids. My god did I feel rubbish. How much did I drink? I don't even remember getting home, I mean to Fiona's. This was usually a bad sign or a goodnight out. I was very uncomfortable, so I looked down at my half-dressed form.

Okay, so I had attempted to undress but only halfway. I had on one boot, my jeans and knickers pulled down to the top of it and all off one leg. My right arm was out of my top and bra, and my hair was still half tied up. I looked a mess and felt it too. I tried to stay in bed but could hear Fiona moving about downstairs (she never gets hungover!). I stumbled out of bed, removing the remaining clothes and climbed into the shower, hoping that this would transform me.

I made my way into the kitchen, where Fiona was fully dressed and looking immaculate. She seemed a little distant. I wondered where she was off too. She said good morning, kissed me on my cheek (normal behavior), said she was out all day, and let myself out whenever and left. Something was up.

She never acts like this. Maybe she met someone last night. Something else was up too. My cheek, where Fiona had kissed me, was tingling and felt slightly odd yet familiar? My eyes grew wide as the memory from last night hit me like a steam train. Everything made total sense. Fiona was avoiding me because I kissed her and almost begged her for sex. Shit, I am such an idiot. Shit, fuck, arse. I had drunkenly let out my secret fantasies of late. What was I going to do?

I started writing a note explaining myself, but then I screwed it up and threw it away, opting for a simple 'sorry' (with a kiss). I left for home to dwell on my stupidity, wondering if I had screwed my friendship with the most delightful person I had ever met—what a mess.

Just over a week had passed and I had not heard a word from Fiona. We talked daily, which I was missing, and now I was sure I had lost her. I missed her and wanted to talk to see if I could help rectify my stupid mistake. After all, I was a straight girl and not interested in sleeping with her - wasn't I? Two girls together are just plain weird! Fantasies are just that. They don't mean anything, and they are usually just something that's out of reach.

I picked the phone up to call her but hesitated. I decided I should see her in person, so I got into the car but hesitated again. What if she wasn't avoiding me but had met someone the other night and was busy fucking her brains out? No. She would have told me that. But what if I go over and this new girlfriend is there?

"Oh, shut the fuck up Zoey, you're cracking up!" I said aloud to myself. I started the car. She lived miles away from me, but I didn't even notice the drive. I stopped at her door. She was out. She must have a new girl. Shit, fuck. While I was sitting in the car and wondering what to do, a shadowy figure came up the road. It was Fiona back from the local shop. Now I had to say something, but what? I opened the door and stood there like the idiot I was. Fiona looked at me quizzically then invited me in to 'talk.' Not good, not good at all.

We stood in her kitchen caressing cups of tea in silence, looking tentatively at each other, hoping the other would open up some sort of dialogue. None came.

"Okay," I said eventually, "I know what I did was wrong on so many levels, but the alcohol just spoke for me, and it's not as if it's very likely to actually happen. I don't even think I want it to either. But I admit, only to you and maybe a bit to myself that it has piqued my interest and maybe into some sort of imaginary fantasy."

I don't know where all that came from. I hadn't admitted that I have a vague girl-girl interest to myself, let alone to her.

"So ... if I kissed you now, how would you react?" Fiona said quietly.

I was quiet, too, fighting my feelings and emotions. Those words sounded quite beautiful, and some weird part of me wanted nothing more.

She slowly took a step forward; she could see the resistance and desire on my face, as plain as day.

"No," I said, "I've never done this before. I have only just realised that I want to." This was another revelation to myself.

"Shh," Fiona said, moments before her super soft, warm lips touched mine, so gently it was almost nothing, but I felt as if I had been electrocuted. My body fired up, and I responded, just pressing back slightly. What the hell was I doing? My body was screaming at me to run, but I was not about to lose this feeling ever!

The kiss stopped, and Fiona stayed close and looked directly into my eyes, searching for some kind of signal.

The signal I gave her was to close the distance and kiss her passionately. I was conflicted with my sensible, rational mind, but I desired to pour out of my soul for the first time. This kiss was better than all the sex I'd ever had put together. It got better. Fiona responded by sliding her tongue across my lips, asking for entry. My mouth responded without thought. The best part was when her arms went around my neck and my arms wrapped around her waist. We were pressing together like lovers, and it felt terrific and somehow so natural and even usual. I relaxed, but only a little.

We slowly made our way to the sofa nearby. I sat, and Fiona straddled my lap. I had never even done this with a guy. I don't know why. It felt good, perfect. No, it was great and sexy and passionate.

Despite the mental conflict, Fiona had lit a furnace in me. I had never known anything like it. I had thought that my rubbish sex-life and track record was my fault. I didn't know that passion could feel this good.

We kissed for what seemed like hours. Fiona brought me to new heights with every movement, caress, and touch. Her mouth was so delicate, sweet, and accurate. She knew what I needed, and indeed what I wanted. She spent time kissing down my neck, over my shoulders, behind my ears. Everywhere I liked and some I didn't even know I liked. It was amazing. If my night had ended there, I would be on cloud nine. But my god, I hoped it wouldn't!

Things started heating up. Fiona dropped the shoulders on the cute dress that I was wearing, exposing my sweet but plain blue bra. She stopped and looked me in the eye.

"Is this what you want?"

"YES!" I exclaimed. "I've never wanted something more; it feels so good." I couldn't believe my ears. Had I said that?

My dress pooled at my waist, thankfully covering my equally plain and not matching knickers (I hadn't planned this). It was a relief as the dress also covered what I was sure was the increasingly wet patch in the knickers.

The kisses moved down slowly over my shoulders, down my chest and soft, warm hands gently, sweetly caressed my breasts softly. My bra slipped off with ease, expertly undone with no fuss.

I felt Fiona's hot, wet tongue slide around my left breast, around the side, underneath over the top avoiding my nipple until, finally, she captured it in her mouth and gently suckled it. My god, I think I was on the verge of cumming then and there. What was this girl doing to me? My other breast was consumed shortly after, and now it was my turn.

I wanted to do that too. I was still in the clumsy stage as sexually undressing a girl was a pretty new experience, but Fiona understood and helped me. She guided my mouth with little gasps and moans while her hands were wrapped in my hair. I think sucking a large soft breast is definitely, the sexiest thing ever. Fiona's boobs are the finest. People talk to them instead of her, and they are the envy of everyone, man and woman—large, firm, and pert. And I was sucking on them! Me. The goody-two-shoes straight girl!

I was so involved in kissing and sucking that I didn't realize my dress was now on the floor and I was on Fiona's sofa in just my plain black knickers, my plain black soaking knickers! Her hands were expertly stroking my inner thighs, edging up slowly and back down again, agonizingly slowly. I had to make her quickly move as I was rapidly getting to the point of needing some release. I needed touching, but she didn't rush, teasing me to the last.

Finally, gently, she stroked me up across my pussy and over my knickers. Again and again. Slowly. Gently. Over and over. The sexy smile on her face told me that she knew what effect this was having on me. I would beg if needed.

"Touch me. Please, please touch my pussy!" I cried out. This had the desired effect (I made a mental note). My knickers were removed expertly and quickly and replaced, much to my surprise and delight, with that soft, warm tongue that had pleasured my nipples earlier. It was exquisite. It was nothing like I had ever felt before. Of course, I had been given oral pleasure, but usually grudgingly and only as a means to an end.

This was different.

She swirled her tongue up and over my clit, flicking across it, and slowly down through my folds, slowly and expertly bringing me to the edge. Again and again, just holding me off until I felt a finger (or two) slide in and with circular tongue motions around my clit.

"HOLY FUCK! OH,OH OH DONT STOP, OOOOOOHHHHHHHHHHH JESUS, OH GOD OH OH OH AAARRRRGGGHHHHH!"

My body convulsed and thrashed around the tongue that slowed but didn't stop. The fingers still moved gently in and out. Peace descended, but briefly. Fiona then curled her fingers up and gently massaged my g-spot while swiping her tongue again across my clit in a different motion this time, and I instantly exploded again. This was the most unbelievable day of my life. What had I been missing?

The next few minutes (or hours I have no idea) were calm and gentle, soft kisses, no urgency, just bliss (from my perspective anyway). I wanted to make Fiona feel this good but the nerves kicked and I realized that I didn't know the first thing about what to do, clearly forgetting that she had the same parts as me so I should know my way around them and I could start with what turned me on.

Thankfully, Fiona saw the look of what must have been horror on my face and smiled kindly. She brought herself up and straddled my torso and over my breasts. I could see her beautiful, swollen wet pussy, and I was in awe. Slowly, she started stroking across it, giving out soft moans as she slid a finger in, and it gave the most satisfying squelch. I breathlessly watched as she masturbated and rubbed, leaving sticky, slick patches over my breasts. It felt marvelous and very sexy if a little selfish. I gathered my courage and slipped my hands onto her gorgeous arse and pulled her up over my face.

I was now staring into her pussy at point-blank range. By this point, I was excited with oxytocin and endorphins, so I just dived right in, licked, sucked, and slurped as if my life depended on it. I imagine it was very amateurish, but it seemed to do the job as Fiona screamed and came hard collapsing over me. Slowly she caught her breath, slipped down to my level, looked into my eyes, and gently kissed me.

We spent a long time kissing and stroking until eventually sleep claimed us.

What would become of me in the morning? Was I no longer curious? Was I even straight? Surely this would question my very being, or was it just a one-off 'incident'?

I hoped not!

Chapter 02

4:29 am

I woke early, subconsciously wanting to savor the feeling of sharing my bed with someone instead of just my vibrator. It wasn't just anyone, though. It was Zoey, and I watched her as she slept peacefully. Did she have a slightly satisfied smile on her face, or was that just wishful thinking? Her hair was a tangled mess; she looked like she'd had a night of wild sex, and she had!

It was hard to resist a slight peek under the covers to marvel at her gorgeous breasts, thinking how only a few hours ago, I was sucking, kissing, and playing with them.

These moments were genuinely beautiful, although there was a real fear at the back of my mind. This was her first time, and she had always been adamant that she was 100% straight. What was going to happen when she woke up? Would she regret everything we had done and run for the hills? Would this destroy our friendship? Why was I so stupid to sleep with my best friend? I had overstepped the line in a moment of weakness. This had all happened before, and it had haunted me for years.

When I was much younger (perhaps to some, too young), my best friend and I spent time, in fact, a lot of time, experimenting with each other, getting more intimate every time. It was regular full-on multi-orgasmic sex. I loved every second of it. It was my first experience of sex and love, and I was head over heels in love with her. The problem was that while indulging in our favorite thing of her grinding on my face. She rubbed my pussy, naked, of course, and just as we were reaching orgasm, her older sister walked in on us. Oh shit. Amongst a string of other abuse, she called us a couple of disgusting dykes and left.

The next Monday morning at school was possibly the worst day of my entire life. Everybody knew. Even the teachers, her bitch sister, had told all. Even my former best friend distanced herself from me. It broke my heart and seemingly let her off the hook. I became the joke of the school and a total social outcast. Even the nerdy kids didn't want anything to do with me. I also struggled with my demons.

Was I gay? I knew I liked looking at girls in the locker room after working out. I also used them in my private masturbation fantasies. I convinced myself that this was normal. I struggled with these feelings and thoughts for a long time, eventually locking them up tight in my mind. Eventually, slowly, things started to get back to near normal.

I dated a couple of guys. I lost my virginity to one of the popular guys at school. However, it was rather unpleasant and uncomfortable, and he then went around bragging how he had converted the lesbian.

Anyway, finally, the school was over, and university life started—a clean slate. After many, many wrong turns, I eventually learned that it was okay to feel these things for me to like girls as more than friends. I had casual relationships but could never really open up after my broken heart.

Anyway, my mind back to my best friend lying in my bed naked after a night of possibly the best sex I have ever experienced.

I gently rolled onto my back and closed my eyes to stop the tears from the impending doom of losing my best friend again. When I opened them, she was lying on her side, looking at me. She smiled and said, good morning. We lay there for quite some time, looking at each other and not knowing what to do.

I broke the ice with the offer of breakfast, which received a hearty nod and another bright smile. I could see confusion and doubt in her eyes; it didn't seem right, but at least she was still talking to me and hadn't run away.

ZOEY

Had I made a huge mistake? I so wanted to try sex with Fiona. I had fantasized about it, not thinking I would ever go through it in a million years. I felt a little uncomfortable about it now, lying naked next to her. She was so beautiful and sexy that I was having a hard time trying not to jump her again. The big problem was that I was straight. Or was I as straight as I thought?

Does everyone have these types of feelings? Maybe I was curious all along. I didn't know. What I do know now is that night blew my mind completely. I had never had sex quite like it, and Fiona took me to places I never knew existed or even imagined. I usually struggle to cum through sex unless I take matters into my own hands. But Fiona had me screaming with ease (I never even knew I was a screamer!). It was quite amazing. So much so that I felt like I wanted more. The question was, 'what does this make me'?

I felt baffled. I was not ready to answer these thoughts at that moment. How should I act with Fiona? What should I say? Should I talk about it, or just try and act normally? Understandably, I wasn't normal anymore; I had just had a wild night of the best sex ever with my best friend.

"I am in need of tea," I said in an attempt at being normal, "and the toilet right now!" before leaping from bed to the bathroom, completely forgetting my state of undress. I felt embarrassed and a bit bashful. Fiona just sat there looking at me with a smile. She knew how silly I felt.

"I am naked too you know," she added, just to make me feel even more silly. I had to laugh.

Sitting on the toilet, I was smiling. I felt pretty good.

When I came downstairs for breakfast, Fiona was cooking up some eggs in the kitchen, wearing only a pair of knickers and a small, tight vest top. It was struggling to contain her very ample cleavage. She looked sexy, and I just stared at her knowing how good her body felt. What was happening to me?

Breakfast and tea were eaten and drunk, and we chatted as if we hadn't fucked last night, both ignoring the tremendous pink elephant that had joined us for breakfast.

I had a family get together to attend, so I had to get going. I was anxious about leaving things as I was still perplexed about these new feelings and concerned that I could hurt Fiona.

FIONA

As Zoey left, I gave her a quick kiss on the lips as a goodbye. I think it surprised her, but she didn't react badly.

"I'll call you later," she called over her shoulder as she got into her car.

I sat on the sofa, wondering if I would ever see her again.

The whole day I spent between horny excitement at having great sex, and depression about the situation.

Zoey didn't call or text or reply to my texts. I couldn't help but fear the worst. That night I lay in my bed, alone, crying myself to sleep.

Monday came and went; no call.

Tuesday, Wednesday, and Thursday passed; no call.

I had calls from friends sorting a night out on the tiles, but I declined as usual. I wondered why they stuck around such a bore.

ZOEY

I knew I owed Fiona an explanation as to my disappearance over the whole last week. I needed some time to think about things. I had no answers but had to see her, and she was still my best friend. After all, I hoped.

On Saturday, early, I knocked on her door. After several knocks, she finally opened the door to me. She looked tired but still beautiful. My heart started beating harder as I saw her, and it dawned on me then that I must have had the hots for her in some way. I had never seen her looking more tired and bedraggled but still found her irresistible and beautiful.

"Can I come in?" I asked, rather meekly.

"Of course, you are always welcome here. Have you lost your key?" answered Fiona with a warm smile.

She seemed to have cheered up all of a sudden. Maybe it was me?

"We need to talk. I am really sorry not to have called. It was so wrong of me. I just didn't know what to say or how to put it. I needed some time to think about things, to know how I felt, and maybe even to understand the confusion. Oh, I don't know."

My thoughts all just came rushing out at once. Fiona just smiled and gave me a gentle hug. It felt so good to be in her arms again.

"Have I messed things up between us?" I asked, while my face was nestled into her neck. I wanted to kiss it.

"Shh, you're here now and we can talk, or maybe just draw a line in the sand and carry on as normal," Fiona said very calmly.

"I love you totally as my best friend and I would never want to pressure you into anything you might be uncomfortable with. What happened the other night admittedly was really good and I can't regret that, but I can't not have you in my life. I need you as a friend."

"I need you too," I quickly replied, "I don't want to spoil things. I don't regret that night either and at least now I know how good you are in bed." I tried to lighten the mood, but it was more a truth. I strangely felt a pang of jealousy towards any future girl who was lucky enough to get a night with her.

"Are you busy today? Maybe we could hang out, get some lunch or something?" I asked, hoping to spend some much needed time with her.

"Sure, that sounds nice," she replied.

We spent the day messing around as usual, and it was fun, and we laughed a lot. Things felt great and happy, and we were our old selves again.

Late in the afternoon we went to the cinema and sat at the back like a pair of teenage lovers. I had to hold her hand as the film was scary (I'm not good at scary), but it felt nice, warm, and soft. I liked it more than I should.

I was planning on staying at Fiona's afterward, and we left the cinema hand in hand through town. It felt nice like she was all mine.

We stopped off for a drink in her local on the way home and chatted with a few of her friends then left for her house. Fiona opened a bottle of wine, and we sat on the sofa close together, murmuring about our fun day.

After a few minutes of silence, I turned to her and said, "Fiona, will you take me to bed?" It felt right - I wanted this.

"Will you disappear again after tomorrow?" Fiona's voice showed concern, but I also knew she wanted it as much as me.

"I won't. I don't know what this all means, but right now, I really want it, more than anything. Please take me to bed and make love to me." With that, I kissed her softly on the lips, and Fiona's hot, soft lips kissed me back tenderly. It was bliss.

The kissing built slowly, softly, with no rushing, just tenderness as our passions rose. Her fingers loosened the buttons on my shirt. Her warm hands slipped under the shirt and swept lightly across my bra covered breasts, teasing my nipples, straining against the fabric. I felt dampness seep into my knickers. I was very quickly a hot, sexy mess.

Let's get into bed," Fiona suggested as we moved together from the sofa.

On the way, Fiona pushed me against the wall and kissed me with a fiery passion, and it took my breath away as she moved on to my neck. I let out a loud gasp and grabbed her hand, and pressed it against my still covered breasts rubbing it around.

After a short moment, she took my hand and quickly dragged me to the bedroom. While kissing frantically, we removed each other's tops, and bras (I was surprised how easy it was to remove someone else's bra - why do guys struggle with them?) Once freed, we pressed up together, breast to breast. This wonderful feeling notched up my desire another 100%. My god, it was so good, soft, warm, smooth, and sexy.

"Fiona, please take my knickers off," I asked breathlessly between kisses. I could hardly wait any longer, surprised by the level of my desire. I had never wanted it this much, ever. This woman was driving me crazy. Lust or love, I didn't care, I was on fire.

My hands were on her enormous, soft breasts thumbs rubbing over her stiff nipples. They felt amazing, and I suddenly knew why guys like boobs so much. As she bent to remove my jeans and knickers, she latched her mouth to my right breast and lapped gently I nearly exploded into orgasm. Wow! I felt on the verge, and we were still half-dressed. This woman has found something in me I never knew existed. She was sexy beyond my wildest dreams.

I felt my jeans falling to my ankles, and Fiona's soft hands gliding up my thighs and across my bum, gently kneading the flesh. After pausing, her hands moved up my back, under my arms, and over my breasts, as she gently swept her thumbs repeatedly over my engorged nipples and then seamlessly slid them down to my over-heated sex. She teased momentarily, slipped her hands around my thighs, lifted me, and gently laid me on the bed with her on top of me.

Her breast pushed against my pussy. I could feel her hard nipple slowly rubbing against my clit. She slowly rubbed it in circles so lightly across and around, gathering the plentiful moisture, missing my clit every so often, teasing me to new heights. I wanted her to carry on, to stop, to finger me, to lick and suck me. I was a sex-crazed bundle of horniness, mostly though, I was acutely aware that she still had clothes on that had to be removed.

I pulled her up to my level, feeling her moistened nipple dragging up my torso. We kissed more, passionately rubbing our breasts together, grinding against each other. My hands reached down and undid her jeans, and I slipped my hands under the fabric across her panty-clad bottom and squeezed, hard. It was gorgeous. Soft, round, and sexy. I brought my hands back out and grabbed the waistband of the jeans and pushed them down. Fiona lifted herself and helped take them off, also taking her very damp knickers with her. Now we were both naked, in bed, passionately rubbing our bodies together. I had never known a feeling like it; it was beautiful. There was a sense of urgency right now for a lot, lot more. We both felt it, and while so far, it had been very unhurried and fluid (in more ways than one), we were both now desperate.

Fiona started kissing her way down my body, slowly and still with a teasing desire, down over my needy pussy and across my thighs. My pussy was on fire, and I could feel the sticky wetness on my inner thighs. I needed more.

"Oh, Fiona, please, please lick my pussy, please?" I whimpered. She didn't need asking twice and immediately went to work.

She ran her tongue gently from the very bottom right up to the top, over the clitoris, and then traveled back down again. Up and down, up and down. She softly nibbled and sucked at my labia then slipped her tongue over my clit while gently pressing two fingers up and into me, lifting them to my g spot. I exploded like an atom bomb.

"OH FUCK! YES, YES OH YYYER ARRGHH FUCK EEEEEGHHH," noises that I didn't even recognize as my own. Spent, I collapsed, gasping for breath. I could hardly move. Fiona still had her fingers deliciously buried in my vagina gently rocking them with no real pressure, while looking up at me, her face covered in my sticky girl cum. Keeping her fingers inside, she moved up the bed to lie next to me.

"You taste divine," she said.

So I leaned over and kissed her hard on the mouth, mixing her saliva with my cum. I often taste my fingers when masturbating, but it was much better from her mouth. She started rocking her fingers more, slipping them in and out in a steady rhythm, making a sloshing sound from my incredible wetness. The desire rose in me very quickly, and I felt an impending orgasm almost immediately. Up, up and over. A deep growling sound emerged from within me, followed by a line of expletives, followed by blackness.

When I opened my eyes, Fiona was lying by my side, gently, lovingly, stroking my face. I felt good and loved and, utterly, spent.

We lay together for a while, cuddling up. It was comfy and warm, and there was no pressure for me to return anything. It was just soft and sweet. At this point, I became restless. Remembering how I licked Fiona last time and how much I enjoyed doing it, I realized I was pretty desperate to do it again. I wanted to taste Fiona, and I wanted to make her cum.

With this renewed vigor, I set about it by kissing her mouth first, then sucking lightly on her breasts, lifting her on top of me, and moving down to her surprisingly wet pussy. Before devouring her, I looked closely at her gorgeous flower. It was swollen and pinky-red with damp folds. It looked beautiful, and although slightly nervous from my inexperience, I could hardly wait to taste her.

I tentatively lapped my tongue across her clitoris, getting a sharp gasp from Fiona, and then slipped my tongue the full length from bottom to top several times. While doing this, I was squeezing her bottom with both hands. Egged on by Fiona's moans, I built-in confidence and lapped away. What I lacked experience, I made up for in enthusiasm. I pressed a finger into her as I sucked gently on her clit, and I could hear her building, her breaths coming in quick succession as I slipped a finger up against her puckered anus (this is something I do sometimes when masturbating as it makes me instantly cum). The response was a loud, guttural gasp as I then pushed, and it slipped in up to the first knuckle. It had Fiona cumming hard, swearing, and panting. I felt a light leak of fluid onto my face, and she then flopped onto the bed gasping. Slowly, easing my fingers from her, I scooted up the bed next to her, and we kissed lovingly and softly.

Satisfied and satiated, we drifted off to sleep, leaving the difficult questions until the morning.

7.22 am

I woke and found myself cuddled up to Fiona's beautiful naked form, looking directly into her sleeping face. I felt totally at peace and happy with no doubt whatsoever.

"Fiona, I think I love you," I whispered. Then happily let myself drift off again, cuddled up and warm.

Romantic Lesbian Erotica
10 Hot Short Romantic Stories for Women
Alana Meehan

All Rights Reserved. No part of this publication may be reproduced in any form or by any means, including scanning, photocopying, or otherwise without prior written permission of the copyright holder. Copyright © 2020

This book is entirely a work of fiction. The names, characters and incidents portrayed in it are the work of the author's imagination. Any resemblance to actual persons, living or dead, events or localities is entirely coincidental.

Story 01

It had been a few months since Darlene and I had gone out together. We always enjoyed shopping, or going to the beach, having lunch. You know, girl things. She left a message on my machine wondering what I was doing Friday and if I was in the mood to go shopping. Well, I quickly returned her call and set our plans for a day of paling around the mall. She wanted to get "something special, something sexy." How could I resist.

Darlene is a few years younger than me. She stands about five foot six inches tall, with shoulder length, wavy blonde hair. Her real 36C breasts are capped by pert nipples that almost always seem to be hard, there is not a single tan line on this woman and she's a natural blonde. She really keeps herself in shape.

Friday arrived and I was rather excited. I hadn't seen Darlene in a while and she'd been a star in more than a few finger sessions of mine from time to time, though we'd never actually had sex. As with all of my friends, she knew very well of my sexual preferences. I'm very happily bi-sexual, leaning more to the lesbian side.

Darlene showed up at my house just before 9:00. I wasn't quite ready when she arrived, I still hadn't figured out what to wear on this shopping spree. This is very important, you know. Clothes to shop in are almost as important as the clothes one is shopping for. The doorbell rang. I answered the door nude. At some people's houses that might seem a bit odd. Not at mine. The pizza boy really likes it. Darlene is wearing a long skirt and a halter top. "Just throw something on," she smiled. "You're not going to be wearing it long, anyway." She followed me into my bedroom and sat on the edge of my bed. I picked out clothes to get in and out of easily, a skirt and a t-shirt, and was looking for a pair of panties. "Don't worry about those, I'm not wearing any." She stood up and raised her skirt so that I could see her beautiful blonde patch. "No bra, either, Sweetie," she said, dropping her skirt and unbuttoning her top. I wasn't sure, but I thought she was trying to seduce me. Her tanned breasts popped out as if anxious to be free. It took a lot of will power to keep from walking over to her and helping her all the way out of her clothes and say to hell with shopping. I put my clothes on, brushed my hair and we were ready to go.

We took her car, a sporty little convertible. It was a wonderful day, so we had the top down. "I shouldn't have worn this skirt," she said, pulling it up to almost around her waist, revealing her tanned thighs all the way up to her pubes. "I can't work the clutch in it." Right then, I knew something was going on in that deviant little mind of her's. I'd seen her drive this car in evening wear and heels. She was trying to show herself off. That's fine by me, I'll play along.

We went to a little French bakery for some croissants and coffee before we hit the mall. We chit-chatted about our lives since we'd last seen each other. It was so nice to see Darlene again. No matter where the day when from here, I would enjoy it.

We arrived at the mall just as the shops were opening. I really like that time of day there to shop. No kids running about, not many adults for that matter. And it's early enough that no one's ruined the salesperson's day yet. Darlene and I browsed through some of the shops, not really looking at the clothes, just browsing. Waiting for that one particular thing to jump out and say "try me."

After a couple of shops, Darlene ventured into a lingerie shop. "Ah. This is what I've wanted," she cooed, as she fondled a couple of very sexy pieces. "Here," she handed something to me. "Let's try these on." We went into the dressing rooms, I was going to take my own, simply because we were the only two in the shop. Darlene grabbed my hand and asked me to share with her, the sales girl smiled and said her name was Tammy and to shout if we needed anything and left us alone.

Darlene was out of her clothes before I could completely close the door. What she had picked out didn't really need trying on, she just wanted to. She had picked out two very sexy black lacy garter belts. The dressing room wasn't really big enough for two adults, so we were very close to each other. As my shirt was going over my head, I felt Darlene's hand lightly cupping my right breast. Once my shirt was off and I could see again, I saw Darlene staring at me as if she were in a trance.

"I have a confession to make," she sighed. "I need your help with something. If you don't want to, I'll understand," her hand fell from my breast. "I caught Mac wanking to some girl-girl pics on the computer. I know he's always wanted to do it with two women, I've just never known a woman I wanted to be with. To tell you the truth, it really turns me on, too, the thought of another woman." She looked into my eyes. There we were, completely naked in very close quarters and a fantasy of mine was coming true. How could I resist her? I reached out and embraced her, lightly kissing her on the mouth.

Our kiss only made us both hungry for more. Not here, though. Not like this. I wanted our first time to be beautiful and sexy and sensuous. As I ran my fingers over her smooth skin, electric shocks tingled at my clit and my pulse raced. I wanted her deeply. It took every once of will power to, again, control myself and put my clothes on. All I said was "We need to go." We purchased the garter belts and matching stockings, black silk with the line up the back.

On our way out of the shop, we held hands and giggled like schoolgirls. My mind was racing. I had always wanted to make love with Darlene. Her husband, Mac, had told me on more than one occasion that she was absolutely wonderful in bed. I guess I was going to find out.

In the car, Darlene explained what she wanted to do with, and for, Mac. "I want to see the lust in his eyes when he sees two real, in the flesh, women making love in front of him," she beamed. She instructed me to open the glove box and take out a piece of paper. It was a picture of two stunning women wearing only black lace garter belts, black stockings, heels and pearls. Their hair was done up elegantly in a comb in back. Their make-up was impeccable. They were locked in a lovers' embrace. I was awed. "This is how I want to dress and that is only part of what I want to do," she said, grinning from ear to ear. She stopped at a red light, turned to me and, in morning traffic, kissed me square on the mouth. The kind of "come fuck me now" kiss that takes you a few seconds to recover from. The kind of kiss that makes the guy behind you honk his horn because the light has changed. The kind of kiss when you ignore the guy honking his horn behind you for a moment.

"Okay," was all I could manage.

Darlene put the car in gear and sped off toward my house. I was finally going to make love with her. The short few miles from the mall to my house seemed an eternity. I hadn't been this excited in quite some time. I was most certainly enjoying it. I told her it would probably be better if she left the top of the car down, my seat needed to dry. She reached over and felt the seat between my trembling legs and giggled.

Once inside my house, I had to get naked. All the way there I pondered just how to do it. Sexily? A slow tease? Help each other out of our clothes in heated sexual bliss? Abandoning all that, I opted for the get as naked as possible as quickly as possible route. My t-shirt was off before the front door was closed and my skirt was off before my t-shirt hit the floor. My screaming to be kissed pussy was soaking wet and my nipples were ready to cut glass. Darlene, on the other hand, slowly unbuttoned her halter, waiting until it was completely unbuttoned before opening it to reveal her luscious breasts. I stood there, mesmerized by her beauty, like a schoolboy looking at his first in-person naked woman. I'd often fantasized about this very moment. Fantasy is wonderful, but reality has got it all beat.

With her halter now off, Darlene massaged her breasts and let out a low moan. Her left hand reached down, down between her legs outside of her skirt and pressed to her mound, fingers out wide and using the heel of her hand for the pressure. Her head was back in bliss. She purred as she found the elastic waistband of her skirt and pulled it down, revealing her beautiful, tanned arse. Now using both hands, she slid the skirt off and stepped out of it. She stood naked in my eyes. One of the most beautiful women I had ever had the pleasure of knowing. I was going to make her cum like there was no tomorrow.

We moved toward each other, eager for the first full embrace. Skin to skin. Breast to breast. Mound to mound. Mouth to mouth. Lust to lust.

We kissed. Nibbles at first, feeling it out, so to speak. We wrapped ourselves around each other as our kiss became deeper, stronger. We moved to the couch. It's a good thing we did, too, or I would've been on the floor shortly after. My knees were very close to giving out. On the couch, we explored each other more as we continued to kiss. The urgency in the room was almost overwhelming. My need to do more, explore more was coming to a head when Darlene broke our kiss and planted her mouth on my left nipple. I came. She licked and sucked and I came some more. She put her hand on my right breast and kneaded that one as she sucked the other and I came some more. I was writhing under her as she played with my tits and all I could do was come. I pulled her face up to my mouth as I sat up and I kissed her and gently pushed her on to her back. I sat back up for a moment and looked at her. There she was, naked before me, nothing to hide, ready to receive my love. I reached out and cupped her right breast in one hand, her left in the other. I tweaked her nipples with my thumbs as she moaned and purred under me. I lowered myself to her, taking her left nipple into my mouth. I licked `round and `round, spiraling up to the erect nipple, then back `round again. Over and over as her moaning increased. I took her nipple in my teeth, not to bite, just a tiny bit of pressure and then sucked her breast like a Hoover to a football. She hugged my head and pulled me closer, holding on for dear life.

It was then that I reached down between her gorgeous tanned thighs and reached for her very wet, very willing, very ready pussy. My finger found her clit and she stepped onto the express lift. Her legs shot open and a hand grabbed my arse and pulled me even closer to her. She started to whimper below me as my finger massaged her swollen clit. I was determined to give her many an orgasm today, so this might as well be the first. I continued to finger her, sliding in and out of her wetness, her hips starting to buck to meet my hand. I still had her breast in liplock and she still had me in a wonderful headlock.

"Oohhh, yesssss, please, please -- oh, please. Don't--don't--(gasp)--stop. Oh, my -- oh, my! OH, MY!!! HERE! HERE! HEEEERRRRRE! OHHHHH!!!!!!!"

She was gasping for air as her orgasm crashed through her like a tidal wave. She held me as she came back down, kissing the top of my head as I lay on her breast, feeling her breathing regain its rhythm. I smiled as I felt the beads of perspiration between her breasts. Sexual perspiration. Sexual orgasm perspiration.

I slowly sat up, enjoying the sight of her in her post-orgasmic glow. Her smile, her eyes, her body, warm and relaxed, back from that place where all women go in orgasm. "You wouldn't believe how long I've wanted to do that," I smiled. "I know," she smiled back. "I've had quite a few afternoons spent thinking about you and this and how it would be--"

Darlene then told me a story about when she was at camp her senior year of high school. She and her roommate would lie on her bunk next to each other and watch each other masturbate. They never made it to the point where they could touch each other. Sad. I hugged her and kissed her. "We've only just started, Love," I said, taking her hand as I stood up from the couch.

I lead her outside to the pool. We swam and lazed about for a while. We sat back on pool lounges and talked, mostly about sex. As we talked, I noticed she was touching herself. "Don't worry, I'll do far more for you than just watch." I reached over and slid between her legs. She increased her rubbing. I moved my face closer and laid my head on her thigh, inches away from her blonde paradise. She spread her legs and her lips and continued to diddle her swollen clit. I could see her wetness between her lips and could smell her musky aroma and that was all I could take. I slid up and kissed her pussy. Her moans and sighs and gasps encouraged my kisses to become more passionate. I kissed her pussy like I would kiss her mouth. A few brushes, then fuller with the lips, then open mouthed with my tongue.

Once I began kissing her pussy, her hand was removed and placed on the back of my head. As I switched from kissing to licking, the pressure from her hand increased slightly. I continued to lick her sweet wetness and the pressure from her hand increased a little more. I had been purposely staying away from her clit. I wanted to tease her and make her orgasm build to the most explosive she'd ever had by mouth. Once I started licking and sucking her swollen, aching clit, she ground my face to her with both hands and bucked to the rhythm of my tongue. The neighbours three blocks away heard her cumming, if they were home. My face was wet to my shoulders when she was done. I absolutely love doing that. I came right with her.

"Let me do that for you now," she begged. We kissed and she tasted herself on my mouth. "I want to please you, Siobhan, I want to give you orgasms. I want to give you what you gave me--

Like I was going to say "no".

I kissed her again and sat back on the lounge. I opened my arms to her for a hug. As we embraced, I whispered into her ear "Do what you wish, my love." We kissed a while longer. She started to move down my neck with her mouth, slowly across my breasts, down to my belly. She slid back some on the chair and wrapped her hands around my thighs as she lowered herself to my waiting, wanting, ready, aching, wet, wet, wet pussy. I spread my legs for her as she lowered her mouth to my little pink slit. I could feel her breath from her nostrils across my patch of red pubes. Her lips touched mine, lightly at first. I could feel her become more at ease with having her face between another woman's legs as she began to kiss and lick at my wetness. It didn't take her long at all before she was lapping at my pussy like she'd been doing it for years. She was enjoying it almost as much as I was. As she kissed and licked and sucked at my pussy, I could feel that familiar, wondrous feeling start to build. I clutched the arms of the lounger as she dove herself into me, licking and sucking at my lips and then, finally, at my screaming clit. She put one hand on my belly and one under my arse as the waves of my orgasm crashed through me. Darlene continued to lick and suck at my clit sending wave upon wave upon wave of pleasure through me...

The rest of our afternoon was spent in my room, in bed, making love, resting, and making love some more. As we lay there, lost in our bliss, Darlene noticed it was well after the time her husband usually arrives home from work. She reached for the phone and dialed up her home number. She called out of love and courtesy. She was almost giggly on the phone. The last thing she said to her husband was "I love you, I'll see you in a little while. Oh, by the way, I bought you a little present--"

Story 02

Part 01

As I drove home from our weekend together, all I could do to occupy myself was to review, for what felt like the hundreth time, the events that had brought us to this point.

I laughed to myself remembering the look on your face the day I appeared in your office....but, true to the professional you are, you maintained your composure. The truly priceless moment was when I told you I had an interview for the new position that had been posted.

I was honest with them, tho....I made sure that they knew that you and I knew each other....just wonder what they would think if they knew how well. Now, after a month of working in the same office as you everyday, I can hardly stand it. I've been so good, not bothering you, not trying to spend every free moment with you. I made sure that you knew that my taking this job and moving here was not to screw up your life......I made sure you knew that I just needed a change of scenery, and wanted someone I knew to be close by, in case something happened. The fact that there was a job available in your office was just a bonus. That, and knowing that if you ever decided to take the chance on experimenting, I would be close by! But, you have to admit, I've been very good about not even making the slightest suggestion that you sleep with me.....

So then this past Friday rolled around. You hadn't said anything about taking the day off, so I was surprised not to see you, and even more suprised when someone told me you had scheduled off. The morning literally crawled by without your face to smile at.... Finally, fearing I'd go nuts, I took myself to lunch. Of course, I ended up eating Chinese....those mean spirited fortune cookies...mine said, "You will have a wonderful suprise!" Hah, with you gone, I doubted my weekend would be much of anything, let alone a surprise....

I guess that's why I was so excited when I got back to work and saw the sealed envelope on my desk with your handwriting on it. I was sorry I had missed you, but ripped right into the envelope, only to find your note that said,

It's time..... Meet me at Bear Creek Lodge as soon as you can after work tonite. Room 27....

I reviewed the directions, and started planning in my head. All the while, I remember thinking that now the afternoon was gonna crawl by, too, but I was strangely energized, and finished the project I was working on by 1:30. When I took it in to the boss, I was rewarded with the afternoon off for all my hard work. HOT DAMN! I thought. I smile, remembering how excited I was to be coming to you, and thinking that I'd never had another fortune cookie that was so accurate.....

It was a long drive, and I kept feeling like people were staring at me....must be the ear to ear grin on my face....

I arrived at the lodge in good time....saw your car sitting there, so I knew you weren't out picking up last minute supplies. I walked into the lobby and was immediately at home.....it was warm and cozy there. I asked for directions to your room, and they said they were expecting me, although not this early, but you had left a key for me. Things were definitely going my way!

I got to the door, very gently set my bag on the floor, and turned the key as quietly and slowly as I could, hoping to surprise you. As it turned out, I was the one surprised...finding you stretched out on the bed, on your stomach, sound asleep. Even with the sheet pulled over you, I could see you were laying there naked. And, I could feel my heart beating so loudly, I thought for sure you would hear it and wake up. I walked into the bathroom to catch my breath, and found the reason you were sacked out....the hot tub showed signs of a recent occupant, and there was an empty beer bottle on the tub ledge. Man, I thought, I may have to have this smile surgically removed......

I wandered back to the doorway of the bathroom, looking around the room, trying to keep from just jumping on you right away. I almost laughed out loud when I saw some "supplies" on the dresser. So, my love, you do have more than just "vanilla" sex planned.....wandering over there, I checked out your arsenal....the ropes, the blindfold, the cuffs, and the vibe... My, my, you were very well prepared, and I laughed quietly, thinking how well these items would fit with the surprises I had in my little bag!

Working quickly now, wanting to surprise you, I tied the four lengths of rope to the legs at the foot and head of the bed. How totally fortunate for me that you were laying spread eagled, your toes dangling over the edge of the bed. Getting the ropes over your feet and around your ankles about shot my nerves, but you didn't stir. I tightened them as much as I dared, knowing that any movement on your part would pull them tighter, so I didn't have much to worry about.....

Moving faster now, I get the ropes for your wrists into position, and then very, very gently, lay on the bed next to you. You have your head turned to the right, so I lean on my right elbow and wake you with a kiss on your cheek. Catching you by surprise was a good plan, you rolled onto your left side, raising yourself on your right arm, which I quickly pulled out from under you and slid into the rope, tightening it with one pull. You brought the left up over your head, trying to turn, and while you were still foggy and trying to find out why your feet wouldn't move, I moved across you, grabbing your left wrist, and slid it into the final loop, pulling it as tight as I dared.

Smart girl, I thought to myself, seeing that you weren't trying to fight. I watched you test how far you could move, and was honestly pretty satisfied with myself. So I laid myself back down at your side, and just smiled at you. I remember telling you about getting away from work early....was making mundane talk, letting the position you were in sink in to that sleep fogged brain. Finally, I looked at you, asked if you were comfortable, offered you some water......

Smiling my most charming and mischevious smile, I looked sweetly at you and told you I was going to take a shower.....

After stopping to stretch my legs and get something to drink, I resumed my drive, and my recollection of our time together......

I stepped into the shower, loving the feel of the hot water across my already hot body, and I found myself moaning in appreciation of the warm shower, and what I knew was to come. I smiled to myself, thinking that I wondered what you thought I was doing.

Truth was, it was hard to resist touching myself lingeringly, but I managed to keep from orgasming right there - I wanted the first time to be with you. After all, I could get *myself* off anytime!

I quickly dried myself, and wrapped myself in one of the terrycloth robes hanging in the bathroom to maintain the shower warmth on my body. I walked back out into the bedroom, and checked your wrists and ankles - looking to see if you were being hurt, but also checking to see if you had been trying to get out. I was pleased to see that you had not even tried. You asked if I had enjoyed my shower, and I just smiled at you.

I lit three candles you'd left sitting on the dresser, placing them in strategic spots around the room, then turned off the light. I was glad you had closed the drapes, it made the room darker. I moved to the end of the bed, standing between your feet. I pulled the sheet off of your body, admiring your back, your ass, and then your legs. What surprised me most was that I could see, even in the light of the candles, that you were already very, very wet. I loosened the belt, dropping the robe behind me, then moved to lay myself on your back. I was still holding myself mostly on my elbows, so I could move my hips across yours, brushing my pubic hairs across your ass. I couldn't resist, thrusting my mound against you. I heard you moan deep in your throat. Again, I found myself smiling, knowing that this was going to be wonderful!

I laid on the bed beside you, and asked if you needed to use the bathroom. You did, so I told you that I was going to untie you from the bed, but keep you bound, and that if you fought me, you'd be punished. You promised not to fight me, so I untied one hand from them bed, then the other, and tied the ropes together behind you. They were loose enough that you could put your hands at your sides, with the rope across your back. I moved to do the same with your feet. I helped you roll onto your back and sit up. I couldn't resist finally kissing you deeply, face to face. I felt your tongue teasing against my lips, and I opened my mouth, drawing your tongue inside, playing mine over it.

I pulled your hips forward so you could stand. The ropes were not intended to bind you, just slow you down. I made sure you were okay, and let you have your privacy in the bathroom.....didn't think we were ready to go there just yet.

While you were gone, I continued the "set-up" of the room. When you came back into the bedroom, I made sure you had been able to reach everything, then asked you to come over and stand in front of me. Taking another rope that I had brought along, I tied the rope between your feet to the rope between your hands. Basically, the ropes looked like two capital letter Y's, bottom to bottom. This had the effect of tightening the space between your hands and feet, but not significantly. I moved to the armchair that the lodge had so thoughtfully provided, and sat down, pulling you onto my lap and putting the chair back in one motion. I hooked your knees over mine, spreading both of our legs. Again, your hands were at your sides, and you could touch me, but with you sitting on the rope that tied your hands to your feet, you couldn't reach far to touch me, even if you leaned forward.

I made sure you were comfortable, then began my seduction. Letting my hands roam across your belly, circling, moving slowly upward to your breast, while beginning to kiss your shoulders, moving up to your neck. I nibbled your earlobes, feeling the weight of your breasts in my hands as I cupped them, pinching your nipples between my thumb and forefinger. I was enjoying your squirming against me, your back rubbing my hardening nipples. I moaned softly in your ear, and whispered, "I want you."

I continued to stroke your body, feeling you writhing on me, your ass pressed against my hot mound.....ummmmm, I knew you wanted to cum badly. I reached down next to the chair and picked up a familiar toy....once you heard the buzz, I felt your breathing quicken. I stroked the vibe across your belly, your breasts, over them, under them, over your nipples, along your neck, down your arms, across your pelvis. The tip of the vibe brushed along your hair line, then down the top of your right thigh, up the inner thigh, then I felt you thrust toward the vibe. I immediately switched it off, hearing you give a small, frustrated yelp. I whispered in your ear that if you didn't wait for your treats in my time, you would be severly punished.

With a resigned sigh, I felt you relax back against my body again. I switched the vibe back on, then ran it again up the inner part of your right thigh, running the tip just oh soooo lightly across your hairs to your left thigh, moving down the inner thigh and back up across the top. I flattened the vibe against your belly, rolling it across your pelvis until it was pointing downward, toward your hard, wet clit.

Slowly, I began to move the vibe downward, and you began moaning softly. As I moved downward, I gently eased the vibe out away from your body, again teasing just barely against your hairs. Sliding it lower and lower....under you and into my waiting pussy....moaning myself at the sudden electric shock that raced through me. With you still on my lap, I began to thrust my hips against the vibe pressed inside of me, wondering if you could feel any of the vibration from inside my body.

I pulled the vibrator out of me, letting the tip of it tease against my clit. I started moaning loudly, telling you that I was about to cum......you whimpered so much that I thought you were in pain, and I switched off the vibe. I asked if you were okay, and you smiled sweetly and told me that you didn't want me to cum yet. Well, that did it. I put the chair back up, using the motion to lift you from my lap and push you face first onto the edge of the bed. Without pausing, I slapped you across both cheeks of your ass, making red marks, then slapped your pussy, hearing that wet splashy/suctiony sound. Hearing you moan, though, I couldn't wait any longer......

I quickly untied your hands and feet, sat back down in the chair, and pulled you onto my lap, facing me this time. Reaching down beside the chair again, I produce the double head dildo that I brought....hearing you catch your breath at the sight. Reaching between us, I put one end inside me, then helped you to settle yourself over me until the other end was deep inside of you.

I wrapped my arms around your body, holding you tight against me, sitting perfectly still until both our bodies adjusted to the fullness inside of us. I kissed you again, my hands stroking your back, down your sides to your hips, encouraging you to begin thrusting. Your movements are what move the dildo inside of me......I lifted you, showing you the motion that makes it good for me, too. You caught the motion, started to rocking forward and back, thrusting your hips, your muscles squeezing....mmmmmm, as you did that, the chair helped push the dildo in and out of my hot, wet pussy, too.....

The momentum grows, you are riding hard, and I'm enjoying every downward thrust you make. I can hear your breath quicken, feel your muscles working hard against the dildo, I know that you are near orgasm, then you start telling me that you're about to cum. That is all it takes for me....I feel the waves of my own orgasm begin. You're shouting by now, saying over and over, "I'm cumming, oh god, baby, I'm cumming." I wrap my arms around you again, pulling you hard against me, holding you still, feeling the shudders of your orgasm go through your body, feeling my body shudder right along with you......

As our breathing slows, I whisper into your ear, "Now it's time to clean you up, Jill, darlin' " I carefully and gently disengage us, kissing you softly. I lift you from my lap, stand in front of you, and move you backwards to the edge of the bed, laying you on your back, gently spreading your legs, all the while looking you in the eye and smiling broadly. Just as I'm about to lower my head to lick you, taste you, take all the juices you have to give me, there is a knock at the door..............

The knock at the door scared us both....you immediately started scrambling further up the bed, pulling the sheet up over you, but the spread had fallen to the floor. I grabbed the robe, and walked over to open the door, barely giving you time to cover yourself. As I open the door, we hear the person on the other side say, "Room service!"

I open the door to see a very attractive woman, about 5'2", deep red hair, green eyes, and a great smile. She wheels the cart into the room, her gaze moving over me, sliding over to see you laying in the bed, obviously naked, barely covered by a sheet. Then I notice that she is seeing the candles, the toys still on the dresser and laying next to the chair, and the ropes. Being a true professional, she shows no reaction.

Stopping the cart, she turns to me and asks if I want the meal set-up. I tell her that I'll take care of it, but also tell her that we may need additional help later. "What time is your shift over?" I ask. She says she's done at 10, and I ask her to come back after she's clocked out. I hold a generous tip in my left hand, my right hand still on the door knob, but keep my left hand close to my body. True to my expectations, she smiles, then reaches for the tip, brushing my breast with her hand, in full view of you. As she walks past me, I use the same hand to smack her on the ass, and am rewarded by another smile and a wink as she turns in the hallway. As I softly close the door, I hear her say, "I will see you both later."

I turn from the door, still smiling, and find you staring at me with your mouth hanging open. You look so shocked, so scared, and just a little jealous. I smile, sit down, take you in my arms, and tell you that I know her from the bar. We've danced and talked before, and I know what she's about. I ask you to trust me, telling you that it will be well worth it.

"Let's check out the food!" I say, trying hard to distract you. I reach under the tablecloth, and pull out an ice bucket with a bottle of champagne nicely iced in it. You ask about the room service, and I explain that I ordered it when I arrived.

Bringing the champagne bottle back to the bed, I have you lay down, and straddle your hips, already unwrapping the foil. I twist off the wire over the cork, then wiggle the cork, aiming it carefully away from us, and find myself rewarded with a loud, "POP" as the cork shoots across the room. The bubbly, true to its name, starts to fizz out of the bottle, dripping on your chest, breasts, and belly. I put the bottle on the nightstand, and lean over to lick the wetness from your body, then kiss you, giving you your first taste as well. Grabbing the glasses, I pour for us both, and toast you, reveling in your beautiful nakedness.

I move to sit on the bed beside you, telling you that the spread on the cart is the fulfillment of one of your fantasies. I move to light the sterno can under one of the pots, uncovering two other containers, and two huge platters. I sit back down, telling you we have to wait for just a bit to make sure the contents of the hot pot are warm enough. I bring the first platter to the bed, and you see that it has Brie cheese, apple slices, and french bread. I begin spreading cheese on apples and bread, feeding both of us. We continue to sip champagne, talking, smiling, kissing each other occasionally, until I rise again to check the pot, cut back the flame from the sterno can to maintain the temperature, and indicate to you that all is ready.

You stand up to examine the cart, finding chocolate sauce warming in the pot, and a huge platter of fruit - apples, strawberries, bananas, raspberries, pineapple chunks, and cherries. Two other containers hold carmel and cream cheese fruit dips. I'm grinning from ear to ear, just watching your face light up, the wheels spinning in your mind.......we both know where this is going, I think to myself.

We both sit on the edge of the bed, and I can tell that you're nervous suddenly. I lean across the cart, reaching for the champagne to refill our glasses. As per usual, I manage to get part of my body where it doesn't belong.....at least I'm naked, so I don't mess up clothes like normal. Reaching for the champagne, I managed to get my left breast in the carmel dip. Sitting back down with the bottle, I may sure to touch your breasts with its coldness, then reach for a napkin to clean up the carmel, but you stop me, looking at me and shaking your head.

I pour the champagne, sip a bit, and suddenly find you pressing my shoulders backwards to the bed, wanting me to lie down. I do so, at your insistence, then you get up and move to the dresser. I watch you pick up the blindfold, and walk back over to me, handing it to me to put on. After I do, I lie back, and you tell me to spread my legs towards the corners of the bed, and to reach my arms straight out to both sides towards the edges. You tell me that if I move from that position, there will be punishment, up to and including you stopping whatever you're doing and walking away from me. Well, honey, I don't have to tell you that I have no intention of disobeying this time.

You're still standing beside the bed, and I hear you moving to the cart, and back again. You ask me to open my mouth and feed me a small slice of apple with carmel dip. Then I feel something being spread over my right breast.....then apple slices laid against the underside of my breast. Ahhhhh, I think - you did get the hint for the fruit....we DO think alike!

Next, you feed me a slice of banana dipped in chocolate, and then I feel you lay 5 slices down the middle of my chest and belly like buttons, but I can tell from the temperature that not all of them are dipped in chocolate. Then, I taste a raspberry in the cream cheese dip, and you move to tuck one under each of my earlobes. I am finding it harder and harder to lie still, much to my amazement - I am getting really turned on by this.

The next morsel you feed me is a slice of strawberry, dipped in chocolate, and you lay two slices on each side of my neck, at the base, in that little hollow spot, followed by three more banana slices down my lower belly. I hear you chuckle a bit, then taste pineapple chunk dipped in chocolate. The next thing I feel is the warm sauce dripping across my left thigh.....I feel you spread my legs and my pussy lips, and place the pinapple right next to my clit. The warm chocolate begins to drip down...warming as it runs towards my already wet pussy. Oh god, I can hardly lie still, wanting your touch.

I keep wondering where else you can possibly place fruit, when I feel you kneeling next to me, offering me a cherry, covered in the cream cheese fruit dip. It's obvious that you're holding the cherry with the stem in your mouth........now I'm REALLY wondering......

I feel you spread my pussy lips with one hand, then suddenly feel you pushing a cherry inside of me, then another, then another. You tug gently on the stems, making sure you have a good hold on them. I can't believe that you've put them there, but I know that you know better than to let go of the stems....don't want another lost fruit story!!!

So, my love, I think to myself behind my blackness, what next? Fortunately for me, I didn't have long to wait. You began by licking the carmel off of both nipples, first the left, then the right, followed by eating the apple slices. I could feel that my nipples were rock hard by now.

Moving lower, you nibble the three banana slices on my lower belly, licking up the carmel and chocolate sauce, making sure you get all of it. Then, I feel you shift your body to taste the raspberry behind my right earlobe.....ahhhhhh god...the chills all the way down my body! And then to the left earlobe....mmmmmm.....even more chills, tingles......

The next item to be consumed is the other banana slices on my chest and belly. You check the cherries by pulling the stems......I almost feel I could orgasm from that, you've got me so aroused. I feel you moving to straddle me, your pubic hair brushing mine....you lean over to take the strawberries, and I can't help but raise my hips to press them against you, wanting to feel your heat. I hear you clear your throat in a warning, and I realize what I'm doing. I lie still, not wanting you to stop now, since I know what the only fruits left are.......

After eating the strawberries, and nibbling my neck a bit, too, I'm just about thrashing all over the bed wanting you..... Finally, FINALLY, I feel you moving your body downward, sliding your arms under my knees. I feel you tug on the cherry stems again, but I know you're doing it with your teeth this time. Then I gasp, feeling your tongue beginning to lick the chocolate, along with a new kind of fruit dip, finally taking the pineapple chunk in your mouth......I manage to resist the urge to thrust against your mouth....but I have to grit my teeth to do it. When you pull the cherries out, I can't help but moan very loudly, turning my head from side to side, whimpering in frustration when I feel you get back up from the bed.

I hear you rustling around, and feel you pressing something against my lips....I open them, and you give me another slice of banana....

I can't help but wonder if your gonna start on my back, instead I feel you on the bed between my legs again.....OH MY GOD....I feel a whole banana against my pussy, pushing gently, sliding inside a short way......then, I hear and feel that you are eating the banana....that knowledge breaks the dam, and the waves of my orgasm pound hard in my head and against the banana, pushing it out. Each bite you take pushes it back in, then the muscle contractions push it out again.....wave after wave of pleasure...I feel I'm about to faint as you finish the banana and cover my body with your own, removing my blindfold and kissing me deeply.

I sink into a stupor, your body laying half on me, half on the bed, your head laying on my shoulder, your arm across my chest just under my breasts. Mmmmmmm....I could keep you here like this forever. After a time, I know not how long, you rouse me and offer to run me a hot bath to clean me up. While you're in the bathroom, I stretch my body, thinking of the things that are still to come.........

Settling into the bath, sitting between your legs, I lean back against you, enjoying the feel of the warm water, the pulsing jets, and your hands stroking my belly and my breasts. I so enjoy the feeling of the backs of your fingers brushing across my nipples, teasing them to hardness.

I sigh, relaxing further against you. It is so wonderful to sit still, cuddling, talking quietly, laughing together. I couldn't have asked for a better way to "clean up." Finally, with you talking quietly in my ear, still touching me softly, I doze off, leaning my head against your left shoulder.

Slowly, like climbing out of a fog, I struggle to wake up, realizing the water is still and a bit cold, and you're teasing along my neck and shoulder with your tongue. I sigh my appreciation for your letting me sleep, and for your gentle awakening of me. Realizing you have to be freezing, I climb out of the tub, grab your bathrobe, and throw it around you, hugging you close to me, rubbing your arms and legs through the terrycloth. I grab mine and slide into it, and we move back to sit on the bed, enjoying more of the fruit, bread, and cheese.

I don't remember you blowing out the candles, but the light next to the bed is on, casting a warm, but small circle of light around the room. The toys on the dresser cast weird shadows on the drapes, and I find myself giggling. Of course, you ask what I'm giggling about, and when I tell you, we both fall back on the bed, laughing, holding each other close.

The next thing we know, it's morning, and the sunlight is streaming in the room.....

Story 03

Part 01

My new friend Coni and I had agreed to spend the weekend at a Bed and Breakfast near Atlanta, Georgia, and to get to know one another more completely. We had arrived on a Friday afternoon, following a full week of work for both of us.

The B&B, as it turned out, only accomodated one set of guests at a time, and was operated by a Lesbian couple who dearly loved sharing their home and their hospitality with an occasional guest.

Following a rather quick, but very gratifying lovemaking session with Coni, we decided to go out to a nice French restaurant in the city for a delicious, candle light dinner. We had both brown-bagged it for a week to save money so we could treat ourselves. It was worth it. We were seated facing each other and just sat gazing at one another. Neither of us was able to hide her desire for the other. About halfway through dinner, I suddenly felt something on my leg, under my skirt. I reached down and discovered Coni's bare foot. She pushed against my hand, so I released her foot and resumed eating my dinner. She inched her foot ever so slowly up my leg until she reach my pussy. We had agreed that neither of us would wear panties tonight, just in case an urge struck, so when I spread my legs apart, she had easy contact with my already wet pussy. She began to rub her big toe up and down my slit. I spread my legs farther apart and she turned her foot sideways and stuck her toes inside me, all the while both of us were smiling and trying to make small talk. She would stick her toes in then bring them out and wiggle them on my slit, occasionally finding my hard button.

I was rapidly losing my concentration - and my ability to make small talk. I reached under the table and grabbed her foot. "Are you almost finished with dinner, dear," I said, making a statement more than asking a question. "We really need to get back before it gets any later." Within ten minutes we had paid the check and were headed to the B&B.

After we arrived at the B&B we chatted for a while with the owners, making tentative plans to join them for dinner on Saturday night, then we "retired" for the evening. When we were settled in our room, I handed Coni a bag containing a gift that I had bought for her -- a sheer black bodysuit in a spider-web pattern. It had spaghetti straps and was very low-cut. The back was cut below the waist and it had a convenient opening in the crotch. When she went to the bathroom to change, I undressed and put on my own gift. I had bought myself a baby blue, one-piece camisole that was cut to my waist in back and had a ribbon lace- up front which opened down past my navel. The bottom was cut very high on the hips and had a thong back.When Coni came back into the room, she took my breath away. Every wonderful curve of hers was accentuated by the suit. We embraced and kissed softy. We simultaneously began rubbing our hands on each other's backs and ass cheeks. As we began to French kiss I squeezed her cheeks and she did the same to mine. We pulled each other close so that our pussies and breasts were smashed together - grinding and rubbing toalmost a fever pitch. "Let's get on the bed, darling," I said.

 We lay side-by-side facing each other, all the while kissing and fondling anything we could reach. We scissored our legs so our pussies were rubbing each other's thighs. We continued this until I felt ready to burst. "Roll over on your back, darling, so I can kiss you better," I said. When she did, I laid on top of her--tit-to-tit & pussy-to-pussy and started kissing her face and neck, then moved farther down. I pulled her spaghetti straps down to expose her now-erect nipples and began sucking them. I sucked on one and then the other until they were hard and wet. Coni was moaning now and writhing her body. I continued my assault on her breasts. As I sucked on one, I rubbed the other one with the palm of my hand and would then roll the nipple between my fingers. She was very hot by now (as was I) so I began to pinch her nipples. I'd suck on one and get it good and wet, then I would roll it and pinch it until she was jerking. I would ease up on the pinching and just suck for a while. Then I would roll and pinch again. I knew she was going toclimax if I kept this up, so I moved farther down. Coni's was now clinching the sheets with her fists and her head was rocking from side-to-side. I kneaded, kissed and sucked her luscious skin through the bodysuit until I came to her swollen mound. I sat up and got between Coni's legs. I folded my legs and had her put her lower body onto my lap. This position made her legs spread apart (lucky me), so when I wrapped an arm around each of her thighs, I had perfect access to heaven. I began to suck and lightly chew on Coni's mound. Every few "bites" I would open my mouth as wide as I could and suck in as much flesh as possible. I began moving down to her slit and to the opening of her pussy, still through the suit. Then I used my hands to pull the crotch opening apart so Icould get to her wonderful treasures. I began by sucking the folds of her pussy into my mouth and then I began to tongue-fuck her sweet hole.I kept this up for what seemed like hours. Coni was moaning now and was writhing so hard that it was getting difficult to hang onto her with my arms and my mouth. "Oh, god," she would moan, "Oh, god, I can't believe this. Ohh, it feels so good. Ohh, do it to me, please. Ohh, ohh!" Ibegan to suck her clit into my mouth. I would suck it, then I would blow on it. I brought one hand under her ass and suddenly stuck two fingers into her pussy. She stifled a scream and immediately began bucking her ass up and fucking my fingers and mouth. She came in wave after wave, moaning loudly, her big breasts heaving, her pussy raised high in theair - it was a beautiful thing to watch.When she calmed down enough, she made me lie back and then returned the favor. She was wonderful. Still turned on by her own fucking, shedidn't waste much time on preliminaries. After literally ripping my top open, she dove into my breasts. She pushed my breasts together and sucked them simultaneously - - sucking and pulling and massaging. She was making a low, guttural sound deep in her throat and her total lack of control was making my already wet pussy even wetter. I brought my legs up and locked them around her waist. She reached down and slid my thong crotch to one side and started rubbing her lace-covered pussy onto my bare one. The sensation was unbelievable! The friction this caused was like lighting a match to my cunt. I squeezed by legs around her waist as tightly as possible and humped her pussy with all my might. She was still clamped onto my breasts and as I began a scream toward my climax, she bit down on my nipples enough to make me see stars. She didn't stop when I climaxed, though, she keep sucking and kneading my breasts and rubbing my sopping pussy. I couldn't believe it when I felt my second climax coming hard. Oh shit, I thought, I'm going to lose my mind right hereand now. I was bucking her pussy hard and I grabbed her head so her mouth wouldn't leave my breasts, but I needn't have worried because she was in her own world of fucking and climaxing. She came as hard as Idid-- her juices flowing through that slit in her suit and dripping into mine. "Oh fuck me my darling girl," I screamed as my heart pounded and my mind exploded into a thousand stars. We stayed wrapped in each other's arms as we came down from our wonderful journey of discovery and joy with each other. We were both exhausted from our efforts and soon drifted off to sleep. But there were other pleasures awaiting us before we would see the sunrise together.

As I sat in the big easy chair, Coni sat in my lap, cradled in my arms with her head on my shoulder. We watched from our window as the sun rose over the garden of the B&B, the early morning mist gathering and the sun sparkling on the dew covered flowers and plants. It was a magic moment in a night that had been filled with magic moments. We had made love almost the entire night, catching naps when we became exhausted from our efforts to please each other - and ourselves. And now here we both sat, naked, in each other's arms watching the glorious pink, yellow & lavender sunrise. I leaned down and kissed her forehead. She looked up at me and I kissed her sweet lips. "Are you ready to get up and about?" I asked. "No," she replied, "but, I am ready for you to touch me again." I kissed her again and she responded by introducing the tip of her tongue between my lips. "My angel," I said, "what do you want me to touch?" "Everything," was her reply. As we kissed more deeply I pulled Coni closer up on my lap, held the back of her head with my left hand and entertwined my fingers in her beautful, long hair. With my right hand I began to lightly rub all the skin I could reach. I rubbed down her back to her plump ass cheeks, down the backs of her thighs and behind her knees. I rubbed back up her side and on her shoulder and down her arm. I kept my touch very light, just skimming her lovely skin. I moved back to her legs, then up the front of her thighs, barely grazing her mound, up to her lower stomach. I began light, circular movements on her stomach and moved up to her breasts, circling her nipples, then up to her throat and neck. We stopped kissing long enough for me to rub her upturned face, eyelids and lips, then I started down her body again. She was already beginningto make little sounds in her throat, so I knew I was on the right track. We began to kiss more intensely. I rubbed her chest and moved lower to her breasts. I was still rubbing her skin very softly, but occasionally I would tweak one of her nipples a little. I moved my hand down to her stomach and circled inside her navel with my finger. As I rubbed toward her mound, her stomach muscles begin to tighten. I raised my lips from hers long enough to look down at her lovely face. Her lips were swollen from our long night of lovemaking (as were mine) and, as my hand continued its journey, she began to chew on her bottom lip and then run her tongue over her lips. I still had my hand on the back of her head, so I drew her face up to mine and began kissing her again,doing a little chewing of my own. Just above her mound I circled my fingers ever so lightly and moved down to the top of her slit. She parted her thighs enough for my fingers to enter and I began to move them up and down her slit, dipping between her folds and finding the entrance to her pussy. I rubbed her like this for a long time, then began rubbing her clit with my thumb. She was really turned on now, her pussy sopping wet, her

nipples tightening into hard nubs as I put my middle finger into her pussy. I moved the finger around inside of her as I continued rubbing her clit. She was beginning to move with me now, raising her hips in an effort to get me inside of her even more. I accommodated her by introducing another finger. I wasn't pumping her yet, just moving my fingers around, feeling and rubbing inside her pussy. Her position in my lap prevented her from moving around too much, and that's what I wanted. I wanted to do all the work and make her come by just using my fingers and mouth. I took my left hand from behind her head, wrapped my arm under her arm and around her back and raised her up so I

could have easy access to her breasts. It was not the most comfortable position either of us had ever been in, but passion had reared its head. I began an assault on her nipples - first one then the other - licking them first and then sucking the hard nubs into my mouth. Coni had thrown her head back over the arm of the chair and was really into this now. She tried to put her feet on the other chair arm so she could arch her hips enough to help me fuck her, but I wouldn't let her. I just kept up my assault on her body. I kept sucking and gently biting her nipples, my fingers still rubbing inside her pussy, my thumb rolling her clit around. She threw her head from side to side, then she put both hands on the chair arm which raised her tits so that they were even more accessible to my mouth. As I sucked and sucked on her beauties, I began moving my fingers in and out of her cunt, slowly at first, then faster, then slower. Occasionally I would bring my fingers completely out of her pussy and rub her juices all over her slit and down to her little anus. Forcing my hand and lower arm between her thighs, I rubbed her hard, up and down, first with my fingers and hand, then with my arm, rubbing her clit and pussy and anus harder and harder. She was beginning to clasp her thighs around by arm so tightly that I could barely move it. "Open your legs!" I demanded under my breath, "And keep them open. I want that pussy of yours wherel can reach it!" She complied as best she could and I continued my assault on her. I rubbed her juices onto her anus and moved my finger in circles on that little hole. This almost sent her over the edge, but I wasn't finished with her yet, so I moved my fingers back up to her pussy hole where I roughly introduced two fingers again. I began to pump in and out of her, quickening my pace by degrees. I glanced up long enough to notice that

Coni had beads of sweat on her forehead and upper lip. She was more than ready. I resumed sucking and biting her tits as my fingers pumped her pussy harder and harder, my thumb still assaulting her clit as she came hard. "Oh please, fuck me, fuck me. I'm cuming, oh god, fuck me!" "I am fucking you, baby," I said, my voicebreaking with emotion. "I'm fucking your sweet pussy. Doesn't it feel good, baby. Don't my fingers feel good in your pussy, my precious baby?" I pumped and pumped her pussy as she climaxed in wave after wave of pleasure, her juices flowing freely from her fucked cunt. I decreased the pumping of my fingers until she had calmed down, but kept them in her pussy long after her climax had completely subsided, loving the feel of her juices on my fingers and the feel of her cunt contracting on them. Coni put her head back on my shoulder and I ask her if it bothered her that I had spoken roughly to her. "Oh, no," she said, "I kind of liked it. I know you would never do anything to hurt me, but it did turn meon, if that makes any sense." "Of course it makes sense, baby," I replied. "There's something about a little danger that is very erotic,as long as you're sure of your partner. My pussy was already wet from fucking you, but the words I said to you made it even wetter. I already feel maternal towards you and you are, after all, my "baby," and we know that "babies" don't always behave and sometimes need discipline. Maybe it's a side of our relationship that we can explore later, when we both feel like it. Would that be something you might be interested in? No pain, of course, but maybe a little domination?" "I think Iwould," she said. "I'm getting a little excited just hearing you talk about it. I want to learn everything and I want you to teach me." (Good answer, my pet.) With that, Coni got off my lap and knelt between mylegs. She pulled my pussy to her face and began to lap up my juices. Of course, it was a lost cause because the more she lapped the more juice she created. I put a leg on each of the chair arms, grabbed her head and forced her beautiful face far into my cunt. She sucked on my already hard clit while she stuck her fingers into my pussy and pumped. Then she put the index finger of her other hand into my little hole. She pumped her fingers simultaneously while she sucked my clit. I came and came as she kept sucking and fucking my holes. Oh my, she's already this good, and I have so much more to teach her! We were going to have so many adventures together, and I couldn't wait to get started.

Story 04

It is a perfect beach day. I've talked you into driving down to see me. I know the ideal spot for us.

As soon as I see you pull up, my stomach does flip-flops and my knees get weak. We walk all the way to the end of the beach. I suggest we settle high in the dunes, out of sight from anyone. My eyes are glued on you. I can't believe how beautiful you are. I watch as you smear oil on your skin. Hmm, I am getting turned on. I tell myself to wait a minute and give you some space, but I see the look you are giving me. I know that look. You lay on your belly and I rub oil on your back and down your legs. I'm getting chills just touching you. I can't help but kiss you as I cover your body. I lay back and let you do the same for me. Your touch sets me on fire. Both of us lay on our backs, taking in the rays. It is hot. I've got cold beer in the cooler. I reach for one and we split it. I'm watching your breast rise and fall as you lay there peacefully. I grab an ice cube and slide it on your belly. You jump at first, but I think you know where I'm headed, so you lay back. I lean over and kiss you deeply. I grab your tongue and suck on it. I tell you I want you desperately. Please. I watch the ice melt and pool in your bellybutton. I roll over and lick up the water, sliding the ice over your mound. I move your bottoms aside and push the ice into your hot moist pussy. You quiver when it enter you. I immediately follow with my tongue, pushing it deeper and deeper. You are moaning loudly. You are getting so hot that the ice is melting rapidly. I suck the water and your juices. The water is running down your thighs, mixing with the oil and glistening in the sun. I reach up and caress your breast. I take one in my mouth and circle the nipple with my tongue. I love your body, the way it looks and the way it tastes. I've got my now soaked pussy wrapped around your leg and humping it slowly as I move my fingers in and out of you and suck your breasts. You like that, don't you? I move down on you sucking your clit as I slide my fingers in and out. I find your rhythm and watch the waves of passion flow through you. You are almost there. I climb on you 69 and put my pussy in your face. Can't you see how wet I am? I slide right down on you, doing the bump and grind. The faster you suck and lick the faster I do. Soon we match eachs motion. Oh I can feel it coming. We start to cum at the same time. You let go all in my face. My face is covered and so is yours. I roll over to face you and we collapse in each others arms. We roll together in the sand kissing, ala from here to eternity. Now we are both covered with sand and oil. I suggest a shower at the bathhouse. We walk kind of wobbly up the beach. I watch your toned body in front of me and I'm hot again. Oh god, woman, you drive me crazy. We climb in the shower and I feel your wet pussy on my ass. I want you to take me in the shower. Tell me what you are going to do to me. Let go...

CJ, has this experienced changed since meeting? I really wanted to kiss you that day, but I knew that you were upset. I could sense you back-peddling and believe me, I understand. Anytime you want to talk, call me,ok?

Story 05

My name is sister sophia. it is the year 1387. a few years ago I took my vows and entered the order of st. catherine. this is not my real voice you are hearing. I have taken a vow of silence. these are the sounds of my thoughts.

I admit that I did not enter the order out of piety. I entered to escape. yes, I am scared of the world. it is a frightening place. I did not want to get married, and I did not want to bring children into this world. so I left the home where my parents lived and came to this nunnery in the foothills, far away from the rest of the world. here in this silent world where we are not allowed to speak, I found peace and solitude, and for the first time in my life I found friends who were not threatening. here I was free to fall in love.

Her name was sister margrette. I noticed her during my first mass here. she was saying her prayers. I was supposed to be saying my prayers too, but I couldn't help but to look at her. suddenly she looked up, as if she had been startled. she noticed me looking directly at her. I noticed her eyes. her eyes were beautiful, pools of water with firey islands blazing from the center of her pupils. she looked directly back at me, looking deep into my eyes. we held the glance, neither of us wanting to look away. until we became too afraid.

She took care of me those first few weeks. she showed me around. gave me a bed and linens. and helped me learn the way of life I now lead. one of the first nights here I became lonely. I missed my old home. she could sense my lonelyness, eventhough I could not say the words. she looked at me and gestured by nodding her head at the board, offering to stay the night with me. I nodded my acceptance. she slipped into my bed. I wrapped my arms around her. the look in her eyes as she looked at me told me not to be afraid. it told me that she loved me. she kissed me on the cheek. I kissed her back and I felt much better.

By day we worked tending the gardens. we would weed the plants and water them. When the summer roses bloomed by the wall I couldn't help noticing how magnificent, how soft, she looked framed by the soft velvety petals where she worked. I loved the way her hands curved around the spade, and her toes dug into the earth beneath her feet. throughout the day we would exchange glances and smiles.

I wanted her. I wanted her sexually. I knew these thoughts were unholy, that the church would not approve, but I knew for the first time in my life that I had discovered what love meant. to not express my love was agony. I wanted to share my feelings, my love, and my life with her. but if I was rejected by her, what would be the consequences? if she revealed my lust, I would be forced to leave the nunnery. but that would be the mildest of punishments, compared to her rejection of my love. I did not fear the wrath of god. I knew my love was holy. I feared her rejection. knew my love was holy. I feared her rejection.

I planned how I would reveal my feelings. sometimes the sisters would go gathering mushrooms in the woods. that would give me some time and privacy. if she rejected me, I hoped that being out there would give me some time to set things straight before returning to the sisterhood. the next time we went gathering mushrooms, I led the way. I went deeper and deeper into the woods, deeper than we had ever gone before. a few times she glanced at me with a questioning look, asking me if I knew where I was going. I just nodded yes and kept going. and kept going.

When I thought we were far enough away, I stopped and turned around, looking directly at her. she was taken back. she did not know how to react. she stood there looking at me. there was sexual tension in the air. I walked over to her and kissed her on the lips. she did not react. she just stood there like a statue, looking straight forward and breatheing heavily. I kissed her again while she just stood almost ignoring me. suddenly, as if a lifetime of inhibitions were suddenly released in a single second, she grabbed the back of my head and forced my lips back on hers. we kissed and kissed. tears came to her eyes. I broke the kiss to look in her eyes. she cried harder, and while her tear filled eyes looked into mine, she reached down and took off her nun's robe. I could only stare. she reached down to grab my hand, and brought my hand up to her right breast. I stroked it tentatively, yet lovingly. she smiled and it was clear that those tears were tears of joy.

We fell to the ground. she slowly disrobed me. she rubbed her hands over my breasts, at first avoiding the nipples, until I couldn't stand it much longer. then finally she pinched them. my god, I was hers. .. then finally she pinched them. my god, I was hers.

She crawled on top of me, her breasts rubbing against mine. I felt the damp earth under me and its moisture seeped into me. I was like a sponge absorbing my environment. her hands were touching me everywhere. she y environment. her hands were touching me everywhere.

She caressed my shoulders, my neck, my back, my stomach. she planted a trail of kisses across my body, starting on my forehead, my temples, my cheeks, my chin, my neck, my chest, across my breasts, down my stomach. I waited in suspense. would she kissed where I wanted her to kiss? she planted a trail of kisses down my leg, over my knee, down to my toes. I wiggled in ecstacy. she kissed up my thigh. she nuzzled my pubic hairs. oh how I wanted her tongue. she rubbed her cheek back over my stomach, and started kissing the bottom of my breast, specifically avoiding my nipples. my god, she was a tease. I grabbed her head and held it over my nipples, she finally licked them. I cried out.

 I pushed her head down to that place that belonged only to her. my womanhood was hers. she planted kisses throughout my pubic hairs. I held her head tighter until she finally licked me. and she did not stop. we lay in each other's arms for hours that day, safe and comfortable. s arms for hours that day, safe and comfortable.

We knew, our love would have to remain a secret. we knew that we could not share our joy with our sisters. but we had our own private little world, a safe world, a loving world. I had found my home. I had found the world between my lovers arms.

Story 06

Infatuation first saw her at a housewarming party. Desire was sitting in the corner, calmly sipping a glass of white wine and observing the crowd. She wore faded jeans that hugged her elegant legs and a white silk blouse with the top two buttons undone. Infatuation could not but help notice the way the sun played on her skin, turning it pale gold. A warm flush crept through her, making her shiver.

"Who is she?", asked Infatuation of her husband.

"I don't know, except that you've got nothing to be jealous about. I'm told that she's a lesbian. A mind of her own. No fun at all." He grinned teasingly.

"Oh."

She kept her eyes on Desire, watching her gracefully put down her glass of wine and talk to some of the guests. A drop of wine rested upon her full lower lip, quickly tasted away by a flick of tongue. Large brown eyes surveyed the crowd, held Infatuation's gaze for a breathless moment, then roved on. Infatuation was not aware of her companion's departure for the bar; she was fascinated by Desire. She found that she wanted to touch that golden skin, feel that graceful body pressed against her own. Cheek pressed against Desire's cheek, breathing her sweet scent. She felt her body grow warm and languid at the thought.

Abruptly, she shook herself. "Am I actually attracted to another woman?" Her face drained white with shock, then red in mortification as she realized that Desire was looking in her direction again. Infatuation quickly turned around and determinedly sought out the location of her husband, refusing to acknowledge the passion pounding in her heart nor the knot in her gut screaming that something was not right. For the rest of the evening, she fiercely ignored the presence of Desire. She did not see Desire slowly move towards her throughout the evening until she felt a tap on her shoulder.

"Hello. I don't believe we've met." Large dark eyes, catching a glint of the setting sun. The touch on her shoulder became the softest caress. Infatuation's breath caught in her throat. "Would you like to dance?"

Confident eyes gaze into confusion. A hint of passion within the confusion, quickly overwhelmed by fear.

"No. Please." Infatuation steps away. "Don't." Another step, then she turns and quickly walks away from Desire.

That night, Infatuation made love to her husband, almost forcefully. It did not occur to her to ask herself why, or what she was trying to prove.

"Hello again."

The soft words floated down to Infatuation. She was sitting on the beach with her eyes closed, breathing in the wild scent of the ocean. This was her favorite spot - at the edge of the cliff looking down to the waves crashing upon the beach. There was a trail behind her that snaked along the edge of the cliff, but it was early and Infatuation did not expect to meet anyone.

She knew that voice.

A long moment, then she opened her eyes to a tentative smile. Desire stood there, elegance personified. A simple shirt tucked into khaki pants. Sandals on her feet. Morning sunlight weaving gold into her dark hair. The smell of spices and lemons wafted towards Infatuation as Desire sat down next to her.

Infatuation did not know what to do. She wanted to run away. She wanted to put her head on Desire's shoulder and be lost in her essence. She wanted to touch, hold, love. "This is ridiculous," she told herself. "I am in love with my husband. I can NOT be attarcted to another woman. I can handle this." Taking a deep breath, Infatuation looked up and met the eyes of Desire.

And saw her passion reflected in Desire's eyes. They stared at each other for the longest time. Then Desire leaned forward and kissed Infatuation.

"What's on your mind, lady?", asked her husband as he playfully nuzzled Infatuation's neck. "You're awfully spacey these days."

"Mmm...not much. Your turn to make dinner, though." Infatuation smiled winningly at her husband. She held the smile until he grinned, then left for the kitchen. Then the smile faded.

Memories. Vivid memories of holding hands with Desire. Laughter, touches, caresses. Shivers as Desire kissed her fingertips. The easy companionship she felt. The scent of spices mingled with their lovemaking in Desire's bedroom. The taste of exquisite ecstasy.

A memory of Desire asking her to stay. They were sitting in the meadow, dining on a picnic lunch and each other's presence. Laughter in the air, slowly being replaced by serious silence. Then Desire asked Infatuation to stay with her. For always.

"I can't, " she had replied.

"Don't you love me?"

"Yes, but I love my husband, too."

"But not like this."

A sigh. "No, not like this. But this is not...real. This is not real love..."

"Are you so sure? Why not?"

"Because it's not right. It's not proper."

"Look around you. Look at yourself. Look at me. Now tell me that this is not real, nor right, nor proper."

Infatuation found that she could not reply.

"I want to be with you, " said Desire.

"Please, don't push me. I can't."

Silence. Then a sigh from Desire. "I love you. How can I not but push you?"

Infatuation stayed with her husband. No words of good-bye to Desire, just a silent refusal to see her anymore. Desire raged at Infatuation, pleading, crying. Each time, she quietly placed the phone receiver back into its cradle and buried her feelings deeper within her. Slowly, the calls became less frequent, then stopped altogether. She refused to acknowledge her pain, but instead told herself again and again that this was the right thing to do.

It was a long time before she could make love to her husband again.

It was an even longer time before she could look into herself and realize that this was not the life she wanted anymore. She began to feel trapped in her marriage.

"What's the matter?, " he would ask her. "Can we talk about it?"

She would be unable to answer, unable to articulate the pain eating at her heart.

Memories of Desire's hands on her body haunted her dreams.

She finally left her husband, and took on many lovers. Men, at first, as she gradually came to terms with herself and her identity. Then, a few women. She would smile, and tell herself that Desire would be proud of her.

"See, I've accepted myself. Now come back to me." Sometimes, she could almost see Desire smile.

Story 07

When I finished the story about Marcia. Kate's eyes were red and full of tears that were spilling down over her cheeks. I was crying too. She gestured for me to come to her and lay my head in her lap. I curled up against her, and Kate petted my hair, rubbed my back, and tenderly kissed my cheeks. Her tears mingled with my own. She softly said, "Its okay Riki, please believe me its okay. Neither one of us thought we would ever see the other again. I thought I had lost you forever. You thought the same."

"I didn't want Marcia, I wanted you."

"I know sweetheart. I know."

"Where did you go? "

Kate was quiet for awhile. She was fingering my hair, my face, my back. She finally took a deep breath and said, "When I left St. Phillip's, I told you I was going back to my mother house in the east to go to school."

"New York?"

"New Jersey, actually. That place had been my home for

many years. My parents were killed in a car accident when I was just twelve."

"The sixth grade?"

"Yes." Kate brushed my hair off my cheek and softly kissed me there. "The sixth grade. I instantly became an orphan. My grandparents were all dead and both my parents were only children, so I was alone."

Kate's voice drifted away somehow as she told me of a very lonely youth. "I already lived at the catholic boarding school next to the mother house, so really not much changed in my daily life, except I stopped getting letters and phone calls from home. When vacations came all the other girls went home, but I stayed at the convent and followed the same schedule as the other nuns. As I finished my high school education I knew I would become a nun. I never even thought about anything else. It was truly the only life that I knew."

"Because I never took a vacation from school, I finished a year early, at seventeen and went immediately into formation training. I took religious classes and education classes for one year and three months, and the following August, I was sent to St. Phillip's to teach the sixth grade. I was eighteen years old and there I was in charge of a room full of sixth grade students." I turned over on Kate's lap, so that I was on my back and could look into her eyes. She let her arm rest across my chest and her hand on my breast,

"I noticed you the first day. You bounded into the room and immediately commanded the attention of everyone, boys and girls. Everyone greeted you. "Hi Riki. How's it going Riki?' I remember now that Marcia gave you a hug. I remember the first day I saw you as if it was happening right now. I didn't know I was attracted to females instead of men. How would I know? I'd never been around a man other than the priests who said Mass and heard my confessions. But, when I saw you, a feeling in the pit of my stomach started gnawing at me that I had never experienced before. It left me dizzy, but I liked the feeling. And then you practically skipped up to my desk and introduced yourself. `Hello,' you said, `I'm Riki Jacobsen. I'm glad you are our new teacher.' You stuck out your hand to shake mine and my hand was damp. You told me not to be nervous, that we would have a great year. Do you remember that day?"

I shook my head, "No not really, I wish I did."

"I remember that day and almost every other day right up until that afternoon in early October when we first were together. I let the growing love and passion I felt for you overrule my good sense. I would see you playing with yourself in class. I wanted to replace your fingers with mine. I wanted to taste your sweet flesh. Riki, I planned that assembly program. I ordered that movie because it would keep everyone in the school busy all afternoon. I wanted to find some way to spend an afternoon alone with you; to see if you felt any of the same feelings as I did. I was so scared, but I was more in love than afraid. When you told me I could touch your breasts, I was swept away in a flood of passion. I have only bits and pieces of memories of the rest of that afternoon. I guess my brain was on hold and my libido was in overdrive."

"Kate, that was the most wonderful afternoon of my life. No matter how many times we have made love, that afternoon is still the most incredible. Everything was new. I didn't understand how intense sex could be. You woke my body up to a whole new experience." Kate kissed me gently, and said, "For me too. I had never made love with anyone before. I was just eighteen and you were my first lover. There hasn't been anyone since I left you."

This time I was crying. "Kate, I am so sorry that I ever got involved with Marcia. Please, please forgive me!"

"Riki, you don't need to be forgiven, you didn't do anything wrong. You were just trying to get on with your life."

"Please, I am so sorry!" Kate pulled me close. Her wet cheek was pressed against mine, "I forgive sweet Riki, I forgive you."

Kate kissed me and a rush of passion flooded my body. I clung to her desperately and kissed as deep and as hard as I could. Our arms clutched onto each other as we tried to make our two bodies one. Kate's hand slid up under my t-shirt and grabbed my heaving breast. She rubbed, and massaged the entire breast while I moaned in anticipation. When she finally took hold of my nipple, I cried in pleasure. She pinched my nipple just hard enough to create exquisite pain and then pulled and twisted it. The sensation coursed through my tit and rushed throughout my body. My pussy was starting to tingle and my juices were seeping through my shorts.

"Stand up, Riki. I want you naked." We both quickly stripped and she pulled me close again. We stood together naked, letting our bare bodies rub against each other for a very long time. "Come over here." She led me to a large rug in front of a fireplace, There was no fire, but the rug was so very inviting. Without letting go of each other, we slowly lowered ourselves to our knees, and continued to hold and kiss each other. Kate lowered me to the floor and lay on top of me. The kissing, the touching, the closeness was so very wonderful. My body was on fire. "Please, Kate, please, I need your tongue inside of me. Please, take me now."

Kate started a long, slow slide down my body, tormenting me by taking time to kiss each breast, to taste each sweaty patch of skin, to suck my navel. She stopped at my belly, and licked and bit the smooth skin there, blowing softly across my hot skin. Finally, she began an even slower descent to my overheated cunt. She nipped at my skin under my bush of hair. She blew into it and let her tongue flicker lightly there. Finally, her tongue just grazed the crack to my pussy. She was taking an excruciating amount of time. It only made me want her even more.

She began to lick my engorged lips with her full tongue making contact. I could tell she was gradually increasing the pressure and without warning she plunged quickly into my fully aroused cunt. Now her tongue was a hard rod and she began to deliberately fuck me. I was near ecstasy, and all I could say was, "Oh god, Kate! Oh my god, Kate. Please, oh please. Oh fuck that is so...damn...incredible!"

Her tongue found my clit and pressed hard on it. She slid two fingers into me to continue fucking me, while her tongue provided the necessary contact to send me over the edge. She used just the tip of her tongue to slide rapidly up and down the length of my clit, pressing hard as she did so. Heat was building quickly at my very core and radiating down my legs all the way to my toes. I felt my lower body stiffen and my toes curl. I sucked in my breath and held it while the pressure built. In one gigantic release, I exhaled and called out to Kate in ecstasy. I closed my eyes and held my breath again as spasms of pleasure caused my body to shudder uncontrollably.

Kate put her arms around me and pressed her cheek against my still throbbing cunt. We were both trying to regain our breath. "Please Kate, please, hold me." She quickly moved up next to me and wrapped me in her arms and legs. Sobs of shear joy wracked my body. Kate held on tightly and rode out the storm of passion that had swept us both away.

Story 08

My Dearest Red,

Happy Birthday Honey! I hope your day is as special as you are! I thought about buying you diamonds or sapphires, or something stunning, but LOL I hate to overwhelm you. *S* In my fantasies I would fly to the west coast to wine and dine you, to meet your friends...(do you think they would like me?)...and spend the night making love in some romantic hotel room. Making love to you all night long, now there is a wonderful fantasy!!

Slow and sweet, hot and passionate, kissing, holding, touching. Touching you darling would be so incredible. I am tingling all the way down to my pussy as I think of placing the palm of my hand on your face, looking into your eyes, whispering, "I love you Red," just before my lips touch yours. I can feel your arms pulling me close as our lips press together, our tongues meet and play gently with each other. My hands slide into your hair as I drive my tongue in deep feeling you suck me into your mouth. Passion takes over, our lips constantly change positions, sucking, nibbling, struggling to be one. My hands hold you tight, pressing against your back, pushing my breasts into yours, my nipples kissing yours. Sliding my hands down your back, cupping your sexy ass, lifting you up, your legs go tight around my waist. Still kissing you, I carry you to the bed, gently lay you down and stretch out beside you. Our legs and arms wrap around each other tightly. My mouth moves to your neck...nuzzling, kissing, sucking, while my hand finds your breast, holding it gently, squeezing, rubbing, finding the nipple and teasing it. Lightly licking your ear babe, whispering,"My god Red, I am fire...."

My tongue traces the outline of your ear while my fingers pinch and pull your nipple, feeling you inhale sharply and moan letting me know I have the touch just right. Licking your neck, moving down to cover your breast with my mouth, sucking at your nipple, the tip of my tongue makes little circles, feeling it get harder in my mouth. My hand slides down your belly, seeking your hot, wet pussy. Cupping it in my hand, rubbing it as I take your other nipple into my mouth. Baby you are so wet! My fingers play with your pussy lips. My lips leave your breast, I kiss each nipple, and slide down your trembling body. Your skin is so hot! My tongue lingers at your belly button as my fingers slide into your dripping pussy. Kissing your mound, I move to between your legs, spread you wide, and press my face to your wet lips. The smell, the heat makes me dizzy lover! My fingers part your lips and I slide my tongue into you. You gasp, as the heat of my tongue touches your inner lips, sucking and licking at them, they are so swollen darling. Using the tip of my tongue, I part your lips, sliding up seeking your clit. You gasp as my tongue makes contact. Damn, you taste so good! My mouth covers your clit and I suck it into my mouth, pulling gently, feeling you arch your hips, pressing your pussy tighter to my mouth. Darling, I want to be inside of you. I want my entire hand deep in your vagina. Babe, you are so wet, ready to take me in. I use my fingers to open your hot waiting hole.

I hear you say, "Yes, Ann, yes, I want all of you" and I am sliding three fingers into you. Feeling your muscle walls stretch to let me enter...licking your clit as I fold my thumb and little finger in tightly, stretching, pushing, slowly, giving your muscles time to relax, allowing me to enter. Finally I am all inside of you baby. Your muscles are so tight on my hand as I wiggle my fingers caressing you from deep inside. Now I start to stroke your muscle walls with my fingers curved upward, just the way you like it. I open and close my fist, slowly, allowing my finger tips to make complete contact with your vagina walls, stretching you with each opening and closing. Its so easy to caress you darling, finding that sweet spot that drives you crazy. Your muscles grab onto me, pulling me in deeper. I just need a small amount of in and out movement. Your muscles pull tight on my hand as I pull it out, before driving it back into you. I continue this motion baby, as I suck your clit into my mouth, pulling it to create tension and letting my tongue lick it, round and round. "Cum for me Red."

I can feel your muscles tense and your clitoris throb. Your back, your body tenses, you inhale deeply and everything seems to stop for a second or two, And then it hits! A huge explosive orgasm rocks your body sending shock waves from your head to toes. The feeling of your orgasm on my hand makes me cum to.

"O god, baby," I whisper, "Happy Birthday." I kiss your belly and rest my cheek there with my hand still inside of you, "and many more."

I love you Sweetheart,

Ann

I sat near the gate, mindlessly flipping through the magazine I'd just bought. Her plane was due in about a half hour, but I kept looking out the window as if it would just suddenly, miraculously appear. She'd only been gone a week. She had to leave in a hurry because of a family emergency and had asked me to watch the house and her dog while she was away. I had no problem in helping her out. I've been in love with her for years.

While she was gone, I corresponded with her web friends Mary and Sue to let them know the reason behind her sudden departure. They expressed their concern and love and I quickly began my own friendship with them. I confided in Mary and she gave me wonderful advice. I thought of her letters as I sat waiting for the plane.

Siobhan and I had known each other for several years and had been lovers for most of that time. If you have read her stories `A Day With Darlene' and `The Show', I am the Darlene she wrote about. She was my first experience with another woman. I'd been in love with her since we met, at least 2 years before we first made love.

The plane arrived and taxied to the gate. I walked over to the doors and waited for them to open and for Siobhan to appear. I was tingling all over. For a week I had slept nude in her bed, wandered nude through her house and swam nude in her pool - without her. It was time for me to do those things with her.

My heart raced as I caught the first glimpse of her red hair as she walked through the gate. I moved to her, and she to me, and I felt every nerve ending in my body scream for her. Not caring about the others around us, we hugged and kissed - not like 2 women glad to see each other, but like the lovers that we are. Our kiss was long and full of passion. Our tongues danced together as our breasts mashed together in our embrace. I looked into her eyes and saw the glow of love - and lust - as we continued to hold each other. We broke our kiss and started toward the baggage claim, arm in arm, happy for her to be home.

I had arranged for a cabbie friend of mine to meet us so neither one of us would have to drive. He was patiently waiting in the pickup area. We climbed into the back seat as he put her suitcase in the trunk. My cabbie friend, Jim, hadn't even gotten into the car and Siobhan and I were kissing passionately in the back seat of the taxi. Jim knew about our relationship, so he wasn't startled by our actions. He did get an eyeful, though.

Siobhan and I share the same feeling toward clothes. They are nice, sexy and not always necessary. When dressed, Siobhan is more of a jeans and t-shirt girl, while I like sexy, showy dresses. We were both wearing our favorites that day. Siobhan was in her fav 501s, white t-shirt and a blazer. She only wears a bra when she `has to' and today wasn't one of those days. Her 36C breasts were straining at the cotton of her t-shirt and her nipples were hard and lovely. Meanwhile, I'm wearing a slinky black dress that I couldn't wear a bra under if I wanted to. My nipples were equally as hard, wanting so desperately to be in her mouth. Once Jim had pulled away from the terminal, Siobhan and I were exploring each other with our hands and locked in a sensuous kiss. Her blazer and t-shirt were off before we were to the Interstate and my dress was off right after that. She managed to get her jeans unbuttoned but before she could get them off, I straddled her legs.

Our hands were rubbing and kneading each other's breasts and rubbing our nipples together as our kiss became more and more passionate. My knees were on the seat on either side of her legs, my open puss between her open legs and my juices oozed from inside. The more we kissed and the more we rubbed, the hotter and hornier I got. My clit was swollen and begging to be touched and I started to hump air. Siobhan broke our kiss, smiled, and moved me back over onto the seat next to her so my head fell into her lap. I reached up and started sucking on a nipple and she put her hand to my flooding puss.

I licked and sucked like a feeding baby as her hand worked over my puss. Her fingers stroked my blonde patch before caressing my labia, stroking and spreading the lips open and closed over my hard, swollen clit. I could feel my juices were running into my ass as she tickled my clit with her finger. That welcome, familiar warmth was building and spreading inside me as I cupped the breast I was sucking. I felt a finger enter me. I moaned and started to push against her to get her finger further in faster as the heel of her hand landed on my clit. Another finger entered me and I was on fire.

I kept hold of her breast with my mouth and hands as she stroked her fingers in and out of me, the heel of her hand applying just enough pressure to my clit. I felt myself burning deep inside as my moans vibrated her swollen nipple in my mouth. Her other hand was caressing my breasts, bringing me closer and closer to exploding. I opened my legs as wide as I could, pressing my clit against her hand, humping against her fingers, hanging on and sucking her breast for dear life as my orgasm flooded through me like a tidal wave.

With tears streaming down my face, my mouth released her breast as I screamed her name! "Oh! Siobhan!!!" I came and came and came, soaking my thighs and ass, Siobhan's hand and the taxi seat. Siobhan brought her fingers to her mouth and licked and sucked my juices from them. She noticed my tears and shushed me and held me. I sat up and tasted myself on her mouth as she kissed me. We whispered "I love you" and stared into each other's eyes.

Jim was just pulling the taxi into Siobhan's drive as she removed her jeans. Jim stopped the car and stared into the rear view mirror for a moment, smiling. Still nude, I leaned forward to ask the fare just in time to see Jim ejaculate into a towel. "I don't think I could've made another mile," he smiled. "This one's on me, ladies." After a moment, Jim put himself together and got out of the car, walking to the trunk to retrieve Siobhan's suitcase. Siobhan and I collected our clothes and got out of the car - still completely nude.

Once inside the house, Jim placed the suitcase inside the door, said his good-byes and closed the door behind him. Siobhan and I were halfway to the bedroom, hand in hand. In the bedroom, I laid her down on the cool, fresh sheets on the king size waterbed and went through the room, lighting the candles and incense I'd placed throughout the room. I had truly missed her this past week and tonight I was going to show her just how much.

Back on the bed, we kissed and rolled in each other's arms. Skin to skin. Breast to breast. Mound to mound. I held her and touched her and caressed her and kissed her and stared into her lovely green eyes. All the things I'd missed over the past week. I rolled her on to her back and started to nibble at her neck. She likes that. I moved my way down her beautiful body, nibbling and planting kisses, her fingers laced through my blonde mane. She squirmed as I kissed inside her hip on my way down to her thigh and then to her knee. I raised her leg and hugged it to me as I licked behind her knee. I looked at her and smiled. There, in front of me was the woman I'd been missing.

I smiled again as I kissed my way back up her leg, alternating between each thigh, kissing and nibbling towards her magnificent red-haired puss. I planted a kiss square on her labia and her fingers once again intertwined in my hair, stroking my head in an attempt to guide me into her. I was going to tease her, bring her ever so close and keep her there. I continued to kiss, but only with my lips to her lips. This was teasing myself, too. I wanted so badly to put my tongue deep inside her and drink every drop of her sweet juice.

Her fingers combed through my hair as I continued to kiss her lovely puss. I could feel her wetness building on her lips, and on mine. I slowly started to lick her. First around the outside of her, her thighs and red pubes and around, closing in on the center of my attention - her hard, swollen, delicious clit.

She bucked as the tip of my tongue touched her clit. I reached around her hips to hold her. We were both in for a wild ride. I started licking her everywhere - her lips, her entrance, her clit. She started to thrust her hips to meet my tongue. With my fingers, I spread her puss open to reveal her throbbing clit. So beautiful! I sucked on it and I thought she was going to hump us both right off the bed. I wrapped my lips around her nub and sucked and sucked and sucked. Her hands her holding my head as she ground herself into my face. She was calling my name as I released the suction from her clit and dove my tongue into her gushing hole. I licked and swallowed her cum as she about drowned me with her orgasm.

I didn't stop there.

As she was cumming all over me, I stuck 2 fingers way up into her. I heard her scream. I finger fucked her and went back to sucking her clit in time to my fingers. She continued to cum and cum and cum, grinding her puss to my face in rhythm to my fast fingering, yelping her pleasure. With one last throaty scream, Siobhan drenched me with her cum and pulled my face away from her puss. I removed my fingers from her spasming canal and a flood of cum followed. I crawled up and held her in my arms, her tear streaked face cradled to my breast, as she convulsed in her orgasm.

I kissed the top of her red hair and whispered "I told you I missed you".

Story 10

I blinked twice and realized that I had been staring blankly at a Ronco Food Dehydrator infomercial for quite awhile. Looking down, I also realized I was in the same pair of flannel pajama bottoms and mis-matched shirt that I had been wearing for the last three days.

"Snap out of it, Jody" I thought to myself and, realizing I was hungry, I meandered into the kitchen and stood in front of the fridge waiting for something to dance. I was munching on a carrot and contemplating the back of a box of rice-a-roni as Tess walked in dragging Max behind her.

"Damn dog was humping the neighbor's poodle again" she growled as she threw her bag on the floor and fought with max to get him through the doorway. Then she saw me standing there and concern clouded her eyes as she walked over and threw her arm loosely around her shoulders.

"How are you doin' hon?" she asked.

I shrugged and walked into the living room with a bag of Frito's in my arms. "Well, I don't have a job. I am running out of money. I haven't changed in three days and since Michelle left me a month ago, my dog is getting laid more than I am. That about sums it up. Any more questions?"

"My pooor roomie," Tess moaned, making me smile in spite of myself. "Maybe if you changed and left the house we could at least work on the getting you laid part..."

"No thanks, Tess. Really. I am just not ready to go barhopping. And not in the mood. Why don't you go?" I offered. "I think I'm just gonna soak in the tub and go for a walk or something. Get out for awhile..."

"You sure?" she asked.

"Yep. Now go on ... scoot. Shake your bootie for both of us, okay?"

--- --- ---

Fresh and clean, polished and pumiced and shaved, I slid into a clean pair of cords and a t-shirt and threw a sweater on against the cool breeze that had been finding it's way into the house all afternoon. I laced up my boots and grabbed my keys off the knob, stopping to stare at myself in the mirror by the front door. "Pretty in a quiet kind of way, " I thought to myself. "Nice lips, nice hair. Nice breasts. I'd date me--" I grinned at myself and headed out the door.

Tess had told me yesterday that two dykes had moved in down the block. I decided that was as good a direction for my walk as any and pointed my toes that a way. I crunched through the piles of leaves as I went, making satisfactory noisy messes all along the sidewalk. Who needs therapy. Just give me a pile of leaves and I'll make it through anything.

So, Michelle had left me. So she had left me for some bitch named Sarah that ran a Domino's pizza -- a fuckin' dominoes pizza, for god's sake! My thoughts wandered through the dark place of my memories, replaying happy moments together. Making love in the car on the side of the road, our heated panting steaming up the car windows ... trying to wallpaper our bedroom and having it all fall off cause we didn't use the right paste ... the taste of the cantaloupe she fed to me the morning after our first night together... Falling asleep in her arms ... our long talks about politics and books and music. Would I ever find someone to share those things again? Part of me knew I would, but the weather called for melancholy thoughts and I was more than happy to oblige.

Turning down Millbrae Avenue, I heard a moan. "What the fuck?" I thought, glancing around me to see where the noise might have come from. Nothing.

I looked up and saw I was in front of the house Tess had told me our new neighbors lived in. Now, anyone that knows me knows I am a nosy bitch, so it shouldn't be any surprise what I did next. I snuck up the front walk and crouched down in front of the window. I peeked in, glanced around me to see who was watching me, then got comfortable and looked through the window. Two women were making love in the living room with the damn curtains wide open. A delicious grin started at the corners of my mouth. This was going to be an interesting night after all.

There was a taller, brunette woman, obviously the dominant one, with short-cropped hair and broad shoulders. She had lovely brown breasts and a thick patch of fuzz between her legs that was peeking out from behind a lovely hot pink strap on. Kneeling in front of her was another brunette. This one had longer curly hair that she was holding back from her face as she sucked on the dildo as her lover moaned loudly. She had pale pale skin and rosy nipples that her lover was pinching between her fingers.

I couldn't believe what I was seeing! And I have to admit, I was getting quite turned on. They were so ... hot. Strap-on woman pulled back from the other's mouth and said one word "Around" and the other turned around on all fours and pressed her ass against her lover's crotch, rubbing and wriggling, as if she couldn't contain herself a moment longer. Her lover cupped her ass in both hands, caressing the soft skin and then suddenly *slap* hitting her hard on the ass. She moaned, obviously in pleasure. Her lover reached down and caressed her cunt, playing lightly with her clit and smearing her wetness around. She leaned over and, spreading her ass cheeks, flicked her tongue against her asshole. She moaned even louder and pressed her hips back against the tongue. MMMmmmmmmmm, I wanted to taste that sweet sexy spot on a woman again.

Pulling back, dildo-gal pressed her hot pink shaft deep into the woman's ass, filling her fully. She cried out and her lover ran her fingers across her back, leaving bright red scratches. She started up a slow rhythm of gently out and quick thrusts back in as her lover's hips began keeping the rhythm with her. Their pitch increased as their moans and gasps became louder and more passionate. Harder and harder she thrust into her lover, slapping her warm flesh against her lovers ass, jarring her whole body forward. I let out a small moan, then quickly looked around me to see if anyone was walking the street and could see me. Just what I need: to be arrested as a peeping tom. I should go, I thought, but as I began to turn away, she pulled out of her lover's ass and turned her over on her back. I licked my lips and turned back towards the window.

She was lying on top of her lover, her weight pressing her into the floor. They kissed and kissed and kissed, passionately licking each other's mouths and tongues and biting each other's lips and tongues and then, necks and shoulders. I couldn't stand it any more. I silently unzipped my cords and slipped my hand into my pants and found myself quite wet already. My fingers stroked and pinched at my clit and pressed into my cunt as the two lovers continued to suck and bite each other's nipples and shoulders and necks. I realized she had slid her silicon cock into her dripping cunt at some point and she was slowly rocking in and out of her, pressing deep and slow and rubbing her clit as she went. Faster and faster they thrust against each other, biting and pinching each other's nipples and shoulders. The one being fucked raised her legs up and draped them over her lover's shoulders so she could thrust deep and hard and fast and she began intermittently slapping her lover hard on the ass as she thrust into her.

Their moans and cries of pleasure were getting so loud, I was sure someone else would hear and come to investigate, finding me here, my hand sliding furiously in and out of my cunt, my own moans stifled behind my lips as I bit down on them to keep them in. But at this point, I didn't care. I wanted to here them come. Wanted to see her thrust deep one last time and cry out, her lover bucking and writhing beneath her. Then, it happened. She let out this slow long sigh and arched her back, heaving her breasts up into the air and cried out "Yes! Yes! Yes! Oh, God! Yes!" and I could see the orgasm roll through her, sending shivers down her torso. Her lover collapsed on top of her, their moist bodies crushed against each other, kissing and caressing and holding each other. I came myself then, silently moaning as my cunt clenched onto my fingers, sending the waves of pleasure out from my stomach. I sat there a moment longer, watching their gentle caresses and kisses as I caught my breath. Standing up, I zipped my pants up and, on shaky legs, I walked back out to the sidewalk and down the street towards my house. I can't believe I just saw that. I can't believe they didn't spot me, a strange face in their window, watching them in their love making. My mind was reeling as I got home and crawled into bed and pleasured myself again, remembering their smooth bodies fucking so hard and so passionately. I curled up in my flannel sheets, smiled, and fell asleep, exhausted.

Sexy Erotic Encounters
07 Erotic Adult Stories for Women (Short F/F Sex Stories)
Alana Meehan

All Rights Reserved. No part of this publication may be reproduced in any form or by any means, including scanning, photocopying, or otherwise without prior written permission of the copyright holder. Copyright © 2020

This book is entirely a work of fiction. The names, characters and incidents portrayed in it are the work of the author's imagination. Any resemblance to actual persons, living or dead, events or localities is entirely coincidental.

Story 01

Thank God this week had ended. Between work and the stress of my routine at home, I felt exhausted from head to toe. Totally drained, I was relieved when I realized it was my monthly appointment for a massage and pedicure. Gathering my gym bag, waterproof Sony Walkman and terry cloth robe, I was out the door and into the car in a flash. Relief from the tension and stress was within reach and I couldn't wait to get on the table to sink into a gently, peaceful state of mind.

Perfectly Pampered was a welcomed addition to our tiny rural community. Most of the residents had little idea what a pedicure was let alone ever envision themselves receiving a full body massage. The town's male population jumped right on the bandwagon at the thought of massages administered by the artful hands of a bosomy female. The women generated fantasies of hugely endowed pectoral zealots gently yet forcefully kneading away their cares and woes. Fantasies ran rampant at Perfectly Pampered and that exactly the product they had intended to provide.

Traffic was light down Main Street and parking would be easier since many had already left work this Friday afternoon. As luck would have it, there was a space waiting for me only 50 feet from the front door. Dropping sufficient change in the meter to cover my 2 hour visit, I gathered my belongings and headed towards the door.

"Welcome Mrs. Danzig," said Sheila, the perky, blonde receptionist who strategically positioned herself directly across from the entranceway.

Sheila had learned early in her customer service career that eye contact made all the difference when it came to clients being satisfied with their service. It provided an air of caring and friendliness that such close body contact and stimulation would seem to dictate. Making the customer feel comfortable in this unusually physical setting was her job and she most certainly did her job well.

"Hi, Sheila. Sorry if I'm a few minutes late. Is Daphne ready for me yet?"

"No, she's got about 15 minutes left on her last appointment if you'd like to change a spend a few minutes in the sauna, I'll call you when shes ready."

"That would be great. I could use the steam right about now. I'm a bundle of nerves today."

Moving back towards the changing area, I looked for a locker to stow my gear. Stripping down to nothing but a pale lavender terry cloth sarong, I grabbed my Walkman and headed for the sauna. Sheila had said I had 15 minutes to soak up the steam but, realizing the time it took to change, the dial was set for 10 minutes in the hopes I could squeeze each and every last minute out of the timer before my time had come.

The sauna had been an additional benefit to the clientele. The management made it available as a means of keeping the waiting room area cleared as much as possible. It also served to soften the skin around the toenails for the pedicures as well as provide some relaxation prior to a massage. Almost everyone tried to arrive a few minutes early just to partake of a few minutes of warm, body engulfing steam. Realizing I was running late, I had feared my sauna time would be lost. Luckily I was wrong.

Not wishing to be make idle chit chat with another today, I was relieved to find the sauna empty. Nestling myself in the far corner, I placed the headphones on and pressed play. On more stressful days, I would find a little Yanni just the perfect touch. Today, that seemed made to order. I leaned back against the bench seat backrest and closed my eyes. I could feel the steam settling quietly over every inch of my exposed skin and I could feel the warmth of it's touch as I inhaled deeply. Such a feeling of security and solitude. Almost like a thick, soft mink blanket caressing my body into peaceful blissful slumber.

"Are you ready Mrs. Danzig?" Said Sheila. "Daphne is just about ready."

"I'll be right there," I said calmly. Not nearly ready I thought to myself but, there was little choice for now. Maybe a few more minutes after the massage.

The hallway between the sauna and the massage area was narrow to maximize the space for as many massage rooms as possible. Daphne was part owner of the business so she was fortunate to have one of the larger areas at her disposal. She had decorated the room with subdued pastel colors and adorned the walls with poster prints depicting relaxing fields of windswept grass and aerial views of statuesque wonders such as the Grand Tetons and Glacier National Park. All relaxing and all soothing.

"How are you today Mrs. Danzig," Daphne asked in a quiet reassuring tone yet, almost as if she already knew the answer.

Daphne fully realized that most of her customers were stressed, exhausted or forever frustrated with their jobs. That's why they were here. They were here to be pampered and put at rest. They wanted tender loving care and wanted to leave with a peaceful mind and a well ministered to body which was also at peace.

"It's been a long week," I said. "I can really use this massage today. Can you also work my lower back as much as possible, I'm having some pain and may need to see a doctor next week if it doesn't subside."

"Certainly," Daphne responded. "Just let me know if I press too hard."

Daphne knew what she was doing. Her degree had been in Physical Therapy from University of Virginia yet, during her final internship, she decided to branch out into massage therapy. Many of the patients she saw during her last 6 weeks of school were going to need short term massage and there were limited trained personnel at the disposal of many of the Physical Therapy clinics. There was a market to be tapped and Daphne received her degree and opened a small clinic of her own. Seven years later, she had doubled the size of the clinic and added 2 additional technicians to help with the growing work load.

"Would you prefer scented or unscented oil today?" asked Daphne.

"Unscented I think. I have a date later this evening and I won't have time to shower in between. "

"Just relax Mrs. Danzig. Do you want your headphones while I work?"

"Please," I said.

Daphne reached below to the lower shelf of the treatment table where I had set my belongings. Extracting the headphones from the towel was a chore in itself but, she managed to free them and I placed them on my head, fiddling for a relaxing FM station. I preferred light classical for a massage and found KKEZ at 105.6 was well suited the duration of my appointment.

Daphne looked at her appointment schedule, then glancing my way, she noted "they have you scheduled for a back massage but since you're my last customer for the day, any interest in a full body massage?"

Thinking I had an appointment later in the evening, I had to be careful about my time but, it had been a dreadful week and the thought of a full body massage was quite appealing just about now.

"If you've got the time," I said, "let's do the full body massage since I know I could use the rest."

Nudging the tray with her oils and lotions off to the side out of the way, Daphne began to work her magic. Cradling my head carefully in her left hand, she began to gently massage the areas around my temples and firmly pressed downward to force the tension lower and lower on my neck and shoulder area. Over and over she rubbed and as she moved to my forehead area, I could feel the relaxation begin to surge within my mind. Gently rubbing in continuous circular motions eased the tension flow and I could feel her long slender yet forceful fingers pressing gently on the upper reaches of my neck just below the hairline.

"Why don't you get real comfortable on your front right now and I'll work these areas first."

Daphne reached for the tray of oils and lotions, squeezing a generous amount of unscented oil to the reservoir created on her awaiting hand. The oil was slightly warm as she began to spread it along the lines of my shoulders and collar bone area. After 6 months of weekly visits, Daphne had gotten to known which areas were sensitive to touch. The areas which exuded a giggle or a twitch, as well as the areas which would lead to that chill or slightly erect nipple. As I laid there, eyes closed, fixating on the touch of each finger, I felt safe. Her hands gently yet firmly continued to press the tension from the back and sides of my neck ever lower over the shoulder and down into the areas of my shoulder blades. I could feel the knots growing as she lowered her hands and began to press harder with each continuing motion.

As her hands ebbed their way along the edges of my armpits, I was relieved I had shaved earlier this morning before work. Daphne had commented that it was difficult to do an appropriate massage with too much hair. It began to pull and was more uncomfortable for the client. I wanted pleasure and no pain and as such, made certain I had removed as much of my body hair as was possible before each visit.

Lower and lower her hands went along the edges of my spine. Additional oil had to be added to make her contact more pronounced and my skin more supple to her touch. I could almost envision the direction of her strokes as she worked her magic fingers across the reaches of my body. The pain was in fact pleasurable and the pressure reassuring. As she approached the area of my waist, I could feel each of her ten fingers pressing strongly on the outer edges of my hips. Circling and pressing, pushing the stress downward toward the tips of my toes. The pressure on my butt was delightful. As she circled each cheek, I could feel her gently separating them and exposing my anal area. Along my rectal crevice went her entire hand as if to press away the tension. To move it lower and lower down. Draining it from my upper body to it's demise.

As her hands passed along the underside of my buttocks, I could feel the additional pressure along the inner most reaches of my thighs. I was glad she had avoided my genital area, I had become wet from her touch and I was embarrassed at my lack of control. She must have been used to that though because she never mentioned my wetness nor commented on it's excitement.

"You've had a difficult week, I can tell," replied Daphne.

She knew I couldn't hear her with my headphones on. All I could decipher was a muffled sound of her gently soothing voice. It continued to relax me as I laid in complete control of her touch.

Down my thighs she went. Round and round. Pressing, pushing, kneading and all the while disseminating the tension and knots which had manifested themselves in my every muscle. More oil, more pressure, more pleasure. Down along my calves she maneuvered. Every finger plunging it's way to the center of the tension. Every circle a ending of tension yet the beginning of pleasure. I began to doze as I concentrated solely on her touch.

"Time to turn over Mrs. Danzig," spoke Daphne in a more demonstrative tone. She knew I was fading into restful slumber and it was time to finish the remainder of my massage.

"Sorry," I said, "I was falling asleep. Your fingers are so relaxing."

"No problem, it happens all the time," she said.

I watched her reach behind to the table of oils and she continued to moisten her hands with a generous serving of unscented oil. Closing my eyes I began to envision the preparations she was making to touch these more sensitive areas of my body. I could feel the heat of her breathing as she leaned over my breasts. Grasping each shoulder around my collar bond she began to gently knead her thumbs into the muscles again forcing any remaining tension from their control. Down along my sides she pressed and in long seductive rubs she motioned the tension below. I could feel her hands gently cup my left breast and as she continued to press, I felt that same chill. Her right thumb and forefinger rolled my nipple tightly between her fingers. I could feel it swell at her touch and I could feel the other nipple on my right breast following in stride. Round and round she pressed. All of a sudden in a start, I felt the warm, moist touch of her tongue encircling my nipple . Awakening in a start, I slightly raised my head and looked directly into her awaiting eyes.

"Do you mind?" Queried Daphne. "I've always wanted to have you."

"No, I don't think I do mind." I whispered.

Daphne kissed my lips gently and then dutifully returned to her task at hand.

I could feel her tongue pressing along the out reaches of my areola. The glands swelling with every sweep of her tongue. A chilling thrill as she breathed on each pass and an excitement I had never felt with a man. Her mouth began to engulf my breast. Down she went pushing as much as was humanly possible into the reaches of her mouth. She had begun to suck -- began to suck hard. I could feel her pulling my nipples farther and farther erect with each sucking motion. It was incredible. Her right hand released it's grasp from my left breast and it worked it's way slowly over to my other awaiting breast. Gently cupping it's body while continuing to suck, I could sense the table lowering underneath me. Realizing I was surprised at the motion Daphne halted her movements and looked over at me.

"Don't worry, I'm just lowering the table so I can climb on."

Daphne mounted the table and me sitting astride my waist. With the angle of my glance, I could see the curly brown hairs of her own mound pressing down gently on my own. They were warm and moist and they felt wonderful. Raising my arms to her own breasts, Daphne showed me where she wanted me to press and she continued my massage.

"Just caress them," she said. "Press the nipples between your fingers and feel their strength."

I did what she had asked. No hesitation, no fear, no embarrassment. It seemed so natural. I felt I knew exactly what she wanted. She most definitely knew what I wanted. Her hands pressed tightly on my sides, moving upward. I felt her hands cup as they rose up towards my awaiting breasts. Her fingers were the scouts and the heels of her palms were the warriors, pushing back the tension and the uncertainly. Lowering herself down upon me she pressed her mouth squarely upon mine and kissed me long and hard. I felt her tongue enter my mouth and as she pressed hard I could feel her thrusting upon my waist.

"Are you ready for me to touch you there?" she said in a gently whisper.

"Let me touch you too," I said.

"Not yet," she said "this is what you are paying for. I'll get mine later. Okay?"

"Okay," I said.

I could feel her body raising as she shifted herself lower on the massive table. As she moved, I could feel the moistness of her tongue as it traced a path to my dark, curly haired soaking wet pussy below. Gently pressing the lower lips of my clit aside she continued her full body massage, this time with her tongue. Up and down, side to side, in and out of my hole. The same motion, the same pressure the same sensual tension reducing motions she had used on every other inch of my soul. All of a sudden I could feel the full blanket of her tongue on my lower lips. She had begun to suck. To suck on my magic button of pleasure. Gently arching to reach her lips more I felt her pull away. As I began to raise my head to see what was wrong, back went her tongue with that same blanket of pleasure and the same suction of delight. How close she was bringing me to an incredibly intense orgasm. Did she realize what she was doing. I think yes.

As gently as she had positioned her mouth, I could feel the release of her lips and the insertion of her middle finger. I think if was her middle finger. It was hard to tell though. Reaching inside as far as it could I could feel pressure. Pressure on my G-spot. Most men don't know about the G-spot and if they do, the majority of them are not as interested in pressuring it. But, Daphne knew how much it would increase the intensity of my orgasm and she searched carefully for it's location. Down came her flicking tongue. Down along the folds of the clit, now riddled with wetness. Completely engulfed with the moistness of my own excitement and the saliva from her own gyrations. Flicking up and down continuously I felt myself heave up into her awaiting tongue. With each rise of my hips I could feel more pronounced pressure on my G-spot and more precision of each flick.

"Not now," I said "Not now."Tearing the headphones from my ears I must have seemed panicked.

"You're okay," said Daphne in her quiet controlling tone. "I won't let you come until we're both ready. I want you to want me to make you come. I want you to need for me to make you come. I want the decision to be in your mind and totally out of your own control."

With that her index finger joined her middle finger inside of me and her remaining hand positioned itself upon my left breast, stroking, tweaking my nipple and gathering it's own pleasure from my excitement. All three areas of pleasure captured the entire reaches of my mind. My breast, my clit and my g-spot all receiving pleasure at once. How incredible this sexual experience was. How much I had been missing from my male friends. What she had given to my life had seemed unattainable until now.

"I want you," I screamed as she touched me.

"You'll have me in time." Daphne commented quietly as she continued her mission.

All of a sudden I felt her fingers release they grip on my vagina. I could feel her thumb being inserted fully into my insides and her middle finger press lightly on the edges of my anus. Gently removing her left hand from my breast I glanced up and saw her locate the tube of KY Jelly from her table. I could feel a small amount being squeezed from the tube atop my anus and gently she positioned her finger inside of my anus. Her middle finger slowly insinuating it's way inside of me, thumb pressing lightly along the lower rim of my vagina, tongue returned to it's flicking and left hand atop my breast -- she was a master. All of a sudden I felt slightly dizzy. I felt her increasing the motions of her tongue up and down, pausing briefly to such my clit hard and then flicking up and down, up and down. Her middle finger had increased the intensity of it's pumping and I was motionless beneath her glorious touch. Longing to come and come hard. I could feel my body rising up and I was unable to control the pleasure.

"It's now," Daphne said. "You can't stop and if you could I wouldn't let you. You're coming and you'll come hard I promise."

Daphne was right. I came long and I came hard. In fact, she had me come at least three times I was conscious of. In what seemed to be miniscule moments in time I had experienced the greatest sexual pleasure of my life. I had been pleasured by the artful hands of another woman and I loved it. Opening my eyes, I searched to meet hers.

Raising herself up, she looked longingly into my eyes and I felt a tear streak it's way down the side of my face. I had been the receiver and not the giver of any of this pleasure. Daphne raised her right hand to my cheek, gently wiping away my tears. She lowered her pleasureful lips to mine and kissed me gently as she had done at first.

"I'd like you to come home with me tonight," she said. "I'd like us to be naked together and make love to each other. Would you like that too?"

Daphne didn't have to wait long for my answer. "I would love that," I said.

Gathering my belongings I reached for my towel and exited to the dressing room to gather my thoughts. Before I left, I poked my head into Daphne's office and asked "where do you live and what time?"

"Go home and relax, I'll call you in an hour." Daphne smiled wickedly and before I was able to leave she remarked "Do you still want the pedicure today?"

Laughing to myself I threw up my hands and said "Maybe next time."

Reaching my car just in time for the meter to run out, I sat briefly behind the steering wheel and sighed. I had no stress whatsoever remaining in my body. I was calm and relaxed and felt truly happy for the very first time in my 45 years. Even before my divorce, I had never felt this relaxed following sex. Grabbing my phone from it's cradle on the dashboard I hit the #4 speed dial button.

"Randy," I asked as the voice on the other end answered. "Can we make it another night, I have a headache."

Story 02

I was out bra shopping with my friend when this happened. I always shop for bras with her because we're the same size and often try on the bras and then throw them over the stall partition to try the ones the other person took. That way we can try more on at one time, without having to go out and get more.

Well, one day when we both needed new bras we went to a lingerie shop at our favourite mall. My friend, Sadie, took 5 in, as did I, but found one after trying just two, so she gave the other four to me. I was just about done trying them on when someone knocked on one of the inside walls of my stall and said, "Hello?"

I answered back with a hi. The woman had a nice voice and then asked me if I'd mind giving her my opinion on something. I didn't know what to say, so I just said yes, not wanting to be rude and not having enough time to think of an excuse. So she told me in a sweet, melodious voice to come on into her dressing room when I was finished and she would leave the door unlocked.

I skipped trying on the last two bras so Sadie wouldn't get upset that I took so long. I wasn't sure what the woman wanted me to look at or how many things she wanted me to see. I put my top back on and grabbed the black bra I wanted to purchase. I hurriedly looked down the aisle to make sure no one was there before I snuck into the other ladies stall. She seemed a lot older than my 16 years, maybe her late 20's, early 30's. She had on snug-fitting hip huggers that showed off her model-like figure and a satin push-up bra that showed off her big, round globes. Her long, straight brown hair was soft-looking and wispy, her bright green eyes big and beautiful. She had a small, neat nose and a pouty, full mouth.

"Thanks a lot for helping me out, sweetie," she said after I had closed and locked the door. She stood there for a minute taking me in. I'm only about 5'4", but I have light blonde hair and green eyes, and pretty good figure, with nice breasts. I guess I'm pretty good-looking, and am in the popular group at school.

She told me she wanted to impress her lover and asked if I'd mind telling her how some things looked on her. I said sure and that I didn't mind at all. And that was the truth! I've read stuff about women having sex and the thought of this thrilled me. I wouldn't mind one bit having this sexy lady model lingerie for me.

She introduced herself and told me her name was Monica and what was my name? "Wendi," I told her.

"Okay Wendi," she said in a sensuous voice, "How do you think this looks on me?"

"Wonderful," I said. It was true, the moistness in my panties could verify that.

"Good, I'm glad you like it. Now I'm gonna try something else." She unhooked the back of the bra, so I turned around while she changed. When she turned around it was all I could do to not grab her and kiss her.

She was wearing a very skimpy, see-through bra, and a matching, low-cut thong. I was so horny for her it was unbelievable. Her long hair tickled the tips of her nipples and her full lips were drawn up into a sexy pout.

"Do you like this?" she asked me.

"Oh yes, you have the perfect figure for it," I said. She looked at herself in the mirror some more, and I took it that she needed more reassurance so I told her she looked so sexy her lover wouldn't be able to take his eyes off her.

"He?" she said with a seductive giggle. "Who said anything about a he?" She studied herself in the mirror for a few more seconds before turning to me again. "One more thing Wendi, and then you can go back to that cute friend of yours."

I turned around and she started removing the bra and thong set. I stole a peak and saw a hint of her round, tanned tits. They were beautiful. Perfect to suck on, I thought. It took her a bit longer to change this time. But oh, it was worth it!

Standing before me was perfection, dressed in a skimpy, erotic torselette of black and red velour. The cups of it were were black lace that you could easily see her boobs through, and her long, muscular legs sported black nylons with a bit of sparkled in them. She had another thong on, this one made of black velour with lace around the edges making it look ever so kinky. I just stood there staring. Monica was clearly enjoying modeling like this for me. I had no complaints either! "You like it?" she asked me.

"Uh huh" was all I could manage. She stood in front of the full-length mirror with a questioning look on her pretty face.

"What is it?" I asked her.

"Well," said Monica, "I guess it looks pretty good, but I wonder how long it will take to get off? I don't want my lover to spend all night taking it off, do I?" She appeared to think about that for a minute before saying, "On second thought, maybe that will make my night more fun!"

She looked at me with a wicked grin on her face. "Wanna find out?" she said to me. With that, she pounced on me, bringing her lips to mine in a passionate french kiss. I felt her tongue feeling the insides of my mouth and then slowly working its way down my throat. I was doing the same to her and thinking that kissing another woman beats kissing a guy one thousand fold. When we finally stopped, Monica asked me if she could see me in the bra I planned on getting.

"All right, but you have to turn around while I change," I instructed in a playful tone.

"Of course," came the giggling reply.

I could see Monica's sexy, firm ass in the mirror, and I rubbed my tits, not quite as large as hers but big enough, as I was putting the bra on because I was so horny. I wanted nothing more than to screw that exquisite lady with the piercing green eyes. When I had the bra on, I told her she could turn around she drew in a sharp breath when she saw me.

"Ohhh," she moaned and came to me like a puppy wanting to lick its owner's hand, except that's not what Monica wanted to lick! She took my hands and placed them on her breasts, moving them around and around. They felt so soft, although I would've loved to have been feeling them underneath her torselette. She then slid her hands up the front of my bra to fondle my tits, getting me very excited. I rubbed and pinched her nipples, enjoying seeing them spring to attention like nipples tend to do.

Monica then unhooked my bra and was about to take her mouth to my boobs. I whimpered with pleasure as she licked around the outside of them, teasing me, before she moved closer to my nipples. When she finally reached the centre, she licked and sucked for all she was worth. Pulling the nipples of my breasts with her teeth made me grab her head and hold on, while I continued to get pleasured. My crotch was on fire and we fell to the ground, Monica on top of me, still furiously sucking on my tits.

When she stopped, I unzipped the torselette a bit, just enough so that her jugs popped out of the top. I had already fondled them, but now was my chance to take them to my mouth. For the first time, I let my tongue come in contact with a part of another woman! Oh, the feelings I got from sucking and licking and biting those perfect globes!

I saw her hand go down to her crotch to remove her panties. I grabbed her and moved her hand to the button of my jeans. She slid my pants down and started rubbing my cunt through my thong. It was sending chills up and down my spine!

I got on top of her, kissing her lovely body from her breasts to just above her mound, over top of the sexy lingerie that she had on. She let out a groan and I told her to be quiet, people might her us, and that if she did it again she might get a spanking.

"Ooohhh, that doesn't sound too bad!" Monica whispered naughtily. Luckily, nobody seemed to be using the change rooms, it was a week day and early in the morning, long before the mall would get busy. I took off the torselette but left her thong on. I could see some of her pussy hair coming out of the sides. She had been playing with my cunt all the while, massaging it through my panties that were thoroughly soaked. I was moaning softly and planting kisses all over her satiny stomach. I'd go down and nuzzle her pubic hair, teasing her and making her think I was going to her slit.

Her hands left my pussy and I wondered where they were going to go. Then I felt them on my ass, stroking it softly and occasionally poking at my crack. All this teasing was getting to me. I couldn't wait to finish what we started. Apparently neither could Monica, because we shuffled around until we were in 69 position. I began kissing and licking her upper thighs, causing Monica to squirm around on top of me. Just then, one if the salespeople came to the door and asked if I was doing okay and would I like another size in anything? I grabbed the torselette and gave it to her, asking if I could have a leopard print one in a size small.

"I'll be right back with that," the saleslady said.

She had no clue there was anyone in there but me, let alone anyone on top of me, and we burst into a fit of giggles.

I started tickling Monica's thighs with my tongue again, then removed her thong, stroking her ass as I took it off. I moved my tongue up slowly, getting nearer and nearer her wet twat. I ran my tongue slowly around her pussy lips and she started moaning "Wendi" over and over again.

I was all hot and wet, and Monica started sucking on nice, firm ass. The saleslady came back and put the item I'd asked for over the stall door. I mumbled a thanks and went back to Monica's cunt. I felt her with my fingers for a little, then inserted three of them into her dripping hole. She put hers inside me, but after a second took them out again. As I kept going, Monica took her fingers and rubbed them around in my juice to get them nice and wet. Then I felt her shove them up my asshole! I gasped in surprise as I felt her fingers move around and although it hurt a bit at first, I knew I was going to include this in all my love-making to come. I ran my hands up and down her leg, letting her know I appreciated it.

I'd been in there with Monica for roughly 10-15 minutes. now and thought that Sadie was probably wondering what the hell was taking me so long, so I stopped my hands from stroking her glorious thighs and she took her fingers out of my ass.

I flicked my tongue at her twat a bit, until Monica called, "Ready?" I said yes, and with that I shot my tongue deep inside of her while fondling her tits, as she did the same to me. I was in ecstasy! Having a woman's tongue inside me was a new experience for me and I can't describe the feelings it gave me, except for that they were wonderful! And Monica's cunt tasted so sweet and good! I now new why so many people were lesbians, although I still liked guys as well.

I gasped as I felt my orgasm coming, like a whole bunch of rockets were going off inside of me! Monica reached orgasm and came inside my mouth. I let myself go and released my come into her mouth. I could feel her sucking up my womanhood, determined to not let a drop get away. I was eagerly doing the same to her and when we finished, we lay there panting.

We got up and I got dressed, putting my panties and bra back on, as well as my jeans and shirt. Monica put the leopard print torselette on and asked my opinion.

"The first one," I said with a wicked grin, "Definitely the first one!" I was about to exit the change room and make my way to Sadie when Monica told me to go back to my previous dressing room and wait until she got back. After about two minutes, a bag from the shop we were in was slipped under the door.

"Thanks for everything sweetie," Monica said. I opened the bag and took out the black and red torselette, the thong and the glitter tights she had had on. The thong was still wet and reeked of her juices. I held it up to my lips for a second and then left the store.

I found Sadie near the front of the store. "What took you so long Wendi?" She demanded. "And what did you buy? I didn't see you go to the counter."

"I'm sorry. You know it takes me longer than you to try on bras and I had to ask the saleslady to get a few things in different sizes. I just bought a bra though."

As we left the store I told her that I thought two ladies were making love in one of the stalls. I wanted to see what she thought about that kind of sex.

"In a public place like that? They could have got a room!" Sadie exclaimed.

As we walked through the mall, I thought to myself that she didn't say it was disgusting. Maybe there's hope for us after all!

We went home with nobody knowing what happened except me and my secret lover. I was having trouble believing that I had sex with _another woman_ in a store change room! I felt the wetness of my panties between my legs and peeked into the bag that Monica gave me that would be a permanent reminder of my little adventure. It had been real and it had been EXCELLENT!

Kris, deciding she has been putting in enough time thinking about personal computers, online personalities, computer problems and how to solve them, read again the MSG she had just received in her mailbox:

You have been selected to judge the comforts of our resort, free of all charges, for a weekend of your choice, No charges will be made for any service, including restaurant, lodging, health club, beaching areas.

It went on, and she read it all, noting she would only be requested to attend a one-hour sales session, and it was not mandatory, she could leave at any time, no one would contact her unless she requested it.

Perfect, she decided, she also decided to leave her portable cpu behind, she would take nothing except pleasurable goodies, and of course her cellphone, for security.

Noting this was a nudist organization, there was no packing to be done, so she showered, changed into a flowing, sheer type of garment to get her into the mood, and set off, thinking about her first encounter in a nudist setting. She pulled in for fuel, letting a young, healthy, firm young lady in tight, skimpy t-shirt & shorts fill her tank, they both noticed the extra time the attendant gave to washing Kris's windshield, while they both appreciated the other's healthy bodies, making warm, gentle comments about the other's appearance, and with the convertible top down, opening the red Mercedes, to the sun, Kris knew she was an erotic spectacle, against the white leather interior. The not-accidental touch while passing credit card back & forth caused static electricity to jump between them, encouraging them to touch again, both taking advantage of the opportunity to make the touch more caress than either would have expected of themselves. An-di, the attendant, laid her hand on Kris's arm, caressingly sliding it up under the sleeve of the sheer material, they talked about how well the material set off both the lighter and darker skin. An-di told Kris how very attractive her shaved pubis appeared, playing peek-a-boo in the material. When Kris pulled out of the station, she regretted not being able to take the delicious youngster along for the weekend, but she did tell An-di where she was going, and in case An-di could get away... Kris was also surprised how easily she was slipping into a pleasure mode, it having been quite some time since her last pleasure outing. She had done this only two other times this year, setting out to pamper and pleasure herself, thoroughly, selfishly, taking in pleasure, recharging herself, for the months of giving to others, as all women do. This started her down the road of remembering how selfish most men are, how childishly selfish, as if they had a biological block, which prevented them from experiencing the pleasure of giving, freely, without obtaining credit to their account, that could be cashed in, used as a lever... shaking her hair flowing in the breeze of the late morning, tossing the heavy thoughts to the wind, letting her cares, her concerns flow from her mind, as the wind flowed through her hair, as she noted the effect she was having on the many males and a few females she was passing, playing tag with a few other drivers, accepting the admiring looks, as she started recharging herself.

She followed the directions, pulling up to the manned gate, registering, and accepting grounds map & lodging instructions, leaving instructions in case An-di arrived. Kris also accepted the admiring looks and comments about her attire getting her into the mood for the weekend, brushing off the instructions that this was a clothing-optional environment, Feeling Natural being the entire point of the enterprise. She did make a mental note that the masseuse/masseur would apply sunblock as the last event of massage.

Kris drove to her condo, parked, and took her keys, in spite of the gatekeeper's contention that no one would touch anything. It seem'd impossible to believe that his statement that "once you disrobe, giving up all your protections and pretensions, you become ONE with the Community". She entered, noting the long curtains flowing in the breeze, closed her eyes, unclasped her wrapping, letting it fall, catching on her upturned nipples, seemingly touching her everywhere as it moved in the breeze, gently sliding down her body, caressing her buttocks, thighs and legs on it's slow decent to the floor. She stepped sideways, hooking her toe into the material, flipping it onto the bed, and turning, was surprised to find a lovely college-aged girl appreciating her, explaining she was to be Kris's guide for the rest of the day, if Kris desired it. Mary was her name, hair auburn, well proportioned, healthy young body, shaved pubis, above long legs, muscles well defined. It was clear Mary delighted in her body, Kris decided Mary would be her guide today. Mary explained she was experienced in massage, and thought a shower & massage would be a wonderful way to start the weekend. Kris too, thought this a wonderful idea, they both headed to the bathroom, completely tiled, the entire floor sloped into the drain of the shower, and what a shower it was, three feet by five feet, two shower bars, each with four spray dispensers, and six foot handheld shower heads, each set opposing the other, Mary explained the water was heated naturally, from the sun, and taken from the shallow lake above the Community, there is no need to worry about rationing hot water, Mary adjusted both spray bars with the constant temperature controls, both women stepped into the spray, Mary soaped a puffer with body shampoo, gently yet firmly, scrubbing every inch of Kris's firm body, except between the folds of buttocks & vagina, and Kris was VERY pleasantly supprised to feel Mary gently slide her fingers between her buttocks, making Kris put her hands on the shower wall, lean forward, allowing Mary very easy access. Mary took her time, caressing, squeezing the firm flesh, running her finger tips the full length of slit, both sighing at the same time, and them both laughing at the coincidence. Mary applied more shampoo to her hands, pressing her body against Kris's back, reaching around Kris to clean her vaginal area, Kris turned her front away from the shower spray, not wanting to wash the shampoo too quickly from her pussy, wanting Mary to take a good, long time, cleaning her cunt. After about five minutes (an eternity), Mary stepped back, and started rinsing Kris, again paying attention to Kris's bodily openings, which Kris thoroughly enjoyed. Mary allowed Kris to rinse her, but after only a minute of attention to each of Mary's bodily openings, she announced it was time for Kris's massage. Finding no towels, Kris followed Mary into the main room, outside to a massage table under specked sunlight, entering through a grapevine growing across the entire twenty foot square trellis, producing a perfect massage area, light, warm, yet accessible to a gentle breeze.

Mary hugged Kris, telling her she was about to be erotically put to sleep. Kris returned the hug, saying she was already feeling very erotic from the shower, asking if Mary wouldn't rather caress each other? Mary smiled knowingly, gently pressing Kris back onto the massage table, saying "You will get all the caressing you can stand, all things in a gentle, unhurried time, naturally". Kris soon found herself lying on a water mattress, face down, a straw in a delightful iced drink, conveniently placed, the tile floor pattern of no discernible image, yet somehow, the quartz patterns somehow seemed to glow, as if lit from beneath, and mirroring her uppermost thoughts and emotions, erotic, somehow.

Kris felt Mary's hands, first in her hair, massaging the bones, cartilage, her neck, the bones, muscles, feeling the natural flow of motion to her shoulders, ribs, sides, buttocks (Mary worked those buttocks with pleasure), down her thighs, lower legs, and her feet. Oh, her feet! Kris was mesmerized by the erotic feel of pain mixed with intense peace(how can peace be intense?), the effect was pleasure, and Kris felt a lacking, when Mary moved on, up the same leg, worked the buttocks (this time lower towards the vagina, pleasurably), down the other leg, to the foot, where Kris experienced the same mixed feelings of the first foot, then back up to her buttocks again, and Kris raised her pelvis when she felt Mary massage (very gently), the uppermost of vaginal opening, moistening her fingertips from the flow of precum, massaging it into the lips, creases, flesh of her most sensitive areas, moaning with pleasure as Mary gently pressed her oiled finger into the rectum, just the fingertip, Mary rotated her finger slowly, gently, bringing Kris to raise her pelvis even more, as a lusty moan escapes her lips, willing the invasion of her virgin ass, suddenly understanding why some women allow this.

Suddenly, rough toweling is rubbed across her shoulder, harshly breaking the spell, Kris mewls in disappointment, as she feels Mary rubbing the oil off her body, hearing Mary laugh delightedly, saying "Not to worry, my Dear, you are done on this side, I am simply preparing to turn you over, and as you will soon discover, you will like this much, much better".

Thinking she would need all her strength, Kris took a long pull on the cold,sweet drink, feeling it cool her feverish mouth and throat, as she swung her legs down & sat up, streatching, arms above her head, Mary smiling, moving between Kris's spreading thighs, looking into each other's eyes, slowly Mary's hands press to Kris's sides, sliding around, cupping the sides of breasts, gently lifting, thumbs rubbing nipples, lips approach lips, tongue touches lip, retracts, touches again, again, finally licking with just the tip of her tongue, Kris feels her lips toyed with, tentatively licked, pinched, caressed, by Mary's lips, and after an eternity lasting only moments, Kris puts her tongue against Mary's, they slide across one other, then Mary steps back, one hand trails down across Kris's belly, causing contractions all along the way, fingers coming to rest, pressing against Kris's pussy, fingers pressed gently but firmly, straight but pulsing independently, middle finger working it's way into the wet slit in the center of Kris's being, her total attention centerned on the middle finger, pulsing in her slit, the hand raising, coating the upper region with precum, pulsing, finding the clit, pressing, pulsing, then caught between two fingers, wetly being rubbed between the pulsing fingers, then Mary stepping back, a wicked smile on her lips as Kris mewls again, watching the most erotic act of Mary slowly raising her wet fingers to her lips, licking Kris's precum, eyes locked on Kris's eyes locked on Mary's fingers, tongue, Kris starts to rise, to come to Mary, and Mary extends her still wet fingers to Kris's lips, Kris grasps Mary's hand, and licks the precum as if it is the most delishious nourishment available, thirsting for more, more, Kris's other hand starts towards her own pussy for more, Mary grasps Kris's wrist, smiles, presses Kris back onto the massage table, licking Kris's lips, her fingers covering Kris's snatch, saying she will make her feel much, much greater pleasure, if she is allowed to continue, and Kris somehow allows herself to relax, her muscles obey Mary's hands, as Mary positions Kris on the table, both looking into the other's eyes, as Mary caresses her hand across the supine body, legs spread invitingly, Mary's hand cups the Mound of Venus, gently, slowly, pressing the single middle finger into the wet, inviting pussy, curling, Mary leans slightly to allow her finger to impale Kris completely, in her search for Kris's Hot Spot...finding it, watching Kris raise her body like a wave, head first, then neck, breast, ribs, back arching, as Mary slides her fingertip, inside Kris, around and around, and just before Kris comes on her finger, Mary slides her wet finger up, out, over her clit, then placing her finger between Kris's lips, Kris, dissapointed, hungrily licks & sucks her precum off Mary's finger, and Mary leans over, lowering her lips to Kris's lips, they both lick and suck the finger, then the finger is removed, and they lick each other's lips, tongues, and face, everywhere the slick jucices have been, slowing, then stopping, they look into each other's eyes, knowing this is going to be a weekend to remember forever.

Story 04

The weather in Southern California was perfect, Hot and Sunny. As I stepped out of the car the heat swept over me. My nipples and clit began to tingle with anticipation of the days events. I was on a new adventure here in Palm Springs. I was going to my first Alternative Lifestyles convention. I really did not know what to expect, but being the adventurous person that I am, I was most happy to let my new experience begin.

Walking into the hall, I saw many booths with all types of sexy things for sale. The first booth I stopped at sold bikinis. I selected a couple of thongs and went into the dressing room in the corner to try them on. The dressing room was filled several ladies all in various states of dress. I squeezed in and found a spot, and as I did the odor of pussy overpowered my sense of smell. I started to take off my dress and as I did I noticed the lady next to me taking off her swim suit bottom. She gently rolled the bottoms down letting the thong pull out of her ass as she bent over. I couldn't help but notice that her pussy hair hung just a little between her legs. I must have had a lusty look on my face, because she turned and gave me a sensuous smile. She finished putting her clothes on and turned to walk out, when she did, I looked down and saw she had left her panties for me! I could not believe my luck. I reached down, picked them up, sniffed them, then I place them in my purse. When I straightened up, she was peeking at me through the curtains. I mouthed, "thank you," and finished trying on my suits. I don't think she was the only one that saw what I just did!

For the next few hours I strolled up and down the aisles looking at each booth. There were sex products for sale everywhere I looked! Along the way I purchase an 18 inch riding crop that I would use to some lady's ass nice and red. My next purchase was a small vibrating egg with a 2 inch point protruding from one end. This will come in handy when Peggy and I get together later this month. As I rounded the end of this row I came upon a man selling Sex Swings. This is a product that you hang from the ceiling and lay back in to enjoy all kinds of different sex! As I approached this booth, the older man caught my eye and yelled for me to come try out this great product. I smiled and said I would. He held the swing and I set down and then moved back into it. Once I was laying back he first came around behind my head and placed each of my wrists into a fitted slot spreading my arms entirely apart. Then he returned to between my legs and lifted each one into a loop which strapped my ankles tightly into place. While he was working between my legs I noticed a small crowd had gathered behind my head. I made eye contact with several of the peepers and saw that they were enjoying the open access they had on my hairy pits. "Now your all in and the party can begin," the man said! With that he began to move the swing around to face me out towards the crowd. Thank God I had on clean panties because several cameras were flashing away. I don't know how many pictures were taken but I know several were made of my hairy pits and the puss hair hanging out from under my panty! I told the man I would take one of these swings and with that he began to undo my hands. Next he swung the swing back around and was again standing between my legs. "How about a 25% discount," he asked? I said sure why not! With that he knelt down and kiss my hairy pussy through my dampened panty. "Thank you," was his response! I asked him to hold my swing till the end of the show and continued with my shopping.

Near the end of the hall, in the far corner, there was a booth with some sterling silver jewelry. I stopped to see what they had. I saw a piece of jewelry that looked like a hairpin with a blue heart shaped stone on the end. I looked up to see if I could get someone to help me. As I did, I noticed a young girl sitting in the corner with one of the hairpins on. My mouth dropped open, because what I thought was a hair pin wasn't at all, it was in fact a clit clip!

This sweet, innocent looking, girl was sitting with one foot up on the chair, leaving her legs wide open for all to see how sweet her hairless pussy looked with the beautiful puss jewelry (Talk about effective advertising). I tore my eyes from her pussy and looked up to see she also was looking at me. She got up and walked over and said "Can I show up anything?" I asked if she could explain the jewelry and she said yes. She turned around and brought out several different color clips and asked which one would I like. (I thought to myself "yours"), but only said I would like to see the blue one.

I asked if there were instructions that would show me how to put mine on. She just smiled, took me by the hand and said, "I'll give you a demonstration." We walked to a nearby dressing room. When we went in, two other women were in it trying on clothes, but this didn't matter to this young girl. She took charge and asked if she could have the chair that they had their clothes laying on. She then told me to set down and lift up my dress. I did. She said, "you'll have to take off your panties." I started to get up and she said, "I'll help." I lifted up my ass and she slid my panties down my legs and discarded them in the corner. She was sitting in front of me and said "just a moment I want to warm my hands", as she started to blow on her fingers before she touched me. I could not believe that I was sitting in this dressing room in the middle of the convention hall with a sweet young girl getting ready to help me try on some pussy jewelry.

I kept looking at her pussy and she reached down and touched herself telling me that this was the greatest piece of jewelry you will ever buy. "This will keep you aroused all day." she continued. "As you can see my clit is sticking out and the pressure just makes me feel like I am ready to cum. Just touch your bud and it will send tingles through you." I could tell when she touched her bud that she liked the sensation. She reached up and gently touched my legs she told me I had a beautiful hairy bush and she wanted to make sure that she did not pull my hairs while she was putting on my jewelry. I sat back and she reached in and gently pulled on my clit and spread my pussy lips apart. She started to slid the jewelry down around my clit. She did not succeed the first time, so she tried several more times. As she was giving me instructions, she commented on my small lips and hairy pussy again.

I was trying to concentrate on how she was doing it, when she looked up, grinned and said, "I am having a little trouble, because you're getting really wet!". With that, she turned and kissed my inner thigh. I forgot all about the jewelry and took her head and gently pulled it to my pussy. She immediately started licking my juices and sucking on my bud. I was oblivious to all the sounds around me, for all I could feel was the great sensations that were racing through my body as I was being taken to a great orgasm. The next thing I felt were fingers moving around my pussy again. I tilted my head back forward and made eye contact with my seducer! "I'm so glad you came in today. I was hoping to find someone that would really enjoy the help I could offer!" she mouthed. "By the way", she said, "my name is Cindy."

Next Cindy sat back on her legs and said she wanted to take a look at her work. As she did her eyes made their way down my thighs and ended up looking at the ankle bracelet I was wearing. "My god," she yelled! "You even got hairy legs!" With that comment, I lifted my arms and replied, "what do you think of these pits?" Cindy's smile grew even larger as she rose from the floor and came to my side. "I just have to have some of this!" she continued. With that I felt her mouth sucking in and licking my entire hairy pit. "You taste so great!" Cindy said.

Next Cindy asked me how many clips I wanted. I replied only one, but asked if I could have the special instructions and her help putting my jewelry on each day? Her reply was a wonderful deep french kiss. I took that for a yes!

Cindy's kiss was very nice as it had the familiar taste of my pussy and pits. That taste was all I needed to push me over the edge. With that I rose from the chair and took her in my arms. I continued my kiss as she slide down onto the chair. I guess I could have pretended that it was my turn to practice putting on one of these clit clips but all I wanted to do was to ravage her pussy! I know that I should have been disappointed with her hairless pussy but at that moment it just didn't matter. I licked and licked and licked and licked and licked until all of her juices were in my mouth. Besides her cum I found that her clit clip was also in my mouth. I then began sucking on her clip and heard her moans get quite loud. I let the clip slip from my mouth and glanced up to see her smiling.

Sometime later we found ourselves setting on the floor and heard two ladies enter the dressing room. I know we shocked them a little. Even though this was a Lifestyles convention, most of the sex went on back in the rooms! It was time so the three of us adjusted our clothing and left the room. We walked Cindy back over to her sales booth and completed the purchase of this clit clip. The other two people working the booth were smiling at us. I leaned over and have Cindy a kiss good-bye.

I headed back over to the sex swing booth to complete that purchase. This guy was most happy to see me and asked if I would like to try out another swing. The time was running late so I declined. I really enjoyed my Palm Springs adventure. Being a hirsute women is a lot of fun!

Story 05

"Oh, honey, that's so good, baby, so good, " I chanted as my husband's hot dick sliced into my pussy. I was just at the brink when the telephone rang to interrupt us. Still inside me, my husband grabbed it, listened, barked a few words and hung up. Wordlessly, he started fucking me again, very hard, and came quickly.

"Sorry, baby, plant emergency. I have to leave now." He plopped out of me and headed toward the shower. I lay there unsastisfied again with his seed spilling from me. Promising to make it up to me, he kissed me lightly and slipped out of the bedroom.

I showered and came back to bed. I tried to make myself cum with on my fingers, but was unsuccessful. Smelling the coffee that my husband had put on, I grabbed a dressing gown and followed its trail down to my kitchen. Restless and unfulfilled, I roamed around the room with my cup in hand. I needed another warm body to satisfy my needs. Damn my husband--again.

The ringing of my front door bell brought me out of my reverie. Looking through the peep hole, I saw our young female postal worker with a clipboard. An idea formed as I opened the door to her. She was a pretty, petite woman of about 22. She had green eyes and a long black ponytail that protruded through the back of her cap.

"Hi," I said holding the door. "It's a scorcher already, isn't it?"

"It sure is, ma'am. I have a special delivery letter for you. Would you sign here, please?" she said, pushing the clipboard toward me.

I signed and put the letter on the little table at the door without glancing at it. "Would you like something cold to drink, Aly? I have lemonade in the kitchen," I said leading her back.

"That would be wonderful. Thank you."

I handed her a tall glass. "Aly, your uniform is sticking to you. I could

throw it in the dryer if you like. You'll feel so much better when you're dry."

"I'm ok. But thanks anyway," she said between gulps.

"If you're worried about being naked, I can get something for you to wear."

"In that case, I'll take you up on your kind offer. I'll just take my morning break here while my things dry."

"I'll get you a robe. You can strip and put your clothes in the dryer. It's right in there," I pointed. I practically ran up to my bedroom and yanked open the closet door. Wanting something sexy for her, I chose a short, thin silk kimono. Her back was to me when I eased into the room. "Hold out your arms, Aly."

Aly slid into the kimono and tied its sash. She ran her hands over the fabric lovingly. "This feels so good. I've never worn anything so nice."

I rubbed her shoulders and whispered close to her ear, "You look beautiful in it." My hands had a life of their own as they slid from her shoulders and lightly massaged her high young breasts through the silk. Seduction was my motive. Flesh was my goal.

Aly tensed. "Ma'am, I'm sorry, but I'm not into this. I've never done anything sexual with a woman."

I continued to rub her breasts. "Neither have I, Aly. My husband fucked me just this morning. But I need something more. You can help me Aly. Would you? Please?" I turned her around to face me. I released the sash on my robe revealing my nakedness. Looking deep into her eyes, I unsashed hers. Her mouth was open and wet as I took her head, removed the scrunchie to unleash her hair and kissed her deeply. Between kisses I mumbled, "I want to taste your pussy, Aly." I maneuvered her to my butcher block table, sat her own the end, spread her legs and dropped to my knees.

Aly was hot and wet to my touch. My mouth and tongue knew what to do instinctively as I ate her sweet cunt. My tongue traveled over, under, inside her folds. My lips sucked her lips as she came, found her clit and sucked it as she came. My tongue pumped into her as she came. Wet-faced, I resurfaced to kiss her. She cupped my pussy and I finally came, humping her hand, glorying at her touch.

I had Aly move to the center of the table and pull her robe aside. Straddling her, I sucked at her breasts until she could take no more. I spread her legs, spread my own robe, spread myself on her. Lustily, I fucked this sweet girl's pussy with everything in me. We came many times as I hungrily bore my flesh into hers, as we screamed, then whimpered in pleasure.

The timer on the dryer went off just as I was sucking the last of our juices from her pussy. She dressed quickly, kissed me at the door, and left. I noticed the special delivery letter. When I pulled out the contents, I found I had been summoned for jury duty!

Sexually satisfied and very happy at having done the forbidden, I went out in the yard to check a rosebush. I came face to face with a pretty young woman selling magazine subscriptions and invited her in. The day was looking up, indeed!

If you do anything worthwhile today, "do it" with a woman.

Story 06

I just had to get back in that nice neighborhood! Women were home all day, probably bored out of their skulls. Besides, I hadn't reached my magazine quota yet. I could sell to these women and give them something in return. Everybody wins.

Pulling into the neighborhood around 10 a.m., I parked, pulled out my packet and large shoulder purse. I was ready to sell and in pursuit of pussy. A tallish brunette in a green dressing gown stepped out of her front door, heading toward a blooming rosebush. Bingo! When she looked up from the bush, I was right in her face. "Hi, I'm from the university--selling magazine subscriptions. Would you be interested?"

"Sure. I'm always willing to help further education. Come on in."

"Thank you," I said following her in and looking at her rear end swinging.

"I could use some self-help magazines," she said browsing through my samples. "Look here on Cosmo--'How to Make your Man Stay in Bed.' I need that! And this--'What To Do If He Fails You in Bed.' She looked at me and said, "I'll bet a girl as pretty as you doesn't have problems with men."

"No I don't," I smiled at her. "I have men as friends, but I prefer women as lovers."

"Do you now? That's interesting. My husband left me so unsatisfied this morning that I seduced the mail lady. She was my first."

This would be easier than I thought. "Good for you. I saw her as I was coming into the neighborhood! You must have done a great job on her. She was practically skipping down the sidewalk."

"Well, thank you. I just did her by instinct. She was reluctant at first but fell right into line with me when I started to lick her pussy," the lady said.

"How did her mouth feel on you," I asked. "The female mouth is the best, isn't it?"

"Well, we never got that far. I ate her--a lot-- and we screwed on the kitchen table, but I didn't ask her to do it to me. Besides, I don't think she would have anyway."

"Would you like me...you know to...I'd be happy to do you right now. You're a beautiful woman and I'd love to fuck with you." I was heating up at the possibility. "I can make you feel better than any man could."

She pulled her dressing gown aside, lifted her leg to the arm of the sofa and gave me a come hither smile. My next smile was in her shaved pussy. I sucked that entire shaved mound into my hot, wet mouth, tongueing it all over. She shivered as I licked her like a lollipop. I blew on her pussy after I licked away the wetness of my saliva and her juice. She moaned as I pulled her lips apart gently with my teeth, gasped as I erected my tongue and plunged it into her flesh. She held my head close--very close-- to her pussy as she squeezed my tongue inside her. Her ass arched from the sofa as she came three times. Then I started on her all over again--very slowly.

"You are better than any man, sweetheart. I didn't think I was capable of multiple orgasms," she said before she leaned over and kissed me. "My own husband is not even in the same league as you."

"Thank you. I can do other things with you that can make you feel just as good."

"Like what," she said teasingly.

"Like this." I rambled through my purse and pulled out the strap-on dick I'd hoped I would have a chance to use. "Ta daah!" When I held it up, her eyes lit up.

"Let's go upstairs." She pulled me up from the sofa and led me upstairs, the dick in my hand. In her bedroom, pillows were strewn on the floor and the bed unmade. The smell of sex still hung in the air. "Get undressed and let me see you put it on." She removed her gown and sat on the bed.

She watched me intently as I stripped down. Grabbing the dick, I stepped into the apparatus. I inserted my half in my pussy and tightened the straps. The seven inch long realistic, vibrating dick that I would put into her protruded from my pelvis. Wordlessly, I walked to her. She took the dick into her mouth and sucked it.

"Lie back. I'm ready for your pussy." She moved to the center of the bed. I straddled her waiting body, turned the vibrating dicks on low--I would do most of the work myself. I could feel mine circling inside my pussy. After spreading her legs and unnecessarily testing her pussy for wetness, I plunged in.

Her body rose off the bed on impact, driving both dicks in deep. I stopped all movement except kissing her deeply and pressing downward. Gradually, she started moaning and screwing lightly, the vibrations helping move the dicks around in us. The kissing and screwing gained a huge momentum just before we came together. Neither of us could have held back any longer. After a small interval, I pulled out, poising my self above her. Then I started fucking her again, but this time forcefully sliding the dick in deeply and almost pulling out completely. She was going wild beneath me, arms and hair splayed out over the messy bed, screaming for release. Totally in charge here, I let her come over and over, but only after I took her to the edge many times.

"It's a shame to waste all this nice hard dick," she cooed between sucking my breasts.

"What do you mean? Didn't I fuck you good with this? "I said stroking it.

"Yes you did. Better than anyone in my whole life. But I've never had it in the ass. He refuses to do it. Can you?" she asked expectantly. "I have lubricant right here," she said, opening a drawer.

"Can I do it? Can I do it? Just watch me, lady. Give me that tube and get on your hands and knees at the end of the bed," I demanded. I lubed the dick really well and stood behind her. I rubbed her ass relaxing her. Then I bent down and slid my wet tongue between her cheeks before applying a generous amount of the lubricant around her hole. I had to steady her because she trembled as my dick slowly eased its way into her asshole inch by inch. I met resistance, but was persistent until I was fully in. Reminiscent of my time with the tutor, I spoke as she did with me, "Did I do it? You're filled up, aren't you, hot bitch?" I asked and lightly slapped each cheek, thrusting lightly. "Do you like my dick in your ass? What?" Slap, slap. "Of course you do. I'm going to fuck you real hard now. Hold on. Your ass is mine."

Turned on by my own words and her sexy moans, I rammed into this woman with everything in me as she whimpered and begged for more. The vibrators in the dicks had long since lost power, but we were making our own. She put her head down on the bed, leaving her ass in the air for me. I opened her cheeks and watched as the dick slid in and out of her screwing ass, giving her a few of the slaps she seemed to enjoy. She mumbled that she couldn't stop coming, but I kept slapping and pumping. After a while, I let myself cum and eased out of her. Pulling her up by the shoulders, still on her knees, I rubbed my palms over her swollen nipples as I sucked a passion mark on her shoulder, the dick poking at her backside.

"Come here," she said sexily after I undid the straps and removed the dick. "I want to suck your pussy before you leave." I squatted over her face and went to heaven--again.

I was exhausted and sore when I left her house. What an excellent, energetic fuck she was and she bought five subscriptions! God, I love this neighborhood.

   If you do anything worthwhile today, "do it" with a woman.

Story 07

Hair here, hair there, hair everywhere. . ... can this really be the midwest? Being hirsute myself, I have no problem with sharing my hairy pits and legs with anyone that wants to take a look. Over the years I have "come out" with my body hair and most times don't even give a thought letting it show anywhere, any time. Today I have notice more and more women in the midwest are enjoying the natural female body and the sensuous life that being hirsute provides. Let me give you a example of what I mean!

Everytime we go to the Loop or the Central West End we truly enjoy the side walk cafes. While setting outdoors, the sunshine warms my body to a nice wet glow which I find exciting. My sweat begins to flow and with that up goes my arms which allows that nice little summer breeze an attempt to cool me off and dry my dripping pits. Of course, this act gives everyone a clear view of my very visible pit hair. I know there are other women that go flat out crazy over even the slightest glimpse of armpit hair. Then let it be soaked with sweat and watch out, hard-core sex is just around the corner. The best part is that on many outings, women are looking and even questioning me about being hirsute. Trust me, these conversations can become very interesting!

On my last shopping spree to the Loop, Debbie bought me a new belly chain and ankle chain. Once in the little shop we were greeted by a young lady with multiple ear rings and baggy pants that were ready to fall off her butt. She asked what I could be showed and as she pulled our the first tray of stones, she easily showed off her fully breasts. Then after she stood up and placed the tray on the table she raised both arms and pulled her hair back into a pony tail. Her pit hair was full, dark and slightly damp. We made eye contact and the smiles flowed just as our pit hair did!

Well the sales pitch continued and after I picked out the various stones needed to complete the chains, I had to be measured. I thought the young lady helping us would complete this task, but with that a lady slightly older than me came from behind the back counter and pulled out a cloth tape. She told me to pull out my T-shirt from inside my shorts so she could get a good measure.

Her first attempt reaching around me placed her nose within inches of my pit. When I felt her hair brush the bottom of my arm I quickly raised my arms fully over my head. Of course I held onto my shirt which as it traveled along with my arms exposed my breasts. What surprised me a little was that she moved still closer to my fully exposed pit and took her time completing the measurement. I took a few glances from other men and women in the store, but I wasn't sure if they were staring at my pit hair or my tits.

I wondered how she was doing when she knelt down in front of me and said that my shorts were in the way with getting an exact measurement and suggested that I loosen my shorts and let them slip down just a little to expose my full waist. So I unbuttoned the clasp and lowed the zipper. I heard a small gasp escape from her throat as I let my short slip down about three inches. Then I remembered that I hadn't put any panties on this morning and my bush was sharing her right in the face. Next she reached around me again with the tape which brought her nose now in direct contact with my pussy hairs. I knew this could not go much further with everyone still in the store, so I let her finish her measurement and then pulled my shorts back up.

As she stood and turned to write down the chain's length, the younger women called out to me and said I should come to the end of the counter and sit in the chair. As I sat I crossed my legs and found this hirsute sister down on the floor in front of me with her own cloth tape. This little sweetie extended my leg holding it with one hand and stroking my hairs with the other. She attempted to appear professional moving the tape up and down my leg looking for the perfect place for the future ankle chain to lie. She smiled her little smile as she smoothed my leg hairs that had been messed up by her measuring. I knew that I felt a little strange with how I was setting in the chair as I realized that she had shifted the leg being measured slightly up and away from the other. This movement had allowed the gap at the couch of my shorts to extend enough that she had a clear and direct view of my bush. This completed the needed measurements and the sale was done.

It took about two weeks for the chains to be completed before I returned to try the on. With very little surprise, upon my return, I was asked to step into the back dressing room to get the best feel of the new chain's fit. As we walked down the long hallway, I shared with the older women our love of nudism and how I planned to wear these chains on the nude beaches in California. Once we arrived in the dressing room, she pulled closed the antique shear curtain. She next suggested that since I would wear these chains in the nude, I should try them on the same way. So I stepped out of my sun dress and placed it on the chair next to me. There I stood completely naked ready to try on the chains. Once again she was on her knees in front of me reaching around to close its clasp. Her nose felt good against my bush so I quickly placed my hands on her head and pulled her into me. She hooked the chain and nudged me backwards setting me down on the dressing room couch. As if still trying to make the sale, this pussy lapper didn't let up until she had her tongue buried deeply. My legs easily spread allowing her full access to my pussy. It only took about fifteen minutes for her licking to bring me off.

Beginning to regain my normal breathing, I opened my eyes and found the young sales lady peering through the curtain. The smile on her face and the hand in her pants assured me that she had enjoyed the sensuous scene between two women. Once again our smiles joined along with our eyes. I nodded and she walked forward stopping once she was seated upon my lap.

She told me that my ankle chain was finished but first she wanted to give me something else. With that she raised her right arm over her head and leaned forward pushing her hairy pit against my mouth. She smelled wonderful. Her hair was about 2 inches long which I easily drew into my mouth. Her flavors were better than I could have hoped for. It didn't take me long to clean this wonderfully hirsute girl. She then slide off my lap and knelt down to place the new chain around my ankle. As she extended my leg, she began a series of long licks starting at my ankle and ending just below my knee. My leg hairs laid strangely different after her loving tongue left its damping trail. She finished licking my entire leg and then returned to the task of placing the ankle chain in its place.

Both ladies then suggested that I stand and look at myself in the dressing room mirror. I must admit that the chains looked great. I looked pretty good too after all of the attention I had just received. I must return to this store again. Yes, this is the midwest.

Hair here, hair there, hair everywhere. . . .can this really be the midwest? Yes, Dorothy, there are hirsute women in the States and some of them live in the midwest. As my friends know, I have no problem with sharing my hairy pits and legs with anyone that wants to take a look. Life is good and not having to shave is my business and mine alone. Not only does it save me a lot of time but to be totally honest, its a real sexually rush when men and women can't get enough of my hairy body! Here's an example of what I mean.

One Saturday night, Debbie and I went dancing at a strip club in East St Louis, MO. We met two other sexy couples there around 11 pm. This is a fun place to party since on Saturday nights they feature a special dance area for the sexy couples that want to dirty dance.

Our evening began with the six of us dancing in a close circle facing and holding each other. Since the DJ plays three song groups, we had time to begin the night's fun. I guess the best way to describe it is to think of an orgy! Each person's hands are exploring someone else's body. A sexy time is had by all caressing breasts, pusses, asses. Now remember that we are not out there alone. Many other couples (straight & gay) are on this dance floor doing the same thing. Sexy bodies everywhere you look on the dance floor and along the edges you can even see couples fucking. Also remember that while we are doing all of this, six dance stages are presenting male and female strippers. So the tone of the evening is very much set. By the third song I found myself getting so turned on that I went to my knees to eat Debbie's pussy. Of course while I was busy enjoying myself, Debbie was also busy grouping tits and ass. After Debbie enjoyed a good cum, I swung around and started in on Michelle. I finished off Michelle just as the last song stopped. The six of us returned to our table to enjoy the drinks.

Since this is a strip club and it was Sexy Couples night most women were wearing very little at all. This also help set the tone for a truly fun filled evening. As the six of us were setting there talking, another woman from a neighboring table stepped up beside me and took my hand leading me to the dance floor. The song had just begun so she did too. This woman was strong and was touching me as if she was my doctor doing a complete checkup. She began by reaching around and rubbing my pussy. Once it was sopping wet, she licked the juice from one hand and moved the other to my ass. I was glad that she took it easy and only caressed my ass and didn't rape it. Now we were into the second song and her hands moved back around to me tits. Of course while she was feeling my tits I was fingering her pussy and rubbing her ass. I remember feeling lost in this moment between two women, but I became alert once again as she moved her hands from my tits to my hairy pits.

By now they were nice and wet which helped her fingers slide around. She also pulled lightly on the long hairs as if measuring their length. Since I was still facing out to the others on the dance floor they were getting a full show of all the attention being paid to my hirsute body. The DJ was into the moment too because I heard him announce he was seeing some really heavy lez action on the couples dance floor and didn't want it to end so he was going to keep the music going right on into the next three songs. With that this woman continued her use of my body still feeling my pits. She then moved around me enough to begin licking my right one. Before her tongue went to work her nose was enjoying the delicious pit odor that had built up. Surprised I felt my left arm being raised above my head and another tongue began licking my left pit. Two women at once were enjoying my hirsute body. This felt really good, but it only got better. Within a couple of minutes, a third woman came up to me and shoved her hairy pit against my mouth! This women must of had some German family lines because her pit hair was very full and black. It too was extremely wet with sweat but this made my sexy snack all the better! This four-way must have gone on for some time because the music finally ended. We all exchanged kisses, several with some really good tongue. Once again I was taken by the hand and lead back to our table. One last kiss there and this wonderful woman was gone.

I grabbed my drink and told Debbie that I needed to pee and I would be right back. When I got to the toilet, there was the normal line. As it moved up past the mirrors I thought I would fix my hair. As I raised my hands to my head, my eyes dropped to my hairy pits. Yes still damp and still there! The young woman standing next to me gasp and smiled. Our eyes made contact for the longest moment. Then she raised both of her arms and showed me her hairy pits. She said she had just begun to let her hair grow after seeing Drew B's hairy pit in a Harper Bazaar magazine. Although only about a half an inch long this young woman's pit hair was very dense. Next another women came up from behind and said she had seen the activity on the dance floor. That brought another big smile to my face. She stood between us and asked to sample both of our hairy pits, you know like a taste test challenge. We both raised our arms and submitted to this request. Now most women not pissing were watching this little show. A few others commented about our sexy pit hair and one additional women spoke up saying "me too"! Our eyes shifted in the large mirror and saw her arms up in the air showing off her hairy pits. Hands down this woman easily won this hirsute contest! Her hair ran about four inches in each direction from the center of her pit. Well the line finally began to clear and it was my turn. The young woman came out of her stall and held the door for me. I quickly walked in and dropped my panties. I started to pee an entire evening's worth of drink. As my stream hit the water, I realized the young woman was still holding the stall door open and was watching me pee. I looked up at her saw her open mouth begin to move. "Could we dance." she ask? "Sure sweetheart," I said taking her by the hand.

Back on the dance floor we caressed each other's body dancing our dance. Although we did feel each other's pit hair, our fingers were mostly kept busy in each other's pussy. Both were still wet with pee and became wetter from our little pulses. Her kiss was sweet and sincere. After the song she followed me back to our table. There I introduced her to Debbie. More drinks were ordered and the evening continued. As we talked, this young woman asked if she could see me again. She continued on by saying that although she was letting her hair grow, her mom and sister thought it was stupid. I could tell she was hurt and was looking for some support. I gave her a hug and told her that she could come visit any time and if she needed to she could even spend the night.

I must have danced another ten dances with various women before it turned 4:30 a.m! Well that was late enough so Debbie and I gave our kisses to our friends and headed home. We go to this club alot. Yes, this is the midwest.

She was tanned and very good looking with the longest dark-brown-hair that I had ever seen. Most everyone in the bar was staring at her as she enjoyed her drink. Although this was my first time in the particular bar I was beginning to feel that this girl was some kind of a regular. So there she sat with a skirt so short that it left nothing to the imagination and a blouse so open that even a blind person could read her nipples like a braille letter. I had just ordered my second beer when the lights started to dim and the house music came up a lot louder. With that I turned my attention towards the back of the room and saw a very sensuous lady pick up the microphone and announce the first act of the evening. "Ladies and Gentlemen, please give a big round of applause for our first act tonight . . . Here is Becky, our most exotic of exotic dancers!"

With a flash the house lights came completely down and the bright spot light shown with a new brilliance directly on the center of the stage illuminating Becky in the cutest little plaid school-girl dress that I had ever fantasized over. Just as I had seen a hundred times before this dancer worked her body with precision hitting every note in the song being played. Becky's hips went right and then left, then she squatted down and smacked her ass lightly on the polished stage floor. Wow, that spread gave me and everyone else in the audience a really good look a her very, very hairy pussy. Her pussy hair was so long and so thick that I was surprised that it wasn't braided. Now I have seen many a stripper but usually they keep their panties or g-string on until the end of their dance. But not Becky, this exotic dancer shoved her hairy nest out to the edge of the stage within inches of the lucky sex hound's nose sitting on their seat edge.

The song continued on and Becky's dancing became even more erotic. She began to trade-off her squatting for a sexy peep show of her 34C breasts. A flash here and a flash there, little by little there was nothing left to anyone's imagination. With her tits already out of the bag [so to speak] Becky began to slowly lift her tiny halter top over her head. Since the bright spot was focused directly on her, not a sole in the entire bar missed this hirsute honey's hairy armpits. They both jutted out as if they were each its own pussy patch just waiting to be ambushed! Now with her halter top off Becky focused upon continuously showing off her bushy armpit play-grounds. The spot light man helped all he could by keeping the light tightly focused and aimed directly where everyone's eyes were already riveted - Becky's hairy pits. The longer Becky danced the more eye contact she and I made. The more she looked at me the more I looked back and smiled as if my life depended on it. I could tell that she was getting a little confused. I mean here I was watching her as if she was the only lady in the world and yet I wasn't setting their at the edge of the stage with the other dollar bill people taking their shots when every possible. Finally her dance song came to an end and Becky left the stage with all of the class like the lady she was.

As I was drinking down beer number four and was thinking I was pretty much through a fun filled evening. Suddenly, and quite unexpectedly, I felt a hand softly touching my shoulder. I quickly turned around and found Becky standing there with a that same big smile on her face. Before I could say anything, she popped out with, "I must ask you why you were smiling so I me?" I answered her back saying, "I was smiling because she was the prettiest and most professional dancer I had every seen." Then I continued my praise by saying, "Although I had seen hundreds of exotic dancers, not until tonight had I seen the ultimate of all dancers!" "Becky", I said, "when I saw that you were a hirsute lady, and saw how proud you were of your hirsutness, I knew that that no other dancer could hold a candle!"

By now Becky had taken me by the hand and had lead me off to a private table. Once there we continued to talk. While our conversation continued, Becky took a moment to slip off her halter top once more. We both knew that she didn't need to do that to show me her hairy armpits so I figured there must be something else that see wanted me to see. Well, fellow hair lover, there was! Right in front of me was Becky's perky 34C tits and each of them had beautiful little dark hairs growing around the nipples. As you can imagine, a big smile came back to my face! Becky told me that she had never had anyone complement her so on her hairiness and in fact, she had had several of the other dancers tell her to shave off that ugly hair! She went on the say how good I had made her feel and that she was so happy to meet someone that really appreciated her.

We continue to talk and finally Becky put a finger to my lips and told me to quite talking. She then smiled once more and said she wanted to do something for me to show her appreciation for my kind and very positive hirsute words. "How about a kiss?" Becky asked. Trust me on this one, I was ready, no more than ready. But at that moment, I asked Becky if she would allow me to nuzzle my nose into both of her hairy armpits and suckle at her sweet forests? Becky said that she had no problem with my request, but said that I would first have to bury my face into her pussy mound. Of course I quickly told her that I was at her total service and with that I got down on the hands and knees and began to work my way towards her love mound.

My trip to hairy pussy heaven didn't take long! Once I arrived I was rewarded with a the most tasty flow of woman drink which was made from a combination of sweat, pee, and cum. While I was feasting at her sex fountain, Becky told me that while she danced, she would enjoy several orgasms and during these orgasms she would leak out a little of her piss. Although I could hear her talking I was very much consumed with the matter [pussy] at hand and did my best to bring her to a full orgasm. It only took a little bit longer for Becky to get off and once she quite squeezing my head with her thighs, I stood up and returned to my chair. Becky leaned forward and gave me a big wet kiss and used her tongue to removed some of the excess pussy juice from around my lips. Then she sat back in her chair and raised her arms over her head and said, "Dive in and eat my pits!" This is what I was waiting for. Here in front of me was two heavily forested armpits which were both dripping with sweat. I didn't want to wait any longer so I leaned forward. First to her right armpit and then to the left. I kissed and licked both of them with even more enthusiasm than I had exhibited when I was eating out her pussy.

Becky began to talk again but this time she was not talking to me. Two of the other dancers had come by to see what was going on. Becky told them that I was a lover of hirsute women and that I was very busy paying homage to her. Since she was satisfied that I had made love to her dirty pits with all of the sensitivity that she demanded, she pushed my head back and told me to move around to the back of her chair. While I got down on my hands and knees Becky turned her chair around and now was leaning over the back with her arms and had scooted her ass almost completely off of the chair seat. Now I felt like some ancient Roman soldier looking at her hairy ass! You know the old saying, "I came, I saw, and I conquered!"

Well, I not sure who conquered whom, as Becky took a second from talking to her two friends to reach back and with both hands, spread her ass cheeks and say, "eat my ass clean!" With that one of her friends moved to her side and squatted down so she could see my tongue lapping at this hairy feedbox. Becky's asshole was smelly and dirty [no shower during this day for sure] but I continued to eat, as I was told to, licking her asshole and ass cheeks to a "just-showered state" of cleanness. My ass eating continued for about fifteen-minutes at which time Becky told me to stop and to pull up a chair and set next to her. As soon as I sat down, Becky reached around me and gave me a big hug and a really nice French kiss. One of her friends was just returning from the bar and brought us each a drink. Almost at the same time the three ladies all said, "we thought you could use something to wash down your meal." With that we all laughed.

Next the other two other dancers began to talk to me about spending some time with each of them. Of course, I ask them both how hairy they were and they said. . . Well, that's another story!

Part 04

I picked Michelle up around 8:00 a.m. and we went straight to the LADY'S DAY OUT, which is a little out of the way boutique that specializes in pampering women in the most creative ways. We walked in their front door and was quickly greeted by Kitty, the shop's owner. Kitty gave us both a hug and a simply, but sensuous, kiss on the lips. I remember wondering that if this was how the day was to begin where was it going to end?

Michelle and I had planned this day as a treat to both of us since we had been working so hard. We were both looking forward to this special day at this uptown location, where each lady is served a glass of wine upon their arrival and then is helped to undress in preparation for their full day of "personalized" body treatments. Some of their "treatments" included; a full body message, which then lead to a soak in a special hot tub, which was followed by deep cleaning enema, a pedicure, a facial, and a wonderful breast message. Oh yes, they also offered a hair cut and style if you desired one. If that wasn't enough, this special day also included a sexy lingerie show, lunch, an afternoon tea, and champagne & wine sampling though out the day. God, I love being a woman!

After spending the last hour looking over every inch of my body, Michelle had become extremely entranced with me. I could tell that Michelle was enjoying watching me receive the full body treatment, but seemed some what surprised to see how many of the shop's employees were coming in and out of our room, all seeming to leave their eyes lingering just a little too long in the direction of my hirsute body.

Michelle became very turned on watching the masseuse rub her hands over my entire body. Mary, the masseuse, was obviously very much in tough with my sexuality and was herself very excited with all of my body hair. Michelle watched Mary's fingers touch and embrace my hairy arm pits, my hairy pussy, my hairy ass crack and then move back up to tweak the little hairs growing out of my tits. I lost track of Michelle for just a few minutes but was brought back to the moment as she joined in with Mary to bring me over the edge delivering the first [I hoped] of many orgasms for this day.

After we all caught our breath, Mary took Michelle and I by the hand and lead us down the walk-way to the hot tub room. Once there we both slide into this wonderfully warm pool and found ourselves smiling like there was no tomorrow. Mary returned with a full goblet of wine for both of us. While we scooted down into the bubbling water, Mary knelt down between us and poured in a small bottle of oil to help soften our skin.

The next part of the day was quite out of the ordinary for me as Michelle and I found ourselves laid out on a strange looking table with all kinds of hoses strung out above it. Val, the enema technician, moved softly around the table as she prepared the hoses. "I have selected a very special nozzle setup for you two," said Val. With that, she opened the cabinet next to our table and picked out a large tub of rose scented lubricant. The next thing I felt was Val gently slipping her middle finger up inside my ass. "This will help your both relax and get ready for this dual nozzle setup." Val continued by saying, "Susan, I can't help but notice your hairy asshole. I bet all of the girls go crazy over this furry little love button!" I think Val took her sweet time administrating the lubricant and the enema but it finally came to an end [pun intended]. Val left Michelle and me alone while we used the antique bed pans to expel our internal fluids.

Feeling better now, and much more empty inside, Michelle and I left the enema room and headed over to the sunny garden room. As we walked inside, we found an assortment of cheeses and crackers alone with finger sandwiches, vegetables, and salad. Best of all there was a wonderful selection of wine just waiting to be enjoyed. We relaxed for over an hour enjoying the food and drinks and each other. We actually found some time that we could spend making out before we were whisk off by Kitty to our next adventure.

Next we found ourselves setting beside a beautiful wooden run-way. As we enjoyed the sweat glasses of champagne Kitty walked up to the stage and announced the first of several models. Each one was more attractive than the other, each also seemed to wear something a little more sexy for their part of the show. Just when I thought our day was beginning to end, Kitty ask us both if we would like to take our try at modeling.

We both jumped at the chance and were led into the dressing room. I wasn't surprised with all of the "special" help we received changing into the sexy lingerie. Kitty picked out a bright red camisole and handed it to two of the models. They told me to lift my arms over my head. As I did they both began to caress my hairy pits. What a wonderful love they made to me. Next I found Kitty kneeling in front of me. I heard her tell me to lift my leg. Thinking that she wanted me to step into a sexy pair of dance panties I raised my leg. But as I did Kitty began to lick my pussy hair. She ate me so deeply that her face seemed to disappear into my hirsute mound. After what seemed like forever, I regained my senses and saw that three other models were having their way with Michelle, I remember thinking how happy I was that there was no prejudice at this establishment.

   Feeling totally renewed, Michelle and I found ourselves alone once again. Smiling at each other we chatted for a few moments recounting the various adventures of the day. "Are you about ready to head home?" I asked Michelle. She answered with a very soft yes. We both had found the special day that we had come in search of. It was now 4:30 p.m..

Extreme Erotica (FF, Femdom)
3 Erotic & Steamy Story Novellas for Adults
Alannah Kieran

All Rights Reserved. No part of this publication may be reproduced in any form or by any means, including scanning, photocopying, or otherwise without prior written permission of the copyright holder. Copyright © 2020

This book is entirely a work of fiction. The names, characters and incidents portrayed in it are the work of the author's imagination. Any resemblance to actual persons, living or dead, events or localities is entirely coincidental.

Story 01

Chapter 01

The applause swelled as I stepped up to the rostrum to accept the award, and my only regret was that my mother and father were not there to share the moment. While I gave my short, prepared speech, I scanned the audience hoping to see my sister, but, despite her promise, it looked as if she had not made it.

It had been a long day, and, as soon as it was polite to do so, I slipped away and took a cab back to my hotel. My mind was still buzzing as I unlocked the door to my room and let myself in, but I was jolted back to reality.

It was not so much the surprise of finding a woman on the bed as the fact that she was gloriously naked with her hand purposefully between her legs. I took in the situation at a glance. The woman had propped up the pillows to make herself comfortable and watched a porn film featuring two German pneumatic blondes who were theatrically fondling one another's breasts.

For a moment, I remained frozen in the doorway, unsure how to react, but then, without missing a beat, the woman turned to me.

"I think you have the wrong room."

"I'm dreadfully sorry!"

Without thinking, I left the room, closing the door behind me, but on checking my pass card, I found that the door number tallied. More confused than ever, I took the lift back downstairs and looked for the concierge.

The desk advised that two keys had been requested for the room, and I, in turn, confirmed that the second one was for my fiancé, who would be joining me the following day. I was ushered through to the bar, where I was presented with a complimentary drink. While the problem was resolved, I was now concerned about her luggage, which had been sent on.

Less than a quarter of an hour later, and with profuse apologies, the concierge escorted me back to the room, which looked pristine. The bed was remade, and a vase of fresh flowers lent a heavy scent. My suitcase, seemingly untouched, stood by the bed.

As I showered, I wondered what had happened and who the woman was, but I was too tired to give it much thought. I slipped into bed and fell asleep almost immediately.

I had set aside the following morning for sightseeing, and to this end, I went down for an early breakfast. I was sipping coffee and catching up on the news when I was tapped on the shoulder.

"Good morning. I guess I owe you an apology."

I was shocked to be confronted by my surprise visitor. The previous night I had wondered if she might have been a hooker who had taken advantage of an empty room. Seeing her now, in an expensively tailored two-piece business suit complete with a Louis Vuitton document case, I realized that I was very mistaken.

She was startlingly attractive. She had close-cropped black hair framing an oval face where her dark eyes shone brightly beneath a pair of perfectly sculpted eyebrows. Her whole appearance screamed high maintenance. Her make-up was immaculate, and, when she smiled, her full red lips opened to reveal Hollywood perfect teeth.

"That's quite alright. These things happen."

She put out a hand.

"Liana."

Without thinking, I took it, and it only was as I felt its warmth that I was confronted with an unsettling image of her as she had been just a few hours previously.

"Would you think it terribly presumptuous of me if I joined you? I'm meeting a business colleague here."

She took a seat opposite, and I was lost for anything to say. In that end, I settled for something foolish.

"Liana, that's a nice name."

"French. My mother was from Limoges."

For the next few minutes, she seemed content to talk about herself, and, despite my initial reservations, I found myself warming to her. She had a manner of speaking that was almost conspiratorial, as though she were divulging secrets to a best friend, and her slightly accented English added further charm.

When she found out that I was alone for the day, she asked if I would care to join up for lunch; her meeting was to be a couple of hours at most, after which she was at a loose end.

I would have refused her offer in the normal course of events, but ignoring my better judgment, I accepted.

For want of anywhere better, we met up in the hotel coffee shop. For an hour, I sat entranced as she regaled me with stories about her job as a clothes buyer for a major department store; it made my career in academia seem so dry by comparison.

After lunch, she invited me up to her room to see some of the samples she had been telling me about and, with childhood memories of dressing up games in mind, I tagged along.

Her room was in a new annex, a long way from mine, and, as we walked together, I wondered idly how the previous evening's mistake had occurred.

"What do you think of this?"

She was holding up an emerald green brocaded top. It was not the sort of thing I would typically wear, and my dislike must have shown.

"You're not seeing it properly. You have to see it on."

Her enthusiasm was infectious, but I was surprised as she quickly unfastened her blouse and threw it onto the bed. Underneath, she was wearing a half cup bra with lace trimming, which hovered between pretty and provocative. Her breasts were a similar size to mine at 34C, and I wondered if I dare ask where she had bought it.

She put on the top and, on her, with her dark coloring. It looked stunning, but she could see that I was still dubious.

"Here, try it."

She took the top off and handed it to me.

"I couldn't."

"Of course you can. Don't be silly."

I took it from her, and instinctively looked towards the bathroom, but she had had no qualms about undressing in front of me, and I did not want to appear prude. I took off my blouse, revealing my altogether more modest underwear, and put it on.

Standing in front of the mirror, I was surprised at how nice it looked on me, and I turned a shoulder to get the full effect.

"That is so you...but wait, try wearing it like this."

As I stood there, she came up behind me and reached around to undo the buttons,

She slipped it off my shoulders and, before I realized what was happening, she had unfastened my bra.

I covered myself instinctively, but she was holding out the top for me to put back on.

I never go braless, but it felt so comfortable. It seemed to mold and supported my breasts and, while my natural state would not be obvious to a casual observer, it brought the top alive in a new way.

As I continued to preen myself in front of the mirror, I realized that I had a problem. The movement of the fabric had brought my nipples to an embarrassing prominence. For a second or two, I conjured up an image of myself wearing this and little else while my fiancé looked on with an expression of pure lust on his face.

Liana stood expectantly, waiting for me to take it off again, and I felt the color in my cheeks heighten but, if she noticed my state of arousal, she contrived to ignore it. Over the next half an hour, we tried on more outfits, and she had no reservations about stripping right down to her panties in front of me. The truth was I felt intimidated by her; she was a beautiful woman with self-confidence to spare, and it was as if I were standing in her shadow.

Having taken off yet another dress, I stood again in just panties and stockings, resisting the urge to cover my breasts. The tension must have been obvious to her because she took hold of my shoulders and turned me towards the mirror.

"You are a very beautiful woman but the real art is to exude it."

She smiled at my puzzled expression.

"You know one of the tricks I use? Imagine you are someone else. Not someone outrageously different, perhaps someone famous, with similar features. It gives you a focus, makes you aware of how you carry yourself. You, you remind me of that actress in the film Grease."

"Olivia Newton-John?"

"That's her."

She held my hair behind my head, imitating a ponytail, and I could see something of a likeness. I shared her blonde hair, blue eyes, and high cheekbones, and I had always thought that I looked younger than my twenty-eight years.

I was still contemplating the image when she shocked me by reaching through my arms and cupping her hands under my breasts.

"She can't compete with you in this department."

She held their weight for a couple of seconds and then released me, but it was time enough for my nipples to react.

Feeling flustered, I grabbed for my clothes and quickly put them back on. I made my excuses, saying that I had to get ready for my fiancé's arrival, and Liana began tidying up.

She saw me to the door and thanked me profusely for lunch.

"Wait."

As I stood in the doorway, she grabbed a carrier bag and began stuffing it with bits and pieces from her wardrobe.

"Free samples, cosmetics mainly, I get given them all the time."

She was being overly generous and must have sensed my unease.

"Please, you would be doing me a favour, I couldn't take them all back with me."

I got back to my room and was surprised to see how late it was. Any thoughts about further sightseeing were set aside as I prepared for Daniel's arrival. As I showered, I reflected, not for the first time, on our relationship's odd nature. We had been together for four years and got engaged after three. In reality, we had probably been in the same country together, at any one time, for something less than twelve months; his career as a field archaeologist and mine as a lecturer conspired to keep us apart.

Even this meeting was contrived. Daniel was on his way to the University of Columbia from Syria, but he had engineered a stopover so that we could be together for one night. Fortunately, his flight was on time, and we were able to meet up at the restaurant as planned.

It had been two months since I had last seen him, and his ruggedly handsome face looked even more weathered, making him appear older than his thirty-four years. We brought each other up to date over the meal, and then we adjourned to the hotel for a furious bout of lovemaking. As usual, after a long period of abstinence, he came quickly but, much to my surprise, I was able to climax with him, and I gave him no respite. I teased him back to readiness and rode on top of him until I reached a second orgasm and was disappointed when he could not manage a third.

He fell asleep, leaving me to ponder my wantonness, and I guiltily concluded that it was the result of the frisson that I had been feeling all afternoon from being with Liana. This set off an awkward train of thought, as I was in no way attracted to other women, and I found that I could not get to sleep.

I picked up my book, thinking that I would drift off after a page or two when I remembered the bag of goodies that she had thrust upon me. I had not had time earlier but now felt quite excited. I retrieved the bag and sitting cross-legged on the floor. I gently emptied it in front of me. It was mainly cosmetics, but there were also some nicely wrapped panties and a pretty scarf. I picked it up to see it better and gasped audibly. Underneath it was an expensive-looking vibrator.

It was large, much larger than my modest model, but, more disturbingly, it was not new. It was fashioned from black plastic, which had dulled with use and looked like an old favorite. I stared at it for a few seconds, unsure what to do, and then, tentatively, I picked it up between my fingertips.

I had a fleeting image of Liana using it, and for reasons I could not explain to myself, I brought it closer to my face and took a furtive sniff. Appalled at my behavior, I was relieved to find that it smelt of nothing at all, and I quickly thrust it back into the carrier bag.

I collected the other gifts together, and, having put them to one side, I crept back into bed. Before long, I drifted off into a fitful sleep only to be rudely awakened by a six a.m. alarm call.

We barely had time for showers and breakfast before the taxi arrived to take Daniel to the airport, and I was left with a familiar empty feeling as I waved him off.

Back in the room, I began to pack ready for my afternoon flight, but I was left in a quandary as to what to do with the vibrator. I could have thrown it away and pretended that I had never seen it, but then there was a possibility that Liana would realize what had happened and might ask for it back.

In the end, and unusually for me, I decided to be bold. I went to her room and rang the bell. There was no immediate answer, and I was about to go away again when the door opened. Liana was standing there in the hotel's complimentary robe, obviously having just come from the shower.

"Oh, I'm sorry."

"No, don't be silly, come on in."

I followed her inside and sat down on the edge of the bed. With a broad smile, I handed her the bag.

"I think you may have been more generous with your freebies than you thought."

I expected her to be embarrassed, but she looked in the bag and took out the vibrator as though it were the most natural thing in the world.

"I thought that must have been what happened. Did you try it?"

I was caught off balance by the casual way in which she said it.

"No, of course not."

"You should have done. It's the best. Boy, did I miss it last night."

As she spoke, she used the robe to towel herself, seemingly unaware that she was affording me a view of her naked body.

"This hotel has a great porn channel."

She must have seen the shock register on my face.

"Oh, come on, you must have taken a peek."

The truth was I had not. Once or twice, my curiosity had gotten the better of me in the past. I found nothing arousing about the manufactured sex that was presented.

"It's not my thing."

"Well congratulations to you if you can get off on your own fantasies."

Her smile became just a little mischievous.

"What does it for you? A threesome? Two guys or a guy and a girl?"

"I don't need that. I have Daniel."

"You're telling me that a feisty girl like you doesn't fantasize?"

She moved closer to me in that conspiratorial way of hers.

"I have a regular boyfriend but that doesn't stop me indulging in a few flights of fancy. In this industry I get propositioned a lot, particularly the girls, you'd be surprised how many of the top models are lesbians."

I thought back to the film that I had caught her watching and started to feel distinctly uncomfortable, but she continued unabashed.

"It's not that the girls aren't tempting I just need a little something extra."

She was now right beside me, almost whispering in my ear, and I could feel her body heat.

"You know what really turns me on?..."

She said it quietly that I turned my head slightly to hear better only to find myself looking directly at her breasts, which had spilled from the robe altogether.

"...I like the idea of making a straight woman go down on me."

I sat immobile, my eyes slightly widened, hardly believing what I was hearing.

"Just imagine. She would be a little unsure at first, a little clumsy perhaps, but I would direct her, telling her just what I like."

She was hovering over me, and I felt like a mouse caught in the shadow of a hawk. I could see the slight dampness on her skin, and I could smell the citrus tones of shower gel.

"What do you think?"

Her voice was husky, almost mesmeric, and the question had so many connotations.

She shifted slightly, and the edge of the robe caught on my knee, opening it further. It was now like a curtain hiding us from the rest of the world, she naked and me staring mutely at the deep pit of her navel.

It was all so wrong. I knew myself to be assertive, self-assured, and, to the outside world, an authority figure, but I sat there awestruck. I wanted no part of what she was suggesting, but she wove a spell around me.

I braced myself to get up, laugh it off, and wish her luck with her fantasy, but I could not move. My world was bounded by her robe and the naked perfection of her body, which moved inexorably closer.

I turned my head to one side. Was it my fault? Had I led her on in some way, and Would my refusal hurt her?

Even as these thoughts crowded in on me, I felt the touch of her skin against my cheek. I remained motionless, listening to her heartbeat, which seemed so much more controlled than my own, and then she leaned forward slightly, enveloping me further, and I could feel the weight of her breasts pressing down on my head.

I was cocooned in warm, comforting darkness, and then I felt her hand stroking my hair with a soothing gentleness. It seemed natural to rest my face against the warm softness of her stomach, and I felt my eyelids droop.

She continued with longer strokes following my hair down across the back of my neck, and I bowed my head the better to enjoy the wonderful sensation. In my mind, I was ticking off seconds, telling myself that after the count of ten, I would get up and pull myself together, but ten became twenty and then thirty. The rhythmic caress disguised the fact that, by tiny degrees, her hand became heavier, and, millimeter by millimeter, I was slipping down the wall of her stomach.

I felt a tickling sensation on my nose and came to with a start. I was poised at the border of her damp pubic hair, and the smell of citrus was underscored by something altogether spicier. I would have jerked but, anticipating my reaction, she stilled her hand to keep me in place and stroked behind my ear with the edge of her thumb.

Very gently, I pushed upwards, testing the resistance, but she did not move. I wanted to tell her that she had misread the situation, but, in some bizarre way, it seemed unladylike to speak while facing the floor.

For a few seconds, we remained static, held in tension, but then her other hand came into view. Her fingernails were immaculately manicured and varnished a deep red. She flexed them in front of my face before grazing them through her nest of curls.

The effect was immediate. A rich, unmistakable scent assailed my nostrils. On one level, I was appalled, but on another, my unconscious mind-forged the association with my memories of arousal, and I felt a warm, undesirable, tingling between my legs.

As I watched her fingers slowly rubbing over her mound, I was almost mesmerized, and I was slow to react when she suddenly cupped my mouth and nose with her hand. I gasped in surprise, but, in so doing, I breathed her essence deep into my lungs.

My natural reaction was to open my mouth to draw a fresher breath, but, as I did so, she slipped two wet fingers between my lips, and my mouth was filled with a taste that was both tart and sweet.

I knew my smell, every woman does, but I did not know my taste. Daniel had often tried to get me to go down on him after we had made love, but I always had steadfastly refused. The truth was that I found no pleasure in the act, but I would do it for his sake as long as he had showered beforehand.

Now I was left to wonder if this was how I tasted; this earthy richness that had my tongue instinctively lapping for more as though it were doughnut sugar on my lips.

At that moment, I tried to regain a grip on reality. I braced myself to push her away, but she anticipated me as easily as if I were a child. With a gentle strength, she pushed my head a couple of inches lower, and, at the same time, she removed her fingers from my mouth.

I was now pressed to her sex, and I was amazed at how coarse it was. Ever since my pubic hair grew, I have loved to run my fingers through it, not in an obvious attempt to stimulate myself but simply to enjoy the silky texture.

I supposed I had reasoned that all women were alike, but Liana's sex was framed by a starkly delineated black Mohican of tight curls that had an almost masculine quality.

"Lick me."

She said it quietly but assuredly and the words, cutting through the enshrouding stillness, worked to even greater effect.

I did not want to do it, and I was reminded of my mother's hatred for "those women," but some devil within me was asking, "who would ever know?".

Like a child eating an illicit sweet beneath the blankets, I tentatively put out my tongue. Her curls seemed to resist me as I pressed uncertainly only to yield suddenly revealing the frightening prospect of her labia.

My sex is almost childlike, and it could in no way prepare me for what I now confronted. Her outer lips were long corrugated folds of flesh clutched at my tongue as if drawing me into a trap. I wanted to free myself but, in that same instant, I caught the taste of her.

The taste on her fingers had been just a hint: now I was drinking from the font. She was hot, syrupy, and the ripeness of it suddenly filled my mouth in a way that no fine wine could ever have done. With vulgar greed, I plunged deeper and closed my eyes as I found the wellspring.

"That's a good girl. Suck me.."

I needed no bidding. I closed my mouth over her sex and drank deep, literally slurping juices through her matted hair. I was like an animal, and she petted my head knowingly. I was overtaken by madness. I had a dim sense of my arousal, but, at that moment, my only concern was to get my tongue deeper.

She indulged my need for a little longer, and then, twining her fingers in my hair, she gently pulled me away. At some point, I had come to my knees, and she stood before me and slowly removed the robe altogether.

Safe now, in the knowledge that she had brought me to an exact state, she moved around me, and it was her turn to sit on the edge of the bed.

I had sat uncertainly, maybe afraid, but her demeanor, by contrast, was assured, almost regal as she opened her legs wide.

"You've had your fun. Now it's my turn. I want you to lick me...nice long strokes."

She made everything seem skewed. I was almost left feeling that I had assaulted her, and now it was incumbent upon me to make amends. I shuffled round to face her, but there was no longer the comfort of darkness. I took in her smile, tolerant, perhaps even a hint of triumph, before my eyes dropped to take in the raw beauty of her sex.

The curls were wet, flattened, allowing her relaxed labia to stand proud. They were like some species of exotic, dusky pink, sea creature sensing their surroundings and at their heart glistened the bright inner lips.

I knew that I should have felt disgusted, but I felt my saliva glands readying my mouth even as I stared. I wanted to devour her again, but I was informed by instinct. Bowing my head, I put out my tongue and touched the tip of it to the soft oyster bed only for her outer lips to enfold me in a beckoning embrace.

The intimacy of it was almost overwhelming. I heard myself groan as I started to lap at her, running my tongue repeatedly along the whole length of her sex, which yielded a little more with each stroke drawing me deeper.

At first, she started to seep, a thin, briny, offering, more the product of sweat than arousal, but then a stronger taste exploding on my tongue.

All the while, she remained aloof, issuing quiet instructions.

"A little slower..."

"Yes...just there."

It felt like a challenge. I knew I was getting to her, every swallow confirmed it, but I wanted her to lose control. At some point, I thought that she had climaxed, as I felt a sudden gushing, but she seemed unmoved.

"Don't stop..."

I lost track of time. I was dimly aware that my knees ached, and there was a dull throb in my tongue, but, at that moment, there was nowhere else I wanted to be.

Her labia had become languid, and she was now totally open to my attention. I licked softly along her exposed inner lips, and this finally bore fruit. She put her hand to the back of my head, stroking my hair encouragingly, and I felt her start to shiver.

Spurred on, I began to lick more quickly.

"Now!...Deeper!"

I thrust my tongue into her molten interior only to feel it painfully clenched as she surrendered to the cramping contractions of her orgasm. It built and built, forcing an involuntary sob from her, and just when I thought it was over, the waves settled, it broke the surface once more.

When she finally released me, my face was wet from our co-mingled sweat, and her arousal and the air felt chill against my skin.

I knelt there, bemused, looking at her sex, which was now a livid red, trying to come to terms with what had just happened. This was beyond my experience, and I had no idea what to say, but Liana suffered from no such uncertainty.

"That was wonderful. Give me a moment."

She stood up on slightly unsteady legs and moved around the bed. She plumped the pillows, and, when she had them just so, she arranged herself on the counterpane with her back propped and her legs open.

"I'm ready."

There was no question in her mind. She knew what she wanted exactly, and my acceptance was simply taken for granted. If I had had a shred of self-respect left to me, I would have left the room. She had subjugated me, but there would have been a minor victory in leaving her wanting more.

I got up from my knees and was at the point of moving towards the door when I made the mistake of catching her eye. For a few seconds, we waged an unspoken struggle, and then she turned her head slightly and raised an admonitory eyebrow. I heard my mother's voice, in an echo from the past, telling me that it was rude to stare and, without thinking, I cast my eyes down.

She had her hand at her sex, holding herself open.

"Come and suck my clit..."

The words, crude, coarse, out of keeping with her well-modulated, accented, voice hit me like a cosh.and, under the weight of the blow I bent slowly to the bed.

For a moment, I lay on my stomach. I looked along the canyon formed by the high peaks of her knees to where her fingers formed the columned entrance to her shrine. Like a supplicant, I crawled forward, and, as I did so, the columns parted slightly, and I held my breath.

Her clitoris bloomed into view, and I could not believe that I had missed it before; it was a swollen bud so much larger than my own. I moved closer still, and her steamy scent filled my nostrils like eastern incense clouding my mind.

I closed my eyes and, breathing deeply, I put out my tongue. It seemed even larger by feel alone, and it had an odd, neutral, smoothness, but I was aware of the pulse of her excitement. I began to move my tongue back and forth and was pleased when she took a sharp intake of breath. Emboldened by this small success, I gently sucked it between my lips and licked more quickly.

I could no longer taste her, but it was as though my tongue was delivering tiny pulses of current. Her body began to shudder almost imperceptibly, but, as I grew in confidence, she jerked violently. Her bucking threatened to bruise my mouth, but I was not going to relinquish control.

At the finish, she straightened her legs and crossed her ankles behind my head, pressing her thighs to my ears. I was plunged into a sudden silence, and then she started to come. I could not breathe, and I felt cut off from the world, but there was a wonderful comfort as I was squeezed to the sopping sponge that her sex had become.

I was aware of a growing heat and the pounding flow of blood in my ears, and then, as suddenly as it had started, it was over.

She unwound her legs, and I gasped for air, but I could see that she too was struggling to bring her breathing back to normal.

She sat up and swung her legs over the side of the bed.

"Oh fuck...that was unbelievable."

I looked up at her needing to make a connection, to make sense of the situation, but she stood and stretched, keeping her back to me.

"Haven't you got a plane to catch?"

Chapter 02

I got back to my room in a state of shock heedless of the odd looks I got along the way. I stripped off my clothes and jumped into the shower, which I set to a punishingly cold temperature and tried to clear my mind.

When I had finished, I toweled myself vigorously, but I avoided looking at myself in the mirror. I could not bring myself to put the same clothes back on, and, in a fit of anger, I stuffed them into the bin, mildly feeling disgusted when I saw just how damp my panties were.

Once I was on the plane back to London, I felt slightly better; after all, I was never likely to meet Liana again, and, hopefully, the episode would soon be forgotten.

In reality, it haunted my dreams for weeks afterward. The part of me that I liked to think of as sassy could see it as one of life's experiences, something I could tick off the list before I settled down with Daniel, but my mother had raised my sister and me in a strong high church tradition, and I could not shake the feeling that I had, in some way, sinned.

Meanwhile, my academic life slipped back into gear with the difference that my lectures were now far better attended. The controversy raised by my paper and the fact that it was recognized with an award had given me a new cachet.

Daniel and I kept in touch over the net every night and spoke at length on the phone at least a couple of times a week. I missed him sorely, and the more so now that I was harboring my guilty secret. There was no way in the world that I would tell him, but I needed to see a reflection of myself in his eyes to make sure that everything was just as it was before.

One thing that did help to distract me was a new commission. I had only been back a couple of days when I received an offer from a publisher. As part of the celebrations surrounding the London "Year of Fashion," they were putting together a one-off magazine that would contain six essays from successful women from different walks of life on the theme of emancipation.

I was very flattered to be asked as I could immediately think of at least half a dozen women in academia better suited to the task. They wanted fifteen thousand words, and they were paying generously. I immediately cleared it with the university bursar and began research.

It took a few weeks to put it together, and I was pleased with the result. It seemed that the publisher was happy too, and I was flattered and excited to be asked along to a session with a photographer so that my picture could accompany the article.

I arrived at the studio in the late afternoon and spent an hour being pampered by a professional makeup artist before being introduced to the photographer. Her name was Trudi, and she quickly put me at ease. She explained that a major fashion house was sponsoring the magazine, and she asked if I would have any objection to being photographed in something from their current range.

She had not intended to upset me, but my thoughts inevitably turned to my rendezvous with Liana.

Trudi misread my mood and thought that I lacked self-confidence. She was a real sweetie, assuring me that I was beautiful, and I have to say that by the time she had me decked out in a daringly short skirt and a blouse which showed off my cleavage to the devastating effect I felt like a film star. When she showed me the preparatory polaroids, I barely recognized the gorgeous vamp staring back at me.

In truth, I was a little worried about what my friends might think, but, on the other hand, I could not help but feel that I was striking a blow for intelligent women everywhere.

The photography itself took very little time, but once it was over, Trudi asked me if I wanted to tag along to the neighboring studio where they were setting up for the magazine cover shoot.

Still enthused with the excitement of this new experience, I accepted her offer and followed her along the corridor to a second, much larger, studio. I have to admit that I had entertained the slimmest of hopes that my photograph might be used on the cover, but when I saw the two models that they did intend to use, I could see that there was no competition.

I guessed that they were both in their early twenties, and both were breathtakingly beautiful. The first girl, a blonde, had had her hair teased into a thick halo of tight ringlets, and she was dressed in a period costume best described as a comely wench. The second girl had black hair drawn back from her face in a neat chignon, and she was dressed in the style of a lady of the manor.

There was much giggling as the wench was placed in a pillory. Simultaneously, the lady of the manor stood imperiously to one side with a riding crop as a prop. The tableau struck me as titillating rather than relevant, but I knew as well as anyone that sex sells.

I watched in fascination as Trudi adjusted the set lighting and posed her models, and in no time at all, the shoot was over. The blonde was helped out of the pillory, and, in a moment of inspiration, Trudi turned to me.

"Let me take your picture in harness so to speak."

I thought she was joking and tried to laugh it off, but the others goaded me along. I did not want to seem a spoilsport, and so I put my neck and hands into the apertures while Trudi lowered the yoke onto the back of my neck.

She took a couple of shots, but then my blood ran cold.

"Liana tells me that you like to play."

She must have seen the look of astonishment on my face at the mention of the name.

"Didn't you know? Liana is the associate editor for the magazine. I understand that it was she who put your name forward."

I now knew why I had been chosen in preference to more esteemed colleagues in the profession, but the knowledge brought no comfort. I began to panic, and I tried to free myself from the pillory.

"Don't hurt yourself. We borrowed it from a historic reenactment society. It's authentic in every detail. Look, you can even adjust the height."

So saying, she switched a wooden lever at the foot of the device, and the yoke began to drop, forcing me into a painful crouch.

"Let me out. I've had enough."

"Oh, don't be like that. I think we can have some fun. Girls, why don't you undress her."

For the next few moments, I put up a futile struggle while the girls, laughing all the while, slowly removed all my clothes. I tried kicking out, but that only increased their amusement and put a painful strain on my neck.

"Please, don't do that."

Now that I was completely naked, Trudi was moving around me, shooting off more film. I tried positioning myself to protect my modesty, but it was all too easy for her out manoeuver me.

"Catherine, let's have you in shot."

The blonde moved in front of me. She was kneeling and presented the plateau of her cleavage to me in a parody of Nell Gwynn. I turned my head aside, trying to avoid her, but that only increased her amusement. Egged on by Trudi, she slowly began to undo the buttons of her stiff top freeing her breasts.

They were a modest size, but it was her nipples that caught my attention. Coral pink with almost no areolae, they were all teat, and they stood astonishingly erect.

For a second or two, I stared without thinking and then realized that she was moving closer to me. She cupped her breast and began to play her nipple across my face, and it felt as if she was using a pencil eraser. I closed my eyes, trying to shut out what was happening, but she knelt up a little higher, looming over me, and brushed a rigid teat over my mouth.

She did it so gently that it tickled, and, as I opened my lips to avoid the irritation, she slipped it inside. Obeying some long-buried instinct, I licked at her breast. It tasted faintly of coconut, presumably from a body lotion, but the tip itself was very slightly salty.

I knew I had to get control of myself, but my tongue seemed to have a mind of its own. The taste was gone, but it just felt so right in my mouth. I licked in a circle, feeling it become even more engorged, and when I gently began to suck, it seemed the most natural thing in the world.

I forgot the others as I reveled in the sensation, and I felt aggrieved when she eventually slipped away, but it was only to feed me her other breast. I accepted it greedily and even began to use my teeth to nip gently, knowing that this was something that I enjoyed when it was done to me.

With my eyes closed, I heard laughter and occasional red flashes against my eyelids, suggesting that Trudi was still at work. Still, I was rapt, and minutes slipped by disappearing into the fog that clouded my mind.

"It's my turn. Get yourself ready."

I opened my eyes to find the dark-haired girl whispering at Catherine's ear.

She seemed reluctant to forego the pleasure I was obviously bringing her, but, with the tiniest hint of impatience, she got back to her feet.

It was difficult to look up at the dark-haired girl from my cramped position, as she stood over me, but things quickly got worse. With a smile best described as cruel, she took hold of the lever and switched it over.

I yelp as the yoke's weight forced me to lower still until I was just inches from the floor. For a few seconds, I lay prone, but I could not keep my head raised sufficiently to ease the pressure on my windpipe. Instead, I was compelled to hunch up with my backside raised obscenely.

"Please, this is painful."

She ignored my plea, and, for a moment, she moved out of my line of sight. When she returned, she was carrying a cushion, which she casually tossed onto the floor. I was still looking at her feet when her period skirt slid down her legs to pool around her dainty, stiletto-heeled, ankle boots to be quickly followed by an all too modern thong.

I should have protested, at least shown my anger, but knowing now that she was standing there as good as naked from the waist down strangely excited me. I even cricked my neck in a covert attempt to cast my eyes upwards.

"Is this what you're trying to see?"

In a single graceful movement, she dropped herself down so that she was sitting on the cushion, and she hooked her long, lithe, legs over the yoke. In this way, her thighs blinkered my eyes, and I was left to stare at her sex, scant inches my face.

"You like?"

Her sex had recently been shaved, and her pudenda were now dressed with a frizz of tiny black hairs. She was already moist, and where the tiny fronds meet over her neat slit, forming a single wet line. The effect was extremely exotic, and my tongue almost slipped between my lips.

Putting one hand behind her to support herself, she used the other to rub over her mound and the faint but audible rasp as she raked her nails through the dark stubble set, my heart beating faster.

My eyes remained riveted, and, as I caught her scent, I was vividly reminded of what had passed between Liana and me.

I was reaching a point of no return. I understood that I had to flee or be drawn into a web from which there would be no escape. The problem was that the pillory made escape impossible.

"Please...this is not what I want."

I knew I sounded pathetic, but that only seemed to delight her further.

"Are you sure?"

As I watched, her sex seemed to swell as though it were being inflated from within. The wet hairs reluctantly parted from one another as her slit slowly opened to reveal a surprisingly moist interior.

She began to slowly rub the pad of her finger along her delicate inner lips, and, in the quiet of the room, I could hear the squelch of moisture. My whole focus became her immaculately varnished nail with its scattering of stars on a dark blue background. As it moved up and down, almost hypnotically, a creamy high tide mark rose slowly up her finger.

She was in no hurry, and, as minutes passed, she rubbed a second finger against the first until they were both equally wet, and only then did she start to push them deeper.

She began to keen, a quiet, almost sad moaning, but there was no sadness associated with it. The brightness in her eyes and the more urgent rise and fall of her chest betrayed her ever-growing excitement, and her fingers began to move more quickly, creating a deep sucking sound.

With a growing sense of urgency, she introduced a third finger and drove them inside herself right up to the meat of her hand. The effort caused a fine sheen of sweat to form on her inner thighs and the heat transmitted itself to my captive face.

She was breathing hard, but she managed a hoarse whisper.

"This is for you babe...it's all for you."

She slipped her fingers free and put her hand out to one side to help support her weight. Her sex remained open a raw, wet, pit, and then her body began to convulse.

When the first hot spurt struck my face, I squealed. As it began to run down my cheek, a second gobbet hit me, and then, over the next few seconds, she carried on ejaculating spasmodically covering my face.

When it was over, she collapsed, completely spent, and I felt dirty and humiliated.

"Give me a moment and then you can clean me up."

I wanted to kill her, but I had to keep my anger in check. I could do nothing while I was still trapped, and I sensed that I would only make things worse for myself if I offended them.

While my tormentress was still recovering, Catherine walked back into view. She had her back to me and was naked but for a network of black leather straps that girded her waist and thighs. They also crisscrossed her taut buttocks forming a stark contrast against her perfect creamy skin.

"Wet it for me."

She straddled her prone companion's shoulders, and I could now see the black phallus jutting out eight inches from her groin. Under other circumstances, I would have laughed at the absurdity of it. If women wanted to do without men, then why the hell did they try to imitate them?

I wanted to ridicule them as she pushed the shaft down so that her friend could take it into her mouth, but I have to confess that, for a brief moment, as I watched her expertly fellating it, I felt an undesired twinge of excitement.

They played out the pantomime for a moment or two, but I was determined there was no way that I was going to lick her to get her ready for Catherine to attend to her with her strap on monstrosity.

How could I have been so naive?

Catherine got up smiling, with the hideous shaft glistening with saliva, leaving her friend to take up her position on the cushion once more. Trudi could see, as I could, that her arms were too tired after her exertions to take her weight and so she put down her camera and knelt behind her to give her support.

This left her free to use her fingers to present her sex, which was now a wet mess.

"Are you ready for a taste?"

Her tone was almost a taunt, and my anger got the better of me.

"Go to hell."

This was Catherine's cue, and I screamed in surprise. She had moved behind me, and I now felt her cool hands on my buttocks and the unyielding shaft pressed against my sex.

"Please!..Don't!"

I braced myself for the inevitable pain, but as she leaned her weight into me, I felt my sex opening to accept the intrusion. Having breached the portal, she paused, and I was left feeling ashamed at how wet I had become.

After a few seconds, during which I raised no further protest, she pushed gently, and I felt the shaft begin to fill me inch by inch.

I have had my fair share of men, and I am not shy about using vibrators, but I had never accommodated anything quite as large as this. By the time I felt the heat of her thighs pressed against my buttocks, it felt decidedly uncomfortable.

I dared not move, but then I felt Catherine's fingertips on the outside of my thighs. Men always seem to feel the need to hang on tight, sometimes painfully so, but Catherine's touch was gossamer light. She stroked lovingly, causing my nerve ends to tingle, and deep inside, I felt my muscles miraculously relaxing.

What, only seconds ago, had been an unwanted invasion now became pleasurable distension. When she began to withdraw slowly, I wanted to move back with her, but she moved her fingertips upwards until they were gently pressing on my buttocks in a clear signal to stay still.

She almost pulled out altogether, leaving me with an empty feeling both physical and mental, and I could not help but groan when she slowly filled me once more.

For the next moment or two, she repeated the process while, at the same time, her fingers continued to tease. I felt like a slut as I reveled in the sensations; the more so when the air was punctuated by a sound like water leaving a plug hole. I was incredibly wet, and Catherine began to pick up speed.

Daniel is a considerate lover, but, notwithstanding his prowess and stamina, there was always the possibility he would race to a finish before I was ready. With Catherine, there was no such anxiety. The shaft would not lose its firmness, but, better still, she found my natural rhythm.

When making love, there is a point at which the pace and degree of penetration are just right and, if I can surf that moment, I know that I can enjoy the most intense orgasms, but men cannot tune into it.

It was as though Catherine could divine my body with her fingertips. She picked up the cadence, and I began to soar but, no sooner had I taken flight than she slowed to a stop. I immediately opened my eyes and tried to look back at her.

"Please..!"

"She'll start again when I think you're doing a good job."

The dark-haired girl, forgotten then, was preening her sex from which the smell rose-like damp clothes in front of a fire. The prospect was unedifying, but I would have done anything to make Catherine begin once more.

I strained my neck. She smiled but, after a second or two, she shifted forward, and I was able to lick. The taste was cold, a little sour, but now that she was assured of my submission, she warmed quickly, and I was surprised at how wet she became given her previous display.

She was pleased with my performance because I felt the tender caress of Catherine's fingers once more, and then the shaft began to move. This time she teased me a little going just slightly slower than the perfect rhythm.

In a demented twist of logic, I licked faster and deeper in the hope that Catherine would pick up on the girls' satisfaction and reciprocate, and so it proved. She moved a little so that I could fasten on to her clitoris and use a hand on the back of the head to keep me just so.

Catherine immediately picked up the beat. She was no longer driving to the hilt, but it was more than deep enough. Beads of sweat dripped from my hairline to form a salty counterpoint to the nectar, which I now craved. As my orgasm built, I was sucking and swallowing hard. Her scent filled my nostrils, and her taste cloyed in my mouth, but I wanted more of it.

Sensing my need, she shifted upwards, allowing my tongue to go deep, and then she began to rub he clitoris at a dizzying speed. In the following seconds, I thought I would go insane with pleasure. The first waves of my orgasm broke over me, and, at the same time, my mouth was filled with a hot flood. I was not so much breathing as snorting.

I started to relax, waiting for the inevitable softening and the warm afterglow, but this was different. Catherine barely paused. She kept up the same powerful, but tender, piston movement.

I thought I had no more to give, but she knew better. She drove deep a couple of times, coaxing me, and I felt the wave rising again. In front of me, the girl pushed her fingers deep inside and then offered them up to my mouth. I sucked on them as though it were the sweetest taste in the world as Catherine took me over the edge once more.

When it was over, Catherine slipped from me, and I was suddenly aware of different pains across my whole body. My neck, shoulder, and back ached terribly, and my knees felt swollen.

The dark-haired girl had got up from in front of me, leaving me feeling exposed, but I was relieved when she reached for the lever.

"Wait a moment."

Trudi had also got to her feet, and it appeared that she had reached a hasty decision. While I watched, she quickly stripped out of her clothes, and I got a sense that this had not been part of the script.

I guessed that Trudi was a year or two older than me, but her stylishly cut blonde hair, with its fetching fringe, made her appear younger. Despite the pale coloring, she had large green eyes, and I suspected that there was some Celtic blood coursing in her veins.

She sat on the cushion and placed her legs over the yoke, but she lacked the natural grace of the two models. That was, perhaps, an unfair comparison; she was a woman who would turn heads. She had breasts that a man would find desirable, but a female might consider just a little too heavy, and if one was critical, she could shed a couple of pounds, but the fact was, like her or not, I was in no position to be choosey.

"Please, I've had enough."

"The sooner you get started the sooner you'll be free."

She had obviously been aroused for some time. She maintained a lush growth of hair, but it was damp and flattened, exposing her prominent labia at the apex of which her clitoris was already exposed.

Over the past half an hour, my face, nose, and mouth had been coated with moisture, and I would have expected my senses to be dulled, but, as Trudi edged forward, my nostrils twitched as they once again picked up on her rich earthy scent.

To start with I refused to co-operate but it availed me nothing.

"I can stay here for as long as it takes...can you?"

The fact was that every muscle in my body seemed to be protesting. I tried moving a little, which brought some ease, but, after a time, I found that I was swapping one pain for another.

Loathe as I was, I had to do as she wanted.

Catherine and her dark-haired companion were standing watching, laughing at my predicament, and that only increased my ire, but pragmatism won out. I extended my weary tongue and began to lick.

Trudi shivered at my first touch, and she literally oozed moisture. It was if she had been holding back all this time, and my tongue was the key to turning the valve. It may have been this that made the taste richer, and I instinctively began to lick with the flat of my tongue seeking out every variation.

Trudi started to moan, sounding like a porn film soundtrack, but nothing was fake about it. I quickly concluded that this was her first experience with another woman, and, knowing that I now exercised a modicum of control, I counted it as a small victory.

I slipped my tongue onto her clitoris, and she drew a sharp breath. It felt firm, like a tiny pebble half-buried in sand, and I licked as if to free it.

Trudi went into an eruption, and I licked lower harvesting the moist product of her heightened arousal. She was breathing unevenly and shifting her position, encouraging me to concentrate on her clitoris once again, but I played out my advantage.

I pushed my tongue inside her, where it was immediately clamped tight. Breathing was difficult, not least because my cramped position applied pressure to my lungs, but each time I breathed out, the warmth excited her even more.

We remained in stasis for a moment or two until she finally forced the issue. She brought her thighs together, pressing uncomfortably against my ears. Now I could not breathe at all, and I felt my face flush in a panicked response. She gave it a few seconds, and no words were needed. She relaxed her muscles, and I capitulated.

I withdrew my tongue and licked her as she wanted. Almost immediately, her body began to shake, and, as her climax began to build, she thrust her pelvis at me, adding an extra strain to my already tortured neck. I licked more frantically, flicking my tongue in tiny movements, and I felt her clitoris swell very slightly. It was then that the dam burst. She thrust herself at me one last time and, with a drawn-out scream, she started to come.

I could hear her hands and feet clawing at the floor as she tried to squeeze out the last ounce of pleasure, and then she collapsed.

I was spent, but I could not escape her sex, which was still leaking just inches in front of me while her heavy breasts rose and fell as she struggled for breath.

Chapter 03

They released me. I got dressed and left.

There were no histrionics. I could have shouted at them. Perhaps I might have struck out, but there were three of them, and what would it have availed me other than to compound my humiliation?

Over the next few days, I could not get the incident out of my mind. I had been kept against my will, I had been sexually assaulted, but I had also experienced one of the most shattering orgasms of my life. Nothing made sense.

Of course, I considered the possibility that I might be a lesbian, but then I had a 'dirty' phone conversation with Daniel. We had done it a couple of times before, but this time I was really into it. We would masturbate while talking on the phone and then describe, in graphic detail, what we were doing and how it felt. The result was that I had a fantastic orgasm; it was almost as if I could feel him inside of me.

When I put the phone down, I was crying. I missed him terribly, but at least I had convinced myself that I was normal.

At the University, we were heading into the exam season, and the longer hours helped me keep my mind occupied and ensured that, once I got to bed, I did nothing but sleep. It was exactly a fortnight later that the incident was forcefully brought back to mind.

I was called in to see Nadine Dexter, my head of department. At best, my relationship with Nadine could be described as cordial. She was a Californian, ten years my senior, but, in my view, my intellectual inferior.

It galled me, and others, that she held the universities chair of psychology, but it had been endowed by her property magnate father who could deny his only daughter nothing. She was well qualified, which was not in doubt. She had published several papers, albeit that allegations of plagiarism lurked in the background, it was just that she had no drive.

Having become one of the youngest doctors ever to hold a chair in an English university, she seemed content to rest on her laurels. Her nickname amongst the staff was 'Sinister' Dexter.

As I walked into her office, I had trouble keeping my eyes off her chest. She had recently been back to California for a couple of weeks, and the rumor was that she had taken the opportunity to have a breast augmentation.

It would not have been her first surgery. She was a beautiful woman, but she was determined to give nature a helping hand. To my knowledge, she had had work done on her eyes and nose, and I had a suspicion that she had handed her surgeon a photograph of Demi Moore to use as a template. Her resemblance to the actress could not be denied.

As ever, her office was impeccably tidy. It was one of the biggest on-campus and overlooked the grassed quadrangle. The walls were oak paneled with original bookshelves, and she had supplemented it, at her own expense, with a large antique desk and leather armchairs.

"Take a seat."

I sat down, assuming that she wanted to discuss exam timetables, but then I saw the galley proofs on her desk.

"I've just signed the release for your article."

I already had a financial dispensation from the bursar, and it galled me that her approval of the content was required. It was a university stipulation as I was writing in my capacity as a lecturer, and the institution was mentioned by name.

"It's very good and this photo really does you justice."

I felt a small swell of pride. Trudi was a bitch, but she was also an exceptional photographer. The finished photograph to accompany the article did make me look a bit of a minx. I wondered how I could get an original to send to Daniel.

"Thanks very much. Is that all?"

I got up to leave, but she pulled me up short.

"Sorry, yes, there is one other thing. I found this amongst the proofs."

She handed me another photograph, and a cold sweat instantly chilled me. It was a shot taken over the shoulder of the dark-haired girl. It was taken in such a way as to suggest that my face was buried between her legs.

"I have no objection to you having a few personal shots taken but I have to consider the universities reputation."

My mind was in turmoil. It was conceivable that the photograph had found its way into the envelope with the proofs by mistake, but it was far more likely that it had been done deliberately. The more I had thought about it, the more I was convinced that the incident with Trudi and the two girls had been orchestrated, and the only name that made sense was Liana. But why had she set out to ruin me? I needed time to think.

"This is somebody's idea of a joke."

"That's as maybe, but what if this got into the press? I think it would be in the best interests of all of us if you were to tender your resignation. You could then sue the perpetrator if you wish and after a decent interval we could consider your reinstatement."

It made no sense. She had approved my article but was now effectively sacking me to save the University's good name. My anger got the better of me.

"Is this something personal? Do you begrudge me my recent successes?"

Her reply was not what I expected.

"Do I begrudge you? No. What I object to is your haughty attitude. I know that you don't like me overmuch but I resent the way that you continually look down your nose at me with that English superiority of yours."

My innate sense of good manners made me feel guilty. I had no idea that she perceived me this way.

"Look, Nadine, I'm sorry, I didn't mean to cause offence. It's obvious that someone is up to mischief I just need a couple of days to find out what's going on."

She said nothing in reply and looked unmoved.

"Come on, you know yourself, If I resign there will be rumours, there always are, this would not be good for me."

"Perhaps you should have considered that before. Besides, people are far more tolerant of lesbianism nowadays."

"I'm telling you I am not a lesbian."

"That's a pity because I was going to suggest a compromise."

I had a hollow feeling in the pit of my stomach, and my worst fears were more than realized as she slowly wheeled her chair back from her desk. She was completely naked from the waist down.

Thoughts tumbled over one another. Her intent was clear, but I could not come to terms with it.

"But you're straight. You're engaged."

She smiled as she leaned forward and laid the framed photograph of her fiancé's face down on the desk.

"What the eye doesn't see..."

I felt unnaturally warm and feared that I might faint. With a final effort of will, I turned away towards the door.

"If you leave now I'll block your article and let the dean know why."

I froze in my tracks and then turned to face her. When I spoke, it took a conscious effort not to swear.

"Why are you doing this?"

"Because I can. If you had the power to make another woman go down on you, knowing she could not refuse, would you exercise it?"

"Of course not!"

Even as I spoke the words, I doubted myself. What if the roles had been reversed?

If it had been me sitting in the chair? For a second or two, I conjured up the vision, and it caused an unnerving tingle between my legs.

I hated myself for the things that I had been recently made to do but, no matter how hard I tried to put it from my mind, one thought kept on intruding. Catherine had revealed things about my body that I was previously unaware of, and I knew that ingénue that I was, I was capable of taking a woman to new levels using my mouth. Now I wanted to know what it was like.

Looking her straight in the eye, I spoke tentatively.

"Look, if that's your price, I'll pay it. I guess you should try and experience everything once before you settle down."

I gave what I hoped was a disarming smile and continued.

"Let's leave early, get ourselves a hotel room, and take it from there. Then, after today, we need never speak of it again."

She did not respond immediately, and I dared to hope. The truth was that the incongruity of the situation was stirring something inside of me. Her office exuded intellectual gravitas, and she, in her starched blouse and expensive silk scarf, was half-tuned to the sober atmosphere, but I could not pull my eyes away from her long, bare, legs.

After an interminable pause, she deigned to reply.

"Don't get me wrong. You're a beautiful young woman but, frankly, I'm your boss and I will not be compromising my position of authority. You, on the other hand, need to make an impression. Now, my fiancé is very good with his mouth, I make sure he gets lots of practice, but I expect you to do even better,"

With that, she slowly opened her legs.

She was always impeccably turned out, her hair always just so; her make up painstakingly applied, and so it was a shock when she revealed her sex. A single faint line of dark hair ran from her navel like sand from an hourglass, and it piled up into an unruly triangle of black curls which overflowed the delta and extended to her inner thighs.

The first, incongruous thought that entered my head was that she must eschew bikinis. The fact was that, on any other woman, it would have seemed unsightly but, somehow, she carried it off.

There was something almost pagan about it, something forbidding, and I could feel my adrenalin pumping priming me to flee, but at the same time, I felt drawn to it for reasons I did not understand.

It was reminiscent of my encounter with Liana, and that too should have been a warning, but now, real or imagined, I could smell her, and my tongue moved in my mouth.

I cannot remember crossing the room. At one moment, I was standing, frozen in indecision, the next I was on my knees between her legs. The room was so quiet that I could tell that she was holding her breath, and I was convinced, at that moment, that she had not believed that I could be brought to do it.

It no longer mattered. I was wreathed in a now-familiar stillness, hemmed in by her thighs, and centered on her sex's magnificence. Almost reverentially, I moved closer, and I began to ruffle her with my nose delighting in the softness of her curls. They were faintly scented with a honey-based soap, but as I burrowed deeper, they released a familiar musky odor.

I closed my eyes and breathed it in; then I could wait no longer. I put out my tongue and began to explore the undergrowth. I expected her sex to be brazen, but it was deeply hidden, a reward for finding the way through to the cave.

At first touch, it was a little dry, but now that she knew that there was no turning back, the tension eased, and an earthy tang soon tinged the wetness of my saliva. I licked slowly, teasing her labia into life, and I could feel them swelling under my tongue.

"Yes!...do it slowly."

I knew what she wanted. Men do it quickly, using their tongue to provide a quasi fuck before racing on to the main event. I was on a voyage of discovery. I spent time surveying the contours of the fleshy uplands and was pleased when her body stiffened with initial waves of pleasure. I then ventured onto the lower slopes, moving carefully over this more sensitive range.

"Oh God!...Don't stop!"

It became hotter between her legs as her excitement grew, and I knew where to quench my thirst, but not just yet. I skimmed over her inner labia, threatening to withdraw my tongue altogether, only to swoop once more.

I felt a mischievous, but guilty sense of pride in taking her to places she had never been before. I sensed that she could orgasm from this stimulation alone, but she was desperately holding back, knowing that, if only she could hold on, the best was yet to come.

"Oh you sweet little bitch..."

For long minutes I teased her lips, which were exuding dew like leaves in spring, and my evident delight as I swallowed it down only served to string her tighter.

Her sex was now as open as it could be without further aid, and I began the final descent to where a creamy line marked the valley floor.

I scooped it up in one greedy lick, and she shivered with excitement, but now I had to have more. With a murmur of pleasure, I speared my tongue inside her. I began to swab the walls of the tight tunnel.

She could take no more. She placed her hands on her inner thighs pulling herself wider and encouraging me to go deep,

We remained there, fused, and finally, it was my panted breath alone, which took her over the edge. She cried tears of joy as the pleasure exploded inside her and rushed to every extremity, causing her to stretch her limbs ecstatically.

When it was over, there was an awkward silence, but then she slid her chair under her desk and became very businesslike.

"You had better go. We'll talk about this later."

I wanted to talk about it immediately, but I did not trust myself not to say something untoward. Instead, I gathered myself as best I could and left the room.

It only was as I opened that door that I spared a thought for Nadine's secretary. None of the other lecturers on campus retained secretaries, but Nadine felt that it added to her authority. Michelle was a brash, eighteen-year-old blonde that she had picked cheaply via a government job placement scheme.

I guessed that I looked a complete mess. My hair was damp with sweat, and my make up must have been shot to hell. I had not even bothered to rearrange my clothing. Thinking quickly, I put my face in my hands and pretended to sob as I dashed down the short corridor that doubled as her office. She could make of it what she would.

I went back to my office and fixed myself up as best I could then, for the first time in my career, I skipped a lecture. I phoned the administration office and pleaded a migraine before grabbing my jacket and dashing out into the park.

I went to my favorite bench at the end of the lake, and for a few moments, I wept quietly. After I while, I pulled myself together and began to try to make sense of what was happening to me.

My life had seemed ordinary, so well planned, but now, I had gone down on two straight women in the space of a few weeks, one of whom I almost despised, and I had been involved in a bizarre lesbian orgy.

It was clear that Liana formed a link between the first two incidents, and the third might have been just coincidental, but I sensed a more sinister influence. Among all of the praise that my article had garnered, some correspondence had vilified my conclusions. I wondered if there was a connection. Still, those who had been the most vitriolic had not given addresses.

The problem was that no amount of speculation could disguise the fact that, to some degree, I had made myself a willing participant, and that was the most frightening thing of all.

We all feel that we know ourselves so well, and I could bring my perspective as a psychologist to my observation, but it seemed I hardly knew myself at all.

The following morning I decided to confront Nadine. My paper, and the well-publicized award, had imbued the faculty with a lot of kudos and, now that I had had time to reflect on it, I was willing to bet that she would not want to rock the boat. She might be envious, but she was also basking in reflected glory.

I walked passed Michelle, refusing to catch her eye and bid her a cursory good morning as I walked into the office.

There was something different, and it took a second or two to register what it was.

The armchairs were pushed back against the wall, and now, beneath the window, there stood a classic psychiatrists couch. I knew that she had studied psychiatry before finally majoring in psychology, but it still seemed to be something of an affectation.

She followed my gaze and walked across to the couch, where she lovingly stroked the antique leather.

"Do you like it? It cost me a small fortune."

"I'm sure it's very nice but I did not come here to discuss furniture."

She remained unfazed by my curt tone as she gracefully took up a reclining position on the couch with her back raised.

"That's a great pity because I bought it with you in mind."

She was wearing a black bolero jacket over a matching calf-length skirt with buttons right down the front. Holding my eye, she slowly drew up her legs, and she began to undo them.

"Nadine, we need to have a serious talk."

She had more than half the buttons undone before she replied.

"Do you like stockings?"

Under the circumstances, the question was entirely inappropriate, but I could not formulate a reply. The skirt had fallen open to form a drape around the couch, and I was left staring at a vision of darkness. In addition to her jacket and skirt, she was wearing a midnight blue blouse and, as I could now see, black stockings with matching suspenders.

She kept herself in impressive shape. I knew that she used the gym every day and watched her diet carefully, and, at that moment, I could have been looking at the body of a twenty-five-year-old.

The problem was that she knew that as well as I. Not only did she maintain her body, she knew how to flaunt it. She had supreme self-confidence, and she exuded it.

When it comes to art, I count myself almost an aesthete, and for the space of a few seconds, I just stood and admired her. My eyes were almost inevitably drawn to the tops of her thighs, the creamy splendor of which was exaggerated by the canvas's dark background.

She could see exactly where my eyes were fixed, and, with a knowing smile, she cast her web.

"Come and lick them."

I was pulled towards her in much the same way that I was upon seeing my first Henry Moore sculpture, and, as then, I began to run my hand over the perfect contours.

"Use your tongue."

I moved around her slowly and leaned in between the deep vee of her legs to place a delicate kiss on her inner thigh. Her legs were perfectly depilated and felt almost unnaturally smooth. They were also deliciously warm, and I began to lick slowly towards the slight slope at the top of her leg.

I paused for a moment, licking in a lazy circle, and she gave a loud hum of appreciation. I was now half kneeling on the couch, and I turned my attention to her other thigh tracing the same languid path from her stocking top to the border of her panties.

They were a translucent shade of grey but made dark by the cushioning of her abundant curls and, even as I watched, a pool of even greater darkness spread slowly outwards permeating the air with her rich scent.

I reached towards her wanting to peel the damp silky material away from her ripe sex, but she gently pushed my hand away.

"No, just lick."

I knew what she wanted exactly, and, in the past life, I would have considered it outrageous, but now, devotedly, I began to work my tongue over the crotch of her panties. Her pubis felt deliciously spongy, and as the material became wet with my saliva, I began to taste her juices in erotic osmosis.

She was leaking copiously, and, with a frenzied craving, I began to suck at her noisily.

"Oh you filthy little bitch."

Her taunting and laughter only increased the madness, and when she finally condescended to pull the gusset of her panties to one side, I fell upon her like a ravening beast.

I was conscious of her looking down at me as I surrendered to my carnal instincts, and I felt like a curious laboratory specimen, but there was no way that I could stop myself. I worked my tongue deep inside her as she relaxed into a powerful, drawn-out orgasm.

I was breathing heavily, and I knew that my face was red with embarrassment, but I suddenly felt a desperate need to get away from her. I started to rise, but she quickly put her hand on my head.

"Not so fast. You're not finished yet. Take them off."

She brought her legs together so that I could remove her panties altogether, and my instinct was to tell her to go to hell, but when I looked into her eyes, I felt completely cowed. Having made that decision, it seemed easier to do as she asked, and it was as though a weight had been lifted from me.

I eased her, now sodden, panties down her legs and let them fall to the floor, and, as I did so, she opened her legs once more. She parted her labia and pointed with her middle finger.

"Nice and slowly...just here."

There, nestled deep amongst the curls, lay her clitoris already stretched free of its cloak. It was a deeper pink than the bed in which it lay, and it almost seemed to pulse with expectation. After a momentary hesitation, I bowed to my task.

As I grazed my tongue over the smooth bulb of flesh, I felt my cheeks and nose tickled by her sleek, wet, hairs but I felt, in some way, secure as if I could use them to hide from the world.

I lost all sense of time, content simply to bring her the pleasure she demanded, but by the time she finally reached a second, more leisurely orgasm, my neck and back ached terribly.

Once more, I made to rise, but she held me in check.

"Clean me up..."

I felt an odd sense of guilt. Why had I waited to be asked? I began to like to groom her pubis with my tongue, not stopping until the taste was clean.

Finally, she rose dismissively from the couch and began to fasten the buttons of her skirt. I bent to straighten my skirt when she pushed her sopping panties down into the front of my vee necked jumper.

"A little souvenir."

She laughed as I rooted them out and dropped them to the floor in disgust, but some traitorous part of me almost made me bend to retrieve them. This final confirmation of my depravity frightened me more than anything, and I fled from the room, not stopping until I reached the sanctuary of the washroom.

In the following two weeks, I began to fear for my sanity. Nadine would pick up the phone, and I would come running. There was no reciprocity; she would lounge on the couch, and I would serve. Not once in our encounters did she completely undress. She would remove her skirt and underwear to give me access, and it felt as if I was not worthy enough to appreciate the rest of her body.

We were both experts in matters of the mind, but I even felt intellectually undermined. What I was doing could not be considered rational behavior, and it worried me that she had somehow found her way to my inner psyche.

I would leave her room in tears but invariably with my panties wet with excitement. The problem was that I could not bring myself to masturbate and thus ease my frustration. I was concerned that if I even began to make the association between my deviant conduct and my sexual relief, there would be no way back.

I found myself phoning Daniel almost every evening, and he realized that something was amiss, but it was not an issue that I could, or would, want to discuss with him. He even volunteered to fly over, but I knew that it was out of a sense of exasperation. I assured him that everything was fine, and we would stick with my scheduled visit to the States the following month.

The breaking point came one morning. The ringing of the phone startled me, but, as it was wont to do nowadays, it set off a Pavlovian surge of excitement. Nadine no longer bothered to keep up the pretense.

"Come along right now. I need a little relief."

When I arrived at her office, she was still seated at her desk. I stood, expecting her to make her way to the couch, feeling a frisson of excitement as I waited to see if she had already removed her skirt,

"Come here. I'm a little pushed for time this morning. You can get on with it whilst I work."

I moved slowly around the desk to find that she was wearing the buttoned skirt again. It was already unfastened and peeled away from her legs. Her condescending tone had irritated me, but my eyes were, by now, fixed at the juncture of her thighs.

I started to go down to my knees, but she shifted a little further back from her desk, and I finally understood. The suggestion was as outrageous as it was demeaning, but I felt a moist warmth between my legs. No more words were needed. I sacrificed the remainder of my pride and crawled under the desk.

The modesty board and the seasoned oak made it a dark, closed, space and, as she wheeled herself back into place, her skirt acted as a curtain shutting out the light. Within seconds my tiny cell was permeated by her scent, giving the lie to her feigned indifference, and I did not have to move far to set about my appointed task.

Above me, I heard the shuffling of papers and the occasional scratch of her pen, but this only incited me to get her to show some reaction. It became an unspoken battle of wills but, after what felt like half an hour, I felt clamped by her knees as she finally went into meltdown.

It was a small success, but she soon put me back in my place. Almost as soon as it was over, she made me start again, and, notwithstanding her suggestion that time was short, she kept me there through a second and third orgasm.

I do not know how long I was confined, but by the finish, my whole body was wet with sweat. Even the air around me felt hot, and every breath that I took was impregnated with her smell. My back ached, and, once or twice, I banged my head as it went into spasm.

When she finally let me go, I had trouble straightening up, and she laughed as I slunk from the room.

I had reached my nadir, and something had to be done. I even contemplated a change of University, but when Daniel finally came to settle in the UK, I knew that he would not want to be based outside of London.

In the end, it was simple. All I had to do was refuse. I no longer feared blackmail, and Nadine did not need to threaten me; from her point of view, I had willingly become her oral whore.

The next morning I ignored the phone when it rang. A little later, when it rang again, I gave a peremptory reply saying that I was busy. After that, I was fearful. If she came for me, I was not sure I could trust myself.

I just needed to get through the day, and then the next day was sure to be easier. I had some essays to mark, and, gathering them together, I made my way to my sanctuary.

In the basement, the University maintained what it chose to call a museum. In reality, it was a rarely visited depository used to store the various gifts bestowed on the faculty. For the most part, it comprised an uncatalogued trove of books and research papers, but there were also oddities like a writing desk that had belonged to Hans Eysenck and a consulting couch used by Sigmund Freud.

My particular favorite was one of the pieces which had found its way from the infamous Bethlehem Lunatic Asylum or "Bedlam" as it was known to the poor souls incarcerated within its forbidding walls. It was a heavily padded chair that would not have looked out of place in a dentist's surgery. I would often come down during my lunch hour and catnap in it for ten minutes without fear of disturbance.

I had barely made a start on the papers before I felt my eyelids drooping, and I decided to rest my eyes for a few minutes. I lazed back in the chair and lulled by the gentle hum of basement machinery pumping air, heat, and water through the arteries of the building I must have fallen asleep altogether.

I awoke with a start, and for a second or two, I could not remember where I was, but then I pulled myself together.

"Hello sleepyhead."

"Michelle? What are you doing here?"

As soon as I realized that Nadine's secretary was standing next to me, I tried to sit up, but I found that I could not move my arms and legs.

"She sends me down here. There's bugger all to do upstairs and she tells me to come down here and make lists."

The chair in which I was sitting was fitted with well-worn leather straps, and she had buckled them tight over my wrists and ankles.

"Michelle, I don't know what you're playing at but I want you to release me right now."

"All in good time. You see, I know what you do...with her."

The fact was that Nadine had been less than discrete, and there was a strong possibility that Michelle had heard her in the throes of passion. My only chance was to bluff it out.

"I hope that you're not suggesting that you've been listening in to private conversations. The University takes a very strong line on confidentiality. It could be a dismissal offence."

"Do you really think I give a shit about this job? It pays fuck all to be bored rigid for eight hours a day. I don't need it."

Her caustic tone shocked me, and I was momentarily lost for words, but I soon found my tongue when she began to adjust the chair.

"What are you doing!?"

At a touch of a lever, the chair began to move on smooth hydraulics until it had transformed itself into a flat bench with me fastened securely to it.

"Michelle, that's enough! Let me go this minute!"

She ignored me completely and, as I watched in horror, she started to undress.

"I've always wondered what it would be like, with another girl, and from what I've heard you are just the woman for the job."

Having taken off her tee-shirt and jeans, she now stood in just her chain store underwear, which she shed with no hint of embarrassment. I could see that she had a good body, not exceptional but still with a youthful tone. Her skin was very pale, and her modest breasts were capped with pale pink nipples, which were almost difficult to discern. What made them startling were the two silver bars with which they were pierced.

I have never liked body modification, especially on young girls, but Michelle was clearly a fan. She had several tattoos, the most prominent of which was a wreath of ivy on her left shoulder, a single strand trailed down to her breast.

She came back to the bench and pulled another lever, which had the effect of moving the bench slightly out of the horizontal plane, lowering my head and raising my feet.

"Michelle, you are in serious trouble. Now if you'll undo me and get yourself dressed we need not say anything more about it."

"Seems to me that you're in no position to tell me what to do."

The bench narrowed towards the top. A padded headrest supported my head. She proceeded to step over it, and she was straddling my face. She looked down at me with a smirk, and then I lost my temper completely.

"If you dare to try anything I will bite you so hard you'll need stitches."

"Well that's a great pity."

Much to my amazement, she lifted herself and walked away, but I felt uneasy when she crossed to one of the cabinets which held other Bethlehem exhibits. She returned, holding something that looked like a spare tire for a model car, and, as I watched, she squeezed it between her fingers, distorting it into an oval shape. I now realized what it was, but I was too late. In a single movement, she pinched my cheeks painfully between her thumb and fingers, forcing my jaws apart, and by the time I had recovered enough to try and close my mouth, she had forced the device between my teeth.

The foul-tasting rubber had a channel running around the circumference, and my teeth sank into it. I could neither open my mouth wide enough to expel it nor close my mouth altogether.

"Neat, don't you think?" One way of making sure the loonies took their medicine, and you're sure as hell going to take yours.

I shook my head frantically from side to side as she stood and laughed, but it would not be budged. When I eventually quietened down, she came and settled over me once more.

I tried swearing but could only produce a dribbling incoherence, but I was determined that I was no going to cooperate.

She slightly shifted so that I could see her sex hovering over me. It was covered with an uneven growth of blonde hair as if she had unsuccessfully tried to shave in a design. Above that was another small tattoo. It was downward pointing arrow, and only someone close enough to be intimate would have been able to read the surrounding Celtic style script, which said 'Gates of Paradise.'

I had no time to ponder this conceit as she lowered herself onto my mouth. In just a few seconds, breathing became difficult, and, feeling the onset of claustrophobia, I drew in such air as I could through my nose.

"I want to feel your tongue."

She wriggled on my face a little to reinforce the point, but I still steadfastly refused.

"Okay, it's your choice."

With that, she reached down and pinched my nostrils closed. In a panic, I tried to breathe through my mouth. But I almost choked on a mixture of rubbery saliva and a taste now very familiar to me.

She did not relent. She stayed in place as my body convulsed, and in a silent scream for mercy, I speared my tongue through the rings' opening. She immediately released my nose and even lifted herself for a moment to let me fill my lungs, but she quickly settled once more.

It was a battle I could not win. I knew that she would not deliberately cause me any permanent harm, but I was worried about what she might do inadvertently. I accepted my fate and put out my tongue again, engaging with her labia.

The ring did not allow for a great degree of penetration, and so she moved her sex over the opening, directing my tongue exactly where she wanted it. It was an odd sensation. At the edge of my tongue, I could taste the smooth bitter rubber while at the tip. I could taste her growing arousal, which was so much the sweeter by contrast.

She was in no hurry. She moved over me like a slow-moving belly dancer presenting her labia and, now and again, her clitoris, which seemed to have grown a tiny bit more each time I was allowed to lick it.

She was a hot young woman, and I was soon sweating within the enclosure of her thighs, which were themselves glistening. Now and again, I involuntarily tugged against my bonds and had to fight down a growing sense of panic, but each time I managed to get a grip and continue.

Above me, I could see that she had taken hold of her nipple piercings and appeared to be pulling at them almost painfully, and I hoped that this was an indication that she was getting close.

I was not wrong. She centered her clitoris over the opening and settled her weight more heavily on my face. As she grew ever more excited, her pubic bone pressed against my nose, threatening my breathing once more, and I licked crazily to bring her to a finish.

When she came, her hips jerked powerfully, and I was grateful for the bench's padding, which helped to take the strain, but then she came to a complete stop as she tried to get her breath.

I twisted my head and grunted, making clear my distress, and she finally found the strength to lift herself.

I waited for her to release me, but she walked across the room and returned with a bottle of mineral water. As she stood gulping it down, I was made aware of my thirst and the fact that my mouth was still filled with the acrid taste of rubber.

She had almost finished the bottle when she finally relented and poured the remainder slowly through the opening in the ring. I almost choked on it with my head down, but I managed to get a couple of swallows.

"Good girl...get yourself ready."

I barely had time to take in the implication before she straddled my face once more. I screamed in frustration and shook my head, but there was nothing I could do. She used her thighs to keep me still and then sealed the opening.

Fortunately, she had not quite come down from her previous high, and so it did not take nearly so long to bring her off, and, at the finish, she took things into her own hands. As before, she let me take her weight, but she worked her clitoris with her finger, and, as she came, she spurted through the opening deep into the back of my throat.

She was still recovering when, without warning, she leaped up.

"I taut I heard sum noise."

The unmistakable voice, with its West Indian patois, belonged to Bernadette, a catering staff member. She had been using the kitchen storeroom, which was situated next to the museum.

Michelle was scrambling to get dressed while Bernie suddenly loomed over me. Everyone on campus knew her, a larger than life Jamaican who was never without a smile, and she had quite the finest set of brilliantly white teeth that I had ever seen.

I must have looked a state, and for a second or two, she struggled to recognize me. Once she did, I breathed a sigh of relief. Not only would I be freed, but I now had a witness to Michelle's assault. It was a shock, therefore, when she spoke once more.

"You de bitch that tryin' to get me sacked."

I shook my head in frantic denial. A couple of months previously, the student body had decided to start a healthy eating campaign. They had formed a committee to which I had very reluctantly been seconded to represent the faculty. Unlike other lecturers, I did not even use the refectory, but, nevertheless, I had drawn the short straw. The campaign was well-meaning but, not unnaturally, the catering staff felt that they were being targeted.

"Seems you got your own way of eatin' 'ealty."

Michelle, now a little more composed, came back into view, straightening her tee-shirt.

"Oh, she is good at eating "

"Me man don't do dat for me; 'im tink it unmanly."

"Well be my guest. She isn't going to complain."

I began to struggle hysterically, making as much noise as I could. If Bernie had heard what was going on, then there was a chance that someone else might be near.

"Me do dat, she get me sacked for sure."

"Well if you know that I wasn't here and I know that you weren't here, what's to believe?"

I could almost hear her thoughts as she pondered the situation. Then she turned to Michelle.

"Get de door. We not wantin' to be disturbed."

Michelle padded off gleefully to lock the door as Bernie reached under her skirt to remove her panties.

I felt sick with fear. I would guess that Bernie was about thirty, but she was a very heavy set woman. She had large breasts and an even larger backside, but, like her many of her countrywomen, she counted it as a desirable asset.

"Ain't dis de damnedest ting."

She was looking down at the ring in my mouth and inquisitively poked a meaty finger through it. I tried pleading with my eyes, but there was a brightness in hers that told me that she was not going to be denied.

"Wassup girl? You ain't never had no black pussy?"

As she said it, she raised the hem of her heavy woolen brown skirt to reveal her sex. She had thick thighs and a mound to match. It was a pronounced hillock covered with a tight mat of black curls and quite the longest slit I had ever seen.

She could not step over me in the same way as Michelle had and so she resorted to standing by my head and then lumbering backward. I was immediately enveloped in the smell of fatty food, with which her skirt was impregnated, and it was hard not to gag. Fortunately, she was tall enough to stand proud of my face, and she had only to relax her legs slightly to nestle into place.

As she did so, she flipped her skirt over my head, depriving me of light and her thighs pressed against the side of my face like plump, warm, cushions. With the darkness came a stillness in which I could hear my measured breathing through dilated nostrils.

It was dreadfully hot, and I was all too aware that I had been lying for some time with my head lower than my feet, but I could not communicate to them the possible danger I was in. I had no choice other than to get it over and done with as soon as possible.

Once again, I pushed my weary tongue through the ring but found that I was only licking curls. A million miles away, I heard a muffled whoop at this first contact, and it was a little while before she fractionally shifted so that I could lick her slit.

I feared her taste, but, to begin with, my mouth burned with the astringent tang of soap. As I pushed a little deeper, and she became more excited, I found that it was a little different from the other women that I had attended upon.

The problem was that, as I presented my tongue, and she moved over me, her scratchy pubis was making me very sore, and I began to understand her husband's misgivings.

Finally, after another round of distant laughter, she moved to present her clitoris, which seemed unnaturally large to my numbed senses. Fortunately, it also seemed incredibly sensitive. I no sooner started licking than she began to exude a richer essence, which filled the tented enclosure of her skirt with an animal aroma.

She had remained almost still up to that moment, but now she began to move, and then, unexpectedly, she raised her skirt to reveal her sweating face.

"Go girl!"

She looked almost manic and, fearfully, I began to lick more quickly. In response, she dropped her skirt again, and then my tongue was forgotten. She began to ride my face, sliding her sopping sex down over my chin and up to my forehead. It was a brutal, pumping, rhythm, and I thought my nose would break. Whether by accident or design, when she finally reached a climax, she came to rest over my mouth, and I was forced to swallow what little moisture she had left to give.

She raised her skirt again and, finally, catching her breath, she laughed.

"I got to get me some more o' dat."

My throat constricted with panic, but, without another word, she levered herself off of me and began to put her voluminous panties back on. Once dressed, she walked to the door and turned back to Michelle.

"Remember girl, we got a deal."

Michelle watched her leave, and then, two minutes later, she unbuckled my wrist and fled the room.

After she had gone, I released myself but not without effort; having done so, I quickly collected my car and drove home.

My immediate reaction was to call the police. After removing the ring from my mouth, I could barely move my jaw, and my nose felt flat but, after a long shower, the only visible damage was my slightly swollen lips, and even they returned to normal within an hour.

The problem was that no one would believe me. It was an extraordinary claim, and if my two assailants were going to corroborate an alibi, how would it look?

The only good thing to come out of it was that it provided the jolt I needed. I loved teaching, but I could not go back. I had plenty of contacts in the commercial sector, and I had often entertained the possibility of setting up in private practice. Better still, I did not need to rush into a decision. When my mother and father died, they left my sister and me well provided for, and I could survive without the immediate prospect of an income.

Thoughts of my sister dragged up old feelings of guilt. We had been very close right up until university. My parents had fully funded my degree in psychology, but they were less generous with Estelle. My father, in particular, regarded her degree in Interior Design as a soft option. I felt very sorry for her, but things got worse. After their tragic deaths, the estate was, on the face of it, divided evenly between the two of us. Still, it became clear that the little things, the photographs, and other family history were bequeathed to me, suggesting that they wanted me to be the torchbearer.

I knew Estelle felt aggrieved, and I offered her any or all of it, but the damage had been done. She got her degree and set up in business on the south coast. Over time she became very successful. She began to be in demand by celebrities, and I felt a swell of pride whenever I saw a magazine photoshoot of her designs, and the fact was, they appeared more and more often.

Over time we became close once more, but our respective locations meant that we did not meet as frequently as we would have liked.

In the next few days, things happened quickly. I tendered my resignation and said that I would forego my salary instead of notice. Almost immediately, I received an e-mail from Nadine pleading with me to reconsider. I think she suddenly appreciated what my loss would mean in professional terms, not least a lot more work for her, and she said she wanted things back the way they were. I presumed that she wanted our sordid relationship to be forgotten.

Shortly afterward, I was visited by the Dean of the University. He, too, was desperate for me to reconsider, and he almost had me convinced, but now that the decision was made, I was looking forward to a fresh start.

Then, finally, I received a phone call from Estelle. My birthday was coming up, and I had been sad that I could not spend it with Daniel, but she invited me down for a celebratory meal and promised a surprise.

The venue was a Thai restaurant and, when I arrived, Estelle was sitting with another woman at a table set for five. The décor was stunning, but so was our dining companion. She was a tall, elegant, blonde with almost hypnotic blue eyes, and I put her in her mid-twenties. I thought that she had to be a model of some sort, but Estelle introduced her as Alex.

Estelle had mentioned Alex during our telephone conversations. She was a fellow designer, and Estelle had spoken of a possible business partnership.

There was wine already on the table, and I accepted a glass while we waited for the other guests to arrive. Any preconceptions I may have had of Alex being an airhead were quickly dispelled, not least when I was told that the décor on which I had lavished such praise was her work.

After ten minutes or so, Estelle got up to greet another guest. I had my back to the door and so had to turn in my seat. As I did so, I dropped my glass to the floor. Standing there, as large as life, and now hugging my sister was Liana.

While the waiter cleared up, Estelle made introductions, but Liana acted as if we had never met. For the next few minutes, I sat unnerved as Estelle explained that she and Liana were good friends who had liaised on several projects.

My mind was in turmoil. I could not understand why Estelle had invited me to a birthday celebration with women. She believed I did not know, and a further hammer blow to my sanity arrived in the shape of our final guest.

Sneaking up behind me, with a huge hug and a kiss, came Daniel. I was so shocked that I could not find words. I barely comprehended as he explained that Estelle had pleaded with him to make the trip to complete the surprise.

Wine flowed, and the meal, concluding with a birthday cake, came and went, but I could still not quite get a grip on reality. All the women warmed to Daniel with his natural charm and rugged good looks, but I just wanted a few minutes alone to take a reality check.

I established that he was staying in a local hotel and, possibly fueled by a little jealousy at his effect on the others, my thoughts turned libidinous; Estelle, though, had other ideas. She insisted that we carried on the party at her apartment and, while I gently tried to turn down the offer, Daniel insisted we went.

I realized then that he and I had done most of the drinking and that the others were in better shape. We squeezed into Estelle's car with me sitting up front, and Daniel somehow winding up as the meat in the sandwich between Liana and Alex.

Estelle's apartment was new, and I had yet to see it, but once inside, I found that it was a true measure of her success. It was a huge glass-walled penthouse space with magnificent views southwards over the town to the sea and northwards to the gently rolling downs.

Set around a low coffee table and facing towards the sea was a huge white, curved sofa which could have comfortably accommodated twice our number. Estelle served more wine and encouraged us to sit, but I somehow finished up in the center next to Liana with Estelle and Alex off to one side and Daniel by himself on the other. Much to my annoyance, he seemed to be dozing off.

We continued to chat, but I still felt distinctly uncomfortable. Liana was a decorum model and said nothing untoward, but I could not shake the notion that this was way beyond the realms of coincidence.

Alex did not help things. She was wearing a remarkably short skirt, and, as she grew more relaxed, she was slumping down further on the sofa, revealing just a little too much of her perfect legs. I tried to put the guilty thought from my mind and looked across at Daniel, but he had tuned out completely.

I looked back to catch what Estelle said, but, as I did so, Liana leaned in close and whispered in my ear.

"She's beautiful isn't she, from a purely aesthetic standpoint?"

Alex could not have heard, but, at that moment, she chose to shake out her long blonde hair. Model or not, she held herself with the bearing and confidence that only the truly beautiful can manage.

Liana was still there at my ear, and I was conscious of her warm breath on the nape of my neck.

"Lovely legs, I'm a little envious."

I could not help but look down only to look up again almost immediately, but in so doing, I unwittingly caught her eye. There seemed to be the tiniest hint of an appreciative smile about her lips, but I could not be sure.

I wanted to move away from Liana, but I did not want to appear rude for Estelle's sake. So I remained where I was and smiled while she whispered again.

"Do you think she's wearing panties? Have you been trying to see?"

I felt myself flush hot with embarrassment. The thought had not crossed my mind but, now that the seed was planted, I could not rid myself of it. It would occur to me to go out without underwear, but would Alex?

Once again, I could not stop myself from casting a fleeting glimpse downwards, but his time, she brought her legs together more tightly and turned them away from me towards Estelle.

I felt as if I had been caught out, and the heat rose in my cheeks once more, but no one seemed to notice. It was just then that Estelle made a joke about a mutual acquaintance, and as we laughed, she slapped her hand gently on the top of Alex's thigh.

She leaned forward a little and continued unabated, but she left her hand where it was. She seemed completely unaware, and yet I could not tear my eyes away. Her words were lost to me as some perverted corner of my mind willed her to move her hand a little higher.

She turned to Alex to make a point, and, as she did so, her hand did inch indeed upwards, lifting the hem of her skirt almost imperceptibly. I felt my heart leap and, with it, a warm tingling between my legs. At the same time, Liana groaned softly at my ear, and I was overcome with a sudden self-loathing.

I thought the episode with Michelle and Bernie had rid me, once and for all, of any Sapphic leanings. But here I was getting aroused by an unintended action on my sister's part and, worse still, with my fiancé in attendance.

I cast another look at Daniel, who had his head back staring vacantly at the ceiling and then decided that the best thing to do would be to go to the bathroom and splash a little cold water on my face.

Liana had not moved, and now, as though reading my mind, she gently put a hand on my shoulder.

"Not yet..."

There was no good reason not to excuse me, but I found myself doing as she asked. I was feeling ever more uncomfortable at her proximity, but neither Estelle nor Alex appeared to notice.

Estelle was still holding the floor, and she chose that moment to make a self-deprecating remark. Alex chided her, giving a flattering reply, at which my sister turned and pecked her on the cheek.

It was perfectly innocent, but it was a revelatory moment. I had never thought of questioning Estelle's sexuality, simply assuming that she was very fickle in her choice of men. She had turned up with different partners over the years, but I never got the sense that any of them were serious. One or two of them had even struck me as slightly effeminate, but I assumed that it was the nature of the art world in which she moved.

Now, for the first time, I looked at her in a different light. A fleeting image of her and Alex together flashed through my mind. To my surprise and embarrassment, I felt my panties moisten.

Right away, I felt guilty at entertaining such an unworthy thought, and I looked down at my knees. It took a few seconds to register that the room had become silent, and when I lifted my eyes once more, it was to find both Estelle and Alex looking at me.

Estelle favored me with an odd smile, and then she half turned towards Alex.

"I think it's time baby ..."

Alex, too, smiled at me and then she got up from the sofa. For the next few seconds, I felt as if I had entered a dream state. She crossed her arms, took hold of the hem of her jumper, and, with a static crackle, pulled it over her head. She discarded it onto the sofa, ran her fingers through her hair, and lifted her breasts. They were larger than I had imagined, but what caught my eye were her dark, fully engorged nipples as they strained against the expensive silk of her brassiere.

I wanted to look at Daniel to see his reaction, but I could not pull my eyes away. Estelle had reached up, and, with a deft flick of her fingers, she had undone the fastenings, but Alex had cupped her breasts in anticipation, and she now teasingly revealed their full beauty.

My heart was galloping, and I had not drawn breath for some seconds. The whole situation was surreal, but I did not want it to end. It seemed as if she was stripping for my benefit. She let the bra spill to the floor and then slipped her thumbs into her skirt's waistband.

She paused for a fraction, just to make sure that I was fully engaged, and then, with a seductive shimmy, she slipped her skirt down her long, supple legs.

I gave a quick, involuntary gasp when I saw that Liana guessed correctly. Alex was wearing pale crotchless hose, and there, centered within the elliptic opening, was the most exquisite sex. At the apex was a consummately sculpted triangular tuft of hair which pointed downwards, beckoning the eye to her prominent labia. They were a perfectly matched pair of vivid pink petals that reverently cradled the globe of her exposed clitoris.

As Estelle's older sister, my duty as a moral guardian dictated that I show my anger at this outrageous behavior; I should have roused Daniel and left in high dudgeon, but the last thing I wanted to do was to break the spell.

My nipples had long since become erect. They tingled, demanding attention, and Liana, demonstrating an eerie prescience, allowed her hand to fall from my shoulder and gently brushed the side of my breast with the back of her fingers.

Alex stood dressed only in her hose, and her high heels and the expression on her face defied me to look away, but I was lost. If she had asked me, I would have gone down on my knees and worshipped at the shrine; it was as if the others no longer existed.

I knew, in that instant, that this was something I could not forsake. I convinced myself that these women had forced themselves upon me, either physically or by the strength of mind, but the truth was that they were feeding a craving that had come to haunt my dreams. Even the trauma of being restrained, seen at this remove, held an unaccountable excitement.

Alex paused, as though following my train of thought, and then she slowly turned her back on me while looking over her shoulder. I tried to look her in the eye, but she knew that my resistance was broken. I hesitated, and then, as she knew I would, I looked down. Framed in pale nylon her behind was as firm and well-formed as apricot, and my mouth watered.

I did not know where this was leading, nor did I care, but what happened next almost tipped me over the edge. With an almost balletic grace, Alex knelt in front of Estelle, who slowly lifted her skirt and opened her legs.

She was wearing a pair of flimsy, pale blue, panties, and, even from where I was sitting, I could see a telling darker area which seemed to spread even as I watched.

I felt faint, almost nauseous. I had always considered my sister to be more beautiful than me, but my feelings, just then, were corrupt. I looked at her face fleetingly and saw in her eyes a look that was triumphant in some way, but my mind was refusing to keep up. I was caught up in an emotional and physical whirlwind, and I was letting it take me where it would.

Alex bowed her head and placed a kiss that appeared almost supplicatory then, with a feline mewling, she ran the flat of her tongue up and over the already dampened material.

Estelle indulged her for a moment, stroking the back of her hair, and then she lay back, lifting her hips slightly. Alex acted upon this unspoken signal sliding her hands slowly up her thighs and then under the waistband of the now soaked panties. She deftly rolled them over her hands and then eased them down Estelle's legs.

Not since childhood had I seen her naked, and it was a rude shock to see her sex dressed with an adult growth of blonde curls. The imperative to look away still acted strongly upon me, but my muscles would not obey.

Alex remained still for a few seconds as though captivated by a gallery painting, and then she leaned inwards.

Estelle hissed in a breath through clenched teeth as Alex lovingly went about her task, and my imagination filled in the blanks as I watched the back of her head, making tiny but deliberate movements.

"You didn't know that your sister was a lesbian?..."

Liana was still poised at my ear, and I resented her tone, but the fact was she knew, and I had failed to guess despite all of my professional training.

"...How could you not? They've been together almost two years."

She was taunting me, but I had no reply. What had come between us such that she felt unable to confide in her sister?

Even while these thoughts churned in my mind, my body continued to betray me. I could see that Estelle was approaching a state of personal ecstasy as Alex used her mouth with a familiarity born of love, and I found my tongue moving behind my teeth.

I did not resist, as Liana's hand moved. She was now cupping my breast and using the inside of her thumb to tease my nipple. It strained against the thin material of my bra to meet her caress.

I almost came myself as Estelle reached her first climax. Alex slowed a little to draw out the waves of pleasure, but she did not pause. Her movements suggested that she was fastidiously lapping up the outpouring, and then she found her rhythm once more.

Estelle settled back with a beatific smile, and I gave a petulant groan as Liana's hand left my breast but, seconds later, she pressed her finger gently to my lips. My nostrils twitched, and I drew the familiar scent deep into my lungs before I put out my tongue and licked soothingly.

Her taste acted upon me like a narcotic, and, like a junkie, I craved more.

"Down on your knees...Olivia."

The use of the nickname that she had tagged me with was intended to be demeaning, but I was beyond caring. I slid down from the sofa and knelt before her.

She made me wait as she slowly rose. She unhurriedly took off her skirt and panties and then simply stood there knowing full well the effect that the sight was having upon me.

I had fantasized about her since that first time. Now that I was confronted by the savage sensuousness of her sex once again, I felt cowed.

The Mohican of dark hair was already damp, and her labia visibly swollen.

"Is this what you want? You want to eat me?"

She ran her fingers over her mound, wafting me with her aphrodisiacal fragrance, and then she sat back down on the sofa with her legs open.

Estelle was groaning her way towards a second climax behind me, but my only concern was seeking the comfort of the humid, tropical grove that lay before me. I moved in towards my goal, but, as I did so, Liana touched a finger to the center of my forehead, bringing me up short.

I remained poised, too ashamed even to look up at her, and then she drew up her legs. She now had her feet flat on the sofa's seat, her heels tucked into her buttocks, which opened her to view to an obscene degree.

The carnal display appalled me, but, at the same time, the hunger within me became almost uncontrolled. They say that, of all the senses, it is the sense of smell that sets down the strongest roots in our memories, and those that run the deepest are usually associated with needs or traumas. It was not in doubt that my first encounter with Liana had been traumatic, albeit erotic, and my brain now processed her unique esters and stoked my unnatural craving.

I moved forward to make real the phantom taste that already haunted my mouth.

"Not yet. If you want that you have to earn it. You know I want..."

For an instant, I was perplexed. I remained stupidly poised, trying to understand her meaning, and then the answer came to me with a hideous realization. Her dark growth was not confined to her pubis. It continued onwards into the next valley where it formed two ever-narrower tracks and there, framed between them, and now plainly open to view, was the tight, ribbed, opening.

It was like the head of a tiny exotic flower with a pink heart shading to dusky gray petals, and her leakage had already made it moist so that it scintillated under the spotlights that lit the room.

I felt frightened by it. It was the ultimate taboo, and it went against all my moral teachings but, even as I stared, frozen in temporary paralysis, I felt a treacherous bead of moisture trickling down my inner thigh.

I could not do it. I could not subject myself to this ultimate debasement, but Liana was an all-knowing puppet mistress. She coaxed her labia with her fingertips teasing out a runnel of viscous sap, which made its inevitable way through the valley. As it approached the heart of the flower, it pouted very slightly as if to sip it in.

It was arousing in a way that I could not put into words. It felt like a current had been applied to the pleasure centers in my brain, and my whole body zinged. I realized that I was hovering at the edge of orgasm, and there was only one way to take myself over the edge.

No longer thinking nor caring, I edged closer and slowly put out my tongue. At first touch, I closed my eyes as I savored her taste, but then I began a curious exploration. The tight rosette was unyielding as if her flesh had been vulcanized, but I could feel the tiny, rhythmic, distensions as my tongue increased her arousal.

"Come on...you know you can do it...you know you want to."

She was still in control, but her voice betrayed the edge of her excitement.

I probed a little more firmly, unsure of what I expected or even what I wanted, but this was a portal that was not to be broached. I could feel the tension of anticipation in her muscles, and I knew I was no match.

Instead, I curled my tongue and gently worked the tip of it at the very center only to find that this was the key. She relaxed momentarily, and I was able to push just a little way inwards and hold my ground.

In a frozen equilibrium, we remained there for a few seconds while my tongue assimilated a briny, baser, taste mixed with the more familiar piquancy of her arousal. At the same time, my nostrils flared in obedience to some primal instinct.

Her whole body was quivering, and I knew she was close. This fired me with an overwhelming need to share in it, and, with an uncredited strength, I drove my tongue all the way home.

"Oh God!"

She started to come, and, as she did so, I was squeezed painfully. Still, I felt every tiny contraction as she worked out her climax with my deep-rooted tongue the focus of her exhilaration.

I could stoop no lower. Saliva trickled from the side of my mouth as I breathed noisily in a process not helped by a flood of moisture from above. I had now come to my senses and wanted to be free, but she continued to grip me tightly simply because she could.

When, finally, she deigned to release me, I was fearful of bringing my tongue back into my mouth, but then I realized, with horror, that Estelle and Alex were seated on either side of her watching me with amusement. I was not sure what was worse, the fact that they had borne witness to my humiliation or that I had been so caught up in this act of corruption that I had failed to be conscious of their presence.

"Well, well, my big sister. Whoever would have thought it?"

The flush of embarrassment in my cheeks turned to the heightened color of anger, but even as I prepared to get up, Liana quickly wrapped me up in her legs, crossing her ankles at the small of my back.

"Not so fast...you're not finished yet."

I felt myself quaking with rage.

"Estelle. What the hell is going on here!?"

She was unfazed by my outburst; in fact, she even smiled.

"Don't keep Liana waiting. I'll explain it all when you've finished."

Liana unhooked her ankles and sat with her legs opened wide, and I cursed my weakness as I could not stop myself from glancing downwards. Her sex was puffy and relaxed due to her orgasm, and I had to make a huge conscious effort not to be deceived.

In looking away, I caught Alex's eye; she had not dressed and sat there radiant in her nakedness. As she held my gaze, she ran the tip of her tongue over her perfect teeth brushing her top lip. That simple gesture caused new flooding in my already uncomfortably damp panties, and for a fleeting second, I entertained a vision of her down between my legs.

Did I dare hope?

I found it hard to accept that I was taking such a perverse pleasure in adopting a submissive role, but it could not be denied. It was almost as if I became, just for a time, another woman, a wanton with no will. In reality, I was reaching levels of arousal previously beyond my imagination. By denying myself, I was only adding fuel to the already fierce flames; but there was more to it.

If I once allowed myself this same pleasure that I now so readily bestowed, I knew that I would be lost. I was hovering at the brink in every sense, and there was still a chance to pull back. I could turn my back on all this and pick up my normal life. Daniel and I could be happy together; all it needed was an act of will.

I remained there, conscious of the three of them looking at me, and then I was undone by a kiss. I looked at Alex once more, wanting a sign, and she slowly pursed her lips. There was a tiniest, seductive pop as she gave flight to it, and I knew that I had to have her even if it meant pleasing Liana once more.

I leaned forward, signaling my surrender.

"There's a good girl...come and eat me."

The scent of her arousal wafted around me, and the air seemed to become denser as I moved closer to her sex, but now I wanted to push my tongue deep inside. I suppose that I was trying to erase the memory of what I had just done for her and get back to 'normal' in this new twisted existence.

As my tongue slipped easily inside, it was like breaching a dam. She was wetter than ever, a creamy offering that seemed to have been drawn up from the very depths, and I let it fill my mouth before swallowing it down. Her whole sex was coated, and I sought it like a hummingbird gathering pollen.

She let me have my way for a moment or two, but then she reasserted herself.

"Go slow....nice long licks..."

I did as she asked, and for the next few minutes, I entered my nirvana.

"She learns remarkably quickly. You would think she had been doing it all her life...Get your tongue inside..."

"I told you she was that way inclined. Our father had suspicions and he always held it against me. I wonder what he would make of his favourite if he could see her right now?"

Her words drifted to me, but I found it hard to make sense of them. Was this what it was all about? Was my father's favoritism based on my sister's sexuality and not on her choice of career as I had always thought? Was Estelle seeking some form of revenge, or was she trying to prove a point? Was she trying to demonstrate that her successful, heterosexual sibling was as just as deviant as she? If so, she had succeeded.

Liana noticed my hesitation as I tried to digest all of this.

"Don't stop...lick my clit."

The abrupt demand made it easy for me to take the easy option. I simply stopped trying to think and focused my attention on her engorged bud. I licked with the flat of my tongue, and she began to shiver beneath my coaxing.

She was in no hurry. They carried on talking while I snuffled away until, finally, she closed her thighs about my face as she erupted for a second time.

It was a while before she relaxed her hold, but when she did, my face was red, hot, and covered in her copious sap. I was suddenly overwhelmed with embarrassment, and I wanted to run from the room, but I simply remained there on my knees with my head hung in shame as I tried to catch my breath.

"Liana, now you've had your fun perhaps you would like to get him ready."

I looked up as Liana crossed the room to where Daniel still lay semi-conscious. Without another word, she began to strip him of his clothing. I turned on Estelle angrily.

"Just what the hell is going on here?"

"You still haven't figured it out?"

"Just tell me what this is all about."

"It's very simple. I always suspected that you and I inherited the same tendencies. It's just that you never dared to explore your feelings; you always did what you thought was right by dad, like getting yourself a trophy boyfriend, for instance.

With Liana's help, we thought that you should be allowed to discover your real self."

"You set that up?"

"It was easy enough. I knew which hotel you were staying in for the presentation ceremony and it was straight-forward for Liana to organize a business trip to coincide. She really is straight by the way. I just so happens that it helped to fulfill one of her fantasies too."

"And the room?"

"A simple lie about a lost key card and a big smile for the concierge; it was easy. You see, you're not the only one who knows a little bit about psychology. I knew that the shock of finding Liana as you did would prime your latent instincts.

"I never realized you could be such a cruel bitch."

Estelle leaned towards me with anger in her eyes.

"You don't think that your paper was cruel. Do you know what you've done?"

This reference to my paper caught me off guard, but then pieces fell into place.

"You and Alex, you want to adopt a child?"

"Do you know just how hard you have made it for couples like us?"

For a second or two, I wondered if any of the hate mail I had received had originated from my sister but decided that even she would not stoop so low. The European Union had originally commissioned my paper. It drew together various strands of research into the psychological impact on children raised by same-sex couples.

I knew that the real plan was to establish if male couples could make good parents, but, for the sake of balance and even-handedness, I looked at children raised within lesbian relationships. The paper reached no hard and fast conclusions, but it did sound a cautionary note.

Gay men were obviously not happy with it, but the backlash from the lesbian community had been both vocal and unexpected. I suspected that they liked the status quo of public opinion, which would just about tolerate the "two mothers" approach, and they now felt that I had tarred both gay men and gay women with the same brush.

"Estelle, I didn't know. It was never intended to hurt you."

She cruelly smiled before she replied.

"Well now you know what it feels like from our side of the fence."

"He's ready."

I turned back to Liana, who now had Daniel completely naked and prone on the sofa.

"What have you done to him?"

Estelle answered as she and Alex rose from the sofa.

"A little sedative, just enough to keep him dreamy."

I suddenly began to get an inkling of what they intended.

"Estelle, you're not serious..."

"Very much so. As you will appreciate this is a little distasteful for Alex and I that's why Liana is here to help and it's fitting that you should help too."

"This is my bloody fiancé we're talking about!"

"To us he is just an inseminator. He's obviously carries the genes for good looks and he has an extraordinarily high intelligence quotient, you told me so yourself, but most importantly he is in the ninth decile on the fertility scale."

I could not believe that this was coming back to haunt me. In one of my e-mail exchanges with Estelle, I explained that Daniel and I did not intend to start a family until later in life, but we had both taken the precaution of having a fertility test to make sure that there would be no problems. I now regretted exulting about Daniel's high scores.

"Liana, I think it's time..."

"My pleasure."

She was still naked from the waist down, and as I watched, dumbstruck, she eased her way onto the sofa. She pinned Daniels arms with her knees as she straddled his head, and then, with studied deliberation, she nestled down onto his face.

I knew that I should have screamed at her, torn her hair out, but I just knelt there watching.

She was facing down his body, and she began to rotate her hips, grinding herself down. Within seconds I heard Daniel give a stifled groan, and then he sprang to an erection.

My immediate reaction was irrational anger that he should allow himself to be so easily manipulated. Still, then my view was blocked as Alex moved in front of me, standing with her legs slightly apart.

"Get me ready."

I looked up at her. She was a goddess, breathtakingly beautiful, and my resistance was straws in the wind. I wanted to run my hands over her sublime curves but felt, in some way, unworthy. Instead, I leaned forward and ran my tongue over her incredibly smooth mound before moving on to the delicate pink ridges.

She was trembling almost imperceptibly, possibly nervous about what was to come, and in some perverted way, I felt it was my duty to calm her. My tongue ached, but I licked delicately back and forth along the valley of her labia each time, drawing a little closer to her already exposed clitoris.

Her sex began to weep, a tiny trickle of clear teardrops that promised sweetness but bore the rich taste of her womanhood. I caught up each and everyone on my tongue and, when I could no longer stand it, I took her whole sex into my mouth and plunged my tongue deep inside.

She took hold of my head with both hands as she started to come, and I did not want it to end. I could hardly breathe, and I think I would have died there, but at that moment, I envied my sister beyond riches.

As she moved away from me, I wanted to reach out for her, but now she was purposeful.

Liana was still on Daniel's face, and he was moaning quietly, but his erection betrayed his excitement. She held it firmly in her hand and stroking the vivid, bulbous head with the pad of her thumb. I was sure I had never seen him quite as firm nor as tightly strung, and now Alex moved towards him.

In my mind, I heard myself protest, but I remained mute as she positioned herself on the sofa with her back to Liana. I could sense a little trepidation, but Estelle came to her, entwined her in her arms, and kissed her fully and deeply.

They were still kissing as she eased down, and Liana did the rest. She guided him home, and then she worked herself on his face once more. Immediately, his body stiffened, and I knew he was coming more powerfully than I had ever known, his cries shut off in the deep canyon of Liana's thighs.

As soon as it was over, Alex slipped from him. She was weeping, a mixture of distress and joy, and Estelle guided her away, closing the bedroom door behind them.

Epilogue

I ran from the apartment, my own eyes filled with tears. Liana was still sitting on Daniel's face as I left, and, to my disgust, he was already coming back to erection.

Within two days, I was in France. I rented a cottage on the hills just south of Les Sables overlooking the Bay of Biscay. It was an area that I knew from childhood holidays, and it offered the solitude that I needed. While still at the university, I had been offered an advance to produce a book, and now I intended to take up the offer. It was not a lot of money, but I anticipated my needs to be simple.

I left a phone number, but not an address, for Daniel, and he phoned almost as soon as I arrived. His memory of events was hazy, and I could not help but wonder if it was willfully so.

I was angry beyond measure with Estelle, not because of the Sapphic episodes, I could no longer hide from myself in that respect, but because I felt that, in raping Daniel, she had stolen my life.

I wanted Daniel to sue for common assault, but he would have no part of it. Looking back, I suppose he was right, who would have believed him, and he ran the risk of ridicule.

After a few days, I recognized my unreasonableness and was prepared to try a reconciliation. I phoned him, and we spoke for a long time feeling our way carefully. Towards the end of the conversation, he suggested that it might be helpful if we were to broaden our horizons. When I pressed him on exactly what he meant, he grew nervous but eventually confided that he would not be opposed to having another female join us from time to time.

Without another word, I put the phone down on him. His suggestion seemed like a betrayal and implied that he remembered more of the incident at Estelle's than he was letting on. There had also been something about his tone of voice, something a little too salacious.

In the days that followed, the idea preyed on my mind, but, at the finish, I decided that if I was going to marry, it was going to be a conventional relationship. I could conquer my aberrant behavior. All I needed was time.

I heard nothing more from him for the next four weeks, but he was often on my mind, and I suspected that I would have gone back had it not been for Monsieur Guillaume. He was my landlord, a practicing pediatrician, who had returned to France from America, after several years, to help restore the family estate of which the cottage formed a part.

He sounded older on the phone. In reality, he turned out to be around forty years old, and he was everything Daniel was not. His features were a lot softer, and he had a thick head of dark hair, shot through with the odd strand of silver, which he kept expensively styled. I never saw him in anything other than dark, designer suits, which he always wore with pastel cotton shirts and very plain silk ties.

He did not wear a wedding band, and, were it not for all the complications, I might have let him charm me. As it was, he became a regular visitor. I made him speak French so that I could sharpen my language skills, and he leaned me books. I managed to get through "Les Misérables" in the original and rediscovered the somber joys of Gidé.

In the second week, he invited me to lunch, and I found it easy to relax in his company. I began to fancy that he was manufacturing excuses to drop by, and I felt that I ought to tell him about Daniel.

I decided that I would tell him on the night of the opera. Knowing my love of music, he had obtained two tickets for a performance of Massenet's "Thais," but, in the event, he was called away to a medical emergency. He apologized profusely and suggested that his sister attends in his stead.

As soon as I saw her in the foyer, I saw the family resemblance. She shared her brother's height and slender build, which was accentuated by the well-cut, black silk, evening gown that she was wearing. As I drew nearer, she fixed me with her large, blue, piercing eyes and flashed me a disarming smile.

The evening went wonderfully. The opera was sublime, but once or twice I caught myself guiltily taking a furtive glance at Sophie's perfectly tanned legs as revealed by the long side opening of her gown. I told myself to snap out of it, and I was a model of decorum as we enjoyed a late supper at the neighboring bistro.

I found her captivating, open and friendly as her brother, and with a great sense of humor. I knew that this was a friendship worth fostering and that I must do nothing to jeopardize it. Any fleeting, unworthy thoughts were banished at the mention of Claude. His name came up in conversation a couple of times and, while I did want to pry, I got the impression that he and Sophie were an item.

The following morning was a Saturday, and I was delighted when Sophie suggested that we had lunch together. I proposed the small beachfront café to which I regularly cycled to take breakfast, but Sophie insisted on a picnic on the small cottage terrace.

She turned up at lunchtime, looking at a different woman. Her thick chestnut hair, which, the night before, was restrained in a sophisticated chignon now hung loosely about her shoulders. The gown was replaced by a daringly short skirt and a "Les Bleus" football shirt, which made it perfectly obvious that she was not wearing a bra. I now realized that she was much closer in age to me than she was to her brother.

She brought freshly baked bread, local cheese, paté, and a salad she had already prepared along with two bottles of the rough but drinkable, local red wine.

Over the following two hours, we chatted like life long friends, and we were well into the second bottle.

I was disappointed when the time came for her to leave, and I only remembered the DVD that I was due to return to her brother. My hands were wet from washing up dishes, and so Sophie went to fetch it from the bedroom where I had been watching it on my laptop.

After a few moments, she had still not returned, and I wondered if I had left it in the living room after all. I dried my hands and followed her into the bedroom, but as I stepped through the low doorway, my heart stopped.

Sophie was bent over the antique pine table that doubled as my desk perusing my journal.

Since entering my teens, I had always kept a journal. I found that writing things down helped me to reach a fuller understanding of myself. Now I stood frozen in horror. Everything was there, Liana, Nadine, Estelle, all of it.

"Sophie..."

I hoped that she would be suitably embarrassed to be caught out in an act unworthy of her, but she seemed unfazed. She picked up the journal and turned to face me.

"Is this true...or some sort of fiction?"

The temptation was to lie and tell her that it was the outline of a story, but I could see, from the look in her eyes, that she already knew the truth.

As I watched, she seemed to transform. She stood a little taller, and her already ample chest swelled. She waited, for a moment, with a single finger pressed to her full lips, and then she spoke again.

"Undress for me."

In an accent that was a subtle echo of Liana's, those three simple words caused an involuntary shiver. I felt a guilty excitement at the prospect that she might find me physically attractive, but there was also the possibility that she now believed that I was there to be used.

I recognized that this was a defining moment. If I wanted a future with Daniel, I had to be strong. As I continued to waver, I even wondered, fleetingly, if I should explore the possibilities with her brother, but then I made the mistake of looking into those deep blue eyes.

My fingers seemed to seek out the buttons of my sundress of their own volition, and I was soon standing naked before her appraising stare. A decision had been made, consciously or otherwise, but I was now willing her to undress. I wanted her to enfold me in her arms, to kiss me in the way that I had seen Estelle and Alex kiss. I needed to know if we could connect on an emotional level.

The next few seconds stretched into eternity, and then I had my answer. She slowly lifted the hem of her skirt to reveal a pair of sheer, drenched, panties.

"Come here and take them off for me..."

Story 02

Chapter 01

Hanging naked while being whipped by a surreally beautiful nineteen-year-old goddess was not how I envisaged spending my thirty-seventh birthday.

She did not appear to be expending any effort, but each casual flexion of her arm seared another painful stripe across my already tortured backside. We agreed twelve, but after seven, I begged her to stop.

She was slightly built, but the form-fitting leather outfit she had chosen to wear imbued her with a sense of latent strength. The phrase "warrior princess" came to mind, and I mentally filed it away for later use.

She walked in front of me, the sharp heels of her boots sounding menacing on the parquet floor, and brushed a stray hair from my forehead.

I have always counted myself blessed by looks, but I had to give second best to this young woman. Her lustrous blonde hair was swept-back and held in a ponytail giving stark expression to her striking facial features.

Her skin was flawless, and her pale blue eyes had an inner radiance that was almost hypnotic. Her nose was cute, forming a contrast with the sensual fullness of her mouth, and she could, under other circumstances, have seriously tested my heterosexual credentials.

I appraised her again, trying to see her as her clients would. Her breasts were full, a fact attested to by the bodice work that held them firm, and her legs long enough to give her an inch or two advantage over me in terms of height. For one so young, she did not lack self-assurance.

I waited for her to release the velcro cuffs that held me bound to the steel bar that hung from the ceiling, but she seemed in no great hurry. She reached out and brushed her gloved finger against my exposed nipple, and I pulled away reflexively.

"I promise you that, given enough time, you would be pleading with me to touch you but, for now, I intend to fulfil our bargain."

I looked at her and smiled.

"I have all I need, thanks. I still don't pretend to know what motivates your clients but I can see that you are very good at what you do."

She returned my smile, but there was a hint of amusement about it as if a joke was told, and I had failed to understand the punch line.

"I think that you've missed a fundamental part of the equation. I don't just do this for money, or the benefit of my clients, I do it because I enjoy it; just as I will enjoy giving you the remaining five that you asked for."

I assumed that she was still in her role and, I have to give her credit; she sounded as if she was totally for real.

"Look, I appreciate your assistance, just unfasten the cuffs and I'll buy you a coffee."

She disappeared from view, and I waited for her to engage the winch and lower the bar. I had mentally relaxed, which made the shock even greater when she struck me again.

It came completely without warning and made everything that had gone before seem tame by comparison. The crisp snap across the taut flesh of my buttocks sounded no louder, but the pain was of a different order. It blazed where she had struck and was then diffused across my whole body.

I stiffened involuntarily and understood that she had only been toying with me up until then. I was so jolted that I could not form the words to protest before she laid another stripe across my already tortured flesh.

For a split second, I felt the precise cut of it, but then the pain merged, and it felt as if someone was holding a steam iron to my skin.

I screamed, and tears started to my eyes, but the pain was unremitting. Some part of my mind insisted that this could not be happening while, at the same time, I understood that she had deliberately warmed me up to maximize my anguish.

There was a long pause with the silence only broken by my sobs and then the sinister creak of leather. The movement of the whip through the air sounded so innocuous, but the effect was devastating. She struck lower this time, catching the crease of my buttocks, and the instant agony was such that I was sure that blood had been drawn.

I wanted to swear at her, but expletives do not come naturally to me, and I howled as I had not done since I was a young girl.

I begged and promised her anything, but the final two strokes were delivered with studied deliberation and even greater severity.

When it was over, I tried to squirm away as she gently used her fingers to check the damage that she had inflicted.

"Get off me!"

She ignored me and, instead, molded herself into my back. The leather she wore felt blissfully cool to the touch, and, for a few seconds, I surrendered to its soothing effects.

The heat was slowing spreading, and she traced its expanding boundaries with her fingertips right around to the front of my thighs.

I twitched anxiously, but she remained close pressed, and then her hand cupped my sex. I was shocked to stillness, and I could feel every tiny movement as she surveyed the shape and firmness of my mound.

I turned my head and murmured.

"Please...don't."

She continued as if I had not spoken her touch, becoming ever surer. I felt a sense of disgust, but, at the same time, I was aware that she was touching me as no man ever had. There is a certain feeling that can only be elicited by your fingers, but she attuned herself to me in only a matter of minutes.

Against all reason, I felt myself becoming aroused, but in so doing, the pain that she had visited upon me was being decreased. My body relaxed a little, and I rationalized that she would stop when she deemed that I was befittingly embarrassed.

That moment came more quickly than I thought. She held up her finger to me, and I could see the leather darkened with moisture.

"Well, well..."

I wouldn't say I liked the idea that she might, in some way, believe that I could take some pleasure from this. It then occurred to me that I might be perspiring, but she forestalled this avenue of evasion by bringing her finger to my nose. The smell of leather was strong, but there was no doubt about the nature of the scent that overlaid it.

She dropped her hand to my sex once again, and I was determined to resist, but her fingers fluttered in such a way that I held my breath in anticipation. She applied the slightest of pressures then teasingly held just at the threshold.

I have enjoyed three long term relationships with men, but I have never been able to achieve orgasm from penetrative sex, and their crude fumbling with their fingers was worse still. The best I could manage was to have them go down on me, but some of the pleasure was lost from constantly having to issue guidance.

The best orgasms were those that I conjured for myself, and I have lost count of the number of times that I have waited for my partner to go to sleep before I could finally find release.

Now, suddenly, here was a suggestion of something more. It was almost as if I was touching myself. The heat of pain merged with a flush of arousal across my whole body.

It seemed an age that she held me there. Her finger barely moved, but almost imperceptibly, I could feel her slowly encroaching and melting my body to accommodate her.

Her face was close to mine, and I was aware of her slow, controlled breathing even as my own became more ragged.

Her finger was inside me now, but she did no more than flex it slightly, allowing my sex to come to terms with the stealthy invasion slowly. Her body supported mine as the tension left my muscles, and it felt as if we were melded as one.

My whole consciousness was focused on that delicious intrusion, and I moaned softly, hoping that she would take things further. I could feel myself getting wetter moment by moment, and I lewdly imagined her glove becoming sodden.

Just moments before, I could have killed her, but now she was asserting her dominion over me in a completely different way, and, if she were to release me, I was not sure how I would react.

Everything in my upbringing railed at what was being done to me. In a darker part of my mind was the thought that no one would ever know beyond the confines of this room.

I gasped as I felt her move slightly, and I feared that she was going to leave me high and dry. She had seemingly done very little, but I was getting frustratingly closer to the edge.

Her finger was sliding away, and I turned my face to hers.

"Please..."

For a few seconds, I watched as she pondered her decision. She could have asked me to beg, and she knew I would have done, and it was her certainty of this victory that tilted the balance.

I felt the pad of her finger at the apex of my sex. It took but a second or two for her to orientate herself, but then she unerringly engaged with my clitoris.

Her touch was perfectly weighted, and I could feel the slight roughness of wet leather each time I breathed. Had it been me, I would have increased the tempo, but there was an exquisite agony as she unhurriedly held me in check until I was made acutely aware of each tiny abrasive movement.

All my pain was forgotten as my focus centered on her fingertip and the resulting pulses of pleasure, which thrilled my whole body and slowly grew in intensity. It seemed absurd that she remained so still while I was panting for breath and sweating with the effort of staying in touch with her.

In the end, there was some semblance of mercy. She increased the pressure fractionally and caressed with a feather-light touch, which had me wanting to thrash my body, but I knew that stillness was the key.

When my climax came, it was slow and assured, bearing me up higher than I thought it was possible to go. I knew that I was crying out, but I knew not what. For long seconds I was transported to a plateau where there was a whiteness about everything, and my body seemed both tense and relaxed at the same time.

It was too perfect, and at the zenith, I blacked out for a second or two before re-emerging frantic to hold on to every last ounce of it before it ebbed away.

When it was over. I groaned as she slipped away from me, leaving me hanging limp and desperately confused.

Chapter 02

I had always envisaged myself as a successful news journalist and, ideally, a foreign correspondent. In my early years, I was moderately successful and even won an award, but I quickly found that, apart from a few household names, journalism does not pay well.

I was able to afford a modest flat of my own, but three failed relationships had put paid to any long term financial security. I joined the profession when staff jobs were on the wane, and the major papers relied upon a pool of freelancers. I was able to sell stories but never the big one, which would make my name.

I was going through a particularly barren patch, both personally and professionally, when one of my friends suggested that I should try submitting a feature article to a magazine. This was anathema to someone who considered themselves a real journalist, but pragmatism won out.

The big buzz of the moment was s&m, courtesy of online book sales, but if I was to tap that vein, I knew I needed a different slant on it. I started researching and found most of it particularly unedifying, but then I chanced upon a website that dealt with the topic of women wishing to submit to other women.

I had never given this a thought, but I found myself intrigued. I eventually lighted upon

Jessica's profile and I were fascinated by her honesty. She set out the services she was prepared to provide and a list of fees, and I was convinced that the photograph was a fake, that is, until I met her.

She stipulated a public place, and I opted for a Starbucks branch where the alcoves offered some privacy. When she walked in, she made heads turn, and my immediate thought was that, if she needed to make money to fund her studies, she could turn her hand to modeling rather than the seedier path she had chosen.

I was clear with her from the start. I just wanted to conduct an interview to discuss her motivations and experiences. If the article was published, I guaranteed her a percentage of the fee. And as much, or as little, publicity as she wanted.

She was happy to talk, but by the end of half an hour, I had no real sense of her. It was then that she suggested that the only way for me to understand fully was to experience it, and so my fate was sealed.

For obvious reasons, the resultant article was heavily sanitized, but it still garnered more interest than I had anticipated. It got taken up by a major domestic magazine and then went on to be syndicated. Even allowing for Jessica's percentage, I still made more money from that single submission than I had in the previous twelve months.

Therefore, it was no great surprise when I received a phone call from the editor asking if I had anything else in the same vein.

It seemed logical to get back in touch with Jessica, but I was forced to question my motivation. Despite her tender years, her experience was much broader than mine, but I could have considered someone else.

I rationalized it by telling myself that I was lucky to find her in the first place. She was intelligent, articulate, and, given the nature of the topic, salubrious.

When I phoned her, she was excited at the prospect. I had given no specifics about her identity in the article. The magazine had been inundated with e-mail traffic, which they had passed on to her, and business was booming.

I thought that she might steer me towards another byway of this strange netherworld, but, instead, she suggested that I could gain a different perspective by watching her in session with another client.

It was an interesting idea, but I wondered if it would make for too similar an article, and there was something else in the back of my mind which would not quite come into focus. I finally decided that it was a question of nothing ventured, nothing gained, and a time was arranged.

When Jessica opened the door to me, I was surprised to find her casually dressed in a baggy tee-shirt, tight jeans, and a pair of well-worn leather sandals. She looked every inch of the university student, and I wondered if her client had cried off.

She assured me that everything was still okay and proceeded to make coffee. I sat across from her and felt slightly disjointed. She spoke about the success of the article in such a way that she was talking about two different people.

When the doorbell rang, she told me that I should follow her lead and not make notes.

I was intrigued to find out what sort of person availed herself of the services of a girl like Jessica, but I was surprised when the woman was shown into the room. Jessica had explained that she was a regular client whom she knew as Linda, but that was not her real name.

I guessed that she was about thirty, and her expensive business attire marked her out as a professional, a lawyer perhaps? I suppose that I expected someone shy and nondescript, but she was a woman who lavished a lot of attention to her appearance.

She may have been a pound or two overweight, but she had a classical hourglass figure, which men currently clamored for. She was very attractive facially; her glossy black hair and dark eyes hinting at some middle-eastern blood in her heritage.

Jessica came and sat beside me on the sofa, leaving Linda standing in the middle of the room. Her expression was neutral, but I could see that her pupils were dilated; she seemed completely unfazed by my presence.

"Why don't you undress for us..."

Linda's hesitation was momentary. She put aside her bag, an expensive Chloé, if I was not mistaken, and took off her jacket.

I sat transfixed, having to convince myself that this was really happening. She slowly stripped to her underwear, and I had the distinct feeling that she was putting on a show for my benefit.

She stood still, allowing me to take in the curves of her body, and I was suitably impressed. Her skin bore a healthy tan, and, despite the odd holiday pound, she looked very fit.

"Don't be coy. She wants to see you naked."

Jessica spoke as if reading my mind, her tone calm but assured. Linda's eyes flicked to mine and then quickly away as she carefully removed her bra and pants and set them to one side.

Her legs were nicely toned, and her breasts more fulsome than they first appeared, but it was her nipples that took my attention. They were a dark shade of brown and so much larger than mine.

"Show her."

I cast a glance at Jessica, wondering what she meant, but Linda knew what was demanded of her exactly. She brought her hands to her breasts and gently teased with her fingertips.

I almost gasped as I watched the teats distend until they were almost an inch proud of her heavily dimpled areola. This display of raw nature seemed so at odds with her professional persona.

She began to pinch more purposefully and gave a low moan as her eyes closed. I could only watch jealousy wondering if her nipples were sensitive in proportion to their size.

The answer came as she reached down to her sex and began to massage her mound while still squeezing vigorously. I knew that, with the article in mind, I should have remained dispassionate, but watching her like this stirred something inside me.

I am no stranger to pornography, but nothing I had seen could have prepared me for the reality I was now confronted with. There was no faking, no cutting away. Here was a woman who enjoyed being watched, at the height of arousal.

She was in no way a model of perfection, but her blemishes only made her more human, more like me.

There was something else, something it took me a moment to grasp; the scent of her was in the air. I felt a little guilty as I deliberately breathed her in noting the subtle constituents.

Her perfume was musky and expensive, but there was also a hint of overworked deodorant and something more. I do not know why it came as such a shock, but the realization that I could smell her arousal startled me.

She was some feet away, but it was sufficiently potent to fill the void, and I wondered if this is how it had been for my various lovers. That thought was no sooner formed than I became self-consciously aware of my sex and felt an almost overwhelming urge to touch my body.

She was becoming more and more heated, but I noticed that she did nothing more than rub herself. If it were me, I would, by now, have my fingers deep inside, but she was demonstrating incredible self-control.

I looked across at Jessica. She had a half-smile on her face, and I suddenly comprehended that it had nothing to do with Linda's powers of restraint; she was waiting for permission!

Now that I understood, I could see that Linda's eyes were not just conveying the arousal that she felt she was also pleading silently to be allowed to go further.

Jessica let her continue for a few minutes more and then quietly said

"Stop..."

Linda did as she was told, but, for a moment, the reality seemed to intrude on her fantasy. She covered herself with her arms as if she was caught in the act. She looked at me with a hint of embarrassment.

Jessica had not explained in any great detail what was to transpire. She told me to come along with an open mind. Now she stood up, stretched gently, and then waited.

Her extreme beauty aside, she radiated something hard to define. There was a certain aura about her, which had a profound effect on Linda. Linda looked at her with admiration. She stepped forward hesitantly, and, in a choreographed movement, Jessica raised her arms, allowing Linda to remove her tee-shirt carefully.

She was not wearing a bra, and my eyes fell to her breasts. They were beautifully shaped with the enviable firmness of youth and nipples almost perfectly circular. Linda stared for a moment before slowly dropping to her knees.

She reached forward, and I could see her hands slightly trembling as she began to work the fastenings of Jessica's jeans before gently working the tight denim down her long legs.

Jessica stepped out of her jeans and sandals in a single movement to stand in just a simple pair of white tanga pants, which made it obvious that she had a very prominent mound.

She was like a work of art to be gazed upon, but I felt a growing compulsion to do more than look. Linda was similarly affected, but I was astonished as she leaned forwards and placed a single kiss.

Jessica's panties now bore the imprint of Linda's lipstick, and it was one of the most erotic images I had ever beheld. I felt my sex growing warmer with each passing moment, and I found myself pressing my thighs tightly together.

No acknowledgment was made, no instruction is given, Linda took careful hold of the flimsy cotton garment as if it were precious silk of inestimable value and stripped it away. I noted that she secreted them with her own discarded clothing, but my attention was now firmly fixed on Jessica's naked form.

I saw that her sex was dressed with a neatly trimmed covering of blonde hair, which came as a surprise, but then I thought everything this young woman did was carefully calculated.

Searching for an adjective to describe her mons, I could not get beyond the word ripe. The perfect upswell was accentuated by the revealed tips of her labia, which had a beckoning quality.

This was borne out as Linda knelt before her looking mesmerized. She moaned almost inaudibly like a desert traveler lighting upon an oasis.

Jessica looked perfectly serene and totally in command of the situation. I knew what was coming, and I could not believe how aroused I was at the prospect. Had anything like it been outlined to me only days before, I would have laughed out loud, but she kept me as skilfully on edge as she was Linda.

Finally, she put a finger under Linda's chin and raised her head.

"Adore me..."

She needed no second bidding. Leaning forward, she began to kiss and lick between Jessica's legs devotedly, but she did not attempt to broach the portal. It was not lost on me that she kept her hands clasped behind her back the whole time.

Jessica looked tranquil, which contrasted with my state of agitation. I was now undeniably aroused, and I guiltily craved the sensations that I knew she could bestow.

She allowed Linda to indulge herself for some minutes, and I felt sure that she was fully aware of the effect it was having on me. Eventually, she bade her stop, and then she came and sat beside me on the sofa.

Her carefree, naked presence rattled me, and I tried desperately to retain some professional integrity, but I was fighting a losing battle. My heart skipped as, with calculated slowness, she parted her legs.

She beckoned Linda forward with a single finger, and she approached on her knees. She appeared transported, and I noted that her nipples still stood fiercely distended.

She paused for a moment, as if waiting at a prayer rail, and then closed the divide. She sealed her mouth to Jessica's sex, and for a brief moment, her cool façade slipped. Her body arched fractionally, and I surmised that this was in reaction to the invasion of Linda's tongue.

She quickly gathered herself, but I could see that Linda was straining to penetrate as deeply as possible, and, for an exquisite instance, it was as almost if I could feel it myself. My sex was becoming uncomfortably wet, but I remained frozen, not wanting to break the spell.

Time stood still, and I became acutely aware of every sound. The background of distant traffic and the hum of the refrigerator from the kitchen, set against this, was Linda's soft murmuring and the lapping of her tongue.

I knew, then, that she would carry on for however long, Jessica wanted, for as many hours or as many orgasms as she wished, and that thought nearly brought me to a climax.

I must have moaned out loud without being aware of it as Jessica turned to me.

"Take off your panties..."

I knew that this was all so wrong, but the world of mores seemed beyond my reach. I fumbled beneath my skirt and was mortified to find that my panties were soaked.

Jessica laughed at my discomfort as I quickly removed them and dropped them somewhere in my handbag's vicinity on the sofa's side.

"Lift your skirt and open your legs."

My hands seemed to belong to someone else as I did as she asked and became immediately aware of the cool air on my heated sex. I had used a depilatory that morning, which was unusual for me as I usually waited until the weekend.

My eyes flitted to Linda only to find her looking back at me, and I realized that, for her, the script had suddenly changed.

Jessica slowly eased away from her sex. She stroked her hair as if she were doting on a pet, before speaking to me again.

"Do you want her..."

Linda looked shocked at the rejection, but I could see that it had spoken to something deep inside her. For my part, I was conflicted. Jessica was offering the use of her, treating her as nothing more than a body slave, and it went against all of my principles, but I reasoned that to deny her might be the crueler option.

In the end, she decided for herself. She moved from between Jessica's legs to take her place in front of me, and the look of lust she conveyed sent a shiver through me.

I felt an impulse to close my legs, reminding myself that this was another woman, but she gazed at my sex with a reverence that no man had ever exhibited. The protuberant labia that had once worried me until I came to embrace them as an adult were, to her, a thing of beauty, and as she began to kiss each side in turn gently, I almost swooned.

She took her time, licking over the whole expanse of my sensitized mound and then returning to take each wing in turn gently between her lips before caressing with her tongue. The feeling was almost indescribable. I did not want her to stop what she was doing, but my body was screaming out for her to be more assertive.

In a lucid moment, it then dawned on me that this was the essential thrust of the article. There was a dynamic at work here that needed to be explored and explained.

By slow degrees, she was changing her approach. She subtly began to apply more pressure and licked along the whole length of my furrow, resulting in a teasing pressure on my clitoris.

I had no control over my own body as it yielded to her sly urging. My sex opened to her, and I felt a welling of moisture.

This was her cue, and she pressed home in a single thrust that robbed me of breath. Her tongue seemed to fill me, but she flexed it to give herself further access.

She was like a musician tuning an instrument as she explored within finding those spots that provoked the strongest response. My fingers clawed at the sofa as she toyed with me, and she had yet to seek out my clitoris.

This was well beyond my experience. Even the men who had professed to enjoy it, most of whom I did not believe, had never come close. Linda had a natural understanding of what it took to bring another woman pleasure, and she was a skilled practitioner. It felt as if we were as one, sharing the same sympathetic vibration.

I could feel myself leaking copiously, but that only served to feed her need. She swallowed greedily, and hearing her increased my exhilaration.

I should have been climaxing, but she denied me the final touch while promising so much. Her tongue found the roof of my sex working a point beyond my clitoris, and my body began to tense. It was an incredible feeling, and not something I had achieved with my fingers.

The strain was a beautiful agony, and when, at last, she gave her attention to my sweet spot, a spring was uncoiled. I felt each tiny, knowing movement centered there and then radiating throughout my body with unbelievable intensity.

I fought to breathe as wave after wave crashed over me, and there seemed no end until I could take no more, and I returned to the here and now. I wanted to thank her, but she had all the thanks she needed as she lapped the warm residue from my thighs and then returned to Jessica for unfinished business.

Chapter 03

The article presented a problem. I could not allude my intimate involvement, and, to satisfy the guidelines of a mainstream magazine, I had to edit it heavily. I believed that I caught the inter-relationship and the nature of dependency succinctly, but I was struggling to meet the minimum word count.

I was discussing this with the editor when I uttered the fateful words.

"If only you could see her..."

The obvious leap to the possibility of a photo-shoot fired the editor with renewed enthusiasm, but I was dubious. Jessica had remained in control in terms of confidentiality, using the magazine as a cut-out, but photographs presented a different problem.

I contacted her without hope or enthusiasm; after all, she was studying at one of the country's most prestigious universities, but her reply took me by surprise.

She was happy to pose, but only if a friend undertook the shoot. I pointed out to her that the magazine used some of the best fashion photographers around and that they would not compromise, but she insisted that I come along and take a look.

A couple of days later, I collected her, and we drove the short distance across town to her friend's studio. I was expecting commercial premises, but we arrived at a residential address, and Jessica led me up to the loft apartment.

Yet again, I was confounded in my expectation. I thought that I was to be introduced to a university contemporary, but Evelyn Proctor turned out to be a Canadian closer to my age than Jessica's.

She was larger than life in every sense. She stood a little taller than me and carried a lot more weight, but she had it in all the right places, and she exuded a sense of good health and vitality.

I was welcomed expansively with a kiss on both cheeks. The intimation that any friend of Jessica's was a friend of hers.

The loft, come studio, was a huge airy space with a large range of expensive photographic equipment. The walls were decorated with her work, which included some original paintings amongst the many black and white photo prints, which seemed her forte.

One photograph, in particular, just inside the doorway, caught my attention. Its composition featured a woman, partly unclothed, secured to the four corners of a bed. The style was reminiscent of a fifties pulp book cover, but the counterpoint was her nemesis who stood over her holding a whip. The second figure was cast in shadow, but there was just enough definition to suggest that it was another woman.

The image was familiar, but I could not quite put my finger on it until Jessica said.

"Your taste in music?"

I then remembered the brouhaha from the previous year. An Australian girl band, whose name was lost to me, were the subject of a massive launch for their first album, but the music itself had become overshadowed by the debate, mainly in the feminist press, about their choice of the cover artwork. The story had been big enough to find some space on the sleazier Sunday tabloids' inner pages.

I looked at Evelyn with renewed appreciation and then noted that the greater part of her oeuvre had fetish undercurrents. I am no art expert, but I could see that there was quite a talent here.

All of her photographs drew you in to examine them more closely with the theme seeming to be things hidden or hinted at in the shadows. In each, she managed to pull off the trick of showing the beauty of her models without identifying them, and I knew, immediately, that Jessica had been right.

Evelyn brewed coffee, and we sat down on a pair of facing sofas. I sat next to Jessica with Evelyn opposite us, and we reached an agreement. I would recommend Evelyn but, once the introductions were made, she would have to negotiate her fee with the magazine. I suspected that she would have done it for nothing just for the exposure, but the magazine stood to gain from her recent notoriety.

The conversation was pleasant, but business-like until Evelyn stopped me cold.

"Do you like legs?"

"I'm sorry?"

"You seem fascinated by my legs. I'm sorry, I notice these things."

I felt a guilty flush start to my cheeks. She was wearing a skirt which had ridden up a little when she sat down, and the exposed expanse of her legs had indeed caught my attention. They were surprisingly toned and shapely, leaving me wondering what she did to keep fit.

Before I could formulate a reply, she spoke again.

"Forgive me. I run an on-line fetish magazine to promote my work. It has been astonishingly successful and I've gained a unique insight into what turns people on. Breasts are probably most popular amongst the general population but, in the community that reads my magazine, there is more of an emphasis on legs and particularly women's backsides."

Her matter of fact tone put me a little more at ease, but then, irrationally, I wondered if she was speaking mainly for heterosexuals. Her works seemed evenly divided between those depicting men with women, and those that I would consider of a lesbian leaning. There were just a few that showed men with men.

It transpired that they knew one another through the magazine and that Jessica had become something of a muse. Evelyn showed me some shots featuring her, and they were quite breathtaking. Even without totally revealing her face, she had captured the essence of her as well as her raw beauty.

Jessica looked at the photographs herself, outwardly lost in thought, and then said.

"Let's take a couple of shots now so that we can show the magazine what we can do."

I took the sheets from her and looked at them again.

"We could just use these as examples."

She touched my hand and smiled.

"No silly, if we are going to do this than it has to be for real. It has to be you and me."

I did not know how to reply. My immediate thought was that I was too shy, but I was vain enough to be flattered that she would even consider me as a potential model. I was also intrigued as to how Evelyn would work with less than perfect raw material.

It became a fait accompli when Evelyn drew the blinds and began to set up her lighting rigs. Jessica drew me across the room, and it was amazing how intimate space now seemed.

When Evelyn was ready, she wheeled over an empty clothes rail.

"Get undressed and hang up your clothes."

I hesitated for a moment caught between the clinical reality and the fantasy I had conjured for myself. It was Jessica who snapped me out of it.

"If you're going to take Linda's part you need to be naked."

I slowly removed my clothes, all the while conscious of the harsh lights. It seemed impossible that this set up could yield such dramatically shaded results. Once I was naked, Evelyn began to circle me taking a variety of shots but never asking me to pose.

As she worked, Jessica took off her clothes and, seeing her naked. I felt that same hollow feeling inside. She sat down on the sofa as if taking a throne and, only then, did it really come home to me what I had agreed to.

Evelyn switched her attention to Jessica, who was a natural in front of the camera. She regally sat until Evelyn changed cameras and nodded.

Jessica slowly opened her legs with a wicked smile on her face and pointed to the floor.

My heart beat faster as I went to my knees, and I immediately noticed that she was professionally depilated. Since our last encounter, this change added emphasis to her mound, which appeared almost burnished.

"She's a Goddess isn't she?"

Evelyn spoke softly at my ear, but I could not reply. I yielded as she moved me closer in, and I barely registered the soft click of the camera. Over the next few minutes, she posed the pair of us, but my eyes remained fixed on the delta of Jessica's sex.

Evelyn asked me to open my mouth and show my tongue, but the truth was that I was breathing through my nose, hoping for some indication that Jessica, too, was being affected. She played her imperious role well, but she was more aware than I gave her credit for.

"Lick me if you want to."

Was I so transparent? Was it something I wanted? Evelyn remained completely unfazed.

"Go ahead honey. I can give you a few minutes and then we can pick up again."

In a state of confusion, I got to my feet.

"I need a break."

Jessica laughed as she addressed Evelyn.

"She's a lesbian but she's still discovering herself."

To hear it put thus, starkly seemed so very wrong. What the hell did this girl know about me! In the past few days, I had done a lot of thinking, but I had convinced myself that I was caught up in the circumstances of this particular job. Another man would stroll into my life at some point, and this would all be put down to experience.

Evelyn put an arm around my shoulder, and her presence was a comforting warmth.

"It's fine baby. I didn't find the faith until later in life myself."

I froze in her embrace. I had not considered her sexuality other than to think that she would have no problem attracting men. My sudden tenseness did not daunt her. She took me in her arms and cuddled me to her ample bosom, and I smelt the soft fragrance of her perfume.

I could, perhaps should, have pulled away, but some deep memory stirred, and I felt a sudden, blissful, sense of wellbeing. She stroked my hair and spoke in a whisper.

"You are so very beautiful. I say that not just as another woman but as an artist."

Was she coming on to me? I did not know, but the bigger question was whether or not I welcomed the advance. She held me for a long time, and I could hear the steady beat of her heart. It would have been so easy to drift off in the comfort of her arms.

Eventually, she eased away and took my face in her hands.

"Do you trust me? I know exactly how to photograph you."

Without waiting for an answer, she began to move lights to the back of the studio, and Jessica took me by the hand and led me across. I immediately recognized the bed from the album cover print and now had an inkling of what to expect.

Evelyn appreciated my unease. She sat on the bed and invited me to sit next to her.

"This will be a private photograph just for you. No one else ever need see it unless you wished."

Even now, I wanted to dissent, but I put up no resistance as she eased me backward. With an evident facility, she and Jessica bound my limbs to the corners of the bed, and my only thought was how white and pure the ropes appeared.

She began to take shots from various angles, under different lighting settings and set me a new challenge.

"I want you to struggle against the ropes. Ignore me, and do it for real."

I started tentatively but found that while the ropes were relatively thick and the knots seemingly innocuous, and I could not free myself. Trying again, I closed my fingers and tried to slip free, but there was insufficient play in the ropes. Now, mildly annoyed, I tried in earnest, twisting my whole body, but I was stuck fast.

"I've had enough now. Untie me."

Evelyn, who had been shooting fast and furiously, put her camera aside and spoke breathlessly.

"Wait just a moment..."

She wheeled across a small trolley bearing a computer monitor. She plugged in the camera, and her fingers flew across the keyboard while she made adjustments with a mouse.

When she was happy, she turned the screen towards me.

"It's not the finished product...just to give you an idea."

Even from my prone position, I could see that it was a beautiful composition. She had caught my face in the half-light so that it was undoubtedly me, but the expression could have been one either of agony or ecstasy.

My body was arched, emphasizing my breasts and the toned shape of my thighs, which I am so proud of. It was as if she had reached inside and learned of the things about me that had the most appeal as far as I was concerned.

What was she said next that completely skewed all of my assumptions?

"I've tried to capture your natural submissiveness..."

In my view, I was a pretty tough cookie. My career seemed like a constant stream of adversities that had to be overcome, and it would have been easy to crumble under stress imposed by my relationships.

Again, in some uncanny way, it felt as if she was following my train of thought.

"There is great difference between the face that you present to the world at large and that which you show to those who know you most intimately."

This continuing presumption that they knew me better than I knew myself was beginning to anger me, and it must have shown. Evelyn touched my face.

"I could prove it to you..."

I watched as she took off her jumper and then started to remove her skirt. She was the only anchor point on reality in this surreal environment, and now the chain was slipping.

For a second or two, she stood in just her underwear, and I noted how much more expensive it looked than mine. A burgundy, lace fringed bra uplifted her impressive breasts matched by a pair of French panties.

With her slightly untamed long brown hair, she looked like a woman out of time; before the waif era, she could have stepped out of a McGill seaside postcard.

For the present, all thoughts of release were forgotten as I waited to see what she would do next. A moment later, with all the grace of a seasoned Burlesque performer, she stripped naked.

She had praised my appearance, but it always felt like a constant work in progress, an ongoing review of diet, fitness, and cosmetics. While looking at her, there was an effortlessness and confidence in the natural beauty she possessed.

She sat beside me again, and I could not help but look at her breasts. They were heavy but superbly rounded with neat, upward-pointing, pink nipples. She saw where I was looking and, in response, she reached out to me.

She brushed my nipple with the back of her finger, perking it to life.

"You have nothing to be jealous of..."

She was so close that I could feel the warmth of her breath, and, for the briefest instant, I wanted nothing more than to feel the fullness of her body pressed to mine.

That thought was made manifest as she seemingly flowed over me with a teasing touching of flesh. I tried to lift myself to meet her, but she gracefully rose above me until her knees slipped over my captive arms.

I was enclosed by the columns of her pale, sculpted thighs, and there, filling my vision was the splendor of her sex.

"I know that you have been fantasizing about Jessica but now I want your total concentration."

Her skin was enviably flawless, and only the faintest tracery on her inner thighs betrayed the fact that she was an older woman. Her sex, set against the expanse of her legs, was surprisingly shy, a smooth mound with a perfectly straight divide.

She let me stare for a few moments more, and then she touched a finger to my mouth.

"You know what I want you to do..."

Of course, I knew, but to hear her say it still came as a shock. I was restrained, it was against my will, why then did I not object?

Slowly, so as not to alarm me, she relaxed and began a measured descent, and every detail was magnified; the increased pressure on my arms and the heat radiating her thighs; the renewed strength of her perfume, which she must have dabbed between her legs. Most of all, the deepening shadow into which I was now cast.

I felt detached from the world; my only reason for being the fulfillment of her desire.

She paused and held steady just millimeters away, and the heated scent of her excitement inexorably filled the void, increasing my sense of space denied.

"Kiss it..."

It was said sotto voice, barely a command, but it chimed in my sub-conscious. Somewhere, coherent thoughts, the makings of a protest, were being formed, but this one immediate need shouted them down.

I raised my head, formed my lips together, and laid a kiss at the center of her mons before falling back.

"Once more...show me your devotion."

They were just words, so why did they have such a disturbing effect? This time my inner turmoil held me in stasis, but she waited patiently, knowing that there was only one possible outcome.

I closed again, this time, it was a longer, fuller, kiss, and as I broke away, I licked the taste of her from my lips.

It was a taste familiar from my guilty fingers, a promise of excitation and fulfillment, and I felt a powerful tingling between my legs.

"Lick me...nice and slowly."

Again, she phrased it as a demand, but where there should have been anger, I just felt more aroused. I had relinquished all control and, in so doing, everything suddenly seemed so simple.

She stayed poised above me so that it required an effort on my part to do as she asked, but, once I began, I was aware of nothing other than that intimate connection between us. I licked her mound, registering its smoothness and pliancy as I began to explore.

I used the flat of my tongue, and each time I crossed the divide, I was rewarded with a hint of what lay within. From time to time, I looked up to find her smiling indulgently safe, knowing that I would do whatever she asked of me.

"Rest you head now. I want your tongue inside and this is going to take a little while."

I laid back my head on the pillow, and there was a momentary alarm as she sank onto my face, but she allowed me time to accustom myself to the increased pressure.

Her sex lay open to me, and I braced my tongue slipping inside her with unexpected ease. As I did so, the taste of her almost overwhelmed me. There was a richness that excited first my tongue and then my whole body.

I probed as deeply as I could craving more, and then there was a new thrill as I felt her skilled muscles holding me in place. I lay there, breathing in the heat and wetness, and I felt as if I had found myself.

She let me remain as I was for a long time, the only evidence of her engagement the occasional welling of moisture into my mouth, but in the end, I lacked the strength to keep my tongue strained to its limit.

As I withdrew, my one desire was to gather myself and try again to see if I could bring this beautiful creature to a shuddering orgasm.

She sighed softly, and I felt a new jolt as she gently squeezed her breasts before speaking once more.

"You've done well, and you'll do more...a lot more...but there is something particularly to my liking. Unfortunately, you may not enjoy it quite so much but you should take comfort knowing the pleasure it brings me."

With that, she eased forward, just slightly closing her thighs as she did so. I was entombed beneath her.

I could hear nothing but the quiet groaning of the bedsprings and the racing of my pulse in my ears. My eyes were pressed closed, and I could only breathe with a concerted effort. It was how I imagined a tropical jungle to be. The enclosed air was hot and heavy with moisture, every breath deeply scented.

For some reason, a recent article I had written came to mind. An American doctor, working with people with dementia applied total immersion techniques using mainly taste and smell to reinforce memories.

She kept me under for a long time, and I sensed, rather than heard, that she was conversing with Jessica. I tried not to panic, telling myself that she meant no harm, but as minutes ticked by, I became light-headed.

When, at last, she moved a little, I thought it was over, but she was only beginning. She settled again and, slowly at first, she began to rock herself on my face.

It was not painful but certainly uncomfortable and grew more so as she leisurely gathered pace. She moved rhythmically and with control as she worked herself from my chin to my forehead.

I should have been outraged, but as she slid ever more easily, smearing me with her essence, I moved my head to the extent that I could accommodate her. I felt like a total whore, but the more she abused me, the closer I came to orgasm.

It reached a point where she became more focused, bearing down on the bridge of my nose, and then she stopped moving altogether. I barely had time to wonder what was wrong when her body began to quiver, and then I felt her climax as it pulsed through her causing her to cry out joyfully.

It took an enviably long time to recede altogether, but she was left drained and unable to move. I remained sealed in, her weight bearing down more heavily and her sex leaking freely.

I was becoming overheated, and I started to squirm anxiously to give myself some much-needed breathing space, but then I felt a firm pressure between my legs.

It could only be Jessica, and within seconds, her skillful fingers were exciting, my clitoris. She knew exactly how to play me, and she brought me to within a hairsbreadth of a climax so that I was breathing hard with every draught of air enriched with humid arousal.

My agitated movements spurred Evelyn back to life, and she raised herself sufficiently to make it clear what she wanted. In a frenzy, I began to employ my tongue while Jessica continued to keep me at a fever pitch.

I did not think that I could hold out, but she eased off only to fire me up time and time again until, finally, Evelyn reached a second climax, and I was allowed to join her exultantly. Our orgasms seemed to feed off one another, increasing the intensity of taking me to a new realm. I did not want it to end, but I was close to exhaustion, and I licked one last time before collapsing, completely spent.

Chapter 04

The new article took on a life of its own. Helped, in great part, by Evelyn's prints, it got picked up by the tabloids, and I was even receiving requests to do television. I was under no illusions; it was not me that they wanted to interview; they were using me as a conduit to get to Jessica.

I wondered if their attitude would have differed had they known that I was the "other woman" in the photographs. The magazine let it quietly be known that models had not been used, and then, from somewhere, a rumor started that the submissive was a person in the public eye.

Evelyn had worked her magic, and, as the guessing game ensued, I was very flattered by some of the names being suggested.

My money worries were dissipated almost overnight, not least because Jessica was on a very modest percentage. Further investigation revealed that she was the only child of wealthy parents and could be considered wealthy in her own right.

I learned that, while her childhood was not unhappy, her parents had not lavished her with affection. Nannies and tutors effectively raised her until she could be packed off to boarding school. She wanted for nothing, but there was an emotional void.

I considered whether or not there might be a third article exploring the psychological origins of her particular preference, but she quickly poured cold water on the idea. Above all else, she wished to preserve her privacy.

I also started to receive calls from friends and contacts who had all but cut me off. In several instances, I took great pleasure in being curtly dismissive, but one e-mail did excite me.

It came from May Eddington at the Femrights publishing house. I knew her from University when her name was May Flowers, and she was the first declared lesbian of my acquaintance. Intrigued by the change of name, I looked up her on-line profile and found that she had entered a Civil Partnership and changed her surname by deed poll.

I still carried a guilty conscience about the way I treated her at University. For my first term there we were room-mates. She was open about her sexuality, and her plain Jane appearance and strongly held feminist convictions reinforced my image of lesbians in general.

In truth, she was great to share with. She was tidy, diligent, always ready to help, and completely respected all of the boundaries. The problem was that I became the butt of snickering rumors, and, after the first term, I asked to be moved, making it clear to everyone that I was uncomfortable with the arrangement.

The inference was that May had acted with impropriety, and nothing could be further from the truth. Nevertheless, a whispering campaign began.

Years later, I was so glad to hear of her success. With more gumption than I gave her credit for, she set up her own publishing house on leaving University. To begin with, it focused mainly on feminist issues but still enjoyed modest success.

At some point, she must have compromised her principles because, seizing the zeitgeist, she started a new imprint and began to publish Chick Lit. For me, the books were total fluff, but she had a knack of picking a winner, and she was now a big player.

In her e-mail, she asked if I ever considered writing a book, invited me to join her for lunch with colleagues, and with thoughts of a chance to make my name and an opportunity to apologize after all these years. I set out to her office.

The building itself was a real eye-opener, a converted Edwardian terrace next to the theatre district on which no expense had been spared. I was taken up to the Board Room, which was an expansively glazed addition to the original flat roof. It gave a wonderfully quirky view over the rooftops of the old city.

"You like it?"

I turned around, and I had to do a double-take. The woman who had walked into the room was May but not the May that I knew. Gone was the mousey hair and the troublesome teenage acne. Even her timorous posture had changed.

This was a confident businesswoman who could have stepped straight off of an advertising hoarding. Her hair was a deep shade of red-brown, expensively coiffured, that harmonized with her dark eyes, which were more beautiful than I remembered.

Her make-up was impeccably applied, and she wore a bright red lipstick that only the most self-assured could get away with.

Throughout her days at University, she had always dressed in jeans and shapeless tops, but today, in her tailored business attire, I appreciated for the first time just how good a body she had.

I was still lost for words, but she filled in without missing a beat.

"I thought that we would take lunch up here. We have it sent in from the deli over the road. It's very good and it allows us a little more privacy."

I was still debating whether or not to shake her hand when she came and kissed me on the cheek.

"It's been a long time."

Before I could say anything more, the food arrived and was set out on the table, and then we were quickly joined by May's colleagues.

"Let me introduce Nalini and Erin."

The two women formed a stark contrast. Nalini looked to be of Indian extraction. She was tall, entirely dressed in black, but her most striking feature was her shorn hair. It was barely a stubble over her whole scalp; cut back as if not to detract from her perfect face.

Erin, despite the Irish name and accent, was a bubbly blonde. She was pretty in a cute way if that was your thing, but her clothes were a triumph of hope over-ambition.

She was a little dumpy but wore a dress that was as low cut on her chest as it was high on her legs.

May poured the wine, and we enjoyed the food while making small talk, which centered mainly on her and I catching up. Given her evident success, I felt like the poor relation, but she was at pains to put me at ease, and she was gushing about the recent articles.

Slowly, the conversation turned towards books, and Nalini came into her own. She was managing editor of the original feminist imprint, but she was very knowledgeable about the industry. She started to sound me out on any thoughts or ideas I might already have had.

Unfortunately, when it came down to it, I was too vague and did not help when Nalini said that a passion for a subject fuelled the most successful books. They were usually the same books that needed the most editing.

At this point, May interjected.

"I've invited Erin here to give an author's viewpoint."

I have to say I was taken by surprise. What little Erin had added to the conversation seemed completely vacuous, and I had not imagined her to be a writer. When she then referred to her recent book, I nearly fell off my seat. She wrote under a pen name and her books sold by the truckload.

It was immediately clear that while one or two of her ideas might be deemed original, her literary skills were almost zero. Her books had to have been edited to within an inch of their lives. The more I listened to the nonsense she spouted the angrier I grew. May must have known that this was the sort of woman that would put me on edge.

I began to think that she was never going to stop, but May cut across her.

"Let's cut to the chase. The book I would like you to write, the book you want to write, should chronicle your descent into lesbian submission."

I looked at her appalled. I was shocked that she would say something like that in the company, but her perception jolted me. She smiled as she continued.

"Do you want to deny that it's you in those photographs?"

I sat trying to come to terms with my confused thoughts, and she continued without waiting for an answer.

"You know the ironic thing about how you mistreated me at University? I knew all along that you were a lesbian even if you didn't know it yourself. I could even have been attracted to you but I chose not to influence you in any way."

It was too much to take in. Had she really known? I tried to get things back onto a normal track.

"Look, I appreciate your hospitality but what am I really here for? Are you offering me a deal?"

"Yes, I am. I think that your articles could be fleshed out into a bestseller. Obviously, you will need to widen your experience and learn more about yourself. That's why Erin is with us."

I took a deep breath.

"With all due respect to Erin, and her undoubted achievement, there is little or nothing she can teach me about writing."

"You misunderstand. Erin is writing a new book in which she needs to describe her heroine's first lesbian experience. Now, in order to help her with that you are going to crawl under the table, you are going to politely ask her permission and then you are going to eat her out until she tells you to stop."

The suggestion was despicable, but the assuredness she had spoken and the unwavering way she held my eye sent a tingle down my spine. I looked at Nalini, but her demeanor was calm as if I had been asked to pour tea.

Inevitably I turned towards Erin and, while she tried to look collected, her eyes were lit with greedy expectation.

The real me resented this, but I felt disembodied hovering over the immoral slut I had become looking to satisfy her depraved craving. When the two recombined, any pretense at rationality was subsumed by the need of the flesh.

I no longer cared as I crouched beneath the table: at least here, I did not have to see their faces. As I crawled towards Erin, she opened her legs, and I saw that she was not wearing panties. She had known all along that it would come to this. Even as she registered my disdain at her empty-headed advice, she knew that I would be humbled.

As I drew nearer, the further evidence hung in the air. The reek of her was strong, attesting a lengthy period of anticipatory arousal.

Her pale thighs were a little plump, but nothing that a little structured exercise would not put right, and her sex looked befittingly plump. Her dusky labia stood proud, and even in the subdued light beneath the table, they shone with moisture.

Saliva filled my mouth, and I swallowed hard. I nudged between her legs now wanting to taste her, but she lifted her skirt and held me still.

I looked up into her triumphant eyes, and she raised a quizzical eyebrow.

In a searing moment of clarity, I saw the insanity of what I was doing, but I could no more prevent myself than stop breathing. I sold what was left of my pride and whispered.

"May I?"

"Be my guest."

There was no finesse. She shrieked with laughter as I fell upon her sealing my mouth to her sex and pressing my tongue deep inside. I was rewarded with a surge of pent up arousal, and I sucked upon her ravenously.

Within seconds my sex began to leak as, somewhere deep inside, switches were thrown, and my mind and body found a new configuration. It felt so natural as if, for years, I had been misaligned.

Once again, her arousal was stoking mine in a symbiosis that I had never felt with a male partner.

It did not take her long to reach a climax, but she did a good job of disguising it from the others. I was dimly aware of their conversation and occasional laughter, but Erin wanted my total concentration as she shepherded me towards her clitoris.

The second was a far more protracted affair as, even as I employed all of my newfound skills, she was determined to savor the moment. My face and her thighs were wet with sweat before she finally melted into another orgasm.

She dismissed me with a deep, satisfied, sigh, and a flush of embarrassment immediately beset me. How had a business meeting degenerated into this, and how was I to extricate myself?

I came out from under the table and, without meeting their eyes, I used a napkin to tidy myself up as best I could. When I was done, I reached for my wine glass and drained the remaining contents in one gulp.

I decided that the best and only option was to get up and leave without another word. They could laugh about it amongst themselves, but I did not have to see any of them ever again.

Not trusting my judgment, I looked towards Nalini, hoping to gauge the room's atmosphere, but her expression was inscrutable. May broke the awkward silence.

"She seems to find you particularly fascinating Nalini. Would you like to use her?"

It took an instant to process the implications of what had been said, but my sex seemed to react more quickly than my mind. I felt a swathe of heat, centered between my legs, spreading out across my whole body.

Nalini looked me up and down dismissively, keeping me off balance, and then stood up.

"I think I will."

As if it were the most natural thing in the world, she stood up, kicked off her shoes, and began to unfasten her designer jeans. With my heart racing, I watched as she eased the black denim free then proceeded to remove her panties.

I guessed that she was touching thirty, but she had the body of a catwalk model. She sat back down again and nonchalantly hooked her long legs over the arms of the chair.

Her casual wantonness almost made me climax on the spot, and when she wordlessly gestured for me to approach, I felt weak at the knees.

I took my place between her legs and saw the motif of shorn hair was repeated on her pubis, but here it was immaculately shaved into a representation of a labrys with the short handle pointing the way down to her sex.

I had taken a Medieval Studies module at University and so its symbolism, and the current usage was not lost on me.

Her skin was the color of rich honey, but her labia were darker still. They stood proud of her cleft like a pair of open wings, and they gradually shaded to an inviting pinkness.

Almost reverentially, I took a turn between my lips. I licked at the fringes, but there was a foretaste of what was to come. In truth, the taste was familiar and exciting, but in my mind, I imbued it with a subtle exoticism.

She did not hurry me, and it was a long time before I relinquished this particular treat and then began a deeper survey. She was incredibly relaxed, and I eased inside her effortlessly to lick the syrupy offering from the walls of her sex.

Even knowing that I was being watched, I felt curiously contented the only problem being an ever stronger need to do something about my state of arousal. As things stood, my panties were going to be beyond redemption.

I felt as if we were conjoined. Her labia clung at my face as I stretched my tongue to its limit, but now she wanted something more. Sensing her requirement, I refocused my attention at the apex of her sex, and here lay a fresh discovery.

Her clitoris had unveiled itself, and it was beyond anything that I had ever imagined. Any fisherman lucky enough to find a pearl this large could have retired with assured riches. I could feel its firm roundness as I used the flat of my tongue, and she began to purr with pleasure.

I became lost in her. The others were forgotten, and time was of no consequence as I continued the act of reverence. There was a simple, blissful relief from all my worldly cares.

I fell into an easy rhythm, licking in a lazy figure of eight, and she touched the top of my head in a silent command to carry on exactly as I was.

The result was a climax almost as majestic as she was. She stayed totally in control of herself regulating the ebb and flowed until the very end when my face was baptized with gouts of warm moisture, which dampened my hair and ran down to soak my blouse.

When it was over, she gracefully unwound her legs, but my work was not finished. I preened her legs and her sex. I was cleaning her of all residue even while her offering was drying on my skin.

She got up from the seat and coolly put her clothes back on, leaving me kneeling on the floor. My tongue was tired, and my jaw was in danger of cramping, but there was one more task to complete, and, to my surprise, I was both prepared and expectant.

I turned to May with a renewed yearning, but she smiled indulgently.

"You have to learn that the cruellest twist of all...is denial."

With that, and without another word, all three of them left the room.

Chapter 05

The formal offer was couriered to me the following day. The advance was eye-watering, but the first draft had to be completed within six months to tap the original articles' interest.

In a side letter, May said that she wanted more in the same vein. She was not looking for any attempt at professional analysis; she wanted my thoughts, impressions, and conclusions. She left it up to me whether or not I wanted to make it a first-person narrative but strongly hinted that she wanted the board room episode included.

From my standpoint, there were two stories to be told. One was the recognition that I had been evading and denying my true sexuality. This was the easy part. The second was the fulfillment that I had found in adopting a submissive role.

The fact was that I was seriously troubled. I could see myself living a perfectly normal life with another woman, but could I suppress this new need I had found within myself?

My immediate reaction was to fix myself up a couple of normal dates and give myself some benchmark. To this end, I signed up with a lesbian dating site, but I found that it was fraught with many of the same difficulties that I had encountered with men.

The women I met up with were not my type; they were not people I would readily befriend, let alone anything beyond that.

My next attempt was to try a couple of lesbian clubs, including one that was BDSM themed. Still, while I found some women, especially those of a dominant persuasion, very attractive, I could not fully engage with what was going on.

The only good thing to come out of it was the provided material, but, at this stage, the book had no coherence. All of my instincts told me to go back to where it all started and speak to Jessica again. But this was now my story and not hers.

It was then, out of the blue, that I received an unexpected phone call. Evelyn called to confirm that she had received her payment and thanked me once again for the commission. She went on to ask me if I would care to join her for a celebratory meal.

I accepted, but I put the phone down with very mixed feelings. I waited for her the following evening in the bar at "Chez Alec" being the most bohemian restaurant I could think of. She arrived ten minutes late, but she entered the restaurant like a force of nature.

She wore a dress that displayed her curves to the utmost, not least her impressive décolletage. She wore her hair up, which helped to tame it a little, and she had applied very minimal make-up.

I was not the only one staring at her impressive legs as she sashayed across to hug me effusively.

With one or two obvious considerations, I felt very easy in her company, and it was several hours later before we got up to leave. I expected her to ask me back. A part of me was hoping for a repeat of what had gone before.

Much to my surprise, she kissed me primly on the cheek, with no hint of our former intimacy, and said very simply.

"I'd like to see you again."

As she departed in a taxi, I felt like a teenager. The prospect of a second 'date' had me stupidly excited.

In the next few weeks, we met up six times, and not once did she come on to me. It was an old fashioned courtship, a slow getting to know one another, and I loved it. Our partings left me as frustrated as hell, but I did not want to force the pace.

Finally, after a night spent at a new gallery opening, she invited me back to her studio. I expected coffee, but she led me by the hand to her sumptuously appointed bedroom. She had me stand beside her beautifully carved four-poster, and then she slowly began to undress me as if I were a precious gift.

As each article of clothing was removed, she stroked my skin, and as she knelt to remove my panties, I thought my legs were going to buckle.

She eased me back onto the richly quilted bed cover and then undressed. I held my breath as her magnificent body was teasingly revealed, but then she surprised me as she put on a short satin nightdress.

She smiled when she saw my disappointment, but she came and laid down next to me.

"Tonight it's all about you."

She rose over me and touched her lips to mine. For a few seconds, we breathed one another, but then she brought our mouths together, and I felt the tip of her tongue reaching out.

The overall impression was one of the wonderful softness. I had always enjoyed kissing but now knew that I had never really experienced it. There was no imperative to bring things to the next stage; it was just a long, languid enjoyment of one another, our tongues dancing together as if we had known each other all our lives.

I became so absorbed that I initially failed to notice as she began to stroke my shoulder before her hand found its way to my breast. At first, she grazed with just her fingertips before more boldly testing its shape and form.

This was not the clumsy fumbling that I was used to. The artist in her had an appreciation of the feminine contours while the woman understood the sensations she could engender.

My nipples became engorged long before she touched them, and when she did, it was with a feather-light caress seeking out the boundaries and discovering how I reacted.

I loved being stroked in this way, but I had never considered someone with such finesse. It was an age before she brought her thumbs into play and began to pinch gently, and my sex felt as if a direct connection had been forged.

I was seeping, and I was eager for her to venture downwards, but she had other ideas. She took my nipple between her lips, and her tongue flitted over the tip as she gently sucked. I felt a lurch in the pit of my stomach and with it the comprehension that she was relentlessly driving me towards the edge.

Despairing of any man, I had tried so many times to bring myself to orgasm this way but always grew impatient and thought it was a myth. Now she was dispelling it. Her tongue circled the whole of my nipple and then came back to the teat at irregular intervals while her fingers worked similar magic on my other breast.

Getting hotter by the second, and I had to fight the urge to fidget, not wanting to do anything that would disturb the equilibrium. I was reeling, and when, finally, she gently nipped me with her teeth and applied a correspondingly dull pressure with her thumb and finger, it was the trigger I sought.

It was not a tsunami but more a series of heavy waves, each, in turn, bearing me up to be held still and then released only to be raised even higher. It was wonderful in itself, but it most certainly left me wanting more.

I had the impression that Evelyn could have produced an even stronger reaction had she wished, but she had only painted the first strokes.

I sighed as she repositioned herself but then stiffened in expectation as she kissed a trail down towards my navel. It is deep-set, and I have always been conscious of it, fearing that it suggestive of a bigger belly, but she began to lavish attention as if it were a mystical cave.

I had never thought of it as an erogenous zone, but her delicate exploration was already rekindling the waves of pleasure, which, I thought, had ebbed entirely. She worked purposefully, and only gradually did I appreciate that she was telling me with her tongue what was to come.

With this understanding, I shifted my hips, wanting her to fulfill her promise, but she stayed as she forced me to relax and be patient. When she deigned to move, it was at a glacial pace, kissing as she went, while all the time, her knowing hands continued to trace and titillate the outline of my body.

By the time she reached my thighs, they were sheened in sweat, and she licked them lasciviously with the flat of her tongue.

She was almost driving me insane with need but still made me wait before she assayed the delta of my sex. She ran her finger lightly along the fringes of my swollen labia and then sucked on it appreciatively. The look on her face as she closed her eyes was pure lust, and I groaned in anticipation.

She replaced her finger with her tongue, and her touch was lighter still, but it was enough to make my sex ooze. Still not to be hurried, she continued to lick as if imprinting every detail in her memory.

My head was clear of all thought except for her and her devoted attention. When she sealed her mouth to my sex, and her tongue worked its spell inside me, I cried tears of joy.

I could not hold back my second orgasm, nor did she attempt to deny me. She read every nuance, increasing the depth of penetration each time I was buoyed up and then relaxing a little as I paused before restarting the ascent.

I could feel myself squeezing hard against her tongue, but she showed no distress. She stayed with me until the dam broke, and I felt a heavenly flooding release.

She continued to lick and swallow for the whole time that it took me to recover, and I feared that I would exhaust her, but I had underestimated her determination.

She resumed her ministrations of my labia, which, if anything, were feeling even more sensitive. My whole body was quickly stirred and, while I would not have thought it possible, I sensed that there was better yet to come.

Over the next few minutes, she changed the point of concentration little by little until she was centered on the crown of my sex. She licked in tightening circles, and my clitoris engorged in response.

I was almost panting with desire, but still, she avoided the gem itself. It was becoming ever more difficult to resist the impulse to use my fingers to open myself up to her, but I forced myself to calm down.

The reward, when at last it came, was almost beyond words. I was acutely aware of every subtle change as she varied the degree of contact and pace in her quest to understand my innermost need.

In so doing, she removed any element of doubt. There was no fear of being rushed or left disappointed as so often in the past. She was perfectly in tune with me reading the rhythms of my body and bringing me to a perfect pitch.

As I reached my orgasm, she helped me retain control, measure, and enjoy each ecstatic increment until my body reached an undreamed-of nirvana. I wanted to hold myself there forever, but my inner strength finally failed me, and I slumped in a state of delicious exhaustion.

I felt very guilty when I found that I had fallen asleep. The room was much darker, and I had been covered up, but I barely had time to orientate myself before I felt a nuzzling from beneath the quilt and the pure delight of a tireless tongue.

Chapter 06

The following morning I tried to apologize, but Evelyn was having none of it. I hoped that we could fix another date, and very soon, but I was to be disheartened. She told me that I had to finish the book and, when it was done, she would be there for me if that was what I wanted.

I managed to leave her studio before the tears started, but in reality, I was more confused than ever. After all that she gave, was she suggesting that I would have to accede to her dominant trait to be with her?

On the journey home, I knew that the previous night had, in some way, been a pivotal moment, and the understanding of it was the key to the completion of the book.

Sitting at my desk, I randomly wrote down all of my thoughts and impressions as well as the questions I was asking of myself. It formed a long untidy list, but somewhere in it, I caught a glimpse of something. I put it to one side, hoping that it would reveal itself if I left it alone for a day or two.

Towards the weekend, I received a call from May. I told her, a little untruthfully, that the bulk of the book was prepared, but that was not her reason for contacting me. She told me that she had a release from the magazine for the Jessica material, but her approval was also needed.

I assumed that her legal people would deal with it, but May told me that these things went a lot more smoothly when conducted informally. To that end, she wanted me to fix up a meeting with Jessica.

I had broached the topic with Jessica at the outset, and she seemed enthusiastic about the project and looked forward to an extended reappraisal of our sessions together. Now, when I told her that the publisher wished to meet, her interest was piqued.

In keeping with her wish to keep things on a casual basis May asked if we could meet at Jessica's house. I fixed the meeting for eight p.m., but when I arrived, May was already there, and the pair of them seemed to be getting along just fine.

Jessica poured the wine, and the formalities were tied up quickly. I have to say that I was impressed with the way that May handled the negotiations. She was slick, confident, and a world away from the woman I knew previously. She even broached the possibility of Jessica producing a book of her own, an idea that left me with very mixed feelings.

It felt more than a little odd to be sitting there, holding a normal conversation with two women who had seen me humiliate myself in quite the way that I had. May even went to lengths to flatter me.

"You write so well. The third person narrative you've employed gives no hint that you were actually the victim. You were the victim, right? You've allowed the reader to put themselves in the place of either participant with equal facility."

There seemed little point in denying it. At heart, I wanted this to be a serious study, that's why I had gone along with the pain that Jessica had inflicted on me, but I was no fool. Conveying an understanding was one thing, but it was the inherent titillation that would ultimately sell the book.

May brought me back to reality when she leaned forward eagerly.

"May I see the room?"

Jessica smiled as she got up.

"Of course."

She was wearing a pale yellow dress that was little more than a chemise. It seemed provocative, but we were in her home, and so who was I to judge. I did notice that May was giving her legs an appreciative glance as she led the way.

When Jessica opened the door, my heart quickened. The room was as large as the lounge. The center was a raised podium above, which was the bar from which I had been suspended.

Around it there was more equipment and, once again, it appeared to me that no expense had been spared in fitting it out. May was suitably impressed.

"Oh my word...Soundproofed?"

"Yes, but the house is detached anyway."

243

May wandered around, examining the various fixtures. The largest looked more like a piece of exercise equipment. It had a recumbent seat set in front of a large padded hummock.

"Intriguing. How does it work?"

Jessica looked as if she was about to embark on an explanation, but then she smiled.

"It's probably easier if I demonstrate."

She turned to me and said as if it were the most natural thing in the world.

"Get undressed."

I do not know if it was the setting, their presence, or the total inconsistency of what she said, but her words hit me like a cosh. I looked at May, but she just raised an amused eyebrow. I stood dumbfounded, but then Jessica took hold of the hem of her dress and raised it fractionally.

It was a simple gesture, but it had a disproportionate effect. It was the hint of a promise, and my tongue moved reflexively in my mouth. I was little more than an automaton as I started to remove my clothes.

Looking back, I told myself that I was trying to avoid coming across as a spoilsport, but it was a feeble avoidance of the truth.

Jessica patted the hummock and gestured for me to lay over it. I did as she asked, glad now to hide my nakedness partially. She crossed the room, opened a cupboard, and said to May.

"Would you like to help?"

They returned, holding an array of leather cuffs and belts, and I began to mildly protest, suggesting that it was time to bring proceedings to a close. Jessica laughed and told me to shush.

They drew down my arms and legs and used cuffs to bind my wrists and ankles to fastenings at the foot of the hummock. Once I was secured, they employed the belts across my back and around my thighs to completely immobilize me, and May seemed to take particular delight in cinching them as tight as possible.

It was an odd feeling. I was helpless, but there was a calmness to be drawn from the fact that I was no longer in control of my destiny. Also, my legs were lewdly spread, and my sex was pressed to the slightly roughened leather surface, setting up sensations that were unwelcome just at that moment.

Now that I was bound in place, it was evident to both May and me, what was to happen next. She looked across at Jessica and asked.

"Would you mind?"

Jessica smiled in response.

"Please. Go ahead."

May did not bother to undress altogether. She looked at me as she casually removed her skirt and divested herself of her panties. A little awkwardly, she settled into the seat and made herself comfortable.

I was left staring down between her open legs at the thicket of dark curls that dressed her sex; this was the first time she had exposed herself to me even though we had previously shared a bedroom and bathroom.

The device left us some way apart, but I could already smell her excited state and wondered what happened next. The answer came when Jessica handed her a remote control.

May experimented with the bottoms and squealed with excitement as the seat smoothly began to move. Within seconds she had it mastered, and she raised herself, bringing her sex to press firmly against my mouth.

"This must have cost you a fortune!"

Jessica touched me on the back as she replied.

"I have a client whom you would recognize. She's a television actress, happily married, but she has certain predilections. She has a young admirer and she brings her here to avail herself of my facilities. She paid to have this constructed and installed."

Amid my anguish, I wondered if I could use this titbit in the book, knowing that the answer had to be no. The press feeding frenzy if such a thing were to come out would not bear thinking about.

May settled more comfortably into the seat and shifted her hips forward fractionally with the result that my nose was pressed deep into her damp fur where her scent was almost overpowering.

The calm that imbued me up to that point gave way to a sudden urge to rebel, but, short of biting her, there was nothing I could do. Some part of me still yearned for her, but, for the moment, I stubbornly refused to cooperate.

A sharp snap, and a sudden pain, made me open my mouth in a stifled scream of anger. It felt as if a hot iron had been set to my backside, and it was immediately followed by a second searing strike to my other cheek.

Jessica came and knelt by my side, showing me the riding crop she held in her hand.

"I'm sure I don't have to spell it out; if I think that you are not putting in enough effort..."

I wanted to protest, but I was suffocated by Mays's sex, which was now appreciably wetter. Jessica disappeared from view, and I braced myself for more pain, but I was given an opportunity to cooperate.

It was galling on two counts. Firstly the fact that I had no choice, but perhaps, even worse, I wanted to do it. I was immersed in her warmth and moisture, and it was acting on me like a drug.

I began to lick, softening the tight curls before applying gentle pressure. Her sex opened to me with almost obscene ease and a deep hum issued from her throat. The sound reverberated through her, and I felt it with my lips.

Encouraged, I worked my tongue a little more quickly, but my awkward position put a continual strain on my neck.

"Is it satisfactory?"

"Not quite, she should be able to get her tongue a lot deeper than that."

The sting of her criticism was matched by two crisp strikes of the crop reigniting the dying pain that tormented my buttocks. I wailed resentfully, but May's response was to mash me more firmly into her heated maw.

Her sex seemed amorphous, and I found it difficult to orientate and establish the best method of bringing her quickly to fruition. Submitting to her urging, I thrust as deeply as I could, releasing an inner pool, the richness of which swamped my senses.

The pain that I felt receded to be replaced by euphoria and an intense thrilling of my nerve endings emanating from my sex. I began to devour her, knowing that, if I could bring her to a climax, it would sufficiently resonate for me to join her.

At some point, Jessica playfully slapped me again, but I was beyond caring. May tried to hold back, but my enthusiasm took her by surprise. She wanted me to find her clitoris, but I stayed rooted deep inside her, where the ever stronger spasms of her muscles betrayed her imminent release.

She came violently, shaking in her seat, and tightly pressed to my face. In response, I opened my mouth wide and screamed inside her as my orgasm strained my restricted body.

Fortunately, she had the presence of mind to ease herself away from a little as I gasped for breath, but she was still close enough to see her sex throbbing as she slowly came down from on high.

She needed Jessica's help to get up from her seat and, even then, she was visibly unsteady on her feet.

"That was really something else!"

"I'm glad you enjoyed it...but we're not quite finished yet."

With that, she eased herself into the seat that May had vacated and slowly parted her legs.

She must have been able to see for herself that I was spent, but it was of no consequence to her. She took up the control pad, but, to my surprise, she moved the seat backward until we were about twelve inches apart.

She calmly raised her dress, to confirm that she was not wearing anything beneath, and then she brought her fingers to her sex. Over the next minute or two, she watched me as she teased herself, and I felt my mouth watering as beads of moisture seeped from her.

My tiredness was forgotten as I awaited the opportunity to serve, and her smile told me that she was fully aware of my longing. Continuing her leisurely manipulation, she addressed herself to May.

"I could do with a little stimulus..."

Her meaning was unclear, not least because May was out of my sight, and I remained enraptured by her total inhibition.

The answer came in a fresh blaze of pain. This was not the sharp sting of the riding crop but a dull, heavy, splat that flared right across my backside.

"Very good...again."

I shrieked in defiance, but the second blow fell, setting up a new burning track on virgin flesh. I turned my head to entreat her, but she was already raising the leather strap for the third time. There was a look of malice in her eyes as she struck me again.

Her technique was unrefined, with the unfamiliar implement, but that made it no less painful. I twisted back towards Jessica, hoping for a show of pity from that quarter, but she now had two fingers deep within while her thumb worked purposefully on her clitoris.

Her eyes brightened with excitement as May continued to set about me, and the tears streaming down my face only seemed to heighten her pleasure. Only when she had reached a climax did my tormentress relent but, by then, I was almost beyond pain.

Chapter 07

For the next ten days, I was a complete mess. The marks on my skin had faded, but the mental scars were as vivid as ever. I came close, several times, to giving up on the book altogether, but the plain fact was that I needed the money. In my darker moments, I wondered if May was aware of this and had used it to her advantage.

Ironically, I was excited about the material I had accumulated, but it still needed wrapping up in some way. One of the major decisions was in deciding whether or not to include my night with Evelyn. She was inextricably bound up with the journey I had taken, but I wanted it to be a different facet.

She had told me to come back when the book was finished, but my need to see her again was becoming overwhelming.

I was researching a new article, which I hoped to sell and so help me out of the cul de sac that the book had become, but I could not entirely focus. After twenty minutes of staring at an all but empty screen, I surrendered and picked up the phone.

My heart leaped when I heard her voice, and she was genuinely excited to hear from me. She suggested that we returned to "Chez Alec," but I felt a pang of jealousy when she said that the waitress was adorable.

I spent a lot of time getting ready, and it felt a little strange, deciding how I could make myself most attractive to her. In the end, I dressed demurely and only later considered whether or not there had been something sub-conscious in my choice.

On this occasion, she arrived first, and it transpired that she had booked the Gide room. André Gide had reputedly lived in the apartment above the restaurant on his short stay to London during the First World War. The dining table was ostensibly the original that he had used as a writing desk, and the room was decorated in period style.

She must have noted my hesitation because, as she stood to kiss me on the cheek, she laughed.

"Don't worry. I'm paying."

The private room provided a delightful intimacy, and in her easy company, I felt more relaxed than I had for weeks. The food, as ever, was simple but delicious and we drank house wine by the carafe.

The only slight discord was that she had arranged for us to be served by the young French waitress that she had commented on previously. I could not deny that she was a lovely young woman, but I wouldn't say I liked the impression she gave, that we had a secret that was safe with her.

We both choose to skirt the topic of my book, but it could not be altogether avoided. When I was sufficiently fortified with alcohol, I brought her up to date. I mentioned the visit to Jessica without going into detail, but she touched my hand and said tenderly.

"Did she hurt you?"

I cried and then told her everything. As I spoke, I recognized my weakness and felt that, in some way, I had been unfaithful to her.

She listened quietly, and, in that way of hers, she took my face in her hands. She kept her eyes locked with mine for long seconds, and then she leaned over and kissed me fully on the mouth. I could have stayed like that forever, but she slowly broke away.

"I don't pretend to understand Jessica. I think she thrives on the theatre of it all, but she seems to take a perverse pleasure in taking money from women who want those things done to them even though her trust fund will see her okay for life.

Her clients? I guess that the pain gives them an endorphin rush, but, like you, the real key is the relinquishing of control."

I wanted her to go on, but the waitress chose that moment to come back in and replenish our glasses. Evelyn paused momentarily and then continued.

"I think you and I are good together, and I hope you feel the same way, but we will need some ground rules. Firstly, there may be some discomfort involved, but I think that you enjoy that; I would never consciously hurt you.

Secondly, I would like to involve others from time to time but only as a couple never by ourselves."

As I listened, my emotions were scrambled. The possibility of being in a relationship with her made my heart soar, but the mention of 'others' left me perplexed.

She could see me wrestling with my thoughts and smiled.

"I think I know you better than you know yourself. It's something that would excite you. Take our friend here..."

The waitress was doing her best to pretend that she heard nothing of consequence, but now Evelyn touched her on the hip.

"... how would you like to come over here and kneel in front of her?"

As so often in recent months, the bizarreness of the suggestion threw me completely off-kilter, but, at the same time, a frisson of excitement surged through me. I looked at the waitress expecting an expression of shock or anger, but all I found was sheer wickedness.

Had she been primed, bribed, even? She was tall but appeared taller still as she cunningly raised her skirt and apron to reveal her long slender legs. My suspicions seemed confirmed when I saw her expensive, lacy, underwear, which did not seem appropriate for a day spent waiting tables.

Once again, I felt disconnected from the real world, and I was almost cramped with excitement as Evelyn stroked the girl's pert derrière.

"She's waiting for you..."

Her voice was hypnotic, and it was like feeling the warm whisper of her words against my sex. I was not sure if I was more anxious to please her or the girl as I fell to my knees and caught the musky waft of her arousal.

It was insane. I doubted if she was yet twenty years old, but here I was, making my obeisance. My hands trembled, causing her to smile as I slid her flimsy panties down to her ankles.

Her sex was adorned with a frizz of dark hair, razor shaped into a sharp triangle, which was in stark contrast to the storm of curls that passed for her hairstyle. I imagined that many men had knelt before this shrine, but I wondered if she was experienced with another woman.

She tried to remain coolly aloof, but her shallow breathing and the slight tension in her posture told a different story. My hands replaced Evelyn's as I cradled her smooth cheeks and drew myself on to her.

There was a moment of hesitancy as I applied my tongue, but, once she was sure that it was going to happen, she accepted me willingly. A mild astringency told me that she had washed in anticipation, but it was quickly replaced by the rich taste of a young woman in heat.

The temptation to push my tongue as deep as I could and sate my own savage need was countered by a subliminal understanding that there were two sides to this bargain. Accordingly, I calmed myself and licked her more purposefully, savoring the warm swell of her labia beneath my tongue.

The compensation for this more considered approach was a gradual increase in arousal as I began to make her moan.

How long we remained sealed together, I had no idea. The possibility that someone might come into the room added to my feeling of debauchery, but I suspected that safeguards had been put in place.

One thing was for sure the girl had now totally abandoned herself to my attention. My face was wet with her offering, and she held me by the head, urging me on.

I did not disappoint. I snaked my tongue inside her, and the contractions I felt confirmed that she was close. For the next few moments, I did nothing more than thrust very gently, but she was becoming crazed with desire, and her legs were threatening to fail her.

I slipped from her eliciting a panicked yelp, but it gave way to an almost obscene growl as I took her clitoris between my lips. I alternated a slow circling with rapid flicks of my tongue, and she was pleading with me not to stop.

She was gasping for breath between entreaties as her climax took hold, and I sealed my mouth to her and began to suck. Her sex was pulsing as she continued to erupt, and I swallowed hard, draining her of all she had to give.

Evelyn had the foresight to give up her seat just in time to allow her to collapse in a state of total dishevelment. She then knelt in front of me and kissed me deeply, sharing the girl's taste before she whispered.

"I hope you haven't tired yourself out. Today it's my turn to be pampered and you have a long night ahead of you..."

Epilogue

After that, things moved so quickly it was like being caught up in a whirlwind. My relationship with Evelyn intensified, and the idea of moving in together came from me. I knew, even before I suggested that it was what she wanted too, but the decision had to come from me. It was the final affirmation of who I wanted to be.

This happy ending also gave the book its final form. It gave me the last chapter, which helped me reappraise and refine all that I had written up to that point.

May was professional in her editing and marketing of the book, and if early sales lived up to their promise, it looked like a best seller. There was already talk of a possible television dramatization.

I was given an advance on a second book, and May took me by surprise when she said that it need not be a sequel. Her faith in my abilities as a writer was warming, and, in truth, I was reluctant, at this stage, to pour out any more of myself onto the printed page.

As I lay on the bed, I was already sketching out a novel with a lesbian premise based on my newly acquired insight into the world of art dealing. If I was honest with myself, the main character was an imagined version of Jessica in years to come, and the thought of her, even now, gave rise to feelings of something unrequited.

I smiled to myself and listened to the voices next door. The room was nice and warm, and there was a strange comfort in lying there naked my limbs bound to the four corners of the bed.

Evelyn was entertaining Hatsue, a buxom Japanese gallery owner, who was completely unaware of my existence. I was left deliciously on edge, wondering whether or not an invitation would be extended for her to join our little game.

Story 03

Chapter 01

The later than normal train had the benefit of some spare seats, and I was glad of the opportunity to stare vacantly out of the window. My visit to the doctor that morning had taken a completely unexpected turn, and I was still trying to come to terms with it.

Having just hit thirty-five, I thought that I needed to pay more attention to my health, so I booked myself for a general check-up. My regular doctor had just retired, having looked after me for most of my adult life, and this was my first appointment with Dr. Addison.

She looked as if she was just out of medical school, but she was proficient and quickly put me at ease. I exercise regularly, eat reasonably well, and know that some consider me beautiful and so I was not altogether surprised when she congratulated me on my general well-being.

It was when she began to address more personal issues that I became less comfortable. I told her that I was slightly stressed at work on occasion and that I was happy living alone. She asked if I had a regular partner to which the answer was no.

She then lectured me on the virtues of safe sex, and I felt mildly offended, telling her that I had no great interest. This was true to a degree. I found men attractive and harbored vague thoughts of motherhood eventually, but I seemed to be missing the spark of arousal.

She asked me straight out if I masturbated, which took me aback, but I answered truthfully and told her that I enjoyed it.

It was then that she broached the possibility that I might be asexual and explained that there was a lot of new research into the idea that a percentage of the population, both male and female, had no interest in sex.

As I continued to take in the passing view, I wondered if it was true of me and, if so, whether or not that made me deficient in some way. I would not confess to her, or anybody else for that matter, that I made use of pornography to fuel my private fantasies, and that, surely, confounded her argument.

The train pulled into the next station, and the platform canopy shaded the sun. I refocused on the window picking up the reflected image of my fellow passengers. My eyes were taken by a young woman engrossed with her phone. For a split second, I thought that she was not wearing a skirt but then saw that, with her legs crossed, it had ridden up to expose her thigh.

My instinct was to turn around to cast a surreptitious glance and see her for real, but I held fast and tried to place her within the carriage. She was sitting opposite in the next bank of seats.

The reflection was imperfect, but I could make out enough to see that she was a very attractive blonde, and I put her age somewhere between seventeen and twenty. It amused me to be able to look at her without her being aware of my attention.

She was wearing a name badge, so I guessed that she was one of the many medical students who used the service. This was borne out as she remained on the train giving me further opportunity to stare.

It was mischievous, but I figured that there was no harm done. It did, however, set me to thinking about how I would react if I thought that someone was checking me out in such a devious manner.

As we pulled into the terminus, I gathered myself and shuffled off the train to find myself following her along with the platform. I wondered if my guess about her had been wrong. She had long legs shown off to devastating effect by her abbreviated hemline, and it hardly seemed an appropriate manner of dress for a health professional.

As the sunlight caught her, I found myself trying to make out whether or not she was wearing a bra. From behind, there was no evidence of it, and I was now intrigued as to what her job might be.

At the barriers, we went our separate ways, her to the bus stand, me to the underground. I gave her no further thought during a hectic day.

That evening I ran myself a hot bath and relaxed with a copy of Vogue. Afterward, I sat up in bed, finishing the magazine when I reached an article on fashion trends in Denmark. The model featured in the photoshoot looked not dissimilar to the girl on the train, and, almost without being aware of it, my fingers idled between my legs.

In recent months I had found myself gravitating towards lesbian-themed pornography. I needed something more than just pneumatic coupling, something a little more believable, and lesbian scenes, particularly those directed by women, at least gave the impression that the participants might be genuinely enjoying themselves.

Now, without being entirely sure why I tried to conjure an image of a desirable man as my fingers worked more purposefully. My new contact at Phelps fitted the bill. He was not the sharpest tool in the box, but he was undeniably handsome and possessed of a certain naïve charm.

The problem was that I could not stay focused, and my mind kept wandering back to my journey that morning. I was still watching the girl's reflection in my mind, but this time, my fingers were brazenly at work much as they were now.

The thought of doing it in public was a novelty, and I found it exciting. Usually, I take a very leisurely approach, but, spurred by this hint of deviance, I rubbed myself more purposefully.

Seconds later, I lifted my hips from the bed and twisted my wrist; I pushed two fingers deep inside.

I was stunned by how hot and wet I was, and I worked myself furiously. I could usually control the onset of my climax, but this time, it remained frustratingly out of reach as though urging me to the greater effort.

My hand ached with the exertion, and I was groaning loudly, which is something I never do. Then, in a moment of frightening clarity, I saw the girl's face as if she was in the same room. She smiled and gently touched my cheek.

"Come for me..."

My orgasm was so intense as to be almost painful. It rolled on and on, and the contractions crushed my fingers, but I did not want it to end. I felt almost delirious as my whole body hummed with the force of it, but, at the finish, I could take no more, and I collapsed on the bed, breathing hard, my skin sheened in sweat.

Some while later, as I tried to come to terms with this aberration, I gingerly touched my sex, still barely believing that it had happened and what had finally triggered it. Almost unconsciously, the touch became a caress, and I began to bear myself up once more.

This time it was more familiar. It was slow and controlled, but it still had echoes of what had gone before. I teased myself for as long as I could and then surrendered to a prolonged-release, which left me with tears of pleasure in my eyes.

I slept deeply and more contently than I had for some time. Unfortunately, it meant that I would be late into the office for the second day running. Usually, I would go to the front of the train to beat the rush on disembarkation, but today, I stood in the middle of the platform putting myself where I had been the previous day when I only caught it.

I could not believe how hard my heart was pounding when, two stations later, I peered out of the window, wondering if she was going to be there. As the train slowed, I felt an unnerving sense of delight when I saw her once again. She was a creature of habit as not only had she opted for the same carriage, but she was once again occupied with her phone.

She was wearing another short skirt and tee shirt combination, and, as she stood caught in sunlight, I realized why she seemed somehow familiar.

I rarely watch television, but one of my guilty pleasures is the show 'Friday Nights Lights,' which some American friends of mine had steered me towards during a recent trip to California.

This young woman was like a petite version of Adrianne Palicki, who played one of my favorite characters in the series.

As she boarded, I willed her to take the same seat so that I could use the window to my advantage. Still, having surveyed the carriage, she obviously decided that, today, the train's shaded side would be preferable, and she sat down directly opposite me.

Taken by surprise, I looked up at her, and she flashed me a disarming smile before settling and continuing with the game she had running on her phone. For a few seconds, I was wreathed in her perfume, which smelt a little expensive for everyday use.

As the train pulled out, I gazed at her reflection and inwardly smiled as I concluded that she would probably look more at home on America's west coast than on a London commuter service. It was a second or two before I realized that she had looked up absently from her phone, and she was effectively returning my stare in the glass.

I felt irrationally guilty and quickly turned my head a fraction before I decided that I was being stupid and told myself to get a grip. I purposefully took my Kindle out of my handbag and tried to engage with my current novel.

The reader had a leather case, and I held it in my lap in the manner of a traditional book.

The problem was that this allowed me to take furtive glances at her bare legs. She had them crossed, as before, and they seemed to go on forever.

It was insane. I read but took absolutely nothing in. I just kept on looking at her, wondering how she kept them so smooth. There was no way she could know where my eyes were fixed, but, as if reading my mind, she slowly unfolded her legs and sat with them fractionally parted.

I immediately felt a prickly discomfort across my skin and, in a perverted twist of thought, I wondered what sort of underwear she had chosen.

I almost admonished myself out loud as I fidgeted a little and desperately tried to focus, hoping that other passengers might get on and reaffirm some sense of normality.

In the event, no one else joined the carriage save two mothers with children who moved to the opposite end. I was still alone with her, and an unwelcomed recollection of my fantasy the night before came to my mind.

Almost without thought, I brushed my little finger over the tight crotch of my jeans concealed by my book. The resulting frisson made me shiver, and I sensed her looking across at me.

I kept my head down and breathed deeply, but, to my acute embarrassment, I could feel myself seeping. The urge to touch me again was almost irresistible, and, to compound my discomfort, she shifted slightly in her seat, parting her legs a fraction more.

I considered going to the lavatory, but we were not too far from our destination, and I decided to sit tight. Over the next ten minutes, I spent almost the entire time staring at her legs, wondering what the hell had come over me.

As the train slowed to a halt, I put away my book and looked up at her. She smiled at me and, perhaps I imagined it, but I thought I caught a knowing glint in her eye. I quickly looked away but not before noting her name tag. She was, indeed, employed at the hospital, and her name was Bryony Bainbridge.

I was still flustered when I arrived at the office. I grabbed my working attire from my locker and went into the ladies. I stripped out of my jeans and was aghast at just how damp my panties were. Fortunately, I kept a couple of spare pairs in my locker but, as I stood there, naked from the waist down, someone entered the adjacent stall. I heard a rustle of clothing, and it became apparent that the occupant was using the space as a changing room in the same way I was.

I wondered who it might be and began to conjure images of one or two of my colleagues standing naked just three feet away separated only by a thin wooden partition.

The next moment, I brought my fingers to my sex and began to rub myself. I was already wet and had to suppress a whimper of gratification. I had never done anything like this before, and it was almost as if I had become another person.

The woman finished up but then spent some while at the mirror outside. I was willing her to leave as they need to complete what I had started was almost overwhelming. My fingers were still busy and breathing fast, and I knew that I could not trust myself not to cry out.

I heard the spritz of a perfume spray followed by the sound of the door opening and closing. The scent left hanging in the air was that used by Grace, one of our young receptionists, and that knowledge somehow tripped me over the edge.

The force of my climax buckled my legs, and I slumped awkwardly onto the toilet seat as the ebbing waves of pleasure made my body twitch and left me murmuring with my lips tightly closed.

Sanity once again prevailed, and I set about tidying myself up. A shower had recently been installed to accommodate the growing number of staff who cycled into work, and I now made use of it. I sluiced myself down and washed my hands guiltily like a latter-day Lady Macbeth.

In the ensuing days, I threw myself into my work. I resumed my early morning commute. It was cramped, overheated; carriages were enough to negate any lustful thoughts. After a regular week, I felt that my uncharacteristic behavior could be put down as a one-off never to be repeated.

They say that hubris will always find you out, and the truth of this was revealed to me just two days later. I work long hours and travel home late, and it is a real pain when there are problems with the rail network.

The unusual number of people on the concourse suggested the worse, and, sure enough, the service was suspended due to signaling problems. I joined a crowd of people around a harassed railway official who thought it would be at least an hour before the problem was remedied.

I had alternative routes, but, at this hour, they were few and far between, and there was not much to be gained. I looked back up at the board and whispered under my breath.

"Shit..."

"Touché"

I turned to see who had spoken and recognized a woman that I often saw on my train. She was about my age, well dressed, and carried herself with a confidence that suggested that she held down a very well paid job.

There seems to be an understanding that commuters do not talk to one another unless thrown together in adversity. This was one such occasion. She checked her watch and then sighed.

"I can't be bothered to go all around the world. I'm going to get a drink and try again later. Can I tempt you?"

For reasons I would have found hard to explain, I cast my eyes down to her left hand and noted that she wore a wedding ring.

I had been a little negligent of late, not keeping in contact with my circle of friends as often as I would have liked, and perhaps it was to assuage that guilt that I said yes to her sociable invitation. She suggested the bar on the concourse so that we could keep apprised of developments.

She insisted on paying, and I found a table while she ordered some wine. When she returned with a whole bottle, I must have looked alarmed, but she laughed as she put it down.

"We're big girls. We can manage three glasses each can't we?"

I immediately warmed to her, discovered that her name was Steph and that she lived with her husband and a two-year-old daughter only about a mile away from me. She was an easy company, and we laughed as we regaled one another with stories of our commuting travails.

It was as she started to tell me about her job with a large shipbroking company that I looked over her shoulder to see what was happening on the concourse. My eyes immediately lighted on the furthest table, and I involuntarily caught my breath.

Sitting with another young woman was Bryony. She was more formally dressed but looked all the more beautiful for it. She sat sideways on. Once again, a twist of fate had set me so that I could look at her without her being aware.

As Steph continued to speak, I cast occasional glances into the distance and wondered what it was that I found fascinating about her. I even lost the thread of what was being said to me until Steph brought me up short.

"She's beautiful isn't she?"

Steph had her back to the table, and so I was left floundering and wondering to whom she was referring.

"I'm sorry, who is?"

"The girl you keep looking at. I see her on the train sometimes; she makes it all seem so effortless."

I was tempted to play dumb, but I decided to cut it short. I drained my glass.

"I guess she does. Shall we go and see what's going on?"

For a second, Steph looked at me quizzically, but then she quickly finished her drink and followed me. Unfortunately, the train situation was still unresolved, and when Steph started referring to her phone, I thought that she was trying to get an online update, but she had other plans.

"I'm ordering a taxi. Can I offer you a lift?"

Even shared the fare was going to be outrageous, but she smiled reassuringly.

"It's after nine p.m. I can charge it to the company."

It was an offer I could not refuse, and ten minutes later, we were seated together as the cab made its way out into the suburbs. It took nearly forty-five minutes to reach our destination, but the time flew by as we exchanged gossip.

We reached Steph's home first, and I was suitably impressed by the large detached property. I was about to ask her about the mechanics of discharging the cab when she touched my hand.

"Do you fancy a coffee? My daughter is staying with her grandparents."

I had a lot to do at home, but it seemed churlish to refuse now that she had paid for the journey. Figuring that I could walk home in fifteen minutes if needs be, I said I would stay for a short while.

She led me to the house, and I was taken with the minimalist décor. She left me in the living room, which looked out on to a professionally tended garden, and then returned with the coffee pot a few moments later.

In the time taken, she had changed out of her business suit and now wore a loose tee-shirt over a pair of baggy cotton shorts. She had also let down her hair, and she immediately looked years younger.

"I hope you don't mind..."

"No, of course not, it's your home."

There was something almost gypsy-like about her. With her dark hair now framing her face, her complexion looked a shade darker, and cheekbones were emphasized. Her large eyes and smiling mouth would not have looked out of place on an Italian film starlet, and she had the hourglass figure to match.

She sat next to me on the sofa, and, as we drank coffee and continued to chat, I could not help but notice that, despite the warmth of the room, her nipples were standing proudly erect. I was beginning to wonder when her husband would be home when she leaned forward and conspiratorially touched me on the knee.

"I have a confession. That girl, in the bar, I saw her on a late night train a few weeks ago and she was kissing another girl! I came home and had the best sex ever!"

To say I was shocked was understating the case. There was the spooky resonance with my recent experience and the feeling that, somehow, she wished me to make an admission of my own. Her eyes gleamed with mischief as she further invaded my personal space.

"Have you ever been with another woman?"

Still stunned to silence, I mutely shook my head in denial. In response, she raised an eyebrow as if she had misjudged me, but then she continued.

"You must have wondered?"

My heart was hammering in my chest, and I felt the color rising in my cheeks. My every sinew was braced to flee, but I remained in stasis unable to move. She held my eyes as she moved closer still, and then she touched her lips to mine.

My whole body was trembling, and I felt like an awkward teenager. This was wrong on so many levels, but I could not clear my mind. All rational thought was overwhelmed by the softness of her mouth and the slight sweetness of her lipstick.

Her touch was light as if threatening to retreat, and I knew that it was entirely up to me. I could pull away, and we would both laugh it off as the result of wine too quickly drunk, but I was already breathing her in.

I caressed her cheek, questioningly admiring the perfection of her skin. Other women have told me that they love the feel of a man's face against theirs, but, in truth, I have always shied away from that abrasive contact insisting that they are perfectly shaved.

This was something so different and, despite all of my misgivings, it felt so natural. In the end, I could not say who made the first move. Our tongues gently touched, as if in a courtship ritual. Her mouth closed over mine, and we were joined as one.

She kissed so beautifully, and there was something indefinably feminine about the way her tongue danced with mine, first leading and then inviting. I could have remained floating at that moment, but she needed to move on.

Almost without me being aware, she eased her arms out from her tee-shirt, and then, barely breaking our kiss, she removed it altogether.

She sealed our mouths once more but guided my hand to her naked breast. I froze, all of my uncertainties resurfacing, but she coaxed me with her tongue lulling me back into a state of detached serenity.

My senses seemed heightened as the shape and fullness of her breast was revealed to me. My thumb slowly strayed, mapping out the dimpled extent of her nipple and then pausing at the rigid teat so much larger than my own.

My touch elicited a muted gasp, and I brought my finger into play. My nipples are extremely sensitive, but I had never found a lover who could attune himself to my needs. Now I began to massage her nipple with a subtly. I would have accorded my own, and, as she whimpered softly in my mouth, I felt unbelievably aroused.

She brought her hand to the back of my head and held me close for a moment, but then she relaxed a little, and the message was clear. I broke the kiss and trailed the tip of my tongue down the length of her neck, leading inevitably to her breasts' swell.

Her engorged nipple was a beautiful shade of dusky pink, and I gently took it between my lips.

Taking her other nipple between my fingers, I began to tease and, while I felt sure that my attempts were clumsy, I was inordinately pleased when she groaned. Encouraged, I carried on for some time at first just using my lips and tongue but then, boldly, nipping her with my teeth.

I felt the tension building in her, and my nipples were achingly erect. I was getting desperate to return the favor, but she took my hand from her breast and eased it downwards.

With her hand covering mine, she slipped inside the waist of her shorts, and I was so shocked by the heat and wetness that I felt immobilized.

"Come upstairs..."

She drew me up slowly from the sofa, and I followed almost mesmerized. She did not attempt to cover herself as she leads the way up to the bedroom, which was at least twice the size of mine. It was finished with white fitted units, with very simple lines, which only pointed up the starkness of the huge bed dressed in royal blue satin.

Letting go of my hand, she slid out of her shorts and stood proudly naked before me. Her body was the product of healthy living and made me feel guilty about my recent lazy attitude towards diet and exercise.

That thought made me hesitate momentarily before beginning to get undressed, and in that pause, she settled on the bed propped by a heap of expensively upholstered cushions.

The word that immediately sprang to my mind was regal. With one knee raised, she looked so assured and desirable.

I was still hesitant, but now for different reasons. I had deluded myself into thinking that this was a voyage of discovery for both of us and that either of us could say no should we feel uncomfortable. I was convinced that she was far more worldly than I had given her credit for; I suddenly felt like her quarry, but I found it exciting for some strange reason.

Not recognizing this facet of my nature and I needed time to think, but she was already beckoning me towards her. I felt wound by an invisible chain as I drew closer to the bed, and then I was there kneeling at her feet.

I wanted her to open her arms, enfold and comfort me, but she spread her legs to either side of my body, putting her sex lewdly on display.

I could smell her now. I am not sure what I expected, but there was a surprising familiarity which of itself only served to increase my sense of arousal. She could see it working on me, and she smiled, knowing I was trapped.

She extended her hand, and, as I took it, she invited me forward but only so far. I hovered over the delta of her gleaming depilated sex, where the shy fringes of her labia shone moistly with promised sweetness.

Until now, I had never considered it as a thing of beauty, but there was an undoubted allure that resonated deep within me. Its warm, yielding incitement was the antithesis of the more familiar threat of thrusting masculinity.

In my mind, I was already justifying my behavior, telling myself that this was an opportunity never likely to come my way again; it would be just this once, and no one need ever know.

She gave no guidance, and I wondered how she would react if I were to walk out on her, but she knew me better than I knew myself.

I leaned in and kissed her inner thigh and then spent a seeming age working my way upwards. Nervousness got the better of me, and I skirted around until I was lavishing my attention on the plane of her stomach.

She sighed, but it was a sound of contentedness and not exasperation. She knew that all she had to do was wait.

I lingered at her navel, beautifully shaped and deep-set, and noted the almost invisible trail of faint hair leading the way downwards. I began to follow it, her scent growing stronger with every centimeter traveled, keenly aware that my hands were shaking.

I began to lick at the firmness of her mound, where her taste was already in evidence. It was unexpectedly tart, but then I caught up a single droplet as it leaked away. The sensation was startling. The rich muskiness filled my mouth and sent a shiver through my whole body.

Craving more, I tentatively ran my tongue along with the exposed tips of her labia, which seemed to swell in welcome. My reward was seepage of oily nectar, and I licked avidly, slowly working my way deeper.

Within, she felt incredibly hot to my tongue, and her excitement was made evident as she began to squeeze, encouraging me to even greater effort. I could not get enough of her taste, but now I tried to read her contractions and adapt to her impending climax's rhythm.

I was sweating heavily, but I was beyond caring. We were moving as one, her hips undulating as she worked her way to the summit.

When the moment came, she put both hands to the back of my head and clasped me tightly. I struggled to breathe, but I gamely licked as she began to melt in a series of barely controlled juddering convulsions.

She cried out, heedless of who might hear, and it was more a command than a request when she told me not to stop. Her climax seemed to roll on forever, and with each passing minute, I was getting desperate for my turn.

When, at last, she had no more to give, she released me and slumped back into the piled cushions. My face was hot and wet, and I was grateful for the cooling air. By contrast, she looked beatific; the only obvious evidence of her exertions was a light flush over her breasts' surface.

Now, once again, I was not sure how to take things forward. It was my turn, but she made no obvious attempt to reinitiate proceedings. Instead, she got up from the bed and touched me on the tip of the nose.

"Give me a couple of minutes."

With that, she went into the ensuite bathroom and closed the door behind her.

I was sorely tempted to get into the bed and cover myself, but I did not want her to think me prudish. I was considering how to compose myself when I heard a sound behind me. It was like the groaning sound that my aging heating boiler made from time to time, but I could not imagine that, in a modern home like this, the boiler would be housed in a bedroom cupboard.

When the sound was repeated, curiosity got the better of me. I padded across to the row of built-in wardrobes and peeked inside. Part of me hoped to find her clothes storage as disorganized as mine, but nothing could have prepared me for lay behind the door.

It would have been hard to say which of us was the more startled, me or the naked Adonis that stood there bound in place. Steph had joked that her husband was a trophy toy boy, and I did not doubt that this was he.

With his dark eyes and thick oiled hair, he put me in mind of a Spanish footballer. It was evident that he was exceptionally handsome, notwithstanding the ball gag that distended his mouth.

His body was toned, and there was not a single hair on it, which only went to emphasize the fullness of his impressive erection. Outside of porn films, I had never seen one quite so prodigious, and I had the sense that it had been straining at the leash for quite some time.

He stood with feet apart, his ankles bound to eyebolts drilled into the floor, confirming that this situation was not new to him. His posture thrust him forward a little, and a quick look showed why.

His arms were held behind him in a single leather sleeve that cinched his wrists to the opposing elbow. The whole arrangement was then attached to another eyebolt set sufficiently high in the wall to ensure a measure of discomfort.

It was hard to read his expression, a mix of surprise, excitement, and perhaps a little fear.

For my part, I was wondering just exactly what I had gotten myself into.

Now that the wardrobe door was open, I could see that the louvered vents afforded him a surprisingly clear view of the bed, and so, not only had he been able to hear everything, he had been able to watch as well.

For some reason, that discovery excited me more than I might have imagined. A mischievous part of me wanted to take hold and tease him by way of revenge, but, at that moment, I heard the toilet flushing.

I quickly closed the wardrobe door and returned to bed. When Steph came back into the room, I looked at her anew. I was strongly tempted to confront her, but something held me in check.

She took up her station reclining on the cushions, and I now understood that she was provocatively putting herself on the show directly in her husband's line of sight. If further proof were needed, she raised her knee and nonchalantly ran her finger along the length of her exposed sex.

Unfortunately, her casual wantonness did nothing to assuage my own desperate need. A fever of lust fogged my mind, and, heedless of the consequences, I prostrated myself once more and sealed my mouth to her sex.

"My, my, you're insatiable."

Her gentle laughter might have been edged with a hint of mockery, but I was beyond caring. It took a while for her to begin to simmer, but I had my plan.

I tucked up my knees and raised my backside. I regard it as my best feature, and now I displayed myself shamelessly as I brought my fingers into play. I found it hard to believe just how wet I was as I pushed my hand as far back as I could, smearing my skin with the product of my arousal.

It was so perverted, cruel even, knowing that he was helplessly watching, but I am not sure that I had ever been so turned on.

Usually, sex, for me, felt disjointed. I could focus on my partner's needs or my own but rarely together. Now it was a perfect symbiosis. The wetter and more aroused than Steph became, the more my body responded.

As I licked and sucked at her, I was driving two fingers deep inside myself. Those two fingers became three and then four. I had never done this to myself before, and my wrist was making a tortured complaint, but my heated savagery subsumed it.

My whole hand was swallowed, and wetness dripped from my forearm as I impaled myself.

I could no longer support myself properly, and I was pressed even closer to Steph's ravening maw. She started to swear, urging me on, and I feared that I would not have the strength, but then she started to come.

My tongue was deep inside her as my climax took hold. Centered on my sex, it reverberated throughout my whole body. It was a tingling sensation that kept on feeding itself, and I did not want it to end, but it felt as if my head would explode with the sheer happiness of it.

At the finish, I almost cried in frustration as I finally had to let it go. I withdrew my aching fingers and, still slumped between her legs. I gently licked the hot sticky residue from her cooling skin.

It took some while for my breathing to return to normal, but, in the ensuing quietness, another unmistakable groan could be heard.

Steph put her hand to my head to hold me still, but then she was a bustle of activity.

"You are going to have to leave. My husband will be home anytime soon."

She ushered me into the bathroom and handed me my clothes, leaving me bewildered. As I quickly tried to tidy myself up, I could only assume that she was trying to save herself the embarrassment of his presence being exposed. Some small part of me was tempted to reveal to her what I had already discovered for myself.

Only later did I consider that she was simply greedy and that she was eager to say goodbye just so that she could take advantage of his pent up frustration.

Chapter 03

For the next few days, my work suffered badly. I found it hard to concentrate as I tried to reach an understanding of everything that had transpired.

In an aesthetic sense, I had always appreciated the beauty and attraction of certain women, but I had never thought of it in terms of defining my sexuality. Before recent events, had anyone suggested that I would be prepared to physically engage with another woman, I would have laughed in their face.

The truth was that I still felt that Steph had used me, but I knew that, if she asked me again, I would say yes in a heartbeat. It had been the most intense sexual encounter I had ever had in my life.

Twice, I found myself taking the later train to catch a glimpse of Bryony, and I berated myself for acting like a besotted teenager. I knew I had to pull myself together, or I was in danger of jeopardizing my chances of promotion to partner.

When I received a phone call from John, the eye candy from Phelps, I decided to put him out of his misery and accepted an invitation to a drink after work. To keep the arrangement loose, I suggested meeting for a quick glass of wine at a bar near the station.

He left the choice to me and, subliminally or otherwise. I suggested, "The Other Side of the Tracks." It was a popular haunt for the after-work crowd and the gay community drawn from the theatres nearby.

Unfortunately, while John attracted admiring glances from both women and men alike, he was a dull conversationalist. He was doing nothing to restore my faith in the male of the species. My eyes kept flitting to the far end of the room where the same-sex couples seemed to be having a whale of a time.

It was a predominantly male crowd, but there were a few female faces, and one, in particular, looked familiar. It took me a few moments to bring it to mind, and then, with a jolt of excitement, I recognized her as the girl I had seen at the station with Bryony.

She was small, dark-haired, and could have been taken for a young teenager, although her full breasts strongly suggested otherwise, and the bar was strictly over twenty-ones. She seemed perfectly at home amongst the raucous theatrical fraternity.

Almost inevitably, as a man confident in his desirability, John made a crass attempt to talk me into something more than just a drink, and at that point, I called a halt to the proceedings. I allowed him to escort me into the station and went on to the platform before doubling back and returning to the bar.

I ordered another drink and took a table closer to the girl and her friends. I was not sure what I was doing or hoped to achieve, as I got out of my laptop to give the impression that I had a purpose.

From the snippets that I managed to overhear, it seemed that the girl had a small part in the musical at the Palace Theatre just around the corner, and I found myself wondering what connected her to Bryony.

After twenty minutes, my drink was almost finished, and, telling myself to get a grip, I began to put away my laptop. I had just switched off my wireless mouse when I saw the girl look towards the door.

I felt a sudden rush of adrenalin and intuitively looked up from my bag to see Bryony enter the bar. She had a look that suggested that she had come straight from work, and the girl broke from the crowd to greet her with a gushy kiss on the cheek.

With all thoughts of an immediate exit dispelled, I turned on my laptop again and tried to put my finger on just what it was that made her seem so attractive. She was not the most beautiful woman I had ever met, but there was a certain something about her.

The general hubbub now made it impossible to overhear what was being said, and I contented myself by taking stolen glances in her direction. At one point, I peered over the top of the screen only to find her looking directly at me, and I quickly cast my eyes down again, figuring that she was checking out the clientele in general.

I was still pretending to be engrossed when I got the shock of my life.

"Good evening..."

Without another word, she took the seat opposite me and presented me with a glass of wine. Close to, her icy blue eyes were almost hypnotic, and I could do nothing about the guilty flush that now reddened my cheeks.

"I'm Bryony...but then I suspect you know that."

She paused to take a sip from her glass and then continued.

"I could almost believe that you're stalking me. Don't get me wrong, it's flattering to be stalked by a woman as beautiful as you but, if I had to guess, you're very new to this."

To be caught out was one thing, but to be made to appear so transparent was unnerving. I desperately wanted to tell her that I was not normally like this, but it would have only served to confirm what she had already surmised. I opened my mouth to speak, but I could find no words.

"If you are interested I can let you have some contact numbers. There are lots of straight women who are curious."

Was she rejecting me because she had determined I was straight, or was she just not attracted? Either way, I felt a hollow forming in the pit of my stomach. My embarrassment must have shown because her features softened into a warm smile.

"Look, what I'm saying is that, for someone like you, I am dangerous to know."

It was such an odd thing to say, and I was intrigued by her choice of words. It felt as if she was trying to belittle me somehow, and I reacted by pushing my glass towards her and snapping back.

"I'll buy my own drinks, thank you."

She looked intrigued, even a little amused, and then she produced a business card. She scribbled an address on the back of it and handed it to me.

"Meet us later, after ten."

With that, she got up and rejoined her group. She left the glass of wine, which I finished quickly, and then I packed up my things. I waited until I got outside to peruse the card, which, to my astonishment, declared her to be a junior pediatrician.

The address on the reverse was in an area that had grown in popularity with the open-air market; I sometimes visited at weekends. On reading it, I felt a frisson of excitement, but there was no way on earth that I was to entangle myself.

It was a pleasant evening, and I decided to take a quick stroll along the embankment to clear my head, but I kept on coming back to the same question. To whom was she referring when she said "us"?

It was later than I thought when I eventually boarded a train, and it was close to ten-thirty as it approached Bryony's station. I only had to stay on for three more stops, and I was home, but my body seemed to move of its own volition.

I told myself that I would not call in; I would take a look at where she lived simply out of curiosity. It turned out to be one of the up-market apartments that looked out over the new canal and its associated green space.

I was building up an altogether different picture of Bryony when, for the second time that evening, I was shocked out of my reverie.

"I knew you'd come."

Standing behind me was Bryony herself in company with the girl from the bar. They must have been on the same train that I had taken. The natural assumption was that they were in a relationship and living together. But, if so, what was their interest in me?

I was almost in a daze as I followed them up to the top floor apartment, and as they opened the front door, I was struck by high ambient temperature. The overall décor had a Scandinavian feel with lots of beech wood and pastel colors, and I expected it to feel cool.

I stepped across the threshold, and Bryony took my jacket. Still, I was taken aback when her companion stood in the entranceway and proceeded to completely undress as if it were the most natural thing in the world.

Bryony laughed.

"I like her to be naked when we're at home."

Alarms were shrilling in my head, but I did not resist as Bryony led me to an open plan living space with windows on three sides. Given the choice of a sofa and two chairs, I took the safer option of a chair. Meanwhile, the girl had disappeared only to return with a bottle of wine and a tray of glasses.

She poured drinks for Bryony and me but not for herself. When she was done, she sat on the floor, and Bryony began to stroke her hair as if she were a favored pet. I was still finding it hard to guess her age, but strangely, without her clothes, she somehow seemed more empowered.

The next ten minutes were surreal as we discussed our respective jobs as though the girl was not even there, but I noted that she was slowly moving closer until she was nuzzling Bryony's legs.

My innate sense of good manners made me want to ask her a direct question and draw her into the conversation, notwithstanding their strange juxtaposition, but she did not attempt to engage with me. Her whole attention was fixed on Bryony.

She looked the embodiment of innocence, but, at the same time, there was an undeniable air of eroticism about her.

For a few seconds, I was jarred back to a state of clarity. I could not deny that I was intrigued by the possibilities of the scene being played out in front of me, but I hated not being in control, and I needed to get a grip on reality.

I put my glass down and stood up to make my excuses but, before I could speak, Bryony forestalled me.

"Leaving so soon? Please sit down, the fun is only just beginning."

Her smile issued a challenge. She had, after all, warned me, but I had chosen to ignore it. I found myself rationalizing that we were both professional women and that this was nothing more than an innocent diversion. What harm could come of it?

I sat back down and unbidden, and the girl refilled my glass; as she did so, Bryony slowly parted her legs, and I quickly looked away as she flashed her panties.

She retained her immodest pose as the girl returned to her this time to settle between her legs. Without missing a beat, she began to tell me how the staff in her Paediatric department were encouraged to dress less formally to make their young charges feel more comfortable. Still, her words were lost on me as the girl began to rub her cheek against Bryony's inner thigh.

If she was seeking my attention, it was undivided as she began to kiss her way slowly upwards. Bryony sat as though it was nothing more than her due, her flow of conversation uninterrupted.

I remained mute as the girl knelt low and completely turned her back to me. She was lost between those enticing thighs as Bryony enshrouded her with her skirt and gently held her in place.

Any lingering pretense at normality was dismissed. I could no longer ignore the growing ache between my legs, and I shifted a little in my seat, causing Bryony to give a quiet laugh.

"Go ahead, touch yourself."

Some last echoes of decorum tugged at me, but my heart was racing, and I could feel my heightened pulse throbbing at my temples. With my eyes fixed on the girl, and my imagination ran wild, I slid my hand under my skirt and deep into my panties.

I was obscenely wet, and my nose twitched at the liberated reek of my arousal. How had I come to this so quickly?

Bryony relaxed into the chair's embrace and sipped her wine nonchalantly while the girl continued her labor of love. From time to time, she spoke to me, but I was beyond cogent thought; my mind was a slave to my primal, physical need.

"Why don't you make yourself more comfortable?"

She left the interpretation entirely up to me, and I felt disembodied as I arose from the chair and began to shed my clothes. I wanted her to look at me, to find me attractive, and her appreciative smile suggested that I had achieved the desired effect.

I sat down once more and caressed myself openly and unrestrainedly. I had never known my nipples to feel so rigidly tumescent, and I was pleased as she lowered her gaze to my breasts.

At some point, the girl had divested Bryony of her panties. Her contended whimpers as she reapplied herself to her task had me leaking jealously. I had no idea where this was headed. There was no little irony in the fact that I was cast voyeur's role and was being given a taste of my own medicine.

I could not believe the degree of self-control that she was exhibiting as the minutes ticked by, and the girl showed no sign of tiring. My fingers were moving ever more urgently, and beads of moisture were forming in the valley of my breasts.

Bryony gave the slightest of smiles as she recognized my state of agitation. I wanted to reach the zenith together with her, but she knew that it was a battle lost. As she stared me straight in the eyes, I sought the final crescendo, and I keened a muted, soulful scream as my climax bore me up and wrung out every last ounce of pleasure from me.

I was left gasping for breath and incapable of movement. She, by contrast, looked serene as she somehow conveyed that the moment had come. The girl gave a greedy groan, and then I heard her softly sucking.

It was clear that the girl was very practiced but, even now, Bryony retained her composure. She melted into a prolonged orgasm with barely a sigh, and it was evident that she was saving herself for much more to come.

In evidence of this, the girl did not move, and I could hear her still gently lapping. That simple sound set off fresh sensations centered between my legs, and I felt my tongue moving in my mouth as I was almost overcome by an aberrant urge to take her place.

As the thought was formed, I caught Bryony's eye, and it was as if I had expressed my desire out loud. She stroked the girl's hair and tenderly eased her away to leave me looking at the majesty of her reddened sex.

That feeling of not being in command of my own body returned as I got up to cross the divide between us, but, as I did so, Bryony rose from her chair, and the girl eased in and took her place.

I looked to Bryony in confusion, but she said.

"It's only fair, do you not think?"

The girl sat waiting with a sense of insouciance. Her legs casually parted. Whereas Bryony was perfectly depilated, the girl retained a light growth of dark curls which were matted with moisture, and her glistening inner thighs bore further witness to her arousal.

Was it possible that she had come without touching herself, simply by the act of ministration?

I badly wanted Bryony, and if this was the price, then I was prepared to pay it. Some part of me balked at her elfin youthfulness, but as I went to my knees before her, I had the distinct impression that she was far more experienced than I.

Once I was settled between her coltish legs, I was enveloped by her scent as it rose from her heated skin, and I began to breathe more deeply. It acted on me at some subliminal level, and I now craved the taste of her.

Looking up, I saw her smiling at me, her pupils dilated, and fully understanding what I was going through exactly. She ran a finger along the length of her sex, parting the wet curls and revealing the lush inner pinkness.

I sealed myself to her like a drowning woman seeking air, and the first taste was rich and full. There was no doubt that she had already climaxed, but she was ready for more spurred on, no doubt, by my perceived inexperience.

Almost immediately, she began to leak a warm, creamy, offering which flooded my mouth and sharpened my senses. I could feel my sex distending, and I wanted to touch myself again, but I knew that, for now, she had to be the focus of my attention.

I began an exploration, mapping her intimate contours, and seeing what she liked the most. Her deep-set clitoris was sensitive, but I did not want her to come too quickly. Instead, I set to squirming my tongue as deep within her as I possibly could, and the resultant gushes of moisture told their own story.

I was becoming lost in her when I felt Bryony put her hand to the back of my head and pressing me tighter.

"Suck her..."

I did as I was told, and I had to swallow repeatedly to keep my mouth clean. Had I been told that a woman could be so wet, I would not have believed it, and I was even more shocked by the extent to which it aroused me.

A series of irregular convulsions were shaking her body, and I could no longer restrain myself. I pursed my lips at the apex of her sex. I began to flick my tongue over her clitoris while simultaneously working my fingers over my own.

Once again, it felt as if her impending climax was, somehow, feeding mine. It was a shared uplifting that guided the actions of my mouth and hand until her sex stifled my exultant cry as I took us both over the edge.

It took an age for us both to recover. I was too weak to move and remained between her legs, panting hard, as her body finally settled to stillness.

I was brought back to reality by an ironic round of applause from Bryony.

"Bravo!...but I think you might want to tidy yourself up."

I got to my feet unsteadily, and she handed me my clothes as she ushered me towards the bathroom. Looking into the mirror felt like beholding a stranger. Sweat had made my hair lank, and my makeup was smeared. I worked my tongue around my mouth, which was thick with the girl's taste, and my face was still wet with her outpouring.

I washed quickly and put some toothpaste on to my finger to freshen my mouth. I decided not to reapply my makeup, and I fixed my hair as best I could.

For some unfathomable reason, I felt embarrassed about going back outside. In handing me my clothes, Bryony had signaled that the evening's proceedings were at an end, but I desperately wanted to see her again, and I had no idea how she felt about things.

When I emerged, the girl was nowhere to be seen, and Bryony gave the impression that we had done nothing more than sharing an innocent glass of wine. I was struck mute as she led me to the door and kissed me chastely on the cheek.

"We must do this again sometime."

Fortunately, over the following few days, my work was demanding that I could hardly spare a thought for anything else. I had been as good as assured that if I could land the Etheridge account, I would be made a partner. Everything had been going well, but, as it transpired, too well.

The Etheridge board were so impressed by my initial pitch, and subsequent presentation, that they asked me to revise my dispositions and dividend forecasts to take into account an investment three times the amount originally postulated. I would have liked more time, but they wanted to take up positions before the end of the tax year.

After a fourth late night, the new presentation was ready, and, for the first time in days, I got around to thinking about my personal life. At home, I checked my backed up messages, many of which were from an ever more frustrated John who wanted to take me out again. I wondered if I could get past his inherent dullness in return for an uncomplicated bout of sex.

The truth was I was hoping that there might be a message from Bryony but then remembered that my number was not included on the business card that I had given her.

Now that my mind was clear of investment strategies, she came to occupy it more and more. I could not sleep without conjuring her image, and, when I did, it was to wake stressed and clammy with my hand between my legs.

The temptation to take the later train in the hope of bumping into her was strong, but I knew that she would see through it. In the end, I did the civilized, uncomplicated thing and gave her a call.

Just hearing her voice sent a thrill surging through my body, and it took a moment to appreciate that she was delicately turning me down.

"...we all had a good time but we are travelling in different directions."

I was left confused; after all, it was she that had intimated that we might do it again.

"Can we meet, just for coffee perhaps, there are things I think we need to discuss."

There was a pause at the end of the line and then what might have been an exasperated sigh.

"Okay, tomorrow lunchtime. There's a Costa Coffee shop here at the hospital. Can you make it for one-thirty?"

The timing was awkward, especially as it necessitated a trek across town, but I said yes, and my heart was hammering as I put the phone down.

The next day I spent an age considering what to wear and the morning at work passed in a blur. The immediate pressure was off as Etheridge had still not given a commitment, but they had undertaken to give their decision within seven days and so there was still time in hand.

I splashed out on a taxi at lunchtime and arrived a little early, but Bryony was already there. She looked different, but no less beautiful, with her hair up and dressed in a white medical coat. She was engrossed in a set of notes, and I stood for a second or two, just staring at her.

She looked up, smiled sweetly, and beckoned me across. The coffee shop had imaginatively divided up some of the floor space into a series of separate conference areas, and she was seated alone in one of the booths.

I kissed her on the cheek and, after a brief exchange, I placed the order for coffees.

It seemed impossible that we could be so formal in one another's company, given what had transpired, but the atmosphere was uncomfortably stilted. Finally, she leaned across and touched the back of my hand.

"Just ask me a question. Anything you want."

I had so many, but I started with something blunt and obvious.

"What's your relationship with your flatmate?"

To my surprise, she pondered a moment before replying.

"I suppose the answer is short term. Gwen is staying with me for the duration of her play's London run. Later this year it goes on tour and so I guess things will come to a natural conclusion."

I felt an irrational sense of relief that they seemed not to be engaged in anything long term, but my question had been double-edged, and she smiled as she continued.

"A little while ago, I was made aware of a group of women, professional for the most part, with little time or inclination to tie themselves down to anyone partner. These women are discrete, discerning, and, in a word, demanding.

In turn, they opened my eyes to another caste of women who have a natural inclination to serve. They are affectionately referred to as "the sluts".

Once I was aware of this, I found that I could pick out these women; perhaps it's a gift or something to do with my medical training. In your case, you remain on the cusp. I do not doubt that your lesbian leanings will win out but, the question is, are you a slut?"

The frankness of her remarks shocked me. It all sounded preposterous, but could I deny the evidence of my own recent experience? The suggestion that I would allow myself to be used in any way was, somehow, insulting; why, therefore, did her choice of words excite me?

I was still trying to order my confused thoughts when we were interrupted, and Bryony smiled at the newcomer.

"May I introduce Grace De Moyes. Grace is a Consultant Paediatrician here at the hospital and she has been acting as my mentor."

Her name sounded vaguely familiar, but had I met her before; I would have remembered her. She was tall and slim with deep brown eyes that seemed to bore into me. Her short dark hair was shot through with the odd silver strand, and faint laughter lines softened her face, which might otherwise have been considered stern. I found it hard to determine her age. She could have passed for the late thirties but might easily be ten years older. Given her occupational status, I guessed that the latter was closer to the truth.

"My pleasure. Bryony has been telling me about you."

I was not sure whether to be flattered or alarmed, but her attention had already switched as she seemed to look disdainfully at her surroundings.

"I'm on my way back to my office. Why don't you both join me? I'm sure I can rustle up something a little more palatable to drink."

I was about to refuse because I needed to get back, but Bryony rose from her chair and took me by the hand. We followed Grace along a crowded corridor before cutting across the grounds to the original hospital building, which, I was informed, was now a medical school.

Grace had "rooms" on the top floor. The outer area was bright, gaily lit, with lots of children's toys in evidence. Her inner sanctum formed a complete contrast. The originally carved wood paneling had been preserved and, but for the phone and computer, it could still have been the 1920's.

Without asking, she poured each of us a glass of sherry from a crystal decanter. It was not something I would normally drink, but I could tell that this was a long way removed from the supermarket offering I was used to.

She took a seat behind her desk and Bryony, and I occupied the guest chairs. Grace asked me about what I did for a living, and I explained about ethical investments and how, in some areas, it had common links with the medical profession. As she listened, I was intrigued to notice that she made a note on a jotter.

I was no fool. The meeting with Grace had been engineered, and I could make a reasonable guess as to why. The real question was why I had gone along with it?

Grace shifted a little in her seat as if she had followed my train of thought.

"Bryony tells me that you are an ingénue and I have to tell you that I find that attractive in a woman...so much so that I want you get down on your knees and crawl to me."

I looked at her in total disbelief, but her face displayed no hint of amusement; rather, there was an expression of purest lust that lit her eyes and lent her a cruel beauty. I had only met this woman moments ago, but I was almost overcome by a need to be kissed by her.

I had never felt this was way about a man. It was as if she had cast a veil over us and created a secret space free from the usual mores that might otherwise inhibit.

I could not tear my eyes from her and could not understand why I felt such an irrational need for her approval. I was not being forced, not even coerced, so why did I go to my knees?

Her desk did not have a modesty board, so her skirt to ride up revealed her legs. As I neared, she parted them a little more, and in the dimmed light beneath the desktop, I could see that she was wearing stockings and suspenders.

It seemed so decadent to be wearing them as everyday attire, but on her, it seemed perfectly natural.

I felt both absurd and demeaned, but an aching need crushed any thoughts of stopping as she lured me further. Her legs were opening inch by inch, exposing the paleness of her thighs above the dark welts.

As I began to kiss her warm skin tentatively, I was infused with a feeling of well-being that I had not experienced since childhood. I stroked her smooth calves, moving up to the solidness of her toned thighs, willing her to beckon me in.

I heard distant laughter and snatches of conversation, but they were meaningless as I was slowly seduced by the prospect that lay before me.

Her panties were dark, expensive, silk, and they were stretched across her mound, which was obscenely prominent. She had applied a light scent to her thighs, but it could not compete with the emergent proof of her arousal.

Driven by an outlandish yearning, I used the flat of my tongue to lick the tight crotch of her underwear, feeling the soft rasp of silk and appreciating the exuded taste.

For a moment or two, I was riding a wave of pure euphoria, but then, she eased her chair backward without warning.

"That's good for now. I want you to come back at the same time tomorrow. Make sure that you free up the afternoon."

The abrupt dismissal hit me like a cosh. Less than five minutes later, I was standing alone on the pavement, having left them together, feeling both confused and bereft.

Back at the office, I could barely function, and I could not fully comprehend what had happened to me. I had prostrated myself for a total stranger in front of a woman I hardly knew, but there was no doubting that I had been excited almost beyond measure.

While trying to take a step back, it seemed that Bryony was showing me how weak-willed I really was and how easily I could be seduced. Now it had been left up to me.

I spent a restless night thinking things through, but by morning I had reached a decision. I still harbored a strong desire to get to know Bryony better, in every sense, but the price was too high to pay. I determined that I would explore my feelings for other women on my terms and, bolstered by this plan, I went into work.

At the office, I spent a productive couple of hours clearing my in-tray, but then I drew a sharp breath as an e-mail from Etheridge arrived.

It was a personal message from Moira Etheridge herself and started with an apology for the delay in replying. My heart began to beat faster as I read on. The Etheridge board was happy with my proposal, and it would now go to a vote of the trustees. She suggested that, with the support of her recommendation, the vote would be a formality, and I gave a muted whoop of delight.

The final paragraph referred to our mutual decision to revisit the tax shelter issues in light of the first year's returns, but Moira asked if I would give a brief outline to one of the trustees who had raised a last-minute question.

I was elated. The tax issue was completely uncontroversial, and there was no way that it would a show stopper. The deal was effectively done. I opened the attachment to get the trustee's contact details, and then I gasped as I read the name. Grace De Moyes.

Chapter 05

I was breathing raggedly, and sweat beaded my forehead. It was a minute or two before I recovered a vestige of composure, and then I frantically called up the Etheridge trust deed on screen.

The trust had been set up by Henry Etheridge, who had made his money in South African mining. His wife, Moira, ran it on a day to day basis along with a board of trustees, all three of whom I had met frequently.

Beneath board level, all organizations that contributed to the investment pool, that Etheridge administered, were represented by one or more trustees depending on the size of their commitment. There were more than one hundred contributors and nearly two hundred trustees entitled to a vote.

Buried way down the list, I found Grace's name as one of two trustees representing a children's charity called 'Compassion.' A further trawl established that she had never attended an Etheridge meeting, nor had she ever registered a vote. Hers was a token presence.

There was no way on earth that this was a simple coincidence, and I angrily picked up the phone. After five frustrating minutes of being pushed around the hospital's telephone system, I was eventually told that Grace was running a clinic and would not be available until later.

I was still seething as, after lunch, I took a taxi to keep our original appointment. I burst into her office without knocking and confronted her at her desk.

"What the hell do you think you're playing at?"

She looked up from the report she was reading completely unfazed.

"Good afternoon."

Her insouciance riled me even more.

"I do not care about your little fantasy life. Anything that happened between us is at an end and you do not threaten my professional role, even obliquely."

She looked at me with mild amusement.

"A little ironic don't you think? Our talk of worlds colliding and here we are, my charity and your asset management company. The truth is the name of your company rang a bell but I could not think why. Finance is not my strong suit."

I bit my tongue, waiting for her to continue.

"I wouldn't even have bothered to check it up except that Bryony and I talked after you left yesterday. You see, Bryony surmised that you had come too far too quickly. She guessed that you would step back from the brink and that you would not keep our appointment today.

Now that, for me, would have been a great pity. So great that I was encouraged to do a little digging and lo and behold..."

I looked at her intently.

"You will phone Etheridge and you will tell them that everything has been cleared up to your satisfaction."

A hint of a smile crossed her face.

"...my satisfaction...yes, I guess it will all come down to that.

I had to check with my accountant. She confirms that your work on behalf of the trust has been exemplary. She even thought that the tax shelter matter had been carefully handled, but I needed something to entice you back."

Only now did I fully understand what this was all about.

"The tax shelter is not an issue at all. I can talk to the Etheridge board and clear this up in two minutes."

She put her pen down and steepled her fingers.

"I have no doubt that you could. I only have a nodding acquaintance with Moira Etheridge but 'Compassion' is a large stakeholder. I'm guessing that I could make a minor nuisance of myself."

Did she know about the tax year deadline? Any delay beyond that left an open-ended completion date and the prospect of other suitors trying to get a foot in the door. I had to get the deal sealed.

She remained silent for a second or two longer, and then she spoke bluntly.

"I want two hours of your time...or, more particularly, two hours of your lovely little mouth and tongue."

I fired back at her.

"I will not be blackmailed!"

She smiled as she replied.

"Think of it in any terms you wish."

Without another word, she got up and left the room, and it was a few seconds before I gathered myself to follow after her. I walked through to the outer office and was stopped in my tracks. She was standing in the middle of the room, having already shed her dress, looking beguiling in her elegant black underwear.

Her lightly tanned, toned, body belied her age, and she was fully aware of the effect that she was having on me. She crossed to the examination couch, which was decorated with nursery motifs, and pressed a button at its head. With a soft hum of motors, the couch reconfigured from a single to a double platform.

Seeing my bemusement, she explained.

"It is sometimes easier to examine a child if the parent lies down with them."

With studied deliberation, she removed the remainder of her clothing and settled onto the bed with her legs parted.

"A quick one to start with, just to ease the tension, and then you can settle down and take your time."

She spoke as if I were nothing more than a concubine, a slave to her desires, and I should have been fired with anger but, instead, the heat within me was transmuting into a pathetic craving.

Her sex was revealed in all its glory by a bank of spotlights that illuminated the couch. The perfectly shaped mound was shaded by a close trimmed covering of dark hair with a few flecks of grey sparked by the light, but it was her labia that riveted my attention.

The swollen lips bloomed languorously already speckled with tiny droplets of moisture, and I swallowed audibly as my tongue awakened to a realm of possibilities.

She said nothing more but lay there confident of the inevitable outcome. I felt irritated, but I had lost all sense of reason. I paused fleetingly, wondering if I should undress, but I could wait no longer.

I lay prostrate on the couch, setting myself between her legs and breathed in the fullness of her scent, which hung heavily in the air. Its muskiness was narcotic, and I began to softly kiss her lips, each in turn, before slyly employing my tongue.

Her taste was all that I could have hoped for, and I was soon lapping greedily along the whole length of her furrow. Outwardly, she retained her cool demeanor, but the heat that radiated from her sex told its own story.

I wanted to work my tongue deep inside her, but she had made clear her desire, and I strained my neck to seek out her clitoris. It needed no coaxing, already standing proud, and as I engaged with her, I could feel the vitality of her pulse.

I was sure that my technique left something to be desired, but it only took a few strokes of my tongue before she began to clutch me to her, and the dam quickly burst. Her body shook gently but erratically as she rode out her climax, coating my face with the dew of her arousal.

I pulled away from her to catch my breath and to cool down a little, and, as I did so, she drowsily turned over onto her stomach.

Now that she was faced away from me, I could her appraise her more fully. Her body was long and lean, and her skin flawless save for two tiny moles high on her shoulder. Her legs would be the envy of many a young athlete. But my eyes were drawn to the surprising fullness of her derrière.

It was beautifully carved, and, without thinking, I reached out and ran my fingers over the taut contours. In response, she gave an appreciative moan and lifted herself a little. I drew my hand away quickly as if scalded, only to hear her chuckle.

"Don't be coy...I want you to lick me."

She stretched with a feline grace opening the divide and putting herself lewdly on display. The tight, puckered, opening was fully revealed, a forbidden shade in a pale landscape.

It would be a lie to say that this was something that I had never contemplated, but it required a degree of intimacy that I had never found in my previous relationships. How bizarre then that I should feel so drawn to a woman I hardly knew.

As I drew nearer, my body trembled, and I took a deep breath to calm myself. I placed my hands carefully on her cheeks as if she were a work of art and then cursed my timidity; I licked clumsily.

I was surprised by the tenseness of her muscles but pleased as she growled approval. I tried again, this time more positively, with a long stroke of my tongue.

I fell into an easy rhythm, causing her to sigh deeply, but then she began to arch her body, guiding me towards the ultimate goal.

Even now, I felt uneasy, my arms rigid, as I dared myself. Each successive sweep of my tongue was foreshortened as I began to focus on the opening itself.

At first, it felt inflexible, but then she held her breath, and there was a tiny but perceptible yielding. Emboldened, I speared my tongue and applied steady pressure.

It seemed a futile struggle for a few seconds, but then she hissed out a triumphant "Yes!" and I breached the portal to be gripped tight within. The initial pressure was uncomfortable, but as I flexed my tongue and probed more deeply, she relaxed and accepted my ministrations.

I registered a brackish taste cut through with the astringent tang of an expensive soap. There was a strong temptation to switch back to her sex, which was weeping copiously, not least because she had brought her fingers furiously into play.

At the finish, it was this evidence of her excitement that kept me in place, trying to drive her ever higher. I lay locked with her for what seemed an age, and when she finally deigned to allow herself a second climax, the cramping of her muscles threaten to painfully crushing my tongue.

For the briefest instant, I felt pathetic, but I knew that, if she asked, I would do it again. Through it all, I hovered on the brink of an orgasm that promised to shake me to the core.

As I finally slid free, she twisted herself and lay slumped on her back. Her mauled sex was a beautiful shade of angry red, and the surrounding wetness spread to her thighs. I needed no bidding. I slowly and slavishly licked her skin clean, working my way inevitably back towards that beautiful oasis.

Her third climax was prolonged. She would stop me from time to time to regather herself and then allowed me to resume. My neck and tongue, in fact, my whole face, ached but I remained tireless in my efforts to please this captivating goddess. My arousal ebbed a little but only to swell again as she joyously shuddered through another series of blissful contractions.

Her two hours had become the better part of three before she cleaned herself up and got dressed again. I was conscious that she looked composed while I looked a complete wreck, and I knew I would have to go home rather than back to the office.

I was almost in a trance as she led me to the door and, as I stood there, wondering what the hell to say, she slipped her hand beneath my skirt. In the space of a single heartbeat, she fleetingly touched my sex and then brought her fingers to her lips. As she sucked them gently and closed the door on me, I collapsed to the floor as I climaxed on the spot.

Chapter 06

The next few weeks passed in a blur. The Etheridge deal was sealed, and my partnership was confirmed.

Setting up the initial investments and putting all of the required reporting into place was demanding, and I had little time for a social life. If I am honest, I was glad of the distraction as it gave me an excuse to duck the personal issues that I should have been confronting.

The one exception was the temptation, on several occasions, to get in touch with Bryony, not least because I noticed that the show at the Palace Theatre had closed as a prelude to the touring production, but cowardice got the better of me.

I had already decided that I would move house to somewhere more commensurate with my new position in life, and I figured that Bryony would fade into a past left behind.

My confidence was further boosted when the other partners tasked me to take a trip to New York to talk to some US investors interested in the Etheridge model.

I decided to tack some well-earned annual leave onto the back of the trip. Ostensibly I would revisit some of the sights I had first taken in as a teenager, but in reality, I was keenly aware that, as a stranger, I could dip my toe into the waters of the gay scene and see where it led me.

As it transpired, my toe-dipping proved to be a disaster. The bar I chose was nice enough, but the clientele made it a pantomime. Every stereotype was to be found there. They were loud, ostentatious, and this was a place to see and be seen. I found some women attractive, but there was no way on earth that I was going to make an approach.

Back in my hotel room, I struggled to formulate what I really wanted, let alone how to go about finding it. I was gazing blankly at my e-mail account when a new message appeared. I took a sharp intake of breath and ran my finger across the address bar on the screen to be sure.

The message was from Bryony.

"I tried to get in touch but I am told you are in New York - lucky you! We'll catch up when you get back but, in the meanwhile you might want to look up a friend of mine."

My heart soared irrationally on reading the simple words, and then I quickly re-read it to ensure that nothing was incriminating given that she had used my work account. My instinct was to reply immediately, but something held me back. Hard as it was, I decided that I would let her wait until I returned home.

A day later, I picked up the phone and dialed the number she had given me.

I asked to speak to "Philly" and was rocked back by the boisterous reply.

"You must be the investment guru Bryony told me about. That English accent is so cute!"

Within moments I had agreed to meet with her at her apartment on the Lower East Side. I dressed as if for a date and then gave some serious thought to changing again, but I finally plucked up my courage and had the doorman hail me a cab.

Philly was something in magazine advertising, and her apartment turned out to be a barn of a place on Stanton. It was a reflection of the woman herself, who seemed larger than life. I guessed that she was at least ten years my senior, and she was heavy in a sexy, curvy, sort of way. Her clothes were tailored to flatter her fuller figure, but her face seized my attention.

She had the most startling blue eyes set above high, rosy, cheeks, and a sultry Clara Bow mouth. The roundness of her features was accentuated by her shoulder-length blond hair set in soft curls.

With a little work, she could be a total beauty, but I sensed that she was more than happy in her skin, and people had to meet her on her terms. She greeted me with a glass of wine, and within minutes, it felt as if we had known one another forever.

It struck me that I would be happy to spend an uncomplicated evening in her company, but we both knew the unspoken ties that bound us. Thus, I was not sure how to react when she asked.

"How adventurous are you?"

I was still examining my feelings when she rose from the sofa and opened her handbag. She took out some lengths of wide white ribbon and showed them to me.

"Would you let me tie you up?"

If she had been a man, I would have refused point-blank but, contrary to every instinct, the prospect of putting myself at her mercy sent a shiver of excitement coursing through my body.

Set in front of the sofa was a full-length Ottoman style upholstered coffee table which doubled as a footstool. As she bent to pat it, I saw how it could be put to another purpose.

"It might be more comfortable if you undressed."

I think I began to take off my clothes to give myself more time to deliberate, but the ribbons looked so innocuous, and her face beamed with naughty fun. Almost in a daze, I laid down on the padded surface and allowed her to fasten my limbs to the table's leg.

Once she had me securely in place, I found that the ribbons were more than equal to the task of holding me firm, and with my legs opened across the table's width, I felt frighteningly vulnerable.

She left me for a moment, and I heard her talking, presumably on the telephone. It only now dawned on me how stupid I had been, but she smiled openly and put me marginally at ease.

She came and knelt beside me and idly teased my nipples to engorgement.

"Bryony wasn't lying. You really are beautiful."

The knowledge that Bryony considered me in those terms caused my heart to flutter with excitement, and I felt like a lovelorn teenager. Philly had a look of understanding on her face as she trailed her fingers down my body, and I became desperate to feel her touch on my sex, but she proceeded with aching slowness.

She had me squirming by the time she began to caress my inner thighs, but each time I thought she was going to put me out of my misery, she would withdraw and start all over again. I lost all track of time, and my body became clammy with sweat, but she was not put off in any way. At one point, she leaned over me and licked a bead of moisture from between my breasts.

That single act sparked a burning desire to have her kiss me, but this too, she seemed to anticipate. She touched her lips to mine for the briefest instant and then returned her attention to my lower body.

I could feel myself leaking, and she whispered into my ear.

"You reek of it you slut..."

What could have been taken as an insult was, from her, an unbelievable turn on? I groaned and felt a further seepage.

When, finally, her fingers began to graze against my sex, it was a gossamer touch that continually skirted my labia. I was, by now, straining against my restraints, and I begged her to be merciful. She smiled, switched her concentration to my breasts, and began again.

I almost reached a state of delirium when I was jolted back to reality by the doorbell ring. Ignoring my protestations, Philly got to her feet and went to answer it. My embarrassment was almost beyond measure when I heard voices and realized that she was showing the newcomers into the room.

From what I could see, with my limited view, there were two of them, and they both looked as if they had just stepped out of a business meeting. The first was a tall black woman. She had the stark features of Grace Jones softened by her long, straightened hair. Her make-up was impeccably applied, and I had difficulty pegging her age.

At first, I thought that her companion was an Asian, but, on closer inspection, her pretty square features hinted at some Native Americans in her DNA. She was slightly built, suggestive of youthfulness, but something about how she held herself made me think that she and I might be of a similar age.

"I see you started without us."

This from the black woman who removed her jacket and made herself comfortable on the sofa to be joined by her companion, who seemed totally at ease with the situation.

Philly poured them each a glass of wine and introduced them to me as Sara and Aponi as if the situation was nothing out of the ordinary. For the next fifteen minutes or so, they made small talk while she continued to toy me. On its face, she was giving no thought to what she was doing, but every caress of her fingertips increased the erotic tension that racked my whole body.

Aponi was the first to finish her wine, and, having done so, she stood up and casually began to get undressed. I was shocked by her sangfroid, but more so as the others were completely unfazed.

Once she was completely naked, she came and stood over me, allowing me to appraise her lithe figure. Her breasts were mere upswells, but this only emphasized the rigidity of her dark nipples. There were almost perfect roundels from which the teats stood almost obscenely proud.

Her hips were youthful, but her swollen mound along with her exposed, puffy, labia suggested a woman of worldly experience.

"Well this is an unexpected pleasure at the end of a tiring day."

There was no further preamble, no niceties as if by divine right, she straddled my face and settled herself down. It took some seconds for me to come to terms with what was happening, but Aponi was already rubbing herself demandingly over my mouth.

Her skin still bore the musty smells of a day at work, but they were quickly overwhelmed by the heated scent of arousal. I was fully aware that I was being both used and demeaned, but, far from being angered, I was turned on even more.

I began to lick her almost frenziedly, and my reward was the wonderful touch of Philly's fingers on my sex. She enticed the inner surfaces of my labia, ignoring the imploring thrusts of my hips, and I was panting with need.

The heat of my quickened breathing helped coax Aponi towards a swift orgasm, but I sensed that this was only the beginning.

She leisurely arose from her throne to reveal Sara standing gloriously naked at the foot of the table like some Amazonian princess. She was a woman who worked with weights, and the muscles of her arms and legs were clearly defined. Her stomach was toned, and her conical breasts were uplifted to the extent that her nipples stood almost perpendicular.

She was a frightening sight to behold, but my eyes were already dropping to her sex, and I wondered how she would taste. She smiled at my appraisal but then turned to Philly.

"Do you have it?"

"Of course, but first things first, there is someone else who wishes to join us."

For a moment, panic threatened to overwhelm me. I had barely come to terms with the idea of three of them taking advantage of me, but now things seemed to be getting out of hand. I was on the verge of demanding that Philly released me when her meaning became apparent.

She opened a large screen laptop set on an elaborately carved escritoire, which was the room's showpiece. Having switched it on, she produced a small cam with an adjustable tripod and carefully pointed it at me.

My immediate, and not irrational, fear was the prospect of the blackmail. She turned the laptop towards me so that I could see myself on screen in all my wanton glory, but then the image changed, and I was confronted with Bryony's smiling face.

"Hi! I hope you're having a good time. I've just settled in to watch the show...I know you're going to make me proud."

My mind was in turmoil. On the one hand, I wondered how dare she, and what it said about her feelings about me, but on the other, I had a ridiculous sense of wanting to be worthy of her.

By the time I refocused on reality, Sara was already preparing herself. Philly had handed her a webbed harness, and only as she stepped into it did I register the double-ended phallus that defined its purpose.

I watched with a mixture of shock and fascination as she eased the thing deep inside herself with a guttural groan of satisfaction. I am no stranger to vibrators, but the threat implicit in this had me shaking my head in denial.

"There, there. Don't fight it. Just relax and enjoy."

As Philly spoke, she eased her finger fractionally inside me, and despite everything, we could all hear the soft suck of moisture.

Notwithstanding, I felt myself trembling as Sara approached like a panther bearing down on its prey. My muscles were tensed, but she was in no hurry. She lightly played the tip of the thing over the opening to my sex, and I could feel my body betraying me. She spent some moments continuing to coax, and I was relaxing involuntarily.

She read the moment of transition as defiance surrendered to greedy desire, and she gently broached the portal.

Even now, we remained barely engaged as she let me get used to the initial intrusion before she pressed herself home with exquisite slowness.

The thing was modestly sized and both warmer and more pliant than I imagined. Sara paused again once we were joined and reached forward to torment my nipples, which had remained almost painfully tumescent.

Her touch was not as skillful as Philly's, but, in my present state of agitation, it was enough to string me even tighter.

She continued for only a short while before she started to concentrate on her own need.

At first, I thought she was withdrawing altogether, but she stopped at the cusp and then gently invaded me once more.

It was a prelude to a series of long, easy strokes, and the glint in her eyes as she held my gaze told me that she was as aroused as me if not more so.

She was beautiful to look upon. Her body's animal quality was enhanced as her skin began to glisten with a fine sheen of sweat, and her latent power transmitted itself through the link that joined us.

There was a thrilling moment of realization that there was to be no softening, no disappointment. She was determined that we would both be fulfilled, and she had both the resilience and purpose of delivering her promise.

Over the ensuing minutes, she gradually picked up the pace, impaling me with the commanding thrusts of her hips. I felt as if I was in the grip of continuous slow-burning orgasm, but I knew that the true climax was yet to come.

She looked deep into my eyes, and I saw in hers a distillation of pure lust. There was an unspoken understanding that we were both ready, and she found a fast and unremitting rhythm that shamed any man I had ever been with.

Her conquering growl as the dam burst triggered an orgasm that shook my whole body and left me trembling long after she was done. She was still now, but the ebbing pulses of her sated sex were conducted to mine, and I fed off them to keep myself aloft until, finally, my strength spent I lay limp and sublimely contented.

The room smelt of sex and expensive perfume evaporated from heated flesh, and I breathed it deeply. I groaned with disappointment as Sara tenderly withdrew, but oddly my thoughts turned to Bryony and what she had witnessed.

Exhausted as I now was, I hoped that Philly would release me, but her smile told another story. She moved closer, making sure I could watch as she slowly undressed.

Naked, she was as impressive as Sara but in an altogether different way. There was a heaviness to her, her breasts, belly, thighs, but her body was beautifully toned. I felt a longing to be enfolded in her arms to embrace her inviting softness.

She stroked my face, giving a sense that all my yearnings would be gratified, but, as often in the recent past, it was a matter of being careful what you wished for.

In a haze of movement, she seemed to flow over me, and then my face was arranged between her thighs as she looked into my eyes.

"I want you to worship me..."

Her choice of words was odd, but it chimed with something deep within my psyche. Entrapped by the fullness of her flesh, I felt cut off from all else, and now she eased forward presenting her sex.

I suddenly felt uncomfortably warm, but my eyes were riveted to the lush delta before me. Like her, it seemed so much larger than life. She was flawlessly depilated, and her labia erupted from within to form dark, demanding, wings on which tiny beads of arousal caught the light.

She had waited a long time, and her scent was rich but far from recoiling my nostrils twitched in expectation.

I put out my tongue, but it was a stretch to reach her, and I could barely run the tip along the edge of her lips.

It was enough to infuse my tongue with the pure taste of her, and it acted on my brain like an ice-cold shot. I strained again, wanting more, and I was dimly aware of her knowing smile.

It amused her, for a moment or two, to watch me trying to satisfy my craving, but then she proceeded to demonstrate her dominion. She slowly eased forward, eclipsing me with the slight overhang of her belly, and then the last thing I was aware of was the mounds of her breasts before all was darkness.

She settled with her sex covering my mouth, and I was acutely aware of the mass of her bearing down on me. My temperature rose within seconds, and breathing became more of an effort until I willed myself to relax.

I reached out blindly with my tongue, but I was unprepared for the sudden heat and wetness. I had penetrated her with ease, and her essence ran down my cheeks.

All my senses were suffused. Her body's warm compression cut me off from the world, offering a sanctuary where my only and task and desire was to please her. The solidity of her thighs blocked my ears, and every breath I took was moist.

I do not know for how long I labored, my tongue exploring the depths of her. At moments her taste was more intense, and the ever more erratic contractions, almost uncomfortable, gave the only clues as to my degree of success.

I had reached my state of nirvana and recognized that I might reach another climax without even being touched.

Finally, her legs parted a little, and I felt her hand on my head, bidding me remain still. She began to move over me, slowly at first, but then more positively. She was using my face, and, contrary to all sense of reason, I welcomed it.

Her movements, like Sara's, were graceful but powerful and assured. She was asserting her womanhood in a manner that left me awestruck.

At last, her orgasm broke over her, shaking her whole body, and my mouth was suddenly flooded with gouts of moisture, which I swallowed with unseemly greed. I did not want it to end, but a lack of air was making me light-headed.

When, at last, she rose from me, Aponi came and kissed her on the cheek, and I felt an enormous sense of pride. My body ached in so many ways, but, on balance, I was feeling wonderfully gratified.

My three tormentresses ignored me while they refilled their glasses, but I had reached a point where I was prepared to relax and see how things played out.

After a few moments, Aponi returned her attention to me and began to release my legs. It now seemed that proceedings might be coming to a close, and I have to confess that I had mixed feelings.

Philly and Sara put down their wine glasses and joined us. Philly knelt and addressed herself to the ribbons that still bound my wrists but, rather than undoing them. She checked to make sure that they were secure.

My surprise at this turn of events turned to shock as Philly loomed over me. Once again, she straddled my face, but this time, I was left staring at the spectacle of her voluminous derrière.

"You know what you have to do..."

From my vantage point, it was, almost literally, a breathtaking sight to behold. Her skin was flawless, and the heavy curves had a beauty all their own, but I was very aware of the implicit menace.

I had already broken this taboo, but that had been on my terms. Now there could be no escape even if I wanted it. Philly reached down and spread her cheeks, revealing a puckered opening that was only a slightly darker shade of pink than her natural skin color.

The angel and demon within me fought for control, the one cautioning the other, encouraging me to indulge my darkest desires.

Philly relaxed a little, bringing herself in reach of my tongue, and then sighed as I made a first, uncertain, foray. Her skin was a little salty, but the taste of leaked arousal beckoned me on.

I licked more positively, and I was repaid when I felt her hand caressing my sex. I wanted to feel her fingers inside me, but she reached lower, spreading my wetness and mirroring my tongue's actions.

I was in a dream state. I could hear them speaking but paid them no heed as I endeavored to satisfy Philly and, in turn, have her please me.

"Are you ready Aponi?"

This from Philly but then, more eerily, the disembodied voice of Bryony.

"A little larger I think."

Philly began to settle more heavily upon me, and I braced my tongue to meet her. With seemingly little effort, we were gradually conjoined.

It felt as if it were always meant to be, but it was an act of total trust as she sealed me in and commanded every breath that I drew.

I could feel the pulses of excitement deep within her, and, in return, she increased the pressure of her finger. After a fleeting sensation of discomfort, she broke through and began a gentle massage, and my state of arousal became incredibly heightened.

I was immediately transported to a hotel room in Paris. I was on a business trip, and, on my one free evening, I had been watching some lesbian porn while stimulating myself with a vibrator. Using her hands, one of the girls had penetrated the other both front and rear and, just for a moment, I was tempted to try for myself but, when it came to it, the opening seemed too tight and the vibrator too brutal and so I chickened out.

Now Philly was showing me what I had missed. She introduced a second finger with such subtlety I did not even realize it was happening, and the feeling of fullness seemed extended to my sex.

My clitoris was crying out for attention, and I pushed my tongue further inside her hoping to engender a similar degree of need.

Philly was beginning to sweat, which only added to the feeling that I was drowning in her flesh, and, great as the pleasure was, I began to wonder how much more I could take.

Divining my moment of crisis, she gently withdrew and switched her attention to my heated sex, but, at the same time, I felt my legs being raised. Where, seconds ago, her warm fingers had been there was now a cool, persistent, hardness.

My howl of protest was smothered as I felt myself being impossibly stretched. My muscles clenched defensively, but Philly began to stimulate my clitoris, and my resistance crumbled. I was torn between the intense pleasure she bestowed and the continuing invasion.

I could take no more, but I was still being filled until I felt the warmth of thighs pressed against me. In light of what had been said, I assumed that Aponi had donned the harness relinquished by Sara, but this seemed brutal by comparison.

She gave me a moment to adjust to the situation, and I appreciated that, in some manner, my sex had become more sensitized. Philly knew from experience exactly what I was feeling as her fingers continued to dance over my clitoris, bringing me closer to the brink.

My tongue was free, just as well as I panted for breath, but Philly gave me no respite from my burial. She remained solidly in place as Aponi withdrew a little only to press home once more.

There was nothing I could do except try and relax, but as Aponi found a rhythm, I was surprised at how readily my body came to terms with the intrusion. Philly's ministrations continued unabated, and I found myself working my hips to meet Aponi's quickening thrusts.

I began to cry out, yearning for release, and Philly did not disappoint. Aponi pressed home one final time, and I sensed that she was lost in the throes of her climax as Philly worked her fingers with a barely credible rapidity and launched me into an orgasm like no other.

I was soaring so high that it was frightening, and my body trembled with waves of pleasure stretching to each extremity. I did not want it to end, and I wept as I finally had to let it go.

I drew a deep breath as Philly finally relinquished her throne, and I was able to watch as Sara helped a spent Aponi out of the harness.

My mind was a whirr of confused thoughts and impressions, and I now just wanted some time alone to try and make sense of everything. Philly smiled at me as if my thoughts were transparent to her and used her fingers to brush my matted hair from my forehead.

"Not just yet sweetie..."

Chapter 07

My 'holiday' left me anything but refreshed, and I returned home feeling more uncertain than ever. It could be counted as a success from a business standpoint, and I had made some useful, and hopefully, profitable contacts.

For the first couple of days back, I buried myself in my work and put together a prospect report for the senior partners.

I spent a lot of time thinking about Bryony, but it was with mixed feelings. On the one hand, it felt as if she had pimped me out, but I had picked up the phone of my own volition, and the excitement of that evening would live with me for the rest of my life.

I had finally decided that I would move forward and leave it in the past when, out of the blue, she phoned me at work. My heart was beating madly, and I had to breathe deeply and calm myself down. The conversation was brief and amounted to an invitation to dinner that same evening.

I accepted but very nearly cried off at the very last minute. She had chosen a modest French restaurant in the center of town, and she was already there when I arrived. As she stood to greet me, I felt like an adolescent on a first date. She was dressed, but her smile left me weak at the knees.

For the first few minutes, we exchanged small talk, which mainly consisted of me chatting about America while pointing out any references to Philly and her friends. She could see my awkwardness, and she put her hand on mine.

"Let's be clear. We are here to enjoy a meal, and I have no intention of inviting you anywhere afterward.

I have some things to say, and I would like you to hear me out. I then want you to take a couple of days to consider and then get back to me."

This was not what I was expecting, hoping? To hear, but she continued without pause.

"I was a gifted child raised by a single mum who meant everything to me. The trouble was that I went off the rails, not least because I struggled with my sexuality. When my mum died of cancer, she left me a healthy inheritance, and I decided that I owed it to her to turn my life around. Choosing medicine as a career path seemed fitting somehow.

I think I have now reached another turning point in my life. I once told you that I would be dangerous for you to know, but the truth is, there is something about you that attracts me in a way that I have never felt before. What I am trying to say is that I want to try a normal adult relationship, and I want it to be with you."

I sat lost for words, unable to think coherently. She smiled and kissed me on the cheek.

"We can still role play together, we could even invite others to join in, but it would be up to you. I think that we are both strong and sensible enough to know where the boundaries need to be drawn."

The rest of the meal passed like a dream. She told me more about herself, and I opened up to her in return.

That night I slept the soundest sleep I had enjoyed for a very long time, and on the train, to work, I could not keep the smile from my face.

I walked into the meeting of senior partners still on cloud nine, wondering what these three women would make of me if they only but knew.

They all sat with a copy of my report in front of them, and Francesca took the lead.

"This is an impressive piece of work but there seems to be something missing...Tell us about your meeting with Aponi."

I felt my face flush and a cold sweat across my body. How the hell had they found out? Had they been sent a film of the proceedings, but who stood to gain?

I remained silent. What did they know, and could I talk my way out of it?

I could feel their eyes boring into me, and then Francesca smiled.

"Very few people even know that Aponi Swan is the power behind the throne at CareCo. It's one of the largest portfolios on the east coast, and we've been quietly trying to get a foot in the door for over twelve months.

We even tried going through Grace de Moyes. She's a minor trustee at Etheridge; you may remember, she raised that last-minute tax question. Anyway, we were given to understand that she was friends with Aponi, but it got us nowhere.

Now, you get to the states, not even aware of our interest, and scoop the pot. She loved you. She wants us to set up an investment pool, but there is one small catch, but we think you'll be more than happy.

She wants us to have a permanent presence in New York, and she wants it to be you.

Lesbian Femdom
Two Erotic Novelette Collection for Women
Alannah Kieran

All Rights Reserved. No part of this publication may be reproduced in any form or by any means, including scanning, photocopying, or otherwise without prior written permission of the copyright holder. Copyright © 2020

This book is entirely a work of fiction. The names, characters and incidents portrayed in it are the work of the author's imagination. Any resemblance to actual persons, living or dead, events or localities is entirely coincidental.

Story 01

Chapter 00

She sat next to the woman on the barstool. Her long black skirt and long-sleeved red top, cut close to her neck revealed nothing of her body. She wore black shoes with black stockings, but only her ankles could be seen.

"So you think you are a slave." the blond woman said.

"yes Ma'am," the girl replied, looking down.

"What makes you think that?"

"My desires Ma'am."

"Understandable. But you said you have a problem."

"Yes Ma'am."

"You are unable to release the passion inside you. You are unable to obey because of hangups that plague you."

"In short, yes Ma'am."

"You can't even bear the touch of another human being." she asked.

"No Ma'am, not more than a handshake anyway Ma'am."

"And how do you expect a Domme to overcome this?"

"I don't Ma'am. I expect to be alone my whole life."

"But you wish a Domme could overcome your problem."

"Yes Ma'am."

To avoid the woman's hard gaze, Grace looked around the room. The bar had glasses hanging from racks over the bar, and lights hanging from the ceiling on the dance floor. There were also toys such as St Andrews crosses, and spanking benches. People were playing at some of the stations, Masters beating their slaves and Mistresses beating theirs.

"What makes you think someone can help you?"

"I don't Ma'am."

"But you hope regardless."

"Yes."

"You have a beautiful face Grace dear," the Lady said.

Grace blushed, "Thank you Ma'am," she replied, looking down.

"Of course you have no idea what I do for a living," the Lady said, "So I shall tell you."

Grace looked at her for a moment, and the Lady went on.

"I am a psychologist, and a hypnosis therapist. I deal mostly with abused women and I have ties with women's shelters in the city."

Grace's eyes widened in surprise, and hope lighted in her.

"That seems to surprise you. Do you find something strange in that?"

"To be honest Ma'am, it does seem strange that a Domme would specialize in helping those abused. Isn't there a fine line between the lifestyle and abuse?"

"Yes indeed there is a fine line. But, there IS a line. And I never cross it, though some in the lifestyle do."

"You seem quite a lovely Lady, Lady Amanda Ma'am. Smart and beautiful as well as a little dangerous."

"Thank you girl. Shall we meet here again tomorrow night?"

"I would like that very much Ma'am."

"Good. Be here at 9."

"Yes Ma'am. see You then," Grace replied as Lady Amanda got up and left.

Grace was impatient all day. She could remember every moment spent with Lady Amanda. The look of Her hair, what She was wearing, and the smell of Her perfume. The nuance in her voice, and every detail of their conversation.

Lady Amanda was just as beautiful the next time Grace saw her. Her long blond hair fell about her shoulders, covering the thin straps of Her black and red calf-length dress. Her makeup was flawless, and her beautiful blue eyes sparkled underneath her powdered lids and long black eyelashes.

"Hello Lady Amanda," Grace said, smiling.

"Hello my girl, instead of sitting at the bar tonight, lets get a table."

"As you wish Ma'am."

Lady Amanda led the way to a small booth table against the back wall and took a seat while discreetly pointing at the ground near her. Grace saw Lady Amanda's finger-pointing at the floor and knelt beside her.

"Very good my girl," Lady Amanda said. "You are paying attention."

"I can but try Ma'am."

A waitress stopped at their table and asked what Lady Amanda would like to drink. Lady Amanda ordered for both of them. The waitress returned quickly and set Lady Amanda's drink down on the table and reached down to Grace with hers. Lady Amanda and Grace thanked her, and the waitress moved off to another table.

"Do you drive Grace?" Lady Amanda asked as they sipped their drinks.

"I have my licence, but I don't currently own a car Ma'am."

"Ok." Lady Amanda replied.

They talked for a long while. When they had finished their drinks, Lady Amanda ordered another round for them but ordered a soft drink for Grace instead of her vodka and orange juice that she had been drinking. And then they continued their talk. The more they talked, the more Lady Amanda smiled, and the more Grace's heart palpitated. She thought about it for a moment in a lull in the conversation, and she knew she was falling for this Lady.

After a couple of hours and several soft drinks, rum, and cokes, Lady Amanda looked down at Grace and said, "Grace, last night I decided that I needed to help you. And I think I can. I am excellent."

"That is wonderful Ma'am," Grace replied.

"I am not finished yet my girl," Lady Amanda said, scolding her smilingly for her interruption. "But I like you very much. There are two ways I could help you, and which way would depend on how our relationship is going to go. But here is the thing my girl. I like you very much. If, and I stress the if, all were to go well, I would like to eventually own you."

Grace's heart rose in her chest, and she blushed and looked down at the floor. "Thank you Ma'am."

"That actually gives me the better chance of succeeding in helping you my girl, but I have wanted to get to know you better in order to decide which way I would go with this. If I hadn't wanted to own you, I would have had to try a different, less personal approach. But I still would have tried."

"Yes Ma'am, thank You Ma'am," Grace replied.

"But you also have to want this. Are you interested in pursuing a relationship with me Grace my girl?" Lady Amanda asked.

"Yes I am Ma'am. I find you to be beautiful and smart and kind, and wise, and wonderful. I am very attracted to you on many levels."

"Good. You may address me as Mistress from now on and we will see where this leads."

"Yes Mistress, thank you Mistress," Grace replied, smiling up at her shyly for a moment then returning her gaze to the floor.

"Good girl. We're leaving. You're going to drive me to your home and we're going to talk in a much more intimate setting."

"Yes Mistress," Grace replied, following Mistress Amanda two steps behind as she got up and headed for the door.

Mistress Amanda led her to a small sporty older model black BMW. "Nice car Mistress," Grace said as Mistress Amanda handed her the keys. "Thank you my girl. I like it. Its fun without being ostentatious."

Grace smiled and unlocked the passenger door and held it open. Mistress Amanda got in, and Grace closed it behind Her, then walked around and got on the other side.

The car drove well, and Grace was impressed. After she began to get used to how it drove, Mistress Amanda picked up their conversation from where they'd left off; the more they talked, the more Grace became attracted to Her, and the more hope rose in her. But she was deathly afraid of yet another letdown, and it showed on her face.

"What is wrong my girl?"

"I have been here before Mistress. I am afraid to hope because there have been others who said they could help. I am hopeful, but scared to hope for fear of being let down yet again."

"I completely understand Grace my girl. There is nothing I can do for the moment to change that feeling. But if I am successful, and I make no promises, then you will no longer need hope. At least not for that."

"I understand Mistress. How are You going to help me?"

"I will not share the details my girl, you don't need to know. But in broad strokes, I am going to help you release the passion within you and help you become the girl you want to be."

"Yes Mistress, thank You."

"You can thank me when I've succeeded my girl. But if I succeed, I think you are going to be a lovely slave."

"Yes Mistress."

Grace wondered and pondered. Mistress was a hypnotist, so that could be one of the methods she used. But Mistress Amanda didn't give her a lot of time to think. She kept asking questions, and the conversation went on until they pulled into Grace's apartment complex.

Grace got out, opened Mistress Amanda's door for her, locked the car, and handed Mistress Amanda the keys. Then they walked side by side to Grace's apartment, and Grace unlocked the door and stepped back for Mistress to precede her into her home.

Grace showed her around her small home and then fixed them a drink and served it to her with both hands on the glass. "Thank you my girl," She said.

"You are welcome Mistress," Grace said, kneeling beside the couch where Mistress Amanda sat.

As they drank, Mistress Amanda asked many pointed questions. About the fantasies, Grace had, about the women she admired and who she thought she might like to be. "I sense a battle within you my girl," after Grace had refilled their drinks.

"I am not surprised Mistress."

"You desire to be free to express the passion you feel deep inside, but the women who do so, lack your respect."

"I am not sure that is entirely accurate Mistress."

"How so?"

"I don't think it is them that I lack respect for," she whispered tears coming to her eyes.

"I know my girl. I know."

Grace took a large swallow of her drink and looked down at the floor.

"But all this talk has given me much to work with my girl. And I have a plan. But it is going to require a lot of trust on your part."

"May I ask, Mistress?"

"You may ask. I may not answer though."

"Of course Mistress, it is not always for the slave to know." Grace paused and looked up at her Mistress and then asked the question, "May I ask what Your plan is Mistress?"

"I am going to create a slut, and then put her inside you my girl."

Grace blushed and looked at the ground as her heart raced, and she began trembling.

"That scares you," Mistress said, deadpan.

"Yes Mistress."

"What else does it make you feel?"

"Anticipation Mistress, and something more."

"What?"

"Desire," Grace blushed and looked at the ground again.

"Good. You admit it. Your desires and needs will be key to the creation of my slut."

Grace's face turned even redder at the thought of being Mistress Amanda's slut, and her ears burned, and her hands trembled as she took another large swallow of her drink.

"Finish up your drink my girl, my plans begin as soon as you're done."

Grace downed the last of her drink, swallowing several times and draining the glass, and then she set it down.

"Ok my girl, I need a chair."

Grace fetched one from the kitchen, set it beside the couch, and waited for what came next.

"I want to see my girl. Please remove that overly modest clothing and stand before me naked so I may inspect my future property."

Grace blushed again but did as she was told. She removed her long black skirt first, then removed her long-sleeved conservatively cut top. She let them fall to the floor and trembled as she removed first her black bra and then her panties. She trembled as if from cold as she stood there before her Mistress.

"You are more beautiful than I had hoped my girl. My slut will have a good home in you."

Grace blushed, her ears turning crimson, and she looked at the ground.

"Ok my girl," Mistress Amanda said, "Lay on the couch please."

Grace did, though her trembling wouldn't cease.

Lady Amanda moved Her chair so that She sat next to Grace, and She took Her girl's hand.

Grace's trembling continued, but she didn't pull away.

"Ok my girl. Before I can start, I need you to do something that requires trust."

"What do You need me to do Mistress?"

"While I will eventually own all of you my girl, and your heart, mind, and body will be mine for the taking and plundering, for the moment I need you to surrender your arms and hands to me."

"I don't understand Mistress."

"That's ok my girl. Just surrender them up to me. Give them to me to be mine to do with as I wish."

"Then they are Yours Mistress, my hands and arms are Yours to do with as You wish."

"Good girl," Mistress Amanda smiled down at Her girl, squeezing her hand a little.

"Do you masturbate my girl?"

"No Mistress, but sometimes I caress myself in the shower, but it makes me nervous."

"That's ok my girl. I want you to touch yourself for me. Just caress yourself as if you were in the shower."

Grace shook, but she did as she was told. Her fingers traced little patterns on her belly and trailed up to her breasts and traced little circles around her nipples. She whimpered a little, and her fingers trembled as she touched herself.

"Now I want you to bring your fingers down to your pussy my girl. Caress yourself there."

Grace trembled and bit her lip, but she did as she was told. She traced her fingers lightly back down across her belly and found her pussy. She lightly caressed her outer lips, and then one finger lightly caressed the place where her lips came together, following the crack up, and then down again. She was blushing beet red, and her ears were burning, and her trembling became more severe.

"Penetrate yourself my girl." Mistress Amanda ordered.

To Grace's credit, she tried to put one finger to her lips and began to push, but her trembling became outright shaking, and she jerked her hand away from her vagina.

"I'm sorry Mistress, I can't."

"That's ok my girl. My slut will do that often for me."

Grace turned even redder, and her breathing became faster.

"You like that don't you my girl."

Grace whispered, "yes Mistress."

"Now I have a harder task for you my girl." Mistress Amanda said.

"Yes Mistress?"

"Give me your hands please," Mistress Amanda said, holding her hand out.

Grace held her two hands up to Mistress Amanda's, and her Mistress grabbed both of Grace's hands by her wrists and held them firmly in Her grasp. "Now I want you to not move my girl. No matter what happens, I want you to remain still."

"I will try Mistress," Grace said with a catch in her voice.

Mistress Amanda held her wrists firmly, almost painfully in her strong left hand. Her other hand moved toward Grace's naked belly. She lightly touched Grace's soft skin with just the tips of her fingers, and Grace began shaking violently. She tried to pull her hands away from Mistress Amanda's grasp, but they were held in her Mistress' firm grip. Mistress Amanda began caressing her belly with the tips of her fingers as Grace shook and pulled. Grace whimpered and cried as her Mistress laid her palm flat on her belly and gently rubbed her, moving her hand in circles, getting closer and closer to her breasts at the top of the arc, and closer and closer to her pussy at the bottom. The closer she got, the more Grace resisted and cried out and tried to pull away. As Mistress Amanda's hand touched the underside of her breasts, her shaking became violent, and when she touched her pussy lips, Grace began kicking her legs, trying to get free. But Mistress Amanda did not let go. She pulled her hand away from her girl, and calmly waited for Grace to calm herself.

When Grace's shaking and crying subsided, she let go of her girl's wrists, and Grace held herself tightly, and Mistress Amanda handed her a tissue and wiped the tears from her eyes.

"Are you alright my girl?" Mistress, Amanda asked softly.

"I will be Mistress. But you see my problem."

"Indeed. It's worse than I had hoped for my girl. But I think I can fix it."

"You can?"

"Maybe. Now you will be required to trust me as much as you can my girl, and do everything I say from now on."

"Yes Mistress. I will do my best."

"I know you will my girl." Mistress Amanda took a shiny gold ring off Her finger and held it up so that Grace could see it.

"I want you to look at this my girl."

Grace focused her eyes on the ring, and her Mistress began to speak. She spoke quietly, her voice calm and pleasant. "Follow the circle of the ring. Move your eyes around the circle following it in its neverending loop. A circle has no beginning and no end, but it is forever. Listen to my voice as your eyes trace the circle of the ring and as you do so your eyelids will become tired. But I don't want you to close your eyes, no matter what, keep your eyes tracing the golden circle of forever."

Grace's eyes traced the gold ring's outer circle as she listened to her Mistress' voice. Her eyelids became heavy and she had to fight to keep them open. Mistress Amanda's voice filled her and comforted her and she felt completely secure despite her earlier panic. her eyelids got heavier and heavier as she listened and traced and she heard her Mistress' voice. "Your eyelids are getting heavier and heavier. In a few moments I will allow you to close them as you must wish by now, but when you do, you will fall into a deep trance. In that trance you will be able to hear my voice, but you will not be able to move or open your eyes again. Once they shut, you will be deeply asleep but still listening." Her Mistress's voice went on and on, and Grace's eyelids got heavier and heavier., She did everything she could to keep them open, but her Mistress's voice lulled her mind and calmed her body, and finally, her eyes shut.

"Good," Mistress Amanda said. "You are in a deep trance now. I want you to imagine you are in a totally safe place. You are safe from any harm from anything and anyone. No one and nothing can hurt you. Do you understand?"

"Yes Mistress," Grace said sleepily.

"You are even safe from your own feelings Grace my dear. Nothing you feel, nothing you think, nothing you do, can hurt you. For this time, your deepest fears are of no concern except as random facts about you. Except as things to talk about so I may help you. Do you understand?"

"Yes Mistress, my feelings can't hurt me."

"No, they can't. In this deep sleep they can't hurt you so they are easy to look at. Do you understand my girl?"

"Yes Mistress, they are easy to look at and they can't hurt me."

"They are no more important right now than what you ate for breakfast yesterday. They are just trivial facts about you that we will talk about. Ok?"

"Yes Mistress. They are unimportant except as trivial facts."

"Good. Now I have some questions for you my girl. You are going to answer completely honestly. But the answers are completely unimportant except as information. Is that clear my girl?"

"Yes Mistress."

"Good. How did touching yourself make you feel my girl?"

"It excited me Mistress and it made me afraid."

"What were you afraid of?"

"I was afraid of doing bad things because of those feelings Mistress."

"Why my girl?"

"My stepfather did bad things because of feelings like that Mistress."

"He hurt you."

"Yes Mistress."

"He raped you."

"Yes Mistress."

"What else did he do?"

"He made me hate myself Mistress."

"Why?"

"I must be bad if he needed to hurt me like that."

"Why do you think that?"

"He told me it was my fault. That I begged for it Mistress."

"What did you do that he said made him think you begged for it my girl?"

"I wore short shorts, skirts above the knee, and light clothing that exposed more skin than he could stand to look at Mistress."

"Is that why you now dress so conservatively my girl?"

"Yes Mistress. If I keep covered no one will know that I'm bad."

"So what do you think about other girls who dress more provocatively my girl?"

"I hate them, and I am jealous of them Mistress. They are free to be who they are, and they are bad."

"Now you know they are not bad, don't you my girl?"

"Yes and no Mistress."

"Explain please."

"They beg for it, yet they are free Mistress."

Grace began to tremble in her trance.

"It is ok my girl. Remember that all these feelings are completely unimportant and can't hurt you right now. Not while you sleep in my trance."

Grace's trembling eased as she replied, "Yes Mistress."

"If I told you that you weren't bad, would you believe me my girl?"

"No Mistress, but I would want to."

"Then I will have to prove it to you my girl. How does that make you feel?"

"Scared Mistress."

"Why?"

"Because then I might have to understand that my stepfather was a bad man even though I loved him very much."

"Is that all my girl?"

"No Mistress."

"What else then?"

"If I let those feelings into myself, I might do bad things like my stepfather did."

"Do you really think you could my girl? Do you really think you could damage a child simply because you felt passionate, or aroused?"

"I don't know Mistress. It scares me."

"I understand. Now I have another question for you and I want you to remember that the answers are completely unimportant facts that can't hurt you in anyway."

"Yes Mistress."

"When I touched you and caressed you, how did you feel?"

"Aroused and scared Mistress."

"Is the fear the same one you already talked about?"

"Yes Mistress."

"And the arousal?"

"Your touch was like passionate fire Mistress, I ached for it to continue. I ached for you to bring my passion to life and make me cum in your hand."

"Good. I want you to know my girl, I am pretty sure I can help you."

"How Mistress?"

"Like I said my girl, I am going to create a slut and then put her inside you."

"How does that make you feel?"

"Scared, and hopeful, and excited Mistress."

"Good. Now I want you to know that you are not going to remember any of our conversation during your sleep. When you wake up you will not remember anything we talked about."

"Yes Mistress."

"But before I wake you there is one more little thing I want to talk about."

"Yes Mistress."

"Now, do you remember that you gave me your arms and hands my girl?"

"Yes Mistress."

"That is what I want to talk about."

"Yes Mistress."

.....

Grace woke to feel refreshed and safe and comfortable despite the cool air of her living room. She yawned and stretched and looked at Mistress Amanda. "What did You do to me Mistress?"

"nothing important my girl. Don't worry, everything is fine."

"Yes Mistress."

"I would like you to please get dressed my girl and fetch a leather bag from the trunk of my car. Would you please do that?"

"Of course Mistress. Thank you."

Grace dressed, and Mistress Amanda watched her, admiring her curves and thinking possessive thoughts.

In a few minutes, Grace returned with Mistress Amanda's bag and then fetched them each another drink.

Mistress Amanda began to pull things out of Her bag. Grace saw that it was a small recording console and a microphone. "May I ask what it is you are going to do Mistress?"

"I am going to give you something to listen to my girl."

"Oh," She replied, knowing that her Mistress had not answered her question, but also knowing that she had done so on purpose. She guessed it wasn't meant for her to know right away.

Mistress Amanda set up Her equipment and plugged it where Grace indicated she should and then said, "I need you to leave the room for a while my girl. I need you not to listen or be able to even hear me. Do you have something you can do for an hour?"

"I can go play on my computer in my room Mistress. And I can put on my headphones and listen to music as I play around on it."

"Perfect. Then please do so. I will come get you when I am done."

"Yes Mistress."

"But before you go, I want you to remove those clothes."

"Yes Mistress," Grace said, smiling as she pulled off her clothing.

"Very good. Now run along," Mistress Amanda said once Grace was once again naked.

Grace smiled shyly and left the room. She sat at her computer in her leather chair naked, and brought up her music player and put on her headphones. She busied herself playing games and browsing the net, but inside she was dying to know what her Mistress was doing. She put that aside. She knew that if Mistress desired her to know, she would be told. She trusted Mistress Amanda more than she had ever trusted anyone. Why she did not know, but she did.

Despite her eagerness to be back with her Mistress, time did pass. After a while she got lost in the game she was playing. Suddenly she felt a tap at her shoulder and turned and found Mistress Amanda standing there. She removed her headphones and shut down her game and smiled up at her.

"Alright my girl. I am done. For now at least. Do you have a portable CD player?"

"Yes Mistress."

"Alright then. Here are your orders regarding this CD," Mistress Amanda said and handed Grace a CD. "I want you to put your CD player on automatic repeat and then put your headphones on and listen to this every night when you sleep. Do you understand?"

"Yes Mistress. perfectly."

"Good. Now, lets go drink some more because I want to get to know my future property and admire her naked beauty while I drink."

Grace blushed and smiled shyly and looked at the ground and replied, "Yes Mistress."

They talked and drank long into the night. Mistress Amanda sat on the couch, and Grace knelt at her feet. Every time Grace showed signs of a lot of pain from kneeling, Mistress Amanda would direct her to sit cross-legged or with her legs outstretched for a while to let the blood flow back into her legs. Grace realized that her Mistress was very concerned for her welfare, and her trust and love for this Lady grew.

When Grace's voice began slurring, Mistress Amanda cut her off. "That's enough alcohol for you tonight my girl. I want you clear headed for sleep."

"Yes Mistress. am I to go to bed now?"

"Not yet my girl. I want your head to clear a little first. I could use another drink though my girl, and if you are thirsty you may drink something soft."

"Yes Mistress," Grace replied and fetched them each a drink.

They talked a while longer, and when Mistress Amanda saw that Grace had sobered up some, she declared it was time for her to sleep. "But I wish to observe you during your rest so that I may be sure this is working properly my girl. Would you be able to sleep if I were in your room watching you and playing on your computer?"

"I think so Mistress. I feel safe in Your presence Mistress, though to be honest Mistress, my mind races about you and my heart beats quickly and I might have a little trouble. Though that would be the case even if you weren't there."

"Well we will try it my girl. I think you will be surprised. The CD should help."

"Yes Mistress."

Grace followed her Mistress to the bedroom and began to put on her pajamas, but Mistress Amanda interrupted her. "I want you to sleep naked my girl."

"Yes Mistress," she replied.

Grace got under the covers and put on the headphones to her CD player and inserted the CD. She hit the replay button on the machine and then lay down to sleep and hit the play button. Mistress Amanda sat at the computer and kept herself busy while keeping an eye on her girl.

In just moments, Grace's eyes closed. Mistress Amanda knew it wouldn't be long before she saw results. She had implanted a post-hypnotic suggestion in her girl to bring her back into trance easily.

It wasn't long before she saw Grace's hands moving. Well, she thought, they are MY hands, and she smiled to herself. Grace's hands moved about her body, and Grace moaned in her sleep/trance. Mistress Amanda watched as her girl's hands moved all about her body, caressing, teasing, and arousing. Grace moaned every few seconds as her hands touched her in sensitive places. After some time, her hands went down to her vagina, and Mistress Amanda could tell that they were doing her work. Mistress Amanda turned the heat in the room up slightly and pulled back the covers so she could see what was happening. Grace moaned louder as her fingers penetrated her lips. Grace's fingers started fucking her pussy. "My fingers," Mistress Amanda reminded herself. She knew Grace would feel as if they belonged to her Mistress.

After some time had passed, Grace's body shuddered, and she cried out in her sleep. Mistress Amanda knew she had cum. Mistress Amanda turned back to the computer, and Grace went to sleep. An hour later, Grace's hands began again. All night long Grace's hands, well, Mistress Amanda's hands as Grace had surrendered them, teased and pleasured her. Grace came to many orgasms that night, and in between, she slept peacefully. Mistress Amanda remained at Grace's computer and bedside all night long. She made coffee and kept herself awake while her girl experienced orgasm after orgasm with periods of real sleep.

Mistress Amanda stayed awake all night, and finally, when the clock was at 9 am, she put the blankets back over her girl and removed the headphones. "Time to wake up Grace," She said. "The slut is done for the night."

Grace opened her eyes and said, "Good morning Mistress, I had such arousing dreams."

"I know you did my girl, I would have been surprised had you not. Good morning my sweet girl, how do you feel?"

"I feel great Mistress, but uhm," she paused for a moment and looked down, "I feel very horny." She blushed and trembled as she said the words, and her ears turned red, and her hands shook.

"You blush so prettily my girl, but it isn't you that feels horny. It is the slut I am creating. Don't let it bother you."

"Yes Mistress."

Grace looked at the clock. "did You stay awake all night Mistress?"

"I did my girl. But I wanted to be sure it would go right. You are important to me."

Grace smiled. "Did it?" she asked.

"It did."

"Would you like breakfast Mistress?"

"That would be lovely my girl."

Grace made her Mistress breakfast and then knelt at her feet and set her breakfast on a chair beside Her. "Thank you my girl, this is pretty good."

"I am glad You like it Mistress, I am not much of a cook but it is hard to ruin breakfast."

"True enough my girl. So, lets talk about the slut."

"About her Mistress? Not about me?"

"I am creating her as a different person my girl. But I will need you to tell me how she is doing and what she is experiencing and etc, because the slut doesn't have her own voice."

"Yes Mistress," Grace said, looking slightly relieved.

"So I noticed a lot of moaning and movement my girl. Did the slut have good dreams?"

"She had horny dreams Mistress. She dreamed that she lay there, unable to move, while you teased and tormented her with your hands, and while you brought her to orgasm repeatedly."

"That sounds like my slut had good dreams then my girl."

"She liked them Mistress. Though she got tired of it after a while and only wanted to sleep."

"To be expected. She isn't much of a slut yet my girl. But she is there."

"But I am concerned Mistress."

"About what my girl?"

"Well, when you finally put the slut in me as you said you would, won't it me be who feels such feelings?"

"Yes my girl. And?"

"Well, I don't want to feel them for just anyone. I don't want to end up being a slut, but only your slut, if you catch the difference."

"I do my girl. And I will see to it that that is the case. You will only be aroused for me. How is that?"

"Thank you Mistress."

"And how do you feel about the slut my girl?"

"She is disturbing Mistress."

"How so?"

"Well, she was obviously having fun, but its scary as well as exciting."

"I understand my girl. Sometimes we are bound in chains that were created in our youth and it takes much to break them."

"I don't understand Mistress."

"You will my girl, don't worry about it. Just remember it."

"Yes Mistress."

Once they finished breakfast, Grace went to clean up, but Mistress Amanda stopped her. "Now I need to sleep my girl. I don't trust myself to drive home, so do you object to me sleeping in your bed?"

"Of course not Mistress. Do you wish me to change the sheets for you?"

"No my girl, I am quite happy to sleep surrounded by the smell of the sluts arousal."

Grace blushed.

"Why do you blush m y girl?"

"Well, she was very aroused Mistress, I'm sure the smell is strong."

"And so?"

"Well, wouldn't you prefer to sleep in clean sheets?"

"No I wouldn't my girl. I like the smell of my sluts arousal. As long as it isn't old. You will change your sheets every other day to keep the smell fresh, but I think even you will come to appreciate the smell of an aroused slut."

"Yes Mistress."

Mistress Amanda could see the war being fought behind her girl's eyes. One part of her wanted what the slut seemed to have, and the other part was afraid. She smiled to herself. Her girl would come around. And she would finally be free of the evil done to her.

"While I sleep I want you lay on the couch and listen to my CD. The slut has a long way to go my girl, and I want her to come into being as fast as I can arrange it."

"Yes Mistress."

"You don't have anything planned for the day do you my girl?"

"No Mistress."

"Good. Now come and tuck me in. I want a good night kiss and hug from my girl before I sleep."

"Yes Mistress," Grace replied, following her into the bedroom. She hugged her Mistress and kissed her on the lips lightly. While her Mistress held her, she trembled but held on anyway.

"That will get better my girl. The slut will help you."

"Yes Mistress," she replied, "sweet dreams."

Grace picked up the CD player and began to leave the room. "Set your alarm for 3pm and you can wake me as soon as you wake my girl."

"Yes Mistress," she replied.

Mistress Amanda got up and made sure Grace was installed on the couch with her headphones on and then. She went back to bed. Her girl's predicament was arousing to her, and she decided to add to the smell the slut had left in her girl's bed. Then she slept.

She woke to Grace, leaning over her and whispering in her ear. "Its three PM Mistress, you wanted me to wake you."

Mistress, Amanda stretched and replied, "Thank you my girl. How are you doing?"

"I am well Mistress, but I am all wet."

"Oh so I see," Mistress Amanda said, looking between her girl's legs to see that the juices had leaked down her legs. "Good. I see the slut has been busy while I slept."

"Yes indeed Mistress. She had more dreams and she got me all wet." Grace replied, looking shamefaced.

"No worries my girl, it is perfectly natural. The slut will get you all wet often. But the slut enjoys that sort of thing. Let's go shower. That will fix your problem."

"Yes Mistress."

They cleaned up, and Grace was very nervous about showering with another person, but Mistress Amanda never touched more than her hands or her hair, which she washed for her. Grace did the same for her Mistress.

"You seem to be ok being naked around me my girl."

"Yes Mistress. You inspire confidence, and aside from that moment last night when you held my hands, you have not done anything to make me fear you."

"I know my girl. But I must tell you that it is hard to not touch you in the way I'd want to touch you if you were free of your chains."

"Will that ever happen Mistress?"

"Yes my girl, it will. I am more confident now. The slut is taking to the training very well."

"Yes Mistress," Grace said, confused.

"You don't understand."

"No Mistress."

"Its ok, you don't need to. At least for now. You will one day though."

"Alright Mistress," Grace smiled.

"They ate a light meal that Grace fixed and served, and then Mistress Amanda said to her, "Alright, my girl, I want to do some things to you and my slut before I leave. I have to go home for the night."

Grace looked disappointed but said, "yes Mistress. Will you come back?"

"Of course my girl. I will be back tomorrow."

Grace smiled. "I will miss you Mistress."

"As I shall miss you my naked girl. For now, I want you on the couch again."

Grace lay on the couch, looking up at her Mistress expectantly. Mistress Amanda looked at her lovingly and then said a word. Grace immediately fell asleep. It was over an hour later that Grace woke feeling fresh and happy and full of energy. She looked at the clock. "Oh my Mistress, how time has flown. I hardly feel like any time has passed."

"I know my girl. Its a side effect of the trance state and my work in your mind."

"Yes Mistress."

"Now I want you to dress and escort me to my car my girl. You may carry my bag with my recording gear. I am going to need it at home tonight."

"Yes Mistress," Grace said and dressed.

Once dressed, Grace carried her Mistress' bag down to the car, following her Mistress two steps behind, and she put the bag in the trunk once Mistress Amanda had opened it.

"I will miss you my girl. And I will miss my slut," She said.

"I will miss You too Mistress, as will your slut I am sure."

"Do I get a hug and a kiss my girl?"

Grace smiled and fell into Her arms and trembled only slightly in her Mistress' arms. "Now, my girl, hold here for a moment while I explain something to you."

Grace stayed still, trembling slightly in Mistress Amanda's arms and listened.

"Do you remember that you gave me your arms and hands?"

"Yes Mistress."

"They are going to be doing things to my slut whenever the opportunity arises. If you need them for any reason, they will be yours to command as it should be, but in moments of quiet, they will be busy working on my slut."

"On me you mean Mistress?"

"Not really my girl. In a huge way you and the slut are two very different people. So I want you to think of her as another person. But you may find it a bit uncomfortable."

"Yes Mistress."

"I left you my email address and cell phone number. If you need me for any reason you are to either call or email depending on the urgency of the need. Do you understand?"

"Yes Mistress."

"Good. Now I want you and the slut to be good girls."

"We will Mistress. I can't wait to see you tomorrow."

"And I can't wait to come back my girl. Have a good night and I will see you tomorrow evening. I will call before I come and you can make supper for me."

"Yes Mistress, I will be happy to."

"Good night my girl."

"Good night Mistress."

And then Mistress Amanda got in her car and left. Grace returned to her apartment and sat down at her computer. She could smell the odor of arousal from the sluts night of excitement mingled with an odor that wasn't hers though she didn't know it. She put on some music and sat at her computer, reading an e novel. As she read, her hands rested at her side, but not for long. Her hands suddenly became her Mistress's hands and began teasing her. Or rather, began teasing the slut. She thought of the slut as an entirely different person, and the sluts arousal didn't bother her in the least. The smell of arousal in the room grew. She continued reading, every few minutes she'd take her hand away from the sluts body as she thought of it and would scroll the page down so she could read further. But after a while, the sluts arousal got to her, and she decided to watch a show instead.

She put on a streaming show she liked on the computer and sat there and watched while her hands returned to their torment of the slut. When the slut came, Grace moaned loudly, crying out, part of her wishing it was her that her Mistress's hands were teasing and toying with. Already in her mind, it was cemented that she and the slut were two completely separate beings. The orgasm over, she returned her attention to her show. And that was how she spent the night. Her eyes would watch the show, while her Mistress' hands would play with the slut, bringing her over and over to orgasm and making her more and more aroused. After a while, the slut began to experience multiple orgasms, and Grace found it hard to focus on the show.

The room's smell of arousal and sex was almost visible when she was ready for bed. She lay down, and the smell of her Mistress was more clear. The slut became aroused by the thought that her Mistress had been aroused in Grace's bed. But Grace didn't think much of it. She put on her headphones and hit play on the CD player and lay down. Almost immediately, she fell into a deep trance to repeat the events of the night before.

In her dreams, she watched her Mistress toy with the slut, who looked exactly like herself. She watched as her Mistress made the slut come over and over again, and deep within her, she felt stirrings that she ignored because they were dangerous.

She woke sweatily and smelling of sex, but refreshed and feeling fantastic. It was 10 am and the day was young. She got up and had some breakfast, and after cleaning up the kitchen, she cleaned the apartment in expectation of her Mistress' visit. When she got to the bedroom it reeked of pussy, of sex, and of arousal. She changed her sheets and put them in the wash and once everything was cleaned up she went and sat on the couch in the living room and watched TV. She realized that she had not dressed when suddenly her hands, or more properly her Mistress' hands began to do their work on the slut again. She wondered why she had not dressed. It was unlike her to walk around naked no matter that she was always alone. She resolved to dress but soon forgot about it as the slut was teased into an orgasm, making Grace cry out.

After the orgasm passed, she got up and went into her bedroom to find some clothing. She reached into her top drawer for some panties (conservative and functional rather than pretty), and one hand slapped the other away. She dropped the panties back in the drawer in surprise. She reached for them again, and again, her other hand slapped her hand away. Ok, she thought, no panties. She reached for a bra. Again her other hand slapped the first away. 'ok, no bra either.' Then she wondered if she would be allowed to dress at all. She opened another drawer and reached for a pair of pants. Again she was slapped. She went to the closet to get a skirt that hung from a hanger, and again she was slapped. Being stubborn, she reached for a top, and again, her hand was slapped away. 'I guess I am supposed to be naked,' she thought to herself, and went and sat at her computer. She pulled up her word processor and began to type without really seeing what she was typing.

"The slut tried to dress today but Mistress' hands taught her she shouldn't. After several attempts to reach for clothing that were prevented with slaps, the slut learned her lesson. she is to be naked except when it is needful to dress. The slut is very horny today and has come many times. in my dreams I watched Mistress tease and torment her and bring her to orgasm over and over. The slut seemed to enjoy it a lot. Watching it touched something deep inside me that was enticing as well as scary. Sometimes I wish I could be a little like her."

Then she saved the document in a new folder titled, "The slut diary," and emailed a copy of the journal to her Mistress. Then she seemed to wake from a daze, and she went to fix a snack. After she had finished eating, she sat at her computer and listened to music and tried to read. Every time her hands weren't needed, they teased the slut. Grace tried to focus on the reading, but the sluts aroused torment, and eventually, teasing overcame her ability to focus, and she gave up. She put on some music and lay on her bed, letting her Mistress' hands do as they would. She knew the slut would have a good day. And the slut did. Mistress's hands brought her to orgasm over and over. Her fingers fucked the slut silly and teased her clit so much it was almost raw. Grace kept an eye on the clock, and as soon as she could, she got up to fix dinner, and the sluts torment/training stopped while she prepared dinner for her Mistress.

She kept her hands busy as much as possible, but every once in awhile, she had to wait for things. Every time she waited, her Mistress's hands got busy on the slut. Then it would be time for something else to be done, and she'd get control of her hands again. Cooking was done, and the table was set, her Mistress place at the table's head, and her place at her Mistress's side. With nothing to do, her Mistress's hands got busy again. She gave in with a sigh and went to lay on the couch and let her Mistress's hands have their way with the slut. She knew there was no fighting it.

Her Mistress's hands brought the slut to two orgasms before Grace heard a knock at the door. She got up and ran to answer it, but realized she was still naked and became cautious. She looked through the peephole and saw her Mistress. She hid behind the door to hide her nakedness as she opened it and said quietly, "please come in Mistress."

"Good girl," Mistress Amanda smiled and closed the door behind her. She put down the bag she was carrying and took her girl in her arms and held her tightly. Grace trembled but was glad of the closeness and felt the strength in the arms that held her. Her trembling eased ever so slightly. She took in her Mistress's scent. She was wearing a perfectly lovely perfume and smelled divine. "You smell lovely Mistress. You look lovely as well."

"Thank you my girl. You look good too."

Grace blushed. "Your hands wouldn't let me dress Mistress."

"I am aware my girl. Part of the sluts training is all."

"So I understood Mistress. Am I correct in assuming that had I needed to go out I would have been allowed to dress?"

"Yes my dear."

"Ok Mistress."

"Your needs will always come first my girl. Unless of course I am there to make the decisions. In which case, I will make them."

"Yes Mistress. Thank you Mistress."

"And how is my slut my girl?"

"She is sore, and horny, Mistress," Grace replied. "She has had many orgasms today and your hands have kept her busy whenever I didn't need them for something."

"Good. Very good my girl. I am sure my slut is well on her way to being properly trained."

"Yes Mistress," Grace agreed without understanding at all. "Supper is almost ready Mistress."

"Good girl. It smells lovely."

"It is just something simple Mistress, but I think you will like it. its one of my favourites."

"I am sure I will as well my girl." Mistress Amanda agreed as Grace took her coat and hung it on the hooks by the door.

"Would you like a drink before dinner Mistress?"

"Yes I would my girl, you may have one for yourself as well if you wish it."

"Thank you Mistress," Grace replied and headed for the kitchen.

She returned in a couple of minutes with two drinks. She served one to her Mistress, seated on the couch, and then knelt at her feet and sipped her own.

"How are you feeling my girl?"

"I, am well, Mistress, but a little annoyed.'

"Why my girl?"

"Well, every time I get to doing something your hands start working on the slut and soon she cums. Not that I mind her cumming but it breaks my concentration and I lose track of what I'm doing."

"What were you doing my girl?"

"Mostly trying to read Mistress."

"Ah yes. That could be a problem." Mistress Amanda paused then went on. "If you like my girl, I can make it so the slut will only cum when I tell her to."

"Oh yes Mistress, that would be fantastic. I might get some peace then for a little while at least."

"Good. I will take care of that after supper."

"Thank you Mistress."

Grace put down her drink, and her hands immediately started in on the slut. Mistress Amanda smiled and watched. "How does my slut feel Grace?"

"She is horny Mistress. She is wet and wanton and is looking forward to another orgasm, but she is sore and her clitoris is in pain," Grace replied. Then the hands released the slut as Grace reached for her glass and took a sip. The moment she put it down, however, her hands went back to their work.

"I can give my hands something that will ease up on the sluts clit if you think it would help my girl."

"Oh please Mistress, she is enjoying herself but her poor clit is rubbed raw."

Mistress Amanda reached into her purse and brought out a small pink vibrator. "I just bought this for the slut today my girl. I am sure she will find it useful and it will keep her clit from becoming raw."

"She thanks you Mistress, as do I."

"I am glad you aren't afraid of it my girl."

"If it were for me I would be Mistress, but that is the sort of thing the slut will like very much."

"I am sure my girl. I want you to understand that it is not for you. You may not use it at all."

"Yes Mistress, not that I would want to."

"I understand my girl, but I want you to keep it near the slut at all times so that when she is to be trained it is near my hands so they can put it to good use. And always replace the batteries when they die."

"Yes Mistress. I will."

"Good. Here are a couple of spare batteries I picked up so you won't have to run out to the store for a while." Mistress Amanda handed her a small package of high-quality double-A batteries.

"Thank you Mistress." Grace reached for the vibrator and the batteries and put them down near her drink. She picked up the drink and took another sip, and when she put it down, her Mistress's hands took over and tormented the slut. Suddenly they grabbed the little pink vibrator and turned it on and put it to the sluts pussy lips and plunged it inside the sluts wet orifice.

"You are welcome my girl. How does my slut like that."

"Your slut likes it very much Mistress, she is mad with desire," Grace moaned.

"Good slut. Good Grace."

"Thank you Mistress," Grace panted.

Just then, they heard the stove buzzer go off, and Grace got control of her hands. "supper is ready Mistress. May I serve you?"

"You may my girl." Mistress Amanda replied, getting up.

Grace followed, keeping the vibrator in her hand. She carried it into the kitchen with her as she followed her Mistress, and she put it down on the chair next to her place setting. Then she served dinner to her Mistress and then served herself,

They talked as they ate, and Grace was very thankful that her Mistresses hands didn't interrupt. "Shepherds pie my girl, I love it. It is one of my favourites as well. And you did it well."

"Thank you Mistress."

Mistress Amanda watched her girl as they ate. She noticed that Grace finally seemed at ease naked in front of her, and she didn't blush nearly so much. They were small gains, but they were gains, and she was satisfied for the moment.

Grace ate eagerly. She was so happy to be with her Mistress again; she just wanted to get the meal over. Mistress asked her questions, and she answered happily. Most of them were about the slut, and Grace happily told her Mistress all about the dreams she had had about watching Mistress Amanda bring the slut to orgasm over and over. But she was eager to have the slut stop cumming so much.

Finally, supper was ready, and she picked up and started to fill the sink to wash the dishes when Mistress Amanda said, "leave that my girl. I need you to dress."

"Yes Mistress." She replied and ran to her bedroom, stopping only to pick up the pink vibrator and carry it with her as she had been ordered.

When she was finished dressing, she returned, still holding the vibe in her hand. she found Mistress Amanda on the phone. "You can bring it up now and I'll show you where I want it installed." She paused. "Yes, thank you. Apartment 216. Good."

"Here hand me that my girl," Mistress Amanda said, pointing at the vibe. Grace gave it to her, and she stuck it in Her purse. "What is going on Mistress?"

"I am having something installed in your bedroom to further the training of my slut my girl."

"Yes Mistress."

Grace was dying to know what it was, but she knew that her Mistress would have told her if she was meant to know. So she sat patiently until finally there was a knock at the door. "Come with me my girl." Mistress Amanda said and went to answer the door. Two men were standing there with something about the width and length of a queen-sized bed but only a few inches thick covered with a blanket. "Ok my girl," Mistress Amanda said, handing her the car keys. "There are a couple of bags in my trunk and a suitcase in the back seat. Take as many trips as you need to and please don't drop anything some of it is fragile."

"Yes Mistress," Grace replied and passed the men in the hallway. It took her a minute to get there, and when she grabbed the first bag, it was heavy. She carried it up to her apartment. The men were no longer at the door, and she could hear the sounds of tools coming from her bedroom. "Don't worry about that my girl. Just set down my bag here in the kitchen and go get the rest please."

"Yes Mistress," Grace smiled.

Two more trips and the task was finished. Mistress Amanda indicated that she was to sit in a chair beside her Mistress as they waited for the men to finish and leave. It didn't take long. Twenty minutes after Grace finished her task, the men came out, and one said, "All done Amanda Ma'am."

Mistress Amanda replied, "Thank you Tom," and handed him some money. Tom didn't even count it, he just put it in his pocket, and the two men left nodding at Grace.

"Ok my girl. I have things I want to do. Here is the sluts vibe to carry with you again," She said, handing the pink toy to her. "Now I want my girl naked again."

Grace stripped off her clothes without hesitation.

"Sit please," Mistress Amanda said.

Grace did and looked at her expectantly.

Mistress Amanda said a word, and Grace fell into a deep trance.

"Alright my girl. Sluts dress a certain way, and they wear makeup and etc, and I want my slut dressed and made up. So that is what we are going to do." She paused and then went on. "But first the matter of the orgasms." She spoke for a few minutes, and Grace promptly forgot what was said.

"Now get up my girl . I want you to remain in trance and not wake up, but I want you to shower and get cleaned up. Then I want you to shave the hair on your pussy. Ok my girl?"

"Yes Mistress," she replied and got up in a trance and headed to the shower.

Mistress Amanda returned to the bathroom with her shopping bag in hand, just as Grace, still in a trance, was finishing her shaving. Mistress Amanda helped her dry off and put the lid down on the toilet and sat her on it. She opened up a package of black nylon stockings and a garter belt and helped her girl put them on. Next came a pair of sexy strappy black heels. The last item was a demi-bra cut so fine as to reveal Grace's nipples.

"That is a much better outfit for my slut."

"Yes Mistress," Grace replied, still in a trance.

"Now for the makeup," Mistress Amanda said, pulling some more things out of her bag. "Come stand in front of the mirror please Grace, I need to do my sluts makeup."

Grace did, still not registering anything but the command of her Mistress as she was still in a trance.

"Now I want you to pay attention my girl. You will have to do the sluts make up every day."

"Yes Mistress."

It took only a few minutes. Mistress Amanda explained each step as she went, and how Grace should use each item. When she was done, Grace was even more beautiful than Mistress had ever seen her. "Now my girl a lot of women wear makeup and they are not sluts. But I want you to always make sure the sluts nipples are rouged well enough to see the colour." She handed Grace the brush, and Grace dipped it in the blush and brushed some onto her nipples until they showed a somewhat more pinkish color. "Good my girl. Next comes the sluts pussy lips. The pink will make them look more aroused and draw attention to them."

Grace again dipped the brush in the blush and then brushed some onto the lips between her legs.

"Good. Now look in the mirror. This is how I want my slut to look all the time my girl."

"Yes, Mistress,' Grace replied, looking into the full-length mirror on the bathroom wall. Grace calmly noted how the slut looked and knew she would always see that her Mistress slut would look like that from now on.

"Doesn't my slut look good Grace?"

"Yes she does Mistress."

"I'm glad you like her. Now follow me. We've got a lot to do tonight my girl."

Mistress Amanda led the way to Grace's bedroom.

Grace saw without seeing, the two cameras mounted on tripods at either side and near the foot of her bed. She noted without seeing the huge mirror on her ceiling with the words, "the slut" at the top of it.

Mistress indicated that she should lie down, and Mistress sat on the edge of the bed beside her. Grace still had the pink vibe in her hand, and Mistress began to talk to her for a long while, giving her instructions and planting post-hypnotic suggestions.

Then she sat at the computer and said the word that would bring her out of it. Grace quickly looked over at her Mistress and smiled, wonderfully feeling refreshed and energized.

"You have been having your way with me Mistress," she smiled. "last thing I remember we were in the kitchen."

"Indeed my girl. Not in the way I would like, but still, it was indeed fun. I want you to focus on the ceiling for a moment please my girl."

Grace looked up and saw the mirror. It was a magnifying mirror, and she could see every detail of how the slut was dressed and made up. And suddenly, her perspective changed; it was as if she were looking down at the slut. As if she were floating above her bed looking at her Mistresses slut who was lying on the bed. She knew it was her Mistresses slut she was looking at because above the sluts head were the words, "the slut"

"Do you see the slut my girl?"

"Yes I do Mistress, she is beautiful. And frightening. She seems so free to be able to dress like that and wear makeup."

"Describe her to me please Grace."

In the bed, Grace's eyes focused completely on the mirror above her bed, but she still looked down on the slut below her.

"She is wearing a garterbelt and stockings Mistress, and black high heel strappy shoes. She is not wearing any underwear. Her bra is barely there Mistress and her breasts and even her nipples are exposed. Her nipples and pussy are brushed slightly pink and look very inviting Mistress. Her face is beautifully made up, black mascara, pink blush and eyeshadow and lipstick and her hair is down about her shoulders rather than tied back the way I would keep my own."

"And what do you think of her my dear girl?"

"She is beautiful and free and dangerous Mistress."

"Why dangerous."

"It is dangerous to be so free Mistress, to attract the feelings of lust by expressing ones own."

"You know that isn't always true right my girl?"

Grace hesitated then replied, "sort of Mistress. If my step father hadn't been who he was, maybe things would have been different."

"That's a step in the right direction, my girl. For now, don't think about it," Mistress Amanda said as she saw Grace's face crinkle in the beginnings of self battle. Grace's face relaxed, and the smile returned to her face as she gazed at her Mistress' slut.

"Ok my girl, I have a task for you."

"Yes Mistress?"

"I want you to tell me everything the slut is doing, and everything she is feeling. You are the only one who can do that because you and she are connected at a very deep level. Will you please do that for me?"

"Of course Mistress." Grace smiled.

"Your slut is smiling Mistress, she is happy, and she is horny. She likes how she is dressed and how she looks Mistress."

"Good. Now watch." Then Mistress said a word and the sluts hands, the hands that Grace had surrendered to her Mistress started moving.

"Your hands are teasing your slut Mistress, they are caressing her belly. They are moving up to her breasts and teasing them, caressing them. Your slut is beginning to get very aroused Mistress."

"Good. Keep going. Describe everything you see to my girl."

"Yes Mistress. Your hands are pinching her nipples lightly, ooo she likes that though it hurts a little. She's got some pink on your fingers now but they aren't stopping. They are caressing her chest, and her neck, touching her face lightly, like fairy wings. ooo Mistress, your slut is sooo horny. She feels so good and so free. Your hands are moving down her body now Mistress trailing passionate fire in their wake, arousing every inch of your sluts skin. Now they are at her vagina Mistress...."

Mistress Amanda interrupted her at that point, "The word is pussy my girl. Say it right."

"Pussy Mistress," Grace said, and she felt her face turn red.

"Your slut is sooo horny Mistress, your hands are teasing her pussy and she wants to moan and writhe beneath your hands, but something is holding her still. Oh, her legs are spreading to allow your hands greater access Mistress. Now your hands are grabbing her vibrator Mistress. They are inserting the vibrator into her wet pussy. She loves it Mistress, your hands are turning her on so much. she wishes she could come for you Mistress. Oh, your hands turned the vibrator on inside her. She feels the buzzing so strongly. She wants to come so bad Mistress. But she can't. I don't know why but she is completely unable to come. She is sooo horny Mistress. Your hands are penetrating her....."

Mistress Amanda interrupted her again, "The word is fucking my girl. My hands are fucking her. Say it."

"Yes Mistress, your hands are fucking her."

Grace's breath was ragged and rapid by this time. "Your slut is panting like a dog Mistress, she wants to cum so bad. "

"The word is like a bitch in heat, my girl. Say it."

"She is panting like a bitch in heat Mistress, she wants to cum soo bad. Your hands are continuing to fuck your slut bringing her ever closer to orgasm, but she cannot reach it. Mistress, why can't she cum?"

"Because you said her orgasms annoyed you my girl. I made it so she can only cum if I allow it."

"Oh," Grace said in a small voice. "I regret that I think Mistress."

"I know you do my girl. But the slut wishes to please you too, not just me. So she was happy to have that done to her."

"Will You let her come Mistress?"

"I might be able to be persuaded my girl."

"How Mistress?"

"The slut doesn't have a voice of her own my girl. She needs someone to speak for her."

"I would speak for her Mistress, oh she is soo close to cumming. Right on the edge as your hands fuck her Mistress. will you please let her cum?"

"I like to hear begging my girl. I like to be begged for little things that for other people would simply be their own choice. Will you beg me to let the slut cum my girl?"

Grace's answer pleased Mistress Amanda very much. "Please Mistress, please allow your horny slut to come. She is in need like a bitch in heat, she is so horny that she feels she must die if she is not allowed to cum. Please have mercy on your slut and allow her to cum."

"That was very prettily done my girl, have you done that before?"

"No Mistress, I have never begged for anything but for my stepfather to leave me be."

"Don't think of that just now my girl, it might ruin the sluts pleasure."

"Yes Mistress," she replied

"I have decided to allow my slut to cum my girl. But I want something."

"What do You want Mistress?"

"I want to fuck her with my strap-on to make her cum."

"Oh she would love that Mistress, she would love to have your body touching hers, to have you causing her pleasure directly."

"Will you beg me to fuck my slut then my girl?"

"Please Mistress, fuck your slut. She desires your touch sooo badly. She needs you like she has never needed anyone in her life. She wishes nothing more than to have you touch her, to lay your body on hers, to feel the fire in your skin as you fuck her and make her cum."

"Very well then my girl, I will, since you asked so nicely."

"Ooo that makes your slut happy Mistress, see how she is smiling through her horniness."

"I am glad she is happy my girl." Mistress Amanda said. She stripped off her clothes and reached into the bag she had left beside the bed.

She pulled out a harness with a 7-inch pink dildo attached to it and stepped into it, fastening it around her waist with the leather buckle. "Continue describing what you see my girl, don't stop now."

"Your slut is eager for your dildo Mistress...."

"The word is cock my girl."

"Yes Mistress, your slut is eager for your cock. She desires to be filled with it. I can see you standing over her at the foot of the bed, with your pink cock sticking out. It looks big and though it would frighten me very much your slut wants nothing more than to have it inside her. I can see You moving toward her, kneeling on the bed between her legs. Your hands have stopped and pulled the pink vibrator out of her pussy and she misses the feeling of being filled with it. I see you kneeling between her legs Mistress, I can't see her pussy anymore, but I see you laying atop of her. Oh, you are inside her, I can almost feel it as she feels so full of your cock Mistress. I can see You fucking her Mistress, your hands, your own hands that is, grabbing onto her breasts, pinching her nipples, oh that hurts her, but she likes it. She's such a slut Mistress. You are leaning over her almost kneeling as you fuck her, she is loving this so much Mistress, she desires nothing more than to be your fuck toy..."

Mistress Amanda's eyes widened slightly at those words. She hadn't expected such wonderfully dirty language from her girl unless encouraged first, but she knew that was an indication that things were going much better than she could have hoped for.

"Oh Mistress, your slut loves Your cock. She loves having you touch her and caress her, and even pinch her pink nipples. Oh Mistress she is sooo aroused, so horny. She feels Your cock filling her, and leaving her empty, and filling her, and then leaving her empty again. She wants you to fuck her harder, please take her like you own every part of her Mistress. she wants you so badly."

"I am enjoying fucking my slut my girl. I am glad she is liking it as well. Are you enjoying this Grace?"

"I like watching you fuck your slut Mistress," Grace replied. "Part of me wishes it was me, but that is a scary thought so I don't go there much."

"I understand my girl. Does my slut want to cum?"

"Yes Mistress, she wants to cum so badly."

"Then she will come my girl since you want it so badly." Mistress, Amanda replied.

Grace went on with her description. "Oh Mistress she is soo close to cumming Mistress, right on the edge...."

Mistress Amanda said a word, and suddenly Grace's head was exploding. 'Oh, she's cumming Mistress, oooooh she's cumming so hard, but you are not stopping, you are fucking her right through her orgasm, and she is coming again Mistress, oooooh she is on fire, her pussy is exploding, her whole body is on fire. Oh, You have stopped and are lying on her and inside her Mistress, and her orgasm is abating. She feels so wonderfully satisfied and happy Mistress, and she feels so relaxed. She feels a fantastic Mistress. Oh, she's putting her arms around you and holding you, and you are holding her and kissing her, I guess, I can't see properly anymore. Oh, now you are pulling away, and I can see a wonderful relaxed smile on her face Mistress. Thank you for making your slut cum. You have made her so happy."

"You are welcome my girl. I was glad to get to fuck her. She's a wonderful slut isn't she?"

"Oh yes Mistress she is."

"Mistress her nipple and pussy blush is gone."

"Alright my girl, come down here then and go put some more on her."

"Yes Mistress,"

Grace's perspective changed, and she grabbed the little vibrator and got up and went to the bathroom to reapply the blush to the sluts pussy and nipples. Once she was satisfied with their pinkness, she returned to her Mistress, sitting in the computer chair once again.

Mistress Amanda looked at her and said, "That's better my girl, thank you for taking such good care of my slut."

"You are welcome Mistress, it is my pleasure."

Mistress, Amanda smiled.

"Have a seat on the edge of the bed for a bit my girl. There is something I want to do."

"Yes, Mistress," Grace replied. She sat and watched as her Mistress plugged a long wire from one of the cameras to her computer. As she watched her Mistress' hands began their work again. Grace tried to focus on what her Mistress was doing, but she felt the slut getting aroused again.

"What are you doing to your slut Mistress?" Grace asked.

"I am training her to be aroused and horny for me all the time my girl."

"All the time Mistress?"

"Yes my girl, forever and ever amen."

"Oh." Grace's cheeks turned slightly red.

"I think your slut will like that Mistress."

"I think you're right my girl."

Mistress went about downloading all the video that had been recorded onto Graces computer as they talked, and Mistress's hands continued their work on the slut."

"Does your slut have a name Mistress?"

"Why do you ask that my girl?"

"Well, I am curious Mistress. We call her the slut, but most people have names, and I thought she might have one as well."

"Well yes my girl, she does have a name."

"Might I please know it Mistress?"

"No my girl, you may not. But you will. I promise. The day you are better, you will know her name."

Grace smiled, the sluts painted lips opened slightly, and her dimples pitted deeply.

"Thank you Mistress. When will that be?"

"Oh full of questions today are you my girl?"

"I guess Mistress, I am very curious."

"Well, it will still be a while yet my girl, but you are further along than I would have expected at this point."

"Oh goody Mistress. Thank you for helping me."

"It is my pleasure my girl. The more I get to know you, the more I want to own you forever and ever amen."

"Oh," Grace blushed, "Thank you Mistress. I would like that Mistress."

"Good."

Mistress Amanda finally finished, and Grace could feel and smell the sluts arousal as her Mistress's hands continued their work.

"Alright my girl, I want you to get the slut in bed and watch her again."

"Yes Mistress," Grace said, getting onto the bed. Her eyes immediately went to the magnifying mirror over her bed, and her perspective changed.

Again, Mistress Amanda, had her describe everything she saw. Grace did so. For over an hour. Grace described every detail of the sluts arousal and everything that was happening to her.

"Mistress, your slut needs to come again, she is on fire, your hands have kept her on the edge of one for soooo long," Grace panted.

"Oh, you beg so prettily my girl. you must like the slut a lot to be willing to beg so for her."

"Yes Mistress I like her. She is free to be the passionate woman she is, without guilt or fear or remorse or evil. Sometimes I wish I was like her."

"I know my girl. Now about my slut cumming. I want something."

"What do you want from your slut Mistress?"

"I don't want anything from my slut right now my girl Grace. What I want, I want from you."

"From me Mistress?" Grace said with a catch in her voice.

"Yes my girl from you."

"Well, if I can Mistress, you know I love you and wish to please you."

"I want you to lick my pussy until I come Grace my girl."

"Oh," Grace said and blushed and got a look of fear in her face.

"The slut is trembling Mistress. I think she is afraid for me."

"What is there for her to be afraid of my girl?"

"I don't know Mistress. Oooo she is sooo aroused."

"I know my girl. But she will not cum until I do."

Grace saw the slut tremble and her lips pursing, and she felt sorry for the slut. "The slut really needs to cum Mistress," she said sorrowfully.

"I know my girl."

"I will do it Mistress," she whispered.

"What was that my girl?"

"I said I will do it Mistress," she said louder.

"Do what my girl?"

"I will lick your pussy till you cum Mistress."

"Good. Now come back down here please."

Grace's perspective changed again, and suddenly, she was sitting on the edge of the bed. Mistress Amanda, still naked from when she had her fun with her slut, sat on the edge of Grace's computer chair and spread her legs.

"Go ahead my girl. I am eager to feel your tongue." She said.

Grace swallowed hard and knelt on the floor between her Mistress' legs. She trembled, but leaned in close and she could smell her Mistress' musky arousal. Despite her trembling, she leaned further and extended her tongue until it touched her Mistress' outer lips. Mistress Amanda put her hands on her girls head and ran her fingers through her girls hair. She did not push or pull or try to force anything and Grace felt comforted and her trembling eased a little. She was afraid and nervous, but she knew the sluts need. So she plunged her tongue between her Mistress' folds and tasted of her. The musky odor was only a precursor to her taste. The taste of her Mistress filled her tongue and mouth as she began licking.

"Oh my girl, this pleases me so much. You have no idea."

Grace's heart lightened, and the fear lessened just a little, and she began licking less tentatively.

"Oh you found my clit my girl. Remember it. It is the little joy button for a woman."

"Mmmm," Grace mumbled as she licked. She licked her Mistress' clit and then went further south and found her Mistress' entrance.

"Yes my girl, use your tongue like a little cock and fuck my hole."

Grace extended her tongue straight and bobbed her head forward and back, penetrating her Mistress' entrance as far as she could, as deeply as she could, and then pulled back, only to plunge in again. She did this for a while and her tongue became tired so she returned to her Mistress' clit and licked and nibbled it.

"Oh yes my girl, lips are made for nibbling on clits."

Grace's heart lifted a little as she came to understand the pleasure she was giving her Mistress, and she redoubled her efforts.

Her Mistress's taste filled her mouth, and her juices ran down her cheeks onto her neck. It wasn't long before Mistress Amanda too was trembling, and suddenly she shuddered and cried out with her orgasm. She grabbed hold of Grace's hair at both sides of her head and lifted her to her feet and kissed her, tasting her juices in her girl's mouth.

Grace trembled and shook, but she didn't pull away. She did find that her Mistress's kiss was arousing, and she felt the slut stirring.

"Very good my girl," Mistress Amanda said, pulling Grace's head back by her hair at the nape of her neck. "For a first time."

"Thank you Mistress," Grace blushed and looked at the ground, feeling shamefaced, but pleased that she had pleased her Mistress.

"Now, about the sluts orgasm."

Grace felt the needs of the slut rise to the surface again from where they'd been forgotten. As they had to have been for her to be able to please her Mistress.

"Get the slut on the bed again Grace and keep an eye on her for me please."

"Of course Mistress," Grace moved, and in a few moments, she was looking down at the slut from above. She never stopped to think about how she was floating above herself. In her mind, the slut was a different person who happened to look just like her. Well, with makeup and clothes on that she would never wear. But she found the slut very attractive if frightening in ways she refused to think about.

She saw her Mistress reach into the bag she had beside the bed and pulled out some rope. "What are you doing Mistress?"

"I'm going to tie my slut up my girl."

"Oh," Grace said. "I think she'll like that Mistress."

"Oh, I am sure she will Grace dear."

Grace watched the slut breathing heavily as Mistress Amanda tied ropes to each of the sluts limbs. Grace's breath caught in her chest as she saw her Mistress tie the sluts wrists and ankles spread eagle to the four posts of the bed. "How is the slut feeling Grace?"

"She's nervous and excited Mistress, and very horny as always."

"Good."

Then Mistress Amanda lay between the sluts legs and did for her as Grace had done for her Mistress.

"Oh she likes that Mistress," Grace said. "She is on fire, her face is blushed with excitement Mistress."

Mistress Amanda pulled away from the sluts pussy and said, "Good girl Grace, I rather thought the slut would like that." And then she returned to what she had been doing.

Grace kept up a running commentary, and Mistress Amanda could tell that Grace was getting very excited despite the separation between her and the slut. Her breathing was rapid and shallow, and her voice caught often, and the tone of her commentary ran faster and faster, and little moans escaped her lips as she spoke. Mistress, Amanda, was pleased. Her girl was learning to express passion. She thought ahead to the culmination of her plans to the day when Grace would embrace the slut and finally be free of the harm done to her. Her breath caught in her chest as she looked ahead. Then she focused on the task at hand.

After a few minutes, Grace's nearly shrill voice said, "Mistress the slut is right on the edge, she is going to cum very soon, ooooo."

But Mistress Amanda didn't stop, and soon Grace was saying, "oooo Mistressssss, she's cummmmiiiiiiiinggg. ooooo."

Mistress Amanda pulled away, slid up her girl's body, and lay on top of her holding her tightly in her arms and kissing her. Grace moaned and mumbled but didn't think about why she was unable to talk as the slut kissed her Mistress back.

After a few minutes, Mistress, Amanda, pulled away and began to untie her slut. "How is my slut doing Grace?"

"She is feeling absolutely wonderful Mistress, she was delighted to have you holding her afterward."

"Good. Now I have more computer stuff to do so I'm going to leave you to watch the slut for me for a while as I work," Mistress Amanda said, untying the slut and putting the ropes back in her bag.

"Yes Mistress." Grace replied.

Mistress Amanda busied herself downloading the video recorded by the two cameras. As soon as the slut had her arms free, Mistress Amanda's post-hypnotic suggestions took over, and the sluts arms began to tease and arouse her once again.

Grace kept up her running commentary interspersed with moans of passion that she didn't recognize as her own. It wasn't long before Grace's commentary was more moaning than speaking though she took no notice. She thought only that the slut was very aroused.

It took Mistress Amanda some time to finish her work at the computer, but Grace hardly noticed that she was completely engaged in the sluts titillation.

Pretty soon, Grace was begging her Mistress to allow the slut to cum again. "Please Mistress, she is in such need. she is burning from the touch of your hands. Could you please allow her to cum to put the fire out, if just for a little while?"

"Nope." Mistress replied. "Though you beg most prettily my girl. I do not want her to cum right now."

Mistress Amanda turned away from the computer and said, "I want you to come down and go fix us a snack my girl. I am hungry. It is getting late and I have plans for my slut after that and then we will sleep."

"Yes Mistress," Grace replied, and suddenly her perspective changed, and she was sitting on the edge of the bed facing her Mistress.

She got up and went to the kitchen and looked through her supplies.

She returned to the bedroom and asked, "do you like ice cream Mistress?"

"Yes I do my girl."

"Would you like a banana split Mistress?"

"That sounds lovely my girl."

"Where would you like to eat Mistress?"

"In here my girl. Just bring our snacks in here when they are ready," then she turned back to the computer.

"Yes Mistress," and Grace left the room.

She returned a few minutes later with a tray containing two banana splits and two vodka and oranges. "I thought you might want a drink Mistress. I brought one for myself as well if that is ok Mistress."

"It is my girl. I am sure you are thirsty after all that talking you've been doing."

Grace blushed and looked down, she put the tray down and served her Mistress in proper slave fashion.

Mistress Amanda turned away from the computer and ate with her girl. Grace sat on the edge of the bed and ate hers, sneaking glances at her Mistress's beautiful naked body.

"Do you like what you see my girl?" Mistress Amanda asked, showing she had not missed the glances from beneath lowered lids.

"You are beautiful Mistress."

"Thank you my girl, as are you, as is the slut."

"Thank you Mistress."

"Why don't you get a good look instead of hiding glances Grace?"

"Yes, Mistress," Grace replied and openly looked at her Mistress' lovely body. Her breasts were large and full and hung beautifully, and her legs were long and muscular, with just a little cellulite. Her skin was smooth, and Grace had a sudden urge to touch her, but suddenly she looked away and blushed, her heart beating rapidly and the old terror rising in her.

"Are you alright my girl?"

"I will be Mistress."

"I know you will my girl."

They finished their snack, and they lifted their drinks. Mistress Amanda raised her glass and said, "Here's to my girl Grace, and to my slut, the best pair of girls a Lady could ever ask for."

Grace chinked her glass with her Mistress and then drank to the toast. Mistress Amanda looked hungrily at her girl as they drank, and Grace felt very self-conscious and fidgeted much.

"Nervous my girl?"

"Yes Mistress."

"Why?"

"Its the way you are looking at me Mistress."

"I like looking at you my girl. You are pleasing to my eyes."

Grace blushed and sipped her drink.

When Grace's glass was down to half, Mistress Amanda said, "Give me your glass sweetie."

Grace did and watched her Mistress put some clear liquid in it.

"Now drink it all my girl." As Grace began to drink, She said, "Don't stop till its all gone my girl."

Grace downed the half glass of vodka and orange in one go and when she was done. Mistress Amanda said, "That's a good girl."

Then she pulled her chair closer to the bed and pushed Grace back, so she was lying down. "Now close your eyes, my girl.

Grace did and waited for what was next. But there was nothing for quite some time. "what are you doing Mistress?"

"I'm looking at you and admiring my future property my girl."

Grace blushed so hard her ears burned.

"What did you put in my drink if I may ask Mistress?"

"something to help me help you. You should begin to feel it in a few minutes. Tell me when you feel it. But until then I'm simply going to sit here and look at your beautiful naked body."

Grace blushed harder and whispered, "Yes Mistress."

They remained like that for a while, and Grace began to feel sluggish and floaty and light-headed.

"I feel light headed and very relaxed Mistress."

"Good. It has taken effect. Then let us begin." Then she said a word, and Grace fell into a deep trance.

Mistress Amanda spoke, but her words did not register on Grace's conscious mind. She dreamed.

She sat on one side of her bed, and Mistress sat on the other side. Between them, the slut lay back on the bed, her hair down about her shoulders, her pristine makeup making her look beautiful and free. The sluts hands worked at her pussy, and she moaned her desire and need as her hands worked furiously on her pussy.

Grace watched, her eyes devouring the slut and her actions and the passion she expressed. She looked over at her Mistress and saw that She too was watching. Mistress looked over at Grace and smiled. "Isn't she beautiful?"

"Yes Mistress," Grace replied in a whisper, her voice trembling.

They watched the slut pleasuring herself for a while, and the slut got more and more aroused, but there was a tone of frustration in her moans, a tone of desperation. "What is wrong with her Mistress?"

"nothing is wrong exactly Grace sweetie. She is just unable to make herself come, no matter how much she desires to."

"Then why does she continue Mistress? She is only torturing herself."

"She doesn't understand that she is unable to find release herself Grace. She doesn't know she needs someone else."

"But surely Mistress, she must realize that something is wrong."

"Her need will not let her Grace love. She only knows that she needs, and she is bringing herself further and further along, but she will never reach her goal by herself. She is powerless to find that release."

"Won't you please help her Mistress?"

"I'm sorry Grace I cannot."

"But. You are Mistress, you have made her cum before."

"True, but here in this place I cannot."

"What will happen to her Mistress?"

"She will remain here in this room, in this place, ever desperate for release, and never reaching it. She will eventually die of heartbreak and frustration in the darkness in which she finds herself Grace."

Grace's eyes teared up, and she whimpered, "but there must be something you can do Mistress."

"No my girl. Not I."

"Who then Mistress?"

"You my dear."

"Me," she asked in a small quivering voice.

"Yes my girl. In this place, only you can help her."

"What must I do Mistress?" she asked, her voice still small. The sluts moans were becoming louder and more desperate. Her eyes were tightly shut, and her muscles were strained with the tension in her body.

"You must make her cum my girl. If of course you wish to help her."

Grace began to tremble with her fear, and she asked in a still smaller voice, almost completely drown out by the sluts moans, "how Mistress?"

"Move her hands away and finish the job for her my girl. If of course you wish to help her. Do you?"

"Yes I do Mistress, she is so needful and desperate. I wanna cry just thinking about her, but I am afraid."

"I know you are my girl, but deep down you know there is nothing to fear."

"I don't Mistress."

"You do my girl. But if you are not able to face your fear, then this is the sluts fate."

Grace blushed hard, and her ears burned as she felt a deep shame for her fear and her apparent inability to help the slut. She swallowed hard and extended her hands. The sluts eyes opened as Grace's hands closed over hers. "Here sweetie, let me help you," Grace said and moved the sluts hands aside. She took a deep breath, and her trembling hands closed over the sluts vagina, no, pussy, slick with her juices. She inserted a finger and then another into the sluts stretched and well-used hole, and her thumb found the sluts clit. She worked her fingers in and out easily the sluts juices lubricating her fingers copiously. Her thumb lightly caressed the sluts clit as her fingers plunged in and out. She fucked the slut with her fingers, and her other hand took one of the sluts hands in hers and held it. The slut looked up gratefully and started to say something, but moans of pleasure were the only sounds that came out of her mouth.

Mistress Amanda looked down on her sleeping girl and watched the girl's hands moving furiously in and out of her pussy. She listened to the moans coming out of her girl's throat and smiled. She was confident that all would be well as things were unfolding better than she could have hoped.

Grace watched the sluts face, and the slut looked Grace in the eyes as Grace's finger fucked her, faster and faster, and harder and harder. she looked at Mistress and asked, "Its not working Mistress."

"You need to encourage her my girl. She is frightened and trapped in a paralysis of self denial."

As Mistress Amanda watched her girl dream, she heard her say in her sleep, "come on pretty slut, you can cum now. Its ok. I'm helping you. Come on pretty slut, cum for me."

In the dream, the slut smiled at Grace as she was fucked, and suddenly she screamed in ecstasy as her orgasm finally reached her pussy, and she shook, and her hand squeezed Graces hard enough that Grace cried out in pain.

In a few moments, the sluts shaking orgasm subsided, and Grace saw her muscles relax, and a soft smile found its way to the sluts lips as her eyes half-closed. "Thank you Grace," she said shyly.

Grace woke up feeling very relaxed but tired and breathless as if she had been doing something strenuous. She looked up at her Mistress and smiled. "I love You Mistress."

"I love you too my girl. How are you feeling?"

"I feel wonderful Mistress, but I am sooo tired." Then she looked up shyly and sheepishly and said, "I made the slut cum."

"I know my girl." Mistress, Amanda smiled.

They talked for a while about how Grace felt sorry for her and liked her but was still quite afraid.

Mistress Amanda was pleased that her girl has passed that challenge. But the next challenge would be tougher for her. Her girl had been able to bring herself to do unto others; to bring pleasure to others. However, she knew that getting her girl to accept pleasure given to her would be the harder task.

"Grace love, my sweet slave girl, I'm tired."

"Yes Mistress, you can have my bed, I'll make up the couch for me."

"No my girl, that's not what I want."

"Surely You don't want to sleep on the couch Mistress."

"No, that's not it my girl, think again."

Grace got up and went to fetch blankets and started to make herself a bed on the floor.

Mistress Amanda stopped her by grabbing a fistful of her hair at the back of her head. She pulled Grace's face close to hers and said gently. "I want to sleep with you my girl. I want us in the same bed."

Grace began to tremble, and she looked down, but she whispered, "Yes Mistress."

Mistress Amanda let go of her girl's hair, and Grace put away the bedding she had set on the floor. Then she made up the bed. "It smells of sex and arousal and wet pussy Mistress."

"That's alright my girl, you can change the sheets tomorrow," She said. She knew the smell might stimulate things within her girl. She hoped it would anyway.

"Undress the slut my girl. I want you naked beside me and we will worry about the slut tomorrow. She is fine for the night."

"Yes Mistress," Grace said, mechanically removing the bra and shoes and nylons. "Shall I wash the sluts makeup off of her Mistress?"

"You can do that in the morning my girl after you shower."

"As you wish Mistress."

Mistress Amanda got into bed and turned down the covers to let Grace in. Grace got in reluctantly, her body trembling as if she were cold. She got into the bed and stayed as far on her side as she could. Mistress, Amanda sighed. "My girl, I am cold."

"I'll get another blanket Mistress," Grace replied, starting to get up, but Mistress Amanda put a hand on her shoulder. "No my girl, I want you to warm me."

Grace swallowed hard but approached her tentatively. She put her arm over her Mistress' body and threw her leg over Mistress Amanda's legs, her body touching her Mistresses all along her front. She shook as if struck with a disease.

"Thank you my girl, that is much better."

"Yes Mistress," Grace said in a small voice and put her head on Mistress Amanda's shoulder.

Grace flinched as Mistress Amanda's arm, enveloped her and held her gently.

They lay like that a long time. Mistress Amanda breathed deeply and slowly as if she were near sleep, but she lay awake thinking and hoping her gentle passivity would encourage acceptance. Grace trembled but did not retreat. Mistress Amanda began to get tired. She knew she couldn't sleep so long as long as her girl was like this. But Grace showed no sign of relaxing. Every time Mistress Amanda moved in the slightest, Grace flinched. Mistress Amanda, however, would not admit defeat. She held her to her desire and her will. She refused to give in.

Time passed, but Mistress Amanda dared not look at the clock. She began to feel exhaustion and a real desire for sleep, but she wouldn't allow herself to sleep unless Grace fell asleep first. So she waited. And waited. And finally, as the light of predawn began to filter into the room, she heard her girl heave a big sigh, and the trembling ceased.

Mistress's Amanda's arm felt leaden. Her shoulder ached. She needed to change positions, but she knew Grace was not asleep yet. So still, she waited.

Finally, she heard her girls breathing deepen, and a light snore escaped her. Mistress Amanda decided to risk a slight change in position. She moved her legs until Grace's knee fell between Hers. Grace flinched in her sleep and stirred but did not wake.

"Even in her sleep?" Mistress, Amanda thought to herself. She began to wonder if her earlier confidence had been misplaced. She ran through all she had seen in her girl, and all that her girl had described. She thought about Grace's reactions and past. She then thought about the things her girl had done, the steps she took and knew she could do nothing else. She also knew that if she had not been able to love the girl, and if Grace had not been able to love her, then she could have done nothing for her. Her heart was heavy. But despite her loss of confidence, she was still determined. Her will hardened. She would win this fight.

Every once in awhile, Mistress Amanda shifted her position slightly to make herself a little uncomfortable. Every time she did, Grace flinched in her sleep. Mistress Amanda let out a sigh, tightened her arm around her girl, and relaxed her arm as Grace flinched again. And slowly, the night passed.

After a long while, Mistress's Amanda dozed lightly. Her eyes stared upward unseeing, and her mind wandered in dreamland, and suddenly she woke from it. Grace had moved. Toward her rather than away. She had snuggled closer in her sleep. It was a little thing. Just one small victory, but Mistress Amanda's heart soared, and her confidence was restored. She knew now she would win. With this victory lifting her, she slept for real.

The sun was shining high, and its light shone down onto the floor at a steep angle when she woke. Her girl was still in her arms, and she smiled. She turned her head and looked at the clock. It read twelve-fifteen. Grace stirred in her sleep when she turned her head but did not wake. Mistress Amanda decided to allow the girl to sleep until she was slept out. She knew last night had been hard on her. And She knew that tonight would be worse.

But she did not have long to wait. Grace's breathing changed and she sighed a deep sigh and snuggled closer. She whispered, "Mistress?"

"Ah, you are awake my girl. Good morning my sweet Grace."

"Good morning Mistress," Grace said happily.

"Did you sleep well?" She asked.

"Yes Mistress. It took me a long time to fall asleep, but when I did I slept hard. I had dreams."

"What did you dream my girl?"

"I don't remember Mistress."

"Ok."

"Did you sleep well Mistress?"

"Yes I did my girl, thank you. you kept me nice and warm all night." She omitted a bit, but she knew she wasn't lying as when she had finally slept, she had slept well, secure in the knowledge that her girl would be healed.

She had a thought. Should she? She asked herself. She wanted it, but her needs were the least of her concern right now. Would it be the right thing? She decided to risk it.

She turned toward her girl and embraced her, wrapping both arms around her and kissed her on the forehead. Grace did not flinch. Instead, she wrapped her arms around her Mistress and lay her head on Mistress Amanda's shoulder.

Mistress Amanda's heart soared. Another victory. She would win. But she warned herself that it was not over yet.

She released her girl and held her shoulders and looked her in the eyes. "I am hungry my girl. What do you intend on doing about it?"

"How about I fix You some breakfast Mistress? In bed?"

"That sounds lovely my girl. You may get up."

"Thank you Mistress," Grace said, sliding out from under the covers and covering her Mistress up before leaving the room.

Mistress Amanda wanted to go back to sleep, but instead, she went over her plans for the day. She was deep in thought when Grace returned with a well-laden tray. Grace waited as Mistress Amanda sat up and leaned back against the headboard, and then she put the tray's feet down and put the tray over her Mistress' legs. "Here you go, Mistress, and I hope you enjoy it."

"Thank you my girl."

"May I get mine please Mistress?"

"Of course my girl. You may even sit beside me in bed."

"Thank you Mistress," Grace smiled and quickly left.

She returned moments later with another tray. This one had no feet, so she lay it on her lap after she sat beside her Mistress.

They ate in silence, each content to be alone with their thoughts. "Breakfast was good my girl, thank you," Mistress Amanda said when she had finished.

"You are welcome Mistress," Grace said and moved to take the tray. "Stay," Mistress Amanda ordered. "Finish your own first. Then you can pick up."

"Yes Mistress," Grace smiled.

Grace quickly finished breakfast and then took both trays to the kitchen. When she got back, Mistress Amanda signaled her to stand still for a moment. She gave Grace a long slow look down and back up again. Grace blushed deeply, but before she could lower her gaze, Mistress Amanda winked at her. Grace giggled.

Mistress Amanda smiled at her girl's reaction and looked at her warmly. "Alright my girl, it is time for us to begin our day. I would like you to shower and then dress the slut and make her up. She has a busy day today as do you. There are more nylons and another bra in that bag," She pointed.

"Yes Mistress," Grace replied and got the clothes out of the bag and left.

She cleaned herself up and dried off, then got in front of the bathroom mirror. She cleaned the remaining makeup off of the slut and washed her face. After her shower, she painstakingly did the sluts makeup just as she had learned to do in a trance, including rouging the sluts nipples and pussy lips. Once she was finished, and the slut was beautifully made up, she dressed the slut in the garter belt, nylons, demi-bra, and heels, and then she returned to her Mistress.

"Very good my girl, the slut looks beautiful, don't you think?"

"Yes Mistress," Grace smiled, "Thank you Mistress."

Mistress Amanda got out of bed and asked for a towel. Grace handed her one from the closet.

"Alright my girl, get the slut on the bed and watch her while I shower please."

"Yes, Mistress.' Grace replied, laying down and looking upward. Her perspective changed, and she found herself looking down at the slut once again. She saw her Mistress leave the room and heard the water running in a few moments, but her eyes were drawn to the slut. With nothing to do, the arms that had been surrendered to her Mistress began their work once again. The slut moaned and whimpered as she was teased and sexually tormented with pleasure without release unending. It wasn't long before the slut was on the edge of orgasm once again, and Grace wished she could cum. She knew the sluts intimately need though she didn't acknowledge that it was indeed her own.

Mistress returned from her shower and sat at the computer and watched the slut. "How is my slut doing Grace?"

"She is sooo horny Mistress. She's been on the edge of an orgasm for several minutes already," Grace moaned.

"That's good my girl. As last night I want a running commentary on what the slut is doing and how she is feeling ok?"

"Yes Mistress," Grace moaned.

As the night before, Grace spoke about what the slut was feeling, how she looked, what she was doing. She spoke a constant stream of moaned comments as she watched the slut pleasure herself.

Mistress Amanda busied herself at the computer playing with a video editor and the footage she had recorded the night before.

It wasn't long before Grace begged her Mistress to allow the slut to come, but Mistress Amanda simply said, "No."

Grace felt a great disappointment but knew her Mistress' will was paramount. She returned to her commentary on the sluts activities and feelings, moaning out the words until they became almost incoherent.

A half-hour later, she again begged her Mistress to let the slut cum. Again Mistress Amanda said simply, "No."

Grace returned to her commentary once again, disappointed but knowing she pleased her Mistress.

She waited almost an hour this time to beg once again for the sluts release. She figured her Mistress would say no again, but the slut was in such need as it disturbed her greatly, though, in the deepest part of herself, she knew the sluts predicament was arousing her.

Mistress Amanda turned toward Grace and asked, "Do you really want her to cum my girl? There will be a price."

"Yes Mistress, I want her to cum. she needs it badly. What would the price be Mistress?"

"I want something my girl. And frankly I doubt you are either brave enough for it, or ready for it."

Grace wished to please her Mistress, but she began to be frightened. "What is it Mistress?"

"I want to watch you cum my girl."

Grace froze, and the slut trembled in empathic fear. Grace's heart raced, and she began to sweat. "I...... Mistress...... I....." and tears began to fall from the sluts eyes.

"I know my girl. Its ok. you are not ready."

The pressure Grace felt on her eased as she realized her Mistress wasn't going to force her.

"Please resume your commentary my girl."

"Yes Mistress," Grace moaned.

After a while, the sluts moans began to intrigue Grace. The pleasure the slut felt was so obvious. Another obvious thing was that the slut was not doing anything she shouldn't. Like hurting people. A part of her began to admire the slut, and her voice took on a loving tone as she talked about everything the slut was doing and feeling. Mistress Amanda could hear the need in her voice as well. Though she knew only that the slut was aroused, Grace needed to cum desperately.

After another hour, the slut was in such need that it was spilling over into Grace. she asked, "Mistress, please?"

"Please what my girl?"

"Please allow the slut to cum, she is desperate, she is even raw from it Mistress."

"You know my price my girl."

Grace's face fell, and she saw that the slut was disappointed too.

With a catch in her voice, Grace said, "but... Mistress....I've never..."

"I know my girl. But don't you think its about time?"

"Don't you see what you've been missing?"

"Yes Mistress, I do," she replied.

"I'll give you a break this time my girl. I will make the slut cum once more. But after that she will NOT cum until you do."

"Yes Mistress, thank You." The fear that had been constricting around Grace's chest let go, and she breathed a sigh of relief.

"Keep up your commentary as I do this please my girl,"

"Yes Mistress."

Mistress Amanda got on the bed and sidled up to the slut. She lay on her side, her naked body touching the slut all along her side. Mistress Amanda put one arm around the slut, cradling her gently. Grace's heart lifted at this, and she found herself a little jealous. She was reminded of the closeness she had finally shared with her Mistress the night before. Which had been the only closeness with another person she had felt that she could ever remember. She knew she must have had, such as a baby with her mother, but she had been too young to remember.

The slut was moaning desperately under the onslaught of the hands that would not stop. Mistress Amanda extended her hands and put them over the sluts and moved them away. The sluts arms lay at her side. Mistress Amanda's free hand cupped the sluts pussy and gently probed her depths. The slut moaned as she penetrated her with a finger. The sluts back arched, and her breath came more rapidly. Grace's voice exuded desperation, and her words were almost incoherent as she spoke. It did not take long for the slut to cum, though. Mistress Amanda inserted two fingers and started fucking her girl with them, and suddenly the slut was cumming, "Oooohhhh she's cummmiiiiinnnggg Misssttreessss," Grace moaned almost hysterically

The slut trembled and shook with a powerful orgasm, and her body shook with the released tension. Her moans finally died down, and Mistress Amanda held her close, wrapping her free arm around her wrapping her girl in her embrace.

"That's so beautiful Mistress."

"What is my girl?"

"You love your slut very much don't you?"

"Yes I do my girl. As I love you."

"I'm glad Mistress."

"Me too my girl."

As Mistress Amanda held the slut she and Grace talked. Mistress Amanda could tell that Grace was desperately in need of the things the slut was getting, but she still wouldn't allow herself the pleasure. She sighed and kissed her slut on her painted lips. She got up and went back to the computer and her work with the video editing. The sluts hands once again began their work on arousing the slut with the little pink vibe.

It wasn't long before Mistress Amanda was finished with her video editing. "Alright my girl," She said, standing up. "Get yourself over here and watch this video of our slut."

"Yes Mistress," Graces replied as she sat up, and her perspective shifted.

She sat in the chair her Mistress vacated and focused on the video as Mistress hit the play button. She saw the slut masturbating furiously and heard her own voice describing what the slut was doing.

"Now be a good girl and focus on the slut and what she's doing."

"Yes Mistress."

As she watched the slut in the video, her Mistress' controlled hands began to play with the slut. She knew the slut was watching too and found what she saw on the screen to be very arousing. Grace watched for a long while, and then she saw her Mistress kneel on the bed with the strap attached. She watched as her Mistress fucked the slut. She saw it from the two different angles at different times, and as she watched, her controlled hands continued their work. The slut was soon on the edge of an orgasm that wouldn't spill over.

The video was about two hours long, and near the end of it, she saw her Mistress perform oral sex on the slut, and she couldn't help but see how much the slut loved it. Part of her wished she could have that. Not that she hadn't seen it already, but the constant exposure to it began opening a crack to let just a trickle of lust penetrate.

And all the time she watched, her Mistress' hands worked on the slut, well, she knew they were her hands, but she had surrendered them to her Mistress that first night. The slut was intensely aroused and desired to cum desperately, but Grace wasn't ready to beg her Mistress to allow it yet. She knew her Mistress would stick to her desire to see Grace cum first. And she was afraid.

She had looked it up one time. It was called malaxophobia - the fear of physical love. She had had it her whole life, well since she had been abused. She had never been able even to love herself. But she wished she could. She hoped Mistress Amanda could help her. The slut seemed to have so much fun, in a tortuous kind of way. She was jealous of the sluts freedom of spirit.

When the video finished, Mistress Amanda indicated that Grace should make supper for them. Which she did. First, she fixed the sluts makeup and rouged her nipples and swollen and red pussy lips. It had been well used. All during the time she was preparing supper, she thought of what she had seen the slut experience. What she had seen of the sluts need. And she wished she was brave enough to experience that for herself.

She served Mistress Amanda and ate her meal, kneeling on the floor. She had little to say as she was deep in thought. Mistress Amanda did not seem to need her to say anything, so they ate in silence.

After Grace had cleared away the dishes, they returned to the bedroom. Grace once more watched the slut get sexually teased and tortured with her Mistress controlled hands. It was too much for her, and finally, she begged her Mistress to allow the slut to cum.

"You know my price my girl."

"but..... I.... ok. but I have a request Mistress, if I may be allowed to make it."

"You may ask my girl, but I might say no."

"Of course Mistress as is your prerogative."

"Then ask."

"I want to cum like you made the slut cum earlier. With you laying beside me, touching me, holding me in your arms. Please Mistress."

"You know that might be too much for you my girl. It might be easier for you to do it yourself."

"I know Mistress, but I want to be loved like you were so obviously loving the slut. I was jealous of her then."

"Were you really my girl? That is sweet of you, but why?"

"You showed her such love Mistress. It was sexual yes, but it was also loving. And that is what I wish I had the most."

Mistress Amanda looked at her with a measuring gaze for a few moments. "Alright then my girl. Lie down and look at me rather than at the slut."

"Yes Mistress," Grace said, slowly moving to lie on the bed while keeping her eyes on her Mistress.

Grace lay there smiling nervously, but holding her gaze upon her Mistress. Mistress Amanda is a gorgeous woman, she thought to herself as she beheld the naked Lady. Her breasts were full and round, and her hips were womanly rather than boyish like her own.

Mistress Amanda lay on the bed beside Grace, her belly and breasts and legs touched Grace's side. She slid Her arm underneath Grace's head and cradled her in a loving embrace. Grace began to tremble, knowing what was coming.

Mistress Amanda leaned down and kissed her on the lips. Grace flinched but moved back into position to allow it. Mistress Amanda's lips were soft and gentle, and Grace felt such passion rising in her that she began shaking. She tried to pull away, but Mistress Amanda held her. She began to panic, and her whole body started shaking. Mistress Amanda broke the kiss and raised her head and looked at her. "Its ok my girl. you are fine. Please remember that."

"Yes Mistress," Grace whispered, the shaking subsiding. "but this doesn't bode well Mistress."

"Not really my girl, but you will get over this. Trust me."

"Yes Mistress."

Mistress Amanda extended her free hand and laid it on Grace's belly. She shivered and trembled a little, but didn't move. Mistress Amanda's hand started caressing Grace's belly lightly, and wherever her hand moved, Grace felt the passion and need in its wake. She began trembling in earnest, and Mistress began whispering in her ear, "you are alright my girl, there is nothing to worry about here, there is nothing here but love. You are alright my girl, you know I love you, and I know you love me, everything is alright," and so on while her hand continued its caresses. It seemed to help as Grace's trembling started to ease. But when Mistress Amanda's hand touched her pussy it all started up again.

Grace whimpered as the passion rose in her, as she began to feel aroused on a level that she had never felt, but had seen only in the slut. She whimpered and cried out in fear, and her trembling got a lot worse. Her legs shook as if she had palsy. At first, Mistress Amanda seemed not to notice, but when Grace began to try and pull away, she stopped and sighed. "My girl, its ok. I've stopped."

Grace began to cry, but her trembling stopped. "I'll never know love Mistress. I feel horrible."

"Its ok my girl. I knew we would fail."

Grace looked up at her in surprise. "You knew?"

"Yes my girl. I knew you weren't ready."

"then why did you allow it?" Grace asked, a hint of anger in her voice.

"I allowed it because I think its an important step to becoming ready."

"How so Mistress?" Grace asked, the anger fading immediately, and her voice instead, full of trust and love.

"I am not going to tell you that my girl. Just accept that I felt it would be beneficial to you alright?"

"Yes, Mistress,' Grace smiled.

"And I do want to point out that you have indeed made progress my girl."

"I have?"

"Yes. Look at us. I am naked beside you, who is also naked. Our flesh is touching. My arm is around you. And yet you are not trembling. Now it is only when I try to pleasure you that you begin to fear. Trust me, you have made progress. There is an end in sight my girl. Trust that."

"You are right Mistress. This has never been possible before. I guess there is an end in sight." Grace smiled and leaned up and gave her Mistress a quick, shy peck on the lips and then drew back with a momentary fear in her eyes that fled the moment she lay her head back down.

Mistress Amanda held her in her arms for a while longer and said, "But you still owe me an orgasm my girl."

"Yes Mistress," Grace said with a catch in her voice, "I guess I do. How is that going to happen?"

Mistress Amanda said a word, and Grace fell into a deep trance. She woke what seemed like moments later, and Mistress Amanda said to her, "you will masturbate yourself to an orgasm for me while I watch my girl. I had thought of getting the slut do to it, but I don't think you could stand to be touched, even by your twin."

"You may be right Mistress. but I have never made myself cum before."

"There is a first time for everything my girl," Mistress Amanda smiled down at her.

"Will You hold me like this while I do it Mistress?"

"Well my girl, I am not sure you are entirely ready for that either. But I promise you that and more will come."

"Yes Mistress."

Mistress Amanda untangled herself from Grace and moved away just a little, so that she lay on her side, near Grace, but not touching her. "you may begin my girl."

"Yes Mistress," Grace replied meekly.

Mistress Amanda watched as Grace began doing the same things she had watched the slut do, her hands caressing, teasing, and arousing herself. Little moans escaped her lips, and her body trembled. She whimpered as the fear rose in her, but Mistress began murmuring to her as she had done before. This time without Mistress Amanda touching her, the words had a calming effect, and the fear subsided. After a few minutes, only the moans of arousal remained. Her hands found her pussy and began doing things she had never done to herself before. She had seen the slut do it a lot, though, and knew how to please herself.

Mistress Amanda watched her with pride at her girl's bravery and efforts to please her Mistress. She watched as Grace's fingers dove into her pussy. She began fucking herself with the fingers of one hand while the other caressing her clitoris gently, slowly increasing her speed until soon she was fucking herself furiously.

Suddenly she was coming, and the release was something she had never before experienced. She screamed in ecstasy. "Don't stop my girl, keep going." Mistress Amanda ordered in a voice that would brook no disobedience. Grace didn't stop, she kept fucking herself with her fingers, and she kept rubbing her clit furiously with her other hand. She climaxed again, and again, and again. She began to become completely overwhelmed with the feelings, and finally, Mistress Amanda said, "Good girl. Very good, you can stop now. I am proud of you my girl."

Grace stopped and sighed heavily, and tears began streaming from her eyes, and she sobbed quietly. Mistress Amanda moved to her and held her, her naked body touching her girls without causing any flinching or trembling. Grace turned her head into Mistress Amanda's shoulder and sobbed, her tears wetting her Mistress' shoulder.

Mistress Amanda held her and comforted her and whispered, encouraging and calming things in her ear. Grace moved slightly, wrapped her arms around her Mistress' neck, and continued sobbing into her shoulder.

Mistress Amanda let her cry. She understood her pain, at least on a sympathetic level. But inside, she was singing. Her girl had made a significant step, and her plan was working—Grace would heal.

After a while, Grace's tears stopped, and she pulled back from her Mistress. "I'm sorry Mistress, I don't know what came over me."

"Its ok my girl. Ones first orgasm can be powerful."

"It was amazing Mistress, I've never felt that before. Look at all the time I've wasted, I could have done that thousands of times in my life."

"There are thousands of times to come my girl," Mistress Amanda said.

Grace laughed at the double entendre. "True Mistress."

"So what is next?" Grace asked.

"Are you in a hurry my girl?"

"Yes Mistress, I want to love you."

"As I want you to love me my girl, and as I want to love you back."

"Then, can we please get to what comes next?"

"Are you thirsty my girl?"

"Now that I think about it, yes Mistress."

"Then go get us both a drink. I find I am thirsty as well."

"Yes Mistress," she said, getting up and leaving the room, walking easily in the sluts heels without even noticing them.

She returned a few minutes later with vodka and orange juice with a splash of grenadine as usual and served one to her Mistress before taking her own.

"I am very proud of you my girl," Mistress Amanda said as they drank sitting side by side on the edge of the bed. "I'm glad Mistress, I'm so slow at this. I feel like I should be able to be with you now."

"Well, my girl, things are what they are, and this will take the time it takes. Don't worry your pretty little head about it, let me do that."

"Of course Mistress," Grace smiled.

When Grace was halfway done, her drink Mistress Amanda said, "Give me that for a moment my girl."

Grace handed her the drink, and she put something in it again. "Drink up," she said and smiled.

Grace did, tipping it up and swallowing over and over until the glass was empty.

"Now lay with me while we wait for it to take effect," Mistress Amanda said, and Grace smiled.

They lay together for about twenty minutes, Grace feeling secure and safe and loved in her Mistress' arms. Finally, she said, "I'm feeling light-headed and floaty Mistress.

"Good." Mistress Amanda said, letting go of her girl. "Now lay back."

Grace complied, and Mistress Amanda said a word. Grace fell into a deep trance. After a while, she dreamed.

Grace and the slut knelt at Mistress Amanda's feet. Each took one of Her feet in their hands and kissed and licked and fondled it. They licked and nibbled her toes, and Mistress said encouraging things to them. How long they remained like that Grace didn't know. But after a while Mistress, Amanda put her feet on the floor and spoke.

"Alright my girls, its time for a bit of fun. Grace, you've made the slut cum, now its her turn to make you cum."

Grace became apprehensive but said, "Yes Mistress," and the slut looked up at her and smiled with a devilish look in her eyes. "Yes Mistress," she said happily.

Grace was nervous, but she lay down on the bed as her Mistress wished. She lay there quietly as the slut knelt over her and began caressing her. She was nervous, but she trembled only slightly. The slut caressed her belly, touching her with both her hands, moving them in circles, and getting closer to her breasts and pussy. Grace trembled, but Mistress began saying encouraging things in a quiet but comforting voice. She tried to relax as the slut caressed her breasts. The slut giggled as Grace cried out when the slut pinched her nipples and then went back to caressing.

Grace's body was on fire. The sluts hands were almost as exciting as her Mistress's hand, and they trailed passion and need in their wake.

When the sluts hands went to Grace's pussy, Grace froze and flinched, but Mistress Amanda continued saying words of encouragement. She relaxed ever so slightly and only flinched slightly when the sluts fingers penetrated her wet pussy. She looked up at the sluts beautiful face, and she painted lips smiling as she gave Grace pleasure, her powdered lids half-closed as she focused on Grace's need.

Grace's arousal mounted, and her hips started moving, trying to impale herself on the sluts fingers. But the slut pulled away, teasing her, and then she plunged them deep into her. Grace moaned, and her hands moved as if to stop the slut, but Mistress Amanda's voice cracked, whip-like, "Stop Grace, put your hands to your sides."

Grace obeyed, feeling dismayed that her Mistress had had to speak to her like that. She was very much afraid that she had disappointed her. Mistress continued speaking words of soft encouragement and love and reassurance.

Grace moaned again as the slut grabbed the vibrator and turned it on and penetrated her with it. The slut fucked her with the vibrator, and she got nearer and nearer the edge. She remembered her orgasm from before, and she felt great anticipation. She moaned and tossed her head from side to side. Her hands clenched at her sides but did not move.

The slut fucked her soaking wet pussy furiously with the vibrating toy, and soon Grace exploded in a deep orgasm that shook her and made her scream with the release. Mistress Amanda said "don't stop slut"

The slut laughed and said, "yes Mistress," and continued pounding Grace's pussy with the vibrator, one hand moving to Grace's clit and rubbing it gently, sending Grace into the throes of another orgasm before the first was even finished.

She came four times before Mistress Amanda signaled that the slut should stop. Grace lay on the bed, heavily breathing drenched in sweat and reeking of sex.

"Good girl my Grace. You have done well."

"Thank you Mistress," she replied.

"Now wake up my girl."

Grace opened her eyes and looked up at Mistress Amanda, leaning over her. "That was wonderful Mistress Thank you."

"I am sure it was my girl. And you did wonderfully."

"Did I Mistress?"

"Yes my girl you did. And I enjoyed watching you be made to cum very much. So I'm going to arrange to see that quite often."

"How so Mistress?"

"You and the slut are going to take turns my girl. You will make the slut cum, and then she will make you cum."

Grace's heart raced. "Yes Mistress," she blushed crimson and looked down.

"You're so pretty when you blush my girl," Mistress Amanda said, which only made Grace blush more.

Mistress, Amanda laughed.

"Alright my girl relax," She said.

Grace lay back on the bed, and Mistress Amanda said a word and Grace fell into a deep trance.

When she woke, she felt wonderfully refreshed and energized, and even aroused. She blushed when she realized how aroused she was.

"How do you feel my girl?"

"I feel great Mistress," she said and quietly added, "and aroused."

"Good. That is something you should get used to my girl. I like that in my slave."

"Yes Mistress," Grace blushed again.

"Now what about supper my girl?"

Grace looked at the clock and saw it was past 7 pm. "It seems like it was early afternoon just a few minutes go Mistress."

"Yes my girl, I've had you under a lot today. Don't worry your pretty little head about it. Just fix us some supper. I'm hungry. And fix us a couple of drinks before you get started please, I'm thirsty too."

"Of course Mistress,"

They went into the kitchen, and Grace got her Mistress a drink and then began working on the meal. The heels didn't bother her at all, and she didn't even notice the clothing she wore. to her, it was all the sluts outfit, and she thought she was simply naked.

It didn't take long to get supper done. She used the microwave to cheat and served her Mistress and knelt with her plate sitting on a chair.

"I feel different Mistress," she confessed, turning red.

"I know my girl."

"What is it Mistress?"

"You are simply feeling those things that you have never allowed yourself to feel on a conscious level my girl. Don't worry about it. It will become commonplace before long."

"Yes Mistress."

They talked of inconsequential as they ate. Grace said she had to go out the next day for groceries and other supplies. Mistress Amanda said, "Ok my girl. I have to go home tomorrow. Well, work first, then home. I have a few things to do but I will come back in a couple of days."

"I will miss you Mistress."

"As I will miss you my girl. But we do have tonight. And I plan on watching you and the slut come many times tonight."

Grace blushed yet again.

When the meal was done, Grace refreshed their drinks, and they returned to the bedroom. "Alright my girl, get the slut into position. Its your turn to make her cum."

Grace lay on the bed and looked up, her eyes glued to the mirror, and her perspective changed. She looked down on the slut who was waiting eagerly to be made to cum. The sluts arms were at her sides unmoving. Grace reached down with her own and began working on her.

It didn't take long before she made the slut cry out with her orgasm. "That was easy my girl," Mistress Amanda said.

"Yes Mistress, the slut was very aroused already."

"I am sure she was. How about you my girl?"

"Oh I am also very aroused Mistress, watching the slut cum only made it worse."

"Good. Time to switch."

Grace moved, and suddenly she was looking up at the slut, smiling down at her. Her arms were at her sides, and she had no power to move them. But the slut reached down with hers and began caressing her.

While Grace saw things as if there were two people on the bed, Mistress Amanda saw the truth. Grace's own hands were doing the real work. What Grace saw she knew, was a figment of her imagination created with posthypnotic suggestions.

"I want you to describe what the slut is doing to you at all times my girl."

"Yes Mistress,"

Grace began a steady stream of commentary. "She is caressing my belly Mistress, it feels good. She is touching my breasts, ouch she pinched my nipples, that hurt. She is touching my pussy Mistress, now she's got her fingers inside me and she's fucking me with them. She picked up the vibrator Mistress and she is fucking me with it, oooo it feels soooo good," Grace's voice was interspersed with moans and whimpers. Mistress Amanda watched the girl fuck herself with the vibrator while giving her a running commentary.

She knew that giving the girl an outlet to experience this arousal, such as the slut, had created a situation that would eventually lead to acceptance of her own need. Grace saw what she desired in "another" and desired it for herself. She had been feeling all of this on another level, making the need strong within her. Strong enough to overcome her fears. She hungrily smiled as she watched the vibrator move to Grace's ass.

"Oh Mistress, she's sticking the vibrator in my ass, oh please make her stop," Grace cried out, but though she sounded a bit panicked, there was no trembling or shaking such as she had previously displayed.

Mistress Amanda replied, "No my girl. I want my girl and my slut to be used to the use of all their orifices. I myself will be fucking your ass with my strap on or sticking things inside both your holes, whenever I wish. So get used to it."

"Yes Mistress," Grace moaned as it penetrated her until it was buried inside her. Mistress Amanda tossed another vibrator out of her bag onto the bed and watched Grace pick it up and insert it into her pussy.

"Oh she is fucking both my holes Mistress, I'm going to cumm," and then she came in a powerful orgasm.

"Would you like a drink my girl?"

"Yes please Mistress,"

"Then go get us each one. And you can fix the sluts makeup while you're at it."

"Yes Mistress."

She returned a few minutes later with fresh drinks and fresh makeup. "The slut looks much better my girl. you could stand to take a lesson from her."

"Yes Mistress," she said and blushed.

"tomorrow when you go out for your grocery shopping my girl, I would like you to wear some makeup. It doesn't have to be quite as heavy as the slut wears, but I want at least some eyeshadow, mascara and a light coloured lipstick."

"Yes Mistress," she replied, looking down at the floor as she sat on the bed, sipping her drink.

When Grace was done, her drink Mistress's Amanda had her, and the slut continue their fun. Every time Grace came, she would have her get them each a drink. She knew all that talking was hard on the throat. Eventually, she declared that it was time for bed. Grace looked at the clock and was amazed that it was midnight. "The time passed so quickly Mistress."

"time flies when you're having fun my girl. Now get the slut undressed and lets get to bed."

Mistress Amanda lay down and got under the covers as Grace undressed. Grace crawled in with her, and Mistress Amanda held perfectly still as Grace snuggled up next to her, her knee thrown over her legs, and her arm draped across her chest and her head lying on her shoulder. She smiled and kissed her girl good night. There was no flinching, so she decided to see if she could get anything more out of her. She leaned close and kissed Grace's lips and nibbled them. At first, Grace responded well. She opened her lips and returned the kiss, but as Mistress Amanda put her free hand on Grace's naked hip, Grace flinched and then froze and began to tremble. She was not ready yet. But Mistress Amanda knew it would be soon.

Mistress Amanda calmed Grace with a soft voice and gentle words, and she lay back to sleep. Grace snuggled close, and it wasn't long before they slept.

In the morning, Mistress's Amanda kissed her girl on the forehead to wake her. Grace looked up at her and smiled. "Would You like breakfast Mistress?"

She looked at the clock and said, "Sorry my girl, I don't have time. I'll stop at a drive-thru on the way to work. But you should eat something after I leave."

"Of course Mistress. Do you have time for coffee?"

"I'll make time for coffee my girl. Please hurry."

A few minutes later, Grace returned to find Mistress Amanda dressed as a professional. She looked dapper and confident in her grey skirt and white blouse with a blazer. She had on neutral-colored nylons and low heeled black shoes.

"You look, great Mistress," she said as she served her the coffee."

"Thank you my girl, I would prefer to wear something a little more casual but I have meetings today with professionals who would be insecure if they saw me that way."

"Awwww," Grace sympathized.

"I want you to be a good girl until I come back my girl."

"Yes Mistress."

"Make sure to spend a lot of time in bed playing with the slut. She will help free you."

Grace blushed, "Yes Mistress," she said in a quiet voice.

"Ok my girl, I am leaving. You may kiss my feet before I go."

Grace knelt and kissed Mistress Amanda's feet at the toe of Her shoes several times on each foot. Mistress Amanda grabbed a handful of her hair, pulled her to her feet, and kissed her hard and passionately. Grace flinched but couldn't pull back. Though she shook and trembled, she tried to return her Mistress' kiss.

Mistress Amanda pushed into Grace's mouth with her tongue and mouth raped her, exploring every part of her mouth. Grace whimpered and tried to pull away again, but Mistress Amanda held a firm grip on her hair, and she was completely powerless to do so. Her tongue explored Grace's mouth, tasting her tongue, and then she pulled back and kissed her gently on the lips.

"I'm sorry to make you afraid my girl, but I am getting impatient and I want my girl."

Grace blushed, "Its ok Mistress, I can't wait till you can have me."

"I know my girl. I am not often so impatient, but you are very attractive. There is so much I want to do to you, and with you. The waiting is getting hard on my nerves."

"Me too Mistress."

"Be good, I'll see you in two days my girl."

"Yes Mistress. I love you."

"As I love you my girl."

And then she left.

The next two days were fun for Grace. She put on some light makeup as directed and took the bus downtown, and did her grocery shopping. People noticed her, and though part of her liked it, part of her was apprehensive. But no one acted in a way they shouldn't, so she relaxed after a while and was smiling on the way home.

Once home, she put away the groceries and got herself a soft drink and then found her feet leading her to the bedroom. Seemingly without a will of her own, she sat on the bed and stripped off her clothes. She took a few more sips of her drink and then found herself lying on her back, and suddenly the slut was playing with her again. When the slut made her cum, they "switched" places, and she did the same for her.

That was how she spent the next two days. She and the slut were both sore but very horny. They stopped only for mealtimes and sleep. At night she put on a CD that Mistress Amanda had left for her, and her dreams involved Mistress doing wonderfully arousing things to her. She woke in the morning and ate and showered and cleaned up, and then began it all again.

Two days later, the slut was about to make her cum when she heard her doorbell ring. She moaned her disappointment, but got up immediately and threw a robe over her to answer the door. She was very excited as she had missed her Mistress greatly and could hardly contain her excitement.

She opened the door, and her breath caught in her chest. Mistress Amanda stood there in a tight leather skirt just above the knee, a leather sleeveless top, black strappy heels, and a leather jacket slung over her shoulder. Grace stood there, gawking at her beautiful Mistress until She finally said, "Well my girl, are you going to stare all day or will you move so I can come in?" but she was smiling as she said it, so Grace knew she wasn't unhappy with her reaction.

Grace swallowed heavily and moved aside and shut the door behind her Mistress after she came in. She knelt at her Mistress' feet and kissed Her black nylon encased feet in their strappy heels. "Good girl, now get up. I want to kiss you," She ordered.

Grace got up, and Mistress Amanda grabbed a handful of her hair, and as She had done before, kissed her deeply and passionately. While she kissed her girl, her free hand pushed the robe off of Grace's shoulders, revealing the sluts usual attire underneath it.

Grace trembled only a little as her Mistress's held her by her hip as she kissed her. Mistress's free hand roamed Grace's body, touching her in her secret places, which aroused her the most. When Grace began trembling more severely, Mistress Amanda pulled her hand away and released her from the kiss.

"Much improved my girl. you are almost there."

"Oh Mistress that makes me so happy. I did really miss you."

"I know my girl. as I missed you. But I am here now and we have a couple of days together again before I have to return to work. And I am hoping that you will be able to go with me."

"Go to your work with you Mistress?"

"Yes my girl. I have plans for you to return to the work place under my supervision. My office isn't huge, but my clinic has a few psychiatrists and psychologists and aids and such. I think you would make a great receptionist."

Grace looked uncertain, "but I have not been able to work Mistress. The doctors said I might never be able to as I had post traumatic stress syndrome from my experiences."

"I know my girl, but I am confident." She smiled.

"Yes Mistress."

"Now, I'm hungry my girl. I came straight here from work."

"I will fix you something Mistress."

"Good girl."

As Grace made supper for them, Mistress Amanda asked all about her two days. Grace told Her all she had done and felt. And when she was on the edge of an orgasm when the bell rang.

"Very good," Mistress Amanda said when Grace finished. "I am not surprised you are making such progress. It wont' be long before I can do anything I want to you without you feeling such terror. At least, not because of my touch."

Grace giggled nervously and blushed.

They ate and talked of Mistress Amanda's plan to bring her into the workforce. Grace began to hope for more than just sexual freedom.

Then dinner was finished, and Grace cleaned up while Mistress Amanda sat and sipped at a drink. When Grace was finished, Mistress Amanda took her hand and led her to the bedroom.

"Ok my girl, bed." She said shortly.

Grace complied.

"Now my girl," She said as Grace looked at Her. "I believe you are ready for the next step."

"Yes Mistress."

"Now I'm going to put you under again," She said, and Grace nodded.

Then She said a word, and Grace fell into a deep trance.

Mistress Amanda asked all the same questions She had asked previously, and the answers were very much the same. Then She asked, "Do you trust the slut my girl?"

"Yes Mistress, she wouldn't hurt me."

"How do you know?"

"I don't know Mistress, she is just a lovely woman and I know she wouldn't."

"Well, you are right. Do you love her?"

"Yes Mistress."

"I thought so. So here is what is going to happen...."

And though Grace forgot her words as soon as she said them, she listened intently.

Later they all sat in the living room. Mistress sat on the couch, and Grace and the slut knelt at her feet, kissing and nibbling her feet and toes. "How are you feeling my girls?" She asked.

"Good Mistress," they replied in chorus.

"Alright lets go to the bedroom." And She led them to the bed.

"Grace, sit at the computer and watch us." She ordered.

Grace did, and Mistress took the slut in her arms and kissed her. The slut responded passionately with no fear, no panic, only passionate response. The Mistress lay her down on the bed and lay beside her. Her hand went to the sluts belly, and the moment She touched it, the sluts back arched in response bringing her belly closer, responding to her touch as if a puppet on strings. Every place Mistress Amanda touched her, she responded with desire and need, as if the only thing the sluts body wished was to be closer to her Mistress.

Grace felt pangs of jealousy then. Her Mistress was having a lovely time with the slut, and there she was sitting on the sidelines. She wished very much to be in the sluts place.

When Mistress Amanda touched the sluts pussy the sluts legs opened wide as if by reflex to give her easy access and to open her secrets to her. Grace watched for an hour or so as Mistress Amanda played the slut like an instrument, bringing her to the edge of orgasm, then letting her fall back, then bringing her back once again. Grace's eyes began to tear up. This is what she wished for herself. She wished Mistress could touch her like that. Could play her body like that. But at the same time, she was becoming very aroused. The sluts responses to her Mistress were very arousing. Her pussy began to leak, and her leather chair became slippery as she fidgeted with her need.

Finally, Mistress Amanda let the slut cum. She leaned down and said softly into the sluts ear as her hand fucked the sluts pussy, "Cum my slut, Cum now," The slut screamed with the release, and her body shook and trembled.

When it was over, the slut lay there with a Cheshire smile on her face looking up lovingly at her Mistress.

Mistress Amanda smiled down at her and then looked over at Grace, "Don't you wish that could have been you my girl?"

"Yes Mistress, very much so."

"As do I my girl. There is a way."

"There is, Mistress?"

"Yes my girl. Come here."

Grace lay on the bed, "Now make love to the slut. Give and take pleasure with her and from her. After you have shared an orgasm, I will tell you what is the next step. It will be a big one so prepare yourself."

"Yes Mistress," Grace quietly said as she leaned down and kissed the slut.

The sluts mouth opened to meet hers and their tongues touched and danced together. Grace was content with this for a time, but the slut had other ideas. She embraced Grace and rolled them over so that it was the slut learning over her. The sluts hands reached for Grace's breast and fondled and caressed first one, then the other. Grace did the same, cupping the sluts hanging globes in her hands and caressing them lightly with her fingers. Grace was just getting used to the touch of the sluts hands on her breasts when the slut lightly trailed her fingers down her belly and found her pussy. Grace was already wet. Inspired and aroused, she reached for the sluts pussy, and her fingers found similar wetness there. It wasn't long before they each had their fingers buried in each other's pussies as far as they would go.

Grace wanted to taste her, so she moved down and slid beneath and between the sluts legs, and she started licking. The slut tasted musky with an astringent aftertaste. Grace devoured her pussy. In moments the slut was doing the same. They lay together in a sixty-nine, and in moments they were cumming.

They sat up and knelt facing each other, and Mistress Amanda got onto the bed and hugged them both close.

"Very well done my girls, especially you Grace. I know that was not as easy as it should have been."

"Thank you Mistress." she replied.

"So now comes the hard part," She said, giving Grace a confident smile.

Grace was nervous, but her Mistress' smile and warmth reassured her.

"Slut my girl, do you like Grace?"

"I love her Mistress."

"I know you do my slut," Mistress Amanda said then looked at Grace, "And do you love her as well Grace?"

"Yes Mistress. she scared me at first, but I have come to love her a great deal."

"Do you wish you were more like her my girl?"

"Yes Mistress, she is free to be as she wishes."

"I can give that to you. Well, she can."

"How Mistress?"

"Take her inside you."

"How Mistress?"

"Do you wish her to be a part of you my girl?"

"Yes Mistress," Grace whispered.

"Alright then slut, crawl into her vagina."

Grace reluctantly lay back on the bed and watched as the slut smiled at her and then put the fingers of both her hands into Grace's pussy. Grace felt a fire in her pussy, and she began to feel passionate and aroused. Grace watched, enthralled as the sluts hands disappeared inside her up to her wrists, and then further. When her elbows disappeared into Graces pussy she began to feel the passion spread to her belly. The slut looked up at her and smiled a loving smile and finally lowered her head, and that started disappearing into Grace's pussy as well. In mere moments, the slut had disappeared to her waist. The fire inside Grace was spreading all over her body. She tingled with arousal and passion, and need.

The sluts hips disappeared inside her and then her thighs, then her knees, and pretty soon, all that was left were the sluts feet and ankles. As she had no purchase to push herself further in, they remained there wiggling. Grace reached down and pushed them inside her, watching as her wiggling toes vanished into her pussy. She felt a great peace. She was relaxed and aroused, and she knew that Mistress had done as she had said she would. Grace looked up at her and smiled.

"Alright my girl," Mistress Amanda said, "you can wake up now."

Grace opened her eyes. Mistress was staring down at her, smiling. "Alright my girl. Tell me the name of my slut."

"Your sluts name is Grace Mistress," Grace smiled.

Mistress, Amanda smiled. "Not for long my girl, but lets see how my slut works."

Mistress Amanda extended Her hand and reached for Grace's belly. Even before it got there, Grace's back arched, and her belly eagerly rose to meet her Mistress's hand. Grace felt her Mistress' touch as if it were a liquid passion. She moaned as Mistress Amanda caressed her belly and then breasts, and then Grace's legs spread wide as Mistress Amanda reached for her pussy. Mistress Amanda played Grace's body like an instrument, and her girl's moans were music to her ears.

She plunged her fingers into her girl's pussy, and finger fucked her while her thumb rubbed her clit lightly. Grace was moaning, and her head shook side to side, and Mistress Amanda knew she was close. "You wanna cum don't you my girl?"

"yes Mistress," Grace moaned.

"Then cum my girl," Mistress Amanda ordered, and Grace cried out as she found release.

Mistress Amanda's fingers stopped and simply sat quietly inside Grace's pussy as she smiled down at her success.

Grace finally stopped cumming, and she looked up at her Mistress a bit sheepishly but with a wide smile on her face. "You did it Mistress. You fixed me."

"I helped my girl. But you did a lot of it yourself. But all is well. We can be together now."

Mistress Amanda took her fingers out of Grace's pussy and held them up to Grace's mouth. Grace sucked them clean, tasting her juices, and savoring them.

"Now we have something to talk about my girl."

"What Mistress?"

"Us. I want you to be mine my girl. All the way mine. With collar and full ownership."

"I want to be yours Mistress."

"Good. Then there isn't a lot to talk about." Mistress Amanda got off the bed and sat in the computer chair. "Kneel before me my girl," she said as she reached into her bag and pulled out a gold necklace that seemed to be made to resemble chain links. "This is my collar you will wear my girl. But first, we need to talk terms."

"I didn't realize I'd get terms Mistress."

"Well, not terms my girl, but things you must abide by as mine."

"Yes Mistress."

"One. You will obey me in all things."

"Yes Mistress, I will."

"Two. I will do whatever I wish to you, including making you forever aroused, and only permitting you to cum when I wish it. Whether that be once in a month or ten times in a night."

"Yes Mistress. As you wish."

"Three. When I decide its time for you to wear the permanent lifelong collar, you will decide then and there whether to remain mine or leave me. But once you make that decision it will be irrevocable."

"Yes Mistress."

"Four. I'm going to make changes to your body as I wish. Whether that be jewelry or tattoos or even a brand."

"As you wish Mistress. I think I'm hoping for a brand."

Mistress, Amanda smiled.

"Five. You have the right to be heard and understood. But I am the one who makes the final decisions on anything."

"Yes Mistress."

"Is there anything you can think of that has not been covered my girl?"

"No Mistress, except that in case of doubt refer to rule number 1." Grace smiled.

"Exactly."

"Will you wear my collar under those terms my girl?"

"I will Mistress, and gladly."

Mistress Amanda smiled and leaned forward and fastened the gold chain around Grace's neck.

"You are mine now, and I name you Amanda's Charity. "Yes, Mistress.' Charity bent forward, kissed her Mistress's feet several times each, then sat back on her heels and smiled up at her Mistress.

"Oooo I have such plans for you my dear Charity," Mistress said with a devilish smile on her face.

Charity smiled, "I can't wait Mistress."

Story 02

Chapter 01

Lauren found her roommate in front of her computer, shocked at what she was seeing. On the screen, some whackjob preacher was talking about how the world was doomed. The preacher said the world would end in a week and a half. Lauren knew her roommate was a bit strange in the religion department, but she had no clue that she was this gullible.

"Oh no!" Christy said as she heard her friend's footsteps behind her. "It's doomsday. Maybe the rapture. I don't know. But we're all done for."

"That's all nonesense Chris and you know it."

"No, it's real. This guy is a real bonafida prophet."

"He's never been wrong."

For an hour, she tried to convince her friend that it was nonsense, but after a while, Christy started becoming truly offended at her attempts to dissuade her.

"Fine!" She finally declared in frustration. "The world is ending. So what?"

And then Christy started crying. Damn, what have I done now? Lauren thought to herself. She knew her friend was rather sensitive, even for a girly girl, but she could usually avoid hurting her feelings."

Playing up to the girl's beliefs, she asked, "Why are you crying? Won't you be happy to go to heaven if it is the rapture?"

"It isn't that Lauren." She looked up at her with tears in her eyes.

"Well," Lauren said softly, "What is it then?"

"I had a life I wanted to live."

"Don't we all?" Lauren said, somewhat regretfully casting a shamefaced glance down at Christy's alluring legs and then quickly back up before her friend noticed.

Christy stood and held her friend as if for dear life and cried on her shoulder.

"But, I didn't want the kind of life most people would expect from me. I'm dirty. Bad."

Now that was something Lauren had never heard from her before. You think you know someone, she thought to herself.

"What do you mean?"

"I can't."

"Can't what?"

"Tell you about it. I'm too ashamed."

"You know you can tell me anything right? We've been friends for four years now. If you don't know you can trust me by now, then I don't know what to say."

"It sin. It isn't trust. I can't say the words. I'm ashamed."

Her friend was so distraught she considered for a moment as the poor girl cried on her shoulder. What she needed was to let go of her inhibitions. At least enough to confide in her. The only thing Lauren knew that worked and was readily available, was.

"Alcohol." She finished aloud.

"What?" Christy asked.

"I'm going to get you drunk my dear."

"Good Christian girls don't drink."

"I know. But the world is ending anyway, so might as well experience it at least once. Right?"

"Well," Christy started, "If I repent in the morning and ask for forgiveness I guess it will be alright. I mean, we're all going to be gone in a week and a half anyway. Right?"

"That's the spirit," Lauren told her, rolling her eyes at her friend's weirdness. She grabbed Christy's hand and led her to the car."

This promised to be an interesting weekend, and she thought as they drove. Christy was silent during the drive, and Lauren was completely flustered as to what to say to her friend. How could she cheer her up without offending her friend's weird beliefs? She had been religious since they'd met. The first night they shared their apartment Christy had tried to convert her bible in hand. It had been a bit awkward for a while, but Christy eventually decided to accept her status as a "sinner" who couldn't be saved, and Lauren chose to do the same for her. And they'd gotten along great ever since.

She often wondered if her friend were a closet lesbian. She didn't date men. Of course, she had her religious reseason for saving herself for marriage, but Lauren was pretty sure a good Christian girl could at least date a man to find out if she wanted to marry him even if the date had to have a chaperone or something. But Christy never even mentioned guys. Maybe she plans on saving herself for Christ, she thought acidly, and with a tinge of regret.

Lauren was a lesbian. In the beginning, that had been a big part of their conflict that made Lauren think she'd have to find a new roommate before Christy's sudden acceptance of the fact that she wasn't going to be converted. That had been a relief. But sometimes Lauren wished she and Christy had been unable to come to terms with each other. She found Christy very attractive and had often fantasized that the woman she was with on any given night was Christy. It was unfair to her lover, of course, but she couldn't help it. It was almost always a test of her self control. It was why her lovemaking sessions were often rough. It was also why she had never gone on more than three or four dates with the same woman. At least not after the first year they had lived together. Even though Christy was such a weirdo when it came to religious belief, she was a good, kind, and caring friend. She did more than her share of the housework. She even cleaned Lauren's room for her once in a while though it was a bit weird at first. She cooks more than her fair share as well. In some ways, Christy was a bit disturbing. She had fallen for the old religious beliefs about woman's place in life. It would be a waste to have her friend marry some guy and live the life that religions like that map out for women.

In the liquor store, she bought a couple of kinds of beer, some sweet wine, vodka, orange juice, tequila, and seven-up. The store clerk had someone help her load it into the car, and Christy showed how naive she was about that sort of thing when she asked, " Will that be enough?"

Lauren laughed. "Sweetie, that could get an army of good Christian girls like you drunk."

Christy's eyes widened.

"I don't know what you'll like so I bought a wide variety."

"That must have cost a lot of money I'm sure Lauren, can I pitch in?"

Lauren knew Christy didn't make a lot of money at her job at the church. But she also knew that Christy was adamant about paying her fair share. She always paid her rent on time, and her share of the bills, even when it meant she had to walk to work instead of spending a little money on bus fare. So she told a little white lie.

"Of course you can dear, your share would come to twenty dollars."

"Exactly twenty?" Christy asked.

"Well, twenty and a bit of change, but what's a few cents between friends?"

Christy smiled and got twenty dollars out of her purse and handed it to Lauren.

Then she blushed and took out another quarter and set it in the change holder mounted in the dash. Lauren smiled and inwardly shook her head.

Once home, the ladies took two trips to get it all inside.

"What do you want to try first?" Lauren asked her as her friend sat on the floor and leaned back against the sofa.

"I don't know. I've never even tasted that stuff."

"Ok, we'll try you on some beer first. It doesn't pack as much punch as some of the other stuff."

"Will it get me drunk? I mean, if I'm going to have to repent tomorrow, I want to have something to repent."

Christy looked a little shamefaced but eager. Lauren laughed.

Christy wasn't her only friend with weird religious beliefs. Her friend Mark was a druid. He was also gay. Of course, that didn't matter to her as she had no attraction to him or him to her, but she often thought it was funny to think of a gay druid. Not that she knew why she found it funny. She loved him a great deal and valued his friendship. He had been the one she confided in of her pain regarding Christy. He sympathized, at least emotionally. He had told her he had once been in love with a straight guy. He had made the mistake of confiding his love for his beloved, which was the end of the friendship.

Lauren grabbed them each a beer and handed one to Christy. "Shouldn't we get glasses?" Christy asked.

"Definitely not." Lauren said, "When you're having an end of the world party you absolutely have to drink from the can. It's an unwritten rule."

Christy laughed. Even she wasn't that naive. She pried open the top and started to lift it to her lips.

"Wait. We need a toast," Lauren said.

"Oh, let me, I've never toasted anything before. Well, aside from bread."

Lauren had to laugh at that. She nodded and waited while Christy seemed deep in thought, and she wanted to make it a good one.

She stood and raised her can of beer and said, "To the end of the world, the shedding of burdens, and the freeing of spirits to find heaven!"

Lauren suppressed a laugh. Her friend was dead serious. Oh well, she thought and wistfully smiled as she raised her can in reply and drank.

Christy downed half the can in one go. Lauren laughed, reached over, pulled the can down, and said, "Whoa there girl, you're going to make yourself sick chugging like that."

"Oh. I thought that was how you were supposed to drink beer."

"Well, maybe the young men do that at frat parties, but anyone with any sense takes it a squitch slower than that."

"Oh."

"So how do you like beer?"

"It's, uhm, icky," Christy said, then burst out giggling.

"Oh. Ya well beer is an acquired taste. Let me get you some vodka. You like orange juice right?"

"Oh, I love orange juice. But I have to finish my beer. Waste not want not."

"Ok then," Lauren laughed. She had never seen her friend act this way. She was usually far more reserved, and it worried her a little.

Lauren avoided asking any serious questions until Christy had drunk two full glasses of vodka and orange. She had, of course, finished the beer as promised even though she did not like it. She knew it was time to begin the conversation when she returned with a third glass of vodka and orange, and her friend was absentmindedly staring at her feet as she approached. She was wearing black open-toed sandals and nylon stockings, and Christy smiled dreamily for a moment as Lauren reached down to hand her the glass.

"You have such pretty feet," Christy said, "And your nail polish is beautiful." And then she giggled.

"Ok, you're definitely getting drunk. I think it's time we talked about what you couldn't say earlier."

"I can't. I can't tell you." Christy said, and Lauren started rolling her eyes. "I'm sorry, it's not in me to say the words. Not yet anyway."

"If you drink too much more my dear, you'll pass out and then you won't have said anything anyway."

"You're my friend. I care about you a great deal and I want you to be happy. Talk to me."

"I can't," Christy shuddered, but before Lauren could express her irritation Christy went on, "but... I can show you."

"Huh?" Lauren asked intelligently as her irritation was replaced by surprise.

"Please come with me," Christy said and stood shakily. She wobbled a bit on her heels before regaining her balance.

"You should probably take your shoes off hon, you're going to fall on your head."

"Ok," Christy agreed readily and gingerly stepped out of them and then knelt and arranged them neatly by the front door. Christy was always a bit of a nut that way.

Finally, she stood again and led Lauren to her bedroom.

She sat at her computer and warmed up. Then she pulled up her internet browser, and Lauren's eyes nearly popped out of her head when Christy pulled up a website full of erotic stories.

Christy was blushing beet red and couldn't look Lauren in the eyes, but she pulled up an author named 'boundinchains' and quietly asked Lauren to read this author's stories.

Lauren was staring at her puritan friend like she had lost her mind, or one of them had anyway, but she moved to the chair Christy vacated. Her friend was obviously in distress, and despite her issues, she wanted to help. But the stories astounded her.

Christy went and got them both more alcohol as Lauren started reading.

The first story was a lesbian romance, with subtle hints of a controlling relationship that seemed to have a few religious undertones. It also had undertones of the BDSM lifestyle that Lauren had flirted with from time to time. There was nothing overtly kinky in the story, but the author's way of writing told her more than what was written.

She downed her drink to try to cool the fire spreading through her body. The thought of her beautiful and oh so puritan friend being turned on by this story. She looked over at Christy, who was curled up on the bed with her eyes gazing off into space, occasionally sipping her drink.

"This is uhm, different than what I'd expect to find you reading sweetie," Lauren started, but Christy came out of her distracted state and said, "Please read them all and then we can talk. I 'm too ashamed."

Christy stood up and said, "We need more alcohol."

Lauren handed her friend her glass and then returned to reading. The next story was more overtly kinky. The religious undertones were still there, but the lesbian relationship was more in line with the 'I say, you do' style of the kinky lifestyle. Lauren's mind was exploding, and she harbored lustful thoughts about her oh so pretty roommate.

Christy brought her glass back full, and she hardly noticed.

Another story later, when Christy brought yet another drink, she realized she hadn't even drunk the last one, though she thought Christy had drunk hers. Christy seemed quite drunk. Lauren wanted to keep her head, and she didn't want Christy to pass out before they had their chat, so she said, "Quit it with the alcohol for now. We'll have more later. Ok?"

"Ok," Christy said quietly, putting her glass down next to Laurens two full ones and lying back down on her bed.

Lauren was becoming hotter and hotter as she read. The stories and there were five of them, were a bit immature in that it was someone inexperienced writing them, but they were imaginative, and they became hotter and hotter and more and more overtly kinky. And they were all lesbian. The last one was all lifestyle all the way through—the relationship between a slave and her beautiful owner. But there was a constant thread of love through them despite some of the humiliating acts that the Dominant woman made her slave do in the last story.

Her juices flowed, and her panties were wet enough that she worried for a moment that she'd leak through her skirt onto her roommate's chair. But as she finished the last story, she turned toward her friend and saw that Christy had her hand down her skirt, but when she saw Lauren turn toward her, she pulled it out and acted as if nothing had happened. For her part, Lauren pretended not to have seen, though that stunned her just as much as the stories.

"Ok Christy," she started, "I've read them all. And I have to say that I feel it's very unkind of you. I haven't been with anyone in a while and stories like this can be frustrating if you're alone."

"I'm sorry, Lauren," Christy said in a quiet voice as she got off the bed and came close to Lauren. She knelt in front of her friend and looked at the floor.

"What are you doing reading this kind of stuff anyway? It's very unlike you. Or is that the problem?"

"I didn't just read them," she replied, and her voice went down to a whisper. "I wrote them."

Lauren couldn't believe her ears, but Christy went on. "I imagine the characters in the story are you and me." She hiccupped as that last part came out.

Lauren felt the world shifting under her feet. "What? Did you want to dominate me then?"

"No. I want you to dominate me. I want you to own me. I want to be your slave. I want to be your toy. Your possession. Your property. I want you to use me, and punish me, and reward me, and love me....At least until the world ends."

Desperate to find some sense, Lauren asked, "I thought this was against your religion?"

"If I'm your slave then it's ok. My pastor told me that as property slaves weren't responsible for anything except in how they served their owners and that they are still honoured in heaven after they die."

"Well slavery is illegal now dear."

"But I have a contract we can sign. And according to the bible if you agree to something, then it's binding."

Lauren felt like she had drunk far more than she had. The world was spinning around her. She figured one of them must have gone crazy, and it was probably her. So she decided she had to talk to someone who was always, well, almost always, sane.

"You stay right there," she said, letting some of her bewilderment out as anger.

She ran out of the room and put in a quick call to her friend Mark.

Luckily he wasn't out or otherwise occupied. At first, he asked her, "Have you been drinking." She replied. "Yes, with Christy!"

"With Christy?" He asked, "What is going on? Did hell freeze over?" Then he had to get her to slow down. She took a deep breath, and she told him everything that had happened. His laughter came over the phone very clearly.

"Why are you laughing?" She demanded. "This is serious."

"Oh, why am I not surprised," He mused. "It's always the ones you least expect," He laughed for a few moments longer until Lauren's irritation peaked, and she said, "Well what the hell am I supposed to do with her?"

He laughed harder and asked, "Why are you asking me? I've never been with a woman before."

"I mean in the long term you idiot!. She's only doing this cause she thinks the world is ending. Her religion has her so messed up that she'll believe any old thing she see's on youtube. What happens if I take her up on this? When she wakes up after the world was supposed to end and finds herself between my legs?"

He said, "The world's got to end sometime."

Then he laughed even harder. Then he got very serious for a moment. "Listen love, she obviously needs this. She has rationalized it with her religious beliefs which are very strong according to what you've told me about her, into something she can accept so that she can be happy. It's something we humans are rather good at. That sort of thing is inevitable. We always do it when needed. Or we break apart into a million pieces. She will in fact find an answer to this need of hers one way or another. Either with you, or eventually, with some stranger who may or may not care for her as you do." He paused and went on, "You do still care for her don't you?"

"You know I do."

"Well, so what is the problem? Haven't you told me of your domination fantasies?"

"Well, I don't know if I'm as serious about it as her stories are," she stopped herself, "that's not the point you idiot. This will ruin our friendship!"

He replied, "I think Christy just took you way out past it and your treatment of her at this point could in fact ruin your friendship. But if you take her up on her offer I'm sure that if you love each other you could come to some balance that pleased you both."

"She's drunk, and she's crazy. Or I am. I don't know which anymore."

Mark laughed again, and she could tell he thought this was all very funny.

He said, "This is the funniest thing I've heard in months. The woman you have secretly lusted for, for the last couple of years, has offered you everything you could ever want from her and you're talking to me on the phone."

She wanted to bitch at him more, but she started to see his point.

He paused in his laughter to quietly ask, "Where is she now?"

"She was kneeling on the floor, and I told her to stay put so I could come to find some sanity, but I haven't found any here, you jerk!'

"You left her drunk and alone kneeling on the floor to stir in her own fear, doubt, shame, and misery, and I'm the jerk?" He asked quietly.

"Omg, you're right. What do I do?"

"Well, the worst that could happen is she changes her mind when the world doesn't end right? What would stop you from setting her free at that point? Or do you want her to go find some stranger who may not care about her well being as much as you do. Though I have to wonder if you really do when I think of the poor girl kneeling on the floor worried to death."

"You.." she momentarily let her frustration out and then said, "Ok, you've made your point. Ass. Bye. Love you."

"Love you too," and then more laughter as she hung up the phone.

She returned to find Christy kneeling where she'd left her exactly. Her head was down, and she was so still Lauren almost thought she wasn't even breathing. She spoke, "I'm sorry Christy, it's ok. I kinda lost my head for a bit and I needed to talk to Mark. We need to talk."

"Ok," Christy said in a quiet voice.

The first question Lauren asked was, "Why me?"

"You've always been kind to me even when I was rather nasty to you trying to convert you to my religion. I care about you a lot. I trust you. A lot of people aren't really very nice even though they act nice toward you when they want something. It's hard to tell when someone wants you because they care, or if they just want to use you without regard for your well being. And I know you aren't like that. And I love you."

"Well, what about a nice man?"

"I don't like men."

"Huh?"

"I never have. All the girls in my church love their husbands, but I never wanted one. I didn't know why until I met you."

"Can I please have a drink?"

Lauren handed her a glass and grabbed one for herself.

"Well, get up. Let's go back to the living room and talk."

"Can I please bring the contract?"

Lauren's eyes widened. "Fine. But I'm not signing it until we talk."

"Thank you," Christy said with a little more cheer in her voice. The hope that Lauren could sign lifted her spirit. She hit print on the computer and tried to stand as the printer spat out the contract, but she found her legs had fallen asleep as she knelt. She fell and spilled her drink on her blouse. Lauren quickly helped her sit on the bed as she suddenly realized just how long Christy had been kneeling there.

As she arranged her friend on the bed, she couldn't help but admire what was showing through her friend's wet blouse. It clung to her and revealed her generous cleavage. Lauren wet her lips as she stared.

"Let's get this wet blouse off you," She said, reaching for the hem. Christy pulled away and said, "No. Not unless you sign. Not unless you own me."

"You're willing to be my slave and do anything and everything I want, but you won't take off your top unless I own you? How does that make sense?"

"I'm a good Christian girl. I can't do those things. But if you own me, then it's your right as my owner."

Lauren rolled her eyes and shook her head. "If you say so dear."

330

She grabbed the printed contract and helped Christy to her feet and led her to the living room where the bright overhead light showed her more of Christy's charms through her drenched blouse. Christy saw where she was looking, and she blushed beet red. And if Lauren wasn't mistaken, did she hear a whimper out of her?

Christy asked, "My drink got spilled, may I please have some more?"

"Of course," Lauren answered, "I'll get you some..." but Christy interrupted.

"No please let me get it. And I'll get you some too. Isn't a slave supposed to serve her Mistress?"

"I haven't agreed to anything yet."

"Well, the end of the world is only a week and a bit away. Would loving me for that short time be so bad?"

Lauren shook her head, but Christy didn't see as she had turned to go into the kitchen.

Christy returned with two full drinks. She put one down on the floor and knelt before Lauren, who had taken a seat on the couch. She reached up and handed it to her. She's done some research if she knows to do that, Lauren thought to herself. She had never seriously gotten into that lifestyle, but sometimes she had wondered if it was only because she never found someone she wanted in that way. But Christy's behavior was appealing to her.

"Thank you," she absently said as she thought back. Christy had always had a knack for being caring and considerate. But looking back with this new understanding of her friend as a lens, she realized that much of Christy's behavior could be interpreted as a form of service. She stared down at her friend, almost as if seeing her for the first time. Her pussy twinged, and she felt her desire for the kneeling girl.

"Sweetheart, as much as I wish I could take you up on this, you're drunk, and it wouldn't be kind of me to take advantage of you...." she didn't get to finish as Christy interrupted with her frustration and hurt evident in her voice.

"I'm not as thunk as you drink I am!" She declared angrily. "I've been thinking about this for a long time Lauren. But I'll make you a deal. Let's sign it, and if in the morning you see that I feel regret over it because you've somehow taken advantage of me, you can rip it up and we can forget the whole thing."

"And if not?" Lauren asked softly.

"Then you own me until the world ends." Christy said happily.

Her frustration got the better of her, and Lauren threw up her hands. "Fine!" She said. "If you want to throw sense out the window until you come back to it then give me the damned contract."

Christy held her eyes down as she handed it and a pen to Lauren, but there was a smile on her face.

Lauren took the contract and gave it only a cursory glance before grabbing the pen and signing her name and dating it on the two indicated lines. She handed it to Christy, who happily smiled as she did the same. Then she ran out of the room.

"Where are you going?" Lauren asked.

"When there is a contract between people then all parties involved have to have a copy right Mistress?"

Lauren rolled her eyes again, but couldn't argue. Christy was too much.

Christy returned and handed the original back to Lauren, and Lauren asked, "And where is your copy?"

"I left it on my bed Mistress. I want to frame it and hang it on the wall over my bed. Is that ok?"

Lauren laughed. Then she had an idea that was sure to make her messed up friend change her mind.

She said, "Actually that gives me an idea slave. Why don't we make a third copy and hang it here in the living room. Right over there where it will be plain for everyone to see that you are mine."

Christy blushed but said, "As you wish Mistress."

She quickly went and made a third copy and returned a short time later with a copy mounted in a picture frame with a glass front to protect it from dust.

"If I may be allowed to get another picture frame when we go out Mistress, I was going to use this one to hang my copy in my room."

"Sure hon," Lauren shook her head again. This seemed so out of character for her friend. Oh well, she thought, she'll wake up tomorrow and feel very differently. Hopefully, we'll be able to laugh it off and go on as we were before.

"Will you hang it Mistress?" her friend asked, interrupting her thoughts. "I'm not good with tools."

Playing along, Lauren agreed, and in a few minutes, the contract was hanging on the wall behind the sofa where she thought it would surely embarrass Christy in the morning.

Lauren turned around, found Christy naked, and kneeled on the floor with her clothes set to one side. Lauren's breath caught in her throat. Oh fuck, I am ever going to make her pay for this, Lauren thought to herself. This is ridiculous. I am soooo freaking aroused right now. She decided to let some of that frustration out.

"Christy, I swear, when we wake up tomorrow and you are embarrassed about all this, I am going ot make you pay for how aroused I am right now."

"Would you like to have your slave lick your pussy then Mistress?" Christy blushed hard, but she had meant it because she started to crawl toward her on her hands and knees.

"Stay!" Lauren ordered, and Christy froze in place.

"Sweetheart, I am giving you tonight to sober up and change your mind. Tomorrow when you are hung over and embarrassed and have changed your mind we can have a good laugh together and then sort things out."

"Awww. As you wish Mistress." Christy said with her disappointment evident. Then she looked up and blushed as she asked, "May I please masturbate then Mistress? I'm really horny."

Lauren looked at her sharply. Ok, she thought, I'll give her one more thing to regret in the morning. Making me this sexually frustrated is going to have consequences.

"Fine," she said, "But I'm going to record you doing it on video."

Christy blushed, but a slight whimper told Lauren that she liked the idea. Shaking her head, Lauren got her phone out of her purse and turned it on. "Ok slave, go," she ordered.

Christy blushed hard, but quickly lay back on the floor and started touching her pussy. She was hesitant at first, but as her fingers explored herself, she found confidence in her explorations.

Lauren just had to twist her a little. "I thought good girls didn't do things like this?"

"I'm not a good girl anymore Mistress. I'm a slave."

"Are you telling me you've never done this?"

"No Mistress, I tried once, " she moaned, "but my mother caught me so I never did it again....I've wanted to though," she added.

Lauren decided not to ruin her friend's moment with what might be painful questions. That could wait until morning when she would have to fix this mess.

She found herself extremely getting aroused as she watched Christy's self-exploration. She wanted so much to join her on the floor. But her integrity, (or was it something else? a nagging voice in her head asked quietly), wouldn't let her. She stared at the girl's pussy that looked like it had never even been trimmed. She wondered what it would look like shaved. It might very well be a very pretty pussy. She shook her head at her thoughts as it was only a short time before Christy began to shake and moan and whimper. She had the cutest little whimper. "Oh Mistress I'm cumming.Ohhhhhhhhh."

Lauren's cheeks were flushed, and she was breathing hard as Christy lay completely exposed on the floor for a few moments and then crawled on her hands and knees to Lauren and began kissing her feet. "Thank you Mistress, thank you," she said between kisses.

Lauren kept the video running and let Christy make a fool of herself for quite a few long moments until she decided she had enough video and stuff to make Christy understand the mess they were now in.

But though she put down the camera phone, she sat there and, (enjoyed? or was it relished?) the attention her friend gave her feet.

Finally, she decided it was enough and got up. "Ok my friend, it's time for bed. We can talk about this all in the morning."

"Yes Mistress," Christy replied and followed Lauren to her room, leaving her clothes in a bundle on the living room floor.

"Just where do you think you're going?" Lauren asked.

Christy looked downhearted and softly said, "I know that a slave doesn't always get to sleep where she wants Mistress, but can I please sleep with you tonight?"

"Waking up naked in my bed will certainly be educational for her," Lauren thought. "Fine. But we are sleeping. Nothing else."

Christy's smile was like the sunshine. "Yes Mistress," she said happily.

Lauren decided not to humiliate her in the morning and reached into her closet for something to wear to bed. She decided on a low-cut, spaghetti-strap silk nightdress that clung to her body and caressed her curves. It reached just a third of the way down her thigh, exposing a lot of legs. She had never worn it before as she had been saving it for a special occasion. It didn't occur to her to stop and ask herself why she chose to wear it.

She pulled the covers back and lay down. Christy was standing there looking like a little girl at Christmas. She patted the bed, and Christy nearly jumped into it. Christy put her head on Lauren's shoulder and draped her arm across Lauren's chest and whispered, "Good night Mistress."

"Good night Christy," She replied.

She was very aware of Christy's arm lying on her chest. Each intake of breath caused a slight movement of her arm, teasing Lauren's breasts. Her nipples were poking up clearly through the thin nightdress. She sighed. It was going to be a long night.

Christy was soon fast asleep. Lauren, however, had no such luck. Torn between her desire and her responsibility as Christy's friend, she pushed away all the lustful thoughts that begged to be considered.

She lay there a long while. Christy was a sound sleeper and didn't move at all, but Lauren was restless. As she became more and more fatigued, she came out of a bit of a daze and found that she had turned her head toward Christy. She could smell her roommate's breath and scent, as well as remnants of a lovely perfume that clung to her, and she could even detect the powdery scent of Christy's deodorant.

She turned her head the other way in frustration. Sometime later, she fell asleep as exhaustion overcame her dilemma.

She was having a lovely dream about an exotic, beautiful lover. The lover was doing wonderful things to her when she started coming out of her fog. She was very aroused.

Her pussy felt wonderful, her lover was a very dedicated pussy licker, and she moaned and sighed as she opened her eyes.

But the feeling didn't go away. Surprised, she looked down and found Christy between her legs hungrily doing her best to please her. The night's events before came back to her in a rush, but she was too far gone to care. Fuck it, she thought, and lay back and enjoyed her friend's mouth.

She didn't have a lot of experience, but her mouth's touch put a fire in Lauren's belly that begged to be fueled, and she moaned. She got closer and closer to orgasm, and after a moment's hesitation, took Christy's head in her two hands and helped guide the girl's tongue so that within a few more moments, her cries filled the room and she spilled over into Lalaland. Christy didn't stop licking, and Lauren's orgasm stretched across the long seconds, and she whipped her head from side to side as her body trembled, and her orgasm crested. Finally, she pushed Christy away and lay there for a few moments, just feeling wonderful. Then reality stepped in, and she asked herself, "So what do I do now?"

She opened her eyes and saw Christy still between her legs looking up at her with a smile on her face. "What was that about hmmmm?" She asked.

"It's in the contract Mistress. 'The slave must wake her Mistress every morning by licking her pussy.'"

: Lauren's eyes widened. "Oh really?"

"Yes Mistress."

"I guess I should have at least read it before signing," she sighed. "I take it you don't have regrets."

Christy smiled. "No Mistress...." and she hesitated.

"Spit it out. I want nothing but the truth from you."

"Yes Mistress. It's just that I wish we could have, uhm, you know, last night."

Lauren sighed inwardly. "I guess I own a girl," she thought. "At least until the end of the world doesn't come."

She shook her head. "You sure are something."

Christy smiled and asked, "Would you like breakfast Mistress?"

Giving in, Lauren nodded her head. Christy smiled and left the room, and the rearview of her attractive roommate turned slave was just as pleasing as the rest of her. Lauren sighed.

After a few minutes, she put on a robe and joined Christy in the kitchen. The girl was still completely naked and standing a bit back from the stove as bacon sizzled in one pan and two eggs cooked in a second. Lauren had a look, and there didn't seem to be a lot of food. "We aren't out of breakfast foods already are we?"

"No Mistress."

"Well, how come you're making so little?"

"This is for you Mistress."

"Well what about you?"

"In my research I learned that slaves eat after their owners and only when their other duties permit Mistress."

"Well from now on unless I say otherwise you are to eat with me. Understand?"

"Yes Mistress," Christy smiled and added more eggs and bacon to the pans.

"You're really serious about all of this aren't you?"

"Yes Mistress."

"Why?"

"Because I've had these urges since long before I met you Mistress."

"Really? But yet, you never even masturbated."

"No Mistress."

"How did you handle it?"

"I prayed."

"Did it help?"

"I prayed a lot."

Lauren's eyes widened again at that, and she laughed with real humor. Her new girlfriend, well, slave, she corrected herself, was full of surprises.

"Well, slave, where do we go from here?"

"Wherever you want Mistress, it's only till the end of the world."

Afraid of offending her girls very touchy religious weirdness and offending her greatly, Lauren let that pass without comment. She would just have to wait until the day after the appointed day to have that conversation. But what to do with her until then? Her mind suggested several things at once, and she looked hungrily at the naked girl cooking breakfast. Fine! She almost yelled at herself in her thoughts. I'm not turning her out of bed after all of this. I'm going to have fun. Her heart sang despite her irritation with herself.

She smiled at Christy. "You look really good naked."

She could almost hear Christy blush, and the girl replied, "Thank you Mistress."

"But I noticed last night that your pussy hasn't been trimmed in a while."

"It's never been trimmed Mistress. I didn't touch myself there because I was afraid I'd give in to sinful thoughts."

"Well, as you said last night. Now you're a slave. I want you to shave that pussy completely bald after breakfast."

"Yes Mistress."

She watched Christy as she cooked, and her mind drew lustful scenario's. Her eyes followed every movement of Christy's body, every ripple of her smooth skin. Christy flinched as the bacon splattered, and Lauren wondered for a moment if she should tell her to put an apron on. Her naughty thoughts suggested something else instead. she said, "Don't stand so far away from the stove, you'll burn breakfast."

"Yes Mistress," Christy agreed and gingerly got closer to the stove. Lauren's pussy twitched. She watched silently as every few seconds; Christy flinched or jumped.

Lauren was lost in her admiration of her girlfriend, (property, the nagging voice whispered,) and it seemed like breakfast was soon ready.

Christy, two hands served her plate, arranged her fork and knife beside the plate on a folded napkin. She then poured Lauren a coffee and made it just the way she liked it. Then hesitantly, she asked, "Do you want me to kneel on the floor to eat Mistress?"

Lauren shook her head in surprise and said, "No eat at the table with me." Then as her mind filled with those thoughts again, she added, "Maybe you can kneel to eat on the floor another time."

"Yes Mistress," Christy said happily and brought her breakfast to the table.

They ate in silence, and Lauren couldn't help but stare and admire Christy's naked body.

For her part, Christy blushed when she saw the way Lauren was looking at her but ate in silence, glancing up every few seconds to see Lauren watching her with raw hunger in her eyes.

When they were done, Christy stood and cleared the table. Then she left the room. Lauren finally had time to get her brain in order without the constant lust for her roommate, (slave, her mind insisted). Christy wanted this. She wasn't unhappy about it. She wasn't at all regretful as Lauren had expected. She seemed to be reveling in her situation. As weird as all this was, Christy seemed more carefree and well, happier, than Lauren had ever seen her.

A few minutes later, Christy came back, and she stood close to Lauren and said, "Mistress, I have shaved my pussy as ordered. Have I done it to your satisfaction?"

Lauren came out of her thoughts and gave her girls pussy a good look. She had been right. Christy had a pretty pussy. Without any hair at all, it reminded Lauren of how she had looked before puberty. She imagined Christy in that same stage. Then getting hair, and lustful thoughts that she had somehow been made to feel were wrong. Then her absolute self-denial for years, until she could figure out a way for her to be herself, and believe what she'd been taught. Damn, Lauren thought, she wants this. And, a tiny voice in her heart said, so do I. Fine! She's MINE! At least until the world doesn't end and Christy wants to go back to the way things were. So. What to do now?

Christy stood there quietly throughout Lauren's blank stare. She started to think Lauren was not pleased that she hadn't done it properly when suddenly Lauren reached out and touched her pussy.

Christy flinched as Lauren's fingers caressed the place that until last night Christy hadn't even caressed. Christy whimpered as Lauren slid a finger up and down, just between her lips. Lauren looked up at her and saw her nervousness. "It's ok, you did a good job."

"Thank you Mistress."

"Now I'm going to play with what is mine."

"Yes Mistress," Christy said in a breathy whisper.

She dragged her finger between Christy's lips, barely penetrating between them, and found she was already very wet. Smiling, Lauren pushed her finger into her girl and felt her muscles clamp around it. She slowly penetrated deeper, and Christy whimpered, and her knees shook. Lauren realized this was not where she wanted to be doing this. She stood and turned, and as she did, she hooked her finger into Christy's pussy and said, "Come with me."

Not that Christy had any choice as Lauren's finger was inside her pulling her along behind. She took her to her bedroom and had her lie on the bed and lay down beside her, regretfully letting her finger slide out as they positioned themselves. "I want your first time to be sweet and tender, not controlling and demanding."

"If that's what you want Mistress," Christy replied, smiling at her.

"That's what I want," Lauren replied softly, leaned in, kissed her, and wrapped an arm around her. Christy replied with passion, and when Lauren's tongue touched Christy's lips, her mouth opened to accept it.

Christy's hand reached for Lauren's hip, but stopped short and started to pull back. Lauren noticed and pulled out of the kiss. "Did you want to touch me?"

Christy looked down and nodded.

Lauren grabbed her hand and placed it on her hip. "I want you to feel uninhibited. If you really think that you shouldn't do what it is you want, then ask. Ok?"

"Yes Mistress," Christy whispered and smiled at her.

Lauren's lips were soon pressed against Christy's and her tongue dancing in her mouth.

Christy started caressing Lauren through her nightwear. Her hand felt delicious through the smooth fabric. But Christy wasn't happy with that for long, and her hand dropped down to below the hem and pulled it up and was soon caressing Lauren's bare skin.

Lauren moaned and began to slowly, and ever so gently, drag her fingers lightly from Christy's shoulder to her chest, teasingly across her breast, and down her belly. Christy whimpered that cute sound she made as her fingers grazed her bare pubic mound.

Lauren teased her a little. She dragged her fingers right down to Christy's lips, and then back to her hips, her side, and underneath her breast. She grazed her nipple on the way by. Christy whimpered again and again. Christy was still caressing Lauren's hip, but she got braver and cupped Lauren's firm cheek and gave it a gentle squeeze.

"Please," Christy whispered.

Lauren knew what she wanted but wanted to tweak her a bit. "Please what Christy?" she asked innocently.

"Please touch me."

"I am touching you sweetie, do you feel my fingers caressing your breasts?"

"Down there Mistress. In my pussy. Please."

"Well, I'm the Mistress right?"

"Yes Mistress."

"What if I don't want to?"

Christy's eyes widened, and she said quietly, "That is your right Mistress."

"But I do want to, silly," Lauren laughed, and her hand cupped her lover's vagina, and a finger found it's way inside her.

Christy moaned, "Oh thank you Mistress."

"You're really horny right now aren't you my girl?" Lauren asked as her finger slowly moved in and out, stopping at her entrance before entering her again.

"Oh God yes Mistress. I've never been this aroused."

"You're beautiful when you're horny my girl." Lauren teased.

Christy whimpered and moaned.

Lauren didn't have to play with her pussy for long before Christy was close. She slowed down and asked, "As I said sweetie, you're really beautiful when you're horny. I don't think I've ever seen you so beautiful."

Christy whimpered and looked into Lauren's eyes, and Lauren could see her need.

"What if I wanted to keep you this way?" Lauren asked. "I mean all the time?"

Christy's eyes widened further, and she whimpered, and Lauren could feel her muscle clamp tightly around her finger. "That would also be your right Mistress. I am your property."

For a long moment, Lauren's finger held itself still. Her mind raced at the thought of keeping Christy in that state for a long time. Forever needing, forever lusting, always eager for her touch, but never quite able to hit the beach on the shores of orgasm. Her darker side laughed, and her pussy twitched.

But she said to herself, "Maybe another time. It could be a lot of fun to keep her like this, or worse, for a week or two."

And then she moved down between her girl's legs and tasted her. Her musky and slightly astringent taste was music to Laurens taste buds. Her tongue devoured her without any preliminaries. She knew Christy was ready, and she was hotter than she'd been in a long while. She inserted a finger, then two, and sucked and nibbled on Christy's clit. She looked up and saw Christy was watching her intently, and her hands were to either side of her clutching the sheets and squeezing them for dear life.

"Mistress, may I please cum?" Christy asked.

Her desires conflicted, and she was caught in a momentary paralysis with the thought of keeping her like this, but she snapped out of it and replied, "Yes my dear, you may. Come on, cum for Mistress." Then she took Christy's clit between her lips and flicked it back and forth with her tongue while her two fingers fucked her harder and faster.

Christy moaned and cried out and almost screamed as she came, and her tight entrance clamped around Lauren's two fingers and spasmed. Her body trembled, and her hands pulled the sheets she was trying to mutilate until the mattress was exposed. Lauren smiled a devilish smile and didn't stop.

Christy orgasmed, and her pussy clenched and unclenched around Laurens, unstopping fingers, and she started begging, "Mistress please, please stop, please...."

"What if I don't want to?" Lauren asked with a grin and returned her lips to Christy's clit.

Christy stopped begging, but her moans and cries continued.

Lauren took pity on her, though, and stopped her tongues movement on Christy's clit, and her fingers jammed into her one more time and then lay still. And slowly, Christy came back to earth.

Lauren finally moved and took her girl in her arms and held her. Christy trembled and snuggled up close and remained still as Lauren whispered her love for her. Finally, Christy moved. She moved down Lauren's body and knelt on the bed at her feet and started kissing and licking and nibbling her feet and toes.

Lauren smiled and mused on the recent events as she watched the girl show her gratitude. It was evident by this time that Christy had meant everything she'd said. Lauren's breath came faster as she watched. Christy's long brown hair fell down the side of her face, down her bare neck, as she kissed her Mistress' feet. Bare neck, Lauren thought. That's not right. What am I going to do about that? She asked herself. She thought about that for a while but didn't bother Christy with it. She found that watching Christy helped her think.

Christy, for her part, didn't stop. Lauren came out of her deliberations with a clear idea of how she was going to proceed and found Christy in the same position. "Alright Sweetheart. Enough."

Christy crawled up and lay down next to her and snuggled against her. "Thank you Mistress. That was..... wonderful."

"You're welcome. But there is something wrong here."

Christy looked up at her and trembled. "What Mistress?"

"something every slave should have, that you don't my girl. And we're going to fix that. Let's go get cleaned up and we'll go out and take care of that."

"Yes Mistress," Christy said, quite obviously not knowing what her Mistress was talking about.

They showered together. Without having to give an order, Christy washed her. She was ever so gentle as if Lauren was made of glass. When she was done, she started to wash, but Lauren took the loofa away and washed her in turn. They rinsed and dried off, and then Lauren went to get dressed. Christy followed her. "Well, go get dressed love, we're going out." Lauren said.

"What would you like me to wear Mistress?"

It had never occurred to Lauren to control what Christy wore. But Christy had surrendered that part of her life as well. And Lauren's mind turned down many arousing corners. "Ok, let's go take a look at your wardrobe," she said to give herself time to organize her thoughts.

Christy's wardrobe was sadly very old maid like. Plain underthings and very conservative styles of the dress made Lauren think that she'd have to have Christy get a whole new wardrobe. At least for when the girl wasn't with her church people.

"Do you have any stay up stockings or a garterbelt dear?" she asked.

"No Mistress."

"Do you have any well, pretty underthings or are they all designed for wear and not show?"

Christy blushed, and that was all the answer Lauren needed. Of course, she didn't have any daring or racy clothing. The girl had been a nun in all but name.

"Ok, we're about the same size give or take. Let's go see if anything of mine fits you."

"Yes Mistress," Christy said happily.

Christy was a little larger in the chest than Lauren, but she had a beautiful bra that never had quite fit right. She handed it to her girl and told her to try it on.

"I think it's broken Mistress," Christy said once she'd got it on. The lacy black demi bra gave plenty of support to the underside of her breasts and seemed to fit well, but what Christy was referring to was the lack of coverage for her nipples. The bra stopped short in a delicate lace edge about an inch and a bit underneath them.

"No sweetheart, it's meant to be that way. And it's perfect."

Christy blushed.

Lauren handed her a pair of nude, stay up stockings, and watched her put them on. Christy's pussy moved in interesting ways as the girl bent each leg and pulled the stockings up her legs.

Next, Lauren handed her girl a black loose-fitting skirt that came to mid-thigh. Not too short, but short enough to get into Christy's head. She had probably never worn one above the knee. "What about panties Mistress?" Christy asked as she pulled the skirt up.

"You're done with panties my girl," Lauren said, smiling. "Except when you are on your menses, or when I want your pussy dressed up, you are not ever to wear panties again."

Christy blushed, but replied demurely, "Understood Mistress."

With just a bit of the devil in her as the old saying goes, Lauren's final piece to the outfit was a white button-up vest type blouse with neither sleeve nor collar that was cut far below what Christy would have worn but was still plenty conservative for most people. It fit ok, though it seemed just a tad tight around the chest, Lauren had a wonderful feeling in the pit of her stomach looking at her girl dressed like that.

"Mistress, you can see my nipples if you look closely."

"Can you? Oh well, Sweetheart, I'm sure no one but me will notice. Now go pick your sexiest pair of heels, then do your makeup. And I'd like you to do your make up a little bit, uhm, what is the word.... slutty. Understood?"

Christy blushed but readily agreed. "Yes Mistress." And she left the room.

That gave Lauren time to dress. She chose black knee-high stockings, black lacey panties, black form-fitting pants, black lacey bra, dark red scoop neck sleeveless blouse. Strappy red two and a half-inch heels that matched her blouse gave her a bit of height and accented her long legs. Then she threw on a black leather jacket over the top. It was autumn and was a bit cool for a sleeveless top.

She left her room and went to the bath to fix her makeup just as Christy was coming out. Besides her foundation, Christy had on dark eyeliner, deep purple eyeshadow, dark red lips, and a little more red-tinted blush than was strictly necessary to accent her beautiful girl's cheekbones. It wasn't what most would call slutty, but for Christy, it was extremely daring.

"Good girl," she said as they met in the hall.

"Thank you Mistress," Christy said, and Lauren knew she was blushing though she couldn't see it underneath the makeup.

"Now wait by the door while I finish getting ready," Lauren ordered easily.

"Yes Mistress," Christy complied.

Lauren did her makeup somewhere between tasteful and dramatic. She didn't usually apply quite this much, but she had an image to present. She grabbed her purse and found Christy standing obediently by the door. She looked at her girl and realized she'd probably be a bit cold in that sleeveless top. "Oh well, she thought, I can always turn the heat on in the car. And then her mind went to naughty places when she considered ways to turn up the heat.

"Alright my girl, let's go."

She locked the door behind them, and they walked to the car. She saw that Christy was walking two paces behind. "Love, walk with me unless I say otherwise, alright?"

"Yes Mistress," Christy said quietly and moved to catch up.

Hmmm, she was calling me Mistress out here in daylight public territory. My girl has guts.

As she opened Christy's door, she noticed that Christy hadn't brought her purse. Of course not, I didn't tell her to, she thought. She filed that away and helped her girl into the car and shut the door.

In the car, she noticed that Christy had goosebumps at the chill in the air. It wasn't exactly cold, but at around fifty-five degrees, she was sure her girl wasn't exactly warm either. She put the key in the ignition and then looked at her girl. "There's something wrong here sweetie."

"What Mistress? What did I do wrong?"

"You didn't do anything wrong my girl, it's just that I can't see your pussy."

Christy blushed.

"It may not be the most beautiful part of you, but it is beautiful. The new rule is, that unless I tell you otherwise, you are to pull up your skirt, and sit on the car seat in your bare flesh."

"Yes Mistress," Christy replied and pulled her skirt up with some difficulty as she was sitting on it.

"That's a lot better sweetie," Lauren said, making a point to ogle her love.

"Thank you Mistress," Christy blushed.

Lauren started the car and drove for a bit. As the car warmed up, she turned the heat on, and she could see Christy felt more comfortable.

They arrived at a shop that Lauren had only visited once or twice. And she had never been quite so serious about the visit as she was this time. She parked on the street and turned the wheel, and then turned the engine off. "You can fix your skirt now hon."

Christy blushed again but said nothing as she removed her seat belt and then pulled her skirt into its usual position. She reached for the door handle, but Lauren stopped her.

Lauren got out of the car and went around to the passenger side and opened Christy's door for her. She held out her hand, and Christy took it and stepped out the car gingerly. Lauren locked the car, and they went inside.

Lauren kept a close eye on Christy as she led her inside. She saw Christy's eyes widen and stare at everything in wide-eyed wonder. Christy had never been inside a BDSM/sex shop before. Lauren smiled tightly and kept a tight rein on herself.

Christy followed her around as she casually glanced at things, but Lauren knew in the main, what her priority was, and waited for a salesperson to approach them.

An older and matronly sales lady approached them and asked, "Is there anything I could help you with ladies?"

Christy blushed, but Lauren replied evenly, "Yes dear, we are looking for slave collars."

"Day collars or play collars Ma'am?" the lady asked.

"Well, play collars at first, dear," Lauren replied. "And then once we figure out what is needed, perhaps a day collar, and perhaps more.

"Right this way ladies," the saleswoman smiled.

Lauren followed her, and Christy, blushing, followed Lauren.

They hadn't been all that far from the play collars Lauren found out. The woman brought them two aisles over and down a bit and then spread her hand and said, "Here they are. Do you know what size you need?"

"The collar is for Christy here. But I don't know what size she is," Lauren replied.

Christy blushed but did not say anything.

The sales lady was accommodating and asked Lauren, "Would you like me to measure her neck?"

Christy blanched.

Lauren replied, "That would be lovely thank you."

"Alright, I'll be right back ladies," and the woman headed down the aisle.

"How are you feeling Christy?" Lauren asked.

"I'm very embarrassed Mistress. Good girls don't come to these kinds of places," Christy answered.

"Well, you're right about that. But what was it you told me about that?"

"I'm not a good girl anymore. I'm a slave, Mistress."

"Do you really mean that?"

"Yes Mistress," Christy whimpered.

Lauren smiled.

It wasn't long before the lady had returned. "Ok ladies, I have the measuring tape. May I measure her neck?" she asked, looking directly at Lauren.

"Please do dear," Lauren replied, noting the casual, but strict adherence to one of the few lifestyle rules she knew was written in stone. 'Always ask permission before touching another person's property. Whether it be a flogger, a sex toy, or another human being.'

The lady took a seamstress' tape measure and circled Christy's neck with it. Christy held herself still as the woman carefully took care not to pull it too tight.

She pinched it at the mark and pulled her hands away from Christy's neck. "Twelve inches. I know right where we can find what you need."

"Lead on," Lauren replied.

"It isn't far," the woman said, stepping about five paces down the aisle and showing them a selection of collars.

Lauren had a look while the saleswoman looked on. She made sure to keep an eye on Christy, who was blushing hard. "Which do you prefer my girl?" Lauren asked, twisting her tail a little.

"I'm not sure..... Mistress, there are so many to look at." She replied, making Lauren very proud of her boldness.

"Take your time slave," Lauren replied, matching her girl's boldness with her own.

"Yes Mistress," Christy replied quietly.

They looked for a couple of minutes, and Lauren saw several that she liked. A couple that was a bit well, extravagant, and a couple of others that were less so. All were utilitarian.

Christy surprised her in her ability to choose one in front of the saleslady. "I like this one Mistress," she said, touching one of the more utilitarian ones. It was about an inch and a half wide and made of black leather. It had a little diamond-shaped studs in the center of its leather band and eight O rings spaced at even intervals for ease of use in binding, well, anything to anything. It also had at it's back a U bolt and slot in its opposite end to lock it in place with a padlock. Lauren smiled. It had been one she had been considering as well. "Well take that one hon." she said to the saleswoman.

"Very good Ma'am, is there anything else I can help you with today?" she asked, smiling.

"Yes there is dear," Lauren replied. She handed the car keys to Christy and said, "Wait in the car slave."

"Yes, Mistress," Christy blushed as she took the keys and started walking away. Lauren touched her, and she turned, "You can start the car and turn the heat on if you like."

"Yes Mistress, thank you," Christy replied and left.

Lauren turned to the saleswoman and explained her needs. She spent another thirty minutes in the store, and then paid for her purchases.

She returned to the car with two bags in hand, to find it running. She put her two bags in the back seat and got into the driver's seat. She looked over at her girl, who looked beautiful in her white sleeveless top with her nipples poking through. But then she frowned. She stared intensely at Christy's skirt covered bottom. Christy noticed where she was staring and blushed and remembered and pulled up her skirt so that her bare flesh was on the seat, and Lauren could see her lovely naked pussy.

"That's better my girl. I do hope I won't have to make an issue of this."

"No Mistress, I'm sorry Mistress, I was distracted. I will accept whatever punishment you wish."

Lauren put her seat belt on and pulled out of her parking space and considered that.

"How did you feel about going into the shop so openly my girl?" Lauren asked.

"My pussy is wet again Mistress," Christy replied and blushed.

"Oh really?" Lauren asked and reached over with one hand while the other remained on the steering wheel. She grabbed Christy's pussy and slid a finger between her lips. It came away slick. "You're right my girl. Now that is a wet pussy."

Christy blushed.

"And my finger is covered in your juices dear. Clean it off."

Christy leaned forward and took Lauren's finger in her mouth and sucked it softly. Lauren didn't want to have an accident, so she didn't prolong it. "Good girl," She said.

"Thank you Mistress."

Lauren smiled at her girl and then returned her focus to her driving and silently planned out their evening.

To see how her girl would react, she asked, "Did you see that guy at the end of the hall looking at you as we were walking around sweetie?"

"No Mistress," Christy said a bit nervously.

"I'm pretty sure he could see what you weren't wearing," she tortured her girl just a little. "In fact, he was staring at you like he was going to bore holes in your nipples," Lauren said casually. Christy blushed deep red, up to her ears, and whimpered.

"What was that Christy?" Lauren asked.

"It wasn't a word Mistress," Christy replied. "It was a whimper."

"Oh? And why did you whimper?"

"Because it made me hot Mistress," Christy said, blushing harder.

"Oh. Ok. Good to know my girl," Lauren said, finally letting her off the hook.

They got home, and Lauren helped Christy out of the car again, and they went into the apartment. As soon as the door was locked behind them, Christy started removing her clothing. Lauren smiled and said, "I'd like you to keep that outfit where you can get at it again love."

"Yes Mistress," Christy blushed as she realized she'd be wearing it out again.

Lauren took her two bags to her bedroom and closed the door behind her, and opened them. She put a few of the things away, but two items remained out. She put one on the edge of the bed, sticking out just a bit, and she grabbed the other and headed for the living room.

"Oh girl!" she said loud enough for Christy to hear her. Christy came out of her room and knelt at Lauren's feet.

"Yes Mistress?"

Lauren pulled out the collar she had bought for her girl and held it up. "Would you like to wear this?"

Christy bent forward and kissed Lauren's stockinged feet. "Yes please Mistress."

"Well, you're going to have to earn it my girl since you disobeyed a rule today."

"Yes Mistress," Christy said, looking at the floor.

"I want you to crawl into my bedroom, and without touching it with your hands, bring me the item that is on the bed."

"Yes Mistress," Christy replied and started crawling.

It wasn't a big apartment, and Christy didn't have too far to go, but Lauren enjoyed watching her girl crawl away from her, her generous ass disappearing into her room for a moment. She didn't take long to appear again, paddle in her mouth, still crawling, and a bit shamefaced.

She brought it to Lauren. She knelt before her with the paddle in her mouth and waited for her Mistress to take it. Lauren smiled at her, petted her head and hair, and said softly, "That's a good girl."

She could see Christy's eyes brighten just a bit. But Lauren made no move to take the paddle out of her mouth. She petted her girl's hair for a few long moments. Then she held out her hand in stop motion, said, "Stay," and left the room, leaving Christy kneeling with the paddle in her mouth facing away from Lauren's direction.

Lauren went to the kitchen and made noises like she was busy. She then silently walked back to the doorway between the rooms and watched her girl. Christy didn't move. She shivered a bit, but Lauren knew it wasn't cold in the apartment.

She let Christy sweat it for a bit, then she silently went back into the kitchen and not so quietly grabbed a kitchen chair. It didn't have arms so that it would be perfect for her needs.

She brought the chair out and set it in the middle of the living room floor. Of course, Christy couldn't see it as she was facing the other way, but she could hear. Lauren took a seat in the chair and said, "My girl, turn towards me."

Christy did, and Lauren could see her girls struggle. Not wanting it to be a hard test, she eased up on the tension. "Crawl over to me."

Christy did and knelt at her feet. Christy's drool was sliding down the edges of the paddle and onto her breasts. Lauren found that quite attractive but didn't stop to admire it long. She held out a hand, and Christy gently placed the paddle in it with her mouth and waited for her to take it.

Lauren took the handle gently and eased it out of her girl's mouth. Christy worked her mouth a little and swallowed a few times as she looked up at her Mistress a little fearfully.

"You know why you brought this to me?"

"Yes Mistress."

"And you know what I must do?"

"Yes Mistress."

"And you know why I must do it?"

"Yes Mistress."

With each agreement, Lauren could see Christy's shame at her failure.

"Crawl onto my lap with that ass in the air."

Christy did, seemingly eager for it to be all over. When she was positioned over her Mistress' knee, with her hands touching the floor on one side for balance, and her toes touching on the other, Lauren gently touched the paddle to her bottom. Christy flinched. She lifted the paddle off her girl's ass and put her hand on it instead, and she caressed it gently and massaged her girl's muscles. She lifted her hand and gently touched the paddle to her ass again. Again Christy flinched, expecting pain.

Lauren lifted the paddle again and brought it down with a "slap!" Christy cried out, more in fear than in pain as the paddle had been louder than painful. Lauren left the paddle sitting gently on her ass for a bit. Then she lifted it and replaced it with her hand, and softly, gently, caressed and massaged her girl's lovely ass. Then she lifted her hand and "SLAP!" Christy jumped and cried out again. It had hurt more this time. Lauren left the paddle on her ass for a minute. Then again, she replaced it with her hand. A few long moments of gentle caresses and soft touches, and then she lifted her hand again. "SLAP!" Christy cried out with real pain this time. Lauren left the paddle on her ass for a few moments and then lifted it. Christy's ass was a bit red. She caressed her girl's ass for a few moments and then said, "The lesson has been taught my girl. Don't make me repeat it."

"Yes Mistress," and Christy started crying.

Lauren pulled her up and led her to her bed and held her. When her cries petered out, Lauren began caressing her—teasing her. Sensuously, delicately, waking her nerves and arousing desire and passion in her. Lauren ran her fingers down her girl's body and began working on her pussy. It was drenched. Her finger slid inside her with almost no resistance. As if her girl were only waiting to open to her touch. She slid in a second finger, feeling the slickness, and the tightness of her girl's entrance, squeezing her two fingers. She fucked her girl with her fingers for a few minutes, and Christy began to whimper and moan and clutch at Laurens another arm. Lauren slid a third finger into her girl, and Christy moaned loudly. She moved down her girl's body and used the fingers of her other hand to caress Christy's clit. It wasn't long until Christy was cumming. Her muscles clamped down around Lauren's fingers, jamming them tightly, and one hand clutched at Lauren's shoulder. At the same time, her other squeezed the bedsheets as her cry of "IloveyouMistress" came out seemingly all in one word, but Lauren understood her.

Lauren held her tightly for a while. "Thank you Mistress," Christy said.

"You're welcome my girl."

"I love you," she whispered.

"I love you too," Lauren replied.

They lay like that for a while.

Lauren looked at her girl, who was snuggled close and sighed. And then she decided to implement her plan for the evening.

"Does my slave girl like games?" She asked her girl.

"Sometimes Mistress."

"I have an idea for a game that my sweet slave might like."

"Really Mistress? What is it?" Christy's curiosity was perked, and she was looking up so innocently that Lauren had to laugh.

"It's a kind of guessing game."

"Oh. I'm not good at those Mistress."

"Oh, I think you might like this one."

"Really? What is it?"

"Well, I really think we should discuss rewards and penalties for playing before I tell you more."

Christy's eyes widened at the word "penalty," "I don't want to be a bad girl anymore Mistress."

"No sweetie, I'm not going to punish you if you fail."

"Oh. Well what kinds of rewards and penalties are you talking about Mistress?"

"Well, here's what I was thinking my girl. You would have five opportunities to figure it out. The sooner you figure it out, the more rewards you will get."

"And if I fail in those five times Mistress?" Christy asked a little apprehensively.

"Then each time you fail I get a reward, which is your forfeit."

"What will the forfeit be Mistress?"

"Let's talk about that why don't we my girl? As well as the rewards? This is supposed to be a fun game so I don't want to go too heavy on the forfeit."

"Yes Mistress," Christy agreed.

They talked about what Christy liked, and then Lauren framed the game. "At the end of the game my dear, we are going to have some ice cream. You do like ice cream right?"

"Yes Mistress," Christy's eyes lit up.

"Ok. Now, you will have five opportunities to figure out the answer to what it is that I want. If you succeed on the first attempt, you will have all five rewards while you eat your ice cream."

"Do I have to eat fast Mistress?"

"No my girl, one of the rules, is that we can have as much ice cream as we want, (within reason), and we can take as long as we want to eat it."

"Oh goody," Christy said eagerly.

"So let's talk about five rewards that you might like." Lauren said.

They decided that Christy's most important reward, would be for Mistress to stroke and pet her hair and head while she ate. So Lauren said, "Ok my girl, then that will be the last reward. You will get that reward if you figure it out on the last attempt or sooner."

"Yes Mistress."

The next to last reward was having her Mistress caress her breasts and belly. "That will be the second to last reward."

"Yes Mistress."

The middle reward was that Christy would get to sit in Lauren's lap.

The fourth reward was that Lauren would caress Christy's clit on occasion, with the hand that was already to be caressing her breasts and belly.

And her last reward, which she would only get if she figured out the game on the first try, would be to have a vibrator turned on inside her as she ate her ice cream.

Christy's eyes sparkled as they discussed it all.

Then Lauren said, "Now, no matter what happens, we both get ice cream. But I get to eat my ice cream first."

"Of course Mistress." Christy agreed.

"Now here are my rewards, which will be your forfeits. Each time you fail to figure it out, out of the five chances you will get, will mean that I get one of my rewards, which is a forfeit for you. Understood?"

"Yes Mistress, but what kinds of things do you want?"

"I will tell you my girl. The most important one is the dish I eat my ice cream out of. I want a very special dish. So if you fail to figure it out on the first attempt, I'm going to have my special dish."

"But Mistress, none of our dishes are all that special."

"I'm going to have a very special dish my girl. I'm going to lie you on the table and I'm going to eat my ice cream off your belly."

Christy's eyes widened, and her mouth opened in a little 'o' shape, and her pussy twitched.

"Now the second most important of my rewards, will again, have to do with my dish. I don't want it moving around and spilling my ice cream. That would be bad wouldn't it?"

"Yes Mistress," Christy said a bit breathlessly.

"So if you fail on your second attempt, I'm going to tie my dish down. I'll bind your hands and feet so my special dish can't move. Understood?"

"Yes Mistress," Christy's breath was coming faster.

"Now my third reward, of course has to do with my special dish." Lauren said, and Christy was enthralled. "I like it that though my dish can't really escape, she might squirm a bit, so I'm going to put a brand new butt plug I bought today into my girls ass while I eat off my special dish."

"Yes Mistress," Christy blushed.

"Now my fourth reward, well, I won't want my dish tooooo comfortable," Lauren said with emphasis. "I'm going to put a pair of nipple clamps on my girl while I eat off my special dish."

Christy's eyes widened, and her breath came quickly.

"Yes Mistress," she breathed.

"And if you fail the last time, I want my last reward to be a very horny dish. So I will be putting a lovely vibrating egg in my girls pussy and a butterfly vibrator on her clit while I eat my ice cream from my very special dish."

Christy whimpered.

"There, now we've got the rewards for each of us. I think I'll get ready for the game. Why don't you go turn the tv on and I'll get comfortable?"

"Yes Mistress," Christy said, her chest still rising and falling raggedly.

Lauren wondered if Christy would want to lose more than win. In any case, she intended to give her girl a fair chance to lose.

She went into her room and stripped off her clothes and put on a babydoll camisole type nightie with no panties. She sprayed on just a bit of perfume, on her neck, a dab behind her ears, and just a small spray of it on her pubic area and around her vaginal lips. She smiled and returned to the living room.

Christy had the tv on and was sitting on the floor. Lauren shook her head and went and got a large cushion and had her girl sit on it. Christy thanked her by kissing her feet. Lauren smiled and petted her hair.

Then she got her purse and pulled out her camera. She used a wire to connect it to the tv, and in moments Christy was watching a little video of a lovely brunette masturbating on this very floor.

Christy turned beet red but watched intently. Lauren sat on the couch and waited until Christy was deeply involved. "My girl?" She said softly.

Christy didn't turn her head away from the scene she found so fascinating, and Lauren smiled. She took her hand down to her pubic area and tapped her pussy twice, making just enough noise. But of course, Christy's eyes were glued to the tv, and she didn't see the movement. She turned her head at the sound, but it was too late to have seen it. Lauren smiled at her. Christy smiled happily and then, with nothing else forthcoming from her Mistress, returned to her watching.

Lauren asked, "Do you like what you see?"

Christy blushed. "Yes Mistress," she said quietly.

Lauren let her get her watch until it ended. "Ok my girl, the floor is getting pretty dirty. Please sweep it."

"Yes Mistress," Christy said, looking up at her with a questioning expression for a moment, but then stood and went to get the broom and dustpan.

Once Christy was focused on the task she had been given, Lauren once again said, "My girl?"

Christy replied, "Yes Mistress?" As she glanced her way and then back to what she was doing. Of course, she missed Laurens double tap on her fair flesh, but she heard the sound once again and looked over at her Mistress with that questioning look. Lauren smiled at her. Christy began to look confused, but when her Mistress didn't do anything else, she went back to her task.

When Christy was done, Lauren thanked her and asked her to bring a chair from the kitchen. When Christy brought it in, she asked her where she wanted it. Lauren looked her in the eyes and held them with her will and said, "Gee, I don't know girl," and then tapped her pussy twice quickly and continued her speaking, "over by the door."

Christy hadn't noticed Lauren's fingers even though she had been looking at her. But she had heard the twin tapping sounds. She began to get very confused and began to wonder what exactly it was that her Mistress was after.

She put the chair down, and then her Mistress said, "No, I guess I don't want it in here after all my girl. Please take it back to the kitchen. "Yes, Mistress," said a poor and very confused girl. She picked it up, and as she had almost made it to the kitchen, her Mistress said, "My girl?"

Christy looked. She looked hard. Her Mistress was looking at her and smiling and asked, "I hope that chair isn't too heavy for you."

As she spoke, she held her girl's eyes and lightly tapped her pussy twice, making that double-tapping sound. Christy had been looking only at her face and hadn't quite seen her hands move in her peripheral vision. But she did look down. But by the time she looked down, Lauren's hand was back at her side. "Uhm, no.... uhm, Mistress. It's not heavy."

Lauren smiled and gave her a few long seconds to figure it out. But when she didn't, Lauren pointed to the kitchen, and she returned the chair. She came back and knelt at her Mistress' feet.

"What do you want to do now Mistress?" she asked, uncertainly.

"I want to eat my ice cream."

Christy's eyes opened wide, and she breathed, "Did I miss all five chances Mistress?"

"Yes my girl, you did."

"Oh," she said and looked down at the ground. Then, "What was it you were doing and why Mistress, if I may ask?"

Lauren spread her legs wide as she sat on the sofa and pointed to a spot on the ground and said, "Kneel right there please my girl and I will show you."

Christy knelt on the spot, which was right between Lauren's legs and about six inches away from where her feet rested.

Lauren said, "My girl?"

Christy looked up at her, and this time, she did notice her Mistress's hand moving. She heard the double taps and finally understood what her Mistress had been doing. Then she sat there for a moment, trying to figure out what it meant. Then her eyes lit up, and she crawled forward between her Mistress' legs and began to lick her pussy.

"That's exactly right my girl, but it will have to wait," Lauren said, taking her girl's head in her hand by the hair and gently pulling her back. "I did that five times already, and you missed it. I want my ice cream on my special dish."

Christy's eyes widened, and the thoughts of her failure evaporated as she looked ahead to what was scary, but also exciting. "Yes Mistress," she breathed.

Christy followed Lauren to the kitchen. Lauren had her wait there while she fetched her bag of toys. "Bend over my girl," she ordered. Christy did and soon felt cold, wet lube on her anus. Her Mistress inserted a finger, and Christy whimpered. It didn't exactly hurt, but she was confused about how it felt. After a minute, Lauren started moving her finger, and Christy decided that it didn't feel so bad after all. The more cold lubricant was added, and then Christy felt something much larger than a finger push into her hole. It was quite uncomfortable for a moment as she stretched and stretched, and then suddenly, her sphincter muscle closed around a part of the plug that was significantly smaller. She breathed a sigh of relief though she still felt it was a bit uncomfortable. But her pussy kept twitching.

"Spread your legs my girl, the egg is next."

Christy did so, and Lauren lubed up a little black egg with a wire on it and inserted it into her vagina with just the wire hanging out. It wasn't on. "Don't let it fall out my girl."

"No Mistress," Christy said, making sure to keep her vaginal muscles tight.

Lauren bent down at Christy's feet and said, "Lift your leg dear." "Now the other."

Lauren then pulled up a little butterfly looking thing, put it in place over Christy's mound, and wiggled it a bit until it touched her most sensitive flesh. It was held on by strings that held it in place directly over her mound. It was not turned on either. But Christy was beginning to be.

Lauren took out the play collar she had bought and fastened it around her girl's neck. It fit perfectly. "I guess that lady knew what she was talking about hmmm my girl?"

"Yes Mistress."

"Up on the table my girl." Lauren said, taking her hand and helping her up there. She lay her girl down with her head at the edge of one end, and her knees bent over the end of the other. She took out a pair of leather cuffs and held one up. "Arm." She said.

Christy held out a wrist to her Mistress. Lauren fastened the cuff around her wrist tightly, but with just a little wiggle room. "Other one." And she did the same to the other. She took a chain and pulled her girl's wrists behind her head and fastened them together through one of the d rings at the back of her collar.

She took a long silk scarf out of the bag and tied it to Christy's arm by the elbow, and then to the table leg and pulled just enough so that her elbow was held away from her face. Then she did the same to the other arm. Another long scarf was used to fasten one leg to one of the table legs, and a fourth, to tie her other leg to the opposite. Christy's legs were spread wide open, and her charms lay completely exposed. Lauren found her girl very inviting but restrained her desire.

She brought a pair of nipple clamps, with rubber covered ends, and a chain that linked the pair out and held them up for Christy to see. Christy's eyes widened.

Lauren set them on Christy's chest, one end resting on her breast's softness, and the other rested between her two mounds. Then she turned to Christy and smiled. "Now to get my ice cream," she said with obvious relish.

She dug around in the refrigerator for a few moments and brought out some stuff that Christy couldn't see, though she lifted her head as much as she could to look. Lauren got the ice cream out of the freezer, double chocolate with chocolate chips, and set it on one side of the table near Christy's hip. She then got a cutting board and placed it between Christy's legs. Christy's eyes were wide open as she saw her Mistress with a small knife. She was unable to tear her eyes away when her Mistress picked up something and showed it to her. A strawberry. "Need to trim these my girl." Christy whimpered and lay her head back.

She heard her Mistress cutting the green bits and stems off the strawberries, and she saw her put one in her mouth and close her eyes. "mmmm these are soo good. Would you like one my dear?"

Christy whimpered, "Yes please Mistress."

Lauren walked over to her head and held a plump and juicy looking just a few inches from Christy's mouth. Christy looked up at her, and Lauren smiled encouragingly. Christy lifted her head and gently took the strawberry in her lips. Lauren did not let go when Christy tried to pull it into her mouth. She looked at her Mistress, who smiled encouragingly, "Come on girl."

Christy started nibbling at it while Lauren held it in between finger and thumb. She sucked at it, and bit at it, taking small pieces of it off the whole, while her Mistress held it. "You're such a good girl," Lauren said as she watched her. After a time of nibbling, sucking, and biting, there wasn't much of the strawberry left. Lauren smiled at her and said again, "Good girl," took the rest of the strawberry, popped it into her mouth, and then returned to the other end of the table to finish cutting up the ones she seemed to plan on putting on her ice cream. Then Christy moaned as Lauren held up a banana. "Do you like banana's my girl?"

Christy whimpered, "Yes Mistress."

"I thought you did. Ice cream is so much better with a few slices of banana, don't you think?"

"Yes Mistress," she said as her breath seemed to catch.

Lauren spent a minute or two workings on the board between Christy's legs and then asked Christy, "Would my girl like a bit of banana?"

Christy smiled and said, "Yes please Mistress."

Lauren smiled in response and returned to her head. She held a healthy slice of banana just a couple of inches above her girl's mouth and looked down at her and smiled.

Christy lifted her head and gently lipped the slice and nibbled at it as she had done with the strawberry. When Christy had managed to eat half the slice through Lauren's fingers, Lauren let her have the rest and petted her hair. Then she returned to between Christy's legs. She worked there for a few moments and then moved the board back to the counter. "This is going to be soooooo good my girl. Don't you agree?"

Christy whimpered and whispered, "Yes Mistress."

Lauren put a few things next to the container of ice cream near Christy's hip.

She leaned over Christy's chest and picked up the nipple clamps. She opened one clamp and slowly let it clamp down on Christy's nipple. Christy squealed, and then breathed deeply. Lauren smiled and did the same with the other. "Owwww owwww owwww," Christy said, and then breathed deeply in and out.

Lauren smiled and then reached over to Christy's pussy and turned on the butterfly vibe. Christy whimpered. Then she turned on the egg. More whimpers.

"Alright my girl, I'm going to show you how I like my ice cream so pay attention."

Christy lifted her head to watch.

Lauren scooped out a large scoop of the ice cream and placed it directly on Christy's taught belly, right over her belly button. Christy whimpered at the feeling of wet cold touched her. Lauren smiled and dug out another scoop and placed it just above that one. Christy whimpered again. A third and final scoop was placed below that one making Christy whimper more. "Now I want my special dish to be careful not to spill my ice cream ok my girl? That would make me very sad, and we might have to start all over."

"Yes Mistress," Christy breathed.

"Now that we've got the ice cream in the dish, we add the strawberries," Lauren said, taking her time selecting just the right spots for five pieces of strawberry. "And now the bananas," she said and did the same with the banana slices.

"Do you think it's ready my girl?"

Christy was shivering a bit, but she didn't know if it was from the pain of the clamps, the cold of the ice cream, or the two vibes. She nodded and said, "Yes Mistress."

"Nope my girl. There is still something missing." Lauren held up a bottle of chocolate syrup. Christy giggled.

Lauren smiled as she poured a generous amount of chocolate syrup on her ice cream, letting plenty of it spill down the sides of Christy's belly, and some dripped down her belly toward her pubic mound. Christy gasped as the cold touched her and began to pool at the top of the butterfly vibe and run down her legs.

"There," Lauren said triumphantly. "Now it's ready. This is going to be sooooo good my girl."

All Christy could do was moan and whimper and shiver and shake.

Lauren sat on the edge of the table and gently inserted a spoon into the ice cream. Very slowly, she took a bit and put it in her mouth and closed her eyes and "mmmm" the come in enjoyment of it. She made a great show of enjoying it while her girl writhed and moaned and whimpered.

"I love this ice cream my girl. And the dish it has been served on is just divine."

Christy whimpered again.

Lauren dipped her finger in the chocolate sauce running down the sides of Christy's pussy and ran her finger through it, very, very, slowly. Then she made a great show of putting the finger in her mouth and enjoying the taste. "Oh my girl, chocolate flavoured pussy cream. Mmmmmmmmmm."

Christy whimpered again, and her body shook as she experienced a powerful orgasm.

"Did my special ice cream dish just cum?" Lauren asked innocently.

"Yes Mistress," Christy whimpered.

"Oh? I guess my dish is enjoying my ice cream as much as I am." Lauren smiled.

Christy lay her head back down on the table and moaned.

Lauren ran her finger through the chocolate syrup dripping down Christy's pussy again and held it over Christy's lips. "Would my girl like a taste of my chocolate flavoured pussy cream?"

Christy whimpered and said breathlessly, "Yes please Mistress."

"I don't know if I should give you any my girl. You don't seem to want it very badly." Lauren said and smiled a thin smile while her eyes laughed. She took another bite of her ice cream with her spoon while Christy began to beg. "Please Mistress, chocolate flavoured pussy cream sounds soooo good. May your girl please taste your magnificent creation?"

"That's much better my girl. I guess you do want some after all. You may lick my fingers clean."

"Thank you, Mistress," Christy said as she leaned her head up and began to lick the chocolate off Lauren's fingers. She was careful not to use her lips or take her Mistress' fingers in her mouth because her Mistress had been very clear in the permission she had given.

Lauren took another couple of spoonfuls of ice cream and ate them while she allowed Christy to lick her fingers.

She had been keeping an eye on the clock, and as she saw that it had been nearly twenty minutes since she put the clamps on her girl's nipples, she reached down with both hands and removed both clamps at the same time in a quick motion.

"Ooooowwwwwww," Christy cried.

"Yes my girl, I have heard that they are more painful coming off than going on." Lauren smiled. Then she returned to eating her ice cream.

She ate slowly and relished every last bite. Christy was shaking, shivering, moaning, and whimpering the whole time. She had two more orgasms before Lauren had eaten all the ice cream and fruit. Lauren smiled, "Almost done my girl, there is just all this chocolate syrup and melted ice cream left." She leaned over her girl and began delicately licking the syrupy mess from her girl's belly. It ran down her sides and down to her pussy and onto the table between her legs. When Lauren was confident that she had gotten enough of it off her girl's belly, she slowly followed the trail of chocolate syrup and melted ice cream down to her pussy. She gently moved the butterfly out of the way and began a proper clean up.

Christy was a moaning whimpering quivering mess. And Laurens tongue only made her more so. In minutes she was experiencing her third orgasm. Lauren pulled her head up and looked at her girl and smiled as her eyes laughed. "All done!" she said happily and turned off the egg. Christy moaned in relief and lay back and began to relax for the first time since the butt plug had been inserted.

Lauren carefully untied her girl, but left the collar on, and left the egg, off, and the butt plug, where they were. She led her girl to the bedroom, cuddled, and held her. She stroked her hair and told her softly how she was such a good girl and how much she loved her. Christy held her tightly at first and then relaxed into her arms and lay there in a bit of a daze and let her Mistress soothe and comfort her, and she knew that she was loved.

Christy didn't exactly lose track of time, but it ceased to matter. She lay there long. Lauren held her, petted and stroked her hair, and touched her gently, and whispered things in her ear for a long while. Then she fell silent and just held her, and the warmth of their love overshadowed the warmth of their bodies.

It got dark. And they remained as they were for a long while afterward. Finally, Christy stirred. She rolled so that she was facing her Mistress and kissed her shyly on the lips. "Mistress?" she whispered.

"Yes my sweet?"

"I love you."

Lauren tightened her arms around her for a moment and replied softly, "I love you too."

They lay there in silence for a bit, and Lauren worried about what would happen when this so-called "prophecy" of the end of the world didn't come. How would her girl react to that? What would her, well, weird, beliefs cause her to feel? How would she react?

That had been the deepest cause for all of Lauren's hesitation, she realized. She loved Christy. And she liked Dominating her as well. More than she had suspected, she could like that role. But there remained that fear of what would come to the day after "doomsday." She could not take it. She had to ask.

"My girl?"

"Yes Mistress?" Christy said, looking her in the eyes.

"What happens, on the outside chance, just supposing, that this prophet you saw was wrong and the world doesn't end in a week and a half?"

Christy smiled and shrugged. "The world's got to end sometime, Mistress," she said, shining brightly.

"That's exactly what Mark said to me my girr....." She looked at her girl hard, suspicion rising, and her heart trembling in fear. Christy smiled and snuggled tightly against her body and whispered again, "I love you Mistress."

Chapter 02

Lauren looked at her girl and pointed to the bed and said, "Stay!" Then she walked quickly out of the room. She put in a call to Mark, and when he answered, she demanded, "Have I been set up here?"

"What do you mean?"

"tonight after much fun and love, I asked Christy what would happen with us if the world didn't end next week. She answered with the same exact words you said to me last night!"

"Don't be angry Lauren dear. There was nothing done to hurt you. You can trust both of us on that."

"So I have been set up then!" she snarled.

"Well....."

"Get your ass over here, I want to talk to you and her together so I can get the straight of this."

"Demanding aren't we?" He said laughing, but before she could retort, he quickly went on. "I'll be right over. We love you Lauren. Twenty minutes."

And he hung up.

Lauren, suspicious and a bit put off, went to her room and said to her girl, "Mark will be here in twenty minutes. Go to your room until he gets here. I want to be alone for a while."

Christy hung her head, knelt, bent down, kissed Lauren's feet several times, and then did as she was told.

Lauren alternately worried and fumed. She turned on the tv and sat on the couch and worried and fumed.

She couldn't focus on the tv. She had no real idea of what was even on. It was just background noise to cover her fuming. Had she been set up? That much was evident at this point. Was it all some cruel joke? Neither Mark nor Christy was like that. But still. She'd been set up.

Almost exactly twenty minutes later, there was a knock at the door. She opened it to Mark, and he took her in his arms before she could say a word and said softly. "It wasn't meant to hurt you. It was meant to help Christy love you."

Lauren started crying a bit, and he held her tightly. She didn't cry long, and when she stopped, she pulled back and looked at him. "I'm going to hear everything, and you, could be in big trouble."

He smiled at her and replied, "If you and she end up happy in the end, I'll take it," He laughed.

She laughed with him and pointed to the couch. "Christy," she shouted, "Mark is here."

She sat down next to Mark on the couch and saw his eyes widen in surprise. She turned, and there was Christy, naked, in the process of gracefully kneeling. She was blushing and had her eyes down.

"What are you doing my dear?"

"Coming to visit with Mark as you wanted Mistress."

"You're not wearing any clothes Christy."

"Yes Mistress, you didn't tell me to put any on."

"What?"

"It's in the contract Mistress. 'The slave is not allowed to wear clothing in her Mistress' home unless her Mistress orders it."

Lauren shook her head, amazed at her girl's boldness.

"Well, I think you should have some clothes on as you've made Mark uncomfortable...." She started to say, and Christy started to get up to get some clothes, but Mark chipped in laughing.

"I think she's made you more uncomfortable than me Lauren," he laughed.

"Oh ya?" She asked, looking at Mark with a fire in her eyes. "Fine. Christy, stay!" She pointed to the ground where Christy was kneeling, and Christy returned to her place there and knelt back down.

Mark blushed red but laughed some more.

"Do you want a drink Mark?" Lauren asked.

"Sure. Beer?"

"Christy, get us all some beer please."

"Yes Mistress," Christy replied, standing gracefully and heading to the kitchen. The butt plug was visible, and Mark blushed and Lauren arched her eyebrow at him as if to say, "Want to play some more?"

"Brave girl," Mark said quietly.

He was smiling gently, and she did the same. "Yes," she replied, her attitude softening. "Especially considering her upbringing."

"Indeed," he replied.

Christy returned shortly with a tray with three beers on it. She knelt on the floor and put the tray in front of her. She picked up one of the bottles and knelt before her Mistress. She bowed her head and held the beer up to her in both hands. Mark looked at Lauren and raised one eyebrow. Lauren shook her head slightly and gently took the beer. "Thank you my girl," she said.

"You're welcome, Mistress," Christy replied and then served Mark the same way. He looked at Lauren, his blush plain, as she knelt before him, beer held in both hands. Lauren raised her eyebrow at him and nodded at Christy. He swallowed and took the beer, and thanked her. "You're welcome, Mark," she replied, then she picked up her beer and knelt back in her place at her Mistress' feet.

Lauren took a sip of her drink as did the other two, and then she held it in her lap and asked, "Ok, Exactly what is going on? You two set me up somehow, and I want the story." She looked at them sternly.

Mark looked at Christy and said, "It's mostly your story dear."

She nodded.

"Ok Mistress, it's a bit long, but I'll begin at the beginning."

"Good idea," Lauren replied sarcastically.

"Mistress, you know what I was like when I met you. Despite that, on the inside I had all these needs and desires that you have helped me free. I wasn't always nice. Anyway, after we settled that you weren't going to convert no matter what, everything went along fine, until I started loving you. It's been what? Four years that we've lived together? I fell for you about two years ago. And it got harder and harder on me and I prayed more and more. But the beliefs my church espouse did not help it go away."

Christy took a long drink of her beer and made a face at the taste. Then she went on.

"Anyway, about six months ago, I met Mark at a store while shopping. I recognized him immediately as he has been here often in the last four years Mistress. And we got to talking. I found out he was an ordained Minister, and was a druid, who believed all spiritual paths that aren't fundamentally evil, are valid. It was a weird concept for me Mistress."

"I bet it was my dear," Lauren said. She looked at Mark and asked, "And you didn't tell me any of this?"

"I couldn't. It all ended up under the seal of the confessional as things went. Even now that is all I am allowed to say as it is still sealed."

Lauren looked down at her naked, kneeling girl and replied, "But she can."

Mark laughed and agreed.

"To make a long story short Mistress, our discussion led to a lot of thinking, and in the end, I decided that my church was wrong about some things. I didn't know quite what to do about it, cause it's my church."

"Mark and I had more than one conversation over the next couple of months. And I ended up telling him my deepest secrets. And he was just as kind as you. And then, one evening I came home from bible group and your door was open Mistress. I peeked in to see if you were there, and you were loving someone. I knew I shouldn't watch, but I couldn't move away. You were quite rough with her. And she liked it. And you liked it. And then afterward, you were so tender. That sealed it in my mind and heart. And my prayers changed from 'help me not be this', to 'help me have this." Christy giggled. "I got my prayer answered."

Lauren laughed.

"Well, what was all this about doomsday then?" Lauren asked.

"Well, A few weeks ago I told Mark that I needed a way to be able to tell you. And he explained to me that you may be denying needs of your own so I might need to trick you into letting you be yourself."

Lauren gave Mark a dirty look. He held her gaze and asked quietly, "Well, was I wrong?"

She looked at him hard for a few moments and then spat, "ass. No, you weren't. I've had more fun with Christy in the Mistress role than I ever thought I could. Jerk." And she smiled to take the sting out of her words.

"But Christy, I thought you didn't believe in lying."

"I didn't lie Mistress."

"Oh no? So that guy on the youtube is a prophet then? And he's never been wrong?"

"I was told his predictions have never failed to come true Mistress."

"Oh? And who told you that?"

Mark laughed. "I did my dear. Then I suggested she not ask any questions about it." He laughed.

"Oh? So this guy is a prophet?"

"I have no idea. He might be. It IS in fact true that none of his predictions have ever been wrong before. But, then, this was his first one." He wasn't just smiling; his eyes were laughing. Lauren often wondered how he managed to be so expressive. His lovers must love that about him. She idly thought as she thought about whether or not she should be angry about the whole thing or not.

She stared back and forth between the conspirators, and finally gave in. "Fine. You're an ass Mark, and Christy, I fucking own you."

Mark laughed and drank down his beer, and Christy smiled up at her Mistress, and Lauren saw the sun shining out of her smile. "Yes Mistress, you do," she agreed.

"And you had better be a good girl, no more of this manipulation, not even if this ass is helping... no, especially if this ass is helping. Or I might have to invite him over for ice cream."

Christy blushed deep red and quietly said, "Yes Mistress."

Mark looked back and forth between the two women. Lauren was looking all hard but with laughter in her eyes, and Christy blushing deep red and looking at the ground but aroused. He knew he'd probably regret it, but he asked, "Ice Cream?"

"Oh do tell our wonderful, meddling friend about the ice cream Christy. Telling him, will be your punishment in your part of all of this, and hearing it, will be his." Lauren had that hard look still, so Christy explained as she blushed harder.

When she had finished, Mark had a poleaxed look on his face. Part disbelief and part wonder. "I may have to try something like that with Greg," He laughed. The two women joined in.

"So I know I'm going to regret this, but I have to ask, what all is in this contract, that Christy came and knelt naked while you ladies have company?"

"I have no idea," Lauren said sheepishly. "I never read it."

Mark laughed and almost spat beer all over.

"You signed it, agreed to it, took her as yours, and you never even bothered to read it? Bit hard by the love bug?" He laughed harder.

Lauren stuck her tongue out at him.

He set his empty beer bottle down and asked, "Are you two going to be alright?"

Lauren smiled at him, "Yes my friend, we are. Thank you for coming. And for everything."

"You are most welcome. And if it doesn't work out in the end, you can always blame your meddling friend."

"Oh I surely will," Lauren laughed.

"Christy, go and see Mark to the door will you? And lock up behind him. I have plans for my girl tonight."

"Yes Mistress," Christy said and got up.

At the door, she blushed and hugged him. "Thank you."

He was careful to only look at her face, but he smiled at her and replied, "You're welcome. I do hope you two will be happy."

She smiled. Then he locked the door after he left.

She returned to kneel at Lauren's feet and saw that her Mistress had the contract in her hand and was finally reading it.

Her face looked stern as she read it. She turned to look at her girl when she was done and asked softly, "Is this all really what you want? Or need?"

"It is what I found to be appropriate for slaves according to the culture Mistress."

"That isn't what I asked you."

Christy blushed and looked down and replied softly, "I am not really sure what it is I need Mistress, except to be yours. So far it has been absolutely wonderful."

"I understand my dear. I will consider this and as we get to know each other all over again. I will refine some of the rules to be more appropriate to us, rather than to convention of so called 'society'"

"Yes Mistress," Christy acknowledged. "It is your right to define and redefine our relationship based on the contract and your position within it and ownership of me."

"For now my girl, I am telling you that if we are to have company, that unless I tell you that I want you naked during their visit, you are to be clothed. You will follow the rules I have given you on what you are allowed and not allowed to wear. I really don't want to embarrass more of our friends." Then she laughed and said, "But Mark got what he deserved."

Christy giggled and replied, "Yes Mistress."

"And what about you my girl? What do you deserve for the plainly manipulative way you sprung that on me?" Mistress Lauren looked dead serious and stern, and Christy's heart leaped into her throat. Quietly she said, "Anything you feel is appropriate Mistress."

"Anything?" Mistress Lauren asked, arching her eyebrow.

"I belong to you Mistress," Christy whispered. "You have every right to do whatever you wish."

"Hmmm, I'll have to think about that," Mistress Lauren said with a twinkle.

"I will leave you to wonder what it is I am thinking. One day I will surprise you with it my dear. And my revenge will be soooooo sweet." Mistress Lauren said after a moment, as she looked at Christy with a raised eyebrow.

Christy blushed but said nothing.

"You know what my dear?"

"What Mistress?"

"You never got your ice cream."

Christy looked up at her with her surprise showing. "I guess after how you had yours Mistress, mine didn't matter."

"Oh yours matters my girl. I did say we'd both have some. And you do like ice cream don't you?"

Christy smiled, "Yes Mistress."

"Alright then, go get yourself a bowl," Lauren ordered.

"Yes Mistress," Christy smiled and stood and made her way to the kitchen, the butt plug still visibly in place.

Christy was gone for some time as Lauren reflected on what had happened. It seemed like a whole new life, and in a matter of a day. Oh well, she finally concluded, life is good.

Christ finally returned, and she had a bowl of the double chocolate, chocolate chip ice cream, strawberries, bananas, and chocolate syrup. Lauren smiled. Christy began to kneel, but Lauren shook her head. "No girl, I want you on my lap."

Christy smiled and sat on her Mistress' lap, the butt plug feeling somewhat uncomfortable in her ass.

"I see you found all my ingredients." Lauren laughed.

"Yes Mistress," Christy giggled, "My dish may not be as fancy as yours, but the ice cream will be good."

Her Mistress smiled and switched on the egg that was still inside her. Christy moaned as she felt it come to life. She looked at Mistress Lauren, smiling, and then she took a bite of her ice cream.

Lauren began caressing her girl's hair with one hand, and her front with the other. Christy moaned and said, "But I lost the game Mistress."

"So? I'm the Mistress aren't I?"

"Yes Mistress," Christy agreed, smiling at her with desire in her eyes.

Lauren caressed her breasts with the one hand while the other petted her girl's hair. Then she dipped her hand down between Christy's legs and caressed her clit, ever so lightly, and when Christy moaned and got distracted from her ice cream, she returned her hand to her girl's breasts. "something wrong my girl? Is the ice cream not good?"

"The ice cream is fine Mistress," she moaned as Lauren's fingers took a nipple between them and rolled them between finger and thumb.

"Then why aren't you eating it my dear?"

Christy blushed and took another bite.

And that went on for quite a while. Christy would just start eating, and her Mistress would pleasure her in ways that begged her attention, leaving her ice cream to melt in the bowl while she moaned and squirmed.

Then Lauren changed tactics. When Christy went to take a bite, Lauren quickly moved to stimulate her clit. Coupled with the vibe inside her, and the hair petting, Christy paused with the spoon halfway to her mouth. Lauren smiled and kept going. Christy moaned and whimpered and looked lustfully at her Mistress as she played her girl. The spoonful of ice cream was forgotten, and it began to melt and drip onto Christy's breasts. Lauren said not a word but stopped so she could finish her bite.

Lauren repeated the process for every bite for the next little while, and though it didn't always work. By the time Christy finished, she was nearly covered in melted chocolate and syrup.

Christy looked at the empty bowl, then her Mistress, and then herself. "Oh no Mistress, I got chocolate all over. Even on you."

"I guess we'll just have to have a shower then my girl," Lauren smiled.

They headed toward the shower, and Lauren undressed and threw the clothing in the laundry. She then removed the plug from her girl's ass but didn't remove the egg. They got into the tub, but instead of turning the shower on, Lauren licked the chocolate off her girl. Christy moaned and whimpered. She longed for it to continue forever, but it was only a few minutes before Lauren was done. She kissed her girl roughly, and her tongue penetrated her girl's mouth, invading, and exploring. Christy responded after a moment of surprise, and they stood kissing each other deeply.

Lauren reached over and turned the shower on. Coldwater sprayed her girl since her girl was standing with her back facing the showerhead. She yelped, but Lauren held her still by the back of her hair and continued kissing her. Christy broke out in goosebumps, but Lauren didn't let her move, and the cold, and the kiss, made her shiver. It didn't take too long for the water to warm, and Christy felt the warmth increase her arousal.

She was getting very aroused when suddenly Lauren grabbed the body wash and sponge and started washing her. Christy moaned her disappointment, but Lauren gave her a stern look, and she stifled it. Lauren gently, and at times, not so gently, washed her girl clean, making her lift her feet and then bending her over so that the water cascaded down her back as she washed her girl's ass. When Christy was clean, Lauren handed her the body wash and sponge, and Christy gently washed her Mistress.

After washing her Mistress's upper body, Christy knelt with the water cascading over her head and down her face and back, as she gently soaped up her Mistress' legs. Lauren lifted her feet one at a time for Christy to wash properly, and she made sure to get between each of her toes.

Once her Mistress was clean, Christy moved to get up, but Lauren grabbed her head and pushed her back down. Christy didn't quite know what she wanted until she saw her Mistress' hand tap her pubic area twice. She giggled and moved forward and began to lick her Mistress' pussy.

Her tongue found her Mistress' center and eagerly lapped up her juices. Lauren's knees felt weak, so she lay with her head against the inflated pillow at the back of the tub. Christy knelt further down to continue pleasuring her, and the shower spray cascaded over her head and shoulders, as well as

Lauren's belly. Lauren moaned. She brought herself out of her pleasure for just long enough to ask, "Are you alright, my girl? I don't want you to drown."

"Mmm hmmmm," Christy hummed in the affirmative without leaving her duties.

"Good," Lauren replied and moaned, sinking back into that moment of heaven.

While her tongue gently licked her Mistress' clit, Christy held her right hand under the falling water and after making sure they had no remnants of soap on her fingers, quickly shoved two fingers into her Mistress' sopping vagina.

Lauren's eyes were nearly closed, but she kept an eye on her girl throughout, and the sight of her beautiful girl licking her as the water cascaded over her head added to her pleasure. It wasn't long before she came. She cried out, and her head went as far back against the inflated pillow as she arched her back. Christy felt her Mistress' opening tighten and spasm around her fingers, and she felt great pride in the pleasure she had brought her.

"Stop," Lauren ordered, and of course, Christy obeyed. She knelt back on her heels and waited while the water ran over her head, down her face, breasts, and back. Lauren lay there with her eyes closed for a few moments and then looked at her girl. Seeing her kneeling in the shower spray tickled her sense of humor, and she laughed and moved to get up. From a standing position, she grabbed her girl's collar and pulled until she too was standing. She shut the shower off, and they dried each other gently and then stepped out of the tub.

Lauren bent her girl over and put the plug back inside her and patted her bottom as her girl stood.

"Come, my girl, I want more," Lauren ordered, and Christy followed her Mistress to her bedroom.

In the bedroom, Lauren pointed at the floor beside her side of the bed. "Kneel there my girl."

Christy knelt in the position she had learned online, her knees spread, her back straight, her chest thrust out, with her eyes down and her hands on her thighs, palms up.

"You're such a good girl," Lauren said softly.

Christy smiled.

Lauren left the room for a couple of minutes, and when she returned, she rummaged around in the shopping bags she had left in her closet.

A few minutes later, Christy could see Lauren's feet as she stepped over to her. "Alright my girl, up on the bed, face down. We're going to play."

Christy smiled and got up onto the bed and lay face down. Lauren grabbed her feet and pulled her until her shins hung over the edge of the bed. Her head was placed in the middle of the bed.

"Hands," Lauren ordered.

Christy moved her hands behind her back, and Lauren attached cuffs just above her elbows and on her wrists.

She attached chains from each wrist cuff to each elbow cuff, and in moments, Christy's hands were effectively bound behind her back.

"You ok my girl?"

"Yes Mistress."

"Good. Feet," she ordered.

Christy lifted her legs toward her ass, and she felt Lauren attach cuffs to her ankles, and heard and felt the various chinking that indicated a chain had been attached between them.

Lauren then dipped her finger into Christy's pussy and found it sopping wet. "Like this do you my girl?" She asked.

"Yes Mistress, bondage has always been one of my fantasies."

"Well, have you heard of predicament bondage?"

"Sort of Mistress. I'm not really sure what that is."

"Well, what it is, is that the Dominant, in this case me, binds the slave, in this case you, in such a way as to create a predicament, that if the slave fails, there are consequences."

"I don't understand Mistress. You haven't put me in any kind of 'predicament.'"

"Not yet. That part is coming. But I want to explain the rules to you first to give you a fair chance."

"Thank you Mistress."

"I am going to tie a string, from the chain between your ankles, to the butt plug. Your job is to keep your feet close enough to your ass that the plug isn't pulled out. That is your predicament."

"I understand Mistress, and what are the consequences if I fail?"

"I'm not done yet my girl," Lauren said. "I am then going to lay on the bed, with my pussy in your face, and you are going to eat me to three, count them, three, orgasms. You must not pull the plug out, and you must warn me if you are about to cum. Because the other rule, is that you are not allowed to cum, before I have cum three times."

"I understand Mistress." Christy said, a slight tremor in her voice.

"Good girl," her Mistress replied and then fiddled with something at her feet and with the plug for a few moments.

"There my girl, you have a little bit of slack, thanks to the chain between your ankles, and from the cord attached to the plug. Make sure to keep still."

"Yes Mistress, and what if I fail?"

"That depends on how you fail my girl. If you cum without permission, you will be punished, and harder than I punished you earlier."

"Yes Mistress," Christy said in a quiet voice, and Lauren went on.

"You are not allowed to remove your mouth from my pussy unless you are unable to breathe. In order for me to know that you are near orgasm, you are to alert me by making three short whimper type noises, but make them loud enough that I can hear them."

"Yes Mistress."

Lauren demonstrated a sound that was almost a whimper, and almost a bark but done without opening her mouth or enunciating sounds. Christy repeated the sounds, and they sounded decidedly puppyish coming from her. "Good girl. That is the sound you are going to make when you get close."

"Yes Mistress."

"Now, the other way you can fail, is to let the plug come out. The punishment for that failure will be to have to wear a larger plug from now on, and no orgasm for the rest of the night. No matter how much more fun we have," Lauren stated, and paused for a moment before going on. "And I warn you my pet, I intend on having a long session tonight. I have been sexually frustrated for a while and I have a lot of sexual energy to release tonight. Any questions?"

"Just one Mistress. Do I get a reward if I succeed?"

"Well, do you consider an orgasm a reward my girl?"

"Yes Mistress."

"Then yes you do."

"Oh goody," Christy said impishly.

Mistress Lauren stripped off her clothes and lay on the bed, with pillows propping her back, and after a few moments of wriggling into a place, she settled on the bed with her spread legs surrounding Christy, and her pussy pressing hard against Christy's mouth.

Christy saw she had something in each of her hands but couldn't tell what without risking losing her mouth's position on her Mistress' pussy so she disregarded it and focused on her Mistress' pussy..

"Lick," Lauren ordered.

Christy began licking and lapping at her Mistress' pussy. Her Mistress' juices tasted wonderful despite a slightly astringent taste, and for a little while, she lost herself in pleasure and was giving her Mistress. Then she felt her Mistress's hands on her head. "In order to make sure you focus completely on your task, I am going to blindfold you my girl." Lauren said, and Christy's vision was darkened as what seemed to be a sleeping mask was hooked in place.

With her sense of sight gone, her Mistress' taste, and smell, and the soft silk that her tongue enjoyed seemed just slightly more than they were. Then she heard her Mistress speak. "I am going to talk to you as we do this my girl. I will not only give you direction and teach you how to lick my pussy properly, but I will discuss fantasies, present scenario's, and ask you questions. When I have asked you a question, or if you like something in particular, you may respond with a whimper in the positive. One simple 'Mmmmm" to indicate the affirmative, or pleasure in the idea. Do you understand?"

Christy replied, "Mmmmmmm," with that positive and pleasant tone that indicated affirmative.

"As well as that, if you need to answer in a negative manner, I want you to whimper the double 'mmm hmm' that most people would take as negative. Do you understand my girl?"

"Mmmmmmm."

"Alright, demonstrate the negative for me my girl," Lauren ordered.

Christy moaned, "Mmm Hmmmm."

"You're such a good girl," Lauren stated with obvious pleasure in her husky voice.

"You really lick pussy quite well my girl."

"Mmmmmmmmm," Christy said.

"But what I teach you, will make you better," Lauren laughed.

For the next ten or fifteen minutes, Lauren gave direction. "Nibble my clit. Tongue my entrance. Long licks, from bottom to top. Suck on my clit, but gently. While you hold my clit in your lips, and nibble it, flick it with your tongue. Faster. Faster."

In each case, Christy obeyed as best she could. As she did, she found herself getting more and more aroused. And she felt a deep feeling of fulfillment in bringing her Mistress this pleasure. Every once in a while, she felt a tug at her anus. As she lost herself in what she was doing and let her feet move too far from her ass, and the cord put pressure on the plug. Each time she moved her feet so that they touched her ass, and tried to focus more of her attention on keeping them in place.

Then as Christy plied all of her lessons on her Mistress' pussy, her Mistress began to let little moans escape her. Christy refocused on her Mistress' pleasure and made every effort to please her.

Then Mistress Lauren started talking again. "Now I know you didn't like being punished my girl, I could tell that easily simply from the hangdog look on your face, but the pain got you wet didn't it?"

'Mmmmmmmm.`

`Now, do you think you'd like it if I occasionally felt like causing you some pain once in a while, just for fun?"

"Mmmmmmmmm."

"Oh you're becoming such a good pussy licker," Mistress Lauren moaned. "Maybe that's what I'll call my slave girl. 'Mistress Lauren's pussy licker.'"

"Mmmmmmmm."

"It's not much of a proper name though is it my girl?"

"Mmm Hmm." And Christy had to bring her feet back against her ass as she felt the tug on the plug again.

"But it is, very descriptive, and accurate."

"MMmmmmmmmmm."

"Oh these sounds you make are so lovely my girl, very puppyish really."

"Mmmmmmmmmmmmmm."

Lauren took note of the length of that expression of pleasure and made a mental note to determine if her girl had any desire for puppy girl play.

And then Mistress Lauren was coming.

"Ooohhh you're such a good pussy licker."

"Mmmmmmmmm."

Christy felt the tug on the plug and jerked her feet back into place as her Mistress' thighs clamped around her ears. She found it a bit hard to breathe for a few moments as her Mistress came, and her body quivered, and her legs trembled as they clamped down on Christy's head.

"Stop," Mistress Lauren ordered when she had more than enough. "Just for a few moments my girl. You have done well."

Mistress Lauren spread her legs wide again, and Christy could breathe easier as her Mistress relaxed. She did not remove her mouth from her Mistress' pussy.

"That is orgasm number one down, and only two to go. But the game will get just a little harder now. Remember the sound you are supposed to make if you are close to coming."

"Mmmmmmmmmm"

"Mmmm, you're such a good girl my pet. I'll have you licking pussy like a pro in no time," Lauren teased her.

"Mmmmmmmmmm," was Christy's reply, and her mouth was unmoving, pressed tightly against her Mistress' pussy.

"Now you may start again my girl, but remember that the game will get harder," Mistress Lauren said.

Christy started licking again, and in a few moments, she almost jerked her head back, and she felt a hard tug on the plug in her ass as her feet moved in response to the sudden feeling of the egg inside her vibrating. She got her legs under control and pressed her feet tightly against her ass, and her mouth continued its work.

The entire situation was making her very aroused. She was breathing very heavily into her Mistress' pussy as she licked and nibbled and sucked. Soon she was very close, and Lauren heard her whimper, "Mmmm mmmm Mmmmm," quite loudly.

Lauren quickly turned off the vibrating egg via her remote. "Is that better my dear?" She asked.

"Hmmmmmmm," Christy sounded as her mouth continued.

A short while later, the egg started again, and Christy had to quickly pull her feet back toward her ass as she felt the plug begin to move. She squeezed her anal muscles and tried to make sure it was set solidly in its place.

This time it did not take long for Christy to give her little whimpering bark. "Mmmm mmmm mmmmm," she sounded, and Lauren turned the egg off and patted her girl's hair. "You're such a good girl. I'm getting really close. Seeing you blinded and bound, and at my mercy, is having an almost narcotic effect on me. I think this is a game we will play a lot."

Then the egg was turned back on. Christy had been expecting it this time, so her reaction wasn't as intense, and the plug did not move.

A very short time later, Christy gave her whimpering bark three times, and Lauren shut the egg off. She left it off only for a minute, and then Christy became a moaning whimpering mess as she licked her Mistress. Lauren was soon moaning and whimpering herself. She almost missed Christy's whimpers that told her she was close and shut off the egg just before Christy went over the edge.

Lauren brought Christy to the edge three more times in maybe seven or eight minutes, and then she was cumming. She grabbed Christy's hair in both hands and pushed her face into her pussy, grinding her nose and tongue. Christy could barely breathe, but she kept on licking. Lauren held her there for only a short while as she soon couldn't take anymore. Then she released Christy's head and ordered her to stop.

"Very good my girl, that's two," Lauren softly said when she came down from her climax. "Now the game will get harder."

"Hhhmmmmmm." Lauren heard a distinctly worried tone in that.

After a minute of rest, Lauren tapped her pussy twice, and Christy started licking again.

Snap! A vicious sting hit her back, and she cried out loudly into Lauren's pussy. Her feet had jerked back some, and she could feel the plug pulling and slipping. She jerked her feet back to her ass, but the plug was no longer settled properly. She squeezed her sphincter around it and wiggled her ass, trying to get it settled.

"Having trouble my girl?" Lauren asked in a sympathetic tone.

"Hmmm."

"It didn't come out did it?"

"mmm mmm." Christy said as she continued licking.

The egg suddenly turned on, and Christy moaned into her Mistress' sex.

Snap! Christy cried her muffled cry but pulled her legs toward her ass this time, and though the plug wasn't quite back in position, it didn't come any further out.

Snap!

Snap!

Snap!

Christy's back was sore from whatever it was Lauren. I was hitting her with, but she was soooo close. "Hmm hmmm hmmm," Christy whimpered, and the egg was turned off.

Snap!

Snap!

Snap!

Christy's cries only served to make Lauren hotter. While she wasn't truly sadist, Christy's predicament and her efforts to please her served to make her hotter than she'd ever been.

"Ok my girl, it's going to get harder one last time. The egg isn't going off again, and I'm going to hit you fast and hard. And I'm not stopping till I cum."

"Hmmmm," Christy moaned in her worried tone again, and her efforts at pleasing her Mistress doubled in intensity. She licked furiously and nibbled and sucked and flicked Lauren's clit with her tongue.

The egg came on, and Christy moaned. Snap! Snap! Snap!

Christy's cries vibrated on Lauren's clit, and her tongue never stopped. Christy's feet were clenched, and her heels were digging into her ass to make sure the plug didn't come out.

Lauren was getting very close now, so she hit harder and faster. Snap! Snap! Snap! Snap! Snap.

Christy whimpered, "hmmm hmmm hmmm," and Lauren knew she was close. But Lauren was close too. It was a race. She figured that since Christy wasn't a masochist, the pain would keep her from going over the edge, so she hit harder and faster. Snap! Snap! Snap! Snap! Snap! Snap! Snap! Snap! Snap! Snap! And then she was cumming. She turned the egg off with the remote as she came and pulled herself out of reach of Christy's tongue, which kept licking thin air for a moment before Christy knew that she could no longer reach.

"You are such a good little pussy licker my girl. And you passed. You get to have an orgasm tonight. Isn't that great?"

Christy whimpered, "Hmmmmmmmmm."

"You can talk now sweetie."

"Thank you Mistress. Yes that's great. I'm soooooo hot right now Mistress."

"I bet you are. I lost count of the times you got close."

"Me too Mistress, but I'm ready to cum anytime you wish to allow it," Christy giggled.

Lauren laughed, "I bet you are."

"But first I want to play another game."

Christy moaned as the egg turned back on.

"What is the game Mistress?"

"It's called, drive Christy to distraction with desire."

"I don't know if I like the sound of that game Mistress."

"Oh but that doesn't really matter does it my girl? I mean, I'm the Mistress and what I say goes. Right?"

"Yes Mistress," Christy replied.

"Good," Lauren said, and the egg turned on. "Don't forget to warn me in your usual way before you cum girl."

"Yes Mistress."

A few minutes later, Lauren turned the egg off when Christy gave her three whimpers. And a minute later turned it back on. And off and on. And off. Lauren brought Christy to the edge of orgasm over and over. Christy lost count of how many times she got close: how many times she gave her little

359

puppy-like whimpers. She became a writhing, moaning, sweaty mess. All she knew was desire, and that she wasn't allowed to cum.

Finally, just as she got close again, she heard her Mistress whisper in her ear. "Cum my girl. Cum for me." This time the egg was not turned off. Lauren reached between Christy's legs and gently caressed her clitoris with her second finger, and her thumb penetrated her vagina and stimulated her g-spot.

Christy came, moaning her climax loudly enough that it was almost a scream. Lauren kept stimulating her clit and g-spot and left the egg on. "Keep cumming my girl. Keep cumming. Let all that sexual tension find release."

Christy's orgasms came and went in waves. But they kept coming, and receding, and returning. Finally, Christy begged, "Please Mistress, I can't take anymore."

Lauren laughed but didn't stop. "First you want to cum, and then you want to stop," she teased as Christy rode another wave until it receded. But she could tell Christy really couldn't take much more, so she turned the egg off and pulled her hand away from Christy's sex. She pulled the plug out of her ass, unchained her wrists and ankles, and then pulled her blindfold off and lay down in bed with her. She took her in her arms and held her trembling girl and comforted her. "I'm so proud of you my girl. You did very well. You're alright now. Everything is ok now."

Christy lay in her arms quietly, her only movement her deep, and somewhat ragged breathing. But after a few minutes, her breathing slowly began calming, and a few minutes later, it was back to normal. She finally moved. She looked up at Lauren and smiled. "Oh my god Mistress."

"Hmmm?" Lauren asked without words.

"That was something. You sure know how to torture someone without a huge amount of pain."

"Well, I did flog you my dear."

"Yes Mistress, but actually that helped keep me from cumming. It was being so close to the edge, and wanting and needing to cum so badly that was the real torture Mistress."

"I could tell my dear," Lauren said with a throaty chuckle.

"And the orgasm was incredible. And then you wouldn't let me stop!"

Lauren laughed again.

"But it was good Mistress. Thank you."

"You're such a good girl," Lauren said, petting her hair.

They lay together with Lauren, petting Christy's hair for a while. When Christy fell asleep, Lauren remained as she was for a long while afterward. Finally, she moved Christy a little to the side, stripped off her clothes and turned out the light and got into bed with her and covered them both with a blanket, and soon was asleep.

Her last thought before falling asleep was a delicious thrill at the thought of how she would be woken up in the morning.

Forceful Lesbians
02 Erotica Novellas for Adults
Alannah Kieran

All Rights Reserved. No part of this publication may be reproduced in any form or by any means, including scanning, photocopying, or otherwise without prior written permission of the copyright holder. Copyright © 2020

This book is entirely a work of fiction. The names, characters and incidents portrayed in it are the work of the author's imagination. Any resemblance to actual persons, living or dead, events or localities is entirely coincidental.

Story 01

Chapter 01

As the plane banked over the Jutland peninsular and made its final descent into Aarhus Tirstrupt airport, I felt the first pangs of trepidation. My parents fully supported my determination to place myself in the hands of Agnetha Madsen. But they were unaware that it was a decision based as much on the current complications with my love life as it was on my desire to become a world champion.

I walked through into the arrivals lounge and immediately recognized Larina, but she did not return my smile. She helped me with my bags and left it to me to make the best of a rather one-sided conversation as she drove the short distance out to the training facility.

She showed me to the room that was to be my home for the next twelve months and then left me alone. It was a little spartan, but it offered a lovely view out over the frost tinged lawn to the lake.

I turned away from the window and caught my reflection in the mirrored wardrobe door. Somehow the image did not seem like the real me, and in some ways, it had not been for the past two years. I had secured sponsorships from a cosmetics company and a major fashion chain, and now it was incumbent upon me to look the part.

To some degree, this is what attracted had me to Agnetha. The girls she was training, Larina included, somehow managed to maintain their femininity while still producing medal-winning performances; for the first time in years, the female robots coming off the Far Eastern production lines had some real competition.

After I had unpacked, I took a deep breath and set off for my first meeting with the woman who would determine whether or not I would achieve my life's ambition.

My room was one of four on the third floor, and as I passed my neighbor's door.

I was brought up short. At first, I thought that someone was in pain, but, as I instinctively stopped and strained my ears, I realized my mistake.

"Oh fuck!...Yes!...Don't stop!"

I smiled to myself, thinking that someone was breaking one of Agnetha's cardinal rules. Her regime was strict; I had been sent a list of infractions, any one of which would lead to my expulsion from the facility. The top of that list was a total ban on male visitors in the accommodation block.

I knew that I should have passed on by, but there was no one else around, so I stepped closer to the door and cocked my ear.

"Oh God!....That's it!....Now!....I'm coming!"

Each imprecation was louder than the last, and it was clear that the girl did not care who heard her slow rise to ecstasy. As she let out a final piercing shriek, I found myself feeling decidedly jealous.

I had not had sex for nearly six weeks, and even that had been a furtively snatched bout before John's wife came to collect him from the gym. Having an affair with my trainer had been a distinctly bad idea, and the more so as I became increasingly convinced that he was lying when he said that he loved me.

I ran my hand firmly over the front of my abbreviated skirt to try and quell the increasing tingling in my crotch, and then I pulled myself together. I skipped downstairs, and less than two minutes later, I was standing nervously outside Agnetha's office.

I knocked and entered, and Agnetha rose to greet me. The office itself was large, light, and airy. The furniture was all bleached pine, and the rear wall was a single huge glass panel beyond which the wooden flooring extended to form a patio deck. Against this background, my new trainer was a dark presence.

She had always kept her hair cropped during her playing days, but she had now grown it out into a heavy black bob, which softened her features. She had used a dark eyeliner to emphasize her deep blue eyes, and her full lips were enriched with a lustrous red lip gloss. It was hard to believe that this beautiful woman was the same player that the press had christened "The Viking."

She was wearing a black tracksuit, which sat a little incongruously with her impeccable make-up, but it was obvious that she still kept herself in great shape. She topped me by two or three inches, but she somehow seemed taller still, and, had I not known that she was twice my age, I would have thought her years younger.

She smiled warmly, asked me about my flight, and then she got down to cases.

"You've heard the rumours, you've seen my stipulations, if you are not prepared to play by my rules you can leave whenever you like. That said, you have a paid a years fees in advance and that is non refundable."

She was talking a lot of money. Her fees were more than double what I was paying in the UK. On top of that, I had to fund my living costs, including accommodation at the center. She was also looking for a larger percentage of prize winnings, but if her record with other girls was anything to go by, I could look forward to more success.

"Whilst you are here you will learn about physiology and sports psychology as well as fitness training and tactics. For your first two weeks you will not touch a racket."

She must have seen the look of surprise on my face as she said this because she leaned forward to emphasize her next point.

"Look, it's your choice, you can either be another Kournikova or you can be a gold medalist. What is it to be?"

The jibe was double-edged. I hated being compared to a tennis player and particularly Kournikova. The press had made much of my resemblance to the young Russian and the danger that, like her, I could fail to achieve but still make a living from endorsements. I had already been offered a small part in an independent British film, and my natural vanity had almost led me to accept.

The next morning I reported to the treatment room where I was introduced to Tamiko, a young Japanese woman, who acted as the center's physiotherapist. For nearly two hours, she talked me through the nature of muscle groups and particularly those governing the wrists and legs. I was having trouble taking it all in and was still confusing the flexor carpi redialis and flexor carpi ulnaris when she told me to strip off and lie down on the massage table.

I lay face down, with only a small towel to protect my modesty, as she illustrated the remainder of her lecture with the movements of her hands. I have had many massages, usually as a prelude to a big game, but I had never experienced anything quite like Tamiko's touch. She talked me through what she was doing, but I was afloat in a world of my own. She was running her fingers just over the surface of my skin so that the tiny, almost invisible hairs erected under a static charge, and then she stroked more firmly, coaxing each muscle group in turn.

It was so relaxing, and I felt like a cat stretching out its spine. As she worked over my shoulders and her fingertips brushed the edges of my breasts, I began to think of John, and I squirmed slightly to alleviate a growing itch between my legs. She cautioned me to keep still, but now I just wanted it to be over so that I could get back to my room and bring myself some much-needed relief.

She continued for another quarter of an hour, and I was growing ever more frustrated. I had never entertained the notion of making love to another woman, but with a guilty inward smile, I wondered what Tamiko would be capable of. Immediately dismissing this unworthy thought, I tried to concentrate on what she was saying.

Our session was brought to a close by the return of the girls from their on-court training, and I dressed quickly in the hope of slipping away, but Tamiko had other ideas.

Larina came through from the changing rooms looking decidedly hot, and with no hint of embarrassment, she stripped out of her sweat-soaked sports kit. I just had time to notice that she was a natural blonde before lying down on the table that I had so recently vacated.

Tamiko beckoned me to her as she began to work at Larina's muscles heedless of the sweat that sheened her skin. She had her eyes closed, but I could see, from the expression on her face, that she was enjoying the magic feel of the Japanese woman's fingertips.

I was still appraising Larina's lean, tanned body when I realized that I was being asked to help. I placed my hands tentatively on the back of her left calf and tried to emulate what Tamiko was doing to the right leg. I was immediately aware of the smoothness of her skin and the curvature of her muscles. She had a superb tone, but it was so very different from a male physique's hardness.

I found my hands moving a little higher, and Tamiko remonstrated with me, but I am certain that Larina gave a tiny sigh. I suddenly felt a little annoyed that she should be enjoying it quite so much as if I were some sort of body slave, but I had to remind myself that I had been in a similar position just a few moments earlier. I resumed my ministrations carefully following Tamiko's instructions.

She had spoken to me about "muscle flutter," the moment when a tensed muscle is coaxed to relax under the fingertips and resonates very slightly. My clumsy fingers could not perceive this subtle change, and Tamiko was showing signs of exasperation.

Her hands were now working the hams in the back of Larina's thigh, and she encouraged me to follow suit. I was feeling uncomfortable, not least because of Larina's nakedness and the fact that Tamiko's fingers were edging closer to the crease of her buttocks.

She was still asking me if I could feel the transition, and I was tempted to lie, but then a frown of anger creased her face.

"Do this."

I watched incredulously as she leaned forward and placed the tip of her tongue high up on the back of Larina's thigh.

She straightened up and stopped what she was doing, waiting for me to give it a try. After a second or two, she clicked her tongue and then spoke to me as if I were a simpleton.

"Do it. Your tongue is more sensitive than your fingers."

I remained frozen for a second or two, but then I copied what she had done.

Larina's skin was slightly salty, but she was immaculately depilated, and it was such marked contrast to John's coarse hirsute legs. Without thinking, I moved my tongue slightly over the surface only to hear an audible moan.

I stood up instantly and caught a slight smile on Larina's face. I stormed out of the treatment area and went straight back to my room. Within ten minutes, Agnetha was on the phone. She told me in no uncertain terms that I was to do what Tamiko asked of me exactly, or I was to leave. Two minutes later, I had most of my items stuffed hurriedly into my suitcase, but then my anger passed, and I started to think more rationally.

I guess that, in part, my anger was fuelled by the fact that, at nineteen, Larina was my junior by only a couple of months, but there was no doubting that her progress under Agnetha's tutelage had been spectacular. I was world ranked eighth, and she had come from nothing to sit just a couple of places below me.

I went back to Tamiko and assisted as she warmed down the other two trainees.

For the next few days, I felt like a nun. I worked with Tamiko during the day and took my evening meals with the other girls in the refectory. They made polite conversation, but I felt the outsider very much. Of course, there was a certain irony in this because I was regularly seeing them naked, and Tamiko had made me repeat the trick of using my tongue to check for tension. I began to harbor the suspicion that they each looked forward to that part of the session, and I could not shake the feeling that I was being mocked.

They invited me into town, but I got the sense that they were simply polite, and so I spent my evenings reading or watching DVDs on my laptop before masturbating myself to sleep. My problem was that, in trying to rid myself of memories of John, I found myself thinking of the treatment room, and particularly the daily massages I received from Tamiko, as I reached a climax.

On the fifth morning, I reported to the treatment room as usual, but something was different. Tamiko, who had, up to then, always presented herself with her hair tightly, and sensibly, bound now wore it loose, reaching almost to the small of her back. Her immaculately pressed white overall had been replaced by a gloriously embroidered blue silk kimono. I had put her age somewhere in the thirties, but now, seeing a hidden beauty revealed, I began to think that I might have overestimated.

As I came through the door, she brought her hands together and made a bow.

"Congratulations. I have told Agnetha that you have reached the required standard. You need now only attend the treatment room for your own conditioning."

For a moment, I felt slightly at a loss. I had actually begun to enjoy the learning process, and I was pleased with the things I could now do with my hands. I had come to know the girls' bodies and was willing to bet that I could tell them apart blindfolded even though they shared a similar physique.

Gathering myself, I thanked her and turned to leave, but she touched my arm.

"This morning, you get a full ritual massage. Get undressed please."

I did not argue. I stripped out of my clothes and lay down on the table, allowing my body to relax into the padded leather surface. I waited for Tamiko to drape my buttocks with a towel, a routine which seemed odd given that the others always lay completely naked, but she made no move to cover me.

Instead, she lit a squat candle which began to fill the air with the scent of sandalwood, and then, standing beside me, she picked up a glass-stoppered bottle and poured a measure of amber-colored oil into the palm of her hand.

She started on my calves, and the oil was cool to the skin, but as she gently massaged it in, I felt a pleasant, rosy warmth. She took her time working each leg slowly in turn and then both at once. Her touch was more delicate than usual; she was not kneading my muscles as much as preening them, and the feeling was deliciously therapeutic.

I felt her hands moving higher as she used her thumbs to manipulate the back of my knees, and I found this oddly stimulating. As she continued, I felt my eyelids growing heavy, but then, without warning, she stopped altogether.

I stayed still, not wanting it to be over, but then I was taken by surprise. Almost before I realized it, she had mounted the table, and she straddled my back. She took her most of her weight on her knees, but I could feel her buttocks pressing lightly on the base of my spine. From this vantage point, she reached down to my calves once more and commenced with series-long strokes up over the back of my thighs.

It felt so nice, but my focus had completely shifted. As she moved rhythmically back and forth, she was gently brushing against my back, and I was not convinced that she was not wearing underwear. I was still wondering if this was in the Japanese tradition when her hands made their first foray over my buttocks.

Her touch was so assured as she spread her fingers and held me firmly while her thumbs did wonderful things at the summit. My instinct was to open my legs, but the pressure of her knees held me in check.

I was guiltily aware that I allowed myself to be affected inappropriately, but I was afloat on an ocean of bliss. I felt almost aggrieved when she finally dismounted and turned her attention to my back. She worked her way slowly upwards from my coccyx to my shoulders, but every now and again, her fingers brushed at the edge of my breasts. She had done this before, in the course of our sessions, but this time I felt my nipples hardening beneath me.

I was still reveling in the sensation when she lifted her hands away.

"Turn over please."

I felt myself blush and was unsure what to do, but I could not just lie there. In the end, I rolled over onto my back with my arm covering my breasts.

She appeared not to notice my awkwardness, and almost immediately, she straddled me once more. Now that she had her back to me, I willed my nipples to relax, but my cause was not helped as she leaned forward and began to work the oil into my shins. Her sleek black hair flowed over her back as she moved, and I could feel the warmth of her on my stomach.

I found myself peeking at the shifting hem of her kimono as she straightened a little and started to stroke my thighs. I needed to get a grip on myself. I closed my eyes and tried to remember what she had told me about the anatomy of the quadriceps. But her magic thumbs had found their way into the dimples high up on the inside of my thighs.

At that moment, I felt an inner heat, and I panicked lest she picks up the embarrassing trace of my arousal, but some personal demon was hoping that she would go further. I began to look for justification to convince myself that it would be just this once, and, after all, I was not being called upon to reciprocate.

My heart quickened at this outrageous thought, and then she stretched forward.

She reached out and began to massage the tops of my feet. In doing so, she shifted back a little so that her weight was centered on my chest. This caused her kimono to ride up. I was afforded a view of her tight, well-formed, behind through the curtain of her hair.

Now each tiny movement grazed my breasts, and my nipples became almost painfully hard. There was no way that she could remain unaware, but she continued with slow leisurely strokes, seemingly unaffected.

I felt the first pricks of sweat on my forehead, and through the miasma of sandalwood and fragranced oil, I was convinced that I could discern the guilt-ridden scent of arousal.

I took a deeper breath, but her hands were slowly making the journey back up my legs, and as they moved.

By the time her hands reached my thighs, she was astride my breasts, and I knew that this was beyond the limits of any ritual massage. I heard myself telling her to get off me, but before I had finished saying it, her hand found my sex.

It was the faintest of touches as she skimmed the neat growth of hair that dressed my pubis, but I felt my whole body shiver. She did it again and again, so delicately that it felt as if gentle wafts of air were stimulating me.

I was desperate for a firmer touch and perhaps something more but, as I raised my hips, she moved with me, keeping up the same tantalizing routine. I groaned in frustration, and I felt a warm tell-tale prickling as I started to leak.

It went on for minutes as she gently rotated her pelvis, creating a pleasing warmth and pressure on my breasts. At the finish, I could take no more. I whispered a plea.

"Please..."

It was as if she had waited for this moment, and two things happened at once. In a single movement, she pressed the flat of her hand gently onto my pubis, allowing her middle finger to penetrate me with sluttish ease. I gave an involuntary gasp, and, as I did so, she slid backward until she was squatting over my face.

My first, irrational thought was that she had got oil all over herself, but I suddenly realized that this glistening moisture, filming the inside of her legs, betrayed her arousal. Without conscious thought, I found myself drawing breath through my nose and found that her scent was almost as familiar as my own, but I had never been enveloped in it to such a degree.

She remained poised, as though allowing me a moment of appreciation, and then her finger did something incredible inside me. I felt a sudden pressure somewhere behind my clitoris, and there was an instant of almost unbearable pleasure. As it surged through my body, my spine stiffened, lifting my head from the table, bringing my face between her legs.

My fastidious nature made me flinch, fearing a wet mess of pubic hair, but there was just an incredible smoothness. As my head fell back again, she slightly shifted so that her sex was directly above me, and I could see that it was as perfect and shiny as a beetle's carapace.

I lay there willing her to continue, and then I felt her finger twist almost imperceptibly. As it did, the second jolt of pleasure stiffened my body, forming my mouth into a rictus, and she brought herself lower.

Her sex was pressed gently to my lips, and a sharp tang invaded my mouth. This was not what I wanted, far from it, but her finger seemed to be vibrating inside of me, and I found myself panting. I was being held on the verge of an incredible orgasm, but she refused to take me over the edge.

In the heat and wetness between her enclosing thighs, I whimpered pathetically.

"Please...please..."

As my mouth formed the words, my lips moved against her sex, and she mirrored the stimulation with her finger. Her meaning was clear, but I could not bring myself to do it. The impasse lasted a few seconds, and then she withdrew her finger, just the tiniest fraction.

I had no choice. I had to surrender; her touch held the promise of a pleasure I had never known, a pleasure I could not forego.

With reluctance, I put out my tongue and touched it to the firmness of her sex. The first taste was unexpected, slightly salty, not altogether unpleasant but, as I started to lap at her, in the way I enjoyed having it done to me, it became richer, exciting more of my taste buds.

It met with her approval because her finger found the spot once more, and I was quickly taken back to the edge.

Now that I had broken the taboo, I found it easier. Her sex began to open, allowing me to discover the petals of her labia and, as they bloomed, so her flow increased.

I do not know when I reached the moment of transition, it may well have been in response to her irresistible palpation of my sex, but at some point, I drove my tongue deep inside her. My initial reluctance had become a craving as I tried to fill my mouth with her essence.

I had tasted myself on my fingers, but it was as nothing to this. Her taste was both subtle and complex, exciting my tongue and firing neurons of pleasure deep inside.

For a few seconds, my gratification was forgotten, but she rewarded this new evidence of enthusiasm with another purposeful movement of her finger.

I thought that I had reached an orgasm, but I realized, with astonishment, that she had simply taken me to a higher plateau that, unbelievably, there was more to come.

At that moment, I would have done anything for her. I opened my mouth wide and formed a seal around her sex, with my tongue buried deep, and then I began to suck. My technique may left much to be desired, but this physical declaration of my devotion was obviously to her liking.

With the final curling of her finger, the air rushed from my lungs; I melted into the be-all and end-all of climaxes. I found myself gasping for breath, but she remained seated on my face as she surrendered herself to a far more controlled orgasm. She was pulsing moisture into my mouth in sync with my attempts to breathe, and my tongue was being almost painfully constricted.

At the same time, as I was racked with pleasure beyond my experience, it felt as if I were drowning, but even in this, there was some distorted fulfillment.

At the zenith, I think I may even have blacked out for a second or two because, as my body jerked with a few final aftershocks, I found Tamiko standing beside me. She favored me with an inscrutable smile before she blew out the candle and left me alone.

I went back to my room and could not believe the mess I was in. My hair was damp with sweat and my face red; fortunately, I had not bothered with make-up.

I took another shower, but even after some minutes under the warm jets, I still felt as if I reeked of Tamiko. I stood there and, as so often when I get agitated, I talked to myself, and this time the question was, "what the hell was I thinking of?"

Thoughts crowded in on one another. Had she set out to seduce me, or had I given some unwitting signal? Had she done this with any of the others?

One thing I was clear about was the fact that it would not happen again.

I had been scheduled to spend the whole day in the treatment room, but there was no way in the world that I was going back that afternoon. Instead, I walked out of the complex and picked up the number nineteen bus, which ran down to the deer park. There had been a leaflet advertising the attraction in the reception area but, fortunately, there were very few day-trippers around. I was able to wander the grounds, keeping myself to myself, and try and put my thoughts in order.

I returned in time for the early evening meal with the other girls, each of us on a slightly different regimented diet, and then I accepted an offer to join them in town. Larina drove, and, as alcohol was expressly forbidden, we headed for a coffee shop in the old quarter.

As we laughed together, we were the center of a lot of male attention. I had grown used to it over the past two years and had learned to ignore it but, that night, I guess I was seeking some form of reassurance. A couple of young, clean-cut, Danish lads kept smiling in my direction, and I did nothing to put them off.

I now knew that my next-door neighbor at the complex was Larina and that she, at least, had sneaked in a male companion, so I was just a little put out when she told me to stop flirting and reminded me of Agnetha's strict rules.

That night I could not sleep. Each time I closed my eyes, I was confronted with yet another disturbing image of Tamiko. I knew that I ought to be disgusted with myself, and I could not get over how she had manipulated me so easily.

The following morning I got up to find that a revised schedule had been pushed under the door. I was to report to the gym after breakfast and then to Agnetha in the afternoon.

For the best part of three hours, I was put through my paces, and it quickly became apparent that the emphasis was to be on cardio-vascular work with only very limited weight training. During the morning, I surprised myself with the self-analysis of my different muscle groups and the way they flexed and contracted; I was far more aware of my limits, and I enjoyed exploring the boundaries.

After the session, I was ready for a shower, but I was caught by surprise when I was told to report to Tamiko. At the mention of her name, I had a hollow feeling in the pit of my stomach and the buzz I had got from the gym work instantly dissipated.

In the event, she was totally businesslike. Dressed, as usual, in a crisp white overall, she was a model of brisk efficiency, and she warmed me down as I had seen her do to the other girls. No reference was made to the previous day, but I found myself on edge throughout the session, wondering if, and when, her hand might go astray.

After lunch, I reported to Agnetha's office. She had two chrome and leather armchairs facing one another by the window, and she told me to be seated. She sat opposite me with a clipboard on her knee.

"This afternoon we are going to cover the rudiments of sports psychology. We are going to talk about self motivation and how we give ourselves an edge over our opponents. Now, all you are required to do is listen, but, whilst you do so, I do not want you to take your eyes off of my legs."

I looked up at her in surprise.

"Not my face. My legs"

I immediately cast my eyes downward. She was wearing a sports kit, and her short white skirt meant a lot of her legs to be seen.

"I watched a video of you losing in the Malaysian Open. Tonight, I want you to watch it too."

It was not a match I was proud of. I had lost to a ranked but beatable opponent. John and I had studied the video to spot the flaws in my game, but his analysis proved inconclusive.

"I want you to notice, particularly, how your opponent keeps looking at your left leg."

Now that she had said it, I did remember it. At first, I thought that the girl was checking me out, there are always a few lesbians to be found on the circuit, but she kept looking throughout the game. At the finish, I wondered if I was carrying my leg awkwardly.

"It's a trick a lot of the Far Eastern girls are using right now. It makes you think that they have spotted a weakness. You end up compensating for a problem that does not exist."

For the next hour, she expounded on what might traditionally be called "gamesmanship," and throughout that time, I kept my eyes on her legs. I knew that, on retirement, she had, for a short while, modeled for a Danish lingerie company, and it was clear to see why. Even now, her legs were enviable, long, well-shaped, and not over-muscled.

From time to time, she crossed them, rearranging her clipboard on her knee, and at least once, I found myself looking a little higher than was necessary. As I did so, I formed a fleeting image of Agnetha and Tamiko together, and I felt a warm but embarrassing tingling.

With the session over, I watched the video and found she was absolutely right. I felt such an idiot to have been influenced in this way.

The next day followed the same routine. I did three hours in the gym, followed by a massage, but there was something subtly different about it. It was nothing I could pin down, but when Tamiko had finished with me, I felt a heightened sense of tension.

I still felt slightly odd as I entered Agnetha's office. She was waiting with the chairs set up as they had been the day before, and I sat without being asked.

"Today, we are going to talk about court commands. During our training sessions I want you to hear my voice and do what I tell you without thinking. Later, we will work on your inner voice. You play an instinctive game and that serves you well, it surprises opponents, but to be the best you need to think through every single shot and the way to do that is to hear that voice."

"Okay, whilst I talk I want you to keep your eyes on my shoulder."

This all sounded slightly offbeat to me, and I was a little put out because I thought she had already proved her point about staring at an opponent's limb. Nevertheless, I did as she asked. The problem was that she had chosen to wear a scoop-necked vest top, and she was obviously not wearing a bra. Every time I tried to fix my gaze, I felt my eyes slipping towards her breasts.

She was well endowed, and my breasts were modest by comparison. Sports bras were all well and good, but I found myself wondering if she found it a disadvantage on the court.

"Do you find them fascinating?"

For a few seconds, I had drifted away and lost what she was saying, and now she was angry.

"Would you like a better look?"

She lifted her top to reveal a pair of heavy gourds crowned with perfectly round, chocolate brown nipples. I should have looked away, apologized, but I simply stared. They were beautiful, in a purely aesthetic sense, but that was no excuse.

She got up suddenly from her seat, her breasts still revealed, and a face like thunder.

"What exactly are you here for? Have you come to learn, or have you been hanging around in the showers with your young friends for too long? Were you trying to find out what a real woman's body looks like? Is that it?"

She moved closer to me, and her tirade became almost concussive.

"Well take a look and then perhaps we can get on!"

She ripped away from the velcro fastening of her sports skirt and allowed it to pool at her feet. Beneath it, she was wearing a pair of flesh-colored panties which struggled to contain her sex.

She had the most prominent mound I had ever see, and it was covered with a luxuriant growth of black curls. I had been exposed to naked bodies throughout my sporting career and the vogue, amongst players, was for total depilation with a few going for a token fringe, but this was beyond my experience.

It had a feral quality, a sense that this was how nature intended things to be, and it seemed so right. Only days before, I had blanched at the prospect of touching Tamiko, but now I felt an unnatural

371

attraction, a stirring deep inside of me. Without conscious thought, my tongue moved in my mouth, seeking out the phantom of a forbidden taste.

I tried to shift my gaze, but, as I did so, she moved very slightly. It was a tiny transition, but it gave her posture a certain arrogance. At that moment, I wanted nothing more than to nuzzle up against her, to feel her warmth, to take in her scent., but she put her hand behind my head and pulled it back slightly.

She looked at me directly in the eyes.

"You little slut."

And then she was gone. She picked up her skirt and refastened it before taking her seat as if nothing untoward had taken place.

"Now, where were we?"

For the remainder of the session, I stared mutely at her shoulder as she elaborated on the court commands that she would be using. My heart rate was raised, and my skin felt clammy, and it was all I could do to avoid fidgeting in my seat. Fortunately, she did not keep me for much longer before dismissing me for the day, and I left the room almost in a daze. I felt chagrined but also an embarrassing sense of arousal.

I was still cursing myself under my breath as I walked into my room, and I was startled to find Tamiko sitting in the single armchair - she was wearing the same blue silk kimono.

"Lock the door."

I flared to anger and told her to leave, or perhaps that was another me because I found myself turning the key, and my pulse pounded in my temples as I slowly turned from the door to face her.

She was sitting with her legs crossed. Her fingers were steepled together under her chin, with a knowing smile on her face.

I remained still, unsure of what to do, and my discomfort seemed to amuse her. She waited some seconds before she slowly uncrossed her legs allowing the kimono to slip open with a gentle hiss of silk.

My stomach lurched as I recalled the sensual skill of her fingers, and I was all too aware of the dampness between my legs. The frisson that I had felt while ensconced with Agnetha was boiling up once more, and I could see, in Tamiko's eyes, that I had no secrets.

I could not look her in the face, and my eyes dropped to her breasts, which were still just hidden by the folds of her gown. At this, she turned slightly, allowing the briefest glimpse of a conical pink nipple before she leisurely lifted one leg and draped it over the arm of the chair.

I wanted to close my eyes in denial, but they were drawn, almost hypnotically, downwards to where her sex glistened. Even as I watched, the firm mound seemed to swell, allowing the pink inner lips to yawn into awakening.

I swallowed audibly, and there was no doubt that she heard. She skimmed the tips of her fingers regally over her sex as though presenting a rare jewel.

"Adore me..."

The air seemed charged as I caught the faintest hint of her scent, and then I was drawn forward as though by an invisible rope. Time stood still, and I felt disembodied as I went down to my knees.

There was no subtlety. I licked broadly over the clear divide of her sex, filling my mouth with her taste, and then I was like an animal. I licked again and again, long strokes, accompanied by a bestial keening. Her sex opened wider as I drove deeper, and any pleasure she took was certainly not as a result of my technique.

Juices and saliva bubbled in my nostrils as I tried to sate my irrational need, and, in those seconds, I wanted to fuse with her, to feel my tongue squeezed in her comforting depths.

And she understood it all.

She put her hand to the back of my neck, applying gentle but insistent pressure. Breathing became difficult, but I welcomed the onset of light-headedness as I swallowed her warm offering.

I do not think she climaxed; she seemed content to let me work out my feelings, but I did not know what I really wanted. At the outset, I wanted her to use her mouth on me to create another of those shattering orgasms, but as I suckled gently at her sex, I reached a state of personal nirvana that seemed to transcend the physical.

At some point, she released me, and I reluctantly fell away from her only to be overwhelmed by an immediate sense of guilt.

She rose imperiously, vouchsafing me one last look at her body before wrapping herself in her kimono and gliding to the door. As it closed behind her, I finally broke down. Tears coursed down my cheeks as I wallowed in self-recrimination and tried to understand what had just taken place.

The next morning I felt no better, and the temptation to give up and leave the complex almost won out, but, in the end, I determined to get a grip on myself and at least wait until the conclusion of the Dutch Open.

I reported to Agnetha, and we sat as we had the day before. As soon as I was in the room with her, I felt my skin flush, and my whole body seemed unnaturally warm. I had a notepad on my lap, and I scribbled away as she spoke but, every now and again, I was taking surreptitious glances at her legs.

When the time came to leave her office, my heart was hammering. I headed back to my room, but I paused at the threshold. For a few seconds, an internal battle waged in my mind, so intense that it resulted in a headache. One part of me desperately hoped that Tamiko would be there while the other was frightened at the prospect.

The room was empty, and I now had to cope with a combination of relief and disappointment, with both feelings being further exaggerated as I collapsed onto the bed and pushed my hand into my panties.

The next couple of days were a repeat of the same routine. I grew heated in Agnetha's presence, especially as she had a habit of opening her legs as she leaned forward to emphasize a point, and then the anticipation as I returned to my room.

I even shunned the company of the other girls, despite repeated offers to join them in the evening, but I felt I just could not trust myself. It was as if I was living a dream, but, in my more lucid moments, I was shaded by a cloud of self-loathing.

Finally, Agnetha allowed me some court time, and it felt comforting, in more ways than one, to have a racket back in my hand. However, I was surprised when we were ushered to the far end of the hall, where there were no nets and no court markings.

On further inspection, there was a single rectangle marked out on the floor. It was about six inches square, and Agnetha made us stand about six meters back from it, keeping it at a diagonal to us. We then spent the whole session lofting shuttles and trying to get them into the defined area.

I could not see the point in this repetitious exercise, but the girls took it very seriously, and my competitive nature kicked in. After an hour or so, Katya was way out in front, but there was little to choose between Larina, Aruna, and I. Just As I began to hope that we were nearing the end, Agnetha shouted out, "Forfeits!"

The girls had told me about Agnetha's incentives, and I certainly did not want to find myself cleaning one of the other girl's rooms or doing laundry for that matter. The problem was that I now tried too hard and that, combined with a lack of racket practice, allowed the others to pull ahead.

As the winner, Katya was allowed to choose my forfeit, and the other girls laughed as she said that she wanted her room cleaned. My immediate reaction was to rebel, but I did not want to appear to be a spoilsport; so, before dinner, I found myself in Katya's room with a dustpan and brush.

As it happened, she was almost clinically tidy, and there was little to do, but I determined not to lose the next day.

The following morning we practiced serving over an imaginary net. In reality, there was a laser beamed across the hall at the required height, and Agnetha could monitor how tight we were to the tape. At intervals, she called out our current standings, and I was pleased when I moved into the lead, but when she shouted "Forfeits," my excitement got the better of me.

I thought that I was doing well, but Agnetha made it clear that I was falling back. At the finish, Larina won, and I was last again. I was sure that I saw her smirk when she said "laundry," but I swallowed my pride and followed her up to her room.

I was glad that she had not asked me to tidy her room. It was a tip compared to Katya's, but I had second thoughts when she handed me a bag of dirty underwear.

"They'll need hand washing."

I hovered on the verge of throwing it back at her, but I checked myself and determined that next time, she would be returning the favor. When I got the bag back to my room, I found that it contained cotton sportswear that certainly did not warrant special attention and so I decided that I would use the communal laundry room and put them in with my own.

I was about to put the bag to one side when I found one final pair of panties at the bottom. They were white silk, tanga style, and clearly very expensive. I wondered if these were what she wore when she smuggled in her boyfriend, and I tossed them to one side, angered at the thought that she wanted me to wash them.

That evening I joined the girls in town and had to put up some good-natured banter about my forfeits, but I was already planning my revenge. When we returned to the complex, I went straight to bed but, not for the first time. My sleep was troubled by images of Agnetha and Tamiko.

As I thrashed, fretfully, in the darkness, I flung out my arm and lighted upon something soft. It took a second or two to realize that I was touching Larina's discarded panties, and I jerked my hand away again but then, for reasons I could not explain, I reached out once more.

The material felt smooth and cool in my clammy palm as I gently crushed them, but, even now, I was telling myself that this was dreadfully wrong. A fleeting image of Larina, naked, came unbidden to my mind, and, as it did so, my free hand snaked its way down between my legs. To my surprise, I was already obscenely wet, and my fingers slipped easily inside.

As I continued to tease myself, I turned my face to the pillow to stifle a groan and drew my hand back into the bed. Without thinking, I began to gently rub the soft silk over my achingly erect nipples, and I felt my climax drawing closer.

With two fingers buried deep, I used the edge of my thumb to caress my clitoris, but my other hand seemed to act of its own volition. My fingers opened, straining the silk, and at the same time, turning them inside out.

I should have stopped, cleared my head, but like a free diver gasping for oxygen, I stretched them over my face and breathed deep. They were impregnated with her scent, and I could not shake the notion that she had made them wet for me, knowing what I would do exactly. It was a rich smell that reached into my mind like an expanding nova, and now I worked my clitoris with unremitting energy. My orgasm wrenched at me, thrashing my body, but every heaving breath was sucked in through wet silk, drawing out the very last taste of her.

In the aftermath, I sobbed, both with pure pleasure and remorse, but less than half an hour later, I was reaching a second shattering climax as I licentiously pushed the bunched panties deep inside myself.

Chapter 03

On the court the next day, I could not meet Larina's eye, but now, I felt I had a chance. We were to play conventional singles, a round-robin series of mini-matches to five points with the points total being accumulated.

I was afraid that I might be a little rusty, but I outranked the other three, and I was determined not to lose. I got off to a good start beating both Aruna and Katya, but Larina refused to be fazed by my powerful style. She deliberately slowed the game down, and suddenly nothing would go right. My serves fell short, and my smashes, usually so accurate, all went wide or went beyond the baseline.

Things went from bad to worse. Aruna and Katya saw what Larina was doing, and they adopted the same tactics; by the end of the second round, I had lost to both of them.

By the end of the session, I was trailing badly, and in my final game, against Larina, I had nothing to play for but pride. I reined myself in and tried placing my shots with the result that I soon had her chasing the game. It was the longest game of the day by far, but, with a final triumphant whoop, I smashed a winner.

Larina's singlet was plastered to her body as she came to the net to shake hands perfunctorily, and she did not look best pleased.

Agnetha told us that she would discuss the session after lunch and told Aruna and Katya to report to Tamiko. With time on my hands, I decided to shower in my room, but Larina caught me up at the lift.

"Do you have my washing?"

I resented her terse tone, but I kept my tongue. I had finished the laundry before breakfast, and I invited her to come and collect it. She followed me into my room, and I caught her casting a critical eye around my scant personal effects.

I handed her the bag of washing, which was still a little warm from the dryer, and only then did I remember the silk panties. I had had to hand wash them twice and had even added a little eau de cologne to the rinsing water. They were hanging up to dry on the towel rail, but now that I looked at them, I could see that they were drying creased.

Larina walked into the bathroom behind me and snatched them from the rail.

"What the hell have you done to them."

She held them up, and then with an odd look, she brought them to her face and sniffed.

"They smell of your perfume. Have you been wearing them?!"

"Of course not. They were a little soiled."

It was a poor choice of words, and I immediately regretted saying it.

"Soiled! I've hardly worn them."

I knew this not to be true, but I could hardly make an argument of it.

She was visibly angry, and I tried to make amends.

"Look, they just smelled as though they needed freshening up."

It was a stupid thing to say. Like everyone, I sniff my clothing from time to time to see if I can get away with not washing things, but it was not something you say about someone else's underwear.

She looked at me oddly.

"You've been sniffing them?"

I brushed past her back into the bedroom.

"Of course not."

She followed me out, refusing to let it go.

"You just said they didn't smell fresh."

"Look, it was just a turn of phrase."

Now her tone turned more mischievous.

"Is that how you get yourself off, sniffing other girls panties? Perhaps I ought to tell the others to check for missing underwear."

"Come on, you've had your fun now I want you to leave."

"You should have just said. I could have let you have a steaming hot pair. Here, how about these?"

She lifted her brief skirt to reveal her white cotton briefs, and I found myself staring. I had seen her naked, but this was, somehow, even more intimate. Her inner thighs were still sheened with sweat, and the panties themselves were damp at the edges where they had soaked it up.

I looked away, but I had lingered a second too long, and I saw realization dawn in her eyes.

She looked directly at me as she unfastened her skirt with a sudden rasp of Velcro that made me flinch.

"Don't be coy. You only had to ask..."

My thoughts immediately sprang back to the day of my arrival when I had listened outside her door; only now did it occur to me that it might have been one of the other girls in the room with her. I found myself excited by the notion, but I had to put a stop to this immediately.

"Please put your skirt back on and leave."

"Are you sure that's what you want...?"

I was about to phrase it more forcefully as she pressed a finger gently to the crotch of her panties. As she did so, a damp circle formed, its circumference slowly widening. I tried to look away, but the sight was shockingly beguiling.

I was unsure on my feet for a second as I willed myself to move away, but the trap was already closing as she took a slow step forward.

"Get down on your knees..."

Her tone was, at once, both tender and demanding, and, with my legs already threatening to give way beneath me, kneeling seemed like a sensible option.

"Good girl."

She stroked my hair, and she suddenly seemed so much older than me.

"Lick my thighs..."

I had heard her say it in my dreams, an echo of Tamiko's massage instruction, but now the context was different. Any thoughts of a clinical exploration were dispelled as I placed my hands on her legs and bent to my appointed task.

I licked the salty sweat from her thighs with broad sweeps of my tongue like a dog on heat. Somewhere above me, she laughed, but I no longer cared. Her skin was delicately tanned and incredibly smooth, and I licked everywhere.

"You little slut. I knew, that first time on the massage table; do you think about me while you masturbate?"

I ignored her taunts as my hands explored the well defined under the curve of her buttocks, and then my fingertips brushed at the cotton of her panties, stretched tight by the perfect globes, as though reading a message for the blind.

She smelt feral. Her delicately scented deodorant was just starting to lose the battle against the day's exertions, and this, combined with the rich reek of her underwear, should have been off-putting, but my mind was clouded by memories of the night before. I could almost feel the silk panties against my face once again.

This association of ideas gave rise to a new madness. Without thought, I lifted my head, and I licked at her sex through the ripe, wet material.

"Don't stop. You really are a little knicker lover aren't you?"

The night before, I had been consumed with guilt as I tentatively touched my tongue to silk, but now I was a ravening beast. I sucked noisily, filling my mouth with the taste of wet cotton enriched with her essence.

For a moment, I had a fleeting remembrance of childhood; my mother was scolding me for putting the collars of my dresses in my mouth. But the image faded almost as soon as it was formed.

I was virtually chewing at her, but the grinding of her hips suggested it was very much to her liking as she entwined her fingers in my hair.

"That's it....just like that...make me come..."

The soaked cotton was rubbing my tongue, but still, I licked, all the while snorting labored breaths through my nostrils. Finally, a jerk of her hips told me that the moment had arrived. It was an unintentionally painful thrust into my face, but she was using both hands now to keep me in place as the tremors shook her whole body.

As she rode it out, her legs threatened to betray her, but she held on tightly with her weight bearing down on me until, with one last gasp, she let me go and then, unceremoniously, stepped back and collapsed onto my bed.

I knelt there, my face wet and red from exertion, and the first, totally irrational, thought that entered my head was that she was going to stain the quilt. It was absurd, but then the whole situation was surreal. I wanted to go and wash, but some part of me felt that she would find it insulting.

She looked at me as she tried to catch her breath and then smiled.

"Just give me a moment."

My mind was in turmoil. I desperately wanted her to go, but at the same time, I was incredibly aroused. Would she? If I asked?

I stayed as I was, daring to hope until she regained her composure, but she then slinked further up the bed until she was sitting up with her back supported by the headboard. She quickly slipped out of her damp tee-shirt and then discarded her bra to reveal her lividly erect nipples.

I wanted to undress, to lie with her, and feel her breasts pressed against my own, but my innate sense of decency still required an invitation. I held my breath, willing her to say the words, and then watched as she raised herself slightly and skimmed her ruined panties down her legs.

She kicked them onto the floor and then opened her legs with her knees raised.

The light covering of blonde hair on her pubis, usually so immaculate, looked as if it had been insanely gelled and her sex itself appeared mauled. Her labia were swollen, and the private pink interior lay glisteningly revealed.

"Okay, I'm ready, take it slow this time..."

I felt a sharp pain, a hurt that centered itself in my chest. Nothing had been said, promised, or inferred but I felt rejected, and it was not a feeling I was familiar with. For a few seconds, I remained rooted to the spot, and then I got to my feet.

I was going to leave the room to make her feel the same way as I did, but as if reading my mind, she put her hand between her legs and pushed two fingers deep inside. They made a rich, inviting, sucking sound, and when she withdrew them, she slowly allowed her fingers to open, revealing delicate syrupy strands.

"Come and eat me..."

I was put in mind of a spider's web, but the truth was, I had no wish to escape. She held her fingers out to me as I drew nearer and joined her on the bed, and then she gently pushed them between my lips.

I closed my eyes as I used my tongue to savor the bittersweet taste, licking between her fingers until there was no more to be had.

She indulged me for a moment or two, and then she slowly pulled her fingers free. I followed, reluctant to let them go, but she coaxed me downwards, and, when they were finally gone, I was just inches from her sex.

I needed no further inducement; I leaned in and formed a seal with my mouth.

Mindful of her wishes and fearful that I had been a little too aggressive at first, I used my tongue to gently trace the contours of her labia, licking in long lazy circles.

"Yessss.....that's nice."

She was incredibly hot, and I found myself wondering if the physical exercise she had performed had any bearing, but that ceased to matter as her sex began to seep a succulent creamy offering.

I pressed my tongue gently to her core, and it was as if I had applied pressure to a membrane. Notwithstanding her first orgasm, she was still surprisingly wet, and I relished the taste as it flowed over my tongue.

Her raised legs seemed to shield me from the world as I snuggled deep in the valley, content simply to lick her as, over long minutes, she slowly tensed herself for a second powerful orgasm.

Her breathing became more ragged, and I took this as my cue to give her clitoris some attention. I pulled back a little freeing my nose from the tender embrace of her labia, and only in so doing did I realize how strong her scent had become. Without thought, I closed my eyes and breathed it in only to feel my sex tingle in anticipation.

"Don't stop."

She pulled me back into place, breaking my reverie, and I used my tongue once more.

Her clitoris was discrete, and, despite my best efforts, I could not coax it completely free, but it did not seem to matter. As I licked softly at the fleshy collar, her body suddenly stiffened, lifting her from the bed.

For the next few seconds she remained bowed, taking her weight on her head and buttocks, until, suddenly, she gave a piercing shriek. I feared that I had hurt her, but then she began to shudder uncontrollably as the pent up pleasure zinged through her.

I wanted to get lower, to swallow everything, but I remained focused on her clitoris teasing out the final ripples until she slumped on the bed, totally spent.

She looked beautiful, with her eyes closed and a high color in her cheeks, mirrored by a vivid flash across her breasts. She seemed totally relaxed and quite at ease with herself as she lay with her legs still wide open.

Only now did I become aware of painful cramping in my neck and an ache in my jaw, which threatened to worsen later on, but still, I was not sated. She was wet with a mixture of her juices and my saliva, and, starting on her inner thigh, I began to clean her up.

"Ummmm... that's nice."

She stretched herself and casually brought her hands to her breasts as I worked my way over her mound and across to her other leg.

I could find no rationale for my behavior; perhaps I hoped, even now, that it would be my turn, but if I gave a signal, it was misread. She reached up and grabbed my pillow, and then used it to raise her hips.

"I'm ready when you are..."

The next morning, Larina greeted me on the court as though nothing had happened, but my tongue, sore to the root, knew otherwise. I had been fearful that she would tell the others, but the practice session started as usual with no obvious sniggers.

Agnetha had us playing with each other while she shouted commands. When my turn came, I was paired with Larina, and I found it difficult to stifle my natural playing instincts as I listened for her voice.

"Down!"

"Get in!"

Agnetha moved from end to end, coaching each of us in turn, and it was as she was instructing Larina that we met at the net in an exchange of drop shots. I had to go low to pick up a particularly good return when Agnetha screamed.

"Force her!"

Something in my mind slipped at that point, and Larina gave me a knowing smile as she hit an unplayable shot to the back of the court. From then on, I could not concentrate. Every one of Agnetha's commands seemed to take on a new, sinister significance, and Larina wound up thrashing me.

A little later, we had another round-robin tournament, but I found myself almost in tears as shot after shot mixed its mark. I excused myself and went to the toilet so that no one would see my distress, but I had only been there a moment or two before Katya walked in.

At twenty-three, she was the oldest of our group, but she displayed a maturity beyond her years. She had a natural gentleness of spirit, but when it came to matches, she was as ferocious as any of us, and I sensed that there was little love lost between her and Larina on the court.

She came over to me and put a comforting arm around my shoulders.

"You have to get used to the court markings."

I looked at her, perplexed at what seemed a cryptic remark.

"Agnetha has the court marked up a couple of centimeters short. It is also a little narrower than regulation width. She wants to condition us to play within those boundaries so that, when we play for real, there is an allowance for the extra degree of exertion that she demands of us."

I looked at her in astonishment. My shots had not been going out. They were simply going where my long years of muscle memory were placing them. Back in the UK, I had sometimes practiced with a slightly heavier shuttle; I found it a waste of time because I was quickly able to compensate, but it would never have occurred to me to play on anything but a regulation court.

I felt such a fool, but I also felt very angry. It was as if I had been duped. Without another word, I went back out to the practice hall and picked up my racket.

I began to play like a woman possessed. With a speed and strength fuelled by rage, I began to smash shots from all parts of the court.

Larina tried to slow me down by playing drop shots, but I simply lofted the shuttle back, inviting her into an exchange that she could not resist. She was no match for me. Having beaten her, I proceeded to finish off the other two with ease.

I wound up the overall winner but, better still, Larina had overexerted herself in her effort to beat me, and she subsequently lost to both Aruna and Katya. I suddenly realized that it was for me to call the forfeit and for Larina to pay it.

Of necessity, Larina went into Tamiko first, but as she passed by, I could not resist whispering to her.

"I'll see you in your room afterwards...be ready."

When it came to my turn, I enjoyed Tamiko's ministrations as much as ever, and she seemed, somehow, tuned in to me. The massage, at first vigorous, developed into something almost sensual, and by the time I got off of the table, to give way to Katya, I was more than ready.

I made my way to Larina's room and knocked confidently on the door. She opened it and looked at me resignedly as she stepped aside to let me in. Following my shower, I was wearing nothing more than a long, sloppy tee-shirt and a pair of flip flops, and, coincidently, she was similarly attired.

My eyes fell to her chest, where her nipples were clearly delineated through the thin cotton, but they were as nothing to mine which excitement had brought to an aching rigidity.

"I'm guessing that you don't want me to clean your room."

I enjoyed my moment of triumph, as I replied.

"That's for sure. We have a couple of hours before lunch but you are going to do a lot of eating before then."

As I said it, she looked over my shoulder, and I turned to find Aruna standing at the bathroom door, her face aghast.

"Aruna has just received a letter from her father. He's found someone."

That explained the tears that were starting from her eyes. Without thinking, I rushed to her and put a consoling arm around her shoulder.

"I am so sorry."

Aruna was born and raised in Denmark and spoke English with the same cute accent as Larina and Katya, but she was of Indian parentage. She was fun to be with, very much one of the girls, but the sword of Damocles hanging over her was the inevitable fact of an arranged marriage.

She held only loose religious beliefs and was happy to drink alcohol from time to time, but on the question of marriage, she felt she had no choice. The rest of us found it a total anachronism and tried to talk sense to her. Men flocked to her, we had even nicknamed her "Paddy" due to her remarkable resemblance to Padma Lakshmi, the Indian supermodel, and would-be actress, but she remained chaste.

For myself, I could not conceive of a life in which I only ever had sex with one man. I knew that, no matter how much I loved someone, my curiosity would one day get the better of me.

I sat Aruna down gently on the bed, and Larina came to sit on the other side of her. Once again, I launched into the same futile argument.

"Look, I'm sure that your parents will make the right choice but you owe it to yourself to make a natural connection. What about that cute guy at the coffee shop? He's obviously besotted with you."

Aruna looked into her lap as she replied.

"I have to be a virgin..."

It was positively medieval, besides which the term virgin was open to interpretation. If an intact hymen was a prerequisite, then Aruna's self-confessed use of sex toys put her on uncertain ground. She even used masturbation as part of her argument, saying that she could always resort to onanism if her husband turned out to be a disappointment.

It was then that Larina quietly interposed.

"She could still enjoy the experience ... it doesn't necessarily have to be a man."

Her words hung in the air, and I felt embarrassed by Aruna's part, but then I suddenly realized that they were both looking at me.

I got up from the bed quickly and fought down a wave of anger.

"Larina, you are one sick puppy!"

Mustering my dignity, I turned and walked towards the door only to be brought up short.

"Are you sure ...?"

My fingers were already on the door handle. A couple more steps would have brought me back to normality, but, like Lot's wife, I made the mistake of looking back.

They were still seated side by side, but Larina had lifted the hem of Aruna's abbreviated sports skirt to reveal her long tawny legs. There was a frozen pause, and then, slowly, Aruna parted her knees.

I wanted to draw my eyes away, but my heart was already pounding, and the more so when I saw that she was not wearing panties. Lush growth of black hair covered her sex, and, for a second or two, I was reminded of Agnetha's display; perhaps it was this that sealed my fate.

"Please...I need to know what it's like."

Aruna's voice was a siren's call but was there something more? The faintest hint of mockery? It made no difference; I had already taken the first irreversible step back towards her.

As I drew closer, she opened her legs wider to accommodate me as I slowly sank to my knees. For a few seconds, I could do nothing but stare. The dark growth was not totally black. As she shifted slightly, the light picked up subtle hints of burgundy complementing the native coloring of her skin and then, deep within, beckoning, a secret, roseate, orchid.

I could smell its perfume, richer than any flora, and I was as captivated as a butterfly. I flitted over the dark canopy, and then I moved closer to dip my tongue.

"Oh God! She's doing it."

I only heard Aruna's voice at the periphery of my consciousness as I focused on my single goal. Her labia were neat and symmetrical, and, as if to proclaim her virginity, they met edge to edge except at the midpoint where they pouted open slightly.

I placed the tip of my tongue on the exposed pinkness and felt her inner heat while she, for her part, remained unnaturally still as she waited to see what I would do next.

For a moment, I was content simply to breathe her in. She favored heavy, musky perfumes, which complimented her exotic appearance, but this was now overlaid by the fresher, animal smell of her excitement. The combination was heady, almost overpowering, but I could not get enough of it.

Her impatience finally got the better of her.

"Do it!"

Her attitude rankled, but, in truth, I was serving my own needs. I applied gentle pressure, slowly peeling her apart, and I registered the first sharp tang, but the deeper I went, the sweeter it became.

"Yess...."

The nervous tension made itself manifest as her body began to quiver, and the motion drew my tongue further in.

She was incredibly tight, but, as I explored deep inside, she finally managed to relax.

"That's so good."

She brought her thighs together, squeezing my head, and I immediately stopped to make it clear to her that it was uncomfortable. Getting the message, she eased the pressure but still kept my head trapped as though fearful that I might suddenly change my mind.

In reality, I was drooling. Her taste was that same rich nectar to which I was becoming worrying addicted, but in my mind, it seemed to have a caramel quality in keeping with her exoticness. I lowered myself slightly so that my tongue was angled upwards, allowing me to catch her flow.

"Oh fuck! I'm going to come!"

I had never quite gotten used to the ease with which this outwardly prim Indian girl would suddenly employ expletives just like the rest of us but, just then, her coarseness excited me to an incredible degree.

She was shifting restlessly, and then her thighs tightened about my ears once more while, in the muffled distance, I could hear Larina urging her on.

"Don't hold back...she loves it."

I started to stab at her with my tongue, my perspiring face sliding easily between her equally slick thighs, and then the dam broke. Her body shook with unexpected violence, but I had no choice but to ride it out with her as she kept me firmly gripped.

When she finally deigned to let me go, I was panting for breath, but she lay back, unheedingly on the bed in a state of beatific exhaustion with her legs still open in wanton abandon.

Her sex looked a little raw but still retained it quaint coyness, and, as I watched, it slowly oozed a bead of clear moisture.

Without thought, I leaned in and scooped it up on my tongue and was immediately goaded by Larina.

"She's an insatiable little slut."

At another time, in another place, I would have slapped her, but the truth of what she said was self-evident. I was already trying to tease more moisture from her, and Aruna did not seem to mind.

"Let her have her fun."

She eased herself further onto the bed so that she was lying prone with her knees raised, and I followed slavishly.

"Make her lick your clitoris, she really is very good."

Following Larina's instruction, she used her fingers to hold herself open to reveal a perfect pink pearl, peeking out from its ochre collar.

"Take your time ...."

I pursed my lips to the inviting bud and kissed it reverentially before bring my tongue into play. For the next few minutes, my whole world was but a span of inches as I teased her clitoris and slowly brought her to a peak of excitement.

She quickly began to groan, and she would periodically thrash her head from side to side, but I kept up the same leisurely pace, only dipping now and again to lap up her ever more copious leakage.

My tongue and jaw had grown used to this exercise, and it must have been fully half an hour before I finally lavished her whole sex with the broad sweeps, which I knew would take her over the edge.

When the moment came, she stopped breathing. Her body slowly bowed upwards until, with a final forceful exhalation and an accompanying string of expletives, she reached a second explosive climax.

Before it was over, I rolled away from her and wiped the back of my hand across my mouth. I tried to come to terms with what had just taken place.

I closed my eyes to avoid the awkward silence that followed, punctuated only by Aruna's labored breathing. When I finally opened them, it was to find Larina sitting in the armchair, gloriously naked, her hand idly toying with her obviously aroused sex.

"I hope there's still some life left in that slutty little tongue of yours..."

That same evening, I once again thought long and hard about leaving, but I finally decided on a new strategy. I determined to become a woman of ice.

I trained with others every day but refused to exchange anything more than courtesies. I declined to associate with them in my free time but most important of all. I refused to go along with the forfeits; after all, they were not compulsory but simply a bit of fun. If Agnetha objected to my attitude, then, as far as I was concerned, she could send me away.

As it turned out, I was able to set the agenda by winning the next two training sessions and refusing to demand a forfeit. The other girls' attitude towards me grew frosty quickly, but Agnetha seemed to find this new statement of intent somewhat amusing.

I trained hard for the next few days, and then we traveled together to Eindhoven, where we joined up with our respective national teams. In theory, I was indebted to the national coach, but it had long since become recognized that the top-ranked players would make their own coaching arrangements. After completing the formalities, I was left to my own devices.

On the day before the event, I trained with my national team colleagues in the Sportcentrum hall where the event was to be staged, and it quickly became clear to me that none of them would be capable of beating any of Agnetha's protégés.

And so it proved. At the third round stage, I was the only team survivor, but elsewhere Larina and Aruna were also doing well. Unfortunately for Katya, she was drawn against the world number three in the first round and was eliminated after a game struggle.

In the quarter-final, I was lucky enough to be drawn against the only remaining unseeded player, and I breezed through, which gave me time to check out the number three court where fate had decreed that Larina and Aruna would play one another.

On paper, Larina should have won with something to spare, but Aruna had, of late, found a new spirit. Much to Larina's chagrin, I began to cheer on the underdog, along with the rest of the crowd, but, while Aruna managed to take the game to three sets, Larina's extra stamina won out at the finish.

In the semi's, Larina was drawn against the world number one and I, the world number two, the night before Agnetha handed me another of her fabled dossiers. Amongst many other details and statistics, it contained DVD highlights of my opponent's recent games and charts showing her favored shots and areas of the court.

As I digested it, I wondered what would have happened if I had been drawn against Larina. I naturally suspected that she would favor her fellow countrywoman, but I was beginning to believe that she would genuinely support the player with the best prospect.

On the day I played beyond myself and, with the help of the dossier, I won through. I was ecstatic, and I came back out an hour later to cheer on Larina, but it was clear from her manner that she was still peeved about my support of Aruna.

To her credit, she put up a titanic struggle but finally lost out after an epic third set leaving me to play the Malaysian number one in the final.

I was so nervous that I had trouble focusing on the dossier, which bore Agnetha's handwritten amendments resulting from the semi-final clash, but I finally got myself to concentrate.

The next morning I just wanted to get on the court and get started, but the game had a new satellite broadcaster, and they were demanding a little more razzmatazz. Following the recent upsurge in interest in women's volleyball, the European Badminton Federation was stealing some of their promotional ideas. This included a troupe of four scantily clad young women who warmed up the crowd with a series of raunchy dance routines.

The girls were stunningly good looking, and I had to pull myself away to avoid unnecessary distractions. But Larina, who seemed to know one of them, was cheering raucously at courtside.

When the game finally started, I lost the first set cheaply, and I realized that, in the excitement, I had reverted to my instinctive game.

For the second set, I played to the dossier, and it was almost as if I could hear Agnetha's voice inside my head. I lost the first few points, but then I felt buoyed up by winning two shots exactly as she said I might. After that, my confidence grew, and I edged the second set.

The deciding set was hard-fought and became a war of attrition, but I had played a much less demanding semi-final, and, to my disbelief, my opponent played one last loose shot, and the championship was mine.

The next few minutes passed in a blur. There were many offerings of congratulations and then a formal presentation ceremony before I was snatched up for a television interview.

When that was over, the crowd gave another cheer, and, still, in a state of euphoria, I turned to go back to the dressing room.

It was then that I saw them. It was a prank that had first seen the light of day at the Hong Kong Invitational, and I suspect it was another TV-inspired stunt. The four dancers had unfastened the net, and now they captured me in it. The crowd shrieked delightedly as the girls ran around me, mummifying me in the nylon mesh with my arms pinned to my sides. They then lifted me and carried me off the court shoulder high.

I could hear the dying echoes of the crowd as they carried me out of the hall, but it took a second or two to realize that we were not headed back to the players changing area. Instead, I was carried into a smaller changing room normally set aside for match officials.

The girls lowered me onto a bench, and I could see that the room was filled with their paraphernalia, including costume racks and make-up mirrors.

I tried to sit up, but with my body and legs bound, I could not quite make it.

"Thanks girls, if you would like to help me up I could do with a shower."

The troupe leader, a large-breasted brunette, leaned over me and put a finger under my chin. Moving closer, she still spoke in slightly accented English.

"You're not going to disappoint us are you? Your friend says you like to play."

I had no doubt that she was referring to Larina, and I was furious.

"Look I don't care what you were told. Let me up right now or I'll scream the place down!"

"That's not very nice. Do you know how good it feels dancing out there? How much of a turn on to know that every man in the room is sitting there with an aching erection wishing he could have you? A girl needs a little stress relief."

I had had enough. I opened my mouth to scream, but she was too quick for me. She clamped her hand over my mouth and turned to the others.

"Give me something to keep her quiet."

I watched wide-eyed as another of the girls quickly slipped off her panties and handed them over. Now, when the hand was removed from my mouth, I kept it firmly closed, but the brunette reached down and squeezed my breast through the netting, causing me to gasp in surprise.

As my mouth opened, she deftly slipped the panties between my lips, and I knew, immediately, that she had not been joking when she said that their performance aroused them. The taste was strong, and, for the briefest instant, I pushed my tongue deeper into the bunched material, but then sanity prevailed, and I desperately tried to spit them out.

The brunette put her hand back over my mouth and pointed at one of the clothes rails.

"Pass me that."

She was handed a single, tan, lycra stocking, and I was powerless to resist as she opened it and then quickly pulled it down over my head.

I felt like a bank robber, but I was surprised at how much I could still see. The problem was that there was now no way I could expel the panties.

I made an effort to scream, but all I could manage was muffled nonsense. The girls gathered around and laughed at my predicament, which only made me more determined, but they knew, as I did, that I was powerless.

I tried to calm myself to see what would happen next, but the steady pressure of the stocking about my head was already making me uncomfortably hot.

"Who's going first?"

The brunette was definitely in charge, but, worryingly, I still had no idea what her intentions were. To begin with, I feared that Larina had told them about my newfound oral talents, but the makeshift gag suggested some different form of mischief.

"Well I guess that I'm ready."

I turned my head to see who had spoken and found that it was the girl with short red hair and pixie looks who had already supplied her panties.

The others gave her room as she approached and playfully pinched my nose.

"I'm going to enjoy this."

Without any further preamble, she stepped over the bench so that she was straddling my face, and I found myself staring at her sex, which was completely denuded of hair. I had scant seconds to take in the dark, protuberant labia and to make the connection with the rank panties that still filled my mouth before she lowered herself.

I began to panic, fearing she would crush me, but she settled lightly, and, immediately, she did so, moisture began to slowly leech through the stocking.

"Squirming's good."

She was clearly enjoying the movements of my head beneath her, so I kept still and tried to calm myself, but, as I did so, she began to move.

At first, the movements were tiny, as she brushed her sex over my mouth and my flattened nose, but as the area of dampened lycra slowly expanded and crept up over my cheeks towards my eye-line her level of excitement was self-evident.

"Go girl!"

With the others egging her on, she gave an exaggerated groan and then began to ride my face in earnest. She was still bearing her weight on her conditioned dancer's legs, but she was rubbing herself from my chin to my forehead.

I had never felt so used in all my life, but there was absolutely nothing I could do about it. The stocking was sodden, but that only seemed to make it easier for her as she began to move ever faster.

I closed my eyes, praying for it to be over, but she was not going to stop until she had reached a climax.

Finally, she took hold of the bench with both hands, just above my head, and, moving from the hips alone, she ground out her orgasm.

She lifted herself reluctantly and nonchalantly adjusted her skirt, leaving me feeling dreadful. My face was flushed with exertion, but there was nowhere for the heat to escape to, and I was convinced that it would swell horribly were it not for the continued pressure of the stocking.

I knew that I was irrational, but I was left with little time for reflection. A second girl, a blonde with a passing resemblance to Reese Witherspoon, was already removing her panties, and any vague hope that my ordeal was over cruelly evaporated.

As she approached, I shook my head in fierce denial, but she simply laughed. It occurred to me then that they knew that they had all the time in the world. I still hoped that someone would come looking for me, but now a new possibility arose. Was my reputation now such that anyone seeing me disappear with four gorgeous dancers would assume that I would want some privacy?

This turn of thought froze me for a moment, and that was all the incentive the blonde needed. She straddled my head, but, unlike her friend, she faced down my body towards my feet.

I could see that she too was depilated except for a tiny fringe at the apex, which looked like a downward pointing arrowhead but then darkness fell as she sealed me in.

She was certainly not put off by the fact that the stocking was already wet, and there was to be no gentle start. She immediately began to rake herself over my whole face, and it was obvious that the first girls' performance had got to her. She was already wet, and the insidious panties soak up her juices up like a sponge.

Breathing was difficult, and I tried to swallow to ease my quickly drying throat, but there was now no escaping the ever stronger taste which had long since lost its allure. I tried to keep a focus by counting, but I repeatedly lost the thread, not least because my tormentress insisted on being theatrical.

She leaned forward, almost lying flat along my body, and then wiggled her tush. The others found this highly amusing, but it resulted in her painfully mashing my face. I growled in frustration, encouraging another burst of laughter, but it resulted in fresh devilment.

Without warning, she pushed her face down into my crotch, and I felt a tiny but insistent pressure as she worked her tongue through the swaddling mesh.

Her thighs were pressed against my ears, but I could hear enough to know that she was making a passable impression of a porn actress. The problem was that it was so near yet so far. I could feel the warmth of her mouth through my skirt and underwear, and my sex began to react accordingly, but it would never be enough to bring me the satisfaction I sought. It was so cruel. I had longed for something like this, but now I was completely powerless.

Cheered on by the others, she hammed up her performance for a few more minutes, but then her own needs overcame her. She sat up once more and began to rub herself over my face with renewed vigor. Her climax was not long in coming, and now there was no acting. She braced herself with the simple expedient of pressing down on my breasts, and then she let herself go.

The panties soaked it up, and now, in my heightened state of arousal, the taste once again acted like a drug fuelling my own desperate need.

I knew there was no escape, they would all take their turn, and they were so at ease with one another that it was obvious that they were not new to this - and that gave me hope. The blonde girl had intimated that she was not averse to going down on me; surely, once they had taken their pleasure, it had been my turn.

The next girl was already getting herself ready. She was the one who had led the troupe in a raunchy mambo routine, and I was guessing from her coloring that she may have been Cuban.

Having slipped out of her panties, she slowly and deliberately removed her skirt and then turned slightly towards me. The wetness of the stocking was making it harder to see, but I could make out the perfection of her taut buns as she no doubts intended me to.

She had long, coltish, legs, and the firm, twin, globes, formed a crowning glory. She shimmied playfully and then approached.

"Are you ready for me?...because I am more than ready for you."

Her pride in her chief asset was obvious as she eased herself into place over my face adopting the same position that her friend had just relinquished. She looked to be the least heavy of the group but, now that she was poised just inches above me, the dark, unblemished orbs seemed to bespeak a menacing weightiness.

She settled slowly, as though aware of the fear she inspired, and as the light gave way to pressing darkness, I felt a sense of claustrophobia that I had not been aware of with the others.

At first, she remained still, demanding admiration, but I desperately wanted her to move; at least then she would not be a dead weight. She had also perspired more than the others, and the tiny pocket of air available to me had a briny redolence.

When, at last, she did begin to move, I immediately regretted it. Her movements were sinuous as she writhed from the hips, and I realized that she was dancing on my face to some unheard tune.

With the others, there had been a predictable rhythm that allowed me to brace myself and time my breathing, but now there was no such luxury. She was grinding out her pleasure, and the coarse tuft of dark hair that ran the length of her sex felt as if it were abrading my skin.

Time seemed to stretch forever, but she showed no signs of stopping, and certainly no sign of an impending climax. I thought I had reached the depths of misery, but I was wrong. Without warning, she lifted herself slightly and reached back to take hold of her solidly muscled rump. The deep, dark, cleft opened a little, and then she lowered herself once more.

She was centered over my face, which now felt as though it were gripped in a vice. Breathing through my nose was rendered impossible, forcing me to draw air through the, by now, fetid panties, and this was all part of her design.

I became aware of a new movement, and it took a few seconds for me to realize that she was masturbating. As well as I could judge, her fingers were moving quickly, but every now and then, she slowed down and leaned forward slightly. I could only guess that she was pausing to push her fingers inside, and then the reason became apparent.

The panties began to take on a fresh taste, which suggested that she had made herself so wet that she was dripping on to them. A fresh outburst of laughter and cheering from the others seemed to confirm this.

This went on for some time, while my head felt as though it would crack beneath her weight. I was by now in genuine distress. I was incredibly hot, but, at the same time, it felt as if I could no longer sweat. Added to this was a craving for fresh air, which manifested itself as a dull ache in my chest.

I was beginning to think that I should succumb and let myself blackout; they would then have no choice but to release me. This was an easy decision to make but much harder to put into practice. I was to find that my body was prepared to fight even though my mind had surrendered.

Fortunately, my last gasp struggles gave her all the encouragement that she needed, and, with a final banshee wail, she started to come.

Her friends shouted approval, and I could soon feel why. She braced herself against my face, and through my sports-top, I began to feel heavy spatters of warm moisture followed by a final series of lingering droplets heavy enough to be felt through the stocking and panties.

It seemed to take an effort for her to lift herself from me, and, once she had, I shook my head in desperation. Had I been capable, I would have begged, but then it seemed my prayers were answered.

The brunette loomed over me, and, using the edge of her fingernail, she slit open the stocking over my mouth. I immediately used my tongue to expel the panties, and when they almost free, she flicked them disdainfully onto the floor.

My mouth was dry and thick with the taste of them, but I was glad just to breathe normally. The urge to swear at them almost overcame me, but I was still helpless, and so I kept myself in check.

If the Cuban girl had been proud of her backside, then the brunette was equally proud of her impressive breasts. As I watched, she proceeded to undress completely and, once naked. She began to tease her already excited nipples.

For a dancer, her breasts were large. They were classically shaped, and each would have fitted snuggly into a champagne saucer, but it was her nipples that really demanded attention. The teats themselves were long and tumid, a dark salmon pink standing proud in the wide rosy fields of her areolae.

"Suck it..."

She bent over me, presenting her breast to my mouth, and driven by some long-buried instinct, I began to lick at it. It felt so right in my mouth, helping me to produce some much-needed saliva, and very soon, I was sucking it gently between my lips.

"Oh sister, you are a natural."

Even after all I had been through, I took a perverse pride in her praise, and when, inevitably, I was called upon to lavish attention on her other breast, I found myself desperately trying to please her.

I think that she would have been content to let me suckle for hours, but I sensed an impatience amongst the others, and she reluctantly withdrew.

I knew what was coming next. It was confirmed as she rubbed her hand over her mound, smearing it with moisture, but I felt that I had made a connection with her. As she looked down at me, I must have appeared pathetic, my red, ravaged face still wrapped in the wet, messy stocking, but I tried to plead.

"Please, I've had enough..."

For a second or two, her face took on a sympathetic expression, but then she smirked with laughter.

"If you think you're leaving me high and dry, forget it. I'm looking forward to some very personal attention."

With that, she stepped over the bench to present her sex to my mouth. But she continued to play the exhibitionist. Looking down, she used one hand to stimulate her nipples while, with the other, she stroked her prominent labia, wafting me with her scent in the process.

"Are you ready? I've made myself all creamy just thinking about you."

Just to demonstrate her point, she opened herself to reveal a wet coral cave strung with gossamer threads, which, even now, made my mouth water.

I do not know if she came to me or me to her, but I thrust my tongue greedily inside and swallowed all she had to give.

For a few moments, she was content, even amused, to watch me in my feeding frenzy, but as my tongue began to have its inevitable effect, she focused more fully on her own needs. She fractionally moved so that I could reach her fully engorged clitoris, and it took very little after that to finish her off.

At the point of crisis, she took hold of my head in her hands, and her weight began to bear down on me until finally, her feet left the floor, and her legs opened in a wide gymnastic vee.

I think that then I finally blacked out.

Once again, when I managed to bring my surroundings back into some sort of focus, my head felt as if I had been repeatedly coshed, and I was stupefied. I dimly registered the brunette, getting dressed in the periphery of my vision, but then a shadow fell over me.

"Wakey, wakey sleepy head. You're not finished yet..."

.They left me in the shower where I wanted to remain forever under the comforting warms jets, but, out in the real world, there was a flight to catch. My body ached all over, and my skin was crisscrossed with the imprint of the nylon netting. By the time I had finished washing my hair, the marks were already beginning to fade.

I feared to go back into the changing area for a moment, but, while their costumes were still there, the room was empty.

I was forced to wear my soiled kit to make my way back to my locker room, but it seemed that, here too, everyone else had left. I dressed quickly and was able to slip out quietly while everyone's attention was focused on the men's final. Under other circumstances, I would have stayed to watch, but I was in no mood.

While the others were to fly back to Denmark, I was flying to London. I had some commercial sponsorship obligations, and I wanted to meet my parents on their return from their three-month sojourn to Australia and New Zealand.

For the next few days, life returned to something like normal. Eschewing my flat, I stayed with my parents, who were overjoyed by my victory but bitterly disappointed that they had missed out on being there to see it by just a couple of days.

On the sponsorship front, my paymasters were equally happy, and there was talk of extended contracts. Everything seemed peachy, but when the time came to return to Denmark, I was a mess of mixed emotions. I now firmly believed that I could go all the way with Agnetha's guidance, but the question was at what cost.

While in England, I had even received a congratulatory phone call from John, my former coach. He was his usual flirty self, and for a few seconds, I felt the return of the old frisson. There was no way that I would start up with him again, but I was encouraged by this evidence of heterosexual yearnings.

Back in Aarhus, I had just two weeks to prepare for Danish Open, and then the plan was for us all to decamp to Anaheim for the World Championship. I quickly found that the atmosphere in our little community had changed. I continued to remain aloof, but both Agnetha and the others seemed to be treating me with newfound respect. Between themselves, they still played out their games of forfeits, but I was left to my own devices.

I trained hard and retired early each night, after which I would normally masturbate myself to sleep. The trouble was that my fantasies seemed centered on the people around me, and I even climaxed while conjuring up images of the abuse I had suffered in Holland. In a determined effort to put things right, I started surfing the porn channels available on satellite TV. While I found the boy/girl imagery arousing, I almost invariably flicked to the German girl/girl channel when I needed to climax.

By the eve of the Danish open, I was badly on edge. When on the court, I found myself looking at the others in an entirely inappropriate way, but, at the same time, I felt so ashamed by what I had already done.

That evening I skipped my meal and went straight to my room. I determined that I would not switch on the TV, but within half an hour, my resolution had crumbled. I was naked with my hands between my legs when there was a knock at the door.

I was tempted to shout out, telling them to go away, but there was a possibility that it might have been Agnetha. I got up, threw on a nightshirt, and quickly washed my hands.

I was surprised to find Katya standing at the door, holding two cups of coffee and a bag of pastries.

"Can I come in?"

I wanted to say no, but the local coffee shop was a fair distance from the complex, and she had obviously put herself out.

It only was as I stood aside to let her enter that it occurred to me that there might still be a tell-tale scent in the air, but she did not seem to notice.

"You missed dinner. I thought you might be hungry."

She took out two Danish pastries from the bag and offered me one. They contravened our strict dietary regime, but, right then, comfort food was just what I needed. What I thought was coffee turned out to be delicious hot chocolate. While we sat and ate, we discussed our preparations for the following day's tournament.

I had warmed to Katya ever since she had revealed the secret of the court markings to me, but I felt awkward because I was sure that she must know about my unsavory conduct. If this was the case, she gave no hint of it, and it was comforting to be able to just chat with her as a friend.

She was almost four years older than me but, with her blonde curls and a face prone to flush easily, she looked younger. It was a lethal combination. She had a curvy, mature figure with a baby doll face, and, when we were out in the town, men of all ages would be drawn to her. In short, she was enigmatic, and I have to admit that, in my more lucid moments, she had featured in my guilty flights of fancy.

I now felt really bad about those improper thoughts. She was a genuinely nice person who was reaching out to me. We talked for another hour or so, but I was becoming conscious of the time; I needed a goods night's sleep, and there was still a little personal matter that needed attending to.

I half stood, dropping a hint, but as she followed suit, quickly trying to finish the dregs of her chocolate, she managed to miss her mouth.

"Shit."

It ran down her chin onto her breasts, which were covered by a white cropped sports top. Reacting quickly and without modesty, she whipped off the top to prevent it from being stained.

I had seen her naked on many occasions, but the confines of my room conferred an uneasy intimacy. Her breasts were so sharply uplifted as to be almost cone-shaped, and her nipples formed a pair of delicate dusky crowns.

"Can I borrow a towel?"

I realized that I had been staring; I watched in fascination as the runnel of chocolate trailed between her breasts and over the pale plane of her stomach before disappearing into the deep pit of her navel only to reappear once more.

I dragged myself back to reality and grabbed a towel from the bathroom. Dashing back, I began to dab at her, but the chocolate had already begun to seep into her pink jogging pants.

"Damn it."

She pulled the waist of the pants away from herself slightly, and I blotted up the mess but not before noticing that she was not wearing panties. She was totally depilated but for a near-invisible blonde furze, which was suggestive of a little laziness on her part, and this now lay revealed by the chocolate.

"That will do."

She took the towel from me to finish off but, without thought, I took hold of the waistband.

"Let me get these into soak, you can borrow a pair of mine."

She refused, saying that she would be back in her room in a trice, but I was already on my knees pulling them playfully, but insistently, down her legs.

In the next few seconds, the frivolous mood evaporated as the aspect of our new juxtaposition made itself apparent. I looked up at her, unable to read her expression, and she remained awkwardly silent.

I wanted her, but I had to do something to ease the tension, and so, without taking my eyes from hers, I leaned forward and licked upwards from the top of her mons to her navel, following the residue of the dark sweet trail.

She whispered nervously.

"I can't do this..."

As she said it, I felt an almost painful twinge of disappointment, but, at the same time, I felt her body shiver with excitement. I trailed my tongue off to one side, and, when she raised no further objection, I slowly followed the curve of her pubic bone downwards.

I am sure that I caught the faintest hint of her natural musk, and I felt my own bodies' sympathetic response, but I did not want to frighten her. I eased my way back to my starting point and felt the sharp prickles of young growth as I gently licked her clean.

She gave an almost unheard groan and placed an admonitory hand on the top of my head, but she made no effort to push me away. Taking this as encouragement, I brought my hands to her hips and

390

slowly eased her jogging pants down her legs. When they were bunched at her ankles, I moved my hands slowly upwards over the gentle curves of her calves and the tensed muscles at the back of her thighs until I was cradling the gentle weight of her cute derriere.

She gasped and then froze for a few seconds before looking down at me.

"I can't ...not with another girl."

I was unsure of how to respond. Did she want to stop altogether, or was she simply saying that she could not reciprocate?

She remained very still. Was I expected to get up, to apologize, perhaps?

In the end, my own need drove me to test her resolve. I started to lick once more but began to range ever lower so that my tongue swept over the tight, reluctant slit of her sex.

"Please...don't..."

Even as she said it, the position of her hand on my head shifted ever so subtlety. It could have been interpreted as a signal to stop or perhaps something else.

Undaunted, I moved lower still so that I was licking at the base of her sex and was rewarded with the first hint of wetness.

I knew then that it was only a matter of time. Having forced my blade between the tight clams of the oyster, I slowly built on my advantage and gently eased it open.

There could be no doubt now. Her hand had found its way to the back of my head and her inner lips swelled to embrace my invading tongue. I responded by licking up and down the whole length of her sex, which was now open to my assault, and my prize was a warm creamy offering, which I lapped up with an involuntary groan.

I could sense her frustration now. The pants around her ankles were an encumbrance; she wanted to open herself to me but was fearful of losing her balance. I could not stop now, so I held her more firmly to me as I began working her interior moisture up over her neat clitoris.

At first so subtle, her scent was now all-pervading, and her taste took on an ever-increasing richness. I thought I could use these signs to gauge her, but her climax seemed to take us both by surprise. Her body rocked back and forth from the hips in an almost bizarre parody of a man being fellated, and in her attempt to hold me in, she only succeeded in turning my head sideways so that my cheek was smeared with her sap.

As it came to a finish, she held me there, clamped tight, as though she did not want to face the reality of what had just taken place. In the end, I had to ease myself up from what was an awkward, cramping, position and I used the towel to clean myself up as best I could.

I turned my attention back to Katya, who was standing head down, unsteady on her feet, as she tried to breathe normally again, and I knew I had to break the ice.

"Would you like to use my shower?"

She looked up at me, her eyes still slightly glazed, and gave an indecisive nod. She teetered the short distance to the armchair and sat down on it awkwardly. She kicked off her slip-on trainers without using her hands and then divested herself of her jogging bottoms.

She looked across to the shower room as though the effort of reaching it was going to be too great, and then she looked back at me. In the next few seconds, she regained her composure, and any sense of uncertainty was dispelled. With calm deliberation, she dipped her finger into the cold pool of chocolate on the tabletop, and then, opening her legs, she drew a trail on her inner thigh.

"I think you missed some."

I should have been angry that this erstwhile, reluctant ingénue now had the audacity to act so suggestively, but I was, once again, caught in the grip of an inexplicable hunger. I suppose that, in turning my head away, she had somehow denied me, but that could not excuse my aberrant behavior.

Like a somnambulist, I moved forward, and I sank slowly to my knees. Putting my tongue to her thigh, I followed the sweet, dark track until I reached her finger, which had paused while she waited for me to catch up - as she knew I inevitably would.

Now her finger moved on, and, like a slave girl on an invisible rope, I was drawn with her. She led me slowly across the shallow declivity at the top of her thigh and then upwards onto her mons, where the taste became more bitter as it combined with the residue of her first climax.

It was hard to believe that she had been so unyielding as she now pushed her finger between her labia with a loud squelch and then twisted it slowly back and forth. When she withdrew it, the chocolate had helped to form an oily coating, and, after a moment's pause, she fed it to me.

I sucked her finger deep into my mouth and cleaned it with my tongue, but now I wanted the real, unadulterated taste. As if reading my mind, she gently freed herself and then used both hands to make herself available.

I opened my mouth and put it to her sex, plunging my tongue deep inside. There was still a slightly unwanted, alien sweetness, but it was soon overcome but the warm, earthy taste that I craved.

She was flowing freely, and as I drove my tongue as deep as it could go, she lifted her hips to meet me. I was caught up in madness, and I slipped my arms under her thighs to get my hands on her tight globes so that she could not escape. Her second orgasm was not long in coming, and as she exploded, I sucked it from her.

She collapsed exhausted, unmindful of the fact that she was pinning my arms, and I was kept captive just inches from her sex as she slowly came back to her senses.

Finally, we peeled ourselves apart, a little clumsily, and this time she did avail herself of the bathroom.

I lay on the bed, listening to the shower running, willing her to hurry up. It was getting late, and I had to be up at six to catch the coach to the competition arena. I must have drifted off at some point because when I opened my eyes, Katya was lying beside me, fast asleep and naked.

I should have woken her, told her to go, but she looked beautiful in the darkness, and she had her arm around my neck in a gesture that I found comforting. I must have smelt rank, but she did not seem to mind as she sleepily brought her face closer to mine.

I surrendered to sleep and uneasy dreams only to be woken by an insistent pressure. I opened my eyes, and it took a second or two to remember that Katya had not left. We were on our sides facing one another, but I had, somehow, moved down the bed a little. My face was level with her breasts, and a hand at the back of my head was coaxing me.

I glanced up, but she still appeared to be asleep, and the slow rise and fall of her breast were almost mesmeric. It seemed the most natural thing in the world to slowly take her nipple between my lips and to tease it with my tongue. Feeling it distend, I drew lazy circles and began to explore the raised dimples of her areolae.

Throughout this, her breathing remained steady and sleepy, but then she groaned and moved a little making me feel that I had imposed myself. For a second, I was almost petulant as she pulled herself away but, as she rearranged herself, she drew up her knees so that she was curled almost fetal, and I found my face pressed against her stomach.

I waited for her to settle once more before easing away, but she shifted once again. This time she arched her back, moving her upper body away from me, but at the same time, her pelvis was thrust forward, bringing her sex level with my mouth.

She had used my shower gel, and her skin was redolent of jasmine but also present, unmistakably, was a deeper undertone which suggested that, asleep or not, I had had an effect on her.

For a second or two, I was tempted, but I had to get some sleep. With resignation, I pecked the gentlest of kisses on her sweet labia only to hear a deep sigh. She was still asleep, I was sure of it, but as I slowly backed away, her body stretched, and she moved with me, her sex opening very slightly in the process,

The light from the window was reflected from a single dewdrop which lay quivering just where I had kissed and, without thought, I collected it on the tip of my tongue.

It was my undoing. I remained there lapping in the darkness slowly and gently, a gossamer touch, which made her sex melt.

I was lost in time, but it must have been at least an hour later before she shuddered into a slow, dreamy orgasm, and even then, I licked on until she had nothing left to give.

Later I was awoken by the piercing shriek of the alarm clock, and it took me seconds to orientate myself.

Katya was gone, my head pounded, and my mouth felt thick and cloying. I struggled to the shower and then rushed breakfast before dashing for the coach. As I boarded, I avoided Katya's eye and sat by myself at the back.

Fortunately, my opening match was late on the court, and I mainlined coffee to bring myself around. By mid-morning, I was feeling a little better, but my confidence took a knock as I watched a clearly under par Katya lose to a rank outsider.

When my match was called, I went on to court nervously. This was an opponent who had never beaten me, but I was making elementary mistakes in the early stages, and I lost the first game cheaply. I fought back in the second, winning a closely contested game, and then went on to win the third, but I knew that I had expended too much energy this early in the tournament.

As I came off court, Larina was there smirking at me.

"Too much bed, not enough sleep?"

I tried not to let the jibe get to me, but I began to wonder if she knew, and then, with my thoughts taking an even darker turn, I began to consider the possibility that I had been set up.

Over the next few days, I let my anger feed me, and I powered my way through to the semis.

In a reversal of the Dutch open, I was to meet world number one while Larina was drawn against world number two. Having already beaten my opponent so recently, I was optimistic. But I was further encouraged when Agnetha handed me a revised dossier, which anticipated the tactics the Malaysian might adopt in light of her defeat.

I was still feeling good about things the next morning when the bombshell dropped. Larina had strained a thigh muscle, and she could not compete. This would give her opponent a bye but, more importantly, an extra days rest. Even if I got through the semi, which would be tough, my chances in the final were slim.

I tried not to let it prey on my mind as I went onto the court, but oddly, it spurred me on. For me, this was now the final; if I beat the number one in consecutive matches, the world would take notice.

In the event, the match was an epic. Games one and two went to tie breaks, leaving us at one game all, but in the third, I felt my energy draining. I gave away easy points and thought it was slipping through my fingers, but, at the turn round, I caught sight of the dossier in my bag.

I remembered Anegtha's prediction that my opponent would play to my backhand as the match went on. As I tired, I tended to hold the racket just a little lower and lofted the shuttle more often.

I focused on this and made myself ready. Sure enough, she started to drive to my backhand at every opportunity and then positioned herself for the loft, but three times in a row, I caught her out with a short crosscourt. The scores were level, and it was now her turn to make mistakes.

Knowing that I stood little chance in the final, I gave everything I had, and after playing one final, winning, smash, I collapsed to my knees.

I accepted the congratulations in a blur but managed to pick out my mum and dad in the crowd before heading to the dressing room.

As I did so, I heard applause from the number two court, and curiosity drew me over. To my astonishment, I saw Larina warming up with her thigh heavily strapped. I sought out Agnetha in the stand.

"She shouldn't be playing."

Agnetha turned towards me.

"I asked her to."

"But she doesn't stand a chance."

"She knows that."

And then the light dawned. She was going to make her opponent work at least so that I stood a chance in the final.

The match took less than forty minutes, and the strain showed on Larina's face from the start, but she made the other girl run. She could not get her balance right to hit power shots, but she could play the shuttle around the court, keeping her opponent moving until, inevitably, she was herself outplayed.

As she came off court, I was the first to greet her.

"Thank you."

"You owe me one, and I intend to collect."

By rights, I should have lost the final the next day but spurred on by Larina's sacrifice, I played beyond my normal limits, and I won my second championship in a row.

Players and parents gathered afterward in a local fish restaurant, and I was pleased when my win was treated as a success for the whole team rather than just a personal triumph. My parents, at first suspicious of Agnetha's methods, now showered her with praise. But loudest of all was Elise, Larina's mother, fuelled by just a little too much Sancerre she, quite rightfully, trumpeted Larina's part in my victory.

I knew that Elise was a single parent, a woman in her mid-forties who had put her career on hold to further her daughter's ambitions, and they seemed to share the same determined spirit.

They could have been taken for sisters. Elise looked young for her years and, while she carried a few extra pounds, her well-cut clothes did enough to compensate. They were also alike facially, sharing the same Scandinavian features; the only major difference was in the color of their eyes. Larina had the blue eyes common to the population, but Elise's were a deep brown, which she accentuated with burnished gold highlights in her blonde hair.

In theory, I should have shared the national team hotel, but, in practice, we formed a team of our own, and we returned to our hotel, booked by Agnetha, for a final drink. Elise was still loudly holding court as my parents finally said their goodnights and went up to their room, and, after a decent interval, I followed suit.

All the girls gave me one last congratulatory kiss, but as Larina pecked my cheek, she whispered in my ear.

"My room...half an hour."

I could have simply ignored her, but I had done some hard thinking in the run-up to the tournament. There was no doubt that I was bi-sexual to a degree, but I was prepared to allow the possibility that the lesbian part of me might be the dominant trait. To further explore, I needed to bring to an end the perverted form of Sapphic indulgence that I had already engaged in and allow for some form of a meaningful two-way relationship.

I was still unsure whether or not Larina was an out and out lesbian but, even if she was, I was not attracted to her in any emotional sense, and I was now determined to make this clear to her.

Armed with this resolve, I made my way to her room and knocked confidently on the door.

"Come in. It's not locked."

I walked into a room, which was the mirror image of my own but then realized it was the wrong one. Reclining on the bed dressed only in brief, diaphanous, nightie was not Larina but her mother.

"I'm dreadfully sorry. I thought his was Larina's room."

"It was, but we swapped. My room had twin beds, this one had a double. We'll be more comfortable here."

I looked at her open-mouthed as the implication of what she had just said sunk in. Finally, gathering my wits, I tried to put things straight.

"I think there's been a misunderstanding."

"Oh, I don't think so. You see, Larina has told me about your scheme of forfeits and I am sure we are agreed that you are in her debt. Let's just say that she has assigned your indebtedness over to me."

It was too much to take in. Her knowledge suggested an unnatural and frightening candidness between mother and daughter. Shock kept me rooted to the spot, and she made the most of her advantage.

As I watched, she raised her knees and slowly allowed her legs to fall apart. Unlike her daughter, she allowed her pubic hair to flourish, and protruding from the blonde thicket was the base of an ivory colored vibrator.

"I've been warming myself up but I understand you are worth the wait."

In the ensuing silence, the loudest sound in the room was a dull insistent hum that slowly rose in tone as the vibrator, at first imperceptibly, but then more obviously, began to slip free until it lay on the bed between her legs in a noisy frenzy.

Her eyes did not leave mine as she slowly picked it up and switched it off before turning it slowly so that its shiny wet surface caught the light.

"Come and clean it for me..."

The suggestion was outrageous, disgusting, but it flicked a switch somewhere in my perverted psyche. I approached the foot of the bed and then crawled towards her as she held it out towards me, only to draw it away as I got closer. I slavishly followed until she held it against her mons like a faux erection, and then I began to lick.

I guess that it was down to pheromones because the taste was Larina. I now knew that a woman's taste was fundamentally the same, but their subtle nuances were determined by various factors. In this case, there was a family resemblance.

"Good girl, but you can do better than that."

She lowered the vibrator just a little, and, rising to the challenge; I took it deep into my mouth. For a few seconds, I sucked on it greedily, but I was soon experiencing the sterile, chemical taste of plastic.

I tried to pull away, but she was amused at my display, and she put a hand to the back of my head while at the same time raising her hips. I thought that I would gag, but she bucked herself playfully until I withdrew with a sudden wrench.

"Oh, I'm sorry baby. I guess you're anxious for the main course."

I was more angry than anxious but, as she put the vibrator aside, I was left looking at her sex, which was already hot, wet, and relaxed. Her labia were loose, thick, folds, which suggested maturity, and I got a sense that she had, over time, made the most of her single status.

As I stared, I tried desperately to pull myself away. It was not that she was a woman, that particular barrier was well breached, nor her age but simply the fact that it felt, somehow, incestuous. It just felt so wrong, given what had passed between Larina and 1, to now be engaged with her mother.

Elise waited patiently, as though she could read my thoughts, and then, in a further display of prescience, she used her fingers to gently peel herself open.

I could now see her clitoris, a plump, tight-skinned, succulent berry, and at the same time, my nostrils were assailed by a strong waft of scent from deep within.

I could no longer resist. I dropped on her like a bird of prey. In one movement, I pressed my tongue inside her, and, at the same time, I nuzzled her clitoris with my nose.

"My, my, aren't you the greedy one."

She was surprisingly tight, and I had to work hard to penetrate the tight sheath of muscle, but my reward was the rich pool of sap that I encountered at the bottom of the well.

I used my tongue like a hummingbird, enjoying the taste on the very tip, while at the same time, she squeezed at me, displaying remarkable control.

I could not last long with my tongue almost painfully stretched, but she was in tune with me, and the squeezing intensified as she quickly worked herself to an initial climax. As it broke, my tongue was expelled, but I licked slowly along her labia as her body shuddered to a finish.

No words were spoken. We both knew that my job was not yet done, and for the next few minutes, I continued to minister to her as she came off of her first high and prepared herself for a second ascent.

"I'm ready babe. Do my clit."

I shifted myself slightly so that I could give all my attention to this particular treat. At the first touch, she shivered, and then I began a languid oral assault. I licked in circles pausing now again to suck it delicately between my lips.

She groaned from time to time and whispered encouragement and particularly so as I licked at the taut collar of the retracted hood. Having discovered her preference, I began to tease her, and very soon, she was pleading with me to take her over the edge, but this newfound power was thrilling, and I found that the more I denied her, the greater my arousal.

This went on for some minutes until I finally relented and did as she asked. Her body stiffened and then shook, and it was as if she were dancing with pleasure on the tip of my tongue. She managed to stretch it out until her body could take no more but, even as she began to relax, I began a renewed attack.

"No more..."

It was a desperate whisper, but she had still not fully descended from the plateau, and it was all too easy to tauten the strings once more. This time I alternated between her clitoris and her cleft, which was seeping onto the counterpane. From not wanting to continue, she had to decide how she wanted to come for the third time.

My skillful tongue had her writhing, and she was desperately pulling at her erect nipples. I suspected that another clitoral orgasm might be too much for her, which was borne out as she grew more desperate.

"Deeper!"

For a moment, I complied, pressing my tongue between her folds but then, in a spirit of rebellion, I move onto her clitoris once more.

"No!"

Her voice, frantic with need, was hoarse, but I ignored her. I clamped my mouth to her and licked frenetically over the whole area at the top of her sex.

She tried to fight me, but her inner craving got the better of her, and she had no choice but to surrender to her pleasurable fate. Her body formed a strained arch, and she became very still, making me think that she had passed out, but then a tiny whimper betrayed the fact that she was caught up in the throes of an orgasm more powerful than the two that had gone before.

She was so drained she could not ride it out to its conclusion, and she collapsed with a frustrated moan, her body twitching for seconds afterward.

As I looked down on her, I slowly became aware of my own desperate need, but something about her whole attitude told me that she was likely to refuse, and I had already suffered enough humiliation. Without another word, I gathered myself together and left the room.

Anaheim. It seemed unreal. I had planned to enjoy myself, to use the tournament to gain the necessary experience to mount a realistic challenge the following year, but now, here I was, with a huge weight of expectation on my shoulders.

Agnetha had done a good job of keeping the world press at bay while we trained, but now there was no escaping them. I was being talked of as the great white hope. I was the first woman in years from outside of the Far East with the potential to win the championship.

I was still convinced that it was too soon. I had won a couple of tournaments, beating the world's best, but they were geared up for this. I had already played beyond myself, but they were bringing themselves to their peak just for these few days.

Agnetha and I had discussed it for hours, and she had convinced me that I could do it. After that, a group decision was reached. We would train as usual, but, with the help of the others, I would be groomed for a run to the final.

I thought that they would be resentful but, without me noticing, they had concluded that I had the best chance and that, as in Eindhoven, a win for me was a win for all of them.

The training itself was more rigorous than ever and professional. There were no more pranks, no more talk of forfeits, and, most importantly, the girls left me alone. It was this more than anything that helped me focus. I had made up my mind to explore my sexuality, but I was determined to do it in my own time, on my own terms, and on a partnership of equals.

By the time the tournament began, I was fitter than ever, and Agnetha had me convinced that I was as good as anybody. Nothing had been left to chance. She had prepared the usual dossiers; she had even checked the sports hall temperature in advance. She knew that it would be heavily air-conditioned to combat the Californian sunshine, and she was concerned that I might cool down too quickly, so for the past two weeks, she had made us train in a hall set to the same ambient temperature.

In the event, I breezed through the first round brushing aside a mid-ranked opponent, but in the second round, I was drawn against Aruna. We were all agreed that, once the event started, we all played for ourselves; there must be no suspicion of collusion.

There was no dossier on Aruna. I did not need one, but she knew me as well as anybody. So it was that our match was closely fought. Technically, she was my equal but what separated us was the instinctive skill that only champions have. I beat her because I could pull off the unexpected.

I was into the quarter-finals but, surprisingly, Larina did not make it. In a cruel twist of fate, she was drawn against Katya, and no one was more astonished than I when the older girl played the match of her life to win through.

If fortune cast scorn on Larina, it seemed to favor me. In the quarter-final, I was drawn against another Brit, a girl I had played, and consistently beaten, through the junior ranks. That gave me a psychological edge, and I used it to my advantage.

In the semis, I was paired against the surprise package of the tournament. The little South Korean girl had never been beyond the quarter-finals of any major tournament, but she had beaten Katya convincingly to take her place in the semis.

I knew very little about her, but Agnetha had produced a fulsome dossier updated with notes from the earlier rounds. The girl was not as muscular as the other girls from the Far East, but she was incredibly quick around the court. Agnetha advised me to keep the rally going and let her blow herself out. This led to a longer match than I was comfortable with, but I finally managed to grind her down.

That set up the final that everyone had been hoping for, the established number one versus the young pretender.

On the morning of the match, I was more nervous than ever before, but the oddities in my personal life of late had put me in situations where I had had to conquer my nerves with alarming frequency, and it was a lesson well learned.

I squeezed myself into my immodest sports skirt and looked at myself in the mirror. The federation had made no official comment on dress code but, taking their lead from ladies volleyball, they were prepared to turn a blind eye to anything that boosted the television ratings. For my part, I knew that it was not just my sporting ability that attracted the sponsors, and I was going to make sure they got their money's worth on this the biggest day of my life.

If I was puffed up with pride, then the balloon was soon pricked. I lost the first game scoring only two points. My opponent was half a second faster and reaching an inch further than the last time we met, and she seemed to anticipate every shot.

At the changeover, I sat on my seat feeling bewildered, but into that void came Agnetha's assured commands. It was almost as though she were at my side telling me what to do. I had to calm down and, contrary to expectation, go on the defensive.

In the next game, I lost the first couple of points, but then my opponent served long. Her dossier suggested that she needed to be in a groove and that if she made a mistake, she tended to make two or three in a row, so it proved. I went three two up, and I could sense that, beneath her ice-cool exterior, she was angry at herself.

From then on, it was close, but, with the crowd behind me, I edged the second game.

At the interval, it was obvious to everyone who had spent to most energy. I was breathing deeply, finding it hard to take fluids on board, while my opponent sipped at her drink contentedly.

In the third and deciding game, I quickly went behind as she casually stepped up a gear, and at the turn round, I was seven three down and struggling. Once again, Agnetha's voice, in my subconscious, came to my aid. I cast my eyes across the small table opposite on which sat the modest trophy that represented the pinnacle of my ambition.

Agnetha had told me to stare at it, to tell myself that the prize was mine and, for I few seconds, I felt my conviction renewed, but, as the umpire gave the ten-second warning, I began to waver. It was at that moment that something drew my gaze upwards. Seated immediately behind the trophy was Agnetha. She had moved out from the bank of seats reserved for officials and was now right in my eye line.

I wondered, fleetingly, how she had contrived to reserve that particular seat, but I was then shocked to immobility. As I looked, she slowly opened her legs, allowing her elegant skirt to ride up just a little.

I was the one person in the arena who would now know that she was not wearing panties, and, as I continued to stare across the hall, the true majesty of her sex was apparent to me.

I knew then what the real prize on offer was, and adrenalin flowed through my veins like an illegal stimulant.

The umpire had to tap my shoulder to bring me back to reality, but when I took to the court, I played as a woman possessed. For the next few rallies, she had no answer to me, and I won six points without reply. After that, the game was more evenly balanced, as my opponent got back to her very best, but I had a new belief in myself. I wanted to be magnificent, to make myself worthy of my mentor, and I reverted to my natural game. I played audaciously, following my instincts, and the unorthodox nature of my shots gave me a new edge.

At match point, I positioned myself to serve high but then dinked a cheeky shot just over the net, and the sheer audacity of it caught my opponent flat-footed. It was an unworthy shot with which to win the world championship, but I did not care.

The crowd roared, and I stepped into a world of unreality. The many congratulations, the presentation, even the press interviews seemed to be happening to somebody else, but I knew, at that moment, that my life would never be the same.

I gathered myself sufficiently to talk to my ecstatic parents, and then I made my way to the showers. I luxuriated under the powerful spray for long minutes while I tried to take it all in, and then I was chauffeured back to the hotel. It was odd suddenly being left to myself, but there were a couple of hours in hand before we were scheduled for dinner, and then I was obligated to stay until the following day for the men's final and closing ceremony.

As I opened the door to my room, I had the premonition, and I was buoyed up and discomforted at the same time.

I smelt her perfume as I crossed the threshold, and then I saw her standing at the window. I paused, knowing that I should ask how she had got in, but no words came.

She made me wait for a space of seconds, and then she turned to me. Her eyes fixed on mine, and I could see that she knew everything.

"Congratulations, we did it"

Her choice of pronoun seemed calculated, and it grated just a little, but she continued without pause.

"I was, of course, a little disappointed at your lack of discipline at the finish but I'm sure I count on you to do as you are told from now on."

The old me would have made a smart comeback, but I was in awe of her. She stood there assuredly radiating a raw, unfettered, sex appeal and all my carefully constructed plans dissipated like dust in the wind.

"Come and undress me."

It was an absurd thing to say, but for her, it was the most natural thing in the world, and she knew there was no question of my saying no.

I walked towards her slowly, and my fingers trembled as I fumbled with the buttons of her blouse.

She made no move to help me. She simply stood there until the last button was unfastened, and then I had to reach up to slip it from her shoulders.

It dropped to the floor with a quiet sigh, and I proceeded, unbidden, to unfasten her bra. Of course, I had already seen her breasts, but it was as if I were revealing treasures for the first time. The undergarment was expensive, obviously made to measure, and provided an arrogant, but becoming, uplift. As I slowly peeled it away from her body, her breasts parted slightly but maintained their desirable resilience, and it was all I could do to keep myself from stroking them.

I could have moved closer to her, reached around her to unfasten her skirt. Instead, I went to my knees. It somehow seemed the natural thing to do.

For her part, she slowly turned around, providing me with access to the one simple button and the long zip, which released her skirt, allowing it to slide down slowly like a theatre curtain.

My heart was beating manically, my face just inches from the sculpted perfection of her behind, which was framed by a simple black garter belt holding up an equally dark pair of silk stockings. I found myself trying to remember if she had been wearing them at the arena but that one long glimpse between her legs had been totally focused on the exclusion of any extraneous detail.

The mere recollection caused my mouth to open ever so slightly, allowing the tip of my tongue to moisten my top lip, and something in the way she held herself made it seem as though she understood what was happening behind her exactly.

For a few seconds, I remained there, unsure what to do next, until she finally condescended to turn around.

"Oh God."

I whispered the words without thinking. Her sex was truly a thing of beauty. Her mons lived up its Latin appellation, forming a high curved prominence, covered in a dense thicket of dark curls with severely defined borders, which suggested some expensive, professional grooming.

Her labia seemed to erupt through the dark covering, and I could imagine her sex as a tight skinned fruit which had split to reveal its contents. The lips were thick, more grey than pink, and suggested a maturity that made me nervous.

"Is this what you want...?"

She moved fractionally closer, causing me to flinch reflexively.

"From day one I knew two things about you. I knew that I could make you a champion and I knew that, once you were, I would have you right here on your knees."

At that moment, I realized. She had groomed me all along. I was in no doubt now that she knew all about the others, starting with Tamiko and, just like my badminton training, she had planned it meticulously - and all to make me worthy of her.

Some small part of me was appalled at the seeming ease with which I had been manipulated. But the truth was that I desired her with a hunger beyond words.

I lurched forward and threw my arms around her legs, nuzzling her sex with the side of my face. I felt the rasp of the tight curls against my cheek and breathed in deeply through my nose, taking in the smell of her. She had used a musky perfume on her inner thighs, which complemented her natural scent as if distilled for the purpose.

She stroked my head for a moment or two, indulging my need, and then she peeled herself away.

"Come over here."

We were staying in the Crusader Hotel, which was subtlety themed in keeping with its name. The centerpiece of my suite was a large coffee table resembling the lid of a casket complete with an etching of a knight in his final repose.

As I watched, she picked up a plump cushion from the sofa and laid it down over the knight's face. This was not what I wanted, but we both knew that, if it was going to happen, it was going to be on her terms. Without further bidding, I moved towards her and then lay down on the table's cold, hard surface.

With my head supported by the cushion, and with my arms by my side, it was as if the table was cut out around me and the association with death, albeit vague, brought an involuntary shiver.

Agnetha stood over me, a slight smile on her face, and then she reached down to clear a stray wisp of hair from my forehead. I shivered once more, this time in trepidation, and her smile widened almost imperceptibly.

For good or bad, I wanted it to begin, but she drifted out of my line of sight only to return with the two larger remaining cushions in hand. Almost ritually, she placed them carefully on the floor at either side of my head.

Still, she made me wait. She lifted her hair from the back of her neck and then let it fall back into place before raising her arms and stretching herself. She was a looming presence, and I was suddenly made aware of the difference in our physiques.

At last, the time had come, and she lifted her leg over the table in a single graceful movement. Her knees were mere inches from the sides of my face, and I found myself staring up into the heart of darkness.

Her sex, which had, until then, been the focus of my desire, suddenly seemed imbued with menace, but I had already come too far. With an almost balletic poise, she began to descend, and I felt the heat of her thighs as her knees slowly sank into the cushions.

She held herself poised, barely touching my face, and then she moved slowly back and forth. The gentle brushing of my skin was almost maddening, but her scent was now all-enveloping, and I was breathing ever deeper.

She was in no hurry. She continued with the same soothing movements, and I felt as if my face was a territory that was being marked and laid claim to.

"Don't."

The gentle admonition came because I had felt the first hint of dampness on my face, and I had put out my tongue. Now I withdrew it and waited.

She became still, and in the closed confines of her thighs, I felt my face growing ever warmer, and my forehead was pricked by the first tiny beads of sweat.

I knew what was coming, and I held my breath. She allowed her knees to relax, and then with almost painful slowness. She came down on me.

Her weight pressed my head deeper into the cushion, and I felt a wave of panic, but she paused, knowingly, to allow the moment to pass. Once my body was relaxed once more, she moved forward slightly, using my nose to split her labia, and then she completed her descent.

The wet folds of her sex mated with my lower face, sealing me in as if it were always meant to be.

The pressure was painful, but I had a sense of well being. I wanted to lick, to get her taste, but this was not the moment. She was asserting herself. I might be the world champion, but she was letting me know that, in her scheme of things, I was still an ingénue.

In the stillness of the room, I was aware of the pounding of blood in my ears, and I realized that it had been some seconds since I last drew breath. Instinct made me try to open my mouth, but her weight prevented it. My eyes closed until then, flew open only to find her looking down on me with an air of studied detachment.

As my lungs started to burn, I braced myself to push her away, but, at the last moment, she lifted herself sufficiently to allow me one single gasping breath before closing the seal once more.

For the next few moments, she controlled my breathing in the same way, and with every desperate inhalation, I was filling my mouth and lungs with the taste and smell of her. She knew, and I was to find out that those moments of panic would burn sensory impressions into my mind, which would remain with me forever.

At the finish, she was very wet, as evidenced by the sheen of pungent juices that now coated my skin, and I feared that she would use my face to ride out her climax but, without warning, she slowly lifted herself from me.

She smiled as she looked down at my red, abused visage, and then she crossed to the edge of the bed and sat down.

"Come here."

I struggled upright and walked towards her; my eyes were drawn to her nipples, which stood out in arrogant arousal. Some vestige of good manners made me look up to her face, which had never seemed more beautiful, and I wanted for nothing more in the world than to be enfolded in her arms and to kiss her lustrous lips.

"Undress yourself."

She said it tenderly, and as I quickly removed my clothes, I finally dared to hope. I stood naked before her, knowing I was desirable, but now desperately wanting to see it reflected in her eyes.

She kept me standing there for a space of seconds, and then, with studied deliberation, she slowly opened her legs.

"Kneel."

With that one word, my world caved in. Her smile told me that we would never be equals, but more, she knew I would not refuse her. Even as my heart lurched, I felt an unwanted heat between my legs as she put her sex wantonly on display.

It looked untamed now. The wet hairs caught the light, and the labia were swollen, demanding attention. I was feet away, but it seemed that I could feel the heat of it.

I went to my knees without even realizing it, and it was on my knees that I closed the gap between us, the scent thickening the air around me as I approached.

"Wait."

I paused, just inches short, my mouth salivating, and I was surprised when she got up. She moved around the bed, and I could see that she intended to make herself more comfortable.

While I remained on my knees, she collected the pillows and formed them into a pile in the center of the bed.

She smiled at the look of confusion on my face only to see it replaced by an expression of apprehension as she slowly folded herself over the pile; she snuggled down, leaving her behind raised high.

I stayed frozen in place, my mouth dry. The inference of this new posture was all too obvious, but surely this was not her expectation?

"Don't keep me waiting."

Once again, she said so much with so few words. Her tone not only confirmed her presumption; it made it clear that there could be no demur.

It was an outlandish proposition, any sane person would see how demeaning it was, but I was already slowly moving up onto the bed.

Her body was positioned in such a way that her tight cheeks lay open and in, some perverse manner, I was pleased to see a tiny blemish, an almost faded spot, which confirmed that she was not a total Goddess.

It was an irrational thought, but more than that, a dissimulation as I tried to come to terms with my feelings.

I had to make an effort to shift my gaze up over the smooth contours and then down into the shallow valley where a new shock awaited. The hair that flourished on her sex formed a classical triangle that only came to a point beyond her well-formed rosette. Even here, it was immaculately shaved into shape, making me wonder not only who offered such a service but, more to the point, what were the expectations of a woman that paid to have this done.

The only conclusion I could draw was that I was far from being the first and that she enjoyed making herself an object of adoration.

It should have been off-putting, but it had a primal beauty that resonated deep within me. The rosette itself was a tight pink elliptical crater that was already thinly sheened with sweat, and I could not resist its Siren call.

As I drew ever closer, I felt almost feverish, and my heart was tripping. I put out my tongue, hesitating in a now or never moment, and then I licked.

My first impression was one of strength. There was no softness or yielding. Her muscles were tensed, and as my tongue explored the open cleft, I was aware of the taut smoothness of her skin.

I licked along the whole length, my tongue registering a salty, slightly musty taste. But it was quickly diluted by my saliva, and, as I grew more confident, it disappeared altogether.

I continued to lick slowly in a series of long strokes from the base of her sex to the sharp point of the sculpted triangle, and I was thrilled when Agnetha groaned with obvious contentment.

My sex was making its demands, and I felt a lazy trickle of moisture on my inner thigh; what I was doing might be considered degrading, but I had never felt more aroused. The urge to touch me was growing, but, for now, my whole world was bounded by those two perfect hemispheres.

Without conscious thought, I began to make each stroke a little shorter, and soon, I was entirely focused on the rosette itself. I was fascinated by its ribbed texture, which seemed designed to draw me ever inwards.

This was the final taboo, but any qualms I might have had had now evaporated.

I pointed my tongue and dipped it experimentally into the very heart, but it was unyielding - and then I understood. She could have relaxed. She could have made it easy with her obvious experience, but she wanted me to work for it.

I placed my hands gently on her cheeks, and at the same time, I applied my mouth tightly over the opening. After a momentary pause, I braced my tongue once more, and then, with a strength born of some ancient animal urge, I began to push.

It seemed impossible for long seconds, but then I felt a tiny easing, and the tip of my tongue gained a hard-won couple of millimeters. It was now being nipped painfully, but I held fast, and then, with one final effort, I was through.

My tongue slipped inside, deeper than I thought possible, and I heard her gasp.

We remained still as we both came to terms, and then I flexed my tongue in a tentative exploration. The opening was extremely tight, but the constriction was strangely comforting. Following my instincts, I withdrew almost all the way and then probed once more, and this time it was a lot easier.

Much to my surprise, the taste was clean. I realized she had prepared for this, and this further evidence that she knew me better than I knew myself made me uneasy.

I began to move my tongue rhythmically in and out, and I was pleased when she started to urge me on.

"Yes...like that...deeper."

At last, I felt that I was gaining a little control, which seemed borne out by the fact that the air was again heavy with the scent of her arousal. Now, with each new thrust, I groaned with effort, and her body began to rock as she matched my rhythm.

I guessed that this would be enough, of itself, to bring her to orgasm, but she knew where she wanted my mouth exactly when it happened.

"Wait..."

Her voice was slightly less self-assured now.

"...let me turn over."

With some reluctance, I withdrew my tongue as she rolled off of the pillows. She grabbed the top one, and I noticed that it was discolored by a large damp patch, but she was heedless of this as she lay on her back and placed it under her hips.

She made herself comfortable, linked her hands behind her head, and then opened her legs wide.

"Make it good."

Her rosy pink inner labia now lay starkly revealed, and they looked invitingly moist, but to me, at that moment, her sex was a shrine, and I bowed my head to worship.

I licked languidly at first, letting the taste of her spread slowly over my tongue, but I wanted more. I applied gentle pressure and parted her labia to find a milky pool, which I lapped at greedily.

Her eyes were closed, and she appeared dispassionate, but her body had started to squirm slightly, and I knew I was getting to her. I pushed my tongue even deeper, where it was squeezed by the wet velvety walls, and I could feel the furnace heat of her increasing excitement.

I worked my tongue inside her allowing her nectar to slowly fill my mouth. Every now and again, I swallowed lazily. My experience was limited, but she was wetter than any other, and her taste was more desirable. It was ripe, peaty, in some way more womanly, and I could not get enough of her.

I do not know how long I remained there feeding my need, and at the same time, stoking up the fires of her climax, but the dull ache in my neck and the first hints of soreness at the root of my tongue suggested that it was quite some time.

She was reaching the zenith, writhing beneath me, and from time to time. She squeezed my head between her thighs, which were slick with sweat.

I wanted to make it special for her, and I now withdrew my tongue and adjusted my position slightly. Her clitoris was deep-seated, a hidden jewel waiting to be discovered, and now I was going to make it mine. I licked at the apex of her sex and then explored with the tip of my tongue until I felt the rounded smoothness.

It was not as large as I expected, but as I began to work my tongue around the retracted hood, she relinquished any final vestiges of control. Her body bucked to meet me, and it was not easy to stay together, but, in a final act of assertion, I drew it between my lips and gently sucked while feathering it with my tongue.

Her body began to spasm, and I was surprised as a spurt of moisture hit my chin. I almost broke away, but her hand was suddenly at the back of my head, and she held me in place as my upper body was anointed with her outpouring.

She was beautiful to behold in the throes of pleasure, and I was disappointed when it slowly but inevitably came to an end. We lay together, her in blissful exhaustion and me with my head resting on her thigh as I watched her sex pulsing the very last drops.

After a few moments rest, I leaned in and licked the leaking moisture from her labia, following the glistening trail downwards until I was once again licking gently at her moist rosette.

With reluctance, I braced myself to get up and to think about a shower, but as I did, she hooked an ankle behind my back.

"We're going to be late for our meal...but you've got everything you want to eat right here... "

Epilogue

I flew to London for a break and to consider my options. In theory, Agnetha was still my coach, and she was keen to extend our contract to take in the next world championship, but I knew that, for the sake of my sanity, I could not return.

She had only to click her fingers, and I would go down on my knees, and she knew it all too well.

Word must have got out because, after the first few days, I received several overtures. Some I might have expected others were a surprise. The biggest surprise of all was a phone call from Ellen Taylor. She had been an established international player and was relatively new to coaching, but, more tellingly, she was John's wife.

She was ten years older than me, and it was hard not to like her. I had been racked with guilt when John and I started our affair, but he convinced me that the marriage was all but over. Only later did I realize how gullible I had been.

She suggested a local wine bar and, while I felt awkward, it seemed churlish to refuse. She volunteered to drive, and at eight o'clock promptly, my doorbell rang. When I opened the door to her, I felt distinctly underdressed. She was wearing a simple but expensively cut, a navy blue dress that set off her enviable figure to perfection. It also appeared that she just come from the hairdressers. Her long, thick, auburn hair had been straightened and styled with a fetching center parting.

I instantly decided to change my outfit, and I left her with a glass of wine while I darted into the bedroom. When I returned, she had refilled her glass and set one out for me.

She sat on the sofa, and I took the armchair opposite. We discussed my recent successes for a few moments, and she seemed genuinely pleased for me, but I could not avoid the obvious question.

"How's John?"

Her face, up to then so radiant, became sad.

"We've split up."

As she said it, I felt a mix of emotions, but I gathered myself to say what was expected of me.

"Oh, I'm sorry. You guys seemed right for each other."

I felt such a hypocrite. Not only did I know at first hand just unfaithful he had been, but I had also become convinced that he had only married Ellen in the first place because she was considered to be one of the most beautiful women in sport.

There was a moment's awkward silence before she spoke again.

"There was someone else..."

In the next few seconds, my heart went cold. I did not know what to say.

"...Anyway, let's not discuss that. How is Agnetha?"

"You know her?"

"Didn't you know? I was over there for a fortnight last year when I was studying for my coaching badges."

I had not known, but I now found myself wondering if Ellen had any idea about Agnetha's true character. I answered neutrally.

"She was well when I left but I don't think I'll be going back."

"She suspected as much."

"You've spoken to her?"

"A couple of days ago."

"About me?"

"Yes. You see, I think you owe me."

She knew. She knew about John and me. Her eyes had become cold, and I felt myself wilting. As I sat trying to find some words, she stood up, and then, to my astonishment, she slipped her dress off her shoulders and let it fall to the floor.

She stood unabashed, beautifully naked, and I felt my mouth go dry.

"I'm going to be your new trainer..."

Story 02

405

Chapter 01

She sat arrogantly, and her eyes conveyed an unspoken challenge. At eighteen years old, she was my junior by fifteen years. For her, it counted for nothing; I represented authority in name only.

She wore her blonde hair in a ponytail scraped back severely from a face with a natural beauty, which she seemed determined to disguise with crudely applied cheap cosmetics. Therefore, it seemed perverse that she was dressed in a manner that was guaranteed to draw attention.

When she walked in the room, her skirt was so short that it threatened to reveal her underwear with every step she took, and a blue lycra top strained to hold her ample breasts in check. I could have taken issue with her and cited the dress code, but I did not want a confrontation before we had even started. She was my very first, and I was determined to get it right.

I kept my expression impassive, but my heart was beating fast, and I looked down at my paperwork to hide my momentary anxiety. After a count of three, I looked up again.

"Laura, you've been told how this works. This will be the first of five or six sessions after which I will make a determination about your future. Perhaps we can start today by you telling me what happened in your own words."

She said nothing for a few seconds, and I sensed that she weighed me up, but I held her stare as I had been trained to do and waited for her to break the deadlock.

"It's on the file. Why do you need to hear it again?"

"I've read the file and I've reviewed the court transcripts but I want to hear it from you."

"And if I co-operate? What's in it for me?"

"Laura, I won't lie to you. You are going to serve a custodial sentence but the length and nature of that sentence will depend on the outcome of these sessions."

There was another silence as she contemplated her choices. She had already seen off two case officers, and it had been made clear that I represented her final option. For a few seconds, I feared that she would get up and walk out, and it was to forestall that outcome that I prompted her.

"She was a teacher, but she was only a few years older than you..."

Laura smiled very slightly at that. I had not been allowed to speak to Miranda Coombes, but I read her testimony and had seen her on television throughout the trial. She was a stunning redhead, and the cameras loved her so much, so she had left the teaching profession and now worked as a news anchor.

Laura would still not be drawn, and I tried a slightly different tack.

"You say she accused you of cheating...."

Her eyes hardened just a little, and then, after a long pause, she spoke.

"I beat her blue-eyed girls and she couldn't take it."

Ironically, in light of later events, it turned out that, despite being dyslexic, Laura had an above-average IQ. There was no reason to believe that her score in the disputed non-verbal reasoning test was anything other than genuine.

"Do you think that justifies what you did?"

"She put me down in front of the whole class. She got what she deserved."

Miranda Coombes' ordeal had lasted for three days. Laura had followed her home to her flat, and, having discovered her address, she turned up on the following morning with her two accomplices.

They had never been found. Coombes had given a detailed description; two women in their early twenties, one blonde, one dark, both medium build with better than average looks. She said that they had distinctive northern accents, but Laura had consistently refused to reveal their identities.

"The police report says that you kept her naked the whole time and that she was spanked repeatedly, all three of you taking turns over three days."

Laura smirked at that.

"The silly bitch should have done what she was told."

I was edging into new territory. Much of the court evidence had been given 'in camera' and was not in the public domain. In the end, this had proved counter-productive and had lead to much lurid speculation in the press.

"What did you want her to do Laura?"

She gave an evil smile.

"You read the papers, what do you think?"

It had been very difficult to tell fact from fiction. What was not in dispute was that Laura had pretended to be Coombes and had phoned in sick. It had also come out that Coombes had spent much of the time handcuffed to her bed.

"Was it an apology? Is that what you wanted?"

"Oh she was ready to apologize as soon as we ripped the clothes off of her."

"But you must have known that you wouldn't get away with it."

"She wasn't going to tell anyone, you can be sure of that. It was just unlucky that her boyfriend turned up."

I have to admit that, for a moment, my interest was more than purely professional, and Laura seemed to pick up on the nuance.

"Do you want to hear me say it? Would that excite you?"

My mouth was a little dry, but I did not want to admit to it, and I left my glass of water where it was on the table. Her smile fractionally widened as if she could read my thoughts.

Her two previous case officers had both been men. Laura had goaded them with sexual innuendo to the point where it was deemed inappropriate for them to carry on. That was why I had been drafted in. My inexperience counted against me, but female case officers were currently in short supply.

As I watched, she casually pulled down on her top to straighten it, but, as she did so, her nipples began to stiffen. I kept my eyes locked on hers, but they were there at the edge of my vision, and they just continued to grow.

My nipples are fairly prominent when I am aroused, but they bore no comparison to Laura's. The long teats looked set to tear through the flimsy blue material.

"It's a little cold in here don't you think?"

The fact was that the room was comfortably warm, but I was suddenly feeling somewhat hotter. When I walked into the room, I was determined that I would not be fazed, and I was comforted by the fact that the interview was being monitored on CCTV, but the unseen audience only seemed to spur her on.

"It's very simple really. I wanted her to kiss my ass."

"Literally or metaphorically?"

As soon as I said it, I wish I had not. The cardinal rule was to keep the language simple. The girls must not think that they are being spoken down to, but Laura was not fazed.

"Well I guess you could say both. Metaphorically, she was going to beg for my forgiveness but, in order to do that, she was literally going to kiss my ass."

"Coombes says that you beat her, that you made her do it."

She softly laughed before she replied.

"We slapped her backside a couple of times, that's all it took, She was a total wimp."

"She says that you made her kneel."

"How else was she going to take down my jeans?"

My pulse quickened just a little. This was something new, something that was not available to me in the transcripts.

"What do you mean?"

"It's very simple. I bent over the arm of the chair. She took down my jeans and panties and then she begged."

At that moment, I was shocked. I had read the papers, but even they had not embellished the story to this extent. I tried to get the interview back on track.

"She did as you asked, and very quickly by your account, why didn't you let her go? It would have been your word against hers; you could have pleaded guilty to assault and avoided the kidnapping charges".

She did not reply for a second or two, almost as if the question had not occurred to her.

"She gave in too easily. She spoilt the fun so I made her beg my friends as well."

"Tell me about your friends."

"Don't be a stupid bitch. I told the police nothing and I'm certainly not going to tell you."

I let the insult pass. It was my fault, I thought that she was opening up to me, but I had misread her.

"Okay so you made her beg your friends as well. Did they undress?"

I hope I appeared clinical, as I tried to understand the ritual, but I sounded slightly awkward even to my ear. Laura looked at me as if I had asked a stupidly, obvious question.

"So what happened next?"

For the first time since she walked into the room, she looked slightly on edge.

"Are you a lesbian?"

I blinked in surprise.

"No, I'm engaged."

Without thinking, I showed her the expensive solitaire on my ring finger.

"It's just that you look like that actress...Portia something"

"Portia de Rossi?"

"That's her."

I could see that there might be a facial resemblance to the lesbian actress, but she probably went a couple of dress sizes smaller than me. It was just intriguing that Laura should think that, because we looked a little like one another, we might share a common sexual orientation.

There was an awkward pause before she continued.

"I'm not a les but seeing that bitch kissing ass made me as horny as fuck. I decided to see how far I could push her."

I tried to keep my expression neutral, but I felt a frisson. She was revealing more than I dared hope, but, in truth, it was not just my professional curiosity, which was roused.

"We had to spank her a little but she got the message. She wasn't that good, she cried the whole time, but what a fucking power trip. She just kept licking until I told her to stop and you better believe that took some while. In the end I came like a train".

I hoped that I projected my disgust. She was clearly out to shock me, but I wanted her to believe that I had heard worse. I said nothing and simply waited for her to continue.

"After that the others wanted some attention. We found some booze and made ourselves comfortable."

I tried to imagine the scene and the fear that Coombes must have felt. I wondered how I would have reacted. I told myself that I would take a beating, that nothing would make me degrade myself in that way, but, then again, I had no real idea what they might have threatened her with.

I was lost in these thoughts for a moment or two, but then my nostrils twitched. The room had a slightly stale, institutional odor, but I was now aware of a new smell, something vaguely familiar. I breathed in again, trying to place it, and then, with a shock, it registered. My eyes opened a little wider, and I saw the amusement in hers.

She had her hands beneath the table, and I realized that I had made a mistake. The rules called for her hands to be in plain sight at all times, and I had not enforced it. My immediate reaction was to snap at her but to do so, then I would have been to admit my error and might be construed as a show of weakness.

I decided to maintain a professional demeanor and ignore it, but I found myself looking at her arms and checking for movement signs.

She slumped a little lower on her seat and picked up where she had left off.

"Well you must know, a sexy woman like you, once is not enough for us girls. We all took another turn and it seemed to go on from there. We didn't even have to leave the place to eat. We just helped ourselves from the kitchen."

Her arm was flexing, barely noticeable, but just enough, and the smell grew more redolent. I should have told her to stop, but I was desperate to hear how her story panned out.

"You've seen her, how beautiful she is, can you imagine her down on her knees in front of you? Her mouth was really hot and her face was so smooth and delicate, not like a man's."

She was trying to provoke a reaction, and, outwardly, I refused to rise to it, but, for a few brief seconds, the picture she painted was emblazoned on my mind. I could see myself looking down at that mane of, now famous, red curls with my fingers entwined, and I could almost feel her tongue.

I shifted in my seat and pulled myself together.

"Let's just stick to the plain facts."

Laura gave a knowing smile, and then I heard it, almost imperceptible, but there was no doubt. It was the sound of the soft suck of moisture.

Despite myself, I felt my cheeks begin to redden. She was sitting there, less than a meter in front of me, with her hand inside her panties. I should have stopped the interview right there and then, but I did not, and from that moment, the course of my life changed forever.

I chose to ignore it, to pretend it was not happening, but Laura knew what effect she was having exactly. As I did, she also knew that the watching camera was situated behind me so that she was only visible from the waist up.

Giving in, I took a much-needed sip of water but, as I put the glass back down onto the table, I glanced furtively at her chest. Her nipples were still obscenely erect and, seen in outline. They were commensurately large. The heavily dimpled areolae were inches across, and they seemed to have a maturity which was somehow inappropriate for one so young.

I took a deep breath and looked her in the eyes once more, but she was still smiling knowingly.

"Like what you see? You only have to ask."

With that, she used her free hand to lift her top, and, for a couple of seconds, her breasts were totally revealed. Without thinking, my eyes dropped, but I looked up again almost immediately.

"Cover yourself up."

She slowly pulled her top back down into place, but the afterimage lingered. Her breasts were heavy orbs crowned with dusky pink nipples so large that they seemed to melt into the surrounding skin, but what stayed in my mind were the teats themselves standing proud enough to cast shadows.

She sat silently, almost sulky, and I tried to draw her out again.

"You stayed in her flat for two nights wasn't that a little reckless?"

"Maybe, but she was getting better and better with practise. Just think about it. She was there to be used; when we woke up, after meals, even when we were watching her TV."

I should have felt abhorrence, not least because of the casual nature of her cruelty, but to my eternal shame, I felt a familiar tingling between my legs.

"Why did the other two leave?"

"They had to get back but I was greedy. We had her handcuffed to the bed, totally helpless, and I couldn't resist one last time...and that's how her boyfriend found us, with me sitting on her face."

"And he arrested you?"

"I reckon he took his time about it. I think the bastard watched until I was finished."

"A little unlucky that her boyfriend was a policeman."

"She wouldn't have pressed charges, she didn't want it coming out, but once he knew what was going on he couldn't turn a blind eye."

I decided to wind things up and reassert my authority.

"Well Laura, I think that's enough for now. I would like to thank you for being so candid with me but I have to say that your description of your victim's ordeal and your obvious lack of remorse inclines me to feel less well disposed towards you right now."

She looked at me coldly, as though she had expected no other outcome, and then she slowly got to her feet.

"A couple of things you ought to know. We didn't take the handcuffs with us, we found them in the flat after we got there...and, yes, we made her beg but she was still begging long after the spankings stopped"

I sat stunned and, as she held her hand out to me, I shook it without thinking.

She knocked at the door and, after the guard came in and escorted her away, I gave her a moment and followed her out. I quickly turned towards the ladies' room and then stood still at the sink.

For a few seconds, I looked down at my hand like Lady Macbeth, but instead of thrusting it under the tap, I tentatively brought my fingers to my nose. I could smell her from inches away, and my first thought was that the scent was surprisingly like my own.

I caught my reflection in the mirror and blushed. I was a trained professional supposedly doing my job, and here I was loitering in the lavatory like a guilty schoolgirl.

The room had two stalls, both empty, and I slipped into the nearest one.

I do not know what possessed me. I had never before entertained fantasies of sex with another woman but, having locked the door behind me, I slowly and deliberately eased my hand down into my panties. It seemed so perverted, almost as if I were rubbing myself against her, but the immediate sexual charge was almost overwhelming.

It was wrong on so many levels. I enjoyed a healthy sexual appetite and had probably had more than my fair share of partners before getting engaged, but I had never got so close to orgasm in such a short time. It was made worse because I knew that it was fuelled by a combination of Laura's outrageous behavior and the story she had told.

I was not even using my fingers. The warmth of my hand and the knowledge that it had been tainted by her touch was enough of itself. I desperately tried to conjure an image of John, currently working two hundred miles away, but all I could think of was that young harlot and, more particularly, her remarkable breasts.

I was jolted back to reality when I suddenly heard a door opening and then the sound of someone occupying the adjacent stall. I quickly rearranged my clothes, flushed the bowl, and walked out. This time I did wash my hands, scrubbing them more vigorously than necessary, but I convinced myself that the whole thing was a temporary aberration. There had been no harm done, and it would certainly not happen again.

Now I wanted to get home and have a shower. After that, I would write up my case notes and get my relationship with Laura Simmons back onto a professional footing.

I looked at my watch and was surprised to find that only a few minutes had passed since the interview ended. I went back down the corridor, the way I had come, and walked into the observation room where I had left my coat and bag.

"Are you okay?"

The girl sitting at the monitor did not look much older than Laura herself, but the fact that she had drawn this duty meant that she was at least one year post qualified. It seemed an odd question for her to ask, but I answered politely.

"Yes, I'm fine thank you."

I found myself checking the monitor, which showed the empty interview room, and, while I had seen it before, I now noted just how clear an image the camera relayed.

"You could have used the chicken switch."

She was referring to the panic button on the desk's underside, which would have brought the guard running.

"I think I had it under control."

She smiled, but I thought I detected the faintest hint of condescension. I then noticed that she was not wearing her clip-on tie, and she had undone the top buttons of her blouse. It would not have seemed out of the ordinary was it not for the new governor's insistence on strict adherence to the uniform code.

Only then did it occur to me that she too might have been affected by Laura's display. She turned around and ejected a DVD from the machine putting it carefully into a case.

"Do you want a copy?"

She kept her expression neutral, but that was just something about how she said it, and I replied tersely.

"I am not entitled to a copy."

She gave a tiny shrug of the shoulders.

"I thought she came out with stuff that didn't come out at the trial."

"Even if she did, it's strictly confidential. She's already been tried and convicted. The purpose of these interviews is simply to assess her suitability to join one of the new rehabilitation programmes."

She looked taken aback by my harsh tone, and I felt a little guilty. In the scheme of things, she was way down the scale compared to my exalted status, but the job she and her colleagues were doing was both demanding and draining. If she were earning a third of what I was getting, I would have been surprised.

It was very easy to see the uniformed staff as drones, but it had to be remembered that they too had had to qualify to do their jobs. From a professional point of view, I found it interesting to see the lengths to which they would go to assert their individuality.

This young woman had adjusted the darts on her standard-issue white blouse to emphasize her attractive bust line, and her skirt had been shortened so that it was probably just on the wrong side of regulation length.

I also noted that she was wearing makeup. This, too, while not strictly prohibited, was discouraged, but hers was very subtle. She had beautiful blue eyes, which she had pointed up with a light mascara and a very pale grey eye shadow. I found myself checking out her full lips. If she had not used lipstick, then she had certainly used a clear gloss.

"I'm sorry I didn't mean to snap."

She smiled genuinely.

"There's no need to apologize, I guess she got us both a little hot under the collar."

I did not know how to reply. It seemed important to repudiate her assertion, even if it held a strong element of truth, particularly as she was now looking at me conspiratorially.

"She's very young. She was just testing the boundaries. She'll come into line."

"Young or not did you hear the things that they made that woman do?"

For reasons I could not explain, I found myself mounting a defense.

"She also suggested that there was some give and take."

She was silent for a second or two and appeared lost in thought. She idly toyed with her hair, cut in a rebellious elfin style while kept to the proscribed length.

"Do you believe her?"

"It's possible. All else apart, some people have a naturally dominant personality and others are perceived as innately submissive. There are innumerable case histories of manipulative personality types influencing others do their bidding".

"But do you think that she could make someone do that?"

I was beginning to find her questions both impertinent and a little intrusive, and my reply was more sarcastic than I intended.

"How would you react if I asked you to come over here and get down on your knees?"

I hoped that my rudeness would bring an awkward conversation to an abrupt end, but she looked neither angry nor aggrieved. Instead, her expression was odd, hard to read. There was a long pause before she replied.

"Is that what you want me to do?"

She was not replying in kind. She said it quietly, and I was shocked to realize that she was framing it as a genuine question. In the next few seconds, my thoughts crowded in on one another, and my heart began to race. My conscience screamed professional integrity, but there were darker forces at work deep in my psyche.

"Lock the door."

The words came from my mouth, but it was as if it was not my voice. There was no hesitation on her part. She rose from the chair, turned the key in the lock, and then waited.

I could see now that she was some inches shorter than me, perhaps five feet four, but she had a slim build, and her body was perfectly proportioned. I knew that I had to act before I lost my nerve quickly.

"Come here."

She took half a dozen steps to close the gap between us, and I noted that she was no longer looking me directly in the eye; instead, she kept her eyes downcast at the level of my neckline.

She stopped in front of me, and I sensed that she was awaiting instructions.

"Kneel down."

I held my breath, wondering if this was a step too far, but she slowly dropped to her knees.

In seven years of psychology training, nothing could have prepared me for this. Had I been asked, I could have given an analytic appraisal citing character traits, natural urges, perhaps even suggestion techniques, but that all seemed a world away.

"Lift my dress."

This was the moment. My panties, already partly soiled by my activities a few minutes earlier, had become damper appreciably in a matter of seconds, and I was inviting this young stranger to witnessing my arousal.

She reached forward, almost reverently, and took hold of the hem of my dress. She paused for a heartbeat and then slowly lifted it.

Almost at once, I could smell myself, and, for an instant, some deep-seated sense of propriety made me feel a little ashamed, but then I saw the look on her face.

My panties had started the day a pristine powder blue, but they were now visibly discolored by a damp patch that was still slowly expanding, and, as I looked down, she leaned inwards.

That which, only a moment ago, had seemed sordid now became shockingly compelling.

"Get closer. I want you to smell me."

For the first time, she appeared to hesitate, as though she might be entertaining second thoughts, but I could not stop now.

"Do it."

My tone was a shade harsher, and it brought the required response. She inched forward until the tip of her nose was almost touching, and then I saw her chest swell as she breathed in deeply.

Only a quarter of an hour earlier, I had hesitantly experienced the scent of another for the first time, and now here I was demanding the same of someone else, and I found it thrilling.

"Keep breathing."

She was holding the breath that she had drawn, but I wanted her to keep filling her lungs; driven by some previously untapped inner arrogance, I was determined that she would never forget me.

She breathed slowly through her nose, and the simple act of watching was enough to make me hotter.

"Take them off..."

I was tempted to add the word "slowly," but it proved unnecessary. She gently took hold and peeled them delicately down to my ankles, allowing me to step out of them and leave them where they lay.

She returned to her station, and her eyes were wide with excitement, and perhaps a little trepidation.

"Take off my skirt."

I turned my hip a fraction, revealing the side zip, and she slowly worked the fastening. As the dark material slid down my legs, I pushed it aside impatiently with my foot.

I now stood with my legs a little apart, and she knelt before me gazing at my sex. In truth, it was a little untidy. John liked me to have regular waxings, but my rebellious streak kicked in when he went away for any length of time.

My protuberant labia now emerged from a young dark growth which, to my mind, conveyed a rightful sense of maturity. We remained frozen in place, but the stillness of my body was not matched by the beat of my heart, which was pounding ever faster.

413

I was going to make her lick me. I knew it, she knew it, and the sense of power was intoxicating. I could feel my sex swelling, opening just a little, and then the prickling of a single bead of moisture as it traced its way down my inner thigh.

Her eyes slowly dropped following its slow, sinuous progress, and then, for the first time since she went down to her knees, she looked up at me. I made her wait for a silent count of three, and then I smile indulgently.

She needed no further encouragement. She bowed down and touched her tongue to my knee and then slowly worked her way upwards, following the silver trail.

Her tongue was hot and the touch slightly ticklish, but I almost swooned with the pleasure of it, and she, for her part, gave a deep purr as she lapped the taste of me from my skin, but as she drew closer to my sex, she paused as though again unsure. Her tongue lingered in the crease than formed the border of my mons. Her nose nuzzled at the undergrowth with a soft rasping.

I tolerated it for a moment or two, but I was, by now, almost breathless with anticipation. I brought my fingers to my sex and eased myself open, presenting the heat and wetness. My scent was stronger than I had ever known it, and it must have wreathed about her face with an almost tangible thickness.

She seemed almost frightened by it, but there was no way I was going to stop now.

"Look at it."

Again there was an unaccustomed edge to my voice, but it had the desired effect. She moved away just a little and stared at my open maw, and I could feel myself oozing beneath her gaze.

"Don't keep me waiting."

I looked down on her as she put out her tongue once more, and, for a second or two, my knees threatened to buckle, but then she eased forward, and I felt the first hesitant touch.

No confirmation was needed; I could tell that this was her first time. She kept her tongue still as she experienced the warm softness and the raw taste before she began to gently probe, testing the resistance of my labia.

The ease with which she was able to slip inside seemed to take her by surprise, and I moaned as I felt her tongue swelling within, but I needed to retain control.

"Not yet...I want you to lick me."

She reluctantly withdrew but immediately began to use the flat of her tongue in a series of broad sweeps from the bottom to the top of my sex.

Her technique left much to be desired, but the fact that she was a woman and knowing that she would do anything I asked was enough to bring me to the edge. Realizing this, she moved a little higher, seeking out my clitoris.

"Take your time."

I could have surrendered to orgasm right then, but I wanted to savor the moment. I knew that my interview was the last booking of the day, and there was little chance of us being disturbed.

She looked up at me with a hint of petulance in her eyes, but she hunched lower and picked up the rhythm once more.

I placed my hand lightly on the top of her head, and, for the next few minutes, I continued to direct her.

"A little slower..."

"Harder..."

"Inside..."

"Taste me..."

She followed each new instruction without demur and seemed gripped by an inner calmness, but I knew that I could not hold out much longer. I let my hand slip a little to the back of her head and then gave one last command.

"Now..."

Her neck was, by now, a little stiff, but she ignored the discomfort and adjusted her stance. I guessed that my clitoris was no larger than average, but, just then, it felt as if it had swollen to twice its normal size, and she found it unerringly.

That first touch was electric, and my whole body shivered with the pleasure of it. I had reached a climax while standing on many occasions, but this was like no other. She was licking with a newfound ardor, and I found myself grinding my sex against her face.

Desperate for relief, I gave up any pretense at control, but my body refused to let go. It was as if it knew that a few more seconds of exquisite tension would bring a reward beyond measure.

I looked down at her again, but her eyes were fixed as she licked ever faster. Her face was red with exertion, her forehead glistening with sweat, and only then did it occur to me that she too was close.

The thought that she could come without touching herself, simply through this act of devotion, was the final trigger. My body stiffened and then shook as jolts of pleasure coursed to every extremity. They radiated from my sex and then surged back to collide with even more powerful tremors so that I was caught in a quaking ecstasy.

It was as quick as it was violent, and this was just as well. I could not have taken much more, and I recognized that the desperately muted screaming I could hear was my own.

As my body finally began to relax, I realized, guiltily, that I had held her pressed hard against me throughout, and, as I released her, she gasped for breath.

Having assured me that she was okay, I slumped down into her chair, but, even now, my body was still shaking slightly. As I tried to compose myself, I idly wondered if she had managed to come herself. She looked washed out, convincing me that she had, which sparked a new train of thought.

I wanted to know, now that it was over if she felt embarrassed or perhaps guilty. I was surprised to find that I felt neither, but I was mischievously determined to find out. I opened my legs, revealing the soggy mess that my sex had become. A mix of saliva, sweat, and arousal had matted the dark growth, and my labia were lewdly relaxed.

She was still looking at the floor, gathering herself, but my spoor was in the air, and it finally caught her attention. She turned towards me, and, as she did so, I stroked a finger over my pubis.

"Come and clean me up."

She appeared disconcerted, as though she misunderstood, and then she looked aggrieved, and, for the first time, it occurred to me that she might have expected me to return the favor. The fact that I was going to disappoint her was oddly exciting, but I knew that it was important to reassert myself.

"Over here..."

I could see, in her eyes, an internal struggle being waged, but I could almost feel her bending to my will. Slowly but surely, her body began to move, and, without getting up from her knees, she came towards me.

No further words were necessary. She began to lick at the salty residue on my inner thighs, and then she began to groom my pubis itself. As she did so, she made a soft, sucking sound, and I felt a growing twinge.

I did not think that I would be capable of more but hearing her as she diligently went about her task was threatening to bring me back to the boil. She understood what was happening and began to exploit her advantage.

Her tongue roamed over my pubis, sometimes returning to my thighs, but she avoided my labia, and very soon, I was squirming. It went on for some time, but finally, I could take no more, and I whispered under my breath.

"You little bitch..."

She looked up at me from between my thighs and smiled broadly, and then in one movement, she clamped her mouth to my sex and sank her tongue deep inside. I was taken by surprise, but then I tensed my muscles and held her in.

Once again, she must have had difficulty breathing, but she made no attempt to free herself, and as I looked down at her worshipful eyes and her buried nose seemingly fringed by my pubic hair, I felt myself start to come for a second time.

This time it was not so intense, but I made it last longer as I rode it out, and the whole time I was aware of her swallowing down my offering.

When it was over, I was breathing hard, and I remained slumped in the chair with my eyes closed. When I opened them again, she was standing in front of me, proffering my clothes. We had suspended reality for a space of time, but now it was back with brutal harshness.

She had cleaned herself up as best she could and was now anxious for me to get dressed. Once more, I became aware of the background noises that marked out the building as a storehouse of misery, and I put on my clothes without a word. We both knew that, had we been caught, we could have said goodbye to our careers, and we parted in conspiratorial silence.

Chapter 03

As I left the room, the insanity of what I had just done came home to me, and I knew that it must never happen again, but that thought brought with it a rueful realization that it had been one of the most exciting moments of my life.

Later I returned to my apartment and took a long shower but, even having had something to eat, my mind was still buzzing with the thrill of it, and I desperately wished that John was with me.

It was a warm evening, and I sat on my bed dressed in a short nightdress while browsing the case papers for the following day. It took about an hour, and I knew that I was simply avoiding the one job that needed to be done.

Finally, I could put it off no longer. I picked up Laura's file and began to think about the case notes. In due course, I would receive a transcript of the interview, and I was mildly amused at the thought of what some poor young secretary was going to be obliged to type up, but for now, I had to jot down my impressions and initial conclusions.

For the first time in my career, I found it hard to remain dispassionate. Her seeming lack of remorse counted against her, but she had thrown out the tantalizing hint that her victim was not totally coerced. My immediate inclination was to not put her name forward for the rehabilitation scheme, but I was convinced that, given time, I could work with her.

Unfortunately, when writing up the notes, it was difficult not to picture her in my mind's eye, and that, in turn, brought me back to my subsequent outrageous behavior. This remembrance brought with it a growing heat between my legs that was becoming harder to ignore.

Taking a pragmatic approach, I put the file to one side and settled back into the piled pillows. Opening the bedside cabinet, I took out my trusty vibrator and switched it on. I would treat myself to one orgasm, and then I would get back to work.

I was surprised to find that I needed little teasing, and I was able to slip the simple white shaft deep inside almost from the outset. I tilted it slightly to touch it against my clitoris, and it was at that moment the telephone rang.

I switched it off but left it inside as I grabbed for the phone. I was surprised to hear John's voice and only then appreciated just how late it was. He was back in his hotel room, having entertained clients for dinner, and he proceeded to tell me about his latest deal.

I loved him, but, in truth, I could have done without hearing the minutiae of his business affairs. I understood how lonely it could get on the road and that sometimes you just needed a sounding board. From time to time, I filled in with details of my day, but he did the talking for the most part.

I must have done it without thinking because, as I continued to listen, I felt the vibrator buzzing deep inside and, before long, I was slowly pushing it in and out.

Lulled by the sound of his voice, I slid a little deeper into the pillows and started to raise my hips to meet the movements of my hand.

I was no longer paying attention to what he was saying, but I tried to picture his naked body. As I grew more excited, the problem was not his image that came to mind, but that of Laura teasing me with her breasts.

I tried to dismiss it, but my efforts were only half-hearted, and each time I surrendered once more, I felt myself getting ever nearer to a climax. At some point, the phoned slipped from my sweaty grip, but instead of retrieving it, I used my fingers to caress my nipples, which had grown painfully distended.

It took a very little longer. I was soon pistoning the vibrator in and out of myself in an uncontrolled frenzy and squeezing my breasts. I tried to stay quiet but what started as a stifled groan became an uncontrolled shriek as I clawed my way to the pinnacle.

It was over quickly, but then there was the sublime moment of knowing that there was to be no softening, that my loyal little friend would carry on untiringly until I decided otherwise.

I eased it out slowly but let the tip of it rest against my pubic bone from where the vibrations were transmitted to my still excited clitoris. From experience, I knew that it would take a long time to come this way, but I also knew that my patience would be rewarded with a second slow, drawn-out climax, which would leave me completely drained and ready for sleep.

As I surrendered to the pleasurable sensations, I guiltily reached for the phone again, but, in dropping it, I must have disconnected the call because all I could hear was a dial tone. I was not worried; John would phone back, and I would apologize for accidentally cutting him off, but in the meanwhile.

I managed to tease myself for nearly an hour, occasionally varying the pressure to bring myself closer only to ease off at the critical moment. But, throughout, I was still plagued with images of Laura and of the other young girl who had brought me so much unaccustomed pleasure earlier that day.

When I finally came, I almost cried with the intensity of it, and when it was over, my body was sheened with sweat. I decided to rest for a few moments before showering once more, but I must have drifted off.

By the time I awoke, the sun was well-risen, and I had to rush to get ready. Only as I was going out of the door did it occur to me that John had not phoned back, but that would have to wait.

The day was particularly busy and passed quickly, and once back at home, I tried calling his mobile. When that failed, I tried the hotel switchboard, but he had requested not to be disturbed. I was not unduly worried, figuring that he would phone as soon as he was able.

I cooked a meal and watched a little TV and, as he had still not called, I tried phoning again with the same results. Only then did it occur to me that perhaps it had not been me that had cut off the previous day's call after all. More worryingly, if he had heard the noise I was making, it was not a great stretch of the imagination to see what conclusions he might have drawn.

I was now seriously worried. At worst, he might think I was with someone else, but even if he could be made to believe that I was alone, it did not say a great deal about my interest in his conversation. I tried calling, on and off, for the remainder of the evening but to no avail. I even considered telling the hotel it was an emergency, but, even now, my pride would not allow me to appear quite that desperate.

At worst, I figured that I could pay him a surprise visit at the weekend; he would not be able to stay angry for long once he saw me in the flesh. With that thought, I went to bed for an early night. I had a long drive the next day, and I wanted to be fresh.

My journey took me eighty miles west for a meeting with Nicola Stoke-Marnes. I was a little peeved that I could not meet her in chambers, which would have involved a short walk across town, but she was still recovering from illness and was only in the office two days a week.

Stoke-Marnes, a junior barrister, had been appointed as Laura's defense attorney; in retrospect, it was probably too much for her. At the outset, the case had been seen as fairly routine with an almost inevitable outcome. Only later, as details started to come out, did the media frenzy begin, and she suddenly found herself involved in one of the most high profile cases in recent years.

Having looked at the transcripts, she had clearly done the best she could, but the strain must have gotten to her.

I was headed for her weekend retreat, a mill cottage, which proved a challenge even for my upmarket sat nav. When it finally came into view, I was immediately envious. It was a fairy tale granite building, dark with age, set in a large garden which graduated from immaculately kept to an unkempt meadow.

I recognized her as soon as she opened the door to me, but she looked so different. The press had made much of this beautiful, intelligent young woman and poked fun at a judicial system that obliged her to appear before the bench in outdated wig and gown. Now, casually dressed in a sloppy tee shirt and baggy jogging bottoms, she looked naturally vivacious.

The strain was still there to be seen in her eyes, but she smiled easily, and it struck me that, she too, would have had no difficulty with a media career if that what was she had chosen to do.

She welcomed me into a living room well appointed with period furniture and offered me tea and cake that she had baked herself. We made small talk for a quarter of an hour, and then I tried to get down to business.

"In order to complete my profile I would be grateful if you would let me have your personal impression of Laura."

The inquiry seemed to put her ill at ease, and she did not answer it immediately. Instead, she responded with a question of her own.

"This profile, it will determine whether or not she stays in prison?"

"No. She has been found guilty and she will serve a sentence. It's my job decide if she would profit from rehabilitation."

"You mean day release? To sweep the streets?"

I smiled before replying.

"No, this is something new. We are choosing candidates whose school records suggest that they might otherwise have been achievers. We will assess their aptitude and then we will give them tuition."

"What good does it do? Nobody is going to employ them."

"That's what makes this different. The candidates will be guaranteed a job, There will be openings in finance, media even the law but it will be tough. They will receive education and training but they must then take and pass the required entrance exams. There is no feather bedding, they will be competing openly and on the same terms as job market applicants but if they pass they're in."

"And employers are going for this?"

"They have nothing to loose. Its good, cheap, publicity. We will meet the salaries for the first two years, including any promotions; if the candidates turn out to be genuinely unsuitable they can be sacked like anybody else."

She seemed to think about this.

"Why do you think this will work?"

"Simply because, as they perceive it, they will be competing on a level playing field for the first time in their lives. It gives them a chance to get a foot in the door and prove themselves."

She paused, and when she spoke again, there was an edge to her tone.

"Laura is not the sort of person you're looking for."

Taken by surprise, I tried to explain further.

"Her guilt is not in doubt. What she did was totally and utterly wrong. Now it's simply for me to decide if there is sufficient potential to work with."

"That girl is evil, I don't think you realize how manipulative she is."

I was about to tell her that such judgment was more in my province when I saw the tears in her eyes. Before I knew it, she had leaned across the sofa and was sobbing freely against my shoulder.

The professional in me wanted to ease her away, but I found myself petting her hair.

"You can talk about it if you want to."

She was probably only four or five years younger than me, but I suddenly felt much older. She sobbed for a little while longer and then sat up and dabbed at her tear-stained face.

"I'm sorry. You don't know what she put me through."

The fact was, I probably did, and for reasons I could not explain, I began to feel uncomfortably warm. She collected herself and continued.

"It was my mistake. When she was out on bail we had to keep her in hiding because of the press intrusion and in a moment of madness I suggested the cottage. My boyfriend is abroad at present, finishing his doctorate, and so I thought it would give an ideal opportunity to put her case together."

Her composure broke once more, and she started crying again. Without thinking, I pulled her to me and stroked her head to try and calm her, and in fits and starts, her story came out.

"She told me what she had done to that poor woman. Her language was crude, as if she was deliberately trying to shock me. I made it clear to her that she was making it nigh on impossible to mount a defense, but that only seemed to amuse her.

That night I had dreams. You have to understand that my career has always come first. I have only ever had one serious relationship, and that is with the man I intend to marry, but I couldn't get the picture out of Laura and that woman out of my mind."

Her tears were making my blouse damp, but I continued to hold her close. I knew what she had been through exactly, but it was clear that she was not as well equipped to cope.

"When I got home the following day, I tried to go through it again. I made it clear that she was not helping herself, but she didn't seem to care. She wanted to know if her story had turned me on.

By that stage, I was ready to give up on her but walking away from my first high profile case would not have looked good. I had trouble sleeping again that night, but at least, when I managed to get off, I was able to dream about Justin.

"I dreamt that he was with me, caressing me; it seemed so real. Look, I'm sorry. It's hard for me to say this..."

"Take your time. There's no hurry."

She was racked with guilt and desperate to confide in someone and, being a doctor. I guess I was 'the perfect choice.' It also helped that I had met Laura and knew how calculating she could be.

"In my dream Justin wanted me to...to go down on him...he pushed my head down and I didn't like it. He was being too assertive and that's when I woke up."

My immediate thought was that her dream was nothing out of the ordinary. Her boyfriend's coercion might have been an unconscious manifestation of the pressure she was under, but it was an otherwise healthy fantasy.

"She was there, in bed with me."

For a second or two, I did not comprehend.

"She was supposed to be sleeping in the spare room but I woke up and found her beside me. I told her to leave but she wouldn't go. I threatened her, tried to push her out of the bed, but she is stronger than she looks and, besides, I have never been in a fight in my life."

Her shoulders shook as she was almost overcome again, but she seemed determined to get her story out.

"She was naked and I was hampered by my night dress. Somehow she got on top of me. She pinned me down. She made me....made me do things."

I think I knew what she was made to do exactly, but the fact that, even now, she could not articulate it suggested just how traumatic the experience must have been for her.

I said nothing, waiting to see if she wanted to continue, but she must have taken my silence as condemnation. When she spoke again, she was defensive.

"I tried to struggle but she threatened my face with her nails. I had no choice."

My feelings at that moment were curiously mixed. On the one hand, I felt for her and wanted to see Laura punished, but on the other, I have to admit that I was faintly but inappropriately aroused.

I tried to set my mind straight.

"Afterwards, you didn't report her, nor did you drop her case."

"I couldn't."

"Did you throw her out?"

"I wanted to..."

I waited for her to complete the sentence, but she left it hanging, and I have to say that I was intrigued. By now, my blouse was extremely damp, and she used her fingertips to gently, but guiltily, pull it away from my skin.

I turned her face towards me, and her eyes conveyed a plea to be understood, but I was still puzzled. It was then that I felt her hand, and, in a moment of blinding clarity, it became obvious.

Her touch was unsure, but she edged her fingers just inside my blouse.

"Oh my God. You enjoyed it didn't you?"

She looked away from me, unwilling to meet the accusation, but she did not take her hand away.

"It was so... different. I never would have dreamt it."

As she confessed it, she was wracked by another bout of guilty sobs.

"You mustn't anguish over it. No one will ever know and you must put it down to experience."

Even as I said it, I felt a total hypocrite. Who was I to give advice after my own recent experiences?

"You don't understand. I love my boyfriend but I have never felt that way with him. After that first time she made me do it again and I couldn't resist her."

Her words gushed from her as the dam broke on her pent up emotions.

"Look, it makes no difference. What's important is, that when it came to it, you acted totally professionally and represented her to the best of your abilities. I've read the transcripts and it was, in part, your defence of her that brought her to the attention of the rehabilitation committee. She was lucky to have you."

For a moment, my words seemed to have the desired effect, and I could feel some of her self-esteem returning, but then she gave way again.

"But she's changed me. I see women now...and I look at them...I...I imagine myself."

"Believe me, it's nothing to worry about. It might just be that you're wired that way. You'd be surprised how many people are."

I tried to project professional confidence, but that only encouraged her to open up even more.

"But how can it be right? Just now, when I opened the door to you, a total stranger, and all I can think about is what a beautiful woman you are."

As she said it, her fingertips slowly slid into the confines of my bra cup, and I suddenly felt myself becoming a little light-headed.

There was no more pretense. She flexed her fingers to make room for herself, and then she gently pinched my nipple, which swelled to meet her touch.

Now was the moment for indignation, but I said nothing and allowed her to continue her exploration. She teased me, circling my areola, and I could feel her warm, gentle breath against my skin.

I was now desperate to feel the touch of her lips, but I had to be clear.

"Nicola, I can't do this for you..."

I expected her to be disappointed, but she simply smiled.

"Don't worry. Just tell me what to do."

It was surreal. Laura's influence was obvious, as it had been with the young woman back at the remand center, and I could not shake the unnerving notion that she had deliberately set events in motion.

For a second or two, I was torn. One part of me wanted to run, to escape the seemingly malign influence, but Nicola chose that moment to run her tongue slowly over her lips, and I could no longer resist.

"Where's the bedroom?"

She smiled and, taking my hand as she rose, she led me through to the back of the cottage. Sunlight streamed into the bedroom through a recently installed set of French windows and reflected from yellow painted walls. There were no curtains, and there was a view across a field to an isolated copse of trees.

She sensed my awkwardness and smiled as she began to unfasten my blouse.

"Don't worry, I own the field and no one ever comes by."

Reassured, I stepped back from her.

"Get undressed."

She needed no second bidding. She stripped out of her tee-shirt and bottoms to reveal that she was wearing nothing underneath. Then she stood almost coyly as though waiting for my approval.

She need not have worried. She was blessed with a beautiful figure. Her breasts, large to begin with, were emphasized by the narrow set of her shoulders, and she had classic hourglass curves. My eyes dropped to her navel, which was pierced and set with a small ruby, and I smiled as I wondered what her colleagues in chambers would have made of this seeming act of rebelliousness.

Her legs were completely waxed, and so it was a surprise to see that she maintained a lush, but well-groomed, growth of dark hair at her sex.

In all, she was a picture of healthy vitality, and I was a little envious, but that passed as I saw the look in her eyes as my own body was revealed.

I have had many men look at me, and they have all shared the same lustful expression. They are appreciative of my beauty but only in so far as it serves to fuel their physical release.

With Nicola, it was different. She made me feel like a goddess, and it was clear that her one desire was simply to bring me pleasure.

She walked past me, gently brushing my shoulder with her hand, and then she proceeded to arrange the cushions on the bed. Six of them were covered in gold satin, and she carefully heaped them to form a welcoming pile.

"Come and make yourself comfortable."

I moved unhurriedly, almost theatrically, encouraging her to gaze upon me, and then I slinked onto the bed. I reclined against the cushions, and, having made myself comfortable, I slowly raised my knees and then allowed my legs to part.

She looked at me and smiled knowingly before her eyes dropped. Her mouth opened very slightly, and the very tip of her tongue touched against her top lip. Her stare was fixed as she came towards me and slowly bowed down to lie between my legs.

"It's beautiful..."

Her long, dark hair formed a silky curtain as she paused inches from my sex, and I could feel my labia swelling beneath the gentle warmth of her breath. She remained still for some time, happy simply to look but then, slowly, she extended her arms and eased them under my thighs.

I felt myself being lifted very slightly before she closed to place a single delicate kiss at the center of my sex.

"So beautiful..."

After that, she continued to kiss, each touch a slow, gentle pursing of her lips, which whispered against my sex.

The feeling was amazing. On the one hand, I ached for her to lick me, but I also felt incredibly relaxed. As the minutes passed, she continued to admiringly murmur as she explored the whole of my mons, which slowly began to weep its appreciation.

My body stretched and squirmed deeper into the cushions, but she did not miss a beat. She rose and fell with me as she teased my inner labia. With each tiny kiss, she drew them gently between her lips before reluctantly releasing them and moving on.

I wanted to stay there forever, and she seemed only too willing to oblige. Time slipped away, but still, she remained unhurried, and I realized that, if she were to continue, she was going to make me come with this simple act of veneration.

With this thought, I felt my sex grow warmer. I was already leaking profusely, but now I felt a fresh outflow, and my scent wafted strongly. As though reading my mind, Nicola chose that moment to look up at me for the first time in minutes. Her mouth did not leave my sex, but she wanted me to see as she flared her nostrils and breathed in deeply.

She closed her eyes, held her breath, and then reluctantly exhaled.

"So nice..."

She looked transfixed, as though she had experienced the rarest incense, and it was this look of devotion that took me over the edge. It was not a jolting orgasm. In fact, for a moment, it was not like an orgasm at all. My body stiffened, and my back slowly arched. I held myself poised for a few seconds, and then I was aware of a tingling deep in my sex. It slowly spread through my body, and I dare not move lest it is lost.

"Come for me..."

Nicola was kissing again, barely making contact, but it heightened state I could feel every tiny touch.

The tingling grew more insistent, and I began to pant as I held myself on a tightrope. To fall was to fail, but the longer I held my balance, the more intense the sensations became. My body was aching with the effort of it, but all the time, Nicola continued to coax.

"Now...let me taste it."

Just one touch of her tongue would have released me, but those gossamer kisses continued to tease it from me in exquisite drawn-out agony, and then, with a final flush of heat across my skin, it began to ebb away.

I slumped back into the cushions, breathing hard, and tried to come to terms with what had happened. I felt relaxed, as I would after coming, but in some way, unfulfilled.

Between my thighs, Nicola was still smiling, and I wondered at her endurance. Her neck must have ached dreadfully, but she seemed unconcerned. She kissed until I was breathing normally once more, and then I became aware of a new sensation.

There was a slight increase in pressure, and then she gave a playful growl. She was running her tongue lightly over my mons, stopping every now and again to gently suck moisture from my sodden pubis.

"MMmmmm..."

I could feel my labia swelling in eager anticipation, but she ignored them as she moved downwards to lick at the declivities of my tensed inner thighs.

Even as she worked to cleanse my skin, I could feel myself welling up once more, but she was in no hurry, and the effect was wonderfully soporific. The comfort of her arms as they held me slightly raised and the warmth of her tongue lulled me into a blissful state of being.

I closed my eyes and found myself quietly moaning. She was slowly bringing me back to the boil, but I felt so relaxed that it would take her a very long time. For a fleeting moment, I felt guilty, but it quickly passed; if she were tired, she would stop, but in the meanwhile, I decided to lay back and enjoy it.

Half an hour slowly passed, and the sun had by now moved across the sky so that we were bathed in its radiant warmth. Her body remained perfectly still, as it had done throughout, and the only movement was the unhurried bobbing of her head as she went about her task.

In the reflected yellow light, she was a perfect symphony of curves from the arch of her back to the swell of her neat derriere and the tapered lines of her sculpted legs. She was a thing of beauty, and she was mine to do with as I wished.

I gave an almost silent sigh of joy, and then I gently stroked the hair at the back of her head.

"Now my darling..."

Nothing more was needed. She shifted her head fractionally, and then I felt her tongue grazing the very edges of my labia. I shivered in delight as she traced the same path over and over again, patiently easing me apart.

Over the next quarter of an hour, she worked her way inwards until her tongue could go no deeper. My whole body felt incredibly hot, but it was being stoked by the furnace that my sex had become.

I felt myself lubricating freely, and every now and again, she would pause to swallow quietly. She continued to dictate the pace, and I was happy to let her. I had been growing a little restless, waiting for her to seek out my clitoris, but she had me so aroused that I was going to come without much further stimulation.

Her tongue was moving inside me as if it had a mind of its own, and I squeezed it welcomingly. She seemed to find pleasure points that I did not know existed, and she started to murmur encouragement. They were not words, simply sounds, but their meaning was obvious.

My body grew tense until I was shaken by tiny convulsions, and the whole time she urged me on. Sensing the final onset, she sealed her mouth tightly to my sex and moaned one last plea. The resonance was the trigger I needed, and my body exploded in a glorious liquid release. It seemed to go on and on, but she was not deterred. When I finally came down from the pinnacle, I was dimly aware that she was still bound tightly to me, willing to take all that I had to give.

At the finish, my legs were badly cramped, and, recognizing this, she slid her arms away, allowing me to straighten them out to either side of her. She did not move but simply looked up at me with a rapturous expression.

"Did you enjoy?"

Her face was covered in my juices, and sweat beaded on her forehead, making her hair lank but, even in this chaotic state, she still looked totally desirable. I reached down and touched a finger to her cheek.

"It was wonderful...the best."

Her eyes lit up at the compliment, and then she smiled.

"Not yet...the best is still to come."

Without another word, she bowed down. I felt her tongue at the apex of my labia, and my clitoris stirred in response. I was exhausted, and it would be an age before I was ready again, if at all, but she was willing to take as long as it took.

Chapter 04

The following day, I overslept and was almost late for my second interview with Laura. When I got there, I was pleased to find that the session was to be monitored by a different warder, which saved any embarrassment.

I gathered my papers together and waited for Laura to be escorted in, and it was a further relief to see that she was dressed far more soberly than before. I hoped that the rigors of incarceration were finally coming home to her, as it was more likely to make her cooperative.

Her school record indicated an aptitude for maths, and intelligence tests suggested that she had well-developed problem-solving skills. She could be well-spoken when she wanted to, as evidenced by her trial, but usually chose to express herself in street argot.

One of the companies offering training places under the rehabilitation scheme was a large firm of Loss Adjusters. I had my doubts about their motives, their chairman being pretty tight with high placed members of the government, but mine was not to reason why.

In truth, I was leaning towards rejecting Laura, but I was still prepared to give it my best. I spent twenty minutes trying to find out from her where her interests lay, but she was irritatingly vague.

At that point, I let her have my opinion and gave an almost mechanical presentation of the skills required in Loss Adjusting. To my surprise, she showed a keen interest and asked several probing questions, some of which were beyond my vague knowledge of the subject.

That we were communicating at all was a big plus, and I began to feel the familiar buzz that came with doing my job well. I was just explaining to her that, at the highest levels, the job required character reading skills, to see through the bullshit that was so much a part of insurance negotiations, when the warder entered the room.

I could not believe that time had passed so quickly, but as Laura turned to leave, she smiled at me.

"I think I'm pretty good at character reading. You've met Nicola, how did you find her...?"

With that, she was gone, and I was left to try and decipher her parting remark. Was it a casual inquiry, or was she toying with me?

If my professional life was back on track, it was more than could be said for my personal life. John had still not phoned, and I was angry with him to the extent that we seemed to have become engaged in a childish game of 'you first.'

I had no doubts that it could all be thrashed out at a face-to-face meeting, but the truth was, I was in no great hurry. The past few days had revealed to me facets of a persona previously unimagined. I had engaged in reckless sex with two women who had been complete strangers to me, and it had excited me in a way that my encounters with men had never come close to.

Had it simply been a case of exploring lesbian sex, then I could have dismissed it as one of life's experiences, something to be savored and then left behind, but this was something different – it was all about control. The thought of going down on a woman still made me shiver, but the thrill of having it done to me and dictating the manner of it induced a high the like of which I had never known.

I had a degree in psychology, but I could not explain to myself the paradox whereby my yearning to be in control was, by any rational analysis, symptomatic of someone out of control.

For the next few days, I threw myself into my work. Laura's was one of only many cases that I was currently running but, for all the wrong reasons, it was the most intriguing. I met her for the third time, and this time she was keen to talk. She wanted more information on a prospective placement with a Loss Adjusting firm, and I promised to get her some background materials.

By the time of our fourth encounter, she was speaking of it as though it was a fait accompli, and I felt a little guilty. I was still not entirely convinced of her suitability and, although she did not know it, the best I could hope to argue her sentence down to would be two years and that, in itself, was dependent on one major factor.

What finally convinced me was her willingness to take a distance learning course during her time in prison so that she could hit the ground running on her release. I reasoned that, if she passed the exams, it would prove her ability to reform.

I began to put the wheels in motion. Without my intervention, she was probably facing five years. If I put her forward for the scheme, it would automatically go down to three, but there was one other possibility.

The government was laying a great store by a new scheme called "Face the Victim." As its name implied, the victim and perpetrator were brought face-to-face so that the victim could explain the ongoing effects of the offense, and the perpetrator had an opportunity to apologize. It was hoped that the scheme would give the victims closure and that the perpetrators, having seen the misery that they caused, would feel suitably remorseful.

It was a very long shot, but I wondered if I could bring Laura together with Miranda Coombes; a positive outcome might just get Laura three years of remission.

In the event, Coombes was a very hard woman to contact. She was now of sufficient stature to be represented by an agent, and, of necessity, I had to be circumspect in my approach. At first, my calls were not returned but then I tried another tack; I submitted the "Face the Victim" scheme not as a personal issue but as a prospective human interest story.

Later that same day, I got a callback. Coombes was prepared to meet me and offered lunch. I accepted but immediately began to have second thoughts. I was not authorized to officially discuss the scheme, and if I revealed the true nature of my interest, she might have good grounds for seeking my dismissal.

In the event, I went anyway. Looking back, I guess I was motivated as much by self-interest as I was by taking the case forward. Laura seemed to exert an influence over people, myself included, and if I could bring all the jigsaw pieces together, I felt that I might just reach a better understanding.

When she walked into the restaurant, I saw that the transformation from teacher to television anchorwoman was complete. She wore a charcoal, tailored, business suit, the skirt of which emphasized her long legs while still maintaining her professional appearance. I also noted that the jacket was cut in such a way that it tempered her large breasts and made them appear more modest without compromising their pleasant shape.

I hated to think about what the outfit had cost, but clearly, no expense had been spared. Her face was her fortune, and her makeup had been professionally applied to highlight her piercing green eyes and the generous proportions of her lips. As she approached, I found myself wondering if she had had some work done on her nose; it looked a little neater than I remembered it from the photographs. All in all, this vision that sat down at the table seemed a world away from Laura Simmons.

At the outset, she maintained a professional demeanor but, as we both worked our way through a salad, she began to open up. I sold "Face the Victim" as a possible documentary, and she seemed keen to cement her claim to being a serious journalist. Throughout the meal, I made most of the running as she quizzed me on my job's nature and my thoughts about the scheme.

It was only over coffee that I alluded to her own experiences, and in the space of seconds, the atmosphere changed. All pretense at friendliness disappeared as she settled the bill and politely, but briefly, said that she would be in touch. As she left, I thought that I had failed and that I would never hear from her again.

Therefore, I was surprised when, two evenings later, the phone rang; it was Miranda. She had just finished the early evening bulletin and asked if I would like to meet for a drink. I hesitated for a second or two, having just stepped out of the shower and donned my nightwear.

She picked up on my perceived lack of enthusiasm.

"Look, if you don't want a drink can I swing by? I'm in your area and I just need ten minutes of your time."

I was now intrigued and gave her directions to my apartment, the address of which she already knew from my business card. I was dressed in scant shorts with a sloppy top and considered getting dressed again, but my skin was still damp, and I decided that she would have to take me as she found me.

As I let her into the apartment, she saw how I was dressed and faltered momentarily, but she quickly regained her composure. I invited her to sit on one of the twin sofas, and then I sat opposite and offered a glass of wine from the bottle that I had open.

I sipped from my glass and waited for her to speak.

"I want you to tell me honestly. Was your approach to me in any way to do with Laura Simmons?"

For just a second, I considered a lie, but there was something in her look, something imploring.

"I'm evaluating her at present."

Her eyes flashed to anger.

"And so our meeting was a pretence?"

"Look, if you want to proceed with the project, I can put you in touch with the right people. They're anxious to publicise the scheme and your personal experience, whether mentioned or not, will give it an added poignancy."

She considered this for a moment and seemed to appreciate the merits before she spoke once more.

"Tell me, in your opinion, does it work?"

"Not in all cases. Some of the perpetrators are beyond remorse but, where they do show it, yes, I think it works. The victims become less fearful and they go on to rebuild their personal dignity. Of course, if you're cynical, you could argue that it gives the victim a chance to gloat but that too can be constructive in terms of rehabilitation."

"Where do the meetings take place?"

"Strictly speaking they should take place in a secure environment, that would usually be a prison, but, if it is not a first degree offence, it could possibly be arranged under guard somewhere of the victims choosing."

There was another pause, and she dropped her eyes. I immediately became conscious of my unfettered breasts, and I awkwardly covered them with my arm. Miranda did not seem to notice.

"You know what she did to me?"

Again, I was tempted to skirt the issue, but I felt it best, to be honest with her.

"Yes, I do."

She looked at me for a long time, and I could see that she was deciding whether or not to confide. When she next spoke, it was with hesitation.

"That girl changed my life. On the one hand, if it hadn't happened, I would still be a teacher, I would not have been able to fulfil my dream but she has taken something away and I want it back."

I think I had an inkling, but I waited for her to continue.

"I was engaged to be married, I wanted all the usual things, I still do, but I'm different now. And do you know the worst of it? My whole career is built on image, I'm in the public eye, I can't explore these new feelings, but I need to know what I have become."

The Laura effect. Monica was fighting the same demons as I was, but I knew that the influence had worked on her in a different way than it had on me. I framed my next question carefully.

"You want to know if it was just her or something more?"

This time there was no doubt; her eyes roamed over my body, flitting awkwardly. My mind was working overtime. She was a victim, as I was—in need of help. The professional in me knew what I should do exactly, but there was, of course, another way.

I rose from the sofa. Outwardly, I remained calm, but my heart was hammering.

"Come with me."

For a second, she had a look of confusion, mixed with a hint of trepidation, but the natural tone of authority in my voice seemed to reassure her. She put down her glass and got up.

I led the way, and she followed docilely but then hesitated at the threshold of the bedroom.

"Come inside."

She stepped forward, almost mindlessly, and I wished that I had had time to do a little tidying up. The alcove containing my desk and computer was permanently cluttered, but I would not normally leave dirty clothes strewn on the floor.

She did not seem to notice. Her eyes were fixed on the bed with its lazily arranged quilt. She remained frozen, and then I remembered something Laura had said. She had commented on Miranda's choice of a pine bed with head and footboards, which made it a perfect choice if bondage was your thing.

Purely by coincidence, my bed was of the same type, a king-sized model which I had bought from IKEA and constructed myself, but I had chosen it for its elegant simplicity.

Up to that point, I had no clear idea exactly where I wanted to take things, but one look at her now made up my mind for me. After an awkward hiatus, she turned towards me, and I gave the guidance she sought.

"Lie down on the bed."

Her hands moved hesitantly towards the buttons of her jacket.

"Don't undress..."

She looked unsure but then did as I asked, lying primly with her hands at her sides.

She was dressed much as she had been at our lunch, another immaculately tailored business suit but this time in a fetching shade of pale grey. As I walked towards the bed, her nervousness was made evident by the uneasy rise and fall of her chest, but I was about to increase her anxiety. I stooped to pick up a pair of discarded 'stay up' stockings from the floor, and her eyes immediately widened.

"Let me have your arm."

She looked at the stockings and then back to me before half rising from the bed.

"It's your choice. I'm not forcing you."

Even as I spoke the words, it occurred to me that it might be the duress that she sought, and I thought, for a moment, that she would not go through with it, but she lay back down and looked at me earnestly.

"No one must ever know..."

"Why would I want to tell anyone?"

She hesitated for a second or two more and then stretched out her arm to me. As I took her wrist, I saw that she was no longer wearing an engagement ring, and I felt a momentary pang of guilt about John, but it quickly passed.

I passed the stocking around her wrist and tied a double knot before securing the other end to the bedpost. I had no experience, but I tied it in such a way that her circulation was not endangered. I then moved to the opposite side and secured her other arm, which she extended willingly now that she was reassured that I would not be too severe.

At the outset, I had intended nothing more than a symbolic restraint, but her helplessness had a greater effect on me than I could have imagined. I opened the drawer in the bedside cupboard and took out a second pair of stockings. She raised her head to see what was going on.

"What are you doing?"

"Shush..just relax..."

She had discarded her shoes before lying down, and I now took hold of her ankle and bound it as I had her wrist.

"Wait...I'm not sure..."

I ignored her as I finished and then started on the other.

She raised her knee in a gesture of token defiance, but she did not resist as I gently pulled her ankle towards the foot of the bed. Now that I had her fully restrained, I felt my heart pounding in my chest. We both knew what must come next, but I realized that it was more than just the anticipation of physical release. Just days ago, Laura had planted a vivid image in my mind, an image that had guiltily haunted my dreams since, and now it had become a reality.

I kidded myself that I was helping her to explore her own darker impulses, but I had woven my own design. Laura had abused a frightened, naked teacher; I had only known the immaculate, professional, journalist, and it was that woman that now lay before me.

Almost without thinking, I ran my hand lightly along her calf, then a little higher until my fingertips grazed the inside of her knee. She moaned, almost imperceptibly, and shifted slightly so that her skirt rode up fractionally. I arched my fingers beneath it with a smile and could now see that she was wearing traditional stockings and a pair of very expensive looking white panties.

"Were you hoping to impress someone this evening?"

She said nothing as she lay perfectly still with her eyes closed, and I suddenly understood that she was frightened that I would take my hand away. I was intrigued by this. It had been no part of my intention, but I allowed my fingers to drift a couple of inches higher.

I was now hovering at the darker border of her stocking top, and she was breathing with increasing rapidity. My own need was growing more urgent, but I held myself in check.

Very slowly, I eased my fingertips upwards onto bare flesh, and she hissed a breath through gritted teeth.

Her skin was very warm, and I was aware of toned muscles overlain by an incredibly smooth softness. I was used to the hard insensitivity of men's bodies, but this was something completely different. I could feel the tiny tremors of her excitement, silently encouraging me to explore further.

Her ankle pulled against its restraint as I removed my hand, but she froze again as she felt me raising her skirt. She lifted her hips a little, but I had no intention of removing it altogether. I simply wanted to see the effect I was having on her, and I draped it on her stomach to reveal her lower body.

The tan straps of her suspenders perfectly matched the color tone of her stockings, and I wondered just how much they had cost as I playfully slipped a finger underneath. Her body tensed at this fresh intrusion, but I eased away again to continue my journey across her inner thigh.

My fingers moved teasingly, and her body began to writhe slowly to the extent that her restraints would allow.

"My, my, who's an eager little slut."

The words sprang to my lips almost unbidden, but they only seemed to excite her more. A tiny damp spot had formed on the crotch of her panties, and, as I continued to take my time, it slowly began to spread.

Her skin now felt slightly clammy beneath my fingers as she grew ever more heated, and the smell of her arousal was rich in the air. As it assailed my nostrils, I remembered my first encounter with Laura and those furtive minutes in a toilet cubicle. I had thought her a monster, but here I was no better than she.

I edged ever upwards and tentatively allowed a single finger to slide into the leg of her panties. As I had suspected, she was completely denuded of hair and enjoyed a smoothness that suggested a lot of professional attention.

"Please..."

She lifted herself to meet my finger, but I had other ideas. I slipped it free, leaving her squirming in frustration.

For some minutes, I continued to caress her upper legs. Every now and again, brushing at the borders of her mons, until her skin was glossed with sweat and her panties were completely soaked.

"No,...please..."

Now that I had brought her to the boil, it was time to address my own needs. I put her skirt back in place and gently, but mischievously, pressed it against her panties. Almost immediately, the grey material began to darken.

"You've had your fun. Now it's time for you to take care of me."

The words sounded alien to my ears. But, even as I spoke them, I felt a pleasing ache between my legs. I stood in front of her and undressed slowly. I wanted her to be fully aware of what was about to happen.

As I cast my tee-shirt aside, I pinched gently at my engorged nipples, knowing that hers, still trapped in her clothing, were crying out for the same attention. I taunted her for a moment or two more, and then I slipped my thumbs into the waistband of my shorts and slowly slid them down my legs.

I was surprised to find that I was almost as wet as she was. Until then, I focused on my mental arousal, but now I was desperately in need of a physical release. I stood for a few seconds allowing her to appraise my body, and I noted, with detached interest, how her look grew almost fearful as she focused on the dark thicket that dressed my mons.

I could wait no longer. I moved up onto the bed and straddled her chest, uncaring of the fact that her jacket would now be soiled to match her skirt. As I loomed over her, she cast an eye at the binding around her wrist and then looked back at me.

"Look...I'm sorry...I can't go through with this..."

"What you do or don't want no longer matters."

It was my road to Damascus moment. There was nothing theatrical in my reply; I had expressed a genuine belief. The fact that she was helpless had fired my arousal to new heights, and I knew that there would be no turning back.

She sensed it too, the point at which when any semblance of professionalism finally slipped away, and there was panic in her eyes.

"Please...let's talk."

"Later perhaps..."

I slid forward, pinning her arms with my knees, and for a second or two, I hovered over her face. Between my legs, she began to shake her head.

"Please...no."

That final, impassioned plea caused my sex to melt. I lowered myself, sealing her in, and, as I came to rest, I was shaken by a climax, which was almost painful in its intensity. My body jerked violently, and I had to take hold of her head to keep my balance. Somewhere beneath me, I was aware of her muffled cries, but they were drowned out by the sound of my keening.

I do not know how long it lasted, but when it was over, I put my arms out so that I could take some of my weight, and I felt her desperately gasping for breath between my legs.

I was overcome by a confusing mixture of feelings. On the one hand, there was a wonderful sense of fulfillment, but this was combined with a sudden, desperate need to understand what had just transpired.

I needed to clear my head, and, ignoring her pleas, I got up and left the room. I picked up a half-full wine glass and drained it in one before immediately refilling it. I feared, for a moment, that I might face an assault charge, but I quickly dismissed the thought. Even if it came to it, nothing could be proved.

The one thing I did not feel was guilt. I knew, deep down, that if the same opportunity presented itself, I would do it again. How ironic that I could now condone the behavior that I had found so abhorrent when attributed to Laura.

My main source of unease was one that I felt sure that I had in common with Monica. The absence of a ring aside, I was almost certain she broke up with her fiancé because of her need to explore her sexuality. Now I too needed to make some decisions. I had convinced myself that this was a passing fad, but it had brought me alive like nothing else before.

After about twenty minutes, when the second glass of wine was finished, I went back into the bedroom. I half expected her to scream and yell, but she remained quiescent. She looked a real mess; her clothes were damp and rumpled, and her makeup was a long way beyond repair.

As I approached the bed, she spoke.

"Why did you do it?"

"I thought it's what you wanted."

"Let's not kid ourselves, that was hardly for my benefit, I told you to stop."

It was not the tone of anger with which she said it but the suggestion that she was somehow in control of me. I was already in the process of loosening her wrist when I came to a sudden decision.

"What are you doing!"

I tugged the stocking drawing it more tightly around the post and stretching her arm into the process.

"Stop that!"

I tied it off and moved around the bed. As I loosened off the other stocking, she started to resist in earnest, but she had no leverage. It was all too easy, using both hands, to tug the stocking around the post and secure it. Her arms were now bound far more strictly than before.

"Let me go or, so help me, I'll call the police."

"Do you think they'll believe you, given your history? Are you going to suggest that I overpowered you?"

This gave her pause for thought, and, in the meanwhile, I tightened the bindings around her ankles.

When she spoke again, she was a little more conciliatory.

"Look, what exactly do you want?"

"I want to help you. You want to know if you're a lesbian, a submissive or both. Let's find out shall we?"

I could not believe that the simple act of tying her more securely could give me such a charge, but I could already feel a tell-tale trail of moisture on my inner leg.

"Please, I can't, not again..."

I was already taking a pillow and putting it lengthways under her head. With that achieved, I mounted the bed once more and straddled her face.

"I'm sorry, about the last time, I lost control. This time all you have to do is lick me."

Seconds earlier, she would have refused, but now I had presented it as the lesser of two evils, and there was a look of relief on her face. She did not respond immediately, so I allowed my weight to settle a fraction more heavily so that her mouth touched my sex.

"Do it for me...like you did for her."

As I suspected, this was the trigger. As I looked down at her, she slowly put out her tongue and made first faltering contact. Her touch was enough to start a flow that oozed over her chin, but she did not demur. Now that she had the taste of me, she grew more eager. She started to attack me with broad sweeps of her tongue, and my labia swelled in appreciation.

The pillow ensured that her neck was not unduly strained, and she adopted a leisurely, lazy tempo. Her technique suggested hours of practice as she licked with just enough pressure to please me but not enough to break the seal; then, every few minutes, she would press her tongue inwards and would swallow the dammed up reward of her labors.

After the intensity of my first climax, the second took a long time to build, but she was tuned in to my natural rhythm and knew just when to increase the pace. Her tongue began to work deeper, giving me that delicious feeling of being filled, and she seemed to make it swell at will.

I moaned my approval, and she arched the very tip to caress a spot just behind my clitoris.

I do not know if she had been taught this or if it was her own discovery, but the sensation was amazing. I kept my body still so that I could focus on that single breathtaking pressure point, but the tension made me tremble. I had wanted to hold off from orgasm, but it was too much to resist. As she strained to the utmost, she moaned hot breath deep into my sex, and then my muscles were no longer mine to command.

I came in a series of frantic shudders, but I managed to hold station as juices seemed to boil inside before exploding into her waiting mouth, which she now sealed tightly to my sex. I saw spots before my eyes but, as I breasted the summit and started my gradual descent, I was again aware of her soothing tongue as she slowed to a gentle halt.

It took an effort to disengage from her, and I flopped exhaustedly by her side. My body was damp with sweat, and it took some time for my breathing to return to normal. I guess I must have dozed because, when I next became aware, I found my face pressed to hers.

"Was it good?"

Her question took me a little aback.

"It was wonderful."

She smiled, and, notwithstanding her ruined makeup, she still looked incredibly beautiful. I immediately felt my heart soften a little, and I suppose I must have looked a little guilty, but she read my mind.

"Don't worry, I don't expect anything from you. I got what I wanted."

I eased away from her and stood up. I stretched expansively and then started to unfasten her wrist. As soon as it was free, she reached down beneath her skirt and gave an almost feral groan as thrust her hand into her ruined panties.

Despite all we had been through, I felt a little awkward watching her, but then she looked at me imploringly.

"Would you...?"

Given our understanding, I stood there uncertainly, but then realization dawned. With a smile, I slinked back onto the bed. For a third time, I straddled her face but this time facing down the body.

As soon as I was settled, I felt her tongue once more, but this time, there was no subtlety. She licked like an animal, my thighs, my sex, whatever she could reach, and her fingers began to work frantically. I could hear the squelch of moisture as she drove them deep inside herself and then saw her frustration as she tried to lift her knees and open her legs wider only to be frustrated by her bindings.

She gave, what might have been, a scream of irritation, but she was now vigorously rubbing her clitoris, and she was not going to hold out for much longer.

Laura had me imagine that mane of red hair down between my thighs but, watching her like this, driven out of control simply by the taste and smell of my sex, was taking arousal to a new level. As she clawed her way to her inevitable climax, I slowly relaxed and let my bodyweight press her head deep into the pillow. A fresh scream of protest, or perhaps of ecstasy, but I did not care as I came on her face for a third shattering time.

Over the next two days, I was tormented by personal anguish. In terms of sex, I had never felt so exhilarated, but I was allowing it to seriously cloud my professional judgment.

I was rapidly coming to the conclusion that I might have to make some serious changes in my life. I knew that I should no longer represent Laura, which led me to re-examine my whole career strategy. More than once recently, I had looked at opportunities in Australia. They were crying out for qualified professionals, and the salaries reflected their desperate need.

If I made the move, I could afford the house of my dreams, complete with a swimming pool, for less than I was paying for my apartment. The stumbling block had always been my relationship with John. I had touched on the subject once or twice, but he was lukewarm. His career prospects would be seriously prejudiced, and he was not a fan of warm climates.

The big difference now was my whole attitude towards my engagement. John had finally caved in and called me, leaving two messages on my answerphone. He sounded hurt and genuinely sorry, but I had still not returned his calls.

More tellingly, I had surfed the net checking the criteria for Australian visas and then, guiltily, tried to find some websites that would tell me the attitude towards gay women.

I was drafting my request to be taken off Laura's case when the telephone rang.

"Hi, it's me Miranda, can you talk?"

"Yes, of course."

I was a little bemused. I had not expected to hear from her again.

"I've been thinking over what you said, about meeting Laura Simmons, can you arrange it?"

I had exceeded my authority in broaching the subject in the first place, but such was the current enthusiasm for the scheme I was sure that something could be done.

"Yes, it shouldn't present a problem."

"Where would the meeting take place?"

"It's up to you. Some people choose to meet in prison others opt for their own home."

"I don't want that bitch to know where I live now!"

The fierceness of her reply caught me by surprise.

"It might be possible to set up a neutral venue."

There was a long pause before she spoke again.

"How many people have to be present?"

"At the meeting itself? There would be three; you and she plus a mediator. In Laura's case there would have to be at least two guards but they could wait outside."

"Could you act as mediator?"

"In theory I'm qualified but I have had no specific training besides which I am not sure that it would be entirely appropriate."

It seemed surreal to be having a conversation of this manner given the nature of our most recent encounter, but when she spoke next, there was a hint of desperation in her voice.

"I have to get her out of my head and I want you to help...you owe me."

I was uneasy with the whole prospect, but she was right; I felt that I owed her something. I also wanted to do the right thing by Laura. She was no longer going to be my responsibility. But if I could be influential in getting her custodial sentence reduced and help her long term career prospects, I would feel better about myself.

It took a lot of string pulling to bring it together, but the date for a meeting was finally set. The venue proved problematic. Miranda was not prepared to visit the prison, and her home was out of the question, but it was she who finally came up with a solution. Her company sometimes used a particular hotel suite for their more prestigious interviews. It had the benefit of being both very central and very secure, and, in presentation terms, the spectacular views across the city, with all the well-known landmarks, afforded a stunning backdrop.

It was booked by the day, and she found a day when filming would be completed in the morning, leaving it free for the afternoon. I arrived early but was surprised to find Miranda already there. She was modestly attired in a fetching blue sundress, and she had a drink in her hand.

"We will need to dispense with the alcohol before they arrive."

She looked at me blankly and quickly drained her glass. I took it from her and set it to one side before joining her at the small conference table. I spent a few minutes outlining the various 'do's and don'ts,' and then there was a knock at the door.

Laura stood there flanked by two smartly but informally dressed female guards, and I could not help but stare. In preparation for the meeting, she had been granted access to a hairdresser, and she was allowed to wear her own clothes. She looked simply breathtaking. She was wearing her thick blonde hair in a flowing shoulder-length style that softened her features, and her make-up was subtly applied to highlight her clear blue eyes and a smile that would be the envy of a Hollywood starlet.

She had chosen to wear a dark, off the shoulder, a-line dress. She must have bought it from a chain store, but she made it look haute couture. She had lost a little weight while on remand, and her tan had completely faded, but that only added to the allure of her svelte figure.

Strictly speaking, the guards should have remained outside the door of the room where the meeting was taking place, but the suite was enormous, and they did not protest when I suggested they make themselves comfortable in the kitchen. There were some magazines on the small dining table, and I told them to help themselves to coffee. I then led Laura through to the living area and closed the door behind us for privacy.

As soon as she walked into the room, the atmosphere was charged. I saw that the change in her appearance was a shock to Miranda as it had to me. I invited Laura to sit at the opposite end of the table to Miranda while I sat to one side between them.

I opened the proceedings by explaining the purpose of the encounter and made it clear to Laura that I would bring the meeting to an immediate close if Ms. Coombes were in any way uncomfortable. I did not mention the word 'apology,' but I trusted that Laura had sufficient good sense to see that the ball was in her court and that she had a lot to gain.

I then invited Miranda to speak. She had her eyes downcast, staring at the tabletop, but she raised them slowly to meet Laura's steady gaze.

"I just want to know why you did it."

"You know why, you accused me of cheating."

Miranda seemed lost for words for a moment but then regained her composure.

"You could have lodged an official complaint. What you did was immoral."

"Would they have believed me?"

The conversation was not going the way I had envisaged. I had expected Miranda to take the high ground with Laura showing, at least, some contrition. Looking at Miranda, I could see that she was getting agitated as she sat with one hand clasped almost painfully around the other.

By contrast, Laura had her hands resting in her lap, but I noticed that she had leaned forward just a little causing her breasts to bulge very slightly against the bust line of her dress. I was immediately transported back to our first meeting and her inappropriate behavior. For reasons I could not explain to myself, I cast a furtive glance towards the large bed visible through the door to the adjacent room.

I mentally shook myself and tuned back into what was being said. I had missed Miranda's next remark but caught Laura's reply.

"But surely that's worth an apology."

"Look, I admit, I may have misjudged you but nothing can condone what you did to me."

Laura paused before replying, and as she did so, she leaned even further across the table. She spoke conspiratorially, almost in a stage whisper.

"If you tell me honestly, that there was no part of it that you actually enjoyed, then I will apologize."

This was Miranda's cue for high dudgeon but, instead, she looked at me almost beseechingly.

I tried to retake control.

"Laura, don't be ridiculous. Your actions amounted to an assault, tantamount to rape. If you cannot see that then I see no point in continuing here."

Laura turned to meet my stare.

"If that's the case then why did you get so turned on when I told you about it?"

I did not look, but I could now feel Miranda's eyes boring into the side of my head as I replied.

"I find your remarks very offensive and you are certainly not helping your case here."

Persistent liars get away with what they do because they are so glib, they can live a lie and almost believe themselves. The rest of us always give ourselves away. It might be a tiny facial gesture or an almost imperceptible change in our tone of voice, but somehow we betray ourselves.

Laura knew, but, worse still, I sensed that Miranda knew too. I turned towards her to reassure her that I was still on her side, but she was looking at me aghast. Before I could say anything else, Laura spoke again.

"My, my ladies. What have we been up to?"

I snapped back at her.

"I think it's time we brought things to a close."

Laura did not move. She looked at Miranda, who could not meet her eye.

"I don't think that Miranda is ready to finish just yet."

I waited for Miranda to back me, but she remained silent.

"Miranda? Are we done?"

Laura laughed as I received no reply and then taunted me.

"You still don't get it do you? She's not here for an apology."

I looked at Miranda and saw it was true. She appeared totally cowed. Without thinking, I took her hand in mine to offer reassurance, but as I did so, Laura rose from her seat. We both sat there, mutely. Without another word, she began to unfasten the buttons at the front of her dress.

I was about to berate her when Miranda squeezed my hand tightly. Things were getting out of control, but I had no idea what to do about it.

Laura had unbuttoned her dress to the waist, and she narrowed her shoulders to allow it to slide down to her ankles. She was left standing in a pair of heels and a matching set of simple black bra and panties. As we watched, she turned slightly towards us, and I saw that even dressed in modest underwear, she was still cover girl material.

The bra struggled to contain her well-formed breasts, and my eye was drawn down to the narrow pinch of her waist and the flared perfection of her hips before appreciating her coltish legs, which were longer than I had imagined.

She stood for a few seconds, and then she sashayed towards the bedroom with us both staring at her flawless backside.

Framed by the doorway, she sat down on the end of the bed, and then she extended a beckoning finger.

I knew it was the moment to draw the line, but I felt powerless as Miranda slipped her hand from mine and got up from her seat. She was like a somnambulist as she walked away from me, and I rose in a half-hearted attempt to pull her back from the brink.

I simply followed her into the bedroom, where she stood in front of her nemesis with her head bowed. Laura glanced at me, fleetingly before addressing herself to Miranda.

"Undress for me."

There was no wavering. She reached for the zip at the side of her dress and pulled it all the way down. She slipped out of it without taking her eyes away from Laura and then started on her underwear. I noted that it was of the very expensive 'show off' variety and, once again, I wondered for whose benefit she had worn it.

Within seconds she was totally naked, standing with her hands at her sides, and I found myself staring at her breasts. They were possibly larger than Laura's, and I suspected that, in years to come, she might need some assistance to hold back the effects of gravity, but, for now, I was envious.

Her nipples were perfect brown roundels pointing proudly upwards, and, even as I looked, they slowly distended. I immediately felt a tingling between my legs, and, with the thought matching the deed, I dropped my eyes to Monica's sex.

It was covered by a closely shaved frizz of red hair which defined a tight, almost girlish, slit but there was obvious dampness at its median. Even as I looked, a distant voice was telling me that her destiny was in my hands, but my physical immobility was matched only by the sluggishness of my thought processes.

As she stood timidly before Laura, I was put in mind of a slave girl of ancient times stoically awaiting her fate, and she was not left in doubt for very long.

"You know what I want."

Laura spoke assuredly, and, notwithstanding my recent experiences, I felt like an ingénue in her presence. It seemed that Miranda was similarly affected as she gracefully fell to her knees.

She started to reach forward slowly, but Laura brought her up short.

"Wait."

She reached behind her own back and deftly flicked her bra open. Then, like a burlesque artiste, she slowly unveiled her breasts.

I had seen them before, albeit fleetingly, but my memory had not played me false. They were as magnificent as I remembered them, and I felt a primal urge to reach out and touch, but I was ignored as Laura settled once more.

Miranda needed no further prompting. She gently took hold of Laura's panties and, as Laura raised herself, she slid them down her legs. Slipping them free, she knelt with them in cupped hands, as if they were priceless vestments, and looked at Laura, who favored her with an indulgent smile.

As I looked on in disbelief, she brought her hands to her face, and I heard her breathing deeply.

"Have you missed me baby?"

Miranda seemed not to hear. Her eyes were closed, and she was gently caressing her face with the warm cotton. It was, at the same time, both repellent and compelling.

"Enough."

Laura spoke the word quietly, but Miranda's eyes opened as if it had been shouted. Reluctantly, she put her trophy aside, but her face lit up when, with calculated slowness, Laura opened her legs.

I found that I was holding my breath and could not shake the feeling that she was toying with us both. The room was silent save for the double-glazed hush of traffic and the low hum of the air conditioning, and so, when Miranda started to groan, I felt the hairs standing up on my neck.

Her eyes were fixed between Laura's legs, and then I saw why she was so affected. Laura's sex was a plump, perfectly depilated mound, which seemed out of keeping with her otherwise lean features. The pale mons had a youthful tightness, which only served to emphasize the proud prominence of her inner labia, which formed a pair of matched ruffles shading from pink to cerise.

Even from a distance, I could see the moist evidence of her arousal, and my nostrils widened involuntarily.

Miranda's upper body was swaying very slightly, and I feared that she was going to faint, but it was simply the strain of holding herself in check until Laura granted permission.

"Go ahead..."

My heart leaped as Miranda fell upon her like a ravening beast. I remembered the feeling of her face between my legs as she lost control, and I felt a twinge of envy, but Laura simply looked down upon her and laughed softly.

"That's not doing it for me babe."

Miranda looked chastened as she stopped and then reapplied herself more methodically. She pointed her tongue and gently swept along the divide of her labia. It rippled as if imbued with a life of their own.

"That's more like it. Take your time. We do have plenty of time don't we?"

While she did not look up, I knew that this last question was directed at me and that it was intended as a taunt. She was letting me know that I could bring it to an immediate halt; it was entirely up to me.

In the next minute or two, I tried to process so many confused thoughts, not least what was best for Miranda, but watching her there and expressing her devotion, it was hard to believe that she would rather be elsewhere.

For my part, I hated being used, but I could feel that my panties were already drenched.

And so I did nothing.

I stood there watching as Laura relaxed, and Miranda continued to moan quietly, content to lick forever. I could almost feel the exquisite pressure of her tongue, and I so desperately wanted to touch myself.

As I fought down the urge, Laura looked across at me.

"Why don't you get undressed? If you're a good girl, or should that be bad girl?, I might let you have a turn."

Her condescending tone rankled, and, under normal circumstances, I would have put her firmly back in her place, but I felt as if I was in a parallel universe. It was with an unearthly sense of detachment that I began to remove my clothes.

I did it slowly, not wishing to break the spell, and then stood naked awaiting Laura's caprice. She had her hand resting soothingly on Miranda's head while, at the same time, making it clear exactly what she wanted. Together they formed a tableau of almost heartbreaking beauty, and I yearned to be enjoined.

Finally, with languid insouciance, she rose from the bed momentarily, leaving Miranda at a loss. She idly brushed at the counterpane with the back of her hand and then picked up one of the pillows. She plumped it up and placed it just so before turning to me.

"Come and make yourself comfortable."

It was an echo of the words that Nicola had used, and it brought a frisson of excitement. I crossed the room, mindful of Miranda watching me from the corner of her eye, and laid myself down.

I looked down my body at Miranda's face, framed by my parted legs, and I tried to read her expression. At first, I feared that she thought me guilty of betrayal, but then I realized that, now she was reunited with Laura, I was simply a distraction.

"Show her what you can do..."

Laura's command brought the tiniest hint of irritation to Miranda's face, but I found that it only made me hotter.

She made herself as comfortable as she could, and then, as if to pay me back, she began to lick at my inner thighs. I groaned and squirmed. It would have taken very little to take me over the edge, but I was no longer calling the shots.

She teased me for several minutes and moved further up my body, where her tongue did things to my navel that no one had done before. Then, each time she moved south again, I braced myself only to have her shy away to give more attention to my legs.

I was soon sweating freely, and I was only vaguely aware as Laura's smiling face loomed over me.

"She's good isn't she?"

As if this was a signal, her tongue trailed down from my navel once more but, this time, she crossed the neatly delineated border of my pubis, and she began to twirl silky blonde hairs with her tongue.

Now that she was so close, the torment was even greater. She preened me with feline grace but avoided my labia, which, stimulated by the close proximity, were screaming out for attention.

I could feel myself leaking copiously, and the scent of my arousal filled the air to an almost embarrassing degree. Any pretense of self-control was long gone as my hips shifted restlessly to make her eat me.

I was so tense that I failed to notice when she finally took mercy and began to lick gently up through my heated furrow; it took an effort to relax sufficiently to appreciate the wonderful new sensations which seemed to buzz through my whole sex.

I felt my climax building with a delicious inevitability but her touch, up to then so sure, became lighter so that her tongue was barely in contact. I raised my hips slightly to encourage her, but she was not going to be hurried.

Over the next twenty minutes, she must have brought me to the brink at least a dozen times only to cruelly withhold the prize each time. I was panting with need, and I was pleading under my breath.

436

Laura filled my field of vision again.

"Do you want to come? Shall I tell her?"

"Make her do it..."

I could hardly get the words out, and the tension in my neck increased as she built me up once again. This time it was so close. I closed my eyes and arched my back, but a sudden pressure in my chest made me fear that I had a cardiac arrest.

I opened my eyes just in time to see Laura slipping her knees over my shoulders and using her weight to press my body back onto the bed. For a moment, I was frozen in panic, but then I registered her sex just inches above my face.

It was obvious what she wanted, but I shook my head in denial.

"I can't..."

"Don't be silly, of course you can..."

Her thighs tightened a little about my head, restricting my movements, and I had no choice but to focus on her sex. It was dry now save for the labia themselves, which had swollen free almost obscenely to pronounce their slippery arousal.

I remembered how it all started. It seemed a lifetime ago, that first tentative sniff of my fingers, and it had culminated in this, impossible to imagine, encounter. Now I could smell her again, but this time there was no escape.

I could still not bring myself to do it, but Miranda chose that moment to flick her tongue across my clitoris. I gasped, but at the same time, my neck jerked, bringing my lips to hers. I immediately fell back, but the taste was now there. My tongue, obeying some long-buried animal instinct, sought it out and found it not entirely disagreeable. I licked my lips again, this time a little more boldly, to find that the taste was slightly musty but with an enticing, underlying sweetness.

I looked up to see Laura staring down at me with a knowing smile on her face. As I watched, she brought a finger to her sex and slid it inside herself effortlessly. She twisted it slightly and then eased it out again, now shiny with moisture. I kept my mouth tightly closed, but she ran her finger over my lips and awaited the inevitable result.

It was like trying to eat doughnuts without licking the sugar from my lips. My tongue had a mind of its own as it slipped out. Soon, my mouth was filled with the rich taste of her.

"Do you like it....of course you do."

I desperately wanted to deny it, but the truth was I did like it.

"Come on...be good to me."

She relaxed a little and softly brushed her labia back and forth across my lips. The sensation was a little ticklish, and I opened my mouth fractionally. I was still uncertain, but all my senses were slowly being overwhelmed. Her legs muffled my hearing; all I could hear, apart from the pounding of my pulse, was the lulling sound of her voice. I could not draw breath without filling my lungs with her scent, and I could see nothing except the almost hypnotic beauty of her sex.

In those warm, smothering confines, it became easier to simply surrender, and she recognized the moment of transition.

"Lick me..."

She said it so softly that I almost did not hear, but I slowly put out my tongue.

Her lips were surprisingly smooth, but they were rich with her taste, and I lapped at them tenderly. At that same moment, Miranda's tongue found my clitoris again, and my arousal instantly soared.

We remained locked like that for a minute or two, but my body was shaking as Miranda took me ever higher. I could no longer stay in control, but I knew what I wanted to do. As I neared the point of no return, I closed my mouth around Laura's sex and pushed my tongue deep inside. The heat, and the pressure of her muscles, came as a surprise. But I was rewarded with a wellspring of moisture.

I started to cry out as my climax took hold, but I kept my tongue in place and drank her in. I did not want it to end, and Miranda used her mouth to entice every last jolt of pleasure from me.

When it was over, I could still feel her tongue helping to slowly ease me down, but Laura was in no hurry to move. She slowly rubbed herself over my nose and mouth, marking out a territory she now knew to be hers.

Finally, she deigned to rise, but, for a moment or two, I could not find the strength to get myself up. I lay there, recovering my breath and trying not to consider the consequences of what had just taken place.

"You don't mind?"

Laura had found the minibar and was mixing a gin and tonic, and, bizarrely, I found myself worrying about the professional consequences of allowing her access to alcohol. Meanwhile, Miranda was still kneeling at the foot of the bed, clearly awaiting further instructions, which were not long in coming.

"I want to watch you two together."

I knew that she was taking it too far, but Miranda smiled slyly and stood up. Any vestige of subservience fell away, and her pose was now deliberately provocative; when she wanted to be, she was very confident of her appeal.

Her face was still shiny with moisture, most of it mine, but I must have looked much the same to her. She held my eye as she knelt onto the bed, and I felt uneasy. I could kid myself that Laura had forced herself upon me, but if I accepted this, there could be no way back.

I raised myself on my elbows, but she was already sliding herself over me, and I felt a delectable shiver as she allowed her breasts to brush over mine. I closed my eyes to try and deny the arousing sensation, but then I felt the warmth of her breath as she closed her mouth over mine.

Her kiss was soft, knowing, and irresistible. Almost immediately, I could taste myself, but, far from being off-putting, I wanted more. My tongue met hers in a slow writhing dance, and, for a space of time, Laura was totally forgotten.

I lay down, allowing her to dictate the pace, and gasped as her thigh eased between my legs. Before long, I was trying to raise my hips to increase the wonderful pressure on my sex, but she rose with me, not allowing me to go too fast.

For a few more moments, we remained joined in an unbroken kiss, and our perspiring bodies continued to move as one. I could feel another climax simmering, but Miranda, too, was growing less composed.

She broke the kiss and looked down into my eyes, and I was struck by how truly beautiful she was. She smiled in an unspoken acknowledgment, and then slowly, sexily, she turned herself around until we were posed in a classical soixante-neuf.

Only moments before, I would have fought against her, but now, with her red-tinged sex poised invitingly, I not only wanted to taste her, I wanted to bring her something of the pleasure that she had already brought me.

I raised my head enough to take a first hesitant lick, and her sex, which had appeared so firm, almost unassailable, split like a ripe fruit. My tongue was welcomed deep inside, and her taste flooded her mouth.

She gave a feline growl and, growing emboldened, I placed my hands on her hips and pulled myself more tightly in. To start with, I was content to probe as deeply as I could but then, mastering the inverted topography; I licked at her clitoris.

As soon as I did so, I felt her tongue engage with my sex, and I almost cried out. She began to mirror my movements, and I became lost in a new depth of intimacy. I had only to let her know what I wanted by using my tongue, and my wish was immediately fulfilled.

I lost track of time as I increased the intensity of my impending climax by proxy, and it was clear that she too was close. She was now lying heavily on me, my face pressed close by her thighs, but I no longer cared. We both began to increase the tempo until, with a final, frantic, fluttering of tongues, we came together bound as one.

It took a long time to recover, with neither of us having the strength to move, and I lay inert with her weight, making breathing difficult but, even now, I was aware of many different smells. There was the dampness of sweat, the clash of mixed perfumes but, overall, there was the hot, raw smell of her sex.

"That was quite a show ladies."

Laura's voice was an unwelcome intrusion, a reminder of a world to which I was in no hurry to return, but, reluctantly, Miranda and I peeled ourselves apart. I sat up, knowing that I should take charge but feeling morally deficient. It took Laura to impose her natural authority.

"Lie down, you know how I want it."

I instinctively turned around, now ready to leap to Miranda's defense, but I was not prepared for the beatific on her face. To my amazement, after all, she had already been through, she laid down meekly on the bed.

Laura, no doubt, fired up from watching us, wasted no time. She straddled Miranda's face and bore down. My tongue and jaw ached, albeit pleasantly, and I was surprised that Miranda could still continue, but a heartfelt groan from Laura told me that she had found the mark once more.

For a second time, I found myself watching, and, after just a few minutes, I became a little jealous. Such was the intensity of Miranda's ministrations that Laura had pitched forward and was supporting her weight on her elbows. This left me with an unhindered view, and to my astonishment, I realized that I was aroused once more despite having just reached two of the most satisfying orgasms of my life.

I was captivated by the uplifted perfection of Laura's twin globes, which were worthy of being preserved in marble. They were tight, unblemished, and called out to the hand. As I continued to stare, I saw that Miranda was now using just the very tip of her tongue to work on Laura's clitoris, leaving the livid gash of her sex clearly on display.

It shone with an inviting ooze and, as if reaching into my mind, Laura commandingly whispered.

"Lick me."

She arched her back just a little more, making her mound even more prominent, and I was drawn like a bee to an orchid.

I moved to lie alongside Miranda, and, without another thought, I began to lick at the luscious opening.

"Oh my sweet little bitches..."

Laura was a mistress of self-control. Even with both of us paying homage, she still held herself in check and issued instructions.

"Kiss each other."

Miranda welcomed the relief. The strain of keeping her outstretched tongue in place was telling, and she welcomed the delicate massage as our mouths closed together, bound by the shared taste of Laura.

It was a short respite. Laura soon had us both back at work as she continued to luxuriate in the attention until, finally, she stretched just a little. As a result, Miranda was encouraged to push her tongue deeper, but it meant that I was displaced.

For a second or two, I did nothing but look on, but then, furtively, I raised my eyes just a little. Something in my upbringing filled me with guilt as, from scant inches away, I surveyed her forbidden valley with warped fascination.

The soft curves of her taut flesh drew my eyes to the very center with the inexorable pull of a whirlpool. It seemed a living thing, this pink rosette with its shaded heart. Almost imperceptibly, it was opening and closing, beating to the rhythm of excitement created by Miranda's tongue.

I continued to stare and then became aware that Laura was looking at me. Her face was a little redder, and Miranda was obviously getting to her, but she gave me that same knowing smile.

"Do it..."

There was no doubting her meaning, and I suddenly found it had to breathe. It was wrong in so many ways, and only days before, I would have found the mere thought repugnant, but I neither moved nor protested.

I felt a little faint, or did I? And my head fell slowly forward.

At first, I remained still, surprised by the heat radiating from her skin, and then, perhaps influenced by Miranda's continued labors, I put out my tongue. I licked softly at her perineum, allowing the possibility of moving back to her sex, but now that I had taken the first step, I could not turn back.

I closed my eyes and trailed slowly upwards, my tongue enlivened by the tang of salt and something altogether more earthy. She was stretched so taut that the valley walls had all but disappeared, but I needed no guidance.

I slowed even more, fearful of the final step, but then I felt it under my touch. It was more solid than I thought, and I was frightened, for a moment, of its hidden strength, but it seemed perfectly fitted for the tip of my tongue.

I played there a little, feeling the tiny contractions, and tried to resist the compulsion to test the boundaries of its resilience. I was winning the fight until, from nowhere, I felt Miranda's hand on my sex.

She still had her tongue buried deep, driving Laura on, but now her fingers slipped inside me, and her thumb unerringly settled on my clitoris.

I gasped and automatically pressed my tongue forward only to meet a solid resistance, but then, degree by slow degree, it began to yield. I was no longer pushing but, rather, was being irresistibly being sucked in.

The tightness was painful, but, at the same time, curiously comforting, and as I got used to it, I was intrigued to feel Miranda's tongue probing across the divide. It was only natural then to forge the final link, and I reached out blindly between her legs. Her sex was hot, wet, and completely open to me, but my position did not allow me to penetrate. Instead, I stroked the area around her clitoris as best I could, and it proved to be enough.

It was as if we were all now plugged into a single energy source, and as we approached orgasm, we seemed to feed one another, supercharging an already overwhelming passion.

My scream, as I reached the zenith, was gagged by my buried tongue. But even before it was done, my heart was stopped by a fresh outburst.

"What the fuck is going on!"

Chapter 06

Miranda and I fell to the floor together, leaving Laura sprawled on the bed. Miranda, aware now of the two guards in the room, clung to me for protection while I tried to grab at the bedcover.

In the next few seconds, I saw not only my career in ruins but Miranda's as well.

The guards stood with a look of astonishment on their faces, stunned to silence, and it was Laura who reacted first.

"Well the meeting was supposed to be convened in a spirit or reconciliation..."

Her words were a jibe aimed at me. I had used the same phrasing when I first mooted the idea to her.

She sat sublimely naked on the bed, and the guards simply gaped. Her hair was disheveled, and a post-orgasmic blush tinted her skin, but, even in this wild state, her natural beauty shone through, and she knew the power of it all too well.

Finally, one of the guards pulled herself together.

"If you ladies would like to get yourselves dressed...I will have to submit a formal report."

Laura got up from the bed unhurriedly, but she made no move to retrieve her clothing. She approached the guards, who instinctively took a step back before appreciating that they had nothing to fear from a naked woman.

She walked right up to the older of the two, a West Indian woman who must have been in her early thirties, and whispered in her ear. As Laura spoke, the woman's eyes widened just a fraction. When she had finished, the woman looked down at Miranda and me before turning to her colleague.

"Just give us a minute."

She took her partner by the arm and led her outside the room where there was an exciting exchange, but I could not make out what was being said. I wanted to get myself dressed in their absence, but Miranda refused to leave hold of me.

They came back and looked down at us before turning to Laura.

"It's a deal."

I was now more alarmed than ever.

"Laura, what's going on?"

She smiled as she came and knelt beside us, and then she spoke a sotto voice.

"Look. It's simple. It makes damn all difference to me, I'm going back inside anyway, but it seems a pity for you both to throw your careers away. Now, our friends here don't want to make waves, they can see for themselves how talented you both are."

The double entendre was not lost on me. I realized, with sudden horror, exactly what she was suggesting.

"Laura, get serious, this ends now!"

"Don't be so hasty. Don't you think that you ought to consult with Ms. Coombes first?"

I turned to Miranda, but it was obvious that for her too, the penny had dropped.

"Miranda, we get up right now, we get dressed and we walk out of here. I'll clean this mess up I promise you."

Her face was a mask of anxiety, and she clutched my arm even more tightly.

"I can't go back. I've worked too hard to give it all up."

For a second or two, I could not think of what to say. Her eyes were imploring me.

"You're prepared to do this?"

She had no hesitation as she replied.

"We have to."

The situation was as outrageous as it was sordid, but it was the one chance for me to rescue my career. I looked up at Laura, and she almost smirked.

"Ladies, I think you've reached a very sensible decision."

The guards looked taken aback, but I guess that they could hardly believe their good fortune. Laura, still unashamedly naked, ushered them towards the bay window.

"I think you'll find the chairs comfortable."

In the bay, an occasional table was flanked by two armchairs, and the guards looked at them uncertainly before the older of the two took charge.

"Let's do this."

Notwithstanding, there was a definite awkwardness as they both stripped off their underwear before sitting down with their skirts raised.

Despite her positive assertion, Miranda was slow to get up, and she stood slightly behind me, leaving me the immediate focus of the two women's attention. I suppose that it was to make it easier on Miranda that I moved towards the older woman. She was slightly heavyset, and she was wearing a wedding band.

Her colleague, a trim blonde, looked to be somewhere in her mid-twenties and, in any other company, would have turned heads, but she paled in comparison with Laura and Miranda.

I was desperate to get it over with, and I knelt quickly between the woman's opened legs, aware, out of the corner of my eye, of Miranda doing the same.

Her clothes had flattered to deceive. I could see that her thighs were thicker than they had first appeared and presented an imposing prospect. As I looked, I was aware of just how much my tongue ached from my previous exertions, but it had to be done.

"I'm guessing that this is your first taste of black pussy."

I did not need this. Why did she have to gloat?

She shifted forward a little allowing her skirt to ride up altogether, and I could tell that she was extremely aroused. Only later did I wonder how much they may have seen or heard before they interrupted us.

"My man would need a lot of weed before he even think about doing this for me."

Now that she was relaxed, her accent shifted towards a pronounced Caribbean patois.

"Momma's waiting honey..."

Her sex was daunting. With an uneven growth of tightly curled black hair, a rounded mound was home to a pair of long, loose labia suggestive of maturity. As I drew nearer, I could see that the dark curtains were parted slightly to contrast with a bright pink interior.

I closed my eyes and braced myself to make a direct assault.but as my tongue made contact; I was surprised by the sharp initial tang.

"How's that taste honey? Sweeter than your white girls I'm bettin."

The truth was that I found it unedifying, but I stuck to my task and pushed through her labia, which melded to my tongue. The taste here was fresher, more in keeping with my recent experience, which made things more palatable.

"Oh yeah, that's one cute tongue..."

For a minute or two, I did little more than leaving my tongue in place, but the novelty of the situation was, for her, sufficiently arousing.

"Go deep babe..."

I did as she asked, bracing my tongue, and pressing further home. She did not have the tone of Laura or Miranda, but the yielding softness was, in its own way, inviting. She was very wet, and the slurp of moisture was soon audible.

"Yeah, that's nice, suck it out of me..."

I closed my mouth about her and pursed my cheeks, but it was almost unnecessary. She was flowing freely, and a distant expletive suggested that Miranda was also working her magic.

"This girl just loves those juices..."

She now linked her fingers behind my head, making me uncomfortable, but I knew that she could not take much more.

"Now babe, find the spot..."

Her voice was unsteady, and her body was beginning to tense. I edged upwards, but her clitoris was impossible to miss. It felt huge beneath my tongue, a smooth, prominent mushroom that felt as if it had burst free from its tight fleshy collar. I licked in tight gentle circles, but she was in no mood for refinement.

"Harder!"

I flattened my tongue and licked broadly as her body bowed up from the seat.

"Oh fuck!"

She started to come spattering my face and neck with gouts of warm moisture before collapsing limply, totally spent.

"Oh, you are really something....clean me up babe."

I almost refused, but a series of high-pitched wails heralded her companion's orgasm, and I knew the ordeal was almost over. I licked her sex clear of juices trying not to raise her level of excitement, but she had had enough.

I sat back on my haunches, grateful just for some fresh air, and saw that Miranda was similarly posed. The atmosphere was severely strained, and it took me a moment to realize what was wrong.

"Where the hell is Laura!"

Epilogue

She had played us all for fools.

A panicked investigation elicited that she had simply walked out of the building headed god knows where.

And so we concocted a story.

We claimed that Miranda was taken unwell during the meeting and that, while we tended to her, Laura had slipped away. We even called a doctor so that the fiction could be embellished, but, as a lie, it was tissue-thin.

Miranda came out of it reasonably unsullied, and the two guards got away with a severe reprimand. As for me, a scapegoat had to be found, and I was invited to fall on my sword. There was no doubting my culpability, but I felt harshly treated. I resigned from the understanding that my references would not be compromised.

It was going to take some weeks to process my application for an Australian entry permit, and, in the meanwhile, I signed with an agency to do some locum work. The confirmation of my pending emigration was enough to finish my relationship with John.

I often thought of Laura, wondering where she was. Of one thing I was sure, she was never going to be destitute. Wherever she had wound up, I had no doubt that she had turned her ability to manipulate to her best advantage.

She had wreaked havoc in my life, turning it upside down, but she still had my grudging admiration.

After the initial brouhaha had cooled down, I met up with Miranda again or, more to the point, she met up with me. She turned up unannounced on my doorstep one evening, and there was little need for words.

The fact that I was going away seemed only to add fuel to our relationship, with both of us knowing that we could enjoy ourselves for a few weeks without the hindrance of commitment.

We reassumed our roles of dominant and submissive, and we explored the boundaries. The problem was that the increasing degree of strictness that I employed was matched only by the growing tenderness I felt for her. I knew for certain that if I allowed myself, I would fall deeply in love with her.

It was towards the end that I had her tied to the corners of my bed once more. We had found a wedding supplier and had splashed out on some white silk ropes with which she was now restrained. I was working from home, and I had left her there for some hours. Every now and again, I would check on her, but at the same time, I used a vibrator to bring her to the edge of orgasm.

By the eighth time, she was screaming for relief, but she knew that she would have to spend a very long time satisfying me first before I decided whether or not she would be allowed to come.

By the early evening, I could no longer ignore my own growing need, and I groaned as I looked forward to riding her beautiful face. I took a shower and donned a robe, but I was interrupted by a ring at the door.

I was not expecting anyone, and I looked through the spyhole to see a young, dark-haired woman that I did not recognize. I challenged her, and she said something but her northern accent was so broad I did not understand. In the end, she simply held up a courier package.

I opened the door to her, and my immediate thought was that she was rather good looking to be a courier. She needed a signature, but her pen was out of ink, so I went to the kitchen to find one. When I returned to the hall, there were two of them just inside the door.

The second woman was a blonde, and an alarm sounded somewhere in my head.

"I don't recall inviting you in."

The blonde smiled, stepped back into the vestibule, and beckoned to someone out of my sight; then, in an accent as broad as her companions, she addressed herself to me.

"There's someone here who wants to see you...I hope you haven't eaten..."

Erotic Females
Three Dirty, Naughty, Steamy Erotica for The Ladies
Emilia Russell

All Rights Reserved. No part of this publication may be reproduced in any form or by any means, including scanning, photocopying, or otherwise without prior written permission of the copyright holder. Copyright © 2020

This book is entirely a work of fiction. The names, characters and incidents portrayed in it are the work of the author's imagination. Any resemblance to actual persons, living or dead, events or localities is entirely coincidental.

Story 01

Chapter 01

Belinda intent on relaxing alone in one of the small steam rooms at her club; she had told her PA she would be unavailable for the whole morning. Membership of this exclusive health club was a perk of the job she used often, her company had its own gym, but she preferred not to have to mix relaxation and work, to put it politely. Her eyes took in her surroundings dreamily; the whole room was tiled in pale blue, relaxing classical music was piped in, and it was wonderfully private. A high, wide platform or ledge ran the length of one wall, and at right angles to these three lower platforms jutted out. Due to the fact today it was an all-female day in the sauna, Belinda felt safe to strip completely naked and didn't bother locking the door even.

Hanging her smaller hand towel on one of the large chromium hooks, she slipped the large towel from around her body and carefully spread it out upon the wide tiled upper ledge. Even in the sauna's warm damp environment, the pastel blue tiling felt quite cold to the touch, and she wasn't going to freeze her arse like some of the other fools did. After adjusting the steam control settings too high, Belinda stepped up on one of the lower seating ledges and climbed onto the towel-covered tiles. Even though the thick towel, she could feel the coldness and shivered a little until her body's heat warmed them a little. Before very long, though, there was a gentle knock upon the closed door, disturbing her solitude.

"Yes?" Belinda called out a little sharply, wondering what this disturbance entailed.

"All of the smaller rooms are occupied so do you mind if I share?" a woman's voice called pleadingly from behind the door.

"No of course not," Belinda called resigned to the fact that she couldn't really deny access; she sat up to see who was coming in, "It's set on hot though so be warned."

When the door opened, a pretty oriental woman peered around and, smiling politely; she introduced herself to Belinda as she entered. Seemingly innocently, she closed the door as she spoke, clicking the lock as she did so.

"My name is Mao Lien but everyone calls me Lien," she smiled. "I am pleased to make your aquaintance." She nodded to Belinda as she spread out her towel on the middle ledge that ran perpendicular to her own directly below then slipped fluidly from her toweling robe.

" Oh I'm Belinda, hello, make yourself at home," she slightly blushed as she found her eyes unexpectedly roaming over the woman's naked body as Lien hung the robe next to Belinda's hand towel.

Watching the woman discretely as she sat down on the lower platform with her back to her, Belinda noted the way the wisps of black hair that had escaped the restrictions of her plait curled in the moist heat. Diverting her eyes momentarily to avoid eye contact as Lien laid herself back on the platform below, Belinda soon looked down once more to gaze at her.

Seeing Lien's eyes were already closed mere moments after laying down, Belinda laid back and tried to unwind. A strange unease grew within her, and Belinda found it increasingly difficult to relax in the other woman's company. After no more than a few anxious minutes had passed, Belinda was intrigued and began glancing over the top at the naked form that lay below.

The woman's smallish firm breasts rose and rhythmically fell as Lien dozed oblivious to her observer. So Belinda, lulled into a false sense of security, began to stare less cautiously at the pretty oriental lithe body. She guessed the woman to be in her mid-thirties but in fantastic shape. Lien's tanned golden skin glowed golden beneath a sheen of sweat as the room's heat gradually built up. Belinda spent a long while gazing at those full pouting lips as they twitched and parted as the woman slept. Eventually, her roving eyes were drawn down over Lien's flat tummy to her crotch with its luxuriant black pubic bush sprouting between the woman's slightly parted thighs.

Drinking in the woman's oriental beauty, Belinda found herself gradually becoming aroused sexually. Without thinking, she began imagining touching and caressing the golden-skinned woman who lay below to feel the excited response. Looking once more at Lien's face, guiltily checking that her eyes were closed behind those thick long black lashes, Belinda returned her gaze to the woman's lips. Her fevered imagination ran amok as she thought of those soft, pouting full oriental lips fastened firmly around one of her own taut aroused nipples. Belinda's vivid imagination was unstoppable; soon, it had built a mental picture of the oriental woman kissing slowly down her pale belly to fasten her small mouth upon her mound.

Lien shifted restlessly in her slumber on the toweled ledge below Belinda, and as she did, one of her legs slipped over the edge of the ledge. Her golden thighs parted enticingly, offering an intrigued Belinda a much better view of the hidden delights between them. Fascinated by the woman, she leaned forward on one elbow, craning her neck out above the recumbent woman to gaze down shamelessly between her thighs. Framed so perfectly within the woman's thick blue-black pubic bush nestled a pair of fleshy red-brown delicately petalled labia that invitingly beckoned her to touch them. Recklessly Belinda leaned even further out, oblivious to everything except the woman's beckoning sex.

A light cough suddenly shattered Belinda's delightful reverie making her gaze flash up to the woman's face, and to her horror, Lien was awake and staring straight up at her. She had just caught Belinda red-handed looking down right between her even now spread thighs. Belinda blushed deep crimson instantly and quickly rolled back on her ledge, cursing her stupidity. Confused and embarrassed, she could not understand the excitement she had felt at the sight of another woman's naked body. Meanwhile, down below, Lien had silently sat up with her back to Belinda, who, in turn, stared shamefully red-faced straight up at the ceiling. An awkward silence descended between the two women for quite some time during which Belinda's embarrassing discomfort subsided very little until Lien softly broke the ominous silence.

"Do not worry Belinda I am not at all offended if you admire my body," her soft voice was unbelievably calm, and it soothed away Belinda's guilt as Lien looked back up over her shoulder smiling.

"I must apologise I don't know what came over me," Belinda stammered, "It's not that I'm a lesbian or anything you know!"

"I know so just forget it," Came the other woman's amiable reply, "You could do me a little favour though would you?" Lien dismissively laughed as she spoke.

"Of course," Belinda hoped she had found a way to extricate herself from this awkward situation.

" I hurt my shoulder in the gym today, could you massage it a little?" Lien coolly asked as if she was unaware of Belinda's recent indiscretion.

"Honestly Lien I don't think It would be a very good idea," she felt panic rising inside her as she spoke. " I mean, I err I don't think I would be any good at massage," Belinda stammered as she tried to get out of the sticky situation knowing inside that she secretly longed for any chance to touch Lien's golden body.

"Nonsense I trust you implicitly," Lien's voice was reassuring; her twinkling black eyes mischievously danced as she spoke, though, "just be gentle with me please!"

"Oh, OK then come here if you're sure?" Belinda gave in though she was still unsure of herself.

Half-reluctant and half-eager, her mind span as she succumbed to the woman's demand and sat up on the upper ledge. Swinging her feet down to rest them on Lien's platform, she nervously clenched her hands together as Lien moved. Turning away again, Lien slid gracefully backward along the lower platform, her towel crumpling behind her as she moved to position herself below Belinda. Then resting back lightly at first against Belinda's knees, Lien waited patiently for her promised massage. Cautiously with trembling hands, Belinda reached down to touch the hot golden skin of the oriental woman's shoulders for the first time. Dry mouthed, she began to gently knead the supple flesh beneath Lien's golden skin with her fingers anxious not to give any indication of her interest away at first. As Belinda's long fingers worked on the doll-like woman's firm muscles, she soon sensed Lien was completely at ease with the situation and began relaxing a little more herself. Belinda got intense satisfaction from her toil. Each time, the woman squirmed against her knees or occasionally gasped with enjoyment as her shoulders and neck were manipulated by her seemingly large hands.

In turn, this both unwound and aroused Belinda, and before long, it seemed to her almost as if Lien was wriggling a little, seemingly deliberately attempting to force herself back between her knees. Despite her earlier embarrassment, though, Belinda cautiously allowed the squirming torso to ease its way between her slightly spreading knees without trying to appear as if it was anything but a sheer accident. Lifting her arms over Belinda's thighs, Lien leaned back between her parted legs and settled back against her inner thighs with her arms hanging limply over Belinda's thighs and knees.

"That's much more comfortable, your knees are too bony!" Lien quietly whispered as Belinda redoubled her amateur efforts at massaging the woman's shoulders.

Once more, Belinda found her eyes gazing down at Lien's breasts, watching them move as her hands worked on her shoulders. Belinda noted excitedly how Lien's brown teats were unmistakably growing taut as she did so, apparently in response to her caresses. Feeling alarmed at how her heart suddenly started pounding excitedly in her breast Belinda's mind was thrown into turmoil as common sense fought with her unnatural desire for this oriental creature. Then as if she was trying to sway the battle being fought in Belinda's confused mind, Lien insistently began to slowly push herself further back between her thighs once again. Belinda found herself willingly allowing the woman to force herself back deeper between her readily spreading thighs. Her struggle to control her desire was dismissed as the gnawing sexual craving built relentlessly deep within, and her legs yielded yet a little more to Lien's insistent squirming. The woman carefully laid herself back between them.

Resting her head back against Belinda's firm ample breasts, Lien reached up and softly stroked her forearms encouragingly. Belinda's heart excitedly skipped as she felt Lien's petite hands grip her forearms firmly just above the wrists and purposefully draw them down towards what was small in comparison to her breasts. Needing no further encouragement, Belinda complied with the other woman's wishes. Her eager, trembling hands slid easily downwards over the slippery golden shoulders to the waiting globes guided by Lien's tiny tugging fingers.

She had never ever considered making love to another woman at all before in her entire life. Normally Belinda would never have imagined any possibility of herself even being attracted to one of her own sex, but this exquisite woman seemed so very, very different. Lien began panting heavily as Belinda's hands slid over her slippery skin to cup her small firm breasts. As Belinda's thumbs brushed tentatively over the hard brown nipples, Lien gasped out with pleasure and began gently kissing Belinda's forearms as her caresses became more confident and bolder. Lien encouragingly rubbed her dark head between her ample breasts and reached up to touch them while Belinda excitedly continued to caress her eagerly. Now totally in the oriental woman's control, she enjoyed the soft caress of the small hands upon her breasts. The long-nailed golden fingers began to nip repeatedly about her swollen areolae, and Belinda squeaked each time excitedly, the delicious pain easily fuelling her uncontrollable desire.

Suddenly Lien was moving, twisting herself from Belinda's grasp; she turned excitedly to face her. Her black eyes danced with lust as she reseated herself between Belinda's open legs. Leaning forward onto Belinda's thighs, Lien reached up to take her large breasts in her small hands before sinking her small mouth over an aroused teat. Belinda felt Lien draw the proud flesh into her mouth to have its tenderness assaulted by a writhing tongue; Lien made her squeal with intense excitement as sharp teeth nipped at the sensitive flesh repeatedly. Belinda leaned back, submitting readily to the woman's advances feeling Lien's small firm breasts crushing against her inner thighs as she leaned forward against her. Her senses reeled helplessly before the onslaught as the mouth moved to her other breast to tease the engorged teat wickedly.

"Oh Lien Oh this is so wrong," she gasped unconvincingly.

"Are you not enjoying it?" her tormentor whispered huskily as her lips broke momentarily away from her eager nipple.

"Yes of course," she whimpered, "But...mmm." her protests were weakened as the woman sucked hard, drawing her nipple deep into her mouth.

Still, with her lips clamped firmly around Belinda's teat, Lien insistently hauled her forward off the upper ledge towards the lower platform she occupied. Looking directly into Belinda's eyes with her intriguing black pupils that flashed intriguing devilment and enticing excitement, Lien made it clear she was in charge.

"Shut up and lie down please!" Lien confidently gestured to her towel as she continued, "Let me show you something."

Unquestioning and enthusiastic, Belinda settled back on the towel-covered platform and excitedly waited to see what Lien had in mind. Climbing onto the tiled platform at her feet, Lien took Belinda's knees and spread her legs apart before leaning forward over her excited body. She kissed her deeply, their tongues writhed and squirmed from one mouth to the other though Lien did not touch Belinda anywhere else.

" Now I want you to experience something incredible my sweet!" Lien whispered after breaking the kiss, "enjoy it... I'm sure you will."

She kissed Belinda lightly once more before her wriggling tongue began an electric journey down Belinda's highly aroused sweat-soaked body. It slithered through the valley between her heaving breasts, eagerly licking her sweat salts from her hot skin as it worked even lower still over her trembling tummy, pausing to probe at her navel momentarily. Lien's small hands easily spread Belinda's unresisting thighs wider, yet as her tongue continued its downward journey, it drew unbearably near to the whimpering woman's crotch. Visibly shaking with excitement, Belinda stared at the tiled ceiling blankly. All her concentration was diverted between her thighs, knowing that Lien would be looking at her enflamed sex.

"Are you ready my sweet?" came Lien's thick husky whisper from below as her breath tickled Belinda's excited flesh.

Belinda raised her head anxious to peer down at the gorgeous oriental woman who crouched catlike between her wantonly widespread thighs. Lien's black twinkling eyes looked back hungrily at her as she licked her lips slowly and sensually. Belinda closed her eyes, unable to watch any more when her lover's full red-lipped mouth sank deliberately slowly behind the thick bush of her dark wiry pubic hair. Her rampant heart thumped excruciatingly painful in her chest as in feverous anticipation she waited for what seemed forever, she trembled all over with excitement, eager for Lien to proceed.

"Yes... Yes!" gasped Belinda pathetically, eager to enjoy the unknown caress of a woman's lips.

Setting her head down, she remained motionless in anticipation of the first touch of Lien's lips on her sex. Belinda couldn't prevent herself from crying out as Lien planted the first wild kiss open-mouthed around her excited swollen lips. The woman started sucking hard, drawing even more blood into her already engorged labia. Lien's tongue began to writhe about wildly against her sensitive flesh deliciously. Unable to hold herself back, Belinda began to grind herself urgently against Lien's face. The oriental woman began expertly biting, licking, and sucking at her swollen labia, easily driving her quickly and relentlessly towards orgasm. Within but a few moments, Belinda felt the first convulsion of pleasure grip her writhing body.

Biting down hard upon her hand in an attempt to stifle her building cries of pleasure, Belinda reeled beneath the sudden intense orgasm that assaulted her nervous system. For what seemed an eternity, she climaxed, convulsing enthusiastically against the still devotedly laboring Oriental's mouth while desperately trying to stifle her cries of passion. She knew that she would be rewarding her lover's efforts with incredible amounts of love-juice; she always did when she came, and the thought of Lien eagerly consuming her bubbling excitement so fuelled her arousal further. In what had been a matter of mere moments, the skillful oriental woman had given her one of the best climaxes she had ever known. Belinda knew that Lien had done so little to her to achieve this fantastic result. Without even probing past her lips or even touching her clitoris, the woman easily had Belinda sobbing ecstatically. Lien had sat back while she recovered her composure, excitedly she sat watching Belinda attempt to cover her embarrassment.

"Was it good?" Lien asked outrightly unabashed.

"Mmm." was all Belinda could manage to reply as she sat up.

They sat there in awkward silence for a few moments, then Belinda smiled and spoke quietly, and her already flushed face reddened further.

"Lien that was wonderful," she averted her eyes, coyly, "Do you want me to..."

"Do you want to my sweet?" Lien cut her short, "I would like you to but only if it is what you want?"

"Oh I'm not sure," she stammered, "I want to but don't know if I can."

"OK my love, do just as you wish and stop if it displeases you." The oriental woman was so understanding, "It would give me great pleasure just to be held in your arms dear Belinda."

So saying, Lien leaned back against the tiles and closed her eyes, allowing Belinda time to make up her mind. Reaching out, she stroked Lien's face gently at first but soon, her nervous hand fell to the woman's breast as she gained confidence. For a while, Belinda was content to cup Lien's small breast in her hand. Soon she had grown in confidence to adventure further still; cautiously, she squeezed the small firm globe in her hand. Gently she began rolling the still hard brown teat beneath her palm to feel Lien twitch in response and whisper encouragement.

"That's so nice," murmured Lien, her eyes still closed.

Belinda looked down at Lien's other nipple, and cautiously, she bent her mouth to it, her tongue reaching out tentatively to taste Lien's salty sweat on its aroused stiff tip. Lien moaned and shifted slightly, and her hand reached into Belinda's wet hair and gently pulled her face closer to her breast encouragingly. Filled with eager fire, Belinda sank her lips around the other woman's excited areolae, sucking it into her mouth and flicking the hard rubbery teat with her tongue. Feeling Lien grip her wrist delicately, Belinda allowed the woman to slowly guide her hand away from her breast down towards her mound.

"Touch me please my love?" Lien whimpered quietly, "Caress me there!" she left Belinda's hand hovering near her pubic hair.

Obediently she slipped her hand between Lien's open thighs, delighted to caress the incredibly wet excited flesh she found there. Eagerly exploring now, her long fingers slithered through Lien's flowing excitement, and soon her long forefinger found the woman's stubby clitoris. Feeling the shudder of pleasure ripple through Lien as her fingers brushed the little hard button thrilled Belinda incredibly. Seeing the startling effect that her touch had on Lien, she began rubbing insistently at it to bring the oriental woman quickly to a whimpering climax quite easily. Pulling Belinda close as she came, Lien lovingly sobbed something softly in Chinese into her ear over and over. Feeling much more confident now, Belinda caressed the quaking woman gently as Lien openly enjoyed her orgasm. Belinda drew extreme satisfaction in knowing how easily she had made Lien come. As she withdrew her come-smeared hand, she decided there and then to go even further. Once more, they cuddled close, and Belinda chose her moment to speak.

"I want to err... Oh could you lay back Lien I'd like to err, taste you?" Belinda whispered, red-faced.

"You really don't have to my sweet Belinda," Lien smiled, "I am satisfied, you have done enough as it is."

"Oh but I want to," Belinda stammered, "I may never have another chance to broaden my horizons like this again."

"Let me think my love," Lien paused deliberately before continuing, "my sweet I have two demands you must agree to before I decide!"

"OK what are they" Belinda was overeager to continue.

"One that we must pleasure one another together and two that you will see me again whenever I wish it to be so," she smiled, knowing Belinda would accept.

"Yes of course," she was so eager she had missed the fact that she would have to wait.

She sat there confused as Lien smiled resignedly then slipped back away from her. As Lien stood up and picking up her crumpled towel, she turned to face Belinda and wrapped it about her golden body. Once it was secure, she bent close to Belinda and kissed her quickly. Lien's attitude had seemed to have taken a strange turn. She suddenly seemed to grow detached, and the tone of her voice altered a little. Belinda increasingly sensed that the moment was over and went to speak, but with a flourish of her small hand, Lien stopped her.

"I have some questions my sweet!" she continued allowing Belinda no time to object.

"Meet me in out the foyer shortly for I must leave soon I'm afraid."

With that, she slipped into her robe and was gone leaving Belinda alone in the sauna feeling stunned and confused. Still incredibly aroused, she sat for a long moment, wondering what had just happened. Should she feel pleased, angry, shocked, or one of many emotions, she couldn't work out! After a few minutes, though, she gathered her wits and slipping on her towel, she grabbed her things then set off in pursuit of the intoxicating woman.

Chapter 02

In the communal changing rooms, there was no trace of the woman at all, and her inquiries about her to the other women there shed no light on Lien's disappearance. Now feeling hurt and bewildered by Lien's sudden departure from the sauna, Belinda changed into her old sweatshirt and jogging bottoms without even showering. Deciding not to return to work today, she would go home, remember what had just occurred, and record it in her diary. Slipping on her aging but comfortable flip-flops, she grabbed her bag and made her way to the foyer. At first, she felt bitter disappointment when there was no sign of the Oriental woman there. Then she realized that she had changed with such haste that if Lien had a private dressing room, she would probably still be dressing. It was a good twenty minutes longer before the woman eventually showed up and apologized so sincerely that Belinda's anger faded at the sight of her enchanting smile.

"I really cannot stay long my sweet," Lien smiled apologetically once more, "I would really like to see you later to carry on where we left off."

"Frankly Lien I'm quite peeved at the way you left me in there," Belinda retorted tersely, "why should I see you later, give me a good reason?"

"Because I fascinate you, you can't resist my charms can you my sweet?" Lien raised her eyebrows and laughed knowingly.

"No I cant!" Belinda blushed, glancing round in alarm at Lien's brazen openness.

"as I said, I must go very soon so here is a list of questions for my filofax," she was quite abrupt but made her request seem so sincere.

"What!"

"If you could fill in the answers for me while I go to ring a cab I'd be ever so grateful Sweetness."

Astounded by the woman's unbelievable audacity, Belinda picked up the card and glanced over the half a dozen neatly laid out questions. Already she knew that if she refused to answer the request, the chances were she would probably never see Lien again. Belinda also knew that Lien knew she was captured and was aware of just how much she wanted to see her again. Already Belinda realized that at the moment, she had probably been no more than a quick distraction and probably meant very little to the woman. Picking up the very expensive-looking pen Lien had confidently left on the table, she answered the carefully written questions on the piece of vellum.

Age 23

Boyfriend/husband- Yes

Live alone- No with boyfriend

Car- Yes

Job- Director of accounts

Salary- £36,500

Sexual likes- Obviously, I like to experiment.

When Lien eventually returned smiling, as usual, she didn't sit down but bent down close beside Belinda and hummed in a pleased tone as she watched Belinda finish her brief questionnaire. Just the woman's closeness and her perfume aroused Belinda, and she sighed with pleasure as a flashback of what had happened between them a short while ago ran through her mind.

"This morning was really great, I mean it, my sweetness," the woman whispered softly into her ear as if she could read her thoughts.

Then as if to confirm her statement, she reached beneath the table and discretely caressed Belinda's inner thigh. To Belinda's surprise, she shook all over in response to the woman's' uninvited touch that ventured dangerously close to her responding pussy. For what seemed minutes, Lien ran her lithe fingers up and down her thigh teasingly as if to torment Belinda, who knew the woman would leave her shortly. Lien's other hand scooped the answered question sheet that lay abandoned on the table, and she perused it as if she had no knowledge of her secretive caress upon Belinda's trembling thigh.

"Meet me at 8 PM in the bar of the Ambassador hotel by the airport and I'll teach you some more, till later Sweetness!" Standing upright, she smiled lovingly and prepared to leave.

"Oh. If you do come tonight, do wear something really sexy for me" her radiant black eyes twinkled, then whisking up her pen, she was gone.

For the rest of the day, the strange excitement she felt refused to fade and gnawed at Belinda relentlessly. Three hours passed, and she seemed to drift through them, not even bothering about going to work or even eating lunch. Early in the afternoon and most uncharacteristically, she went shopping for clothes. Subconsciously recalling what Lien had said, she started by buying a low cut slinky red dress. Some black stilettos, black Dior seamed stockings and sleek red satin panties, and a suspender belt followed, all paid for on her boyfriend's credit card. While passing the jewelers, she saw a lovely triple string pearl choker, and impulsively, she bought it on her boyfriend's card as well.

"If he cant take a joke then fuck him," she laughed to herself uncharacteristically, "Perhaps when Lien was finished with her she'd let him fuck her as a treat when she got home."

When Belinda finally went home, she spent over two hours in preparation bathing and grooming herself for the coming evening. Deciding to wear her curly dark hair up, she pinned it high on the back of her head and fluffed it up before dressing in her new clothes and jewelry. The temptation to masturbate as she dressed was close to intolerable, and it almost overcame her because she was so excited at the possibilities of what may occur this evening. She spent some time trying hard to ignore her arousal by preening herself before the wardrobe mirror checking herself over continually as she put on each clothing item.

Driving towards the airport, she felt so nervous and practically convinced herself that Lien would most likely not turn up anyway. If the woman didn't show, John would be in for the fuck of his life tonight, she decided. After parking her car, she adjusted her dress and, feeling very panicky, headed for the bar on trembling legs. The constant interest and attention she got from many of the men in the bar boosted her confidence and ego quite considerably, but she ignored them. She wandered around and around the bar for quite a while before eventually spying Lien sitting in a quiet booth far away from the hubbub surrounding the bar area. She felt sure that Lien had not been there earlier on her previous circuits. Lien's jet black hair was tightly plaited and pinned up on her head; she wore a very expensive looking deep red trouser suit.

"I was becoming quite worried you wouldn't show up tonight Sweetness!" lied the oriental beauty then laughed. "You look absolutely ravishing."

Belinda smiled coyly and blushed a little as she sat opposite Lien, watching her intently as the woman ordered two drinks from the ever so attentive waiter without even asking her what she wanted. In just a few moments, two large Brandies had appeared before them, and Belinda laughed.

"I bet we wouldn't be so well looked after if we sat here in track suits or ragged jeans?" she smiled at Lien.

Taking a sip of brandy Lien spoke quietly, "I rather thought we could have a meal first before we make love?"

She glanced almost shyly at Belinda, who reddened instantly embarrassed by the woman's open frankness. Without waiting for a reply, Lien had stood and carried their drinks off towards the restaurant gesturing for Belinda to follow her. The hotel restaurant looked very exclusive, it was dimly lit, and the discretely placed tables were draped with beautiful heavy tablecloths that almost reached down to the thick piled carpet. Every single table in the room was adorned with flowers, candles, and silverware. They were seated in a vacant, fairly secluded area close to the windows that looked out over the airport, whose myriad multicolored lights twinkled in the gathering darkness.

"To be honest Lien I must tell you that I really don't think I can afford to eat here," whispered Belinda, slightly embarrassed.

"Don't be silly darling, I'm paying, well sort of, you see I'll charge everything you want to my hotel business account as I stay here quite regularly," Lien exclaimed, smiling warmly.

"Oh, are you staying here tonight then?" Belinda asked.

"No Belinda, WE are staying here tonight, that is if you want to?" the quiet reply caused a shudder of excitement to run through Belinda.

"You know I want to or I wouldn't have turned up," Belinda glanced coyly at the woman lifting her eyes from her arriving starter for a few moments.

"God those shy looks really turn me on," Lien's voice was low and husky. "I want you so badly I don't think I can wait!"

The conversation thrilled her, and Belinda repeatedly blushed as Lien paid her so many compliments as the evening slowly progressed. Just watching the incredibly sensual way the woman ate her food amazed Belinda, so it came as little surprise that she felt Lien's barefoot begin rubbing her foot beneath the table while eating their ice cream. The soft touches she accepted with a receptive smile even when the exploring foot began running up and down her shins and calves. Lien smiled knowingly at Belinda, and her almond-shaped eyes danced mischievously beneath her fringe, openly relishing the sudden look of alarm that spread over Belinda's face as her wriggling foot forced its way between her knees.

"Relax my Sweet no one can see," she reassured her, "Do not resist me please, I insist."

Allowing the woman's exploring foot to slip up beneath her dress Belinda blushed again, desperately hoping her reddened face would not give their secret away to anyone. Within her breast, Belinda felt her heart begin to race excitedly as recklessly she yielded to her lover's advance, and she felt the hot barefoot wriggle up tenaciously between her stocking-clad thighs as she parted them. Noting that the restaurant was quite empty anyway eased her misgivings slightly, and she found the whole idea of allowing Lien to tease her so in public very stimulating. All the same, her guilty eyes constantly shifted around the few people there she could see through the foliage and screening to ensure they were all quite oblivious to their little game. Excitedly she parted her legs wider as the foot slipped passed her stocking tops to press gently against the front of her lower tummy.

"Stockings, Mmm that is sexy," Lien cooed none too quietly. "I adore girls in stockings!"

"Lien you're embarrassing me!" Belinda hissed in an urgent whispered tone, trying to sound annoyed to no avail.

She could only sit there staring in terrified disbelief at Lien's calm face, only her dark eyes that twinkled mischievously betrayed her partner's intent. Belinda froze as she felt the foot move lower until the toes pressed deliciously against her ripe sex through her red satin panties, vainly she tried to clamp her shaking thighs together to no avail around the invading limb. She was powerless to prevent Lien and terrified of drawing attention to them, Belinda tried not to move or betray her excitement at Lien's intrusion. In turmoil, Belinda sat hopelessly attempting to eat her dessert casually while the foot began to massage her sex delightfully under cover of the long tablecloth. Meanwhile, on the other side of the table, Lien casually resumed eating her dessert as she manipulated Belinda skilfully. Nimble toes easily squirmed their way beneath the elasticated lace edging of Belinda's panties gusset to wriggle inside. They slithered against the slippery mess of her wet excited flesh, occasionally making her grunt involuntarily with pleasure despite her anxiety. Trying really hard to keep up the facade of normalness, they were enacting above the table convincing Belinda trembled. Her hands relentlessly shook as she toyed with her ice cream, watched all the time by her beautiful tormentor.

"No Lien STOP!" Belinda tried to make the whisper sound as authoritative as she could.

"I won't!" was the simple reply Lien gave her with which her big toe asserted direct pressure against Belinda's clitoris for the first time.

"Fuck Oh! Shit!" exclaimed Belinda trying to make as little noise as she could.

"You don't really want me to stop do you my sweet?" Lien's insistent quiet voice brimmed with confidence, "Just relax and enjoy it."

Her shaking hands clenched her cutlery as Lien's dextrous toes slowly rubbed her to fever pitch, and Lien gave no respite to her helpless victim. Their eyes were intently locked as Lien carried on masturbating her and behaving as if nothing was happening. To anyone who may be watching, only the strange flushed twitching of the European woman could betray their secret's intimacy. Fortunately, the resultant orgasm was a small discreet, controllable affair that saw Belinda slightly bent forward over the table. She would seem in pain to anyone watching as her convulsing thighs gripped around Lien's foot as she bathed it with her copious issue. Unfortunately, this drew the waiter's attention, who came over to inquire if there was a problem.

"No just a little indigestion," Lien cut in, "she is very prone to it."

"Can I bring you any thing Madam?" he enquired, concerned as Belinda straightened.

"I'll be OK now thank you!" stammered Belinda embarrassed at the unwanted attention they received.

The waiter's intrusion was terrifying for Belinda, but at least Lien's foot was gone from inside her now sodden panties. After a moment, the waiter smiled and bowed before he left them to finish their meal. Taking a sip of wine, Lien cocked a knowing eyebrow at her and smiled sweetly. In turn, Belinda stared back her face, annoyed, but despite her acute embarrassment, she was clandestinely ecstatic by what they had just done. They finished the meal in awkward silence as Belinda still felt embarrassed, and Lien did not want to risk upsetting her further. Lien ordered liqueurs. When they arrived, Belinda had calmed down enough for Lien to realize that the uncomfortable atmosphere was lifting and broke the silence.

"Belinda," pouted Lien, she seemed concerned, "are we OK?".

"Yes of course," now her discomfort had subsided, Belinda tone was apologetic, "It's just that I am well, normally a little more reserved about sex than you shall we say!"

"Don't worry I'll try and control myself from now on," a giggle escaped Lien, then she hissed, "the trouble is your so damn sexy I can't leave you alone!"

"Lien shush!" whispered Belinda nervously, glancing about.

"Sorry," hissed Lien apologetically, "there I go again!"

"Oh Lien I feel so stupid it's not your fault, I'm just really shy that's all," Belinda smiled then added, "I tell you what, to show I mean it we'll do what ever you want!"

"Do whatever I want eh?"

"Yes anything!" smiled Belinda, immediately catching on to how Lien suddenly acquired a greater interest in her statement with slight alarm.

"Do you know what I really wanted to do earlier?" leaning forward as if to tell a great secret, Lien whispered enthusiastically.

"No tell me then," Belinda smiled, almost completely forgiving the smiling woman for her earlier indiscretion.

"I wanted to slip under this table then eat your hot juicy pussy for dessert whilst you sat there acting so prim and proper!" Lien smiled a cool, measured smile.

"Mmm that would have been very nice but a little conspicuous don't you think if you suddenly just disappear and reappeared with all your sexy red lipstick smeared over your unexplainably dripping face!"

She cocked an eyebrow at Lien. For some reason, Belinda felt quite bold and insanely thought she could try and outplay or embarrass the ever-cool oriental. At first, Lien laughed with her and didn't even seem to rise to her comment. Soon enough though Belinda realized that her attempt at cleverness had backfired, alarm filled her as she watched Lien look casually around the room. Once she was sure no one was looking, she carefully eased her chair back and dropped under the tablecloth obscured from view by the heavy linen.

"Shit Lien I was only mucking about" Belinda felt quite horrified but extremely excited by the prospect of what could happen to her.

Only a meaningful silence came from beneath the table in reply as she felt the woman's hot hands slip up her legs beneath her dress. The small, nimble hands felt so good sliding up against her nylon-clad thighs that she didn't want Lien to stop, well almost. Anxiously she grasped the liqueur glass between both hands mainly to stop them shaking and tried to dissuade her tormentor from proceeding further. Lien's fingers were now snaking relentlessly around her hips, grasping the sides of her panties.

"Lien please don't!" she begged in a frantic whisper as the fingers began tugging down her panties, "Oh shit Lien what if the waiter returns?"

"Help me here will you?" was the only whispered reply.

Knowing that Lien would take no notice at all of her protests, Belinda decided to comply, refusing would probably result in Lien doing something insane to draw unwanted attention to them. Obligingly she eased her bum slightly off the seat to help Lien with the removal of her panties. Slouching in her chair, Belinda responded to the furtive tugs that insistently drew her to sit perched on the very edge of her seat. She was putty in the oriental girl's hands, fear of discovery enflamed her excitement many times over. While her panties were still stretched between her ankles, she felt Lien spreading her unresisting knees wider apart. Above the table, Belinda drew in a deep breath then tried to gather her composure and look as if she was relaxing after her meal. Sitting almost stone-like, Belinda could feel Lien's hands carefully lifting and folding back her dress to fully expose her pussy.

Constantly she found herself surveying the other patrons in the room. Belinda realized the danger of being caught heightened her excitement incredibly. Feeling Lien's narrow shoulders pressing hotly against her thighs, she coughed in alarm when she accidentally caught someone's eye. Belinda smiled politely and nodded, and they turned away the exact instant that without warning, Lien slipped her tongue quite deep into her wetness. As Lien's probing tongue speared her delightfully,

Belinda knew instinctively if the woman was allowed to carry on that the resulting climax would be far too intense to keep secret in such a public place like this. Lien had begun writhing her long firm tongue in circular movements as she thrust it into Belinda, sending shivers of pleasure through her. Wanting to let her lover continue for just a little while longer seemed so tempting, but she knew that it would be their undoing. Lien's long squirming exploratory tongue was doing something wonderful to her, but she must be stopped. Common sense burst Belinda's approaching ecstasy, and she began trying to dislodge her lover discretely.

"Lien stop now for fucks sake!" she whispered desperately, "All right you win I'll do anything you want if you just quit it"

To Belinda's relief, Lien must have decided that she had taught her a lesson because Belinda felt her move away and allow her to shut her legs. Lien busied herself out of sight by readjusting Belinda's dress beneath the tablecloth for her. Lien's nimble hands then slipped Belinda's soiled panties from around her ankles, and shortly, she heard her lover whisper.

"Is the coast clear my love?" Lien affectionately squeezed her foot.

"Yes be quick," Belinda felt panicky, "Hurry that was too scary for me!"

"Here I come ready or not!"

A red-faced, slightly flustered looking Lien reappeared in her seat, her lipstick was smeared, and her lower face glistened. Her black eyes twinkled with devilment, and she laughed wickedly at Belinda before lifting the red satin panties to her face. Using them first as a napkin to remove Belinda's spent fluids and her own ruined lipstick Lien then pretended to put them on top of the table just to enjoy the look of horror on Belinda's face. Slipping them somewhere out of sight, she then casually began to finish her liqueur slowly and silently, making her conquest wait. The waiter was summoned, and the bill was put on Lien's room, and once their drinks were finished, they left.

"Right then my sweet," laughed Lien wickedly as she stood up, "time for you to pay me back with interest!"

Chapter 03

They left the restaurant, and Belinda was hurriedly escorted to Lien's rooms. Even before the door had even clicked shut behind them, Lien was ripping off her silk trouser suit, kicking her shoes across the room as she did so. They were still in the small hall. Belinda stared admiringly beneath the suit. Lien was naked, and she turned to Belinda and spoke in a hard, desperate tone.

"That excited me so much!" she hissed, "on your knees now, suck my cunt, slut!"

The degrading way Lien spoke to her excited Belinda, and she fell readily to her knees as Lien advanced upon her with savage flashing eyes. Belinda sat in the hall on her heels, drawing in a big breath just before Lien grabbed her hair and plunged her face between her thighs. A total novice, Belinda attempted to kiss the hot wet flesh that was thrust urgently into her face.

"Lick me, bite me, suck me you bitch," Lien gasped desperately above her "make me come whore!"

Obeying her requests, Belinda attacked her lover's distended flesh with newfound vigor, eagerly filling her mouth with the pleasant musky juices of Liens excitement as she eagerly ate her out. Sucking and blowing as she manipulated her lover as best she could, gasping for breath whenever she got a chance—yelping into Lien as the woman dug her nails into the back of her head. She was crushing her face more insistently against her mound as if she was trying to suffocate her lover. Realizing the woman must already be close to coming, Belinda targeted her clitoris for her undivided attention. It was little more than moments before sudden floods of come burst from Lien as she squealed, shuddering to climax, releasing her grip on Belinda. Not taking her chance to break away, Belinda intended to completely satisfy her partner, enjoying using her newfound skills, hoping that Lien would allow her to practice more. Content to stay knelt there exploring Lien with her tongue and relishing the woman's tangy flavor, Belinda worked on her lover long after the woman's climax had subsided.

As soon as she had recovered sufficiently from her orgasm, though, Lien stepped back and drew Belinda to her feet. Without her shoes, the barefooted oriental woman's head hardly reached as high as Belinda's breasts. Lien stretched up in an attempt to kiss her on the lips. To make things a little easier for the shorter woman, Belinda removed her high heels only to be stopped by the tiny oriental.

"No, Belinda. I want you to keep them on."

"But I thought..."

"Don't worry my love we've all night!" Lien broke away and moved off into the warmly lit apartment.

Following the naked woman, Belinda allowed herself to be led to the bedroom, watching Lien seat herself delicately on the edge of a huge four-poster bed. Shaking with excitement, she drew close to Lien, who smiled mischievously; the woman appeared doll-like upon such an immense bed.

"I've never done anything like this ever, you know?" stated Belinda sounding so eager though almost apologetic.

"It is extremely delightful isn't it?"

"Ohh yes," Belinda blushed, glancing about the room as she replied, "I feel so good."

"If you wish to go further we could really show you something." Lien smiled as if to relieve her lover's uncertainties.

"I don't think I understand what you mean but I must admit I'm more than a little curious," Belinda looked at Lien slightly perturbed, but her voice betrayed her eagerness to please the oriental beauty.

"We must talk my love!" Lien patted the bed beside her.

Still fully dressed except for her wayward panties, Belinda felt more than just a little self-conscious as she sat next to the naked golden-skinned woman. The woman gazed into her eyes adoringly, disarmed by those deep black pools Belinda knew that she was putty in Lien's experienced hands and loved the idea. Slipping her arm about Belinda, Lien drew her close. She settled against the woman anticipating the pleasure the coming night could offer.

Musing to herself for a moment, Lien realized how much she enjoyed procuring such delicious beauties for her appreciative employer. She smiled knowingly at the unwitting beauty that sat oblivious to her lovers' true intentions, and nervously slipped her long arm around Lien's waist.

"Be honest with me Belinda," Lien started, "I wish to learn a little about your likes and dislikes before we continue."

"OK no problem Lien," Belinda smiled, obviously a little reticent about revealing any fantasies if she had any.

"You could have desires hidden within that we could bring to fruition." Lien whispered as if telling a secret, "Do you not agree?"

Twice now, she had used "we" without Belinda showing alarm. Perhaps the younger woman thought she meant we to mean them both, so for now, she could think that for a little time at least. Belinda seemed to take a while to formulate her reply before blushing again as she calmly spoke.

"I mean yesterday, I would have flatly denied even the slightest possibility that I could desire another woman. But look at me tonight, sat next to a beautiful naked woman with her most intimate taste still fresh on my tongue."

"Yes tell me about it," Lien encouraged her to reveal more, "tell me what you fantasise about or what arouses you, don't be shy."

"Oh Lien," she blushed, "well I err quite enjoy giving head if I'm in the mood and John and I have experimented a bit with various ideas, some of which I found quite interesting."

"Enlighten me," Lien appeared intrigued as Belinda carried on.

"Let's see now, once we tried anal but I didn't like that at all, we've dressed up and all that kind of lark of course, that's about it really."

"My you poor thing you have led quite a sheltered life!" mocked Lien jokingly, "Lets try and spice tonight up a little shall we?"

"Like I said I'm fairly willing to try something a bit different."

Playing Belinda along, Lien pretended to think what to do, standing up, she paced the floor purposefully catlike, knowing Belinda was eagerly waiting to please her. Every whim she toyed with her wickedly—watching the lissom naked oriental woman parading herself was stirring Belinda's passions slightly once more. By the time Lien decided to make a suggestion, Belinda would be eager for any attention that she would offer her. Lien timed everything perfectly, deliberately eyeing one of the bedposts with obvious interest before turning to make a suggestion to Belinda.

"How about a little bondage, haven't you ever tried that?" Her soft voice was so persuasive that Belinda wanted to say yes just to please her.

"Err, I don't know Lien, It's not something I've ever really considered." She felt genuine concerns about being helpless and under a stranger's control.

"Ohh pity!" Lien sighed; she was disappointed.

"Why?" Belinda unexpectedly felt stupid and guilty at refusing her lover's idea, "we could try something else."

"Because my love I once was an innocent like you, I've experienced the pleasure and I would of so enjoyed giving a helpless gorgeous woman like yourself the chance to be brought the peak of ecstasy!" the sly oriental beauty fluttered her long eyelashes and pouted.

Putting just the right amount of disappointment, hurt, and dashed enthusiasm into her voice, Lien felt confident; she knew that Belinda would give in to her before the unfortunate girl did herself. Belinda stared guiltily into Lien's hurt moistening eyes, and before long, she had decided to let Lien have her way though she would set certain conditions, of course. As if she could read her mind, Lien put on a pleading puppy dog look at just the right time that was pathetic, making Belinda laugh.

"Oh fuck it," she giggled, "you only live once I suppose there's no harm in trying it; just to please you of course."

"There is no reason to be scared Belinda," reassured Lien convincingly, "I won't hurt you at all, I promise on all I hold dear!"

"I trust you Lien my love," she smiled bravely, feeling stupid for making such a sentimental statement, though she felt more than a little apprehensive about what may be about to occur, "how do you want me then?"

"Lying on the bed I think my love," Lien was blatantly brimming with glee, "on your back with your head towards the bottom I think, I can tie you to those very convenient bedposts with something!"

"Lien you promise you won't hurt me?" Belinda sought reassurance before she would commit herself.

"I promised didn't I silly?" Lien flashed a wicked grin at her, "now my love lie down please, quite soon you will realise true sexual ecstasy, I promise!"

An incredible mixture of fearful foreboding and escalating arousal filled a highly bemused Belinda with anxious excitement as she watched Lien furtively hunting through the drawers looking for something to bind her to the bed with. She found that just thinking about being unable to resist Lien's advances caused her to feel highly excited, more exhilarating than what happened earlier this evening in the restaurant, and that had been unbelievable enough. Lien was returning towards her with her arms full of silk scarves, stockings, suspenders, and belts eager to find which would best serve the task at hand. Such was Lien's performance that she made Belinda almost believe the oriental woman was almost as new at this as she was herself.

As Lien approached, Belinda climbed onto the bed; her heart was in her mouth as she laid back and straightened her skirts. Positioning herself as Lien had instructed on the bed, Belinda watched full of excitement, apprehension, and anticipation as Lien securely but comfortably repeatedly looped then knotted a long silk scarf. Lien tied her wrists with practiced skill, then moved to do the same with her other. Belinda couldn't deny her growing excitement as one after the other; her wrists were secured to the thick oak bedposts. Now she was truly helpless, though her bonds were not tight enough to cause her any real discomfort. They certainly prevented her from moving very much at all. The bed was so large that her now outstretched arms reached nowhere near the bedposts.

"Are you OK?" inquired Lien, bending her face close to Belinda, "tell me when you want to stop."

"Mmm it's quite stimulating actually."

"Belinda, you are a slut aren't you?" Lien laughed, but the tone of her voice commanded respect, as she repeated, "Aren't you?"

"Yes!" Belinda realized that she was expected to answer Lien subserviently, "I'm a slut!"

"I'm going to bind your ankles now slut!" strange as it seemed, the woman's insults thrilled Belinda.

She lay there unmoving as Lien casually fastened a long silk scarf to each of her slender ankles. As with her arms, her legs were bound in turn with the scarves but to the posts at the head of the bed this time. Still fully clothed, she lay comfortably spread-eagled and helpless and had to admit it aroused her incredibly. She gazed up trustingly at Lien, who now stood over her smiling smugly.

"Is it good,?" Lien sounded extremely authoritative now, "to be helpless, does it excite you slut?"

"Yes," whispered Belinda nervously, noting the highly satisfied flash in Lien's eye when she added, "Yes Mistress."

"Good.. good, I see you're learning some respect you whore!"

Trustingly Belinda watched Lien lean over her; she reached down to touch her helpless breast. Without warning quite hard, she began tweaking one of Belinda's already stiff nipples through her dress, making cry out quietly in response to the delicious pain the woman was inflicting upon her. Then her wicked lover's hands swept down over Belinda's clothed torso, and as the woman's breasts descended, Belinda raised her head, clamping her lips about an angry brown teat eagerly. At once, Lien stood up and glared down at the confused woman below.

"Did I permit you to do that you slut?" she snarled

"No I just thought..."

"Shut up whore!!" Lien whirled away.

"Lien I'm sorry."

"Shut up whore!" came the stern reply.

"Lien...." Belinda cried out. She was becoming frightened by the woman's growing aggression.

"That's it, if you will not obey me then I am going to have to shut you up you dirty bitch!" the woman returned and bent over her.

"No Lien I'll be quiet," Belinda tried to dissuade her.

"Too late my love, far too late!" Lien held Belinda's panties above her face. "Open up now there's a good slut."

She knew what Lien intended as she watched the woman roll Belinda's soiled undies into a tight ball, she offered them up to her tightly clamped mouth. Oh, how Belinda wanted to refuse, but her twisted excitement compelled her to obey the beautiful oriental getting a real scary thrill from Lien controlling her. She watched the Oriental's dark eyes intently as the ball of rough, perfumed moist material was pressed insistently against her mouth. She relented, opened her mouth obediently as the garment was offered up to her lips again. She could taste her distinct essence on them as Lien pushed them firmly deep into her mouth before kissing her passionately. She could not respond but ground her mouth feverously against Lien's until the woman eventually broke away.

"Lift your head please!" this command was spoken softly by her tormentor, but she obeyed instantly anyway.

She felt a little panicky as Lien wrapped a length of silk bathrobe sash tightly about her face to secure her gag. Now though Lien seemed very attentive, she carefully arranged everything, putting a small pillow beneath Belinda's head, she smiled down reassuringly at her. Belinda did her best to watch Lien as the woman moved around the bed, silently nudging her hips, gesturing for Belinda to lift them from the bed. When she did so, she felt Lien inserting some pillows beneath her bottom, and she settled back onto them. She felt the oriental carefully rearranging her dress and felt puzzled as to why she would bother. Lien finished her careful preparations and returned to kneel by the bed's foot, her lips close to Belinda's excited ear she began to whisper to her.

"Isn't this exciting you incredibly?" Lien smiled, watching Belinda as she eagerly nodded in agreement. "You're so aroused aren't you, you slut?"

Lien's hot breath teased her ear deliciously; the woman was so close that her lips brushed lightly against Belinda's cheek as she whispered. Writhing in her bonds, Belinda tried desperately to convey the extent of her arousal and readiness to the other woman. Lien seemed strangely content just to talk to her captive for the moment.

"It's almost time for you to experience the ecstasy sweetness," Lien's voice oozed with excitement, "Oh my love you look so delectable laid there I wish I could devour you myself!"

"Mmmm..." was all Belinda could manage as she fearfully began to realize all might not be so well after all.

"Yes that's correct you slut." Laughed Lien as she witnessed the sudden alarm that flashed in Belinda's eyes, "you poor fool, I drew you here not for myself but for another that I worship! Don't fear my pretty darling for you will bring one another such unimaginable pleasure as I could only dream of giving you!"

From around the rolled-up panties, Belinda tried frantically to plead with Lien to free her to no avail. As her muffled pleas were blatantly ignored, real terror took a grip, and she began to cry. Scared witless, Belinda screamed but quickly realized her cries for help were all but silenced by the highly effective make-shift gag. Terror gripped her, a terror that held her so that she did not even struggle against her bonds, admitting to herself that it would be futile.

"Goodbye dear Belinda I may see you in the morning, perhaps!" Lien blew her a kiss as she swept away, leaving the very scared, excited, and confused woman bound to the bed helpless.

At first, Belinda wanted to believe it was a ruse, one of Lien's sick jokes as she heard Lien moving about the other room as the Oriental redressed. Now she was scared and struggled half-heartedly as the lights went out in the other room, leaving her bathed in the soft dim glow of the bedside light. After the door clicked shut and apart from the creaking bed, the complaining silk of her bonds and her pounding heart and labored absolute breath silence fell, then she realized the truth, she was defenseless and soon likely to be at the mercy of a total stranger. Unbelievably as her terror waned a little, she found her predicament quite arousing. As her panic subsided, she stopped her futile, struggling in vain and lay there quietly, contemplating her fate. In the overwhelming silence, her pulse sounded strong in her ears; she began fantasizing about the unknown stranger, perhaps Lien would return in disguise or even send up that dishy waiter to fuck her senseless. As her imagination began to spin more fantastic possibilities, her sense of panic and trepidation subsided somewhat.

Her fantasies suddenly shot from her mind, and her pulse quickened when she heard the key turn in the lock; someone entered the darkened outer room quietly, closing the door behind them. Craning her head back to watch the black abyss that was the door, Belinda felt a delicious thrill of excited anticipation and fear course through her fraught nervous system. Silently the shadowy figure emerged into the soft light and entered the bedroom. Belinda gasped beneath her gag in awe as the dim light fell upon the stranger.

If she thought Lien was beautiful, this girl was far more impressive than even her imagination could conjure up. With her upturned eyes, Belinda examined the stunning stranger who was dressed in a long black kid-hide trenchcoat and carried a doctors style black bag. Wide-eyed Belinda stared up as without even glancing down at her; the girl began unbuttoning her trenchcoat in silence. Belinda thought she was exquisite; her fine tanned features set off beautifully by her incredibly long thick black hair that she wore loose. Bright green eyes glittered menacingly as she finally glimpsed for an instant at the bound woman awaiting her attentions on the bed. The briefest of looks from those intense emerald orbs had Belinda trembling with awesome anticipation of what may happen.

As the girl slipped off her coat, Belinda swallowed hard, for beneath it, she wore an extravagant black leather bodice covered with buckles, straps, and vicious-looking studs. Long strapped and studded tight black leather boots reached right up almost to her hips and were buckled to the bodice with short leather and elastic straps. She wore long fingerless studded black leather gloves on her arms, which were also fastened to her bodice at the shoulder by short buckled straps. Over these gloves, jingled myriad glittering bangles of various precious metals. Excitedly scared, Belinda watched as the stranger who paid her no attention at all now as she carefully prepared herself. Once she decided she was finally ready, the girl turned and approached the bed to carefully examine her defenseless excitable captive. Smiling coolly down at her, she spoke softly to Belinda, crouching low over her as she did so.

"Satisfy me and you have little to fear Belinda," her smile faded slightly, "I feel sure you will have little difficulty doing so."

"Mmm.." grunted Belinda from beneath her gag in turmoil.

"Lien the slut-catcher has done well tonight, you look like a wanton little whore to me. I feel we can bring each other immense pleasure before the night is over, I hope you think so too."

Nodding enthusiastically as delicious fear and the very nearness of the leather-clad girl enraged her untameable arousal beyond reason, Belinda squirmed restlessly on the bed, eager to be the wanton little slut she was expected to be herself.

Seeing how enthusiastic her helpless victim was to comply made Raven smile. Lien always found ways of making the pleasure variable and interesting for her. She thought that such pathetic willingness in such a beautiful captive was so enticing. Gazing down on the voluptuous long-legged beauty tied to the bed, part of her just wanted to take the girl then and there. Her aura was intense, but resisting, knowing how much pleasure she could extract from her, how much sweeter the life-force would taste when the woman was deliberately brought to the very peak of ecstatic endurance. Even so, she allowed herself to savor the woman's pent up excitement and fearful emotions, allowing them to sweep into her in an intoxicating wave.

"You really are a delectable morsel!" she sighed resignedly to the squirming woman below her.

At last, though, Belinda, the girl, was making her move as she came towards her gliding around the bed. She nimbly clambered over Belinda and crouched catlike over her upper thighs. Belinda watched enthralled as the girl's long-fingered hands reached out to caress her shoulders. Staring wide-eyed, she couldn't believe the girl's blood-red nails' length as the girl's hands approached. Almost gently, she ran her widespread fingers over the exposed tingling flesh of Belinda's shoulders. The long fingers traced the lines of her collar bones then suddenly swept down to cup her breasts. Beneath the gag, Belinda moaned low in appreciative response as her aching responsive boobs were fondled.

As the girl settled her weight lightly upon Belinda's thighs, she felt the cold, sharp studs of the girl's boots digging into her flesh through her thin dress. Something seemed to take her over, out of control, she began writhing and grinding herself against her tormentor. Raging lust took over her, and she cared nothing about her predicament, only desperately wanting this woman to use her however she wished. Her earlier devotion to Lien was already completely dismissed from Belinda's mind. She surrendered herself fully to the complete stranger that stared demonically into her eager eyes while painfully crushing her responsive nipples deliciously between powerful fingers and thumbs.

Belinda cried out in delicate anguish behind her gag as the girl's fingers took hold of the neckline of her dress and unhurriedly tore the top half apart straight down the front. For a moment, her ample breasts jiggled as they spilled from the ruined garment's confines before the girl's full red lips descended over one. The girl's long black mane cascaded over Belinda's torso like an inky wave as the girl squirmed her face firmly into her breast. As her teat was sucked up into the girl's hot mouth, Belinda went frantic, bucking her hips in a primal reaction to her intense excitement as full lips suckled upon her aching nipple. The girl fell upon her heavily; even the pain of the many pointed studs that dug deep into her couldn't lower Belinda's insane enthusiasm.

As Raven worked her way down over Belinda's writhing body, she proceeded to slowly tear her overexcited captive's dress further still as she wriggled down over the helpless woman. With a final effort, she tore through the hem of the dress and cast the tattered red fabric aside while furtively kissing along the top of Belinda's red satin suspender belt. The smell of the woman's arousal was intoxicating and beckoned her to sample it. Despite the urge's insistency, she resisted temptation and rose from her crouched position between Belinda's legs. Kneeling on the bed, Raven stared down upon the squirming woman's beautiful naked body, and an intensely delicious shiver of expectant hunger quivered through her.

In turn, Belinda was so aroused her body seemed to scream out for relief as she craned her neck to watch the girl that knelt between her thighs eyeing her vulnerable body ravenously. Her eyes pleaded in vain to the girl as she watched in disbelief when the gorgeous creature sprang catlike from the bed. Fascinated by her tormentor, she anxiously watched the girl cross the room to pick up the long doctor's bag. Solemnly the girl moved back toward the bed, pointedly carrying the bag in an almost ceremonial manner before her as she approached her; once she was standing almost directly over Belinda's head, she opened it. The sharp click of the bag's clasp seemed so loud that the only other noise in the room was Belinda's ragged excited nasal breathing and heartbeat. Creaking the stiff leather bag open, the girl then slipped her slender hand inside to retrieve something unknown.

She knew the delightful terror her victim would be enduring expecting a dagger or worse to be revealed, and so to maximize the tension, she dawdled and made the great theatre of the simple task. She secretly watched the bound girl as she writhed in anticipation below her, absorbing every fearful overwrought emotion that the girl emitted voraciously. Finally, though, she withdrew the surprise from the bag. As she casually discarded the bag, her gaze and interest were solely on the girl.

Anxiety waned, a wave of relief spread over Belinda when the contents of the bag were unveiled to her, but what she did see still terrified her somewhat. Fearfully Belinda couldn't help but stare in wide-eyed astonishment at the huge black shiny phallus the girl had drawn from the bag. Obviously, for her benefit, the girl held the ebon gargantuan directly over Belinda's upturned face while casting the bag down beside the bed. Despite her fears, Belinda found her eyes were hopelessly drawn to stare at the monster as the girl's slender fingers caressed its lustrous titanic gnarled length. She trembled with a twisted mix of anticipation and dread as her gaze ran up and down its robust extent. It was truly a masterpiece of sculpting, enormous as it was in all directions, Belinda felt sure that she could never accommodate it.

Seeming to be in no hurry, the girl held it over her while she made a show of examining it closely herself. Belinda's eyes followed the girl's fingers intently as she touched and caressed it lovingly, the surface of the phallus's long curving thick trunk beneath the bulbous head was a mass of smooth raised convolutions. To her, the girl's hand that held it seemed tiny in relation as it hardly encompassed half its circumference. Two long and two short leather, chrome studded straps hung from its wide base, obviously for attaching it to something or someone, and of course, she knew who was going to wear it and who was going to be impaled upon it before the girl moved away slightly to stand a little from the bottom of the bed.

Tilting her head back, Belinda watched the girl avidly; with a knowing confident smile on her lips, she was leaning back against a chair back with her legs spread. To Belinda's terrified delight, she had begun to fasten the monstrous appliance on. The two short straps were secured to two of several unused buckles along the front edge of her sleek bodice. Passing the other longer straps back between her thighs in turn, the girl secured them to other buckles on the bodice above her buttocks and adjusted the fit of the dildo till she was satisfied. Watching the girl finishing her adjustments, excitedly Belinda's fears about the immenseness of the glistening dildo were absorbed into her overwhelming arousal. She sidled over to the bed once more, Belinda's eyes were fixed on the heavy bobbing phallus that meaningfully proceeded her.

"Belinda oh pretty Belinda!" groaned the girl huskily, rubbing the huge black shaft meaningfully as she came to tower over her.

In morbid fascination, Belinda stared up at her gorgeous countenance past the menacing phallus, her breath came shallow and fast, and her whole body craved the girl's attention. In response to the girl, all she could do was nod.

"Oh how I want to hear your cries of pleasure," sighed the girl, "Lien advises me you're quite responsive!"

"Mmm!" nodded Belinda over excitedly on the bed, "Mmm... mmm...!"

"Dare I remove your gag, I wonder?" the girl quizzed then added in a sterner tone, "if I do I hope you'll be good, for your own sake!"

"Mmm... mmm...!" she nodded back frantically.

"OK!" the girl did not attempt to mask the warning tone in her voice, "lift your head for me."

The head of the huge dildo descended just millimeters from Belinda's face as the girl bent to undo the gag. As soon as the girl untied and tugged the strip of restraining cloth away, Belinda tried to force the ball of sodden fabric from her mouth with her tongue. After being trapped virtually immobile for some time, her muscles complained painfully and failed to dislodge the obstruction. The girl hooked them out instead, softly laughing as she did so. The painful relief Belinda felt upon the removal of the panty ball from her mouth as she gently moved her jaws once again made her hope the girl wasn't going to make her attempt to suck on the shaft. Thankfully the girl stood upright again, easing her concerns for now, and Belinda appreciatively drew in gulps of cool air through her dry lips into her aching mouth.

"If you speak I'll put it back on do you understand bitch?" there was no trace of leniency in the girl's strict tone. She clearly meant it, and Belinda nodded in response, already aware of what disobedience meant.

"Good I can see Lien taught you well."

As the girl moved around the bed, yet again Belinda bit her lip in an attempt to remind herself to stay quiet. Feeling the bed jostle about, she lifted her head and watched as the girl took station kneeling between her feet. Her excitement was at fever pitch, the feel of the girl's fingers as they caressed her stocking-clad ankles around the knotted scarves was electrifying, and she struggled to contain a squeak of pleasure. By now, Belinda was quivering visibly with excitement; she fought to control her most basic impulse to cry out with obscene desire as the girl's gentle caresses reached her knees. She knew it would be impossible to control herself very soon but vowed to try to last as long as it was earthly possible. Throwing back her head, she tried desperately to block out the delightful sensations as the girl lowered herself between her thighs. The girl's hands slipped up to her hips, grasping her around her suspender belt firmly, and her incredibly long jet mane cascaded over her sensitive thighs and belly.

"All I wish to hear are your cries of pleasure you filthy whore!"

She could feel the girl's radiant heat upon her inner thighs as she crouched close to her molten sex. Unable to prevent herself, Belinda wailed quietly through clamped lips as she felt the girl kissing along the bare strip of her right thigh above her stocking top-edging tantalizingly close to her aching pussy as she did so. Moving to the other thigh, the girl repeated the sequence to full effect. Purposefully then the hot, firm lips moved up onto her flat abdomen, kissing and licking the sweat-salts from the sensitive skin above her pubic hair, making her moan in frantic despair. For what seemed an eternity, Belinda was teased like this, kept highly excited by the girl as her wicked lips circled agonizingly close to her blossoming dripping wet pussy planting wonderful firm kisses as they went.

Waiting for the first wondrous kiss on her heated flesh, once more, Belinda was left in ecstatic despair as the black-haired girl began to slither up towards her face, still kissing her exposed skin as she rose. The pain in her limbs and studs raking over her tender body was forgotten as the girl slithered up to plant feverous kisses between her jiggling breasts. She whimpered pathetically when she suddenly felt the cool tip of the huge phallus pressing insistently against her burning hot crotch. Squirming herself eagerly against the bulbous head of it as best she could, Belinda gasped and moaned as she was teased by the girl who withdrew each time she was in danger of entering her. After what seemed ages but must have been but a few moments, Belinda felt a definite shift in pressure, and it was gradually eased into her eager flesh at last. Squirming and crying aloud, she attempted to accommodate its hugeness as it invaded her. As the giant monster was progressively forced into her seemingly inadequate orifice, she reeled, overcome with a strangely welcome pulsating pain that rippled through her from fingers to toes. She couldn't help but cry out ecstatically when the crown of the huge head eventually popped past the barrier of her overstretched but a wantonly eager opening.

Above her, pitilessly staring down at her helpless victim with her magnificent green eyes, the girl began to fuck Belinda at a leisurely pace, easing the oversized shaft delightfully deeper and deeper into her with each successively determined thrust. The sensations Belinda felt were indescribable as the immense gnarled shaft bore into her sensitive overstretched but still yielding vagina again and again. As the girl fucked her deeper, their faces drew closer together, and Belinda watched the girl intently knowing that her face was openly showing the girl all the incredible pleasure it was causing her. Whimpering and moaning with increasing excitement, she instinctively drove her hips upwards in time with the girl's thrusts. They almost face-to-face now, somehow she had managed to accommodate the enormous phallic titan. Perspiring heavily beneath the leather-clad girl Belinda frantically ground herself upon the phallus as best she could, taking into consideration the restriction of her bonds, fervently gazing up at the other girl's face as she did so.

The girl's facial expression seemed very distant, almost detached as she deliberately fucked Belinda intensely slowly with the huge shaft so proficiently. Hidden behind the seemingly disinterested face, though, Belinda could see the furious excitement burning fiercely in the girl's exquisite emerald eyes. The wild intensity she saw boiling there sent a delicious thrill down through her already overloading the nervous system, and in turn, she tried to coax the girl into revealing her hidden pleasure fully. All the pleading looks and pouting had no effect, and the girl even ignored Belinda's attempts to stretch up and kiss her. The knowing, wry smile that sneaked onto the girl's lips failed to alert Belinda that something was about to change anyway.

Withdrawing the dildo almost entirely from her, the girl paused, causing Belinda to stare in puzzlement into her wickedly dancing eyes. Gyrating her hips, the girl slowly twisted the head of the massive phallus around just inside the tight rim of her already obscenely overstretched vaginal opening and unbelievably distending her further. As she did so, she ran her long-nailed fingers through Belinda's moist, tangled dark mane and took a firm hold of the top of her head. Totally unprepared, Belinda screamed aloud uncontrollably when the girl suddenly tensed, arching her back, she rammed the shaft deeper into her than ever before like a piston. Gripping Belinda's head firmly, she immediately set a furious pace that had her reeling beneath the powerful onslaught. Screaming with each rapid, pleasurably agonizing thrust that tore relentlessly into her barely accommodating flesh Belinda spun rapidly out of control to what she realized would be an earth-shattering climax. Insanely she tried to hold back the unstoppable storm that threatened to overwhelm her; her tormenter could read her like an open book.

"Do not hold it back slut! let yourself go, let yourself go!" the other girl cried out in encouragement, "let yourself go NOW!"

Doing as she was told, Belinda let her climax free. As the first convulsion took hold of her, a liquefying crimson wave of ecstasy overwhelmed her, and then everything seemed to slow down. Seemingly detached from her own body, a small part of Belinda could hear her cries of ecstasy over her pounding heartbeat as her body began to shudder. At first, she believed she was about to blackout and stared up at the girl fearfully, but as wave after wave of pleasure spread through her, and the threatening darkness receded, she wailed with delight. Leaning back, drawing her head away, the girl drove the phallus relentlessly into her. She imagined she could feel its immense head trigger every receptor in her manic pussy as it slid unstoppably past, intensifying the climax almost beyond Belinda's endurance. Her heart slowed, pounding noisily in her heaving breast deliriously as ensnared her eyes watched the girl reach for her throat. For a brief instant, she felt the girl's long talons rasp against her burning skin; then, they pulled away. When she felt her pearl choker snap, cascading bouncing pearls everywhere in insanely slow motion, Belinda watched them scatter until her eyes were inexplicably drawn to the girl's full red pouting lips.

Still writhing in her inexplicably extended orgasm, her body was out of her control. Still, despite the furious fucking she was receiving, her interest and eyes were focused on the exquisite girl's face. The look of intense, hungry anticipation that spread over the girl's face made Belinda realize that all was not well, and she panicked. Sensing something beyond her comprehension was happening here, Belinda suddenly wanted to scream but was unable to; something inside told her she could do nothing to save herself. Unbelievably despite her terror, she continued to convulse in orgasm in total contrast to and almost overwhelming her understandable fear. The girl's vigorous pelvic thrusts slowed to an almost lethargic crawl through their effects did not diminish, she was still kept at the peak of orgasm as the girl dipped her face close to hers once more and whispered quietly to her.

"Oh my precious morsel, how your pain and excitement complements your life-force perfectly," her silky voice alarmed Belinda, "your exquisite fear is like the having the finest spices sprinkled upon the sweetest dessert!"

"No... Ohh! please... Ohh, augh, stop fucking about!" gurgled Belinda in terror between groans of obscene rapture as the girl continued to fuck her.

"I see you do not yet comprehend your position do you?" the girl's flaming green orbs sank closer still to hers, rich, spicy breath permeated her nostrils.

As the girl's thick black hair fell in curtains about their heads, Belinda gazed up at the beautiful shadowed face and couldn't conceive how such a gorgeous sight could ever produce such exquisitely exciting fear as she now felt. Particularly aware of the incredible fucking she was still receiving, Belinda gasped at the electrifying touch's intensity when with her fingertips, the girl took hold of her chin almost lovingly. The girl's mask fell away, revealing the hunger that had seethed beneath to Belinda; she felt a perverse thrill sweep through her to add to the torturous storm that consumed her. Deliberately slowly, the girl lowered her lips towards Belinda's ready and welcoming. The perfumed black mane fell over her sweating face sticking to it as her head was suddenly turned aside quite forcefully as their lips brushed.

Given no chance to resist, all she could do was scream as the sharp fangs sank deep into the side of her exposed throat. As the sudden pain hit her, she screamed in absolute terror for an instant before undreamt of ecstasy overwhelmed her. The unbearable pain of the creature's bite and the pain of the many studs that tore at her vulnerable flesh was forgotten as her heart furiously delivered her enriched blood to the feeding creature that writhed above her helplessly bound body. The intense gratification she unexpectedly felt by giving herself to the creature overcame any other thought in her head, even that of her possible demise in doing so failed to frighten her.

"Ohh my love, ohh my love!" she gasped over and over as her blood was drained.

Even when her head began to spin deliriously and the world began to explode in Technicolor flashes, she felt no fear urging the creature on. Her heart pounded eagerly to deliver the last drop of her blood to the creature until the threatening darkness gradually enveloped her failing consciousness. As she blacked out, her tortured senses were still aware of the feeding creature fucking her relentlessly.

The gentle touch on her forehead awoke her, and she stirred groggily. As consciousness slowly overcame her, Belinda became aware of the aches and pain that stabbed at her from her whole body. Still bound to the bed, she looked up weakly to see Lien smiling down upon her. In silence, the woman began bathing her face with a delightfully cold wet flannel. As her senses came to life, Belinda became aware of the heat of the leather-clad girl curled up snuggled against her side like a child. The full realization of what occurred before completely escaped her mind leaving her aware of only the pleasure and satisfaction she felt. Looking down upon the peacefully sleeping girl, she was overwhelmed with adoration that seemed to ease her discomfort. She realized life could never be the same again, and guiltily thought of her boyfriend.

She could hardly move when Lien untied her and helped her stand, the woman attentively removed what remained of her ruined clothing. Still, in a semi-stupor, Belinda thankfully allowed the woman to guide her to a wonderfully hot bath that she had ready for her. Every muscle throbbed, and every tortured joint ached as she was led slowly from the bedroom. Belinda gasped as she sank into the luxurious warm bath water, the chaffed skin where her bonds had bitten into her limbs, and the myriad scores where studs had torn at her stung and a not unpleasant way. In an instant, she was once more asleep, overcome with exhaustion. Despite the noise Lien made clearing up the rooms and caring for Raven, she slept through the morning. She was so weary that even when Lien topped up the hot water, she did not stir. When she eventually woke, the leather-clad girl was gone, and Lien stood patiently waiting above her.

"So my sweetness you survived the night then?" the oriental woman's eyed danced knowingly.

"Everything seems fuzzy, I feel incredible but very odd," she mumbled weakly, "can't really remember what happened Lien!"

The woman helped her from the bath. Belinda felt so weak and exhausted as Lien guided her back to the bed. She lay down naked and only semi-conscious as Lien covered her with the heavy bedding.

"Who was that girl?" mumbled Belinda sleepily.

"That's Raven for you, she can really take it out of you," laughed Lien stroking Belinda's head as her eyes drifted shut, "now sleep!"

Story 02

Chapter 00

I looked out at the brightness through my frosty window. From the guttering, icicles descended, glistening in the wintry sunshine. I opened the window slightly, inhaling the crisp air. "So beautiful," I whispered as I snapped off the longest icicle and dropped it, watching its spear into the snow below. "Mmm, perfect murder weapon!" I giggled. I pulled my fleece blanket tightly around my shoulders as the cold air drifted in on a slight chilly breeze. "Finally we will have a white Christmas..." I heard a familiar Christmas song echo through the speakers on the radio. I instantly began to whistle and hum the tune.

I closed the window and made my way downstairs and headed towards the front door. I opened it quickly, wanting to be out there, to feel the cold surround me and take me back to childhood. At thirty-three, I am still a child at heart. We haven't had snowfall like this for sixteen years. Every year I pray for snow and especially at this time of year. As I recall, I don't ever remember snow at Christmas, and here it is, a day before the best day of the year. Or is Christmas Eve the best day? I think it might b—the anticipation of what's to come. Seeing the smiling faces of nieces and nephews opening their presents, a sight of melting the biggest snowdrift.

The snow takes me back to when I was younger. Hours were spent building a snowman, the beginning of which was a snowball the size of a tennis ball. My friends and I would take turns to roll it from one house to another along the pathways. As we reached the middle of the avenue, the snowball was the size of a football. We trudged through more snow, picking it up as we went, from a football-size to a basketball-size and bigger still. We had so much fun rolling the huge ball around and around the avenue and through the playing field. In the end, the ball got so big that it took three or four of us to roll it back to my garden.

We managed it, though, and when we got to my house, we all rushed in, hoping to find my dad to measure how tall the ball of snow was. Poor dad, we didn't give him time to get his coat and gloves on. When he got outside and saw the body of our snowman, the look on his face said it all. It was by far the biggest we had ever made. He measured it and announced that it was three feet and four inches high. My friends and I jumped up and cheered. We rolled the ball into the right position and headed across the road to start on the other side. It was time to make the head of the snowman.

I smiled to myself as I stood out on the doorstep. I looked down and saw the icicle standing upright in the snow. Dare I step out a little further and get harpooned by my murder weapon falling from the gutter, I thought. I glanced down the road and saw a figure walking towards my house. The only sound was the trudging of their boots as they sunk into the snow. I knew they were heading for my house. There were no other houses nearby. They lifted their arm and waved. I waved back, still not recognizing who they were, although I was sure it was a woman. Long dark hair flowed past her shoulders, dancing in the breeze. She was dressed in jeans and a creamy colored chunky woolly jumper. She must be freezing.

She opened the gate and cautiously walked towards me. As she neared me, she held out her hand. "I'm sorry to bother you, but my car has got stuck in the snow. Can I borrow your phone? I really wasn't prepared for this weather!"

I took her hand, and she held it tightly. Her hand was freezing, and I was surprised she could still move her fingers. "Yes of course you can, come in and I'll get you a warm drink. Is tea ok?"

"Yeah thanks. I stayed at my sisters last night. She lives in the next village. The snow wasn't that bad when I left there, but you seem to have it quite bad here. I'm sure they didn't forecast it, but you know what they say about the British weather..."

We both looked at each other and simultaneously announced, "unpredictable!"

She rubbed her hands together, bringing a little life into them. "I'm Alex by the way. I was a little worried as to who might live here, you're pretty isolated here." She seated herself at the kitchen table, continuing to rub her hands together.

"Isolated yes, but so damn pretty on a morning like this. Don't you agree? Do you have milk, sugar?"

"Milk, please and no sugar..."

"Sweet enough eh?" I teased. She smiled, and her eyes smiled with her. I poured out our teas and placed them on the table, then sat opposite her. Her cheeks were red, and her eyes were glazed over. Oh god, those eyes. They were a shade of green with a delicate hint of blue—piercing. I placed my hands on hers and massaged them. "Jesus, you have frostbite I think. We'd better get you warmed up. I'm Chrissy by the way."

"Nice to meet you, Chrissy. I don't want to be too much trouble. I shall go when I've made my call."

"You aren't going back out there just yet. As lovely as it is, you are not dressed for it!"

"What about your husband, won't he mind your Christmas eve being interrupted?"

I smiled. "There's no husband. I live alone. And it will be good to have a little company. It doesn't look like I will be going out anywhere."

"Where were you going?"

"Oh just visiting my parents and meeting up with the rest of the family. Depending on how it went I might have stayed the night with them. Still, its beautiful here now that we have snow."

Her eyes cut into me again. I have never seen eyes that color before. I hadn't noticed, and neither had she, but my hands were still on hers. I had stopped the massaging and was now lightly stroking her soft skin. I could feel it warming up in my palms; she smiled and parted her lips. "That feels good, my hands are warming up."

I slowly took my hands from hers and placed them around my mug of tea. "Come with me, its warmer in the living room... and the phone is in here too." She took her mug and followed me into the adjoining room. "Are you hungry?"

I looked over at Alex, and she was looking around the room. "I hate to be a bother, but I am a little hungry. You've decorated it wonderfully, Chrissy. I love the coordinated look, but I can never quite manage it, and I end up with an array of colors on my tree and everywhere else." She sat down on the long sofa, her eyes following the silver tinsel as it sat neatly around the edge of the walls where they meet the ceiling. A frosted garland draped over the mantelpiece with static white lights entwined through it. The tree stood about eight feet high and sat proudly in the bay window. Clear lights twinkled through the frosted lilac baubles. She placed her mug on the coffee table. "Did you do all this by yourself?

"Yes I did. I love Christmas. I decorate nearly every room." I leaned down and picked up the firelighters. "I'll get this going then I'll do us something to eat. The phone is just behind you."

"Thanks, I'll call my sister in a minute."

I lit the firelighters, and soon, the crackling of the dry logs could be heard. "You can't beat an open fire!"

She smiled at me with a look of warmth and friendliness. She was stunning, a little taller than me, and maybe a little thinner. I would also say she was a little younger than me. Her bust was smaller than mine, but she had a definite handful! "I'll just call my sister, her husband will help me out."

"I'll go get us something to eat."

She lifted the receiver as I turned toward the kitchen. "The phones dead... no ring tone... or anything!"

I couldn't help but raise a little grin, and my belly somersaulted. "I take it neither of us are going anywhere then. Good thing I have plenty of food in. Won't be turkey for us though... more like pizza or something. That ok with you?"

"Chrissy I can't intrude on your Christmas."

"Sure you can, I'd love for you to stay. But there's a drawback."

Alex looked a little worried. "What drawback?"

"You will have to put up with Christmas music and as we are home, you will have to help me decorate the outside of the house. I wasn't gonna do it but as we are snowed in, the lights on the tree outside will look beautiful. You will help right?"

"I would love to... but I have no clothes... or anything!"

"Well, I guess you are a tad smaller than me, so any of my clothes will fit you. If you don't mind wearing my gear that is?"

"Not at all... I would love to spend Christmas with you."

"Well I will just get you some clothes to change into and while you take a shower I will do breakfast... how does a full English sound?"

"That sounds delicious."

I made my way upstairs and found some comfortable clothes for Alex, a pair of navy leisure trousers and a cream sweatshirt with a logo on it and now for the underwear, something simple—a black pair of bikini knickers and a bra top. I know damn well she won't fill out my bras, but the bra top will do. I laid the clothes on the spare bed in the guest room, then went into the bathroom and ran the shower for her. I draped a huge jumbo size towel over the radiator and hung a bathrobe over the door.

I skipped downstairs and stood in the doorway, looking at Alex. She leaned back against the sofa. Her eyes were closed. She looked so sexy sitting there. I pondered at the thought that maybe she was married, or was she single. Who would ever kick her out of bed? I know damn well I wouldn't. I couldn't help but stand and stare at her. Her long dark hair framed her face perfectly. It was lightly curled like you had twisted it around your finger.

The fire suddenly crackled and startled both of us. Alex spoke first. "I think I must have dozed off. It feels so comfortable and warm."

"Your shower is running and I left you some clothes in the guest room on the bed. I hope they are ok."

"Oh thanks... where is the guest room?"

"Up the stairs, first door on the left. The bathroom is the next door on the left. I'll start breakfast!"

Alex went upstairs and took her shower as I began to cook breakfast. As the sausages cooked, I pulled out the table by the window in the sitting room that looked out to the back garden. I made fresh tea and put the orange juice on the table then went back to the kitchen. The smell of fried eggs, bacon, and sausages wafted through the house. I had just put the food on the plates when Alex strolled into the kitchen. I looked at her and nearly dropped the plate. She smiled at me and took it and went to sit herself down at the kitchen table. "I thought we'd sit in the living room and watch the snow. It's just started to fall again."

"Ok... that sounds wonderful."

"Let's eat, we have a busy day!"

Over breakfast, we learned a lot about each other. Alex was single and had been for a while. She was engaged a few years back but called it off. She never knew why; she just said it was a gut feeling, and that was that—no explanation or anything. She appeared to be a tough cookie, but there was a sensitive side to her. When she talked about personal things, her beautiful eyes glazed over. I reached over and placed my hand on hers, my thumb falling between hers and her index finger. I lightly stroked her, and she tenderly squeezed my thumb. Her sea-green eyes smiled at me, and she released her grip on my thumb. I slowly edged my hand away and stood up to clear the table.

Alex followed me, and we placed the plates and cups on the worktop. She was standing close to me, and I could smell my soap lingering in the air, and when she turned her head, I could smell the fragrance from my shampoo. She stepped closer and put her hand on my shoulder. I looked into her eyes and watched her move closer to me. It felt like it was slow motion, and I couldn't do anything about it. I froze. She kissed me softly, our tender lips brushing against each other. A bolt of electricity passed through, and she must have felt it too. I parted my lips and took her top lip into my mouth. I sucked it between my lips and tenderly released it. I did the same to her lower lip. I felt her softly moan, and I reluctantly pulled away.

I brushed her twisting curls from her face. "Why did you kiss me?"

"To say thanks for your invitation and for the scrumptious breakfast."

She took a step back. After that kiss, I can't let her go. I placed my fingers just under her sweatshirt and pulled on the waistband of her trousers. I pulled her towards me. "You felt it didn't you? The kiss. There was more to it than a thank you." I looked deep into her eyes. This time it was my blue eyes that held her stare. "Tell me you felt it Alex or we'll just forget it happened." She looked down, not wanting to look at me. My heart skipped a beat, and my stomach started to churn. Had I read it wrong? Have I just made a terrible mistake, turning a simple kiss into something more? My finger whispered along her cheek. "Alex, tell me?"

"I felt it Chrissy, it was electric. I have never kissed a woman before. My intention was to just kiss you on the cheek, but, when I stood here, opposite you, I wanted your lips." Her eyes glazed over again, and a tear crept out and slowly made its way down her cheek. I pulled her into me and held her face in my palms. I softly kissed the tip of her nose. I kissed her cheek, then a little higher. I placed my lips on the path of her tear and tasted its saltiness as it hit my taste buds.

"Promise me you will stay for Christmas even if the phone lines get fixed."

"I promise." She smiled.

My lips returned to hers, softly at first—tasting each other, feeling each other's moist tongues twirl around in our mouths. My arm reached around her, and I pulled her into me. Her hands were now in my hair, and her long nails scraped the bottom of my neck. I moaned into her. Our mouths now opened and closed with a new urgency. She flicked the tip of her tongue along my lip, and I sucked it in. My fingers crept up inside the cream sweatshirt, and I felt the curve of her breasts. They were bigger than I thought. My hand trailed down her stomach. Oh god, she was perfect. She had a taut stomach, so flat, so unlike mine. My fingers glided back up and fondled her breasts through the bra top.

She grabbed my hair and turned my head to the side. Her probing tongue flicked my neck, all the way down my throat, and she kissed me in the sensitive dip at the base. Her kisses moved back up, and she brushed them on my ear. She gently nibbled it, and I felt her hot breath on my skin. I softly spoke with an edge of breathlessness. "Alex... I. "Her tongue edged inside my ear. Lightly licking it, swirling her tongue in and around it. "Mmm, I want you Alex."

She pulled her tongue away and purred into me. "You can have me." I turned to face her, and with both hands, I tugged at her trousers and pulled them down to her ankles. The knickers quickly followed. I grabbed at her waist and lifted her on to the worktop. "Oh god, Chrissy what are you doing?"

"You said I can have you...so I'm having you, here and now!" I gently but firmly spread her knees, and I teasingly licked the inside of her thighs. Her hands immediately grappled with my hair as I moved closer to her pussy. Her scent was intoxicating, heightening my arousal to the highest level. It passed through my nose and down my throat. I could taste her even though my lips and tongue hadn't yet crept between her swollen lips. As I kissed her thighs, I could see her full pink lips glistening with her juices. I looked up at her beautiful face, and when her gorgeous eyes met mine, I made direct contact with her clit.

"Ohhh god..." She cried out as she leaned back against the wall. She opened her legs wider and higher. Her pussy was open, begging me to lick every orifice my tongue could find, and god I was going to search. I flicked the tip of my tongue on the underside of her full lips. I moved further along, flicking it faster and harder. I could hear her breathing become heavier, and every inhaled breath carried a moan on it. I swirled my tongue over and under her lips. I hungrily devoured her pussy and moved to the delicacy at the tip of my tongue. I licked and sucked it into my mouth. Her hands in my hair were now guiding me. She pulled on my head and tugged at my hair. My tongue lay hard and flat on her clit, and I began to grunt and groan as she ground herself on my tongue. "Oh god, oh god... yes Chrissy... baby don't stop... I'm cumming... god yesss!" She jolted into me. "Ohh yess." Another jolt. "Ooohhhh god yessssss!"

I lifted myself, smiling at her. "Kiss me, taste yourself on me..." She bent forward slightly and hesitantly placed her lips on mine. Her tongue crept out and licked my lips. She licked my nose and my cheeks. She kissed my eyelids—short sharp kisses covered my face closely, followed by short, moist licks.

"Mmm, I have never cum so hard in all my life. That was something else."

"No baby, you were something else." I kissed her then gently lifted her off the worktop. I got on my knees and pulled up her knickers and trousers. "We have work to do, it will be dark in a couple of hours."

"But what about you?" You haven't cum!"

"All in good time hun. We have the rest of today and tomorrow. And maybe even Boxing day."

I grabbed my boots and a spare pair and gave them to Alex. From the top of the airing cupboard, I grabbed two pairs of thick socks. I rolled up a pair up and hurled them at Alex. "Duck..." I shouted. She didn't do it in time and got hit by the socks. "You will have to be quicker than that baby." I jested at her.

"We'll see." She giggled as she unraveled the socks and began to ease her toes into them.

I took a fleece jacket from the hanger above the back door and handed it to Alex. "It will be a bit big for you, but it'll do." I then took my jacket, and we both made our way down to the shed. I removed the ladder from the hooks and gave it to Alex. She waited as I grabbed the big box of lights from the shelf. "Come on then... if we get time we'll do the hedges out the back too!"

"You really love all this don't you?" She smiled.

"How did you guess?"

We made our way to the front of the house, passing the snowy hedge as it led to the wooden gate. "It's really beautiful here Chrissy, I could quite easily fall in love with it." She looked at me and raised an eyebrow. Her piercing eyes pulled me closer to her, and I placed my lips on hers. Our eyes never closed, looking deep into each other's souls. I could see faint ice blue lines spurring out from the pupils; I could feel her warmth and tenderness oozing through her gaze and her soft kiss.

I slowly pulled away and led us down the path. I took the ladder from her and leaned it against the tree. It stood about twenty foot high and had thick, sturdy branches. We then walked towards the slightly open kitchen window. Alex opened the box of lights and took the plug out, and reached up towards the window. "When you see the plug fall below the window you won't need to push anymore through." Alex fed the cable through the window, watching intently as the plug descended. "Now it's the fun part... come on baby!"

"Snowball fight..." Alex shouted, and before I could turn away, she threw a large ball of snow at me. It thudded as it hit my shoulder and broke up into a trillion crystals. "You have to be quicker than that." She laughed.

I ran towards her, giggling, and scooped up a handful of snow. "I'll get you back my little snow angel..." She stood there laughing as I bound into her, knocking her over, patting the snow on her head and ruffling it through her hair. I was now on top of her; I began to lick the snowflakes off her cheeks, forehead, and nose. She moaned as my tongue met her lips, and again, we kissed with intensity. Surrounded by snow, but all I felt was warmth.

"Chrissy, this isn't helping to get the lights up." Her eyes twinkled, and she looked up towards the guttering. "You know they would make great murder weapons!"

I giggled at her. "Yes I know they would... let's get up before we both get murdered!"

I got up and gave her my hand to hold. "No wait... I want to do something that I've never done before." Before I could say anything, she began to move her arms and legs back and forth. "Now I really am your snow angel."

I offered my hand again, and this time, she took it. "Indeed you are baby."

We carefully unraveled the cable and wrapped the spare wire around the tree's trunk until the first bulb could sit on the lower branch. I placed the ladder against one of the sturdy branches while Alex passed me the lights. I twisted the lights around the branches. I climbed a little higher up the ladder and stepped off it onto a thick branch. From there, I was able to wrap and curl the lights around each branch. She let go of the final bulb, and I curled it around and between two thin branches. I stepped back on the ladder and slowly made my way down. "That's it baby... now do you want to switch them on or shall I?"

"Oh Chrissy can we wait until it gets a little darker. It would look so much better." Her cheeks radiated, and her smile was beautiful. "I know why you get so excited about it now. I have never put lights on the outside of my house. It's going to look beautiful."

"Yes it is... do you want to decorate the hedges and trees out the back?"

Her eyes opened wide, and she broadly smiled. "Can we? Do you mind?"

"I don't mind at all, ... and later it will look beautiful no matter what window we look through."

Her gaze caught me again, and she pointed at her eyes. "And what about my windows that I'm looking through now. I can see beauty already." She leaned into me and ran her finger down my cheek. "I'm so glad I'm here."

"I'm..." She interrupted me with her warm tongue on my lips and gently parted them. Her warmth spread through me, melting the barrier around my heart. I pulled back, wanting to say something but afraid to do so. Other words stumbled out between what I really wanted to say. "We have... about half an hour of light left I guess. We better hurry!" Alex stood and looked at me, blankly. "What's up?" I whispered.

"Oh nothing, I thought you were gonna say something else... let's get these lights up. I can't wait to see how it looks." Alex turned and walked quickly ahead, carrying the empty box while I trudged behind her, holding the ladder. I hooked it back up in the shed as she spoke to me. "Don't we need that?" I looked at her, but she wouldn't look my way. She turned and went to walk out, but stopped as she heard my voice.

"We don't need this for the trees. As you can see they aren't that tall." I grabbed two boxes off the shelf, and we both walked towards the porch at the back of the house. "There's two sockets just inside, if we feed them through the small window we can plug them in down there." Alex took the plugs and slipped them through the window. She opened the door and located the sockets just inside the door.

She plugged them in then trudged through the blanket of snow to where I began to guide the lights through the hedging. "Can I do the other side?" She gave the look of innocence as a child asking.

"Yeah sure, when you get to that furthest post, cut across the garden and weave them through the trees. I leaned in and tenderly kissed her cold red nose. "If it's foggy tonight, Father Christmas will have to make do... I'm not letting you go, Rudolph." She giggled, and I was pleased. The tension from a few minutes ago had dissipated. "I'll race you to the trees..."

One by one, we both hooked up the string of white lights through the hedging. I noticed Alex a little way ahead of me and decided I would slow her down a little. I packed a snowball in my palms and rested it on the hedge. I repeated it until I had six snowballs lined up. I shouted, "Alex..." She turned around, and I threw them one after the other.

She screamed at me. "Stop... that's not fair. You bloody wait..."

"Yeah yeah..." I carried on quickly as she brushed the snow from her clothes. "I'm beating you, I'm gonna get there first."

"Ohhh I will get you back," she teased.

The light was fading fast, and as we neared the center of the trees, the temperature appeared to plummet. "I better get some more logs ready, that's gonna be freezing later. Can you finish my lights off?" Alex smiled and nodded at me as I turned and sunk into the snow and walked to the log store on the left of the wall. I lifted the lid and pulled out some logs. As I bent over, I heard Alex behind me. "You finished the lights baby?"

"Yeah..." I felt her fingers caress my bum. I moaned and pushed further back. "Ohh you like that yeah?" I moaned again into the log store. I felt her fingers slide between my thighs. "It's warm down there baby... have you been having nice hot thoughts... or have you been having ice cold thoughts?" I was just going to answer her when I felt her hand reach up under my jacket and under my jumper. I screamed as she squashed a handful of snow into my back. I jumped up and dropped some logs on the ground, and they rolled between our feet.

"God, you little bitch... shit, that was cold."

"I told you I'd get you back didn't I?"

"Ok, we're even now... no more." After the initial shock, I began to laugh. "It's dark enough now, we can put the lights on." Alex jumped up and clapped her hands in the air. I put my arm through hers, and we walked to the porch. "You wait out here... I'll switch them on." As I passed in front of her, I tapped my finger on her nose. "Is that ok Rudolph?" She smiled that heavenly smile. I crept inside the porch and flicked the switches. The only indication I had that the lights were on was the gasp coming from Alex.

"Ohh god, look... it's... it's so beautiful, enchanting even." I stood behind her and rested my head on her shoulder and wrapped my arms around her. She lifted her arms and caressed my damp hair. "Chrissy, thank you for letting me stay."

I kissed her ear and whispered. "No problem baby. I'm glad I asked you. Come on, let's get these logs inside and we can switch on the lights out the front."

We both picked up an armful each and placed them just inside the back door. I shut the door, and we walked hand in hand, pass the hedge, and through the gate. We headed straight for the front door and stood in the doorway. I knelt and flicked the switch.

"Ohh... wow... all the colours. Look how it appears on the snow. It's like..."

Simultaneously again, we spoke. "The northern lights."

"Yes Chrissy, it's so romantic." Alex began to walk towards the brightly colored tree. "Come with me... hold me under our northern lights." I skipped through the snow and held her tightly. "Kiss me Chrissy..." I planted my lips directly on hers as my arms again wrapped around her body. Her hands came up and held on to my head. Her fingers twisted in my hair, and she pulled me in closer, our lips touched. She devoured me, ravished me under the lights. I was moaning into her, and she was gasping between each breath. "I want you..." Her lips now on my neck were gently nibbling on my soft skin.

I felt her fingers move lower down my arms, onto my lower back and along the waist of my jeans. She spun me around, and my back was up against the trunk of the tree. I felt my jeans become loose and her cold fingers edged inside. Her other hand tugged at my zip, and when it was lowered, her fingers came back up to my face. "I have wanted you since that first kiss." She kissed me hard and bit along my lips. I gasped as her icy fingers slid inside my knickers, the coldness against my warm moist crevice. "Mmm, baby, you are soaked." With two fingers, she rubbed me and slid inside my pussy. I shrieked at the contact, and after a minute or two, I began to shake. "Are you that close?" I nodded, and her fingers retreated from my pussy and flicked my clit.

"Ohhh shit...don't stop..." My legs began to buckle, and my arms reached up, holding on to the branch above. The snow fell off the branches and sprinkled us in whiteness, and it glistened a thousand colors as it fell on her face and in her hair. I rocked back and forth on her fingers. "Uhhh... ohhhh... ohh god. Alex, make me cum." Her fingers were relentless. They strummed on my clit, getting faster and faster. I could feel it building. The tingling and numbness crept up my thighs. Inside, my body clenched. Every muscle tightened. "Ohh baby, yes... yeah." My knees began to fall again. "Harder... do it harder." I panted.

She pressed hard into my clit and frantically rubbed. "Ohh god yeah... ohhhhhh goddddd." I couldn't say anymore, I mumbled. "Mmmm." She kissed me hard as I came, ravishing me. Feeling my orgasm rip through every nerve in my body. I felt my clit throb against her fingers. They lightly rubbed against my quivering flesh until the pulsing subsided. Her kisses became less urgent, and she licked along my lips. My breathing slowly recovered as I looked at her, smiling at me. The reflection of the colored lights twinkled in her eyes, and I was speechless.

She whispered on my lips. "I think we better get inside, don't you?" I nodded and placed my hands in hers. "Shall I make the tea while you do the fire?" I smiled and kissed her cheek, and we walked to the house and removed our boots and jackets. Alex looked towards the fireplace. "The fire is nearly out... will it take long to build back up?"

I lifted some logs from the kitchen floor and carried them to the hearth. "It won't take long baby... you gonna make some tea and I'll do us some soup shortly."

By the time Alex had made the tea, the fire was roaring again. It loudly crackled as we sat at the table. The living room had a warm glow to it, and the Christmas tree finished the ambiance completely. I took her hand in mine and looked out into the beautifully lit garden. "We did a good job out there today. Thank you... for everything!" I squeezed her hand just before she pulled it away and lifted it to my cheek. She brushed the back of her hand down it, and I leaned into it. I bought my hand up to hold hers against my face. "You hungry?"

She shook her head slowly and whispered, "no."

I stood up and took her hand. "Shall we move to the sofa?" She followed me and sat in the same place as she did earlier on in the day. It seemed like so long ago. She sunk into it, letting the cushioning surround her, hugging her; I settled beside her, fidgeting, trying to get comfortable.

"Why don't you lay down and put your head on my lap."

"Do you mind?"

"Course not." She whispered as she patted her thigh. I rested my head on her leg and watched the flames dancing as Alex ran her fingers through my hair. Her touch was soft and delicate. My fingers were tracing swirling patterns, over her knee and down her calf; her other hand dropped from the back of the sofa to my arm. She stroked it lightly. As time went on, her fingers edged closer to my breasts. They crept over my heavy mounds and toyed with my nipples.

"That feels good..."

"I have never felt another woman's tits before. It does feel damn good."

I bought my hand to my breast and covered her hand. I pressed it into me—squashing my breast with our hands. Minutes passed, and her hand pulled away, and her fingers stopped their twirling in my hair. "You ok Alex?"

"Yeah... can I ask you something?"

"Sure, go for it!"

"How many women have you been intimate with? I mean you are obviously experienced after what happened on the worktop earlier."

"Truthfully, only two, the last one being about nine months ago!"

"Chrissy, look at me!" I turned to face her, and she leaned down and kissed me tenderly. "Will you make love to me? You know, really make love to me." She looked deep into my eyes. I could see the flames flickering in them. "Can you do that to me?" I smiled at her and lifted my head. I kissed her, edging my tongue out along her full lips. God, they are so kissable.

"Wait here baby, ok…" I eased myself from her and went upstairs to my bedroom. I opened the bottom drawer and took out the harness and the dildo; I hadn't used it in a while. I began to panic, thinking maybe this was not what she expected at all. I sat on my bed, contemplating as to whether this was the right thing to do or not. After a few minutes, I decided to take my chance then made my way down the stairs.

I had just walked through the doorway and was entranced by what I saw. I stood dead in my tracks and stared at her beauty. Alex was naked, standing with her back to me. The flames of the fire flickered on her taut skin. The glow of the flames silhouetted her body. She began to turn slowly, and I stepped back and stared at her through the door's thin gap. Her breasts fell down as she bent over and pulled the fleece blanket from the chair near the Christmas tree. She turned again and placed the blanket on the floor in front of the hearth. She stood and reached for the large cushions and scattered them on the blanket.

She walked around the room, blowing out the candles. n The only light in the living room now was the orange and red glow emanating from the fire and the soft white lights from the Christmas tree. My breathing had slowed, and I inhaled a deep breath as she walked towards me. God, please don't catch me spying on you. It could ruin everything. Just as I was about to show myself to her, she veered off and went to the chair near the window that faced the back garden. I breathed out then heard her talk softly. "This is so beautiful…" She lifted the throw from the back of the chair and began to walk away from me. As my eyes drank in her beauty, I noticed a tattoo on the base of her back, just above the crevice between her cheeks. She dropped the throw on the floor and sexily lifted her arms and ruffled her hair. She lowered herself, and she pulled the throw over her.

I casually walked into the living room. "You look comfortable down there… are you naked under that blanket?" She looked up and smiled. No words were needed as she peeled away the throw, showing me her breasts. "I guess that answers my question." We giggled as I placed the harness and dildo on the sofa. "This is what you meant yeah… making love to you!" Her nod was all I needed to push my doubts aside. I quickly undressed. I couldn't wait to be near her. "I hope its warm in there. It's freezing upstairs."

She possessed a wicked grin and flirtatiously spoke. "I'm sure we can generate our own heat… now get yourself in here!"

I wasted no time in pulling back the throw and sliding myself in next to her. My hand swept over her belly. I caressed her soft skin, stroking circles around her belly button. From where we were lying, we could see the colored lights from the tree outside. It did look beautiful. I leaned into her face and kissed her tenderly. She let out a moan as I parted her lips. I kissed her top lip, followed by the bottom. As I kissed her, my hands crept up and fondled her breasts. I alternated between each one, lovingly stroking and gently twisting the nipples as she lightly gasped in my mouth. I pulled away and kissed her cheek, ear, and her neck. My tongue found its way between her breasts and swirled itself in moist circles over her firm mounds.

She sighed and moaned as I took her nipple into my mouth. I gently tugged it with my teeth, and she arched her back, feeding me her breast even more. I sucked on it and flicked my tongue over it. Her hands were playing in my hair, getting rougher by the minute. I didn't want this to be hurried or rough, I wanted to give her what she wanted, so I eased my caresses' pressure and softly began to kiss her. Her playfulness in my hair receded to lightly stroking my curls. I kissed her again and brushed strands of hair from her face. She parted her lips, and her voice was barely audible. "Make love to me, Chrissy."

"I would love to." I whispered. "Are you sure though? We don't have to."

"I've never been so sure about anything." Her eyes twinkled. Numerous colors reflected in them; they merged together like the northern lights. "This is so special, laying here. The fire, the lights… you!" I kissed her. I had to. At that point, I was ready to cry my heart out, overjoyed at having this beautiful woman in my arms.

I reached above her and took the harness and the dildo from the sofa and knelt between her legs. Her look was that of bewitchment. She intently watched as I fastened the straps around my thighs and hips. She giggled a little as I positioned the dildo and tightened the straps. I bent forward and lowered my lips to her knees. I kissed and licked them, working my way to her inner thighs. I looked up at her, and her eyes tell a variety of feelings, nerves, excitement, and maybe a hint of fear. We smiled at each other, and I lowered my face to her pussy. I flattened my tongue and licked it with long strokes. She moaned with every lick; she felt like velvet on my tongue. I gently teased her clit, and she grabbed my hair. "Don't tease me, please… I need you!"

I grinned at her and shuffled between her thighs. I kissed her belly, then her breasts. I lowered my bum down and guided the dildo into her pussy. She gasped as I entered her, moaning as I edged it in a little further. She spread her legs wide and lifted them higher, inviting me to go in further. I pressed my hips onto her and was now all the way in. I kissed and held her close to me as I made love to her. A rhythm was building, and she was breathing heavily into my mouth as we kissed. Our breasts became one as they squashed together, our nipples rubbing. Her hands squeezed into my back, pulling me to her. I felt her hips rise to meet mine. I gasped as I felt her nails dig into my skin. "Ohh Alex, I love that..." I was getting breathless. We were coated in beads of sweat; I licked up her cheek and over her forehead. My hips pulled back and forth, and her moans surrounded my ears and echoed right through me.

"Oh Chrissy, it feels so..." She couldn't finish her words as I steadied the pace. Her moans were becoming deeper. "Don't... uhhh.... stop." I lifted myself a little and lowered my mouth to surround her nipple. Again she arched her back, giving herself to me. Her breathing began to quicken, and incoherent words oozed from her. I moved my hand between us, and my finger gently rubbed her clit, causing her to shriek and buck her hips into me. "Ohh god...." My finger flicked her clit harder as I moved a little faster in her pussy. "Chrissy... I'm gonna ex...plode... Ohhhhhh godddd... yes... yesssss." I slowed down the pace, watching her writhe beneath me. I could feel her whole body trembling against me.

Her eyes glazed over, and a tear fell from each one. I softly kissed her cheeks and licked her salty tears. "Baby, are you ok?" She nodded and smiled. I smiled too and eased myself out of her. "You looked gorgeous as you were cumming. I couldn't take my eyes off you."

She kissed me, tenderly and softly spoke. "I don't ever want to leave you."

She had captured me, and warmth spread throughout my body, evaporating my already weakened barriers. "Then don't leave..." She held me tightly against her, my cheek against her breast. Our breathing slowed, and our eyes closed as we drifted off in the glow of our northern lights and to the sound of the crackling fire.

Story 03

Chapter 01

Angela spent far too much of her time watching what was going on in the cul-de-sac for her own good, at least that's what her husband Lionel always said. She couldn't help herself though, her marriage was a sham, and her life otherwise had little to interest her, so she spent most of the day and a great deal of the night watching her neighbors. It had become an obsession over time without her realizing; she even had sets of powerful binoculars strategically placed about her house. It was an expensive area, and the large, expensive houses were well spaced apart, all apart from hers, and two others close to the main road were bungalows.

As for her marriage, it was one of convenience; it had suited both of them, masking their differing sexual tendencies, which could otherwise ruin Lionel's career. They did love each other, though; he was a kind and thoughtful man, and she was never short of funds or wanted for anything. He often treated her to new toys like binoculars or a better telescope. For the next week, she would be alone. Lionel was away for a few days again; coincidentally, so was her next-door neighbor, Laura's husband. The younger, gorgeous blonde woman had caught Angela's eye when the couple moved into the spacious bungalow some time ago. Despite her attraction to Laura, Angela would not be foolish enough to envisage playing around on her doorstep.

Besides that, she had watched the pair closely, too closely at times as they made love by or in the pool, which she had a good view of. They were clearly in love and didn't mask it or shy away from demonstrating their affection. At least though, she could watch the striking blonde knowing her intimately to look at, at least, and fantasize about her. Something about Laura had come to her attention, though. For the past few months, each and every time her husband went away, the same stunning young tall red-haired lady driving a sleek black sports car visited her. Usually, the car didn't move from the drive overnight on occasion for days at a time. Pursuing her hobby, as usual, Angela saw Laura's hubby leave this afternoon; intrigued, she wondered if the redhead would appear tonight.

Normally the woman arrived somewhere around eight and nine; Angela would be at the ready. After a short workout, she showered and slipped into her bathrobe. As she toweled her hair dry, she checked the clock. It was ten to eight; distractedly, she watched the road's length from her darkened panoramic bedroom window. Sat right at the end of the well-spaced street on the top of the hillock, the three-story house gave her quite a vantage point to view her fellow citizens' activities in both her street and neighboring streets as well. An extensive arsenal of optical devices helped as well; she mused as she dusted the powerful telescope lovingly. Her pulse quickened as a flare of bright light caught her eye as a car turned into the street and slowly crawled up the street towards her. It passed drive after drive as she settled in behind the scope and focused in on it. Smiling to herself, Angela chuckled as she recognized both it and the occupant, it was the flash black job belonging to Red as she had christened the woman.

Nevertheless, a little early tonight, just as Angela expected, it swung into Laura's drive; this time, however, the garage door slid open, and the car coasted inside. This was something new, she thought, watching the car lights go out. Changing magnification, she zoomed in on the car door, dressed in a long camelhair coat the redhead slithered from it. Fascinated, Angela watched the woman slink around the car to the boot and retrieve two cases from it. One was the small bulky and a clearly heavy suitcase that she always brought; the other was new to Angela. Over a meter and a half long, she watched Red wriggle it out of the confined space, tubular and quite thin, it was one of those plastic tubes for carrying rolled up artworks. She slung it beneath her arm and walked around the car towards the back of the garage, where Laura appeared to meet her. Dressed casually in loose-fitting jeans and sweatshirt Laura ushered her guest inside, smiling warmly to her as with a flick of the remote, she closed the garage door behind them. Angela couldn't help but notice the excitement on her neighbor's face at seeing her guest.

What did they get up to in there, she wondered again just as she did each time she saw the woman arrive. She was scanning the house with her binoculars repeatedly; her brain whirred as she watched for any sign of them. What seemed like hours later, Angela saw what she knew to be Laura's bedroom light come on. From her high vantage point, she could see into many of her unsuspecting neighbor's bedrooms but not Laura's, unfortunately. Putting down the binoculars, she paced the room; over a short time, interest turned to fascination and then turned to intrigue, finally becoming an obsession. She had to know, had to find out, a plan formed in her mind.

She had to know! What could be considered crazy thoughts and ideas flashed into being, it was late, gone nine-thirty at least by now and already fairly dark, the chances of a passer-by were minimal at best. If she wore black, she would be virtually invisible, between their houses, she didn't even have to set foot on the pavement. She knew her surroundings well; also, she knew the layout of Laura's house and her garden very well too. After dressing in a black fleecy jogging suit and trainers, she headed downstairs and had two straight whiskeys to calm her nerves. Even so, as she slipped out of the back door, a knot of exquisite terror gripped her.

Keeping to the shadows, she flitted over the distance between the houses in no time at all. Catching her breath, she crouched down in the shadow beside the garage wall then crept around the outbuilding till she could make out the illuminated window of Laura's bedroom window. Hunched close to the wall a few feet from the window, she leaned back against the wall once again. She steadied her nerves; she was shaking with euphoric excitement. Already the act of sneaking around spying on her neighbor was giving her such a kick; she listened intently for sounds that would let her know where they were. Wondering what they were up to, she listened harder. Her heart leaped as she heard the faint, slow rhythmic slapping noise and what sounded like a faint mewling cry that followed each well-spaced crack.

Intrigued by the sound, she desperately needed to see what was happening and edged closer to the window frame. Still, with her back to the wall, Angela stared across at the lawn and hedge; what she saw made her almost jump for joy. She had to suppress an excited giggle as she saw the faint stripe of gentle light that softly illuminated a thin vertical strip of the garden; the curtains were not properly closed.

Ducking beneath the windowsill, she looked up at the four-inch gap in the curtains, the light that spilled from it was low; if she stayed back from the pane, she would probably remain unseen, or so she hoped. Taking a moment to bolster her courage and recall the room's layout, she steadied herself before she stretched up to peer in. This was Laura's bedroom; her king-sized bed would be side on to the window; if they were on the bed, she would have a ringside seat. Staying well back out of sight, she cautiously raised her head and peered in, all the time ready to make a bolt for her house.

What she saw left her speechless; it took a few moments to comprehend the scene that was being acted out before her shocked eyes. Across the room facing the window, the redhead arrogantly struck a domineering pose facing her. To Angela's amazement, she was dressed in a shiny black skin-tight catsuit that perfectly clung to her wondrous pert form. Her head was hooded; it masked the top half of her face apart from her delicate green eyes. The woman's long red hair swung in a ponytail from an opening at the hood's apex each time she moved. Her face's pale skin accentuated the fullness of her pert, cruelly smiling mouth that occasionally twitched with obvious delight. Totally enthralled by the transformed, highly erotic creature, Angela watched astounded, the woman's every lithe move captivated her. As the redhead began to raise her PVC clad hand, Angela's gaze snapped to it. She stared transfixed at the cat of nine tails that hung there for a brief moment then seemed to swing lazily down in a slow arc. Angela's heart raced as her eyes followed the flogger on its lazy trajectory to its target, Laura' unprotected up thrust red striped bare buttocks.

Such was her interest in the latex-clad redhead Angela hadn't even noticed her neighbor until that moment. Her eyes widened in disbelief as she saw the young woman. Crouched face down on the messy bed facing the very window Angela was peering through, her pretty neighbor appeared far too distracted to even notice the dimly lit strip of a face peering at her open-mouthed in the gloom outside. The totally naked and excitedly writhing girl's arms were under her probably bound to her ankles, Angela surmised by her strange position. Her head was flung up crying out, Laura's pretty face was contorted in an expression of weeping agony for a brief moment as the tails struck home before slowly assuming a state of delirious bliss as it sank back to the bed. Fascinated by what she saw, Angela watched avidly as Red methodically whipped an increasingly excited Laura's reddening buttocks for a seemingly long time.

In all her voyeuristic capers, Angela had never encountered anything like this; she had expected or at least hoped to maybe get a glimpse of some furtive lesbian activities, what she witnessed instead blew her away. The scene being played out before her was incredible, and any thoughts of melting away into the darkness were dashed. Watching Laura receiving her strokes, she grew increasingly aroused herself. She squirmed uncomfortably as both her mind and body responded disturbingly quickly to the performance she was elatedly witnessing.

The redhead's blows began to change direction and shift target. They subtly changed from an overarm stroke into an underarm swing, and the target was hidden from her sight between Laura's thighs. As the first blow struck, Laura threw back her head, crying out in anguish, Angela felt her stomach tighten with fevered excitement as she eagerly awaited the next blow. Her eyes flicked impatiently to the latex-clad bitch as the woman shifted position to get a better swing of her arm. As she turned to stand side on to her, Angela noticed that the woman wore an impressive black strap on phallus over her catsuit. From her vantage point, Angela guessed it at a good twelve inches long; it's impressively thick convoluted shaft curved upwards menacingly to its bulbous ridged head.

Crouched low close to the window, Angela's hands rested high on her thighs, almost subconsciously they rose to brush her overexcited groin. The semi-accidental contact through her clothing felt so good that she pressed a little harder and was soon absentmindedly stroking herself through the thick fabric. Before her eyes, Laura had appreciatively received several blows to the pussy, and Red had paused her assault for the moment at least. What happened next made Angela groan with envious excitement; placing the flogger across Laura's back, Red fell to her knees, and her face disappeared behind the bound girl's buttocks. Even though most of her head was hidden behind Laura's glowing derriere, it was obvious to Angela that moments later, the redhead began to eat the helpless girl out. A mere three feet from her, Angela fascinatedly watched the pretty blonde's face contort in rapture as she writhed in ecstatic pleasure while the redhead worked on her. Her cries and groans of intense delight reached Angela through the double-glazing, and they tortured her.

It was no good she had to do it, besides who was going to see her crouched here in the darkness. Feeling incredibly naughty, she slipped her hands into her jogging bottoms and, without hesitating, plunged her fingers into her heated wetness. Sighing appreciatively, she watched the show unfold as she stroked her hot slippery flesh.

After a couple of incredible minutes from behind, Laura rose Red, she stood erect slowly, her lower face glistened with her lover's excited secretions, and she licked her lips appreciatively. Allowing Laura little respite, she gripped the phallus in her hand, bending its rigid length down, and she forcefully plunged it deep into the vulnerable girl. Laura's head whipped up again, and she shrieked wide-eyed, staring directly at Angela for a moment. Outside the window, Angela's heart lurched, and dread filled her, even as distracted as she was, the girl must have seen her, she thought. Wanting to run, she reeled away, staggering back a few paces in terror but felt compelled to stay, to see if Laura had seen her, and if not, she didn't want to miss the spectacle.

Moments passed slowly; no cry of alarm had been raised; there was no flurry of activity behind the curtained window. Returning nervously to her vantage point, she peered through; they were still at it. Red was giving Laura a hell of a pounding, and the young blonde was being pulled back and forth like a rag doll. Surely Angela reasoned with herself if they had seen her, they would have either given chase, desisted from their perversion, or drawn the curtains at least. Before long, the scare was all but erased from her mind, and once more, her hands were busy inside her joggers, pleasuring herself furtively.

Unknown to Angela, she had been seen by Laura. They had been aware of her for some time as the camera picked her up, sent a signal to the small remote that beeped out of the window's sight. The small monitor on the dressing table had popped into life at the same time to show the performers their quarry had taken the bait. Angela was blissfully unaware they were scheming about how to deal with her even as they fucked. Alicia had been well informed about Laura's voyeuristic pervy neighbor. They had found her quite amusing and knew that one day she wouldn't be able to resist trying to find out what they got up to during Alicia's visits, they had long ago formulated a plan to deal with her. For weeks now, concealed night vision cameras, even Laura's husband was unaware of, had been installed around the garden, the trap had been set, knowing the prey would eventually take the bait.

Inside, the action appeared to be slowing; to Angela, they appeared to be tiring somewhat; eventually, the redhead withdrew the glistening monstrous phallus from Laura. After caressing the bound girl's mottled buttocks, Red untied her lover and graciously allowed Laura to roll over. Totally engrossed, Angela watched as Laura immediately sat up and drew her tormenter to her urgently by the hips. Angela stared in astonishment and moaned in envious appreciation at Laura, sinking her mouth over the latex monster's head, wantonly sucking her secretions from its glistening surface. Clearly, a dirty little sex kitten, Laura was well versed in performing oral sex and gave a good display of her talents until Red pulled her lover's head back and broke away. The woman turned and left the room, saying something and laughing as she went to Laura, who nodded and giggled.

Somewhere in the house, music burst forth; it was a loud rock with screaming lyrics and thrashing guitars. On the bed before her, Laura began to perform instantly, grabbing Angela's attention. Without looking, she had swiveled to sort of face the window in her naked splendor. Angela watched mesmerized as the blonde caressed her pert breasts intimately, imagination running riot. Angela mimicked her actions playing with herself in time with Laura as the younger woman's hands slid lower. Watching the blonde's fingers sink between her thighs and begin stroking herself, Angela followed suit, assaulting her own exquisitely aching clitty. Before long, she was breathless, totally absorbed, and very close to coming when she noticed Laura was smiling directly and very wickedly at her. For the briefest moment, she was confused; it was then she realized the true precariousness of her situation.

Blackness suddenly enveloped her as a heavy thick fabric hood was pulled over her head. In an abject panic, she struggled, a hand clamped the confined airless hood about her mouth as her unseen assailant pushed her roughly to the ground, effectively muffled her screams of terror. Disorientated, Angela was unable to struggle as her stronger assailant sat squarely upon her back and cuffed her wrists first and then her ankles. Her fear was such that her voice failed her and her terrified shrieks came out as a weak squeal until the hood cord drew tight about her throat, almost cutting off her air. Pulled unceremoniously to her feet, she was dragged at speed far in excess of the restricted steps her bonds allowed. She stumbled along pathetically, shaking with panic and would have fallen several times had her assailant not held her up.

It grew warmer; the music was louder; she was aware they were now inside the house. Her fear stunned mind whirled, unable to form a rational opinion; her only clear thought was that she had been caught by her vice. She wondered what the hell they intended to do with her. The hood was removed, the room was pitch dark, she tried to make things out but couldn't. There was a noise she recognized through the cacophony of rock music, duct tape being peeled then torn off a roll. In moments she found herself gagged with it then blindfolded, thankfully not with the duct tape.

"Well, well what have we here?" from behind an unknown icy cool menacing voice hissed close to her ear that must belong to Red, "don't move a muscle bitch!"

"Looks like we caught us the local peeping Tom here Laura," the voice continued just as menacing, "or is it peeping Thomasina perhaps?"

"It's that nosey bitch Angela from the big house next door, I told you she would come poking around one day didn't I?" Laura shouted over the music.

Shaking with fear, Angela wished she could plead her innocence or beg for forgiveness, but she couldn't even make any intelligible sound past the fast stuck tape and just breathing through her nose in the hot room was difficult enough. Dim light crept around the edges of her blindfold as someone clicked the light on; the music fell to a much softer volume shortly after that.

"Well, Angela, you've caused us quite a problem," Came the soft, menacing Red's tone, "I really don't know what to do for the best!"

"We could call the cops and hand her over, couldn't we Alicia?" chirped Laura helpfully.

"Yes but they may take a dim view when she tells them what she was watching you silly girl!"

"We can't just let her go though!"

"True, very true, Laura," mused Alicia, "what's her name?"

"Angela, nosey bloody parker from on the hill!"

"What to do, I wonder?"

"If we clear everything up and you change, we could tell the cops she was trying to burgle the house, they would never believe her story!"

"Yes they would silly," Alicia scolded her lover, "besides I might have a much better idea."

"Oh," giggled Laura, wickedly alarming Angela, "tell me then!"

"I need to talk to our guest first to educate her to a few home truths."

Dread filled her as she sensed the closeness of the woman, the heat of her breath on her face, and the pressure of the strap on dildo thrust menacingly against her hip, which oddly excited her despite her fear.

"Well Angela, naughty Angela," came the woman's matter of fact tone as she began to explain, so close Angela felt the phallus thrusting against her belly, "how do you think this will look in the papers once it leaks out, it could wreck your social standing somewhat!" "I don't think you want that do you?"

Angela nodded vigorously in agreement with her.

"Good," she felt the presence of the dildo disappear as Red continued, "the thing is Angela, we cannot afford to let you off scot-free after your transgression, so I'm going to give you two choices, understand?"

Once again, Angela was only too happy to nod her acceptance, slightly relieved at being given a possible reprieve. Whether the police would accept her story, she would still face the humiliation of exposure as a peeping tom and all the damage that would do. Already she knew she had little choice but accept whatever punishment sexy Alicia chose for her; the thrill that coursed through her at the thought of submitting to the dildo wearing redhead was quite delicious. Holding still, she made no attempt to resist as if to persuade her she felt what could only be the head of the dildo being eased between her legs. A shiver of exquisite anticipation ran up through her as she felt it slide slowly deep between her thighs, its natural curve forcing delicious contact with her traitorous pussy through her joggers.

"As I see it and I'm sure Laura would agree I have no choice but to punish you myself unless you wish to visit the police cells, the choice is yours Angela!"

With that, she pulled the duct tape away from her mouth in one sharp yank making Angela yelp in pain as it was ripped off.

"Well, have you decided?"

"I don't have a choice do I?" whimpered Angela forlornly as Alicia rode the dildo back and forth slowly against her, "I suppose a generous offer to ransom myself would be rejected?"

"It's not about money you silly cow, will you accept the punishment or is it the cops I call?"

"Why would they believe you?" she gasped breathlessly as, despite her predicament, she relished the thick insistent intruder thrusting back and forth between her thighs.

"Didn't I tell you about our new security cameras Angela?" giggled Laura mocking her, clearly relishing the look of horror on her face, "wanna see the latest footage?"

"Well!" sighed Alicia close behind, thrusting the phallus against her tender flesh so hard. Angela gasped, "what do you say, you never know you may like it, bitch!"

"What do you mean by punished?"

"Why should I tell you and spoil the surprise," Red laughed, "by the time I finish with you Angela I'll have two clients on your street!"

"Clients?" gasped Angela, shocked, "you mean Laura is your...?"

"She is my customer, yes," chuckled the woman interrupting her and seemingly highly amused by Angela's astonishment, "why, you thought we were lovers did you?"

"Yes, yes I did, I never imagined anything like this," Angela spurted in amazement, "if what you say is true and I see no reason to doubt it, you give me no choice but to agree to your demands!"

"Excellent, prepare her Laura."

Trembling uncontrollably with dreadful anticipation of what she had just agreed to, Angela's heart lurched, she sensed Alicia move away, taking the tantalizing phallus with her to Angela's surprising dismay. Soon enough though she was distracted from her thoughts, Laura had drifted up to her; she recognized her neighbor's distinct citrus perfume. Angela jumped as soft fingers lightly touched her lips, sensually drawing the bottom one down, making her shiver with delight.

"Open up Angela," giggled Laura softly as she obeyed her demand without thought, "nice and wide, there's a good girl Angela!"

The plastic ball felt cold and resiliently hard as Laura pushed it deep between her open jaws in one sharp movement. Her tongue was forced back, causing her to gag, Angela's heart fluttered excitedly, she was close to panic as the straps were secured tightly about the base of her skull. Before she could adjust to the intrusive gag, she felt the hood being slipped over her head once again. To her relief, though, this time, it was not fastened anywhere near as tight as it had been earlier.

In another moment, she felt the zip of her sweat top being undone. She began to shake uncontrollably in fear, which oddly excited her. The heat built up under the confined hood as she felt herself redden with embarrassment; beneath her top, she was naked. The garment was pulled down her arms as far as the handcuffs would allow forcing the cuffs down over her hands somewhat painfully. Her complaints were unintelligible and ignored as her wrists were bound tightly together behind her quite skilfully, then her arms were bound again at the elbows equally tightly. Rummaging through the crumpled sweatshirt, Laura undid the handcuffs and discarded both them and the garment.

Inevitably she knew what was coming next, as she expected, her bottoms and panties were pulled unceremoniously past her knees, shame, embarrassment, and fear overwhelmed her. She began to cry, great sobs wracked her, but it did no good, and she felt Laura's hands pushing her down by the shoulders, forcing her to her knees. Wasting no time at all, Laura had her trainers and socks off in a flash, the cuffs around her ankles followed soon they were joined by Angela's joggers and panties.

"Don't fucking move," giggled Laura excitedly from behind her, "or you'll wish you hadn't been such a nosey fucker!"

She had no intention of risking making things worse; how could she. With her arms bound and unsighted, she probably wouldn't even be able to stand up without falling over, never mind attempt to escape and so knelt obediently as Laura returned to bind her ankles then knees tightly together. Once Laura was happy with that, she bound Angela's wrists and ankles together, then Angela heard her move away, leaving her kneeling helplessly in the middle of the room. Without warning, Angela felt a blow land as a foot pushed hard against her shoulder. Screaming more from shock than the pain, she toppled onto her side and lay trussed up and helpless.

"Bitch is ready Mistress," she heard Laura call-out above her.

"I'm almost finished here," came Alicia's distant reply that drew closer as she returned, "ohh Laura that's a pretty good job there, she's trussed nice and tight."

"Come help me lift her," laughed Alicia evilly, "the cars ready, there's a nice warm blanket in the boot. We'll get her nice and snug then we can go whenever we're ready!"

Futilely she tried to struggle as they lifted her; she was wracked by terror at the thought of what they had said. Foolishly she had believed she would have been punished there in Laura's house and never imagined anything other than a good flogging, and a bit of debasement was coming her way. Helpless, she was carried through the house and into the garage where she was lifted into the boot of the car where she was doubly secured to the cargo rings on the floor of the boot, after which she presumed was a blanket thrown over her. She lay in silence; her heart thumping restlessly in her breast was all she could hear for a moment.

"Mistress?" she heard Laura's plea and realized they were still there, "this is very exhilarating, isn't it?"

"Does the thought of what we're gonna do to her turn you on?"

"Oh yes Mistress," she heard Laura coo pleadingly, "please Mistress, please fuck me before we leave?"

"I'd love to you little slut but do we have time?"

"All the time in the world Mistress!"

"Come here then," Alicia oozed, "bend over the car."

"Oooh! Aurgh! Mmm!" Angela felt the car begin to rock rhythmically around her with increasing movement.

"Tell me Laura," Alicia enquired without losing momentum, "How do you know we have so much time?"

"I oooh, met her husband the other ugh, day Mistress," Laura gasped between thrusts, "told me he's out of town all week, won't be back till Sunday!"

"All week, oh my!"

The glee in Alicia's voice terrified Angela. She was out of options and lay there stifled by the hood, pathetically crying as Laura was brought to orgasm so close above her, which should have excited her so. Eventually, the car stopped moving, the boot lid slammed shut, startling her. Her heart sank as she heard them walk away, then silence fell as the garage door clamped shut, and she lay in silence, her mind a flurry of activity. She convinced herself gradually that everything would be okay, they were just trying to scare her, and they had done a damn good job so far.

Despite the painful restriction of her bonds, her thoughts turned to what they might do to her, watching Laura receive her strokes it had aroused her. Perhaps she was going to get the same and hopefully a good fucking to boot. Her imagination ran riot, making her more and more randy; she was aching for release and anticipating the coming hours as she dozed off to dream of Alicia and her foot-long friend.

Chapter 02

The car jiggled slightly as two thumps resounded through the vehicle, waking her groggily from a restive slumber. How long she had dozed, Angela had no idea, shortly after though she heard the engine start, surely they were still winding her up, tormenting her for her indiscretions. Angela found it hard to believe they would dare take to the streets with a trussed up naked woman in their car's boot.

It was incredibly hot and stuffy here; she had been stripped, gagged, blindfolded, hooded for good measure, and then bound tight enough to prevent her escaping. Then she had been carried to the garage and secured to the luggage mounts on the boot floor of the sports car; they had covered her with a thick blanket, which made it even hotter in such a confined space. The hood and ball gag on top of all this made breathing quite difficult though not dangerously, so she was glad of that at least!

The engine burst into life, vibrating the floor beneath her. Angela cried out hopelessly, muffled by her gag, hood, and the car itself as her panic returned. Then, even more, terrifying for her, she felt the car lurch around her as it pulled away. Even now, she truly believed they were winding her up; they would drive to the end of the road and return, wouldn't they? She moved to the left against her bonds as the car swung right out of the drive, soon she would be pushed right as the car turned to return up the street, wouldn't she? Moments later, she cried in shocked dismay as she felt the car turn left and accelerated up the main road. She screamed in disbelief, how could they be so foolhardy, if they got stopped or had an accident, how could they explain this.

Within a few minutes, she was very glad of the blanket they had thrown over her as the air around her began to cool rapidly. Her mind was in turmoil, fear, and terror washed back and forth in a battling tide with excitement and arousal as her bonds bit into her with each bump or turn in the road. Despite the blanket, she shivered and for a moment wondered where the draught was coming from, soon though her mind returned to more pressing matters.

Everything was her fault she found herself considering; if she had resisted the temptation to pry and left them alone, all this would never have happened. Of course, Angela realized it had been a trap. She had been lured into it quite skilfully; if she hadn't been so nosey though, she wouldn't be here now, so it was her fault. She wondered how many times they had baited the trap, how many times they had hoped to catch her, how determined had they been?

With that, her thoughts went back to what she had been witness to a short while ago as she had peeked through Laura's bedroom window. She saw it all so vividly and felt that delightful ache between her tightly trussed thighs, despite or because of her lack of control and fear about what was going to happen, Angela found this all very exhilarating.

Time passed, a lot of it, or at least it seemed a lot before the car finally stopped, and the engine died. She lay shivering with cold beneath her blanket as she heard heavy doors slamming shut. Sometime later, the boot was opened, and her blanket was removed. Overly warm air rushed in to waft over her as someone undid the ropes that bound her to the boot floor. Angela felt herself being lifted from the car. She was bodily carried for some distance to be laid on what felt like a concrete floor. Wondering where the hell they had taken her, Angela sniffed the air that seeped into her hood. It smelt thick, oily, or greasy, definitely somewhere industrial. The rope securing her wrists to her ankles was undone, and she was lifted and maneuvered into a chair.

"Don't move Bitch," came Alicia's cold, emotionless voice, "please don't make things any worse for yourself."

Surrounded by the inky blackness, she nodded her hooded head to show she agreed; it would be pointless to try and make her voice understood around the ball gag. Trembling, she sat perfectly still as her legs and arms were undone quite quickly. They both worked in unison and had her free in moments. The hood, however, stayed in place, unfortunately, and she couldn't stifle the moan that escaped her as her joints moved for the first time in what seemed ages. She wailed pitifully as pins and needles wracked her arms and legs as both circulation and warmth returned to them. Her arms were cuffed behind the chair back before they retreated. Sitting in silence, she could hear them talking and laughing close by too quietly though for her to make out anything useful as they busied themselves doing god knows what. A good five minutes passed before they seemed to pay her any attention at all, three minutes for her to imagine what was about to happen.

"Stand!" barked Alicia authoritatively, nervously, Angela obeyed, rising slowly to her feet.

A hand gripped her none too gently by the back of the neck, forcing her to move; she stumbled blindly in the direction she was forced. The intensity of the dread that overwhelmed her was exquisite. Angela felt her pulse racing excitedly. Her gagged mouth was incredibly dry as she was forcibly maneuvered to stand exactly where they wanted; her cuffs were removed.

"Right bitch, hold out your arms, don't try and do anything stupid!" came a barked order; compliantly, she held her arms out before her.

"To the sides you stupid bitch!" it was Alicia who did all the talking.

Almost instantly, Angela felt them wrapping heavy thick, what felt like leather bands around her wrists and securing them tightly. She could hear the jingle of loose buckles as her wrists were bound. Angela was amazed by how well they worked together, chains rattled over concrete and metal, alarming her, and she felt the heavyweight pull downwards upon her outspread arms as they fastened them to the wrist cuffs. She hoped she did not have to stand like this for too long, for the weight seemed to grow heavier with each passing moment. The heavy sensation did not last long at all, however, for, with rattling clinks from both sides, the chains were drawn tauter, utilizing ratchets, they were drawing Angela's arms out directly to each side of her. If she had wanted to flee at all, the thought of which had never entered her head as a viable option until now, it dawned on Angela that she was unable to.

Her mind span in turmoil, as Angela realized there was no escaping the inevitable; she must endure whatever they had planned for her. Confused by her emotions, part of her wanted to scream, to flee in panic or withdraw in fearful denial, but another darker side hungered expectantly for the unknown. It grew restlessly excited, imagining sensations and emotions she had not yet savored or endured. This side of her psyche grew stronger with each passing moment and ruled her misgivings at the moment without contest.

To her sides, more chains rattled, Angela felt the chill of cold steel against her skin this time about her ankles as the chilly links of steel were wrapped around them twice about and secured. Shortly after, as ratchets clanked and the chains pulled at her ankles, forcing her feet relentlessly apart, she trembled once more. Angela unsteadily wobbled as they forced her to adopt the position they wanted her in. Totally helpless, stretched spread-eagled, gagged and hooded, enveloped in total blackness, Angela realized her punishment was probably about to be delivered. Real fear gripped her, fear of what they were going to do, fear of the pain she was to endure, and mostly fear of why it was stimulating her so much!

"Ohh Angela," laughed Alicia menacingly, causing a ripple of wonderful fear to add to her tense state, "you look so vulnerable like that." "God, you don't know how much I'm going to enjoy this you bitch!" she hissed, terrifyingly enthusiasm sparkled in Alicia's voice.

Unexpectedly the hood was popped off Angela's head, free from the stuffy confines of the hood; she relished the cooler on her face. She drew in several deep lungs full of the oily scented cool air before her blindfold was removed. The light was quite subdued; the main overhead fluorescent lights were out. What illumination there was, came from small lamps set here and thereupon some of the high workbenches, but to her newly exposed retinas, even those seemed really bright. No one was in sight both her abductors were behind her somewhere out of her field of vision; instinct told her it would be smarter to keep her head forwards and not turn to look around too much. Squinting around without moving her head much, her captors allowed her a moment or two to take in her surroundings. To Angela, it was quite obviously a car workshop; she had been secured stark naked between two of the upright posts of a four-post hydraulic car lift by heavy link chains.

From both sides at once, they moved to stand directly before her. Angela stared wide-eyed in shock; if she had been able, her jaw would have dropped in astonishment. Before Angela, her tormentors stood, both were naked apart from tight scarlet latex hoods that covered the top halves of their faces to just under their noses and spike-heeled boots. With heels of six inches or more, both the women towered over her. Alicia's boots are exotic thigh length and match her mask perfectly in color, while Laura's boots are simpler, black, and only calf-high. As she had witnessed earlier, Alicia wore her auburn hair hanging loosely through a hole at her hood's apex, but Laura's blonde shorter tresses were crushed beneath her hood.

They made a very erotic vision and stood side-by-side together, holding each other loosely in a very sensuous manner, which thrilled Angela. Still quaking uncontrollably, Angela's heart lurched as they began to move. The women parted to move to each side close to the car lifts posts and begin to adjust the ratchets on the chain, drawing her arms quite some tauter until she was stretched just enough to prevent her moving without hurting herself. Her stomach knotted in gloriously tense apprehension as Angela waited with bated breath; her current predicament is one of the most highly exciting experiences she has known. Angela's already fraught nerves go into overdrive as Alicia drew

485

very close to look deep into her eyes, something her tormentor saw there made her smile smugly, her icy green eyes mere inches from Angela's.

"Dirty bitch," whispers Alicia quietly so that only she hears, then louder and more aggressively, "you dirty filthy bitch, I know you want this, you may think not but I see it in those filthy whore slut eyes!"

Shaking with absolute terror and extreme excitement, Angela shook her head in an attempt to deny it. Stepping back, Alicia laughed and nodded. She knew she could see it so easily. Helpless to resist, Angela had decided to enjoy what she could and endure what she had to in order to get this over with, at least that's what she had tried to convince herself and Alicia had seen straight through her. Laura meanwhile had wandered away behind Angela somewhere. Though Angela paid the woman little attention as her eyes were drawn to her delectable red-headed, green-eyed tyrant and her verbal abuse as she drew closer again.

"You appreciate why you are to be disciplined don't you Angela?" she nodded once to show she understood, her throat constricted, and she fought to hold back tears.

"I must ask you to be truthful now," Alicia's eyes sparked with malice, "do you deserve disciplining?"

Once again, she nodded after a brief hesitation; she was so close to her Angela could have licked her face if she had not been so securely gagged. Alicia smiled, pleased with her response. To Angela's surprise, the woman cupped her breast making her shudder involuntarily as the fingers drew together to tease her already distended teat. She wanted to cry out, to ask the woman not to stop but could only garble unintelligibly past the gag. As if she knew, Alicia took her other hand and slid it between Angela's legs to cup her aching pussy lightly. Throwing back her head, she wailed incomprehensibly around her gag as Alicia's middle finger speared her oozing flesh very precisely. The delightful intruder sank as deep as possible into her sucking wetness and gyrated several times. Such was her excitement that within moments she was close to climaxing and shook uncontrollably, this time solely through pleasure.

"Feels good, ehh," purred Alicia sexily as she fingered her to the brink.

Focusing on the woman's highly amused eyes, Angela stared pleadingly at her, visually begging her to allow her to come. Of course, disappointment was to be her reward as Alicia withdrew both hands at the critical moment, she held up the fingers that had been in Angela's sex close between them and sniffed the dripping middle finger.

"Dreamy," she purred, holding it below Angela's nose; her musky scent pervaded her nostrils, "here try it."

The woman smeared the thick, copious secretions around her nose. Every breath she now took would reek of her own pungent aroused pussy juices. Angela watched the woman lick her fingers clean with her long pointed tongue and moaned in frustration. All this time, Laura had been busy behind her, and Alicia slid away, laughing to join the other woman out of Angela's sight. Taking deep breaths as best she could through only her nose Angela steadied herself only too aware of the whispering and laughing behind her.

Closing her eyes, she calmed herself down as best she could; her pulse considerably slowed as she took full advantage of their apparent distraction. Something soft gently landed across her upper arm and shoulder, startling her from her composure settling exercise. Looking down, she squealed behind the gag for fanned out across her pale flesh was the soft scarlet leather tails of a flogger. In a wicked way, Alicia played the flogger lightly over her as she ducked beneath Angela's arm and stood before her. Almost tenderly, she flicked the flogger against Angela's belly, flinching each time Angela shrieked unnecessarily in fear expecting worse than Alicia gave her. Confusion reigned within, her eyes widened in horror, but her body ripples with anticipatory excitement of the unknown that was to come as she watched the scarlet tails slap lightly against her. The sensations she felt were incredibly perverse; she knew she was about to be hurt, but she longed eagerly for the torture Alicia had selected for her in a sick way.

"You ready Angela?"

To her amazement, Angela felt a hint of defiance surface. She just stared back at her tormentor, her face a mask of expressionless calm. Alicia refused to be phased by her pitiful show; almost an anti-climax Angela had expected to be struck, but Alicia made no move immediately; instead, she winked, goading her prey. With a flourish of the wrist, she set the floggers fronds whirling in a circular motion and smiled nastily at Angela. Confidence evaporated, the shakes had returned, she could not control them, whether, through excitement or terror, Angela could not tell she was so confused. Time marched on, and she was kept in suspended anticipation for so long she cared not what happened as long as something did.

"Show me you want it Bitch!" hissed Alicia coldly, "show me or by my word you'll be so sorry!"

Her brief defiance confidence dissolved before the threat, and nervously Angela nodded to show she accepted.

"Excellent we got that on camera!" smiled Alicia pointing behind her with her free hand, the flogger still spans lazily in her other.

At first, in disbelief, Angela stared where Alicia is, indicating, and true enough. There is a security camera with a blinking red light pointed straight at her from a top corner of the workshop. How could she be so stupid? She cursed to herself; the bitches were filming this, fuck they'll probably blackmail her. Visions of her oh so comfortable world evaporating clouded her mind but only for a moment.

Before her, Alicia stood beyond striking range. She was smiling evilly, flourishing the flogger in a lazy figure of eight, captivating Angela's focus. Almost daydreaming, Angela was caught unaware of watching Alicia playing with the flogger. Behind her, Laura made the first move swinging her flogger in a gentle arc to strike Angela across the buttocks. Alicia laughs wickedly at her as the unexpected blow landed; the blow was fairly light, but it still hurt her unsuspecting flesh like hell. In shock, Angela reacted instinctively, attempting to throw herself forwards away from the attack. As she lurches forwards in the chains crying out in pain and shock to no avail, Alicia strikes her across her belly; she lurches back only to be struck again from behind. To her, the level of pain is intense. She bursts into tears, wailing ineffectively around the ball gag as they abuse her. All this time, both the evil bitches laugh as they flog her, thankfully not too hard for ten strokes each then stop.

As the pain faded to a bearable ache, she realized how good it felt perverse and how exhilarated she felt as her buttocks and belly burn in the afterglow. Alicia stood hands on hips before her, breathing heavily from her exertions, a light sheen of sweat on her top lip. Foolishly Angela believed it was over up to the point when she has suddenly plunged into darkness again. The fear she feels as her sight is taken from her is extremely arousing; her wait to find out what comes next was very short this time.

A flogger blow struck her hip from the front; it is copied straight away by a blow around her other hip from behind. She can sense this by the way the tassels strike home. The next blow came from the front; it hit across her lower leg to be similarly copied from behind. Blows then struck her upper arm, lower arm, and so on. Blow after blow was landed all up to her sides, and on top and bottom of her arms. Her nerve endings cry out; her body feels on fire as her senses were battered for what seemed an age.

"Halt, change over you lead now," Alicia called out, she sounded almost breathless.

If they were tiring though they did not show it from behind, Laura struck her inner thigh above the knee, Alicia did likewise from the front. To Angela's dismay, the next blow was a double sideswipe and returned across her waist, Alicia copied across her the tender taut exposed expanse of her belly. The agony was incredible, but more was to come. The next was harder back and forth across her upper back. Angela steeled herself, understanding the pattern she knew instinctively where the next double blow would land. Even though she was gagged, she screamed, anticipating the pain long before it occurred. Of course, Alicia followed suit, whipping the flogger quite hard across her jiggling tits as she writhed in her bonds, futilely attempting to avoid the blows.

The pain was intense, but she was given no respite; she screamed on almost panicking, choking on her saliva as from behind the flogger hit upwards between her thighs its ends lashing her exposed pussy agonizingly. Alicia followed suit with a similar blow from the front Angela wailed in anguish at the lashing only to be rewarded evilly. Several tassels hit her tenderest flesh on both strokes, causing searing flashes of pain to burst through her. The ache left behind was exquisitely unbearable. Blows began to rain upon her at random; she pathetically lurched as she was struck with varying force from any angle on any part of her body or limbs. Such was her inability to control her body that she pissed herself; the urine stung the many weals on her legs as it gushed from her in an unmanaged spurt. Her torturers laughed but showed mercy or no sign of halting at her distress. Her feet slipped in her mess as she lurched about under the beating, furthering her discomfort, causing her to swing helplessly in her chains until she regained her footing.

Truth be known, that last assault only lasted less than a minute, but she was close to collapse when they finished with her. Sweat poured from her, her body burnt in exquisite agony as sweat and piss soaked into her whipped skin. Quite exhausted, she hung limply in her chains as the hood was removed, and Alicia stood before her smiling victoriously at her. Once more, she could breathe a little freer, and after several painful breaths with her eyes closed and head hung low, a little energy returned. Looking herself over as best she could, Angela saw there was no part of her body or limbs left unmarked by the floggers.

"Learnt your lesson nosey parker?" came Laura's giggly voice behind her; all she could do was nod weakly.

Her head was incredibly heavy, she stared down at Alicia's red boots and the piss flooded floor they stood on. She could hear Laura scraping and banging about behind her and tried to turn her head to see what the bitch was up to.

"Oh no, keep those pretty eyes on me!" purred Alicia menacingly enough to make Angela raise her aching neck to stare woefully at her tormentor.

She dare not look away for a second; something in Alicia's gaze warned her to look away was extremely ill-advised. The chains holding her left arm slackened, allowing it to fall halfway to her side. She heard Laura walk across to her right, and her right chain was similarly loosened. Her legs were left secure wide apart as they had been as one at a time; her arms were undone. Working swiftly behind her, Laura left the cuffs left on and secured together behind Angela's back. To her ears came the familiar sound of a ratchet working, and she became aware that her arms were being drawn upward behind her, forcing her to bend forwards a little more with each turn of the ratchet just to keep her balance.

What the fuck had they planned for her now? The still aching pain and discomfort they had inflicted upon her already had left her very aroused; she quite fancied the prospect that Alicia had brought that brute of a dildo and was going to finish her torture with that. Her heart raced as if reading her thoughts, Alicia disappeared for a moment and returned sure enough with the big black strap-on in her hands. Enthralled, Angela excitedly stared as Alicia slipped the device on and adjusted it to give a comfortable fit right in front of her highly excitable trembling victim. Angela watched the bobbing bulbous head of the dildo as Alicia crossed to one of the workbenches to pick up something lying there. Returning, she opened her hand to show Angela two small screw cramps laid there. Angela was puzzled for a moment, but not for long.

Holding one in her mouth, she teased Angela's already erect right nipple furthering distension. Angela moaned with pleasure as her tortured teat was expertly plucked. Once Alicia was happy, the nipple was at full erection, she screwed the clampdown on Angela's tender flesh. The pain was not as bad as Angela expected, but she winced none the less, the action was repeated on her left nipple moments later. What hurts her more than the clamps was the stiffness in her back at being held so awkwardly.

Totally unexpected, she felt Laura undo the gag and remove it. As she moved her mouth, she wailed, the ache in her muscles was incredible, that gag must have been in place for hours.

"Is that better, bitch?" purred Alicia quietly.

"Yes, yes thank you," moaned Angela hoping despite her intense arousal that the pain was over.

"Ready for more?"

"Please no! I thought that," she pleaded pointlessly, "please let me free, I've learnt my lesson, I'll do anything you ask of me Alicia!"

"I know you will you whore!" Alicia smiled confidently, "and the answer to your plea for clemency is no."

"Please, please let me go!"

"Fuck you!"

It was all too much for Angela, and once again she burst into tears, showing no pity, Alicia slackened the clamps momentarily, allowing the blood to return to her starved nerve endings. Angelica whimpered as the pain flared in her breast then squealed as the clamp was then secured even tighter. She raised her head once more to implore Alicia for mercy in time to see the redhead nod to Laura behind her. Her heart fell like a stone; she expected an imminent assault with the flogger. Instead, the ratchet rattled into life, and her arms were drawn up higher above her back, forcing her head down and her unprotected rear out further and further. Her shoulder sockets screamed out in protest as she was hoisted into such an unnatural position.

Clamping her lips tightly together, she managed to absorb her distress without crying out. Alicia's hateful comment sparked something inside. Foolishly perhaps Angela decided not to let them get the better of her, well to try at least. Fighting back the tears, she hung her head so that Alicia would not see the hurt in her eyes, she hoped. Pain and humiliation may have fuelled her anger, but she was sensible enough to hold it under control; she wished she could say the same thing about her wayward libido. In all her experiences through the years, she had never been so sexually energized or felt so free, which was so ironic seeing the situation she had got herself into.

For years she had thought secretly spying on her neighbors and fantasizing about lesbian trysts with them had been thrilling, but her obsessions had pushed the boundaries far beyond what she could have ever imagined herself ever experiencing. Her obsessions had nearly got her into trouble on a few occasions, but her husband had sorted things out, usually financially. This, however, was a far different affair; she had stepped beyond his help. She was on her own here. What horrified her most was that despite the abuse, fear, and pain, or even because of them, she found herself reveling in her plight. Had she lost her mind?

Raising her head a little, she saw Alicia's scarlet booted feet before her, about fifteen inches apart. Looking up a little further, she admired the woman's toned thighs above the boots. Alicia's stance was one of extreme confidence; the upwardly curving immensity of black latex phallus was there right before Angela's eyes; she stared at it mesmerized by its menacing bulk. She shuddered at the thought of it penetrating her, bit her lip in anticipation of it stretching her pussy walls as Alicia fucked her and let out a faint sigh of longing. Above her, Alicia chuckled, reaching down she stroked Angela's cheek; it felt so good that Angela looked up and smiled encouragingly at her gorgeous oppressor.

"You want it don't you?" purred Alicia; how could someone sound so menacing and erotic at the same time thought Angela as the woman continued, "you want me to fuck you like I fucked Laura when we caught you, don't you?"

"Yes," her voice trembling and tiny fluttering from her like a tiny bird, "ohh yes!"

"You've been incredibly brave so far Angela," soothed Alicia crouching to look her in the eye, taking a firm grip on Angela's chin in the palm of her hand. The timbre of her voice hardened, she demanded Angela's attention, "you can scream if you want to!"

"Why!" was all that Angela managed; she was puzzled; the pain had not that bad after all.

For a split second, only she vaguely became aware of high zipping noise, sharp pain erupted across her buttocks, the shock almost made her scream as her backside felt like it had exploded. Her eyes widened, and she watched Alicia smile down at her smugly. The bitch had distracted her just enough by offering her a good fucking to allow Laura to attack unnoticed. The next time she heard the crop slice through the air, she knew what it was, but she did not have time to brace herself. Another resounding crack flared agony through her vulnerable rear and, despite her resolve, nearly gave in and almost cried out. Her breath was ragged as she gulped in air, petrified she was waiting for the next stroke.

With both hands, Alicia grasped her hair tightly at either side of her head; she held her securely and moved closer. The immense phallus rested against her face; she could smell its faint plastic odor along with another muskier earthy odor that excited her. This was the dildo that Alicia had fucked Laura with; it was soiled with the woman's dried secretions.

"Lick it you slut!" hissed Alicia, her voice shaking with excitement.

"Yes," whimpered Angela wincing as another blow stripped her enflamed rear, it suddenly seemed right to add, "yes Mistress!"

"At last, you show some respect slave!" Alicia laughed condescendingly, "now lick it!"

Tentatively at first, she proceeded to obey Alicia, staring up at the redhead who watched her intently while guiding her head up and down the bittersweet bulky shaft. Soon, she was enjoying the humiliating task her mistress had given her, but such was the agony she felt with each stroke of the crop across her already well-beaten buttocks that she could not stop herself crying out even before the stroke landed. Her head was gripped even tighter as she began to shudder. The pain and anguish were almost too much mixed with her excitement; she was drowning in the total disarray of mixed emotions.

Alicia held her mouth close to the phallus's head, and Angela snaked her tongue over it, looking up, she stared at Alicia. Angela was shaking with excitement at the aloof coolness the woman emitted as she fellated the dildo. Fingers snaked through her hair to grip the top of her head firmly; she knew what Alicia intended her to do and whimpered excitedly as her mouth was forced to hover directly over the glistening crown of the phallus. As the next blow landed harder than before, Alicia pushed her head down firmly. With no choice in the matter, her scream of pain was snuffed out as her eager mouth is forced to consume inches of fat black latex. This is so humiliating but so fucking exciting that Angela is on the verge of orgasm. Furiously Alicia forced her to accommodate more and more in her mouth as Laura whipped her into a frenzy.

As if taken over by a demon, Angela starts to bob her head of her own accord and was unaware that Alicia had even released her grip on her head. With each stroke of the crop, she was spurred on obscenely by her desire to be a complete slut. Forcing her head down until she gagged, she moaned and gasped for air whenever she could. She was a dirty bitch, a dirty fucking slut; she kept telling herself excitedly as she sank deeper into depravity.

Such was her state that she never noticed the beating had stopped and was only partially aware of the long-nailed fingers scratching across her battered ass cheeks. In oblivion, she fellated the latex cock as a thing possessed. Laura spread her cheeks behind her and, with a well-greased hand, lubricated her puckered ring carefully. That was something new; she thought unalarmed as Laura's finger entered her arse. It felt very nice, she was unsure what the woman was doing, but it felt oh so good, and she was more than distracted wantonly feasting on Alicia's pseudo cock. I'm a slut, a dirty slut. I want it, I deserve it, she repeated to herself as she endured the latest defilement they inflicted upon her eager body.

Interfering fingers vanished, but she cared not as hands gripped her weal crossed hips and something big pressed against her anus, she moaned in surprise as whatever it was pressed on relentlessly, she tensed. A new achingly perverse pain flared through her, she wailed and gripped the phallus in her mouth with her teeth, more pain as whatever it was that was being poked into her bum hole was forced deeper. It took only moments, though, for the pain to fade as her body accommodated the intruder, Laura began to fuck her arse, slowly sliding the strap on deeper and deeper into her with successive strokes. It was disgusting. She never imagined submitting to anything so sickeningly perverse, but it felt good. It felt so good, so unnatural, so sick, so perverse but so very, very good.

Alicia pulled away and allowed Laura to get on with abusing Angela. Such was Angela's excitement she gasped and swore obscenities rained from her and alternatively mewling like a cat as she was defiled so deliciously. The pain caused by her bonds was forgotten as Laura screwed her until, at last, she came. Screaming their names, she was wracked with delightful spasms of pleasure as Laura wrung every drop of pleasure from her. Almost hysterical, she tottered on unsteady feet as Laura withdrew with a loud plop, sweat ran freely over her as she struggled to compose herself and recover.

"So good," she mumbled incoherently, "so good Mistress Alicia, thank you, thank you Mistress Laura!"

"Shut the fuck up Angela," Laura laughed in disbelief.

Such was her state that the pain of returning circulation when her clamps were removed failed to register. Wasting no time, the two women began to free her; she cried out as her arms were lowered and unable to stand, she slumped to the floor as she was let down. They worked quickly, unchaining her legs and arms before lifting her between them and dragging her limp form away. The women dragged her to an empty workbench, like a limp rag doll, she fell where they placed her face down with her legs hanging limply over the edge. She lay inert as they secured her to the bench with cords; her legs were pulled around the sides and secured to hooks to fully expose her rear again. In a wonderful dreamy reverie, she drifted only half aware of what was going on. She was soon wrenched back into awareness.

Something was eased into her pussy, something big, she moaned as she was stretched deliciously to the max. Lolling her head around, she saw Alicia up close behind her; she would get her fucking after all. Thrusting deeper, Alicia built up speed forcing inch after inch of delightful fat latex cock into her molten pussy. Pulling almost completely out, then thrusting downward with every fast-paced stroke, the head and rippled shaft stretched her cunt and ground against her G-spot relentlessly as it tore into her again and again. Unsurprisingly she came in minutes very intensely and very reactively. Even as she came, Alicia gave her no respite fucking her writhing shuddering body more violently still. Thrashing against her bonds, she wildly convulsed until she calmed somewhat and enjoyed the relentless pounding the redhead was giving her. It took not much longer for Alicia to have her helpless victim climax again just as intensely, if not more so than the last time. This time Angela's head felt like it would explode as she came, lights swam around, and she pathetically wailed as she strained against her bindings. Weak as she was, she thought she would pass out before Alicia finally stopped, she did sort of.

When she came around, she was sitting on a chair dressed in her joggers and sweatshirt; she was very aware of the smarting ache in her buttocks. Alicia and Laura, now dressed in jeans and sweatshirts, stood over her, smiling. Alicia offered her a readily opened bottle of water, which she accepted, drinking it eagerly. She felt battered, weak, and tired beyond belief. At the same time, she felt so fulfilled and sated, so peaceful and happy in the quiet after the storm. Laura handed her a Mars bar until then; she was not aware of how hungry she actually was.

"Come on lets go," Alicia said softly, "its almost morning!"

"Are you taking me home now Mistress?" Angela inquired, feeling mixed emotions, not wanting to be alone.

"To your home no," The redhead laughed, "no my little slave, you are coming home with me!"

"Ohh, I thought," she began only to be silenced.

"You don't think now," scolded Alicia softly, "I think, not you!"

"Ohh, I see Mistress!"

"I have six more days to enjoy you before I have to return you to your husband, but for now we must all rest!"

Standing unsteadily, she stretched her aching back, looking around, there was no evidence at all of last nights shenanigans. How long had she been out, she wondered as Laura gripped her arm and drew her along.

Six days! Six days before Alicia would allow her to return home, what had the redhead planned to do with her for six days she couldn't imagine? Her pulse wildly raced as she followed Alicia to the car, Laura climbed into the excuse for a rear seat, and she was allowed the honor of sitting in the front. As she sat outside the workshop waiting for Alicia to secure the building, she tried to imagine what the next six days would hold for her.

"What you smiling for?" Laura hissed from the back seat.

"Ohh nothing." Sighed Angela settling down in the seat, purposefully crushing her bruised cheeks against the seat to enjoy the ache.

Erotic Women
4 Erotic, Romantic, and Wild Lesbian Erotica
Emilia Russell

All Rights Reserved. No part of this publication may be reproduced in any form or by any means, including scanning, photocopying, or otherwise without prior written permission of the copyright holder. Copyright © 2020

This book is entirely a work of fiction. The names, characters and incidents portrayed in it are the work of the author's imagination. Any resemblance to actual persons, living or dead, events or localities is entirely coincidental.

Story 01

Have you ever felt like life has this weird way of working? Well, that's what my life feels like time and time again. You think you have figured out the right life, and then BAM it slaps you in the face when things are too perfect.

I'm 26, sitting outside the house of the girl I'm totally in love with, waiting for her and her girlfriend to finish "getting ready" so we can all go out. The third wheel, no not really, we're going out with a friend of mine, Jenna. She's been with me since middle school and is currently sitting next to me in the car, nagging me about why I put myself through this and don't just get over her.

It's easier said than done, wouldn't we all agree. It's been three years since the day I met her, back at our college graduation. She was a Psychology major as was I, and yet we had never met. Surprising but I always took morning classes, working evenings, as she worked mornings and took night classes.

I walked onto the field where we were all supposed to wait. It was about 10 of us when I got there. See if your family wants decent seats and all together, you have to get there super early as did mine and they made sure I was there at the same time, her family had done the same to her. How early, an hour and a half early.

"Mercedes, Psych and you are?" She put her hand out to shake. I'm left-handed, so it was a bit awkward.

"MJ, Psych also."

"Like Michael Jackson, Michael Jordan, Mary Jane?" I couldn't help but laugh at how different all of them were.

"Um, no, no and no, Marilyn Jean."

"Nice your mom or parents were a fan of Norma Jean, but just Marilyn Monroe or Norma Jean was too much so they went creative with it?" How could anyone know how impossibly crazy my parents could be about Marilyn?

"Yea actually that's exactly what it was, are you a Marilyn fan?"

"No but I did do some research on her for a paper. MJ it suits you, are you a spider-man fan, you know Mary Jane?"

"No actually Superman all the way." And that's how we started our first argument.

"Why doesn't he just kill Lex Luthor? He's just a mere human."

"If he killed him, he would be evil like the villains he fights to protect the world from."

While we waited for our ceremony to start, we talked about everything possible. Ultimately we exchanged numbers and sat next to each other laughing like old friends during the ceremony. Since that day, I've been totally into this girl.

First, it was just friends, you know, and we would hang out sometimes, movies, dinner, clubs, but never anything more than friendship. Her smile made me smile, and her voice brought joy because it meant she was near. Seeing a car similar to hers made me wonder what she was doing. She was amazing, perfect in every way possible.

Anything she needed, anything she wanted anything I could give was hers. What's worse is she never took advantage of it. You know when someone's a jerk to you, you can try and get over them because they're jerks. But with her, she was the perfect friend, never a taker, and always a giver. A great listener and always had time for me as I had for her.

Why didn't I ever go for it? Simple, in my life, great friends are hard to come by. Hell, good friends are hard to come by period. I wasn't just attracted to her because of her looks, and we were friends above all.

I had seen her go through shitty break-ups with girls who didn't deserve her, and all I could do was hold her and tell her it would get better. She loved with all her heart, and when it broke, it was hard on her. I was the one who held her hair when she threw up from drinking too much after a break-up. My bed was the one she shared when she didn't want to be alone. Now here she was again with another girl who didn't deserve her and treated her like crap.

I could tell you every detail about her and never miss a beat from her toes to the top of her head. Long brown wavy hair, always done. When she has a hard day, she pulls it back into a ponytail. Her eyebrows arch into a sharp peak, and her eyes are soft and brown in an almond shape, giving her an exotic appeal. She has a tiny scar on her nose that she hates, but I love it. I have a similar one on my chest. Her lips are so fucking luscious, not that I would know right. But I mess with her all the time I tell her she's Jay-Z's cousin because they're so big. Damn, I would give anything to bite down on one of those.

Her breasts are so beautiful and perfect a handful each, definitely smaller than my own. She's envious of my large breasts that I say are each as big as my head. My only answer is she can have them any time she wants. She always laughs, but I'm so serious. She's perfect the way she is, and I would never change anything about her.

I finally saw her come down the stairs from her place and she smiled when she saw me. That smile makes my heart warm, and I smile automatically. She was gorgeous in black skin-tight jeans and her Burberry Brit Shawl-Collar Belted Coat. I was with her when she bought it, and I had wondered what she would look like with only the coat on and nothing underneath. The outfit was completed with a pair of solid black Louboutin Heels. She was wearing almost a whole paychecks worth of work for me, her birthday present to herself.

Laura, her girlfriend, looks pissed as usual. Like most women I know, Mercedes likes to look good when she goes out and takes forever to get ready. When I wait, I play video games to pass the time. Over the last three years, she has bought me a Wii and a PS3 to entertain myself when I wait for her. Laura, on the other hand, just goes around grumbling about how long she's taking. She's not allowed to touch my toys.

"Hey Jenna, hey Doll." The only person who calls me Doll. I don't think I've used her name since we first met actually. She's shorter than I am standing at 5'3" and I'm 5'8", so her way of greeting me is not the usual kiss on the cheek. She wraps her hand around my neck and kisses it.

"Hey Sugar, Laura."

"MJ. Jenna" No, she doesn't like us.

"Hello ladies, everyone ready." Mercedes jumped in the back seat and Laura walked away, wasn't she coming, not that I minded if she didn't. "Laura?"

"Nah."

We didn't like her so Jenna, took off with nothing else said. It turns out Laura had a job that night, she was an on-call security guard and had to work a concert tonight. We had fun without her, and I later found out that Mercedes was done with her and her crap. It had become obvious to Mercedes that she would only be on-call to work when Mercedes wanted to spend time with her outside of the bedroom. So she was done with her. Fine by me.

That night she stayed in my bed after we all came home from the movies and dinner. Jenna was my roommate and stayed in her room. I had a guest bedroom, but I knew she preferred to sleep with me. This part is torture on me, but what can I say? I'm a glutton for punishment. Every time it's always the same, she wakes up curled into me, with my arms around her, and won't let me out of bed until we have to.

"Sugar let me up, I have to go to the gym." She's practically on top of me with half of her body on my right side, her leg wrapped around my right and her right arm on my stomach, yup she was making it difficult not to feel aroused, horny, WET.

"No, you look fucking amazing Doll, toned, tanned and trim as perfect as can be." Now she was tracing the muscles on my stomach.

"If I stayed out of the gym every time you wouldn't let me out of this bed, I wouldn't look this good." She laughed and looked into my eyes. Why can't she see how much I want her?

"I wouldn't love you any less." She kissed my neck.

"Sugar please." I tried to move, but she's so quick to hold me down. "I really can't stay." I tried to roll away.

"But baby it's cold outside." Please don't call me that I can't take it.

"I've got to go away, it's time for me to leave you know that." I was pleading, begging for her to understand what she was doing to me. Why was she so comfortable with me?

"But baby it's cold outside." Snow will never keep me indoors, and she knows that better than anyone.

"It's nice enough for me to workout." Now I was caressing her back, and I don't think this is getting me any closer to the door.

"I had been hoping that you'd stay. I'll hold your hands, they're just like ice." I'm cold-blooded, Doctor's say I have poor circulation; however, she is like an oven all the time nice and warm, makes my skin instantly feel better.

"I should really get going." I tried to roll her over, but she just rested more of herself on top of me.

"Beautiful, what's your hurry, listen to the heater roar. Doll, please...don't hurry." Why couldn't she see how much I wanted more than just words and hugs but her lips on my own. Her body in my arms for me to make her feel loved and protected, but because I was more than just a friend.

"How about some lattes?" She instantly sat up, and she knew my weakness. She made the best lattes, and I bought her an espresso machine, at her request, for her to have at my house.

"Put some music on while I make your favorite." She had fallen asleep in my dress shirt from last night after I had taken it off, and she had undressed into her undies. It barely covered her upper body and enough of her lower area to see her panties.

"Just a quick cup, I really have to go."

"Baby, it's bad out there." She leaned on the frame and gave me her best pout. Those lips were the death of me, and those big puppy dog eyes could force me to do anything.

She went out, and it took all of me not to want just to touch myself in this bed she had just vacated. I could smell her wonderful scent, lavender, and vanilla, I have no idea how she does it, but that's how she smells. My shirt will have her scent when she takes it off. I can still feel the warmth of her touch on my skin, and legs wrapped around mine. I could feel the moisture from her lips on my neck. I had my chance to leave and get ready, and I didn't.

I didn't need to go to the gym, but I had to get away from her. If I expected this friendship to stay intact, I needed to make a run for it. She had a key and could lock up when she left, hopefully before I got back. As I got up to shower and got dressed, she came back mugs in hand. I didn't even manage to get off the bed, so I sat on the edge and turned on a playlist on my iPhone, whatever was on my playlist last.

"Say, what's in this drink?"

It was her favorite playlist, of course, right, not to mention the best music for being romantic.

"No way you're going anywhere. You know your eyes are like jade stones."

I wish I knew how to break this spell. Why is she saying this and just watching me?

"You roll out of bed, your red hair looks amazing and perfect."

"What are you up to Sugar?"

"Mind if I move a little closer."

At least I'm going to say that I tried to keep this friendship safe, but she's just irresistible.

"What's the sense in hurting my pride."

I smiled and patted the bed next to me.

"I really can't stay."

"Baby don't hold out." She set both of our cups on the nightstand.

"I simply must go." I knew that I should leave, but I wasn't moving; on the contrary, she held my hands in hers.

"But, Baby, it's cold outside." She placed her right hand on my neck and kept my hands in her left.

"You're so nice and warm."

"Look out the window at that storm." I was so occupied with leaving I hadn't noticed I wasn't going anywhere. It was snowing a lot.

"Jenna will be suspicious." What am I saying?

"Man, your lips look so delicious," Tracing them with her thumb. "Strawberries with whipped cream waiting to be licked." I was just staring at her lips as if she was describing the thoughts in my mind. "Gosh your lips look delicious."

"Maybe we should finish our drinks." I placed my hands on her thighs, the hem of her panties, to be exact.

"Never such a blizzard before." She took her free hand to my neck, begging me to look at her, but I wanted nothing more than to take off that shirt and kiss her entire body.

"I've got to go."

"Oh, baby, you'll freeze out there." But I'm burning up in here. "It's up to your knees out there."

"But don't you see."

"Your eyes are like emeralds, look at me, let me see." I looked up at her big brown eyes, pleading for her to see what she was doing, begging her to let go of me. Never had she been this insistent. Never had she been this intimate, this close. This couldn't be, she was lost for sure, she didn't know what she was doing to me.

"How can you do this thing to me?" She took my hands in hers and placed them on her waist, returning hers to wrap around my neck, pulling me to her as I placed my leg up on the bed.

"My life has been a long sorrow, do you know why?" She was fine, calm, and collected, while I was a bomb ready to blow.

"I really can't stay."

"Get over that. It's cold out there." She was begging me for something I couldn't see, but the tear-filled eyes rooted me to this bed. "Can't you stay a while longer baby?"

"Well... I really shouldn't." I looked away from her, and she pulled my head right back.

"I'll make it worth your while baby." She leaned in, and my world was flipped upside down in that one instance.

Her lips were everything I had wished, soft and delicate, hesitant but persistent. I wrapped my arms around her waist. She pushed herself onto me, and I used one hand to set us down gently never to disturb our lips; once on the bed, I rolled on top of her.

Holding myself up on the one hand and undoing her shirt with the other, she was mine today if tomorrow she ran away, today she was mine. The first few buttons from the bottom led me to her soft stomach, sensitive as she felt my cold fingers on her warm body. A moan escaping her mouth into mine. Going straight to the consciousness of my mind, letting me know she wanted more.

I worked the rest of the buttons and felt her silky soft skin, the tops of her bosom, extracting a moan from me at being so close to having the woman I had dreamed of for so many restless nights. Was this really about to happen, but I couldn't just let it happen. I didn't just want one time, and if that's what it was, I had to stop.

"Open your eyes Sugar." I was worried about the answer I might get, but I needed to know. I stroked her face with my free hand.

"MJ, what's wrong?"

"What are we doing beautiful?"

"I thought it was obvious."

"We're friends, I don't want to lose you."

"Then don't screw me over and just screw me. I know it's taken us a while to get here but damn it I've wanted this from that day three years ago when you walked onto that field."

I needed nothing else. We were just too lost to find each other then, but we're here now, and she won't regret waiting.

I thrust my hips downward, applying direct pressure to her mound as I kissed her with all the love and lust I had for her.

"Ahh, do that again..." Damn the way, her eyes roll back and stretch her neck, leaving one luscious piece of her exposed neck. I just had to bite down as I worked my hips one more time and sucked hard.

"Are you sure that's how you want it?" I whispered into her ear, then nibbling on her lobe.

"No...damn I want you....I'm not sure of anything but that I love you." She loved me how many times has she said that, and I had hoped to hear it in a different context.

"Fuck, are you trying to make me fall in love with you, because let me tell you I've already fallen." She finally looked at me with a sincere look of happiness I hadn't seen in a while.

"You better be good in bed, because I don't plan on ever being with anyone else."

I worked my hips in a circular motion with a downward thrust, making sure to hit the spot to make her know she would not be let down.

"I'm not one to brag but you're gonna have to call in tomorrow and the day after. I've been dreaming of this for 3 years Sugar. Believe me I'll be better than good."

I sat and admired her gorgeous body, sexy with curves in all the perfect places, the exact opposite of me. I pulled my shirt over my head as she sat up and took off hers. I was going for my pants when she kissed the first one, then the other nipple. There was a look of awe in her big brown eyes. She held my breasts in her hands tenderly massaging them both, gently squeezing, but never going back to my nipple. Finally, after I thought she could not have been any more delicate, she was hungry for more.

She looked up and a big smile formed on her face, she was going for her prize. My nipples had been waiting patiently for their turn, well they were standing at attention to be exact. She took one into her mouth and bit while instantly pinching the other, I gave up on sitting up and fell forward, she never stopped lavishing attention to either breast. I was in a state of bliss, and every moan escaping my body was a testament to her skill. She closed her eyes and just had her way with me, and I realized I would let her do anything to me as long as she was in my bed.

I finally pulled away, she began to pout, and I stood to pull off my pants. Then I took off her panties. She was mine. Everything, her hips, her thighs, her lips, she would be mine, and I would bring her pleasure and adore her body.

"I have never seen a tastier looking pussy in my life." She looked hungry, and I was definitely on the menu.

"I have, it's between your thighs."

As I went to enjoy my breakfast, she stopped me just as I was about to taste.

"No, I know how I want it...our first time." The sincerity in her voice was exceptional. "I want to see your face, I want to feel your body on top me, I want to feel as much of you as possible."

She pulled me up, and I rested my body on top of hers, placing one leg between her thighs and working my right hand to her neck. I leaned down and bit her neck, and I was claiming my prize, marking my territory. I ran my hand down her body as my lips found hers.

There was a need now, a hunger it wasn't tentative or new it was the want to have more. I found the small strip of hair, leading me to the land of treasures. I moaned instantly, feeling how wet she was. Inserting one finger into the slickness that was her juices, so lost in the sensations that when she lifted her knee into my pussy I moaned her name.

"Fuck me. Say that again." I worked two fingers into her center, feeling every inch of her that was available to me. "Please Doll, say it again for me." I was done; from this day forward, I would never find anyone else who could make me do anything they wanted.

"Mercedes, make love to me."

"I am so in love with you." The way her breath sounded next to my ear was music to my fingers. She was starting a rhythm, forcing her body to dance with me. Her fingers found their way inside me, and we became one. She danced on this bed, making love playing the music from our hearts for our bodies to move.

Our bodies were moving together, harder, faster, reaching every inch of pleasure attainable. I could feel her body tensing, and her fingers jerking forward inside me. She was going to push the button and make me cum all over her hand. As if she was listening to my thoughts, the dam inside her burst.

"YES, YES, YES!" Sending me into a world of euphoria.

"Oh God, MERCEDES!" Her fingers managed to keep moving inside me, and I felt my body react to her. Grinding down on her hand, working my hips downward, applying pressure to my hand inside her and hers inside me.

She had a mischievous smile as I worked my body on top of her.

"Fuck, what's with the smile sugar?"

"Uhh, I am never letting you out of this bed."

"Good there are so many things I wanna do to you."

"Uhhh, yes...yes.....yes......fuck yes. Harder baby me cum."

Reaching for her clit with my thumb, I worked three fingers inside her making her arch her back into my body, bringing us even closer. This was the moment I knew I would never need anyone else. Just as I was cumming, she bit down on my shoulder, forcing pleasure and attention elsewhere from where her fingers were wreaking havoc on my body. Her free hand was digging into the skin on my back. I never thought I would like it rough but damn me to hell I hope she leaves her mark somewhere.

I rested on top of her body as she pulled her hand from my pussy, bringing it to her lips. She was one sexy woman sucking those fingers, cleaning my juices off. Curling my fingers forward, she placed those same fingers into my mouth, and I sucked on them like it was her clit. She pulled them out and pulled my head forward, kissing me with force and a pang of hunger I had yet to see. I thrust into her pussy and touched that wonderful spot. I stroked her insides, and a few moments later, my hand and knee were soaked.

I held still within her waiting for her to calm down, ever so slightly moving my fingers, feeling her body twitch with every movement. As I smiled at her, I had a power trip making her body twitch with every touch, it was wrong, oh so wrong but it felt good at the same time.

"Stop baby."

"I don't want to stop, I wanna make sure my first impression on your pussy is perfect. I'll see you soon."

I forced myself out of her embrace, and she turned her body sideways.

"Oh baby you obviously don't know me well enough do you?"

"Why do you say that?" She was laughing, thinking she was hiding from me, hiding her pleasure zone. I got her to roll onto her stomach by tickling her sides, leaving that gorgeous ass exposed.

"You must have never caught me staring at your ass, because or else you would have never left this perfect asssssssset exposed to me." I straddled her legs, not letting her turn around.

"fuck! What are you gonna do?" She was laughing, but she knew she was in for it.

I laid my body on top of hers, stretching her hands to the side. I kissed and nibbled on her ear, as she moaned and wiggled herself underneath me, allowing pressure to stimulate my already sensitized clit.

"I...my love...." (bit her neck) "am gonna show you" (licked the spot I had bit) "how much I love you." (bit her other ear) "You.." (bit her neck, grinding down on her ass spreading my juices onto her body) "are going to be loved.." (kissed my way down her back) "all" (kissed each cheek) "day" (licked from the bottom of her slit to the top) "long."

Her moans of pleasure were my sign of continuing.

I slid down her body and stood at the edge of the bed. I kissed my way up her legs from her ankles, calf, thigh, to her assets' curve, into her crack up down and back across the other curve down her legs. As I worked my way across her body, her legs slightly parted. Then I licked and bit a similar path over her legs and backside. Getting close to her pussy, her legs again parted a little more for me.

This time I knelt between her thighs.

"That's as far as you're gonna get Doll." She tried to use a serious tone.

"Of course my love I understand." I feigned indifference.

I started at her neck this time, kissing all of her back down to her delicious globes, gently kneading them with my hands and again her legs parted just a bit more as I spread my knees with them. I started tracing her back lightly with my fingertips alternating by using my nails, and I saw goosebumps start to form. I massaged and caressed her body, and she started to squirm, unknowingly opening herself up to me.

As I caress, lick, and kiss her body, I willed her body to open up to me and lift herself off the bed and onto her hands and knees. I tried to avoid removing any skin to skin contact, allowing her too much time to think about what I was doing. I slipped underneath her and dropped my legs to hang off the bed as I worked my upper body between her legs. I did one full sweep of her pussy lips with my tongue, holding her ass, not allowing her to move. I was only able to sneak in because her eyes were closed. When she realized what was going on, she had a beautiful smile across her face.

"I better be careful with you. You have this way of sneaking up on me, first my heart then my pussy."

"Sit up for me and go for a ride. I'm not sneaky you know, I told you I was gonna show you how much I loved you. It's not my fault you didn't believe me."

She sat up and rested herself on my abdomen. She grabbed my hands and entangled our fingers.

"As for your heart well I'd have to say you're pretty sneaky yourself because from the day we met you took little bits of it. I was lost when you weren't around me because you had my heart baby, you always have and always will."

She had tears in her eyes, and I wondered if I had said something wrong, or maybe it was tears of joy. She leaned down and kissed me, moaning when she tasted herself on my lips. She sat up again and pinched my nipples.

"Don't make me cry. You have a lot of making up to do for that." She was smiling."

"Don't bull shit baby just tell me 'I want you to eat my pussy'." She laughed and tweaked my nipples harder, and I was smiling. I just wanted to lighten the mood. "I promise Sugar, with me, you'll never shed another tear of sadness or pain because of me. Now mount up and let me show you how your pussy deserves to be treated."

"With pleasure." She sat up and damn it felt good to taste her again.

She was so wet, licking one lip then the other. I looked up, and her eyes were closed as she bit her bottom lip. Fuck she was sexy. I cradled her breast in one hand and held her ass to me with the other. She tasted so good, she held herself up and opened her pussy entirely to me. Licking her juices from her lips, I worked my tongue from her cute little ass to her clit, circling her clit but staying away.

She started working her hips to my rhythm, she wanted control, but I knew she just wanted release. So she brought her clit down to my lips, and I sucked her button into my mouth. She collapsed forward, holding herself up by her hands.

"Are you ok?" A muffled 'mmmhhhhmmmm' was all I could offer to reassure her that I was right where I loved to be.

Bringing both hands to her ass, I held her down onto me, sucked her clit between my lips, and flicked it with my tongue in circular, sideways, and back and forth motions making her body spasm. She was close, and I wanted everything she had to give. I thrust two fingers into her slippery tunnel, looked for her sweet spot, and a loud 'FUCK' from her mouth was music to my ears.

She gushed all over me, and like a starving woman, I drank up her juices. Her body jerked every time I took a long swipe, actually no matter what I did. She jerked and twitched. I let go of her, and she rolled onto her back. I got up and went to drink my coffee, noticing we had been together for the past two hours, making sweet love on my bed, not to mention the juicy wet spots. I was so busy finishing my cold coffee, and I almost spit it out when she reached over and licked my mound.

"My turn to eat, get on this bed. Now!"

"First we talk beautiful." I sat on the edge of the bed, and she straddled my lap. She wrapped her arms around my neck and whispered as she licked my earlobe.

"No, I want breakfast " She was pouting and kissing my neck.

"Please baby?"

"Only if I can sit here while we talk."

"Deal. Were your serious when you said that you didn't plan on ever being with anyone else?" She blushed and hid her face in the crook of my neck.

"I'm sorry but I was."

"Why are you sorry?"

"Maybe I was being too forward?"

"Look at me beautiful." When those big brown eyes looked at me, she had tears in her eyes.

"For three years we hid our true feelings for each other and now that I know, I'm not holding back. I'm in love with you Sugar. I have been since day one. You complete me in a way no one ever has. You make everything better when you're around. I haven't had one successful relationship since we met, because none of the girls were you. In my eyes you're perfect just the way you are, you don't have to change for me and it would be an honor to have you by my side. I promise to treat you right baby each and every day."

"Promise me you won't change, that you'll continue to be my best friend. Promise me that you'll never take me for granted. That's all I want, for you to be the same person you are now, the person I fell in love with. The person who has always appreciated me. Please baby can you promise me that."

"I promise baby, I'll always be your best friend before anything. I'll be the person you fell in love with."

"Then I promise to love you forever and ever." As her lips touched mine, I couldn't help but moan as it sent an instant bolt of pleasure throughout my body. I pulled her to me, holding that glorious ass that was now mine. I would never have to share her with anyone. Her tongue inside my mouth was searching for something, anything, it could have everything it found.

"We should probably go eat something before we go again, Love." I pulled away as we took a quick breath.

"Say it Again." She held my face in her hands.

"Love." I bit her lip.

"Mmmm, I love the sound of that baby."

"Come on get dressed baby, I'll take you to lunch." She pushed me back onto the bed with a wicked grin.

"But, Baby it's cold outside."

Story 02

To say that I have always been shy is an understatement. Still a virgin at 17, two days shy of my 18th birthday it is not because I haven't had loads of offers from guys to get in my panties and pop my cherry as they so eloquently put it, it is just that I don't get the warm fuzzy vibes from guys. Girls and women of every shape and size, however, have always sent my heart racing, and I didn't know what to do about it, so for all my life, I have just observed, lusted, and fantasized about making it with a loving woman.

I guess there is no other way to put it than I have always been a short-haired athletic shy dyke wannabee. I can remember attending a slumber party at 13 years old and was silent as the subject turned to boys, the way they kissed, and their penis sizes. I excused myself and went to the bathroom, and there was a hamper of dirty clothes. Curious, I looked in, and there was a pair of Stacey's silky white panties with light yellow stains across the crotch. I hesitated as my heart began to beat wildly, and looked around the small bathroom as if anyone was watching, then with shaking fingers, I slowly removed them and brought them to my nose. I took a very short sniff then threw them back in the hamper, berating myself for being such a pervert. But after a brief pause, I picked them up again, and returned them to my nose, inhaling deeply and feeling my young pussy juice up for the first time. The smell of sexy Stacey's dried urine and vagina secretions was intoxicating, and with closed eyes, I took in her wonderful sent for a good 30 seconds.

I was disgusted with myself, I tossed them back in the hamper, then sat to pee, berating my scummy lowlife self for my sick behavior. I wiped, then joined the other girls, inwardly feeling like I had written across my forehead "sick and demented" for everyone to see.

That incident was only one of the hundreds through the years of making me feel like a lost demented outcast with deep hidden secrets and desires for women that no one could ever understand.

Through my experiences, I learned to sneak peeks at my classmates, teachers, and other beautiful girls and women, keep my lusting thoughts to myself and be satisfied with my vivid fantasies.

The internet and my lustful imagination provided my only sexual outlet. I surfed the lesbian sites and printed out beautiful women making out, locked in tight embraces, licking each others' pussies and fucking each other with big dangling strap-ons. I would hide these pictures under my mattress and take them out to finger myself as I envisioned one of my classmates or sexy teachers locked in a similar embrace.

Two days later, the big day arrived. I turned 18 and was "legal." But legal for what I wondered. I wasn't gorgeous at 4'11" and 105 pounds, but I wasn't ugly either. I had always been referred to as a little pixie and "adorable" or "cute as a button."

My tiny little flat breasted, slightly muscular body, though, did have one advantage. It made me the perfect candidate for gymnastics, and I excelled at it, my one claim to fame. In addition to loving throwing my body through space, I loved looking at my naked classmates in the locker room and shower after a meet or after practice. Today was no exception.

We had a tremendous sweaty practice session preparing for an upcoming dual meet, and I loved looking at my beautiful teammates lather up their hair, breasts, and hairy or shaved pussies. Every one of them was in incredible shape from all our hard work. Coach Jo Summers, the most beautiful woman on earth and stringent taskmaster, put us through grueling workouts and made sure that we were all in fantastic shape.

I watched the last of my teammates head back to the locker room to dry off and dress, so I was ready to turn off my shower, when I heard, "Okay Reynolds".....that's me.....Kathy or Kat Reynolds. "Let's move your ass. Maintenance will be in to clean in 20 minutes."

I turned and gasped audibly. Coach Summers was bare assed naked, placing a towel on one of the hooks, and ready to shower. She NEVER had showered with us before but decided to work out today, so I guess she got sweaty.

I knew she had an incredible body, but seeing it without clothing was beyond any fantasy I had ever experienced. She was about 5'6", maybe 135 pounds of sleek feminine muscle. She reminded me of the beautiful bodybuilder from years ago, Rachel McLish, or Maybe Cory Everson.

She caught me staring when she turned, stopped with an exasperated look on her face and her hands on her bronzed hips. "Stop your frigging gawking and finish your shower."

I was never more embarrassed in my life, and all I could say was "Right coach" and turn back to the shower.

I didn't reach for the Fawcett to turn it off, though, and instead reached for the soap to lather myself up again. I just had to buy more time to look at this beautiful goddess.

Facing her shower, I watched her beautiful biceps relax and flex as she washed her short brown hair. Her bubble butt ass was perfectly formed and had indentions on each side, accenting their tight muscularity. Her thighs and calves were also perfect, shaped wonderfully from years of gymnastics competitions and coaching. Her toenails were painted a bright scarlet letting it be known that this muscular Amazon was also 100% woman. Her beautiful round breasts did not need a bra as they were perfectly shaped from pull-ups on the uneven bars. Her areolas were a deep rich brown, and her pubic patch was thick and black, though nicely shaped.

Suddenly she stopped lathering her gorgeous body and turned to look at me again, and caught me staring once again.

"Reynolds! What the fuck...pardon my French, is wrong with you? Quit staring and finish up."

"I'm sorry Coach. I'm just about done."

All I could think of as I turned to wash off the remaining soap was how beautiful Coach Jo was, and what an incredible fuck up I was for my ogling her.

"I heard some of the girls talking to you about it being your birthday. Is that right Reynolds?"

"Yes Coach."

"Got any plans to celebrate?"

"No, my Mom is a nurse and will be working the night shift, and I never knew my Dad."

"That sucks Reynolds. No one should celebrate their 18th birthday alone. Finish up, and get dressed and you and I will hit a bar I know."

I couldn't believe my ears. Was I being asked out? Almost like a real date? Okay, maybe it wasn't a date, but as I have said, I do have a rich fantasy life. My imagination began to run wild as Coach, and I exited the shower, and she went to her office, and I went to my locker.

Once reaching my locker, I continued to be a nervous wreck. I grabbed my panties and examined them to make sure there weren't any brown skid marks or yellow piss stains. What the hell do I think would happen? Did I imagine Coach Jo ripping off my undies and making mad passionate love to me? My friggin' imagination was in overdrive.

I quickly dressed, then went outside the locker room to wait for Coach. My eyes must have been the size of half dollars, and I believe my jaw dropped as I saw Coach Summers exit the locker room dressed in black leather from head to toe, complete with a pair of spiked black patent leather heels.

Coach caught me staring again and smiled at my look of admiration and casually said, "Just something I keep in my closet for when I feel like partying. Come on, let's go."

With her hand on my back, she guided me to her Civic, unlocked my side, and opened the door for me to get in. Then she got in her side and opened the glove box and pulled out a pack of Marlboros and a couple of CDs.

I was shocked when she withdrew a cigarette from the pack, lit it up, and let out a long exhale of smoke from her mouth and nostrils. Don't look so surprised. I smoke when I hit the bars. I would offer you one Reynolds, but you are in training, and I KNOW your coach would kick your ass if she caught you smoking. I couldn't help but laugh, and couldn't help think how sexy she looked smoking in her hot leather outfit.

I watched as she studied the cigarette in silence, and finally, she spoke.

"Reynolds, I made have read you wrong, but I have noticed through the season how you look admiringly at your teammates, and how you kept stealing looks at me in the shower today. I've never seen you with a guy, so correct me if I'm wrong, but I think you like women as much as I do."

I immediately turned red, and shyly looked down at my lap. "I didn't know I was being so obvious Coach. I'm sorry if I made you uncomfortable looking at your body."

"Hell Reynolds. Don't act like you committed the crime of the century. It's not every day that a 33 year old lesbian is admired by a sexy little eighteen year old. I am very flattered."

"Really Coach?"

"Damn right Reynolds. I've always had the hots for your sexy firm little body, but being your coach and teacher, and you being a minor, I was smart enough not to make any moves. Now that you are a legal 18, you are open season if you want to be. I don't want to force myself and my beliefs on you."

I suddenly felt like a dream had come true, and I couldn't believe what I was hearing. It was hard for me to fathom that this beautiful woman could be attracted to my tiny boyish body.

"One of the best things about teaching and living in Falls Church, Va, is that it is so close to DC, which has a great Lesbian community with ample entertainment. If you are up for it, I would like to take you to one of my favorite places in DC called Phase 1. It's an awesome lesbian bar in Southeast, and I can treat you to dinner and beer since you are legal now."

I was so happy I think my smile could have lit up all of Northern Virginia. Good things just don't happen to Kat Reynolds. I didn't want to wake from my wonderful dream, though, so I quickly said I would love to go.

"Good" Tossing her cig from the window, she started the car, popped in a CD of "Tegan and Sarah" and off we went.

We stopped off for dinner around 7:30 at a HOPS restaurant, known for their good food and a huge assortment of beers. Coach got the stares as we entered, but they didn't seem to faze her, and I felt so awesome being seen with her.

We were seated in a booth, and Coach told the waiter to bring us two Powder Horn Pilsners. After the waiter left, we studied the menu, and the coach recommended the ribs, which were 'to die for.' I took a chance and ordered a half rack and Coach a full rack when the waiter returned with our drinks. I couldn't believe this was happening as I sipped on my first brew.

"Like it?"

I smiled, which was becoming contagious around Coach, and said, "Yeah, it tastes great" as I downed almost half of it."

"Whoa lady! Slow down a little. I don't want to have to carry you out of here."

"Sorry Coach. It just really tasted good to me."

"Well we have a full night of partying ahead of us, so just take it slow and drink it with your meal. It will affect you less on a full stomach."

Coach lit another cigarette and exhaled a beautiful plume of smoke, then sipped her beer. I knew it was unhealthy, but I never wanted to smoke more in my life. I wanted to dress in leather, say fuck and what the hell, and become this woman of my dreams.

The waiter brought our ribs and fries with a plentiful supply of napkins. The coach was right. The sauce they use was incredible, and the meat was so tender it fell off the bones. The only problem was they were super messy, but that only made it more fun and sexy. The coach would slowly move her long tongue over her mouth to wipe the sauce away, and then slowly lick her fingers erotically.

I didn't want to be outdone, so I mirrored her actions, which brought a smile and chuckled from her face. "Now you're learning Reynolds."

I was floating. The delicious food, beer, and Coach's wonderful company made it the best meal and birthday I had ever had, but it was only beginning.

After putting the bill on her charge card, we headed back to her car, and once again, she opened the door for me and then went to her side to get in. We hit Southeast DC around 9 PM, and there was a big circular sign outside a building, reading Phase 1.

Soon after we entered, the tattooed butch Manager, named Syd, approached us and smiled and embraced Coach. I was shocked as they put a lip lock on each other complete with visible tongue action.

Finally separating, Syd looked at Coach and said, "You've been mighty scarce Grrl, but you are hot as ever. Who's your little play friend? She's quite a cutie."

Coach put her had on my back and slowly rubbed up and down, sending warm erotic waves through my body. "This is one of my favorite athletes I coach, and we are celebrating her birthday....and possibly her coming out tonight. Am I right Reynolds?"

I shyly smiled and took Syd's hand to greet her and answered a quiet "Right Coach."

The place was already a buzz of activity with women of all shapes and sizes and forms of dress, eating, drinking, dancing, and making out. It was as if I had died, gone to heaven, and finally found a place where I belonged. I couldn't remove the smile from my face as I took it all in.

Syd led us to a booth, and I slid in and was thrilled when Coach slid in beside me instead of sitting across from me.

"What do you think Reynolds? A little crazy eh?"

I felt like a surprised kid on Christmas morning and looked around with my same goofy grin, saying, "Crazy, maybe... but I love it."

"Good Kiddo, because I want to make this a birthday you will never forget."

Coach ordered us two "Buds" and an order of chips, then an emcee came on stage and got the crowd worked up announcing that "Killer Katie" would be taking on "Dynamite Donna" in a winner take all Jell-O wrestling contest.

The crowd hooted and hollered as the warriors entered the arena below, topless and dressed in the skimpiest of panties. Both women looked sexy, athletic, and buff, and both scowled at each other with fierce looks of determination.

The match started, and I had never seen anything so sexy. This wasn't staged, and both women knew some moves in addition to being extremely well built.

Coach leaned over and yelled in my ear about the roaring crowd, "My money's on Killer Katie."

They continued to give and take for 20 minutes until finally, Dynamite Donna ran out of gas and gave a verbal submission, which brings more roars from the crowd.

As things settled down to a gentle roar, I turned to our coach, and feeling a bit of a beer buzz said, "Bet I could kick your ass in a match Coach."

"Think so Tiny Lady?"

"I may be tiny, and you be strong as an ox, but I have great stamina, am YEARS younger, and can move like greased lighting."

"Okay big talker, let's see how you get out of this hold," She moved her head in to join our lips in a gentle kiss. Seeing that I put up no resistance, she moved closer and began to probe with her tongue, causing my body to feel like an electric switch had been thrown to ignite all my lustful senses. Eighteen years of dreaming of my first kiss created an explosion in my body as my fantasies could have never lived up to the wonderful feelings I experienced.

Coach explored my mouth aggressively with her talented tongue and then removed it, so my tongue could follow into her mouth. When she trapped and began sucking on my tongue, I thought I would pass out. All of my defenses had vanished, and all I could do was give little girl moans and squeals of sheer bliss.

Coach took her advantage and did not let up for a second as she placed her strong fingers at my crotch and began to rub up and down, causing my legs to spread as I gasped for air. I never dreamt it could be so heavenly with another beautiful woman, and then she ended the kiss leaving me weak and spent.

"Still think you can kick my butt little Grrl?"

"God Coach. You are the undisputed Champ and there can be no equal."

Coach laughed and said, "Whadda ya say we finish our beers and have a dance? A slow one should be coming up next if your game."

"I've never danced Coach, but if you will lead I am willing to give it a try."

"That's my Grrl.

We polished off our beers then headed to the dance floor, with Coach stopping and holding out her arms for me to join her.

I moved into her embrace tentatively, but once she wrapped her strong arms around me and began to lead me around the dance floor, I felt more relaxed and secure. I never wanted the song to end or our embrace to stop. When the song ended, Coach leaned into me and whispered, "Do you have any problems in getting out of here and going to my place for a nightcap?"

This is what I had waited for all my life and what I had spent countless nights fantasizing about, and now that it had arrived, I was thrilled and scared shitless. I had seen countless pictures of women making love but had never actually come close to it. I was so afraid of doing everything wrong and letting Coach down.

I looked down and gave a tentative, "Okay Coach."

Coach read my apprehension wrong and said, "We don't have to go Reynolds."

"It's not that I don't want to go Coach. It's just that I'm scared."

Shocked, Coach said, "Do you think I would harm you in any way?"

"Oh hell no!!! It's just that should we become romantic....which would be great, I am so inexperienced that I know I will screw it up and just disappoint you."

Coach drew me in and lifted my chin, so I was staring into her beautiful big brown eyes. "We all have our hang-ups Little Bit. I worry that I am too old for you and that I will have to corrupt a cute young girl on my conscience for the rest of my life.

"Oh Coach. Never feel like that. Even at 33 you are the hottest female alive, and I have waited my whole life to find love with another woman, so don't think of it as corrupting me as much as being an answer to an endless prayer."

"In that case, let's hit the road and let the chips fall where they may."

I tried to relax, but I think both of us were a little tense as we were mainly silent most of the way to her condo in Falls Church. It was a lovely one-bedroom at Park Towers, and we entered and walked down the hall to 613 with her hand on my lower back, guiding me and probably trying to reassure me that everything would be fine.

I was so thankful that Coach knew what she was doing and how to proceed. As we entered her unit, she closed the door, and to prolong the anxiety, she took me in her arms and once again kissed me, slowly at first, then going deeper and deeper until I felt like my knees would buckle from the arousal I was feeling.

Coach felt as if I was faltering, so without breaking the kiss, she picked me up and guided my legs so they would be wrapped around her. Her strength and beauty continued to amaze me.

Both of our tongues slowly dueled and danced in a circular motion as I gasped for air and sucked down her delicious saliva. The sandals I was wearing slipped off my feet, so I joined my bare feet in a tight embrace, which my spread pussy rubbing against her stomach driving me crazy with the friction.

Coach broke the kiss, and I was almost relieved to gulp some air, but she continued her attack by slowly moving the tip of her tongue up and down the inside of my ear while breathing warm, intoxicating air. Then she moved her tongue into the center hole of my ear, causing me shriek, "Oh my God!" I never felt anything so incredible.

She nipped and bit at my earlobe, continuing to bathe my whole ear with her talented tongue, then she would slowly move to my neck, taking gentle bites and sucking on my sensitive flesh. I was writhing, closed-eyed, and swaying under her assault, and had to taste her delicious flesh once again, so I tried to follow her lead as closely as I could.

I explored her ear with moist hungry lips, tongue, and teeth, in awe of my newly found intoxicating behavior. I was losing all control as I licked and bit her neck, perhaps a little too roughly, but was thrilled when I heard her sigh "Oh yeah Babe. Fantastic."

I wanted to explore and taste every inch of this delicious woman as I ate, licked, and attacked her flesh while digging my fingernails into the back of her neck. I trailed a line of bites and kissed up her neck and attacked her yielding mouth having changed from a meek little naive child into a hungry, aggressive animal.

As I continued to devour her tongue lips and gums, she continued to hold me with one hand supporting my buttocks and the other hand, removing my button-down shirt, which quickly fell to the floor, followed by my bra. I no longer cared that I was flat as a plank. All I cared about was satisfying my uncontrollable lust.

The coach had no problem with my 32A cup breasts as she circled my hard pink nipples slowly, then gave them a sharp pinch bordering on pain, causing me to cry out in pleasure as we continued to kiss.

She then unsnapped my pants and pushed then down over my tiny ass. I had to straighten my legs in front of her for them to fall away, then quickly slid the panties down and now totally naked, I once again wrapped my legs around her body.

I never wanted the intoxicating kiss to end, so I did my best to remove her leather top. Fortunately, she wasn't wearing a bra, and I was finally able to finally feel the beautiful round full breasts I had been mesmerized by earlier in the shower.

I circled her hard nipples with my forefinger, then pinched the as she had done mine, while simultaneously biting down roughly on her tongue. It caused her a sudden moan of pleasure, which sent a thrill through my body, seeing that I could give this beautiful creature back some of the pleasure she was offering me.

Both of us were building to a feverish pitch, and Coach continued to kiss me as she carried me naked to her bedroom.

Setting me down on the floor, I refused to release her hot moist lips as I undid leather pants and, with some effort, pushed them down to her feet. I did have to release the kiss to remove her shoes and pants the rest of the way. As I bent before her, I realized she wasn't wearing any panties either, and as I completed the task of slipping off her pants, I was once again in awe of her magnificent body.

On my knees, I was hypnotized by being eye level with her red-brown hair pussy, moist and glistening from our past 25 minutes of uninterrupted passion. I had never been so close to another woman's pussy, and had never smelled another woman except for the times when I could dig through a dirty hamper or locker. God, she smelled hot and magnificent. I looked up with questioning eyes, and it was if she read my mind, smiling at me, so I slowly moved my mouth to her bush and gently kissed all around the furry triangle.

I looked up once again, and she had closed her eyes and thrown her head back, moaning "Mmmmm...nice."

She drew my head into her body. I licked with long, even slow strokes from the bottom of her opening to just below her clit. I was hoping to save the best for last. I didn't want to waste a single drop of her golden nectar as I greedily savored and swallowed all of her warm tasty love juice.

I licked every delicious inch up and down, then shoved my tongue deep into her hot wet hole, causing her to ram my face hard into her pussy as she screamed, "Yeeeesssssss! Fuck my Pussy"

I proceeded to ram her hard repeatedly with my long probing tongue as I now began to diddle her clit in circular and up and down motions, just as I had always done when I jacked myself off.

I knew she was about ready to cum as she flexed one magnificent biceps behind her head as she moaned with pleasure and gasped for breath, while ramming my head into her pussy, my hard tongue fucking her faster and faster. I knew I was going to die by either drowning in her love juices or by suffocation from having my face rammed into her pussy, but I felt like right at that moment, my life was complete, and I would die happy.

Just when I thought my tongue and face couldn't take any more, she let out an ear-shattering "Ohhhhhhhh...Fuck Yes...yes!!" and I tasted a further gushing of her love juice.

After about 30 seconds, her spasms and breathing became normal once again. I had finally found my community and where I would fit in and had given a gorgeous woman an orgasm in the process. I knew that Coach did not like to be outdone, and I saw from the look in her eyes that she was going to take on my pussy and devourer as no other woman could. Yes, this was going to be one hell of an eighteenth birthday.

Story 03

"Ahhh, the great outdoors," said Meghan breathing deeply. "It's good to get back to nature."

"If you say so, "said Christy. She slapped at the mosquito that had landed on her arm and continued pulling gear out of her car's trunk. They had packed enough to camp for a few days in the mountains, so there wasn't much to unpack. The sun was almost at full strength, and Christy had discarded her jacket on the ride up. She felt exposed in a white tank top and cutoffs after being covered up all winter long. "Remind me why we're doing this again."

"Why? We're doing this so that we can enjoy the fresh air and the smell of pine," said Meghan.

"We can also enjoy pine sap and the smell of bug repellent," replied Christy.

"We can sleep under the stars and roast marshmallows," said Meghan.

"We can see snakes and experience a lack of hygiene," said Christy.

"We're getting away from our routines," said Meghan

"We're also getting away from cell phone service," said Christy.

"Best of all, it's the perfect way to get out of town and forget about that jerk you used to date," said Meghan. "Besides, where else can we relax in our lawn chairs and enjoy these?" She pulled a cooler out of the trunk and opened it. Inside were three bottles of wine, a couple of six-packs of beer, and a bottle of vodka.

"Good Lord! I was wondering what was in there. You do realize that we're only going to be gone for a few days, right?" asked Christy.

"Then I guess we better get drinking," said Meghan reaching for a beer.

"Not so fast! First, we set up camp. When that's done we can dig into the cooler."

"If you insist," said Meghan with a shake of her golden curls.

Within a half-hour, the women were lounging in lawn chairs wearing their sunglasses. Meghan and Christy had a couple of empty beer bottles at their feet and another couple in their chair cup holders. The sun was beating down on them, and the only sound was the buzz of insects.

"By the way, I really like your new look. It makes your green eyes really pop. I'd cut my hair into a bob if my hair was dark like yours," said Meghan as she took off her sunglasses.

"And give up your blonde bombshell persona? The public wouldn't allow it! I'm glad you like it, though. You seem to be the only one," said Christy.

"What's-his-face didn't like your hair? Shocking. Oh well, that just another reason why you're better of without him," said Meghan.

"Brian preferred long hair like yours. Actually, he made sure to mention that he preferred your hair."

Meghan rolled her eyes. "I don't know why you put up with that guy for as long as you did. You are smart and sexy and he didn't appreciate you."

"You think I'm sexy?" Christy asked.

Meghan smirked and put her sunglasses back on. Christy stared at her friend; Meghan's comment had taken her by surprise. Christy had always thought of Meghan as the sexy one and that she was just the sidekick. She wasn't tall, and tan like Meghan and men's' gazes seem to glide right over her to land on Meghan. With her blonde hair and warm, brown eyes, Meghan had always attracted a male following. She had the outgoing, bubbly personality to match Christy envied her for that. She wished that she could be that carefree.

She looked at her friend with admiration. Only Meghan could look buxom on a camping trip; her khaki shorts rode up on her long, lean legs. Her camp shirt stretched against her shapely breasts, and Christy realized that it was very sheer, too. Meghan's nipples were hard and poked through the fabric.

"Meg, are you wearing a bra?" Christy asked.

"No," Meghan replied with a smile, "I'm getting back to nature and I take it very seriously. Undergarments are far too restricting."

"I suppose that means you're not wearing any panties, either."

"That's right, I'm not wearing any and it feels great."

"That must be nice," said Christy.

"You should give it a try," said Meghan.

Christy thought it over. She had always wanted to be as carefree as her friend, and now she had her chance. Meghan was right: being in the great outdoors could be liberating. Suddenly, all her worries seemed so trivial. It was difficult to worry while listening to the rustling of trees in the wind and the chirping of birds.

She eyed her friend and imagined how it must feel to feel the sun warming her skin through her clothes. She couldn't help but picture what Meghan's body looked like underneath her clothes. She imagined that her breasts were full and smooth. She could also picture her erect nipples and wondered what it felt like to take them into her mouth.

Christy tried to clear the images out of her mind. Meghan was her friend, and she shouldn't be thinking about her that way. That didn't stop her from thinking about letting her mind wander to the smooth curves of Meghan's hips and her flat stomach. Christy blushed as her mind dipped a little further.

"I think I will," said Christy, summoning her courage. She stood up and turned to walk towards the tent.

"Where do you think you're going?"

"To change out of these undergarments."

"There's nothing from stopping you from doing that right here," said Meghan. She motioned Christy to stand in front of her chair. "Show me what you got," she challenged.

"Oh, what the hell," said Christy. She stood in front of Meghan and turned away from her. She slipped off her tee and tossed it at Meghan. She slid off her cargo shorts and kicked off her shoes and socks until she was clad in just a pink racerback bra and a polka-dot bikini. She faced Meghan and struck a pose.

"Va-va-va-voom, " said Meghan. She gave Christy a whistle, and Christy turned away to remove her bra and panties. As she reached for the front clasp her clasp bra, Meghan stopped her.

"That's it? Are you going to tease me without showing me the goods?"

Christy laughed nervously and turned to face Meghan again. Meghan grinned at her.

"That's better. Now let's get started," said Meghan. She spread her legs a little and beckoned to Christy. "Dance for me. Take it off real slow," she joked.

At first, all Christy could do was rock back and forth. She took deep breaths of the crisp mountain air and felt braver. Christy gently rocked her hips and leaned forward to give her shoulders a shimmy. She closed her eyes and continued to twist her body, laughing as she shook her head.

When she opened her eyes, Meghan stared at the sway in her breasts, and Christy's mood turned sober. She reached behind her to undo the clasp of her bra and felt a flush that reached her toes.

Christy locked eyes with Meghan as she reached between her breasts and unhooked the clasp. She slid it off and ran her sweating hands over her breasts and tilted her head back in ecstasy. She hooked her thumbs around the waistband of her panties and pulled them down, and then she tossed them over to Meghan and noticed that they were damp and heavy. Meghan snatched them up and brought them to her face.

"Getting a little excited, Chrsity?" she asked as she brought them to her nose. "Of course, I could tell that just by looking at you," Meghan said. Her eyes lingered on Christy's firm breasts, where her nipples were pointing out almost painfully, before traveling down to the tuft of hair between her legs. Christy looked down to see that the inside of her thighs was slick and shiny. Meghan stood up and sauntered over to Christy and knelt in front of her.

"This is why I can't understand why that boyfriend of yours didn't treat you right. You have such a sexy body. Take your breasts, "said Meghan. She slipped a nipple into her mouth and twirled her tongue around it. "How could anyone resist doing this? They're so receptive." She sucked hard and grazed the nipple with her teeth. Christy's hips bucked forward, and a moan escaped her lips.

Christy guided Meghan over to her other breast, and Meghan sucked and twirled her tongue around it. She trailed a string of kisses from Christy's chest down to her stomach. "And who could resist tasting every inch of this creamy skin?"

She dipped her head even lower until she had her nose at the lips of Christy's pussy. She stroked the neat triangle of dark hair on her mound. She inhaled deeply, closing her eyes and relishing the aroma. She stuck out her tongue and gently ran it up the length of Christy's slit. "God Christy, your so fucking wet!" Meghan exclaimed. She slowly circled Christy's clit with her tongue.

Christy groaned and stroked Meghan's hair. "We shouldn't be doing this here," she told Meghan between moans.

Meghan looked up. "Do you want me to stop?"

"I just think we should move to the tent," said Christy with a grin. "It's more comfortable there."

The women raced to the tent and collapsed onto their sleeping bags. Meghan wrenched open Christy's legs and lapped at her pussy lips. Christy's pussy was engorged, and Meghan had no trouble sliding her fingers around her hole. Before she could even slide a finger inside, Christy began to buck.

"Oh God! Meg, I'm coming!" Meghan gripped Christy's thighs and buried her face into Christy as her pussy convulsed with pleasure. Christy spasmed, and Meghan felt her face getting soaked. Christy grabbed Meghan's hair and pushed her face harder into her slit. She ground her clit into Meghan's face until her convulsions subsided.

Christy collapsed onto the sleeping bag, and Meghan released her grip. Meghan crawled up Christy's body, slipping a nipple into her mouth. She let it go with a pop and kissed Christy on the lips.

"Was that your first time with a woman?" Meghan asked.

"Yes! I've never done anything like that," laughed Christy.

"How was it?" Meghan asked with a raised eyebrow.

"Oh, it was wonderful! In fact, it was so wonderful that I'd like to return the favor," said Christy. She helped Meghan get out of her clothes and marveled at her friend's body. Her breasts were even more perfect than she'd imagined. Her nipples were tightly puckered and were coral-colored. She rubbed her thumbs over them, and Meghan groaned.

"Rough me up," Meghan purred.

"Yes ma'am," said Christy as she dove for Meghan's breasts. She fondled Meghan's breasts as she teased the nipples with her tongue and teeth. She reached between Meghan's legs, but Meghan stopped her.

"Not so fast. I've got a little something, said Meghan. She reached for the backpack that was in the corner of the tent and unzipped it. She pulled out a vibrator and handed it to Christy.

"Now let's get back to business," said Meghan as she spread her legs. Christy turned the toy over in her hand. It was shaped like a penis and was made of a pink rubber that was firm yet smooth. She flipped on the vibrator and sunk between Meghan's legs.

She lightly touched Meghan's clit with the tip of the toy, and Meghan sighed. Christy sunk a finger into Meghan's pussy and spread juices up Meghan's slit. She caressed Meghan's puffy lips and stroked her shaved pussy.

Christy felt herself getting wet again as she played with Meghan. She moved the vibrator along Meghan's slit and bent down to suckle on her stiff clit. She slid the vibrator into Meghan and watched for Meghan's hungry reaction. She slid the vibrator in further and pressed the head against her g-spot.

Meghan caressed her breasts as Christy slipped the vibrator in and out of Meghan's pussy. Meghan shuddered and arched her backed. She pinched her nipples harder, and Christy held the vibrator inside Meghan and tongued her clit.

Meghan's thighs clamped around Christy's head as she climaxed. She moaned and lifted her hips to meet Christy's mouth. She cried out and squeezed her breasts one last time before her body relaxed. Christy turned off the vibrator and tossed it aside.

"Wow," gasped Meghan.

"Tell me about it," said Christy.

"Have you changed your mind yet?" Meghan asked.

"About what?" Christy asked.

"About camping, of course," said Meghan, propping herself up on her elbows.

"I have seen the light. Thank you mother nature! I'm definitely going to like getting back to nature," she said as she leaned in to kiss Meghan on the cheek.

Story 04

I really don't know where to start, so I guess I will start at the beginning. Okay, here goes.

My name is Zara, and it's a Dutch name. Well, the first name is. My father was a Canadian construction worker working in Holland when he met my mother and hard for her. My parents came to this country from Holland 15 years ago, when I was barely eight years old. Mama and Papa didn't have a lot of money, so I am an only child. They worked hard to put me through school, and now I'm going to try and become a Pastry Chef.

In High School, I was friendly but kept mostly to myself. But I did manage to make one good, true-blue friend. That's Danielle, or Dani, as some call her.

Dani and I hit it off immediately. She once told me she thought my accent was sexy, and it certainly seemed to attract the boys. Dani and I never lacked for dates, although she got a bit more attention than I did.

Okay, you all probably want to know what I look like, right?

I'm a pretty brunette of medium height, with a slender build. I've got beautiful breasts that suit my figure perfectly if I do say so myself. I know I have good legs and a sexy little ass – which I've used to my advantage by adding a wiggle to my walk. My hair is brown, sometimes auburn, sometimes Chestnut-brown, like now. I like long hair, and mine almost reaches my butt, but why should I cover up one of my best assets though?] I have full, pouty lips, but mine is natural, no collagen. My eyes are blue, with a hint of Grey.

I like to wear stiletto heels, short skirts and one boyfriend told me he liked it when I wore tight, white pants. I don't have a lot of money, but I do have some nice thongs. I've always wanted to own a beautiful collection of lingerie, as Dani does.

Dani's the kind of girl that draws your immediate attention when she walks into the room. She has a wonderful personality, with good looks to back it up.

Danielle is almost 6 feet tall, almost all of its leg. In heels, she's breathtaking, and she knows it. So she almost always wears heels. She also likes wearing her hair long, and hers is a cornsilk blonde, also nearly down to her butt. Her face is so lovely, and she's always smiling. She has cornflower blue eyes, beautiful mouth with even, perfect teeth. She's got MUCH bigger boobs then I do, and she likes to wear sheer blouses with lacy lingerie underneath, or something low cut. Dani almost ALWAYS wears skirts too, and she has the money to buy stockings, which she looks great in. Her favorite outfit is a sheer black top, black lace bra underneath, and her black leather mini, with silk stockings and black stilettos, the ones with the silver tip. I've always thought those stilettos were so sexy, and I wanted a pair. Every time Danielle and I would go shopping, and I'd look in the shoe store window and stare admiringly, knowing I wouldn't be able to afford them for a while. One of these days, I thought to myself.

There are many reasons why Dani is my best friend in the world, but one of them is her party-girl nature – she's a wild one and loves life – and her big, wonderful heart.

With Dani, pretty well anything goes. She's well-traveled, her folks have wads of money. They own a very well-known Travel Agency, so Danielle gets around. When she came home from her last trip, she had a little surprise in town: Racquel, her new girlfriend.

Dani had gone on a "Party Trip" to Vegas with some of her girlfriends. It was one of those "whatever-happens-in-Vegas" trips, and Dani took full advantage of it. She drank a fair bit, danced until dawn, gambled and got laid quite a bit. As Dani put it, laughing wildly, "I got my brains fucked out, Zars!"

While she said that, she was holding Racquel's hand. Tight.

I had never suspected my best friend liked women sexually, and it surprised me for a split-second. But Dani is a free thinker, so as she and Racquel sat on the couch across from me, I listened to their story.

Dani and some of the girls went to a very exclusive Strip Club, and you had to dress up in your finest to get in. Dani would put on her favorite silver-lame top and mini – I know the one she meant, it's hot. The group of women watched the guys, and the girls whooped and hollered and made complete idiots out of themselves. A few of the girls started getting horny, hitting on the dancers – male and female alike. Dani was slightly embarrassed for her friends and apologized to the waitress who'd been serving them. The pretty waitress was wearing a French Maid uniform, and it looked very sexy on the attractive girl.

Who happened to be Racquel.

Dani said that Racquel smiled and she saw that lovely face for the first time. Her heart was thumping. Racquel was talking to her, but Dani couldn't hear her, she was fascinated with her. It wasn't hard to see why.

Racquel was beautiful. Even sitting across from me, in a white silk blouse and blue jeans with boots [also stilettos], you couldn't get your eyes off her. Yes, she was that beautiful.

Racquel had shoulder-length hair, a lighter shade of Chestnut brown than mine was. A sweet, lovely face, with high cheekbones and brown eyes, even a cute, upturned nose. Breasts that were round and perfect, you'd swear she had a boob job [she didn't] And man, those legs – and that ass! Round, bouncy – perfect!

When Racquel got up to get a coke, Dani caught me watching her walk and laughed, saying, "See?" Racquel called out from the kitchen and said, "Was she checking me out?" She came back into the room and snuggled beside Dani.

I blushed a bit, and Dani filled me in on the rest of the story.

In her little-girl soft voice, Racquel had said to Dani that she was getting off work in an hour, and she wondered if Dani would like to have breakfast with her, she'd love the company. Looking over at her group getting more inebriated by the second, Dani agreed.

Dani told me she could barely contain herself, and she found Racquel so appealing. She stayed in the club until Racquel finished her shift, but she stopped drinking. She wanted to be sober and enjoy her new friend's company to the fullest.

Racquel came out of the backroom, now she was wearing a short white skirt and had her hair tied in a ponytail. Now, she was cute and fresh-looking. Dani told me she found Racquel so sweet and appealing, and she'd never been this attracted to anyone before, man or woman. She was sure her nipples were hard, and all she could think of was how scrumptious Racquel was. Dani told me she'd had a few experiences with women in college – which I didn't know about – but it took all her self-control not to pounce on Racquel.

Racquel was nuzzling Dani as Dani was recounting the story. She was pretty, and I couldn't help but notice. She had an air of sexy, fun, and even I was attracted to her. I wasn't into girls, I had never been attracted to a woman, but I pictured her naked for a fleeting second. Oh, how yummy. I thought, feeling flushed. Then I shook my head and tried to listen to the rest of Dani's story.

The girls went to Denny's and had the Grand Slam – how cliché, huh? - and talked for hours. Dani was going nuts with the desire to act on Racquel, but she also genuinely liked the girl. How could she not? So she played it cool, not wanting to risk offending her new friend.

After a few hours, they wandered out of Denny's and walked the strip. It was Racquel who finally broke the ice and took Dani's hand in hers. They walked some more, but Dani finally turned to her pretty companion and asked for a kiss.

Racquel broke in, "I thought the silly girl would never ask."

Dani smiled. "She has the softest, sweetest lips. The first kiss was gentle, but it took my breath away. The second – well, let's just say she has a pretty agile little tongue. We stood there kissing for a few minutes until we realized we were attracting quite a bit of attention. Two hot chicks in the middle of the strip, making out – we were drawing a small crowd of onlookers." She laughed that wonderful laugh of hers and Racquel spoke up again.

"Your friend was squeezing my ass and we were getting a little passionate. So I asked her to come home with me. My roomie and I work opposite shifts, so I knew we'd be alone."

I was trying hard – and failing – not to get turned on by the story, squirming a bit in my chair. Racquel went on.

"Once we were in the door, we were ripping each other's clothes off. Dani was so obviously into me, and I couldn't wait to taste her pussy. I was kissing her neck, squeezing her big tits, running my hands up and down her legs and stroking her pussy through her panties. Zara, your friend is the hottest woman I've ever known – and I lived in Vegas.

We kept kissing, all the way to the bedroom, stroking each other, babbling, really turned on! Dani told me she liked my skin, and I told her she had the sexiest tan. Her nipples get so big when you suck them, Zara, like silver dollars. I could smell the scent of her pussy, and I wanted to suck it more than any girl I'd ever been with!

When Dani and I got into my bedroom, she started kissing me all over, fingerfucking me, really aggressive. God, was I turned on! She was thrusting her fingers in and out of my pussy, hard, biting my tits, she was telling me what a hot bitch I was! Dani was wild, what a night that was.

Oh, but I gave as good as I got, didn't I Dani? I got out my favorite vibrator and dildo, strapped it on and fucked the hell out of her. She loved it, Danielle did, she was yelling for me to fuck her harder. I slapped her ass a few times when I was fucking her and when we finally stopped, we ached all over. But neither one of us was complaining, were we babes?"

I was mesmerized by this story. I knew Dani was wild, but this was the wildest I had ever imagined her being. Biting, screaming, being fucked by a fake cock – it was all so nasty, but despite myself, I found the images flashing through my mind very, very sexy. I wished I could have been there and seen it all, but I wasn't into women – was I?

The girls gave each other a soft kiss, and Racquel laid her head on Dani's shoulder. "When Dani was ready to leave Vegas, she asked me to come with her. She told me she was nuts about me, but I didn't think I could give up my job."

"So I offered her a new job – with some extras incentives!" Dani giggled as she nibbled Racquel's ear.

I hugged Dani as I left and accepted one from Racquel too. She seemed so lovely, but I couldn't help but be a little jealous. I'd been Danielle's best friend for so long, and now she had another woman in her life, one who had a part of her I'd never know. Every time I looked at Racquel, I could imagine her and Danielle naked and in the throes of passion. At times, I even thought of myself in Dani's place, but I tried to put those thoughts out of my head.

Over the next little while, I spent a lot of time with them. We met for lunch rather frequently; they were as inseparable as a pair of newlyweds. It was hard not to like Racquel, she had a bubbly, infectious personality, and she seemed to make Dani very happy. Dani told me that she and Racquel both still dated men but were happiest together, and we weren't dating as often. I was one of the few people who knew they weren't merely "roommates."

To cement a more solid friendship between Racquel and myself, Dani suggested we start meeting for coffee and lunches, alone. Racquel thought that was a great idea, and she had great taste in food. I teased her that I was going to get fat, she responded that nothing could ruin my adorable little body. Oho, so she paid attention to other girls, did she? I was somewhat intrigued and somewhat flattered at the same time. We also spent a fair amount of time window-shopping, especially lingerie and shoe stores.

Life continued. I tried to concentrate on my studies and dates. I never seemed to spark with anyone, though, and I found myself enjoying my times with Racquel and Dani a hell of a lot more. I looked forward to the "girl's nights" where we'd just sit around, eating junk food and watching dopey, sad movies.

My birthday came up, and I was invited out for a wonderful evening. Dani and Racquel had pooled their resources, took me out for a fabulous dinner, drinks afterward, and danced in one of the area's better clubs. Lots of men – and a few women – were hitting on us, but we stuck to our own company for the night.

Dani had rented a nice Hotel room for the evening, knowing we'd all be a little too intoxicated to make the drive home. "Besides," she said, slightly drunk, "We have your birthday present upstairs."

"Oh Dani, Racquel, that wasn't necessary. This has been a wonderful, fun evening, you didn't have to get me anything!"

"Yes, we did!" Racquel said, flashing that million-dollar smile. At times like this, it was easy to tell why Danielle had fallen for her. "Come on, let your two best girlfriends spoil you rotten!"

We rode up in the elevator together, and I could hear the pair of them whispering and wondered what the heck was going on. I mused that it was true; I now had TWO girlfriends and realized my jealousy had vanished long ago. I liked Racquel, she made Dani happy, and that was all that mattered.

The room was – well, let's just say luxurious was an understatement. You could have held a Gala Reception for 50 people in there. Sometimes, I forget how much money Dani has. I looked around the room and in the corner, saw a pile of boxes from local boutiques, including Dani's favorite lingerie store.

"ALL of those are for me?" I asked incredulously. Both women nodded.

I felt like a kid in a Candy Store. I practically tore the wrapping off, the girls clapped their hands and laughed along with me. Oh, my! They'd bought me nightgowns, teddies, bustiers, basques – the most decadent, seductive clothing I'd ever owned. Silk, lace, but all of it luxurious and sexy. Then I noticed a sly smile on both the faces of Dani and Racquel. "What's up?" I asked them both.

From behind her back, Dani brought out one final, smaller box. "We both KNEW you'd like this gift," she said with a warm smile.

I took the box from her hand and gasped. Inside it was a pair of black stilettos, the silver-tipped ones I always thought were so sexy. That's when the tears started coming.

Danielle grinned at me again, Racquel was standing beside her, her arms around her. "You must have mentioned them a dozen times!" she said, as Dani nodded.

I just HAD to try them on, and the girls said they made me look so sexy. "You have the legs for them!" both Dani and Racquel both told me.

I blushed and told them that I agreed, it was too bad that I had no-one to wear all this finery for.

"W-e-ellll, that's not quite true," Dani grinned.

I didn't know what she was talking about, and the confusion must have been evident on my face. "What, did you hire me a Male Escort or something?"

"No."

I had never seen Dani at a loss for words until then. "We were – kind of – hoping ..."

Racquel cut in. "Oh, for God's sakes, we were hoping you'd like to wear them for us!"

"You?"

Racquel nodded. "We've talked a lot this last little while, Dani and I. We love each other, I can't imagine my life without her. But we both think you're hot ... so we discussed it and decided to take the risk of asking you to go to bed with us."

"What do you think?" Danielle asked.

"What if I say no?"

"Well, we both will love you as a friend. I love you Zars, so does Racquel. You're my best friend, but I have been wondering what you'd be like as a lover, so has Racquel --- and I think you might be curious too!"

I mulled it over, but only for the briefest of seconds. It was like a puzzle where all the pieces fell into place. I was in love with Dani, I knew it then – it is why no man could measure up, why I had been so jealous of Racquel. But Racquel's warmth had worn down my resistance, and if I wasn't in love with her too, I was undoubtedly extremely fond of her.

I choked and nodded.

I don't think I had ever seen Danielle smile that broadly. She and Racquel leaned in and kissed me on the cheek and then one, followed by the other, on the lips. It was like being touched by the wings of butterflies, and I have never known kisses like that.

They pulled away, and my eyes were still half-closed. "Ohh, myyyy!" I sighed. "What next?"

Danielle took one hand, Racquel took the other and squeezed. "Well, we both were thinking that we'd all change into something sexy, pile into the big bed and both of us will teach YOU how much fun making love with a woman can be. Sound good?" Dani asked.

"Yes." I went into one of the en-suite bathrooms, Dani took the other, and Racquel stayed in the bedroom. I knew which outfit I wanted to wear – and I was darned sure going to wear those stilettos, I had waited my whole life to wear shoes this sexy!

I came out of the bathroom, shyly at first, and gasped when I saw Racquel. She was lovelier than any fantasy I had ever had, exquisite with her hair down, diamond-drop earrings, and sexy, white lace, silk-embroidered teddy. She wore matching white stilettos, how appropriate. I sat by her on the bed, and we kissed, tentatively, while we waited for Dani to emerge from the other bathroom.

Danielle was well worth the wait. She came out in a long, black silk nightgown, with a slit up the side that revealed her best asset, long, tanned legs. She was wearing these sandal-like shoes that crossed a good way up her legs, very sexy, very vampy. Her shoes also had stiletto-points.

Bet you're all wondering what I wore? From the second I saw it, I knew the black, sheer bodystocking was for me. It molded to every inch of my slim frame, and the little rosette patterns were so sexy. It dipped down low in the back, just above my cute little ass, and it also had an opening at my pussy. It was designed for sexual play, and I am sure Dani and Racquel bought it for such a reason. I felt very sexy and desirable, and I'd made up my eyes with a smoky mascara and accentuated my lips with a dark burgundy lipstick. I looked pretty hot myself!

Dani joined us on the bed, and I was sandwiched between them. Dani took my face in her hands and kissed me, much more sensually this time. Her tongue slid across my lips and into my mouth, my heart raced, and I could feel my nipples stiffen immediately. I felt Racquel's fingers on my other cheek and turned towards her, and she was an even better kisser than Dani. She had this way of kissing, it was like her tongue massaged your lips, and I could feel the heat radiating from her. I just let myself go and be drawn into the moment.

"You're so sexy, so very sexy!" I heard Dani murmur as she caressed me through the bodystocking. "I think I've wanted to do this for a long time, I'm so glad you didn't run away!" she said, tears glistening on her cheeks.

I kissed her tears and ran a finger through her blonde hair. "I would never have run, you're my best friend, I love you silly!"

"Hey lovebirds, there are 3 of us in here!" Racquel said teasingly, jolting us back to the moment. "Hey you, are you trying to steal my girlfriend?"

"Maybe," I said teasingly and felt myself being gently pushed down onto the bed. Racquel was the first to be on top of me, and I felt her firm, round breasts pressed into mine as she kissed. From the corner of one eye, I could see Dani caressing her legs, massaging her ass, stroking her pussy lips as she pulled Racquel's tiny white thong to one side. I had never seen anything so blatantly sexy, but I figured the best was yet to come.

Racquel's gentle, knowing hands ran down the sides of my body. I could hear panting as if from somewhere far away, then realized it was my heavy breathing. I was excited, so excited I could barely think, just went with the new sensations coursing throughout my body. Racquel moaned, and I looked over again, seeing Dani bury her face in Racquel's soft pussy. She even moved up and licked Racquel's round, sexy ass from time to time.

"Oh, Fucking God, you know what I like baby, eat my cunt!" Racquel yelped her voice practically a growl. I knew I was getting slightly wet at her evilness, and I was beginning to see what Dani found sexy about her. She was a sexual animal, and I was experiencing that first-hand.

Dani lifted her face from between her lover's thighs and winked over at me. "She has the sweetest, tightest pussy – wait until you taste her Zars, you're going to love it!" She went back down between her girlfriend's legs and ate her as I felt Racquel's soft lips on my own again. She was beaming at me.

"Are you ready for me to do that to you?" she smiled. Oh God, WAS I?!!

"Please, yes," I practically begged. "Please Racquel, eat my pussy. Lick my cunt!" I yelled, getting into the spirit of things.

She gave me this almost-leer and moved down. "Pretty little pussy" she purred as she moved between the opening in the body stocking. In a flash, I felt her tongue on my pussy, and she began to lick me. She was slow for a few seconds, but that's all. Racquel began eating me voraciously, really sucking on me. I could feel the juice trickling out of my pussy, and my clit was throbbing, she suckled at that too. Her slender fingers slid into the depths of my pussy, and I wailed in delight, arching my body upwards as she devoured me.

"SOMEONE is having fun!" Dani giggled. "Okay lover, my turn!"

Racquel got out from between my legs, and Dani moved close to me. "I love you, Zara, I think I have for a long time. I"m glad you're here with us."

She grazed my lips with her own, and I saw the tender look in her beautiful baby-blues. "I love you too!" I smiled as she cuddled me close. She made love to me differently than her lover, with more urgency. She kisses were fiercer, more demanding. She squeezed me all over, while she was kissing me, she ran her fingers in and out of my pussy, I could hear how wet I was while Dani fingerfucked me urgently. It was almost as if she was out to prove I was as naughty as she was.

I felt like an entirely different person, more alive, sensual, and more in tune with my sexuality. As Dani continued sucking my pussy, I could see Racquel standing over in the corner, running a vibe over her pussy and nipples. The lights highlighted the sexy black silk on Dani's form. I reached up and cupped her big, round tits. I knew I had wanted to do that for a long time. They were so big, so heavy and damn! So sexy.

Racquel smiled over at us on the bed. "The lingerie's nice girls, but think we should all get naked?" Dani nodded.

"Okay – but keep on the stilettos – I, ummm, kinda have a thing for them!" I said, with a slight edge of embarrassment.

"Oho, we've found the girl's weakness!" Racquel teased as she slipped out of the teddy and rejoined us on the bed. She helped her girlfriend get out of the black silk number, leaving me still in lingerie. This time, she and Dani both were kissing me, our tongues meeting and dancing together in an erotic ballet.

"Someone's not naked yet!" Dani teased.

"I thought my two hot babies would like to undress me!" I said, trying to keep the mood light and sexy. Both of them smiled.

Dani slipped off my shoes, took my feet into her mouth, kissed each toe, and sucking them gently. I squealed and laughed as Racquel helped me get the body stocking off. Teasingly, Dani took the tip of my stiletto into her mouth and licked it before she handed it back to me. Fuck, that was a turn-on!

This time, we were all flesh-to-flesh. I saw Dani's body close-up, her skin tanned, her breasts round and full, her stomach flat and smooth. She was flawless, and I was in awe of her.

I turned and saw Racquel staring at me, a palpable hunger in her green eyes. "You're breathtaking, Dani was right!" she sighed.

"You've talked about me?" I said, turning back to Dani.

"Constantly." Racquel told me, giggling. "Didn't you know you're her fantasy girl?"

"Really?" Dani looked down at the floor, blushing slightly. She then looked up at me and nodded. I hugged her, and Racquel hugged me, and the three of us tumbled back on the plush bed.

"What next?"

"We've eaten your pussy, why don't you eat one of ours?" Racquel suggested. I responded by saying I would love to but hadn't a clue where to start. Dani instructed Racquel to move to the top of the bed and spread her long, sleek legs wide apart. Her sweet, neatly trimmed bush beckoned at me, I wanted to taste her so badly to feast on her cunt's juices.

"Baby, just kiss the lips of her pussy, part it with your fingers. You can't go wrong, Racquel's very sensual. She loves to be touched, don't you baby?"

Racquel smiled and nodded; I eased my body forward. I decided to be a little bold, I licked HER stiletto heel and began kissing up her legs, her skin was smooth as silk. I'd never experienced emotions like this, but I wasn't about to move backward now. As my lips reached her pussy, I went for it, diving in and kissing her. I must have been doing something right, she gave a loud squeal, and I was rewarded with a gush of juices on my licking tongue. I didn't stop, and I began licking in circles, up and down, flattened my tongue against her clit and laved her pussy. I knew what guys liked, I was no sexual novice, but making love to Racquel was a learning experience.

Dani made her presence known a few minutes later. I felt her hands on my ass, parting my cunt's lips and in went her tongue. That slithery, delicious tongue licked me, all over my backside, reaming me, making my senses explode. This, in turn, caused me to eat out Racquel's cunt even harder. My nipples ached from stiffness, and I had never been so awake sexually in all my life.

Their styles of lovemaking were different. Dani was noisy, and it was fun. She slurped and sucked, and her fingers were practically drilling into my pussy as I made love to her girlfriend. This was a birthday I would remember for the rest of my life.

"Fuck, oh fuck Dani, Zara, I'm cummminggggg!!!!"

I felt Racquel's sleek form tense and release, and she collapsed on the bed. I moved you for a kiss, feeling the same kind of affection for her that Dani did.

"Did I do okay?" I asked, still slightly nervous.

"Okay? Fuck Dani, she wants to know if she was okay? Babies, this little bitch is a natural!"

"My turn."

I turned to face Danielle, my dearest friend. This was it, and my life was going to change forever. I knew I would always love Danielle, but I was still terrified. I took in all of her body as she moved to the place where Racquel had formerly lay. She opened her arms wide, and I snuggled on top of her, my head resting on her big boobs.

Dani and I just lay there for a few minutes, running our fingers through each other's hair, taking in the beauty of the moment. Then, I pulled away, gave her a teasing peck, and proceeded to blow my best friend's mind.

I had already figured out that Dani liked her sex wild, passionate, and kinky. I squeezed her beautiful tits, practically mauling them. I bit on her nipples as I felt Racquel's tongue gliding over my now-dripping pussy. I slapped at Dani's luscious tits and rubbed her body all over, going to town, pinching her nipples, marveling at how responsive Dani was to my novice overtures. I felt a swell of pride, knowing I was pleasing my new lovers, the shy little girl making the horny lesbians cum.

When I saw Dani's pussy close up, it was one of the prettiest things I'd ever seen. She was so fair, it didn't look like she had any hair on it at all, but it was so light and delicate. I inhaled the rich scent of my best friend's quim and was transported to a state of lust I'd never known before. I didn't want this night to end, I moved my tongue into Dani's cunt and began feasting on her. My fingers rubbed all over her pussy while I ate her simultaneously. She groaned and moaned, "Eat it, you gorgeous, fuckable bitch!" she hissed. Me, a gorgeous fuckable bitch? High praise from my beautiful, stunning friend.

My tongue lashed out, swabbing her pussy over and over and over again. I was in heaven, and I loved eating pussy. I still wasn't sure if I was bi or lez, but I wasn't worried about it anymore. Why put labels on it? I was having a wild, nasty, kinky sex with two people I loved and adored; no one was going to tell me it was wrong.

Racquel's fingers were sluicing in and out of my wet cunt, which kept my passion at a fever-pitch. I didn't lose sight of my goal, though, to make Dani cum by eating her and fingering her.

"Yes, oh fuck yes, I'm cummming, I'm cummminggggg!!" Dani yelled, and I was rewarded by the flood of pussy juice on my lapping tongue. She fell back on the bed, limp and smiling, obviously satisfied.

Racquel stopped eating my pussy and hopped off the bed. She went into the other bathroom and brought out a bottle of champagne and three glasses. Dani sat up and hugged me, and we drank a toast.

"To our new relationship!" We clinked glasses and drank.

I looked at the two beauties beside me, sexy, leggy in their stilettos, warm and passionate. I felt a flood of emotion, and the tears started again.

"Hey you, what's wrong?" Dani wanted to know.

"This night – was magic!" I said, still sniffing a bit. "I wish it didn't have to end, I have never been this happy!"

"Who says it has to end?" Racquel said, hugging me close.

"Yeah, who says?"

"I don't get it."

"Silly girl, both of us adore you, you adore both of us. Why not keep doing this whenever we want?" Racquel said, grazing my erect nipples with her manicured fingernails.

"As a matter of fact ... " Dani said, sucking on the other nipple " ... why not move in with us? We've got plenty of room for another person – although you might suffer from sleep deprivation!"

I sighed. It was too good to be true - a beautiful place to live, sexy new clothes and shoes to wear, two people I adored.

"Hold it. Your apartment's big, but it only has one bedroom. Where am I supposed to sleep?"

The girls just looked at each other and giggled. Then it dawned on me.

"You want me to sleep with both of you?"

"Why not?" Dani said.

Racquel smiled and took my hand. "Sweetie, this isn't just some rash decision. We both love you, very much. We love spending time with you, this just seems a natural extension of the love we feel for you."

It made sense as she said it, but Dani had more to say.

"Zara, you will have the time of your life. You'll have more money for sexy clothes — if I don't buy them for you — you'll save money on rent, you'll have all the sex you can handle — it's a win-win situation. Besides, do you know what this little slut said to me the first time she saw you?" she asked, indicating Racquel.

Dani continued. "She said `I have GOT to fuck that little hottie', really Zars, she did!"

I looked over at Racquel and then at Dani. "Well, you haven't fucked me yet, now have you?"

Racquel was grinning from ear-to-ear, so was Dani. I gestured to Racquel and said to her, "C'mere baby, let Zara make your dreams come true."

Racquel smiled, then she gestured. "Just a minute, sexy. Dani, did you bring them?" Danielle nodded at her — no, OUR — lover. She went into the bathroom and came out wearing the sexiest, trashiest, HOTTEST pair of stiletto-heeled, black leather "Fuck Me" boots I have ever seen. I was practically salivating as she sauntered back to the bed and got on top of me.

"I want you to fuck me," I softly whispered, feeling Racquel's pussy rub against my own horny, dripping cunt. She writhed atop me, our clits stimulating each other while Dani fingerfucked herself in a nearby chair. I was fascinated with Racquel's arsenal of lesbian love tricks, but I sure wasn't tired of them. These sexy boots were icing on the cake, and I knew I'd never get tired of these two playmates of mine.

She fucked me hard as a man would, I climaxed underneath her, feeling loved and desired. Dani walked over to the bed and sat on the edge, kissing Racquel first, then me.

"Okay baby, we have some more fun planned. I want you and I to eat each other, are you ready for that?" I sure was, I had been fantasizing about a `69' with Dani since this kink fest began. My best friend moved on to the bed but insisted that I be the person on top. I was more than happy to oblige my sexy Dani, and as she straddled me and lowered her glistening, sexy pussy on to my face, I wasn't even hesitant. I gripped her hips tight and pulled her cunt down on to my face, eating her out with pure glee. When her tongue connected with my pussy, I climaxed. I had never had an orgasm like that, she kept eating me, and I exploded repeatedly.

Our funky partner joined us on the bed, cuddling close. I felt loved and protected lying between them, knowing they were mine if I wanted this. I did. More than anything, I wanted to be their lover.

"Okay, who's going to help me move?" I giggled as Racquel began licking my tits again, and Dani's fingers began straying towards my pussy once more.

That was a while back. We go shopping almost weekly, buying naughty toys, sexy undies, and of course, stilettos. We've formed the "Stiletto Club" and added a few new members, including the salesgirl at the shoe store, Racquel's former roomie, a hot Asian named Tobi, and my new conquest, a hot black girl named Denyce, who has legs to die for.

But the best times are when we're home, showing off for each other and playing. I've found the place I want to be, and I couldn't be happier.

Exciting Lesbian Experiences
05 Erotic, Steamy & Short Sex Stories for Women
Emilia Russell

All Rights Reserved. No part of this publication may be reproduced in any form or by any means, including scanning, photocopying, or otherwise without prior written permission of the copyright holder. Copyright © 2020

This book is entirely a work of fiction. The names, characters and incidents portrayed in it are the work of the author's imagination. Any resemblance to actual persons, living or dead, events or localities is entirely coincidental.

Story 01

"Hi, baby, Flame is my name, what's yours?"

"My name is Doris, nice to meet you!" It was Saturday night, so I must be in the 'Bad Girl Bar' because that's where I went every Saturday night! I sat next to Doris at the bar and bought her a drink. She was cute, white, and had brown hair and eyes. As we talked, I guessed that she was about 25 years old, 5'4" with small but perky breasts, and the slit in her skirt revealed shapely legs.

Noting that the bartender knew my name, Doris said, "You must come here often. It seems to be a popular place; this is my first time.

"That's why I've never seen you before! I'm here every Saturday night; I like the band and meeting sweet things like yourself." I liked the way she blushed, 'refreshing to meet someone that had not become hardened by the night life.'

The band played a slow song, and we danced; I held her tight and could feel her body tremble. I was pleased to feel this little white girl melt in my black arms. As I held her tight, my black hand slid down to her shapely buttocks. Doris looked up at me with fear in her eyes. I was unaccustomed to that kind of reaction.

We returned to the bar, and I asked her what was wrong. "This is all so new to me and I am quite nervous. Please, have patience with me!"

"I don't get it! What is new to you? Have you ever been with a black woman?"

Her pretty face was blushing again as she said, "I've never been with a woman! I've thought about it, fantasized about it, and wanted to try, but have never been able to get up the nerve to do it!"

"Wow!!! I'm sorry but we are in a lesbian bar and I just took for granted that you were a lesbian! Then I thought that perhaps it was because I was black. Do you find me attractive?"

"Oh, yes, you are beautiful; I couldn't imagine anyone that I would rather be my first woman lover than you! I'm sorry; it's just that I am so aflutter. I am wet, just looking at you. I want you so bad, but I am scared!"

"I too am wet! Come home with me and let your desire overcome your fear. Don't worry, sweet thing, I will be gentle. You are in good hands!" I got her out of there as quickly as possible; we walked to my apartment.

Sexy music was playing, drinks were served, and we danced in each other's arms. I felt confident now that we were in the friendly confines of my home. We kissed, tenderly at first and then more passionately, out tongues entwined, my hand squeezed her buttocks. I felt her warm body pressing into mine. I dropped her skirt and slipped a finger under her panties and into her wet pussy. Doris was moaning in passion and lost in lust, and I knew that she was mine!

I removed her top, brassiere, and her panties. She was sexy, in nothing but her stockings and high-heel shoes. Wanting to establish my dominance over the white bitch, I sternly told her, "Now take my clothes off, do it slow and let me see the yearning in your eyes when you look at my voluptuous ebony body." Her eyes were filled with desire as she nervously disrobed me.

I kissed her neck, her perky little white tits, and down her stomach to her thighs, and my fingers explored her dripping honey hole! We were standing near a large mirror. I told her to look and observe the contrast of skin color, my big tits, and her tiny tits, and me towering over her at 5'11". I told her that opposites attract and make it so much more exciting.

I dropped to my knees and licked her moist pussy lips with my long serpentine-like tongue. While flicking my tongue in and out of her pussy, I inserted three fingers in her horny hole and sucked on her stiff clit. With tongue and fingers, she was brought to a quaking and shaking orgasm.

I sat on the sofa and pulled her up on my lap. We kissed, and I told her to taste her pussy on my lips! Then I hand-feed the sweet girl my huge ebony breasts, and she nursed on them hungrily. I pushed her to her knees and told her to taste the chocolate treat between my long black legs. Doris kissed my thighs and slowly worked her way to my smoldering pussy! The white girl was kissing my pussy lips the same way she kissed my mouth! Then she began to French kiss my flooding cunt. I grabbed her hair and forced her face tight to my burning pussy and cried out, "Yes baby, that's it!! Stick your tongue as far up my love tunnel as you can. Suck my clit, oh, yes, look up at me while you suck my cunt, I want to see your eyes when I cum all over your sweet face. Lap up all of my cum, bitch, worship my black pussy!" Between me squeezing my long black legs around her head and pressing her face to my soaking cunt, the poor girl could hardly breathe, but she kept sucking my clit!!

I picked her up and carried her to my bedroom. I plopped her ass on the bed and lay next to her. I asked her, "Well sweetie, how did you like the taste of my black pussy? For your first time you did a good job. Tonight I will give you more practice and soon you will be a great little cunt lapper!"

"It was scrumptious; I love your black pussy and want to please you. It was even better than I thought that it would be!"

"Good girl! Now get between my legs and worship my pussy some more."

Doris eagerly licked the sopping black cunt to several orgasms. The white girl feasted on the luscious black cunt and lovingly licked up all of the love juice. She sniffed in the aroused pussy's aroma and became beguiled; she licked and sucked the steaming pussy with enthusiasm.

I told her, "Very good. Now I have a reward for you for being such a good little pussy licker!" I went to my closet and got out a 12" black dildo and strapped it on. I enjoyed the fear in her eyes as I spread her creamy legs wide! The big fat black dildo plowed deep into her pink slit and had her moaning and groaning in no time at all. Soon she wrapped her legs around my waist, and her white feet rested on my black buttocks as I pounded the fuck out of her. I lost track of how many times the bitch climaxed!

As I took off the dildo, my pussy twitched at the lewd sight of her stretched and leaking cunt! It was amazing how the sweet young thing now looked like a total fuck-slut! She told me that she was divorced and offered to let me move to her house in the suburbs. I advised her to take it slow and just concentrate on becoming my obedient fuck-slut. I made it clear that if she wanted to feast on my delicious cunt that she would have to learn to obey my every command. "Yes, I will do anything you say, just let me please you!"

"Good girl, that's a fine start; now, get the fuck out of here and let me get some sleep, leave your number on the table and I will call you. I will wait awhile before I call you; I want the desire for my cunt to build until you can hardly stand it. I want you to crave my cunt so much that you will cum from just smelling it. Oh yeah, from now on you will address me as Mistress Flame, now go!"

"Yes Mistress Flame, I will be waiting for your call." After she left, I chuckled to myself, thinking how easy she was. It was the best night of sex that I have had in a long time. I enjoyed my friends at the lesbian bar but realized that seducing straight women was much more exciting. I made up my mind to pursue, seduce, and dominate straight white women. At thirty-two years old, I should be thinking of settling down like some of my friends, but to hell with that shit!!!

Sunday night, I took my eye-catching ass to a trendy straight bar to see what I could get into. The place was packed, mostly couples, mostly white, but there were some singles. I sat next to a 5'2" brunette; her tits were small, but she wore no bra, and I just loved her large brown nipples; they stood at attention from my gaze; I couldn't help but wonder what they would do at my touch. Then her husband returned from the restroom.

We talked, and they introduced themselves as Helen and Paul. They asked me how I got the name Flame. I got closer to her, looked her straight in the eyes, and said, "My name is Flame because I am so fucking HOT! Maybe if you get too close to the Flame you will get burnt. Come on, Helen, dance with me." She started to make an excuse, but her husband urged her to dance with me.

As we danced, I held her face to my big black boobs. Then I whispered in her ear, "You are one sexy little white bitch! I want to fuck you! Trust me baby, this Flame can light your fire!" She was embarrassed and told me that I was worse than her husband. When we got back to the bar, Paul told us that we made a beautiful couple? Then he shocked me by inviting me to their house for night-caps.

Once we were seated in their living room, the drinks flowed freely. I explained to them that I used to be a stripper but hit the lottery and retired young. Paul begged me to strip for them, and I happily obliged. When I got down to my brassiere and panties, I took Helen's hand and urged her to strip too! She was very reluctant, but Paul pushed her into my arms and asked me to show her how to strip. I held her petite frame to my seductive ebony body and unzipped her skirt. We were all feeling our drinks, and Paul excitedly exclaimed, "Maybe my fantasies will finally come true!"

I said, "Tell me about your fantasies Paul. What is it that you desire?"

"I have always wanted to see Helen make love to another woman and something tells me that you are the one!"

"You got that right; I already told her that I want to fuck her. Tell us Helen; what do you think about all this? Have you ever made it with a woman? Are you ready for a night of sublime rapture? I can make your hot little volcano erupt, when I get through with you, your pussy will itch for me to scratch it again. You will be on your knees begging me to cum back again and again." I slipped two fingers under her thong and into her soaked slit!

She wiggled and pushed back at my black fingers. I guess that answered my question. I sucked on her rubbery nipples, and my long tongue licked down to her burning cunt! Her pink pussy was soaking wet, and she shook to a violent orgasm when my long tongue probed her horny hole! Helen could hardly stand, so I laid her on the floor and straddled her sweet face and lowered my sopping black pussy to her waiting mouth. I fucked her face furiously; her tongue and nose were up to my hot snatch! When I finally lifted my dripping pussy from her well-fucked face, it was red from the friction and glistened from cum and pussy juice!

I glanced over at Paul, and his cock was out, his hand and pants were cum-soaked! No need to ask him if he enjoyed the show. Before I left, Paul gave me their number and invited me to please come back soon. I helped Helen to her feet and asked, "What about you little girl; do you want me to come back and fuck you? Do you want to feast on my delicious black pussy again?"

"I...I guess so, if you want."

"Not good enough baby, I need more encouragement than that. Oh well, goodbye."

Before I got to the door, she called out, "Yes, please come back; I want you to come anytime you want. I would love to be with you again!" I just smiled as I walked out the door. That was fantastic! The white bitches love my juicy black pussy, just as much as I loved them worshiping my cunt with their mouths and tongues!!!

I let a week go by and did not call Doris or Helen; I was tempted to make a call when a night on the town came up empty!! Hey, even Babe Ruth struck out sometimes. But I did not call them because I wanted them to miss me and build on their desire for me, but I was horny as hell.

I went to the gym to work off some steam. While lifting weights, my attention was drawn to an adorable blonde with big green eyes. She was struggling with her weights, so I went over to give her some assistance. I would rather give her something else!! Nothing like a good piece of ASSistance! I grabbed her bar and helped her lower the weights, making sure that she got a good look up my loose gym shorts. ¬

She thanked me and was out of breath. I suggested that we took a break and offered to buy her a drink at the juice bar. She had an adorable accent, her name was Susan, and she was from Ireland. The 26 yr. Old beauty explained that she was here on holiday visiting her married sister.

The poor girl has never been out on the town. Her sister had four children, and one of them was sick, so they could not take her anywhere. I told her that it would be my pleasure to take her out for dinner and show her the town. She said that she couldn't let me do that, but I talked her into it.

We had a divine dinner, and I took her to the 'Bad Girl Bar,' we sat at a booth, and her big beautiful green-eyes were shining with the sights that she had never seen. We danced, and the slender girl felt good in my arms. She was 5'8" and had 36 C breasts. I kissed her ear and neck, let my hand slide down to her shapely buttocks, and looked into her eyes for her reaction. She appeared puzzled but did not say anything. Finally, she asked, "Why are no men here? Is this a lesbian bar? Are you a lesbian?"

"My, my, you are full of questions aren't you? The answer to all of your questions is 'yes'. If you are upset, we can leave and I will take you home."

"No, I'm not upset; we can still have fun but I want you to know that I am not a lesbian!" Susan loved the band, and she sure did love to drink. We even danced to some fast music, and she did know how to 'shake that thing!' I swear that she was teasing me when she rubbed her sexy body against mine. The more she drank, the better my chances were to seduce sweet Susan! When the bar closed, we went to my place for more drinks; Susan wanted to party, and I assured her that we could continue drinking and dancing at my place. Moisture formed in my pussy. I anticipated getting in her panties and seducing the sweet thing!

We stumbled into my apartment and immediately opened a couple of beers. While sitting on the sofa, I accidentally on purpose spilled a beer all over her pink sundress!

I led her to my bedroom, told her to take off all of her clothes, and I would wash them and gave her a flimsy black satin robe to wear. Her breast looked great on that slim body, and the blonde hair on her pussy was a turn on for me. I explained that there was beer on my clothes too and would wash them with hers. I took my time putting on a white satin robe and noticed that she could not keep her eyes off my ebony body! She stumbled and her black robe opened as I caught her.

I looked into her green eyes and could not resist kissing her. Our tongues were slapping each other! I squeezed a firm tit with one hand, and with the other, I slid two fingers into her soaking fuck hole! She pleaded, "No, please don't do this. I told you that I was not a lesbian. Please stop!"

"Susan girl, the lips on your mouth are telling me no, but the lips on your hot little cunt are screaming, 'YES!!!' Now which set of lips am I to believe?" I kissed her neck and worked my way down to her firm tits; I nibbled on her tiny nipples and sucked on them with vigor. I kissed and licked my way down to her sweet honey pot, I now had four fingers furiously pumping her hot little-hole as I kissed her thighs and smelled her aroused cunt, and she oozed love juice. Her sweet pussy was aflame, her face was flush, and I knew that there was no way that she could turn back now. My little Wild Irish Rose was consumed with lust, passion, and desire. This lovely flower was mine for the picking!!

Her long slender legs were wobbly, and I feared that she would fall down. I guided my precious bundle of burning love to the bed. My lips meet her pussy lips, my long tongue invaded her flooded love tunnel, and my fingers continued slipping and sliding in her soaked pussy! "She screamed out, "Ohhh, No. Please don't do this!! It's wrong; please stop!!"

Knowing damn well that she could not stop now; she was so close to orgasm, I removed my fingers from her blazing pussy and lifted my face from her soaked slit and told her, "Ok, that's it, if you don't want to cum, it's alright with me!! Fuck you bitch! Get dressed and I will drive your sorry-ass home!"

"But my dress is not washed yet. I want to stay with you but please, don't make me do this."

I smiled as I now completely understood her. I was reading between the lines, it was obvious that she wanted to play, but by having me 'make her have sex,' she was relieved of all burdens of guilt. She wanted it but didn't want to feel guilty. Very well then, if she wanted to be dominated and forced to do things, she came to the right place!

I plunged right in and gobbled up her sweet pussy, I stirred her still waters and made them flow freely! Her smoldering slit dripped hot honey, and it tasted luscious. My Irish Rose lost control and shook and quivered to a rocking orgasm. My fingers left her juicy cunt and poked their way up her tight ass-hole. Susan reached another intense orgasm and screamed out in sublime ecstasy!!!

Now it was time for me to dominate the white bitch and turn her into my submissive cunt-lapper!!! We snuggled and kissed; I wanted her to taste her pussy! I roughly pushed her pretty face to my bosom and demanded that she suck on my big black tits. I could see the lust and desire in her beautiful green-eyes when she stared at my humongous ebony breasts. Her red lips kissed my black mountains lovingly; then she feverishly sucked my nipples, for a moment, I thought she would draw milk!

Then I pushed her down to my waiting pussy and spread my long black, beautiful legs wide for her. Susan breathed in the seductive scent of my hot pussy, and the sweet bouquet mesmerized the girl. As if in a trance, her eyes stared at my fat pussy lips, and her mouth opened wide when she watched my clit emerge and grow before her eyes. My pussy opened for her like a morning flower covered with dew!

Susan slowly licked my hungry cunt and was drooling! I grabbed a fistful of blonde hair and forced her face to my burning cunt. In an authoritative voice, I demanded, "Eat my black pussy, bitch, chew on my fat pussy lips, suck my clit like it was your boyfriend's little dick and wiggle your tongue all the way up my carnal canal! Stop trying to act like miss goody-goody and show me what a depraved, shameless little slut you really are!" Her tongue licked faster, she sucked my clit and ate my pussy with fervor!

"That's it bitch, lick up all of my pussy juice! Yesssss, suck that cunt.. Show your big black momma what a filthy, vile little white fuck-slut you are!!! Oh Susan, I'm going to cum all over your white face; gobble it all up, you greedy little pig!!! Oh shitttttt, here it comes, lick up every drop. I can feel it dripping down to my ass-hole, lick it out, Yesssss, eat my ass out, your big black momma is going to cum again!! Oh shit, you are a good little white girl; you have a mouth like a fucking vacuum cleaner!!!"

I got out my 12" black dildo, strapped it on, spread her creamy legs, and rammed it up her tight little white pussy. I could feel her cunt stretch, her eyes were rolling, and she screamed out in rapture. I turned her over and fucked her doggy-style. The beautiful blonde girl squealed like a stuffed pig and fucked back hard. I put two fingers in her ass and then, with a sloshing sound, pulled out of her now sloppy cunt and fucked her ass!! Her pussy juices supplied all the necessary lube.

At first, she cried out in agony. I pulled her blonde hair back and pumped her ass furiously; the pain gave way to pleasure, and she humped her butt back at the big black invader!!! I wanted to demean her and tauntingly said, "That's it, you like that big black cock up your shitty ass, don't you slut? From now on, you are my bitch!!! You are a piece of worthless shit and you will obey my every command! Do you understand me? Address me as Mistress and I will call you my little white-fuck-slut! Is that clear?"

"Oh yes Mistress, I am yours and will do whatever you want me to do. I am your bitch and you are my black love goddess! Please keep fucking my ass, it feels so good! Oh my, I am going to cum again, Oh, oh, Yesssss!"

After I fucked the shit out of her, my little white fuck-slut worshiped my ebony body with her mouth and tongue. I loved it when she looked up at me with those big green-eyes while she sucked my sopping cunt!!! She said that she loved me, and I told her to do the wash! I drove Susan to her sister's home, and when I learned that she was going back to Ireland in three days, I realized that there was no time to play the waiting game with her. We made a date for the next night.

When I got home, my mind was filled with thoughts of Susan; she was so fucking Hot! I felt pangs of regret when I realized that she was going back to Ireland and out of my life. I knew that I would miss her! I cursed myself for becoming attached to her so easily, but she was very special, and even though I wanted to continue seducing other women, I did not want to lose her!

The next day, I called Paul and Helen and asked if they wanted to party? They were thrilled to hear from me, and Paul was excited when I informed him that I was inviting two other women. Next, I called Doris and invited her; she was all fired up and ready to go!

I picked up Susan, and when she sat next to me in the car, I kissed her and said, "Hi, angel eyes, you look breathtaking tonight."

She laughed and said, "Angel eyes? I thought you were going to call me white fuck-slut bitch and I was to call you Mistress Flame." I told her that stuff was just for when we were having sex because I knew that it turned her on so much and that when we were out, I would treat her like the gorgeous young lady that she was. Her captivating smile made my heart do flips and my pussy twitch!

When we arrived at Paul and Helen's place, I was pleased that Doris was already there. Susan gave me an astonished look when I introduced her as my love. We drank, danced, and chatted. Paul slyly suggested that I give all of the girls stripping lessons. I told him, "You just want to watch us have an orgy, you want to see us naked and you want to watch your wife get totally fucked, don't you?"

His answer was concise, "Hell Yes!!!" I began dancing and stripping; the other women watched me and did the same. Helen told Paul he could watch but warned him not to touch any of the women. Susan and I enjoyed an orgasm filled sixty-nine. Helen and Doris did the same. I bent all three white bitches over and furiously fucked them with my big dildo. I pulled their hair, called them sluts, and slapped each ass hard until they were all red. Then I tore them new ass-holes, telling them that they would not be able to shit right for a week. I reprimanded them for soiling my beautiful black dildo and made them tongue wash it. Paul asked if he could use one of their mouths. I permitted him to use all three, but he could only cum in his wife's mouth!

After the orgy, I drove Susan to her sister's house and wanted to know if she could stay and not go back to Ireland? She said that she must return, but we could keep in touch and 'who knows what the future holds?' I drove home and thought that at least I had two more days to convince her to stay. I felt a strong need to keep this sweet thing in my life!!!

Sharon stood in front of her closet, sliding hangers one way, then the other. She really had no desire to go out tonight, but Jeff had made it very clear, this evening was important. If he were ever going to make the right connections in the company or have any chance of moving up the Corporate Ladder, this would be the first rung. She'd been to dozens of these parties, and it was always the same. Middle-aged women wearing heavy cologne that choked the very air from your lungs, while their paunchy husbands groped at whomever and whatever was closest. She sighed and finally pulled out her black sheath. A single strand of pearls and her hair pulled up in a tight French knot should be just the ticket. Jeff always wanted her to look like a "showpiece," and tonight would certainly be no different. "Make them look twice, honey." She'd heard it a hundred times before."this ought to do it." Sharon laid the dress across the bed and headed for the bathroom. Jeff would be home in just over an hour. He'd barely have time to change his clothes, and she wanted to be out of the shower before he got home.

She was just stepping out of the shower when she heard his car pull in the drive. "Perfect timing," she smiled to herself and headed back toward the bedroom to start the process of becoming "provocative but elegant." The dress clung like a second skin, so it was important to pay attention to every detail. She slipped her legs into the black satin thong, then a matching black satin bra. Sheer black stocking and her favorite strappy heels, and the outfit were nearly complete. Her make-up was light. Just a touch of blush on the cheeks and some shadow and mascara to highlight her already striking green eyes, and that was all she needed. She smiled as Jeff came into the bedroom. "You better shake a leg, honey. We have less than an hour to be out of here if we're going to make an entrance." Jeff nodded and headed straight for the bathroom. "Quick shower and I'll be ready." As the bathroom door closed, Sharon looked back into the mirror, satisfied with the result, then began to knot and twist her long auburn hair. She chose a pair of faux pearl hair clips and had created a perfect knot at the back of her head. Once again, she sought approval in the vanity mirror.

As she slipped the black sheath over her arms and reached back for the zipper, she heard Jeff calling from the bathroom.

"Lay out my gray suit, will you please, honey?"

Sharon finished zipping the dress and opened the closet door, muttering to herself. "Gray suit....gray suit...ahhh, here we are."

She chose a soft blue dress shirt and striped tie. With onyx cufflinks and tie tack, this would be perfect. She laid it all out across the bed, smoothed the suit coat with the palm of her hand, then proceeded to slip her high heels on. She gave a quick glance in the mirror, turning one way then the other, running her hands down over her backside. She smiled at the result. "Not a single line." More to herself than anyone else.

"What was that, honey?" Jeff questioned as he emerged from the bathroom.

Sharon did a quick turn in the middle of the floor. "Well, what do you think?"

Jeff's smile broadened with approval. "Perfect! Absolutely perfect."

They arrived at the country club right on time. As they entered the private ballroom, Jeff was immediately flagged from across the room.

"Get yourself a drink, will you honey?" he motioned toward the bar and was gone. He disappeared into the sea of people so quickly, Sharon couldn't even begin to find him. With a hopeless sigh, she made her way to the bar and slid up onto a nearby stool and ordered.

"Bourbon and coke, please." The bartender smiled as he poured the amber liquor over ice and then topped it off with nothing more than a splash of cola. Sharon smiled as she took the first sip, then placed the glass back on the bar, turning to scan the room for her husband. With still no sign of Jeff, Sharon once again turned her concentration back to the bourbon in her hand.

"Well, that's a discouraged look if ever I saw one."

The voice was soft but low. Sharon turned to see a familiar face and smiled.

"Oh thank God! I was beginning to think I'd be stuck here alone on this damn stool all night."

Janet Driscoll was around the same age as Sharon. Their husbands had come to work for the company at the same time, and over the last few years, they'd met at several of these social affairs.

Janet's smile was warm, friendly. No matter how much time passed between their encounters, they always seemed to enjoy each other's company.

"Not a chance, lady. I'm bored beyond words. Charlie disappeared into that labyrinth almost half and hour ago and I've been wandering around here lost ever since. When I saw Jeff in the midst of the madness I knew you had to be here somewhere."

Sharon laughed as she spoke. "So you figured I'd be here lushing at the bar, huh?"

Janet chuckled as she picked up Sharon's bourbon and helped herself to a gulp. "Care to get the hell out of here?"

Sharon smiled. "You don't have to ask me twice! Where are we going?"

"Anywhere but here, sweetheart...anywhere but here," Janet laughed as she made her way out the door into the lounge.

It was Janet who spoke first as she flopped into an overstuffed chair. "God, I'm really beginning to detest these things."

Sharon looked over at the woman and nodded. "Beginning? What took you so long?"

They both laughed as Janet fished a pack of cigarettes out of her purse, lighting one then handing the pack and her lighter to Sharon.

Sharon pulled the slender cigarette from the pack, lighting it and handing them back to Janet. "There has to be a better way. All this "climbing the corporate ladder bullshit is enough to drive me to drink." Sharon laughed as she took another hard gulp of her bourbon.

Janet looked over at the woman she had become so fond of. Although they really didn't know each other well, Sharon had always been the one she seemed to gravitate toward. She liked Sharon's ease, the way they clicked almost instantly. "I have an idea." Janet stated, almost emphatically. "Follow me."

Sharon watched as Jan made her way toward the door, then stood and followed her out into the parking lot.

"They'll never miss us." Janet said with a grin. "And I know just the place to spend a nice quiet evening.. We'll take my car, and leave yours for Jeff and Charlie."

Sharon giggled, realizing she was still carrying the bourbon in her hand and followed Janet to the car.

"Where the hell are we going?" she questioned between giggles.

"C'mon. It's a surprise." Janet laughed as she unlocked the doors of her SUV and convinced Sharon to climb in.

"Okay, Jan. Whatever you say."

Janet liked the sound of that and grinned. She was glad it was dark, and Sharon couldn't see the look on her face as she pulled the car out of the lot.

It was less than a 15-minute drive before Janet shut off the engine. Sharon looked around. Everything seemed to be in total darkness. "Where are we?"

Janet smiled then turned the headlights up. In front of them stood the most darling little cabin Sharon had ever seen.

Jan continued to speak. "We bought this place a couple of years ago, so we could get out of the city on the weekends. What a joke. Charlie never has time to get up here. Seems as though the only time it gets used is if I come up here myself, just to get away from the rat race and make sure the place is still standing."

Sharon opened her car door and slid out of the front seat. She felt her dress slide up her thighs and smoothed it back down as she walked toward the door.

"It's adorable! God, I'd be here every weekend if it were mine."

Jan smiled. "Well you're always welcome, sweetheart. Anytime you want to join me, just say the word."

Janet unlocked the door and turned on a dim light in the main room of the cabin. The room was fairly large and well decorated. Janet had such good taste when it came to things like this. She had been in the woman's home only once but had fallen in love with the décor. Janet just seemed to have a flair for making everything feel warm and homey.

"Gosh, it's just darling, Jan." Sharon bubbled as she walked around the room. "Can I see the rest?"

Janet smiled as she led Sharon thru the cabin. "There isn't much more to see. The kitchen has a small eating nook and there's 2 bedrooms in the loft."

Janet looked up as she spoke, flipping a light switch near the bottom of the stairs.

Another dim light came to life in the loft.

"Shall we?" Jan smiled and motioned for Sharon to make her way up the stairs.

Sharon stepped quickly, making her way to the top of the stairs, then gasped as she looked down over the railing.

"Ohhh, Janet! It's just wonderful." She was almost gushing as she took in the entire downstairs from high above in the loft.

Jan smiled as she walked toward the master bedroom and flipped on a light. "This is our room."

Sharon gasped at the décor. The room was a soft blue, the trim, and bedspread matching patterns of Hydrangea.

"Oh Jan, it's simply beautiful. You really have a knack for this."

Sharon ran her hand across the quilted hydrangeas and sighed.

"What's the matter, honey?"

Jan's voice was soft as she spoke. Her footsteps were barely audible in the thick carpet as she moved closer to Sharon's back.

She had already kicked her heels off, and as she stood behind the woman, she was still nearly as tall. Her hands were soft, her fingers long and slender, and her desire to reach out for Sharon was almost overwhelming. It was at that moment, Jan decided. "If I don't do this now, I never will," and in a split second, her fingers were gently pulling on the zipper of Sharon's dress. Her breath was warm against the woman's shoulders as she stepped in closer. Sharon's sudden air intake made her stop briefly, fully expecting the woman to turn and tell her to "stop."

When it didn't happen, Jan simply smiled and finished slipping the zipper the rest of the way down.

The woman's hands felt like velvet as they slipped the black sheath from Sharon's shoulders and slid it down over her body's curves. When it landed silently on the carpet, Sharon never made a sound, but stepped carefully out of the dress, feeling Jan's fingers at the back of her bra. It seemed as though the hooks nearly opened themselves, and without a word, Sharon slid the straps down her arms and let it fall to the floor beside her dress.

Sharon stood in silence, feeling Janet's warm breath on the back of her neck as the woman began to place soft kisses along the strand of pearls. Without a sound, she felt Janet's hands slide around her and gently cup the roundness of her breasts, her nipples immediately responding to the soft brush of Janet's thumbs across them. As she closed her eyes, she felt every inch of her body begin to tingle. It was almost as if Jan could read her mind as the woman continued to tease at her stiffened nipples. Her fingers were soft but strong as she pinched and rolled them to complete erection. Sharon's moans cracked in her throat as she felt her arousal grow hot between her legs. Her whole body had to come to life the minute Jan touched her, yet all she could do now was stand in silence and feel her body giving in.

Janet's touch was strong, controlling as her hand slid up the middle of Sharon's back. With a complete submission, Sharon found herself kneeling in the center of Janet's antique iron bed.

Janet moved silently around the room, dimming the lights, and finally peeling away her clothes. Wearing only a pair of black lace panties, Jan placed one knee on the bed's edge and reached for Sharon's arm. Again, the woman's touch was gentle, but there was a command to the way she took Sharon's wrist in her hand and reached for the iron headboard.

Sharon quietly whimpered as she watched the woman slip a soft velvet band around her wrist and fasten it securely to the iron post. Then, without a peep, walk around to the opposite side of the bed and repeat the same movements. With her mind racing, Sharon watched as Jan crawled onto the bed. Her hands strong, yet gentle as they caressed Sharon's tits as they dangled freely underneath her. The sudden sharp pain of being pinched sent a current from Sharon's nipples straight to her clit.

"Oh God," she heard herself moan as Janet twisted and tweaked each nipple between her thumb and index finger.

Janet never uttered a word, but hooked her fingers into Sharon's thong's string and slipped it easily down over the woman's hips. Sharon felt the small strip of fabric slide between her thighs and down her legs. Completely vulnerable now, she could do nothing more than lower her forehead to the pillows. A small helpless whimper escaped her throat as she felt Janet's hands caressing the round fullness of her ass as it raised in the air.

Sharon's whimper quickly turned to a soft scream as she felt the sting of Janet's hand on her ass. The slap of Janet's hand sent a jolt through her body as she had never felt before. Only in her wildest fantasies had anything ever come close to feeling this good. Only in the darkest corners of her mind had she ever allowed herself to be here, yet now, it was no fantasy, and the dark corners of her desires were coming to life.

It was barely a whisper as Sharon heard her words.

"Janet, please."

Again, there was only silence as she felt the woman's hands on her ass's cheeks. They tugged gently, parting the soft mounds of flesh, exposing more and more of Sharon's desire. Her juices glistened on the soft lips of her pussy. Her tight pink hole quivered as she felt Janet's hands tugging, stretching the puckered rim of her tight forbidden hole.

Soft moans were the only sound that filled the room as Sharon felt Janet's tongue start to make a path between her cheeks. Her asshole quivered with pure delight as she felt the woman's tongue drag across it then circle gently, hot saliva wetting the rim with each slow lap of Janet's tongue. As she felt her body give in to the soft pleasure of Janet's tongue, the sudden sting of the woman's hand sent another jolt through her body that seemed to end directly on the swollen tip of her clit. Her pussy felt as hot as the skin on her ass, and all she could do was moan and beg for more.

"Janet...oh Janet please!"

It was the softness of Jan's fingers at her neck that sent a shiver of goosebumps down the middle of her back. She felt the strand of pearls slip easily from her neck, and her immediate reaction was to reach up toward her throat. It was then that she was reminded of the velvet bindings around her wrists.

She would have never imagined those pearls giving her so much pleasure, but as she felt Janet's hands once again start to part the cheeks of her ass, her breath drew in quick and deep. One by one, she felt the smooth round pearls penetrating her. One by one, Janet placed them at the tight puckered hole and pushed gently, the soft tip of her finger probing carefully as the strand slowly disappeared. With her forehead low and her ass high in the air, Sharon's moans were muffled by the pillow, until once again she felt the sharp sting of Janet's hand. Her head lifted instantly from the pillows, her back arching hard as she let out a scream. Her mind was reeling as she felt the heat of Janet's handprint on her ass.

"Oh, God. Oh my God!" Sharon managed to whimper thru short gasps for breath.

It was Janet's hand tugging at her hair that jerked her head from the pillows this time.

With her head pulled back and her body arched hard, Sharon only whimpered. Her clit was throbbing almost painfully, and the ache in her pussy went so deep she thought she would lose her mind wanting to be filled.

Janet's fingers felt strong as they slid along Sharon's pussy. Her juices coated them almost instantly, and it was with ease that the woman entered her cunt with three long slender fingers.

"Ahhhh God, yes!" Sharon moaned as she felt the penetration.

"Oh, yes, please Jan...please. I want it. I need it so badly."

A deep, steady rhythm took Jan's fingers in and out of Sharon's wet throbbing pussy. Her hips rocked slowly at first, then harder as she felt the bindings tug at her wrists. Sharon groaned with pleasure with each thrust of Jan's hand, urging the woman to enter her again and again. With each thrust, Jan's fingers made their way deeper and deeper, until she could feel the throbbing walls of Sharon's cunt tighten and squeeze down around them. Sharon's moans turned to pleas as she heard the words escape her throat.

"Fuck me, Janet...oh God please.! Fuck me hard!"

With thrust after relentless thrust, Janet plunged her fingers in and out of Sharon's dripping pussy. Sharon's puffing was pure pleasure as she felt her friend's fingers pumping harder and harder into her tight throbbing cunt.

"Make me cum...oh God, Jan make me cum!"

Through clenched teeth, Jan's voice finally echoed in Sharon's ears.

"Want it bad, Sharon? Want it real bad?" Jan moaned. "Mmm...such a naughty little slut aren't you Sharon?" Jan teased as she plunged her fingers back into the woman's wet pussy.

Sharon groaned as she listened to the low rasp in Janet's voice.

"Oh, yes, Janet. Yes! I'm a slut. I'll be your slut. Just please, make me cum!"

It was the sting of Janet's hand on her ass yet again and the sudden pull of her hair that brought Sharon's body arching off the pillows again.

"Beg for it, Sharon. Beg like the slut you are!" Janet demanded. "I want a slut in my bed tonight!"

Sharon's whimpers became almost sobs as she felt the pain inside her. The need to release was making her pussy ache as once again she pleaded with Jan.

"Do it, Jan. Anything you want. Make me your slut and let me cum!"

Once again, Jan's fingers thrust their way deep into Sharon's cunt, this time her thumb pressing in hard around the woman's swollen pink clit.

With each drive of Janet's fingers into her pussy, Sharon groaned and pushed her hips back to meet the woman's hand. With each thrust, Sharon felt Jan's thumb press in harder on her clit.

"Jan, Oh God, Janet please. Let me cum. I'm begging you, please! Let me cum"

It was the feel of Janet's fingers against her warm tight asshole that finally sent Sharon over the edge. One by one, Janet slid the strand of pearls from Sharon's tight puckered ass. One by one, they popped against the rim, opening it gently, then letting it pucker shut before the next little bead made its way out.

It was the sudden fullness that Sharon never expected. With both hands planted firmly on the woman's ass, Janet pulled Sharon back toward her. It was the thick hard latex strapped to Janet's hips that made Sharon's body jerk and arch. The entry was hard and deliberate. Jan's hips slammed hard up against Sharon's thighs and ass, and the rhythm was immediately deep and steady.

"Take it, Sharon. Take it hard!" Jan commanded as she pumped the woman's cunt full with the stiff latex hard-on.

With thrust after unmerciful thrust, Janet plunged the toy in and out of Sharon's pussy. With thrust after thrust, Janet felt the pressure against her swollen throbbing clit.

The slap of Jan's hand on her ass only urged Sharon to rock back harder. The growl in her friend's voice drove her back on the cock again and again.

"Fuck it, Sharon. Fuck my hard wet cock with that hot slippery pussy!"

Jan's own body was on fire. The way Sharon gave in to her. The way she seemed to know what Jan wanted and needed from her exactly.

As she felt her thighs tense and tighten, Janet pulled back one last time, then lunged forward with the full thrust of her hips.

It was the full pressure against her clit that sent her over the edge. Her body went rigged as she felt the orgasm take over. At the same time, Sharon felt Jan's thighs slam up against her ass, and the head of the cock drives into her g-spot and the full tip of her bladder. The sudden hot spurt from between her legs almost sent her flying. The warm trickle down the inside of her thighs felt so good she wanted to scream, but not a sound came from her throat except the low deep groan of her orgasm. As her body shuddered with relief, she felt the thick pool of cum between her thighs and her body collapse against the cool crisp bedclothes. With her wrists still bound, she lay silently waiting.

Jan's legs were trembling as she made her way to the bed's head and began to release Sharon's arms from the iron posts.

Her voice was once again soft as she lifted Sharon from the pillows and kissed her gently. "Get dressed honey. We don't have much time."

Sharon looked at the clock on the nightstand and picked her clothes up off the floor, trying desperately to resituate herself into the black sheath and stockings. With her hair down and tousled, she ran her hands quickly thru it and brushed it into place as best she could.

"Okay, I'm as ready as I'll ever be." Sharon giggled as they made their way back down the stairs.

Jan stopped at the bottom of the staircase and smiled at her friend.

"Funny, about an hour ago I was thinking exactly the same thing."

Story 03

I'd heard about the parties at Jeni's. Everyone had. It was a small liberal arts college, and six-foot-tall plus blonde lesbians were not exactly falling out of the trees. Everyone seemed to know who she was and that she was "that" way, both she and her nearly equally tall and beautiful roommate, Veronique. Veronique had also been pregnant in their freshman year, which caused even more talk and suspicion, but neither girl seemed to be bothered by being the subject of gossip and innuendo. They were from well-off families and were at the college to have as much fun as was humanly possible while getting their degrees. Well, Jeni was. Veronique didn't come back after that first year.

No one knew how exactly you came to be invited to one of Jeni's parties. Not everyone wanted to be, of course. There was no drinking, for one thing, and no drugs. And no men. Ever. I'm not gay or anything, but I still wondered what went on there. There was a girl in my hall who was rumored to have been to one. I didn't know her well, but she seemed glassy-eyed and semi-dazed the day after. And such smiles she had.

So, there I was in the student union, not bothering anybody, not looking to be invited to a party or anything when this girl sat down next to me and said hello brightly. She was alright, kind of pretty, I guess; I wasn't much of a judge or anything. She knew me, though, from some lecture we shared. At first, we just drank coffee and did homework and all. She kept looking at me every couple of minutes like she was trying to bring something up, and, of course, she was.

"Want to go to a party?" she finally asked.

"Sure," I told her. I liked parties; I was a party girl. I hadn't gone to college to become a nun. And I hadn't had a boyfriend since the end of summer.

"It's not a regular kind of party," she went on. "It's a Jeni party."

I looked at her. What, did she think I was queer?

She smiled nervously and shyly. "I know what you're thinking—you're not that way. I'm not that way either. I love guys." She seemed to think it was important that I believed her and that she liked guys.

She paused like she was waiting for me to tell her I loved guys too or something.

She sat back, kind of slumped over and all, like, you know, she didn't want to admit what she was admitting, even to herself. "But, I mean," she breathed, "haven't you ever wondered? College is all about curiosity."

I shook my head. "I'm not that curious."

She seemed disappointed. "I've never, ever," she went on. "But I got invited and I was told I could ask a friend. But, how do you ask a friend to that kind of party.?" She laughed, but it was hollow and embarrassing. "I just asked the cutest girl I know instead."

"Oh, wow," I answered. "That is like such a nice thing to say." It was. I didn't think I was all that cute. I am tallish and rangy, with only slight curves. I have nice hair, though. I call it calico because it is no one color: some red, some blonde, some brown.

"Come with me," she pleaded, leaning forward and taking my hand in hers. "You don't have to do anything. Just come, please? I don't know if I will ever ever get invited again."

I was about to tell her that I didn't even know her, but I stopped myself. That was a good thing, not a bad one, in this case—a free pass to a wild lesbian party. No commitment, no ties, well, I could just watch, couldn't I? I might be at least that curious. I mean, I had seen lesbian porno and all. Did real women act like that? Suddenly, going to this party seemed like fun. Wild and carefree, and so what if it got around? I'd be more exotic, wouldn't I? Besides, everyone does it once, right? And I didn't even have to do anything. No one could make me.

I looked into her eyes as I squeezed her fingers. "Okay. But I probably won't do anything but have a look."

I was afraid she was going to whoop, but she caught herself and just smiled big time. "Oh, thank you, Kelly. Thank you, thank you, thank you! Here's the address." She scribbled something on my rhetoric notes. "I'll meet you out front at 8:00 on Friday."

She scooped up her books and sashayed off, her hips swinging like she was in heat. It wasn't until she was gone that I remembered I didn't know her name.

Friday came finally. I am afraid I was more excited about it than I wanted to admit. I did the happy hour thing at one of the bars, downtown in the afternoon, but I didn't drink a lot. I went home to the dorm about six, showered, and got ready for Jeni's party. Shaved my legs and elsewhere a bit did my hair, tried on all the clothes in my closet, and finally settled on a short skirt that showed off my long legs and a loose top that hid that I wasn't too well endowed but hinted at the idea I at least had breasts. Finally satisfied, I walked the six or seven blocks from my dorm to Jeni's off-campus apartment. I checked my watch when I got to the front of the building. I was a little late, but my mystery friend was not out front waiting. Surely she had not gone inside without me. She was as nervous about this whole thing as I was. She was just late—only a couple of minutes. Then like 15 minutes. A couple of girls passed me and went on in. They didn't look at me. Finally, after standing outside for half an hour, I decided mystery friend had gone in without me, and I climbed the stairs and approached the door of Jeni's apartment.

The apartment is what I expected, but it was the penthouse of the old converted building—the whole top floor. For a girl living in a dorm room barely 12 by 12, it was huge. Heck, it was huge for my mother's house.

When I knocked, the door was opened by a tall blonde girl wearing nothing but a shawl tied around her hips. She smiled and invited me on in—the infamous Jeni. For a well-known lesbian, she looked really young. She didn't seem to be the least bit concerned that she was only wearing a shawl around her hips or opening the door that way. Maybe she always came to the door like that. God, she was confident. She led me in, chatting casually and easily, telling me where to drop my coat, where the refreshments were, the bathrooms. Then she was off, chatting with some other girl. I scanned the place for a mystery friend, but she was nowhere to be seen. I could not believe that she had stood me up.

I wandered around, got something to drink, and had some food. There was not a lot of sex or anything going on for a lesbian orgy. Two girls were kind of making out on the couch, but they had their clothes on. There was one of those soft-focus DVDs on the TV, the kind where the actresses have their breasts and do a lot of bumping into each other to music with a lot of basses—not the kind where you see everything.

I moved out onto the balcony. It had a wonderful view of the campus and part of downtown. I was a little cold in the fall air, but I liked being cold more than the idea of going back in there to get my coat. I thought I could spend a few more minutes there, then just go, and not seem too impolite or anything. While I was out on the balcony, two girls came out too. They were breathless and laughing. I thought the black-haired one, with the ponytail, was quite pretty. I thought it was funny that I was thinking of other girls that way, just because of where I was. The other one dug a ciggie out of her pocket and offered one to me when she noticed I was standing there. "No smoking in the apartment," she explained as she lit up. They stood close together and kind of pawed each other.

Their attention to one another got more intense, and the one girl's cigarette was left to burn in the ashtray there as they made out. As I watched, they began kissing deeply, and the one girl with her hair pulled back in a ponytail slipped her hand into the other's blouse, caressing her as their legs entwined, and they rubbed their bodies together. The pony-tailed one caught my eye over the shoulder of her girlfriend and winked. They didn't much care I was there, but they weren't making any moves on me either, which I appreciated. Her smoking friend had begun to unbutton the pony-tailed one's blouse, and I was treated to the sight of the black-haired girl's right breast before the smoking girl lowered her lips to the nipple. Feeling like a voyeur, I moved back into the big, sprawling great room.

Jeni was smiling across the room. Unlike many tall girls, she stood up very straight, and her breasts swelled from her chest dramatically. Great breasts too—round and full, they were capped with pale areolae from which her nipples stood up more darkly. Obviously, nudity was no big deal with her. The rumor was that her mother was famous and gorgeous and had been in Playboy and some movies. The rumor was that Jeni was the bastard daughter of a famous rock star. The rumor was that she was insatiable. The rumor was that she liked doing straight girls. Well, I was a straight girl. Not that I wanted Jeni to do me. But she sure was pretty. She dropped to sit on the floor, the shawl parting to show off her long legs.

They were getting ready to play spin the bottle if you can believe that. I stood at the edge of their circle of about five girls and just watched. I was still going to leave before long, just staying long enough to be polite. A girl spun, small and strawberry blonde in a super tight top that hugged her full breasts. The bottle stopped at an attractive blonde in jeans, who knelt with her legs apart. The redhead crawled to her, brushed her lips shyly across the other girl's, and moved quickly back to her spot. It was so innocent-seeming. The blonde girl smiled, spun the bottle, and sat back on her heels. It stopped at Jeni. The girls clapped like they knew the game had started now.

Jeni moved forward, crawling forward upright on her knees, making the other move to meet her—no dry brushing of lips this time. Jeni wrapped the other blonde up in her arms, crushing her bare breasts to the other girl's through her blouse, leaning in, opening her lips, and meeting the other girl. I found myself audibly gasping as the kiss deepened, and, before I knew it, I was rubbing my thighs together. It was the sexiest kiss I had ever seen. Jeni drew it out as she opened the girl's blouse, pushing it off her shoulders and baring her breasts before pressing her own back on top of them. This other girl was really pretty, too, with a lush figure and bright brown eyes.

"Gawd, Jeni," the girl said as they finally broke apart, "you make me so fucking wet." She kind of collapsed back into her place, her nipples pointing out from her full breasts. Jeni's nipples were standing up, too, I saw.

The girls in the circle clapped again, and one said she was wet from it too, and they all laughed. The couple from outside had come in and found places among the others.

Jeni smiled and tossed back her long blonde hair, which made her breasts sway. Bending, she twisted the bottle and sat back on her thighs, waiting for it to stop. The other players all seemed to catch their breath, each hoping it would fall to her, each wanting a kiss like the one Jeni had given the now topless girl in jeans. I wondered who would get lucky, smiling as I caught myself thinking that way and deciding I wanted to see Jeni kiss the curvy brunette to her left. Maybe she'd take off her top, and we'd all get to see her boobs too. They looked really big, and I was curious.

Then it was silent, and I looked down to see the bottle pointing between two girls in the circle on either side of me, between them, pointing at me. Jeni rose from her knees and started toward me. I protested that I hadn't even been playing. I took a step back. Jeni gently took my hand and led me into the circle. "Just a kiss," she murmured.

Just a kiss. Just a kiss?

Even barefoot, Jeni was three or four inches taller than I was in my heels. Her soft hands fluttered to my face, cupping me softly, lifting my chin, leaning into me. I felt her hair falling on my skin. Her lips were soft on my own. With a little flick on her tongue, she opened them gently. Lord, I was kissing a girl! She was gentle and soft, but insistent and urgent too. Her hands left my face as I opened my mouth to her. Gliding her arms around my waist, she pulled me closer, and those naked breasts fell on top of mine, pressing against me. Oh, they felt so nice. Her hands dropped, cupping my bottom, and she wriggled her hips and touched me intimately. We kissed, and her fingers inched up my short skirt. I broke the kiss to tell her, no, not to.

Before I could, she growled and laughed, "Panties," and caught my lower lip with her teeth, smiling fiendishly but so prettily before kissing me again. Fingers, not Jeni's, reached under the hem of my skirt where it wasn't lifted and tugged at my underwear. I released my hold on Jeni to stop them, but she caught my hands, interlacing her fingers with mine and kissing me again, letting it go on and on as she rolled her shoulders to drag her breasts over my chest. My panties slipped down, dragged off by insistent fingers. I stepped out of them as they fell to my feet. I mean, the other girl was left topless. I had only lost my panties. I still had on my blouse and my skirt.

"She's wet!" one of the girls announced, lifting my panties to her face. Jeni released me, stepping back and taking her place in the circle. She was smiling. The girl, with my panties, tossed them to someone else. Fine. Get off sniffing my panties. I was wet, though. Really wet. From a kiss by a girl.

"It's your turn..." Jeni said, still smiling at me, but also asking my name again.

"Kelly," I told her and smiled back. I saw how the game was played now. Leaning forward, I reached for the bottle and twisted it. I kept my eyes on Jeni as she watched the bottle. When it stopped, I followed her eyes to the girl it pointed to. She was not really pretty and had a poor complexion, but I was only going to kiss her. We met in the middle of the circle, and, as our lips touched, I reached for the hem of her tee and pulled it up. There was applause for me. The girl just raised her arms and broke the kiss just long enough for me to lift it free of her face, and then she attacked me with her mouth again. We rubbed our boobs together, hers now covered by just her bra, mine still covered by my blouse but bare underneath it.

I moved back to my place, the place made for me between the girls I had been standing behind earlier. I knelt, boldly letting my thighs part, knowing, maybe hoping, someone might see my naked pussy under my skirt. Girls kissed, clothing fell away. Breasts were bared, and every one of us hoped the bottle would land on Jeni. We loved seeing her kiss the other girls, but we each wanted to be the one she kissed. The curvy brunette won applause when she untied Jeni's shawl as Jeni took off her bra. That girl's boobs were bigger than Jeni's, and her areolae were large and brown. I didn't find them attractive, even though I'd wanted to see them before she took her bra off. My eyes shifted to Jeni, who was now nude. Her bottom was nice and round, more so than my little one, and she was blonde between her legs too. Not a lot of hair there, but some. I shook my head to force my eyes off of her. I felt drunk, even though I hadn't had a drink in hours.

Jeni spun the bottle again, and once more, it stopped before me. I stood up, still dressed, while all the other girls were semi-nude and moved toward Jeni. I took a deep breath, afraid of being naked in front of these girls. I opened my arms and closed my eyes, trying to be brave, wanting her to kiss me again and make me wetter. She moved into my arms, but it was not her lips that touched mine. Arching her back, up on her toes, she lifted her chest and touched a nipple to my mouth. I gasped as her hands cradled my head, pulling my mouth lower and closer. I moaned, then flushed as I heard myself. Her nipple stiffened under my lips and on my tongue as my mouth molded around her breast. I know how I like my nipples kissed, and I did to her what I love. Jeni moaned too, not shyly, but happily and with excitement at my touch. That was so cool, I thought. I was making a woman moan— what fun.

Gingerly, Jeni lifted my lips from her left breast and moved them to her right nipple. I tongued and kissed her there too, eagerly, enjoying the sensation of having her nipple grow in my mouth. The soft hug of my arms intensified, and my fingers began to knead the round, plump, softness of her bottom. Jeni pressed her hips toward me, rolling them as she once more ground her sex to my tummy's lower curve. Her bottom was wonderful to touch. I rolled my fingers into her skin, loving the way her flesh moved under my ardent caress.

Some of the other girls began to tease us that it was time to stop, but I didn't want it to. That heady feeling I had before was stronger, almost like I was dizzy, but I didn't want it to end. Jeni pressed her breast to my lips firmly, and I flattered myself that she liked what I was doing. She pressed forward; her weight was bearing us down. I let her lower me to the floor, not letting go of her nipple as we slipped from our feet to our knees and further until I was on my back. I lay under her, knowing my skirt was bunched up around my hips as Jeni bore down on me, but I didn't care. My thighs parted, and Jeni glided between them, holding herself up on her arms as I continued to make love to her breasts.

Suddenly, I heard a sharp clap. "Enough, already," someone said. Jeni laughed and lifted her breasts away from me. The tall brunette with the big areolae had smacked Jeni's bottom to break us up. "Truth or Dare time," she said.

Jeni lifted from between my open thighs and sat back beside me, cross-egged, reaching to lift her fair hair from her out of her face and took several deep breaths. "Okay," she said. "Truth or Dare."

I lay there on my back, my skirt up around my waist and my aroused sex on obvious display to all the girls if they wanted to look. I caught my breath and struggled up to sit too, cross-legged like Jeni, knowing I was still showing off my pussy and kind of liking that I was showing off like that. Like Jeni. She caught my hand in hers, leaned over, whispered something in my ear, and then turned to the circle. "Who goes first?"

I could barely pay attention to the idea of a new game. Jeni had so aroused me with the way she had given me her breasts to love; I could barely stand it. And then that whisper as she sat back again, "I want you.". Jeni wanted me. Oh, god, what now?

The brown-haired, big breasted girl volunteered to go first, as she had suggested the game change. "Kelly," she asked, "Truth or Dare."

Me? Oh, why? I had just gone. "Truth," I murmured, barely able to speak.

The girls all growled with disappointment. They wanted dares. Dirty ones. Nasty ones.

"Okay, Kelly," the girl said, thinking of her question. I was sure she already had a dare in mind. "If you could do any famous woman, who would you be with?"

I had never thought of being with a woman. Not really. Oh, sure, there were actresses and singers I thought were pretty, but I had not had sex fantasies about any of them. I didn't know how to answer. "Um, I guess, Heather Graham."

There were howls of delight and disagreement. The girl who asked the question rolled her eyes, and it made me wonder what I was supposed to have said. "Your turn to ask then," she said.

I looked around the circle, not sure what to do. The strawberry blonde who had been the first to kiss in Spin the Bottle was, I thought, one of the cutest girls, besides Jeni. I looked at her and asked if she wanted truth or a dare. Her blouse was off, and her round breasts swelled under a too-tight bra.

"I'm Heather. Not that one." She laughed at her joke. No one else did. "Dare," she selected smugly. The girls in the circle all clapped happily. Ugh. What was I going to do now? "Um," I hesitated, then decided to be bold. "Take off your bra."

There were some groans, but most of them seemed to think it was an okay dare. Heather reached behind her and unhooked it, then shrugged her shoulders and let the cups slip from her full breasts, the straps gliding down her arms as she shook herself free of it. Oh, she had lovely breasts too. There were red lines where you could see its outline where it had dug into her skin. I licked my lips, then caught myself doing it and flushed, but I don't think anyone noticed as they were all looking at her. She arched her back, grinning and preening for her audience. Heather loved showing off.

"Okay," she said, sitting back again, "my turn." She grinned and looked around the circle for the girl she would ask.

A lot of ridiculous questions followed when a girl would pick truth, always bringing a chorus of groans because she hadn't accepted a dare. The dares were tame enough to start like mine had been. I realized that I was probably not the only shy one there. Most of the girls lost more articles of clothing for their dares as the game went on. The pony-tailed girl got dared to prove she shaved her pubic hair. Finally, the girl I had kissed after Jeni gave a dare to the pretty blonde in no longer in jeans to kiss the bottom of one of us.

The blonde girl smiled, pointed to me, and smiled. I flushed again. Jeni let go of my hand—we had been holding hands all this time—and nodded for me to get up on my knees. As I turned over, I felt her lift my skirt to reveal my ass. I rested my head on my crossed hands on the floor, my bottom high in the air, exposed to the looks of all the other girls. The dared girl came to me on her hands and knees. I felt her breath on my skin, then her lips on my ass, kissing me there. I was sure that was all that would happen. Then her tongue shot out and swept between my cheeks. I felt a shiver and arched my back, unconsciously pushing my ass to her mouth. Her hands caught my hips, and she pulled her face between my cheeks, licking between them, then down, then there. I cried out, surprised, and turned on too. No one had ever done that to me. It was kind of dirty, and it felt terrific too. I rolled my hips to show everyone that I liked it.

Too soon, she stopped, her dare done, and she moved back to her place. I rolled over again, settling back next to Jeni. She took my hand again.

The dares got more risqué after that, with more sexual overtones to them all. I was dared to take off my skirt and then my blouse, and I did, finally, doing a little dance for them because that was what I had been dared to do. They had all seen my pussy by then, but I was a little shy about exposing my breasts. I looked at Jeni as I slipped out of my top, wanting her approval, wanting her to think I was pretty. I wanted her to still want me after she saw me naked. Finally, I stood nude in front of them, my small breasts swinging away from my chest, and their nipples standing up with excitement.

Jeni smiled as I sat next to her again, sliding her arm around my naked waist. Her bare hip nestled next to mine, and it felt so thrilling to feel her skin on my own. I looked around the circle and noted that similar pairings off were seeming to form. Then the girl with the large brown areolae asked Jeni a truth or dare. She surprised us all by taking the truth.

"How many dicks, Jeni??

Jeni laughed. "Oh, you all know that one. Three." She seemed to act like the other girls knew what she was talking about exactly.

While the other girls were still groaning at the tameness of her answer by taking a truth, she shifted slightly next to me, her full naked breast scoring lightly across my bare arm.

"My turn," she said quietly. "And I dare Kelly to let me take her into my room and do her."

There was silence.

She hadn't given me the choice of truth. The dare hung in the air while everyone waited for me to answer.

I swallowed. "Okay."

Jeni gracefully rose to her feet and helped me to get up too. I hadn't taken off my heels, and it felt very sexy to be standing in a group of semi-nude young women wearing nothing at all but shoes, while the most beautiful girl ever was standing next to me, her fingers laced between mine. Then she led me off, letting me trail slightly behind her as the girls in the circle hooted and clapped.

Her bedroom was huge, as befitted the rest of the penthouse. Dominating it was the biggest bed I had ever seen. The door closed, and I was in her arms, feeling her body touching mine with nothing between us for the first time. Our lips met, and she kissed me again with that soul-presenting presence that I felt with a surging twinge between my legs. We embraced, kissing, at the edge of her bed, arms around one another, holding close as the kiss went on and on.

"Kelly," she said finally, barely pulling her lips from mine, "the only thing is to just do what feels nice. That's all."

Easing away from me, she slid onto the bed, sitting across one crossed leg.

"I've never..."

She shushed me by pulling me to her on the bed and kissing me. We fell together onto the mattress, and her fingers captured my breast and teased me. The girl knew how to kiss. Kissing is so important. We lay together, pressing our bodies to one another as we kissed, and fingers teased across bare flesh. She was in no hurry, like some people I had been with were. When her thigh slipped between mine, I found myself pressing my pussy to her, eager, and desirous of her touch. I felt her smile in our kiss, then she drew away, kissing her way to my neck, nipping and licking. I trilled, pressing my pussy to her thigh. Her lips moved down between my breasts. Her fingers intensifying their touch on my right breast, and her tugging of my hard nipple as her mouth sucked in the left one. Her thigh moved against my sex, easily gliding because I was so wet by then. I ran my hands into her long hair, wanting her to do what she was about to do.

She knelt between my open legs then, once more, reaching to lift her hair from her face. She smiled.

Oh, Jeni's tongue. She touched me. A slow, easy lick swept over my lips, and I cried out from its thrill. Her arms slipped around my thighs, and she pulled her pretty face closer to my sex. Her tongue moved on me so sweetly, having opened me, she dipped her pointed tongue inside of me, then curled, drawing out my cream. She laved my clit with it, her tongue circling around. Watching, listening to me, intuiting from my sighs and whispers just which touches drove me crazy.

Oh, and I came. My thighs tightened, and I pointed my toes as orgasm rose within me. Pretty Jeni licked and licked, and her tongue raised me. Clawing the sheets, I raised my ass to give her more of me, and she slipped her hands under to pull me closer, still using that tongue. I felt myself flush again, my chest reddening, and my breath tearing as I screamed in absolute pleasure. Jeni laughed with delight and kept licking, her lips molding around my clit and tugging me into her mouth. I bounced up and down on the bed, and she followed and raised me higher again as she took me there again. I gasped for breath and cried out, digging my nails into the mattress and rolling my head back and forth as she delighted me.

Finally, she relented, rising and coming up and over me, as she lay softly atop me and once more kissed me, her lips and tongue thick with my cream. I tasted my orgasm on her and liked it. Wrapping her in my arms, I held her close, feeling the wonder of her soft bosom pressing to mine as my thighs rose to hug her tightly as she nestled her sex over mine.

"Jeni," I started, unable to know what to say. "Jeni." I murmured and sighed and just kissed her.

"Ohhhhhhhhhhhhhhh," she purred. "That was wonderful."

I laughed with delight. "Oh, it was more than wonderful." I kissed her again, licking her lips and caressing her long back under my hands, sweeping down to caress her bottom. Feeling bold, I eased us both over, letting her fall onto her back as I attacked her lovely breasts with my lips and tongue again. It was fabulous to adore her breasts, feeling their soft sponginess, and how her pretty nipples responded to my lips and tongue. Her breasts were so much larger than my own; it was remarkable to experience their difference. I turned my eyes to catch her as I played as she laid a hand on my head and ran her fingers into my hair. I knew she was hoping I would lick her, but she was not going to demand. She didn't need to.

Rising to my knees, I kissed my way down her tummy, curling my tongue into her navel and then moving lower still. She had very fine hair on her mound, and I caught it in my lips and tugged it playfully as I took a deep breath. I was about to put my mouth to another girl's sex. Imagine that. With a cool, long look into her half-lidded blue eyes, I extended my tongue and ran it along her labia, just as she had done to me, licking softly and feeling her blossom under my touch. That was amazing. Her skin moved and responded to my touch. I wriggled my tongue into her, tasting pussy for the first time, really tasting it, not just my taste on another's lips or a cock that had been inside me. She was powdery, almost dry in taste, yet tart. Very interesting. As she had done, I used my tongue inside her, then drew it out thick with Jeni cream and moved to her clit.

My lips formed around her there, tugging gently, and she raised her hips to follow my mouth. I had a sudden fear that a girl as experienced as Jeni would find my lapping insufficient, but the soft touch of her fingers in my hair encouraged me. She began to moan, exciting me that I was arousing her, and I released her clit and moved my tongue around her clit, circling, then flicking it. Her body surged, rose to me, and I knew she wanted more. My tongue danced with her clit, moving her and caressing her. Her moans grew more intense, and her thighs tightened around my head.

"Kelly!" she cried out. "Kelly!" I used my tongue feverishly, wanting to make Jeni cum. Oh, and she did. Her body tensed, and she held her sex to my mouth hard as her orgasm shook through her. Her hands in my hair held me still as she came, and I knew to just hold her clit in my lips as she shook. Just as she began to relax, I licked again, wanting to take her back there again. My arms pulled her thighs tighter to me. I dug my tongue into her, fucking her with it, wanton in my desire for her. Jeni bounced and cried out, coming again even harder a second time. And then a third. And then again. I was so powerful at that moment.

Jeni finally slipped out from under my tongue and urged me back into her arms. We kissed again, happy to be there in just that moment. I wondered at how I felt, having done what I had just done. It was certainly a surprise.

We were still kissing and cuddling when the door opened a crack. A head poked in, smiling. "About time, you two," big areolae said, then the door swung wide, and the other girls bounded into the room with us. They were all undressed now, and suddenly I found myself surrounded by warm, naked flesh. Heather, the pretty strawberry blonde, kissed me and moved her fingers between my legs, invading me suddenly. I was amazed at how good she felt inside me, both her tongue and her fingers. Before I could barely breathe, she was making me cum again.

Somewhere on the bed, big areolae were kneeling between Jeni's legs. She wore something around her hips, and I realized with a jolt that it was one of those strap-on dildos. Lifting Jeni's hips, she put the thing inside her and began bobbing her hips to move it in and out of Jeni. As I watched with amazement as the two girls fucked, I felt the fingers in me drawing out and a tongue replacing them. The blonde girl who had been wearing jeans was between my thighs, licking me. Oh, my. Then Heather was straddling my face and lowering her sex to my lips.

I was going to just have to find out the names of these girls, but how was I to ask now? I mean, how did I get where I was, anyway? Me, right in the middle of a lesbian orgy. I licked and licked at Heather above me, wanting her to cum, even as the girl licking me brought me off to another heavenly orgasm of my own with her mouth. I felt myself being moved, raised, kissed, fondled, caressed. I didn't even know who was who. My fingers touched a pussy, one with no hair at all, and I thought she must be the girl with the black ponytail or the one with the bad complexion. Both had lost their pants before Jeni had whisked me away, and revealed they were bare. Whoever she was, her sex was interesting to touch, her labia much more prominent than either mine or Jeni's or Heather's. I wriggled a second finger into her, fucking her by moving them in and out as she cried out with happiness. She was quite wet, and it was so interesting to see how she took my fingers so easily.

The pretty girl, Heather, sitting on my face, came, crying out and clutching her breasts as she writhed on my mouth. I tasted her as she came, then she was gone, abruptly torn away as she sought another to make love with. I knew Jeni had come again from the fucking by big areolae. She seemed to like being done with the dildo. I knew what she sounded like when she came now.

Coming up, I looked at the bed. All the girls were there, making love to one another. I shook my head to clear it and my hair cascaded down my chest over my excited nipples. I had licked two of them to orgasm. Who would believe it? I felt a breast touch to my arm and turned to see big areolae grinning at me. I reached over and cupped one of her huge boobs, pressing my fingers to her skin. It felt so different than Jeni's or my own did. What wonderful things breasts are. All so different. Turning my face to her, I took a nipple into my mouth. For all the great size of her, her nipple was smaller than Jeni's was. I sucked it past my teeth and heard her draw in her breath with excitement. God, this was fun. She pushed me onto the mattress and climbed between my thighs, aiming the dildo at me. I laid my head back and found it resting on some other girl's breasts as she lay on the huge bed. I felt myself being fucked, the thick dildo moving in and out of me, but it was a different rhythm than when a guy did me. I rolled my hips, wanting more. A hand found mine and squeezed, and I recognized Jeni's touch. We were still together.

A body moved over me, lowering to my lips. I looked up at the face of the girl with the black ponytail. I hadn't paid much attention to her during the game, as she seemed paired up with the one smoking on the balcony. She was pretty, and her pussy was bare of all hair. As I flicked my tongue over her lips, I decided she felt different than the girl I had fingered before. How many had I made love with? Jeni, of course. Heather. Jeans girl—Lindsay—had licked me to orgasm. I had fingered bad complexion girl, Anna. Big areola, Sarah, was fucking me. And now I was licking black ponytail, Caitlin. Did that leave only smoking girl? No, there was one other, somewhere, Ashley.

It went on and on. One or two or three of us might rest, even doze, while the orgy was going on around us, then we would rise and take the place of one of the others as she rested. I found my way back to Jeni, and we fingered each other until we came while kissing and bumping our breasts together. It was different that way, but still nice too. I didn't think I could stand much more when Jeni eased us down onto the bed again, and she began to lick me once more. Lindsay moved her sex to my mouth, and Sarah settled in to lick her lips. It was amazing, as no one planned it, but one after another, the girls found one another with their mouths pressed to pussies. Anna to Sarah, then Caitlin, then smoking girl, Ashley, then Heather, then Jeni, then me, then Lindsay, then Anna, we completed one another. Cries and squeals filled the air, along with the scents and smells of aroused girls. Someone came, moaning her happiness until echoed by the screams of someone else—me. We all came.

And that seemed to mark the end. Jeni and I nestled together, with Lindsay snuggling against my back and Heather on Jeni's other side. I don't know where the others slept, but the four of us were together when morning came. There were several other bedrooms, I think. I awoke lying on Jeni's arm, Lindsay's lips on my nipple, with Heather's head on Jeni's breast. All of us had wild hair, and the scent of sex was heavy in the air still.

The phone rang, and Jeni fumbled over Heather to answer it. Managing to get to the edge of the bed, she spoke softly into the mouthpiece.

Lindsay curled me into her arms. "It's the girlfriend," she whispered as she kissed my neck.

"What?" I asked.

"Jeni's girlfriend. Veronique. She flunked out because she was pregnant last year, but she calls Jeni every Saturday around noon to see how the party went."

"Oh," I mouthed. They were still together.

"Yeah, there was a really nice new girl named Kelly," Jeni was saying quietly into the phone. "Yes, we did."

We did what, I wondered. Have a nice time? Fuck? Is that what the girlfriend had asked?

Gingerly, I eased out from under Lindsay and slipped into the bathroom. As I sat, alone for the first time in over 12 hours, I smiled at the silly girl I had been when I arrived: I would only watch. Ha. I chuckled at my naivety. I stayed there until I no longer heard Jeni speaking on the phone, then delayed a bit longer still.

When I returned to the bedroom, Lindsay was resting against Jeni's arm in my place. All three seemed to be sleeping again. Biting my lip, I looked at how pretty they were, and I almost climbed back into that bed. But I didn't.

Carrying my shoes, I tiptoed out to the great room. I searched out my clothes and slipped into them. Well, my skirt and blouse, anyway. Who knows who had my panties. I checked my reflection in the mirror over the fireplace and groaned. Combing my fingers through my hair, I tried to make myself look a little more presentable, but I thought I looked like a girl who had spent the night fucking. Well, I had. Oh, well.

Quietly, I opened the front door and made my way out. From the sidewalk, I looked up at the penthouse windows, thinking of the girls still inside. Jeni was wonderful. Lindsay was wonderful. And so were Heather, and Caitlin and Sarah and Ashley and even Anna and the smoking girl. The sex had been phenomenal. Every girl ought to take part in a lesbian orgy at least once. I laughed at myself to think that way and made my way back to my little dorm room.

The stupid photographer said I was not interesting. Stupid jerk. So superior and snooty.

I am over six feet tall; I have blonde hair down to the middle of my back and a good figure. How could he say I was not interesting? I tossed my bag down onto the couch and stalked the apartment, feeling like I needed to do something and not knowing what. I don't drink. I don't smoke. There was nothing for me to do that I had seen other people do, to deal with their anger, and I sure as heck was not going to break anything.

I don't cuss either. Did cussing make girls interesting? I had never thought so, and I spent a lot of time with girls. From the time I was a young teen, I knew I was a lesbian. That is interesting, isn't it? I could tell him about the 127 girls; then, he wouldn't think I wasn't interesting. Or maybe he would. Tall blonde lesbians probably floated out of his studio every day. That was interesting, I thought. I plopped on the couch and felt sorry for myself as I pulled a pillow to my chest and pouted. What did he know?

Bill was not coming over. He was out playing in some honky-tonk later. He expected me to join him, but I just wasn't sure I could get myself together to be the adoring girlfriend. Yes, girlfriend. After nine years of dedicated homosexuality, I had a boyfriend. None of my old friends could believe it. My parents couldn't believe it. I met him when he joined in with some friends of mine that I'd gone out to see play music. He was just sitting in, so he and talked at the bar while he waited. He is about my dad's age. We have nothing in common. But he made me laugh like no man ever did before, and only a few women have. He said something charming about not being the kind of musician girls threw their panties to when I asked him about it. I told him I would if I liked him. I already liked him.

While he was getting set up to play, I went to the ladies' room and took off my thong. It was a tiny little thing that I really liked; it was so pretty. In the middle of his second song, I edged my way into the crowd at the edge of the dance floor and tossed it at him. It went about five feet and fell among the dancers; he didn't even see. Thongs are not aerodynamic. But I told him about it after, and in the lacy white dress I was wearing, it was not hard to prove to him that I wasn't wearing any panties any longer. He already knew I wasn't wearing a bra because he had been staring at my boobs all night. Well, not staring, but looking when he had the chance. He was trying to tell if he really could see my areolae through the material or not. We talked about it later. Surely that is interesting, isn't it?

What if I told about that photographer of Bill's taking me home and fucking me so I couldn't walk?

What was I doing going to a photographer anyway? I have skills. I have talents. I don't need to take my clothes off to make money. Well, I needed to make money. I haven't had a job in six months. And taking one's clothes off in front of a camera for money runs in my family. My grandmother did cheesecake and naturist magazines in the 50s and 60s. My mother did a major men's magazine in the 70s; her sister, my aunt, did a couple of porn movies back then too.

I wished Bill was home so I could talk to him and feel interesting. I wished Veronique, my darling lover, who broke my heart, hadn't moved to Ireland. I wished she hadn't broken my heart too. I wished the other 126 girls would come over.

Having sex with 127 girls should be of interest to someone. But whom? Does that seem like a lot? I'm 23. Is that a lot? I just had fun in college.

I made a rotten dinner for myself and wished Bill were home. I did three guys before Bill. One a few years older than me, who took my virginity, such as it was. And two other older guys. Lots older than me. I wished one of the two of them would come over and find me interesting. And bring his wife or significant other.

I knew what I needed when that desire occurred to me. A girl. A woman. Someone without a penis. I love Bill and all. I am pretty sure. But nine years of lesbianism can't fade away after one year of monogamous heterosexuality, can it? I took a shower, dressed to be looked at, and headed out the door for Christie's.

Gol, a year away, and I felt like I didn't know the place or anyone in it. I used to come often enough to be a regular, from the time I moved to Nevada. It was eerie. After a while, I saw one or two women I recognized as people I had seen there before. And the bartender remembered me because I didn't drink. She smiled at me, and I took my soft drink and wandered over to the dance floor. I like dancing, but I am not good at it. Bill is a great western swing dancer, but I still haven't picked it up well. All elbows and knees. Not interesting. There were some pretty women on the floor, and I watched one in particular until I felt a presence at my side. I was holding my drink in my left hand and the straw in my right. As I took a sip, I looked sideways at her between my fingers and the straw and my hair that was falling in my face.

She was nearly as tall as me, which is unusual enough. It wasn't that that made me gasp, though. She oozed power. Simply, she was the most confident person I had ever met, and I hadn't even met her yet.

"I could get her for you, if you want her," she said. I looked at the dancing woman I had been watching, then back at the power woman.

"If I want her, I can get her for myself," I told her. I can be pretty confident when not lolling in self-loathing because I am not interesting.

The power woman laughed softly. "It is a good thing you don't really want her then, is it not?" she whispered and slid her arm around my waist. Her scent was alluring, even though the smoke and other smells in the room. "My name is Rustina," she said, not really whispering, but not speaking out loud either. She pronounced it Roos-tina, in a European sounding way. I tried saying it to myself, but in my head, it sounded like I was an American girl trying to sound like a European girl. I went to boarding school in Switzerland and spoke French and German fluently, but Roos-tina, surrounded by hard American vowels, sounded silly.

"Jenifer," I told her and rolled my hips under her arm, letting her know I didn't mind it being there.

I have been with two older women, but it was when I was also doing the older guys. I had never just been to bed with a woman much older on my age. I decided it was going to be interesting. Power woman was so sure of herself; she had to know a thing or two. I lowered my drink and looked at her. She had silver hair cut just below her shoulders and blue eyes that were as hard as diamonds.

"I want you to do something for me, Jenifer," she said, her voice still at that low pitch. "I want you to lower the top of your dress."

"Right here?"

"Of course. What fun would it be otherwise?"

"They'll throw me out."

Her laugh was like water in a rapid. "I do not think so."

I believed her. "What if I don't want to do that?"

Her arm moved, and her hand slipped down to my bottom. It moved as she caressed me gently. I liked having her hand there. "What you want doesn't matter."

"A photographer I posed nude for today told me I was not interesting," I told her. It felt nice to confide in someone, even a stranger.

"I will hold your drink for you." She took it without waiting for my permission.

"You'll have to unzip me," I told her, turning my back to her. Her hand rose from my bottom, and sure fingers nudged the zipper tab down. I was wearing another white dress, but this one was short, sleeveless, and form-fitting. I reached up with both hands, draping my hair over my chest, and eased the shoulder straps down my arms, feeling my full breasts swaying as the tight material fell away and bunched at my waist. I turned to her and took back my glass.

Rustina laughed again in that water pouring over rocks way. "I was not sure if you were the one," she said, "but it seems you are."

"What one?" I asked, feigning innocence. I haven't been innocent in this millennium. "I'm just a girl who was told she was not interesting naked, compounding that problem by standing around in a lesbian bar with my boobs hanging out. See? No one even cares. No one has even noticed."

"True enough," power woman agreed, turning to smile at the women passing in front of us who were looking at my hair covered breasts. "What does matter is that I have bent you to my will."

I turned to look at her sideways, drawing back so I could look down my nose at her. "Oh? And where was I when this happened?"

More water pouring over rocks sounds slipped out of her. "You are standing on the edge of the dance floor with your dress bunched at your waist while every woman here is wishing you would move your hair. And you do this simply because I told you to do so."

"Do you think this is the first time I have taken off my top in a bar? It was my turn to laugh.

"Probably not. But this is the first time you have done so because I told you to do so."

I lifted the straw with my right hand again and sucked up more diet Coke. "Which 'one'?" I returned to her earlier comment.

Rustina's hand on my bottom moved, caressing me once more, teasing me. "Tell me, Jenifer, have you ever been whipped?

I swayed my shoulders to signify no. My breasts moved under my hair.

"I think you will like it quite a lot. I shall bind you first, as you will not be able to control yourself if I do not. Not without experience. And I shall not be harsh, merely cruel." Her fingers moved off my bottom and up my back, onto my bare skin, where her nails grazed lightly.

"What makes you think I will let you whip me, Rustina." I made myself say it correctly.

"What makes you think you have a choice, Jenifer?"

I'd been tied up before and liked it. And Bill has these nipple jewelry things he likes to press onto me. They are really fun. He wants me to get my nipples pierced, but I told him to pierce his darned nipples first, and we would talk about it. So far, he hasn't, and I am glad. More because a middle-aged man with pierced nipples would be more silly than that I would have to go through with it, myself.

Being whipped would be interesting, I thought. But would it make me interesting? In my darkest fantasies, I had allowed it. In the cyber play, I had flirted with it. Being whipped, I was attracted to her. She offered me the fulfillment of that darkness. Of course, I was going to let her. I was wet as soon as she said it.

"You aren't even going to offer to buy me a drink?" I asked coyly.

"You are drinking a soft drink."

"You aren't even going to ask me to dance."

"If you wanted to dance, you would be dancing, not watching others."

"Just going to take me home and whip me?"

"My home is in France. I plan to take you to my hotel."

I nodded. "Why me?"

There was that laughter again. "I find you interesting."

A nude German girl was kneeling on the floor of her suite as we entered. Unlike the power woman and me, she was slight. Her breasts were very small, but each nipple bore a ring through it. She had no hair in the body, either.

Rustina turned to me as we entered, barely, and said simply, "Undress." I fumbled behind me for the zipper of my dress, trying not to pay too much attention to the naked girl who rose from her knees and began helping Rustina out of her clothes. She was pretty, whoever she was, with fine light brown hair that came to her shoulders and a striking face. She looked really young. Younger than me anyway. Had I met her at Christie's, I might have tried to talk to her. I slipped out of my dress and tried to be graceful as I eased my thong past my hips and my legs. Then I stood there, just naked in my low heels with two strangers—kind of like college.

Rustina was gorgeous. Her breasts were high and full, as large as mine, but with the low sling of an older woman. The German girl knelt and helped her out of her skirt, and I was interested to see she wore a belt and stockings, but no panties. I didn't know older women went out clubbing without panties. Rustina turned to me, still in her stockings and heels, and I saw her pubic hair was also silver. I wondered what color it had been when she was younger. She moved easily and gently, with poise I liked and wished I could emulate. Usually, I was the confident one, as most of the girls I had been with were less experienced than I, at being naked around another girl. This time, I knew I was the one with something to learn.

"Bind her for whipping," she said to the German girl. She was looking at me, her hands drifting lightly over her nude body. Her smile was gentle and soft. I let the girl direct me, leading me across the room and fitting cuffs around my wrists, then connecting them with a short chain. Her fingers moved over me, taking liberties for someone whose name I did not know, fluttering over my breasts, across my hips, over the fluff on my mound. "Sie hat das Schamhaar," she said to Rustina. "She has hair on her pussy."

"Es ist nicht so wichtig," Rustina said. "It doesn't matter." I wondered why or why not. The German girl pulled what there was of it, fluffing it where my panties had crushed it down. I don't have much hair, really.

The German girl moved away from me and got a chair. She stood on it and pushed my arms until I raised them over my head. She led a rope from a hook in the ceiling through the chain between my cuffs and sharply pulled until I stood up straighter, realizing I had little room to move with my arms so high over my head. She pushed my head between my arms, so they were behind it, and pulled the rope again, forcing me to my toes. Stepping off the chair, she pulled my hair back and wound it into a bun and tucked it out of the way. I shivered, out of the way of the whip. She was making sure my body was uncovered for the whip. I eased down onto my heels again, just barely. There was a hook in the ceiling. Of a hotel suite. Quite accommodating of her, weren't they?

"Sie tut mir Leid," the girl said. I don't think either of them knew I spoke German.

"Sie hat nichts zu melden," Rustina muttered, taking a whip into her hand. She didn't care if the girl felt sorry for me.

"Schaden ihr."

The whip was short, about 18 inches or so, from the handle to the tips of the leather strips hanging from the end. It looked like it was braided leather, but I couldn't see it well. I had seen similar whips used by equestrians.

"Der Sauhund ist bereit, meine Göttin." The cunt was ready for her Goddess.

I took a deep breath, tired of being ignored and spoken of as a cunt and a thing. I was better than that. I looked at Rustina, standing there naked in her stockings and heels with a whip in her hand. I decided to be brave.

"Auspeitschen mir, Göttin." I said bravely. Whip me, Goddess.

Rustina smiled, knowing that her conversation with the girl had been understood. She raised one hand to the girl's fine hair and petted her. "Kiss her nipples, Birgit. Tease her. I want her excited first."

Birgit moved to me. I was so much taller than she; she could take my nipples between her lips without bending over at all. Her eyes rolled up at me, studying me as her mouth made love to my breasts. It was divine. I arched to feed her more of me, her tongue curling around one stiff tip, then the other. Her lips curled into a smile around my nipple as I dropped my head back, loving the overwhelming sensation of being bound, almost up on my toes, with a pretty girl sucking my nipple. And her presence warm and close. Rustina was somewhere behind me, waiting. She was in no hurry. I doubted she was ever in a hurry.

I cried out as Birgit's teeth closed into my flesh, scoring my nipple. Her hand was between my legs then, touching me, feeling the heat of excitement that I felt, and my pussy betrayed. She touched me. Her fingers were sure and confident as she caressed me. It was gentle and insistent, soft at first as she teased my lips into an opening for her, then she flicked her finger into me, fucking me as I stood before her.

"The bitch is wet, Mistress," she murmured around my nipple, in English now. Her accent was strong, stronger, perhaps by being half-muffled by my breast. I didn't like her calling me a bitch.

Rustina laughed softly, off to my left. I heard rushing water in it again. "Of course she is, she is about to be whipped."

I lifted onto my toes as I heard her say that. Was it true? Surely, I was wet because a beautiful girl was making love to me. A beautiful slave of a girl, with a shaved cunt and rings in her nipples and clit hood, was adoring my nipples and finger fucking me as I stood with my arms bound over my head. That was what was making me excited.

The first lash stung and startled me, falling on my unprotected ass with no warning. It was followed by a second that danced the whip's tail fully over my round bottom, getting my attention more than anything. It was light and soft, a kiss of a touch.

My back arched, despite my conscious efforts not to move. It was a reaction to the touch, not to any pain. I flushed, embarrassed by my body, acting out of my control. I heard Birgit laughing at me as she lifted her mouth from my nipple and her finger left me. She stepped back, raising her finger to her lips and sucking my cream from it as her smile mocked me.

"The bitch tastes good, Mistress, but she has no control."

"How could she," Rustina said, her voice chiding. "This is her first time."

The whip cracked against my flesh, stinging sharply this time. I arched again, feeling pain as the leather-wrapped around me. I whimpered, despite myself, then the whip wrapped around my waist, scoring my soft skin as it snapped. The tips caught my tummy and stung me. I hadn't expected that;

544

I had thought a whipping would be only on my back—silly me. The whip left me again, and I stayed tensed, up on my toes, afraid of where it would fall again, dreading it and still wanting it. I found myself biting my lip in anticipation; then my body gave out, I had to relax my taut muscles. I let myself down, flat-footed, taking a deep breath, and then she struck again when I was unready.

I cried out loudly this time, the cruel whip smashing across my back, falling between my raised shoulder blades. She hurt me.

"Breathe, Jenifer," she whispered in my ear. Her lush body pressed to my whipped back. I could feel the softness of her breasts grazing my skin. "Breathe in, slowly, absorb the pain. Take it in and control it. Own it. Make it yours."

I nodded, slowing my breathing, counting as high as I could before stopping the inhalation, then trying to count down to 0 again as I let it out. Rustina let me take two or three deep breaths, waiting until I was calm again. That little bitch Birgit was standing nearby, still smirking at me in my distress. I hated her for that.

I let my head fall back between my arms, breathing slowly, once more in control of my own body. My eyes closed, and I cleared my head.

Searing pain burst through my breasts. My breasts! She had whipped them. My head strike forward, all thought of breathing gone as pain seared through me. I jerked my bonds, fighting to be free. I had never felt pain like that before, ever. Before I could even think of recovering from the first lash, she was at them again, kicking the tips of her evil little whip across the soft, full roundness of my boobs. I cried out again, feeling my eyes welling with tears.

I knew she was standing in front of me. She must have pushed that mean little bitch out of the way to be able to whip my breasts as she did. I forced my eyes open, clouded as they were with tears. There she was, legs spread wide in a steady stance, the vicious whip dangling from her right fist. That long white hair was falling in disarray over her nearly naked body, a thin sheen of sweat lighting her, stray wisps of hair clinging to her skin. She was smiling.

"Jenifer." She said my name to clear my head. "Jenifer, you must ask this time. Do you understand?

I shook my head, understanding all too well.

"Yes, my darling. You must." She closed to me, raising her left hand to my cheek, laying her open palm there, calming me and soothing me as she spoke softly and clearly. "You must and you will."

I looked at her through my tears. She was so beautiful. How could I not?

"Whip my breasts, Rustina."

She smiled and leaned in to kiss me, her lips full, soft, and warm on my own. I wanted it to linger, and I reached for her with my tongue.

"It makes you wet, doesn't it?"

I focused my thoughts again. Did it? I was wet. Very wet. I was dripping. Without even being free to touch my self, I felt I was.

"Yes."

I could hear the smile on her lips as she went on, "Open your legs."

I was stretched so, I didn't know how I could, but I edged my feet apart and spread my thighs open. I forced my breathing to slow, fearing what was to come, but craving it too. The lash across my skin hurt so, but the sting excited me too.

Suddenly, the whip was wrapping around my upper body, tightening to my skin as she flung it at me. I cried out at the touch, the harsh, evil bark of leather on my softness. Rustina raised her hand again, letting the whip fall, hitting my swaying boobs as my body fought the sensation, trying to draw away even as my mind tried to gain control and hold still for her assault. Tears ran down my face as the pain gained the upper hand, and I started to close my thighs to get a better stance.

"Open, you stupid girl," Rustina hissed, her voice harsh and cruel, not the laughing brook of earlier. I forced my long legs open again, and she brought the whip up between them, crashing down on my sex. My eyes clouded over with waves and flashes of red and black as the most extreme pain I had ever felt surged through me. I screamed and begged her to stop, but the whip landed again, again, and again.

Then it stopped, and my senses sorted themselves out. I was aware of the lingering pain, the gasping of my lungs, the awkwardness of my position, arms high over my head, legs apart, body heaving. I tried to maintain position even through the agony of it.

There was the sound of something heavy falling to the floor and Rustina's voice from somewhere away from me. "Release her." After a moment, I felt Birgit lowering my hands and unfettering them. I lowered my aching arms, now tingling as if asleep, and they hung heavily at my sides as I sobbed.

My pussy felt like it was on fire. Waves of residual pain throbbed through me. I could barely stand, but I had no orders to do anything else. Sniffling, I turned, my hair sticking to my face where the tears had wet it, and I saw Birgit kneeling between Rustina's legs, licking her slavishly. I wanted to release myself, to be licked, to lick too. Rustina's hand rested lovingly on her girl's head as the girl adored her sex. Rustina barely raised her eyes to me and tilted her head in the direction of the door.

"You may go, Jenifer," she said, her voice once more the sound of water flowing over rocks.

Through the tears, I searched the floor for my discarded dress, seeing the whip lying where she had dropped it as easily as she was now dropping me. I stepped into the dress, shuddering as the material touched to my aching flesh. I didn't even think of trying to zip it or finding my panties. I stumbled toward the door, reeling from the humiliation of it all. Her voice had left no question that I was only to go. I was too proud to beg. Wasn't I? Behind me, I heard her crying out as the German girl pleasured her.

At the door, I paused, barely uttering one word. "Please?"

Her orgasm drowned me out.

Reeling down the hallway, I crashed into one wall and leaned heavily into it as I waited for the elevator. My hands reached under my dress to touch my pussy, caressing my clit, rubbing to bring on my orgasm. I was in such need I cared nothing for fear of being seen getting myself off in the hall; I only needed to cum. The orgasm crashed through me, robbing me of breath, and I collapsed heavily to the floor, fingers inside of my hurt puss.

I collected myself as I heard the elevator door open. Getting my feet under me, I wobbled into the box, glad it was empty. Crying, sighing, reeking of sex, I looked at myself in the mirrored walls, seeing my striped back for the first time under my still open dress. My hair was mussed, and my face a horror show of dried tears and smeared make-up. I did what I could but still could not close the dress for the pain. My hair mostly covered me, though.

Scurrying through the lobby, I got to my car and drove as fast as I could to where Bill was playing, dying for the touch of his big hands on my brutalized flesh and the bliss of his cock filling my pussy with love and adoration.

But I sat in my car and cried once I got the parking lot of the joint where Bill was playing. My body hurt, and I knew I looked horrid. How was he going to react to his girlfriend showing up freshly whipped? I slowed my breathing and let the tears stop. I managed to clean my face and work up the zipper of my dress with a little effort, cringing as the tight material closed over my scored flesh. My thighs were sticky.

I ran a brush through my long hair. Eventually, I eased out of the car and walked gingerly into the nightclub. I didn't see Bill right away, so I made my way to the ladies' room and did a little more clean up there. I didn't look quite the mess any longer, but I was glad the dancehall was dark, and no one would get a good look at me. Turning, I lifted my hair from my back and saw where I was marked with a crisscross of dull red welts above the low back of my dress. One livid red welt was visible across my left breast above the neckline in the front.

It was later than I had thought. When I left the restroom, the lights were coming up, and Bill and the other musicians were packing up their instruments. I silently stood as I watched him working, the hurts in my body throbbing. He saw me and smiled, coming over and taking me in his arms. Bill is a big guy, and his hugs are firm and strong. I usually love them, feeling so secure when wrapped up in him.

This time, I shied away, afraid of what his touch would do to my hurts. Bill was surprised. I had never avoided him before. "What's the matter, Jeni?" he asked with genuine concern. Taking a deep breath, I told him. I told my boyfriend I had been feeling small and insignificant and had gone to a lesbian bar and let an older woman pick me up, take me to her hotel, and whip me before turning me out like a dog. I said it all in a rush to get it over with. I couldn't lie to him; I didn't want to. I wanted him to know what his girlfriend had done. I was flushed and embarrassed and crying by the time I finished. I had never been so humiliated in my life, and yet I was so fucking wet. I could feel myself dripping.

Bill slipped his arms around me gently and lovingly. He didn't say anything, taking time for just the right answer, as is his way. I wasn't sure if I wanted him to say anything or not. I was afraid he would condemn me. I feared he would call me names I didn't deserve. Or maybe I did deserve them. Finally, he slipped his fingers through mine and picked up his guitar, and we went out of the bar.

The parking lot was nearly empty. The last cars were pulling out, although there seemed to be a fair number of abandoned ones, left overnight for collection in the morning. Bill's truck was around the side, parked against the wall almost at the rear, and he walked slowly waiting for me as I moved gingerly. He carefully stowed his guitar in the back, then turned to me.

"Whipped?"

I couldn't look at him. I only nodded.

He didn't say anything, something I have gotten used to with him because he often takes a long time to give an opinion. Not the sort to just blurt something out.

"You're okay?"

I wasn't expecting him to ask that; I nodded again. He moved closer and gently touched my face. He was so gentle.

"Please," I whispered, turning my back and lifting my hair. "Unzip me. My dress is so tight it hurts."

The relief was immediate as he ran the zipper down, and my body was released. I even pulled my arms out of the sleeves and let the entire top fall down. It reminded me of how bold I had been only hours before when I had done the same thing in the other bar at Rustina's instruction.

I shivered as I stood there before my lover, my whipped boobs for him to see.

"Bill, I don't know what to say. I'm sorry... I don't know..."

He silenced me with a kiss. His big hands covered my breasts as our lips met. They felt wonderful, soothing away the pain lingering there. And his touch intensified the sensation too. It felt both good and bad. "How could anyone whip such beautiful breasts?" he asked as we kissed.

I let him kiss me, loving how masculine he was, even in kissing. "I..." I started, our lips separating briefly. "...I liked it."

"You did?" he murmured on my lips. His fingers pressed more deeply into the flesh of my breast. The feeling was intense, fierce, a mingling of ebbing pain and tenderness.

"I did."

I liked it so much that I had to show him how much. I moved closer to him, sliding over one of his legs, pressing my sex to him. I ground myself to him, so horny at that moment; I was sure it was going to kill me. My fingers worked open his cowboy belt buckle, unbuttoned his jeans, and reached in to find his cock. It was hard, and I had to wrap my fingers around him and twist and pull to get him out. I wanted him in me.

Leaning my shoulders against the wall of the dancehall, the only part of my back I could safely touch to it, I lifted my dress to my waist and spread my legs. Bill was inside of me with a single thrust. A touch to open my lips, and he was inside. God, I was wet.

"You liked having your big tits whipped?" Bill hissed as he fucked me. Because I am so tall, he could do me standing up by simply rocking up and down on his toes, driving that fine cock of his into my sex, and rolling his hips as he filled me, stretching my clit and bumping it with each thrust. I rose up and down on my toes too, my heels giving me extra height so that I could also bend my long legs just a little to slam down harder onto his cock.

He broke the kiss, waiting for my answer. "I loved having my big tits whipped."

He slammed into me again, lifting me and scrapping my shoulders against the wall, forcing my back to it, and I shivered with the pain. And it felt good.

Drawing back, Bill slapped my left boob. His hand stung across the welts of Rustina's whip. I lurched forward, and my breast slightly dangled as he smacked me again. I forced myself up again, arching my back, thrusting my breasts up, open to his abuse. His hand came down on my other one, from below, lifting it as he came up. It stung, and I ground my cunt down on his cock as it dropped after the blow and swayed. Then he did it once more, the smack echoing across the empty lot as his hand crashed against my bare, tender, soft, naked flesh.

"Fuck me, Bill," I moaned. My nipples ached, they were so hard. I rose on my toes again, as he lowered, and we came together hard, my pussy filled up with him and my clit pressed at the base of his cock, and I came. I didn't even care if anyone heard me.

I fucked him back, clawing at his back through his shirt. He lifted me up, off my feet, my long legs dangling as I was flattened against the honky-tonk wall and fucked silly. I came again, shivering and shuddering against him as I raised my legs around his hips and took him into me as deeply as he would go. The head of his cock bumped roughly on my cervix, but I didn't care this time.

He kissed me again, and I laid kiss after kiss on him as he hammered me ruthlessly, up against the wall. I needed this. I needed the orgasms born of pain. I came again, rearing up on his cock, rolling my shoulders across the wall, and I felt him slam into me one more time, all the way in as he got off too. He held me there as he spurts into my cunt, holding me to the wall he had fucked me up against.

We kissed as my legs finally slipped from him to support my weight again, though I needed Bill's help to stand. He was a little weak-kneed too. He stayed in me until his erection softened.

"I love you," I said. I really did.

"I love you too, Jeni," he told me.

"Even if photographers won't hire me and lesbian Dommes whip me and reject me?"

He lifted from my body, easing away from the wall, and led me by the hand to his truck, while I wore my dress bunched around my hips, whipped boobs and ass visible for all to see. The parking lot was deserted, though. He helped me inside the cab, and I winced at the touch of the seat on my ass and back as I slipped my dress off. I'd ride home nude, and we could pick up my car later.

Bill swung into the truck and leaned over to kiss me. One of his big hands covered my right breast, and he caressed me lovingly for a moment or two. As he started the truck and backed us out, he dropped his hand between my legs and began to tease my clit. I was making a mess of the seat, but I doubt he cared. His fingers smeared my wetness over my clit and got me all excited.

I put the truck into gear for him.

"Yes, Jeni. Even if. I find you very interesting.

I came.

Story 05

I had a date on Friday with a boy I had seen a time or two before. I liked him well enough to see a movie and dinner, but there were no sparks between us. I hadn't slept with him, so this date was kind of the point where we either were, or we weren't, and I just wasn't sure whether we would. Then he called and asked if it were okay if we doubled with a friend of his and another girl. I wasn't sure that sounded like a good idea, but also he suggested that the four of us might drive up to the ski resort on Friday to ski Saturday and Sunday. I love skiing, so I agreed.

I was watching from the window as they pulled up in front of my dorm to pick me up in a gray Jeep that looked horribly familiar. Austin hopped out of the passenger seat and ran up to call for me. The driver stepped out, and I just cringed. It was Tom, the last guy I had dated, the one I liked so, but who just been interested enough in me. Oh, great. And then a girl got out of the rear passenger seat. She was blonde and pretty, and I had seen her naked. Her name was Lindsay, and she and I had met at a very intimate party about two months earlier.

So, of the three of them, the only one I hadn't done it with was my date.

That should make for an interesting weekend. I thought as I rolled my eyes and answered Austin's knock. My skis and bags were already waiting in the lobby, so I grabbed my coat and headed down to face a very awkward situation. I could just imagine the introductions. "Oh, sure, Austin, I do know Tom. In fact, I've had his cock up my butt. Oh, and Lindsay? Yes, she's lovely. I've had my tongue in her pussy too." I could just see myself batting my eyelashes ingenuously at that.

It was much easier, with both of them acknowledging that we knew one another without either letting on just how well. Well, Tom smiled more than he might have. Lindsay was just precious. She squeezed my hand to let me know she was happy to see me again.

The snowstorm we ran into an hour out of town was beautiful at first. Then the road started to cover over, and Tom had to drive more slowly, even after putting the Jeep into four-wheel drive. Still two hours from the resort, it became obvious that we should get off the road. When we saw a sign for a motel up ahead, Lindsay suggested we do just that. The boys argued for going on, but even they had to admit stopping somewhere was a good idea when we were forced to slow to no more than 20 miles per hour. A lot of other travelers had the same idea, and the parking lot of the motel was jammed. We were lucky to get one of the few rooms they had. Even so, it was only 4:00 in the afternoon.

We took in our luggage and looked at the two beds and the close quarters and wondered what we were going to do until morning. The snow had filled up the satellite dish, and so TV reception was horrid. Tom had brought a twelve-pack of beer, which was gone within the first hour in the room. The motel pool was drained for the winter. We had no playing cards, only two books (mine), and, within two hours, we were about to drive each other crazy. Tom looked like he wished Austin and I would take a long walk so he could fuck Lindsay, but he was way too polite to say so. Lindsay was quiet and looked generally uncomfortable.

I decided to take a shower and wash off some of the day and the road. When I came out, I slipped into a tee and jeans in the bathroom nook out of the boys' sight. Lindsay joined me there and stripped off her clothes, slipping past me and into the shower too. Her bare breasts grazed over my thinly covered ones as she did. I quivered with delight as we touched. I kind of felt funny about it, though. I dried my hair while looking at the blurred outline of her naked body through the shower door's frosted glass. Finally, I moved to sit on the empty refrigerator so that I could still sort of see her and look out the window overlooking the parking lot as well. It was still coming down.

Watching the snowfall got old fast, Tom was reading one of my books, and Austin was watching the snow on the TV screen, trying to find a channel that would come in. I combed my hair out and stared at the four walls and the two boys and finally Lindsay as she stepped out of the shower wrapped in a towel and began to blow dry her hair while standing before the mirror in the bathroom alcove. I could see her nude all along one flank where the towel parted and fell away as she leaned over from where I sat. I didn't think the boys could see her, though. I bit my lip as I looked at her, my tummy fluttering as I realized that seeing her like that was turning me on. Another girl was turning me on. Again.

"Oh, hell," I said finally, "let's just all just fuck."

The boys stared at me. Lindsay laughed. It was a light laugh, but one that showed she was glad the tension had broken. She turned off the hairdryer and stepped out of the bath nook. Then into the room with the rest of us.

"What," asked my date, Austin, "all of us?" He looked at Lindsay and Tom.

I nodded. "Yes, all of us. You and me, him her, me and her, whatever." I pulled my t-shirt over my head and free of my hair and cast it away.

"You're not serious," Austin said, still not believing it. Tom was looking from me to Lindsay and back, smiling.

I wasn't wearing a bra, so the boys and Lindsay got a good look at my breasts as I got up from my chair and began to slip out of my pants. I am tallish and slender, with small but nicely formed breasts. I think they only really look good when my nipples are hard, though, and they were hard right then. I held out my hand for Lindsay, and she came to me slowly. Once she did, I looked directly into her eyes to see if she would go along. She gave me a look that said she kind of liked the idea and wasn't quite so sure too. Well, I wasn't so sure it was a great idea either, but what was there to do? Besides, it was all her fault, turning me on like she did and all.

A strange question occurred to me. Was it seeing a naked girl that had turned me on so, or was it Lindsay herself who did?

Reaching out, I untucked her towel and let it drop. Lindsay shivered, turned to look at the two boys briefly, and came into my arms. She was warm and soft and fresh from the shower and felt wonderful as I touched my bare skin to her.

The two of us let the wonder of two naked girls standing in each other's arms wash over the two boys. I brought my lips to Lindsay's neck and kissed and licked her there. She cooed and purred, wriggling to me before turning her face to mine and kissing me.

"Well?"

Tom was up and out of his pants in an instant. His sweater flew across the room. He was up and tearing the covers from one of the beds in just his jockeys.

I sashayed over to Austin and tugged him to his feet. The boy was in shock; it seemed. To have his shy, demure, never-more-than-a-little-hand-holding-and-a-quick-peck-goodnight date standing before him in just her panties was a bit much for him, so say nothing of the curvy blonde holding my hand. I helped to pull his sweater off, and Lindsay opened his pants and tugged them down. Giggling, we pushed Austin onto his butt on the bed and worked his shoes off, and took his pants down. As we held his legs, I looked right into Lindsay's sexy brown eyes and let her know I wanted her again. Her eyes said it all. She knew. We let go of Austin's legs and moved a step closer. Curling her fingers around the hip band, she tugged down my panties and helped me step out of them.

Leaning in to barely whisper to me, she said heatedly, "I want you." Her head pulled back again, and a huge grin split her pretty face. I looked at her, and she nodded, then she kissed me deeply and longingly. We held the kiss for a moment, out bodies touching. And then all too soon, she rose and moved to Tom on the other bed. I saw her flow down to her knees and dip her head between his open legs. I turned away before I saw her take him into her mouth. I mean, this whole group sex thing had been my idea and all but seeing her give him head was more than I could stand right away. Maybe ever.

Meanwhile, in our bed, nothing was happening yet. Austin lay across it, stretched out on his back, and so I moved over him, my hands stroking his bare chest and up and down his body. His skin was warm under my touch, and I bent my head to lick and taste him. He shivered a little as I curled my tongue around his nipple. Behind me, I head Lindsay and Tom doing it. No longer was she sucking him. They were fucking. She was crying out as he did her, as he fucked her and made her cum. He was inside her, but I didn't want to turn and see him inside of her. I needed a bit more time before I could stand seeing my ex-boyfriend making love to a girl who had made love to me. I wrapped my fingers around Austin's cock and stroked him, feeling him hard and smooth under my touch. I could hear Lindsay cumming again. I lifted my leg and slipped over Austin's body, holding his cock up to my sex and touching the head of it to my wet lips. I rubbed against him, slipping the length of him along my pussy to my clit. Austin groaned at the touch of me on him. I rolled my hips, grasped his cock, and held it up straight to take him inside. The head of his thing pushed inside of me. I drew back, wetting the head with my cream, then pushed down again, taking him further into me this time. I rose again, leaving his cock shiny with my excitement.

I kept on fucking to him, taking him a bit deeper into my pussy each time I slid down onto him until finally I rested my clit on the base of his cock and rolled my hips, trying to get that exquisite feeling

I can sometimes get that way. I was rewarded with the least little tingle, then I rose, feeling the tug of his prick dragging out of me, stretching me, and then I fell on him again, his penis shoved deep up and filling me. I leaned over him and dragged my stiff nipples over Austin's chest. We began to move together, with me now lying across his body. I was in no hurry, and, being on top like that, I could slow the boy down when I felt him getting too excited. We moved leisurely together, just fucking. It was nice.

My ass came up as I drew off his cock, and I felt a swish across it. I turned to see what it had been, and Lindsay was grinning at me, her brown eyes dancing with fire. Leaning down again, she swiped her tongue across my skin. I blew her a kiss and turned back to Austin, gripping his shoulders and crushing my breasts to his chest, giving Lindsay as much access to my bottom as she chose to take. Mmmmmmmm. The bed moved as it took her weight. Her little tongue crept between my cheeks again, and she wickedly lapped at my dark star. She had done this once before, and I had really liked it, even though it had seemed so strange for someone to do to me. Kind of dirty, you know?

I began thrusting my hips, rotating my pussy around Austin's cock high up inside me and trying to find just that right pressure on my clit as Lindsay pointed her tongue into me and pressed. I groaned and moaned and gripped Austin tighter. Lindsay wetly sponged my ass with her tongue, exciting me. Then, abruptly, her tongue was gone, and I felt her breast graze my back as she brought her mouth to my ear.

"Kelly, darling, do you think you can stand this?" she whispered. Then I felt Tom behind me. His thighs brushed mine as he stroked his cock along the cleft of my bottom. I was scared but excited too. Were they planning what I thought they were? Lindsay kissed my lips and moved back again. I felt her hair softly on my ass as she rested her head upon it and took Tom's cock into her mouth. She was wetting him too, wetting the both of us so she could join us together. I felt her head roll, and her tongue once again swept across my skin, found my star, and wriggled against it. Her lips pursed as her tongue pushed a dollop of saliva into my butt. Then the head of Tom's cock touched me there, along with her tongue, and I held still on top of Austin as he began to push into me.

I looked into Austin's eyes as I felt Tom begin to enter me. He must have seen so many things in mine if he cared to see them. At first, the little sharp pain as Tom stretched my ass, and he entered me, Lindsay's hand guiding his cock into my ass. Then the incredible stuffed sensation as I took him deeper inside of me. Lust. Desire. Depravity. I hooked my arms under his and wrapped my fingers over his shoulders from behind to give myself more support; then I pushed down onto Tom's cock. And onto Austin's cock. Oh, god. I had never felt anything remotely like that before. I grunted and growled and howled and made all kinds of un-girly noises, I am sure. I pulled forward, feeling the two cocks leaving my body. I pushed down again, and the two of them rose into me once more. Tom's hands caught my hips, and he began to guide me, setting the rhythm now, taking me.

"Oh, god, Kelly, you have Tom's cock up your butt," Lindsay whispered in my ear. "And Austin is in your cunt. Can you stand it?" I nodded as it was starting to feel really, really good. Amazingly good. Fantastic. God! She kissed me, shooting her tongue into my mouth and fucking my face with her passion. She pulled her tongue back, grinning wildly again, and said, "I've never kissed a girl who was having her ass fucked before."

I giggled and then grunted. "I've never kissed a girl while having two cocks inside of me."

She kissed me again. "Oh, Kelly," she cooed around our joined lips, "you are so fucking beautiful right now. A cock in your pussy and one up your butt. How do you feel?"

"Full?" We both laughed, and I felt Tom increasing his thrusts into me, and I moved to slam down onto Austin with the same enthusiasm. Then Austin cried out and grabbed my boobs as he came, lifting his hips off the bed and filling my pussy with his hardness. I ground down onto him and Tom and finally felt that sweet spot as my clit rubbed just so to the base of Austin's cock. I lost it. I found it. I reared back, tossing my hair as I did so that it fell over Tom in a calico cascade, and came. I lay my head on his shoulder and pushed my ass down hard onto his cock. He reached around and covered my little breasts with his big hands, flattening them to my chest and holding me tight as I rode out the magnificent orgasm that tortured my body with such delight.

Lindsay caressed and kissed me again as I gasped. The feeling in my body was terrifying in its intensity. I couldn't breathe. She peeled away one of Tom's hands from my breast and covered my stiff tip with her lips, sucking my nipple as my breathing returned. Austin's dick wilted inside of me, but Tom was still hard and wanting more. I rose and lifted one leg so Austin could slip from under me. I knelt on the bed, leaning down onto my elbows and pushing my bottom at Tom's cock once again.

"You're insatiable," Lindsay laughed, then shimmied around so that her sex was right there under my chin. Her fingers caressed my face, leading me down to her, and I kissed her pussy softly as Tom continued to do my ass. I used my lips to tug gently on her hair. She had dark pubic hair. I felt the heat rising in me again. I had come before from his fucking my ass when we had dated. I was sure I was going to again. Lindsay stroked my hair and lifted her hips a little as my tongue followed the line of her labia. I licked gently, still quite new to this whole pussy-licking thing. Pointing my tongue, I slipped it into her. She reached for my hands and intertwined her fingers with mine as my tongue slipped between her lips. I swept up with my tongue, over her clit, flicking there because I remembered she had once done that very thing to me. I think it was her, anyway. Her body trilled in response, shuddering, and dropping back onto the bed. I lapped again, the throbbing sensation in my ass growing as Tom hurried his thrusts again. That Tom. I swear, he could fuck all night without coming, just to please his lover again and again. His hands were on my hips, bounced me up and down on his hard cock, and I felt another orgasm growing up inside of me.

I clutched Lindsay's hands hard in mine and closed my lips down over her clit, pressing down and tugging, letting the suction of my closed mouth pull at her skin. Softening, I repeated the touch, all the while, feeling Tom driving hard and fast into my ass. Lindsay's hands left mine as she wrapped her fingers tight around my wrists and dug in. I licked at her pussy still, then gasped and opened my mouth as I felt Tom push hard into my ass and then held, the thing he always did when he was coming. I pushed back hard to him, letting my body take his cum, hearing him gasping and crying out his pleasure as he blew off.

I stopped tasting Lindsay for that moment, concentrating on Tom and his marvelous cock and what it did to me. I came again, shuddering around his hardness in my softness. I am loud when I come, and I tried to stifle the noisiness of me by pressing my lips to Lindsay's pussy again, but she caught up my hair and lifted my mouth free.

"No, darling, I want to hear you," she said softly. I looked into her eyes again, and she smiled her wicked smile once more. I cried out freely, my body alive with such bliss and sensation at that moment.

Lindsay turned and lay her head on Austin's lap, catching my eyes again as they opened, and she slipped her lips over his soft cock. She drew up, released him from her mouth, and wrapping her fingers around his shaft as she mouthed, "I taste you," to me. She pushed her lips onto him again, taking his erection in her mouth. I didn't mind seeing her suck Austin's cock at all, though the idea of the way seeing her suck off Tom earlier had made me turn away. I wasn't in love with Tom or anything, but he had dumped me, and I guess I was hurt still. I didn't know why he dumped me that he had taken up with Lindsay, who is blonder and bustier than I, struck a chord with my insecurity about my looks and a small chest—danged old busty blondes. Who do they think they are anyway?

This particular busty blonde must have thought she was a pretty fine little cocksucker; I'll say that for her. She had Austin hard again in moments and twisted her luscious body around so that she could bob that blonde head up and down on his cock with abandon. I had never seen anyone giving a blowjob before in person, so it was quite fascinating to watch. Added to that was the sensation of Tom's cock softening in my ass and eventually slipping out. Good old Tom. He was excellent about that, always leaving his cock in me after we fucked and came. Some guys do you and come and then take it out and collapse on the bed next to you and, you know, it just leaves me feeling so fucking empty afterward it almost makes me want to cry.

Austin had just seen his date get butt-fucked and lick another girl as/after he had fucked her himself for the very first time. That is probably a little much for most boys, I suspect. Lindsay was reassuring his guy ego with a bj from heaven. If you are going to have a group sex, it helps to be part of the group, you know? By making him shoot off in her mouth, Lindsay both gave herself to him and included him. I pressed my lips to her pussy again as she raised her left leg for me. I wanted so to make her cum on my lips and tongue. Slipping two fingers into her, I curled them up and wriggled. Lindsay cried out, lifting her head from Austin's dick to gasp for air before taking him in again and bobbing her head up and down urgently.

Tommy had gotten out of bed and was washing his cock in the bathroom sink. He always did that after anal sex, just in case any girls wanted to put it into their mouths or pussies. Such a polite boy.

Austin came as sweet Lindsay moved her mouth up and down on him. I hoped that she, too, was relishing the moment as she pressed her face into his pubic hair and held him deep in her mouth. Her eyes bulged when she felt him cum, and I saw her throat muscles moving as she swallowed. I reached up to clear the hair from my eyes, wondering if that was how I looked when I swallowed. Maybe I should look in a mirror while going down on Tom sometime and see.

A little cold chill hit me as I realized I had that thought about Tom and not my date. Tom had a girlfriend now. Okay, so that girlfriend had my date's cock buried in her mouth at the moment with her throat working his cum down into her tummy, but that was just for tonight, right? It wasn't like the four of us were going to ever do this again. But what about three of us? What about that?

Pretty Lindsay drew herself up off of Austin's penis and came to me, kissing me and taking me into her arms. Her warm, soft breasts pressed wonderfully to mine, and my arms went around her, touching her and caressing her. Lying back, we sprawled over the bed as our bodies responded to one another. Her tongue opened my lips and slipped between them as it sought out my own. Under my fingers, her nipple stiffened. So, here I was in the arms of a girl again. IT was different this time, but darkly the same as that earlier time in the fall too. At that moment, in the motel room, it was just we two girls. The boys were witnesses, not participants in this expression of our desire.

I tasted Austin's cum on her lips and felt delightfully wicked to be doing so. She had just sucked off a guy, and here I was kissing her mouth and tasting him. I still hadn't even gone down on Austin, and he was my date. I had lost sleep after the last time I had made love to Lindsay, from the whole magnitude of that experience, because of what I had done, homosexuality being such a dirty word to so many. Lesbian. Just what all parents want their little girls to grow up to be. I didn't think I was a lesbian, though. I mean, I had just fucked two boys, after all, as much fun as holding Lindsay and kissing her was. I wondered what was going to make me lose sleep this time. The girl-to-girl thing or doing two guys at the same time? Guilt sucks.

I gave myself over to the experience, telling myself it didn't matter, that kissing Lindsay was making me excited and wet and who cared why. She pressed me over on the bed, onto my back, and my legs just opened so naturally to her. She broke the kiss, grinning that wicked grin again as she straddled my face and lowered her sex to my lips once more. I extended my tongue to lick her. Down below, between my open legs, she dipped her head and touched her lips and tongue to me. Her dangling hair fell and tickled on my naked thighs and ass as she moved her tongue. I cried out at her touch, right into her pussy, hearing my passion muffled by her pussy. Then that bad girl licked lower, to my bottom again, her pointed tongue wriggling into my dark star.

While licking me, there was something Lindsay liked to do, and I decided it must be something she liked to feel herself. And if she was dating Tom, knowing that boy likes to do girls in their bottoms, there was a pretty good chance that he had fucked her there. I lowered my lips away from her sex, tilted my head back, and reached up for her hips, pulling her down to me and pushing out my tongue to touch her there. I had never, ever, licked anyone there. I was a little afraid, but I wanted to give her the pleasure she had now given me three times in that intimacy.

Taking a deep breath, I pushed my tongue up, tasting the tart, mustiness of her there, finding it was not so bad at all, for all of its nastiness to think about. There must be a name for what I was doing, probably dirty ones. I laved her ass with my tongue, and I was rewarded with the response of her luscious body, shivering above me as I did. She cried out and curled on top of me, her breasts dragging over my tummy, teasing me with her nipples as they pointed with pleasure. Her ass lifted, and she moved her sex back to my mouth, wanting me to bring her off, I could tell. My lips closed over her clit, and I massaged her with them as my tongue pressed to her. She began to bounce lightly, everything in the way she moved, telling me to go on, do just that, and take her away.

Her mouth moved to, doing to me as I did to her, first licking at my pussy with long, broad strokes, circling my clit, pushing and moving me in ways that made me cry out again and want exactly more of that very thing. Her orgasm surprised me, empowered me. It was different than I expected, her thighs stiffening around my head, and she held her body still as it grew rigid as sensation swept through her. Then I felt my orgasm reaching up and rushing through me under her tongue. I fell back from her pussy, keeping my mouth open and gaping as that ultimate pleasure filled me up and emptied me.

I lay there, gasping for a moment, unable to breathe once again it seemed, unable to think, unable to do anything but feel. And I felt so very good.

The bed moved around and under me, and Tom knelt above me, straddling my face, his cock hard and stiff and clean. He pointed it at Lindsay's pussy, stroking her lips with the head, like a painter with a brush, wetting it in her. Then he pulled back and dropped it to me, to my lips. I reached for it with my tongue, curling around him, tasting the tartness of girl on his skin. He eased his cock past my lips, moving in and out of me gently. Taking himself out of my mouth, he touched his cock to Lindsay's pussy again, this time pushing all the way into her. I watched as he pulled back, that long, clean shaft coming out of her shiny with her cream, then disappearing into her again as he thrust forward. It was fascinating to see, going in and out of her, stretching her. Her sex opened and pulled, the shape of it changing around him as he fucked her.

I raised my head and let my tongue run over his cock as it came out, caressing him before moving into her again. I licked lower, over his balls, but I knew he didn't like having his balls sucked. Some guys do. Not Tom. Instead, I swept my tongue up, licking behind his balls, to his ass, pointing my tongue to press it to him there. He tasted different from Lindsay, more male, I guess, not bad at all, just totally different. On and on we went, me licking, him fucking, Lindsay mewling softly with pleasure as he did her. That cock had been in me. In my mouth. In my pussy. More recently, in my ass. I loved that cock; I wanted that cock. And that pussy. I wanted them both so.

I felt the power of their fucking growing as he slammed into Lindsay, taking her away again, her orgasm surging through her body until she wrapped her arms around my thighs and buried her mouth in my sex. I felt her pressing to me, holding me as she came again, loving that she was coming. Tom held his cock deep in her until her body quieted again, then he stroked her gently, keeping himself hard in her. She drew off of him with a deep sigh and slipped from atop me, falling onto her side and curling, reaching out to touch me gently.

I rolled up onto my knees and took Tom fully into my mouth, eager for him, using lips and tongue to give him pleasure. He was coated with the essence of her. Inside my mouth, I wrapped my tongue around his shaft and dragged it over his length as I drew my head back and then pushed forward to take him inside. Lindsay reached up to caress and fondle my boobs as I knelt on the bed, and I curled my back to press them to her, wanting more.

The bed behind me moved again, and I felt Austin touching his cock to me. I rolled my hips in invitation. Unlike the first time I had taken him inside of me, he filled me with just one thrust, going all the way in past my wet lips and stroking deep. I marveled at this new sensation too, once more with two boys inside of me, one in my mouth, one in my pussy, pushing and pulling, filling me up. My, oh my.

I felt supremely sexual at that moment, making love with the three of them, being made love to by the three of them. The boys stroked in and out of me, neither in a hurry to come again. Each of them has come at least twice already. They were going to last this time. I didn't mind. My fingers reached for and found Lindsay. It slipped between her legs to tease her, my fingers going in her, and fucking her. I was eager for her to be part of this moment too. Then I caught movement somewhere away from us, and I twisted my eyes to see what it could possibly be. In the large mirror over the dresser, I saw us. A tall, slender girl with calico hair in complete disarray with a boy fucking her from behind and another boy pushing his cock in her mouth while a gorgeous blonde girl slid under her body to catch her nipples and suck them. We looked amazing. I liked that I looked that way. Sexual. Sensual. Daring and bold.

I felt Austin speeding up again and knew he was about to let go inside of me. I wanted to meet him there, to cum with him. I wanted Tom to shoot in my mouth, too; I wanted to taste his cum and swallow. I bobbed my head faster on him, working him with my tongue as Lindsay's fingers began to strum my clit. My fingers were between her open thighs too, wanting her to be there with us. I twisted my head again, looking at our reflection. Austin grunted as he came, slamming deeply into my cunt. I whined as I tried to match him, not quite there. Then Tom pushed in and held my head to him, and I watched in the mirror as he came down my throat, and I saw the way my throat moved as I swallowed cum.

I was so close and eager. I spun away from the boys and found Lindsay again, replacing my fingers with my mouth as she scrambled beneath me to lick me all the way there.

I came, vocal and loud once again, crying out as her mouth delighted me so. I wanted to give the same gift to her, and I found her clit, slipping fingers up and inside of her once more, curling to find that spot, to the roughness that tells fingers that is just the place to rub. Lindsay's cries mingled with mine, filling the air, falling like the snow still wafting from the sky outside our room.

I became aware then that all was quiet. Then I heard breathing all around me, irregular and rasping, then slowing and becoming even. I lay down beside Lindsay and cuddled her, pressing my breasts to her back, sex to her bottom, and lips to her neck.

I sighed deeply.

Austin, my date, lay his body up behind mine, his soft cock nestled to my bottom. On the other side of Lindsay, Tom, my lover again, reached around to caress one of Lindsay's breasts and found my fingers already there. We laced fingers together and fondled her as one.

Sexy Best Friends
5 Short Sweet & Wild Lesbian Erotica (FF, FFF)
Emilia Russell

All Rights Reserved. No part of this publication may be reproduced in any form or by any means, including scanning, photocopying, or otherwise without prior written permission of the copyright holder. Copyright © 2020

This book is entirely a work of fiction. The names, characters and incidents portrayed in it are the work of the author's imagination. Any resemblance to actual persons, living or dead, events or localities is entirely coincidental.

Story 01

I'm a cook. I love my job: the heat, the pace, the pressure - all in a good day's work. If you've ever worked in a restaurant, you know how it can be. Tempers run high, but at the end of the day, all is forgotten.

At my particular restaurant (and I'm sure many others), closing is left up to one or two servers and a cook. Those nights are often slow and afford a lot of time for socializing. Recently, my favorite nights have been closing with Natalie. We both got hired at the same time, but she went home for the summer. Then, three months later, she came back, and she got HOT. Of course, I spent most of my long closing nights sitting out in the bar with Natalie, just bullshitting.

"Hey gorgeous, come here often?" I asked with a grin as I slid onto the barstool in my usual spot. That greeting always got a smile and a giggle.

"Hey stud, tough night?" came Natalie's typical response.

This little exchange, our nightly ritual, was just the tip of the iceberg of our flirting. It drove the guys nuts that she flirted with me and hardly batted an eye at them. What they didn't know was that we'd known each other before. We went to school together. We were never close, but when we started working together, we instantly bonded.

"So what are you doing after work?" I asked.

"I got wind of a great after party at Therapy."

"Yeah? Looking for company?"

"You up for it?"

"Of course."

We would often accompany each other out, even though our taste in venues was often different. We'd go to clubs and parties with each other, and if we ever couldn't get rid of an undesirable companion, we were each other's loophole. It was a handy, if somewhat cliché setup. Therapy was one of our favorite bars. Being one of the only bars open after hours, from 2 am to 6 am on Fridays and Saturdays (well, technically Saturdays and Sundays), it attracted crowds from both the straight and gay clubs looking for more party time. It was the right mix for both of us.

"Cruising for guys tonight or are you just looking to chill?"

"I could stand to get some," Natalie said with a wink.

"Well if that's an offer, I'm sure it can be arranged," I winked back.

"I wish MJ could hear this....I'd love to see the look on his face," said Jill from across the bar, referring to the cook with the biggest crush on Natalie.

"That boy needs to get laid more than any of us, I think. One of these days I'll be nice and teach him how to pick up girls," I said as I sipped on my 'cape codder, no vodka' (a.k.a. cranberry juice...no drinking on the job).

"Yeah, 'cause that's working so well for you," laughed Natalie as I threw a pretzel.

"So I've had a dry spell. Picking up straight chicks isn't easy, ya know, and it's been a long time since you've been my wingman," I retorted, now dodging the pretzel I'd just thrown.

"Well, stud, start living up to your reputation!"

And on it went. This is how we passed the boring nights until closing. Then we bust ass for a half-hour cleaning, and head out to whatever late-night party we've chosen that week.

This week I was dressed in my tight low-rise Guess jeans and my "give blood play rugby" t-shirt, as if anyone needed further validation of my dyke-ness. I had a blazer in case it got chilly, but in mid-may, it was unlikely. I'm a tall, thin, athletic type with short red hair. I keep it that way, mostly because of my job; it's a lot easier to keep it short enough so that I don't have to wear a hat. A lot cooler too. And I can cut it myself. I have five tattoos (well, ten if you count all the Japanese words individually). I like to keep my body toned, and when I have time to work out, I like to go rock climbing.

Natalie is pretty opposite. Long, chocolate brown hair and matching eyes, curves in all the right places, unbelievable cleavage. She wore her tight black serving pants (she says she makes more tips when her ass looks good) and a simple, clingy red v-neck top. She could make simple looks that look unbelievably sexy. It's hard not to stare - sometimes I still do, and then I get teased about it for days.

Jill, Natalie, and I walked through the parking lot together to where the employees park. At 1:30 in the morning, you can't be too careful. We said goodnight to Jill and Natalie, and I headed to Therapy.

"Ready? You think you can keep up with me tonight?" asked Natalie as we walked into the club.

"Oh, I'll drink you under the table tonight. Better yet, I'll drink you into bed with me," I replied over the thump of the music.

"Oh really...we'll see about that..."

We walked up to the bar, and I put my credit card on the counter as the bartender started on our usual - double southern comfort on the rocks and bass for me, sambuca shot and a cosmo for Natalie. We started on our drinks and surveyed the room.

"Guy in the black blazer just gave you the twice-over," I said.

"Check out the hottie in the little school girl skirt...looks like she's wearing a garter belt," she said, knowing my weakness for garter belts.

"Mmmm...yeah. Straight. I tried that one 3 weeks ago."

"What about him? In the ripped jeans...oh what an ass!"

"Queer as a football bat honey."

"Damn. You know, you should just get a sex change. That would make my life so much easier."

"Hey, just because I don't have a penis doesn't mean I can't make your life easier."

"You keep trying....let's go dance." And off she went, pulling me on to the crowded floor. We had more drinks and danced for a while before she wandered off with the guy in the blazer. After 20 minutes, I headed back to the bar, figuring that was it for the night; usually, she'd have come for me already if she needed me. I had a couple more drinks when she suddenly appeared at my side again.

"Ok, so he's a loser. A very dense loser. Help." And she walked off. That was my cue, time to be the backup. I made my way over to the table they were at, and she grabbed my hand.

"Oh, Jim. This is Ari, the girl I told you about."

"Right. Your....roommate? Pleasure," he said, shaking my hand.

Natalie pulled me down on the bench and put her hand in my lap. I tried to disguise my surprise and said, "yeah, my roommate."

"So what college do you two go to?"

"What?" I asked, "Oh...no...not that kind of roommate."

"Then what-" Jim started to ask but was distracted when Natalie grabbed my face and kissed me. I felt her tongue work its way deep into my mouth and again tried to hide my surprise. We'd kissed for effect before, but never with a tongue.

"That kind of roommate," Natalie said when she broke the kiss. "Goodnight Jim, nice talking to you." And she motioned to me that we were leaving.

"Oh did you see his face? That was priceless!" Natalie laughed as she stumbled out of the club.

"Well it was nothing compared to the face I wanted to make when you put your tongue down my throat!"

"What, you didn't like kissing me?"

"No, I liked it a lot. I was exaggerating. But seriously, if you don't want me to follow you home and jump your bones, that was not the best plan of action."

"Well who says that's not what I want? Here - I'm not driving. Poor Jim bought me 5 more cosmos," Natalie said, handing me her keys and wobbling slightly. I stood there for a second, unsure of what to think, then helped her to the car.

I drove us to a diner - I had the drunk munchies, and she needed to sober up some. We'd have to pick up my car the next day. After a little while, and a large stack of pancakes, Natalie stopped wobbling so much and started speaking more coherently, so I suggested we head to my place and sleep in my guest room.

We got to my place, and I went to take a shower. Natalie had been there enough to know her way around. When I got out of my shower, I was surprised to find her sitting on my bed. I went into my closet to get ready for bed.

"So I've been thinking about that kiss..."

"Yeah?" I said as I pulled on boxers and a t-shirt. Natalie was already in (my) pajamas.

"Yeah. It was nice."

"Yeah, it was." I got into bed, and she got in next to me. My heart was pounding. I thought I must be dreaming. So many times, I'd fought with myself to push aside my desire for her and reminded myself that she was my best friend. So many times I'd lie awake wishing I could have brought her home instead of some jackass from a club. And here she was.

"Maybe....maybe we could do it again?"

I searched her face for any signs that she was teasing me, or still drunk, and found nothing but burning lust in her eyes. She must have seen it in mine too because she put her hand on my cheek and kissed me again. Slowly, deeply, her tongue explored every inch of my mouth. Then she broke the kiss and started laughing.

"What?"

"You always said you'd drink me into bed with you...and here I am."

"Here you are..." This time, I kissed her, massaging her tongue, my hand going for the buttons on her (my) pajamas. I moved down her neck, leaving a wet trail of kisses as I went. I undid the buttons slowly and kissed each new bit of flesh that was revealed. She sat up and pulled the top off and grabbed my face and kissed me hard.

"I want you..." she said between kisses.

Any hesitation I still had evaporated. I rolled her over, so I was straddling her, still locked to her delicious mouth. Her hands were at my waist, tugging my shirt up. I let go of her lips long enough for her to pull my shirt off. Her hands trailed up my back, lighting my skin on fire. I leaned down to kiss her neck, starting at her ear and working down. I bit down slightly on her shoulder, at which she gasped. I kissed further down to her left nipple and took it between my teeth. I pulled on it gently, and Natalie gasped louder, arching slightly off the bed. I licked little circles around her nipple, eliciting a moan from her lips before I bit down again, drawing another moan out of her. I licked my way over to the right nipple and started sucking on it. At this point, Natalie's hand moved to the back of my head. She moaned and arched up into my mouth as my tongue flicked rapidly over her nipple.

I replaced my mouth with my hand, gently caressing both breasts, and kissed my way up to her mouth again. I wanted to taste her so badly, but I didn't want to rush. The look in her eyes told me she was ready and didn't want to wait. I got off the bed and said, "you need to be naked." She smiled and pulled off what remained of her clothing. God, she was sexy. She looked at me and spread her legs, giving me a full view of her gorgeous shaved pussy. I climbed back onto the bed and kissed up her luscious legs, alternating from one thigh to the other. By the time I reached her pussy, her hips had rocked, and I could see her glistening wetness.

"God, Ari, just eat me....Fuck I can't wait any longer!"

I was more than happy to oblige the beautiful woman in my bed. I lightly licked her pussy lips, my first taste. She tasted so sweet. I tickled her labia with the tip of my tongue before plunging it deep inside her as it would go. Natalie released an animal moan and thrust her cunt into my face. I reached up to massage her breasts as I fucked her with my tongue - as deep as I could. I loved the sound of her moans. I replaced my tongue with two fingers, which made her moan even louder. She certainly was a screamer. My tongue moved up to her clit and flicked little circles over it. I could feel her pussy walls clench around my fingers.

"Oh FUCK! I'm cumming!" Natalie screamed as I pumped my fingers in her pussy. I closed my mouth over her clit and sucked gently, flicking my tongue over it. Then her body tightened, and she arched off the bed with a scream. I licked her clit until she pushed my head away.

She grabbed my head and pulled me up to kiss her. "Holy shit, that was amazing! Where did you learn that?"

"Practice."

"Oh my god you have the most incredible mouth..." and she kissed me again. When her breathing returned to normal, she flipped me over with a smile and said, "your turn."

And with that, she began kissing my neck, my chest, my stomach, then up to my right breast. She sucked my nipple into her mouth as her hand worked its way down my stomach. She pushed past my boxers, and I reached down to pull them off for her. Her fingers trailed lightly over my labia. She slowly pushed one finger inside of me and worked it around, massaging my walls. Soon it was joined by a second, thrusting in and out of my cunt. She kissed her way down my stomach and blew gently on my clit. She was driving me crazy. My hips were rocking against her hand, and I was moaning her name loudly. She licked a slow circle around my clit, not making direct contact.

"Oh fuck Natalie, don't tease me anymore!"

"She licked my clit rapidly, back and forth, not relenting, causing my orgasm to build quickly. Her tongue moved faster and faster until my orgasm crashed over me, wave after incredible wave of pleasure hit me. Natalie licked me through at least two, I'm not sure, not stopping until I pulled her up next to me and kissed her, tasting myself on her lips.

"Are you sure you're new at that?"

Natalie laughed and said, "definitely my first time." And she lay down next to me, and we drifted off to sleep.

=====

The next morning I woke up alone, which wouldn't have struck me except I was naked. The night before flooded back and I got a little worried, thinking Natalie may have freaked out.

I pulled on my boxers and t-shirt from the night before and went downstairs. I was comforted by the smell of coffee brewing.

"Hey stud, want some breakfast?" Natalie appeared from the kitchen, wearing my pajamas again.

"Yeah, smells good...I'm glad you're still here."

"You think I'd leave?"

"I wasn't sure. I'm not sure of many things that I thought I knew."

"Oh. Right."

"I mean, we had a good balance...a good friendship...and I'm not upset about anything. I just worry that you might be."

"Well I realized last night, when we kissed, that there was no reason it couldn't be you...in fact you were the reason I couldn't find a decent guy. I liked what we had so much that I didn't want anyone to come between us."

"So...what happens now?"

Natalie walked over, sat on my lap, put her arms around my neck, kissed me ever so gently, and said, "well, I'd love to be your girlfriend."

I looked in her eyes, and she took my breath away, I was incapable of speech. So I kissed her slowly and passionately. She understood my answer.

"Excellent. Now, how about some breakfast?"

I ate my fill of French toast and bacon and coffee and then pushed my chair back. I watched Natalie finish off her plate. Her hair was slept in, and her makeup from the night before was a bit streaked, and my pajamas were entirely too big for her - and she was more beautiful than ever. She caught me staring and flashed me her incredible smile.

"Well," I said, "that was good. I'm going to take a shower. Then we have to go get my car, and you have to go to work."

"Are you kidding? I'm not going to work. I traded with Jill, I'm working for her tomorrow. Today it's all you and me baby."

I laughed as I walked to the bathroom for my shower.

After a nice hot shower, I headed back to my bedroom. Natalie was sitting on my bed again, looking like the cat that ate the canary.

"What did you do?" I asked, walking over to the bed.

"You know what would be really hot?"

"Um...120 degree weather?"

"No...You know how I always loved you in drag?"

"Yes...but hon, that takes a while to do..."

"No, I don't want you in drag. But I do think it would be hot if you wore this," she said, pulling out my strap-on. She must have found my box o' fun.

I took the strap on from her and kissed her on the lips lightly, "all day?"

"As long as I can stand, then I'll drag you back here and fuck you silly."

"Ok," I said, putting it on and adjusting the straps, "what are we doing today?" The dildo she chose was one of the smaller ones they sell for harnesses - 7 ½", and it had an extension that went below the harness to go inside me so that I enjoy using it as much as the woman I'm using it on. This was undoubtedly going to be an exciting day.

"Well Jill wants us to come by for lunch, and I need to go shopping for my sister's birthday party, so that's a start."

Natalie showered, and we got ready to go out. Lucky for me she's a dress-and-go kind of girl, doesn't spend too much time getting ready. After the quick run from the club to get my car, we were on our way to the party store. Shopping with Natalie was an exciting experience. When nobody looked, she would caress my crotch, heightening my constant arousal from the dildo inside of me. We had to get all the essential party supplies - streamers and balloons and all that jazz. Her sister was turning 24, but Natalie had chosen to do a kid's party with a twist. She was getting ice cream cake and pizza and everything you'd expect at a kid's party, but her sister didn't know that it would be a sex toy party. You know, with one of those companies that send representatives out with trunkloads of sex toys and they go to your house and show them all. I found the whole idea pretty funny.

A couple of hours later, we were finally done and went for lunch. We sat in a booth with Jill, who joined us on her break. Once again, Natalie's hand went straight for my crotch. She slowly stroked the dildo, which made the one inside me move rhythmically. I hoped Jill couldn't tell what was happening, and by her steady conversation with Natalie, I was sure she couldn't. After we ate, I excused myself to the bathroom. I went upstairs to the employee bathroom - it was cleaner, and besides, I didn't want to deal with walking into a women's bathroom with a noticeable bulge in my pants.

When I walked out, Natalie was waiting for me in the break room. Without a word, I grabbed her hand and led her over to the "cage" - what we call our dry storage area. It's pretty much exactly that, a cage that locks, inside there are shelves of all our dry goods like cans, napkins, take-out containers, etc. It's not exactly secluded, but it's easy enough to hide.

She was thinking the same thing I was because as soon as we got to the far corner, she unzipped my pants and lifted her skirt. I lifted her, and she guided the dildo into her pussy. She must have been thinking something like this would happen because she wasn't wearing any underwear. She wrapped her legs tightly around me and grabbed onto a shelf as I started thrusting the dildo in her. I was so aroused already that it was all I could do to stifle my moans.

"Oh my god I've wanted your cock all day," she whispered, her lips brushing against my ear. She started moaning very softly in my ear with every thrust, and I could feel my orgasm building. Then, suddenly, she stopped. She lifted herself off, straightened her skirt, and said, "I've got a better idea."

She walked out of the cage and went and opened her locker. She got her keys and opened up the manager's office (all closers have keys to it, just in case). I closed the door behind me, and she sat down on the desk, spreading her legs wide. I knelt in front of her and dove into her cunt. I licked her clit furiously and hoped nobody came upstairs as her moans got louder and louder.

"Fuck! I want you inside me now! OH!"

I stood up and guided the dildo inside of her hot pussy. I kissed her hard, and she worked for her hands up my shirt and pushed my bra aside. She pinched and rolled both nipples as I fucked her hard and fast.

"Cum with me, baby, OH I'm so close!" She moaned.

I thrust a few more times, and her legs stiffened around me. Her cries of pleasure as her orgasm hit her was enough to push me over the edge. My pussy clamped around the dildo, and I shuddered as a huge orgasm rushed through my body. As we came down from the orgasm, I pulled the dildo out of her, and then took my pants off to pull it out of me. I was too sensitive to leave it in any longer. Natalie took it from me and licked it clean and put it in her purse. I put my pants back on, and we left, locking up the office just as the second shift started arriving. We looked at each other and laughed as we walked out and headed back to my apartment.

Susan and I had been best friends for the past four years. We had met at a previous job and had hit it off very quickly. Our lifestyles were very different. My husband is a successful sales rep for a major computer company, and hers is a construction laborer. We live in relative comfort while they live the life of the lower middle class. My husband is hardworking and attentive; hers is often drunk when he is not at work. But despite the differences, we genuinely liked each other and enjoyed each other's company.

Only in our looks were we similar, both being 39, about 5'6, and a little overweight: both blonde, though mine came a little more naturally than hers. My size eight clothes fit her nicely, and I often gave her clothes that I no longer cared for. She can even wear the same 36D bras that I have.

Even though our husbands had very different jobs and work ethics, they both had to travel a great deal in their respective jobs. It was not unusual than when Susan called me one afternoon to say that Randy was away and that she was bored.

"Carl is gone too," I told her. "Want to try to get together and do something tonight?"

"Sure. Say, Julie, want to watch some chick flix while the men are gone?" she asked.

I immediately thought about some of my favorite movies that my husband hated. Chick flix like "Sleepless in Seattle" or "Waiting to Exhale"; movies that just made Carl roll his eyes or go find something else to do while I got out the tissues for the tearful ending. This sounded like a pleasant way for us to spend time together.

"That sounds like fun. You bring the videos and I'll make the pop corn and break out some wine."

The rest of the day was spent tidying up the house and generally being domestic. I gave very little thought to what I should wear for an evening of Melanie Griffith, Meg Ryan, or Meryl Streep. I simply put on a pair of light cotton lounge pants and a matching tank top. Susan and I were comfortable around each other, so I did not bother to put on a bra.

At about 6:30, I poured myself a glass of wine and puttered around. The first glass of wine tasted pretty good, so I had another. At 7 PM, the doorbell rang. I answered it, and let my best friend in. She had a bag with the movies in it in her hand. She was wearing sweat pants and a t-shirt.

"Oh good," she said, hugging me warmly, "I'm glad to see you are dressed 'casz', too."

"Hey, it's my house, I'll dress how I like!" We both laughed, and she hugged me again. It felt nice to feel her sincere warmth. We broke apart. "You want some wine?" I asked her.

"Sure, that would be great, Julie."

"Get the movie set up, and I'll get some for you."

"I was surprised when you said you would watch chick flix with me. I normally have to watch them alone when Randy is gone." She said.

"I know, Carl doesn't like them either. I go through about a ton of tissue when I get to watch them," I laughed.

"You too?" She giggled. "Ain't it great? I'll get one going. Bring me my wine, garcon."

We both laughed. It was so lovely to be spending time with a friend. I poured her some wine and headed to the rec room where the entertainment center was. We also had a TV and VCR in the living room, but the rec room had a big overstuffed sectional couch that you could just sink into.

"Movies started!" she yelled at me.

I stepped into the rec room and turned the corner. I was expecting to see a familiar title on the screen like "Out of Africa" or "Steel Magnolias." Instead, I heard a twanging guitar riff, and saw the title "Blondes in Heat." Behind the titles, two naked women were tonguing each other's mouths and fingering each other's pussies. I stood transfixed, watching the scene. My mouth dropped open.

"Oh, thanks," Susan said, taking the glass of wine, oblivious to my shock. "I picked out a couple of really good chick flix for us to watch. I didn't know what type you usually watch alone so I picked out this one, and another called "Lonely Wives" since that seemed appropriate to us tonight," she giggled. "What with both our husbands being gone."

I sat down at the far end of the couch from her, but still only three feet from her, unsure what to do. I had seen lots of porn before and enjoyed a good deal of it with my husband as part of our lovemaking. It dawned on me what the confusion was. The term chick flix meant something very different from my best friend. How to handle this?

I looked down at the other end of the couch. Susan was reclining back, her feet curled under her, looking very relaxed, and watching the movie. I could see her nipples had hardened under her t-shirt, so I assumed she was enjoying the video already.

I looked up at the screen. Two blondes were sitting on a couch, kissing, their tongues exploring each other's mouths. Their breasts were flattened each to the others. They each had a finger gently probing the pussy of the other. Their kisses strayed from their mouths and moved to cheeks, necks, and lower. They were lying side by side now, kissing and sucking the tits of the other. Next, they were kissing tummies, belly buttons, and lower. Their thighs parted like a carefully choreographed dance. They were then licking, sucking, and loving the pussy of the other. Their tongues probed pussies; their fingers probed ass holes. Their moans filled the room.

"This movie always gets me so hot. I go through a ton of tissue, just like you said. You got any handy?" I looked at her. I could see the lust in her eyes as she watched the lesbian scene. I could tell her breathing had increased by watching her hard nipples rise and fall inside her t-shirt.

"Uhmmmm... yeah, sure" I got up and got a tissue box from the bookshelf and handed it to her.

"I get so wet watching this stuff, my panties will soak through to my pants if I don't keep it wiped up. You too, huh?" And with that, she took a tissue in her hand, reached down inside her sweat pants, and wiped her pussy.

This was the first time I knew I had to address what was happening. She had asked me a direct question, and there was no avoiding it. A thousand thoughts ran through my mind in a flash. I wasn't offended by what was on the screen. I was just shocked by the situation. This was all just a simple misunderstanding of the term "chick flix." Susan was my best friend and was grateful to have someone that she thought understood her intimate needs, needs her husband did not understand, and someone that she trusted to share them with. The last thing I wanted to do was embarrass her. I decided that no harm could come of us sharing this experience as best friends.

"Sure, the damn thing is just like a faucet," I replied and smiled.

She giggled. "Ain't it great? Looks like you like this video alright." She was looking at my chest.

I looked down. My nipples were visible under my tight tank top. The video so far had had a pronounced effect on me. There was no denying what her eyes could see. I shrugged, smiled, and said, "Well, I have my fine points."

"So I see," She giggled.

By now, the scene on the video had changed. Two different tall blondes were in a kitchen together. One was fucking the other with a cucumber while sucking her delicious looking tits. The vegetable stretched her cunt lips wide. She worked her hips to meet each thrust.

Susan looked at me. "If only cooking dinner was always that much fun. I would never leave the kitchen." She giggled. "Need a tissue yet?"

While the video was making my pussy moist, I was not to the point of dripping. She took another tissue, reached down inside her sweat pants, and wiped herself. I could see a slight shudder pass through her as the soft tissue rubbed over her labia. She laid the tissue on the coffee table in front of her with the other one. I could see her wetness glisten on it. But I thought this could embarrass her if it is just a one-person thing. I reached out and took one. I had never touched myself in front of another woman. She had seemed so un-self-conscious when she had wiped herself. I took the tissue and reached down inside my lounge pants. My hand was met with rising heat and musky aroma from my pussy. I ran the tissue over my pussy lips. I caught my breath as I did so. It felt better than I had planned.

Back on the screen, the blonde holding the cucumber and fucking her partner was now on her knees. Her tongue was flickering over her partner's openly displayed clit. The woman being licked was leaning back and tossing her long blonde hair over her shoulders. Whether her cum was real or acted, I couldn't tell, but it seemed convincing.

"Wow," I heard Susan whisper. "That is awesome... and beautiful, isn't it?"

I heard my voice whisper hoarsely in response, "Yes, it is." I looked down at the other end of the couch. My best friend was looking at me. Our eyes met and held; the tension was incredible. I could see her hard nipples poking out on her soft tits. I looked down, and I could see a wet spot between her thighs! She was looking at me in a way she never had. We both giggled nervously at the same time.

"Need another tissue?" I asked, trying to break the tension even more.

"Shit, too late now," Susan giggled. "I'm soaked through already. You got a blanket or something for me to cover up with?"

"Sure." I got one for her assuming she would simply cover her lap. She draped it over her lap, but then she wiggled under the blanket and pulled out her sweat pants. Her t-shirt followed almost immediately. Seconds later, her panties appeared in her hand.

"There. Now I don't have to worry about getting them wetter. This is much more comfy. Just like I watch at home."

My senses were starting to overload. My best friend was now sitting under a blanket, only three feet away from me, completely naked. Not only naked but completely turned on while watching a very exciting lesbian porn video. I had to admit that she wasn't the only one turned on. My pussy was now in full flow. I could feel the moisture build at the entrance to my cunt, the moisture condenses to a liquid, and the liquid began to run down from my lips toward my ass. It tickled. This time I did need a tissue. Susan intently watched me pick one up. As I slid the tissue over my pussy lips and into the crack of my ass, I could not help but shiver at the delicious sensations that passed through me. Pleasure radiated out from my pussy to all points of my body and back.

Susan could not help but see my reaction. "Did that feel good or are you cold?"

"Maybe I should get a blanket too," I laughed nervously.

She held up a corner of her blanket. "Want to share mine?"

I couldn't see all of her naked body, but I could see her graceful shoulders, most of the breast closest to me, her feminine curved side, and her very smooth thighs.

"You normally stay dressed when you watch these alone?"

I was so turned on by her beauty, her warmth, her friendship, and the intimacy of our situation, that I no longer cared about the mix up about watching "chick flix." I smiled at her and simply said, "No."

I pulled my tank top up over my head; my tits were rising firmly and proudly as my arms went over my head I smiled at her, and she smiled back, her tongue sliding over her lips as she saw my tits for the first time. I hooked my thumbs into my lounge pants and pushed them to my knees. Gravity took over, and they fell around my ankles. I stepped out of them and stood nude in front of my lust-filled best friend.

I sat down next to her, and she draped the blanket over me. I snuggled up to her, thrilling at the feel of her warm, soft skin against mine. My tits were rubbing against her arm. Our hips were pressed together.

"Mmmmm.... This is nice," I whispered. I tilted my head up and lightly kissed her on the cheek.

"Yes, it is." She looked at me, and we let all the final inhibitions crash away. Her lips met mine. Our lips parted, and her tongue was in my mouth. I sucked hungrily, passionately on it. My hand found her tits at the same time her hand found the inside of my thighs. I caressed her nipples. She ran her finger up my pussy to my clit. We both gasped at the touching. I leaned over and took her nipple in my mouth, kissing it, sucking it, and loving it. She parted my pussy lips and began to finger my cunt with the first one and then two fingers. Her fingers explored deep in me, sending waves of pleasure throughout me. I had to touch her as she was touching me. While I sucked on her tits, my hand dropped to her thighs, and she parted them eagerly. My face rose back to hers, and our mouths pressed together. I was finger fucking my best friend, and she was finger fucking me. There was no embarrassment or self-consciousness. There were only two women, best friends, caring for, and pleasing each other.

I could feel my orgasm start to build. I could feel her cunt grow hotter and tighter on my fingers. Her fingers probed deeper into me as my hips thrust against her hand. My hand became covered with the incredible amount of pussy juice she was secreting. Magically, we came at the same time. We moaned and whimpered into each other's mouth as our cunts exploded on each other's fingers. I could feel her nipples pressed into my tits, and she could undoubtedly feel mine in return. We kept each other high on our mutual orgasm, hips working together, pussies exploding together, lips and tongues pressed together.

And then, like the lesbians, we had seen only a short time before we began to shift our position. We were lying side-to-side, able to devour the other's tits, biting, pulling, sucking, kissing them. Without a word or a signal, we were suddenly kissing each other's tummies, playfully licking each other's belly button. And then we took the final step. Her pubic hair tickled my nose as I moved the last few inches toward her pussy. I could already feel the heat and smell her intoxicating oils; there was no hesitation now.

My face was right at her pussy. Hers was at mine. I gladly reached around her thighs and spread them. Her pussy opened up in front of my mouth. I could feel her do the same to me. My mouth covered her pussy, and, like a lover, I began to French kiss it. My tongue probed into the mouth of her cunt in the same way it had probed her mouth seconds before. Her tongue was exploring my pussy, teasing, and caressing my clit. I put a finger into her as my mouth found her clit and began to suck on it. I felt two of her fingers slide into me, thrilling me. Then one of them was removed, and I felt it press lightly at my ass. I mumbled some sort of encouragement, muffled by her pussy, humping my face. I felt her finger break the seal of my ass, and then she began to double fuck me with her fingers, one in my cunt and one in my ass.

The triple stimulation of her tongue and two fingers took me higher and higher. I took her clit in my mouth, sucking it, licking, and caressing it with my tongue and her hips worked feverishly on my face. It was though we were both racing to see who could help the other cum first. She won. As my orgasm washed over me, waves of incredible pleasure hitting my cunt, my hips thrust hard against her hand and face. I tried to concentrate on pleasuring her, but my orgasm won out, and I rose, pressing my cunt hard down on her face. My hands came up and grasped my tits hard, and I pulled at my nipples, trying to create every possible sensation of pleasure I knew my body was capable of. I rubbed my freely flowing pussy all over her face. I could feel her tongue trying to catch every drop of my juices.

In her passion, she reached up and roughly grabbed me by the shoulders and pulled me back down to her pussy. Her roughness was induced by her need to cum, and I knew this. As I was still gasping from my intense orgasm, my mouth once again found her clit. Two fingers slid easily into her saturated but unsated cunt. I licked. I sucked. I finger fucked her. I could feel her gripping my hips, licking my ass, and I could hear her begin to moan more loudly. I wanted to please her the same way she had pleased me, even more, if possible. Her hips worked up and down to meet the thrusts of my fingers. Her hips swiveled back and forth to enhance the actions of my tongue on her clit.

"Oh god, oh god, oh god..." became her mantra of pleasure. Then she came to me. Her hips thrust up hard and froze. I could feel her cunt muscles contracting around my fingers, and her hot juice gushed out, coating my hand. Her clit hardened under my tongue. Her breath came to a stop as she became frozen in time and pleasure. Then she simply melted into a limp body below me.

I pulled my fingers from her and licked them clean. I turn back around and lay next to her, partially draped over her. Our tits met, and our nipples kissed. I gently kissed my best friend on the lips.

"Watching chick flix has never been like this before for me," I whispered to her.

"Yeah," she said as our tongues teased, and her hand found my still demanding pussy. "Ain't it great?"

Story 03

I first realized that I liked members of my sex while a junior in high school. I was sixteen, and it was several hours before my first date with Todd Michaels. It would have been my first date ever. My friend Lindsey was over, and I was asking her questions. You see, she had been on dates before and gave me advice on what to do and what not to do. I had just asked her what should I do if he tries to kiss me. She told me to let him kiss me, but nothing more than that. Of course, being as this was my first date ever, I wasn't too confident about my kissing skills. Yes, just like in that movie "Cruel Intentions," when Sarah Michelle Geller's character kisses Selma Blair's character, my friend Lindsey had me practice with her.

She told me just to relax and not to worry about anything. Then we kissed. I didn't realize why at the time, but for some reason, I felt something. I know now that what I felt was similar to what guys call "getting a hard-on." But at that moment, all I wanted to do was kiss her. I never mentioned this to her, and to this day, I am thankful to her for doing this. I'm still friends with her, and yes, she knows that I am a lesbian. But she has no idea it was a result of her. She thinks it was because of a girl I met during my freshman year in college. She is still my best friend, outside of my lover, and has been very encouraging concerning my choices.

My name is Vicki Green. I am now 19 years old, and I am finishing up my freshman year. I am studying to be a high school teacher, preferably in mathematics. And maybe I will offer to run a sex education course once in a while. I am dating a girl by the name Shannon. Shannon is one of the most beautiful girls I've ever seen. She could be a model if she wanted too if it weren't for the fact that she is only 5'6". She is just an inch shorter than I am. She has long red hair, about breast length, and her breasts; Wow! My breasts look pathetic compared to hers. Whereas I wear a 34B, she wears a 36C/36D. She wears both sizes, depending on how comfortable they are on her. Some bras feel comfortable with 36C, but some need a 36D, or else it is a bit tight. She has the stomach of someone who works out religiously, yet she doesn't. And her ass is perfect in all ways. I sometimes have wondered why she is with me, but she assures me that I am the one for her, and I believe her. And to top it off, she works at a local Frederick's of Hollywood. Can you say a discount? Last time we checked, she weighed 112, while I was 131.

All in all, I love her, and she loves me. And the sex couldn't be better until two nights ago.

We are in that stage in a relationship where sex seems to consume us. We have done it in numerous ways and locations. We have experienced almost all you could experience, outside of another partner and some things that are just too sick even to try (you freaks who do such disgust us). And yes, we have done it several times a day. Oh, and if you might be wondering, we are members of the "Mile-High Club." We have considered three-ways before but never could decide on whom we should invite over to join us. I could tell you how we met, but it would be a repeat of what you hear about other sex stories. We meet, one person makes a move, the other doesn't back down, la-de-da, la-de-da. Same story I've read or seen hundreds of times. I'm not here to do that. I'm here to tell you about a recent event that has changed our lives. We finally had a three-way.

Now, I have to lay down what was happening. Lindsey was over, as she often is, and the three of us were watching TV. The three of us are huge "Friends" fanatics, and we all get together every Thursday night to watch it. "Friends" was already over, and we were watching something else when it happened. Shannon was between Lindsey, and I. Shannon reached over to put her arm around me, but accidentally put her arm around Lindsey instead. She told me later that she forgot that Lindsey and I had switched sides earlier that night. The surprising thing was, Lindsey, didn't do anything. When both of them realized what had happened, and Lindsey just looked at us with a smile, Shannon turned to me and put her other arm around me. I just scooted over closer to her and leaned forward to kiss Lindsey. She didn't resist. She leaned in closer. Imagine my surprise. My best friend, the person who unknowingly turned me onto women, and who has always profoundly professed to be straight, encouraged me to kiss her even more. Shannon was just sitting there, holding us together, and smiling. Little was any of us to know that this would be the best night of our lives.

When Lindsey and I finally broke off the kiss, we had one more quick peck before going our separate ways. Lindsey went up while I went down. As Lindsey and Shannon began to kiss, I moved off the couch and onto my knees between Shannon's legs. Rolling her skirt up to the waist, I forced her legs apart even further. Moving closer, I didn't even bother pulling her dark blue pantyhose down. I didn't have too. Shannon prefers crotchless pantyhose. I pushed her black lace panties to the side and began rubbing her clit. I looked up to see Lindsey helping Shannon out of her tight red v-neck shirt

(I love that shirt). Lindsey pulled her black lace bra down below her breasts, and she did her first exploration of another woman's breasts. I refocused myself on Shannon's pussy as I entered the first one, then two fingers into her pussy, still massaging her clit with my other hand. As I began to finger fuck her, her hips began to move around to go along with my movements slowly. Every once in a while, I would lean my head forward to lick her clit. I even nibbled it a few times.

Looking up again, Lindsey is now standing behind the couch. Shannon is leaning back, sucking on Lindsey's bare breasts, while Lindsey is leaning forward and sucking on Shannon's breasts. All of this is starting to affect Shannon, as she quickly became wetter and wetter. Inserting a third finger, I quit massaging her clit and began sucking on it instead. It didn't take long after that before I heard a quick yelp from Lindsey, and Shannon's juices flowed onto my fingers and chin. I quickly began sucking it all up. When I finished, I stood up and quickly kissed Shannon. She has always enjoyed tasting her juices. I have caught her tasting herself after masturbation. I kissed Lindsey next, as Shannon removed my jeans. After kissing Lindsey, I grabbed her arm and pulled her around to the front of the couch. Noticing a bite mark on her left nipple, I sat down, spread my legs, and had her work her first pussy. As she bent forward to begin playing with me, I silently directed Shannon to work on Lindsey. Encouraging and directing Lindsey, I decided to play with my breasts. As I began to massage my breasts, Lindsey gets startled by Shannon moving around beneath her. Now Shannon knows how to work a pussy, and it was noticeable as Lindsey was so distracted that she forgot about me. I had to work my pussy while Lindsey was fully introduced to lesbianism

This went on for about two hours. Then, Lindsey spent the night with us. The three of us spent every night together for the rest of the semester. Lindsey tells us that she hasn't given up on men yet. Once in a while, we see her hitting on men, but it never seems to go past that. Yet considering the amount of time that she spends with us, the thought of her with a man wouldn't cross your mind. We all plan on staying in this city and getting an apartment once school lets out. Keep a lookout, as you might hear from us again.

Story 04

Hey there everyone, my name is Tammie, and this is the story of my best friend, Jody and me.

Now granted, we have been best friends for years, and neither of us ever sexually thought about each other. But that all changed one hot summer night by Jody's pool.

We were lying out in the dying heat, trying to relax after a long day at work. The night air felt good over our bikini-clad bodies, but neither of us wanted to get into the pool.

We talked about the customers who had come in to pick up their prescriptions and any difficulties we had during the day. All-day long, we both had been trying to get a hold of various doctors but to no avail, and we were frustrated. Then the subject turned to sex and the lack of it.

"I'm sorry but right now if I don't get laid soon I'm going to go nuts." Jody said. "I'm wetter then hell most of the day and staring at all the hunks that come in and out all day doesn't help. What about you?"

"Oh yeah. It's been too long since me and Kirk broke up. I need to feel a guy inside me again. Now the vibrator helps but god to feel the real thing again." I said. "God just talking about it is making me wet and horny."

Jody glanced at me, and I looked at her, both of us had a look of hunger in our eyes.

I could tell her nipples were hard and that she was getting turned on. And I think that she could tell me the same thing from me.

"Um, I don't know about you but I'm suddenly feeling really hot. I think I'm going to go take a dip in the pool. You up for joining me?" I asked her.

"Yeah I'm coming in with you."

With that, we both dived in at the same time, making a huge splash.

I surfaced right behind her and pinched her behind as I came up for air. When I did that, I felt a rush of liquid between my legs. I knew then that her body was turning me on.

She turned and looked at me and smiled. And to this day, I don't know how we ended up in each other's arms and kissing, but we did. And let me tell you something, it got hot and heavy really fast.

We pulled apart, and she said, "Lets go over to the steps I want to feel all of you."

We waded over there and continued to make out and touch each other. She undid my top and pulled it down to expose my perfect 36D breasts. I undid her top to reveal her 38D pierced breasts.

She leaned down and started to suck them and massage them. I couldn't help but moan. She felt so good. As she sucked my nipples, I massaged hers into a complete harness. They were at the point of rock hard by the time she came back to kiss me.

As we kissed, she continued to massage my nipples, and I started to grind my pussy into her leg. I leaned down and took her nipples into my mouth. I played with her nipple hoop and teased her unmercifully with my tongue.

She slid her hand down into my bottoms and slid a finger up inside my dripping pussy.

"My god you're so wet. I want more of you. Lets move over to the chaise and strip naked. I want to see you and I want you to see me. I want to devour you." She said, panting with want and desire.

We managed to get over the chaise and strip each other of the rest of the bikinis. By this time, we were so into kissing and touching that we didn't notice the pool's temperature drop.

We lay down in a sixty-nine position to devour each other's steaming wet shaved pussies.

I have my clit pierced, and when she saw that, she just went after it with her tongue. I started thrashing around as she licked and flicked it with her tongue. I sucked her clit into my mouth and moaned against it, causing a little vibration. I could tell she liked that by the way she continued to attack me clit.

I started to run my tongue up and down her pussy, teasing her with it. Then when I finally stuck my tongue inside her, she came like nothing I had ever felt. I couldn't help but lick up all that love juice. She was doing the same to me, and I just came in buckets. I love being eaten out, and I always cum hard.

I was getting to the point where all I wanted was to feel her against me. So I turned around and faced her.

"I want to feel your pussy against mine. I want to grind against you. Do you want to keep going out here or do you want to move to your room?" I asked, panting.

"Lets just stay out here. I don't think I can move. I'm so horny right now." She moaned out.

I kissed her softly, moved down, and turned onto my side. She did the same, and then we slid together. As soon as I felt her pussy touch mine, I came right then. I couldn't help it, and she felt so good.

We just started rubbing each other's pussies with fingers and clits trying to stay together. Both of us bucking wildly. I managed to slide two fingers inside her, and she slid two into me. We both started to moan and buck even more.

"Oh my god I'm so cumming right now." She said as she flooded my fingers and pussy with cum. "God why haven't we done this sooner? I really love this."

I couldn't talk because I was cumming so much and so fast. All I could do was shrug and cum.

When we finally calmed down and disengaged from each other, we just kind of lay there and panted. I somehow managed to crawl up to her, take her in my arms, and kiss lightly.

After that, I don't remember much except waking up in her arms outside. We woke up because of the cold coming in, and we both decided to go to her room to continue what we had started.

What happened there, well that's another story. I'll have to tell it to you some time. That is after I am done cumming so much with Jody.

Story 05

Chapter 01

Sandra hated this. She really hated it. It wasn't that she disliked sharing her bed with her best friend...no...it was that she liked it too much. The black-haired woman tried relaxing her body, reminding herself that Kimberly was straight, and had just come out of a bad relationship...which was why she was staying at Sandra's for the time being sleeping in her bed with her.

Ever since they'd been teenagers, Sandra had felt this attraction for her best friend, yet knowing that Kimberly was as straight as a stick, she'd kept her hands to herself and her girlfriends a secret. Many of them had been angry at her and jealous of Kimberly. She had unknowingly been the reason why Sandra's relationships never seemed to last long.

And now here they were, lying in the same bed, both in skimpy little night dresses. Kimberly sleeping and Sandra, you might ask? Well, Sandra was fighting a battle with herself not to molest the younger woman in her sleep.

Kimberly's low groaning caught Sandra's attention, and she wondered what was happening in the other woman's dreams. She leaned in closer, trying to hear what Kimberly was whispering in her sleep, but it was too low for her to hear—and anyway—being close to Kimberly's face had caused her to forget why she'd leaned in, to begin with.

Suddenly Kimberly's foggy eyes blinked open, and she blinked some more, trying to clear her vision. "Sandra?"

Being this close to Kimberly caused Sandra to lose control. Before Kimberly could even speak, Sandra was straddling her and had descended her mouth down to devour the woman's soft lips.

The feeling of Kimberly's shy lips moving willingly on hers caused a thrill to rush through Sandra's body. This was too much and too good to be true. She slipped her tongue into Kimberly's mouth and swallowed the moan that elicited from her friend. And Sandra's hands hadn't been useless all this time, no, they had been unbuttoning the girl's shirt, watching in fascination as her pink bra came into view. Unhooking it from the front, Sandra pulled her mouth away from Kimberly's watching her glorious breasts, before descending her mouth on one of the breasts.

Kimberly cried out with the new and exquisitely torturous sensations that ran down her body like lightning, and pooled in her nether regions, fueling moans and groans from her as she threw her head back and tightly closed her eyes. "S—S—San--." But she didn't have the strength in her voice as her body began growing in heat, and her passion rose. Kimberly's hands buried themselves in her friend's hair, arching her back to give Sandra better access.

Sandra playfully bit down around Kimberly's nipple but didn't do so hard enough to break the untainted skin. A smirk covered her face when she heard Kimberly cry out her name. Flicking her tongue over the rock hard pink bud, she used her free hand to begin pushing away at the sheets covering Kimberly. "You don't know how much I want you." She huskily whispered as she began to lick around the tortured breasts slowly.

"You do?" Kimberly's breathy question.

"Yes, Kimberly, I do." Her licks began to descend in direction. She smiled evilly as Kimberly's stomach muscles rippled at the touch of her wet tongue, which was drawing small circles, slowly going lower, and lower, until she'd reached Kimberly's navel.

"S—Sandra--."

"Shh, my love." Sucking on the navel, Sandra began to thrust her tiny pink tongue inside of it three times, giving her lover a hint of what she soon planned on doing with that tongue.

Kimberly groaned when Sandra slowly parted her thighs and went to sit between them. She was about to say something, anything, when she felt fingers brushing softly against her clit, causing her to cry out. Never had she been so aroused, so sensitive and slick that a mere touch would cause her to

writhe. Before she could tell Sandra this, Kimberly lost her breath as those talented fingers began teasing her clit ruthlessly, causing her body to writhe in animalistic pleasure. "Sandra!" She cried when she felt a finger enter her without warning. Her eyes rolled back momentarily as pleasure filled her body, and groaning as Sandra added another finger.

It was hard for Sandra to wait for Kimberly to adjust to having both fingers inside of her while having her clit tortured, but the woman did her best to be patient. After all, this was her wish come true, and she didn't want Kimberly and her first time to be painful for the beautiful woman. Sandra wanted this experience to be something that Kimberly would remember for the rest of her life - for the rest of their lives together.

Then, when the older woman couldn't stand the waiting any longer, she rapidly thrust her fingers into Kimberly. Maybe she should go slow since this was Kimberly's first time, but her passion dominated her...and when Kimberly began bucking against the fingers, Sandra's smirk grew, knowing that the other woman wasn't complaining one bit. On the contrary, she was now writhing with undeniable passion, crying out loud, and begging for Sandra to go harder. And Sandra wasn't one to let her lover go unsatisfied with her performance.

The pleasure was too much for her, and she couldn't handle it anymore; it was going to explode. In seconds Kimberly arched her back and dug her nails into the sheets, screaming into the night as she came into Sandra's pumping hand.

Her body fell limp, and Kimberly yawned. She then looked down at Sandra, her cheeks turning pink all over again. "I've been menaing to tell you something for a long time now, Sandra." Her voice became a whisper. "I —I love you."

Snuggling against her lover, Sandra smiled happily. "I love you too."

Chapter 02

Smiling, Kimberly couldn't wait to see Sandra. She'd gone to see her parents for a couple of days. She was hurrying back to her love as soon as she could. Ever since that first night, Sandra and herself hadn't been separated, and they now had an apartment of their own where they happily lived together.

Entering the apartment, the young woman locked the door behind her, smiling because she knew that the love of her life was sleeping peacefully unawares in their bedroom.

When she entered, Kimberly was stunned at the erotic picture Sandra made—sleeping on top of the sheets, the moon bathing her glorious body with its magical beams. Sandra's long hair had been let out and was cascading like dark silk on the pillows. And the nightgown? Well, it had ridden up her body, giving Kimberly a good view of shapely legs and a scandalously naked bottom. The woman hadn't worn any underwear!

That little minx must have known I'd be coming back tonight. How she always knows is beyond me.

She walked towards the bed as silently as she could, leaning over the sleeping woman. My poor baby looks so tired. I'm just going to kiss her...I. 'm only going to kiss her...god; she smells terrific.

What had begun as 'only a kiss' had sparked into the familiar unquenchable desire Kimberly only experience when with Sandra, and she slowly lowered herself onto the bed, crawling over to Sandra and mounted her, running her fingers through those beautiful locks. It felt like silk to her fingers, soft, shiny, beautiful. All of those words described Sandra.

Tangling her fingers in that hair, Kimberly pulled back Sandra's head and plundered those soft lips. She was stunned slightly when the lips reacted to hers, and she'd pulled away, realizing that Sandra was still sleeping. The smile of a predator appeared on her face as she began licking down the raven-haired woman's neck, hands cupping and slightly squeezing the large breasts beneath hers. Under the cool silk, Sandra's nipples were rock hard, so aroused that Kimberly knew that her soft pinching most hurt slightly.

Even though it was downright sexy, the gown was only being a hindrance to her. The schoolgirl growled very much like a possessive male would, before freeing a breast from the restraint and looking at it hungrily. Licking her lips, Kimberly's eyes bore into the breast. She wanted to taste Sandra's skin. It had been too long since she'd been able to taste her, and Kimberly couldn't keep herself under control anymore.

Lowering her mouth to one of the nipples, she gave it a slight flick of her tongue, before running her wet tongue around the nipple in slow, teasing circles. She loved the taste of Sandra's skin. It was musky, erotic, irresistible, and addictive.

"Kimberly?" A groggy yet utterly sexy voice asked.

"Yes my love?" Kimberly whispered in Sandra's ear once she'd managed to tear her mouth off of Sandra's perfect breast.

"I missed you." Yawning slightly, Sandra rubbed at her eyes. "A girl can get used to being awaken like this."

"I missed you too. But for now...shhh..." Lowering herself down Sandra's body, Kimberly ran a finger teasingly on Sandra's clit and was shocked with awe to find moisture...a lot of moisture. A smirk appeared on Kimberly's face. During the day, Sandra was the accomplished warrior in court. Yet, during the night, she succumbed and submitted herself to Kimberly's authority. Putting her thumbs around the clit, Kimberly leaned down and blew on the clit, a smirk growing when Sandra moaned and squirmed slightly.

"Kim---." Sandra whispered.

"Shhh." Kimberly then lowered her mouth to the wet slit and sucked hard.

"---berly!" Sandra cried softly, her hands digging into the bed desperately.

Swallowing her lover's moisture, Kimberly licked the slit slowly and then began to suck on the sensitive bud before thrusting a finger inside of Sandra without warning.

"Kimberly....Kimberly!" Sandra cried softly over and over, withering on the bed, moans, and groans of passion, heating her body.

Adding another finger, and another, Kimberly stopping sucking the clit for a second, and the thrusting of her fingers, feeling in awe as Sandra's insides stretched greedily around them. The feeling was unreal. A smirk appeared on her face when she heard Sandra's growl of frustration and felt Sandra thrust urgently against her fingers. "Getting a little anxious, aren't we?"

"Oh just shut up and fuck me." Sandra ordered rather breathlessly, and Kimberly found it arousing.

"As you wish." Thrusting the three fingers painfully hard, she watched as Sandra struggled to keep from waking the people sleeping in the other huts with her cries. Returning to her hard sucking and teasing, Kimberly rammed her fingers into Sandra over and over again, feeling as the black-haired woman met every thrust with one of her one.

Soon Sandra's insides clenched tightly around Kimberly's fingers as Sandra made a strangled sound in her throat, and she came into Kimberly's hand.

Licking up the cum on Sandra's jewel and thighs, Kimberly swallowed it and licked her fingers clean; a smirk appeared on her lovely face. "I kept tasting you in my mouth during my visit with my parents. It drove me crazy." Before she could continue, Sandra pulled her into a passionate kiss.

Extreme Lesbian Erotica

4 Spicy & Steamy BDSM Erotica

Jennifer G. Steen

All Rights Reserved. No part of this publication may be reproduced in any form or by any means, including scanning, photocopying, or otherwise without prior written permission of the copyright holder. Copyright © 2020

This book is entirely a work of fiction. The names, characters and incidents portrayed in it are the work of the author's imagination. Any resemblance to actual persons, living or dead, events or localities is entirely coincidental.

Story 01

I guess in a way it was bad what we did to Susie-at least on the surface. But to tell you the truth, I don't feel guilty about it at all. Maybe after I explain what happened you'll understand why.

My name is Morgan and I'm a junior at the University of Washington. I live at an apartment off-campus with my roommate Angelina, who had also been my lover since we shared a room on campus in our freshman year. Angelina's an Italian girl with beautiful brown eyes, olive skin, and long black hair, about 5'5" and very curvy and delectable. At the beginning of sophomore year we decided to move into this apartment together, and it's been a perfect arrangement for us. Both our families would have flipped if we'd wanted to move in with a boy, but since neither of them knows that we like girls, they had no objection to our living together.

We get along really well and we fuck often-alone or in threesomes (or more)-but we keep separate bedrooms and we don't have an exclusive relationship. We have an agreement that we can sleep with other girls whenever we want to as long as we always tell each other the truth about it. We figure we're too young to be tied down to one person, and there's just so much to experience out there. It's nice to have someone to live with, though, someone who's always there for you.

I'm a little taller than Angelina, about 5'8", and I'm skinnier with a slightly smaller chest. My hair is naturally blond but a lot of the time it's dyed red or blue or something. I've been having lesbian sex since I had an affair with my cousin the summer before my senior year in high school. I'm studying Chemistry and I manage to do pretty well in school in between all of my other activities.

Anyway, at the beginning of this year, a new girl moved in across the hall. She knocked on our door and introduced herself while Angie and I were sprawled in the living room, studying. She told us her name was Susie and that she was a freshman at our school.

We introduced ourselves but I was so blown away by her that I could barely remember my name. Susie is an absolutely stunning redhead with a round face and these gorgeous, giant green eyes. It was a warm day, too, and she was wearing a black half-T that showed off her phenomenal breasts and silky-soft belly, and a pair of tight cutoffs that looked unbelievable on her. She was wearing her hair in a ponytail and she had just a touch of baby fat left on her, but it only made her sexier.

Angelina and I exchanged glances and I knew that we were both thinking the same thing: I have just got to get a piece of Susie. But we put on our best behavior and greeted her warmly, inviting her in for some lemonade. I tried to converse calmly about normal things, though I couldn't help myself from surreptitiously stealing looks at her tits. In the back of my mind, I was already picturing what Susie would look like naked and imagining the things I would do to her given the chance. I got pretty wet as we sat there chatting, and as soon as Susie went back to her apartment, Angie and I attacked each other and 69ed for about an hour, just to calm ourselves down.

We didn't talk about it, but I knew that we were both thinking about Susie and about whether it would be possible to get into her panties. I'm pretty good at telling which girls are beddable and which aren't, but it takes a little while. I knew that we'd have to take our time and not blow it by rushing things.

Susie kept pretty much to herself at first but was always friendly when we saw her. I tried to figure out what I could about her. The apartment that she lived in was a pretty big one-bedroom and she lived by herself, and she drove a BMW convertible, so it was obvious that she was pretty well-off. We'd find out later that her father was a fairly well-known conservative congressman.

Angelina and I took every opportunity to invite Susie over to our apartment for coffee, or dinner, or a movie, or whatever. Initially she turned us down often but as time wore on she started hanging out at our place fairly regularly. It turned out that she was very sweet and fun to be with, as well as being fantastic to look at. But whenever I talked to her my mind would wander as I pictured myself kissing her belly button, her stomach dotted with fine beads of sweat, burying my face in her furry red bush, and moving down between her legs...

Then I'd shiver to shake off the vision and try to pay attention to the conversation, try not to stare. I didn't want to scare her off, just in case there was a chance.

Angelina and I never came right out and told Susie that we were dykes, but we didn't hide it, either. From our conversations it was pretty hard to miss; and, after all, Susie lived right across the hall, and Angie and some of the other girls we brought home could be quite loud at times. Despite her father's politics, Susie seemed to have a pretty liberal frame of mind and never looked shocked, though she would be a little embarrassed at times.

Of course, Angie and I were always studying Susie closely, trying to gauge her reactions. About a month after school started, we sat down and compared notes. Susie knew that Angie and I were lovers, but hadn't stopped hanging out with us, which was a good sign. And we hadn't seen her with any guys, which was a very good sign. She was always friendly and laughed at our jokes, and could get a certain kind of flirtatious look in her eyes when she was around us. And she often dressed very sexily-wearing tube tops, short skirts, tight T-shirts, and so on.

Angelina and I decided the signs were good-that it might just be possible to seduce Susie. We got ourselves so excited and carried away talking about it that we decided to make a bet on who could get Susie into bed first. The loser would have to be the winner's slave for a week-that way, even though winning would be better, losing wouldn't be so bad. There were two conditions to the bet: the winner would have to tell the loser everything, and would do everything in her power to get Susie into a three-way with the loser.

I could feel my temperature rising as we discussed the terms of the bet; my hand crept under the kitchen table, up Angie's leg, and into her panties. I slipped a finger into her moist cunt as we concluded our negotiations. She squealed and leaned over to kiss me. In a matter of seconds I had her spread out on the table and was going down on her. We had some of the hottest sex we'd had in months, all fueled by the thought of Susie.

After that Angie and I started being a lot more obvious when Susie was around. We took every opportunity to be caught in our underwear, or even topless, when Susie showed up at the door. Angelina in particular was shameless; if Susie and I were in the living room, Angie would emerge from her bedroom in nothing but panties and go into the kitchen to pour herself a glass of milk. We would rent movies starring beautiful women and make lewd comments about them, Angie and I mock-secretly groping each other in the half-light and moaning softly but audibly. Though Angie and I were in competition, the most important thing was getting Susie heated up enough that one of us would get to her, and quick. Having her around the apartment, as hot as she was and showing all that skin, was driving us crazy.

And it was working. I could tell by looking into Susie's eyes. There was a certain hunger there when Angelina and I kissed, or when Angie walked by displaying her beautiful tits. And she was definitely flirting with us now, standing very close, giggling girlishly, looking raptly into our eyes and then shyly looking away. I started to get very excited; this might actually happen! It would really make my year to finally make love to Susie after so much effort and patience.

Finally, one Sunday night Angelina had to go to a study group and Susie and I got together to watch a movie by ourselves. I chose Bound for obvious reasons. I wore an extremely short skirt and a bikini top and cracked open a bottle of white wine for us to share. Susie showed up in tight, faded jeans and an equally tight striped T-shirt that showed off her body to stunning effect; I was so beside myself with lust that I could barely speak. "This is it," I thought. "She's ready and I'm going to have her tonight."

We sat next to each other on the couch. I was eager and nervous but tried to play it cool, commenting on the movie from time to time. I made sure to drop into conversation the fact that Angie and I had a nonexclusive relationship. I watched Susie closely when Jennifer Tilly and Gina Gershon made love; she tensed a little and nervously sipped her wine, but never took her eyes from the screen. When the movie was over, I flipped off the TV and we sat there in the dark, talking and drinking wine. I was a little tipsy and flushed with the heat of Susie's body so nearby. Finally there was a quiet moment; I felt Susie's leg warm against mine, and I leaned over to kiss her. I felt a sense of unleashed desire as her mouth met mine forcefully. My heart leapt with joy; she tasted delicious and I was going to win!

Our tongues intertwined and explored each other's mouths. I kissed Susie's ear and then her neck, and finally I reached down a to caress one of her breasts...

And she was gone. My caress got nothing but air. The room was very dark now, but I could sense her across the room, panting audibly. "What's wrong?" I asked.

Her voice was weak and broken, shaking with the beginnings of a sob. "I'm sorry," she said, pausing for breath. "I'm not gay. I wanted to- I didn't mean to-" She broke off. "I'm sorry." And she turned, opened the door, and left, just like that. I was stunned. I'd seen the promised land, had it within my grasp, only to be denied. As I sat there in the dark, I felt sure of one thing-the desire I'd felt in Susie had been real. She just didn't want to admit it.

I didn't see Susie again until I ran into her in the hallway a few days later. She wouldn't meet my eyes; staring at the floor, she said "I'm sorry about what happened the other night," then quickly changed the subject. She obviously didn't want to talk about it, and I didn't want to make her any more uncomfortable, so I went ahead and chitchatted idly with her for awhile.

Things got pretty much back to normal after that. Susie still dropped by the apartment once in a while, though she looked edgy a lot of the time. We never mentioned what had happened between us, and I didn't want Angelina to know that I had apparently blown my opportunity. But I now wanted her more than ever, having gotten so close. Sometimes it was all I could do to keep myself from physically jumping her.

A few weeks later, the three of us had dinner together on a Friday night. Around 10 Angie left to meet some friends of hers at a club downtown. I told Susie that she could take off if she wanted to, but she said she'd stay and help out with the dishes. We cleaned up and sat down to watch some TV. As time passed, I noticed that Susie seemed to be edging closer to me on the couch. By midnight we were nestled very close together and I couldn't resist anymore–I again leaned over to kiss her. We necked for awhile, even more passionately than before, and then slowly, gingerly I reached for her left breast with my right hand. I got a nice, round handful and felt a painfully erect nipple pressing into my palm. Then Susie bolted again. She retreated to the doorway and wouldn't respond to my perplexed look.

"I'm sorry," she said again. "You're really nice and all. This... this just isn't for me." The door opened and she was gone.

I was mad this time. This was the second time she'd gotten me all psyched up and left me wet and frustrated. Cursing, I lit up a joint and pulled off my jeans and panties and fingered myself, picturing the sweet red head that should have been between my legs. After coming a couple times, I calmed down, but I was still pretty bummed. The worst part was that I could feel that Susie wanted it as badly as I did–she was just holding herself back, unwilling or unable to let go. Probably for some stupid reason like her dad or what she had been taught growing up. I just sat there for a long time smoking and brooding, and finally about 4 a.m. Angelina walked in. "What's up?" she asked.

I was too depressed and stoned not to tell the truth, so I said, "Susie. We started kissing, she seemed like she was all into it, and then..." "She took off?"

"Yeah. This is the second time it's happened."

"Really?" said Angie. "The exact same thing happened to me! One night when you weren't here, we started making out. I got all hot and bothered, and then she bailed. Said she wasn't a dyke. But I'm not buying it."

"Yeah," I said. "She really wants to, but she's afraid."

"It just about killed me."

"It's driving me out of my mind! There's got to be something we can do. We want her, she wants us. There has to be a way to make her forget whatever's holding her back."

So Angelina and I decided to call off our bet and, talking until dawn, we came up with a plan. And this is where the story gets kind of iffy, like I said. You might say our plan seems questionable, and objectively I'd have to agree with you. But to have such a tasty morsel, so close at hand...we just couldn't help ourselves. Here's what we did:

We waited until things had cooled off with Susie and then, the next Friday night, we invited her over for dinner again. She turned up around 9, wearing blue denim overalls that showed her bare arms with her hair tied back, looking phenomenally cute. Angelina fixed this great dinner of garlic chicken and we sat and talked, but I kept breaking out into a lustful and nervous sweat, knowing what we had planned.

See, we had slipped a sedative into Susie's wine. So when the three of us retired into the living room after dinner, not 10 minutes had passed before Susie fell fast asleep on the couch. Angelina and I exchanged sly grins. Susie looked so gorgeous and innocent snoozing there, her red head resting on one of the arms. Her overalls had shifted so that we had a good look at the bright red bra she had on underneath them.

I walked over to the couch and stroked Susie's hair. I was very tempted to just tear her clothes off and have my way with her right then and there. But that would have been crossing the line. Angie and I had worked out our plan very carefully and decided what we did and didn't consider

acceptable, under the circumstances. So we picked up the unconscious redhead and moved her into Angie's bedroom, where we had made preparations beforehand. It was a matter of just a few minutes to get everything ready; then we sat down and smoked a joint, watching our lovely captive breathe, waiting for her to wake up.

When Susie awoke, she found herself standing with her hands cuffed behind her back around one of the posts of Angelina's canopy bed. I saw her eyes register surprise and she started to say something, only to find that she had been gagged. She looked over to the corner of the room where Angie and I were reclining, watching her. Getting an inkling of what was going on, Susie then looked down at herself, but found that she was still wearing her overalls.

I smiled and stood up, walking over to stand by Susie. She stared at me wide-eyed and questioning, struggling briefly with the handcuffs, then quickly discovering that it was useless. I paused, savoring the sensation of power over this sweet young thing. Then I felt a twinge of guilt as I saw fear in Susie's eyes and I spoke up, trying to put her at ease. "Hi, Susie," I said sweetly. "You can relax, nothing's going to happen to you. You're going to be tied up there for exactly one hour. When the hour's up, if you want us to let you go, we'll let you go. Do you understand?"

Susie nodded. I grabbed Angelina's alarm clock and set it for one hour later. Now it was showtime.

Angie went over to the stereo and put on some music. It was this album called Dr. Octagon, weird and funky rap. As the bass started to throb, I had a seat on Angie's recliner in the corner. Angie jumped up on her desk and started to dance for us-me in the dark corner and our captive audience by the bed. Angie was wearing a leather jacket over a black lace bra and a short leather skirt over black fishnet stockings and a garter belt. Her lips were fiery red and her long black mane had never looked so great as she ground her hips and bent down to show Susie her chest. As the second song began, Angelina took off the jacket and tossed it aside. She played with her breasts for our benefit, cupping them, pressing them together, stroking her nipples.

Next Angie took off the bra, baring her beautiful tits. She resumed fondling them, pulling on her now very erect nipples and wetting them with saliva. Then she unzipped the skirt, shook it down to her feet, and stepped out of it. Now she was dancing in just the stockings and garter and the black lace panties she had on over them. Angelina slid a hand down into her panties, We saw it move down between her legs and she stroked herself, thrusting her head back and her chest out.

I looked over at Susie. She was staring intently at the shape of Angie's hand as it moved under the lace.

Another song started and Angie hooked her thumbs into her panties and slipped them down over her hips, thighs, knees and ankles. Her pretty black bush was now on display. Her hand quickly returned to her crotch, running through the hair and sliding down between her legs again. The pink of her pussy was just barely visible in front.

After a few minutes Angie sat down on the desk and spread her legs wide, showing us her cunt. Although I had seen her exquisite snatch many, many times before, it had never looked so perfect. I could see that she was incredibly wet from the way the light reflected off her lips. Slowly, seductively, she removed the garter and rolled the stockings down her legs and off. She was now completely naked, and she lay back on the desk with her legs apart. Parting her pussy lips, she slid a finger up into her slit. Writhing in time with the music, she began to move the finger in and out. I could see that she was totally into the moment now, and she had begun to sweat a little bit as she stabbed more fingers into her hole. Her fingers found her clit again and again and she came, spasming and then laying still, a look of rapture on her face, glistening with sweat and juices.

I looked over at Susie again. She was completely bug-eyed, her gaze focused on Angelina's exposed crotch. I let Angie recover for just a minute; then it was time for the second part of our little show. I walked over to where Angie lay on the desk, planting a big wet kiss on her mouth. I helped her stand up and then, producing our other pair of handcuffs from my pocket, cuffed her hands behind her back. I put my hands on Angie's shoulders and gently pushed her down till she was on her knees. Then I snapped a collar onto her neck and attached a short leash. I led Angie by the leash as she crawled on her knees until I had her situated in front of the recliner.

I smiled down at Angelina on her knees before me, bound and naked. This had to be working on Susie. It was sure working on me.

I stripped off my blouse and leaned down to feed Angie first one breast, then the other. I pulled off my jeans and panties and sat on the recliner. I slowly opened my legs, exposing my pussy to Angie and to our audience. I started to pull Angelina's head in toward it and she extended her tongue in anticipation, but then I got ahold of her leash and held her just a few inches away. She let out a moan of frustration and it was painful for me too, but I kept her there straining against the leash, sticking her tongue out as far as it would go to try to reach my snatch. Gradually I let her get closer and closer and finally I felt her warm tongue against my lips. I let go of the leash and forced Angelina's head tight up against my crotch as she drove her tongue inside me. Angie's always passionate but she was absolutely mad as she devoured my orifice. She had me coming inside a minute and made me come three more times before she had to come up for air.

Angelina smiled up at me devilishly, her nose and mouth covered with my juice. I was losing control by now. I pushed her onto her back and straddled her head, grinding down onto her face as I lay down on top of her, stabbing my tongue between her cunt lips. I almost forgot where I was and what I was doing, intoxicated by Angie's taste and aroma, until I looked up and saw Susie. Then I remembered our big finale.

I disappeared into the bathroom for a minute and when I returned, I was wearing a foot-long strap-on dildo. Kneeling in front of me, Angie licked and sucked it till it was nice and wet. Then I walked around behind her, bent her over and penetrated her. She let out a yelp and exhaled audibly as more and more of the dildo disappeared into her hole. I fucked lovely Angelina with all my strength, her face against the carpet as she lifted her ass into the air to meet me. I swear that I could feel the dildo, I could feel myself inside her, filling her completely. I fucked Angie to a giant, screaming orgasm that seemed to be happening to me too. And then the alarm went off. It was the moment of truth.

I uncuffed Angelina and took off the dildo. Together we walked over to where Susie stood, handcuffed to the bed. I took just a second to behold her loveliness, gently stroking her cheek. I removed her gag.

At last, I asked Susie the question I had been waiting to ask.

"Do you want us to let you go?"

There was a moment's pause before she responded, a quiet, electric moment. Time seemed to stop.

Looking at the floor, Susie shook her head. "Say it," I told her.

Only then did she look up and meet my gaze. "No."

Angie and I smiled at each other, savoring our victory. Then we dove at our little redhead, kissing her on the mouth and neck and ears. She squirmed and gasped and drove her tongue into our mouths. We unstrapped Susie's overalls at the shoulders and rolled them down around her waist, fondling her tits and stroking her jutting nipples through the red lace of her bra. The bra came off soon after and we finally beheld Susie's tits naked and unfettered. We knelt and began to lick and suck those delicious globes, me on the left and Angie on the right.

After awhile we found ourselves being drawn downward, kissing below Susie's tits, her navel, her hipbones. I caught a whiff of arousal drifting up from her crotch and nearly passed out from happiness. We pulled Susie's overalls down around her ankles and off; now she was wearing only red lace panties matching her bra and a pair of cute black-and-white striped socks.

We kissed Susie's knees, her thighs, her lace-covered mound. She moaned and shivered as our tongues caressed her flesh. I looked up at her and she spoke softly, breathlessly. "Please."

Angie grasped one side of the waistband and I took the other, and we slid the panties down over her hips, her thighs, her knees, her calves, her ankles and her feet, and off. Susie's lush red bush was right there in front of us, just inches from my eyes. I kissed it, then Angelina did, then we ran our tongues through it and across the soft skin next to it. We held Susie's legs and pulled them up and open until her right leg rested on my left shoulder and her left on Angie's right shoulder. There it was before us-paradise. It was all I'd been thinking about for months, and now here it was, mine for the taking-the pinkest, wettest, most beautiful pussy I'd ever seen.

I wanted the moment to last forever, and Angie and I held back, admiring, keeping Susie waiting, for as long as we could. But it wasn't really that long before we could wait no more. We slid our tongues up Susie's inner thighs until they met at the center of her sex, touching as they darted between her petals. Her fresh young cunt tasted like the sweetest nectar. Susie let out a long womanly wail and thrashed her hips as Angie and I ate her like shipwreck victims having their first meal in months. Our tongues moved frantically across her lips and as far up inside her as they'd go, meeting each other in their paths. then flicking against Susie's clit. In a frenzy we made her come once, twice, three times, then again and again, feeling her spasm against us. At long last-it could have been hours later, I couldn't say-we lay back on the floor, heads swimming, our faces covered with Susie's honey and loose red pubic hairs.

When I felt able to stand again, I uncuffed Susie and the three of us embraced. She was smiling broadly and kissed me hard on the mouth. All her shyness seemed to be gone. She looked into my eyes, then over at Angelina. "I want to do you now," she said.

I nodded at Angie. "You first," I said; I wanted to watch and anticipate. I took a seat as Angie reclined on the bed. I lit up another joint as I saw Susie's lips close around one of Angie's breasts. I watched happily as Susie's red head made its way down Angie's body and our little neighbor began to lick my roommate's pussy-her first. Judging by the helpless noises Angelina was making, she must have been doing a pretty good job. After a time, Susie lifted her head from Angie's crotch and looked at me. I motioned for her to come over. She knelt in front of me as Angie had done earlier; I kissed her and gave her a toke. I put one breast into Susie's mouth, then the other, feeling her soft lips play across my skin and her tongue caress my nipples. I slipped a finger into my twat, wetting it, then put it into Susie's mouth; she sucked it as eagerly as any baby with its bottle. She looked so sweet and innocent and also so dirty there, nude on her knees before me, nursing blissfully on my finger. I spread my legs and drew Susie's head down between them. It felt like an electric shock when her tongue penetrated me. I closed my eyes and savored the feeling as Susie enthusiastically gave me head. She had me exploding in no time, but I only pulled her tighter up against me, eager for more.

When I opened my eyes again it was to the beautiful sight of sweet Susie's head between my thighs; then I noticed that Angie had joined in, sliding underneath Susie to lap at her cunt. So this is heaven, I thought. The three of us made love in every possible combination until dawn and finally fell asleep in a heap in the morning sun, exhausted and inconceivably happy.

So, as you can imagine, I really don't feel that bad about it.

Story 02

I imagine that when she awoke, it was 7:30 and I was gone.

She'd never been alone in my apartment before. She wants to snoop. She can't. There's a note by the bed. Darling Alana, it starts, and the rest is instructions to wait until I return. She looks out of the window and sees her reflection in the sunlight. The next building is ten feet away. She waits for someone to walk by, to catch her. No one does.

She remembers the first night she came to my apartment. We'd just met, but I'd known immediately what was going to happen. I'd said I would feed her, and to follow me, so she did. I told her it was a dinner party, but when we got there it was just she, I, and a refrigerator full of leftovers. She hadn't been surprised. I took her coat and hung it up at the door. She walked slowly into the living room, looking around somewhat absently. I walked up behind her and slid my arms around her, pulling her to face me. I watched her eyes widen suddenly, her lips parting slightly. I took her head in my hands and brought her lips to mine, sucking her lower lip into my mouth and biting gently. Alana drew in breath and smiled softly, pulling me closer and kissing me hard, licking the inside of my mouth passionately. I think she'd been expecting this. I started to move against her, wanting her more and more, stroking hard all over her body. I slid my hand between her legs, biting her lip and thrusting my tongue into her mouth. Alana began to breathe heavily, her lips parted and flushed. She started to writhe against my hand, kissing me hungrily. I moved my hands up to her shirt, took it between my fingers and slipped it over her head, letting it drop to the floor. I couldn't think about anything except the way her body felt against mine. I pulled her against me quickly, licking and biting her neck, hearing her cry out. The feeling of her soft flesh giving way under my teeth was overwhelming. I wanted to fuck her.

Wrapping my arms around her, I unhooked her bra, pushed her over to the bed, and began kissing down between her breasts. I slid my hand roughly between her legs, running my tongue over her breast. I heard her mumble "so good, Mira", panting audibly. Unbuttoning her pants with my free hand, I bit down gently on her nipple, running my tongue softly over the tip. I felt Alana arch against my mouth, eagerly helping me unbutton her pants and slide them down to her knees. Sucking her nipple suddenly into my mouth, I ran my teeth over her, sucking her hard into my mouth again and again. I slid my finger lightly between her legs, feeling the wetness spread rapidly.

I felt her breath on my neck as she panted and whined softly, squirming under me. Sliding my arms from behind her back, I slid them down her arms, and held her hands down by her sides. I bit quickly down her stomach, my teeth sinking hungrily into her flesh, my head spinning. I could feel the pull of how much she wanted me. I pushed her leg back a little, licking and biting urgently up her inner thigh. I raised my eyes a little, seeing Alana's nails digging into her thighs. I slid my hands over hers, sliding my tongue over her, licking her hard. Running my teeth over her sensitive flesh, I sucked her clit into my mouth again and again, moaning at her taste in my mouth. I listened to Alana draw in breath and cry out sharply, watching her hands grip the sides of the bed in an agony of lust, fluid running down the insides of her thighs. I ran my tongue over and inside her again and again, biting down on her, listening to her moans and greedily swallowing as much of her as I could.

I heard her crying out over and over, "yes...yes, Mira...don't stop."

Unable to contain myself, I drove my fingers into her as deep as I could, my thumb sliding over her clit, my free hand reaching up and holding her hands tightly above her head. I looked down, watching Alana's eyes grow wide, hearing her cry out in stunned and aching pleasure. Her eyes staring intensely into mine, she arched her back and rode my fingers as hard as she could. Shifting my body forward, I pushed her legs back, fucking her faster and harder, moving my wrists in small circles. I felt fluid running down my fingers, pooling in my palm and running down my wrist. I watched in stunned pleasure as Alana screamed my name, tightly closed her eyes and bit her lip hard enough to draw blood. Moaning painfully, I tightened my grip on her hands, bending to take her lip in my mouth. I sucked deeply on her lip, the metallic taste of her blood filling my mouth, rhythmically driving my fingers into her as fast and hard as I could. I could feel her tightening around my fingers. I could feel her moans passing through my body like electricity.

My eyes locked on the white curve of her neck, arching back. I could feel the tension pulling through her body, stretching toward release. Thrusting deeper inside her, suddenly her eyes met mine.

Gasping, she cried, "I'm yours...Mira, please...I belong to you."

Closing my eyes in ecstasy, a deep moan crept over my lips. I pushed Alana's legs back further, fucking her harder, my wrist moving in quick tight circles. Alana began to tremble violently. I could feel her begin to spasm against me. I could hear the urgency in her low throaty moans. I released Alana's hands from above her head, quickly lowering my mouth to her. Continuing to thrust my fingers rapidly inside her, I began to lick her clit quickly, biting down gently. Moaning at Alana's taste in my mouth, I heard her crying, "yes...yes". I sucked her clit into my mouth, licking and biting her hard all over, my mouth pressed against her hot flesh as hard as I could manage. I felt myself trembling, overwhelmed by Alana's taste all through my mouth and the amazing wet feeling of slamming my fingers deep inside her. A moan welled up from deep inside me. I could feel her complete trembling adoration in rippling waves that began with her exquisite cries of pleasure and passed through my entire body. I felt my senses reaching fever pitch as Alana arched firmly to my mouth, releasing in gushing spurts that ran down my chin and over my wrist. I moaned happily over and over, licking her greedily all over and fucking her slowly, gently.

"Oh, darling," she gasped.

I could feel her blood pounding. She was mine. I heard her breath coming in great ragged gasps as I emptied her with my fingers, cleaning her gently with my tongue. I wanted more. It was all I could think about. When I felt her body completely relaxed and satisfied beneath me, I took her clit into my mouth, sucking very gently, and began to move my fingers quickly inside her. To my great surprise and delight she came again, filling my mouth with silky white fluid. I left my fingers deep inside her for a moment, feeling the strong pulse of her blood and cleaning her happily with my tongue. Slowly the shivers faded and she lay very still, making soft, pleased noises.

I licked her slowly over and over, sliding my hands over the warm skin of her thighs and stomach. I felt her becoming mine, more and more. I heard her whisper in a barely audible, satisfied purr, that she loved me. A smile passed over my face. I pushed her legs open wide and slid my tongue inside her. I could feel her tighten around me immediately, her taste making me dizzy. I heard a deep throaty sigh and Alana began to move slowly against my mouth. I pushed my tongue as deep as I could inside her, sliding slowly, gently in and out of her. The feeling of her hot, soft, smooth muscle around my tongue made me lose myself in the consuming need to possess her. I felt Alana's hands cradling my head, holding my mouth against her. She was riding my mouth as slowly as she could stand.

I could feel how excruciating it was for her, how much she wanted to use me. I loved that feeling. I felt warmth spreading achingly between my thighs, and I began to move my tongue faster inside her, pulling her tighter to my mouth. She began to thrust against my face gently. I could feel her clit swelling against my upper lip. I moved my hands from her hips and opened her more with my fingers, thrusting my tongue even deeper inside her delicious wetness. Alana spread her legs wider, giving me more room to deepen the urgent thrusts of my tongue. I could hear her breath coming faster and faster, driving me on. I moved the index finger of my left hand over her engorged clit, sliding gently over her in small circles, my tongue pulsing inside her. Slowly, she began to try to shift her position on top of me. I pulled her desperately on top of me, impaling her on my eager tongue. I heard her gasp, crying out my name. I loved the way my name sounded when she said it.

I ran my hands over her thighs, urging her down hard on top of me, moving my tongue as quickly as I could deep inside her. I was starting to think that I would lose control over myself completely if she didn't fuck me. I wanted the feel of her inside me. I wanted her to fuck me so hard, to push me. Alana quickly turned around and raised her body slightly, offering me her clit. I closed my mouth around it, sucking gently, running my tongue softly over her. Suddenly, I slammed two of my fingers inside her violently. Alana cried out loudly and started to move harder against me. She began to stroke my sides. Alana slid her body slowly down mine, still moving against my mouth, kissing and licking my lower abdomen. It was all I could do to keep from pushing her off of me and taking her mouth, but I was enjoying the way she was moving on me, and the feeling of being denied. I moaned deeply, sliding my teeth over her clit and licking in small quick circles.

The feeling of her smooth, hot, wet clit under my tongue was making me lose control. Alana's taste filling my mouth and her delicious kisses all over my abdomen and thighs were slowly pulling away my reason. I bit her again gently, enjoying the sound of Alana crying out in pleasure. Sliding my tongue down quickly, I drove it inside of her hard, lingering for a few seconds to enjoy the feeling of her tightening around me. Then I slid my tongue back up and sucked her clit into my mouth, moaning desperately. Alana pressed her clit hard to my mouth, and I whined loudly, rolling my tongue all over her. She moaned softly and sucked my clit into her mouth, her face tight between my legs. My body arched back, pulled taught like a bow, trembling. I cried out, Alana still pressed tightly to my mouth, moving hard over me, raking my teeth over her hyper-sensitive skin. Writhing against her mouth, I closed my lips around her clit, biting down on her and sucking as hard as I could. I had lost control completely.

584

The feel of Alana's mouth on me sent ripples of pleasure shooting through my tense, trembling body. I gasped as Alana excitedly forced her hard tongue inside of me. I felt myself quivering and moving my hips involuntarily, desperate for more, for the wet, hot feeling of her tongue moving hard over me and inside me, for her lips closing around my clit, for her fingers digging into my thighs. I could feel her body sliding achingly against mine, her breasts and stomach running teasingly over me. She began to move her hips over my mouth faster and harder, covering my mouth with fluid. I could feel the delicious urgency ripping through her body. The heat from my body was nearly unbearable. I could feel fluid draining slowly, luxuriously out of me. I slid my tongue deep inside her as hard as I could. I moaned in a frenzy of pleasure, licking her hard, closing my teeth around her clit and sucking frantically, my tongue dancing over her. I felt Alana's moans vibrating through my body. She drove her tongue into me powerfully, filling me up. I felt her tongue growing soft inside me, lapping my wetness into her mouth, hearing her moan softly. I felt like I was spinning. She felt so good. I slid my hips against her eager mouth, pressing myself tightly to her, my tongue pulsing inside her quickly. Suddenly, Alana grabbed my hips with her hands, fucking me hard, her tongue a blur as she slammed it into me again and again, so deep inside me. Gasping, I let my head roll back a little, crying out painfully. I dug my fingernails into her legs as hard as I could, slamming my tongue hungrily into her again and again. My breath started to come faster as my body tensed, coiling like a spring under Alana's mouth. I pushed my tongue deep inside her once again, moving it in hard circles. Crying out sharply inside her, feeling my legs spasming, electric waves of pleasure soaring through me, I felt Alana slamming her tongue quick and hard deep inside me, her whole body shaking on top of me. I sunk my teeth into her hot swollen clit, licking fast and sucking rhythmically, feeling myself so close to release, my clit throbbing painfully. Suddenly, Alana started fucking me harder with her tongue, pushing me easily over the edge. I came so hard, crying out ecstatically, feeling Alana frantically trying to swallow as much of my come as she could. I could feel it trickling gently over my thighs. I sighed deeply, enjoying Alana's pleased moans.

"Good girl", I whispered under my breath.

I licked her all over, my tongue sliding easily over her, lapping her wetness into my mouth. She slid slowly off my mouth, her body glistening beautifully, her cheeks flushed. She slid down between my legs and continued to clean me, breathing heavily. I was enjoying the feeling of her tongue, moving slowly, meticulously all over me, listening to her barely audible, satisfied moans. I looked down at her, her hair falling softly over her face, her eyes closed tightly.

"She belongs to me", I thought.

I ran my hands through her hair, watching it shine, enjoying the feeling of it slipping gently through my fingers. I ran my finger down her cheek, taking her chin in my hand and raising her head, her eyes meeting mine.

"You're such a good girl, Alana. I love you.
"

She smiled, a pleased, sleepy smile and rested her head against my hand. I pulled her toward me gently, so that her head rested on my shoulder, her body wrapped tightly around mine. She lay like that, her eyes closed lightly, her face relaxed and flushed. I stroked her body gently, enjoying the small pleasure sounds she made. Soon, Alana fell asleep, her breath growing slow and regular, a satisfied look on her face. This was all going perfectly. She was just what I'd been looking for. I slid her head carefully off of my shoulder, laying it on to the white pillow. I eased her body back a little, so she rested comfortably in the middle of the bed, her head turned to the side, her red hair falling over the white pillow, her arms resting across her body. I slid off the bed and stood back for a moment, admiring her. I got something from under the bed and then ran my fingers lightly over her left leg, down to her ankle. I slipped the cuff onto her ankle and cuffed her to the lower left bedpost, taking care not to wake her. When I was certain that she was tied securely, I stepped back again. I slid a sheet over her body, sliding it up over her shoulder and smoothing it gently over her body. I loved the way it fell over her. I bent down and kissed her softly on the lips, licking her just a little. I pulled back once more. She looked so beautiful. I kissed her twice more, causing her to moan very softly and shift a little. Not wanting to wake her, I stepped away quietly. I reached down and retrieved something else from under the bed. It was a letter. I lay it next to her on the bed. I reached over and took a rose out of a slender blue vase on my bedside table. I turned back the sheet a little, making sure to keep it resting on her shoulder. I slid the rose into her arms, so that it rested lightly against her breast. I looked at her carefully for a moment. Perfect. I told her that she was a good girl and tip toed out of the room.

As I walk up the front steps, I think about what she's felt in the hours I've been gone. I know she isn't afraid. I wonder perhaps if she is still asleep. I imagine how I would like to wake her. I quickly abandon that idea, deciding that she has probably been awake for about an hour, lying there in the bed. I imagine her reading the letter I'd left, admiring the flower. I imagine her realizing that she is cuffed to the bed. A small whine escapes from my lips at that thought. I imagine her lying in bed, thinking about our night together, growing hungry. I know that she can see the door from where she is. I imagine her watching it, waiting for me. I reach the door and unlock it quickly. I smile in anticipation, opening the door very slowly. I step inside, careful not to look into the bedroom yet. I bring my bags into the kitchen, quickly putting my things away. I walk to get a bowl out of the cabinet. She is awake. I can hear noises coming from the bedroom. I nearly drop the bowl, trembling with excitement. I take a deep breath. I needed to seem in control. I filled the bowl with raspberries, putting them on a tray with a chocolate bar, papaya juice, and a muffin. I put the tray on the table, walking quickly to the mirror on the wall. I checked myself carefully. I replaced a strand of hair that had fallen out of the pin that was holding my hair. I took the tray and walked to the bedroom. She was just as I'd left her. I smiled, my eyes brushing adoringly over her. She must have replaced the rose and returned the white sheet to it's original position when she heard me come in. I could see that she'd read my note. It was folded in half, lying on the floor by the bed. She was lying in the same position that I'd left her, except that her arms were wrapped around her. She was smiling faintly. She gazed at me softly, adoringly, her eyes sparkling. I could see that she was a little nervous. I'm sure she was curious about what exactly was going to be expected of her. I wanted to reassure her. I walked over to the bed. "Good morning, darling." I smiled broadly, looking down at her warmly. Her eyes grew wide and sparkled playfully. "Good morning, Mira." I put the tray on the small table by the bed. Sliding my hand behind her head, I kissed her deeply. My tongue danced over hers teasingly, thrusting deep into her mouth. The kiss seemed to go on and on, growing more and more intense. When I finally managed to pull back from her, I was nearly breathless. I hadn't expected to want her so much. Pulling myself together quickly, I sit on the bed next to her. I stroked her body over the sheet, slowly, watching my hand moving over her.

"Did you read the letter, love?"

She nodded. "Yes, Mira" I was pleased to hear how she was using my name.

It was so good to hear. I asked the next question already

knowing the answer. "Do you understand?" "Yes." She said, quickly.

"I belong to you now". I ran my fingers over her lips with nearly overpowering longing.

"Are you hungry, Alana?" I pulled the sheet off of her, letting it drop to the floor. My eyes rake across her body appreciatively, examining her closely. I could feel that she felt a little uncomfortable, but I was enjoying her too much to care. The curve of her hip was gorgeous. I wanted to kiss her there, but I decided to wait.

"Yes, Mira" Her eyes stray to the tray by the bed. "Good. I'm going to feed you now."

" I stood up, taking my jacket off, enjoying her eyes on me. I decided that I would undress for her later, as a reward. I stroked the length of her body gently, bending to kiss the curve of her hip. I ran my tongue lightly over her, kissing her again and again, enjoying the softness of her skin. I took the cuff off of her ankle, and instead cuffed her hands together.

"You were such a good girl last night, Alana. You've pleased me very much."

I helped her to sit up, placing a pillow behind

her. I kissed her softly on the lips again. I broke off a piece of the muffin and put it in her mouth, letting her lick my fingers a little. An expression of delight appeared on her face. "I did? I pleased you?"

"Yes", I cooed. I brought the papaya juice to her lips, watching her drink. To my surprise I felt pleasant warmth between my legs. I moved closer to her, opening her legs wide, so they hang off either side of the bed. I rubbed my body teasingly over her, whispering my love for her in her ear. I began to feed her some of the raspberries. While she was eating them, one of my hands caressed her inner thighs gently. She moved toward me, opening her legs more to me. I slid one finger gently over her, placing a piece of chocolate into her mouth and listening to her moan under her breath. Even with my fingers just barely brushing over her, I could feel her tantalizing wetness. I wanted to taste her. Sliding my index finger over her clit and massaging it firmly in small overlapping circles, I brought the juice to her lips again, watching her drink. Alana moaned warmly, some of the juice trickling out of her mouth. The subtle movement of her throat as she swallowed made me want to bite her there. I wanted to mark her as mine. Still massaging her clit, I drew closer to her, and licked the juice off of her neck, up over her chin, and to her mouth. I slide my tongue over her soft lips, dipping it inside her mouth briefly, and then pulling back. I needed to have her. I knew I needed to show her that she belonged to me. I drove one finger suddenly inside her, moaning in surprise at her delicious wetness. Deep inside her, I moved my finger in wide circles, watching Alana's eyes roll back in pleasure, seeing her pant lightly.

"You like that, don't you, Alana?" I was so excited, so pleased with how she was responding to me.

"Yes", she cried immediately.

I pulled my finger out of her briefly and then quickly slammed two fingers into her as deep as I could. Alana drew in breath sharply, a warm, syrupy moan erupting from her. I started to fuck her, completely overcome by consuming lust. My fingers disappeared inside her again and again in slow powerful thrusts. I told her to tell me that she belonged to me over and over. She obeyed me quickly, to my delight, her voice growing louder with each thrust. Her eyes opened wide with surprised pleasure one moment, and then closed tightly the next. Great, rich, luxurious moans escaped from her lips. As I watched her body banging against the headboard with each thrust of my fingers, I felt hot fluid running down my thighs. I fucked her faster, using my free hand to help push me deeper inside her.

"Good girl. You're my little whore, Alana. Do you like that? Do you like being my slut?" Alana gasped in pleasure, crying, "yes" again and again. I made her say it to me again and again, enjoying how obedient she was. I could feel how aroused she was, how much she wanted me. Her moans interrupting her smoky voice, she purred, "I'm your slut, Mira" and "fuck me, Mira" as the thrusts of my fingers intensified.

I knew I'd lost control. I couldn't think of anything except the way she was tightening around my fingers and the silky wetness of the fluid starting to run down my fingers.

"You're such a slut, Alana...my good little slut. You like that, don't you? Mm, you like it when I fuck you. You want me to fuck you hard, don't you, Alana?"

I drove another finger deep inside her, fucking her harder and harder. I watched her body quivering and trembling in pleasure, her eyes locked on mine, sending agonizing waves of pleasure through me. I moaned loudly as Alana let her head fall back, screaming my name, over and over.

"You're going to come for me like a good slut, aren't you, Alana?"

Hovering so close to release, she didn't answer me, instead crying out in gorgeous ecstasy. Quickly I reached up, pushing Alana's face back down, her eyes meeting mine. I drew my hand back and slapped her lightly across the face. Her eyes grew very wide. She gasped, moaning deep in her throat and started to move hard against my hand.

"Answer me!" I demanded.

Quickly, Alana stammered, "Yes, Mira...Yes, I'm going to come for you...like a slut...like your good slut, Mira." Unable to control myself, I fucked Alana as fast and hard as I could, twisting my hand inside her, panting with the effort. Her ecstatic, gratifying cries drove through me, filling me with numbing pleasure.

"Come for me now!" A cry of indulgent

pleasure so violently loud escaped from Alana's throat, that I feared she might worry the neighbors. Her body trembled alarmingly with the power of the orgasm. Murmuring my adoring encouragement, I continued to fuck her, bending down to taste her. Her amazing taste flooded my mouth as I slid my fingers smoothly inside her, emptying her slowly. I removed my fingers, letting her finish in my mouth, moaning happily. Her body relaxed and she fell softly back onto the pillow as my tongue ran gently over her, lapping every drop of her cum into my mouth. I adore the little sounds Alana makes after I fuck her. I rose from between her legs, my mouth and chin still wet from her. I knelt on all fours in front of her. My eyes locked on hers, a bolt of electricity passing between us. I raised my hand to my mouth, wiping it off with the back of my hand, my eyes never leaving hers. In a surprisingly confident half growl,

I heard myself say, "Good girl, Alana. Thank me." She obeyed immediately, thanking me breathlessly.

I leaned toward her, kissing her mouth lingeringly. I pulled away, crawling off of the bed and walking to the middle of the room. I turned and looked back at Alana playfully.

"Such a good girl, darling"

I took the edge of the soft blue tank top I was wearing between my fingers, pulling it up over my stomach very slowly, moving teasingly. My eyes laughing, I pulled the shirt over my breasts and over my head, throwing it to her. Alana laughed quietly, smiling at me. Bending over, my eyes never leaving Alana's body, I slid my pants very slowly down to my knees. I stepped out of them with one foot and then the other, throwing my pants to Alana. She giggled again. I left my boots on and walked slowly toward her. I pressed myself hard against her, biting her neck hard enough to leave a small red mark. I uncuffed her hands and turned around, instructing her to unfasten my bra. She did so quickly, fumbling a little. She slid my bra over my arms and let it drop onto the floor. Her hands slid over my breasts, pulling me against her. She sighed happily, kissing my neck and sliding her hands all over my torso.

"You feel good, Mira." she whispered.

I was impossibly wet. I wanted her mouth. She slid her hand between my legs, running her fingers back and forth over me. I moaned softly, feeling dizzy. I enjoyed the feeling of her hands for a few moments and then pulled back. I turned to face her, grabbing one of her legs in one hand and slapping the inside of her thigh hard, causing her to whimper softly.

"I didn't tell you to do that, love. Try to remember that you have to obey me." She apologized quickly, and I nodded, smiling at her. "It's all right, darling. Just don't forget."

I stood up and turned around, telling her to take my panties off. Alana took them in her teeth, guiding them down my legs with her hands. I stepped out of them, bending down and tossing them aside. I turned to face her; happily watching her eyes move over me.

"Good girl, Alana."

I crawled onto the bed, kissing her mouth hard, my tongue sliding hotly over hers, her teeth raking over my tongue. I slid my body hard over hers, hearing her sigh heavily. I rained little soft kisses all over her body. Listening to her whispered moans, I lingered for a long time kissing and nibbling her soft, white neck. I pinched her almost translucent skin between my teeth, listening to her whimper softly, squirming under me. I slid my tongue back in her mouth, kissing her softly, lovingly, her lips soft and warm against mine. I pulled back and looked into her eyes.

"I want your mouth, Alana".

She drew in breath, writhing a little beneath me.

"How?" she purred.

I pulled her body gently behind me as I knelt on all fours. Quickly I felt her tongue sliding slowly over me. I had to bite my lip to keep from crying out. I held myself very still as Alana's tongue slid all over me, so slowly. I heard her moaning softly, tasting me. Her tongue moved down to my clit, now throbbing dully. I felt her lips close around it as she began to suck gently. Unexpectedly, she began to suck my clit very hard, slamming her tongue into it over and over. My body spasmed violently, responding to the relentless surges of pleasure wracking my body. I moved my body hard against her mouth, pushing her tongue deeper inside me. She felt so good. I felt an unbearable ache deep inside me melting slowly into a frenzy of indulgent pleasure. I moved my hips in hard circles over her mouth, moaning deeply. I heard myself crying out her name over and over.

"Fuck me, Alana!"

I felt her breath on my thighs as she pulled back a little.

"Yes, Mira. I want to fuck you."

I could feel the quivering, torturous tension of Alana's need to have me. I felt fluid trickling slowly down my legs.

"Yes...please, Alana"

I was enjoying how this game made me feel so much. The delicious feeling of playing that I belonged to Alana when I knew that she was really mine was terribly exciting. She entered me quickly with one finger, sliding deep inside me. I moaned warmly, tossing my head back and tilting my hips up to let Alana fuck me deeper. My body shook with each thrust of Alana's fingers. I turned my head over my shoulder to meet her eyes, and was startled and pleased by the intense look of frenzied desire and lust in her eyes. She met my eyes for a moment; her eyes narrowed slightly, her teeth biting down on her lip. Then, she leaned forward, and drove her tongue into me again, cradling my hips in her hands. Suddenly, she flipped me over on to my back, sucking my clit quickly into her mouth and pushing her tongue over me punishingly hard. I gasped in shocked ecstasy, quivering against her, my mouth open wide, my eyes shut tightly. Alana slid two fingers hard inside of me as she nipped at my clit with her teeth, fucking me in hard deep circles. It was exactly what I wanted. Alana sucked my clit greedily, twisting her fingers inside me unbearably hard and fast. I felt a steadily growing heat deep inside me. In one swift motion, I rolled over on top of Alana, her fingers still inside me, pinning her down with my body. I bent over and retrieved a collar from under the bed. I slipped it softly around her neck, gazing down at her possessively.

"You belong to me, now, Alana. Do you understand?"

Alana's lips parted slightly as she drew in a quivering breath. She nodded slowly, eagerly, her body moving in slow tantalizing movements under me. "Yes, Mira", she barely whispered, her fingers still pulsing gently, insistently inside me. I whimpered helplessly, pushing myself down harder onto her fingers, grinding her fingertips relentlessly inside my body. I had been keeping myself from release for so long, and could hardly stand the pressure building inside of me. Growing clumsy with desire, I pulled myself up to Alana's mouth, bringing her lips to my clit. I sunk my teeth into my lip as Alana brought me almost effortlessly to orgasm. I let out a great sob of pleasure, my eyes widening in surprise as Alana seemed to empty my body, my thighs trembling uncontrollably. I feared that I would collapse on top of her. I was amazed at how quickly she was learning how to please me. I eased myself down next to Alana's body, in awe of the way she seemed to shimmer in the soft light of the bedroom. Little pleased moans slipped softly over my lips, my body still trembling.

"Good girl, Alana" I breathed, "I'm going to reward you."

She blushed deeply and cast her eyes down. My fingers trailed playfully up and down her body, running lightly over her neck, circling her left nipple softly. The muscles in her stomach jumped at the slight touch of my fingertips. I kneaded her thigh and stretched up to take her earlobe in my mouth, sucking briefly.

"I want you to sleep now. I'll be back soon. I want you to dream about me now. When I come back, you'll tell me everything you dreamed about."

A smile spread briefly over her face, and she closed her eyes.

I'd been watching Alana for about an hour before she woke up. I had intended to wake her up immediately upon my return, but when I got home I decided that I'd prefer to let her wake on her own. So, once I'd arranged everything satisfactorily, I pulled a chair in from the living room, and sat across the room, watching her. I enjoyed looking at her while she slept, replaying the last few days and fantasizing about what I would do that evening. It was a lovely sort of torture, thinking about all of the things that I wanted to do with her, but not allowing myself to touch her. Several times I almost went over to her to wake her with my mouth, but I decided that it would be much better if I simply waited. Finally, I saw her body bend into a luxurious stretch and her eyes opened. She whined sleepily, and blinked a few times. She looked down at the gown that I'd dressed her in while she slept. It was a rich burgundy evening gown. Her fingers ran softly over the shimmering fabric, a look of confusion crossing her face. She smoothed the full skirt around her hips. Her fingers strayed to the thin black collar around her neck and she grinned softly. I leaned forward a little in my chair, and she noticed that I was there for the first time. Her eyes widened a little and her face grew red.

"I didn't see you."

I stood up from the chair and walked over to her. I attached a thin black leash to her collar and pulled her gently into a sitting position. I slid my hand down her back and gave her mouth a lingering kiss. My tongue brushed softly over hers and I felt a shiver go through her.

"Are we going somewhere?" she said.

I nodded slowly, a playful smile dancing behind my eyes.

"We'll leave soon."

I ran my fingertips over her collarbone, bending down to nip softly at her neck. It was growing dark when the car pulled up outside. I tied a black silk scarf tightly over Alana's eyes and led her outside. I could see that she was nervous. I hadn't told her where we were going. I helped her into the car and sat down next to her. I'm not sure if she was aware of the other people in the car. We were silent during the ride. I slid my hand up her leg and massaged the top of her right thigh, feeling her writhe gently against my hand. The car stopped in front of a beautifully landscaped old brick house. There were people moving inside. I stepped out of the car and pulled Alana gently after me. It was a warm night and there was a nice breeze. There were two lilac trees on either side of the large front door, and I watched as Alana inhaled their fragrance deeply. I brushed her face lightly with my hand. I led her up the walkway and inside. Past the heavy wooden door was a dark hallway, furnished only with a thick deep red carpet and a few old-fashioned brass wall sconces. There were four mahogany doors on either side of the hallway. We could hear the muffled sounds of people speaking all around us, but I couldn't discern any particular voice.

"What's going on?" Alana whispered.

I pushed her against the wall and covered her mouth with my hand, pushing her head back and licking hard from her collar up her neck. She gasped a little and was silent from then on. I continued down the hall, pulling her after me. I stopped at the last door on the right, and went in. I had to blink against the brightness of the room. It was a large room with high ceilings and great wooden beams crossing over the ceiling and down the walls. There was an enormous stone fireplace at one end of the room, but there was no fire. There was the same red carpet on the hard wood floors and lights on the wall that had been in the hallway. There were four small, black armless couches at various angles around the room. The only other furniture was several large, cast iron candelabras. There was one by each of the couches and one in each corner. The hardwood floor that was not hidden by the carpet was covered in small white burning candles. There were heavy red curtains over the three large windows, but the light from the wall sconces and candles lit every corner of the room. I wondered what Alana was thinking.

She couldn't see anything from behind the blindfold. I'm sure that she could smell the burning candles. She was walking slowly, tentatively behind me. There were a number of people milling about among the couches, talking softly. Most of them were drinking wine or eating food off of large platters that three women in identical black dresses carried. Some of the guests were naked, others wore masks, others formal attire. A young naked woman was kneeling on top of the couch closest to Alana and I, facing the back of it, her legs tied with thin black straps to the legs of the couch. A girl in a black mask that covered her face down to her nose kneeled on the floor in front of her, biting the woman's inner thighs. Her deep, desperate moans floated above the murmur of the people walking about. I led Alana through the crowd, passing a man fucking a blond woman, her head lolling off the edge of the couch, her breath coming in ragged groans.

I sat down on one of the unoccupied chairs, pulling Alana against me impatiently. I turned her around quickly, grasping the zipper on the back of her dress and unzipping her dress down to her lower back. My hands slid up over her shoulders and pushed the dress down around her ankles. I grabbed her leash again and pulled her around to face me. I ran my hands all over her body, whining and biting my lip. From a small black handbag at my side I produced a pair of black handcuffs. I snapped them on to Alana's wrists behind her back. I raked my fingernails down over her breasts and stomach. I told her to kneel. She quickly dropped to her knees, and I grabbed her shoulders and pushed myself hard against her mouth. My legs tensed and my head rolled back as Alana's tongue plunged inside me. A squeal of pleasure escaped her mouth and vibrated inside of me. I could feel how excited she was. She was fucking me so quickly, her tongue driving deep inside me. I could feel my fingernails cutting into her. I slid one hand behind her head and forced her deeper inside me. I moaned breathily, over and over, grinding my hips against her. I grabbed at the couch, the pleasure rising steadily inside of me. Alana's tongue darted all over me, teasing my clit, sliding down over my ass, pushing deep inside of me. I felt her teeth raking over my clit, biting me quickly. I cried out, my back arching, my legs beginning to spasm as I started to come. I could feel people's eyes on me, but I couldn't think of anything except the feel of Alana's amazing mouth on me. I moaned raggedly, feeling the cum run slowly out of me. Alana lapped at me quickly, emptying me. I fell back against the couch, exhausted. I felt Alana's tongue licking softly over me. I looked up and pushed her back from me gently. I could see that the blindfold was started to fall off, so I removed it. While Alana was adjusting to the light in the room, I pulled her up onto the couch by her leash. I could hear her panting a little. I took the handcuffs off and pulled her onto her hands and knees. I kneeled behind her, slapping her thighs and her ass. I arched up over her and bit into her side hard. She cried out in surprise and I smiled widely. I pulled her legs apart wider and teased her gently with one hand while I reached into my handbag and pulled out a knife with a clean, sharp edge. The handle was made of inlaid ivory. I rubbed the end of the handle hard against her clit. Over her shoulder I saw her bite her lip hard and her body began to spasm as I rubbed her clit faster and faster. With one quick motion I slammed the handle of the knife as deep into her as I could. Alana gasped in surprise and moaned so deeply. I felt myself getting so wet watching the smooth ivory sliding in and out of her wet cunt.

"Such a wet little slut, Alana" I growled.

"Yes!" she cried out.

I was surprised by the loudness and the urgency in her voice.

"Tell me you belong to me, slut."

She responded even before I had finished giving the order. I was growing dizzy with wanting.

"Tell me you love me." I purred. "I love you, Mira."

Her voice was thick and heavy with pleasure. I fucked her harder, moving the knife in quick small circles, knowing that it must be hurting her a little.

"Louder, you little whore!" She nearly screamed it.

I was panting with desire. "Such a good girl, Alana. I love you. You belong to me." I grabbed my wrist and started fucking her as hard as I could. Her whole body quivered against the force of the knife. I could feel that she was getting close to orgasm. The knife handle was covered with silky white fluid. I slid the handle out as slowly as I could stand, listening to Alana whine. I took the handle in my mouth, licking it clean. Then I reached up and cut a thin line in her back. The blood rose to the surface and trailed down her back. She cried out in surprise and frustration. "You're mine, Alana. Say it." She obeyed quickly. "I'll let you come soon, darling." With three swift motions I carved my initial into her back. She cried out softly. Thin trails of blood flowed down her back. I arched up, one finger gently teasing her clit and licked the blood off of her. The taste was overwhelming. It was strong and a little sweet and it reminded me of her taste. I crouched down and took Alana's clit in my mouth, sucking as hard as I could and tracing the words 'I love you' over her as hard as I could manage. I licked back up to her ass and then plunged the knife handle back inside her. She began to move against the handle, helping me to fuck her deeper. I pushed the ivory against her sensitive muscle, watching her begin to spasm. I almost didn't notice when a woman dressed in a long black dress approached us and ran her hand along Alana's body. When I saw it, I drew my right hand back and slapped her hard in the face.

"Get away. She belongs to me."

The woman staggered back, glaring at me. I renewed my efforts, letting my eyes fall indulgently over the gorgeous lines of her back and the smooth roundness of her ass. I fucked her as quickly as I could, rubbing her clit with one two of my fingers. I felt Alana's body begging me for release.

"You good little slut. You're going to come for me, aren't you?"

She answered me with a great moan. I fucked her harder and faster still. I heard Alana's fingernails clawing at the fabric of the couch. I slid my body just underneath hers, enough so I could still fuck her. I told her to fuck me. She reached back quickly, sliding two fingers hard into me. I nearly screamed, I wanted her so much. I started moving the handle in wide circles, plunging deep inside of her wetness. I could see fluid running slowly down the top of her thigh. I wanted to lick it off. Alana's fingers pulsed maddeningly inside me. The whole room was spinning. I felt her beginning to come, her body jerking and quivering, her cries full of the ecstasy of release. I felt my own body coiled like a spring under her touch. I arched my back and let myself orgasm, biting my lip and moaning through my teeth. I slid the ivory slowly in and out of her body, letting the cum run so slowly out of her. Alana collapsed onto the couch, her legs splayed behind her.

I heard her whispering, "I love you" softly each time she exhaled.

I lowered my mouth to her thigh, gently licking her clean. I proceeded to lick slowly all over her and inside her, sucking her clean. I wanted to fill my mouth with the taste of her. I whispered that I loved her. My heart was pounding. I pulled myself up on top of her. We lay there panting together for quite some time. When one of the women with the platters of food walked past us, I took a bunch of grapes from the platter. I rolled Alana over and helped her sit up. There was a faint smile on her face. I looked into her large, soft eyes, and felt like crying. I loved her so much. I fed the grapes to her, watching in delight as her shimmering lips closed around my fingers each time. While I fed her she closed her eyes. I leaned forward and kissed her softly all over her face. I ran my hand along her cheek, down her neck, and over her breast. I sighed at the feeling of her warm, soft breast in my hand. I kissed her passionately on the mouth.

"Let's go home, darling." She smiled warmly at me and nodded.

I helped her back into her dress and we walked together out into the cool night air. Everything looked so beautiful. Alana's face glowed in the moonlight.

"I want you forever, Alana." I whispered. She turned and gazed into my eyes. "Yes, Mira. I want that too." I pulled her close and kissed her so deeply. We were silent in the car on the way home

Story 03

A hotel corridor late at night can be a lonely, intimidating place. This one was no exception. Jay felt distinctly uneasy as she walked nervously across its thickly carpeted length with its subdued night-lights between each anonymous door. As Jay passed one of these darkened recesses where cleaning ladies are wont to keep their trolleys, Jay suddenly felt a presence and almost immediately felt herself grabbed from behind, her arms pinned behind her by another, stronger pair of arms. Before she had time to speak or think her assailant shifted position so that Jay was in an inescapable arm lock.

"Don't struggle and do as you're told and no one will get hurt" hissed the voice in her ear. It was a voice with an authoritarian ring to it, and it was female.

Jay was quickly bundled through one of those anonymous doors. The other woman who was clearly stronger than Jay and obviously trained to handle herself threw Jay to the floor and ordered her to stay there. Jay was aware vaguely of a bed and several candelabra burning at several points in the room.

As jay lay there, not daring to resist, she heard the other woman start to undress. She heard the sound of a zip and of garments being tossed onto a chair. The woman then began to walk around the room, moving objects, making rustling sounds. As she walked past Jay's prone position she crossed Jay's line of sight revealing that she was barefoot and wearing black stockings over what appeared to be a shapely leg.

Presently the movements ceased and the woman ordered Jay to her feet. Jay at last could see her captor-she was seated in a large leather armchair completely naked except for the black stockings and matching suspender belt. She was clearly of Mediterranean extraction, possibly Greek. Her olive skin seemed to glow by the candlelight. As she sat there almost regally, her hands resting on the arms of the chair, Jay could see her small, pert breasts with dark almost black nipples-small but very erect. Her slightly parted breasts revealed the bushiest black triangle Jay had ever seen.

"Get undressed, " said the woman in a tone which did not invite disobedience.

As she complied and started to strip for this woman Jay felt strange, as if it was another Jay meekly obeying the command. It was a warm summer evening so there wasn't much to remove. The blouse was followed by the bra and as Jay stepped from her skirt she stood there in just her panties, aware of how her own large breasts with their hugely prominent nipples contrasted with the other woman's.

"I meant everything! " came the command from the chair, the emphasis on the word " everything " was all Jay needed to meekly comply, stepping from her panties to reveal a closely trimmed blonde pubic bush, so unlike the other woman's.

"Now I am clearly stronger than you and as you know by now I can easily overpower you" said the woman, " So you will be obliged for your own sake to obey me. Is that clear?"

"Yes " replied Jay.

"Yes, mistress! " barked the woman. " Say it! "

"Yes mistress. " repeated Jay.

"I shall either call you nothing or bitch, is that also clear? " said the woman icily.

"Yes, mistress" answered Jay.

"Now bitch, walk over to the foot of the bed, stand facing the bed head and lean forward with the palms of your hands on the bed."

Jay did as she was told. It was in that position that she felt the woman approach her from behind.

"Spread your legs, bitch!"

Jay spread them. She felt the woman's hand between her legs-she was being examined. The most intimate of her body was being spread open to this woman's gaze. She seemed to keep Jay spread like this for an, just looking, occasionally probing one opening then the other, until she had had her fill.

She then crossed to another part of the room, there was the sound of a drawer being opened and closed, the woman returned and began to stroke Jay's buttocks very gently.. Then without warning she brought the palm of her hand down hard making Jay yelp with pain.

"Did you like that bitch? " came the question.

"Yes, mistress. " was the reply, Jay knew the answer she must now give.

Further hard slaps followed, Jay trying hard not to cry out as she obediently received a spanking. Suddenly the spanking stopped. There was a pause. What next? Jay felt a cold flat object placed across her buttocks. Jay had no sooner worked out that it was a ruler than two swift, smarting blows made her cry out loud.

"You are still liking this, bitch?"

"Yes, mistress."

"Well, we'll see about that! "

Again the sound of a drawer being opened, then Jay gasped as the other woman reached underneath to grasp Jay's dangling breasts and attach what appeared to be a heavy metal clasp to each nipple. The sensation, not really pain, shot from Jay's breasts to her pussy. She felt her clitoris tighten. She became wet. She was becoming aroused.

Standing by Jay's head, the woman grabbed Jay's hair, twisting her head around so Jay was forced to stare at the other woman's pussy. In between that black, hairy bush Jay could discern two very dark brown, swollen lips and a very large, hard clitoris protruding between them.

"I think it is time to stop your fun, bitch! " said the woman-with that she released Jay's hair and gave her breasts a slap causing them to sway into each other, the weights pulling them down caused Jay's juices to flow even more.

The woman now moved to another part of the room and returned with a candelabra. She removed one candle, holding it above Jay's buttocks. As the first drops of hot wax fell onto Jay's unprotected flesh she gave a whimper, she was experiencing both pain and pleasure.

"Want more, bitch? " said the woman.

"Yes, mistress."

Suddenly the woman blew out the candle and Jay felt the blunt end between the cheeks of her buttocks. The woman applied a gentle pressure, as if to penetrate and then, without warning changed target and plunged the candle deep into Jay's gaping cunt.

It went in easily, Jay's lubrication was flowing copiously as the slurping sound witnessed as the woman worked the candle in and out.

The woman's mood seemed to change. She removed the nipple clamps and instructed Jay to lie spread-eagled on the bed. She had obviously pre-planned this as Jay's wrists and ankles were quickly secured by ropes previously tied to the legs of the bed. From a bedside cabinet the woman produced a soft leather cat o'nine tails.

Jay tensed as the first blow fell across her breasts. To her surprise it was not a hard blow- more of a caress. A very erotic caress at that. The woman worked Jay's body over expertly- the liquid oozing out between Jay's legs leaving no doubt about the effect it was having.

When the woman at last laid the whip aside, she mounted the bed and straddled Jay across her middle facing Jay's feet.

In this position she reached forward to part Jay's dripping wet cunt, and after pausing briefly to study the effects of her handiwork, began to fondle Jay. Jay moaned as she responded to the other woman's caresses. The woman's breathing was becoming rapid and deeper. Suddenly she moved backwards still facing Jay's feet, but this time her knees were at either side of Jay's head.

In this position she lowered her streaming wet cunt over Jay's face. Jay's tongue was like a snake-darting in and out of the other woman's pussy, gently lapping at her hugely aroused clit, the smell and taste of sex was overwhelming. The woman could last no longer-she exploded into an orgasm of such intensity that her whole frame shook to it's foundations. Her juices flooded over Jay's face-she was sobbing with pleasure as she collapsed forward onto Jay, her full weight crushing Jay's still form. She lay like that for what seemed an age, motionless, sometimes letting out a groan or a sob. At length she rose like a prizefighter dragging himself of the canvas and dressed herself.

She stood over Jay and released the ropes, and as she did so she pushed an object into Jay's gaping wet pussy.

As she opened the door the woman paused, " Same time next week, bitch?"

"Yes, mistress."

After the door closed, Jay removed the object from her pussy. It consisted of ten fifty- pound notes, tightly rolled and secured with an elastic band.

Jay's best client had indeed been very generous.

Story 04 (Bonus)

It was our first date and I could see how much she wanted me. She was peering deeply into my eyes, wanting to feel my lips against hers, lusting so urgently. I enjoyed teasing her so 'innocently'. Leaning forward to give her peeks of my cleavage, bringing our faces together to hear her over the dinner crowd. She looked so intensely at me that my nipples got hard and my pussy~that deep heat making me so wet. It was a difficult ride home as we discussed some rather kinky parties she had attended where some hot chick had needles imbedded along her body and somehow fire was involved.

New to my world~that's for sure! She invited me in to talk...and to show me her leather wrist restraints. I know my eyes lit up when I saw them and handled the leather. I asked her to demonstrate for me. She wrapped the left one on and I put the right one on and clipped them together in front of her. She pulled a little to show me how secure they were and I lifted her arms over her head. It was the perfect height for her oak coat rack and I hooked the restraint over an arm of it. She smiled at me as I leaned in to kiss her...hard and ravenous, hungry for her, wet for her. I grabbed her generous tits in each hand and squeezed, massaging and rubbing and kissing her so hard and wet, our tongues playing. Her nipples get so hard and long between my fingertips as I pull and pinch to my hearts content, harder and twisting and pulling them as she moans into my mouth.

I step back and look at her beautiful round face and those delicious tits hanging out of her blouse. Nipples so hard and pink. I slap at them, stinging them as she shakes them for me. "Oh yes baby, shake your tits," and I slap her nipples back and forth, so hard, tits flushed red. She breathes heavy thru clenched teeth pushing her tits out at me, god what a sexy slut she is for me. I grab her cunt thru her leggings, oh my, pussy all wet. "You little wet slut"

I push her panties down and shove my fingers into her dripping pussy and I bite at her nipples, pulling them between my teeth. Her moans move into words "Yes bitch, bite me...oh god yesss, suck my nipples, oh harder....yessss"

Her juicy tight cunt swallows my fingers as I pump them in harder and faster, sucking and biting her nipples, back and forth, rubbing them all over my face...feeling her juice up, shaking her generous ass, thighs quivering as her pussy grips me in waves, flooding my hand and arm. Her titties fill my mouth as I suck them well after her orgasm. She shakes in my arms, standing with her arms overhead, tits hanging out all wet from my mouth and red from my teeth, panties and leggings around her knees and pussy juice all over her wet cunny and thighs...and me. I removed the hook on her restraint and led her to the bedroom...she smiles at me calling me her mistress. I push her down on her bed and roll her face down, legs apart. I fasten those leather restraints onto her bed. I kneel behind her and pull her pants the rest of the way off. Her pussy juice has run down her legs down her calves. I use the tip of my tongue to clean her up, devouring her tasty juices and her thoroughly wet thighs. She squirms under me,

gyrating on the corner of the bed. I pull her legs further apart and see how she humps the mattress. I bring my mouth to her cunt and thrust my tongue inside...oooooohhhhhhh, and again. Over and over as she humps and squirms and fucks the corner of the mattress. I pull her ass cheeks apart and lick the lengh of her hot pink slit and up the that puckered little ass...so hot. And all over again. I push 2 fingers into her sloshy we cunt and fuck for a few mintues and them slip one into her ass and double penetrate her fast & furious, licking her ass cheeks and pussy lips as I fuck her hot ass and wet pussy, making myself cum whem she does.

Time to roll her over...

Erotic Flame (FF)
03 Lesbian Erotica Collection for Adults
L. J. Orellana

All Rights Reserved. No part of this publication may be reproduced in any form or by any means, including scanning, photocopying, or otherwise without prior written permission of the copyright holder. Copyright © 2022

This book is entirely a work of fiction. The names, characters and incidents portrayed in it are the work of the author's imagination. Any resemblance to actual persons, living or dead, events or localities is entirely coincidental.

Story 01

Sometimes Friday nights suck. It was a little after 9:30 pm, and I was stuck at home. No date. No party. No friends. Just my CD player, a book and me. All of us were sprawled on my bed on top of the silky pink spread. My dark blonde hair was pulled back in a simple ponytail. I've been told I look somewhat like Elizabeth Shue, only with a fuller figure. I had my sleep clothes on, a gray designer label half shirt that just barely covered my boobs, and a pair of powder blue baggy boxer shorts, also designer label.

I was tapping my foot and rereading the same sentence for the third time when Jackie burst into my bedroom. Jackie is my best friend. Our birthdays were only 11 days apart, and four weeks ago, we had a combined party to celebrate turning 18.

"Jesus Christ!" I gasped as I ripped the headphones off. "You scared the crap out of me!" I hadn't been expecting her. She was supposed to be on a date with Brad, her boyfriend for the last few months. She was dressed to kill, with a satiny red miniskirt so short she didn't dare bend over. The side was cut open almost to her waist and held together with three taut strings. The only panties you could wear with it was a thong unless you wanted them to show through the slit. I certainly wouldn't have the guts to wear a thong with a skirt that short and tight.

Her halter top was a matching red with black streaks and sharp-edged swirls. The material was loose and clingy at the same time. Although it could be worn with a halter bra, Jackie chose not to. Her nipples were clearly visible, poking through the thin material. Her B cup boobs were a little smaller than my C cup breasts, but they still jiggled and moved freely underneath the halter top. I've always thought she looked like a young Demi Moore before the boob job.

Her deep brown hair was done up nicely, framing a face that was puffy and red from crying. Mascara and eyeliner streaked her face. She clutched a used tissue tightly in her hand. Her face looked like she was finely balanced between anger and despair.

"Oh, Michelle! Brad is such a bastard!" she cried out. Jackie fell into my arms, sobbing on my shoulder.

"What happened?" I asked. I was hoping to calm her down. My parents went to bed at 9:00 most nights, and I didn't want her to wake them up. I usually locked the house up around 10:00 pm after letting the dog out one last time. Jackie released me, and we sat side by side on my bed. The shoulder of my top was stained with her mascara.

"I guess it's not really Brad's fault, but I'm still mad at him."

"Okay, but you still haven't told me what happened."

"Well, you know we were supposed to go dancing. When we got there, the DJ was really lame and the place was half empty. We hung around for a little while to see if we were just too early. Brad finally asked me if I wanted to go back to his place. His parents were out of the house playing bridge or something."

"That doesn't sound so bad. You've been wanting to get into his pants for a while now."

Jackie had lost her virginity two years ago. Since then, she had screwed most of the guys she dated, although she and Brad hadn't gone that far yet. She said sex was the best thing about having a boyfriend. I was still a virgin, but I got to live out some pretty wild fantasies through her stories. She always told me what happened on her dates, with all the juicy details. When she left, I would masturbate while thinking about her beautiful naked body writhing underneath her latest muscular hunk.

"I know. I didn't get a chance to tell you about yesterday. We were parked in his car making out. He was playing with my tits and teasing my nipples. You know how sensitive they are. Well, I unzipped him and took out his cock. Michelle, it was bigger than Ray's!"

"Oh my God!" Ray was two boyfriends ago, and he was hung like a horse. Unfortunately for Ray, he wasn't very good at using his tool, and she dumped him.

"Yeah! Well, a cop drove up just as he was getting my pants off. We got our clothes back on just in time. The cop told us to move along and Brad took me home."

"You are so bad!" I giggled. Jackie was smiling now as she told the story. Just talking to me had helped calm her down.

"Well, I was so horny tonight. I even wore my 'fuck me' skirt for him."

I glanced down and saw that her infamously short skirt with the slit was failing to hide her pussy. The thin gauzy material of her thong was partially exposed, and the lower half of her plump pussy lips were clearly defined underneath it. I blushed and looked back up at her face.

"Yeah. Brad had that reaction too," she said with a wicked grin. The effect was spoiled somewhat by the red, puffy eyes and streaks of mascara.

"Anyway, we were sitting on the sofa in his living room. He was sucking on my nipples. God, Michelle. I love it when guys do that." Jackie's hands cupped her boobs, her thumb and forefinger squeezing her nipples through the thin fabric. Jackie suddenly realized what she was doing and dropped her hands back into her lap. She only blushed for a moment, though. Jackie had almost no hang-ups about sex. I had always been jealous of her. Making out with guys was fun, but I never seemed to get aroused the way she did.

"So anyway, his hands start playing with my thighs and ass. And I am just going out of my mind. He finally gets to my pussy and gets underneath my thong. I am so wet and hot by now that I just spread my legs wide for him. His fingers are playing with my clit and I am ready to cum. Then his parents walk in the door. They start yelling and screaming at him. I'm trying to get dressed while his father is just staring bug-eyed at me. I'm told to leave and Brad and his parents are still yelling at each other as I get in my car. Thank God I drove instead of him."

"Wow! No wonder you are so upset."

"Michelle, I am so horny right now. Two days in a row Brad has gotten me all worked up and both times he leaves me with blue balls."

"Shouldn't it be blue nipples for a woman?" I giggled.

"I think red nips would be more accurate. That's what they look like right now," she smirked.

"Why don't you go clean your face off and we can listen to CDs and bitch about men."

"That's the second best offer I've had tonight, " she said, smiling wanly.

I could see her from behind in the bathroom. As she bent over to wash her face, the lower part of her ass cheeks was clearly visible. Her thong was riding high, leaving a barely visible wedge of red squeezed between her smooth thighs.

With her face cleaned, she stared into the mirror, lost in thought. I saw her hand creep down her waist and up inside her skirt. She shuddered and leaned forward, her weight supported by her other hand on the edge of the sink. I watched as the muscles of her arm and shoulder flexed and released. The poor girl was so horny she was masturbating in my bathroom! Jackie pulled her hand out of her pussy and hung her head. I heard a softly muffled sob, and then she washed off her hand. She obviously wasn't aware that I could see her.

She sat back down on my bed, and we talked about boys and sex while listening to our favorite CDs. She sat cross-legged, which would have been obscene if she hadn't kept one of my pillows on her lap. She kept shifting positions, moving her hips and ass every minute or so.

"I can't stand it," she finally burst out.

"What?"

"Michelle, I've gotta get some relief. I know this sounds weird, but would you be upset if I...uh...you know, masturbated?"

"Oh! Uh...I..."

"You can just sit there if you want. I mean it probably won't take long. If you thinks it's too gross you won't hurt my feelings if you go in another room either."

"I suppose it's okay," I answered slowly. "It's not gross. I mean I do it too. I've just never done it in front of anyone. I mean nobody has ever done it in front of me. Actually, both."

I was flustered now and beginning to babble. I didn't want Jackie to think was she was doing was gross or bad. I guess I also didn't want her to think I was a prude. She had so much more sexual experience than I did. I also didn't really want to go stand in the dark hall.

"Thank you," she said, giving me a quick hug. Without wasting another moment, she began stripping off her clothes. The halter top was first. I had seen her breasts many times before, but not under these circumstances. She was right. They were red and stiff; her areolas were large and dark, matching her almost black hair. Her boobs looked larger than their B cup as the bounced fee. I felt my mouth go dry. I hadn't realized she would get totally naked.

The skirt was next. It was so tight she had to shimmy back and forth to get it down off her hips. Her swaying breasts with their erect nipples mesmerized me. Once the skirt hit mid-thigh, the rest was easy, and it was whisked off. Now she stood there wearing just her high heels and the smallest scrap of red gauze hiding her pussy. I only had a moment to look at her narrow waist with its firm stomach and the swell of her hips. It was ten times sexier than total nudity. My face felt hot and flushed.

The thong and shoes vanished in a heartbeat. Jackie flung herself down on the bed. She pulled her feet up close to her ass cheeks and let her knees fall wide open. I could see she had trimmed her pussy hair for Brad. The lips were smooth and bare. A dark triangle of close-cropped pubic hair pointed straight at her clit. Her lips were slick with moisture, red and engorged with desire. Her clit was swollen and poking out from its hood. Everything was laid bare and wide open for me to see; I was having trouble breathing. I was caught up in the sensuality of the moment, unaware of my growing passion.

For all of her rush to strip naked, Jackie now moved slowly. Her head was thrown back, eyes closed, and her back slightly arched. She took her tits in her hands and squeezed the nipples. A shudder rippled through her, and her nipples grew even larger. She slid her hands down her stomach with a smoothing motion. Her fingers bypassed her pussy and slid down her thighs toward her knees as far as she could comfortably reach. They dipped down to cover her inner thighs and slowly slid back up toward her pussy.

I watched as she took the fingers of her left hand and sank them into the slick folders of her pussy. Jackie inhaled sharply, and another shudder rippled across her body, making her tits shake like jello. She pulled her fingers out and traced circles over her outer lips. They quickly became coated in her slippery juices. Once the whole area was lubricated, her fingers slipped between her inner lips and began to slowly stroke her distended clit. Her right hand was gripping the sheets, white-knuckled with tension.

My head was swimming, and my nipples ached. I looked down and saw that they were poking through the thin material of my half-shirt. I wanted to cover them up, but that would just draw Jackie's attention to them. I tried to hunch forward to open a space between the material and my jutting nipples, but it was no use. I casually let my hair down so that the tresses covered my condition.

Jackie stroked her clit for an eternity, emitting the occasional moan. She seemed to be having trouble finishing.

"Michelle," she gasped breathlessly. "Play with my nipples. Please"

"Huh?" I answered, drawn out of my fog by her question.

"I'm so close, but I need help."

I watched as my hands took on a life of their own. They rose as if lifted by invisible spirits and softly cupped Jackie's breasts. The flesh was warm and smooth. Jackie groaned and arched her back, pushing her tits into my palms. Wait, what was I doing? How had I let things go this far? Why was I turned on by this scene? My mind was filled with confusion, but my hands were filled with the soft, supple flesh of Jackie's rounded tits. I struggled to find myself while my fingers rolled her nipples. I wanted so badly to stand up and flee, and at the same time, lean down and kiss her beautiful breasts. Paralyzed, I did neither.

"Oh...Michelle!" Jackie moaned. Her hips were gyrating uncontrollably as her wet fingers caressed her throbbing clit. I could see it peeking out between her swollen, enflamed pussy lips, alternately hidden and revealed by Jackie's trembling finger. The blood rushed to my head, and I inadvertently squeezed her nipples hard.

"Uh...fuck!" Jackie wailed softly as an orgasm rocked her body. Inarticulate sobs wracked her body as her hips spasmed around her fingers. I watch, mesmerized as a second orgasm followed on the heels of the first. Ripping my eyes away from her wantonly exposed pussy, I looked up at her face. Her gorgeous features were distorted with lust and ecstasy. Her skin was flushed red and slick with a thin film of sweat. She was biting her lip to stop from crying out.

Jackie's eyes opened, staring into nothingness, glazed over and unfocused. With an effort, she found my eyes and locked her gaze onto them. I could see longing and desire shamelessly flowing from them. Suddenly I realized that I was still squeezing her nipples mercilessly between my thumbs and forefingers. I desperately wanted to look down at my hands on her tits but was unable to tear myself away from the heat of her stare.

"Michelle...Michelle..." she whispered as one last orgasm was ripped from her. Her eyes rolled back in her head, and I was freed. My hands flew away from her tits as if recoiling from a hot stove. I could still feel the soft warmth of her flesh against my palms. A peaceful, happy glow crept over Jackie's features as she gasped for air.

I was light-headed, almost to the point of being dizzy. I collapsed next to her on my back, our shoulders pressing lightly against each other. What had I done? I covered my face with my hands, hiding my shame. I could smell the faint aroma of Jackie's perfume and the subtle musk of her breasts on my hands. My nipples were rock hard and throbbing. My pussy was wet and overheated. I desperately wanted to finger myself the Jackie had.

Was I gay? Why did Jackie playing with herself affect me like this? Why on earth did I grab her tits? I knew part of the answer. Because she asked me to. A second reason floated in my thoughts. I almost sobbed out loud. I also did it because I wanted to. I started to tremble and shake with the realization that I had feelings for Jackie that went way beyond being her best friend. I had always idolized her, but now I knew that was just a mask for a deeper longing.

I felt something warm and wet brush my exposed belly. I was so wrapped up in my own inner turmoil it took me a moment to figure out that Jackie was gently kissing my stomach. I kept my face hidden behind my hands, frantically trying to decide how I should react. I felt her hair tantalizingly brush my skin, and another warm, moist kiss caressed my skin. My legs became weak, and I was grateful I was already lying down.

A pair of hands glided up and down my sides as slower; soft kisses rained down on my stomach. Her tongue traced small, tender circles on my skin. It was the most erotic, loving experience I had ever had. I felt my soul melting as my pussy heated up. I lay still, silently surrendering to her knowing touch, my face hidden behind my hands.

"You are so beautiful, Michelle," she whispered, planting a soft kiss on my navel.

"Thank you for helping me," as her fingers delicately stroked my ribs.

"Your hands felt so good on my nipples," a gentle lick traced the outline of my belly button. I gasped involuntarily.

"I love the way your skin feels and tastes," another kiss and more sliding fingertips. I was on fire. I could feel myself trembling, my skin vibrating with each touch.

"I want to touch all of you," she whispered. Her hands slowly pushed my half-shirt up toward my neck. The lower edge of the material caught for a moment on my erect nipples before sliding up to expose my large breasts.

"Oh! They are beautiful." Her hands slowly caressed the sides of my breasts. I bit my lip silently.

"Your tits are larger than mine, and so soft." Her fingers traced lazy eights along the sensitive undersides.

"I love how large and pink your nipples are," she breathed. Her hot breath was just below my breasts. I could feel her hair brushing the undersides.

"Your nipples are so hard. I bet they will get even bigger in my mouth."

A weak whimper escaped from behind my hands. I had never wanted anything more in my life than to feel her sucking on my nipples. I felt hot breath wash over my left nipple. I stifled a groan. The hand on my right breast eased up the fleshy slope and captured my right nipple between two fingers. The sensation made me squirm beneath her.

I was unprepared for the liquid heat of her mouth as it closed over my left nipple. I gasped and arched my back. Her lips and tongue toyed with the stiff nubbin like a cat with a fresh mouse. Jackie switched her mouth to my other nipple, and her other hand took possession of my wet, engorged nipple. Time lost all meaning as I dissolved into a haze of sensual lust and desire. I writhed slowly beneath her, unable to lie still any longer.

Eventually, her mouth left my breasts as she trailed soft kisses back down my stomach. Both of her hands toyed with my swollen red nipples.

"You liked that, I could tell," she whispered. I groaned my agreement, undulated uncontrollably.

"I loved the way your nipples tasted. I could feel them getting bigger and harder in my mouth."

Her tongue began to trace random figures on the skin beneath my navel but above my baggy boxer shorts. Her hands were fully extended and holding onto my quivering tits. Her hands left my tits and slid down my sides, raising goosebumps wherever they roamed.

"Your skin is so soft," Jackie murmured.

I felt her shift on the bed. Her head left my lower stomach. Her hands gently gripped my knees and spread my legs while simultaneously pulling them up. With my knees half bent and partially spread, I felt her shift positions again so that she was between my legs. I couldn't tell if she was sitting or kneeling.

"You have gorgeous legs," she said throatily. Hearing that telltale of desire in her voice made my legs tremble. Her hands slid down the insides of my thighs, stopping at the edge of my boxers. They glided back up to my knees and then back down my thighs; this time, they stopped a couple of inches inside the briefs. Up and down, each time moving closer to the heart of my passion. Each journey ended in slow circles traced on my quivering thighs.

"I love the way you feel right...here," she said as her hands stroked the very tops of my inner thighs, just shy of the hollow that formed next to my overheated pussy lips. I moaned behind my hands. My hips and legs were shaking with need; I wanted her to touch my hot, liquid center.

"This is so deliciously sexy," Jackie murmured. Her hands began to wander, explored all my upper thighs and lower belly. Her fingers traced the exposed curve of my ass cheeks; it dipped into the hollows at the tops of the thighs. She caressed every part of me except for my aching pussy. I was grinding my hips, desperately trying to find her fingers.

"I wonder if you look as hot as you feel?" Jackie asked. I could hear the hungry grin in her voice. Her hands left my hips, and I cried out softly in disappointment. She gripped the elastic waistband and began to pull them off of my hips. My knees had to come together, and she shifted backward to make room. I heard her gasp as my pussy was revealed. I hate body hair and keep myself completely shaven at all times.

The boxer shorts were gone. I lay naked before her, wearing only my half-shirt, pushed up around my neck, leaving my tits fully exposed.

"Oh my God, Michelle," Jackie said, her voice breaking. "You are so hot. So goddamn sexy. So absolutely fuckable."

She gently pried my knees open again, much wider this time. I was aching for her to touch me. I needed her fingers to caress my pussy like they had caressed her own. I had been kept in a state of constant arousal for so long that I was on fire. Her hands slid up my thighs once more. No games this time, but straight to the very edges of my pussy. I silently begged her to move those fingers inside of me.

I was not prepared for what she did next. Her tongue eased apart my puffy lips with a single long stroke. I cried out and snapped my hips up off the bed. Jackie's arms snaked underneath my legs, and her lips fastened onto my pussy.

I shook and writhed on the bed as her tongue lazily licked my pussy. She started low, on the small strip of skin just below the lips. Wide and flat, she licked up and over my clit, taking her time with each lick. After each lick, her lips would capture one of my labia and gently suck it into my mouth. I was riding the waves of this sweet torment, climbing higher and higher.

Jackie's hands gripped my forearms just below the elbows. Inexorably she pulled my hands away from my face. I kept my eyes tightly closed, my head thrashing from side to side. Jackie had described what it felt like when her boyfriends went down on her. But this was so much more than what I had imagined.

"Look at me," Jackie whispered, her mouth leaving my heaving pussy. I frantically hunched my hips, trying to reattach myself to her tongue and lips.

"Please, Michelle," Jackie begged. "Look at me."

Reluctantly, I opened my eyes and looked down at her. There, framed between the twin peaks of my tits, Jackie lay between my legs. Her arms were wrapped around my upper thighs, her mouth barely an inch above my glistening pussy. Her eyes stared deeply into mine as she lowered her face down into my pussy. Her tongue and lips sought out my clit, massaging and flicking at the throbbing flesh. I exploded. Jackie's eyes held me pinned as the powerful orgasm washed over me like a tidal wave.

Jackie returned to the long slow licks and gentle nibbling on my lips as I descended from the height of pleasure. It wasn't long before I was rising toward another orgasm. She drew it out this time, and I came again as her tongue dragged slowly over my clit. Jackie kept up her tender ministrations while I rode crest after crest of orgasmic pleasure. Finally, I could take no more and pushed her face away.

"Please," I gasped. "I can't take any more."

"I believe it," Jackie said as she rose up from between my legs. "I didn't know a girl could cum that much."

"Neither did I!" I said, trying to catch my breath. I curled up on my side, exhausted and content.

Jackie crawled up behind me and laid down facing my back. I could feel the soft curves of her breasts and hips against my back and butt. She pulled the sheet up over our naked bodies. She snuggled in close and snaked her arm around my stomach. I felt the gentle warmth of her breath on my neck as I drifted off to sleep.

I woke early. The events of the night before flooded my brain, and a mild panic settle over me. I had sex with another girl. No guy had ever gotten further than feeling up my boobs through my shirt, yet I had let Jackie lick my pussy.

Jackie stirred behind me. Her hand slid up my stomach and cupped my breast; her hips moved languidly against my naked ass. It felt so good and so natural and so right.

"Mmmm," Jackie murmured. She planted a soft kiss on the back of my neck that left my skin tingling. Another just like it sent shivers down my spine.

"Roll over," she whispered.

I spun in place to face her, our boobs touching under the sheet. Jackie eased her top leg over mine, snugging her hips up against mine. I found myself staring into the deep brown pools of her eyes. Last night those eyes had mesmerized me more than once. It was the same this morning. Her hand reached up to caress my cheek. Her face was only an inch from mine. With the slightest lean forward, Jackie placed her lips on mine. Our mouths opened, and our tongues met in a slow, soft dance.

All of my worries vanished. This was what it was. There was no point in over-analyzing it. Why should I put her or myself into that box or this one? It didn't matter if I was bi or gay or straight. I was Michelle, and she was Jackie, and that's all I needed to know. I accepted the situation for what it was.

Jackie's eyes closed, releasing mine, as her kiss became more ardent. Her hands stroked my back, and her leg pulled me in tighter. I was drowning in her kiss. My arms instinctively went around her neck and back; her lips and tongue explored my willing mouth. It was the most exquisite kiss I had ever had.

I don't know how long we lay there kissing, but finally, Jackie pulled away. I pursued, urgently wanting more. She relented with one last, long kiss and then slid her hand between our mouths.

"We should shower," Jackie whispered as I rained kisses on her palm. "I'm a sweaty, sticky mess, and I bet you are too."

"Okay," I answered. "But you have to come in with me."

"Oooh! How can I resist an over like that," she said with a grin.

We climbed out of bed; I looked down at our naked bodies. Jackie was right. Both of us were sweaty, sticky, and decidedly disheveled. I recognized a glow on Jackie's face. She called it her "fresh fucked" face; I had seen it a few times after some of her more exciting dates. A glance in the mirror over my vanity told me that I had that same look.

I grabbed bathrobes for both of us, and we headed for the shower holding hands like two giggling schoolgirls. As soon as we stepped into the hot water, we were in each other's arms, kissing passionately. I could not get enough of her sexy mouth. Her hands slid down and gripped my ass, almost causing us to fall down.

"Let me wash you," Jackie said, pulling away from my embrace.

She lathered the soap in her bare hands, ignoring the washcloth. She cupped both of my breasts, hefting the large mounds and gently squeezing them. Her slippery fingers found my nipples and pulled on them until they were stiff and erect.

"I love your tits," Jackie said coyly. "They are so yummy!"

Her hands left my tingling nipples, causing me to pout comically for her. She washed my shoulders, arms, and belly. Silently, she turned me around and began on my back. Her hands reached my ass, coating the firm globes with soap. She took the blade of one hand and slid it between my ass cheeks, pushing deep into the crevice.

"Got to make sure you're clean down here," she muttered into my ear. Her hand moved up and down between my cheeks, causing strange new sensations. It was exciting and forbidden, and it was turning me on. I leaned forward and planted my hands on the wall of the shower stall. I quivered with each stroke of her hand across my asshole. It would never have occurred to me that it could be an erogenous zone.

"Well, that seems to be nice and clean, for now," Jackie said. "But I think we need to clean you up in a few other places."

Her hand moved lower and up between my legs, cupping my hairless pussy from behind. My knees almost buckled as her fingers stroked my outer lips. I move my knees apart to give her easier access. She slid her middle finger between the lips while still stroking the outside with her other fingers. Her middle finger went right to my clit and began to trace soft circles around and over it. In less than a minute, I was cumming all over her hand, shaking and crying out softly. Jackie turned me around and let the shower water clean my slick pussy.

"Well, I know why you like sex," I quipped breathlessly. I reached for the soap, determined to return the favor. I started with her breasts, just like she had. Jackie's boobs were firmer than mine and a little softer. Her nipples grew hard and stiff under my tweaking fingers. Remembering her reactions last night, I pinched them carefully while pulling away from her chest.

"Uhhh...god..." she whispered. "How did you know I like them pinched?"

"Just lucky I guess."

I pulled and rolled her nipples for a little while, watching her eyes begin to glaze over. I slid my hand down her belly until I could feel her close-cropped pussy hair. I toyed with it for a moment, teasing her with what was to come. Moving down, my fingers opened her pussy lips wide. I could feel the slick oil of her pussy juices mixing with the hot water. I let my fingers explore her heated, slippery inner flesh. I let my finger circle her clit. Jackie moaned and put her hands on my shoulders to steady herself. I kept up the slow circling motions until she collapsed into my arms, her hips hunching into my hand as her orgasm flooded her senses.

"I've never touched a woman's...you know, down there," I said, suddenly embarrassed.

"Damn, that felt good," Jackie said, quivering. "It's my pussy. I hate the word cunt, and vagina sounds so clinical."

"Okay. I've never touched a woman's...pussy before."

"You can touch mine any time, so long as you do it like that."

I laughed and helped her clean off, without the sexual hijinks this time. We toweled each other dry, taking care to spend extra time on all the best parts of each other's body. I had never imagined I would feel this comfortable with someone else's body, or even my own. I wasn't embarrassed to stand naked in front of her or to have her naked body fully exposed to me.

"Can I borrow some clothes?" Jackie asked. "All I have here is that micro mini and the halter top. I don't want to give your dad a heart attack."

"Sure. How do baggy shorts and a T-shirt sound?"

"Okay. But I'm going to have to go commando because I don't have any panties or a bra."

"Sounds fun," I said boldly. I rarely went out without proper underwear.

"Then you should too."

"But I have underwear I can put on."

"You just said it sounds like fun. I wouldn't want to be the only one having fun."

Trapped by my only logic, I put on a T-shirt, baggy shorts, sans panties, and bra. It did feel kind of sexy and naughty. We headed downstairs for breakfast. Mom and Dad were at the table eating breakfast, and we dropped into the chairs on the other side. Actually, he was reading the paper with a plate of eggs in front of him, and she was cooking some for herself.

"I didn't know Jackie stayed over," my Mom said. "I have some eggs cooking. Would you girls like some?"

"Actually, I'd rather have one of those oranges and some toast," Jackie said. "I'm trying to watch my figure, unlike some people here." She poked me in the ribs as she said that, and I squealed.

"I'll have some eggs, Mom," I said. "I don't need to watch my figure." I poked her back, and she yelped.

"You'd think the two of you were 12 years old," My Dad said, grinning. "Play nice or I'll have to send you back up to your room."

"Oh, no!" Jackie said with mock horror. "We would want to be sent back up to the bedroom." She dropped her hand directly into my crotch and gave my pussy a gentle squeeze through my thin shorts. Her touch made me gasp, and I playfully slapped her arm. She shifted her hand to my upper thigh but didn't remove it.

"You two got a any plans for the day," my Dad asked.

"Naw," I said. "I figured we'd just hang around the house."

"Don't forget, your Mom and I are spending the day at the Antique Mall in Springfield. We probably won't be back until dinner time."

"Okay."

Jackie's hand slid up my thigh and under my shorts. The edge of her fingers came to rest on my naked pussy lips. I clamped her hand between my thighs. I turned and gave her the wide-eyed 'what the hell are you doing' look. She gave me the 'whatever are to talking about look.' I mean, we were right at the kitchen table with my parents!

Even trapped between my legs, her fingers managed to worm their way between my pussy lips and began to stroke the sensitive inner flesh. I tried to casually push her arm away, but she was stronger than I am. Jackie wasn't even looking at me. She was slowly eating her orange in her other hand and reading the back of the paper my Dad was holding.

Her fingers were working their magic on me, sliding up and down through my slit. I was getting turned on quickly. Mom and Dad were chatting with each other, so I didn't have to pay much attention. I felt my pussy beginning to moisten as Jackie's fingers caressed my inner lips. Damn that girl for talking me into not wearing any panties.

I was just getting ready to stand up so I could get away from those dancing fingers when my Mom plopped a plate of eggs in front of me. I mumbled a thank you, completely unable to focus by now.

"Why don't you spread them?" Jackie asked innocently.

"What?"

"Spread them," she repeated, pulling on my leg to make her meaning clear. "Spread the eggs around on your plate to cool them off."

"Oh."

I gave in to her and spread my legs wider, freeing her hand to move any way she wanted. She immediately repositioned her fingers to get to my clit. I bit my lip and aimlessly pushed my eggs around on my plate. Her fingers were delicately stroking my clit, while occasionally exploring my totally wet and slippery inner lips. I was terrified my mother would catch us. For some reason, that fear gave an extra sense of urgency to what Jackie was doing. I wouldn't be able to hold out for much longer.

I mechanically ate a bite of my eggs. My left hand was gripping the edge of the table tightly. My legs were trembling; I was having trouble keeping my breathing even. Jackie wasn't even looking at me. She was still reading the outside of the paper; I put another forkful of eggs in my mouth.

"Mmmm," I moaned as a lovely orgasm rippled outward from my pussy.

"What, dear?" My Mom asked.

"Mmmm," I moaned again. "Good...mmm...eggs, Mom."

Mercifully, Jackie pulled her hand out of my liquid pussy.

"I didn't do anything special," Mom said. "But I'm glad you like them."

Jackie pulled her hand out from under the table, her fingers coated with my shiny juices. Looking me straight in the eye, she slowly licked them clean. Watching her sent a tingle down my spine. My parents didn't even notice.

"Are you girls cold?" my Mom asked. "I can turn down the air-conditioning."

My Dad looked up at us. His gaze flicked over to Jackie. His eyes widened slightly, and a flush rose to his cheeks. Suddenly he found a very interesting article in the paper. I glanced over at Jackie. Her nipples were fully erect and poking holes in her T-shirt. I realized mine was in the same condition. No wonder Mom thought we were cold. I shoveled two more bites of eggs in my mouth and stood up from the table. I could feel a trickle of fluid leaking down my leg. I hoped there wasn't a wet spot where I had been sitting.

"You don't need to change the setting, Mom. We'll just change into some warmer clothes."

I grabbed Jackie's hand pulled her up too. Hand in hand, we headed for my room. As we rounded the corner of the living room, out of sight of the kitchen, Jackie pushed me up against the wall. Her mouth frantically sought mine, and we locked lips in a fierce, passionate kiss. Her hands pushed up under my shirt and cupped my aching tits. Mine pushed under the elastic of her shorts and gripped the firm round cheeks of her ass. God, she had a nice ass.

Our mouths were devouring each other; our tongues were dueling like fleshy fencers. Small moans and groans were swallowed up by the other's mouth; her fingers were pinching and pulling on my nipples. My hands were squeezing and caressing her ass. This was not the gentle, timeless lovemaking of the night before; this was a reckless need, fueled by wanton lust. Our hips ground together, desperately seeking pussy to pussy contact.

I moved on hand off of her ass cheek and up under her shirt. Her fully erect nipples were easy to find, and I groaned into her mouth as I rolled it between my thumb and forefinger. In the distance, I could hear my parent making meaningless noises in the kitchen. Jackie's hands left my tits and moved down to the waistband of my shorts. With a quick push, she had my pants down, the elastic barely holding them on my upper thighs. I mimicked her, pushing her pants down as well. They pooled at her feet.

Our now naked hips pressed urgently against each other. Her thigh slipped between my legs and my between hers. She gripped my ass tightly in both hands and began to hump my leg. I moved my hands to hold her quivering ass cheeks and began to frantically rub my hairless pussy against her smooth, muscular thigh. Our mouths were still locked in an intense kiss.

I could feel her tiny patch of pubic hair lightly scratching my thigh. Her pussy fluids were quickly lubricating it. She shifted positions slightly, and I could suddenly feel her spread pussy lips directly on my leg. The hard little knob of her clit was tracing a line up and down against my flesh. Imitating her, I spread my knees a little more and hunch up and into her thigh. My pussy lips split wide, and I could feel her whole thigh against my hot, wet inner flesh. My clit was rubbing directly against her smooth skin.

Jackie began to moan loudly in my mouth. I did everything I could to swallow her scream as her hips jerked spasmodically against my leg. Her fingernails were digging into my ass, and then I was cumming too. I hunched frantically against her as my clit slid through the slippery trail of juices on her thigh. And then I was ignited. I hung to Jackie for dear life, and I spasmed against her leg. My hands on her glorious ass cheeks pulled her tight into me.

Our orgasms slowly receded, and we clung to each other, as much to prevent us from falling down as for the wonderful feel of naked flesh pressed up against our skin. Our hungry kisses turned soft and loving. I sucked gently on her lower lip, and she traced a circle around my lips with her tongue. Our hands played with each other's naked ass cheeks. In many ways, the afterglow of sex was every bit as good as the event itself. My shorts had fallen down around my ankles at some point.

"Have you seen my keys?" I heard my Dad say from around the corner in the kitchen. Amazingly they hadn't heard the noises of our lovemaking.

"They're in the living room, dear," my mother answered.

Oh my God! Any second now, he would be coming into the room with us. Jackie and I scrambled to climb the stairs to my bedroom. With our pants around our ankles, we were staggering forward. I pulled mine halfway up, almost falling over in the process. Jackie just stepped out of hers and raced up the stairs ahead of me, her firm round buttocks churning. We managed to get up and out of view just as my Dad entered the living room. Giggling like kids, we collapsed on my bed, safe behind the closed door.

"You are an animal," I accused. "What kind of a pervert has sex three times by breakfast?"

"They you must be the pervert," Jackie quipped back, smiling. "I've only has sex twice this morning. You're the one that's done it three times."

"I guess we're both just horny sex fiends. Do you think you can keep your hands out of my pussy long enough for us to get dressed for real this time?"

"Oh, fine. If you want to be boring, I suppose I can."

We cleaned up and got dressed for real, although Jackie still had to go commando. Lying together in my room, holding hands, I heard my parent's car pull out of the driveway. We had the run of the house.

I'm not even sure what we did for the next few hours. I know we watched a bad movie on cable and listened to some music, but mostly we just talked. We were lying on an overstuffed comforter on the floor in front of the TV; it was turned off.

"Jackie, was last night on purpose, or did you plan that?"

"A little of both. The stuff I told about Brad really did happen."

"So he really did leave you so worked up you had to...you know...do yourself?"

"Oh yeah," Jackie said emphatically. "I was a wreck."

"Oh."

"Michelle, I've had a serious crush on you for months. There were a lot of times I had to leave the room just so I wouldn't kiss you."

"I had no idea."

"Yeah. You know how sexual I am. I think I've told you about every single thing that's ever happened in my sex life. Sometimes when I would be telling you those stories I would be hoping that you would get so turned on you would make the first move."

"No way! Sorry, but I'm not as brave as you are. I would never have had the guts to make that first move," I said, shaking my head.

"Well, last night I couldn't take it anymore. You were sitting there watching me play with myself and I just had to have you touching me. Are you okay with this? I mean with the two of us?"

"I was scared at first. I mean, I was worried that I was a lesbian or something. I'm still not sure about that. But being with you feels so right, I don't care."

"I hate those labels. It's like being lesbian or bi says more about you that how you treat people, or how smart you are, or anything else."

"I was thinking the same thing last night. When I stopped worrying about what box people would put me in, it became a lot easier to just be who I am. And who I am is a girl that wants to be with you."

Jackie kissed me tenderly on the mouth. "I want to be with you too, Michelle. I've wanted to for a long time. If I had know what a good lover you are, I would have done it a long time ago!"

"So I'm better than all those boys you screw?" I said, teasing. "Even Jay?" I knew I had been a bad lover.

"Oh please! My dog is probably better in bed than Jay. He'd certainly last longer." We both laughed.

"So are you going to break up with Brad?" I asked, suddenly nervous. This was important to me. Was she serious about wanting to be with me, or was it just sex?

"I have a date with him tonight."

"Are you going?"

"I think I have to."

I wasn't brave enough to beg her not to go. I didn't even have the courage to ask her why. If she wanted to be with me so badly, why did she need to go out with Brad? The thought of her dumping me for him was terrifying. It was bad enough having to wrestle with the alien idea of being in love with another woman.

Whoa! Was I really in love with Jackie? There hadn't been time to think about the depth of my feelings for her. I had known her for years as my best friend, and I had loved her platonically for a long time. What separated love with a little 'l' from Love with a big 'L'? It was more than just sex, I was sure. I guess I really did Love Jackie.

"Hey, you're suddenly quiet," Jackie said.

"Sorry. I was just thinking."

"About what?"

My courage failed me again. I have never been a brave person. "Oh, just last. It was the most amazing sex I've ever had." That was true.

"I thought you were a virgin?" Jackie teased.

"Well, okay. So it is also the only sex I've ever had, but it was still amazing. I never imagined it could be that good."

"Well I was serious when I said you were the best lover I've ever had."

I snuggled up close to her, throwing a leg over hers and draping my arm across her back. I inched in closer and laid my head on her shoulder.

"Mmmm. That feels nice," Jackie purred.

I leaned in and softly kissed her ear. She made a low noise in her throat. I kissed her ear again. I let my tongue trace the edges of her ear and play with the soft, dangling lobe. When I tired of that, I pulled her dark hair away from her neck and planted a soft kiss on the smooth skin. I was rewarded with some goosebumps and another soft noise.

It was getting tough to reach her neck while lying next to her. So I swung up and over to lie on her back. My knees straddle her buttocks. I held most of my weight on my hands and knees and only allowed my hips to apply and significant pressure on her. From here, I could easily kiss all over my neck, which I proceeded to do.

I took my time, remembering the sweet, slow torture she had put me through last night. I alternated soft brushes with my pursed lips and tracing lazy figures with my wet tongue. I could feel her ass cheeks clenching and releasing underneath my hips.

Having reached the edge of her shirt, I tugged the hemline up, and Jackie helped me strip it off her. Now her whole back was exposed. Jackie has flawless skin, smooth and with almost no blemishes. I picked up where I had left off, kissing and licking my way down her back. I took my time, enjoying every shiver and goosebump. When my mouth went dry, I sat up and stroked her back with my fingertips, tracing abstract patterns on her skin. I let my fingers brush against the exposed sides of her breasts, causing her to moan softly. While I was sitting, I stripped off my shirt and bra.

I slid down her legs and went back to the kisses, but much lower this time. My mouth finally reached the dimples in her lower back, just above her pants line. As a tease, I swiped a long, wet trail all the way back up to her neck. I let my erect nipples drag along her naked back and then lay full on her, kissing her neck repeatedly. Jackie groaned and writhed underneath my weight.

Reversing course, I trailed a path back down to the edge of her pants, my nipples trailing their twin paths ahead of me. Her pants were definitely in the way. I had to climb off her to peel them down her legs and off. Because she wore no panties or bra, this left her completely naked. I could smell her desire. She didn't look up but just lay there compliantly. I was reminded of my hiding behind my hands last night, except that this felt much more natural. I quickly shucked my pants and panties so I could be just as naked.

Facing her feet, I kissed and stroked my way up her left leg. I paid extra attention to her gorgeous, tanned thighs. Reaching the cleft between her leg and ass, the aroma of her passion was unmistakable. I transferred my attention to her firm, round ass cheek, kissing and licking it all over. Jackie was having a difficult time lying still. Her ass would clench and release, and her legs were trembling ever so slightly.

Knowing I was being a tease, I moved back down to her right calf and repeated the entire treatment. By the time I was kissing and licking her wonderfully bare ass cheeks, Jackie was practically squirming. I climbed between her legs, forcing her to spread them. Placing a hand on each check, I spread her wide. I could see the puckered pink ring of her anus, slightly distorted by my pressure. Below that was her glistening pussy lips. We would have to wash the comforter when we were done. A small, wet stain was spread below them.

"You are beautiful," I croaked. Jackie just wriggled.

Release her cheeks, I slid one hand down between her legs and stroked the moist outer lips of her pussy. My fingers danced along her innermost thighs and caressed her puffy pussy lips, but they never opened them up. Jackie was writhing more and more. I could tell she wanted me to touch her where she needed it the most.

"Roll over," I said softly.

Without hesitating, Jackie flipped over, arranging herself so that her legs were on either side of me. Her eyes were bright with lust and desire. I scooted down to where my mouth could reach her knees. I alternated kisses on each of her inner thighs, moving steadily up toward her hot center.

I knew what I wanted to do. I wanted to lick her pussy just like she had done to mine. I wanted to give her that indescribable pleasure of feeling a hot, wet tongue sliding between her labia and flicking across her clit. I was scared I wouldn't like it. I was frightened it would taste horrible and that

I wouldn't be able to do it. I mean, before today, I had never even touched another woman, let alone put my mouth on her pussy.

I found my courage in my need to hold onto Jackie. I was more frightened of losing her to Brad than I was of performing oral sex. I desperately wanted to make love to her so passionately that she would come back to me and not go to him. I resolved to love her with my mouth with as much tenderness and passion as she did to me.

I tentatively licked her outer lips, causing Jackie to inhale sharply. The mildly salty, musky taste was intoxicating. My next lick was right up the center of her cleft. Jackie moaned, and I could see her head rocking from side to side. I hadn't realized that the taste of a woman's pussy isn't what is important. It's that marvelous texture. Encouraged, I explored all of her marvelous folds with my tongue. I slithered between the inner and outer lips, delighted with the different textures.

Jackie's hands were gently stroking my hair. I slid both of my hands under her firm, quivering ass cheeks. The feel of those globes was exciting. I continued to tenderly lick her pussy all over, loving how it felt and loving how she was reacting to my kisses. Her moans and groans were accompanied by occasional twitches of her hips or undulations of her entire body. Her stiff, throbbing clit was easy to find. I gently sucked it into my mouth and curled my tongue around it.

"Oh, yeah!" Jackie cried out. "That's it baby. God, your tongue is driving me crazy."

I began to quickly flick the tip of my tongue over her clit. It only took seconds for her to cum. Her whole body went rigid as she cried out. Then she was flailing uncontrollably on the floor. I snaked my arms around her upper thighs and held on for dear life; I continued my assault on her clit. Her gently stroking hands gripped my hair fiercely. Her cries turned to sobs as her body continued to shake and quiver.

Finally, her hands weakly tried to push my face away, but I held on tight. However, I did stop with the rapid tongue flicks. Releasing her clit, I resumed the long slow licks. I loved the feel of her inner flesh on my tongue. I used my lips to gently massage her pussy lips. Jackie was still groaning and writhing in slow motion.

I settled into a pattern of long, slow lick with the flat of my tongue. Each one started with the tip of my tongue just inside her vagina; it ended with the full pressure on my tongue gliding over her clit. Her body began to shake with a second orgasm, gentler but deeper than the first. I kept the pace slow and gentle but insistent and unrelenting. She had several more of those deep, rolling orgasm. I was too engrossed in what I was doing to count them.

"Michelle, please stop," Jackie finally begged. "I don't think I can take any more."

"Just one more," I pleaded, lifting my face from between her legs for a moment. "I want to give you one more."

"Oh, God," She said, flopping her head back on the floor.

I tenderly sucked her clit back into my mouth, gently massaging it with my lips.

"Oh, shit!" Jackie hissed. Her entire body tensed. I kept milking that tiny knob until she came with a wail. Her hands were clutching at the comforter and at my head. Her back was arched, and her hips kept jerking underneath my face. As this last, powerful orgasm subsided, I released her clit and rained light, gentle kisses on the outer lips of her pussy, avoiding the over-stimulated inner flesh. Jackie's whole body was shaking, and I could hear her crying. I knew those were tears of release, not of sorrow.

"Come up here," Jackie begged hoarsely.

I crawled up her body, feeling the full press of her naked flesh against mine. Tears were streaming down her cheeks. Once again, I knew they were tears of joy and passion, not sadness or anger. She pulled my face down to hers, holding my cheeks in her hands. We kissed passionately over and over. I could feel the wet, sticky juices that coated my face rubbing off onto her lips and face. She didn't care.

We lay there naked, hugging and kissing for the longest time. No words were spoken. I'm not sure Jackie could have managed a coherent conversation. Strangely, I did not feel the least bit horny. Everything I had done was just for her, to show her how much I loved her.

"I have to go," Jackie said. We were still twined together naked on the comforter in my living room.

"Please, stay with me," I begged, my voice breaking. "Don't see Brad tonight."

"I need to."

"Buy why? Don't you love me?"

I realized I had stepped over the boundary. I had used the L-word. Jackie had been my lover for less than 24 hours, and I just implied I was in love with her. It didn't matter that it was true. Even I knew that the surest way to lose a new lover was to push your emotions on them too soon. Now Jackie probably thought I was some sort of lovesick cow.

"Michelle, you're very special to me," Jackie said. "I don't want to hurt you."

I began to cry. It just wasn't fair. I was going to lose her because I couldn't keep my big fat mouth shut. My crying was only going to make matters worse, but I couldn't help myself. My tears were half misery and half anger at my own stupidity.

"Then don't go," I said angrily.

"I don't think I can explain it in a way you would understand or accept. I just know I have to do this."

I rolled away from her and buried my face in the comforter, sobbing uncontrollably. Jackie moved over and draped her naked body over mine. She gently kissed my head and my shoulder.

"Why don't you just go. If being with Brad is so fucking important to you, I wouldn't want you to be late," I said. I rarely used foul language, and Jackie knew it.

"I'll come back," Jackie said, her voice trembling. "I'm not going to let it end like this. I really do care for you Michelle."

"Fuck you!" I screamed and burst into more tears. I knew I was driving her away. The pain of my rejecting her was more bearable than the pain of her rejecting me. She left the house without another word. I lay there crying for a long time. When I heard my parent's car in the driveway, I listlessly picked up the comforter and my clothes and took them to my room. I didn't come down for dinner, claiming to have eaten earlier. I told Mom I was really tired and just wanted to go to bed.

Something touched my cheek. Half buried under the covers. I slowly drifted into wakefulness. Someone kissed me on the cheek again. This time I was awake enough to know it was a kiss. I managed to pry my eyes open and saw Jackie kneeling beside the bed, her face only inches from mine. My heart skipped a beat.

"Good morning beautiful," She said, smiling. "May I join you?"

Then I realized she was stark naked. Even after she betrayed me, I knew I couldn't shut her out. Silently I held up the covers, and she slid in next to me. She put her arms around me, but I resisted the urge to put mine around her. She kissed the tip of my nose.

"Are you still mad at me?" Jackie asked.

"That depends," I answered sulkily. Oh God, please let her tell me she wants me.

"I broke up with Brad last night. That's part of what I needed to do. I wanted to do it in person. It wouldn't have been fair to do it over the phone."

"What else?" I asked. I knew that couldn't be all. If all she needed to do was break up with him, she could have told me that yesterday. Never the less, my heart was singing, and I put my arms around her. I moved in closer and laid my head on her shoulder.

"You're too damn smart. The rest is harder to explain."

"So try."

"I needed to know for sure."

"I don't understand."

"Yesterday was wonderful and scary. I've fantasized about being with you for long time, but I never realized how intense it would be. That was pretty scary. I've never felt like that with anyone else before. I needed to be with someone else one more time just to make sure."

"That doesn't make any sense."

"I know it doesn't. But feelings aren't logical, at least mine aren't. I think I was just scared Michelle. I didn't know who I was. I was drowning in you and it was scary."

"So I'm scary?" I asked, lamely attempting some humor.

"Yes. You're also smart, funny, caring, and sexy."

"Stop trying to butter me up," I said with a wan smile.

"Ooh! That sounds yummy," Jackie said with a twinkle. "I would just have to lick it all off you."I pinched her ribs playfully. She yelped and squirmed underneath me. So far, I like the way this conversation was going, but I was still wary.

"You probably aren't going to understand this, I'm not sure I do. I just hope you can forgive me," Jackie took a deep breath. "I fucked Brad last night."

We both lay very still. She was waiting for my response. So was I. I decided I needed to hear more.

"Why?"

"I had to know. I was having trouble separating sex from feelings and boys from girls. I told you it didn't make sense. I was hoping that if I fucked him I would be able to figure out if what was between us was more than just sex. I was also hoping to figure out if I liked girls better than boys."

"Okay. So what have you learned?"

"Well, for one thing, Brad is a really good lay. You probably didn't want to hear that, but I want to be totally honest with you. Sex with him was really good, but I don't have any deep feelings for him. I do have deep feelings for you. I guess I also learned that for me sex and emotions don't have to go together. I can fuck someone and have great time, with multiple orgasms and everything, and it doesn't have to mean anything. I could walk away and still be friends. I'm also pretty sure I'm just as much into guys as girls, at least sexually."

She had deep feelings for me! I could live with the rest of it just knowing that.

"So making love to Brad was the same as making love to me?" I asked.

"God, no! Brad and I fucked. You and I make love. Just because I can have sex with someone and just enjoy the physical part of it doesn't mean that's the only way. First of all, you are a much better lover than Brad. Second, my feelings for you make having sex so much more intense. That's what scared me in the first place. Right now, I don't want to be with Brad. I don't want to be with anyone other than you."

I grabbed the hem of my sleep shirt and pulled it up and off. Next, the short followed, pushed down deep under the sheet. Naked, I crawled on top of Jackie and kissed her passionately. Our bodies are molded into one another. Her tongue caressed mine as her arms held me close. I loved the way she kissed. I could feel her nipples stiffening against the soft flesh of my breasts. I'm sure mine was doing the same to hers.

"Does this mean you forgive me?" Jackie asked after several long deep kisses.

"Are you done with Brad?" I asked. "I don't think I would like it if you did any more experiments with sex like that."

"No more Brad. No other boys. No other girls even. Just you and me. However, that means you are going to have to satisfy my insatiable sexual appetite," she said, grinning.

My answer was to force my leg between hers. Trapping her thigh between mine, I ground my hips suggestively into hers. I could feel her patch of pubic hair grinding against my upper thigh. She purred appreciatively. I pulled my leg out and squirmed high up onto her body.

"Tease!" Jackie chided me.

I sat on her stomach, pinning her to the bed. Leaning forward, I dangled my pendulous breasts in her face. She cupped each of my generous mounds in her hands and directed my left nipple into her mouth. Her tongue slathered my nipple, tracing circles around the areola. I sighed as the heavenly feeling of her mouth stirred lust in my loins. Jackie switched breasts, drawing the other nipple into her mouth. Her fingers found my other nipple, all wet and stiff from her lips and tongue. While she sucked and licked my right nipple, her fingers tweaked and rolled my left nipple. I shivered as sparks of pleasure shot through me.

She continued to play with my breasts until I was humping my hairless pussy into her stomach, leaving a wet streak across her belly. Jackie released my nipple from her mouth and gripped both of them between her thumbs and forefingers. She pulled on them gently but insistently until I gasped. She kept pulling, forcing me to lean further over her. She began to kiss my upper stomach just below my breasts. Her tugging forced me to scoot up toward her head.

Jackie let go of my nipples and reached down to grip my ass, now easily within her reach. She kept kissing my stomach while pulling me forward. I didn't know what she wanted, but I was willing to do anything for those magic hands and wonderful mouth. When I got to the point where I was straddling her chest, she scooted underneath me so that her face was directly underneath my soaking wet pussy. Now I understood. She pushed gently on my ass until my pussy was plastered over her mouth. This position felt so sexy and dirty all at the same time.

Jackie's tongue stabbed deep into my vagina. I gasped as my legs turned to gelatin. She rimmed the inside of my hole, making me quiver with delight. With a firm grip on my ass, she maneuvered me off her tongue. And then down so that her lips could play with my clit. Her gentle sucks and tender licks were quickly raising the heat of my passion. I was having trouble holding myself up on my arms.

I was riding on the brink of orgasm when she released my clit. I cried out in disappointment, undulating my hips to try and recapture her tongue. She teased me with her mouth, keeping me on the brink until I was desperate to cum. Finally relenting, she sucked hard on my clit while simultaneously sliding a finger deep into my ass. I shrieked as a powerful orgasm broke across my body like a tidal wave on the shore. Her finger moved in and out of my ass while her lips and tongue-lashed my clit. I humped her face uncontrollably, drowning in sensation.

As my orgasm subsided, her lips and tongue caressed the folds of my pussy, avoiding my overly sensitive clit. Her finger remained buried deep in my ass. I wriggled on her face, and she pushed it in deeper, sending strange waves of pleasure coursing through my body. I would never have thought to put a finger in my butt. I certainly wouldn't have thought it would feel good. Jackie's finger felt wonderful buried deep in my ass.

With a push and a roll, her finger popped out of my bottom. I rolled over onto my back, grateful to not be supporting my weight on my arms anymore. Jackie got up off the bed and went into the bathroom. I heard the water running for a minute, and then she returned.

"It's always a good idea to clean up right after doing that," Jackie said as she slipped back under the covers with me.

"Damn! Where do you learn all this stuff?" I asked. "Every time we make love you show me something new that I didn't know."

"Brad did it to me last night," she said. "It felt good, so I thought I'd try it on you."

I reached for her and pulled her into a deep kiss. I trailed my hand down to her breasts. My fingers twiddled her nipples while my tongue explored her mouth. As soon as her nipples were fully erect, I moved my hand down further until I felt the small patch of pubic hair right above her pussy. My middle finger slipped easily into the wet, slippery folds. Jackie moaned into my mouth and spread her legs in encouragement.

"Want to try something else new?" Jackie asked, pulling her mouth away from mine.

"Sure," I said, flicking my fingertip over her clit.

"Uhhh!...Oh, Michelle...I love it when you do that."

So I did it again. And again. Jackie clamped down on my wrist.

"You're going to spoil my surprise if you keep that up."

"What? Are you hiding something in there?" I asked mischievously.

Jackie reached down off the side of the bed and retrieved a big rubber penis. My eyes grew wide when I saw it. I had never seen an erect penis before, and even though this wasn't the real thing, it looked huge.

"This is Mike," Jackie said. "I named it after you, but with the masculine version of Michelle."

"Is this what a penis really looks like?"

"It's pretty close, but the color is wrong. Also it's bigger than most guy's cocks."

"Damn! I hope so."

"I want you to use it on me. I want you to fuck me with it. It will almost be like you are a guy fucking me with his cock. This way there isn't anything that they can do for me that you can't."

Jackie had a pretty twisted way of looking at things sometimes. She had sex with a guy to prove to herself that she wanted to be with me. Now she wanted me to use this rubber penis on her to prove to me that she wouldn't have any reason to leave me.

I moved down between her legs, and she shifted to give me room. She spread her legs wide, her knees up high. I put the head of the rubber monster on the entrance to her vagina. I had to use my other hand to spread her lips out of the way. Jackie was very wet, and her juices lubricated the head of the dildo. I pushed it in half an inch or so and then pulled it back out. The head glistened with her fluids. The second time it went in deeper. With each stroke, more and more of the dildo vanished inside her vagina.

"Wow! This whole thing fits inside of you."

"Oh, yeah...all of it. Now fuck me with it Michelle."

The sight of this artificial penis moving in and out of Jackie's pussy mesmerized me. Her eyes were closed, and her breathing was heavy and erratic. Her pussy lips seemed to cling to it as I retracted the dildo. Then I remembered something I had read in a magazine once about a woman's G spot. I tilted the base down slightly so that the head would rub up against the roof of her vagina, right where the G spot was supposed to be.

"Oh...Oh!...Oohhhhh!" Jackie cried out as an orgasm raced through her. Her head was thrashing from side to side, and her white-knuckled hands were clenching the bed covers. When she began to calm down, I slowed down the motion of the dildo.

"Where did you learn that trick?" Jackie asked breathlessly. "I've never had a guy hit my spot like that before. That was amazing."

"I guess you're not the only one that knows a few tricks," I said proudly.

"Turn it on."

"What?"

"Twist the base. Mike is just a dildo, he's also a vibrator. Turn it on."

I looked at the base of the dildo, still stuck halfway up Jackie's pussy, and saw that she was right. I twisted the base, and the whole unit began to hum. I could feel the vibrations all the way up to my elbow.

"Shit!" Jackie cried. "Fuck me, Michelle. Fuck me with it."

I moved the vibrating toy rhythmically in and out of her pussy. Jackie was lost in another world, a place of ecstasy and euphoria. She was trembling all over, arching her back as the vibrator brought her closer and closer to another climax. Then she pushed over the top. Wailing and crying out, she writhed on the bed before me. Giving the girl, I loved this much pleasure was the ultimate aphrodisiac. I pumped the vibrator in and out of her pussy until she couldn't take any more.

"Stop...please stop," Jackie gasped. "I can't breathe!"

I turned off the vibrator but left it embedded in her pussy. I had an idea for something else I wanted to do, but I needed her to calm down first. I moved the dildo in and out of her pussy in a slow, lazy rhythm. When Jackie could focus again, I laid down between her legs. She looked down at me with disbelief.

"You want more? Michelle, you are even more of a sex fiend than I am."

I put my mouth over her pussy and gently began to play with her clit. At the same time, I angled the dildo to reach her G spot again.

"Oh my God...Michelle...you little demon...you're going to rip me apart!"

She was rising fast under the double stimulation of my tongue and the dildo. That's when I turned on the vibrator. Her whole body went rigid at once. Her hands wrapped themselves in my hair, and she grunted and shrieked as one last powerful orgasm rocked her world. I could feel the juices on my face as her clit throbbed underneath my tongue. The vibrations from the toy buzzed my chin and face. Jackie was pawing at my head, trying to escape the unrelenting ecstasy. When I felt her body collapse weakly on the bed, I turned off the vibrator and sat up.

With a cat's grin on my face, I looked down at her still twitching form. I had given Jackie something no guy, and I hope no girl could ever give her. I looked closely at her and realized that she had passed out. That last orgasm had been too much. I knew then that she would be mine for a long time.

Story 02

The Lady Abigail Rodgers stood at the rail of the sloop of war HMS Indomitable. She was a small woman with flaxen hair and pale blue eyes. The dark dress she wore made her appear even smaller with its wide skirts and voluminous petticoats. She was the very picture of an English Lady out to get some air on a long voyage, but this was no pleasure trip. Each passing moment the fast little ship was carrying her towards an uncertain fate. The deep azure blue of the Atlantic had already given way to the blue-greens of the shallower Caribbean.

Soon St. Eustacius will be in sight, and not long after that, the end of my world, she thought bitterly. Even the sea seems to pity me. Why must my father do this to me?

Her father was the Governor of the tiny island and had arranged a marriage for her. Abigail and her father had never been close. He was a cold man, stubbornly prideful and very ambitious. When her mother died in an outbreak of the plague, he left his only daughter in the care of her grandparents and gone overseas. Abby had been seven at the time and was now a beautiful young woman of nineteen. She did not know him, save for the infrequent letters she had received over the years.

She had grown up under the care of her grandparents at a small estate in Yorkshire called The Brambles. Her grandfather had been a vigorous man in his early fifties. He had made the family fortune privateering in the Caribbean during one of the many protracted wars between the colonial powers. He had returned to the islands after her grandmother died, and Abigail finished her schooling with an aunt in France. She could still remember crying as she left the old manor house, grief over her grandmother's death, her grandfather's departure, and the selling of the old estate to strangers all mixed to form one of the saddest days of her life. Now her wedding day would take the place of that day she feared.

She was betrothed to a most horrid little man, the scion of a wealthy family on St. Eustacius. Sir Gerald Abercrombie had come over to personally escort his pretty bride back home. He was a vain, shallow, arrogant man in his mid-thirties. Thin and short with milky white skin and a scraggly black beard that grew in patches on his heavy jaw, he looked less like a man than one of the mangy hounds her grandfather's neighbor used to keep. He was an odious toad in Abigail's opinion, and the lecherous stares he gave her left little doubt that he was anxious to truly claim his bride. Abigail felt her stomach turn just thinking of physical contact with the man.

Her father had no concern for her as a person, for her likes or dislikes. She felt that to him, she was nothing more than a pawn to be used to gain an advantage for himself as he tried to be elevated to the peerage. She would not be allowed to marry for love, and after nearly three months in Gerald's company, Abigail had come to believe she would never love any man. The members of the crew were all animals, scum taken from Liverpool's docks and jails. They had seemed nice a first, but she had quickly realized they wanted her for the same reason Gerald did. The Captain was a fat man, pompous and prideful. He seemed to have more interest in polishing the many brass buttons on his Royal Navy waistcoat than he did in any of the day-to-day things on his ship. Her entire trip had been one of fear and aching loneliness.

Her dismal reverie was disturbed as her betrothed exited the small cabin he occupied and approached her. He wore his sailor's outfit today, the white shirt open to reveal a shrunken chest covered in a patchwork of hair. Lace decorated the cuffs and collar, and the breeches were of velvet. Abigail cringed as she imagined his body close to hers, and she looked around quickly, hoping for someone nearby to talk to, anything to avoid him.

"Sail Ho!" the sailor in the crow's nest called out.

The crossing had taken nearly three months, and all heads turned towards the distant spec curiously. Gerald went to speak to the Captain, mercifully sparing Abigail his presence. She stayed at the rail, watching the spec slowly grow, first to a sail, then to a toy-sized ship, and finally to a majestic Barque built on the Spanish model. It was beautiful to behold as it danced across the calm sea, leaving a frothy white wake behind. The lines were clean and sleek, and for a moment, she was reminded of the hunting hounds Lord Tort kept on his estate in France. The ship was definitely a runner, built for speed. It was carrying full sail now, the white cloths filled with the gentle breeze that Indomitable had been fighting all morning. She flew the Dutch flag, which Abigail found curious since the Dutch usually used fat, squat trading vessels.

All hands were watching when the Dutch flag came down, and another was raised, a red flag with a blackbird of prey on it. Abigail was trying to make out what kind of bird it was when a horrified shriek behind her announced, "It's Black Lissa!"

She recognized Gerald's panic-stricken voice as the sailors exploded into action around her. Black Lissa? She thought. The notorious pirate? The one they called the Queen of the damned? Even in her sheltered life in England, and later France, Abigail had heard of Black Lissa. She was Spanish or French. No one knew for sure. Brought over to be a "companion" to a Spanish Governor, she had been taken by pirates when the ship she was on had been seized. She had proved to be more than the pirate captain had bargained for and killed him when he came to claim her. She was a classically trained swordswoman and had killed several crewmen before the others backed down. By some obscure rule of pirate etiquette, she had become Captain.

For the last three years, she had been the scourge of the Eastern Caribbean, raiding as far as Trinidad in the South and Bermuda in the north. Horror stories of the way her crew brutally dispatched prisoners vied with stories of how she took captured women to her bed as a man would in the lurid press of the times. Abigail discounted much of what she had heard; no one person could have done so much mischief in so short a time, in her opinion. Still, men spoke the name Black Lissa with a dread that only Lucifer could rival, and she had certainly killed many people. Abigail felt the cold fingers of fear clutch at her heart.

She made her way amid the chaos to where the Captain, Mate, and Gerald were holding a heated conversation.

"We will stand and fight," the Captain said.

"Fight? You idiot! That's Black Lissa!" Gerald nearly screamed. His face was ashen, the small bit of color drained from it, and he was obviously terrified. Abigail thought she had already seen the worst in him, but he was more afraid than she was, and it sickened her.

"Quite right, and that is why we will fight. This is a ship of the line and she is a wanted pirate,"

"She has the deadliest, blackest crew at sea! This ship stands no chance against her. You are supposed to see me safely to St. Eustacius, or have you forgotten?" Gerald whined. The fat Captain got mad then and struck Gerald with a backhanded blow.

"This is a ship of her majesty's fleet, not your private yacht! Man the cannons!" he roared.

Gerald ran screaming to his room as the first shots were exchanged, totally forgetting Abigail in his panic. She watched the battle from the rear of the ship, not sure whom she wanted to win. If the ship were lost, she would be in the clutches of pirates, but what could they do that would be more loathsome than marriage to Gerald Abercrombie? She thought.

The battle was short and brutal; the Indomitable exchanged a broadside with the pirate ship as the two passed. The guns roared, and thick grayish smoke obscured everything, but Abigail was sure that neither ship had sustained much damage. She felt her pulse quicken, and the thrill of it all nearly overwhelmed her. The pirate ship, called the Raven, tacked quickly to bring her guns to bear from the rear.

Captain Wilkinson may have been a pompous windbag, but he was no fool. He ordered his own ship to mirror the pirate's turn. This kept the sloop ahead of the Raven and thus out of her main gun's deadly arc. However, it did not protect his ship from the lethal fire of the cannonade mounted on the pirate's forecastle. These small cannons blasted the sloop with a withering volley of shots that left several crewmen down. Their bodies were shredded and had great holes torn in them. The screaming was frightful, and when the blood began to run through the scuppers, Abigail turned her head and vomited.

The sloop was smaller and faster, but the wind was with them, and the barque was able to keep up with them using her extra sail. A second volley of cannonade killed more of his men, and Captain Wilkinson ordered the sloop to heave to. Apparently, he planned to tack back across his track and brave a broadside from the barque. Once clear, the little sloop would have an advantage as the barque would have to fight upwind, something she could never hope to match the sloop in.

As Indomitable tried to tack grapnels shot out from the Raven, men jumped to cut the lines with axes, but the pirates kept up a deadly fire on the rails with muskets. Unable to break the lines, the sloop lost steerage and was dragged inexorably closer to the pirate ship. Abigail moved to the far rail, hoping she would not be shot by accident.

"Prepare to repel boarders!" the fat Captain roared over the noise of battle. His men all armed themselves and waited. When the two ships crashed together, a flood of humanity washed over the rails. Abigail watched in horror as the pirates swarmed on board; they were a motley collection of men dressed in outlandish clothing. There were tall men with blonde hair from Scandinavia, short, swarthy men from the Mediterranean, even a pair of giant Negroes. Every race and country seemed to be represented in their company, and they were all brandishing swords, pistols, billhooks, or even more fantastic weapons.

The crew of the Indomitable was outnumbered but suffered from an even greater handicap. Black Lissa's crewmen were known as some of the most depraved, sadistic, evil men on the high seas. Their fearsome reputation unmanned many of the sailors; these threw down their weapons at the sight of the pirates. The pirates looked as fearsome as their reputation, and the battle was short and relatively bloody where those men who chose to fight made their stand around the forecastle. Around Abigail, the Englishmen dropped their weapons and begged for quarter, individually and in small groups. In fifteen minutes, the survivors were all rounded up, and the battle was over.

Several wild-eyed men speaking a host of languages confronted Abigail. They leered at her and made obscene gestures that were universal and needed no translation. She was terribly frightened but remained quiet. That changed when a short, swarthy man boldly stepped forward and roughly grabbed a handful of her hair. Abigail screamed as he viciously pulled her to the deck. She felt hands all over her then, pulling at her bodice, ripping away pieces of her petticoats, and forcing her legs apart. She screamed again as she was rolled over onto her back. She found the swarthy pirate on top of her. His leering face was ugly and filled with lust.

Suddenly a second bloody smile appeared on his throat, as if by magic. His startled eyes filled her vision for a fraction of a second, and then he was dragged bodily off of her, splashing her bodice in blood. A tall, lithe figure hefted the smaller pirate above its head and threw him overboard. The figure turned a baleful eye on the men gathered around her.

"Get back ye dogs," the woman commanded. It was a woman, and what a woman, Abigail thought. She was at least six feet tall, and her flaming red hair was tied back under a black kerchief. She wore a black silk shirt that was stuffed into black breeches and tall sea boots. The outfit seemed to cling to her curves, and her legs seemed impossibly long and shapely. Instead of a sash, she wore a belt of black leather with a Rapier and dueling dagger hanging from them and a brace of pistols tucked under the belt. Abigail had never seen anyone so handsome, so elementally powerful, and so commanding in her short life.

"Aww Cap'n, we wasn't gonna hurt her, we just wanted a little sport," one man volunteered.

"Fools, do I have to do all the thinking here as well as the fighting? That's Governor Rodger's daughter. Unspoiled she will bring us a handsome reward, but if she is damaged goods he probably won't even want her back,"

"It's not like she is going to admit the whole crew had a go at her, Cap'n."

"Nay, but that skinflint Rodger's will probably demand she be examined. Are you willing to risk casks of doubloons for a roll with the wench?"

The assembled pirates muttered under their collective breath, but none made any move to voice his objections if he had any.

"Pete, take her to my cabin and watch the door," The Pirate Queen said as she drew her sword, "Or perhaps one of you would care to argue with me about it?"

The men seemed very unhappy, but none seemed willing to take her up on that offer. A grizzled old man grabbed Abigail by the arm and practically dragged the dazed Englishwoman aboard the Raven. He led her into the Captain's cabin in the aftercastle of the ship and closed the door.

"Are you hurt?" he asked in a thick Irish brogue.

"No," she replied in a whisper.

"It was an ill wind that brought you here lass. I will do what I can for you, but my advice to you is to do whatever Lissa wants and stay out of trouble until your father can pay for you,"

"Why would you help me?"

"My name is Peter Lewllen and I came here on the Shark nearly thirty years ago,"

"The Shark? My grandfather's ship?"

"Aye lass, had the Captain not told us who you are I would have never known. Since I do know I will try to help you, I knew your grandfather well. God rest his soul,"

"He isn't dead. He lives on Manservant now. My grandmother is the one who passed away, God rest her soul,"

"Indeed? Then I shall have to go and see the old liar. He was always good to me, and I am getting to old for this line of work," the old man said with a grin, "Now you be a good lass and mind Lissa. She isn't as bad as you have heard, but she has the devil's own temper," he said as he left through the only door to the room.

Abigail wandered around the large room. A big four-poster bed sat on one wall with a night table and a washbasin beside it. A writing desk and chair were on another wall with a sideboard that held a crystal decanter and goblets on a silver tray. Two small cannons were set up facing outward, and Abigail realized that during the battle, they would be manned like any others. There was a heavy sea chest at the foot of the bed and a wooden table with four chairs. The room was richly appointed, but Abigail was surprised at how messy and mismatched it was. She would have expected it of a man's quarters but not a woman's; it definitely needed what her grandmother had always referred to as "a feminine touch."

She strayed to one of the stained glass windows and discovered that it would open, and she pushed against it and found herself looking out at the deck of Indomitable. The survivors were in a small group surrounded by pirates; she recognized Gerald, the Captain, Ansil, the cabin boy, and a few others. The mate was not among them nor the old cook. Lissa was pointing at Gerald with her sword and speaking.

"What on earth is that?"

"Damned if I know. Its dressed like a woman but I don't see no teats," one of the pirates jeered.

"Can't be a man so it has ta be a woman, but damned is she ugly," another called.

"Only one way to find out, strip it," Lissa ordered casually.

Gerald yelled and fought weakly as several pirates ripped his expensive clothes from him. When they stepped back, he was naked. His skin was even whiter under his clothes and reminded Abigail of a fish's belly. She had never seen a man naked, and her curiosity overcame her reluctance as she glanced between his stick-like thighs. His member was tiny and a bluish-purple color. It reminded her of the worms that she had seen floating in puddles of water after a rainstorm, and she was sorry she had looked.

The pirates all laughed and jeered. They were throwing insults at the nobleman, who stood there with his hands over his privates. Abigail was a sensitive soul, and even though she hated the man, she felt sorry for him. No one should have to face such humiliation. After a while, the tall woman spoke again.

"Enough, we have to get the booty aboard and get out of here,"

"Should we kill them all?" a burly pirate asked.

"Nay, I am in an expansive mood. Put them on the longboats and give them food and water for five days,"

"Aye, Cap'n"

"Now get the loot aboard and fire the ship, we are bound for the Tortugas."

A raucous cheer went up, and the pirates began to haul aboard everything on the small sloop they could use. Abigail watched as the men worked like ants, swarming from ship to ship with arms laden. In a little under three hours, they had stripped the sloop completely. A thin pirate descended into the hold with a lit torch and came running out to leap aboard the pirate ship as his mates hacked the lines, and the Raven began to pull away from her victim. Abigail watched the sloop from the window as flames began to lick up from below decks. Soon the beautiful little ship was engulfed in a raging inferno as pitch, tar, sailcloth, and wood succumbed to the hungry flames.

She heard the pirates calling out curses and insults as Raven overhauled and passed the two longboats. The Captain and his sailors refused to be baited and did not look up from the oars as the swift pirate barque overhauled them and then left them behind. Abigail said a prayer for the men in those boats.

She had just finished when the door opened, and the Captain sauntered in. She ignored Abigail and went to the sideboard, where she poured herself some of the amber liquid in the decanter. She then leaned against the sideboard and stared at Abigail. The eyes were green and deep, and the frank admiration in them made Abigail blush.

"You are far too pretty a prize for the likes of them," the pirate remarked at last. Her voice was softer now, still raspy but not harsh. The words were spoken in English with just a trace of a French accent.

"What are you going to do to me?"

"I think I will take you to my bed, at least until I tire of you. It shouldn't take long for your father to pay the ransom for you. He needs you to marry off to some fat, limpdicked heir no doubt,"

"You wouldn't dare!" Abigail said indignantly.

"Aye, why not? You're a pretty enough lass. Or perhaps you would prefer it if I turned you over to the crew?" the Captain replied, with just a trace of the harshness returning to her voice.

So the rumors are true, she thought. Abigail had never imagined doing anything with another woman. The scriptures forbid such relationships as unnatural and blasphemous. She felt trapped. Old Pete's advice had been to do what the Captain wanted, but did he know this was what would be demanded of her? For that matter, how far could she trust him? Her grandfather had never mentioned a Peter in his sea stories.

The pirate put her drink down and, with startling suddenness, crossed the few feet between them and pressed Abigail against the wall. The Englishwoman found her hands imprisoned in one of the pirate's and she felt the Captain's hard lips pressed against her own. She felt the redhead's tongue pressing against her lips, demanding entry, but Abby held hers tightly together. The Captain's free hand roughly seized one of her breasts and began to knead it. Abbey wanted to fight, but it felt wonderful, and she was powerless in the larger woman's grasp. When Lissa's fingers found her nipple and squeezed, Abbey gasped. Her lips parted for a fraction of a second, and the other woman's long tongue darted between them. Abbey was shocked, but as the warm tongue began to explore her mouth, she felt herself beginning to respond.

As the kiss continued, Lissa's other hand released her wrists and traced down her arm, producing a delicious tingling sensation. The pirate relinquished her hold on Abby's breast, and both of the pirate's hands journeyed down to her rear. Abigail gasped again when Lissa's seized a globe in each hand and dug her fingers into the yielding flesh. Abigail's own hands went to the pirate's chest to push her away, but Lissa pressed her thigh between Abigail's thighs. The contact with her cunny caused Abby to moan, and her arms slipped around the pirate's neck seemingly of their own accord. Lissa pulled away from her as suddenly as the attack had begun and laughed deeply.

"You English women are all the same. So prim and proper, but underneath lives the soul of a harlot. I have things to do, but I will be back this evening. You have until then to decide where you would prefer to spend your nights. I promise you my bed is more comfortable than the hold,"

After she left, Abby sat heavily in one of the chairs and began to cry.

Evening came all too quickly for the captive. She was in such a state of emotional turmoil that taking her own life occurred to her as the only way out. Knowing that it was a one-way trip to hell, she had discarded the idea and realistically assessed the two options that Lissa had given her.

On the one hand, she could stay with the handsome woman. While it was a blasphemy, it meant decent food, a warm bed, and at least some protection from being abused. On the other hand, she could be turned over to the crew. There was no less sin involved in fornication with all those men than there was in lying with a woman. The choice seemed very simple.

The problem was in her feelings. Abigail had never experienced anything like that single kiss with the Pirate Queen. In her sheltered life, she had not even kissed a man, and the few experimental kisses with her friends at the academy had been nothing like the exciting kiss of Black Lissa. While she could easily rationalize the choice she made and even ask forgiveness, she realized that she wanted to feel the tall woman's hands on her again. She had been in a state of excitement since the pirate had left her, and she wanted more. Does that make it more of a sin? She thought. I'm sure I can be forgiven if I'm forced into such a deed, but what if it isn't against my will? God help me.

The door opened, and she started, but it was only old Pete with a plate of food. He placed it on the table before her and turned to go, but then looked at her curiously and stopped.

"Are you all right lass?"

"No. That wicked woman wants me to join her in her bed! What shall I do?"

Old Pete looked at her and smiled. "Is it such a terrible fate? Most of the men in these Isle's would give their right arm for such an invitation,"

"But I am not a man and it's blasphemy!"

"Blasphemy doesn't go out here," Pete snorted, "For better or worse you are in the Carribs, if you want to survive you had better put your bible away. This isn't genteel society, its dog eat dog, and while you may lose your soul, if you try to play it by the good book you will definitely lose your life. Now eat up, if the Captain is going to tumble you, you will need the energy,"

Abigail picked at the food after the old man left. He seemed totally unconcerned with her plight. Abigail found her mind returning to the Pirate Queen and that single kiss. Just thinking of it caused her to flush and her breath to quicken. The priests had always told her that women were wanton creatures, and she was ashamed of the desire she felt.

The door opened again, and the tall pirate entered. She sat at the table across from Abigail and drank deeply from a bejeweled flagon. She seemed amused by the fear and trepidation she saw in Abigail's expression.

"Well my pretty, have you decided?"

"Yes," Abigail hesitantly said as she lowered her eyes.

"And?"

"I will stay with you," she murmured.

The redhead laughed softly, "I somehow thought you would," she said, "Come sit in my lap,"

Abigail rose slowly and moved around the table; the pirate turned her chair slightly and opened her arms. Abigail daintily seated herself in the woman's lap. Lissa's arms snaked around her waist and held her tightly. She felt the Captain's breath on her ear and then those soft yet hard lips on her shoulder. She felt herself shiver despite the warm night air.

"Your skin is so soft," the pirate whispered. Abigail shivered again as the warm breath of the pirate was replaced by the tip of her tongue. She felt a strange sensation in her stomach, a tightening that seemed to be almost painful, but not quite.

"Have you never shared your body with another woman?" Lissa whispered.

"No, never," Abby replied. The redhead's hands moved up to cup her breasts. She could feel their warmth through her chemise and dress. When Lissa gently squeezed them, Abby groaned.

"Relax then, I will show you everything," the pirate breathed, and then Abby felt Lissa's lips on her neck. This is so wrong, she thought, but the thought fled under the intensely pleasurable sensations Lissa's mouth and hands were causing. Abby was aware that something was happening to her, her nipples felt stiff and ached while her stomach was tight, and her cunny felt hot and itchy. Abby arched her back when she felt those wonderful hands gently pinch her aching nipples.

"You see?" the pirate whispered.

"Yess," Abby hissed.

The redhead's hands slid down her sides to her hips and then to the juncture of her legs. Abby was not sure what to do with her own hands and finally placed them both on the chair's arms to support herself. The pirate queen was slowly pulling her skirts up, and soon they were bunched around her waist. Only the thin linen of her pantaloons covered her most precious treasure now. Lissa cupped her sex then and pressed in gently with her fingers.

"Oh!" Abigail ejaculated as the strong bolt of pleasure shot through her.

"Have you never touched yourself there?" Lissa asked, sounding incredulous.

"No,"

"Good God woman, are you a nun?!"

Before Abigail could answer, the pirate's hands tugged the drawstring on her pantaloons' lose. Abigail felt one of the pirates' hands slide into her waistband and across the luxurious down of her pubic triangle. The Captain's fingers on her bare skin sent an electric charge through her, and she bit her lip to keep from crying out. A long, stiff finger pressed against her slick lips and then into the warm furrow of her slit.

"Oh God," Abby groaned.

"God can't help you now," the pirate said with a smirk. She then proceeded to gently stroke Abigail's cunny, making sure her finger brushed the Englishwoman's clit with each stroke. Abigail felt like she was about to explode. The tension was building in her, starting at the knot in her belly and radiating outward. She heard herself whimpering pitifully.

That finger, Abby thought. That finger is driving me insane. What's happening to me? Her hips began to rock of their own accord in the pirate's lap. Abby tried but could not stop them. Her breathing was ragged and punctuated by small squeaking sounds she had never made before.

The small woman shuddered once, violently, and then cried out as the damn burst and her first orgasm rocked her. A powerful contraction in her loins set it off, and then thick, heady waves of pleasure pulsed through her. Abigail tried to fight the rising tide, but it was too much. As the pirate's finger continued stroking her, Abigail was carried away on the tide of sensation and only slowly returned to her senses.

Abigail's first reaction was shame, but that did not last. Nothing had ever felt so good in her life. She blushed just remembering it, and then an aftershock rocked her small frame. If this is sin, then I am doomed, she thought.

"That's what your priests are trying to protect you from," the pirate said quietly.

"I never..." was all Abby could manage.

"No, but tonight you shall," Lissa said with a laugh. The pirate stood up and led Abigail to the bed, where she began the complicated procedure of undressing the English lady. Abigail felt the pirate's fingers deftly undoing the small buttons of her dress. Once it was loosened, the tall woman helped Abby out of it and attacked the complicated ties of her petticoats. Abigail cringed when she saw how much damage the pirates had done to the delicate garments. Once they were removed, she felt the exquisite relief of her corset and stays being removed. When she stood in her pantaloons and chemise, the pirate hugged her tightly from behind.

"Quite a bit of digging to get to that buried treasure,"

Abigail blushed then. She had been so impressed with the woman's skill in removing her clothes she had not even realized she was almost naked. The redhead's strong arms around her waist made her feel safe and protected, as well as tingly. Lissa gently nibbled on her ear, and Abigail felt that strange, but no longer frightful, tightening in her belly. The pirate released her and stepped back from her, and Abby turned to face her. Lissa caught hold of the hem of her shirt and whisked it over her head. The Captain's upper body was bronzed, like her arms and finely muscled. Her breasts were tiny, almost flat against her chest. Abigail could easily make out the ribs and the bands of muscle that crossed the tall woman's abdomen.

Lissa smiled and removed her sword belt, placing it over a hook near the headboard. Abigail realized that the hilt would be close to the woman's hand, even when she was sleeping. She also noticed a brace of pistols on the night table. Apparently, the Captain trusted her crew none too much. Lissa then sat on the bed and held her leg out.

"Help me off with these boots,"

Abigail held the toe and heel as the pirate pulled her foot out and then did the same for the other. Abby took both boots and carefully sat them at the foot of the bed, noting that Lissa seemed amused by this. The pirate untied the strings at her ankles and then stood and undid the drawstring at her waist, the breeches fluttered to the floor, and Abigail found herself staring. The pirate's legs were very long and shapely. Her hips were slim and almost boyish, but the fiery red pubic thatch and pouting lips of her sex left no doubt she was a woman. Abigail was stunned by the woman's beauty and by her aura of power.

Abigail's eyes seemed to be drawn to the woman's sex. Like a moth to a flame, she could not help herself. Abby had never seen another woman's cunny before. Even in school, she had been very sheltered. Abigail found herself staring at it in fascination.

"I apparently meet with your approval, how 'bout showing me your charms?"

Abigail blushed like mad and quickly averted her eyes. The small blonde had not been naked in front of another person since she was a child. It took a great deal of willpower for her to remove the little she still wore, but she had known this was coming and had been preparing herself for it all evening. She slowly raised her chemise over her head and folded it. When she turned back to face the pirate, she heard Lissa's sharp intake of breath.

"Go on,"

Abigail shyly undid the drawstring and let her pantaloons fall to the floor. She stepped out of them and stood naked before her captor.

"Gods, woman. With a body like yours how can you be so inexperienced? You were made for pleasuring," Lissa exclaimed.

Abigail smiled despite her fear; Lissa's praise made her feel so good. She had never received many compliments, and the pirate's admiration was welcome, even as it caused her to blush. She knew she should be ashamed, but curiously, she wasn't.

The pirate stepped forward, enfolded Abigail in her arms again, and bent her head to kiss the Englishwoman. This time her lips found Abigail's soft and yielding, and her tongue slipped easily into the sweet cavern of her captive's mouth. Abigail's arms twined around the redhead's neck. She was unsure of what to do, but her tongue seemed to know, and the kiss quickly became passionate and mutual.

When this kiss broke, Abby noticed that it was the pirate's face that was flushed. Lissa stooped, picked her up, and then fell on the bed, her body on top of Abby's. Abigail wasn't used to someone's weight upon her but found that she liked it. The pirate began to kiss and lick her neck, and she felt herself getting excited again.

Lissa's hands moved up her flanks to her stomach and then to the domes of her breasts. Abby groaned when Lissa took a tit in each hand and began to massage them. Lissa's mouth trailed down her chest, and when it engulfed one of her nipples, Abby cried out in pleasure. The pirate's mouth was warm and soft, and as her tongue began to flick over Abby's nipple, she moaned. It felt indescribable, a warm pleasurable feeling punctuated by jagged shocks of a more powerful nature with each caress of the redhead's experienced tongue.

Lissa moved from one nipple to the other while her hands continued to knead the soft flesh that surrounded them. Abigail wrapped her hands in the Pirates' luxurious hair and held her tightly to her breast. I hope this goes on forever, she thought. It was not to be, and soon the pirate's mouth traced down the bottom of one breast and along her sensitive tummy, stopping to nibble at her navel. She moved lower, then, kissing and licking towards the juncture of Abigail's thighs.

"W... What are you doing?" Abby managed. Her voice sounded husky and breathless.

"I am going to lick your cunny," the pirate said between kisses.

"Oh! You can't possibly! That's so wicked!"

"Aye, and you are going to love it, too, my little tart,"

Abigail tried to move, but the pirate lowered her face and kissed the top of the blonde's slit. Abigail's entire body spasmed, and her thighs gripped the pirate's head tightly. For a moment, she was paralyzed by the shock, and Lissa took advantage of it to force her tongue between the slick lips and gently drag it across Abby's clit.

"Oh my God," the blonde babbled.

Abigail was unprepared for the sensation that shot through her body. She cried out inarticulately as the redhead's tongue danced over her sensitized clit. Her hands clutched at the comforter as the gripping sensations tore at her sanity. This is so wrong, her mind screamed, but her body didn't care. Abigail felt like she was being devoured alive; the pirate's tongue seemed impossibly long and soft. She felt the now familiar clenching and unclenching of her inner muscles that announced her climax was near.

"No," Abigail moaned. She fought to keep herself from enjoying it. She knew she couldn't give in to the pleasure without losing her immortal soul, but it felt so good. In the end, she shrieked in pleasure as the bottle burst, and her orgasm ripped through her. She was swimming in a red tide of pleasure, but Lissa did not stop the stimulation, and before the powerful contractions had died, a second orgasm tore through her. She screamed then, a feral scream that startled her that it could have come from her lips. Lissa continued to lash her clit, and she felt another orgasm building.

Can she do this to me forever? Abigail thought. She was doomed now; she had enjoyed the pirate's blasphemous caress. Abigail ceased to fight and rode the waves of pleasure, oblivious to the deeper implications. Her final coherent thought was, God, help me. I never want this to end.

When she returned to herself, she was still on the pirate's bed on her back. Lissa was holding her and kissing her eyelids. Abigail remembered the pleasure, remembered what she had done. The shame was great but not as great as the wish to do it again.

"How do you feel?" Lissa whispered.

"I feel wonderful,"

"Good, now it's your turn,"

"My turn?"

Rather than answering, the female pirate disengaged herself and swung a leg over Abigail's head. Abby found herself looking close up at the woman's sex. Lissa's cunny was fat, her mount easily larger than Abigail's own. Her lips were prominent and a coral color that contrasted with the bronzed skin. They gaped open to expose the inner folds, which were very bright pink. The whole area was covered in the glistening sheen of her juices.

"I don't know what to do," Abby murmured.

621

"Just stick your tongue out and lick, I will make sure you find the right spots," the pirate said. Her fingers traveled down to pry her sticky lips apart, and she lowered herself until Abigail's nose was touching her pubic hair. Abigail tentatively put her tongue out and licked. The pirate's skin was velvety soft and glided beneath her tongue easily. Abby became aware of a strange flavor, one she had never tasted anything like before. It was sweet but tangy with undertones of salt. She could not believe it, but as her tongue returned to the pirate's lips, she admitted to herself that she liked it.

Abigail continued to lap at the Frenchwoman's slit like a cat, unsure if she was doing it right. She had given up on saving her soul and now just wanted to make the pirate feel as good as she had been made to feel. Lissa adjusted her hips and groaned.

"Yes, just there, but leave your tongue out," she hissed.

Abigail continued to lick, following the pirate's instruction, and soon Lissa's body stiffened, and she began to quake. Abigail remembered how good it had felt when Lissa continued as her orgasm rocked her, so she did not stop but redoubled her efforts.

"Yess... There... Oh! Oh gods, yes... Like that..." Lissa ejaculated. She then grabbed Abby's hair and began to grind her cunny into the Englishwoman's startled face. Abigail felt like she would drown as her nose and lips were covered in the pirate's copious juices. Eventually, Lissa calmed down and released her head. Abigail licked her lips tentatively, and then with more determination, she could not seem to get enough of the pirate's cream.

Lissa fell off of her and curled up into a ball. She shook as she hugged herself and then slowly uncoiled to stretch out on the bed. "Damn woman! I have been with harlots who couldn't make me feel like that!"

Abby moved to the pirates' side and smiled when Lissa enfolded her in her strong arms. It may be wrong, but I don't care, she thought. She took the pirate's rough words as praise, and for the first time in her life, she felt like she belonged, was wanted, and was appreciated. She drifted off to sleep with Lissa stroking her fine blonde hair.

Two days of clear weather and smooth sailing followed the night of her surrender to Lissa's caress. Abby was withdrawn and introspective, her mind in such turmoil she spent the days in a trancelike state or mechanically cleaning the stateroom to keep busy. Lissa seemed to understand and initiated no more physical contact, although when they ate, Abby could feel the pirate's eyes on her.

She awoke alone in the big bed on the third morning out. The room was too dark, and the ship creaked ominously. She hurriedly pulled on her dress and opened one of the windows. The sea was a roiling mass of angry gray waves. The horizon was lost in a haze, and the sky was the same leaden gray as the sea. She knew something was wrong, but her passage had been unusually calm, and Abby had never seen a storm at sea.

Throughout the morning, the size of the waves increased, and with them, the rocking of the ship. Abigail soon became violently ill and frequently vomited into a bucket. By the time the rains began, she was lying on the floor, holding onto the bucket, and was so weak she thought she would faint. The door opened, and the storm blew a spray of water in as Lissa entered. Abby was too sick to look up and just closed her eyes. She expected some rebuke or laughter, but all was quiet, save for the howling wind and creaking of timbers. Abby barely opened her eyes and found the prate gazing at her with pity on her face.

Lissa walked to a cabinet on the wall and took out a vial with a greenish liquid in it. She left then but returned shortly with a steaming jack of ale. Abby watched her through silted eyes. She was curious despite her misery. Lissa knelt next to her and gently lifted the blonde's head. She held the jack to Abby's lips, and when the smaller woman refused to drink, she pinched her nose shut. When Abby was forced to open her mouth to breathe, the pirate poured the warm ale in. Abby had no choice but to swallow, even though her stomach protested violently.

Lissa murmured endearments to her and gently stroked her hair. She cleaned Abby up with a wet cloth and then picked her up like a child and carried her to the bed. Abby impulsively hugged her, and the pirate stiffened and then stood up straight.

"Rest girl, let the medicine do its work," she said and stalked out of the cabin. Abigail was confused at the woman's reaction. It was almost as if she had been embarrassed that Abby had seen her being tender.

For three long days, the storm battered the ship. The wind howled and shrieked, and the waves crashed. Abby was sure it was divine retribution and waited for the sea to drag them under with a fatalism that was second nature to her. Whatever the Captain had forced her to drink, it was amazingly potent. Abby's seasickness abated, but she slept even through the worst of the storm, and when awake, she was very drowsy.

Sometime during the third night, the storm died out. Abby awoke to sunlight streaming in through the stained glass windows. She rose and relieved herself and was just straightening her dress when the door to the cabin opened, and Lissa stumbled in. She looked like she was dead on her feet, and when she stumbled again and caught herself on the corner of the table, Abby ran across the cabin to steady her.

The tall pirate was soaked to the bone and shivering. Abby began to work the heavy brass buttons of her waistcoat loose. Lissa tried to stop her, but Abby swatted the pirate's hands away and continued. The heavy fabric was soaked, and it was almost all Abby could do to get it off the tall pirates' shoulders. Once it was off her shoulders, it fell to the floor and lay there in a soggy pile. The white silk shirt was soaked too, and Lissa's breasts were easy to see through the nearly transparent fabric. Abby hesitated only a moment and undid the laces at the throat.

"Arr^t! Ne pas me toucher!," Lissa muttered. Abigail ignored her and pulled the silk shirt over the pirate's head. She dropped it onto the floor and started to work Lissa's belt, trying to ignore both the weapon and her captor's breasts. Lissa protested weakly but seemed incapable of doing more than slurring epitaphs. The belt came off, and Abby went to work on the drawers; these, too, were soaked, and she had a great deal of trouble with the knot. When it gave, she gently pushed Lissa, causing her to fall heavily into the chair behind her. The blonde knelt and removed the pirate's boots and breeches then, leaving her nude.

Now Abby was forced to look at Lissa's body. She had figure out how to get the taller woman into her bed. First, she found a semi-clean towel and dried the pirate's skin. She could not help but look, and to her intense shame, she found her eyes wandering to Lissa's cunny. She felt knotting in her stomach but tried to ignore it as she tried to lift the pirate from her seat.

"Vous etes une salope," Lissa muttered and tried to pull away from Abby. The little Englishwoman flinched at the harsh words but managed to get her arm around the pirate's back and hoist her to a semi-erect position.

"Vous ^tes une chienne"

"I am not a dog! I am trying to help!"

"Vous filth. Vous l'animal sale,"

"Oui, je suis!" Abby said matter of factly. This simple statement caused the pirate to stop, and then she grinned weakly. Lissa straightened somewhat and tried to help Abby get her to the bed. Abby staggered towards the big bed, supporting most of Lissa's weight. Like two drunks, they groped their way to the bed, with Lissa leaning heavily on poor Abby's shoulder. By the time she managed to let Lissa collapse on the bed, Abby was panting. She was not used to such exertion.

It was another two minutes of shoving, pushing, and coaxing before she finally got Lissa under the heavy blankets. Lissa was shivering even under the heavy blanket, and her skin was hot to the touch. She was calling out in French now and babbling in a mix of French and Spanish. Abby knew that high fevers sometimes made people delirious but could not remember what was to be done. She was not at all sure what to do next but decided that she had to stop Lissa from shivering first. Abby crawled into the bed and snuggled up close to the pirate. The thin linen of her chemise did little to block the heat radiating from the pirate's body.

Abby lay there holding the tall woman tightly, and slowly the Frenchwoman began to relax. Her shivering slowed and then stopped as their combined body heat made it almost unbearably hot for Abby under the blanket. She held Lissa tenderly and whispered comforting words to the pirate until she seemed to go to sleep. Abby lay there a long time, just holding Lissa close and listening to her ragged breathing. At some point, she must have dozed off, for she came suddenly awake to find the room suffused in dim light. Evening or Morning? She asked herself. It was impossible to tell. She was lying with her head in the crook of Lissa's arm but did not remember when the tall woman rolled over. Abigail propped herself up on one arm and looked at the woman next to her.

Lissa's hair was a tangled mess, but it was very beautiful, framing her angular face and softening it. Her breasts lay flat against her body with the long thick nipples standing out from the puckered aureoles. She looked so soft in sleep, so feminine without the swords and boots. Abby reached out and very gently traced her fingertip around Lissa's left nipple. Her skin was so soft, it felt like the finest silk to Abby, as her finger glided across it. Abby continued to gently trace her fingers around the stiffening nipple until Lissa moaned softly in her sleep.

Abigail was now curious, as well as aroused. She carefully slipped the blankets off the pirate, hoping not to wake her. Once the blankets were off, Abby took in the sight of Lissa's long shapely legs. The Englishwoman's eyes traveled up toward the juncture of her captor's legs, the treasure that was exposed there. Their first night together, there had been very little opportunity for Abby to really examine Lissa's cunny. Now she found herself drawn to it, her curiosity overcoming her reservations. Lissa's mound was plump and ripe, standing out prominently from her body. Her outer lips were full and gaped open slightly, allowing the inquisitive English woman to make out soft pink folds of the inner labia.

Abby carefully crawled between the pirates' legs, almost unconscious of what she was doing, gently moving them open until she could get a really close up view. She was now lying between Lissa's legs on her stomach, with her arms resting on the pirate's thighs. Abby very carefully pulled the pirate's lips apart and gazed at the bright pink of her most secret place. She examined it curiously, eventually zeroing in on the clitoral hood. Abby remembered how good Lissa had made her feel when she concentrated her tongue there. At least, Abby was pretty sure that this was the area where it had felt so intense.

Abigail felt strange, a tingling sensation from head to toe and the almost overwhelming desire to touch Lissa. Her mouth was watering, and she found herself sucking on her lower lip. Somewhere deep inside, a battle was raging, one of the heart's passions versus the ingrained teachings of the head. Two days of internal strife worked itself out in two long seconds. Screwing up her courage Abby lowered her face to Lissa's sex and gently ran her tongue along the satiny furrow. The flavor was different than she remembered, less sweet, tangier, with definite overtones of saltiness. When her tongue grazed Lissa's partially exposed clit the pirate groaned, and her eyes snapped open.

"Que est-ce qui a pass,?" Lissa murmured sleepily.

Abby started and blushed crimson. "I'm sorry, I didn't... I mean I don't... I..."

"Its all right ma cher, go ahead and take your time," Lissa said softly and spread her legs wide. Abby looked intently at the redhead's face, but the green eyes showed no contempt, only a tender amusement. Abby smiled unsurely and settled back down between the pirate's silken thighs. Her fingers gently explored the outside of Lissa's flower, stroking her mound and reveling in the soft feel of her skin. She noticed that Lissa's cunny was becoming damp, and a strong, musky aroma was beginning to become evident. Abby traced her finger along the pirate's lips and found sticky wetness on her fingertip. She brought it to her nose and daintily sniffed at it. Abby wrinkled her nose, causing Lissa to chuckle.

Abby looked up, hoping for some instruction, but the green-eyed woman was merely watching her. The little blonde touched the tip of her tongue to her finger, and the strong flavor of Lissa's cream filled her mouth. She moved her face back and began to lap at Lissa's cunny, searching for more of the magic elixir. After a while, the pirate's sex glistened with the mixture of Abby's saliva and her juices. Abby noticed that Lissa's hips had begun to make small jerking motions. Abby looked up again to see Lissa's head was thrown back, her eyes closed, and a dreamy, far-away expression was on her face. Abby thought she looked like she was in heaven and returned to her feast.

Soon she earned what she really wanted, for the pirate uttered a few exclamations and then tangled her hands in Abby's flaxen tresses. Lissa firmly guided Abby's mouth to her erect clit.

"There, little one, right there, Mmmmm yes,"

The small organ was erect, smooth, and slick, like a pebble coated in oil, Abby thought. She licked at it tentatively, producing a shudder from the redheaded pirate. Abby remembered the pirate's tongue lashing back and forth over her bud and emulated it, moving her tongue frantically as Lissa's hips began to bounce.

"Oh... Gods!... Ohhhhh..."

Abby sucked hard, pulling the button completely from its cave, and pressed her lips tightly over it. Lissa shrieked, and her whole body seemed to quiver. Abby felt a flood of wetness on her chin but refused to release her hold on Lissa's clit. She kept at it, driving the pirate to a second orgasm and then a third. Finally, Lissa pulled her head away and sat up. Wrapping Abby in her arms, she lay back, dragging the smaller woman on top of her.

"Mon Deau!"

Abby lay there, cradled to the pirate's breast. After a while, Lissa begun to stroke her hair and gently rock her. Abigail had not realized how anxious she had been over Lissa's health or how much the constant emotional turmoil had taken out of her, and she fell asleep almost instantly, with a contented smile on her face.

After that night, Abby's life fell into something resembling a routine. She woke each morning to go help the cook get breakfast ready for the crew. His name was Enrico, and he was from Madrid. They became fast friends when he discovered she could speak Spanish. He seemed to enjoy conversing in his tongue. He was not a bad man, but rather an unlucky one who had crossed the wrong man in the matter of a lady. His choices had been piracy or the goal.

After that, she would clean up the stateroom and then spend some time on deck watching the men and the sea. She got to know many of the crew and was startled when she realized they were nothing like their evil image. They were happy men, who sang and danced, joked with one another, and generally seemed more of a family than any she had known.

Rolf, the first mate, had come out on a Dutch trader and spent two years in a Spanish goal for smuggling. He was a taciturn man but had a kind heart, which he infrequently showed her. The navigator was a Scotsman named Cavendish who certainly could look fearsome, but he also laughed easily and played the harp at night for the men. There were a few bad ones, but Abigail avoided them, and they steered clear of her. No one seemed ready to brave Lissa's ire, and Abigail sensed she was something of an oddity to the crew.

In the evenings, after dinner, she would sew or read. The hold was filled with booty, including many books. She learned from one of the men that Lissa expressly forbids them to damage books. Once the late watch came on, Lissa would come to her. Every night it seemed the Frenchwoman would take her to new heights of passion, and Abigail slowly learned to bring her captor as much if not greater pleasure.

One day she decided to give the Captain's stateroom a feminine touch or two. It grew from a bit of cleaning to a major project. She made several changes, even enlisting some of the men to help her move furniture around. When she was done, the room looked very nice while remaining comfortable. Lissa seemed amused by her efforts at being a homemaker but said nothing. That night the sex was better than it had ever been, and Abigail went to sleep very content.

The next evening they sighted a ship, and when it hailed them, men were sent out in the longboat. Abigail watched from the forecastle as the little schooner with the white flag raised took the pirates onboard. The party returned with a paper that Lissa read. Abby would find cause to wonder what it said, for everything changed, and her happiness was slowly crushed out of her from the moment that letter arrived.

That night Lissa was demanding in bed and seemed irritated. Nothing Abby did was right, and after a short while, the pirate threw her from the bed and went to sleep. Abby spent a miserable night curled up in a chair. She was uncomfortable, but what really made her miserable was Lissa's anger.

It got no better the next day. Lissa confined her to the stateroom, and when she forgot and went up on deck, it was bad. The tall woman saw her and bounded across the deck to deliver a stinging backhanded slap. She then proceeded to kick, curse, and beat her as Abigail frantically tried to get back into the Captain's quarters. Lissa stripped her and stowed her clothes in the sea chest with the big iron lock.

"Go out like that whore," she sneered as she left.

Abby cried for hours, her world had been turned upside down, and she had no idea why. She didn't have the slightest inkling of what she had done wrong or how to make it right. All she knew was that she hurt, was embarrassed by her nakedness, and was wretchedly lonely.

Lissa stalked in late that night, reeking of rum; Abigail looked fearfully at her. The green eyes burned with a strange intensity that only frightened her more. Lissa did not say a word but crossed to where Abigail was sitting and forced her to her knees. The Captain undid the drawstring on her breeches and then dug her hands into Abby's blonde locks. Lissa pulled the scared girl's face tightly against her cunt and began to grind it against Abby's lips and nose. Abby was so shocked she didn't even protest as Lissa ground herself to orgasm and then pushed her away. The pirate pulled up her breeches and stalked out of the room, leaving Abby in a daze on the floor.

For the rest of the week, it continued in this fashion. Lissa would use her whenever she seemed to want it but would otherwise avoid her entirely. Eventually, even this contact ceased. The pirate took to sleeping on deck and not even coming to the stateroom for sex. Abigail felt lonely, trapped, and utterly miserable.

This is my punishment, she thought often. My punishment for enjoying that woman's blasphemous caress. Abigail found it even more unbearable because she longed for the Frenchwoman's touch. Even the short, brutal, one-sided attacks were better than being totally ignored.

Lissa came in one morning nearly a week later. She opened the sea chest and tossed Abby her dress and petticoats.

"Get dressed. A ship lies off the beam and your father has brought the ransom,"

Abigail dutifully dressed and followed the pirate out onto the deck. The sun was brilliant, and it stung her eyes after the long period indoors. When they had adjusted, she saw a large Brig anchored off a beautiful little cove. There was a pretty white beach with lush green foliage behind it. She recognized the union jack flying from the masthead of the Brig. She was none too gently lowered into a longboat, and the men began to pull on the oars. Lissa sat across from her and stared ahead, seemingly lost in thought. Once they were aboard the Brig, a man she recognized as her father met them.

"Are you hurt child?" he asked in that cold voice she remembered from childhood.

"No father, I am fine,"

"Then they have not..."

"Her maidenhead is intact," Lissa interrupted, "She is still fresh as a daisy for her waiting husband."

"Is this true?" her father asked.

"No man has touched me father," Abigail said with her eyes downcast. She knew her face was crimson. It was discomforting to be talked about as if she were not human but a breeding animal.

"Very well, there is your ransom pirate. Enjoy it while you may. I will personally come to see you swing from the yardarm when they catch you,"

The pirates hauled the chests aboard the longboat while both parties stood facing one another in uncomfortable silence. When the ransom was aboard the longboat, Abigail watched them row back to the ship. The Raven's sails unfurled, and the ship moved quickly out of the cove. Abigail watched until it was just a dot on the horizon. Even with the abuse, she knew her heart was still on that ship. She wept then, finally giving vent to the emotions she had tried to keep in check all morning.

Tomorrow was her wedding day, but Abigail was past caring. She had been in her father's home for over a month now, but she had not found the ability to smile. Her days were haunted by the constant presence of her husband to be, who survived the long trip in the longboats. Her nights were haunted by the Pirate queen who had opened her eyes to sensual pleasure and stolen her heart.

She sat at the vanity in her room, idly brushing her hair. She had dismissed Rosa, the Spanish girl her father had hired to be her maid. She looked up as the door opened, and a gray-haired man entered.

"Grandfather!" she exclaimed, rushing into the old man's arms.

"How is my little Angel?" he asked after the embrace broke.

"Miserable."

"Oh? This is supposed to be the happiest time of your life. Sit down and tell me all about it child."

Abigail sat on the bed and told the old man everything, omitting only the nights of passion with Lissa. When she finished, the wise-old eyes stared at her. She felt he knew what she had left out exactly and blushed a deep crimson.

"And you met the Black Queen herself?"

"Yes, grandfather."

"What did you think of her?"

"Old Pete is still alive. I never would have believed it," her grandfather said when Abby hesitated. He seemed to know that questions about the pirate captain would be uncomfortable to her and avoided them. She wished her father were more like his father.

"Why have you never spoken of him?" she asked.

"He was my first mate. I never spoke of him because it wasn't good form. I was a privateer lass, but I also took a prize here and there that warn't Spanish. You see child, I was a pirate as well. Your grandmother knew of course, but it was a secret we kept from the rest of the family,"

"Grandfather, I don't want to marry this man. Isn't there anything that can be done?"

"That, my child, is up to you," the old man said, rising, "If you have any of your old Grampy in you, you will not stand for it, but rest now. I will speak to my son and see if there is naught I can do,"

Her wedding day was upon her. Abigail had given up all hope when her grandfather had returned and said her father was adamant. He would not allow her to break her engagement even when the old man threatened to cut him out of the will. So now she boarded the carriage that would take her to mass with her betrothed. Gerald wore his finest outfit, a broadcloth waistcoat and velvet trousers with a ludicrously large codpiece. Her grandfather was standing there as they boarded the fine coach; he waved at her and then gave her a wink. The same one he had often given her when she was a child, and he had sneaked her outside the house to play behind his wife's back. She wondered what it could mean.

After mass, she would return to the big house and don her wedding dress. From there, she would ride to the church and be married. She didn't dare contemplate what would happen after that. In all honesty, she had almost made up her mind to take her own life rather than face eternity as Lady Abercrombie.

The carriage rolled slowly out into the street. It was a big day, and people crowded the plaza to get a look at the blushing bride. Abigail was staring out when she saw a familiar face. She turned her head to get a closer look and recognized Enrico. The pirate cook gave her a wink. Abigail recognized others in the crowd, Rolf, Old Pete, and Diego among them. She looked forward and sat back, not sure what she should do.

"Is something the matter my pet?" Gerald asked.

"Nothing," she responded automatically.

"I know it is a lot of excitement," he said as his hand rested on her knee. "But soon it will be just the two of us in our bedroom," The unwanted contact and his lecherous smile made her want to slap him.

With a sudden shout and the firing of a pistol, the pirates attacked the carriage. Rolf grabbed the horses and held them steady while Diego knocked the driver unconscious. Enrico bounded into the carriage and grappled with Gerald. Old Pete pulled the footman off the back and held the onlookers at bay with his other pistol and cutlass.

Gerald fought like a man possessed. He had been humiliated once, and against the small pirate, he seemed to feel he had the advantage. Abigail was pushed onto her back as the two fought.

"Hurry up ya damned fool!" Pete exclaimed as the surprise of the attack started to wear off, and the men of the village began to approach.

Gerald managed to throw Enrico to the floor of the carriage and draw his sword. He was standing on the seat and, with a vicious laugh, prepared to run the small man through. Abigail reacted instantly and shot out her leg. Her delicate boot impacted upon the large codpiece, and Gerald was flung over the seat with a screech. Diego and Rolf snapped the traces, and the horses began to run. Old Pete discharged his second pistol causing the men to dive for cover.

"Thank You, Senorita," the little pirate said as he sat in the seat next to her.

"No, thank you. But why have you done this?"

"Captain's orders," the little man grinned, but would answer no more questions.

Abigail was surprised when the carriage stopped near a small bay, and she saw the Raven riding at anchor. They had been riding for over three hours, and she was totally lost. On the beach, a longboat waited to take them to the ship. Once aboard, she was ushered into the Captain's cabin. She noticed the men all smiled at her and seemed happy to have her back aboard. It made her feel good inside to be back among those she considered friends.

Inside, Lissa stood staring out a window at the sea with her back to Abigail. She wore her customary black outfit, but curiously not her swords. She did not turn to face Abigail, and after a while, the silence became unbearable.

"Why have you brought me here?" Abby blurted out.

Lissa sighed heavily and collapsed into the plush chair behind her writing table, the very chair Abby had slept in that first bad night. Abigail saw it then, the lines in her beautiful face and the bags under her eyes. Her whole body spoke of deep fatigue, and her eyes were red.

"I am a child of the sea lass. Always she has been my mistress, and never have I longed for any other. Then I met you. After having you with me the sea has lost its charm, the once vibrant blues are pale. I ransomed you to your father without a thought, but as the days passed I realized that I missed you, more than I could ever have foreseen,"

"I thought you hated me? You beat me and then ignored me?"

"I tried to treat you like a thing, to make you less than human. I was afraid of what I felt for you, afraid of the consequences, but when I heard you were to be married off to some fat plantation owner's son I grieved. I became listless and my control over the crew began to slip. Old Pete held them together until they had reached the breaking point. He came to me then and sobered me up, told me what I knew but didn't want to admit,"

Abigail was confused. She had never seen Black Lissa in any state other than completely in control. While she was a prisoner here, again, she suddenly felt as if she were the captor.

"What was it you admitted?' she asked finally in a quiet voice.

"You really don't know do you?" the redheaded woman asked with amusement and sorrow both showing on her face.

"No, I don't," Abby admitted.

"Then I am lost," the woman said, a tear forming in her eye. Abigail saw how red they were. It had not been a trick of the light.

"I... don't understand,"

The tall woman sighed heavily and stood up. She moved to stand directly before Abigail and then spoke in a quiet and utterly defeated voice.

"Then I shall tell you. I am in love with you Abigail Rodgers. I had hoped to rescue you from a forced marriage. I thought to keep you as my prisoner, as I had before, but I cannot. I never wish to hurt you again."

Abigail was shocked. She could not believe she had heard a profession of love from this woman. She simply stood there in stunned silence. Lissa stared at her with an expression that spoke of forlorn hope. When Abigail did not respond at all, the woman's face returned to the sorrowful expression Abigail had seen when she was first brought before the pirate queen.

"I will have my men return you to the island," Lissa said abruptly and turned on her heel. Her hand was on the door before Abby found her voice.

"Wait!" she called out.

Lissa turned and looked over her shoulder, "Yes?"

"I do not wish to return,"

"As you will. I will take you wherever you wish to go, even back to England if that is your desire."

"You misunderstand me, I do not wish to leave this ship, or your side. I have never known such happiness as those days when you were kind to me. I love you too, but I will not be beaten and abused. If you truly want me for your own, then I accept, but only as your. God, words fail me,"

"Wife?" the pirate asked with an arched eyebrow.

"Yes, blasphemy as it is. Only as your wife, not as your concubine,"

"Very well. A wedding was planned for today, and a wedding there shall be!"

In a small cove on the north end of the island, the Raven rode at anchor. The ship creaked and groaned in the slight breeze. Small breakers caused the great ship to rock gently, like a crib in a mother's hand. It was a very good omen, as old Pete would say.

Abigail had spent the rest of the day and most of the evening in the Captain's quarters. At dusk, the mate and some sailors had hauled a large bronze tub in. Enrico had smiled at her and backed out after it had been filled with hot water. Fragrant oils had been added, and the steam smelled deliciously like roses. Abigail had been unable to resist the urge to take a relaxing bath. She had dozed in the warm, sweet-smelling water and awakened only to find the water cold.

She rose and began to dry herself when she noticed the dress on the bed. It was beautiful, made of the finest lace and brocade. It was a wedding dress, and she wondered just where it had come from. Probably booty from a captured ship, she thought with the trace of a smile. Whoever had ordered, it had had a penchant for lace and brocade; she had never seen such an elegant gown. She carefully dressed herself then, feeling excitement and apprehension as well. The underthings were also of the finest materials and felt exquisite against her skin. She had just pulled her veil down when there was a knock at the door.

"Who is it?"

"Tis me mi'lady. Old Pete,"

"Come in," she said and laughed when she saw the old pirate in a fine waistcoat and breeches. He looked so totally uncomfortable that she was unable to keep from giggling.

Pete smiled back and led her to a longboat that rowed them to the shore. All the men wore their best, and all smiled at her and wished her happiness. Once onshore, she saw that a large fire had been built. There were a lot of people around it drinking and eating, many were prostitutes, but she recognized a few women from town who apparently had lovers among the crew. She also recognized many of the people who had traveled from other British possessions to be at her wedding. Try as she might, she could not explain that to herself.

One man, she did not recognize. He wore a black cape and kept away from her, always in the shadows. He seemed familiar, but she could not quite put her finger on his identity. Cavendish played a few songs, and she danced with many of the men and soon forgot the mysterious stranger. It wasn't the formal wedding she had always dreamed of, but it was infinitely nicer.

She caught a glimpse of Lissa as she and several of the pirates approached the fire. They seemed to be leading a captive, but she wasn't sure. When Lissa came into the firelight, Abigail forgot all else. The tall pirate wore a broad-brimmed black hat with a plume. A velvet waistcoat of Navy blue with lots of shining brass buttons and black breeches. She also wore her sea boots and swords. Abigail smiled when she noticed Lissa also wore a codpiece. She was without a doubt the most handsome creature Abigail had ever seen. Lissa held up her arms, and the music ceased. All eyes were upon the Pirate Queen.

"My friends, you have come here today to witness my wedding. My bride as many of you know is a God fearing woman, and so we have to do this right. Bring the padre," she called. The man who had been held captive was brought forward. He was obviously a priest of some status, and Abigail blanched when she realized he was the very priest who was to have married her to Gerald.

Lissa looked at her then, with those green eyes sparkling. Abigail was touched; she knew the pirate did not believe in her God. This then was totally for her. It made her want to burst with the affection she felt for the handsome pirate.

"You cannot expect me to do this!" the priest protested, "Tis blasphemy of the vilest sort!" Lissa turned on him and glowered. The fat priest took a step backward, his indignation seemingly less powerful than Black Lissa's stare.

"My dear father, tonight there will be a wedding or a funeral on this beach. You may preside at the wedding or be guest of honor at the funeral. The choice is yours," Lissa said easily.

"Even black hearted rogues of your sort would not kill a man of the cloth!"

"Of course not. Luckily I have two men in my crew who don't see you as a priest," she said, indicating the two giant Negroes, "they see you as a white devil,"

Abigail knew the two men somewhat. They were brothers from Africa, but both had been educated in France. They looked fearsome but were two of the gentlest men she had ever met. She had liked them both but never had learned their names. It seemed they were unpronounceable in English.

When the priest saw them, he swallowed hard. He started to speak again, but Lissa nodded to the blacks, and both drew their swords. In the flickering firelight, the taller of them winked at Abby.

"Well, since she is a good daughter of the church I suppose I must do all I can to help," the priest said, visibly paling.

"Of course Padre," Lissa said with a smile. She walked to where Abby was sitting and offered her hand. When she rose, they stood before the priest, who was busy getting his vestments on.

"A final surprise for you my love," Lissa whispered. Abigail was not able to ask what it was for the priest who had begun the ceremony. He seemed rushed as if he wanted to get this over with and get away. When he came to the part in the ceremony where he asked, "And who gives this woman away?" a silence fell.

Abigail had assumed Old Pete would give her away. He was the closest to her of the crew, but the old pirate just smiled at her and shook his head when she looked at him.

"I do," a strong voice called, and the mysterious stranger stepped into the light. Even before he threw off his cape, Abigail recognized him, "Grandfather!" she exclaimed and rushed into his arms.

"Of course," the old man smiled, "Did you think I would miss my angel's wedding?"

The old man took her hand and led her back to where Lissa was standing with a radiant smile. He gently placed her hand in the pirates. When the ceremony ended, Lissa pulled back Abby's veil and kissed her tenderly. A great cheer went up from the crowd, and soon the music was going again as rum flowed into every cup.

Abby drank little and spent most of the evening just holding Lissa's hand. The pirate received the congratulations of each crew member, and from several people, Abigail recognized now as friends of her grandfather. She understood now that her grandfather had gotten word to Lissa of what was going on. He had given the pirates the time when they could best take her without bloodshed. She had always loved the old man, but now she loved him even more than ever.

It was late in the evening when Lissa led her to an awaiting longboat. Her grandfather was there and hugged her once more.

"Thank you," Abigail said with tears in her eyes.

"No tears my angel. This is a happy time. I will see you again, for my home in Monserrat overlooks a sheltered cove. Now go with your beloved and may God smile upon you both,"

"Do you think he can?" she asked suddenly serious.

"Of course he can child. He made you both, and allowed you to meet and fall in love. If he did not intend it to happen it would never have been so."

She hugged him again and took Lissa's hand as the pirate helped her into the boat and then joined her. The four crewmen pulled at the oars and the warm Caribbean night surrounded them. She could smell the saltwater and hear the wood creak and waves lap against the hull. Abigail leaned against Lissa and felt deep contentment. Her grandfather's words dispelled the last of her reservations.

Soon they boarded the Raven and made their way to the Captain's cabin. Lissa opened the door but stopped Abigail as she started to enter. Abigail looked at her questioningly and was startled when Lissa scooped her up in her arms.

"I believe tis customary for me to carry you across the threshold, is it not?"

"It is indeed," Abigail said with a smile.

Once inside, the pirate gently placed her on the deck. They went to the sideboard, where she poured them both a drink. She handed one goblet to Abby and then raised her own, "To us."

The amber liquid turned out to be a rich peach brandy. Abigail took a second sip and then a third. Soon her goblet was empty. She felt excited and flushed but curiously shy considering all that had passed between herself and the dashing Captain. For her part, Lissa seemed nervous and ill at ease. They both stared at each other for a long time, and then Abigail began to giggle. Lissa laughed too and embraced her tightly. Their lips met in a passionate kiss; Lissa's tongue explored Abigail's mouth while the smaller woman sucked gently on it.

When the kiss broke, Lissa retrieved a small wooden chest and placed it on the table. She opened it to reveal an unbelievable number of gemstones. Abby saw diamonds, rubies, emeralds, and all manner of lesser gems. Lissa smiled and said, "This is my wedding gift to you,"

"There must be a king's ransom there. I could buy The Brambles with that," Abby blurted out, "but I have no gift to give you!"

"Really?" Lissa said with an enigmatic smile, "I was under the impression that you do, but we shall see."

The tall pirate stepped closer and enfolded Abby in her arms. Abigail looked up in time to see the redhead bend to press her lips against Abby's. At the first contact, Abigail's lips parted, and the Frenchwoman's tongue slipped between them. As Lissa's tongue unhurriedly explored her mouth, Abby gently caressed the pirate's tongue with her own. Abby tentatively pressed her tongue against Lissa's, and the pirates withdrew. Emboldened, Abby thrust her tongue into Lissa's mouth. The pirate's mouth tasted of brandy and rum, and soon Abby's tongue was tingling, but she also found small pockets that tasted all together different; she sought out these pockets as her tongue explored Lissa's mouth. She felt the pirate's teeth, caressed her pallet and the insides of her cheeks. Lissa groaned and thrust her tongue back into Abby's mouth. Their tongues twined then, pressing and slipping against one another as their embrace tightened.

"Gods! You set my blood on fire," Lissa exclaimed when the kiss finally broke. Abby smiled and kissed the pirate queen's chin.

Lissa bent, gently kissed her nose, and began to undo the many buttons and ties of the dress. Abby felt like it would never come off and helped where she could. In no time, Abby was standing in her stockings and boots with her clothes strewn on the floor about her. Lissa picked her up in her arms and kissed her again as she moved to the bed and dumped Abby onto it. She stood back and removed her hat and sword belt.

Abby could not take her eyes off the handsome pirate as she stripped off her shirt and removed the codpiece. Lissa stared at Abby as she undid the drawstring of her pants and eased them down.

"My God!" Abby exclaimed as she stared. Around the pirates' slim waist was a broad girdle. Attached to the front of it was a large black phallus. Lissa laughed at her bride's embarrassment and stroked the large shaft.

"Like it?"

"I... Where... How?"

"The crew had it made for me in Tortuga. Their wedding gift to us. I flatter myself that the size of it reflects their respect for me,"

The pirate moved to the bed and sat holding a leg up. Abby quickly helped her out of her high sea boots. Lissa spread her legs, and Abby knelt to examine the dildo. She touched it carefully and felt the smooth, warm leather.

"How does it work?"

"Well, it serves as a substitute for the real thing. Men who have been maimed have them made as well as ladies of a certain temperament."

Abby traced her finger along the thick shaft, "Can you feel that?"

"No, but watching you do it is certainly exciting enough."

"If you can't feel it how does it work?"

"Well, it sits upon the seat of pleasure," the Captain replied, indicating the base. "When we are in the act it should feel very good rubbing against me."

"Should?"

"I have never used one before. I have never wished to be a man in bed, until I met you. I hope to be the husband you have dreamed of," Lissa said earnestly. Abigail searched her face for some hint of mockery but found none.

"Will it hurt?" she asked quietly.

"Yes. The first time is always painful, and you may bleed a good deal,"

"Then why use it? You know how to make me feel so good without it."

"Because you are my bride, and I intend to claim you. After the first time it will not hurt and you will grow to love it. At least most wenches I know who have been on the receiving end of one have."

Lissa reached down and caught Abby's hands, and gently pulled her up. She then fell backward onto the bed, dragging the smaller blonde on top of her. Abby yelped in surprise and then giggled before they kissed again. As the pirate worked her tongue into Abby's mouth, the little woman could feel Lissa's hands on her ass.

Lissa's hands were warm and slid across the satin flesh before digging into each globe to roughly massage them. Abigail groaned as Lissa continued to work on her behind, first a deep rough massage, then feather-light stroking. She had no idea that part of her anatomy would react so strongly to the pirate's touch. Abby nearly bit Lissa's tongue in surprise when the pirate's finger began to gently massage her rear entrance. The sensation was at once stimulating and relaxing. The big pirate probed at Abby's rear with her finger, slowly working her finger against the Englishwoman's sphincter until it relaxed enough for her to push her finger in up to the first knuckle.

Without warning, the pirate rolled over, taking the smaller woman with her. Abby found herself on her back with Lissa lying on her. She had been in this position before, but she was very aware of the long hard object that was pressed against her belly. Lissa's mouth moved from Abbey's lips to her neck and slowly downward, stopping to lick, suck and nip seemingly without any rhyme or reason. Abby felt that delicious tightening sensation in her belly, the one she had at first dreaded but now relished. Her time away from the pirate had only made her want it more, and she laughed when she realized how wanton she was becoming.

When Lissa's mouth captured a stiff nipple and began to suck and worry it with her tongue, Abby forgot all else. She sighed and moaned, tangling her hands in the thick red tresses of her lover as the sensations grew from mildly pleasurable to intense. Lissa moved from one to the other, licking, sucking, even using her teeth to nip and tug at Abby's nipples until the Englishwoman felt she would go mad. Lissa made her feel wonderful in the past. But the pirate seemed determined to drive her insane on this, their first night as husband and wife.

Lissa moved lower, tracing her tongue down Abigail's sensitive skin to the pubic triangle and then even lower. Abby was beside herself now, and her hands stole to her breasts to roll and massage her nipples. The redhead attacked her slit with tongue and mouth, working the entrance, the lips, and the soft inner folds but avoiding the stiff clit. Abby was moaning continuously now and tossing her head from side to side. When her hips began to jog involuntarily, it seemed to be the signal the big woman had been working towards.

Lissa rose to a kneeling position between Abby's splayed thighs and situated herself. Abby watched through silted lids as Lissa grasped her cock and began stroking it slowly up and down Abby's inflamed lips. Abby was mildly concerned about the size of it, but it felt so good caressing her that she didn't even think to protest.

When the head was slick with her juices, Abby felt Lissa probing the entrance to her body. By now, all thoughts of pain and fears were secondary to the burning desire she felt. She concentrated on relaxing her body and holding still for her lover. Lissa lined up the big cock and held it on target with one hand while she slowly worked her hips forward. She seemed to be having trouble keeping it where she wanted it and getting enough pressure to force it forward. Lissa changed her angle of approach and, with a frustrated snort, forced her hips forward.

Abby gasped when the bulbous head forced past the inner lips and into her virgin channel. It seemed to be huge, filling her and stretching her. She felt fear clutch at her heart then; surely it would rip her open? Lissa seemed to sense her fear and did nothing more, just holding it there and gently stroking her thighs until her bride adjusted to having the head inside of her. The tall pirate carefully leaned forward, supporting her weight on her hands until she was looking directly into Abby's face.

"Abigail, you must relax. Twil hurt for a short span of moments, but not long if you relax. If not there will be a great deal of pain. I promised myself I would never hurt you again, you have to help me here."

Abby nodded, and Lissa smiled down at her. Abby saw such love and concern in those green eyes that it made it feel as if her heart would burst. Lissa was still smiling, talking quietly to her when she drove forward without warning. Abigail had never felt such pain, a tearing pain deep inside of her body. A second lunge and the big dildo tore through the last shreds of her maidenhead and buried itself deep inside of her. The pain subsided to be replaced by a sensation of being filled that was strange but pleasurable. Abby became aware of Lissa kissing her cheeks and eyelids and murmuring endearments to her.

"It's all right," Abby managed.

The worried look in her pirate's eyes was replaced with the love and happiness she had always longed to see there. Abby forgot her pain and wanted only to please this woman for the rest of her life.

"The deed is done. We can stop now and let you rest if you wish," Lissa said softly.

"If you stop now, I will never speak to you again," Abby said, smiling. As the memory of the pain faded, the arousal of having Lissa so close reasserted itself. She still felt a throbbing ache deep within her loins, but the fullness she felt was partial compensation, and the electric contact of her skin with Lissa's was too delightful to dwell on the pain.

Lissa smiled down on her and carefully reset her legs. She drew back a bit, causing the cock to retreat a bit, and then let her weight take it back. Abby gasped, not sure if it was pain or pleasure that she felt.

"Wrap your legs around me. It will make it easier and reduce the pain," Lissa whispered. Abbey did as she was bidden and found that it did seem to make it less painful. Lissa slowly got used to what she was doing and established a rhythm of sorts. Her motions were still tentative and experimental, but with each passing moment, she became more bold and confident. Abby gritted her teeth but refused to let Lissa see her discomfort. If it were important to her lover to do this, then Abby would not let her down.

As the dildo slid in and out, it became coated in her juices. The lubrication eased the friction until it was sliding in and out without the painful friction she had felt earlier. The sensation of being full, then empty, then deliciously full again soon became extremely enjoyable, and Abby found herself pushing her hips upwards to meet Lissa's downward thrusts. Now both began to enjoy the pleasure of it without having to worry about pain. Abby heard herself begin to moan and whimper, and the peculiar squeaking sounds began again. Lissa had her eyes closed. It was evident to Abby that she was enjoying it and was fighting her climax to prolong Abby's pleasure.

Abbey would never know how long it went on. A minute? An Hour? An eternity? All she knew was she was riding the waves of pleasure towards a shattering orgasm, and when it came, it was overwhelming in its intensity. She screamed when the dam burst, a scream of pleasure so loud it totally eclipsed Lissa's shout of joy.

When they came down, they were still entertained. Lissa was gently stroking her hair. Abby heaved a great sigh of contentment. Lissa was still inside her, but the dull ache was nothing compared to the joy she felt. She was almost sorry when her lover pulled out and rolled over next to her.

No words were exchanged, just kisses and a warm embrace. Abby fell asleep with her head in the crook of Lissa's arm.

She awoke alone in the big bed. The sheets were gone, and she was shivering. The rolling motion told her Raven was no longer at anchor, and the sounds of the sea against the hull made her sure they were in the open sea. Abby donned her dress as quickly as she could and made her way onto the deck. A stiff, cool breeze filled the sails and caused her to shiver again.

She made her way to the aftercastle, where Lissa stood at the wheel. She wore breeches and a shirt of linen today, both white as the sails. Her red hair was flying free, and her sword belt was back around her hips.

Abby moved next to her and was grateful when Lissa removed one hand from the great wheel and pulled her close.

"The whole world is ours my love. We have but one thing to do and then we will go wherever your heart desires."

"My heart is happy, as long as I am with you I care not what our destination is."

The men on deck were all looking at her, and Abby felt a bit self-conscious. It was then that she noticed the bloody sheet was flying where a flag usually did. She colored furiously and looked accusingly at Lissa.

"Tis Tradition," the Pirate Queen laughed, "but it serves a more important purpose today than showing my virility or that you came to me chaste."

"What Purpose?"

Lissa pointed to a spit of land, "Tis the entrance to the harbor. When we sail past, there will be no way your father can miss the ship, or the flag. The whole island will know you have been taken to wife."

"Why do you embarrass me so?" Abigail asked. She was blushing from head to toe and felt a burning humiliation.

Lissa kissed her then, a loving kiss, not filled with passion, but filled with love. "I do not do it to cause you pain my love. As long as he believes you are still chaste your father will spare no expense to have you back. Once he, and all the eligible men on St. Eustacius know that you are no longer suitable to be wed, he will not spare any of his precious money to have you back. I am sorry to say it, but he is a callous man."

The great ship flew past the entrance to the harbor. A few shots from the forts guarding the entrance fell short of the mark, and with startling suddenness, they were away and running in the open sea. Abby stood next to her husband, cradled in the pirate's arm. The sea had never seemed so beautiful, and the sun smiled down with greater promise than it ever had before.

Epilogue:

Three years later, the Pirate ship Raven was sunk off the coast of Bermuda by the Frigate HMS. Courageous. The British records record the Captain as a tall blonde man, and no mention is made of any women being aboard.

The Yorkshire estate known as The Brambles was purchased by a wealthy Frenchman named Le Raven. He brought his small blonde wife to live on the estate, and they were a popular couple among the local gentry. He is listed in the records as being tall with red hair and green eyes and noted for the fact that he was fastidiously clean-shaven and never seen in public without his East Indies style waistcoat. She is mentioned as being a good daughter of the church and is noted for her many donations to the area's poor. Her gravestone can still be seen in a small Yorkshire churchyard. The inscription says simply: Abigail, loving wife.

Story 03

Clia Johansen sat at the very back of the darkened auditorium, fighting to keep her eyes open. At the podium, Professor Roberts rambled on about Alexander the Great or Hannibal or some other long-dead person that Clia really couldn't care less about. She had been dumped in this class to fill her history core requirement and hated it with the same passion she hated Algebra and Biology. Clia was going to be a writer, and she detested wasting her time in mundane courses when she felt she should have been taking more important things. Unfortunately for her, the school had a large number of journalism majors, and all the good classes were filled with upperclassmen before she was allowed to register. Her faculty advisor, an old bat named Mrs. Krieger, had suggested she knock off a lot of her core classes and worry about the writing classes when she was a junior. So instead of sharpening her skills as a writer, she was the only sophomore stuck in an auditorium full of freshmen and one of several students trying not to fall asleep while the professor droned on.

Clia had chosen the second to last row on purpose. Partially to avoid the notice of the prof, she was sure she would be sleeping away many of his lectures and partially to avoid unwanted attention. She had avoided the very back row because she knew in classes like this, the Profs often had TA's patrolling to make sure the students weren't napping.

Clia was tall and had blonde hair, a big bust, and fair skin that were a gift of her father's Swedish forbearers. Her mother's only real contribution to her looks had been the dark eyes and soft features of her Greek ancestry. She was exotically beautiful and wore baggy clothes and no makeup to downplay her looks. Clia told herself she wanted to be known for her writing and not her looks, but secretly she had never been comfortable with the attention the young men had been giving her since high school.

Whenever she thought of this, she was forced to grin. Here she was, hoping to be a writer of love stories, and she had never even been in love. She had won a few local awards for her erotic poems, and she had never even more than kissed anyone. I should be in a class learning about writing, not wasting my time in this godforsaken auditorium, she thought. I hate history.

"Why?"

The softly accented voice behind her startled her, and she turned towards it without thinking. The speaker was a girl seated behind her and one seat to her left. She was small and had a very lush figure with dark curls and dark eyes. The indirect light made her olive skin seem to shine, and the short skirt and poet's shirt accentuated her heavy breasts and wide hips. Her long legs were bare and beautifully sculpted. From her vantage point, Clia could almost see up the girl's skirt and blushed in confusion when she realized she was trying to do just that. The girl's dark tresses were held back by a green hairband with tiny golden leaves embroidered into it. Her dark eyes seemed to be bottomless and very wise for someone so young.

"I'm sorry, did I say that out loud?" Clia stammered.

"No silly, I read your mind," the girl replied in that same softly accented voice. It was musical, melodious in its own way, but deeper than Clia would have expected, and the accent was very sensual.

Clia wasn't sure if the girl was being sarcastic or not. Obviously, she has said it out loud. She felt like she should be angry but was unsure of exactly what she should be angry at.

"You still haven't answered my question, why do you hate history?"

Clia glanced around to make sure no one had noticed them talking in class, but everyone seemed oblivious to them both. She felt like she should resent that last statement. The implication that she was expected to answer annoyed her, but she found herself fascinated with this girl and her strange accent. She wanted to impress her for a reason she could not define. Not wanting to sound like your average college kid complaining about classes and professors, she thought about it a moment before carefully wording her answer.

"I am going to be a writer. I don't need to know all this stuff, I mean really, it's not pertinent to my life,"

"Indeed? What exactly do you write that is so brilliant that it allows you, an author, to claim a right to ignorance?"

"I write love stories, epic romances, love poetry, I don't need to know anything about history for that. I mean, they are all long dead so who cares? And I am not ignorant!"

The girl chuckled softly and picked up the single book on her desk. It was a large volume, like an unabridged dictionary. She slipped it into the simple canvas bag she carried and picked up the black instrument case on the floor by her desk.

"Ignorance is not becoming to anyone especially an author," she said.

"Stop calling me ignorant!" Clia exclaimed as her anger finally overrode whatever power had been in possession of her before.

"As you wish," the girl said as she stood up, "class is over, by the way, Miss. Know-it-all,"

Clia turned to find Professor Roberts gone and most of the students as well. She turned back to find the dark-haired girl had vanished as well. Wondering how she could have missed an auditorium full of freshmen bolting for the doors like a cattle stampede, she grabbed her books and walked briskly out the double doors.

By the time she reached the quad, Clia knew she was cutting the rest of her classes. She wasn't feeling quite right and wanted nothing more than to get to her apartment and lie down. The long walk to day-student parking left her feeling even stranger, her skin was tingling, and she was short of breath. The interior of her little Celica was broiling, and by the time the air conditioner finally began to make some headway, she was bathed in sweat.

Once home, she stripped off the sticky clothes she had been wearing and turned the small window unit in her room to full. Something was wrong, but she could not decide what it was. It was a feeling the likes of which she had never known. Clia decided to take a quick shower before putting on clean clothes. She started the water and waited for it to get hot. Her father had always teased her about liking hot showers, even on the hottest of days. He was second generation Scandinavian and loved the cold. Clia took after her mother there and preferred it to be warm, but she didn't tolerate it being hot well either. She climbed in and pulled the curtain, letting the hot steam engulf her. There was nothing in the world that relaxed her like a hot shower, and soon her mind began to wander.

Who was that strange girl, she thought. Why have I never noticed her before? What kind of accent is that anyway? Clia remembered what the girl looked like, the dark eyes, beautiful skin, heavy breasts, and long legs. She was startled to hear a low moan over the pounding spray of the shower. She was even more startled to realize she had made it. She was shocked to find her left hand gently massaging her pubic mound. Confusion, embarrassment, and arousal all mingled to leave her standing as still as a statue under the spray. Clia forced the girl from her mind and quickly finished her shower.

She dried herself briskly and returned to the now cold bedroom. Clia put on a comfortable bra and panties and pulled her big nightshirt on; she curled up in the bed and closed her eyes. She was asleep almost instantly.

She was standing on a beach with incredibly blue waters lapping at the shore. In this distance was an island that was dark. It was close to the water, and it resembled a woman in repose. The sun was directly behind it, lighting the sky in a series of layers, purplish at the horizon, turning to a rosy red, then a fiery red with yellows and oranges above that and the deep blue of the heavens on top. Clia could not tell if it was rising or setting, but it was breathtakingly beautiful. A woman sat on the edge of the sand before her, her back resting on a large moss-covered rock. She had a stylus in her hand, and a tablet across her knees and penned lines occasionally with a dreamy expression. Her clothing consisted of a simple white dress cut in a style Clia had never seen before, although it seemed very archaic. The woman's eyes never seemed to leave the island, and Clia's eyes were drawn back to it. As the sun fell, she realized it seemed the island had changed. It still resembled a woman, but she seemed to have moved now, and the small knoll that was her bust seemed more prominent.

Clia sensed a presence behind her, but try as she might, she could not turn her head from the scene of the writer and the beach. She started when long, olive arms slipped around her waist, and a soft pair of lips grazed her exposed shoulder.

"What? Who's there??"

The arms pulled her back against a warm, soft body with large breasts and wide hips. The lips kissed up the rise of her shoulder and then up her neck while the hands gently stroked her hips. It felt so sensuous and so nice Clia was caught between fear and enjoyment. She struggled to turn her head, but all her efforts were in vain. When the lips reached her ear, small sharp teeth seized her earlobe and firmly nipped, causing her to gasp.

"Ohhhh, please, what's going on?"

"Shhhh, it's just a dream child," a vaguely familiar and softly accented voice whispered in her ear.

"Why can't I turn around?"

"It is not time yet for you to see me. Now, relax, no harm will come to you I promise," the voice whispered seductively. The warm breath on her ear sent a shiver through her. And when the soft tongue returned to lightly trace her earlobe, a stab of excitement shot through her.

"Where am I?" she asked, the question seeming inane as soon as it left her mouth. In a dream, you idiot, she answered herself.

"On an island in the Aegean sea," the voice replied as the hands traveled up her body to cup her breasts. Clia gasped when they began to gently knead her tits, and she had to bite her tongue to keep from moaning out loud when the thumbs grazed her nipples.

"Who is that woman?" she managed to ask, trying to find something to focus on other than the magical hands and sensuous lips.

"She is a poet, from long ago," the voice replied in a breathy whisper. It returned to delicately tonguing her ear, and Clia found it hard to think. The hands on her breasts were gentle but firm, and they slowly built the pleasure of their manipulation until her nipples ached.

"Which poet?"

"What does it matter? She died a long time ago," the voice replied before the lips slipped back to her neck.

The writer's face was now rapt, and Clia was shocked to see the woman's hand had left the tablet and was now rubbing gently between her legs. Clia gasped again when one of those magical hands slipped down her tummy to massage the crotch of her panties. She felt certain her expression mirrored that of the poet.

"Please, I have to know, who is she?"

The hand rubbing her crotch slipped under the waistband of her panties, and the contact of that soft skin on her excited flesh nearly made her cry out. The index finger forced its way between her now slick lips and began to deftly stroke her clit. Clia's pelvis humped involuntarily against that hand.

"Ohhhhhhh.. please," she moaned. Clia was no longer sure if she was begging for the woman's identity or for release.

"You would know her as Sappho, this is the Isle of Lesvos, and perhaps history is not as uninteresting as you think?" the voice said. There was amusement in the tone, but before Clia's reeling mind could put all of the information together, the fingers suddenly squeezed her clit.

Clia came awake as the dying echo of her scream reverberated around her room. Her nightshirt was up over her bust, and one hand was squeezing a breast. Her other hand was wedged between her legs and still furiously stroking her throbbing clit. Her hands slowly ceased their attentions as the powerful waves of her orgasm passed. She felt so calm, so relaxed, and almost drifted back into sleep before her mind put all the pieces together.

Sappho! Lesvos! Those lips and hands! That voice! She sat up violently in her bed while her eyes were darting around the room, seeing nothing. In her mind's eye, she was still seeing a sunlit beach, with a small woman masturbating as she wrote. As the image faded, her bedroom slowly replaced the beach, and her breathing returned to normal.

"What a dream," she muttered to herself.

Friday was the worst day of the week for Clia. Not only did she have to contend with the anticipation of the weekend making her classes seem longer, but also she had four in a row, and she detested them all. She looked at the stack of books on the dresser as she rose and winced. Algebra, Biology, Chemistry, and Statistics books sat there, seeming to taunt her. She cursed her adviser and herself as she stripped off her nightshirt. While it was true that she would have all of her math and science requirements filled after this semester, she was beginning to doubt she could pass them all. Looking at the books again as she stepped out of her panties, she realized she hadn't done her algebra homework again. She was saying a quick prayer that the prof wouldn't take up homework when she noticed the telltale stains on the crotch of the pink garment.

The dream flooded back into her head as vividly as it had been the evening before, and Clia blushed deeply. She rarely masturbated, and never while thinking of a woman. The entire episode left her feeling confused and a little disconcerted. The panties in her hand were stark evidence of her excitement and pleasure, and she quickly tossed them in the hamper by the bathroom door. This brought her eyes to the clock on the wall, and she realized she was going to have to run or she would be late. The prof always took homework from late students, and she just couldn't afford a zero in his class.

Clia ran a quick shower and threw on the first things that she pulled out of her drawers. A red bra and panty set, tight jeans, and a white tee shirt. She was already in the car on her way when she noticed that her bra could easily be seen under the shirt. There was no time to turn back, and the day student parking was almost full. Clia jogged to class and made it a full fifteen minutes early. This class had assigned seating, and she had just settled in when she noticed several guys in the front row whispering conspiratorially and looking her way. The sniggering, obscene gestures, and hungry looks made her want to find a hole to hide in, and she had never been so happy in her life to see the professor come in and call the class to order. The moment she dismissed the class Clia practically ran out of the class and from the building. She couldn't bear the thought of one or more of those guys approaching her.

Biology was in an auditorium, and she sat near the back. It was dark, and she received none of the stares that had so unnerved her in the smaller classroom. It was cool and dark, and as the professor droned on about mitosis, she began to nod off.

She was standing on the beach again, but it was darker. The sun smoldered on the very edge of the waters, turning them a molten red. The poet was still there, her hand still inside her toga, but she was no longer staring at the island. Clia followed her eyes to see two nude figures entwined on a blanket that had been thrown carelessly on the white sand. The two figures were writhing in each other's embrace as the poet watched. Something was different this time, and it took Clia a few moments to realize she was alone this time, her phantom lover was not there, and she could turn her head and examine things freely. She glanced back to see towering cliffs, but her attention returned to the poet.

As Clia watched, she said something in a language Clia did not recognize, and the two figures on the blanket changed positions. The poet's free hand slipped inside the neckline of her gown to caress her breast as she watched the two figures on the blanket. The motion of her hands was slow, sensuous, and unhurried, but it belied a pent up intensity. Clia felt that the poet would bring herself to the edge of bliss but would not allow herself to cross over. Once in that heightened state of arousal, she would take up the tablet and write. Clia had used the same technique, minus the visual aids, in her own erotic poetry.

The strange scene before her piqued her curiosity. Clia wondered just what it was that the poet found so engrossing and so powerful that it could move her to write verse that was still held in the highest regard centuries later. Clia moved closer and closer, intently scrutinizing the poet as she played with herself. Her expression was indescribable, a mixture of abandon and concentration, while her dark eyes were wild, euphoric, and dreamy all at once. Clia stood close to the writer now, and she observed the soft rippling of the woman's small breasts under the tunic. Clia could see the thick black pubic hair that covered her mound and could smell the musky aroma of her arousal faintly on the breeze. The woman's hands moved quicker now, but as Clia had predicted, the poet tore her hands from her body before an orgasm overtook her. She snatched at the tablet like a drowning woman would grab a live preserver and began to write at a frantic pace.

The poet's eyes lifted from the tablet to the two figures and then back to the tablet as more lines poured from her hand. It was then that Clia realized she wasn't visible; the poet had looked right through her. Entranced by watching the artist at work, Clia had totally forgotten the figures behind her until a ragged moan eclipsed the sound of the surf and brought her attention back to them. It was no surprise to Clia that both of the nude figures were women. In the position they were in, she couldn't see either of them well. They lay one atop the other, but inverted, so that she could see the woman on the bottom's long legs and only the top of the other woman's head and her back.

Clia felt drawn to them and moved closer, making no more sound than the wind across the sands. The woman on top was small with a thick head of dark curls. She lay on atop the other woman, with her arms under the other's thighs and her head buried in her lover's crotch. Clia could see nothing of the woman on bottom save her long legs; even her sex was hidden from view by the brunette's hair, which obscured her hips and inner thighs. As Clia watched, the woman on bottom began to thrash and moan. The smaller woman kept her face glued to the bucking hips of her lover, and without warning, an animalistic howl rang out. The long legs tensed fiercely and then slowly relaxed. Clia had moved closer, or perhaps it was just a trick of the dream, but she was looking down on the pair when the brunette's head came up.

Clia gasped and sat up straight in her seat. The students near her turned to look at her. Many smiled sympathetically and returned their attention to the blackboard. Clia wrote furiously, trying to get all the notes on the board that she had missed, but her thoughts were disjointed and slow. Only with great effort could she keep her thoughts off what she had seen in her dream. The face she had seen when the brunette had looked up continued to float before her vision. It was beautiful and soft with lovely dark eyes and a rapturous expression and glistened in the red light with the juices of her lover. It was none other than her mysterious classmate.

Clia stumbled through the rest of her day in a dreamlike trance. She could not seem to make the distinction between reality and her suddenly very vivid dreams. Everywhere she looked, she would see her mysterious classmate. She was always a face in the crowd or a glimpsed figure moving just out of her line of sight. If she stopped moving or stopped making her mind focus on something tangible, she found herself on that beach drenched in the red of a fading sun, like liquid fire.

She found herself in the cafeteria at a table by herself. She was unsure of how she got there and of how long she had been there. A plate of food was sitting in front of her and a half-empty mug of coffee. She sipped the coffee and found it to be cold, as was the food. Clia noticed that the place was nearly empty, and the janitorial crew was already at work. She glanced at her watch to find it was nearly 4:30. Her last class had been over before noon, and she was almost certain she had been to it, but try as she might, she could not recall the lecture or the intervening hours.

Once she got to her apartment, she felt the overwhelming need to write. On rare occasions, she had felt this need, the frenetic, the nearly delirious feeling had led to some of her best works. Writing in this manic state, where ten pages in an hour were not uncommon, Clia had discovered a joy that was almost orgasmic. She started a pot of coffee and then grabbed a fresh composition book and several pencils and sat down at the dinette in the kitchen. She opened the composition book and picked up a pencil, and fully expected to explode into a frenzy of writing, but instead, she just stared at the blank page. She started several times during the next half hour but never got farther than a sentence or two before she crossed it out and tried to begin again.

By evening she was becoming frustrated and angry. The feeling was there, her body thrummed with it, but the words would not come. Clia passed on going out with her roommates and stayed at the table. She felt certain that inspiration would hit her at any moment, and she did not want to be far from her tablets when it did. The hours passed slowly, and nothing happened. By three o'clock that morning, she had finished two pots of coffee and had two pages of starts crossed out. She was startled by the door opening and her roommates returning from the clubs.

Sharon was drunk, as usual, and hanging on the arm of some blonde guy. Shelly was less inebriated but was also with a guy Clia had never seen before. Beth was the only one who seemed sober, and as usual, she was alone. Clia was in no mood to deal with them or make small talk with guys who only had one thing on their minds. She was thankful that they barely spoke to her before heading down the hallway. Only Beth stopped to ask how she was doing. Clia's frustrated growl of a reply seemed to convince the petite brunette that it wasn't a good time to talk, and she retreated to her room.

Clia's apartment was one of the many new ones put up to house the burgeoning population of the university. The walls were paper-thin, and soon, the muffled sounds of sex drifted into the kitchen. Bedsprings squeaked and the occasional muffled groan filtered to her ear. The sounds seemed to act as a catalyst, and she found herself on the beach of her dreams again. Sharon's crying out jerked Clia's mind back to reality. Clia shook her head and went to get more coffee.

I have such odd roommates. She thought as she made her coffee. Sharon was a tall blonde and a complete slut, a different guy every night, never had a relationship that lasted more than a few rolls in the hay. Shelly was shorter and stockier than Sharon but still tall for a woman and platinum blonde. She had just been dumped by her high school sweetheart and was almost as bad as Sharon, but she seemed to be looking for more than just a one-night stand. Beth was the oddball in almost every respect. She was a small, petite, brunette, very quiet, though not shy. She went out with them every weekend, but to Clia's knowledge, she had never brought anyone home or gone home with anyone she had met. She was closest to Clia in temperament and was probably her best friend at the university. They could talk, but the enigmatic girl seemed to live apart from the rest of the world, and Clia often found her unapproachable. There had always been something there, lying just beneath the surface that Clia could never quite grasp.

Clia returned to the table and her open composition book. The house was quiet now, and the rhythmic ticking of her grandmother's clock seemed to be beckoning her to sleep. Neither sleep nor words would come, and Clia was wide awake when first one and then the other guy slipped out of the house. Time dragged on, and her false starts came less and less often. She was still filled with the urge to write, but the words seemed to have deserted her.

The sun was already up before she finally gave up and padded down the hallway to her bedroom. She passed Beth's doorway just as it opened, and Beth stepped out into the hallway. She was bleary-eyed, and her mused hair and dazed expression lead Clia to believe she must have just woken up. Beth wore only a thin t-shirt and black silk boxer shorts, Clia had seen her dressed like this many times, but today she seemed different. Clia noticed Beth's small breasts and how they stood up and strained against the thin material of her shirt. She found her eye attracted to the gentle curve of the brunette's hips and noticed for the first time the girl's firm and shapely legs. Clia's eyes returned to Beth's face. The girl was very attractive; there was no doubt about that. She was staring, and Clia was startled to realize Beth was speaking.

"Cli?"

Beth's voice startled her, and Clia felt her face flush. Rather than respond, she turned abruptly and hurried to her room. Clia could feel the brunette's eyes on her back all the way to her room. Clia's attempts at sleep were thwarted by the restless energy and feeling that she should be writing. The disturbing encounter with Beth also left her feeling restless and edgy. She tossed and turned in her bed until she finally gave up and returned to the kitchen and her writing tablet.

Clia barely noticed anything going on around her until Sharon asked if she was going out with them. Clia begged off and was actually relieved when Sharon didn't push the issue. She watched her roomies leave for the evening from her place at the dinette. Sharon wore a tight red mini dress that showed off her figure and left her long legs bare. Shelly had on a white western shirt with a string tie, and black flared skirt, and cowgirl boots. Beth wore a green bodysuit with a short black fringed jacket and blue jeans. She also had cowboy boots on and her black Stetson. It must be Bronco's tonight, Clia thought.

She studied her roommates with a detached view that she only achieved when on an insomnia binge. Sharon was pretty, but not overly so. She made up for it by dressing and acting in a way that exuded sex. Guys flocked around her almost as if they could smell sex, and she reveled in it. Shelly was a little heavier than Sharon and not quite as pretty. When she had first moved in, she had been as shy as Clia, but her boyfriend breaking up with her had changed her. She had become as wild as Sharon and just as brassy. Clia felt like it was a knee jerk reaction and that she would calm down some over time. Beth was dressed the least sexy, but to Clia's eye, she was the most attractive of the three. She didn't exude sex appeal, but there was a faraway quality to her, something intangible, that Clia found extremely appealing.

What am I thinking? She asked herself. She realized her scrutiny hadn't gone completely unnoticed. Sharon and Shelly were chatting away about this guy and that, who would be out, where they would go if Bronco was dead, but Beth was staring at her curiously. Clia felt herself blush and looked away. She didn't look up from her blank comp book until she heard the door close.

By the time they returned, Clia was close to tears. She had never experienced writer's block like she was now, and that powerful need to create was making it even worse. On top of that, her mind would not stay focused and returned repeatedly to her mysterious classmate and, if she could have admitted it to herself, to her small roommate as well. The swirling emotions, lack of sleep, sexual frustration, and buzzing need to write all culminated in a whirlwind that left Clia wanting to curl up in a corner and sleep.

Sharon was draped over the arm and shoulder of a huge guy with a crew cut. Clia decided he must be on the football team from his huge muscles and obvious athleticism. Shelly was with a short, swarthy guy with black hair and black eyes. Clia took an immediate dislike to him. He had the arrogant look of an abusive bastard, and since that was the kind, Shelly went after Clia had no doubt he was just that. Beth was alone as usual, but she seemed far less sober than she normally was. She wasn't drunk, but just in that giggly state of being buzzed.

Shelly and Sharon made no attempt at conversation; they both had one thing on their minds and retired to their bedrooms without more than a casual hi to Clia. Beth started a fresh pot of coffee and leaned against the counter; she was staring at Clia with an expression that left the tall blonde hot and flushed. She made two cups of coffee, then sat down and pushed one across the table to Clia.

"Soooo, whats up?"

"Nothing," Clia said, hiding her discomfort by looking down to sip her coffee.

"Nothing?"

"Nothing, why do you ask?"

"Well let's see, You have been walking around in a trance since Thursday, you haven't backed out on us going out two days in a row since you were sick last semester, You haven't eaten or slept in two days, you tell me," Beth said with amusement evident in her tone.

"Two days?"

"Who is it hunny?"

"Who is who?"

"Oh come on, you can tell me. Is it Bobby? Or Jordan?"

"What are you talking about?"

"Cli, you have a crush on someone. It's so obvious. You can tell me, I'm your best friend,"

"A crush?" Clia asked. It all became so clear to her then. Beth was right. She did have a crush on someone, and the someone she had a crush on caused her to feel sick to her stomach.

"Okay, so not Bobby or Jordan, a guy in one of your classes?"

"Oh God," Clia exclaimed. It all came pouring out then, the girl, the dreams, everything. Clia was sobbing by the time she had finished. Beth said nothing, simply listened until Clia had no more to say. She moved to the chair next to Clia and held her as she sobbed.

"Shhhh, it's not as bad as all that. It's going to be all right," she whispered.

By the time class started Tuesday, Clia was a nervous wreck. She didn't know what to say or what to do. She found herself torn between praying the girl wouldn't be there and hoping she was. Clia arrived in class a half-hour early and took her normal seat. She started each time someone entered the room, twisting in her seat to see who it was. Dr. Roberts arrived to call the class to order, and there was still no sign of the girl. Clia was not sure what she felt, disappointment, of course, but also a curious relief. On the other hand, she had to wonder if the girl had ever existed outside of her imagination.

Clia found herself listening to the lecture today and actually enjoying it. Rather than being boring, she found her mind conjuring up images of times long past. She found her fertile imagination beginning to place characters of her own design in among the historical personalities. She felt the creative energy begin to build inside of her, and she hastily pulled out her notebook and began to scribble down ideas.

"You needn't write so fast," a soft voice behind her said. Clia stiffened and then slowly turned her head. The girl with the dark eyes was sitting behind her. Today she wore a simple white dress with a modest neckline and hem that fell to mid-calf. Clia felt her breath catch, she had never seen anyone so lovely, and her heartbeat quickened in her chest.

"I...I mean..." Clia stammered.

"I am going back to my apartment after this class. Will you come with me?" the girl asked in that soft voice Clia had come to love. Clia tried to respond, but no words would come. Her heart was hammering in her chest, and it hurt to breathe. She was so confused, pulled in so many different directions, and so unsure of her feelings and of herself. This strange girl was inviting her back to her place, and Clia felt sure she knew what for. She was not at all sure she was ready for this, but she knew she could not refuse either. In the end, she simply nodded her head.

The class was almost over, but the last few minutes seemed to last an eternity to her. When the professor closed his book and gave out the homework assignments, Clia felt herself becoming incredibly nervous. She was sweating and shaking and suddenly not at all sure she could go through with this. The auditorium emptied out quickly, and soon it was just Clia and the girl. The girl was standing, her book already in her bag and holding the black case Clia assumed held an instrument of some kind. Clia felt her resolve melt, and she tried to think of a way to get out of going. She started to say something, but her eyes caught the girls, and she felt her will to resist fade away like ice under the Aegean sun. She followed the girl out of the historic building and across campus in an almost trance-like state. She did not hesitate to get in the girl's car with her, and throughout the short drive to her apartment, not a word was exchanged.

The apartment was small and tidy, very comfortable and pleasant. The girl fixed drinks and sat on the sofa next to Clia. It was only then with their bodies so close together that Clia could find words.

"I don't know what I am doing here, I must be mad,"

"You are here to begin a great adventure. I, not for what you are now, but for what you can be, have chosen you. In a very short time we shall see if you are worthy of the gift I can bestow,"

"I don't understand,"

"No, but you shall," the girl said as she stood. A gleaming light seemed to come from her body, and as she disrobed, Clia could only stare in fascination. The light became intensely bright, so bright Clia had to shield her eyes when it faded, she was awestruck. The woman who stood before her was not the Greek girl she had known but a tall, statuesque woman with unearthly beauty and the wisest eyes she had ever seen.

"What?"

"Do you not know me?" the woman said in a voice that was both musical and wonderful.

"No, I don't,"

"I am Clio," the woman said simply.

"Clio? This has to be a dream,"

"No little one, it is no dream. I am the muse and I have chosen you,"

"But, I don't even like history," Clia protested. Somewhere in her reeling mind, it occurred to her she was arguing with a figment of her imagination. It seemed so real, but so had the beach dream. She wondered if she was dreaming in Professor Robert's class at this very moment.

"No, but you do not know history, or yourself, but that will change, NOW!"

The final word echoed like a thunderclap, and the world spun away in a dazzling kaleidoscope of colors and tints. Swirling patterns of light and color coalesced around her, and she had the sensation of falling, but not fast, almost floating downwards. This seemed to last forever and yet happened in an instant. The paradox was such that she nearly blacked out from the influx of stimuli. She closed her eyes and tried to block out the colors, but it did not work, and she became aware of sounds. Millions of sounds, the roar and clatter of battle, the gentle patter of summer rain, the voice of a man crying out in pain, the scream of a woman overtaken by ecstasy, the cry of a newborn infant, the dirge of a funeral, and so many others. She heard each with clarity, but at the same time, they were one cacophonous roar in her ear. She felt as if she would lose her mind, and then suddenly, all was still.

Clia found herself standing on the beach of her dreams. There was no poet this time, only the Greek girl from her class. She was sitting on the rock that the poet had been leaning on and staring out at the sea. Clia approached her carefully. The girl looked at her and smiled.

"Clio?" Clia asked.

"In one of my many guises. This is the one you are most comfortable with is it not?"

"Yes. Where are we?"

"You have asked that once before, but I will answer again, we are on the Isle of Lesvos, in the Aegean Sea," she replied with amusement evident in her voice.

"Why?"

"History has no beginning child and no end. If I am to be your guide I had to start somewhere. Your own latent potential and desire lead us here. So it is here that we will start,"

"Start what?"

"Your grand adventure. I am going to show you history, show it to you in a way you cannot imagine, and in doing so give you the unique insight into it that will mark you as one of the greatest of writers," the muse said.

"Why me?"

"You have the potential, you lack only the direction and inspiration. You are also unknown to man and you must remain so. Should you ever have intercourse with a man, my gift is wasted,"

Clia was unsure of what to say. She had always planned on getting married and having children one day. That dream was a nebulous one, with no particular husband in focus. For that matter, she realized she was more enamored of the concept than any particular dream or plan. Five days ago, she would have laughed if someone had broached the quaint idea of her having a muse. Now she believed with all her being that the mythical patron spirits of creativity existed.

The bargain Clio offered was one that many people would have refused out of hand. Clia weighed the options, but she knew before she finished what she would do. She had always felt a deep commitment to her craft. Now she was being offered the chance at inspiration beyond mortal ken. There really wasn't that much of a choice to make.

"Show me then," she said at last.

Clio smiled and nodded. She climbed down off the rock and motioned for Clia to come nearer. Clia approached without fear or trepidation this time. The pretty girl gently touched her shoulder and the world dissolved around her again. The sounds and colors engulfed her again, and she struggled to keep her sanity.

"Relax," the soft voice of the muse urged her, "trust me and let go. No harm will come to you,"

Clia forced herself to relax. The swirling colors and cacophonous sounds crashed in on her, and for an indefinite period of time, she lost herself in the storm. Slowly the colors began to coalesce into scenes. The sounds wore away to a soundtrack, and time began to flow past her like a river. She was everywhere at once and saw everything that had happened through time. An impartial observer, unaware of her existence as a single being, she watched the rise of Greek culture, and it's fall. She saw huge empires rise and fall in the dense jungles of South America and the long voyages of the Vikings. There was far too much for her to ingest it all. But some things remained clear in her mind even after years had passed. Clia sensed the guiding hand of her muse, directing her attention to specific events and people. The muse's choices in scenes that stuck out seem capricious, but Clia detected a common theme. They were always scenes involving women.

Clia watched the mysterious workings of the cult at Delphi. She saw the high priestess of an Assyrian cult conducting an orgiastic ceremony where all the participants were women. In the far north, she watched a woman rise to lead a tribe of Celts on a bloody rampage, and she saw a pharaoh's daughter control the mightiest empire in the world from behind the scenes. In every case, Clia witnessed women in positions of power and authority, women who made significant contributions to art, literature, statecraft, and civilization. She was conscious of the fact that none of these women had ever appeared in any of her history lessons.

Clia felt the gentle urging of her guide pulling her attention towards England. She felt her mind slowly focusing first on the island, then on a particular castle, then on one room in that castle. With a suddenness that was disconcerting, Clia found herself standing on the cold flagstones in a large room. Clio stood behind her, taller now and no longer wearing the guise of her classmate. She could see the muse, but she somehow knew that the occupants of the room could not see her.

The room was huge. Its vaulted ceiling is lost in shadows. Tapestries decorated the walls, and a large fireplace held a roaring fire. A large poster bed dominated one wall. It was made of intricately carved redwood, and the canopy was made of a white gossamer. The coverlet was black and appeared to be silk or satin. Across from the bed, a woman sat at a vanity, peering into a burnished steel mirror. She wore a gown of gold brocade with a skirt, so full Clia wondered how she managed to sit. Two servant girls were busy brushing out her long golden tresses.

The heavy oaken door swung inward, and a woman walked into the room. Clia was instantly struck by the woman's air of command and power. She was tall and very slim with almost no hips or breasts. Angular was the word that came to Clia's mind. There were no soft curves, just planes, and angles. Even her face seemed sharp and predatory without being unattractive. She wore a simple black dress with a scooped neck that showed off the small amount of cleavage she did have. It was cut high on her hips and slit so that one could see flashes of her bare legs when she walked. Her eyes were dark, and so was her hair. Something in those eyes sent a thrill through Clia, a thrill that was part fear and part desire.

Both of the servants turned their heads to glance at the newcomer. Each of them froze, and Clia felt they were both feeling the same thing she did, but more acutely. Their impassive faces lit with a hungry look Clia recognized from the faces of the many men Sharon and Shelly brought home. It was pure lust, and Clia wondered if her countenance looked the same.

"Leave us," the woman said in a commanding tone. Both girls released the blonde woman's hair and hurried out with their heads down. The dark-haired woman watched them go and then sauntered over to the vanity. The blonde never said a word, but her shoulders were hunched, almost as if she expected a blow.

When the dark-haired woman took up a brush and ran it through the seated woman's hair, the blonde flinched as if burned. The brunette smiled a wolfish grin but continued to gently brush out the blonde's hair. She did this for a few minutes in absolute silence and then pulled the woman's long tresses out of the way and scraped her nails along the blonde's shoulder. A hiss escaped the woman's lips, but nothing more.

"Come dear sister, is that anyway to greet me?" the dark-haired woman said. She emphasized the word sister in a way that made it seem ironic.

"Half sister. And only in law," The blonde said. Her voice was tremulous and had a quality to it that invoked pity in Clia. The dark-haired woman smiled and lowered her face to the blonde's exposed shoulder, where she gently traced her lips over the alabaster skin.

"Morgan, please, No..." the blonde whimpered. The brunette paid her not the slightest attention and continued to kiss and lick along her shoulder and her neck. The blonde's hands fluttered to her breast and back to her lap ineffectually. She seemed powerless to stop the dark-haired woman from taking such liberties as she pleased. "Poor little Gwynevere," the brunette whispered, "your words say no, but your body says yes,"

"Morgan? Gwynevere? This isn't real, it's just legend," Clia said as she turned on Clio to find the muse smiling at her. The scene before her was frozen, like a move on pause, but unlike it as well. Her mind was reeling, and things seemed to have more than one meaning and definition.

"This is your first real lesson, Child. Legends abound and so do myths. In every legend, every myth, every parable however there is a grain of truth. These people existed, as did Arthur, Lancelot and Galahad. They were not necessarily anything like the characters you know but they lived, breathed and died nonetheless. For the historian getting to the truth behind the legends is important. Separating historical fact from popular fiction takes diligence, research and above all a willingness to accept that the legend or myth may be totally factually correct. Watch now what happens here and learn a few of the secrets that have been lost to time,"

The scene before Clia began to flow again as the voice of the muse faded.

"Morgan please. We can't!" the blonde implored.

"Bah, just because you chose to marry my simple minded half brother is no reason for me to stop taking my pleasure with you,"

"We can't Morgan, we just can't."

The dark-haired woman growled, and Clia saw anger flash in her eyes. She hurled the brush across the room and grabbed the blonde by the shoulders, bodily jerking the smaller woman to her feet. The blonde tried to pull away, but the dark-haired woman spun her around and caught a handful of her long blonde hair. Morgan jerked her head back and fiercely pressed her thin lips to the blonde's full soft ones, effectively stifling her protests. The blonde's hands were balled into fists, and she smashed them against Morgan's chest weakly. After three or four times, her hands slipped around the brunette's shoulders and her body melted into the embrace.

Clia could see the brunette's tongue exploring Gwynevere's mouth, and she felt her own body responding. Morgan released Gwynevere's shoulders and scooped the startled queen up into her arms. Gwynevere kicked her legs, and under the white petticoats, Clia caught flashes of her stocking covered legs. Morgan unceremoniously dumped the queen on her bed and stepped back. She kicked off her sandals and grasped the hem of her dress, pulling it up and over her head. She was naked underneath, and Clia found herself staring.

Morgan's body was tight, muscular, and lithe. She had almost no fat on her, and Clia could count ribs and clearly see the woman's pelvic bones. Her pubic bush was thick and black, and it covered her labia and most of her pubic mound. She was not at all soft or lush, and her breasts were barely B cups, but she was elemental and powerful and all together sexual. Clia felt the muse's arms slide around her waist, and she stepped back against the woman's body without thinking.

Gwynevere was staring too, and Clia could see the flush on her cheeks. Morgan climbed on to the bed and straddled Gwynevere's hips. She began to kiss the queen's neck, lips, cheeks, and eyelids, all the while her hands plucked at ties, undid buttons, and efficiently loosened the queen's gown. The blonde still seemed hesitant, and she struggled against Morgan's hands, but the fight was not very convincing. The gown seemed to take forever to get undone, but Morgan's mouth was busy, and her hands often stopped to caress and knead. Clia was still a novice, but she had the impression Morgan was deliberately taking her time, slowly working the blonde to an ever higher state of arousal and need.

Clio's hands and lips were not idle either. Clia felt the soft lips on her neck and the magical hands caressing her hips, but where Morgan seemed intent on immediately arousing her partner, Clio seemed to have the opposite intent. Her attentions were exciting and sensuous but not urgent and did nothing to take Clia's eyes or attention from the scene being enacted before her. Morgan dug her fingers into the gown and pulled it down. As it slid across her body, Gwynevere planted her feet on the bed and raised her hips. Morgan slid all the way down her body until she was kneeling at the foot of the bed with the rumpled gown in her hands. The brunette tossed the garment to the floor and licked her lips as she stared at Gwynevere. The blonde looked simply delicious. She wore only her white stockings, which ended at mid-thigh. Her pale skin and those stocking lying on the black comforter formed an arresting contrast. Where Morgan's body was all planes and angles, Gwynevere was all curves. Her breasts were large, almost as large as Clia's, and capped with delicate pink nipples. These were hard now and stood out from the small aureoles. Her hips were wide and lush, and her pubic hair was as blonde as that on her head. Her bush was thick and luxuriant, but the pouting lips of her labia were easily discernable.

Morgan clucked in her throat and then threw herself on top of the supine woman. Their lips met, and Morgan began to hump her hips, forcing her mound to rub against the queen's mound. Gwynevere began to respond, her hips pushing up to meet her lover's thrusts, but as soon as she responded, Morgan stopped.

Morgan sat up and began to stroke the blonde's hips. Her hands lightly traced along the blonde's skin, brushing her mound but not giving firm contact.

"Perhaps you were right, maybe we should stop,"

"Nooo," Gwynevere wailed.

"No? But you said we shouldn't," Morgan teased as her fingers moved to the queen's now soaked slit and began to slide up and down it. Gwynevere moaned and thrust her hips up, but Morgan kept the contact to just a feathery tease.

"Please," the blonde whimpered when she realized Morgan was not going to give her any release.

"Changed our mind have we? Well, you know what you will have to do now,"

"I can't," the blonde whined.

"Too bad, your little kitty seems to be aching for some attention," Morgan said as she slipped one long finger just inside the slick lips. Morgan pumped her finger slowly in and out of the queen's pussy. Clia watched in fascination, and the long digit became slick and coated with the queen's juices. In and out, it sawed with maddening regularity. The blonde humped against it, trying to drive it deeper. Morgan crossed her fingers and pushed them both in. The queen gasped, and her hands slid down her body towards the juncture of her thighs.

"No!" Morgan commanded. The queen's hands seemed to stop of their own accord and then withdrew.

"If you want to spend, you are going to have to earn it little cow," Morgan said as she grasped one of Gwynevere's tits in her free hand and roughly manipulated it.

"Please," Gwynevere gasped.

"Are you ready then?" Morgan asked in a too-sweet tone.

"Yes,"

"Then beg for it, little trollop."

"Please, can I lick you? I am dying to taste your spendings," Gwynevere groaned. Morgan laughed and withdrew her fingers. She moved up the queen's body and placed a knee on either side of the blonde head while her ass rested on the slope of the queen's tits.

"Very well your majesty," Morgan said sarcastically, "get to work and lick my quim like the harlot you know you are,"

As she said this, Morgan rose up and then pressed her pussy directly to the queen's quivering lips. Clia could only see the blonde's eyes and nose, but from Morgan's contented sigh, she had to assume that the queen was indeed eating the sorceress's pussy. Morgan leaned back and rested her hands on the queen's full tits. She began to pinch and pull the little blonde's nipples as she started to rock back and forth.

"That's it harlot, use your tongue. Mmmmm, you are such a talented licker, even better than your serving girls. Maybe I shall have you service both of them, in appreciation for all they do for you. Would you like that? I think you would."

Morgan moaned and began to thrust her hips back and forth on the queen's face. She moaned again and then sighed as her hips went into a paroxysm of wiggling, and she came. When she finished, she slid down the queen's body. Clia couldn't take her eyes off Gwynevere's face. The blonde's chin, lips, and nose were covered in Morgan's juices. In the strange light, they glistened, and Clia was caught between being slightly repelled and wondering what it tasted like.

Morgan settled between the queen's legs and forced two fingers into the blonde's snatch. She started to pump them in and out furiously while her free hand massaged the upper part of Gwynevere's mound. The queen began to jog her hips and make small noises that Clia found very erotic. The Queen's hands went to her breasts and kneaded them as her orgasm approached. With little warning, a cry burst from her lips, and she tensed. Her body thrashed violently on the bed, and then slowly, she relaxed.

Morgan slid up next to her and held the queen in her arms, gently stroking her hair. Gwynevere's eyes fluttered open, and she smiled contentedly and then frowned.

"What are we going to do my love? This cannot last forever,"

"Do not worry my little dove. I have taken steps to insure that Arthur looses interest in you. It will be hard on you at first, but trust me. In time you will be held up as the model of virtue and tragic love, while I will be reviled as a temptress, perhaps even a sorceress."

"You're no sorceress, unless one counts the magical way you make this cold body respond to you," Gwynevere said. Morgan laughed softly, and while she smiled and tweaked Gwynevere's nose, Clia could detect the sadness in that laugh.

"Men must find a reason, and a scapegoat. I do not mind the iniquity I shall have heaped up on me, as long as you are mine,"

"I shall always be yours. No man can stir me to such heights. But tell me, why do you think you will be reviled?"

"I am not without some skill at scrying my love. That old fool of a court magician has shown me a few tricks. But that is neither here nor there. Those idiots are still at the tournament at Trielle so I have hours in which to pleasure you,"

With that, Morgan gently kissed Queen Gwynevere, and Clia found herself floating back into the altered state of consciousness where she, Clia, did not exist. Time flowed once more, and Clia watched England enslaved by the Romans. Her eye roamed far and wide, always drawn to the scenes Clio wanted her to witness first hand, but also aware of all that transpired. She saw a redheaded queen lead the Celts in an uprising against Rome, witnessed the orgies and degradations of that fabled city, and saw it fall. She saw what really went on in the convents of the dark ages and the nightly escapades in the boudoirs of the nobility. She saw the Spanish enslave the new world, watched fleets of treasure ships sunk, and saw England rise to prominence. She was there when an anonymous Corsican woman gave birth to a boy child. She watched this child grow to rule all of Europe.

Suddenly she was herself again, standing on a rainy street in London. She was less disconcerted this time, more comfortable with the drastic shifts in her state of consciousness. A solitary figure, wrapped in a voluminous cloak, moved purposefully down the dimly lit and empty street. From the seductive sway of her hips, Clia knew it was a woman. The figure stopped outside the doorway to a large home and entered after a moment's hesitation.

Clia was instantly inside the home, watching as a liveried butler closed the door behind the woman. He then gestured for her to follow him and led the way into a richly appointed parlor. A woman was sitting on the settee and glanced up from the book she was studying.

"Your guest has arrived Mi'Lady," the butler said stiffly.

"Very well Codsworth, you may take the rest of the evening off," the woman on the settee replied.

"As you wish madam," he replied and withdrew, drawing the doors shut behind him.

"Do you have them?" the seated woman asked.

The cloaked figure produced a roll of parchment and said, "All is there. Ships complements, sailing times, ordinance and commanders" Her voice was sharp and had an air of command as well as a musical quality, but the accent was soft and undoubtedly French.

"Give them to me, I must get them to Horatio as quickly as possible," the seated woman said, extending her hand.

"Not so fast ma Cherie, there is the little matter of payment,"

"Very well, name your price,"

"You know my price, do not play coy with me. This information is vital and you have no time to waste in coquettish games,"

The seated woman nodded and stood up. Her hands went to work removing the dress she wore while the cloaked figure sprawled in a wingback chair and watched. As the dress fell away in parts, more and more of her lovely body was exposed. Finally, she stood before the cloaked woman in only her stays. Her body was lush and soft with wide hips, pendulous breasts, and long trim legs. Her pubic hair was as thick and curly as the long dark tresses on her head; the seated woman held a finger up and made a circular motion with it. The aristocratic brunette pirouetted slowly on her toes. Her ass was full and shaped like a teardrop. Clia found the woman attractive, but she did not cause a quickening of her heartbeat like the sorceress had.

The seated woman hooked both of her legs over the arms of the chair and pulled her cloak up. She was naked underneath. With her legs spread wide over the arms of the chair, her fat labia were exposed. The sparse hair covering her mound was dark but seemed to have reddish highlights that made it look auburn when the light hit it right.

The finger beckoned, and the other woman dropped to her knees and crawled between the widely splayed thighs. There was no hesitation on her part. She used her fingers to pull the prominent outer lips apart and exposed the bright pink inner folds. The brunette pressed her face tightly against the seated woman's sex and began to lap delicately at the soft flesh. Clia was reminded of a cat tasting something for the first time.

The seated woman sighed and cooed, allowing her body to relax while pressing forward with her hips until her ass rested on the very edge of the chair. Clia watched as the seated woman's pussy became wet and swollen. The aristocratic woman continued to lick at it, concentrating her efforts on the now erect clit. The cloaked woman's hands tangled in her lover's hair and pulled her face tightly against her dripping sex. Her voice became throaty, and her breathing ragged as she murmured exhortations in French. Soon her hips began to jog, and the aristocratic woman pushed a finger, then two in, and began to pump them in and out as she licked.

This seemed to be all the added stimulus the cloaked woman needed. She mumbled something unintelligible and then moaned loudly as her body began to shake. The brunette redoubled her efforts, driving her fingers in wildly and sucking the erect clit in to lash it with her tongue.

Slowly the aristocratic woman slowed her attentions as her lover came down from her orgasm. She continued to tongue the seated woman's slick lips, but it was gentle now and seemed more of a soothing caress. After a while of this gentle attention, the seated woman sighed and sat up straighter.

"That was delightful as always Ma Cheri," she said in the husky but musical voice that Clia was growing to love.

"And you taste as divine as you did when last we met my love, but I really need to send that information on," The brunette replied seriously.

"Very well Ma Cherie, I shall let you take leave for a few moments to get the information on its way, but only if you will allow me to take you when you return,"

"As if you could escape without doing so," she said as she rose and took the papers. She stuffed them into a leather pouch and hurried out of the parlor. The cloaked woman did not stir from the chair but waited patiently, her hand idly stroking her pussy. After a long time, a horse was heard galloping away from somewhere behind the house. Moments later, the brunette came in, pulling a dressing gown off her shoulders and tossing it over the back of a chair.

"Now my dear, how do we wish to proceed? Do we have time to adjourn to the bedroom?"

"No ma Cheri, it will have to be quickly. My ship must depart while it is still dark for obvious reasons,"

"Damnable war," the brunette said, and she got on the settee on all fours. She then let her weight fall onto her elbows, which forced her posterior high into the air. Clia could see her pussy clearly; it was open and exposed and also had a slight sheen to it.

"Yes, Damnable," the cloaked woman said as she approached and sat on the settee. She ran her hands up the brunette's thighs and then caressed the fleshy cheeks. With a gentleness Clia had rarely seen, she pried the aristocrat's cheeks apart and then began to tongue her wide open pussy. This continued for some time until the Lady began to moan and squirm.

The cloaked woman sat back then and slipped a finger into the other woman's pussy. She worked it in slowly, taking her time, and then pumped it in and out for a few strokes before she added a second finger. She continued to gently frig the brunette with two fingers while Clia watched over her shoulder. When both fingers were slick the woman's copious juices, she pressed her two fingers together and laid her index over them to form a triangle. This she pressed forward slowly, forcing it into the woman's spread pussy. A groan was torn from the brunette as the three fingers dilated her opening. She groaned again and whimpered softly as the cloaked woman's fingers finally sank all the way in.

The sight of the woman's spread pussy with all three fingers buried in it had a strange effect on Clia. She felt her breath quicken and her nipples harden. The sight was so erotic and so strange, three fingers inside with just the pinky and thumb outside. The cloaked woman gave her lover time to adjust and then began to slowly fuck her with her fingers. As the brunette's moans grew more and more urgent, the cloaked woman slammed her fingers in with increasing force and speed. Clia was fascinated by the spectacle of the aristocrat's pussy holding onto those fingers, almost as if it did not want them to leave. Soon the room was filled with liquid sounds and the moans of the brunette. When her hips began to jog, and Clia was sure she was close to coming, the cloaked woman suddenly stopped. She withdrew her fingers until just the tips were still inside, and Clia was stunned to see her pull her pinky in under the others and press forward again.

"Ow!" the brunette gasped.

The cloaked woman ignored her and pressed her hand forward. The tight ring of muscle resisted for a short time and then yielded. The fingers sank to the first knuckle into the tight space, and Clia found herself leaning forward to see close up. Clia felt the muse's hands on her hips, pulling her ass back against the muse's pelvis, but Clio added no stimulation. She merely rested her chin on Clia's shoulder and watched the show with her.

The cloaked woman was now working her fingers deeper into the brunette's pussy. She seemed to be walking a thin line between being gentle and overcoming the resistance to the intrusion.

"Relax ma petite, "she cooed in that husky but musical voice.

The brunette groaned but exhaled, and Clia saw her body relax. The cloaked woman pressed harder, and Clia watched in awe as her fingers slowly disappeared. When the wide part of her hand reached the ring of muscle, there was the briefest pause, and then her hand sank in until her thumb was the only finger visible. With her free hand, she stroked the brunette's ass and whispered endearments to her. Clia watched the aristocrat's muscles gradually cease to tense and relax as her body adjusted to being so full.

The cloaked woman began to slowly pump her hand in and out, but adding a twisting motion as well that seemed to drive the prostrate brunette wild. In no time, she was thrusting back to meet the cloaked woman's hand. Her moans were continuous now but punctuated by little squeaks and groans. The cloaked woman worked her lover up to an almost frenzied state and then pulled her hand out again until Clia could see each finger up to the first knuckle. Clia couldn't believe what she was seeing when the woman's thumb slid under the other fingers, and she pressed back into the brunette's quivering cunt.

The Lady gasped then, making a sound that was half surprise and half encouragement. Clia watched as the fingers slid back in, back to the point where the widest part of the hand was caught on the ring of muscle. Clia could see the strain as the muscles in the woman's forearm stood out.

"My god," Clia exclaimed.

Before she could say anything more, the tight ring of muscle gave and the cloaked woman's whole hand, right up to her wrist, disappeared in an instant. The brunette let out a squeal that Clia could not categorize as surprise, delight, or pain. It seemed, rather, to be a melding of all three.

"Ohmygod," the brunette hissed, the words running together into one stream of sound. Her haunches were quivering, and the muscles in her stomach and sides were knotting. The cloaked woman held her hand there and did nothing more. Slowly the aristocrat relaxed and ceased making anything but mewling noises and little gasps. Only then did the cloaked woman begin to work her hand in and out, twisting it as she drove it in. Clia was rapt as she watched it, the small muscled in the woman's forearm stood out, and Clia realized she was flexing and spreading her fingers inside her lover. The brunette's moans and groans rose to a howl of animal lust as she began to orgasm. Her juices poured down the cloaked woman's hand in a torrent as her cunt contracted and spasmed around the fist inside it.

When the cloaked woman withdrew her hand, the brunette collapsed on the settee and rolled up into a fetal position. The cloaked woman rose and wiped the copious juices of her lover on the outside of the dark cloak.

"That was well worth it," the cloaked woman said, "but now I must go,"

"Wait!" the brunette said, mastering herself and sitting up.

"Oui?'

"The information you brought will surely allow Horatio to best the French and Spanish fleet. I have been seeing you for over two years now and have never seen your face, or learned why you betray your country or why you demand carnal pleasure with me as the price of your betrayal. In truth I no longer care, I have found ecstasy in your arms that no man, not even my Horatio can bring me. Will you not answer my questions?"

The cloaked woman stood in deep thought for a while, and then she spoke. She was hesitant at first, as if trying to find the words but became more confident as she went on.

"Very well, dear Emma, I will answer your questions. You have held your tongue long enough and I think you are ready for the answers. First the why. Napoleon controls the continent, but he cannot rule the world as long as the English fleet thwarts him. A man who rules the world has no need of a woman, but a man kept from his goal will always need someone to cry to. It is in my best interest that Napoleon controls most of the world, but never all. My price was at first simply a whim, something you could afford to pay for the information I wanted your country to have. That has changed. I have found that sex with men no longer satisfies me and I yearn for my next meeting with you even as I moan in their arms to satisfy their egos. As to my identity, have you not guessed already?"

With that, the woman threw back the cloak from her head. The Lady Hamilton gasped, as did Clia, while Clio, the muse, chuckled.

"Josephine!" the Lady exclaimed in shock. The scene froze, like a movie again, and Clia looked to Clio.

"Your second lesson. Inexplicable things often occur for a reason. Rarely do the strange twists of fortune so many put down to chance actually depend on luck. In your studies keep an open mind and never accept the trite explanations of so-called experts. Nelson's victory over the French and Spanish fleet was indeed due in large part to his valor, genius and determination, but he also had the great advantage of the papers you saw exchange hands here. Always look beyond the trite and you will find that fact is often far stranger than fiction."

Clia nodded and looked back once again at the figures frozen before her. They began to move again, but they were no longer in sharp focus. Her perception expanded, and she was once again the impartial observer as time ran by. Wars were fought, empires rose and crumbled, the boudoirs of the nobility were just as jaded, and a lot of the common folk were just as full of sexual escapades as they had ever been. Everything changed, but nothing really did. Clia saw the millions perish in World War One, where men fought for days over a few feet of muddy territory. She saw the vileness, corruption, and utter disregard for life of the Nazi regime. She witnessed the repression of the Communists and found herself unable to separate the two. She watched the agonizing fear of a world living under the threat of nuclear extinction and the build-up of the cold war to its crisis point over the small island of Cuba.

She found herself standing in a conference room. There was a large table with many chairs around it at the center of the room. Seated alone on one side was a tall blonde woman in the dress blue uniform of a U.S. Navy Captain. On the other side was a tall brunette in the drab green uniform of a Soviet Colonel. The blonde was speaking, and Clia became aware of the words in that disconcertingly sudden way.

"You'll never win Colonel, if those ships don't turn back we will board them and if necessary sink them,"

"Bah, you Americans. So self-righteous, so proper. But you know your blockade is illegal, no one in the world community supports you," the brunette countered in a strong voice with a charming Russian accent.

"It isn't a blockade, it's a quarantine,"

"Play your semantic games, it is the same thing,"

"You are going to start a war," the blonde said ominously.

"We are going to start a war?!" the brunette said, jumping to her feet, "you are about to start a war!"

"You're the aggressors here!" the blonde shouted as she rose to her feet.

"Aggressors?! I'll show you aggressor you bitch!" the Russian shouted and practically leaped across the table, riding the blonde woman down to the floor. Clia was sure they would come to blows, but instead, the blonde giggled.

"No fair!"

The brunette was sucking and licking her neck while her hands plucked ineffectually at the American's coat. Frustrated in her attempt to open it, she took each lapel in her hands and ripped it open, sending brass buttons flying. Clia could see the large mounds of the blonde's breast heaving under her starched white shirt.

The blonde pushed the Russian woman up and ripped her coat open as well. They stared at each other a long moment, and then both laughed. When they had mastered their mirth, the Russian woman gently kissed the American and then stood up. When the American woman gained her feet, there was an awkward silence.

"Are you sure about this solnishka?" the Russian woman said.

"Absolutely," the blonde said in a sorrowful voice.

"Very well, the rules are the same as last time?" the Russian woman said as she began to unbutton her blouse.

"The same," the blonde said as she unzipped her skirt and stepped out of it. The two women continued to disrobe in silence until they both stood nearly naked. The Russian was tall and had an olive hue to her skin. Her dark eyes and dark hair gave her a sultry and exotic look. Her breasts stood out proudly and were larger and fuller than even Clia's. Her hips were slim, and her dark pubes were trimmed into a tight triangle. The pouting outer lips of her pussy were visible, and Clia again felt her arousal at the sight of this lovely creature.

The blonde was even more spectacular. She was shorter than the Russian but had an even fuller figure and massive tits that a stripper would have envied. Her blonde pubes were trimmed neatly, and her pink lips pouted open slightly. Long legs, wide hips, and flawless skin set off her blue eyes. She was intoxicatingly beautiful, the kind of beautiful that aroused a pang of jealousy in Clia. She still wore her black garter belt and stockings, which only seemed to add to her sexiness. The two women stared at each other for a few moments, and then the Russian removed a coin from her jacket pocket.

"Flip of the coin for first position?"

"I won last time so I will grant the option to you," the blonde said with a wink.

"I'll take top then," the brunette said as she tossed the coin onto the pile of clothes at her feet.

The blonde nodded and retrieved her briefcase. She set it on the table and turned the dials on the combination lock set into the cases front. When she opened it, Clia could not see what was inside, but both women giggled.

"The worlds greatest instrument of diplomacy," the blonde intoned with mock solemnity.

"Is that the same one?" the Russian asked.

"No, it's a new one. The old one was thinner. You had unfair advantage with it cause your used to Yuri's moose cock. This one is even wider than he is,"

"But the advantage is still mine is it not? If it is wider than my pig of a husband's tool it is far wider than your husbands noodle,"

"That's true, Bert is such a looser in bed, but you get no advantage,"

"Really? And why is that?" the Russian said as she arched an eyebrow.

"I been practicing," The blonde said and began to giggle.

Clia's curiosity got the better of her, and she moved around the big table to see what they were talking about. When she did, she burst out laughing. The inside of the briefcase was red velvet and held a massive double-ended dildo with two bottles of lubricant in a side pocket. The blonde pulled it out and smiled at the Russian.

"Table of floor?"

"Table, the floor allows you to squirm too much," the Russian said, smiling.

The blonde nodded, and her face suddenly became blank, like the expression men used when playing cards, Clia thought. The Russian's face was just as blank. The blonde handed the dildo to the brunette and climbed up on the big conference table. She lay on her back and spread her legs wide. The Russian handed her the bottle of lubricant and watched impassively as the blonde squirted a large portion into her hand and worked it into her pussy. The Russian took the second bottle and worked a generous amount into her pussy before adding copious amounts to each end of the dildo.

The Russian girl climbed onto the table and slowly forced a good bit of the dildo into the American. She then straddled her opposite and fed a good portion into her slippery pussy. She looked down on the American girl and rode up and down a few times experimentally. She adjusted her position slightly and tried again, and this time seemed satisfied.

"Whenever you're ready," the blonde said between clenched teeth.

"Go," the Russian said and immediately rode down hard on the thick dildo. The blonde groaned. The Russian woman quickly established a rhythm that was to her liking, driving her hips down and thrusting forward in the same fluid motion. The blonde adjusted her hips to allow the dildo to slide more freely and relaxed. Clia watched the game with interest. She had already guessed that the first one to orgasm would lose.

The Russian girl continued to drive down on the dildo, forcing it deeper into the blonde and herself. The blonde groaned and stuck a finger in her mouth, which she began to suck. Clia was fascinated with the Russian girl. She was like a machine, driving down and forward in a seemingly tireless rhythm. Her brow was knit in concentration, and Clia could see she was doing her best not to enjoy it, but Clia could see that each thrust drove the fat dildo as deeply into her snatch as it did into the blonde. Her large nipples were hard, and Clia could see the sheen on her lips that was no longer just lubricant.

While the Russian girl seemed to be intent on not enjoying what she was doing, the blonde seemed to have taken a different approach. She moaned and sighed around the wet finger in her mouth, producing little sounds that were very erotic. She seemed to be totally into the fucking she was getting, and Clia felt certain she would cum very soon. The Russian girl reached out and roughly massaged one of the blonde's large breasts, which caused the blonde to gasp and then moan louder. Her hips began to buck upward, meeting the Russian girl's thrusts so that only a small portion of the big dong was visible.

The blonde's bucking caused the Russian to release her tit and use both hands to steady herself. She increased the tempo, and a smile creased her face. It was obvious to Clia that she knew she was close to winning. The blonde moaned louder and arched her back, apparently on the very brink of cuming, and Clia saw the Russian's face relax. It was almost as if she had said to herself a few more strokes and this bitch is cuming.

A few more strokes and the brunette moaned loudly, the first sound she had uttered since the word go. The blonde responded in an instant. She jerked the finger from her mouth and forced herself up on her elbows. With an almost lightning quickness, she reached forward and cupped the Russian's pussy in her hand. The finger she had been sucking and wetting slipped between the thick lips and started to furiously stroke the Russian girl's clit.

"Neyt," the Russian gasped. She was driving too hard to stop. Both of her hands were tied up in keeping herself atop the blonde. A few more strokes of her sensitized clit and the Russian girl screamed and went wild, riding down on the dildo with rapid, jerky thrusts of her hips as she rode out her orgasm. When it subsided, she collapsed on the blonde and lay panting.

"No fair," she huskily said after she had regained some of her composure.

"All's fair in love and war," the blonde responded with a smile.

"I should have known something was wrong, you never get hot that fast,"

"Not true Natasha, just seeing you naked gets me going. That is neither here nor there however, you lost and I won. Another victory for capitalism,"

"Yes, you won, fair and square. I will return to the consulate and prevail upon Yuri to convince the chairman that you Americans are serious and a diplomatic solution is the only possibility of avoiding war,"

"And I will give Bert a nice blowjob tonight and convince him to tell Bob that we are not prepared to fight a war and he should convince the President to offer some face saving options to the Russians,"

"Ugh, I cannot stand the though of your lips upon that man," the Russian girl said, making a face.

"It doesn't exactly turn me on to be going down on you when I know Yuri has been there either love," the blonde said with a rueful smile.

"Solnishka, I am tired of being apart. Let us do this one last thing to save the world and then leave it in the hands of others,"

"What are you proposing?" the blonde asked in a suddenly soft voice.

"I will defect. I have already made all the preparations. I am prepared to never see mother Russia again, but I can only make that sacrifice if it means having you as my own,"

"Oh Nat! I thought you would never ask. As soon as this is over I will start divorce proceedings with Bert. I have proof he's fucking that little cunt Lieutenant secretary of his,"

"I will meet you in London in six months then. I am defecting through the offices of the British secret service. Where will we go from there?"

"I don't care," the blonde said, hugging the brunette tightly to her, "as long as I'm with you anywhere will be heaven,"

The scene faded, and Clia found herself standing in blackness. She looked around in a panic, but Clio was there beside her.

"My time grow short little one. Do you know what lesson this taught you?"

"Ummm.. That I have to pay close attention to the minor players. History is filled with great people making earth shattering decisions, but often it is not they, but the nameless faceless people who do the most?"

"That's very good and true, but not what I wanted you to take from this," Clio said with a smile.

"I don't know then," Clia said.

"The lesson here is that love can move mountains. Any divide, even that as great as east and west can be bridged by love. Even the gap of social acceptance. This last lesson was a personal one. There is someone in your life who loves you desperately. Whether you choose to accept that love or spurn it is up to you. You will always have my guidance and inspiration, but you will never reach the peak of potential you have unless you are happy and fulfilled in life. This lover can bring you such fulfillment and happiness," the muse's voice seemed to come from farther and farther away.

"Wait! Don't leave me!" Clia shouted. She could no longer see her guide in the inky blackness.

"I shall always be with you, but for now I must go. There are laws even the Gods cannot break. Fair the well!"

"Clio? Wait please! Who is it?" Clia screamed almost hysterically.

"Cli? Clia please wake up!" the insistent voice called.

Clia opened her eyes to find Beth looking down on her with an expression approaching panic. The little brunette was shaking her violently.

"What the...?"

"Thank god you're awake! Are you all right?"

Clia looked around and realized she was lying on the floor in the kitchen of her apartment. She sat up slowly, tuning out the frantic questions Beth was asking.

"How did I get here?" she asked at last.

"I don't know. Professor Roberts stopped me in the cafeteria and asked if you were all right. He said you got up in the middle of his lecture this morning and walked out of class in some kind of trance. I was worried sick,"

"I am all right," Clia said, getting shakily to her feet.

"Are you sure?"

"Yes, I just need to get some sleep," Clia said as she made her way to her bedroom. Something made her turn her head as she was closing the door. She saw Beth standing in the hallway, wringing her hands with a look of concern on her face that was heart-rending.

Clia slept all of the rest of Tuesday away and straight through Tuesday night. It was sometime in the early morning of Wednesday that she felt the presence of Clio. The muse was behind her again, and Clia only made one attempt to turn her head. When she couldn't, she relaxed. Clio's arms slipped around her waist, and she shivered when soft lips planted a light kiss on her shoulder.

"Hello little one,"

"Mmmmm, so this is what you meant by seeing me again? In my dreams?"

"Yes, whenever you are troubled or at a loss for words I will know,"

"And now?"

"Now you are troubled, but I cannot help you. I can only say that you should trust your heart,"

Clia nodded and felt those wonderful soft lips on her shoulder again. She sank back into a deep sleep, and into dreams, she could not remember upon waking.

Wednesday, Clia woke early and called each of her professors. She told each she was cramping very badly and couldn't make it to the class. All of them were very sympathetic and told her not to worry. She used this excuse about once a semester when she really needed a mental health day. She had discovered, quite by accident, that it was the perfect excuse. Her female Professors all understood and immediately sympathized, while her male teachers were all so embarrassed by the subject that they gave her no trouble at all.

Clia was sitting at the kitchen table writing down things she remembered from her journey with Clio when Sharon stumbled into the kitchen and poured herself a cup of coffee. Without her makeup and the false smile she always wore, she looked older than her years. Her eyes had a hard edge to them that Clia associated with girls who slept around a lot. Rather than the semi contemptuous feelings she had always harbored against Sharon today, she felt only pity. Her trip through time had shown her far too many women who simply couldn't be happy with themselves. They needed to have their ego's propped up by attention, and sex was certainly one way to get attention.

Sharon said good morning and returned to her room. Beth came into the kitchen about an hour later as Sharon and Shelly were walking out the door. The two blondes had a 7 AM lab together in Butler Hall on Wednesdays and always rode in together. Beth avoided looking at Clia, got her coffee, and returned to her room. She came out dressed for the class about half an hour later and quietly exited the apartment.

All day Clia wrote, filling Comp book after Comp book with notes, ideas, remembrances, and impressions. At 1:00, Shelly and Sharon came back in. Both were chatting and in a bubbly mood; Clia remembered the concert was tonight over in Monroe. Clia was forced to answer the door a few minutes later. The tall, athletic guy and the shorter guy from the weekend were standing there. Clia let them in and motioned them to the sofa with a distracted wave. She returned to her writing, and after a few monotone responses to their questions, the guys stopped trying to make conversation.

Shelly and Sharon came out, and the four of them left without even attempting to disturb Clia from her writing. Clia barely noticed them leave; she was so engrossed in what she was doing. It only was when she heard the door open around three that she looked up from her nearly full comp book. Beth walked in, looking very tired and very down. She started off towards her bedroom with her eyes downcast, but Clia felt the urge to talk suddenly.

"Beth? Are you all right?"

"Hmm? Yes, I suppose I am," the small brunette replied.

"Ya sure? You seem very down,"

"I'm fine. How did it go with your classmate?" she asked with a half-hearted smile. Clia could see that the smile was forced. She was suddenly very curious about Beth's reason for asking. Clia chose her words with care, watching the smaller girl for her reaction.

"It didn't pan out. She is not staying in school, in fact I won't see her again I am sure," Clia said slowly. Beth's face showed conflicting emotions, but to Clia's now practiced eye, they were as readable as any of her beloved books. There was sorrow there that things hadn't worked out, but also elation. An elation that was filled with hope renewed. How many times had Clia seen that same mix of emotions in her trip through time? A million? More? She would never know, but for the rest of her life, she would be able to read people with an uncanny precision that amazed her friends. The only question left unanswered was why the expression was there.

"I'm sorry Cli, I really am," Beth said.

"It's all right. I'll get over it," Clia said. Beth nodded and started down the hallway but stopped. Clia watched her as she seemed to be fighting some inner struggle. Finally, she turned on her heels and blurted out, "Cli, you wanna go out tonight and get some dinner or something?"

"No," Clia said. Beth looked crestfallen, but before she could say anything or turn around, Clia continued, "I would rather stay in tonight, but how about we get some Chinese?"

Beth smiled and nodded. The smile was so radiant and happy that Clia found herself smiling. She returned to her writing, and Beth disappeared down the hallway. Clia stopped writing and puzzled over that smile and Beth's strange reactions. It was then that the words of the muse came back to her.

"The lesson here is that love can move mountains. Any divide, even that as great as east and west can be bridged by love. Even the gap of social acceptance. This last lesson was a personal one. There is someone in your life who loves you desperately. Whether you choose to accept that love or spurn it is up to you. You will always have my guidance and inspiration, but you will never reach the peak of potential you have unless you are happy and fulfilled in life. This lover can bring you such fulfillment and happiness,"

The words were the same, but the puzzle behind them was suddenly undone. The final veil of naivety was lifted from Clia's eyes. Everything made sense to her now. The looks, the glances, the compassion, and concern, as well as the unapproachability at times, all made sense. The someone who loved her desperately was Beth. Clia smiled and shook her head. What a fool I have been, she thought to herself. She realized she had also been very cruel, albeit unintentionally. Clia giggled then. Perhaps I can make up for that tonight, she thought.

Clia stepped out of the shower and dried off. She looked at herself in the steamy mirror and frowned. She was getting nervous already, and that boded ill. Clia shook off her apprehension and finished drying off. She combed out her hair and then took the make up case from under the sink. She did her makeup slowly and carefully. She already knew what she was going to wear, and she knew exactly how she wanted to look. Once she was done, she eyed herself critically in the mirror. She released a long sigh and hugged herself tightly. I have no idea what I am doing, she thought.

Clia shrugged off her misgivings and made her way to her dresser. She had never tried to dress seductively for anyone before, and she wasn't at all sure how to go about it. Most of her underwear was functional and comfortable rather than sexy, but her eyes were drawn to the white satin set her mother had given her on her last birthday. The set was still in the gift box, and Clia took it out and opened it. She pulled out the tissue paper and took out each piece. First was the white lace garter belt. Clia had not worn one since her Jr. Prom. To this, she attached the white stockings that were packaged in a separate box. Over the garters, she pulled up the panties, which were high thighs. The bra was a demi-cup and took a few adjustments before it was comfortable.

Over this, Clia pulled on her school sweatshirt and a pair of loose fit jeans. She had thought about something dressier, but it wasn't a date, and she didn't want to seem out of place. She sat on the bed and was tying up her sneakers when she heard the door close. Clia walked out of her room to find dinner on the table. Beth had killed the main lights and lit a few candles.

"Hey Cli, dinner is served," she said and smiled.

They ate dinner and talked about school, friends, the idiosyncrasies of their roommates, and a lot of other things. It was nice, and Clia didn't even feel like declining when Beth produced a bottle of wine after dinner and poured them both glasses. The conversation turned to more intimate things and then life, their plans, passions, and ideas. After her second glass of wine, Clia was a bit tipsy, but she also felt very mellow. She had forgotten how easy it was to be around Beth, how comfortable the little brunette made her feel, the very reasons they had become such good friends in the first place.

"How bout a movie?" Beth asked.

"I think I have seen all the ones we have a dozen times at least,"

"I have a couple in my room I don't think you have seen,"

"Like what?"

"Just let me pick one," Beth said with a chuckle and headed to her room. Clia walked over and sat on the sofa, curling her legs under her and snuggling into her favorite corner. Beth came down the hallway with a DVD in her hand and popped it into the machine.

"So what is it?"

"Be patient, It's a romance,"

Beth sprawled on the sofa, leaning on the other armrest with her legs stretched out under the coffee table. Clia tried to watch the movie, but it became apparent to her quickly that neither she nor Beth was spending half as much time watching the movie as they were watching each other. She was at a loss now, unsure of what to do. She had no experience at initiating things, and Beth seemed so scared that she was going to do something wrong she was paralyzed.

Clia looked at the smaller girl then. She was absolutely beautiful. She was also so nice and caring and supportive, the epitome of what Clia wanted in her life. Clia made a tough decision then. She decided to go against every reservation she had and try to initiate something. She scooted closer to Beth and curled up next to her, resting her head on the brunette's shoulder.

Beth looked shocked but quickly placed her arm on Clia's shoulder and held her tight. Their eyes met, and for a long time, they just stared. Clia's eyes darted to Beth's lips and then back to her eyes. Beth leaned forward hesitantly, and Clia did the same, their lips touched almost by accident. Both of them drew back like they had been burned, and Clia blushed furiously. Indecision was written all over Beth's face. She started to speak, then to lean close again, stopped herself, and then licked her lips.

"Cli, I want to kiss you more than anything in the world, but I don't ever want to hurt you. Are you sure it's what you want?"

Clia couldn't speak. She was shaking like a leaf in a summer storm. Finally, she managed to nod. Beth leaned forward again, and Clia closed her eyes. She felt Beth's soft lips upon her own, and it sent a thrill through her body. For a few breathless seconds, their lips were simply touching, but then Clia felt the tip of Beth's tongue swirl gently over her lower lip. Clia's lips parted, and Beth's inquisitive tongue was soon exploring her mouth. Clia was enjoying the kiss when Beth worked her legs under her and then pushed Clia back on the sofa, levering herself on top of the blonde. Through the whole maneuver, their lips never parted.

Clia twisted her lower body, so her legs were out of the way, and Beth settled down between her thighs. Beth's kiss became more demanding, and her hands slid down to pull Clia's sweatshirt up. Clia just held on to Beth's shoulders and kissed back. Her small hands found the large soft domes of Clia's breasts and began to squeeze and stroke them. Clia felt the blood rushing to her center and her back arched. She felt a tenseness building in the pit of her stomach and rising into her breasts. They felt like they would be torn from her chest by the power of the sensations. Clia moaned into Beth's mouth, which seemed to arouse the brunette tremendously. Her small hands dug into the firm flesh of Clia's breasts and roughly massaged them while her pelvis rubbed against Clia's. This new stimulus provoked a small squeal from Clia, and Beth instantly ceased all her attentions and broke the kiss.

"I'm sorry Cli. I don't want to go to far or too fast. I know it's all new to you, but God you turn me on so,"

"How far do you want to go?" Clia asked when she caught her breath.

"As far as I can get away with," Beth said and then smiled.

"Seriously, Beth,"

"Seriously?" she replied as her brows knit. She seemed to be fighting an inner struggle over what to say but reached a decision and took a deep breath.

"I want to fuck your brains out Cli, I have since I first met you,"

"Fuck my brains out? How would you go about that?" Clia asked. Beth smiled and kissed the tip of her nose.

"Never you mind. Suffice to say I could if you would let me, but I don't expect that from you, at least not yet,"

"How?" Clia asked seriously. Beth started to laugh but managed to keep it to just a chuckle.

"Your naivety is so refreshing. I have a strapon dildo I use with the girls I'm with. I'm what they call a butch. I am attracted to pretty feminine girls. I know I don't look like what you probably associate the word to mean, but I am,"

"What am I then?"

"Confused," she said with an impish grin, "And one hundred different kinds of sexy,"

"Seriously," Clia said as she wrinkled her nose.

"You are what's called a femme,"

"Which means?"

"It means you dress and act in a feminine manner. Femmes are usually attracted to butches, but not always. Femmes can be attracted to femmes or to both,"

"So I am a femme and you are a butch,"

"If you need labels, yes,"

"I don't think I need labels," Clia said in a small voice. Beth's face turned serious, and she lowered it until it was just inches from Clia's.

"What do you need?"

The evening had been so nice and comfortable. Clia had enjoyed herself without having to think ahead, but now was the moment of truth. With the question of what she wanted staring her in the face, Clia found herself utterly serene.

"I need you to fuck me," she whispered.

Beth pushed herself up on her arms. She looked down on Clia with a strange expression.

"Cli, I... I have dreamed about hearing you say those words to me, but are you sure? You don't have to do anything, I am content with just the evening and the kiss," she said earnestly. Clia felt her resolve melting. She had not expected Beth to have reservations.

"If you don't want to I understand," Clia said.

"Don't want to? Are you out of your mind? I have spent so many nights dreaming of taking you to bed it isn't even funny. I'm so in love with you. Watching you fall for someone else was awful, but I at least consoled myself with thinking you were Het. When you told me it was a girl I wanted to crawl up in a hole and die. I spent hours kicking myself for never having had the courage to hit on you," she said. The words were coming hesitantly at first but then becoming a rushing torrent.

"Now, you are lying here under me, like I have dreamed so often and saying the words I have longed to hear. And instead of jumping at the chance, I am acting like a fool. Worrying about how you will feel in the morning if we do. I must be loosing it!"

"No, you aren't loosing it. Well no more than anyone else who falls in love. Beth, I should have seen it but I never did. Now I realize it and recognize it in myself. I love you too," Clia said.

Beth seemed too stunned to move. She just held herself there staring. Clia laughed and pulled her back down, feeling the slight woman's weight on her. She pressed her lips to Beth's and, after a moment, felt Beth's tongue slip back into her mouth. This kiss was long, sensuous, and unhurried. Beth's tongue explored every millimeter of Clia's mouth, and Clia's did the same. Beth tasted sweet, like the wine but even sweeter and Clia found she couldn't get enough of that taste. She stabbed her tongue into Beth's mouth and searched out pockets of sweetness until there were none to be found.

When the kiss finally broke, both Beth and Clia were flushed and breathing heavily. Beth stood up and caught Clia's hand. She pulled her up and led her down the hallway to her bedroom. Clia had only been in here a few times, but now she saw things that had never made an impression before. The lack of anything overtly feminine impressed itself upon her. The room was tidy and clean but almost Spartan. Beth didn't give her a lot of time to look, though; she led Clia to the bed and gently pushed her back onto it.

Beth caught the hem of Clia's sweatshirt and pulled it over her head. Her eyes were glued to Clia's ample breasts, but her hands fumbled with the buttons of Clia's jeans. Once open, Beth tugged them off and tossed them on the floor in a ball. Her hands were trembling as they undid the hooks of the bra. Beth made a sharp intake of breath as the bra came way in her hands, and Clia's tits were exposed to her view. She gently stroked them for a moment but restrained herself and stood up.

The small girl quickly shed her own shirt and the sports bra she wore. Her breasts were small but beautifully sculpted and capped with a tiny pink aureole and hard little nipples. Clia barely had a chance to look at them before Beth shucked her jeans and stood before Clia clad only in her black silk boxers. She smiled and slipped the boxers off. Clia's eyes were drawn to the juncture of Beth's legs. She caught only a glimpse of her roommate's pussy before Beth turned and opened the drawer to her nightstand. From it, she took out a black harness with a sturdy black dildo attached to it. She expertly pulled it on and tightened the straps at her hips.

Clia stared in fascination; the sight was very strange but undeniably arousing. Beth stood before her with the dildo bobbing obscenely in front of her. She looked so feminine and lovely, save for that large black weapon jutting out from her slim hips.

Beth knelt between Clia's legs and, with one hand, pulled her panties aside. The little butch wasted only a moment to drink in the sight before she attacked Clia's pussy with her tongue. Clia had never felt anything like it. It was both soft and hard, gentle and demanding, smooth and rough. It was all of these things and more, but most of all, it was always at exactly the right place to make her feel the most wonderful. Beth quickly brought Clia to the brink of orgasm but always stopped just short of taking her over the edge. With each trip to the edge of bliss, Clia was more and more aroused until finally she was crying and begging for Beth not to stop.

Beth stopped again, leaving Clia pounding the bed with her fists in frustration, but the little butch gave Clia no chance to protest. She stood quickly and brought the head of the dildo to Clia's slick lips. Stroking it up and down just inside her lips drove Clia wild with desire. She moaned loudly, and her hips bucked.

"Ohh, looks like my baby is ready for some of this," Beth said in a husky voice. Clia only groaned in response.

"Tell me what you want baby, I have wanted to hear it for so long, come on, tell daddy what you want,"

"I want you to fuck me!" Clia nearly screamed. Beth smiled like the Cheshire cat and drove her hips forward, the big dildo stretched Clia like she had never been stretched before, and she gasped when it bumped against her hymen. Beth drove her hips forward again, apparently not grasping the reason for her access being thwarted.

"What the fuck??!" she growled in frustration. She grabbed the dildo and held it tight, and seemed about to ram it in when she stopped stock-still. Clia's whimpers were the only sounds in the room.

"Cli? Are you still a virgin?" Beth asked in a small voice. Clia could only nod. The full feeling of the dildo and the peak of sexual excitement her dreams and now Beth's tongue had taken her too were too intense for words.

"Cli are you sure about this?"

"Don't start that again," Clia said through clenched teeth.

"Cli, I can't. It's going to hurt you,"

"Please Beth, I want it to be you," Clia said. Beth nodded but still seemed unsure. She braced her legs apart and held the middle of the shaft, and then looked at Clia.

"I have never done this before, so bear with me," she said quietly. Clia just nodded again. Her pussy was beginning to get used to the intruder, but it was still an uncomfortable feeling. Clia closed her eyes and held her breath. She felt a tiny bit of movement and then a ripping tearing pain that caused her breath to shoot out of her. The pain was accompanied by a feeling of being full that was totally alien to her.

Her breath had been knocked out of her. She struggled to breathe, fight the rising panic, and adjust to having the big dong inside her. She was finally able to inhale and slowly got her breathing under control. The pain was still there but had faded into the background of her consciousness. The thing that was foremost in her mind was how the feeling of fullness had gone from uncomfortable to pleasurable.

"Are you all right?"

"Mmmm-Hmmmmmm," Clia hummed as she wiggled around on the bed, delighting in the sensation caused by the dildo moving slightly within her.

Beth smiled and experimentally jogged her hips, causing Clia to gasp. With that reassurance, the little butch caught Clia's hips and began a slow in and out motion of long strokes. To Clia, it was heaven; she could feel every inch of the big dildo as it slid in and out of her. The sensation of being full, then empty, then full again was addictive, and she was sure she would never want it to end.

Clia was rapidly approaching orgasm when Beth slipped her arms under Clia's legs and lifted them onto her shoulders. The angle of entry changed and the amount of stimulation to her clit as well. It took only a few driving thrusts before Clia felt her inner muscles grip the plastic cock. Moments later, an orgasm so powerful it blotted out all else washed over her. She had barely begun to regain her senses when she realized Beth was still plowing into her with reckless abandon. The little butch's hands found Clia's sensitive nipples and began to roll them between her fingers. The added stimulation sent a second orgasm crashing over her. This one was so intense she blacked out.

Epilogue

Clia's fingers were cramped, and her face hurt from wearing a smile for eight hours solid. She hated book signings, but it came with the territory when you made the NY Times bestseller list for the third time in as many years. Her newest book Emma & Josephine, was a new rage and had a set of scholarly debates across Europe and the Americas too.

Clia glanced at the line, at least another hour, she thought. Her eyes darted to the reading area where Beth sat quietly. Beth never missed a book signing or anything else. She was still beautiful to Clia after the years together. Beth caught her eye, glanced furtively left and right, then spread her legs widely apart and stroked the outline of the strapon she wore under her leather pants. Clia was forced to smile, which in turn made Beth smile. It was just the inspiration she needed to get through the rest of the fans.

Clia Johansen, a world-renowned author, signed many more books that day, but her mind was on the little Brunette and the fucking she knew she was in for as soon as the door to the limo closed. There are many forms of inspiration and many muses, Clia thought. She glanced again at Beth, including small brunette ones who packed large strapons. Clia smiled a real smile and signed another book. I name you Beth muse of happiness, she thought as the last hour ticked by.

Beach & Lesbians
03 Short Erotica Collection for Women
Sandra R. Galaz

All Rights Reserved. No part of this publication may be reproduced in any form or by any means, including scanning, photocopying, or otherwise without prior written permission of the copyright holder. Copyright © 2022

This book is entirely a work of fiction. The names, characters and incidents portrayed in it are the work of the author's imagination. Any resemblance to actual persons, living or dead, events or localities is entirely coincidental.

Story 01

Chapter 01

You must imagine yourself on a beach, a beach enclosed in a cove on three sides by towering walls of rock. Huge blooms explode from wild shrubs that grow on the slopes. There must be a path up to the top, or else how did you get here? Perhaps you arrived by boat. You could be anywhere in the world - anywhere that's scorching hot and not too popular. The beach is mysteriously deserted. Perhaps it's a private beach. It doesn't matter. The important thing is that you are utterly alone; nobody can see you.

As there's no one around, you have removed your bikini — on the face of it, to get rid of your tan lines, also to give your body a sense of liberation. This is your holiday. Without a backward glance, you have allowed the rest of your life to slip quietly from your mind. Nothing else matters but the immediate present and your immediate surroundings.

Lying flat out on your front, on a huge white downy towel, you can feel the lick of a mellow breeze from the sea blowing across your body, touching parts that never normally feel the elements. You are drowsy in the heat, and maybe a little woozy from a glass of white wine at lunch. You are feeling faintly horny too, but not excessively so. That wind was grazing your bare ass - it kind of turns you on, in a gentle, take-it-or-leave-it way. And anyway, you are feeling way too chilled out to touch yourself.

Your legs are slightly parted, but not too much. In case someone does come along, you don't want just anyone seeing what you're hiding between them. Although in the privacy of your slumber, you are dead certain that no one will come. Almost absent-mindedly, you note a trickle of sweat dripping down the crack between your legs.

This is the life. This is the way life should be lived. Always.

Through half-open eyes, you see two sandalled feet tramping across the sugary glaze of the sand. You hear them more than seeing them because you really aren't all that awake. But through a half-open eye, you do notice the silver glint of an ankle chain as it catches the sun. And dark pink nail polish on slender toes.

The two feet are heading towards you.

They don't belong to a man. You suppress an urge to look pull the towel over your ass if it's a woman.

The feet pass out of view, behind you. Someone must be heading for the sea, you think. But then the sound of sandals crunching in the sand comes to a halt. That's odd, you think. The heat, and your state of extreme relaxation, have reduced your heartbeat to a reluctant trudge, but you are interested to notice it accelerate into the merest skip. Yes, you are curious, but you're still too sleepy to look up. You close your eyes and slip back into some kind of semi-sexy dream.

And then something happens. Something that you weren't expecting. You can't quite tell if it's in your dream or happening for real—a drop of liquid lands on the tanned left cheek of your ass. Slowly the drizzle drifts across to your right cheek. To start with, it feels slightly cold, but the sun soon warms it as it begins to slide and slither down towards the crack in the middle of your ass.

Then a touch. Soft delicate. A hand. It wipes the oil over one side of your ass. Then another hand lands on the other side and rubs the oil over you. At one point, you feel the scratch of long nails as the person behind you grates the tips of their ('her?') fingers from the back of your knees. It went up to your slightly parted legs over your oily rump and stopped in the small of your back. It happens again. You shift your legs almost without moving; the slight parting is now very slightly wider.

It occurs to you that this is just what you wanted—someone to touch you. The hands start to rub and knead and mold the flesh of your butt. You're getting a massage on the beach, just what you were praying for in your sleep, and it's free. The hands seem to know what to do exactly. Your ass was already warm, despite the breeze from the sea, but now the friction is heating it up, and the heat is transferring from one part of your body to another.

You lie there, and you let it happen to you without moving a single muscle. Why should you? You're on holiday after all.

The hands start to get a little stronger. And a little closer to the middle as they play with your girl flesh. But then they stop. You think it's all over. You knew it was too good to last. Damn.

Suddenly a faint surprising drizzle lands right in the crack. With agonizing slowness, it works its way down into the sweat between your cheeks until - bang - you feel it run over the rim of your puckered little asshole. The sensation ratchets up the tension in your body.

You can feel yourself involuntarily pulling your legs slightly more apart. Just in case something really good happens next.

The oil resumes its journey south until it trickles to the edge of your—but you try not to think about that, to prolong this delicious slow-burning agony.

Without even realizing it, you raise your hips maybe a few centimeters off the ground as if your butt is begging and begging. But, begging for what? What can possibly come next?

It's the gentle feminine hands that come next. They pull apart the cheeks of your ass until you feel fingers and thumb of one hand holding them open. Suddenly a part of your body that never sees the sun is pointing at the heavens. You can feel the baking rays heating the oil. Wow.

You are really starting to enjoy this new and thrilling sensation when something definite happens. There's no imagining this, no dreaming it. A finger is teasing your asshole. You've been vaguely wanting to do this yourself but were too lazy to move.

Now the finger suddenly works its past the resistance of your opening, and you feel your muscles relax. In it comes. A finger, sliding easily in on a river of hot oil. Someone is penetrating you - it must be a woman - you've never seen. You can feel her finger probing around inside you, tickling the walls of your insides. And it's driving you fucking wild.

You lift your ass properly this time, begging her by your movement to push her finger in further. But what does she do? She pulls it out. The sensation as the finger leaves your ass is overpowering, but then she's back, this time with two fingers. It's tighter, but you like it as she starts to push in and out in a rhythmic motion.

This is better than any ass action you've ever imagined. You are being finger-fucked in the sun, and you've never been so turned on.

So you go for it. Nervously, but determinedly, you spread your knees wider. Unless the girl with the thin sexy ankles and the magic touch behind you is blind, she is now going to have the best view in the house of your hot, aching, dripping, pulsing pussy.

She can have it. It's hers to do with as she wishes. But what will she do?

Chapter 02

So where are you? You are on a deserted beach in the middle of a scorching afternoon. Waves are lapping gently against the shore in the distance, caressing the sand. You notice that the tickling sound of the tiny breakers is chiming with a rhythm in your own body. Yes, the mystery woman behind you - because you're in no doubt at all that she is a woman, though you daren't look back just in case she turns out not to be - the mystery woman behind you is pressing her fingers into you in time with the waves. You lucky girl: you are in sync with nature.

It occurs to you from her gentle thrusts that you've never had anything quite so deep inside you. You've never had a cock go this far. In fact, in this story, you've never had a cock in your ass at all. You don't understand how her fingers can reach so far in, as they can't be that long. Maybe it's the way you're ramming your rump backward to swallow every last millimeter of those two fingers as they glide in and out of you. The pleasure is indescribable. So new, so full of surprise. You never suspected this part of you had such a delectable secret. Of course, it took a woman to find it. No man would ever know.

If anyone could see you now from the side - though God knows you wouldn't want that to happen - what would find before them? A girl with her head on its side, shoved into a towel, her inverted back curling upwards towards the sky, legs half splayed, and the crowning glory, two glistening hills of flesh rising above the sand. If the tide came in, the rest of you would be swamped, but there'd be an island of oily ass gleaming out of the water.

You know you mustn't look. But can you touch? Can you touch - if not the other person - then yourself? You bring your right arm out from under you and slowly send a hand backward towards a place it knows how to touch. This is going to be a big moment. You can't wait for your mysterious new friend to help you out, so you are cutting to the chase. You're going to help yourself. You're going to take advantage of yourself.

Just as your fingers reach the edge of the trimmed thatch of pubes, something happens that you weren't expecting. Those fingers, so seductively slipping in and out of your asshole, are suddenly removed. The sensation as they are pulled out so sharply makes you catch your breath. And squirm.

You're so taken aback that your right-hand stops where it is before it reaches its destination. What the hell's going on? You were enjoying that. You loved it. You're just about to send a single middle finger down again when you feel a hand grabbing hold of your wrist, quite firmly, and sending it back to where it started. There seems to be no argument with this. You've been banished. Whoever this woman is behind you, she doesn't want to interfere. If anyone's going to give you pleasure, it's her.

It could be worse. Frustrating, yes. You are - frankly - desperate for your pussy to be touched by someone, anyone. But it can't be put off forever. You know it's coming sometime soon. And in the meantime, there's another surprise for you.

She's feeling around your asshole again. You've never felt more relaxed after that, the gentle widening the stranger has performed on you. But you can feel more oil being poured into your crack. More oil? Why more? It feels like there's been a spill down there already. This time it's less ceremonious, less flirtatious. And there's more of it—a lot more. It feels like half the bottle is being emptied onto you. Into you. Some of it dribbles uninterrupted down your pussy's sides; some of it drizzles speculatively over the little ribs and ravines of your pussy. As if it needs it. But the bulk of the oil is reserved for your asshole, which with two fingers she is actually holding open. She is pouring oil into you. You can feel the burning heat of it seeping in.

What can she be up to?

You pluck up the courage to move your head ever so slightly, and out of the corner of an eye, half-open in the sun's glare, you catch an arm, brown and slender, the brief flash of a thin silver bracelet. It matches the one on her ankle, you think. But then you have to shut your eyes, and not because of the sun.

It's a shock when a third finger is introduced. This time it's tight. No question. You feel the scrape of a fingernail against your insides as she pushes a new thickness very very, very slowly inside you. As a bunch of knuckles meet the muscles at the opening of your ass, you can feel them quiver in protest. This is pain. But not bad pain. Good pain. It's an exquisite pain. Pain that's almost impossible to tell apart from pleasure.

For the first time since this extraordinary new thing happened to you, you make a sound. It's almost as if you haven't been breathing, and now as a fingernail delicately scratches against the roof of your insides, you can't help it. Wordlessly, you squeal. Oh my god. You never knew that such a delicate touch, the merest scrape, could send such a shockwave around your system. You can almost feel the nail in your throat as the touch deep inside your reverberates through your body. You shiver. It may be hot. You may be hotter than you've ever been. But just for a moment, you shiver uncontrollably.

And now the three fingers start to move. Harder than the two fingers earlier. The emphasis is not on pushing them in, but pulling them out so that with every motion, you feel as if you're about to be turned inside out, to have some inner part of yourself drawn forth. It feels like a form of violation, but one you never knew you wanted. The pain is now forgotten as the slippery motion of this clump of fingers gets quicker. And that's not all that's forgotten. It's such a massive, all-conquering feeling that - miracle of miracles - you've forgotten all about your pussy.

This is too much; you can't hold it in. You start to moan.

But it's not some little girly moan; it's not high-pitched. This moan comes right from the pit of your stomach. You can feel it working its way up from the bottom of your lungs: a deep exhalation of breath with just a ghost of a sound to it.

You are being fucked hard, from behind, in your virgin asshole, by a woman.

And you can't even see her.

It's a double initiation. You've never felt the touch of a woman before, and no one has been this far inside you. What the hell else is the afternoon going to bring?

A feeling of ecstasy starts to rise in you, like a wave gathering momentum far out at sea. This has a look, the feel of something pretty big. Something phenomenal. In the small part of your brain that is still available of rational thought, it occurs to you that you've never had an anal orgasm before. In fact, you didn't even know they existed, but something tells you that such a thing may well be about to happen to you like the three fingers with their ridge of knuckles ride and ride and ride and ride and ride and ride in and out and in and out of that gaping, giving, sopping asshole of yours.

You want to say something. But what? You are now next door to heaven, damn near to nirvana. There's nothing to say, apart from the obvious, which is to ask for more. It's hardly necessary. More is what you're getting—more than you've ever dreamed of.

Fuck me.

You think about it, but you don't say it.

Fuck me. Fuck me. Fuck me.

In time with her thrusts.

Fuck me.

Fuck me.

You're no longer in tune with nature. If you could hear them in the deafness of your ecstasy, you'd notice that the waves are still ambling in at their own pace, but your insides, your secret place, your whole body, is writhing to its frantic rhythm.

Fuck me harder; fuck me harder. Fuck me.

And then you actually say something. You hardly know you're doing it, but you can't help it. Your groans now formulate into a single word.

More.

Out it comes softly. It's almost too much of an effort to push the word out. So you push harder.

More.

She's never going to answer you. But still, you say it.

More.

More!

MORE!

You can feel that wave inside you swelling, and swelling, and swelling. Pretty soon, there's going to be no holding it back.

MORE!!!!

For an instant, the three fingers come out—just an instant. For that split second, you panic. Not now, you think. Don't, for God's sake, stop now. You can feel your open wound clamping shut like a reflex. Christ, is that it?

But your fears are allayed as - BANG - she pushes in a fourth finger. It must be the fourth finger because you can feel yourself straining to let her back in. It's as if you are being ripped half-open. And that's all you need to shove you over the edge. As you feel half a hand jamming violently into your asshole, that wave inside you rears magnificently up to its full majestic height. It pauses for at the crest for the briefest moment to before it comes comes comes Comes Comes COMES COMES smashing down in an almighty detonation of noise and power and might.

You practically faint as it hits you, and she rips her fingers out of you one final time.

You want to say thank you, but you can't. Your head is out of oxygen. You can't even begin to focus as strange shapes swim around in your eyes. Your brain has obliterated all other sensations from your body but the one overwhelming message: a shattering pleasure.

And she hasn't even touched your pussy yet.

Chapter 03

That was some orgasm, you think, as you feel your body slacken. The tension drains out of your shoulders, your back, your thighs. Those oily haunches of yours are still thrust up towards the sky, and it occurs to you that you could now happily lie down, happily turn over, and very happily set eyes ~ at last - on the mysterious woman behind you.

How much do you know about her? You tot up the facts. Two chains: one on an ankle – you can't remember which; another on the right wrist. A pair of sandals. Some dark toenail polish. Long fingernails. Two firm hands. One, two, three, four fingers. She has scarcely touched you at all, apart from your insides. You idly wonder what the rest of her is like, what she's wearing - if she's wearing anything. You can't remember ever thinking quite so clearly, and so consciously, about a woman's pussy before. What it looks like. What it feels like, what it might taste like. This is a new territory for your imagination, where it is trespassing very close to the frontiers of reality.

This concrete thought causes you to stir. The time has come. Let's draw back the curtains, you think and reveal the seducer. Let's take off the blindfold. You raise yourself onto your elbows and are just pushing up onto your hands when you feel a hand on the back of your head. It seems to be staying you, lulling you. Something inside you objects or doesn't believe her, and you push yourself up onto your hands and start to turn your head. Promptly the hand grabs a hunk of your hair and restrains you. It doesn't hurt. It would if you moved, but you don't. You are stock still as the hand pulls tightly enough on the hair for the pecking order to be firmly re-established. You are not in charge. She is. Whoever she is. She must be standing directly behind you; you feel a tingle in your stomach work its way downwards. You have never surrendered to anyone before. Not like this.

She holds your hair for perhaps half a minute, just long enough to underline the hierarchy. The slightest hint of resistance, of mobility, and she'll tug your hair tight, like a rider sitting astride a horse and pulling on the leather reins. So you submit.

No sooner has the parallel with a horse and a rider occurred to you than you can feel it happening for real. Two quick steps and her legs are straddled on either side of you. Not that she's touching you, but you know because on the edge of your vision, you see those two feet again. There's one planted next to each of your knees. You notice that the sandals have gone. So she's definitely taken something off.

Gradually she eases her grip on your hair and starts stroking it instead, pat it, pulls it back behind your ears. This is the gentlest she's been with you so far, and in its own way, it's just as intoxicating as the savage fucking that, in the grip of this new sensation, your body is only now starting to forget. If it's possible to lust after someone you can't see, why can't it be just as possible to fall a little in love with them too? That's what you're thinking as she stands over you, caressing your hair and kneading your scalp with her fingertips.

For the first time, you think that she must be your friend. To show this much tenderness, she can't just be your lover. In that instant, you are overwhelmed by a longing to kiss her.

Kiss me.

You say it out loud.

I want to kiss you. Please. I want to feel your lips. Are you going to let?

Big mistake. There is a sudden movement behind you. The hands abandon your hair. You can feel a sudden movement behind you, a flick of thin material grazing your hindquarters, and then before you know it, darkness has descended. A piece of cloth of some description has been placed roughly over your eyes. You can feel your head tugged back as she ties a knot and secures the cloth tightly. You have been blindfolded for real. She has punished you for your curiosity, and now you really can't see a thing. In an instant, the mystery has deepened.

Slap. The next thing you feel is a palm on your ass. Not too hard. But not too soft either. She must be rebuking you—tingle ripples from your butt around your body. You emit the slightest moan. To your surprise, you rather enjoyed a firm smack on your ass.

Slap. Harder this time, on the other cheek. It stings deliciously, but moaning is not allowed for now. Could you pussy be any wetter?

What the hell do you do now? You can't move, you can't see, you can't speak or make any sound. Your options are severely limited. All you can do is hear. And smell. And most importantly, feel.

You feel a touch of a hand on your shoulder. She is pushing you down. You obey. There is no further point in disappointing this forceful woman. The next thing you feel a hand gripping each ankle. In turn, she pulls on one leg, then the other. The instruction seems to be to lie down, flat. Again, you do as you're told. You are back in the position she found you in. perhaps, it occurs to you, she's going to leave, that the blindfold is only there to protect her identity while she retreats across the sand to wherever it is she sprang from. Your heart misses a beat. You were rather hoping she hadn't finished. Below decks, you feel a squirming sensation at the thought of abandonment.

A hand now touches you on your right side, then another hand. You can feel yourself being pushed. You are being urged to roll over onto your back. Slowly, rather hesitantly, you comply.

Your whole body now undergoes a radical shift. It's one thing to be lying naked on your front. Quite another to be exposed in this position. Suddenly you are available to be seen. An instinctive attack of shyness assails you, and you raise your hands to cover your breasts, tilt one thigh inwards to cover your pussy.

As expected, she won't hear of it. A hand, reasonably gentle, pushes your leg back into place, then methodically pulls your arms out wide. You look as if you're being crucified, it occurs to you, lying there in the sun with arms outstretched and legs pinned together. But no sooner has the thought danced into your head that you feel a hand grabbing hold of one knee and lifting it away from the other. You don't even wait for her to grab the other knee but push it into the same position. It's a small victory that you've managed to do something for yourself. You are not quite the slave she thinks you are, you tell yourself. However, your self-congratulation is cut short as she puts a hand on each knee and pushes your legs far wider apart than you think they've ever been before.

She lets go, and your legs can't help closing slightly. She pushes them back again. This performance is repeated two or three times until you realize that you will have to make an effort to obey. Which you do, on the assumption that you will get what you've been waiting for.

Now, you think, lick my fucking pussy, seeing as you've opened it so fucking wide. Just lick it. You gorgeous dominatrix-bitch.

No woman has ever run her tongue along the slippery slopes of your pussy before. You always assumed it would feel different. Now you want to find out. You can't wait. But you do wait. You wait, wet, for your wish to be granted. She doesn't seem to be listening to the speech inside your head.

Nothing happens. There is silence.

Just at the moment where you think of closing your legs in protest, you feel hair falling over your face, followed at once by a tongue licking your lips. But not your pussy lips. The lips of your mouth. It's wet, the tongue. As it moistens your lips, you open your mouth and send your tongue out to meet hers. In an instant, predictably, she withdraws her tongue, her whole mouth, her hair. You feel a hand gripping your jaw, pushing it to shut, while the other hand pushes down on your forehand. She doesn't want you to open your mouth. Message received and understood, you tell yourself, as the hair comes back to caress you. It smells beautiful, you notice, as she plants a kiss on your lips — your first kiss from a woman. You decide to take courage into your hands and respond. Nobody, after all, wants to kiss and not be kissed back. So that is what you do. You respond to her wet warmth as if this is the first time you've ever kissed anybody, which is what it feels like anyway — your first time kissing a woman. It feels utterly different and utterly wonderful. Does she taste of sugar and spice? Surely not. But she definitely tastes different.

Her lips have a fullness to them that makes you want to meld with them. Soon her tongue has flicked out again and this time, as her grip on your jaw slackens, she lets you join her. Searchingly, softly, your two tongues begin to dance and pirouette around each other, licking each other, hardening, softening until suddenly you can feel her tongue jammed deep into your mouth. You respond in kind and start to kiss with frenetic energy.

You lose track of time, but as you feel your heart slowly melting, you do what any normal person would do in the heat of an embrace and start to raise your arms. You want to wrap this faceless woman into you. You want to drag her on top of you and pull her body into yours.

You know it won't be allowed. But you try anyway. You raise a right arm and place it tentatively on her left shoulder. To your astonishment, you are not rebuffed. You raise your other arm on the side; she's crouching and pull it up over her back. You feel the thin slip of some skimpy T-shirt. You push your hand under the material to stroke along her vertebrae, then push on to her neck. Her hair, you calculate, must be quite long, certainly over the shoulders. It's ringlet and, you guess, dark, probably black.

As you carry on kissing, a miracle happens. She pushes an arm under your back, another under your neck, and slowly pulls you up towards her. The kiss has melted into an embrace. As you hold on tight, it only now occurs to you that there is soft flesh pressing into you under her top. She feels quite big, though you can't be sure, and you are suddenly desperate to find out. You've got an animal urge to feel a woman's breast in your clasp. You pull your right hand from her back and slowly drag it around under her T-shirt towards her front.

You are about to push your hand into place when – bang – everything changes. The arms withdraw the tongue, the lips, the mouth—the gorgeous hair. Your arms are pushed firmly back into place.

The kiss is over. You think you can hear her stand up.

You are back to square one, not knowing what will happen next. The only advantage you have now is the knowledge that she's probably not far out. She's probably got some other filthy titillation swilling around in that bitch Goddess's mind of hers.

Story 02

Chapter 01

While sitting in that damp sand, between the water and the dry sand, my legs spread wide so that the waves could lap at my crotch, I thought about Brenda. I thought about how she liked doing that to me. I looked around, and I was alone. I felt alone. Deep down, I was alone. I lifted my bottom and slipped the bottoms of the suit past my ass and over my feet. I held them to my face and inhaled deeply, smelling the mixture of saltwater and my juice—how I missed sharing myself with Brenda.

It was the first of June when my Aunt Peggy called and asked if I wanted the beach house for the next three months. It seems that she had been unable to rent it out this summer. How the hell could I turn such an offer down? We had never been close, but this was what I needed at this point in my life exactly. I had no classes to teach until the fall, so I said I would. I laughed at my luck the whole time I packed.

Just past the toll bridge onto the beach, I took the top down on my Jeep CJ so I could enjoy the next 10 miles of the sun. The last few miles, I was glad I was driving a 4-wheel drive as I plowed through sand-drift after sand drift. Sometimes I wasn't even sure where the pavement was. The house numbers passed, 6824, 6826. There it is, 6886. Wow! It looks like at least 20 homes are gone. The others look empty. Peggy's place was all that is left at the end of the road. I guess I'll have plenty of privacy.

For a few weeks each summer, my parents used to bring me to her place when I was growing up. It had been built in the '50s on a concrete slab with concrete blocks painted pink and jalousie windows—not a popular part of the beach back then, filled with several rows of houses each parallel to the water. Now, after the past several years of hurricanes, many of the houses were gone, only some scrap wood, a few pilings, and a few slab foundations—nothing else. Of course, there had been a pink flamingo out front. The pink flamingo was now gone.

At least the key she gave me still worked. The old windows were now replaced with larger windows. What a mess the place was, it looked like no one had been here all winter to even check on the place. I tried all the faucets, and the water seemed to work, even the hot water. I was surprised that the electric hot water heater was actually working after seeing the place's condition. I was not one to complain, though. I used the broom from beside the fridge to sweep the terrazzo floors. It would be stupid to have carpets in a beach house. It was nice to feel the coolness of these floors on the bottoms of my feet. Nicer than vinyl, and prettier than plain concrete.

A quick survey of the place made me feel like this would be just what I needed this summer. Maybe I could get a start on the book I'd planned to write for several years. Yes, that desk, with a view through the front window towards the ocean, would be the perfect place to plant my butt and my laptop. I hadn't told anyone exactly where I would be, so I didn't have to worry about any friends deciding to surprise me with an extended visit.

Three trips were all it took to carry in my belongings and supplies. I had enough food to last me the first few days. I had seen a small grocery store, still in business and open, about 5 miles before I got to the house so I could make a run for more, as I needed.

Laptop on the desk, clothes put in drawers, sheets on the bed, food in cupboards, and dishes washed, now I stood in the doorway looking at the ocean. I unbuttoned my blouse and let the cool salt air filled breeze blow it open. The warmth of the sun was shining on my breasts now. I pushed on the elastic waistband of my short pants until they fell around my ankles. With a little kick of my foot, they flew up, and I caught them with one hand. How wonderfully wicked it felt to stand there nearly naked.

I grabbed a towel and walked towards the water. Looking around, I realized just how solitary this part of the beach had become. It was like a ghost town. With the tall sand dunes, I couldn't even see any other houses, not even the closest ones, only Aunt Peggy's. This encouraged me, maybe more than I should have let myself become. I carried the towel in my hand with only my unbuttoned blouse to provide any cover.

As I walked away from the houses towards the end of the point of land I was on, through the highest reaches of the incoming waves, only my footprints were to be found. They didn't last very long. A few seashells and some seaweed littered the beach, not much else. It was like I was the first person to discover this piece of shoreline. The solitude was almost overwhelming, much nicer, refreshing compared to the sounds of the city and the university I'd left behind. Now all I could hear was the lapping of the surf as it rolled in and the squawk of a few seabirds. I could hardly wait for tonight as the heavy surf of the incoming tide started crashing hard against the beach.

I spread my towel, tossed my blouse on one corner, and lay on my stomach, my firm ass smiling at the sky. I'd always liked my ass, and several girlfriends had often remarked how they'd like to have theirs be just like mine. The skin on my back warmed, and I felt myself about to fall asleep. I fought to stay awake, knowing the last thing I wanted was a sunburn on the first day.

The nakedness of my body, the fact I was laying this way out here, stirred some primitive feelings between my legs. No, they were not new ones, not at all. There weren't many kinds of sex I'd not participated in. Probably only sex with a guy was all that I'd skipped. I slipped my hand under me and let my fingers play with myself, just casually touching and not really trying to drive myself into an orgasm. I was just enjoying my nakedness myself and out in nature.

Without a watch, it was hard to tell how long I'd laid there, but it seemed like it had been maybe too long. I didn't know why I needed to, but I felt compelled to at least slip my blouse back on, even if I didn't button it up. It is strange how some customs and habits are difficult to not do.

It had been a very long drive and the late afternoon was warm. I could still feel myself in need of a nap, maybe just a short one. The bedroom windows had been opened earlier while I cleaned, and the room was filled with the sensual smell of the sea. I lay naked on my back, lazily diddling my pussy with my finger as I drifted off to sleep.

It was dark as I awoke and sat on the edge of the bed. The nearly full moon was hovering almost above the horizon, a tiny piece of the bottom still hidden by the surf. The air was cooler now, not cold, but just enough to make me put on a long-sleeved t-shirt that covered me to the tops of my thighs. Just before walking out the door, I grabbed a cold bottle of beer to sip as I plodded and splashed through the edge of the water.

The moon was now higher in the sky. The feel of the water up to my knees, sometimes higher, often lower, was almost hypnotic. A breaking wave dampened the bottom of my t-shirt, and I held it up around my waist, the waves now splashing against my bare bottom. I thought about how nice it would be to have someone to hold hands with, to share these moments with. I also thought about how nice it was to be alone for a change.

Back at the house, naked at my desk, I flipped on my laptop and stared at the screen. No great inspiration sprung forth, but the effects of the beer could definitely be felt. I gave up and shuffled to the bedroom. Listening to the sounds of the huge waves of the incoming tide, I quickly drifted off to sleep while my fingers strummed my clit.

I forced myself to follow a routine to make sure I wasn't spending too much time on the beach and not getting anything done on the book. During the next few days, I made some progress on my book and took more walks along the beach.

It was not until the fourth day that I saw my first human on the beach. Some man with a fishing pole and a bucket for whatever he caught. I just happened to not be too exposed, thank God. He tipped his hat, the one that said 'Fish or Die.' He ignored the obvious bulge in his pants. I did too.

That first trip to the grocery store was a bit of a surprise. It looked much, much bigger than it actually was. I was able to get everything I needed, so that was good. Everyone that worked there was either in high school or over 55, mostly later. All were nice; all asked me where I was living, what I did, and how long I'd be around. I left with three bags of groceries and more beer.

The end of the first week had come and gone, and I was still enjoying my time alone. I was still enjoying lying naked on the beach too. Other than the fisherman, I'd not seen a soul on the beach. Today was no different as I lay on my stomach, loving the warmth of the sun on my bare skin.

"Like some company?"

The voice was soft, feminine, and quite sensual. It still startled me. I looked around as I got my heart to beat again. There were women's feet, nice looking feet, close to my towel. I looked up, but the sun was in my eyes. Whoever it was had already seen my naked body, and covering up to no longer made any sense. I sat up, and with my eyes shielded with a hand, I could see more of her.

"You're the second person I've seen out here in a week."

"I parked a few houses up the road and walked along the water. I was surprised to see someone. Like a morgue around here."

"Join me. I'm Karen. Staying in that house." I pointed toward my Aunt's house.

She spread her towel next to mine. "I'm Brenda. Mind if I take my suit off?"

"Help yourself." Not that her suit covered all that much of her anyway. Besides, I was naked already.

As she moved, so she was not directly in the sun, I began to realize just how nice she looked, not a raving model kind of woman, but a lot like me. You know, that mid-forty-year-old look. Body not so firm anymore, but definitely not even close to being chubby. Her hair long, in a ponytail, pulled through a baseball cap. Breasts nice, not huge, and not so large, they overwhelmed her chest. As her suit bottom slipped over her hips, I could see she, like me, didn't have any hair between her legs.

"So Karen, you must be enjoying the quiet. Sorry to interrupt it."

"Don't be. I guess this morning I'd even thought it would be nice to see someone today."

"And here I am." She giggled as she held her hands out wide. Her eyes scanned my body, checking out my breasts, my pussy. "Hope you don't mind if I say how nice you look. Some women our age have a difficult time."

I reached over and opened my small cooler and pulled the other bottle of beer out of the ice, the ice that left the bottle dripping wet, wet like I was becoming. My thumb popped the top. It spun up into the air and landed in the cooler. As I held it out, she took it, letting her fingers brush against mine.

"Likewise. Guess I was checking you out too." I laughed. "You married?"

"Heavens no, just a few lady friends along the way, but nothing currently. And you?"

"Same here. I teach at a university, but off for the summer. I'm trying to write a book. Nothing very heavy, just some erotic fiction about love between women."

"Ah, good smut." She smiled.

"Yeah. Cunts, tits, moans, and such."

My mind began to race with thoughts of her big filling places in the story I was working on. It was not a big leap for me to also see her filling the empty spot next to me in bed as well.

"Sounds like more fun than writing software. I'm staying about 10 miles back towards the bridge at what seems like the only hotel left on the island. Me and about 10 other guests."

She lay on her side facing me, a hand rested on her mound, a finger lightly rubbed her labia and her clit. I watched for a few moments, not saying anything, just watching how casually she played with herself in front of what was a total stranger. I was fascinated by how relaxed she seemed to be doing that.

It was not long before I could no longer resist, and I touched myself in a similar manner and at a similar pace. She watched me as I continued to watch her. Our eyes occasionally looked at each other's face, then returned to prior glances. I was so-o-o turned on.

She lay back, and her mouth fell open. "Ahh..." was the only sound she made. Eventually, she removed her hand, and I did too. It was clear that we both had an orgasm while watching the other. I took it as an unspoken sign that we could do to the other whatever was desired. I think she did too.

I sat up. "Need some lotion?"

"Please."

I squeezed a large drop on her back, and she jumped a little. I knew it would be cold. I really wanted to start with those cheeks of hers. What a nice butt she had. I could only imagine what was between her legs and how that would feel against my fingers or my lips.

It started as a light rub of suntan lotion on her back but soon became a firm massage.

"Now that does feel good." She said with more of a moan than just regular talk.

"Just enjoy it."

Another plop of lotion just above the crack of her ass caused her to squeeze her cheeks tight for a moment before relaxing them. As I kneaded her cheeks, my lotion covered finger dragged deep between them over her anus.

She moaned. "I hope you're not just teasing me."

My fingertip pressed against it, but never went inside. "Maybe later." I whispered deeply.

From the back, my hand slipped between her spreading legs, and the fingers worked their way inside her pussy.

"This is what I want to do now." I leaned forward and kissed her neck. "And a lot more."

"Baby, I hope a very lot more." She rolled over, forcing my hand away for a second. Now on her side facing me, she took my hand and placed it back over her pussy. "Lay down here with me and let's have some lip action."

We held each other tight, the sand caught in the suntan lotion, acting like sandpaper as our skin rubbed back and forth. Our lips spread wide-open as they pressed against each other, our teeth clicking together. Our tongues were moving back and forth like sabers striking through the wide-open space of our open mouths. Her mouth closed enough that my tongue was forced to stay in her mouth by a strong vacuum as she inhaled.

I could feel her fingers grasp my mound, as I had done to hers not so long ago. The tips of her fingers pulling my pussy lips apart, then sliding inside, an edge of probably a thumb working against my clit. A single-digit was rubbing against the roof of my cunt, searching for the tender slab of skin that would unlock much passion. "Fuck Yeah!" I almost screamed as she touched it. She concentrated her touches there until I could no longer breathe, could no longer do anything. "No more." I begged. It did no good. I thought my heart would stop. I had rarely been here this long. "Oh please..." I begged again. She held me at this peak for almost too long, then slowly let me fall back down into a more normal state of being.

Her tongue slammed into my mouth as I inhaled hard. I could almost feel it rip from her mouth, but I knew it had not. All I was trying to do was let her know how much I'd enjoyed her intense touch.

I stared into her eyes. "Are you sure that you didn't just fall from heaven?" I stuck my tongue deep into her mouth so she could not reply right away.

Her fingers squeezed my clit. "Fuck me baby. You're really good." She paused for a moment. "Maybe you should take notes for your book."

"Maybe we will just have to work out a few episodes. Several times each." I giggled.

"Let's go rinse this sand off and I can show you what I like to do the most."

"Hopefully it is eating my pussy."

"A mind reader too. Exciting."

As I stood up, I grabbed her suit bottom and held the crotch to my nose, inhaling deeply.

"You like?"

"I like. I can't wait to inhale the real thing."

The water was running cold by the time we left the small metal shower with spots of rust on the white walls that rattled as we bumped them. It barely held us, neither cozy nor romantic, just functional at best. It was hard to picture my Aunt sharing this or any shower with someone. I knew she had not considered that when choosing this shower.

On the bed, we simply laid down with our faces pressed against the other's pussy. No foreplay, no romance, just straight to business, the business of eating pussy. Alternating between intense licking, fingering, sucking, and just light touching, we rolled through countless orgasms and near misses. Sometimes she was on top, or I was. Sometimes we lay side by side. Everything was good. I loved the feel of her pussy grinding against my face, sometimes my chin. I would respond in a similar manner too.

When we started, the sun was high in the sky. Now it was almost touching the ocean. My thigh was coated with her dried juices from grinding against it more than a few times. I could feel my mouth covered, as well.

She turned and looked intensely at me for a moment before gently kissing my lips. She stopped. "God damn you're good."

"Didn't think I had that many orgasms in me. What will I do tomorrow if I want to have one?"

"Guess I could come back."

"Or just stay."

"Really? Maybe I should go back to the hotel tonight and plan to stay tomorrow night."

"Actually I think you should stay tonight and checkout tomorrow morning."

"We just met."

"I have a good feeling about us."

"Often those initial feelings suck."

"I know. Usually for me they do. This feels different. Besides, how long had you planned to be at the hotel?"

"Two more nights."

"We don't want to waste those precious few nights then."

"Is there a place we can have dinner?"

"I've got some salad and 2 turkey dinners in the freezer. Several cold beers too."

That night had come straight from a romance novel - great company, some dinner, too much to drink, and lots of good sex. Brenda was good for my soul. I'd not ever known someone quite like her. I don't know how we'd been tossed together, but I was savoring every moment. I also was trying to ignore that this would all come to an end far too quickly. I half heartily hoped she wouldn't leave. I knew I could not expect that.

We made love most of the night, and as the sun rose, the bed looked like there had been a massive orgy played out there. An arm rested over each other. Our lips lay inches apart. I could feel her breath blowing against my lips, and didn't bother to open my eyes, just leaned forward until mine touched hers. She automatically responded, and our tongues greeted each other 'good morning.' Probably before we were completely awake, they were deep inside each other's other mouth, and our arms squeezed a little tighter around us.

"If you still want me to stay..."

"If you try to leave, I'll handcuff you to the bed."

"Well I need to go checkout. Come with me and I'll buy you breakfast at the hotel."

I picked up a comb. "Let me run a comb through my hair. Not sure we have time to shower."

"Gag. It's can't be 10:10?"

"Afraid it is." I tossed her a pair of shorts and a t-shirt so she wouldn't have to wear a still-damp bathing suit back to the hotel. "Sorry, no uns."

"Who wears them?"

As we passed her car in my Jeep, she yelled, "Hey, the rental car is still here."

I reached out and grabbed her hand. "Glad you're sitting right there."

"Me too."

And I truly was glad, but my heart ached that the clock was ticking and she would leave. I replayed last night over and over in my head as the pavement passed under the car. Her mouth on my clit put me in a place that I didn't get to go often enough. Those fingers inside of me played me like a fine instrument, and it didn't take me long to get tuned up.

The tall blue water tower was always both a welcoming sign and an exit sign for me as a child. Even painted white now, I could see it not very far ahead. That was the first thing everyone saw as they came onto the island just off the toll bridge. It had been there forever. None of the hurricanes that had torn up the island had ever damaged it. It was like the thing that screwed the island to the earth.

The hotel Brenda was staying at was one of the only big hotels that had been rebuilt and reopened. The others looked like they had been through war; empty parking lots filled with debris, no windows, lots of plywood tacked everywhere. Whatever damage they had suffered, they faired much better than the old one and two-story motels that had been the staple for so many years. They were all leveled now, just concrete slabs and sand-covered parking lots remained.

"Breakfast?" the hostess asked.

"Still serving?"

"For another 5 minutes."

"Great!"

The dining room was nearly empty, and she sat us at a table with a wonderful view of the ocean. The waves were a foot or more and breaking with a crash as they hit the beach. I guess it was still too cool for some, but there were maybe 25 people brave enough to venture out scattered here and there in chairs and laying on towels.

Brenda's head turned as a lovely woman with a golden tan, and not much material covering it walked past our windows.

My eyes traced the path from her eyes to the woman. "Very lovely. I used to have a body like that."

"There's nothing wrong with your body Karen. Nothing at all."

"You're too kind Brenda."

Her Eggs Benedict and my waffle with strawberries arrived.

"Those eggs look good all of a sudden. Wish I'd ordered that."

She cut a portion off and pushed her plate towards me. "For you sweetheart."

I reached over and took her hand in mine, giving it a light squeeze. "You're special."

"Just sharing with someone I had a great time with yesterday and still this morning."

I dropped her off by her rental car. "Careful of the sand drifts." I waved as I pulled ahead.

I parked in the carport, she behind me. As she turned the ignition off, I leaned in the open car window and kissed her. "Welcome home." I kissed her again.

She laid a small suitcase on the bed next to me and unzipped it. Inside there were two more bathing suits, a few blouses, and a single pair of shorts.

"Looks like you travel light."

"Yup. It does. Didn't think I'd need much more at the beach." She held up the bathing suits. "May not need these."

"Babe, don't need to cover that body."

Brenda turned and wiggled her butt at me then slapped it. "Glad you like it."

"Like it all. Sweet tasting pussy too."

She zipped the suitcase up and sat it against the wall. She was lying next to me, her face resting on her palm, elbow on the bed, she lazily rubbed a finger over my breast, my nipple, as she looked down at me. "How did I get so lucky yesterday?" Her hand slipped under my t-shirt and rested on the same breast that she had just been touching.

I pulled her down on top of me, and our lips met, our tongues pressed inside our mouths. I could feel the button on my shorts pop as she pulled on the waistband, followed by her hand sliding inside. "Yes," I moaned loudly, the fingers of her hand rubbing back and forth across my mound on their way to their goal. I was already sopping wet as the first finger entered me quickly, followed by the second and third making a slurping sound as each went in. My hips thrust hard against her hand. "Fuck me!" I screamed, knowing that even with the windows wide open, the sea breeze blowing across our nearly naked bodies, there was not a soul for miles to hear me beg, plead for this to not stop.

Brenda stopped tugging on my shorts suddenly. "What?"

She fucking well knew what I had said. Her hands slowly pulled my shorts down a little more, stopping with the waistband resting under my hips. She moved, so she sat beside my shorts, her hands pulling a little teasing me that she was trying to get them completely off. I even lifted my hips to make it easy.

"Does she want me to pull these nasty shorts off her?"

I held my hips up still as I made a pouty expression and nodded my head yes. "Put your fingers back in me ... please."

Her face lowered until it touched the space between my stomach and the top of my pussy; she began kissing while she pulled my pants from my hips.

"Love this part." Her mouth moved lower. "And this part." She repeated that each time she moved her mouth and kissed again. I was close to grabbing her head and forcing it where I wanted it to be as she repositioned herself, so she was directly between my legs. I spread them as wide as I could make them go. She grasped the backs of my thighs and pushed them up so she could kiss the bottom of my cunt. She twisted a little, so she was at an angle and licked across the opening, catching a piece of skin with her tongue. Her lips gripped and pulled, her tongue now sliding inside me.

I was close to coming as her lips pulled on my clit, several fingers probing deep inside me, my hips humping against her face, my juices pouring out me like a tsunami. Each time my hips landed against the sheets, I could feel the puddle that was building under me.

Hand in hand, we walked along the edge of the water. Brenda stopped and jumped. As she landed, the water splashed high.

I laughed and jumped. "You win." I exclaimed. My splash was far smaller than hers.

She rested her hand over my ass and pulled me against her. "Great day."

It was too. Probably in the top 10 days of my life.

We continued our walk in silence, an occasional glance, and a smile. Sometimes we would swing our locked hands back and forth. We were just enjoying each other. It was obvious that we both were having a nice time.

Suddenly she kissed me then pulled off her clothes, tossing them to me before running into the water. I watched as she floated on her back in the shallow water over the sandbar just offshore. A large wave broke on top of her making her disappear for a moment. I knew she would disappear tomorrow for real. I tossed her clothes and mine on the sand, and I joined her in the waves—the water above the sandbar shallow enough that we could lie down. The saltwater on her body tasted good as I kissed her skin.

The next morning after breakfast, I helped her put her suitcase in the car. We embraced, held each other, and then kissed goodbye. As she backed out the driveway, backing out of my life, we waved to each other for the last time.

In the bedroom, I found her bathing suit lying neatly on the bed, still damp, still smelling like her. I put it on and walked out to the water. While sitting in the waves, waves lapping at my pussy, I thought about her.

Chapter 02

The water over the sandbar lapped at my legs just above my ankles. I stood remembering that day not so long after I came to the beach at the start of summer, that day, Brenda and I kissed and held each other right here. Now it was the end of summer, and tomorrow I would be leaving.

I was wearing the bathing suit she had left behind. I pulled it off in a single motion and stood there with it wadded up in my hands. I held it to my nose and took a deep breath. Her smell was gone, just like she was. I walked further out until the water was up to my shoulders, and then heaved it out further into the water. My chest heaved in a huge sob. Tears flowed down my face.

"Fuck me, it was only a fling," I screamed over the roar of the surf, "she was just here a few fucking days!" I tried to comfort myself by wrapping my arms around me as I shook from the uncontrollable sobbing. I stood in one place for the longest time, unable to pull myself together, unable to stop crying, unable to stop the huge sobs. I could no longer see Brenda's bathing suit floating on the water. The last piece of her was now gone. I turned and started to walk back to the shore.

On the edge of the surf, I kicked the water.

"You okay?"

I looked up, and it was the guy with the 'Fish or Die' hat, the first person I'd seen at the start of summer. I was barely covered then, my blouse unbuttoned. Now I was standing in front of him with no way to hide my nakedness. He was wiping his face with a bandana, the front of his shirt was dripping wet; I assume from the water that I'd just kicked.

"I guess. No not really." Another big sob overtook me, and my body visibly shook.

He put his bucket and pole down and walked towards me, then stood in front of me. His old rough hands with gnarled fingers rested on my shoulders.

"This is about your lady friend from the start of the summer isn't it?"

"Yes. You..."

"I wasn't spying. I just happened to see you two walking on the beach one afternoon. I could tell you both cared for each other. I had a lady friend once. I still remember those times."

"Guess memories are all that I have."

"Enjoy them. Sometimes they are better than the real thing."

Those words rolled around my mind as I looked down. His cock was pressed against his shorts, much like that first time I saw him. He noticed what I was looking at. I could feel his hands grip my shoulders a little tighter for a moment. I don't know what came over me, but my hand brushed against the bulge.

"No. It wouldn't be good for you." He gave me a small peck on the cheek. "You'll find another lovely woman and I'll have a nice memory of you." He walked back, picked up his things, and then continued down the beach.

I lay in the edge of the surf where I'd just been standing, my arms and legs spread wide. The small waves broke over me; a few broke harder, some just between my thighs. My hand covered my pussy; a finger worked its way inside as my mind drifted with thoughts of the summer.

-

The ink of the Sharpie flowed over the square of the calendar as I made another 'X.' It was my third week here, almost two weeks since Brenda left. I cried as I lifted my hand from the page. It wasn't the first time and surely not the last time I'd cry over her loss. It was strange that she could come into my life for a few of the best days of my life, and I would just let her walk away. I knew from the start that she was just a stranger. She had even told me she could only stay a few days. Goddamn, it had been years since I'd had a girlfriend, one that I was really attracted to. This was supposed to be just a summer just for myself. What a pickle I'd gotten myself into.

In the refrigerator, all that remained was a single beer. Not even a frozen dinner for tonight. On the counter was an empty bread bag. I pulled my clothes on and then drove to the small grocery store five miles up the road toward the bridge.

It was maybe the third time I'd been there. Everyone that worked there was very friendly, some more than others. I was looking through the apples for just the right four.

"How about this one?"

My hand didn't stop moving until it landed on a hand.

"You have such soft skin," the same voice said.

I left it there as I looked around. It was Susan, the woman that stocked the fruit and vegetable section. She had always talked to me for five or ten minutes each time I'd been there, probably the friendliest woman. I had thought she might have even watched me from a distance as I shopped.

"Hi Susan, how are you today?"

"Hope you don't mind me saying this, but nicer at the moment."

I looked at her trying to read what she was thinking. I knew what I was thinking. I was trapped in a moment of deep sadness, and I wanted to feel someone lying next to me so very much. That half-hour of masturbation this morning didn't do much to take the edge off either. Susan wasn't a knockout, but not bad looking either. Her lying next to me would probably be quite nice.

I rolled my hand over and wrapped my fingers through hers. "Not at all. Would you like..."

"I'd love to. When?"

"Now?"

"I'll meet you at your place in half an hour."

I told her the house number, and she wrote it on her arm.

-

With my cutoffs and t-shirt still on, I sat the single bag of groceries on the counter. I put the frozen dinners in the freezer and a new six-pack of beer in the refrigerator. As I removed the top from the former lonely cold bottle of beer, a car pulled into the driveway. I leaned against the front door's doorframe holding the screen door open with my outstretched arm as Susan got out of the car.

I looked at her differently now, not the woman in the vegetable section of the grocery store, but as someone, I was about to make love with, well at least have sex with. I tried to picture her naked in my arms, what she might feel like, and how she would respond to touch, a kiss, or a nibble. She was probably in her fifties, maybe five or more years older than me. Age had been good to her, and she was still slim; at least she wasn't even close to being overweight.

About halfway to the door, she called out, "Hey Karen!" It didn't take more than a few more seconds until she was standing directly in front of me, her arms wrapped around me, and pressing her lips against mine. I could feel her tongue forcing its way between my lips. I was so horny I didn't care; this was what I wanted and needed so badly. This was like a drug I needed to take.

My hands held the back of her head, my fingers intertwined in her hair. My tongue welcomed hers; they made love as they rubbed against each other. Our faces parted long enough for her to say, "I wanted you the first time I saw you." I responded, "I need you."

I led her to the bedroom. We both watched with a sense of anticipation as we undressed, then lay next together, our hands touching each other all over.

She suddenly drove several fingers deep inside me. I yelled, "oh yes ... fuck my pussy." She began rapidly working her fingers in and out. Within seconds, my first orgasm started. As it began to subside, I moaned, "Baby, you're good." I kissed her deep and hard on the lips. She pulled her hand up and shared the moisture on her fingers between each of our mouths.

I turned, and without bothering to kiss any part of her body, I put my face directly between her legs. With a forceful lick, I dragged my tongue through the folds of skin at the opening to her pussy. She was very wet, and she tastes delicious. After a few more licks, I pulled her clit up with my tongue and sucked it into my mouth. "Yeah ... suck my clit," she begged. I did too. I could see her twisting her nipples between her fingertips, and she started humping my face. "Here it comes." Her hands pressed my head tight against her pussy, her hips held high above the bed.

We lay with our bare skin pressed against each other, her hands on my ass, and the moisture from our mouths were dripping down our faces as we kissed a very sloppy kiss.

It had been quick but satisfying. I rested on my side and watched Susan standing by the bed as she finished pulling her panties up around her hips.

She looked back at me and smiled. "That was just what I needed."

Her hand disappeared inside the panties for a moment before she put her fingers in her mouth and licked them clean.

I squeezed my nipple. "Maybe you can come over again?"

She paused with a pained expression. "I..." She stopped and pulled her dress on.

"I know. It would be easy to fall..."

"You will leave at the end of summer and I'll still be here."

I knew she was right. After all, I had fallen hard for Brenda, and I didn't want to now fall for Susan. "Could we just do this a few times a week ... just for pleasure?"

Susan sat next to me and put her arm around me, pulling me closer. "I'd like that."

She walked across the concrete of the driveway to her car; she paused and turned. "Maybe Thursday evening?"

"I'd like the company."

I waved as she drove away, wondering if I was making a mistake if I could hold onto my heart and just have sex, sex that was not nearly as good as with Brenda, but adequate. Well, maybe it was the physical contact that made it better than just masturbating. What was I doing?

Still naked, I walked through the kitchen. I grabbed the bottle of now warm beer from the counter and took a swig, letting it swish around in my mouth before swallowing it. I could taste a mixture of Susan's juices and the beer in my mouth. With my towel draped over one shoulder, I walked out to the ocean.

I loved to stand in the shallow water and let the waves splash against me. Facing away from the shore, I kicked a wave, and the water flows into my face. I kicked again, my mouth open, and the salty water filled my mouth. I let some of it go down my throat. I didn't quite know why, but that taste flooded my mind with thoughts of Brenda. The salty ocean water on my face was quickly replaced with salty tears. As I cried, I walked away from the house toward the point of land at the end of the beach. Every few steps, I stepped hard, splashing the water the way Brenda and I had done that day. It wasn't as fun now.

-

It was dark as I sat at the desk with the laptop's glow screencasting a strange light through the room. In the silence between the breaking of the waves, I could hear the keys tapping as I wrote more of my book. Originally I was going to write a series of short stories, but now I was working on a whole book about my summer. I could feel the moisture flow between my legs as I wrote about Brenda and what she had done to me in bed.

The moon was half full as it rose above the ocean. Wow, six thousand more words! Some days the words just flow. I shuffled my feet across the cool terrazzo floor to the bedroom and flopped onto my back on the soft mattress. The dim glow of the moon illuminated just my breasts as I rubbed my fingers slowly across my nipples. A sensuous tingle, not quite an orgasm, flowed through my body, and I drifted off to sleep.

My eyes blinked as I tried to wake up, and I could not quite focus on the large orange numbers of the clock. I wiped the sleep from my eyes and finally saw it was 10:17. The sun was well up in the sky, and it felt like it could be over 80 already, another hot day for sure. I lay on my back with my knees in the air, a finger flicking my clit lazily back and forth. Suddenly I could feel an unexpected tremble wash over my body. A finger from the other hand snuck inside me and rubbed around quickly, turning the tremble into something more like a gentle orgasm.

The solitude of this part of the beach continued through the summer, and I was more than willing to take advantage of it. Part of my morning routine had become a naked run out to the clear turquoise water and diving into a wave. I loved the feel of the warm saltwater on my body and in my hair. The beach and the ocean bottom were made of wonderful white sand that felt nice against my skin, too.

-

I wore only a long t-shirt as the headlights flashed across the room from Susan's car pulling in the driveway. Standing in the front door, much like the first time, I watched as she got out of her car.

"Hey lover!" I called out loudly, knowing there wasn't anyone around to hear other than Susan.

"I'm already dripping wet thinking about you."

I pulled the hem of my t-shirt up and dragged a fingertip through my pussy lips. "Me too."

Susan grabbed my hand and pushed the finger that had just been in my pussy into her mouth and sucked on it. "So good." She kissed me as she cupped her fingers over my pussy. "Tonight we have plenty of time."

"All night if need be." I cooed. My t-shirt was off before the door shut behind us. Her dress landed on the floor about halfway to the bedroom.

We lay next to each other, just looking at each other as our fingers traced little paths over the soft skin. Little nibbles and tugs on our lips became tender kisses. Soft touches turned into deep probes inside us. Her open mouth blew a warm breath on my face as her breathing deepened. "You ... making ... fucking come," she moaned with broken gasps.

The numbers on the clock read 2:11 as we paused for the third time and held each other.

"I have to work today."

"Sorry. I was having a nice time."

"I need to go home and get some sleep."

"I understand."

"Monday?"

"Sure. Sooner if you want."

"Still trying to not get very used to this."

Naked, I waved as she backed out of the driveway.

By mid-August, my last week here, I'd finished the draft of my book that was ready to send to my editor. I was pleased with the results, 400 pages, and lots of hot sex, tender moments, and a good romance. The double spaced pages were tucked inside the addressed brown envelope on the desk as I leaned back with my arms stretched over my head.

I could not believe how I'd become used to not wearing clothes. How strange it would be to go back home and have to be dressed. Here I'd only worn anything the few times I ventured out to shop, maybe a few other times.

Susan and I had been meeting twice a week for a few hours of sex. Our interludes were pleasant and nice stress relievers. It was a little strange when I'd go to the grocery store as I walked through the vegetable section and see her. There were times I would almost imagine seeing her standing naked next to the cucumbers, pulling one from between her legs, and then offering it to me.

The summer had been a real change from past summers, something I sure could get used to. There had been moments I'd dreamed of buying the place from my Aunt. Of course, there wouldn't be a way to support me, so that would be impossible. Well, next year, I would sure try to have the place for the whole summer. Would it be as deserted? That would be great. I think I'd only see five people the whole time. I could see some developers coming in and bulldozing all these homes. That would be a shame.

-

"Is my sexy friend ready?" Susan called out as she walked through the front door.

I skipped across the floor and hugged her. "Only if your pussy is sopping wet."

"That it is baby."

She pulled me by the hand into the bedroom. Her dress was off in a blink with nothing under it. She flopped on the bed. "What's keeping you?"

"Just watching someone looking like a horny teenager."

"You light my fire honey." Susan spread her legs so wide I thought they might break off at the hip. "Just eat me," she begged as she spread her pussy wide with her fingers. "My clit needs your mouth on it."

I, too, had turned into a sex-starved teenager. I loved to eat her pussy and have her eat mine. Lately, we had started foregoing any foreplay and just leaping into sex. I was almost relieved we were doing that since it helped keep us, well me, from developing much of an emotional relationship. I knew I was kidding myself about that.

My tongue lapped up the juices puddled in her pussy and let them slide down my throat before I wrapped my lips around her erect clit and began sucking and nibbling on it. "Just like that," she screamed, her orgasm already peaking. Her hand slapped the mattress as her hips bucked and heaved. "Fucking great," she moaned, her head lifted so she could watch me eating her cunt.

We twisted our bodies around and put our legs on either side of us, so our pussies were together. Our hips rocked back and forth, grinding our cunts, our clits, together. I pulled on her ankle, keeping her pressed hard against me. I started to orgasm. "Hell yeah! ... Fuck me baby!" I yelled.

For the next few hours, we fucked, sucked, and fingered each other in many ways. We fell backward, limp from exhaustion, our arms outstretched. Silent, we just lay next to each other, with brief glimpses in the other's direction.

I knew just like she knew. Our time together was near the end. Probably tonight should be, would be, the end. I could feel the tears forming in my eyes, and I could see them already rolling down her face. I pulled her close and kissed her. Our hands touched each other in all the places that become so familiar, not for pleasure this time, but more like to say goodbye.

"Hard to think this is the last time." Susan wiped at the tears with her fingers but unable to keep up with the flow.

"I was afraid to start this. I knew my heart, our hearts, would be broken when we had to stop."

"Me too. I just was having such a good time."

"Maybe we can just remember those times then?"

"Kiss me. Just for a moment. Then I'll go."

We kissed passionately, our hands roaming over each other, touching in ways that would only make it harder to part. We lingered during some touches. Our tears lay on each other, as we pulled apart and stood. She pulled her dress on and her panties up along her legs.

"Karen ... I'll reme..."

"I will too. You helped me though this summer."

I held her hand as we walked through the house to the front door. I stood and watched until I could not see the taillights of her car.

Back in bed, alone now, I fingered myself through several orgasms as I tried to put Susan out of my mind. All I could do was think what a fool I was for letting myself get even slightly attached to her. We were so different, not at all like Brenda and me. Brenda was my soul mate, and I'd let her go. I cried myself to sleep.

-

The last afternoon at the beach, I lay naked on my towel in the very place I was when Brenda first spoke to me. The sun was now much warmer than then, and as I fingered myself, I became hotter. My clit flipped up and down as my fingertip strummed it. I was in perfect tune, and the music of my orgasm was a fine love song filled with Brenda images. The third orgasm was over, and I lay on my back with my eyes closed, almost asleep.

"Like some company?"

I thought it was just a crazy dream. I forced my eyes open enough to realize someone was standing next to me. How could I forget that voice? It was from Brenda. I jumped to my feet and stood in front of her. Her hair was gone; her right arm ended closer to her shoulder than her elbow. She was still Brenda. Brenda was back. Oh my God, she was back. My heart pounded like the surf not so far away.

"How did you know I was turned on by bald women with one arm?" I smiled a devilish grin, my silly sense of humor taking over for a moment.

I wrapped my arms around her and kissed her for several minutes. She kissed me back. We were like long lost lovers seeing each other again.

"And I thought I just did it so there would be more room in that tiny shower." She giggled and almost laughed. I could tell she was uncomfortable talking about whatever had happened.

We pulled back a little and stared at each other.

"It is so wonderful to see you again." I smiled as I looked into her eyes. "I thought I'd only have a dream to hold onto."

Hand in hand, I led her towards the house. As I took a step, I pushed my hip towards hers and made contact. On her next step, she did the same. We giggled like little girls as we turned our heads to look at each other. It was almost like she had never left.

I held the door open, and Brenda walked ahead of me into the house. She must have read my mind and pulled me towards the bedroom. All I wanted to do was to trade kisses all over our bodies. We sat next to each other as I pulled her tank top over her head. As we lay next to each other, our breasts pressed against each other, we kissed and sucked on each other's tongues. My hand slid along her side, unfastened her cutoffs, and slipped them down her thighs.

My fingertip dragged through her pussy lips and pulled her clit out into the open. I leaned over and gave it a few sucks and licks.

"Goddamn how I missed this little piece of you!"

"I'm such a mess." She paused. "You saved my life."

I pulled myself back up along the side of Brenda as she kicked her cutoffs off her legs and onto the floor. Our bare skin rubbed against each other, sending chills through my body, almost like a mini orgasm. I lightly kissed her lips, and she stroked my cheek with the remains of her arm. I turned my head a little and kissed the end, trying to let her know it was okay. We traded kisses on our lips for several minutes, but I could see the tears starting to form in the corner of her eyes. My fingertip wiped them away.

"Brenda darling ... it's okay. You're next to me now and that is all that matters to me."

"But you let me go so easily?"

"I thought it was just a fling for both of us. I was so wrong. I hurt all summer. I often slept with your bathing suit and held it to my face until I couldn't smell you anymore. It wasn't until this morning I threw it far out into the ocean."

"Before I met you, they found a tumor in my elbow. I was told it was surgery or a short time to live. The day I first saw you, I was actually at the beach that day to take a one-way walk out into the ocean. I don't know why I talked to you, but those few days with you gave me a reason to live. I just didn't know if it was too late to do anything about the tumor. I was afraid to say anything."

"It isn't too late ... whatever time I can have with you is precious to me."

"You're so sweet. That was something I loved about you, the way you always said the right thing. They said the surgery and the chemo has left me cancer free."

I rolled on top of Brenda, her legs wrapped around my hips, and we ground our pussies together. It didn't take long before she was moaning loudly. "I needed you ... to make ... me ... cum so badly," she said, almost in a scream, the pauses filled with gasps. Her hand reached behind my head and pulled my face against hers. Her tongue was forcing my lips apart and searching for my tongue. They touched and rubbed against each other. Her mouth opened wide, and an almost silent "fuck" escaped, followed by a less silent one as her orgasm began to rack her body. Her legs squeezed me tighter, and I continued to rub my pussy against hers. As she began to relax, I felt my muscles tighten as a pleasant orgasm flowed over me.

We twisted our bodies around until we were kissing the other's pussy. I could feel her lips around my clit, that feeling I had missed all summer. It was like Susan had never been between my legs. Brenda's tongue parted the folds of skin and licked the moisture that was ready to flood from me.

I stopped and watched. Her baldhead was moving up and down as she licked me. Her hand rested on one thigh, the end of her arm on the other.

"You're so beautiful."

"Do I need to get you a white cane and teach you Braille, or maybe two eye patches?"

"Too me you are beautiful. I don't care what others might think. I just want you with me."

She looked at me with disbelief. I sat up, reached towards her, and pulled her up towards me. She sat between my legs, her back rested against me, my arms wrapped around her waist. I kissed the back of her neck, and I cradled her breasts in my hands, my fingers rolling the nipples between them.

"Brenda..." I paused for a moment. She turned her head enough she could kiss me. I continued, "We lost each other once. We almost lost something that should not have been lost. I won't let you go this time."

"That's why I came back."

As she lay back down, she pulled me down beside her and kissed me, her tongue stroking my lips and rubbing my tongue. Her hand was touching me all over. Her fingers paused a moment to touch my nipples. I could feel her hand slide across my stomach as it worked its way between my legs. My legs spread wider, making sure there was nothing in the way of her touching me. "I love you," she whispered as she nibbled on my earlobe, and just before her fingers entered me. I could feel my thighs tighten as her fingers went deeper inside me. I tried to kiss her, and she said, "just lay there." She pressed her fingertips up and rubbed that delicate place just enough to make me lose control and drive me into a heavenly state of being. My hands gripped the sheets to keep me from flying off the mattress as I began to buck and slam my hips. "That's it baby ... come for me ... I've dreamed of this many nights." I begged her to stop, and she just shook her head while she smiled at me.

We rolled over, and while we kissed, she humped my thigh with long strokes. Her head lifted, and her mouth opened wide as she obviously started an orgasm. "Oh darling, I'm not letting you get away again." An unintelligible few words escaped her mouth, followed by a deep moan as she finished her orgasm, then she collapsed on my chest. She lifted her head just enough to look in my eyes for a few moments. "I am so lucky to have you next to me."

That night we walked naked on the beach and splashed in the water as the full moon hung just above the horizon.

Story 03

The Law firm Samantha worked for, Johnson, Bollocks, and Hymen, had recently expanded their practice into other cities. They were moving outside their corporate Los Angeles location and opening two new office locations in Australia and New Zealand, Sydney, and Auckland.

Samantha had caught wind that the managing partners were looking for people within her office to relocate and temporarily live in between Sydney and Auckland for three to five months'; assisting in getting both new offices up and running.

The buzz around the office started to refer to this expansion effort as project Down Under.

Samantha decided to throw her name into the hat, letting her boss know she was interested in the opportunity and the chance to expand her paralegal career.

Samantha's motivation to move wasn't only vocational. She had personal reasons, as well. Samantha was recoiling from a relationship that had recently ended badly with her boyfriend, Jake.

It had been a painful break up for Samantha. She was still wounded from the break, and she described the pain as a constant, low, and throbbing ache that was eating away at her stomach from the inside out. Moving out of town for a while would surely give her space and the time she needed to heal.

Within one month after learning about project Down Under, Samantha was told that she was one of the ten employees chosen to go. She had exactly one month to get her ducks in a row, so-to-speak, and ship out.

Samantha was thrilled to learn she was chosen, excited about the opportunity.

She had decided to sublet her downtown Los Angeles apartment out to her best friend, Beth. The timing couldn't be better because Beth was also in the midst of an unraveling relationship, and she was looking for a place to live. Beth also agreed to take care of Licorice, Samantha's soot-colored female cat.

Samantha and Beth had known each other for about six years. They met at a campus rally when they were both sophomores in college at UCLA.

Samantha was in between classes the afternoon she met Beth, stretching out her long, sinuous legs on the grass and checking out the scene. Bookbag close by, she perused the area for hot looking guys and girls while only half-listening to the speaker talk about students' rights.

Samantha saw lots of great looking students that day, but her eyes became fixated on what she considered to be one of the most beautiful women she had ever seen; Beth.

Beth had luscious, thick and black, curly hair that framed her delicate face; the ends brushed against her small shoulders. Beth was standing against a metal railing about 100 feet away. Samantha stared at her for what seemed like an eternity until she finally looked away, only to find herself drawn in. She was staring at her all over again, like a moth to a flame.

Beth was standing next to a short and stocky, pixie-haired, platinum blond. It appeared they were together as a couple. Beth noticed Samantha was staring at her, and she looked straight at her, flashing a devilish grin. Samantha smiled back, and the apples of her cheeks burned, bright red, blushing.

Beth smiled at her again, and this time, the stocky, platinum blond noticed the flirtation and shot Samantha a cold stare. The blond said something to Beth and then stormed away, leaving Beth standing there alone.

Samantha looked away again, feeling responsible for having caused a rift between them. Samantha looked up again, and Beth was no longer standing against the railing.

When Samantha turned to grab her bookbag, Beth was sitting right next to it. Beth smiled at her and lifted her hand, offering a "hello."

"Hi." Samantha said, surprised and smiling; her large, sapphire-colored eyes greeted Beth.

"Hi. I thought I should come over and introduce myself, considering we kept staring at one another for past 30 minutes." Beth said, looking at Samantha with her big, dark chocolate-colored eyes that had just a flicker of honey running through them, adding to her mischievous good looks.

"Hey, I'm sorry if I caused any problems with you and your friend. My name's Samantha, Sam." She said.

"Please, don't worry about her. She's just moody; getting her period, I think. I'm Elizabeth, Beth." She replied.

They talked for a while, and quickly realized they had some of the same classes together and shared similar interests.

Beth was an avid runner and surfer, like Samantha. They started to spend more and more time together, and before too long, they were like two peas in a pod, nearly inseparable, unless, of course, one or the other started dating someone. Samantha was experimenting with her sexuality, dating both men and women, whereas Beth only dated women.

"I read somewhere that July 14th is National Nude Day in New Zealand, and you know the men and women down there are supposed to be fucking hot, Sam." Beth said while taking another swig of Mexican beer from the bottle she was holding; she watched Samantha try and get organized and packed for her trip.

Beth sat cross-legged on the edge of Samantha's bed, wearing a white, cotton, polo dress. The white contrasted against her deep, dark tanned and muscular skin. She was bra-less as usual, and her full, C-cup breasts swayed freely inside her dress; erect nipples rubbed up against the cotton grain.

"National what day?" Samantha asked, pursing her pouty lips while pushing her long, pencil straight, blond hair behind her ears, exposing the freckles that ran over the top of her small, button nose. She grabbed another handful of clothes from one of her open-chest of drawers in her bedroom, searching for space in her suitcase.

Samantha was wearing a pair of washed out, green, cargo shorts that buttoned down the front with a drawstring waistband and they sat low on her narrow hips.

Her small, perky breasts pushed up against a tight, racer-back, white tee-shirt; the front and back advertised surfboard wax. Her wide, muscular shoulders, lean, powerful arms, and the tops of her well-developed thighs were sun-kissed golden, brown from jogging the palm tree-lined streets of Santa Monica Boulevard and surfing the break at rock pile, a local surfing spot.

"You might meet someone down there and maybe he or she will take care of you, down there." Beth said, smiling, revealing the dimples in her cheeks, while she pointed at Samantha's crotch. Beth had a wide mouth and naturally plump, red-colored lips. She had a long, pointed nose and high cheekbones.

Men were captivated with both Beth and Samantha's small, athletic build and natural good looks. Beth was never interested in any of the men that were attracted to her, making her even more attractive to them. Samantha would get a kick out of watching men try time and time again to impress her best friend, but Beth would barely bat an eyelash at any of them. Beth simply wasn't interested.

"I can't even think about meeting anyone new right now. I still feel sick to my stomach over this break up with Jake, Beth." Samantha volleyed back, her brow was furrowed, and her big, blue eyes were welling up with tears.

"Oh, Sam. Don't start crying over him again. He's not worth your tears, girl." Beth said, standing up, walking toward Samantha.

"I'm going to concentrate on work, Beth, not men, at least for awhile." Samantha said as Beth moved closer and hugged Samantha tightly; their breasts' and pubic mounds' were aligned, pressing together.

"I'm really going to miss you, and miss us." Beth muttered into Samantha's ear.

"I'm only moving away for a few months; I plan to come back. Besides, with all the hot women living in SoCal, you'll surely forget all about me in a couple of weeks'." Samantha responded, pulling back a little to look into Beth's eyes and also to regain her composure; she felt aroused by Beth's presence; felt a stirring sensation in between her legs whenever Beth would get a little too close.

Somewhere on a subconscious level, Samantha knew there was a lot more than just friendship between her and Beth, but as you know, sometimes things have a way of staying hidden until we're ready to see them.

"Yeah, okay, whatever, Sam, but did you know your nipples are hard? Beth responded, swatting the back of Samantha's hamstring with her hand.

"Oooh, baby; playing rough, eh?" Samantha jokingly said as she moved away and grabbed more clothes, finding room in her suitcase.

Later that night, after Beth had left, Samantha lay on her couch; listening to the sultry voice of Nina Simone on her CD player; Licorice was curled up in her lap, purring. Samantha started reminiscing about her life; her move out of the country, her break up with Jake, and her long-term friendship with Beth.

As Samantha sunk deeper into her couch, she closed her eyes; her thoughts carried her back; focusing on one specific and extraordinary day she had shared with Beth.

* * * * *

They both loved to find new surfing spots, and Samantha remembered when she and Beth found a secluded beach, a cove was hidden by the steep cliffs above, and on that particular day, the waves were breaking perfectly.

Samantha and Beth were the only two on the beach. After they both surfed for two straight hours, they both agreed the next wave they caught would be their ticket back into shore.

They wanted to take advantage of the gorgeous, sunny, and warm morning; perhaps indulge in a little topless sunbathing. Once they reached the white, sandy beach, Beth and Samantha peeled off their board shorts and short-sleeved rashguards; their standard surfing uniform, underneath they had worn string bikinis.

Beth and Samantha stretched out onto their towels; both surfboards lay horizontally beside them. They were lying on their backs, letting the sun warm their bodies. Beth reached her arm behind her back and untied her string and triangular bikini top, exposing her perfect, round breasts and succulent, erect nipples.

Samantha stared at her breasts; the sunlight reflected upon the light-colored sand pebbles that had stuck to the soft tissue of her breasts.

"God. You have the most amazingly perfect boobs, Beth." Samantha said, opening her eyes for a moment and looking at Beth's bare breasts.

"I love your small, perky breasts, Sam. I love how your nipples are always hard; poking through your tee-shirts. It's so erotic." Beth responded; her eyes were closed.

Beth's thoughts of Samantha's breasts were from her memories. Memories of stolen glances when Samantha would change out of her wet, surfing clothes and into her dry street clothes; often while Beth drove the car, hurriedly racing to get them back home in time for work.

Beth would adjust the rearview mirror, so she could see Samantha's bare breasts and hard nipples, her flat stomach, or the delicate and soft, light brown hair that she kept trimmed and neat, like an airplane strip in between her legs.

"Oh yeah?" Samantha responded, almost as a dare, and she untied her bikini top and flung it over to Beth, directly hitting her in the face.

Beth raised one of her arms and removed Samantha's partially damp, string bikini top from her face, opened her eyes, and moved her head to one side, looking over at Samantha.

Samantha's breasts reminded Beth of lemons that were cut in half; her nipples were elongated, like soft, pink rosebuds. Like Beth's breasts, Samantha's breasts were also covered with tiny particles of sand that stuck to her skin.

Instinctively, Beth reached over to Samantha and brushed the sand from her breasts; Samantha's nipples quickly hardened at Beth's touch.

Samantha opened her eyes and looked at Beth; her full breasts ascended like her nipples were kissing the sun. Samantha would often tell Beth that her natural breasts were probably the envy of every plastic surgeon in Beverly Hills.

Beth's beautiful levitated breasts weren't filled with silicone implants from a surgeon's agile scalpel, but instead, it was a rigorous exercise that lifted and shaped her breasts.

Over the years, Beth spent hours paddling out on her surfboard, out against the pounding surf and then hoisting herself up and out of the water, catching a wave on her board as she made her way into shore, attributing to toning and shaping her breasts.

Samantha reached for Beth's breast and gently rubbed her palm across her nipple; Samantha felt Beth's nipples harden in her hand.

Both women moved from laying on their backs to their sides now; facing the other; each fondling the other's breasts, saying nothing, while the sounds of the waves gently crashed onto the beach, and the wind rustled through their dampened hair, and seagulls cried out around them; searching for morsels of food.

"You know that I love you, Sam." Beth said, hearing Samantha's breath quicken, somehow knowing Samantha's pussy was wet and feeling her pussy become juicy while Samantha stroked and massaged her breasts.

"Yes. I do know. I love you too." Samantha responded as she moved her hands down and across Beth's flat and tight, six-pack abdominals; fingertips felt the smoothness of Beth's soft skin and the light dust of hair that ran down just past her belly button; leading to the very top of her string bathing suit bottoms.

As Beth's one hand grasped Samantha's breast, her other hand reached down and untied the strings to her bathing suit bottoms, pushing the bottoms down until her pussy was exposed. Samantha didn't object; she lay on her side, completely naked.

Her slick, well-manicured pubic hair, round, tight ass, and washboard stomach greeted Beth's eyes and hands.

Samantha glided her hands down along Beth's soft, olive skin, meeting the outside swell of Beth's breast, her ribs, and the indentation of her small waist, stopping once she reached the curve of her shapely hips.

Samantha took a deep breath in and pushed her fingers down further until she touched the inside of Beth's suit bottoms, feeling the wetness of her pussy and the luxuriously soft and thick, full bush that covered her pubic mound.

Beth shuddered with excitement; felt her heart beating faster at Samantha's touch. Samantha's fingers began to explore her best friend's slick pussy. Beth ran her hands over Samantha's body, massaging her shoulders, breasts, and the cheeks of her ass, while Samantha pushed her fingers deeper inside Beth's bathing suit bottoms.

Samantha moved her fingers past the silky hair covering her pussy; touching her outer lips, her vulva, and then pushing her index finger into the slippery, wet cleft; lightly circling Beth's throbbing clit. Beth hissed with pleasure.

Beth pushed herself up and off her towel, moving forward and toward Samantha; kissing her on the lips; her tongue probed deeply into Samantha's mouth.

She pulled back, smiling at Samantha as Samantha lifted her arms around Beth's neck, pulling her down and on top of her body. Samantha rolled from her side and onto her back; Beth hovered above her, kissing her lips, her neck, her nipples, moving her mouth over Samantha's salty, sandy body.

Beth alternated between circling her tongue and sucking and nibbling each of Samantha's hard nipples. Samantha moaned in pleasure, and Beth would suck harder. Samantha pulled Beth back up to her lips and kissed her again, this time their lips press harder.

Samantha lifted her hips and began circling them, pushing her pussy and pulsating clit into Beth's crotch. Beth reached down with one hand and pushed her suit bottoms down and off.

They were both naked, and they ravaged the other. Their sopping wet pussies embraced; thrumming pussy lips kissed; clits rubbed back and forth, and back and forth against the other.

Both women gyrated their hips up and down and around and around; grinding into the other's hot, thrumming clit until Samantha screamed out into the deserted beach that she was cumming; cumming hard.

Her body spasmed and shook as she felt the waves of her orgasm take over her. She opened her eyes and looked at Beth, who hadn't climaxed yet, but she was close, and Samantha watched as Beth slide her fingers in between her legs and rubbed her fingers back and forth across her clit, moaning "Ooooooh. Ooooooh." Beth closed her eyes as her body spasmed toward the release of orgasm.

* * * * *

Samantha's body jerked as she awoke from her groggy daydream state. She could hear Nina Simone singing, Here Comes The Sun in the background.

Maybe it was the memory of having sex on the beach with Beth, or maybe it had something to do with her recent breakup. But, as I mentioned before, the universe has a way of presenting things to us when we're ready to see them, even if something has been standing right in front of us the whole time.

Whatever the reason, Samantha found herself lying there that night on her couch, acknowledging to herself for the first time that her feelings for her best friend were far greater than just a long-term friendship, and she wanted to do something about it. It was as if a light bulb had been turned on above her head.

"God, I don't want to lose her. I love her." Samantha said to herself, reaching down and feeling for Licorice curled up at her side.

Samantha reached for her cellular phone and hit the speed dial button for Beth, "Beth. Hi. Remember that time you and I found that secluded beach; where the waves were kicking and you and I...well, do you remember? You do? Well, what would you think about you, me and Licorice celebrating National Nude Day in Auckland together...?"

Erotic Beginnings

5 Hot Erotic Lesbian Stories for Adults

Sarah Rodgers

All Rights Reserved. No part of this publication may be reproduced in any form or by any means, including scanning, photocopying, or otherwise without prior written permission of the copyright holder. Copyright © 2020

This book is entirely a work of fiction. The names, characters and incidents portrayed in it are the work of the author's imagination. Any resemblance to actual persons, living or dead, events or localities is entirely coincidental.

Story 01

I am a young, very successful professional woman, 5'3", 105 lbs., natural blonde and, I'm told, considered quite attractive. I have a nice figure, which I work very hard to maintain and all- in-all, I consider myself very fortunate. Except when it comes to men. With the exception of two married men with whom I've had incredibly passionate affairs before we went our separate ways, my love life and, consequently, my sex life, has been one bad experience after another. Until now.

I had had my fill of men, both literally and figuratively, so, about a year ago, I made a conscious decision to become celibate. I still dated, frequently, but I no longer jumped into bed with my dates as quickly as I did before. I felt I wanted the men in my life to be friends first, then, if a true, loving friendship developed, sex would follow naturally. I'm still

waiting.

Celibacy, by definition, has one inherent drawback: no sex, no relief. Consequently, I became an incessant mastabateur. I found myself buying (through anonymous mail order catalogs) a variety of dildoes and vibrators which I began to use religiously. But as much sexual relief as these marvelous devices provided, I still craved the warmth and comfort of a gentle, caring body next to mine.

About six months ago, after a particularly horrendous episode with an over-amorous date who tried to rape me, all of my anger and frustrations suddenly boiled over and I found myself crying uncontrollably in, of all places, the laundry room of my apartment building. One of my neighbors, a striking Japanese woman whom I had seen often but never really knew, found me and took me back to her apartment which she shared with another woman I had also often seen. After about half an hour, I finally calmed down and, embarrassed, I apologized to these two wonderfully caring and thoughtful women, Neiko and Linda, thanking them profusely for their genuine concern and comfort and I left to go back to my own apartment.

The following night, Neiko knocked on my door to inquire how I was feeling. She invited me back to her apartment for tea and conversation with Linda and her boyfriend, Mark, and I gladly accepted. It was a delightful evening with truly delightful people. I learned that both she and Linda were registered nurses in the famous research hospital not far from our building and Linda's boyfriend, Mark, a tall, extraordinarily handsome man, was a resident in the same hospital. Mark had to leave early, but Neiko, Linda and I talked long into the night about anything and everything. From there, our friendship blossomed. And it was wonderful. Occasionally, Mark would join us for a pizza and I could easily appreciate Linda's attraction to this man. But something else was going on; something I never would have suspected or expected.

We had joined a woman's health club together and after one particularly grueling workout we all longed for the warmth and relaxation of the sauna. The three of us marched into the sauna wrapped in our towels, but once inside the incredibly hot room, Neiko and Linda unselfconsciously shed their towels and stretched out, completely nude, on the long wooden benches. Being ridiculously modest, I kept my towel on, but my eyes were continually drawn to their exquisitely naked bodies. Stranger still, I slowly realized that I was not only fascinated both by their beauty and their warm, casual manners, but I was actually being attracted to them. Sexually attracted.

Neiko was petite and slender and practically flat-chested. Her tiny mounds were really no more than just puffy red areolas with exceedingly large nipples. She had the tiniest waist which flared out into wonderfully rounded hips and a flat, well defined stomach which sloped smoothly and gently to the extremely sparse, straight black baby-fine pubic hair that framed her pussy. Linda, on the other hand, was a tall, Nordic, athletic woman who, although not nearly as delicate as Neiko, had a perfectly shaped figure with extremely large yet firm breasts, crowned, like Neiko's, with very large nipples. As we talked, I'm sure they caught me staring, but neither Neiko nor Linda, to their credit, indicated that to me. So as casually and as nonchalantly as I could, I let my eyes sweep over their glistening nakedness, getting increasingly more aroused and excited every minute.

As the weeks went on, I continued to date, with the usual, predictable, negative results. I continued to be celibate and I continued to masturbate, but with increased frequency and intensity. But the strange thing that was happening was that the objects of my mastubatory fantasies were Neiko and Linda; individually and together as I had seen them in the sauna. My fantasies were, I'm sure, uniquely naive. As a girl in college I had experienced some "flirtations" with several other girls which culminated in an occasional bump and tickle incident, but I had never experienced a truly fulfilling lesbian affair. So my fantasies involving Neiko and Linda were extraordinarily arousing.

About a week after the sauna incident, I was returning a suitcase I had borrowed from Neiko. After knocking on the door and getting no answer, I let myself into their apartment with the keys we had exchanged. I stopped at the door and called their names. Still getting no response, I put the suitcase down and was about to leave when I heard music coming from Neiko's bedroom. I thought she had left the stereo on so I naturally went back to the bedroom to turn it off. The moment I entered the bedroom, I saw Neiko and Linda, nearly nude, on the bed, making love. To say I was shocked would be a gross understatement. I was amazed. Flabbergasted. Speechless. Yet instantly and incredibly aroused. My first instinct was to leave as quietly as I could; but I was transfixed. I couldn't tear myself away from the sight of my two beautiful friends lovingly entwined in each other's arms.

Linda was lying on her back while Neiko, wearing a black garterbelt and black stockings, was lying on top, between Linda's legs which were wrapped around her thighs. Linda's arms encircled Neiko's back, hugging her tightly as Neiko's hands lovingly caressed Linda's face. And they were kissing passionately, moaning softly, delighting in each other's lips.

I have no idea how long I stood there watching, it was probably only seconds, but, sensing my presence, they suddenly stopped kissing and both looked in my direction. I was so embarrassed I could have died right then and there. I stammered an apology or something, I don't remember what, and they smiled at me. Linda said something like "now you know" and Neiko added something like "I hope you don't mind." I just shook my head. I was so torn; I desperately wanted to leave, to collect my thoughts, but I couldn't. And then Neiko said, very softly, "please, Amelia, why don't you join us."

I couldn't answer. My heart was racing, my mouth was absolutely dry and I could feel my whole body shaking. Sensing my conflict, my overwhelming apprehension and desire, Linda and Neiko got off the bed and moved across the room to me. I can vividly recall how gracefully Neiko moved and how sensuously Linda's large breasts swayed as they approached. Their bodies glistened with a patina of perspiration and I quickly noticed how stiff and erect their nipples were. I also noticed that unlike in the sauna, Neiko's pussy was now shaved clean and smooth.

Linda and Neiko both took my hands in theirs and held them gently as we spoke. Linda told me that she and Neiko often talked about how beautiful and sexy they thought I was and they wondered if I was bisexual. I told them about my few fumbling experiences, but that I really didn't consider myself bisexual. Then, smiling warmly, Linda took my hand she holding and brought it to her breast, pressing my hand against her warm, damp flesh and said, in a whisper, that there was nothing frightening about touching another woman's body, it was the most natural and beautiful thing in the world. Then, still guiding my hand, she slowly moved it around her breast, underneath it to feel its weight and firmness, then up to her swollen nipple to feel its firm, spongy resilience. "It feels so nice, so warm, so smooth, doesn't it," she whispered? And it did, it really did.

I had a catch in my throat and couldn't answer; closing my eyes, I barely shook my head in response. I was so suddenly excited and aroused, my legs became weak and rubbery. I could feel my own nipples growing and hardening beneath my clothes just as I could feel a familiar wetness seeping out between my legs and soaking my panties. Linda removed her hands from mine and raised them to my face, but my fingers remained on her breast, nervously stroking her long, rigid nipple. And then, while Neiko gently squeezed my hand, Linda slowly leaned in and kissed me.

The touch of her mouth on mine was absolutely electrifying. Linda's lips were so incredibly soft, her breath so sweet and her touch so tender, it was so different, so unlike any man's kiss. And I wanted more. I pressed my own mouth firmly against hers, kissing her back, tentatively at first and then more passionately. I could feel her lips part slightly and then felt the tip of her wet tongue slowly wash over my lips. Following her lead, I opened my mouth slightly and allowed her tongue to enter, gingerly touching it with my own tongue, absorbing her warmth and wetness. After a second or two, Linda pulled away and smiled. "We want to make love to you," she whispered and I nodded; I knew, at that precise moment, I was irrevocably committed.

Still holding my hand, Neiko led me to the bed, turned me around and the two of them began undressing me. While Linda pulled my tank-top over my head, Neiko deftly unbuttoned my jeans, pulled them over my hips and slid them down my legs. On her hands and knees in front of me, she slipped off my shoes and helped me out of my jeans. I stood between them, stripped down to my bra and soaked panties, discarding my modesty as quickly as my clothes. In a daze, I freely allowed Linda to unclasp the front closure of my bra and peel the lace away from my breasts. My nipples, although not anywhere near as large as Linda's or Neiko's, were rock hard, jutting out from my swollen areolas like two ripe cherries. Still on her knees in front of me, Neiko reached up and slowly eased my panties down my legs. I willingly stepped out of them and stood there, completely and unashamedly naked as their eyes drifted all over my body.

They eased me down on the bed, fluffing a pillow under my head and then laid down on either side of me, pressing their bodies against mine. Their warmth and their softness and their tenderness were magnificent. My excitement was so intense, it is difficult even now for me to recall exactly what transpired. I felt as if I was consumed by a fog of pure, exquisite pleasure unlike any I had ever experienced. I know we kissed. Long and deep and passionately; first Linda, then Neiko and then the three of us together, painting each other's mouths and lips and tongues with hot, sweet saliva. And as we kissed, their delicate, practiced hands moved sensually over my body, exciting every nerve fiber their fingers trailed over, from my thighs to my neck and face and then slowly down to my thighs again.

They had eased my thighs apart and each wrapped their legs around mine, pressing and rubbing their wet pussies against my flesh as we continued to kiss. Their hands found my breasts and squeezed and stroked and fondled and massaged them in unison. I could barely breathe and talking was absolutely impossible. My cunt was inflamed and throbbing deep within my womb, and I could feel my juices flowing like a slow lava stream down my thighs. I have no idea how long we continued like that, but all too soon, I felt, they pulled their lips from mine. Hungrily, I tried to reclaim their mouths, but Linda smiled, whispering words of comfort, and helped me up, shifting our bodies. Linda moved to the edge of the bed and sat up, cradling my head and upper body in her arms above her lap. My cheek pressed against her soft, smooth belly while her enormous breasts swayed above my face. This was going beyond my wildest fantasies and the feelings I had were so exquisite, I prayed it would go on forever.

With my free hand, I reached up and touched Linda's breast, gently stroking its full, sloping underside. As I did, I could feel Neiko's hands on my breasts again, sliding up and squeezing my nipples between her fingers. Except for my clitoris, which one lover described as a "hair trigger", my nipples are especially sensitive. And Neiko knew exactly how to touch them. She rolled them between her fingers, gently tugging and pulling them upwards. I moaned loudly, twisting away, but Neiko kept a firm grip on my engorged buds and pinched them again. My whole body shuddered and I lost my breath. No doubt encouraged by my reaction, Neiko slid her hand down my breast, and, squeezing it upward, sucked my nipple deep into her mouth. My tit just melted into her mouth and she lapped and licked and sucked my sensitive nipple as no man ever had. I squeezed Linda's breast harder, trying to share my pleasure and joy. She moaned softly and leaned forward, pressing her long, stiff, fleshy nipple against my lips. Eagerly, I parted my lips and drew her thumb-like nipple deep into my mouth, wildly sucking it, making her groan with unrestrained pleasure. I could feel her nipple pulsate on my tongue and I swirled my tongue around it even more frantically.

As Neiko sucked me, I continued sucking this beautiful woman's tit like a starving baby. And then it happened; a strange, hot, sweet liquid suddenly coated my tongue. Thinking I drawn blood, I quickly pulled my face away and looked at Linda's nipple and then at her face. Her eyes were closed and she had the sweetest smile on her face. When I could speak, I stammered something like "did I hurt you?" Linda just shook her head and giggled. "No," she whispered, "I'm lactating. That was milk." I was stunned. Then Neiko lifted her face from my tit and giggled, too. It was then that I noticed that while she was sucking my nipple, she was squeezing her own and there was a tiny droplet of white milk on the tip of her nipple as well. "We're both lactating," Neiko gushed, "it's one of the greatest joys of being a woman, don't you think?"

I was in no condition to think. I gasped "oh, my God" and lifted myself from Linda, looking first at their beautiful faces and then their breasts which they were both now holding. I looked at Neiko and suddenly found myself muttering, "I want to see. Show me."

Both Linda and Neiko were only too happy to oblige. Shifting positions again, Neiko sat upright against the headboard and Linda knelt down next to her. I positioned myself on Neiko's other side and watched as Neiko stroked Linda's head and guided her to her fascinatingly long, thick nipple. I held my own breasts, in empathy, I suppose, and stroked my tender nipples with my thumbs.

As Neiko continued to lovingly stroke Linda's thick blonde hair, Linda held Neiko's tiny mound in her hand, opened her mouth and placed the flat of her tongue against the underside of Neiko's swollen nipple. Then, squeezing Neiko's puffy red areola between her thumb and forefinger, she began milking her nipple slowly and rhythmically while tenderly lapping and licking the tip of it. Then slowly, very slowly, Linda lowered her lips over the other woman's nipple and drew it deep into her mouth. Linda's cheeks hollowed as she sucked and Neiko just closed her eyes and sighed.

It was immediately obvious that these two women had done this many times before. They knew each other's nuances and responded accordingly. As Linda continued to coax Neiko's nipple with her fingers and mouth, Neiko spread her stockinged legs and slid her long, slender fingers along her smooth, hairless slit, rubbing her elongated clit in concert with Linda's sucking, milking movements.

Watching them, I was so turned on, I began squeezing and kneading my nipples so hard they began to throb painfully. And then I saw it; Neiko's milk, a thin white stream, snaking down from the corner of Linda's suckling mouth.

I couldn't stand it any longer. My face went to Nieko's breast, my lips to her other turgid nipple and I drew it deep into my mouth, sucking it feverishly. In a matter of moments she began flowing, squirting jets of hot, salty-sweet, creamy liquid against my throat, filling my mouth. Nieko groaned and gasped as Linda and I both sucked her tits wantonly.

A few moments later, Linda pulled away and I had Neiko all to myself. With complete abandon, I drew her entire tit into my mouth and continued sucking and milking her blazing nipple and then, almost simultaneously, our hands found each other's sopping cunts. Neiko's delicate fingers barely flicked over my throbbing clit sending bolts of electrifying sensations through my entire body. I completely lost my breath and had to pull away from her breast just to draw a taste of air into my burning lungs. But Neiko didn't stop. Her magic fingers continued to electrify my clit. And then I felt Linda between my thighs, lowering her face to my cunt. A second later, her soft-stiff tongue replaced Neiko's fingers, licking, sucking, flicking, swirling around my clit.

My hips had a life of their own, bucking and gyrating uncontrollably against Linda's hungry mouth. I don't know how she held me down. Her fingers pried my cunt lips open and she plunged her stiff, wet tongue into my hole, screwing it deeper and deeper into me. Neiko shifted, pulling herself up, covering my mouth with kisses as she squeezed and kneaded my tits. She kept saying "come, baby, come, baby, come." I was on the edge. I was never so turned on, never so hot in my entire life. I could feel my orgasm building like a rumbling volcano deep within me. I screamed, I gasped, I held my breath...and then I came. Once. Twice. And then a third time like a shuddering explosion, losing myself completely to wave after delicious, exquisite wave of indescribable pleasure. And still Linda lapped my cunt as if it was her last meal. My clit was unbearably sensitive; even her hot breath on it made my entire body shake and quiver.

Totally drained, I had to pull away. I had to catch my breath. I had to regain some semblance of consciousness. I begged Linda to stop. And then I begged her for more. And yes, more was to come. This was only the beginning

Story 02

A sudden flash of lightning filled the small cabin, causing the transistor radio to momentarily crackle with static. A few seconds later, the June night was filled with a resounding crash as the sound of thunder caught up with the light. The storm had been raging for a little over two hours, alternating between violent clashes in the sky and the steady patter of rain against the windows.

"That was a good one!" Exclaimed the dark haired girl as she clapped in appreciation of the sudden illumination.

"You wouldn't think so if we were out there." Replied her companion as she pointed out the large bay windows to the lake beyond.

"But we're not, are we?" The first girl retorted in an exaggerated pout. "Sometimes you can be such a worrier."

"You're right." The first girl answered. "But one of us has to have some sense. Otherwise you'd have us out on the lake because you'd get a better view."

"Hey that's an idea." Robyn said in mock seriousness. "We could take one of the boats down by the dock and..."

"Don't even think it...." Valerie cut her off in a dead stop tone.

Both girls then broke in laughter.

All in all, watching the storm and snacking on popcorn and the wine they had snuck out of the liquor cabinet wasn't the worst way the two 17 year olds could spend the night. Of course it wasn't what they had thought it would be when they come up to the lake two days before.

Robyn Grayson and Valerie Carter had been friends for 12 of their 17 years, ever since they had met on the first day of kindergarten. Back then, they had both been pudgy little girls more interested in games and dolls than anything else. With slight variations, that had continued right up until they began to hit puberty.

In Robyn's case, womanhood sprung upon her with a vengeance. She lost all her baby fat and in a single summer went through a growth spurt that cause her to fill up and out at the same time. Instead of the semi-plump tomboy, she found herself a very attractive young lady with a figure that drew boys like moths to a candle. It was during that summer that she finally appreciated her mother's insistence that she let her hair grow. Robyn had wanted to cut it short because it kept getting in the way. It now stretched down to a few inches below her waist.

Valerie also began to fill out that summer but unlike Robyn, she lost none of her childhood fat. She added more than a few inches to her height over the last few years but with them came more pounds than she liked to think about. Today she hit the scales at 160. Thankfully it was spread throughout her body giving her a mature full figured look.

Both girls sometimes wished that they could exchange bodies, at least long enough to see what it would be like. Valerie wished she could be as slender as Robyn . In turn, Robyn wondered what it would be like to have a 38D bust like Valerie's instead of her own small 34C.

Yet despite the physical changes, both girls had remained steadfast friends. They had seen other friendships fall apart when one friend became one of the popular crowd and then no longer wanted to associate with former friends. Robyn had become part of the in crowd, a head cheerleader and the girlfriend of the star quarterback. But she made it clear to anyone who even suggested that it would look better if she "dropped" Val, that the crowd, the cheerleaders and even the quarterback would go before her friendship with Valerie did.

In fact, the hardest adjustment to their friendship over the last few years hadn't been Robyn's rise in stature but Valerie's. Between both of them, Valerie had always been the smarter of the two. At least as far as the books were concerned. A constant presence on the honor roll, the short haired girl had finished the requirements for graduation six months early. And since she had also aced her SAT's, she'd been allowed to take courses at State this last semester.

Valerie had been home only a few days when her mother had announced that they were going up to the cabin for a few days and wouldn't it be nice if she invited her friend Robyn to come along. It would give them a chance to catch up on the last six months.

The first days of the trip had been pretty uneventful, just swimming in the lake, a little boating and barbecuing with the neighbors. Then this afternoon, Val's 14 year old brother, Bobby took a fall and twisted his ankle while climbing a tree. It had swollen up pretty good and her mother though it a good idea to take him into town and have it x- rayed, just to be sure.

Since Val's father couldn't make the trip, heading into town would leave the girl's alone, but Mae Carter said she would be back in a few hours. If they had any problems in that short time, well the closest neighbors were only a quarter mile away.

The wait in the small hospital turned out to be a lot longer than Mae had expected. By the time they were finished the storm was just beginning to hit. Since the old country roads had a tendency to wash out rather easily, especially the small bridge over Dobson's Creek, the safe bet was to stay in town until morning. So she had called the girls and told them that Bobby was fine and that they'd be back in the morning and not to worry. They'd assured her that they'd be fine.

"I bet you wished you'd stayed home this weekend." Valerie said as she took drained the last of the wine from her glass.

"I don't know, this is kind of fun." Robyn replied as she quickly refilled Val's glass.

"More fun than Sally Kellerman's Graduation Bash?" Valerie countered as she looked at the now empty wine bottle. It seemed like they'd just opened it. "That was tonight wasn't it."

"Yeh, I think so." Robyn said in a somewhat unconvincing tone as she stepped over to the bar and pulled out another bottle. "But I really wasn't planning to go to that anyway."

"Oh sure, the biggest party of the year filled with the most popular people in school and you were just going to stay home and do your nails." Val said as Robyn refilled her own glass. "If my mom hadn't waited until we were up here before mentioning it, I never would've asked you. It wasn't fair to put you on the spot, not wanting to say no to this trip. Its not like I'd be angry if you wanted to go to the party instead."

"I mean it, I really wasn't planning to go." Robyn insisted as Valerie looked on unconvinced. "I guess I'm finally beginning to realize what really stupid assholes some of those people are."

"Well, what do you know?" Valerie called out. "There is a brain in that pretty head after all. Sometimes you can open your mouth and speak up."

"Go to hell!" Robyn shot back in mock anger. "There are a lot of times I open my mouth."

"Yeh, but then it's usually to attach it to some dumb jock!" Val returned.

"Oh how sharp the tongue of a friend." Robyn laughed.

"Speaking of heads and sharp tongues, maybe we should go a little easy on this stuff." Valerie suggested as she indicated the glasses they both held. "Wouldn't do to have mom come back and find us sloshed."

"You worry too much." Robyn said. "By the time she gets back tomorrow we'll have had a good nights sleep and be fine."

"Today you mean." Valerie corrected as she looked at the large clock on the fireplace mantle and noted that it was one in the morning.

"Whatever..." Robyn said, grabbing another handful of popcorn.

"Does this new asshole category include Brian?" Valerie asked, drawing up a mental image of Robyn's on again off again quarterback boyfriend.

"Brian's both a prick and an asshole!" The long haired girl replied. "Turns out he was screwing both Jenny Davis and Helen Williams."

"That would be on the nights you were seeing someone else?" Valerie asked.

"Yes, I mean, that was different..." Robyn replied. "Of course." Val smiled.

"What about you?" Robyn quickly asked, changing the subject. "You haven't said one word about the guys at State. You can't tell me you've been celibate all this time."

While Valerie hadn't Robyn's experience with boys, she was far from a virgin. There had always been guys who realized that she was cute in her own way and would rather date a girl who's idea of an intelligent conversation wasn't what new store was opening in the mall. That and the desire to get a really good look at those big boobs that filled out whatever she wore. Jocks, Nerds or somewhere in between, guys were still guys.

"Well I've been really busy these past few months." Valerie said, looking more than just a little uncomfortable. "College course are a lot more difficult than high school."

"Bullshit!" Robyn yelled back. "I can tell when you're lying. You're seeing someone."

"Well......actually...." Valerie hesitated, she was finding it hard to say the words that floated unbidden in her mind.

"Come on, we're never had secrets from each other." Robyn insisted. "Didn't I even tell you when I screwed Mr. Peterson after he took me home from baby-sitting that night."

Valerie remembered all to well how excited Robyn had been when she called her up on Val's private phone one night after midnight to tell her she'd just been fucked by Robert Peterson. A successful businessman in his late 30's, Valerie still wondered what drew a man like that to take such a chance with an 16 year old. She'd seen his wife many times and she was a very attractive woman. Some things she just would never understand.

"Yeh, I remember." She answered quietly, staring into the glow that blazed in the fireplace.

"So you know you can trust me. Come on." Robyn insisted.

Valerie turned her gaze from the fire to her oldest friend. She could see in her hungry eyes that Robyn was possessed by a need to know. Still, the words wouldn't come.

"Is it a teacher, or a professor isn't that what you call them?" Robyn asked. "Are you sleeping with one of them?"

"No." Val simply replied.

"Is it someone that's married?" Robyn quickly continued.

"No." Val repeated.

"Then why can't you tell me?" Robyn asked once more.

Valerie stood up and walked over to the fireplace, again loosing herself in the warm glow. She ran her hand through her short black hair and sighed. It'd been a real long day, and the need for sleep and the wine was beginning to be felt.

"Why don't we just drop this and get some sleep?" She said.

"Cause I want to know, that's why!" Robyn said. "I want to know what it is that you can't share with someone you've been friends with since we were five."

"Because you wouldn't understand, that's why?" Valerie replied.

"What wouldn't I understand?" came Robyn's reply. "A guys a guy. God knows I've slept with a few jerks. So what's the..........."

Robyn suddenly paused in mid-sentence. She brought her hand up to her still opened mouth in surprise. The reason Val didn't want to talk about it suddenly seemed crystal clear.

"Oh shit," She exclaimed. "He's black isn't he. You're sleeping with a nigger! What's your mother going to do if she finds out?"

Valerie just shook her head. It was bad enough that Robyn couldn't let the matter drop without her letting her narrow minded prejudices create all kinds of wild fantasies.

"No, he's not black, or brown or yellow or for that matter white." Val finally answered, no longer caring how her friend would finally react. "If you really, really have to know - he is a she!"

A pregnant silence filled the cabin as Valerie caused Robyn to be speechless for the first time in her life. She was certain she had just flushed a dozen year friendship down the proverbial toilet. Staring once more into the comforting flames of the fire, Valerie found that she really didn't care. She was tired of hiding it. If her friend couldn't handle the truth, well then maybe their friendship was a mistake in the first place.

"What's her name?" Robyn asked.

"What?" Val asked, not actually hearing Robyn.

"I said, what's her name?" Robyn repeated.

"Your girlfriend, or am I supposed to call her your lover?"

"Whatever you're the most comfortable with." Valerie finally responded, surprised at her friend's calm reaction. "Her name is Beth Moskowitz."

The name brought a sudden image of a tall dark eyed girl in Valerie's dorm. She had been introduced to her when she had gone up to State during spring break to take a look at the school. "I remember her." Robyn said. "She's very pretty."

"Thanks." Val answered, unsure what else to say. "But it's already over between us. She wants someone who can be out in the open about our relationship. I'm not sure I'm ready for that."

"I'm sorry." Robyn offered. The emotion in her voice showing the sympathy was genuine. "You want to talk about it?"

It had been a good long time since the two women had really sat down and had such an intimate conversation. It felt good to the both of them. Surprisingly neither of them felt tired anymore.

"I should apologize for that nigger remark." Robyn said. "I should know better than that, but sometimes the prejudices you're surrounded with are hard to ignore."

"Actually I'm pretty surprised the way you've taken this whole thing." Valerie said. "I almost expected you to call me a dyke."

"I'm not that bad, am I?" asked Robyn.

"I guess not." Val smiled.

"True, lesbianism isn't really a subject that comes up a lot in my circle of friends, but I'm not totally ignorant." she went on. "I know there's a lot more to a woman's interest in other women than the idea that she simply can't get herself a man."

Actually, that little tidbit was the core of most of her friends thinking on the subject. Dykes, as they preferred to call them, were ugly girls who couldn't get a man and so turned to each other.

Inevitably, some of their late night chat sessions would turn to sex. Robyn had always found it laughable as to what was considered acceptable and not. It was always ok to talk about how you fucked your boyfriend or a new position you tried. In fact, she could recall a night that Betty Lieberman demonstrated on a banana the perfect blow-job. Yet there was another night that Sally Keller asked one of the other girls how best to masturbate and found herself shut out of the group. Evidently, that was too close to sexual contact between one girl and another.

Part 03

"Was Beth a one time thing or are you defiantly into women now? asked Robyn.

"I don't know." came Valerie's reply. "I still find guys attractive, but I'm also attracted to girls too. To be honest, I've been attracted to girls for a couple of years. This was just the first time I had the opportunity to do anything about it. If Beth hadn't been so open in her sexuality, I'd still be thinking about it."

Robyn studied the face of her friend. The revelation that she had been attracted to girls for years sent her mind racing along a new track. It was almost a minute before she asked the question that repeated over and over in her head.

"Were you ever attracted to me?"

Valerie waited almost twice as long before answering. Just saying the words seemed to take a great load off of her.

"I've been in love with you since I was 14." Valerie said

"Why didn't you ever say anything?" Robyn gushed.

"What was I going to say?" Valerie asked

"Do you think you could've handled it?"

"Probably not." the long haired girl said after a moments reflection. "I'm not really sure how I'm handling it right now."

"Do you want to let this drop and turn in?" Valerie asked as she looked at the clock. "It's almost one - thirty."

"No, I'm not tired." was Robyn's quick response.

Robyn took a long hard look at her long time friend. Most of their life, they had been closer than sisters. Had one of them been born a man, they would've undoubtedly been lovers. Now that little hinge of fate seemed to have been removed. If that was what they both wanted.

"What's it like?" Robyn asked. "Making love to another woman?"

"I could say it was softer, gentler than being with a guy." Valerie began. "But I don't think that would really describe it. I really can't put it into words."

"I didn't think so." Robyn smiled. "Then I guess you'll just have to show me."

"What...?" Valerie responded in disbelief.

"Do you know what your saying?"

"Maybe, maybe not...." Robyn grinned. "But I do know I love you too. This is about the only thing we haven't done together. I've always had a certain curiosity about it. That much I'm sure of."

Valerie was taken a little aback, unsure what to make of what she was saying or what to do next.

"Besides, I've gone to bed with guys for a lot less reasons." She laughed.

Valerie knew that much was certainly true.

Robyn leaned over and kissed Valerie. It wasn't the first kiss they had ever shared. There had always been the hello and good-bye as well as the holiday kisses. In addition, they had once practiced kissing one night back when they were 15 and they were just beginning to date guys. Robyn's first french kiss had been with Valerie. But all of those had been mechanical. Technically correct but lacking the feeling that you put into kissing a lover. This kiss had that feeling.

A second kiss followed and this time Valerie opened her mouth as she felt the soft pressure of her friend's tongue against it. Many nights over the years she had dreamed of this moment. More than a few times she had been in bed with Beth and she had imagined it had been Robyn instead. Now the unexpected reality of it all as their tongues met was enough for a sudden moisture to appear between her legs, and any sense of caution to be tossed to the wind.

The night sky suddenly erupted with the most violent thunderflash yet, one so close that the boom of its fury followed before the light faded. The windows shook as the sky opened up once more.

"Wow, that was some kiss!" Robyn exclaimed. "I can't wait to see what the rest is like." Valerie merely grinned back, feeling a pleasing warmth filling her soul.

Now it was Valerie's turn to initiate a kiss. As she pressed against the softness of her friend's lips, she reached up and caressed her breasts through the blue nightshirt. Her hand closed and cupped one breast, sending a soft sigh from Robyn's lips.

"Let me take this off." Robyn said as she grabbed the bottoms of her shirt and pulled it over her head.

Gazing with admiration as Robyn's pert breasts bounced free, Valerie found it funny that even though she was the one with all the experience in this sort of thing, it was her neophyte lover who seemed the more aggressive. It was like the old saying that there was no one more passionate than a virgin who had decided to give up her virginity.

"Now your turn." Robyn said as she tossed her nightshirt aside and gave a little tug on Valerie's. Robyn's eyes widened as the red shirt lifted and she looked down at Val's much more ample bust. She couldn't even begin to imagine how many times she had seen her girlfriend naked over the years, between sleepovers, school showers and such. This time it was different. It was the first time she looked at her body with a sexual lust. The girl wondered if the warm flush she felt was the same thing a guy felt when he first saw those melon sized mounds.

Unable to restrain herself any longer, Robyn immediately reached out and ran her hands across Val's breasts, rubbing her fingers against her wide dark aureoles. It sent an even more powerful rush through her body. She couldn't believe how warm her skin felt to the touch. It was as if she were running a fever.

Valerie was indeed consumed with a fever, a heat that had simmered over the years. She reached over and cupped Robyn's breasts, lowering her head at the same time. Passionately, she began to cover them with kisses before taking one of the nipples into her mouth. Her tongue played with the hard little tip, sending little shivers of delight through the smaller girl.

"Oh that feels nice." Robyn gushed as Val moved to her other breast, at the same time still caressing the first breast with her hand. Valerie's touch was so unlike that of Brian, her most recent lover. In fact she couldn't compare it to any of the men she'd be with. She only knew that it felt great.

Valerie continued to suckle at Robyn's breasts as she reached down and rubbed her fingers against the long haired girl's wet panties. Robyn responded by pushing down her panties, giving her friend greater access to her pussy. Her response to the invitation was first one finger, then a second, deep inside Robyn's love canal. It wasn't long before her ministrations brought forth a wet, sweet response that covered her fingers.

Robyn now tried to duplicate Valerie's skill with her tongue as she lifted one large breast to her lips. Of course she didn't have Val's skill, but she had tried this on a boy or two. At least those who didn't freak at the idea. For some reason, guys seemed to associate having their nipples licked or someone playing with their ass with homosexual acts, even if it was done by a girl.

Still, she put everything she had into it as Valerie gave her a reassuring moan. Valerie's fingers continued to slide in and out of her as she moved to Val's left breast.

After giving Robyn the time she needed to satisfy her mammary urges, Valerie guided her to the floor in front of the fire and spread her legs. Robyn knew what was coming next and smiled at her new lover in anticipation.

The skillful tongue that had so caressed her breasts now began it's work on her sexuality. Robyn let out a loud cry of pleasure as she felt the slick appendage slide in and out of her. She reached down and put her hands on the back of Valerie's head, guiding her to her most sensitive spots.

The clock on the wall ticked away as wave upon wave of delight spread out across her body. She closed her eyes and let herself become lost in the ecstasy. The soft cries that escaped her lips every now and then brought an increased desire to Valerie. Tonight was a hundred nights dreams become reality. The honey dew that covered her tongue was like nectar of the gods. She scooped it into her mouth eagerly.

"I've got to try this!" Robyn exclaimed as she shifted her body until Valerie and her were in a sixty-nine position.

The scent of Valerie's womanhood filled Robyn nostrils, making her slightly lightheaded. She parted her friend's lips with her fingers and reached out for her first taste of another woman.

It was, she decided, tantalizingly tangy. Closing her eyes, she relished the sensation, even as she reached out for more. More that Valerie was all too willing to give.

The larger girl pressed her now pulsating mound deeper into her lover's face, even as she mashed her own mouth into Robyn's virgin pussy. She was driven by the idea that this would be her friend's first orgasm by another woman. A woman who had loved her for so long and had dreamed of this night.

It soon became a game of dueling tongues as each tried to outdo the other. Valerie obviously had the experience, but Robyn was driven by an enthusiasm that just wouldn't quit.

They rolled back and forth, their heads buried between each others legs. Nothing else mattered except the climax that each was driving the other to.

A thin film of sweat covered both girls as their hearts began to race. Never had either of them had ever felt so excited. Valerie felt that she should be crying out how much she loved Robyn, but she couldn't bear to tear herself away from the luscious banquet she was feasting on, even for a moment.

Robyn, on the other hand, couldn't help but let out moan after moan as her lover's skillful tongue reached up and into the core of her sexuality. No guy had ever brought her to such an ecstatic state. Fast as the waves of passion were now ripping through her supple form, she knew she was on the verge of a memorable climax.

So powerful were the ripples causing her flesh to quiver and quake, she was having a hard time trying to keep up with Valerie. She just couldn't concentrate on what she was doing. Finally, she just gave up and surrendered to the fire of Val's desire.

Valerie felt the absence of her lover's tongue but she didn't mind it a bit. She was overjoyed to have had her try as hard as she did, it was more than she could've imagined. She slid a free hand down between her own legs and began massaging her saturated mound, taking up where Robyn left off. She was determined that they climax together, even if she had to bring the both of them off herself.

It didn't take long at all. It was almost impossible to tell which of them exploded first. Valerie felt Robyn's body stiffen in her arms, then a loud gasp filled her lips. A second later, she felt her own body erupt as well.

At that moment, as if a sign from the heavens that they had fulfilled their destiny, the night sky erupted in a final flash of luminance, followed seconds later by a roaring thunderclap. A detonation so powerful it caused the walls of the cabin to shake as well. It was the last burst of a tempest which had finally blown itself out.

Like the storm, both girls had expended the last of their energy in that final explosive moment. Robyn collapsed against Valerie, resting against her rapidly cooling flesh. Exhausted as well, Valerie gently stroked Robyn's hair. In a soft, weak, voice she spoke.

"I love you, Robyn."

Still catching her breath, Robyn couldn't summon up the strength to answer. Instead she leaned over and kissed Valerie's breast. The meaning of the non-verbal message was all too clear.

It was impossible for either girl to tell how long they just laid there. Neither was aware of anything but the beating of their own hearts and the cloud of euphoria they found themselves floating in. Occasionally, one would stroke or gently kiss the other.

Gently, the excitement of the night, coupled with the cool breeze that had come up in the wake of the storm, lured both of them into a dream filled slumber. There, the image of their love was replayed again and again.

Sunlight had long filled the cabin as the two girls slept on. Still naked, they had become entwined during the night. It was only when the sound of a car coming up the driveway filled the room that Robyn's eyes slowly opened.

She smiled as she felt the warmth of Valerie's skin against her cheek. Her lover's breasts had served as her pillow. The new sound of a car door slamming and voices outside caused her eyes to now rapidly open and she jerked her head upward.

"Easy, Bobby," said the woman's voice from outside the window. "The doctor said you have to take it easy on that ankle."

"Oh shit!" Robyn reacted to Mrs. Carter's voice as she began to shake her friend awake.

"Just five more minutes." Valerie said in response to her girlfriend's shaking.

"Val, your mothers back." Robyn said softly. "And we're naked."

"Oh shit!" Valerie said as she repeated Robyn's reaction.

Both girls scrambled for their nightshirts and quickly pulled them on. There was no time for anything else as they heard the front door opening.

"Honey, we're home." Mae Carter called out as she stepped inside.

The tall woman paused as she saw the two nightshirt clad girls. She was surprised to find them still not dressed at ten thirty.

"Hi mom." Valerie said.

"Hi indeed." Mae said. "I would've expected the two of you would've been up hours ago."

"Well we kind of stood up pretty late last night." Valerie explained. "The storm and all...."

"And we got to talking," Robyn cut in.

"Catching up a little."

"I see." Mae commented.

"Hey mom," Bobby called out from behind her.

Mae turned around and saw what Bobby had found. There, spread out on the floor, were three empty bottles of wine. As well as two glasses still half full.

"The storm huh." Mae said as she gave the girls a hard stare.

"Well...." Valerie replied, the ambiguity in her voice telling Mae that she knew they had been busted.

"It's my fault, Mrs. Carter." Robyn interjected. "I opened the wine. I was a little scared of the storm."

Mae though about it for a minute. Her expression remained stern. Then, it slowly began to soften.

"Well it was a bad storm." She began. "And as long as you both understand that alcohol should never be used as a crutch."

"Yes, mother." Valerie quickly said.

"You don't have to worry about that, Mrs. Carter." added Robyn. "I'm positive that we'll never need alcohol again to get us through the night. Not as long as we have each other to depend on."

"Good, now get some clothes on." Mae smiled. "I've got a car full of groceries out there. I'll start breakfast while you unload them."

Her attention already on the kitchen and the mess she would probably find there as well, Mae missed the smiles and meaningful looks the two girls silently exchanged. Yet even had she noticed them, there wasn't a chance in the world she would ever guess the meaning behind them. Or ever understand how their relationship had changed - on a dark and stormy night.

Story 03

"Ladies and gentlemen, this is the Captain speaking..." Said the strong male voice over the cabin intercom. "We're about to start our approach into Los Angeles International and should have you on the ground in about twenty minutes."

"On the ground in 20 minutes," Kelly thought as she stared out the tiny window at the countryside rushing by below, ignoring the Captain's comments on the weather and such.

"And then a three hour layover until I catch the 6:30 to San Diego."

The 39 year old redhead sighed as she thought of the long wait in an airport lounge with absolutely nothing better to do but watch people come and go. Of course she could go over her presentation one more time, but she really figured that an even dozen times in the last two days had been enough.

"Forget about inflight movies," She said to herself as her seatbelt closed with a snap. "They should have a theater or two in the airport so that people could kill a few hours."

Originally, the layover in Los Angeless was going to be the best part of her trip. Her Internet lover, Michelle, lived up near Oakland. When she had first learned she was going out to the West Coast to personally present the new marketing campaign she had helped develop, Kelly had seized at the opportunity to fullfill a person desire on her stop over here. San Francisco or Oakland would've been better, but the tickets had been bought for L.A. before she had even been given the assignment.

According to her original plan, Kelly was going to have a full day here and Michelle was going to make the drive down from Oakland. The two woman had never actually met, but had been exchanging emails and gifs for a few months now.

Kelly was an up and coming advertising executive for a New York firm. On the fast track for a Vice President's slot, this trip was going to be a feather in her cap. 5'3" with short dark red hair, the first thing most men took in upon meeting her was her 38 inch bust. It usually put them off guard and Kelly was just aggressive enough to take advantage of their distraction. By the time they learned there was a lot more to her than just a big set of boobs, she had usually passed them on the ladder to the VP's chair.

Michelle on the other hand was 32 and a career military woman. A Lieutenant Commander in the U.S. Navy, she was as aggressive in her own field as Kelly was in hers. She had bucked the boy's club mentality and flew multi-million dollar jets for a living. Currently she was stationed at the Alameda Naval Air Station up near Oakland.

Both women were married, both were mothers with small children. And both had discovered in the last few years, an interested in other women.

They had met one night on the Internet when Kelly responded to a note Michelle had posted on a bi newsgroup. The fact that they lived on opposite sides of the country just gave them the freedom to be totally honest with each other in their almost daily correspondence. The friendship had developed quickly.

Within an hour of learning that she was going to make the presentation herself instead of Bill Sullivan, her immediate superior, Kelly had fired off an email to Michelle. They quickly worked out a plan were as Michelle would take a 48 hour leave and meet her in Los Angeles. Then they would have a full night and day together.

Then a lousy twist of fate intervened in the form of one Janice Zimmerman. Janice was the pencil pushing travel budget coordinator at Kelly's firm. Known as "old nickels and dimes", she took great delight in trying to find new ways to save even a few dollars, no matter what the inconvenience to the traveler.

The pleasure she got from her discoveries, and the chaos they caused the unfortunate traveler seemed to be almost sexual in nature at times. At least that had always been Kelly's impression. It was probably the nosy old bitty's only such enjoyment.

So it was that Janice took great delight in changing Kelly's travel plans so that she had to fly to San Diego tonight instead of tomorrow. In doing so, the company would save fifty dollars on air fare and a whole nights hotel accommodations. Their clients had no problem moving up the meeting a day and Janice had further booked Kelly on a flight home tomorrow that would mean she would have to go right from the presentation to the airport. This would save another night of hotel expenses. The fact that Kelly would be totally exhausted by the end of this two day marathon didn't really factor into the equation.

Kelly could still see the excited gleam in Janice's eyes as she devastated her plans. It was almost taken as an article of faith in the office that Kelly had a hand in the scandal that resulted in the sudden firing of Bill Sullivan a few days before. In truth, she had nothing to do with the anonymous phone call that had led the night security guard to Bill's office late Friday. Of course, she wasn't sorry that he had been caught screwing one of the college interns on the couch. No, she hadn't made the call, but had she known about the tryst, she wouldn't have hesitated to have made it.

As she felt the wheels bounce on the hard concrete of the runway, Kelly against cursed the fact that her chance to finally meet Michelle was slipping out of her fingers. The Navy Officer had told her that even if she broke every speed limit on the way down here, she wouldn't arrive until just before Kelly had to leave. As much as she wanted to finally meet her in person, the Ad Exec wasn't selfish enough to ask her to drive all the way down here just to wave good-bye.

As people all around Kelly took to the aisles and began to gather up their belongings, she just continued to stare out the window. It wasn't like she had to hurry to make her next connection. Then, with only a few other people left onboard, she got up and removed her carrybag from the overhead compartment.

The flight attendant gave her a pretty smile as she thanked her for flying Southwest Air. Kelly smiled back at the young blonde, wondering if she'd like to help her kill a few hours. A silly thought really. Even on the remote chance that the tan suited woman was also into girls, the ground crews were already loading food and fuel onto the plane for their next flight. She would be out of here and on her way long before the New Yorker was.

Savoring the idle thought of how the flight attendant would've looked in a skimpy red bra and panties, Kelly exited the cabin and walked down the long passageway into the terminal.

"Guess I'll get something to eat." Kelly said to herself as she strolled down the walkway, ignoring the many people around her. "Although I can't imagine the food being any better here than on the plane."

Lost in thought and oblivious to her surroundings, Kelly didn't notice the short haired blonde woman she'd just walked past.

"Hi stranger," The blonde said with a smile. "Buy a lady a drink?"

Then the woman leaned over and kissed her on the cheek.

Caught off guard, Kelly jumped back. The look of alarm on her face quickly changed to astonishment as she focused on the woman who had kissed her.

"Michelle!" She exclaimed.

Standing 5'6" with blonde hair and baby blue eyes, Michelle was wearing a sleeveless cotton blouse- and matching shorts. The thin material of her shirt and the tight fit of her shorts outlined the well-defined muscles of her calves and arms. A well tanned body showed that she was an outdoor person who loved to soak up the desert sun.

Smiling ear to ear, blushing just a little, the younger woman held out a small bouquet of flowers to her Internet friend.

"These are for you, Kelly" She said quietly. "I can't tell you how much your letters have meant to me over the last three months. I looked forward to them every day. Thanks for being my friend, you're really someone special."

Taking the roses in hand, Kelly finally found her voice.

"But how...? You said that it was impossible for you to drive down in time." Kelly stammered, still a little shocked by Michelle's sudden appearance.

"Honey, I'm a Naval Aviator." She laughed in a deep rich voice. "We don't drive.....we fly!"

Michelle explained how she had hitched a ride on a transport flight and had only arrived a half hour ago.

"This is wonderful!" Kelly beamed. At least we'll be able to have dinner together."

A wicked smile appeared on Michelle's face. She stared at the beauty of her cyber-lovers face and quickly lost herself in the richness of her deep brown eyes.

"I had something a little better than dinner in mind." The Navy Officer quipped.

With that, the taller woman led Kelly down the corridor and through a locked door that read "Security Only."

"Were are we going?" Kelly asked curiously.

"The Security Chief for the airport is a Reserve Officer and a friend of mine." Michelle said as she closed and locked the door behind them. "He had a small office that he converted into an apartment some time back. A place where he could rest up during emergency situations. It's not the Hilton but it sure beats a cot in the storage room."

Michelle continued as they proceeded up a long flight of stairs.

"I called him yesterday and explained that I had a rather special friend passing through here today and I'd really like to be able to spend some private time with them." She said as they reached the top of the stairs and Michelle unlocked yet another door. "Since you only had a few hours, heading out to one of the local motels was out of the question. He immediately offered me the use of his apartment."

As she stepped into the rather spacious room, Kelly wondered if Michelle had mentioned that her special friend was another woman. Given the military's rather silly obsession with same sex relationships, she guessed she hadn't.

"Here we are, home sweet home." Michelle pronounced with a sweep of her arm.

"At least for the next couple of hours."

Taking a good look around the room, Kelly couldn't help but be impressed. The Hilton it might not of been, but it sure as hell had the Holiday Inn beat by a mile.

"We've got champagne, various appetizers and such." Michelle said as she gently placed her hands on Kelly's arms. "But first, something I've wanted to do for the longest time."

Pulling Kelly tight against her, Michelle kissed her again. This time it was full on the lips. Kelly responded quickly to the warm, soft pressure against her lips, and the taste of Michelle's tangy red lipstick. Opening her mouth as she felt the tickle of Michelle's tongue against it, Kelly drew it inside her.

"Mmmmm" Michelle purred as tongue found tongue.

The reality of countless night's dreams brought a warm feeling to both women. Kelly felt a soft touch against her breast as Michelle slipped her fingers beneath the folds of her blouse.

"Lets get more comfortable." Michelle said as she kissed her a second time.

Slowly, the two woman began undressing each other, continuing to stroke and kiss as they did. Michelle quickly lost her blouse and shorts, displaying an perfect tan that continued even beneath her undergarments. Nude sunbathing was a passion with her. If you wanted to enjoy the kiss of the sun, why let a few silly scraps of cloth get in the way.

Kelly had been wearing a blue blazer with matching blouse and skirt, very conservative and business like. Michelle was more than eager to help her out of the jacket, running her hand across the outline of her breasts. The soft motion was enough to cause the quarter size aureoles to shrink and harden, exciting Michelle even more. She considered ripping it open in a burst of passion, but the idea that any other clothing Kelly might have had was locked away in her luggage finally prevailed.

Filled with excitement, Michelle quickly unbuttoned the blouse and in one quick snap, unfastened the Victoria Secret's black lace bra her favorite spot out in the desert and taught her wonderful feeling you got from frolicking au natural.

"Let just me get the rest of this off you." Michelle said in a commanding voice.

The authority in her tone and her willing reaction to it took Kelly by surprise. She wasn't used to taking orders, especially from another woman. Her bisexual experiences had been with women more or less her own age. The first had been after a long endless night working on a report when she had been guided into the pleasures of girlsex by her administrative assistant. It had been an eye-opening experience. Yet in the end, she was somewhat relieved when Donna had quit to take a job with another company. Kelly's world might not have been as oppressive as Michelle's regarding lesbianism, but it wasn't that open either. She wouldn't loose her job over being exposed, but it would certainly bar her from the vice president's office. After Donna, all of her affairs had been far from the office and usually with women who had as much to loose as she did.

What really surprised Kelly was that she was actually enjoying a submissive role for a change. Usually she had to exert her dominance in every aspect of her life, but she could feel the energy in the woman undressing her. It excited her and she wanted to just see where it would take her.

In no time at all, Michelle had undressed both Kelly and herself. Kelly watched with approval as the Navy Officer had carefully placed her traveling suit over the back of a chair, careful not to wrinkle the clothing. At least she was considerate enough to realize that she could hardly show up in San Diego in crumpled clothes. Deals had fallen through over less.

Michelle couldn't keep her hands off Kelly's huge breasts. Once, while she was pregnant, her own breasts had been close to this size, but had shrunk back to normal afterwards. Still, one does what they can with what they have. She gently caressed Kelly's mounds with her hands and swirling fingers, making imaginary circles around the now swollen nipples. Her soft touch excited Kelly greatly, her nipples had always been extra sensitive. Michelle could hear her lover's breathing began to quicken, causing the blonde's own juices to collect between her legs.

Her tongue replaced her hands and like a babe, she pulled the large nipples deep into her hungry mouth. Strong fingers kneaded the abundant flesh, playing an erotic symphony on Kelly's body.

Kelly reached out with her own slender fingers and played with Michelle's breasts in turn. Truth be told, she actually wished she had mounds like that, having always believed that her's were oversized. She lifted up each breast to her mouth and ran her tongue across the stiff and tanned nipples and kissed each in turn. This sent little shivers of pleasure across Michelle's chest.

In response, Michelle slid one hand down across Kelly's thigh and between her legs, delighting in the deep wetness she found there. Skillfully massaging the stubby clit she found there, she began to steer Kelly toward her first orgasm. A single finger became two, then three. They slid in and out faster and faster, adding fuel to the fire that raged deep inside.

Kelly continued to work on Michelle's breasts, kissing, teasing, and biting them over and over. The conflagration that radiated from her own womanhood made her more and more aggressive. She began to heave back and forth as she felt her first small orgasm, the wetness of which covered Michelle's fingers.

With her free hand, Michelle jerked Kelly's head back and kissed her forcefully, sucking the force of Kelly's orgasm into her. Her tongue pressed firmly against Kelly's. The kisses continued, becoming softer, longer and much wetter. There were few things Michelle loved more than sharing french kisses with another woman, and from the response, Kelly shared the passion.

Now it was Kelly's turn. She led Michelle back to the large bed, the size of which made it obvious that Michelle's friend used it for a lot more that a quick nap. She spread her long muscular legs wide and immediately dropped her head between them. Kelly had been delighted to see that Michelle had indeed kept her pussy as bare as a teenage girl's as she had mentioned in her emails. She had never been with a woman who shaved her hair, it was an immense turn-on.

Michelle moaned as she felt the soft wetness of Kelly's tongue as it slid up and into her love canal. Hitting all the right spots, she began to drive the younger woman up the ridges of her own climax. It wasn't long before Michelle's heart was racing and the same electrical surges that Kelly had felt a short time before now ravaged her own body.

Grabbing the back of Kelly's head with her powerful hands, Michelle pulled her deeper between her legs. So forceful was her grip that Kelly couldn't even catch her breath. Not that she cared at the moment. All that concerned her was the small trickle of juices that she was eagerly lapping up with the tip of her tongue. A trickle that she knew would soon be a flood.

She didn't have long to wait as Michelle's naked form, covered with sweat, began to buck and quake. The larger woman let out a loud cry of joy as she exploded in and across Kelly's mouth. Kelly would've joined in the shout but she was too busy lapping up her reward.

"Oh God, that was great." Michelle panted as the two woman laid side by side.

The two spent long minutes just silently kissing and licking each other clean. No further words were shared, just an occasional shared laughter.

Finally, looking up at the large 18 inch clock on the wall, the military woman noted that they had already been at it for over a half hour. Time was running so fast.

Kelly meanwhile was oblivious to the passage of time, she was having to much fun. She never realized how good it could feel to just let someone else take control, even if just for a little while.

"I've got a little surprise for you." Michelle laughed as she reached under the bed and pulled out her flight bag.

Kelly watched, first in fascination, then in shock, as Michelle produced a large 9" dildo from the dark blue bag. In her own luggage, she kept a smaller vibrator, but nothing like this. It was the strap on kind, and it was obvious that Michelle planned to wear it.

"I don't know about this..." Kelly said with more than a touch of hesitation in her voice.

"Didn't you say in your emails that it's always been your fantasy to be fucked by a monster cock?" Michelle asked as she jumped back onto the bed. "How you always dreamed about it but would never do it with a man other than your husband."

Kelly bit down on her lower lips as she studied the formidable rubber phallic. It had been her fantasy to be totally ravaged at least once in her life. She loved her husband, she really did. Yet sometimes she so much wanted something more than his 7" in her.

"I guess that sometimes you can fantasize about something knowing its never going to happen, that way its a safe obsession." Came her reply.

"All right." Michelle said, a little disappointed. "I'll just put this away then."

"Wait...." Kelly said, taking the time to measure her words. "I'd really like to try it....honestly."

The look of disappointment on Michelle's face instantly turned to joy. It resembled nothing else if not that of the cat that ate the canary. She quickly secured the straps of her artificial manhood around and between her legs. She held out her hand to Kelly and guided her to the floor, it was always more fun down there.

She again started with kisses, first her cheeks, then her mouth. She continued down her body, taking the time to once again enjoy the fullness of Kelly's breasts. Eventually she reached her still moist mound, glistening with shiny droplets of her earlier eruption.

Spreading her cunt lips, Michelle wasted no time in exploring the inner reaches of her new lover's sexuality. The scent of their recent sex filled her nostrils as much as the taste of it filled assaulted her tongue. Michelle took a firm grip on Kelly's buttocks and pulled her closer.

"Oh yes.." Kelly said as the frequency of Michelle's withdrawals and re-insertions increased with each passing moment.

Michelle continued with her oral ministrations, always aware of the ticking of the clock above her. And with each passing minute, Kelly's moans became louder and louder. Michelle was pleased that she was having such an effect on her lover, but was becoming concerned that someone might hear her. True, they were in a private section of the terminal, but there were still workers in the building. What if someone heard them and decided to investigate?

"Not so loud!" Michelle commanded as she paused for a moment. "We don't want to draw company."

Kelly nodded in agreement and obeyed for a few minutes. But finally the wet, moist tongue buried inside her cause her to resume her cries, in an even louder volume.

"Oh God...oh my God...oh it' s so good... faster...faster...!" Kelly suddenly yelled so loud that it caused Michelle to jump.

In all her letters, Kelly had never mentioned that she was a screamer. Michelle immediately realized that Kelly couldn't help herself. As the woman beneath her let out a second equally loud shout, Michelle grabbed the closest thing at hand off the floor and pushed it into Kelly's mouth. What it turned out to be was her own panties, still wet with her anticipation over Kelly's visit.

"Kelly, you have to quiet down..." She said in her most commanding tone. "If you can't stop I'll have to leave that gag in place...either that or we'll have to stop. If I leave it there, then you can moan as loud as you want. Do you want me to take it out and stop?"

Kelly shook her head side to side in a violent motion. No matter what it took, she wanted Michelle to keep on going.

Assuming the classic missionary position, Michelle took hold of the large rod dangling between her legs and positioned it at the entrance of Kelly's now very lubricated pussy. She pushed forward ever so slightly, opening wide the folds of her womanhood.

Kelly let out a grunt that was heard even through her makeshift gag. She was far from a virgin having lost that distinction some 23 years before, but she had never ever taken anything that big inside her before. Michelle looked up from her view of the cockhead disappearing inside Kelly's pussy at the sound. She looked into Kelly's brown eyes to see if she wanted her to stop. It only took a second for Kelly to bob her head up and down for Michelle to continue.

Over the next several minutes, Michelle slowly entered and re-entered Kelly, measuring the force of her thrusts with the display of discomfort shown on the businesswoman's face. She really didn't want to hurt her and was relieved when her facial expression changed from one of determined acceptance to one of enjoyment. If the blonde haired woman needed any other encouragement, she felt Kelly's hands against her ass, pushing her inside her.

Now freed from that worry, Michelle began to pump away in earnest. Faster and faster she thrusted, driving almost the full length of her fake cock into her lover. The pressure of the small protrusion on the underside of the rubber that caressed her own clit, sending oscillating waves through her own form. Thus each powerful stroke was felt by both women.

Michelle had started with the missionary position because it was the easiest for entry. Now to was time to just really have fun. She pulled out of Kelly and barked out an order that would've made her instructor back in basic training proud.

"Get on all fours!" She commanded.

So wrapped up in the wonderful feeling she was getting from Michelle's robust penetrations, Kelly quickly moved to respond. Without really taking the time to think about it, she flipped over and assumed the position, lifting her bottom up into the air as to invite easy access. She just wanted Michelle back inside her.

In that she wasn't disappointed. Michelle grabbed her legs and spread them even wider. Then with a lust filled thrust, rammed the cock back inside her. Harder and harder she pushed, taking both of them to the heights of passion.

Both women could feel the rising explosion that would consume them both. Kelly was more than content to just lie there and await it, but Michelle was determined to meet it head-on.

Pushing Kelly's head to the floor, Michelle straddled her, planted her cock ever deeper with each effort. Now it was Michelle who was grunting ever louder as sweat poured from her pores and her breasts bounced back and forth. Kelly was totally pinned, she tried to shift to a more comfortable position was helpless against the younger woman's strength.

It was Kelly who erupted first. Michelle could feel her pussy contract around the fake cock as she pulled and pushed it in with a single fluid motion. Her own orgasm followed two strokes later.

They collapsed upon each other, drenched in a combination of sweat, sex and exhaustion. They just laid there for about ten minutes, trading soft touches and little kisses.

The clock on the wall told them that Kelly's plane left in less than forty minutes. They had to get cleaned up. Reluctantly they lifted themselves off the floor and kissed one more time.

Standing naked a few feet from each other, they laughed at the sign of each other. Neither resembled the woman who walked into the room a short time before.

Thankfully, the makeshift apartment had a shower large enough for two and it wasn't long before they had washed each other clean. Time was now the enemy as they dressed and gathered their things. Since Michelle had a change of underwear in her bag, Kelly asked to keep the ones that had served as her gag as a souvenir. She quickly shoved them into her jacket's side pocket.

They had to race down the corridor to make the last call for the flight. Flashing an id given to her by the Security Chief, Michelle went with Kelly all the way to the plane. Kelly suddenly pulled her to a stop just a few feet from the cabin door. Quickly looking right and left to make sure they were alone, she leaned forward and kissed her. It was a brief but satisfying kiss.

"I love you." Kelly whispered before she turned and ran into to plane, afraid that if she waited any longer she might not get on.

Michelle watched as the attendant secured the cabin door behind her. Her eyes searched the small windows as the plane pulled away for some sign of her - to no avail. Before turning and heading back down the passageway, she whispered to herself.

"I love you too."

Kelly felt both happy and sad as the plane pulled up and into the sky. Happy at what Michelle and she had shared, it was an experience she would always remember. Sad at the knowledge that it would never be repeated. They were of two different worlds and neither would give up their world to live in the others. They would always remain friends. That, and the memory, would be enough.

Three days later, Michelle got her first mail from Kelly since they had met. She agreed with Kelly's assessment of their relationship. It was enough that they'd had that moment in time. As she got to the bottom of the letter she burst into laughter....

"...and the client in San Diego couldn't believe how relaxed I was after traveling cross-country the day before.

 By the way, you'll never believe what happened while I was away. They fired Janice Zimmerman. It seems that all the while she was saving the company those nickels and dimes, she was diverting the nickels to her own personal account. They're even thinking of pressing charges against her. I almost feel sorry for her, after all, it was because of her the trip turned out like it did. Think I should send her a thank you card?

Love Always,

Kelly

XOXOXOX

Story 04

The snow gave way to a world that was waking after the long slumber of winter. The air was warmer, the grass greener and more people were outdoors. Yet in this world of new beginnings and light, I had something heavy in my heart. I wasn't quite sure what it was but I felt restless somehow. Although I loved my husband more than anything else in the world, I wanted something more, I wanted to explore - I didn't know what. Bobby and I had fallen into the same old habit - he was away a lot and worked all the time. I taught high school English and also worked on my Master's degree. I wanted to have fun and do something thrilling. I hadn't been out with my girlfriends in months, and I even tended to stay home on the weekends when Bobby was working. I was bored and funky.

I felt like that the day I met Sherri. I had just come home from school on a very warm Saturday. I had an mid-morning class so it was only 2:00 PM when I got home. I slowly trudged up the stairs to the bedroom and stripped off my clothes. I then jumped into the shower to wash off my makeup and clean up. Just as I was getting out, I heard the doorbell ring. Soaking wet, I slipped into a terry cloth robe and ran to the door. Forgetting my usual cautions, I swung open the door, and there she stood, one of the most beautiful women I had ever encountered.

She stood there in white short shorts that showed off her long, tan legs. A tight tank top showed every curve of her slender torso and firm breasts. I stood there and stared for what felt like an eternity. Finally, she spoke in a quite, husky voice. "Hi, my name is Sherri. I just moved in to an apartment in the house across the street. I love your house and when I saw you drive in, I wanted to introduce myself." I felt awkward in my robe with my dripping hair, but I told her my name was Bea and invited her in. I offered her a drink and went to fridge and grabbed a bottled water and then ran to the bathroom to finish combing my hair.

I came out and sat at the other end of the couch. We began talking about where she was from and how long she had lived in town. I felt this strange feeling in me, her face and eyes just drew me into them. I was extremely attracted to this woman. I tried to dismiss these thoughts as a product of my mood, but found I couldn't. We talked for almost an hour about ourselves.

When she told me she had to get home, I stood from the couch. While I had been sitting, my robe tie loosened. I didn't realize it until I followed her gaze and looked down. I blushed furiously and covered myself with a slight giggle. But when I looked at her, she was searching my eyes for something. Her own nipples had grown hard under her tank top.

"Well, it was very nice meeting you, Bea," She said breathlessly. "I've been wanting to go out dancing and see the sights of Rochester. Would you like to go clubbing or something soon?"

I thought for a minute, and asked her if she would like to go tonight. "I'd love to," she exclaimed. "Only this time, don't get so embarrassed when you become uncovered. You really do have nice breasts." I stood there stunned as she walked toward the door. "How about 9:00 PM," she asked. At that point, anything was fine to me. I knew that I wanted this woman in a way I had never known. She closed the door softly, and I went to start getting ready. I felt anticipation growing between my legs...

I was so anxious as I began doing my hair. Curl after curl, I anticipated the night to come not knowing what to expect. What could Sherri have meant when she talked about me not covering myself later. I knew my imagination had gone wild, and that she probably only meant to help me get over my embarrassment. But I couldn't stop the fantasies that were running through my head. I put on my makeup a little heavier than usual and it looked really good. I hardly noticed that I had lost five pounds until I slipped into a skirt from six years before. It was a tight little black and white mini that showed too much when I bent over. The air was still warm outside, and so I put on a pink tank top that showed my midriff. Every curve showed to perfection and I admired my reflection for an instant before the doorbell rang. I slipped into some heels and ran to the door. There Sherri stood, wearing a short peach skirt, and a form fitting body suit. Her breasts were bare underneath her top and her nipples protruded through the cotton. Our compliments became a little excessive before we realized it and we laughed the awkward moment off.

Sherri offered to drive and we slipped into her red '95 Miata convertible, top down of course. Her skirt had come up a little and revealed a small patch of brown hair between her thighs. I felt a distinct wetness creep between my thighs. I was glad I hadn't worn panties either. After a long while, I stopped staring at her and enjoyed the ride. We were almost to a bar someone had recommended to her. She knew I had been looking at her and admiring her. By now, I was dripping wet, and slightly embarrassed by that fact. But I had never felt so attracted to a woman before.

We arrived at the bar and walked in. The room was crowded and dim. Smoke curled towards the ceiling and was sucked away by the ventilation. It was cool enough to send shivers up my spine, and blood to my nipples. I realized it was going to be an interesting night when I noticed...most of the couples were women...

I looked around apprehensively. I had never been in a bar like this before. Sherri just looked at me and smiled. She led me to two open bar stools and we ordered drinks. We stayed on those seats for over two hours, laughing and talking. Then she asked if I wanted to go out on the dance floor. It was a fast song, and so I agreed. The more we danced, the more fun we had. We sat back down, hot and sweaty. She inquired if I had ever had a bi-sexual experience. I truthfully told her no, but added that it has always been a fantasy of mine. She told me she could make my fantasies come true.

A slow song came over the speakers, and she took my hand and led me to the dance floor. She put one arm around my neck and the other around my waist. I mimicked her. I could feel my pulse racing, while wetness filled my pussy. She held me close to her as she moved her hips against mine. Then it happened. She leaned over and gently kissed me. I gasped at the softness of her lips. I locked my fingers into her soft hair and kissed her back. I couldn't get over the way her lips felt against mine. Her lower hand was caressing my ass. She asked me if I wanted to leave and go back to her place. I quickly agreed and was positive that the wetness was about to run down my legs. We hurried to the car and got in...

We reached her apartment shortly. My senses were heightened by my nervous anticipation. Her beautiful body pressed gently against mine as she tenderly kissed my lips. So slowly, so softly. She looked into my eyes. I could no longer stand it, I pulled her mouth to mine and kissed her firmly. Her tongue searched for mine in a desperate effort to become one with me. I held her hair twisted between my shaking fingers. She moved to my side and began caressing my nipples and breasts with her long fingernails. She continued to kiss me and our tongues swirled with a fiery passion. We lay back on the bed. She pulled her head away and looked into my eyes for a seeming eternity before she traced my nipple with her tongue, leaving a damp ring around the dark area. Her other hand began stroking my stomach. My body tensed at her touch. Extreme pleasure shivers controlled my body. Hesitantly, I reached for her breast when she suddenly took my hand and put it there for me.

"Squeeze my nipples," she said in between her teasing licks. I obediently began to squeeze and pinch gently, then firmly then gently. Quickly her nipples became taut in my fingers. Her fingers began exploring lower and lower. I felt her pull delicately at my hairs. I couldn't breathe I was so excited. She knew exactly what to do. I squeezed her breasts with my hands, firmly and longingly. Her tongue began taking the same path as her fingers. Down, down my stomach... she left a damp streak of pleasure. Her tongue soon reached where her fingers were still playing with my wetted matte of pubic hair. I could no longer reach her breasts so I began to play with my own.

As I softly caressed my orbs, Sherri took the plunge. Moving slowly down one thigh, Sherri used her tongue, moving ever towards my center of passion. The bedspread beneath us began soaking up the results of our intense embrace. I reached...reached between Sherri's legs and felt a warm tingle between mine. I worked my way slowly past her lips until reaching her small, hooded bud. I gently pushed and squeezed her awakening clit between my thumb and fore finger. Suddenly, Sherri became a thrashing figure as she moaned in a low, ecstatic tone. Waves of pleasure washed over her. I watched Sherri, breathless as I continued to press her button of pleasure. This was unlike anything I'd ever experienced before. The waves just wouldn't stop and I thought she would be jolted by the electricity forever.

I felt my own heat mount as Sherri finally lay spent on the bed in front of me. She pursed her luscious lips and then looked deep into my pure azure eyes. "I hardly know you," Sherri said sheepishly, "yet here I am lying naked next to you." A cool breeze whooshed through the open window of the room. Outside the sun was blazing gloriously but the blaze below was unrelenting. "Well," I giggled, " I hope we have a long chance to get to know each other even more." Sherri looked back longingly and then smiled and said, "Like what are you doing in the next few days, weeks and years." I flashed a bright smile and beamed it her way. "Only you." I said with delighted glee.

Story 05

I was hot, horny and prowling for pussy as I stepped into a dark little bar on Fifth Street. I needed some intense pussying and what better place to start than at a lesbian bar.

I sauntered in wearing a short, tight red spandex dress, three inch high red pumps and no underwear. I wanted to be ready at a moment's notice. My long blond hair was knotted on top of my head. I looked the consummate, cool bitch, but I was hot as hell for some pussy.

The place was packed with women in all kinds of clothes from jeans to evening gowns. I sat at the bar, ordered a drink, then turned to survey my options. My legs spread with a hint of my treasures revealed.

A "biker chick" in full leather walked over to me. "You are one hot pussy," she said looking between my legs. "I want all of that."

She was beautiful behind all that leather and bravado. My pussy began to juice as she looked at it. "I'll bet you do good pussy. Do you want to touch it now?"

She didn't hesitate as she reached for me. "Oh, yes, shit, baby, you are hot and wet for me. I want your shit right now! I will fuck you up!"

I rise from my stool and follow her to one of the fucking rooms in back. She closed the door quickly as I stepped in. She immediately rammed two fingers up my cunt, pushing me against the door. I gasped with pleasure as I knew I was in for the good, hard fucking that I craved. She removed her fingers from me and licked them, looking into my eyes. She grabbed my ass roughly, jammed her tongue in my mouth, and ground her leather crotch into my pussy. I was on fucking fire as she humped me against the door.

"Get on the bed, but keep the dress on." I obeyed. "You need for good hot pussy? Well, baby I'll give that pretty blond cunt the fucking it needs." She removed only her leather pants and moved towards me. She spread my legs on the bed and ate me roughly, biting and sucking my clit and lips as she thrust fingers inside my pussy and my asshole.

"Fuck my shit," I moaned as I thrashed my head from side to side. My hair spilled from its knot and spread over the pillow. After I came three times, I screamed, "Get on top of me now! I need to feel your pussy. Screw me hard. Now!"

"Damn, you are one hot chick," she mumbled as she brought herself to me. She fucked me hard and deep with her dark-haired pussy. "Is this what you want?" she asked grinding into me as she looked into my passion-filled eyes.

"Yes, baby, fuck me, fuck me harder. I need your pussy so bad."

"I fucked all this pretty blonde hair down," she said running her fingers through it after letting me cum again. She lifted my breasts from the scooped neck of my little red dress and sucked and bit at them, fanning the flame in me all over again. This chick knew what I liked.

She kissed me hard and fast then pulled away from me to get something from her backpack. She came back with an awesome looking double headed dildo. I watched as she slowly inserted one half in her pussy. "Are you ready to be filled with my dick, baby? You do like it hard, don't you? You look delicate, but you like your fucking hard don't you? I'll fuck you good and hard with this. I'll have you cumming up the walls," she promised as she pumped the tool into her own pussy.

"Oh yes, baby, fuck me until I scream, make me sore, then keep on fucking me."

She climbed on me and rammed the other half of the dick in my pussy. My ass thrust up to her at impact driving her half deep into her pussy. "Oh shit, shit, honey," she moaned as I screwed her. Filled with each other's dicks, we pressed together until our pussies touched and began to fuck in earnest. She sucked my tongue as she moaned. I dug my nails into her ass cheeks as she ground deeper into me. Inspired by her fucking, I became bold as I wet a finger in my mouth and pressed it into her asshole. She rode me harder and deeper.

"You are one good fuck," I tell her looking into her eyes as I thrust my pelvis to her. She lost it then. Her tempo speeded to maniacal. Never had anyone fucked me so hard and so fast.

"You're making me cum, bitch," I started my dirty talk tirade. "Your fucking pussy is burning up. Fuck it harder, harder. Give me all your shit you leather-clad, pussy eating dyke. Shit, bitch, fuck it, fuck ittt!" I screamed as I came on her. She was right behind me as I came and rammed up and into her. Our mutual dick was vibrating with our spasms.

"Never have I been fucked like that in my entire life," I said out of breath.

"No other woman will ever fuck you like this again--except me. I'm staking my claim on this pussy right now, do you hear?" she said into my eyes as she began screwing me again. Suddenly, she stopped and pulled from me awaiting my assent. "Do you understand? I want your pussy all for myself. Every Thursday night right here. Ok?"

"Yes, yes, yes! you bitch. All yours.

"Right answer darling," she said as she fucked me taking me over the edge again.

No more pussy hunts for me, I thought. She's all I need and more. I pushed up into her as she came on me again. I hope my husband never discovers my little affinity for good cunt. I will not give up the best pussy I ever had--no fucking way.

Hot Lesbian Beginnings
05 Super Erotic Stories for Women
Sarah Rodgers

All Rights Reserved. No part of this publication may be reproduced in any form or by any means, including scanning, photocopying, or otherwise without prior written permission of the copyright holder. Copyright © 2020

This book is entirely a work of fiction. The names, characters and incidents portrayed in it are the work of the author's imagination. Any resemblance to actual persons, living or dead, events or localities is entirely coincidental.

Story 01

Sharon stood up, "I'm going to shower then I'll show you the rest of the place." She said as she turned toward the door that lend to the showers and pulled off her top. She turned giving me a good look at her firm tits, "Come and talk to me while I change." She disappeared through the door. My pulse quicken as I walk toward the door, part of me screaming to leave, most of me wanting to stay. When I went through the door I entered a locker room. Down one side were full length lockers, in front of the lockers were several low padded benches, on the other side were showerstalls, sinks, and a couple of toilets. Sharon was facing away from me, bent at the waist sliding the jogging shorts down her legs. She was wearing panties after all, thong style, I could see the waist band around her hips and the strap that went down the crevice of her ass. After she removed the shorts, she stayed bent over and removed her shoes, then she stood, looked over her shoulder and blew me a kiss. Then she hooked her thumbs in the waistband and slowly eased down the skippy panties bending over, giving me a wide open view of her creamy smooth ass, her puckered asshole and wet slit. I let out a moan, Sharon straightened, turned around and came to me. Her arms went around my neck and she hugged me. Her mouth closed mine and her tongue darted through my parted teeth. My hands caressed her back, and sides as I returned her kiss.

My hands found her tits and began to knead them till my fingers found her rubbery hard nipples. I pinched, pulled and tweaked her nipples, marveling at smoothness, weight and texture of another woman's breasts. My own tits were still confined in my bra, aching to be touched, the cups felt rough to my sensitive nipples. Our kiss broke, both of us short of breath. I pulled my blouse over my head and dropped it to the floor, reach behind me and unfastened my bra. Sharon pulled my bra off and let it fall. She ran her hands over my shoulders and neck, down the slopes of my tits, along the sides down to the top of my slacks then back up. Her hands barely touched me as they moved over my tits, never quite touching the nipples. I stood eyes closed concentrating on the feeling, after the third time she over my front her touch became heavier, squeezing, stroking, kneading but still not touching my nipples. My panties were sopped, my whole pussy throbbed, my nipples actually ached to be touched. Sharon pulled me to her, my nipples pushed against her soft warm tits, a shudder went through my body and I groaned. As she held me against her I could feel the hardness of her nipples, the softness of her breasts, and the heat from her twat.

My mouth was against her neck, I kissed did, licked. Sharon's hands were on my shoulders, slowly she moved my mouth down. I licked and kissed her tits, running my tongue over the soft skin, tasting the underside of each breast, circling my tongue slowly around one nipple, then the other. Her hands were in my hair now, she guide my mouth to her nipples, I flicked it with my tongue, then licked gently, when it was cover in salivas I blew air on it. The nipple puckered. "Suck it." she commanded. I took the nipple into my mouth, sucking in as much of her tit as I could. My tongue swirled around the nipple as I gently bit the tit in my mouth. Then I started to bat the Nipple back and forth with my tongue. I felt her body stiffen against mine. "Now do the other one". My mouth went to her other nipple, I flicked it with my tongue and then bit it softly before sucking it in my mouth.

Her hands pushed me lower, down to my knees, I licked her tummy as my mouth went down her body. I felt the tickle of her pubic hair on my chin and resisted for a second. I could feel the heat of her, the scent of her sex filled my nostrils. I brought my arms up and hugged her, holding my face just above her bush. My hands trailed down the cheeks of her ass, squeezing, weighing them. I stoked the backs, then the insides of her thighs. Then I moved my mouth down, licking around her bush, rubbing my nose through her red curly hairs. Then I tasted the juices that had leaked from her, what was left of my inhibitions s broke. I darted my tongue into the heat of her cunt. My nose pushed at her clit as I tongue fucked her. I pulled her against me with one hand while with the other I massaged the flesh between her cunt and asshole. Her hands spread her cunt lips apart and I licked my way to her clit. I flicked gently with my tongue then harder. My mouth closed on it and I sucked it as hard as I could. Sharon was withering against me, grinning her pelvis at my mouth. I bit her clit done too softly and she moaned. I started flicking my tongue up and down on her clit. Sharon went stiff and made a series of grunting sounds. As I felt her cunt start to spasm I jabbed two finger into her slippery cunt. When her spasms quit she took a deep breath and sighed. Then she helped me to my feet and kissed me long and deep, licking her juices from my face. "God that was good, now for a shower" She said.

"What about me? I'm so horny I can't stand it." I pleaded

"Do yourself." She replied.

"I've never done that, please you do me."

She turn and looked at me. "You've never gotten yourself off? I do believe someone has neglected your education." She walked to her locker and took out her purse. From it she took a cloth bag about 10 inches long. "This is a vibrating dildo, this is my phone number" she took a card from her purse.

"Call me about midnight and I'll help you get off. We'll finish your tour Saturday. I've got a date for dinner and you need to get home before it's too late." She kissed me softly and gave my tit a gently squeeze.

Then she headed for the showers. I picked up my blouse and put it on, then bent to pick up my bra, I saw her g-string laying on the floor, with a glance toward the showers I grabbed them. I stuffed the dildo, g-string and bra into my purse and head up the stairs to the bar. On the way out Linda waved me over. "We'll see you Saturday." She pulled me over and whispered, "I didn't notice what nice tits you have, glad to see you took off your bra." I turn red, I couldn't think of a thing to say. I look quickly around then noticed Linda had the erect cock of the guy sitting next to her in her hand under the bar. I stood up straight, my breast brushed her arm and she smiled at me. The guy beside her was no more than 20. I head for the door.

In the car I removed the dildo from it's bag. It was about 8 inches long rubber, and looked like a real cock. I took out Sharon's panties and sniffed them. The scent of her sex was very strong. I put everything back in my purse and headed home. I drove with one hand. With the other I gently fingered the damp crotch of my slacks.

When I got home my folks were watching TV. I told them I had a job lineup as a bartender. Both of them were a little opposed till I told them it was at the Inn Between. My dad said that would be okay cause Linda ran a tight business and looked out for her bartenders.

I went to my room, and lock the door. I started to undress and take another shower. As I peeled down my pants i caught a whiff of my sex juices and decided not to. I turn off the light, got the dildo, and Sharon's G-string. I lay down on my bed and sniffed the G-string, then rubbed my fingers through my pubs inside my panties and sniffed them. The smells were different, but both were definetly sexy. I took the dildo out, it felt like a real cock, only, cold. It smelled faintly of Sharon. I wondered how often she used it.

I dozed off for a second and woke with a start, looked at the clock, it was a little after 11. My twat still had a dull throb. I reached down, the crotch of my panties was still damp. I thought of Sharon, the things she had done to me and made me do to her. I didn't love her, I felt, I don't know, something for her.

Finally it was midnight. I turned on the lamp by my bed and dial the number she had given me. It rang a couple of times before she answered.

She didn't even say hello.

"Are you in your room?" she ask.

"Yes." I replied.

"What do you have on?" she asked next.

"Just my panties."

"Turn on all the lights in the room and open the blinds and curtains." She ordered. I did as I was told, holding the reciever between my cheek and shoulder and carrying the phone. Looking out the window I was glad my room was in the back of the house facing an empty lot instead of in front facing the street. Still it would be easy for someone to see me standing in front of the window in my panties. "Now get someting to blind fold yourself and lay down on the bed. Get my G-string you stole and the dildo. Blinfold yourself." As I followed her orders I felt my nipples harden and my twat start to warm up. Using the belt to my bathrobe I covered my eyes, wrapping it around my head twice. I used the loose ends to tie the phone near my ear.

"Squeeze your tits, push them together. Play with your nipples. Lick your palms and rub them wet across your nipples." My hands moved to her commands, controled by her voice not by my mind. I could feel my breast heat, my nipples hard. " Pull on your nipples." I pulled until I moan in pain and lust. "Stop! Smell my G-string. Think of my cunt, how you licked it, how it tasted. Now lick my dildo, does it taste like me? Imagine it's RC's cock fresh from my cunt waiting for you to suck it. Lick it up and down the shaft, suck just the head into your mouth. Flick your tongue across the head, pump the head in and out of your mouth. Now suck in as much as you can, think of RC's cock sliding in and out of your mouth." My cunt was dripping, the crotch of my panties was soaked, I could feel my juices oozing down my ass. "Take it out of your mouth. Spread your legs. Now touch yourself through your panties, lightly, just with your finger tips. Run your hands down the inside of your legs, bring them back up running just your nails over the skin." The muscles in my legs twitched, my hips started rocking on their own, heat spread from my sex over my whole body. "Cover your cunt with one hand, trace your slit with one finger, press the palm against your bush rub it agaitn your clit. Poke your painties as far as you can into your cunt. Are you wet? tell me how it feels."

"Yes I'm wet, my panties are sopped. It feels so good."

"What feels good!"

"My finger."

"What's your finger doing!"

"It's playing with me."

"Be more graphic or I hang up you little cunt."

"I'm fingering my cunt through my panties, I'm so horny, it feels so good. My clit is throbbing, my cunt is gribbing my finger. I want sometihing bigger, deeper in my cunt, I want to cum."

"That better, you really want to be a slut don't you?"

"Yes oh yes."

"Good cause that's what you are. Now bring your hand up and lick it clean. Suck are your juices off it. Tell me how it tastes."

"It tastes like you almost, like sex."

"Use your other hand now. Pull your panties up into your slit so you can touch the lips on either side with your fingers. Now rub you middle finger over your clit, down your slit, to your asshole. Rub your asshole gently, think of RC's finger up your ass, how it made you cum. Rub you finger back and forth from your clit to your asshole and tell me how it feels, what's going though your mind."

"I'm burning, my cunt and ass are on fire, my finger feels good, I wish it was a tongue or a cock, I want to be fucked, or licked, I just want to cum."

"Take off your panties. Pull your cunt open as wide as you can, use the index finger of each hand to trace your slit. Imagine your showing your cunt to RC, show him how pink and wet it is. Push a finger in, fuck yourself, use two fingers. Rub your little asshole with the other hand, sho him he can fuck it too." For an instant my mind went to the lights being on and the open curtains, I didn't care. Maybe somebody was watching, the thought set a spark through my clit, someone in the dark watching, seeing the slut putting on a show. "Talk cunt."

"I hope somebody is watching, I hope RC is watching, seeing how much of a slut I can be. He can fuck me, my cunt, my ass, my mouth anything he wants."

"What about me bitch, what if I want you?"

"Anything, I want to suck your nipples, lick your cunt, have you lick me, anything you want."

"Just like a little bitch in heat. Pull your legs up till the touch your chest." I could feel the hot points of my nipples against my thighs. The pressure sqashed my tits, it felt good. "Rub my dildo up and down your slit. Get it good and wet. Push it in your cunt, slowly, all the way in. Now pull it out, in again, out, slowly." My whole body twitch and jerk as I slowly fuck myself. "Push it all the way in, roll over. Up on your elbows and knees, rub your nipples back and forth on the bed. rest your head on the pillow so you can use your hands. Fuck your cunt with my dildo, imagine it's me doing it. Fuck your asshlole with your finger, feel the dildo sliding in out of your cunt as you finger fuck your asshole. Turn on the dildo."

"How?"

"There's a switch on the bottom cunt." I found the switch and pushed, the vibrations jolted through my cunt, I buried my face in my pillow to muffle my gasp and moans. My whole body jerked and rippled as I came and came.

My body was covered in sweat, my finger was still in my asshole the dildo lay buzzing on the bed between my legs, the blind fold had slid up off my eyes. I rolled over on my side, there at the window was the blur of a face, then it was gone. I jumped off the bed and turn off the light. I crouched down and crawled over to the window no one was there. I crawled back to the bed and picked up the phone, the line was dead. I turned off the vibrator and put it in my purse, picked up my panties and started to put them in the hamper, then had another idea and put then in my purse also. Picking up Sharon's G-string I crawled into bed.

I fell asleep sniffing her scent and stroking my slit.

Story 02

This is a story about how I discovered myself. I am a lesbian. I know that now. but I did not always know that. I was not always honest with myself. but she taught me a lesson I will never forget. she taught me to be honest with myself. this story is as much her story as it is mine. I had known her since high school. we were not best friends or anything. although we did have some good times together in high school. we were in the school choir together, and our choir would travel throughout the state of florida. I liked those times. the choir was 80% female which gave me a chance to get away from my old man. I liked just hanging out with the girls.

She was a good friend in the choir and we would spend a lot of time together. on some of the choir trips we were too far from home to return the same evening. so we would usually get a room for the night. the two of us would sometimes share a bed. I remember waking up in the middle of the night, looking over at her and wanting her. I did not understand these feelings. afterall I was heterosexual. I told myself that I wanted men. but I would sit there and fantasize about having lesbian sex with her. needless to say it never happened. but these feelings scared me. a few weeks later I talked to my grandmother about these feelings and she told me not to worry, that it was just a stage that I would out grow. as a result I never acted on these feelings.

When june came around we graduated and I did not see her for a few years. during this time I married a very nice man. he was sweet. I liked him very much. together we had a daughter, a beautiful girl with brown eyes and dark hair.

Sex with my husband was normal, I guess. what is sex supposed to be like? I don't know. the problem I had and I never admitted this to my husband was that to orgasm I always had to fantasize about a woman or about lesbian sex. for this reason, I always tried to avoid intercourse. I prefered him to go down on me. that way, I could fantasize that he was a woman. then I could get off. I also did not feel any spiritual connection with my husband. he was a nice guy. and I liked to hang around him. but I guess deep down inside I knew that I could not spend the rest of my life with him. I needed some excitement, some romance.

One day she came back into my life. I happened to bump into her in the super market. I was lucky to catch her. she had moved to north carolina after graduation. she just happened to be in florida visiting relatives for the holidays. we talked for some time. I told her about my husband, and my daughted. she told me about her little cottage up in the north carolina mountains. she told me about how she loved the peace and quiet of the mountains. after talking for about an hour she asked me if I would like to go out with her for a drink that night. I accepted.

I told my husband that I was going out with an old friend from high school that night, and he did not think much of it. he was happy to spend the evening with our daughter. he really was a loving father.

She picked me up at 10 o'clock. she was beautiful that night, as usual. she was a natural beauty. she did not wear any make up. she did not have to. as we pulled out of the driveway I looked over at her and my heart sunk. I knew at that moment that I was in love with her. and that if I could have a lesbian affair with her, I would go for it in a moment.

We went to a dance club, and had a few drinks. as I started to get a buzz, and my inhibitions were lowering I kept on imagining ways to come on to her. but I was scared. I thought she was straight. she had given me no reason to suspect otherwise. I kept on looking at her, looking deep into her eyes for a clue, but all that I got in response was a deep gleeful grin. I did not know how to take it. I don't know if it was my imagination or what but I kept on noticing that she would look up whenever a woman in a skimpy outfit would walk by. I imagined, hoped, that she might be gay, or at least bi. but I had no way to know. at the end of the evening, she dropped me off at home, gave me a peck on the cheek and invited me to visit her in north carolina. my husband was asleep, so I slipped into the bathroom and masterbated fantasizing of making love to her.

The next week I could not stop thinking about her. I constantly found myself fantasizing about her. I wanted her. eventually, I broke down and called her. on the phone, she once again invited me up to north carolina to visit her. naturally, I could not resist. a few days later I loaded up my car, told my husband that I was going to visit an old friend, and left early in the morning, taking my daughter to north carolina. the 12 hour trip was very hard, but I just wanted to see her again. I still thought she was probably straight, and that nothing would ever work out. however, even if we would only be friends, I had to see her again. she was my passion. I fantasized that we would take a backpacking trip into the mountains. then when it was dark, I would snuggle next to her and start kissing her, teasingly. so that if she reacted negatively, I could tell her that the whole thing was a joke. I fantasized about holding her hand in the supermarket and letting all of the country hicks gawk. I fantasized that maybe she would take the first move and come on to me. afterall, I am a beautiful woman, I thought to myself as I tilted the rear view mirror to look at myself. I am attractive and she ought to be attracted to me, I thought.

We got to her house late in the evening. she told me to put my daughter to bed on the living room couch and join her in her bedroom. she only had one bed in her cottage, so she offered to share her bed with me. I naturally accepted. we talked late into the night about old times, about our lives, etc. but she never mentioned her sex life. I decided to let it be.

We finally got to bed around 3 am. after she was asleep, I snuggled next to her arm. feeling her arm against my cheek was very erotic. I fell asleep in this position.

She woke me up at 11 o'clock. I guess she woke up at 7 o'clock and found my daughter awake. during that time, she had feed my daughter and taken her outside to play, in order not to wake me up. she was so thoughtful. when she woke me up, she was serving me breakfast in bed.

The three of us spent the day together. it was wonderful. then that night, she asked me if I would like to go out for a drink. that sounded good to me, so we dropped my daughter off at a babysitter's place. and my friend invited two of her friends, sara and rama, to come along. on the way over to sara and rama's place, she suddenly became very serious and told me that there was something about sara and rama that I should know. she then told me that sara and rama were lovers who had been living together for 5 years. I don't know what kind of reaction she expected from me, but I just smiled and asked her if she was gay. she looked over at me and told me that she was. my heart fell through the floor, I was so happy. so I laughed and asked her if this was then a double date. She got the biggest smile on her face, and said,"i thought you'd never ask."

Half a minute later, we pulled up to sara and rama's place, but I was not about to lose this moment. I reached over and kissed her tentatively. she then reciprocated with a full on french kiss. we kissed for about five minutes before she suggested that we better go inside. as we were walking up to the house, guess who was peeping out the window but sara and rama. they had seen us kissing. I was a little embarassed, but it made me feel mischievious and romantic, too. for the first time in my life I felt as if I was in love. not only was I in love, but I was also completely out of the closet. as far as sara and rama knew, I could have been out of the closet for years. I was drunk on my new found lesbianism.

The four of us went dancing at a local pub. then before it got too late we went back to sara and rama's house, popped in a video on the vcr and snuggled on the couches. sara and rama took one couch and we took the other couch. I snuggled next to her, letting my hands and arms rub up against her sexual parts. I had never been so excited in my life. I had an orgasm right there, just from the build up in excitement.

Later that evening, we picked up my daughter, went home, and put her to bed on the couch. Finally, my lover and I were alone together. she was on the other side of the room looking at me. she asked me about my husband. I looked at her a laughed. "do you really think I could go back to him after what had happened tonight," I asked her. she looked at me with those beautiful eyes and without a word, she took off her top in a single motion. my fantasy had come true. I went up to her and pushed her on the bed. she wrapped her hands around me and I suckled from her womanhood.

I have to go back a few years, I was 16 at the time, and still naive to much of the world of love. It's not that I hadn't gotten a lot of attention, but of course it had all been from guys. As a matter of fact I got pretty popular with some of the older guys, which confused me for a long time until one of my "boyfriends" confessed that my first lover, (at 13), had spread the word around about what kind of girl I was. My first lover, what a laugh. It wasn't exactly romance but if you want to hear about that one you can let me know. Hell it might even be therapeutic to write it down. Not that it wasn't hot, it was definitely that and more, it's just that it isn't the kind of thing that people think of as normal. (But then who among us is really normal anyway, Newt Gingrich??? find them all and shoot them for the rest of us....please!) I think you have an idea what I'm talking about, but for the more dense among you, my brother Daniel was the first to get into my pants, and he was none too gentle with me on my deflowering day.

Soooo anyway, I have this older sister, Laura, she's really kinda cute and we were always really close even though she is almost 7 years older than me. The relationship got closer as I got older and it gave me the chance to meet and "hang" with some of her friends. Welllllll, I got to know Laura's best friend, Lisa, pretty well over the years. She always seemed to be around when Laura was home on vacation and we had lots of opportunities to talk and ended up getting pretty close. Lisa got married right after she graduated and I went to the wedding. It was fun, her husband David is really a nice guy and actually gave me a lot of attention at the reception, which was fun for a 15 year old girl! Little did I know what HE was thinking!!! I remember having mixed feelings about David, I can tell you what it was now even though I didn't have a clue then...I was jealous.

David and Lisa had a baby girl almost instantly! I guess I can't blame her for that, I mean he is pretty hot and seemed to be fun and all. Anyway, I started baby-sitting for them when the baby was about 2 minutes old. I mean really, they were always going someplace and it seemed like I was spending more time at their apartment than my own home! Each time I would come over, Lisa would always take some time and talk to me about something or other while David just seemed to drift in and out of the room.

I remember thinking at times how sexy Lisa is and got nervous that she might notice me staring at her breasts or ass every chance I got. She would often sit close to me and find a reason to put an arm around me, once even touching one of my breasts on the pretext of measuring hers against my rapidly developing bust. Finally David would come strolling into the room and offer to drive me home, I never remember wanting to leave...ever. On the drive home David ALWAYS asked about my boyfriends and if I liked dating and would comment on how I was growing up soooo fast and all that bullshit, I knew he was checking me out, I mean come on! Well, the moment of truth arrived (finally you said?), when Lisa asked me to lunch on the pretense of helping her with the baby. We had a nice lunch and went shopping at Victoria's Secret and some other shops where Lisa bought some very hot stuff while I wandered around with Holly. I can still remember how excited I was when Lisa called me into the dressing room at Victoria's Secret to see one of her outfits. She asked me if I thought David would like the outfit, well shit who wouldn't, she was wearing one of those Merry Widows. I thought I would die! I told her she looked great and she did! You would never know this woman had a kid. Her breasts were still firm and full and her belly was perfectly flat. I think I kind of stammered something like "very nice" and left pretty quickly, the whole time wondering what was wrong with me, I was dripping wet and shaking with excitement.

I was relieved in a way to be on the way back to Lisa's apartment, I was pretty confused about my feelings but I found myself staring at her as she walked in front of me, or leaned over me. It also did not escape my attention that Lisa was taking every opportunity to touch me as we talked and walked along. If all this happened to me now there would be no doubt in my mind what was going down but back then I was clueless. I still remember today what she was wearing like it just happened yesterday. Those black stretch pants and tube top with that little vest were definitely for my benefit and I loved watching the way her hips moved as she walked in those high heels. This was a definite "fuck me" outfit.

Things got interesting when we settled in at her apartment. Lisa surprised me by offering me a glass of wine. She had been drinking since lunch and was obviously buzzed. I put the baby down for a nap while Lisa prepared a snack. When I returned to the living room Lisa was sprawled out on the couch with a glass of wine. There was a glass for me and I did what any horny, nervous, sophisticated 16 year old would do, I sucked that thing down in about 30 seconds! Lisa got up almost immediately and got me another, with a little grin, telling me that I didn't have to worry about getting home right away and to just relax.

I couldn't keep my eyes off of her, she seemed to shift and move so sensually. I know she was watching me and noticed me staring at her legs and breasts, but I couldn't help myself. I could blame it on the wine but I knew that something was going to happen, and I wanted it badly. I got up to get something in the kitchen, god knows what. When I turned to head back into the living room Lisa was right there in my face, looking down at me with her blue eyes looking into my soul, laughing, leering, loving me. I stood there, frozen looking from her eyes to her boobs to my toes, shaking inside.

Thank god Lisa knew what to do or I think I would still be standing there now. I could feel her breath on my shoulders, and could smell her perfume, it was such a turn on, I was really shaking when I felt her hand on my arm. She slowly tightened her grip until I knew she wanted me to look up at her. When I lifted my eyes to hers I could see that she wanted me. I mean, here I was 16 years old alone with this 23 year old married woman and I was dripping wet, thinking about things that were so new to me, but I wanted it, I knew I wanted this more than anything. Things started happening quickly after that and I apologize if my memory of the events become less complete but I was having a lot of trouble concentrating at that point.

Lisa put her arms around me and told me that she had been wanting to be with me for a long time. I mumbled something stupid about enjoying my time with her. Then she kissed me...I was finished. I nearly jumped out of my skin. My legs got weak, my heart was pounding in my chest and I started to tremble. I opened my mouth almost on instinct and Lisa immediately began probing my mouth with her soft tongue. I whimpered into her mouth and she released me for the moment, leading me into the bedroom by the hand. I thought, "my god, I'm going to make love to a woman....at last!"

I remember her hands on my breasts and the soft touch of her fingers everywhere. I touched her breasts and she moaned into my mouth. My hands slid down her side and rested on her butt covered in those tight stretch pants. She pulled me in close until my boobs were pressed into her tight belly then she asked me the question that changed my life. "Will you love me Vicky? Will you love me like a woman?" At least that's the way I remember it. I realized suddenly that I wasn't breathing! My response came out as a kind of sobbing, moaning, animal noise.

I remember kissing her long and hard as we fell back on the bed. Her hands on my young body, everywhere, under my blouse, on my ass, between my legs. I responded in kind, stroking her back, playing with her big breasts and tentatively groping her tight ass. I was sooo hot I was moaning and crying out my passion for my new found love. Lisa was obviously experienced in this, but I had no way of knowing how experienced. I can tell you now that she was playing me like a concert pianist, and hitting every chord on the mark!

This was something so totally new and exciting for me, there is no way in hell to describe it. Lisa's hands were doing things to me as she moaned and kissed me then I realized that my top was off and my pants were unzipped, and I was shaking like a leaf. I remember having an orgasm when she put her hand down my pants for the first time.

I had orgasms before and lord knows I had been masturbating daily (usually 2 or 3 times a day) for years, but this was so totally different I decided that I really didn't know what sex was until that afternoon. Lisa's fingers running through the soft hairs on my pussy, down between my lips and sliding up and down my slit, slowly circling my stiff little clit, then gently pumping into my aching hole. I must have been moaning, grunting or something because Lisa was stroking my hair with her free hand and telling me that she loved me, that I was wonderful, that she wanted my body...etc. I came again while she stroked my pussy, I would have done anything for this woman, and did.

After my second cum we rested a moment, really it was an opportunity to remove the rest of our clothes. I couldn't wait to see Lisa naked. She seemed to sense my need and teased me terribly. First she helped me take off the rest of my clothes, touching me everywhere while she did. My whole body was super-sensitive and each touch, every stroke would cause me to jump or groan, almost cumming when her fingers would stray between my legs. I was trying to hump her hand, her leg, anything that got near my pussy, until I was finally lying there naked...and waiting for the next act in the most exciting day of my life.

Once she had me naked I reached out for her but Lisa stopped me telling me to be patient and she wanted to get me excited, just to watch. Well hell, I thought if I get any more excited I'll explode!! She got up from the bed and looked down at me with a wonderful smile on her face and a look in her eyes that betrayed her lust. She told me that she had masturbated many times thinking about this moment. Her hands were rubbing her tits through the tube top and occasionally dip between her legs and she would squeeze her legs together and shiver. She told me that she loved my body, my responsiveness to her caresses. She asked if I liked her body. SHIT! All I could do was nod my head and mumble yes. She pulled off her tube top and began pinching her nipples. My hands must have gone to my own tits by themselves because Lisa just moaned and said that I should do it with her just like that.

I wanted her back in my arms but I didn't dare move. Lisa turned her back to me and ran her hands over her butt. It was soo hot, I know I moaned something. Then she bent at the waist and began to slide her stretch pants down over her round ass. I was hypnotized. My entire world consisted of that beautiful ass and my hand sliding down between my legs. When her pants were off she slid her fingers between her legs from the front pulling aside the little band of cloth of her panties so that I could see her playing with her pussy lips. She slid a finger into herself then took it out and licked it, then slid it back in with a moan. Now THAT got me VERY hot!

She removed her finger and hooked her thumbs into the waistband of her panties, slowwwwwlllly sliding them down over her hips, still bent at the waist. Her entire sex was now visible and I was surprised to see that she had absolutely no hair on her pussy. It was beautiful. Even though I had never done this before, all I could think of right at that moment was putting my lips to her pussy lips. When her panties were off Lisa began playing with her pussy again, this time sliding several fingers into herself, holding her lips open for me to see, then pulling out and rubbing her clit, which she completely uncovered so that it was poking straight out between her spread open lips. I think she came right then.

Lisa started rubbing her juices all up and down her crack, sliding her fingers in her pussy, then running them up the crack of her ass, then back again, occasionally stopping and circling her little bottom hole then moving on. What really caught me by surprise was when she slipped her finger up her ass and started pumping it in and out and grunting. She was kind of humping herself back onto her own finger while she did it giving the impression that she was getting fucked by someone or something else. Now I could understand why she kept her nails shorter than most women, (something that I have adopted for convenience as well). I think she had another orgasm while she did this because she was playing with her clit with her other hand, but anyway, she finally stopped and stood up, turning to me with a with a searching look, I guess trying to determine if what I had seen had excited me or turned me off. I must have passed whatever test she had given me because I was laying there pounding 2 fingers into my drenched pussy and pinching my nips. I also noticed that she wasn't completely shaved, there was a little tuft of hair just above her slit, it was really cute.

Lisa climbed back on the bed with me and asked me if I liked the little show. I must have gotten my voice back because we talked for a while about what we liked to do in bed. My comments were very short, hers were very enlightening. She explained to me about what she likes to do with other women, and I wanted it all. When she got to the part about anal sex I was totally lost. It looked like she really got into it but it was a completely foreign idea to me then. She told me not to worry, if I didn't care for it we could skip it, or I could do it to her and she would love that but not try anything like that with me. The whole time we were talking she was playing with my tits and pussy, or just rubbing different parts of my body, I was in heaven. Now I got to touch all of her naked charms as well. I found myself totally absorbed in her pussy, she pushed my hand away several times telling me to go slow, but I would always move back after a short visit to some other part of her.

Basically, I told her I wanted to do everything with her a lover could do. My response must have pleased her because she hugged me to her and kissed me hard on the lips. I could taste her pussy on her lips from her playing before and it only served to excite me further. We hugged and groped each other for a few minutes when she started kissing my breasts and biting the nipples gently. I held her head in my hands and directed her from one tit to the other. She would grab one and squeeze the nipple between her thumb and finger while licking the other nipple, then switch, getting a little rougher each time, until I could feel her teeth on my flesh constantly and was experiencing an exquisite aching and occasional sharp pain that would immediately turn to pleasure as she would bite down on my swollen nips. I was moaning constantly and often yelping or screaming when she would bite me.

Without letting go of my breast Lisa began to lick down my heaving chest to my stomach, then to my bellybutton, which she probed and poked with her tongue. That was strangely exciting and I started humping at her again, waiting and hoping that she wouldn't stop there. Finally finished with my bellybutton she continued to lick down to the beginning of my hair line. She ran her tongue through the little ringlets of hair there. Because I am natural blond, my pussy hair is very light (when I let it grow in), and she seemed to enjoy running her tongue through my little patch.

Now I should tell you that this was not the first time I had experienced a tongue in my pussy, however, I was in no way prepared for what Lisa was going to do me. I had let 2 of my boyfriends lick me before on several occasions and even had a few orgasms (and thought it was wonderful at the time). The hell with that! Lisa fucking devoured my cunt! I went from feeling like I had one giant tongue laving me from my clit to my asshole to thinking that Lisa was actually trying to climb inside my pussy, tongue first. I later realized that Lisa does have a rather long tongue...and I love every inch of it! She would slide the entire length of her tongue into my pussy then run up and tease my clit, then back and forth and slowly enter my ass (which became an incredible turn on) then back to my clit and on and on and GOD I couldn't believe it....THIS IS SEX!!!!!!

At some point I started to cum and I knew it was going to be a big one, but then it hit and I was flailing around, half screaming, but it didn't stop. I kept cumming, and Lisa kept eating me, and I kept cumming, and screaming louder (now into a pillow to keep from waking Holly) and Lisa was pumping 2 fingers in my pussy, and I kept cumming, I clamped my legs together and Lisa grabbed them and pushed me way back completely exposing my ass, and I was just starting to come down when she drove her tongue up my asshole. I immediately came again. Not like the previous cum, a totally different feeling.. The previous cum was intensely mind shattering and almost unbearable, this one was not as intense but more animalistic or something, I needed her to keep pushing into me. I began pumping my ass back on her tongue and grunting out for her to keep going She had my legs in her hands, pushing them back, I reached down and grabbed my legs and pulled them even further open, spreading myself for her. Lisa spread my ass with both hands and drove her tongue in and out of me until I finally begged her to stop. She didn't stop until I had asked several times, and when she did it was with reluctance, but I was completely exhausted and immediately collapsed when she removed her tongue from my ass.

I started crying and didn't stop for a long time. Lisa came up and held me and I guess she was scared that she had injured me or something, but I wasn't in any pain. It was just an emotional response to the most emotionally, physically, and mentally draining experience of my life. I had died and been reborn. When I could speak I tried to tell her this, but neither of us can remember what I really said, I'm sure it was close to incoherent. Lisa was eventually satisfied that I was okay and we just laid back for a little while and relaxed. I did go down on Lisa later that afternoon and she said it was wonderful, but my inexperience and exhaustion made it less than a stellar performance. I have gotten LOTS better since then I promise. The most memorable part of that scene was when she asked me to fuck her ass with a dildo while I ate her pussy. I was shocked when she took the whole thing pumping in and out of her ass and was banging her butt on the fake balls trying to get more. I was amazed that it was possible then, now I would be itching for my turn....but I guess that's yet another story

Story 04

Part 01

Sharon Byrnes hummed an old 60's tune as she walked the streets of Greenwich Village. Never mind that the song had been recorded two years before she'd been born, it always made the 27 year old feel good. And today was definitely a day for feeling good.

She had been hired by a large local clothing manufacturer to set up a new computerized inventory system. Her contract with the firm had called for her to have the system up and running in four weeks. Instead, she had finished it in three, making the fourth weeks salary a bonus. Walking down the street, the tall brunette drew the glances of several male passerby's. She gave them no notice. She was far too interested in the warmth of the sun on her face and the feel of spring in the air. It felt so good to be able to shed that heavy winter coat and finally walk the streets in just a light blouse and skirt.

So fine was the weather and with it her mood, Sharon had canceled her late afternoon appointment and spent the last few hours exploring the local stores. It'd been a long time since she had visited this part of lower Manhattan, but she always remembered it as a place where you could find something totally new with the turn of a corner. So it was that a small sign on a walk down storefront caught her attention. It simply said "Violet Rose."

Unlike most of the shops along the way, no wares filled the windows. Instead, the whole window display consisted of a single violet rose laying on a white silk pillow.

Intrigued, Sharon started down the steps. She was surprised to find the door locked. Perhaps the store hadn't opened yet. She was about to retrace her steps back up to the street when a buzzer sounded and the door opened with an audible click. Stepping inside the small foyer, Sharon noted a small video camera hanging from the ceiling. She had seen similar security setups in jewelry stores. Wondering what kind of store this could be, she opened the second door.

Once inside, Sharon saw a long u-shaped glass display cases that ran alongside the interior of the store. It reinforced the idea that this had once been a jewelry store. But the items in those cases as well as on the walls caused her to take a step back. Filling every case was the most extensive collection of sexual paraphernalia she had ever seen. Some of the wares were familiar to her, having seen them in mail order catalogues. Others were so strange to her that she couldn't even begin to imagine what they were used for.

Her blue eyes ran across the collection of leather goods, oils and lotions. Then across to the wall behind it and its large display of S & M gear. Still standing at the entrance, Sharon was trying to decide if she wanted to stay or leave. Then she saw the rather large selection of vibrators and dildos in the far display case.

"What the hell." she thought to herself. "I could use a new toy." she added, feeling just a little naughty.

Running her fingers across the display case as she crossed the room, Sharon smiled as she crossed over an assortment of handcuffs and other restraints. That was just a little too kinky for her tastes.

"Can I help you?" A voice from behind Sharon said.

The tall young woman jumped at the sound of his voice. She hadn't noticed the salesman before.

"Oh, you startled me." Sharon said as she turned.

The salesman smiled. He was incredible, Sharon thought. Muscular, over six foot tall, with curly blonde hair. He couldn't be more than 20 years old. Clad in a form fitting T-shirt that emphasized every muscle, the young man sent a quiver between her loins.

"Well, I'm looking for..... I mean I was interested in..." Sharon began, suddenly feeling embarrassed.

Seeing her face turn red, the young man smiled even broader. It was a common occurrence in the store. People were really funny sometimes.

"Were you looking for a vibrator or a dildo?" He asked.

"Well, I'm not sure." came Sharon's response. "To be honest, I really came across your store by accident."

"Then maybe you should look around a little and let me know if you find something you like. My names Mark by the way." he replied before turning and walking away.

Sharon couldn't help but lean over the counter and admire his ass as he walked away. He had a really great ass.

Sharon spent the next twenty minutes exploring the various cases and displays. If nothing else, she was getting an education in erotica. At the same time, she was getting up her courage to perhaps ask that hunk behind the counter out for a drink. It wouldn't be the first time she'd pick up a guy, but this had to be the most unusual place she'd ever considered it.

Sharon was about to walk over and strike up another conversation when she noticed him buzzing another customer in.

It was another woman. About 5'5" and 160 lbs, the woman looked to be in her early 20's. She had a stocky build but her weight was so evenly distributed that Sharon wouldn't have described her as fat. Her face was rather boyish and she wore no makeup. Short black curly hair added to that image. Despite the fact that she had tremendous breasts, clearly visible through the plain white T-shirt, she didn't wear a bra.

With great familiarity, the woman walked across the store and behind the counter. The salesman smiled at her, obviously happy to see her.

"Could they be lovers?" Sharon thought as she looked at the mismatched pair. She'd seen stranger couples in her life.

A feeling of reassurance filled her when Mark kissed the new arrival on the cheek instead of her lips. Friends yes, lovers no.

The two spoke for a few moments as the woman glanced in Sharon's direction. The long haired woman quickly looked away, pretending to examine the selection of anal probes in the case next to her.

Then Mark left the new arrival and disappeared into the back room. Sharon watched out of the corner of her eye as the woman walked over behind the counter and stopped opposite her.

"Mark thought you might be a little more comfortable if I helped you." she said in a soft melodious voice that really didn't seem to go with her appearance.

"I think that would be better." Sharon smiled.

"Now what can I interest you in today." the saleswoman continued.

"Well, I was thinking I'd like a new toy." Sharon mused. "Actually, this is a spur of the moment thing. I only found your store by accident."

"We are a little out of the way." the short haired girl said as she and Sharon strolled back to the dildo and vibrator section. "And most of our advertising is done sort of word of mouth

"It is a nice shop." Sharon said for lack of anything else to say.

"Well I like it." came the response.

Ok babe, I'm out of here." called out Mark as he emerged from the back room. "I'm going to meet Peter at the gym."

Ok dear, have fun." the salesgirl called out as Mark quickly crossed the shop and out the door.

"That is one good looking guy." Sharon commented, not even realizing she'd said it out loud.

"That he is," the woman behind the counter agreed. "But I'm afraid you'd be in the wrong ballpark with that one."

Sharon looked a little confused. "He's gay." she clarified.

"You're kidding." Sharon said.

"Ok, I'm kidding. He's not gay - only his boyfriend is." was the reply with a smile.

Sharon cursed her luck and really didn't hear what the salesgirl said next.

"So what's your pleasure this afternoon." she repeated.

"I think he just walked out that door." Sharon said under her breath. Then she replied in a louder tone. "I'm still really not sure, maybe you can suggest something."

"Certainly." came a cheery reply. "Can I interest you in a vibrator?"

"Hmmm." Sharon murmured as she looked down at the samples. "I actually have one of those, and all of these seem to look pretty much like it. Unless you've got something a little more powerful. You know, something that Black and Decker might make, a super-vibrator with four D-cells."

"No, I'm afraid they haven't gotten around to that yet." she replied laughingly. "It's a pity though. I'm sure their missing a untapped market. I know I'd buy one."

Sharon laughed. "Well I guess a dildo then, I don't have one of those."

"Ok, lets see what we can do then." said the salesgirl as she brought a tray of samples out and put them on the counter. "We pride ourselves on our selection."

Sharon was impressed by the woman's demeanor. Regardless of her occupation, she took her work seriously.

"Have you been doing this long?" Sharon asked as she picked up a small dildo and examined it. "Been a salesgirl I mean?"

"Oh I'm not part of the hired help like Mark." she grinned. "I own this place."

"Really?" a surprised Sharon asked.

"Yes, really. My names Violet Carey. Violet Rose to my friends."

"Nice to meet you, Violet Rose." Sharon said as she extended her hand, to be met by a firm handshake. "Sharon Byrnes."

Somehow, she had thought that a store like this would be owned by some businessman who hid his name behind a screen of dummy corporations. Someone who wanted the profits but didn't want his name associated with this type of enterprise.

"So now that we've been introduced, what say we get down to business." Violet said. "Would this be for personal use or where you planning to use it on someone else. If so would that be vaginal or anal use."

"I'm afraid I don't understand." Sharon said.

"Well its quite simple actually." Violet

explained. "Would you be using this on a man, say your husband or boyfriend?"

"Oh, no chance of that, I'm afraid." Sharon answered. "Both categories are pretty empty these days."

"I see. I asked because that would give me an indication as to size." Violet said. "Do you have any preference as to color. Quite a few woman seem to like this model. " she said as she held up a large black hued rubber phallic. "Although I'd bet none of their lovers ever see it."

"I've never had an interest in that direction." Sharon said as she admired the craftsmanship and detail that had gone into the product. It even had tiny veins on the sides.

"It was just a thought." Violet said as she put down the dark rubber cock and picked up another to show Sharon.

The two woman chatted as they went. Sharon found it amusing to be buying a sex-toy in a store like this. Violet acted like she was selling a scarf in Macy's. After examining a few more models, Sharon asked if Violet had a personal preference.

"Sure," Violet said with a broad grin. "Wait a second, it's behind the other counter."

Violet returned a few seconds later, holding a rather large piece of rubber. She dropped in on the counter. Sharon was taken aback by its size, it had to be at least 10 inches long and thicker than any she had seen so far. It was also a strap-on.

"I think that's a little too big." Sharon said as she ran her gaze up and down it's length. It was as detailed as the smaller black one she had admired earlier. "I'd never be able to handle anything that big." she admitted.

"Oh you'd be surprised at what you can handle." Violet said as she ran her fingers across the dildo. "As long as the right person is on the other end of it."

Sharon looked deep into Violet's enveloping smile. She'd have had to have be pretty stupid not to have noticed that Violet was as gay as she said Mark had been. And that she had been coming on to her since she'd come into the store.

Not that Sharon felt awkward in being hit on by another woman. Back in her college days, she'd experimented a little with girl-sex. After that, she'd had a brief lesbian romp with a girlfriend following her divorce. But those had all been with girls that she would've described as feminine. This was the first time she'd drawn the attention of a butch. An attention that she found herself enjoying.

"It does sound interesting." Sharon said.

"But since I don't live in the city, I'd hate to buy something that I'd have to come all the way back to the city to return. That is if you can return such things."

"Well there's an easy way around that." Violet said beaming.

"And that would be?"

"I'd be happy to give you a demonstration."

Sharon's face now also beamed.

Violet led Sharon to the back room. Surprisingly, instead of the storeroom she expected, Sharon found a small one room apartment. It had a couch, television, refrigerator and microwave. All the comforts of home.

"Do you live here?" Sharon asked as she looked around.

"No," Violet said as she pulled the blinds, flooding the room with sunlight. "It's just a place to crash when someone needs it."

"Pretty nice, I......."

Sharon was cut off in mid-sentence as Voilet abruptly grabbed her and pulled her against her large breasts. Any cry she might've wanted to make was cut off by the crush of Violet's lips against her own.

The kiss was forceful, aggressive, more like that of man than a woman. Yet at the same time, it was exciting and intoxicating. It had been a very long time since Sharon had wanted to be taken forcefully by someone. Violet had connected with a primitive desire that was usually buried deep inside.

Continuing their exchange of lust filled kisses, Violet slid her hand beneath Sharon's blouse and fondled her smaller breasts. With practiced ease, she undid the front clip of her bra, letting her round globes fall free.

Sharon moaned softly as strong fingers played with her nipples. Violet's touch was a combination of both rough and gentle. Almost immediately, both nipples were rock hard.

Pulling against the yellow blouse, Violet ripped it open, sending several buttons popping to the floor. Sharon didn't have time to worry about how she was going to repair the damage to her outfit. Grabbing one of her now free hanging mounds, Violet lifted it to her eager mouth.

"Oh God, yes." Sharon sighed as she felt the alternating pain and delight of Violet's teeth and tongue working on her sensitive tips.

"Oh, baby, we're just getting started." Violet laughed as she turned her attention to the other breast.

Sharon ran her hand through Violet's short curls as she held her head tight against her breast. Not that the younger woman needed any encouragement. She found the feel of the short hair enticing.

Not were Violet's much larger mounds to be ignored. Already covered with sweat, her large thick nipples pressed out against her thin shirt. Sharon reached out with her one free hand and took hold of as much of one as she could.

Even through the material, Sharon could feel the warmth of Violet's skin. She couldn't wait to get past that thin cotton barrier.

She didn't have long to wait. Violet released her hold on the older woman and took a long step back. Grabbing the bottom edges of her shirt, she pulled it up and over her head. Her gigantic orbs bounced heavily as they fell back into place.

Freed of what little restraint her shirt had offered, Violets breasts were larger than Sharon had guessed. Her nipples were almost a quarter inch in length and the dark pink circles around them measured nearly three inches wide. Sharon's eyes riveted on a small violet rose tattooed on her left breast.

Violet took a heavy breast in each hand and lifted each in turn to her mouth. Her nimble tongue reached out and tickled the tips, then she took each rose petal into her mouth, whole.

Sharon was getting incredibly turned on by Violet's exhibition. Her hands slid down across her now exposed breasts and stomach. Then she lifted her blue skirt and reached for the already wet mound beneath it. Thankfully, she rarely wore panties.

A familiar feeling filled her as she felt her fingers glide inside her. It'd been a long time since she'd found herself this wet before anyone had even touched her sex. She played with herself for a few minutes, her eyes never leaving the sign of Violet suckling herself. Finally, Violet left her breast slip from her mouth and lifted both of them outward. Inviting Sharon to partake of their delight.

Never one to let an invitation grow cold, Sharon reached forward and cradled Violet's left breast, planting her first kiss right on her tattoo. A second kiss quickly followed, then a third, fourth and fifth. She quickly worked her way across the soft flesh until she felt the large nipple slip into her waiting mouth.

Violet sighed as she felt Sharon's tongue make contact. She'd had her pegged right from the moment she first seen her. Like a child with a favorite piece of candy, Sharon rolled her wet tongue around and around the dark pink circle, sending tiny jolts of rapture up and across Violet's ample bosom.

"God, I'd forgotten how good this could feel." Sharon thought to herself as she shifted her attention to Violet's other globe and began to feast on that .

Even as the younger woman delightfully moaned in response to Sharon's efforts, Violet slid her hand down between the brunette's legs. The carefully trimmed bush she found there was already wet. Instinctively, she slid two fingers in between her lips and began to pump them in and out.

As Violet's fingers began to move in and out, faster and faster, the taller woman was unable to keep up her mammary ministrations. She released her mouths grip on Violet's nipple and let it fall free. Violet eased her back onto the couch and spread her legs wide. In a quick motion, Violet's mouth replaced her fingers. She only paused long enough to lick the tasty juices off her fingers.

A few minutes under the tutelage of Violet's talented tongue was enough to bring Sharon almost to the edge. It'd been such a long time since she'd felt this good.

"Oh God!" she yelled out as she felt Violet's warm tongue reach up inside her once more. "Don't stop! What ever you do, don't stop!"

Yet only a few minutes later, Violet did stop. It took a few moments for Sharon to realize it. Her eyes opened wide and sought out her lover. She found her a second later. Violet was now totally nude and was in the process of adjusting the strap on the strap-on she had shown Sharon earlier. Hanging down between her legs, it looked even larger than before. Strapped tight, a small nub at the base of the rubber cock extended into her own pussy, rubbing against her clit.

"Now the real fun begins." Violet smiled. A sudden feeling of apprehension filled Sharon at the thought of being penetrating by that monster. It was bigger than any man she had known. She opened her mouth to say something but something held her back. Sharon remained mute as Violet reached out and pulled her up off the couch.

"Over the edge!" She ordered in an authoritative tone as she bent Sharon over the arm of the couch.

From a tube in her hand, Violet smeared a large amount of clear lubricant over the cockhead of her dildo. Then she pushed her slippery fingers down between Sharon's legs and up into her already lubricated pussy. She pushed all five fingers in, stretching the opening.

"Oooo" moaned Sharon as she felt the initial intrusion.

Violet pressed her naked body up against the back of Sharon's own. She lifted her hanging cock and positioned the head against the now saturated tunnel.

"Spread those beautiful legs, honey." Violet whispered into Sharon's ear as she nibbled at it.

"Cause you're going to love this." she added with a kiss.

With that she began rubbing the round tip of her cock up and down the length of Sharon's pussy before taking a firm grip and pushing it within her.

"Aaaaa!" Sharon yelled as she felt herself being penetrated .

"Relax." Violet said as she eased the dildo out a little, before pushing it back in twice the depth of her first attempt.

Violet reach around and rubbed her fingers against Sharon's clit. Doggy style was her favorite position, it gave her such a feeling of superiority. Her frantic motions against the small nub at the top of Sharon's cunt helped distract her from the pain as Violet began to thrust deeper within her with an ever increased frequency.

Gradually, the pain lessened and gave way to an increasing pleasure. Even through the artificial cock, Violet could feel the walls of Sharon's cunt grabbing hold of her as she thrusted inside her one more time.

"You love this, don't you?" Violet asked between thrusts as she grabbed both of the taller woman's hips and pulled her ass hard against her.

"Oh yes," Sharon panted as she began to match Violet's rhythm and draw the dildo deeper inside her.

Violet slid her hands up and down Sharon's body as she continued to fuck her with ever increasing ferocity. Her fingers closed tight against her breasts as she used then to pull Sharon against her time after time. Violet always got off fucking other women in this way. All of that sensitive lover crap might've been ok for others, but she loved to be in control.

As short a time ago as this morning, Sharon would've never entertained the suggestion that she would let someone use her like this. Like just a pussy that was there for someone's pleasure. Yet that was exactly how she was letting Violet use her. And to Sharon's astonishment, that understanding was turning her on in such a way that she couldn't explain.

Violet pushed Sharon's head and shoulders down across the arm of the couch, giving her greater access to the depths of her pussy. The constant rubbing against her own love button was sending her into pre-orgasmic fits as well. Hot sweat covered each of their bodies as both shook with the energy and passion of unrestricted sex.

Words between them were no longer possible, the best they could manage were animalistic grunts. Yet even those were being constantly interrupted by frantic gasps for breath.

Totally lost in the fury of her passion, Violet grabbed Sharon's long hair and pulled her head back. With a fierce fire in her dark eyes, Violet pressed her lips hard against the helpless girl beneath her. The taste of their tongues as they intertwined was enough to push her to within an inch of the abyss.

"Deeper." Sharon gasped as Violet's tongue slid out of her mouth.

Try as she could, it would've been physically impossible for Violet to get any more inside Sharon. At least in the position they were in.

"On the floor!" Violet commanded as she pulled the dildo all the way out. "On your back!" Not even giving Sharon time to comply, the younger woman pushed her onto her back. She followed her a moment later and rammed the large rubber cock between her outstretched legs. Sharon screamed in ecstasy as Violet drove the dildo it's full length within her. Violet's massive mounds pressed hard against Sharon's smaller globes, causing an electric tingling as their nipples touched.

Burying her temporary manhood deep inside her new lover, Violet's body quaked in anticipation of the explosion she knew was imminent. Beneath her, Sharon was lost in a similar state.

Continuing to pump away with all of her strength, Violet was taken by surprise when Sharon reached up with her legs and wrapped them around her buttocks, allowing her to penetrate to an even greater depth. Her arms also wrapped around her, binding them together in an unbreakable lock.

"Fuck me!" Sharon screamed at the top of her lungs. A cry so loud that for a moment Violet wondered it she could be heard out on the street.

One final thrust was enough to unleash the explosion that had been building within the two of them. Both bodies jerked violently as they were consumed by the bodyquake that ripped through each of them.

Sharon drove her nails deep into Violet's back as an orgasmic paralysis gripped her. Violet continued to plummet the captive pussy that was pressed so tightly against her own. Until she too was gripped by that same loss of control.

Their journey through the endless ether of sexual bliss was both instantaneous and timeless. Fireworks filled the sky and rivers of joy caressed their quivering forms. Soft, quiet moans filled the air as hearts raced uncontrolled.

As has been written many times, all good things must end and eventually the fire that had claimed both women cooled and their sweat drenched bodies began to untangle from each other. Sharon was still aware of the massive cock-toy still filling ever inch of her cavity. The feeling was so unlike that she had after a violent love session with a man. Usually she was faced with a small feeling of disappointment as she felt his cock soften and slip from her. Instead it was now a constant reminder of the joy she had just experienced.

Violet was simply too exhausted to even pull her strap on from within Sharon. Instead she simply stoked her now cool skin and planted a gentle kiss on her lips. The fires of aggression had cooled within her, and now all she wanted to do was rest.

The late afternoon sun had already slipped beneath the tall buildings when Sharon emerged from the small shop. Thankfully the small apartment in back had been equipped with a hand held shower. She would've really hated to have had to make the long trip home with the unmistakable odor of sex clinging to her.

Over the next two hours, as she rode first the subway and them the Long Island Railroad, Sharon gave little notice to the multitude of people around her. Instead her thoughts were focused on the narrow ten inch package she clutched to her breast. That and the promise that if she ever needed another demonstration of it's use, she merely had to ask.

With that idea, her smile grew ever brighter.

Story 05

Chapter 01

It began the fall of my second year in grad school, at Ann Arbor, Michigan. I was twenty-three years old, a young woman living on my own for the first time, my life dedicated wholeheartedly to the study of physics, which I immersed myself in till my dreams were full of conversations between quarks and neutrinos. I knew Joanie from the weekly department parties. She was the wife of Jack Holcombe, esteemed professor of mathematical physics, who taught my tensor calculus course. Ex-wife, I should say. About half-way through my first year, the news came that they were separating. But after fifteen years as a faculty wife, Joanie was as much a part of the department social life as Jack was, and so no one found it odd that she kept coming to the department parties; it was Jack who dropped out.

For a woman in her fifties, Joanie was quite attractive. Take it from a woman who's spent a lot of time fantasizing about other women. She wore her long silver-grey hair pulled back in a neat braid or pony tail. And if her round face was creased with laugh lines, it was because Joanie laughed often, easily. She was short and rather heavyset; but to my taste, she was heavy in just the right places.

Now, as for me, I have short brown hair, slightly buck teeth, and big brown eyes. In high school, my nickname was "Gopher." I'm fairly petite, not very well-endowed in the chest department; though I have rather wide hips for my build (like a bottle of salad dressing, a girlfriend once said). I've been called cute more than once; though only Joanie has called my beautiful.

I began to realize I was a lesbian in junior high. I had a miserable, protracted love affair with Karla Gringold, which began in seventh grade, and didn't end till tenth. Mostly it consisted of me hanging around her like a devoted puppy, while she ignored me. Just when the pain got to be too much to bear, and I pulled away from her, she would suddenly turn into Ms. Sex Kitten around me, and we would feverishly kiss, touch, and -- when we got a little older -- lick and suck. Then she'd turn back into the Ice Princess. I never figured out what game Karla was playing with me, but when I finally broke up with her, I resolved to play it "straight", date boys, and channel my passions into my studies -- and so I did through the remainder of high school and, aside from a couple of flings, through college as well (though by then, I'd given up on men as well). But as I say, that didn't stop me from fantasizing.

I could fantasize about Joanie Holcombe, over a glass of white wine, from across the room, watching her gab with the senior faculty ... admiring the radiant smile that periodically flashed across her face ... admiring the generous curve of her hips beneath her denim skirt, the heavy swell of her bosom straining against her blouse. But Joanie was straight -- not to mention old enough to be my mother, and I don't have a general thing for older women. She was friendly enough to me, asking me how my research was going, telling me not to let Dr. So-and-so intimidate me, and so on. But she belonged to the world of the senior faculty: overlapping with, but far above my own world as a grad student. And so, it never occurred to me that I could actually have this woman as a close friend, let alone lover.

It was a few days before the Thanksgiving break. The party was winding down. I bade my farewells to the host, and headed out the door to my car. Joanie was parked behind me, trying to start her car.

"Molly," she called to me, "do you happen to have jumper cables? I must have left the headlights on." I didn't. We went back inside. It turned out that nobody there had jumper cables. "Um, I'd be glad to give you a ride home Joanie," I eagerly offered. "Your car will be safe here till tomorrow."

"Are you sure it's not too far out of your way?"

And so she climbed into my rusty Toyota, and we headed off into the frosty November night.

"This is really very sweet of you Molly. I owe you one for this, OK?"

"Oh, come on," I protested, "I'm just giving you a lift."

"Well, how about if I cook you a nice dinner sometime. You know, living by myself now, I miss being able to cook for other people." The loneliness in her voice was palpable.

"That'd be great," I replied, trying to sound nonchalant.

"Say," she suddenly lit up, "are you going to be around for Thanksgiving?"

I was. I didn't say that I would probably be spending Thanksgiving hunched over my readings, eating a turkey TV dinner.

"Well then, it's settled. Why don't you come over in the early afternoon."

As I pulled up in front of her house, she thanked me again, then kissed me on the cheek.

"See you Thursday," she smiled.

Chapter 03

Now, despite my impending "date" with Joanie, despite the kiss, despite the fact that this magnificent woman had asked me to share most of Thanksgiving day with her, I spent the next couple of days determinedly keeping cool, reminding myself that Joanie was straight, she was understandably lonely around holiday time after her divorce, and that she undoubtedly saw me as, at most, an ersatz daughter.

Thanksgiving morning, I showered twice, and finally settled on a dark-grey blouse and slacks. The color reminded me of her hair. At 1:30 I took off for her place in my Toyota.

When she met me at the door, we both burst out laughing. She was wearing the exact same outfit, the same shade of grey. She made a joke about our "nun's habits", and ushered me into her house. Her house was small, simply decorated, but comfortable; and at the moment the atmosphere was filled with the comforting smell of roast turkey and stuffing. Vivaldi was playing on the stereo.

"Now then, the turkey will be done in about a half hour, and everything else is under control; so until then I suggest we park ourselves on the sofa and have a martini or two."

"Um, OK, I'm not exactly used to drinking martinis though."

"Well, neither am I," she laughed, "But you and I have some ice-breaking to do; and for that, I think at least one martini per person is required."

One martini per person later, she had told me about her degree in musicology, what Jack had been like as a young man, her work in the university music library, how the physics department had changed over the years.

"I'm sure you know that they all think you're their brightest student in years," she dropped. I sat for a moment, digesting this piece of news, feeling my head swell.

And then I came out to her.

"I thought you might be gay," she said quietly. "You don't flirt with the men. You know -- hang on, this is gonna take another martini." She poured herself one, took a sip, then resumed. "You know, I slept with a woman once. A few years ago. I've never told this to anyone before. She was an art historian visiting from another university. I helped her find some library materials, and then she took me out to lunch. I don't know how to make sense of it: she just swept me off my feet; and completely on impulse, we went back to her hotel room and made love. She went back to California that evening. I got a few cards from her, but I haven't seen her since."

As she told me this, a tingly feeling shot down my spine, right into my cunny, which suddenly had become quite moist.

"Is that why you and your husband split up?"

"It was a contributing factor. Not that I ever told Jack about her. We had already drifted pretty far apart by that time. After my experience with Jeanne, I realized there was a part of me that was never going to be satisfied in a heterosexual marriage; but you know, a marriage can keep going for a long time on inertia, because it's familiar, and the thought of actually severing the ties is painful. Then one day Jack told me he was having an affair with a woman he'd met at the APA conference, and he asked for a divorce."

I took her hand. She sat silently for a moment. Then her eyes popped open.

"Oh, damn! The turkey's burning."

We rescued the turkey in the nick of time. As we sat down to dinner, I must have looked dazed: in truth, my mind was reeling from the martini, and from the bombshell she'd just dropped. Joanie took my hand.

"Molly, I'm really glad you're here and that we're getting to know each other. I've wanted your friendship for a long time. I ... well ... I didn't know how to approach you without making you worry that I was ... coming on to you or something."

"I've wanted you too. I mean ... I've wanted your friendship," I stammered, turning crimson. Then I ran to the bathroom and threw up my martini.

"Are you OK?" she intoned from the bathroom door. "I feel awful for making you drink that martini."

"I'll be fine in a minute," I replied, rinsing my face.

"I don't suppose you feel like eating a heavy dinner right now."

"Not really. Could I borrow a toothbrush, to get this taste out of my mouth?"

Luckily, she had an extra one, unused. I brushed my teeth in her bathroom sink. She told me she would wait to eat too. Then we sat back down on the sofa. Strangely, I felt emboldened: I'd survived the embarassment of thowing up in front of Joanie Holcombe, and I felt I could face anything.

"Joanie, what do you think would happen if you did come on to me?" I traced my fingers over her cheek.

She was silent for a long time, looking down at her hands. "I'm a good thirty years older than you, you know."

When my lips found hers, she did not pull away, and she soon began kissing back.

"Molly darling, when I invited you over, I honestly wasn't setting out to seduce you. But, God, now that you've started, please don't stop."

I had no intention of stopping. My lips were getting drunk on the warmth of her skin, and my panties were sopping. As I kissed my way down her neck, her hands began touching my breasts through my blouse. Now, as I explained, I'm rather flat-chested; but I have big, extremely sensitive nipples; and Joanie's fingers were driving me crazy.

"Joanie, take me to bed: I want to see you naked."

Our arms round each others' waists, she led me back to her bedroom.

Chapter 05

We fumbled with buttons, zippers, sleeves, and pantlegs, until she was in her bra and panties. She unbraided her long silvery hair, and it fanned out over her back like a waterfall. I unhooked the bra, it sagged forward, and she slipped it off her shoulders. Her untrammeled breasts seemed even larger than I had imagined: they hung down almost to her navel, a delicate tracery of blue veins visible beneath the skin, capped with large, brownish-pink nipples. Her rounded belly seemed soft and inviting. It was the body of a mature woman: there were stretchmarks and wrinkles and flab; but I fell in love with it on the spot.

"You undress too, love," she whispered, stepping out of her panties.

Taking off my clothes had never felt so deliciously erotic before. I felt proud and powerful, as her face registered admiration for my body. She took me in her arms then, and the shock of her warm, soft body against my bare skin sent me into an altered state. I could feel her thick erect nipples grazing my ribs, my tingling nipples rubbing against her skin. My hands travelled down her back and over the immense, soft roundness of her ass. Cupping one of her heavy breasts in my hands, I lifted it to my mouth, and began to lick and suck on the nipple. Her excited moaning suddenly became a sharp cry of pleasure, and her knees buckled. We staggered backward and flopped down on her bed.

"I came," she beamed, "just from you sucking my titty. God, look how excited you've gotten me."

She guided my hand down to the thick dark jungle between her thighs. As I rubbed her, my hand immediately became wet with her juice. I had to taste her. I clambered between her knees; taking her broad hips in my arms, and burying my face in that luscious grove, I drank deeply. Her honey tasted so good, I couldn't stop till she had come several more times.

Finally, she pulled my head back. "Now it's my turn," she growled.

She rolled me on my stomach, and began kissing the back of my neck, giving me delicious shivers; leaning the full weight of her body upon me, so that I felt engulfed in her warm softness.

"I've wanted to do this ever since the Christmas party last year," she said huskily.

She kissed a wet trail down my spine, down to my tailbone. Her hands began massaging my ass cheeks, spreading them apart and squishing them together. I felt uneasy: no one had ever done this with me before; and in fact, I wasn't quite sure what she was going to do next. But I didn't want her to stop either. Then I felt her hot, wet tongue travelling down between my cheeks, and my inhibitions went out the window. Her tongue circled around my madly contracting anus, then down into my sopping wet cunt. I heard her slurping loudly. A moistened finger was touching my anus now, slipping inside, and I bucked against it, taking it in deep. Her tongue was slip-sliding over my clittie. Other fingers were filling my vagina. The orgasm started like a gentle wave that picked me up, then intensified, carrying me higher and higher, till I felt I was riding a tidal wave, or rather a series of tidal waves that buoyed me up, one after another. Gradually, they subsided. I opened my eyes. The bedroom seemed to be suffused with a soft rosy haze, and through it, Joanie's face was beaming down at me.

"How about a hot turkey sandwich?" she asked.

Chapter 06

She brought me dinner in bed. We both lay there naked, feeding each other forkfuls of turkey and mashed potatoes. Then she brought in apple pie and coffee. Food had never tasted so good before; though perhaps it seemed so because I was falling in love with her. When she asked me to spend the night, I wasn't about to turn her down.

"What can I do for you now?" I asked her. She thought for a minute, her arms folded behind her head. Then a smile lit up her face.

"I feel like taking a bath with you. Would you wash me?"

"Oh honey, you bet I will!"

I was delighted by her deep Japanese bathtub, big enough to hold two adults comfortably. As the tub filled, and the water heated up, we soaped each other up outside the tub, Japanese style. I paid particular attention to her nipples and the undersides of her breasts, before my soapy hand travelled down her belly and between her legs. She leaned back against the side of the tub, spreading her legs to give my hand better access. Soon three of my fingers were twisting and thrusting inside her honey-filled cunt. She was so beautiful like this, and the sounds she was making were driving me crazy; but I wanted to give her more.

"Turn around," I growled. Her back now toward me; she bent over the side of the tub, presenting her magnificent ass to my hungry gaze. I ran my fingers from her honey-hole to her anus, back and forth, till her whole between-the- cheeks area was lathered with soap, and with her honey.

"Please, Molly, touch me inside my ass," she whimpered. "I need you there." I did. Three fingers in her cunt and one in her ass, I thrust in and out of her, as I showered her beautiful broad buttocks with my kisses. I felt the beginning contractions of her orgasm against my fingers, fore and aft. Leaning over her, I murmured in her ear,

"Joanie Honey-comb, Honey-woman, I love my Honey-woman. Make honey for me... "

"Ooooooooouuuh, Molllyyyy, I'm cuuuummmmmmminnnnnggg!" she keened.

We sank down on the floor together. "Whew!" she said, when she could breathe again. "I've never come that hard before. God you're sweet."

We slipped into the tub then, letting the heat of the water envelope us. I wanted to hold her, so I sat behind her, my thighs wrapped round her waist, as she leaned back against me. My fingers brushed lazily over her stiffening nipples.

I admitted I'd had a crush on her for a long time. She was surprised.

"Our age difference doesn't bother you?" she asked timidly. "I'm not exactly ... well ... I'm an old woman, Molly. And you're so young and lovely." "No, Joanie, don't think that. Your body's fantastic. When we made love just now I felt so happy just looking at you and touching you, you took my breath away. And you make me come like gangbusters. Does it bother you that I'm an inexperienced kid?"

"Molly, I'm so happy, so blessed, to have you as a lover." She turned back and flashed a knowing grin at me. "And I wouldn't exactly call you inexperienced."

We sat in the tub, kissing, laughing, holding each other, till our fingers and toes were wrinkled. At last we crawled out and towelled each other off. Joanie put on her bathrobe, and lent me a nightie. We went into the kitchen and she made us some tea. I sat drinking it, happily watching her, as she put away theThanksgiving leftovers. Then we did the dishes together. I felt so comfortable with her, so natural. When we finally went back to bed, I joyfully cuddled up to her, smelling the wonderful scent of her body.

"I'm falling in love with you, Joanie."

"I love you too, Molly. I've never been in love like this before. I never loved Jack like this; even when we were happy together, it wasn't like this." She turned to face me. "Can you stay with me tomorrow? I have the day off." She started to kiss her way down my belly.

"Mmm, yes. Maybe we could go to the art museum together? Ahhhhh! There's a new surrealist show- ohhhhhhhhhhhh!"

I'm not generally an early riser. But when I awoke at 6:45, I was too excited to fall back asleep: it was going to be our first whole day together. I got up silently, put on my nightie, and found my way to the kitchen. After a fairly exhaustive search of the cupboards, I found the coffee and the coffee pot, and started it going. There were some eggs in the fridge, and some milk, some tomatoes and onions. Soon I whipped up an omelette, made some toast, found the tray from last night. Proudly, I carried the tray of breakfast back into the bedroom to my sleeping Joanie.

"Molly?" she murmured sleepily; then she opened her eyes and sat up. "Have I died and gone to heaven? Darling, this is wonderful; nobody's ever brought me breakfast in bed before. Nnn, don't kiss me, I have morning breath."

I kissed her on her forehead. Her radiant smile melted my heart. If she smiled at me like that, I'd gladly make her breakfast every morning for the rest of her life. I sank down beside her and began to feed her bites of omelette, and she did the same for me. We drank our coffee slowly, and formed our plans for the day.

After a quick shower together, we stopped by my place, so I could get some clean clothes and some toiletries. Then we headed downtown to the art museum. I insisted on paying for her ticket -- so it would feel like a real date. We strolled through the museum together, holding hands when nobody was looking. I liked the dreamy quality of Chirico's paintings. Joanie filled me in on all the artists, and what the surrealist movement was about. Apparently, she knew about painting as well as music.

Outside the museum, we ran into my best friend from the department, Ken, with his girlfriend Sarah. They were heading in to see the show, but Ken, intrigued at this unexpected social development, persuaded Sarah that we should all go for lunch together first. We settled on an inexpensive Italian place nearby. I hung on to Joanie's arm proudly. Later, Ken told me I was grinning like the Cheshire cat. "You might as well have been carrying a sign: 'Look at the babe I just landed!'" he teased.

After lunch, we left Ken and Sarah at the museum, and headed over to the park. It was a brisk November day, but the sunshine and movement kept us warm. Here we could wander, holding hands, nobody else around. In a secluded corner, we huddled together on a bench, and made out. Unfortunately, it was too cold to do what we really wanted to do without risking frostbite.

After a while, we set off to find a find a cup of espresso and a place to pee. Later, as we walked back to the car, she suddenly told me to wait, and dove around the corner. A minute later, she came back and presented me with a single red rose. "For ardent love," she said. I kissed her on the mouth, right there, standing on the sidewalk, in front of everybody. "Goddam dykes," some guy muttered. Joanie glared at him and he slunk away. We walked quickly back to the car. The raw hatred in that jerk's comment shook us both up a little. But in the car, Joanie said, "I know there's a price to be paid for being 'out' as a lesbian. But I'm not gonna let that stop me from loving you." I felt safer after that.

We went home, and Joanie made up a delicious turkey- vegetable soup from the leftovers in her fridge. It was piping hot, and it thoroughly warmed me up.

"Stay again tonight?" she asked. I nodded happily, sinking into her arms.

"I've been waiting all day to make love to you, Honey- woman. Let's go to bed now."

"Oh, Molly, I get so wet when you call me that ..."

In the bedroom, I undressed her, savoring the softness and the fresh smell of her, kissing her all over her body, slowly treasuring every dimple, every freckle, every hair.

"I don't want there to be an inch of you I haven't kissed," I growled possessively.

After a while, Joanie whispered, "Darling, my cunny, please..." And I moved down between her legs and began to lap up her honey. She came easily and powerfully for me, again and again; I felt so proud of my ability to give her pleasure.

Eventually, I crawled back up beside her. She sat up in bed, cradling my head against her ample bosom, as her fingers found their way down between my thighs. I took her nipple into my mouth, sucking hard, as I felt her fingers slipping between my dripping lips, sliding over my tingling clit, filling me up deep inside, frigging me hard as I bucked and shuddered against them. All the while, she murmured into my ear, "Come for me, darling, come give it to me, give it to your Honey-woman..."

I moaned into the fat breast that filled my mouth as I came and came for her till I was exhausted.

We fell asleep, cuddled together, my head pillowed on her soft warm bosom; happy, dreamy smiles on our faces.

Chapter 08

After a few days like this, it was obvious that I had no more use for my own apartment; so I terminated the lease, and moved my computer and books into Joanie's house. She set up part of the study as an office for me, and my life as a grad student continued. At school, Ken teased me something terrible about Joanie: I was trying to sleep my way to the top, he laughed, but I'd made the mistake of sleeping with the professor's wife instead of the professor. Really, though, he was very supportive of my relationship with her, and when I sometimes had arguments with Joanie, I would go to Ken, and he would help me to cool down and and then go back and make up with her. The rest of the department, as far as I could tell, shrugged their shoulders and paid our relationship no mind. Jack Holcombe never said anything to me about Joanie. That spring, he anounced he was taking a job at Stanford. Joanie told me that that was where his new girlfriend was. Soon, I was typing away at my dissertation, while Joanie practiced away at her cello pieces.

My parents weren't as supportive as Ken. They met Joanie at my graduation. I introduced her to them as "my partner," but I guess they thought that was some kind of academic relationship, like research partners or something. Anyway, at the graduation party, my mother saw Joanie put her arms around me, and she screamed, "Get away from my daughter, you freak!" I quickly bustled my parents out the house.

"Listen to me! I yelled at them. "Joanie and I love each other: we're a couple. If you can't respect that, you just get the hell out of our house." And that's what they did. Without a word, they got in their car and drove off.

Joanie came out and took me in her arms. I collapsed against her, sobbing.

"I wish," she said, "my love could wipe away the hurt. I wish I could be your mother, so I could tell you what a wonderful daughter you are, and how proud I am of you."

"You're my real mother now," I bawled. "You're my family. You're the one that loves me."

She took me back inside. "Should we keep the party going, or do you want to be alone."

"'Lone, with you."

She graciously sent my professors and friends away. When she sat back down next to me on the couch, I sniffed, "I need some good loving from my Honey-woman."

"Your Honey-woman wants you to take your clothes off, Dr. Molly Steiglitz," she whispered in my ear. "Right here." I obeyed. She kissed and licked the tears from my face while her deft cellist fingers thrummed a concerto on my bare nipples. Soon she was kneeling on the floor, her head between my legs, while I rode her face to orgasm, bursting through the tears, surfacing into the sweet warm sunlight of pleasure. She took me to bed, tore off her clothes, and climbed in with me, cradling me against her warm naked body, lulling me to sleep with the sweet pounding of her heartbeat beneath my cheek.

I've barely had a word from my parents since that night, though it's been ten years.

Chapter 09

I was offered several post-docs. When I suggested taking the closest one, so that I could drive home on weekends, she shook her head.

"Darling, I'm ready to retire from the library. I can sell the house. You take the post-doc that you want, wherever it is; and I'm coming with you." I hugged her long and hard for that.

I took the MIT post-doc. Joanie and I found a lovely little apartment right in Cambridge, which she began decorating with great glee. She told me she was happy to have a home that we were building together. She delighted in the rich classical musical scene in the Boston area, and soon joined a string quartet. Around the spring of my first year, the chair told me that a tenure-track position was opening up in the department, and encouraged me to apply. A few months later, I learned that I had gotten the job.

The night she took me out to celebrate, Joanie told me we'd gotten an eviction notice. It seems the landlord was planning to tear our building down and put up offices. I checked the figures in our bank account: we had a large amount from the sale of Joanie's house, on top of our substantial savings. The next day we walked into the landlord's office and bought the building out from under him, a hundred percent down. Instantly, we were the heroes of the other tenants. We promptly fired the property management company (it specialized in forgetting about repairs, and losing rent checks) and Joanie took over as property mangager (she bopped me on the head when I called her "Mrs. Worth").

   The other tenants love her. We've never had a single problem from a tenant. Recently, various neighborhood groups have been urging Joanie to run for city council. If she ever decides to do it, I'll support her a hundred percent, and I know she'd be great for the community; but I'm not crazy about the idea, because I'm afraid it would cut seriously into our time together. And so far, Joanie has refused to run.

Joanie's sixty-five now, and I'm thirty-four. Before I met Joanie, I suppose I thought that sixty-five was way over- the-hill as far as sex is concerned. But that woman's appetite for sex just gets stronger and stronger. And her body is as beautiful and dear to me as it's ever been. My Honey-woman: I get wet thinking about her heavy breasts, and that special honey that flows for me in her secret place.

I know that our remaining years together are limited; that I will probably survive her, and have to face a long rest-of-my-life without her. So I savor the time we have left; and it makes our pleasure together more poignant. But who knows: maybe Joanie's going to be one of those feisty old ladies who lives to be a hundred ten. And I'll be an old lady sitting beside her in the rocker, with my hand up her dress, searching for honey

The Naughty Beginnings

4 Erotic Hot Lesbian Short Stories for Women.

Sarah Rodgers

All Rights Reserved. No part of this publication may be reproduced in any form or by any means, including scanning, photocopying, or otherwise without prior written permission of the copyright holder. Copyright © 2020

This book is entirely a work of fiction. The names, characters and incidents portrayed in it are the work of the author's imagination. Any resemblance to actual persons, living or dead, events or localities is entirely coincidental.

Story 01

Becky looked up from her work as Mr. Barringer and the woman walked into her office. Becky was surprised. Mr. Barringer rarely came into her office; she usually reported to the senior partner's office not the other way around. The woman was someone new to her. She was older than Becky, probably about twenty-nine, but younger than any of the other women in the office. She was small, about 5'2", with a good figure and good taste in clothing.

"Becky, this is Katherine Martin, our new associate," said Mr. Barringer. Turning to the new woman he continued, "Becky here is our law clerk. If you need her to look anything up for you, just ask her, but clear major research projects with Ms. Riegger."

The two women shook hands. The new woman smiled and said to call her Kate, followed by a pleasantry about getting together for lunch, then Mr. Barringer took Kate off to introduce her to the rest of the staff.

Another woman in the office, and someone closer to her own age, Becky was glad. The legal secretaries were all over forty and they had little in common with Becky. With the exception of Kate, there were no female lawyers in the firm. The partners were all much older and, while nice, did not socialize with her. The two other associates were in their twenties, but once she made clear that she was not interested in going to bed with them they stopped talking to her about things other than business. There was no one to chat with, and the office was kind of dull.

* * *

After Mr. Barringer had finished taking her around to meet the staff, Kate settled into her office. While she was organizing her things, she assessed her new job. It looked like a good office. It was a small, conservative firm. She wanted a small firm, and this one made lots of money. The four partners all had excellent reputations and they seemed like nice people, albeit in a solid, WASPish, Republican kind of way. The other two associates were typical young, ambitious lawyers. They were probably jerks, like most young men, and would undoubtedly hit up on her, but given the reputation of the firm, they were probably excellent lawyers.

The support staff seemed pretty typical, but older and with little in common with a young, ambitious female associate. That Becky was a luscious number though. About twenty-three, svelte, creamy skin, long black hair, small breasts, she was absolutely stunning. Kate caught herself. It was not good to be thinking like that. This was a small, conservative firm. Sexual relationships in the office were not good for the career. Besides, Becky was probably straight. Kate's breakup with her ex-, Jeannie, had been rough, and she did not want to do anything stupid that would sacrifice her career for a fling on the rebound from a long relationship. She would have to make friends with Becky though. Her sanity would depend on having at least one confidant in the office.

* * *

The next day at about noon Becky's intercom buzzed.

"Becky, this is Kate. I was wondering if you were up for having lunch today, my treat. In return for picking up the check, I expect you to give me the lowdown on the office, a perspective on what it's like for a young woman to work here."

"Sure. When would you like to go?"

"Why don't you meet me at the reception desk in about fifteen."

Becky enjoyed the lunch. There was not much she could tell Kate about the office. It was a good place to work; the worst thing about it was that there was no one to talk to on breaks, or to have lunch with. She warned Kate about the other two associates, too late. One had hit up on Kate already.

Becky told Kate about herself, how she worked at the firm during the summer and a few hours a week when law school was in session, how she got the job through her dad who was a tennis partner of Mr. Barringer. Becky found herself opening up to Kate, saying things about her personal life that she never thought she would tell a stranger. She never talked to anyone about her sex life, but she did it with Kate. This was more evidence that she really needed someone with which to talk.

Kate did not learn much about the office, but she did learn a lot about Becky. Her gaydar was pinging throughout the meal. Becky was an athlete, a softball player. Her body showed it. She was thin but had broad shoulders and well muscled, but still very feminine, arms and a knockout ass and pair of legs. She had been brought up in all-girl, Catholic schools and attended an all-woman college. Becky talked about her boyfriend, but somewhat shamefacedly admitted that they did not have sex. Becky was waiting for marriage, a self-described "old-fashioned girl."

Kate came away from lunch fairly certain that Becky was approachable. She would not act on this belief, however. If she was wrong it could be disastrous. What Kate took to be lesbian traits might just be Becky's strict Catholic upbringing repressing a heterosexuality. She reminded herself that not all softball players were lesbians.

* * *

That night, Becky was feeling lonely. Her lunch with Kate had made her itchy for companionship. She called Peter, but his roommate said he was at the library and would not be back until late. She thought about leaving a message telling him to come over, but decided against it. If he came over late, he would stay the night, and every time he stayed the night there was pressure for them to have sex.

Peter was very good; he never pushed. He clearly wanted to fuck her (a chill went through Becky's spine when she thought the word "fuck," it made her feel dirty), but he respected her wishes. They usually just necked and when Peter slept over they played spoons, but little else. Occasionally, when she got him especially excited, she would give him a handjob (and rush to Confession the next day). She would let him play with her breasts, little as they were, but never let him touch her "down there."

Becky often wondered if this were unnatural. Peter was a really nice guy, and she liked spooning, feeling the warmth and closeness of his body, but she just did not want anything more from him.

She was embarrassed that she had confided so much in Kate, a complete stranger. She had not told her about details like the spooning or the handjobs, but she did admit to not having sex with Peter. There was something about Kate that inspired trust. Maybe it was her openness, her smile. That laugh she had, it was infectious.

She was a beautiful woman that was for sure. She was an athlete, like Becky, but not into sports. Kate said she worked out in a gym, lifting weights mostly. Becky thought about her own body and wished she were curvy like Kate. Kate had real hips, an hourglass figure, and breasts. Becky was embarrassed about her breasts. She was very flat-chested. Kate's breasts were not particularly large, but they were nicely proportioned to her smaller frame.

Becky realized that as she had been thinking about Kate, her hand had slipped down between her legs and she was absent-mindedly rubbing herself. She stopped. Masturbation was bad enough, but thinking about a woman while doing it, that was sick.

This was not the only time she had had thoughts about other women, though. Those thoughts and he apparent lack of sexual desire had worried her. She had read some psychology books on the subject, and once even asked a priest about it. Both the books and the priest assured her that occasional thoughts about members of the same sex were normal, and not to be worried. It did not mean anything. Becky was worried though, the thoughts came a little too often to be considered occasional. Still, she had a boyfriend, and although they did not have sex, that was because she was saving herself for marriage, not because she did not like men.

She had never acted on any of these thoughts, and that reassured

her some. A woman had even hit up on her once, and she had done nothing. It had been freshman year in college. After softball practice, Lori, the first baseman, had asked her to pitch some extra batting practice. They practiced about forty-five minutes later than the rest of the team and the locker room was empty when they entered it. Even the coach, who usually stayed late, had left.

In the shower room, Becky could not but help look at Lori. She had large breasts, and Becky wished that she had breasts like that. Lori noticed Becky's glances and came over to borrow some shampoo. As Becky handed her the bottle of shampoo their hands touched. It was as if an electric shock ran through Becky. Lori stepped closer, touched Becky's shoulder and ran her hand lightly down her arm. Lori stepped even closer and leaned forward letting her lips brush against Becky's.

Becky closed her eyes and started to return the kiss, then suddenly, overwhelmed with fear, stopped and pushed Lori away. Becky apologized, telling Lori that she was not "like that." Lori said that it was her fault and that she should not have made a pass at her. That was the end of it. They quickly finished showering and never spoke of it again.

Going to an all-women's college, Becky knew lots of lesbians, some were even good friends of hers, but none ever came on to her after that incident in the shower; Lori had spread the word that Becky was straight.

As she was thinking of the incident with Lori, Becky's hand had wandered down between her legs again. She was quite wet. She sighed and gave up, too horny to resist. She pulled off her pants and underwear and started masturbating in earnest.

She rubbed her fingers in small circles around her clitoris with her right hand and stroked her labia with her left. With eyes closed, she forced herself to think of Peter. She would give in to masturbating, but not to thinking of other women.

She wondered what it would be like to take his penis in her mouth. In her thoughts the penis changed into Lori's breast. She was sucking on the nipple, licking around the areola and flicking the tip of the nipple with her tongue. Again, she forced her thoughts away from Lori and back to Peter. What would it taste like if he came in her mouth? She brought her left hand up to her mouth and tasted her juices. Would it taste like that, she wondered? Would it taste like a woman?

Peter had nice, broad shoulders, like Kate, but his body was hard and straight, not curved like Kate's. She wondered if spooning with Kate would feel any different. She tried to imagine it. Kate kissing the back of her neck, rubbing her breasts, then slipping her hands down between her legs. It was something she never let Peter do, but in her fantasy she let Kate do it. She imagined turning to face Kate, kissing her on the lips and letting her hands run down the other woman's body. Becky could no longer control her thoughts. Peter vanished entirely, his place taken by images of Lori and Kate. As both hands furiously rubbed her clitoris, a strange, but very pleasurable, sensation began to well up from within her. It grew in intensity, uncontrolled. As the contractions of her orgasm began, Becky imagined her legs intertwining with Kate's and the two of them grinding together to a simultaneous orgasm.

As the waves of her orgasm crashed over her, Becky almost blacked out. She had to stop touching herself; she was suddenly too sensitive. She was sopping wet, and a puddle of liquid had formed on the couch. Becky lay panting. Gently, she brought her right hand back between her legs. The sensitivity was fading; she could touch herself again. She slowly stroked herself, amazed at the wetness. She did not masturbate often, and it had never been like this before.

Was that an orgasm? She had thought she had had orgasms before, but evidently not. It was incredible. Maybe she was really missing out on something, saving herself for marriage. She thought that it would be wonderful to do that for real.

Suddenly, she went chill. "For real" would be with another woman. It all fell into place. Her choice of an all-woman's college, the incident with Lori, her longings for Kate, the lack of interest in sex with Peter, her first orgasm happening to thoughts of another woman, it all pointed to one conclusion.

No. She refused to believe that she was "like that." She was not a ... lesbian. She hesitated before thinking that word. She had used it before without embarrassment; everyone who went to a woman's college had, but she had never dared apply it to herself.

Becky avoided Kate as much as she could for the rest of the week. She could not bring herself to face the woman of her fantasy. Kate, busy as she was, did not notice the avoidance, but she did notice that Becky was disturbed about something.

At lunch with the other two associates, one of the men mentioned that Becky was upset about something and asked what it was.

"Boyfriend troubles," answered the other man.

"We can only hope," said the first. It was an article of faith between the two that Becky would sleep with at least one of them if not for her boyfriend. The remark made Kate angry. She did not enjoy male-bashing and had nothing against men; she just did not want to sleep with any of them. Remarks like this, however, just fulfilled the stereotype of the man with a one-track mind.

It was not until later that she realized the true reason for her anger was that she had had the same thought.

* * *

That Friday, Becky invited Peter over. She intended to sleep with him. She had to prove to herself that she was not a lesbian, and expressing her desire for Peter would be a good way to prove it.

Peter arrived. She kissed him hello, but he seemed nervous, agitated. He refused to sit down at first. Finally, they sat on the couch together, he took her hand in his and said the fateful words:

"We have to talk."

He wanted to remain friends, but their relationship was stagnant. He apologized. ClichŠ stumbled over clichŠ. He did not want to pressure her into sex, but he had needs. It was better if they just called it quits.

Becky was stunned. She could not come on to him now; it would seem like an obvious attempt to keep him, and Peter would turn her down. He was really a nice guy, she knew that throwing herself at him would be futile. What really disturbed her though, was that she was not upset about losing Peter. She was upset about losing something that protected her from the world, or herself.

Peter left. She picked up the bottle of wine she had bought for the evening and threw it into the fireplace, where it shattered against the bricks. She tried to call some friends, but they had gone out for the evening. She toyed with the idea of calling Kate, even going so far as to fetch the home phone list the firm published, but fear stopped her. She was afraid that she would be unable to control herself, and that Kate would be disgusted with the knowledge that her coworker was a dyke. The only thing left was to get drunk.

Unfortunately, she had no liquor in the apartment. She had just smashed the only bottle. With no alternative, she headed out the door and down the street, toward the liquor store.

The bell above the door rang as she opened the door to the liqour store. She managed a smile at the owner behind the counter who was ringing up another customer. It took her a moment to realize that the other customer was Kate.

* * *

Kate smiled and said "Hi," but then she realized that something was wrong with Becky. She had been crying and was visibly quite upset about something.

Kate pulled the younger woman away from the cash register and the owner and asked her what was wrong.

"Peter and I just broke up."

"Oh, poor thing." Kate hugged her. "If you need someone to talk about it with, I'm here."

"Thanks, but I just plan to get drunk."

"That's not good. You shouldn't get drunk alone. The best thing would be to go out and get drunk in a public place. I know some good clubs, you would be with people, but no one would notice that you were upset."

"No, thanks. I just could not face people tonight."

"What about just one person? A shoulder to cry on? We could go to my place, or yours, and get quietly drunk."

A warning bell went off in Becky's brain. This was what she feared and desired above all else, being alone with Kate. She was afraid that she wouldn't be able to control herself. She should refuse the offer.

"I'd like that, but I wouldn't want to ruin your Friday night," Becky found herself saying.

"Oh, it's no bother. I was just going to spend the evening

watching TV."

Kate had no ulterior motives in offering her shoulder for Becky to cry on; she was just trying to be a friend. The fact that Becky was a highly desirable woman did not even cross her conscious mind. In accepting Kate's offer, Becky was aware of the desires she had for the older woman, but wanted her company not because of them, but because she truly did not want to be alone.

Becky bought another bottle of wine and the two women left the store, heading for Becky's apartment which was closer.

* * *

Once at her apartment, Becky offered Kate dinner. She had planned an intimate dinner for two with Peter, and if it was not eaten it would only go to waste. While Becky finished preparing the meal, Kate cleaned up the glass and spilled wine in the fireplace. They ate in the kitchen, Becky had set the table with candles for her dinner with Peter and Kate asked Becky for matches to light them. The younger woman tensed at the thought of a candlelight dinner with Kate, but the older woman obviously had no ulterior motives in lighting the candles.

Over the flickering glow of the candles, Becky unloaded on Kate. She told how she was finally ready to have sex with Peter, when he broke up with her. She was confused sexually. She avoided any mention of her fears of being a lesbian or her desires for Kate. All the while she was slugging back the wine; it made it easier to talk. After dinner, they left the dishes on the table and went into the living room and continued the conversation on the couch.

For her part, Kate mostly listened, making understanding comments where appropriate. She was aware that Becky was holding something back, but it did not matter. It was not her place to pry into Becky's private life. She was careful with the wine, though. With Becky drinking so much, it would be unwise to get drunk, too.

The alcohol finally got the better of Becky and she started sobbing. Kate opened her arms and Becky leaned on the other woman, crying into her breasts.

Becky's crying eventually gave way to gentle snuffling and that to gentle breathing. She felt safe and warm in Kate's arms. The older woman was gently rubbing her back, and Becky could feel the softness of Kate's breast against her hard shoulder. This felt right and good. She turned her head and looked into Kate's eyes. They were soft and warm and a small smile played across Kate's face. Becky raised her head and slowly brought her mouth towards Kate's.

When Becky started crying, Kate did not know what to do except hug the younger woman. Kate, never one comfortable with emotional scenes, was just glad that words were unnecessary. She just rubbed the younger woman's back and literally took on the role of a shoulder to cry on. Gradually, Becky's crying ceased, replaced by steady breathing. Kate thought she had fallen asleep when the younger woman turned her head and looked at her. Becky's blue eyes were soft and bleary from the crying and the wine. Kate smiled.

Becky's kiss took her by surprise. Not knowing what to do, she returned it. She felt Becky's hand on the back of her neck pulling the two of them closer. The kissing grew more insistent. When Kate felt Becky's tongue try and find its way between her lips, she knew it had gone far enough. The younger woman was far too drunk for this. Kate broke the embrace. When Becky tried to reinitiate it, Kate took the younger woman's head between her hands and gently kissed her on the forehead.

Kate looked at her friend. Becky was clearly confused, but also on the verge of passing out. Kate somehow managed to get Becky to stand and led her into the bedroom. Becky collapsed on the bed. Kate took off the other woman's shoes and drew the bedclothes over her.

* * *

When Becky woke it was still dark outside. She needed to pee. She stumbled to the bathroom. Halfway there, the headache kicked in. By the time she reached the toilet she was nauseous as well. Her stomach made a few feeble attempts to expel its contents, but nothing came up. Becky swallowed a few aspirin, swearing that she would never get drunk again. She sat down on the toilet, relieved her bladder, and tried to remember what had happened the night before.

Clearly, she had embarrassed herself in front of Kate; she remembered the crying. She was still wearing her clothes from the night before, so she had passed out without undressing. She had also had this disturbing dream, at least she hoped it was a dream, of her and Kate kissing. Getting drunk had not changed anything, she still desired the other woman.

Becky headed back to the bedroom, intending to go back to bed and sleep off the hangover. She stopped short when she saw that Kate was lying on the other side of the bed. She was facing away from Becky, and the covers over her were rising and falling slowly and steadily. She was asleep. Becky nearly panicked, then realized that she was being silly. She had passed out, and Kate, who had probably drank a lot too-although Becky could not really remember-had simply crashed in her bed as well.

Becky undressed down to her underwear and slipped under the covers, trying not to disturb her friend, but as she did so Kate turned, and still asleep snuggled up to Becky. The younger woman, gave in to her own desire and tentatively returned the embrace. Kate sighed in her sleep and murmured the name "Jeannie."

Becky stiffened. While she had not accepted her desires for Kate, she had grown accustomed to them, but she had never imagined that Kate might be capable of returning the affection of another woman. It was a dangerous idea. If Kate was a lesbian, that would make it more likely that a physical relationship would develop. That was something Becky was not sure she was ready for. It was comforting though, the chance that the desire might be mutual. It made her feel less alone.

Becky snuggled closer and closed her eyes. She heard Kate sigh contentedly in her sleep as Becky drifted off.

Kate awoke somewhat disoriented. She was in a strange bed and there was a warm body intertwined with hers. It was Becky; she was asleep. Kate flashed back to the night before. Nothing had happened. A drunken Becky had kissed her then passed out. She had put Becky to bed and then, it being late, climbed into the other side of the bed to get some sleep herself. Maybe she should have gone home.

Sometime during the night, Becky had snuggled up to her. She enjoyed the moment, lying in the other woman's arms, but knew she had to get up. Becky was not ready for this; she was probably not even a lesbian, just confused.

Kate gently tried to untangle herself from Becky's limbs without waking her up. The attempt was unsuccessful. Becky stirred, opened her eyes, and seeing Kate smiled.

"You stayed the night."

"Yes, I was a bit worried about you," replied Kate. "You were pretty drunk. How do you feel?"

"Like shit. I will never drink again."

"That will teach you. Will you be all right if I leave?"

"Yeah. I just have to lay here until the hangover goes away. Thank you for staying."

"No problem. It was too late to go home anyway."

Kate rose out of the bed. Becky lay there watching her friend dress. Kate was aware of the younger woman's eyes upon her. As she finished dressing Becky spoke again.

"Do you want to do something together this evening?"

Kate looked at Becky. The younger woman was nervous, almost shaking, a pleading look in her eyes. Kate sat down on the edge of the bed.

"Are you sure you feel well enough?

"Not now, but by this evening the hangover will be gone."

"Okay. Why don't you come be my place about seven. I'll have dinner for you."

"That would be great."

Kate decided that it was time to cross the line the two of them had been skirting. It was risky. Becky's drunken lunge the night before and her cuddling up during the night might only mean that the younger woman was confused and in need of companionship. She leaned in to kiss Becky to find, to her relief, that the other woman had risen up to meet her halfway. Kate grasped Becky by the shoulder and pulled her in tighter. Lightly, her tongue probed past Becky's lips, finding no resistance. Kate felt Becky's hands tug at her back, moving up and down without conscious control. After a few moments she broke the kiss and looked down into Becky's face. Her eyes were still closed. Then they slowly opened revealing satisfaction and long suppressed yearning.

"I'll see you at seven," said Kate. Then she got up and let herself out.

* * *

Becky had trouble going back to sleep, her excitement overcoming her need for recuperation. She lay in bed thinking about the kiss, thinking about what it would mean to sleep with Kate.

She was a bit frightened, but not like before. She was not frightened at the discovery that she desired another woman. She had accepted that, now. This was a nervousness akin to her first date in high school, only different in that she had not felt sexual desire for the boys that had taken her out. In high school she had been nervous because she wanted the boys to like her. She wanted to date, to be a normal teenager. Not knowing better, she confused this with sexual desire.

Briefly, she considered what her parents would think of this. They would be shocked and hurt, blaming themselves for not bringing their daughter up right. She did not want to hurt them, but this was so right she would not give up the pursuit. She no longer had any doubts. She still did not know if she was a lesbian or not, but she did know that she wanted Kate, wanted her more than she had ever wanted anyone.

* * *

The doorbell rang. Kate took a quick look in the mirror; she looked fine. She had considered meeting Becky wearing only a robe, but that would be moving too fast. Becky had had all day to change her mind.

Kate opened the door and Becky, holding a bottle of wine, stepped inside. Kate closed the door and the two women kissed. It was almost chaste, lingering only a moment too long to be just a friendly greeting.

Dinner slipped by. Kate and Becky spent time in the kitchen, preparing the meal and chatting about work. They moved into the dining alcove with the finished meal and ate and continued talking. Talking about anything, but what had happened last night and that morning.

Kate had deliberately "forgot" the wine. She did not want Becky to get drunk again. After dessert, they left the dishes on the table and went into the living room. Kate put some music on the stereo and "remembered" the wine. It was late enough to give Becky the chance to back out sober, but the alcohol would help remove any lingering doubts. Kate replayed this logic in her head as she opened the bottle. The cold calculation of the seduction excited her.

The two sat on the couch, drank the wine, listened to the CD, and continued the talk about work and the people in the firm. As they talked Kate leaned toward Becky. The conversation ended in a moment of awkward silence. Becky looked silently at Kate. Kate reached over and took the glass of wine from Becky and set it on the table. She set her glass next to Becky's.

Kate then leaned in toward Becky, cocking her head and bringing her lips to those of the younger woman's. Becky returned Kate's kiss, slipping her tongue between the older woman's lips. For a while, Becky became the aggressor, placing her hands on Kate's shoulders and pushing her onto her back. The two kissed wildly, nibbling at each other's ears and necks. Kate's hands roamed around Becky's body, but Becky, for her part, could not bring herself to bring her hands to any parts of Kate's body except her shoulders and arms, at least not yet.

After several minutes of furious necking, Kate realized that she would have to make the move to bring their lovemaking to the next level. She placed her hands on Becky's shoulders and pushed the other woman back up to a sitting position. Becky just sat there, looking at Kate, her shoulders heaving and nostrils flaring.

Becky was wearing a pullover blouse. Kate placed her hands on Becky's waist and tugged at the blouse until it came out of her pants. She then slid the blouse up, and with Becky cooperating, removed it and tossed it aside. She then reached around Becky and undid the fastener holding the bra on. The bra followed the blouse to the floor. The older woman then paused and admired Becky's upper body. She was nearly flat chested, her breasts making only the slightest bulge. Becky was not very curvy, but with her long, dark hair falling about her shoulders, she was very, very feminine. Kate then leaned in and bit Becky lightly on the neck, sliding her teeth down the younger woman's breast until the right nipple was in her mouth.

Kate flicked her tongue around Becky's nipple, feeling it stiffen. She lightly nipped it with her teeth, drawing a gasp from the younger woman, and then moved across and did the same to the left.

Kate then sat up and took Becky's hands in hers. She drew the younger woman's hand up to the top button of her blouse. Slowly, Kate thought too slowly, Becky fumbled and unbuttoned each button working her way down to Kate's waist. Kate had to take Becky's hands in hers again and bring them back up to her shoulders. Becky finally got the idea and removed Kate's blouse. Without further prompting, Kate's bra followed.

Becky hesitated. Kate wanted the younger woman to lean down and suckle her, but she did not cooperate. So, Kate stood up and held out her hands. Becky hesitated again for an instance, instinctively realizing this was the moment of no return. Up to now they had just been necking, what would follow would be sex. Slowly, hesitantly, Becky placed her hands in Kate's and allowed herself to be raised up until she was standing. Kate then led her into the bedroom.

The two women, naked from the waist up, stopped at the foot of the bed. They kissed again for a moment, and then Kate slowly dropped to her knees, running her lips down Becky's chest and navel.

Kate unfastened the button on Becky's jeans and then lowered the zipper. She reached up and tugged at the waistline and slipped the jeans over Becky's hips and onto the floor. Only the thin, moist fabric of the panties separated her from Becky's sex.

Kate looked up at Becky's face. The younger woman was looking down expectantly. Kate tugged the panties down over Becky's hips and they followed the jeans to the floor. The tart, tangy aroma of Becky's sex assaulted her nose. Kate breathed it in; it was delicious. Becky's pubic hair grew wildly about her crotch. Kate parted the hair with her fingers, and finding the clitoris, she planted on it a quick kiss, and then stood up.

"Now, you take off my pants," Kate told Becky.

Becky hesitated, then she kneeled and removed the Kate's jeans.

"Now the panties," directed Kate.

Kate's panties were soaked through. Becky could see the matted pubic hairs and the lips of Kate's pussy beneath. She tugged at the panties and pulled them down the older woman's legs. Like Kate before her, Becky breathed in the aroma. It was pungent, but pleasant. Like her own, but slightly different. Kate's pubic hair was shorter than her own, and was neatly trimmed. The idea of Kate trimming own pubic hair, preparing for a lover, excited her.

She wanted to reach out and touch Kate's pussy. She wondered if she should kiss it, like Kate had done to her, but she could bring herself to do neither, not yet. She stood up.

As the two women kissed again, Kate maneuvered Becky so that her back was to the bed and her calves were pressing against the mattress. Kate pushed her lover gently back, so that she was lying on the bed. She then knelt on the floor, between her lover's legs and started kissing Becky's inner thighs and legs.

Becky closed her eyes. This was almost unbearable. She was so excited, but Kate would do nothing to release her. She was just being teased by Kate's lips and tongue.

Finally, Becky felt Kate's tongue part her lips and lap up some of the juices that were oozing out of her. A minute or two of this and she would come to orgasm. Then, suddenly, Kate's lips locked around Becky's clitoris. The pleasure was unbearable. Becky sat up and screamed, grabbing Kate's head and mashing it hard into her crotch. She dropped back onto the bed as the orgasm continued to crash over her.

After the contractions were over, Becky let go of Kate's head. The older woman continued to suck and lick Becky's clitoris, occasionally darting her tongue down between her pussy lips to lap up her juices.

Becky opened her eyes and looked down at her lover. Their eyes met. Becky could see that Kate was smiling as she licked and nibbled. Becky leaned back, closed her eyes again, and allowed Kate to bring her to a second orgasm. It was not as intense as the first, but it lasted longer.

Sometime after her second set of contractions ended, Becky felt Kate nibbling at her ear. The older woman was now lying beside her. She opened her eyes and looked at her lover. Kate's nose and mouth glistened with Becky's secretions.

Becky moved towards Kate and kissed her, tasting her own juices on her lover's mouth. After a moment, Becky broke the kiss.

"That was wonderful. I never knew it could be like that. Thank you."

"Don't thank me," said Kate. "I loved doing it." And then she said rather pointedly, "I'll bet you would love doing it too."

Becky took the hint and smiled. Where there had been hesitation before, there was none now. She wanted to bring Kate to orgasm like nothing she had ever desired before. She kissed Kate again, a long, lingering kiss. Then, when the kiss broke, she kissed Kate's left shoulder, and then her upper chest, a series of kisses that ended at Kate's left nipple.

Becky halted her downward movement at Kate's breasts for a while. She suckled at Kate's left breast, and then moved to the right, running her tongue in circles around the nipple. After a few minutes of this, Becky started her downward movement until she was between her lover's legs.

Kate was sopping, and the aroma was strong down here, but Becky reveled in it. She leaned into her lover and quickly licked Kate's clitoris, just once. Kate shuddered and grabbed Becky's head with both hands. Becky leaned in again and ran her tongue along Kate's lower lips, from bottom to top, scooping up her lover's juices. Then Becky began her attack in earnest, alternating between the lips and the clitoris.

It was a bit frustrating for Kate. Becky was clearly inexperienced. Becky would suck at her and just as the as the pleasure would begin to mount, Becky would shift down to her vagina. Then as Kate started to build toward a vaginal orgasm, the younger woman would move back to Kate's clitoris. Becky was lapping wildly, undisciplined.

Kate sighed and leaned back. She thought about saying something, about directing her inexperienced lover, but then thought better of it. There would be plenty of time for instruction later. Don't spoil her first time. It might take longer, but she would come. Kate just closed her eyes and let Becky work.

Becky saw Kate lean back and doubled her efforts, moving back and forth between clitoris and vagina faster and faster.

For Kate, the orgasm slowly built. She didn't notice the first signs, faint and deep as they were. It was taking longer than usual, but it was happening. She began to clench Becky's head in her hands, forcing the woman's mouth deeper into her vagina. The orgasm crept up on her. Before she knew it, she was in the throes of the most violent contractions since Jeannie had left her.

When it was over, she looked down, between her legs. Becky was looking up, inquiringly, her face glistening with smeared vaginal juices.

Kate pulled her new lover up, and they kissed again. Becky embraced her, burying her face in Kate's breasts. Kate absent-mindedly ran her fingers back and forth along Becky's arm. They both drifted off to sleep.

They both awoke a little after midnight. They talked for a bit, Becky admitting that she had been scared at first, but was now certain that there was nothing wrong in what they had done. Kate told Becky of her loneliness since she had left Jeannie to take this job. They made love again, this time Kate giving Becky the gentlest instructions. Becky was a quick study.

In the morning, they awoke in each other's arms and they made love again in the light of the morning sun that was streaming through the window.

Story 02

"Damn," Doreen Doyle said under her breath as the sunlight from the open window forced her to open her eyes and greet the new day. Rolling over in bed, the 26 year old was immediately reminded of the indecent amount of alcohol she had consumed at last night's teacher's party. Sitting up in the bed, she discovered that her head still hurt a little. Who'd have ever thought that a bunch of teachers could party so hard. Doreen hadn't felt so wasted after a party since her senior year of college.

Still it had been fun, at least as much as she could remember of it. When she had been selected as a delegate from her home town of Parkerston, Indiana, the brunette had expected to spend four days listening to boring lectures and maybe having a little time for sightseeing. After all, a free trip to San Francisco was worth a little sacrifice.

What she had found instead was a few quick, quite interesting meetings every day, followed by a nightly party. Every night being a little wilder than the last, with last nights being the grand finale. She wondered if every conference was like this. If the school board knew of it, they'd never foot the bill to send anyone next year. It then occurred to her that was why every teacher who had attended an earlier conference had given her the same advise. "Just go there with an open mind and enjoy yourself." She had thought at the time they were referring to opening her mind to different theories of education.

Moving to the edge of the bed, Doreen noticed her clothes from last evening scattered across the floor. She must've really been out of it when she dragged herself back to her room. Usually she would at least pile her clothes on a chair or something. She had also been surprised to find she had slept naked, something she didn't even do with her boyfriend back home. Sliding her lower body from beneath the sheets, she was presented with an even greater shock. All of her pubic hair was gone.

"What the hell did I do last night?" She asked herself as she ran her fingers across the now smooth skin between her tighs.

Before Doreen could ponder the question too long, the sudden sound of running water from the bathroom made her jump with a start. There was someone in there. Grabbing her glasses from the night table, she took a good look around the room. While the room was almost a mirror image of her own hotel room, there were enough small differences to tell her she was in someone else's room. A quick glance at the other side of the twin bed showed that someone else had slept there. The inescapable conclusion was that she hadn't spent the night alone.

Rubbing her head, Doreen tried to remember what had happened last night. Now fully awake, pieces of the puzzle fell into place. It wasn't the fact that she'd slept with someone that upset her so. She had, after all, been sexually active since she was 17 and slept with her boyfriend Tim on a regular basis. It was that she couldn't remember who it had been.

The image of Billy Thompson suddenly filled her mind. The delegate from Seattle had been trying to hit on her since day one. Was he the guy from the other side of the bed. She did remember him trying to buy her a drink last night. The sound of running water from the bathroom abruptly stopped. In a few seconds, Doreen would see if it was Billy or not. Hopefully it wasn't someone worse.

Doreen's eyes nearly popped out of her head and her small mouth dropped open in shock as the bathroom door swung open and a tall form walked into the room. Walking over to Doreen, the blue clothed figure bend over and kissed her. It was a warm touch, but Doreen was too much in shock to respond. As her mystery lover moved away from her, Doreen barely heard herself being asked to lock up behind her as her lover in blue was late for a meeting.

The hotel room door closed behind her lover before the reality of the situation fully hit Doreen. Her lover had been tall, blonde and gifted with an incredible body. In addition, her lover had been the last person she could ever have imagined coming out of that door. Her name , Doreen remember now, was Evelyn Howard. Doreen had spent the night with another woman.

"Oh shit, oh shit, oh shit!" Doreen thought as she jumped out of the bed. "What did I do last night?"

Grabbing the various pieces of clothing scattered across the floor, Doreen quickly made for the bathroom and after a quick wash proceeded to dress. As she buttoned up her blouse, she noticed a small razor in the sink, still covered with small brown hairs.

"Guess that explains were my hair went." She noted as she ran her hand through her long dark hair.

Exiting the bathroom back to the main room, she carefully opened the outer door and looked into the hall. Thankfully it was empty. Closing and locking the door behind her, she quickly moved to the elevator and hit the up button. During the short two floor ride, Doreen felt like every person in the small elevator was staring at her. As if they all knew what she had done. When the doors finally opened on the twelfth floor, she almost ran out them.

It wasn't until the 26 year old was safely in her room that Doreen was able to relax. Thankfully her assigned roommate was already out for the day, attending some conference or other. The school board back home hadn't been willing to pay for a private room so she had been forced to share accommodations. She'd had little contact with her roommate, only having met her twice. A tough old bitty twice Doreen's age, she'd made no secret of her dislike of the night time parties and was usually already asleep by the time Doreen made it back to the room.

"I need a shower." Doreen said to herself as she began to strip out of the clothing she had so hurriedly put on only twenty minutes before.

The hot water felt good against her skin as the fog in her mind began to clear. She began to remember images from the night before and by the time she had toweled dry, was forming a good picture of the events that had led her to Evelyn's bed.

Wrapping herself in a warm robe, she dropped onto the unused bed and closed her eyes. As her thoughts drifted, the last ten hours began to replay in her mind like a movie.

The noise of the Flamingo Room filled Doreen's ears, thankfully drowning out the sound of Billy Thompson's voice. The grammar school teacher from Seattle had been going on for almost twenty minutes on some subject or other, all the while stealing glances down Doreen's blouse whenever he could.

Normally, Doreen liked showing off her breasts. They weren't very big, only a 34C, but she worked hard to keep them firm and pert. It was just that Billy Thompson, while sort of cute, was also an incredible bore. Over the last few nights, she tried every way she could think of to let him know she wasn't interested. She'd mentioned her boyfriend back home at least a dozen times, but still he kept coming back. Eventually she was just going to have to tell him to bugger off, something she really hated doing.

"So I was saying to the Principle........" Billy went on as he took another deep look down Doreen's shirt.

Doreen had finally had enough. Filled with liquid courage, she opened her mouth to tell Billy off when a tall blonde woman stepped alongside her. There were plenty of empty seats around the bar so it was obvious that she wanted something from one of them.

"Maybe she had the hots for "Mr. Rogers" here and is going to take him away from me." Doreen thought hopefully. "Maybe she's a long lost girlfriend."

That hope faded as quickly as the annoyed look on Billy's face appeared. Whoever this woman was, she was no friend of his.

The blonde in the bright green dress looked at Billy for a moment, then turned to Doreen and smiled.

"Sweetheart, I've been looking all over for you." The older woman said in a musical tone. "I thought we were going to meet in the Kiki Kiki Room."

Doreen hesitated for a moment, then quickly replied.

"Oh my goodness, I'm such a airhead at times. I've been having this fascinating discussion with Billy here, by the way, have you met Billy Thompson from Seattle. I must've lost all track of time. You will forgive me, won't you?" Doreen put all she could into the statement, trying to convey the idea that she was indeed supposed to meet this woman. It would've helped greatly if she knew her name. She'd seen her on a couple of discussion panels but really hadn't paid that much attention.

"Oh course my pet, how could I ever stay angry at my little pearl."

"I thought you said that you came to the Conference all alone?" Billy said to Doreen.

"I......I ..err....did." Doreen replied. "But ......"

"Doreen and I are very old friends." The blonde said as she reached out and took Doreen's hand in hers. "Very close friends...." She added with a special emphasis that couldn't be mistaken.

"I see.....I mean I didn't know....." Billy stammered as his face turned a bright crimson. "I....have to go.....excuse me."

With that he was gone.

"I hope that's what you wanted." The older woman said as they watched Billy disappear from view. I've seen him following you every night and you looked like you'd just about had enough."

"Oh yes." Doreen gushed as she smiled at the woman. "I just can't believe you got rid if him in a few minutes. I've done everything but write him a note spelling out that I wasn't interested."

"Evelyn Howard, from San Diego." The tall blonde said as she reached out and again took Doreen's hand, this time for a firm handshake.

"Doreen Doyle from Parkerston, Indiana." Doreen replied as she returned Evelyn's firm grip. "My friend's call me Dee Dee."

"Well the first part I got right away," Evelyn grinned.

"You're still wearing your name tag."

Looking down, Doreen grimaced on seeing the small name plate clipped to her blouse. She quickly removed it. At least that explained how Evelyn had known her name.

"Well anyway, I'm grateful." Doreen said as she slipped the tag into her pocket. "Can I at least buy you a drink."

"Certainly," Evelyn replied. "But lets move to a table. Standing at the bar attracts too many guys."

By the second drink, Doreen and Evelyn were fast on their way to becoming the old friends Evelyn had fictitiously created earlier. Evelyn, Doreen learned, was 39 and the assistant principle at an junior high school back in San Diego. This was her fifth conference and she sat on three of the permanent discussion groups.

The conversation turned away from education and Doreen talked a lot about her boyfriend, Tim, back home. He was a nice enough guy. A lot of fun, both in and out of bed. But she really wasn't sure she was ready to settle down. This was only her third trip outside of the state, and the other two had been supervised. There was so much to see and do.

"Well no one is watching over you on this trip." Evelyn said. "And there are a lot more interesting people to meet than that bore from Seattle."

"Your right," Doreen said as she lifted her glass in a toast. "To so many men and so little time."

So intent was he on draining her glass that she didn't notice that Evelyn didn't share in the toast.

"How did you ever come up with that idea to get rid of Thompson. I never would of thought of it." Doreen asked as she put her empty glass on the table and signaled for another.

"Well, sometimes with people like that, all you have to do is present them with something they just can't deal with."

"Imagine," Doreen said as the waiter replaced her empty glass with a full one. "Pretending to be a lesbian and that I was your date."

"Oh I wasn't pretending," Evelyn said calmly. "I am a lesbian."

Doreen nearly dropped the drink she had lifted halfway to her mouth.

"It was only my date with you that I was pretending about."

Doreen slowly placed the glass back on the table, her face still registering surprise.

"Is that a problem?" Evelyn asked. "I really wasn't trying to pick you up or anything."

No, of course not." Doreen stammered out. "You just caught me by surprise."

For the moment, Doreen took a long look at Evelyn. Lesbian. The word had never been part of her vocabulary. Back home in Parkerston she had never even know anyone who had ever met a lesbian. At least no one who had ever admitted to it. Of course there were always those rumors about Sylvia Johnson back in high school, but she had moved away right after graduation.

Evelyn had said that she hadn't been trying to pick her up, but just the same, Doreen began to wonder if the older woman was attracted to her. While she never considered herself beautiful, she knew that men found her pretty. Was a lesbian attracted in the same way men were?

A few moments of awkward silence covered the table until Evelyn finally broke it.

"I can leave if you like, I don't want to make you feel uncomfortable."

"Oh no, please stay." Doreen responded. "I'm sorry for staring but you really don't fit what I always thought a lesbian would look like."

Without thinking, Doreen had whispered the word lesbian. Just like she sometimes heard the old women in her family lower their voice when they wanted to say something about someone. Like "they drink you know" or "They had cancer surgery". It was usually something unpleasant.

"You really don't have to whisper the word, Dee Dee." Evelyn said. "I don't hide the fact that I'm a lesbian. It's not some kind of disease."

"I'm sorry, I didn't realize I had done it." Doreen apologized. She really felt kind of foolish. After all, she was so far from home, who would ever know she had drinks with a lesbian.

As the conversation went on, Doreen found herself being captivated by the woman on the other side of the table. More and more she found herself staring at Evelyn's ample breasts, wondering what it would feel like to touch them. It had been a long time since she had such thoughts. Back in her sorority in college, it was rumored that a few of the girls engaged in lesbian practices, but Doreen never found out if that was true. There were a few nights when she saw girls sneaking into one another's rooms, but she had never been invited. Sometimes she wish she had, just out of curiosity. Finally, the bartender called last call, and the two women got up to leave. Doreen felt a little unsteady on her feet, a combination of the alcohol and the strange excitement she felt from being with Evelyn. She knew the folks back home would never approve.

Waiting for the crowds by the elevator to thin out, Doreen continued to stare at Evelyn. In return, the tall blonde seemed to be ignoring her gaze. Finally Doreen concluded that Evelyn might be thinking that she was looking at her as if she was some kind of curiosity and decided to stop. She was curious it was true, but it wasn't fair to treat another person as such.

As the two women entered the elevator, they were joined by another man. Doreen noted that Evelyn hit the button for the tenth floor while she hit the twelfth. The stranger had pressed four.

No sooner as the doors closed on the fourth floor behind the man, when Evelyn stepped over to Doreen and abruptly kissed her. Caught totally off guard, Doreen instinctively opened her mouth to protest, only to have the protest stifled by Evelyn's probing tongue.

Then as abruptly as it had begun, Evelyn broke the kiss and stepped back.

"All evening, you've been wondering what that would feel like." Evelyn said as she smiled. "I could see it in the way you kept staring at me. So now you know."

Doreen was still too taken back to respond. It was been both abrupt and exciting she had to admit.

Anything she then wanted to say was cut off by the chime of the elevator door's opening on ten. As Evelyn stepped off the elevator, she paused for a moment and turned to Doreen.

"If you really want to see what it's like, I'm in room 1005."

She said as the doors closed behind her.

While the elevator moved upward, a dozen thoughts ran though Doreen's mind at once. Could she do something like that? Who would ever know? Would she ever get another chance? What would

Timmy think? Did she even care?

The doors opened on twelve and she took one step out, then hesitated. Taking a deep breath, she stepped back in and pressed the button for ten.

Over ten minutes passed as Doreen stood outside the door to room 1005. What am I doing, she asked herself for the tenth time. The elevator chimed down the hall as she heard a few people getting off on this floor.

Thankfully, they went in the other direction and entered their own room. She could tell they were drunk and hadn't even noticed her.

"Can't stand here all night." Doreen said to herself in a low voice. "Either go forward or back."

Taking a deep breath she finally knocked on the door. Long seconds passed and she thought Evelyn might have already gone to bed. She was thinking of leaving when a voice called from behind the locked door.

"Who is it?"

"Doreen...." She managed to stammer out.

A second later, the door swung open and she stepped inside.

The room wasn't much different than her own. Same color, same furniture, same boring art on the walls. Her head turned as Evelyn locked the door behind her.

The tall blonde was now wearing a blue terrycloth robe. Her hair had been unclipped and combed out, hanging loosely around her shoulders. It was also slightly damp, telling Doreen she had just come out of the shower.

"Did you forget something?" Evelyn asked as she smiled.

"I was thinking about what you said in the elevator." Doreen said, her eyes fixed on the soft valley between Evelyn's breasts that was visible through the folds of the robe.

"And......? Evelyn asked.

"And, I think I'd like to know more." said Doreen somewhat hesitantly.

"You think.....?" Evelyn said in a strong voice. "Either you do or you don't. Now which is it?"

"I want to learn more." Doreen said, this time with conviction.

Evelyn smile grew larger. She reached out and ran her fingers down across Doreen's cheek. The school teacher from Indiana found the touch unbelievably erotic. Her long index finger slid down across Doreen's face and caressed her small lips. Evelyn slid her finger into Doreen's mouth and let her suck on it for a few moments. Pleased with the young woman's willingness, Evelyn removed her finger and took a step back. The bright smile grew to it's fullest.

"I told you in the bar that I was a lesbian." She said as she took the same finger and ran her tongue across it. "What I didn't mention was that I'm also a dominant. Do you understand what that is?"

Doreen had seen the word in a few books, she wasn't totally ignorant. She nodded a yes.

"Tell me what you think it is?" Evelyn demanded.

"I would guess that it's someone who's into Slave and Master situations." Doreen said, proud of her being able to answer.

"A person who was a ....." She hesitated a moment as she tried to remember the word. ".......Dominatrix." She finally remembered.

"Very good." Evelyn said. "But there are various levels and situations that go with that."

Doreen looked confused for a moment, her reading hadn't covered anything like that.

"I'm not into whip, chains, leather or anything like that." Evelyn laughed softly as she now ran her finger down the deep valley of her 38D's. She could feel Doreen's eyes glued to it's journey. "I just enjoy the feeling of being in total control. Do you think you could handle something like that?" Doreen thought about it for a few long seconds, her eyes riveted on the drop of saliva running between Evelyn's mounds until it disappeared beneath the robe. If Evelyn had asked her this a half hour ago in the elevator, Doreen was sure she would've ran as fast as she could. Now after taking the giant steps which had brought her this far she only felt exhilaration instead of fear.

"Yes I could." She replied in a solid tone.

"Really now?" Evelyn countered.

With a flourish, the taller woman turned and walked over to the edge of the bed. She motioned for Doreen to follow. Standing at the edge of the bed, Evelyn hiked her left leg up onto the bed. She pulled loose the sash around her waist, allowing the robe to fall open. Doreen took a long hard look at the naked body that had just been unveiled. It certainly wasn't that of a 20 year old, but neither was it that of a woman pushing 40. Her large breasts were still full and only sagged a little. They were capped by silver dollar sized aureole, which in turn were topped by erasure sized nipples - already hard and erect. So enthralled by Evelyn's endowments, the younger woman didn't notice at first something she hadn't seen since junior high school gym. A totally nude pussy.

A wicked grin on her face, Evelyn reached down and spread her vaginal lips with her hand, drawing Doreen's attention to it's bareness.

"I want you to lick me!" She commanded. Doreen dropped to her knees without a moments hesitation, so compelling had been the command. She looked up at the tall blonde and saw a pair of piercing blue eyes bearing down upon her. Then she looked forward into the pinkness stretched open in front of her.

"Last chance to back out..." Doreen said to herself as she dropped her gaze to the floor and removed her glasses.

Then with less hesitation then she showed the first time she took a boy in her mouth, the 26 year old grammar school teacher reached out with her tongue and stroked the sex of another woman.

"Mmmmm, this is pretty nice." Doreen thought as she explored the inner reaches of Evelyn's canal.

The young woman found it pleasantly surprising that she actually liked the taste that now filled her mouth. Prior to this moment she had never sampled the juices of a woman, not even her own. Based on the comments of both her boyfriend Tim and two previous lovers, she had expected it to be somewhat gross. At least that was the excuse they had always given for not doing it for more a few minutes. Just enough to help get her wet before intercourse.

After giving Doreen ample time to become comfortable with exploring her womanhood, Evelyn took a gentle grip on the back of Doreen's head and helped guide her tongue to the most sensitive spots.

"Not bad for a novice." Evelyn chuckled as she pressed the brunette's face deep between her legs.

Doreen took that as praise and increased the motion of her tongue. Her face was now smeared with the sticky juices, but she didn't care. Without even checking, she knew that her own pussy, still covered by her panties, was also wet.

"I guess you can handle it." Evelyn said as she released her grip on Doreen's head and guided her back to her feet.

As soon as Doreen stood up, Evelyn pulled her close and kissed her again. This kiss was much more aggressive than the one in the elevator. Evelyn really loved the taste of her pussy on another woman's lips and after running her tongue along the interior of Doreen's now willingly open mouth, she began to lick it off her cheeks.

Part 04

"Strip for me." Evelyn whispered in Doreen's ear as she nibbled on the lobe. "Make me hot for your body."

Doreen took a big step back and reached behind her for the zipper of her dress. She had never stripped for anyone before. Usually the men she'd been with wanted her naked as quickly as possible. She remembered an old adult movie she had seen in a motel she and Tim had once spent a few hours in. Incredibly, he had switched on the television after their lovemaking and watched part of an adult film for the last hour of their stay. Dropping her dress to the floor, she tried to copy the woman she had seen that night.

Cupping both breasts in her hands, Doreen played with them for a few moments before releasing the front clasp. Then with an exaggerated shimmy, she let the plain white bra fall away from her mounds and drop off her arms. She returned her hands to her breasts, now running her fingers across the nipples. The girl in the film had breasts large enough to pull up within reach of her own tongue, Doreen knew she couldn't duplicate that. Instead she wet the tips of her fingers and rubbed the last remnants of lovejuice from her face, then spread it across her nipples.

Evelyn had laid back against the headboard and was playing with her own breasts with one hand and sliding two fingers of the other into her pussy.

"That's right." She purred. "Put on a show."

Doreen's slip followed the bra to the floor and she stood only covered by a cheap pair of cotton panties. She slid both her hands beneath the waistband and let out a loud sigh. Then thrusting her shoulders back and her chest out with each motion, she began to rub her own clit.

"Take it off!" Evelyn encouraged from the bed. Doreen continued to rub herself, now adding pelvic thrust to her gyrations. Then with as much strength as she could muster, she expanded a previous small tear in the material and ripped her panties off. Now totally exposed was a wild growth of bushy brown hair.

No sooner had the now torn material hit the floor when Evelyn jumped from the bed and grabbed Doreen's shoulders. With a powerful shove, she tossed the smaller woman onto the bed. Then lifting each of her legs up and outward, she dropped down and buried her head between them.

"Oh God!" Doreen exclaimed as she felt the wet touch of Evelyn's tongue. It was like a spark of electricity that shot up and throughout her body. The first jolt was followed by a second and a third, until it became a constant wave of delight. Evelyn's skillful use of her tongue instantly showed years of experience. In only a minute she had brought Doreen to a place she had only imagined before.

The pressure against her sex increased, driving her further and further into a euphoric state. Her breathing quickened as she forced air into her lungs in short gasps. She gripped the sheet beneath her, balling it up in her closed fists. Doreen could feel the crest of an orgasm fast approaching, far faster than she could have ever brought it on herself.

Rocking the bed she began to lunge her pelvis against Evelyn's face, trying to match the blondes own thrusts. Finally her body began to shake as indescribable pleasure filled her existence.

"Ooohh Goddd!" She yelled in a high pitched voice.

Evelyn took a firm grip on Doreen's ass and practically lifted it off the bed. She ran her tongue up and down the hair covered opening as fast as possible, finally sending her new found lover over the edge.

"YYYeeeessssss!" Doreen now screamed at the top of her lungs, not caring who heard.

The shout was music to Evelyn's ears.

A few minutes later, the two woman laid side by side, regaining their strength. A look of bliss covered Doreen's face. She looked into Evelyn's blue eyes and finally spoke.

"That was the most incredible moment of my life." She said in a quiet little girl tone. "I wish it could've lasted for hours."

"That was just a warm-up." Evelyn laughed. "We still have a long way to go."

Doreen's smile grew brighter.

"But first, why don't we do something about this mess." The older woman said as she ran her hand across Doreen's cum stained pubic hair.

"Sure, I'll only take me a minute to clean it up." Doreen replied as she started to get up.

"Actually, I was thinking of cutting it all off." Evelyn interjected. "I don't think there's anything sexier than a woman who's bare." She added as she spread her own legs and let the overhead light shine on her own bare beaver.

Doreen didn't even stop to think about it. If Evelyn had said they should go downstairs and run through the lobby naked, she would've given the same answer.

"Ok." She said in that same little girl voice.

Ten minutes later, Doreen stood in front of the full length bathroom mirror and admired her newly saved cunt. Evelyn had handled the razor with precision and not even a small scratch was visible. On her own, Doreen couldn't even shave her legs without drawing blood. She ran her fingers across the now exposed skin, giggling at it's softness.

"Mmmm, that's much better." Evelyn said as she embraced Doreen from behind and cupped her small breasts. Playing with her nipples, she kissed first her neck, then pulled her head around and met her lips with her own.

This time the kiss was soft and gentle, and for the first time, Doreen was able to appreciate the warmth of Evelyn's kiss. A second kiss followed, then a third. All the while, the blonde played with the smaller woman's breasts, bringing her nipples to a stiff attention.

Evelyn took a seat on the bowl and pulled Doreen to her. Her face now level with the small firm breasts, she kissed each nipple in turn. Just a peck at first, then a little harder. Soon Doreen's entire mound was covered with wet kisses.

Pulling the brunette tighter in her embrace, the kisses turned to love bites as Evelyn's teeth glided across the soft skin. Then her attention turned to her nipples as first one , then the other disappeared into Evelyn's mouth. Doreen had never realized her nipples could be so sensitive, or that the simple act of sucking on them could feel so good. So distracted was she by this new revelation, she jumped when she felt two of her teacher's fingers slide between the folds of her now nude womanhood.

The faster her fingers slid in and out, the harder Evelyn sucked. In a mixture of pain and pleasure, she brought her junior right back to the excited state she had enjoyed a short while before.

As if hypnotized, Doreen began to again gyrate in time with the penetration. If Evelyn kept this up, she wouldn't last another ten minutes.

As Doreen once against approached the edge of an orgasm, Evelyn suddenly stopped.

Rising from the seat, she put her hands around Doreen's waist and helped her hop up onto the vanity. No sooner as she settle her ass against the cold countertop when Evelyn replaced her fingers and began to again finger-fuck her.

The advantage of this new position was that Evelyn's large breasts were now face level with Doreen. A fact that the history teacher wasted no time in exploiting. Immediately she lifted the right breast and guided the nipple to her waiting mouth.

Like a babe at her mother's tit, the 26 year old woman suckled. The rising heat from between her legs just increased her desire to bring Evelyn the same pleasure that she had given her.

"Oh yes, baby." Evelyn said as she pulled Doreen's lips tighter against her breasts. "You're doing fine.

Moving to the other breast, Doreen continued to stroke the saliva soaked nipple with her hand. What she lacked in experience she more than made up in enthusiasm.

"Let's go back to the bed." Evelyn suggested as she pulled her breast away from a reluctant Doreen.

Back on the bed, Evelyn laid out on her back and invited Doreen to get on top of her. Instead of going face to face, she swung her body around and again offered her moist pussy to Evelyn.

"I knew you'd be a fast learner." Evelyn quipped before she was silenced by the weight of Doreen's sexuality as she pressed it down against her mouth.

By the time Doreen had moved her own head down between Evelyn's legs, the blonde was already fast as work with both her tongue and fingers. It only took a few minutes for her to whip Doreen back to a teetering edge. Try as she could, she couldn't keep up with the more experienced woman, but she would give it her best effort all the same.

With her tongue pressing around and around Doreen's clit, and her fingers now covered with shiny lubricant, Evelyn abruptly switched hands. While her dry fingers soon became as wet as those they replaced, Evelyn ran the wet hand up across the curve of Doreen's ass and pressed the tips against her tightly closed pucker hole.

First with one finger, then with a second, she pressed forward and gained entry. Once her hole has been stretched enough to hold two fingers, Evelyn applied enough pressure to force them both inside.

The result on Doreen was immediate and explosive. Her anus had always been incredible sensitive. Once, a long time ago, a had performed analingus on her and she immediately fell in love with the act. Unfortunately, none of her later boyfriends would have anything to do with such a practice. Except for Billy who had once tried to have anal sex with her, but had been such a clod that it hurt too much to even get it inside.

Now with Evelyn finger-fucking both her pussy and ass, as well as licking her clit, Doreen realized she was on the threshold of the orgasm of her life. She gave up any attempt to try and bring Evelyn off and instead simple shut her eyes and allowed herself to drift of the currents of ecstasy ripping outward from her crotch.

Finally in such a burst of raw energy that she thought she might be having a seizure, Doreen climaxed as she had never before. For the first time in her life she actually gushed, covering Evelyn's pretty face with the products of her eruptions.

Evelyn of course was more than happy to accept the gift, continuing to both pump and lick away until she felt the woman on top her began to go limp with exhaustion. Evelyn had no intention of disturbing Doreen as she lay drained, her now totally saturated cunt still resting an inch above her mouth. she gently removed her fingers from both holes and with a gentle motion of her tongue, continued to partake of the fruit of her efforts. Evelyn liked nothing better than the taste of a satisfied woman.

They made love once more that night, with Doreen finally bringing Evelyn to orgasm. After that, they both slept the sleep of the dead until Evelyn's bodyclock wore her up a scant 15 minutes before her meeting.

* *

The relentless drone of an unanswered alarm flooded Doreen's consciousness. The flood of the memories that had replaced the alcohol induced haze abruptly stopped as she opened her eyes.

"Oh my lord," She said to herself as she pulled herself up into a sitting position. "Was that really me last night?"

It had been, she was forced to admit to herself. It would be easy to blame it on the booze. Simply say she had way too much to drink and had gone way over the edge. But while that lie could come easily enough, it wouldn't be true.

It had been fun, and yes it had been exciting. Doreen couldn't remember the last time sex had been so exciting. But the thing to do now was admit that it had been both fun and exciting and put it all behind her.

After all, tomorrow morning it would be back to Parkerston, Indiana, population 4,425. Back to the Eisenhower Elementary School were she was expected to set a moral example to the community and "lesbian" was a word not used in decent company.

Yes, that was definitely the best thing to do. Just chalk it up as another little adventure that was better left forgotten.

"Well better see what's on the agenda for today." Doreen said out loud as she walked over to the desk and picked up the brochure her roommate had left.

Circled on it were discussion groups about various subjects by various well known and really incredibly boring educators. No doubt her roomie would find them fascinating. Since the closing ceremony for the conference was scheduled for 4:00 in order to allow many people to head home tonight, there wouldn't even be a party tonight.

"Well at least I have a morning flight, no rushing to the airport tonight." She said to herself as she looked at the pile of suitcases her roommate had piled by the door. Her roomie had a 6:00 flight back to New Mexico, but insisted on attending as many discussion groups and lectures as possible. According to her plan, she would attend the final comments and then race like the devil to the airport to catch her flight.

"Well I wish her luck." Doreen thought. "Because if she misses her flight she'd be stuck her until tomorrow and I'll have to put up with her again."

Looking at the clock, Doreen remembered that she told Tim she'd call him about this time to confirm what time her flight would get in. That way she could be sure he'd be there to meet her.

As she reached for the phone she realized that was a really silly thought. Of course he'd be there to meet her. And if she knew Timmy, he'd take her straight to his apartment for a little between the sheets action. After all, he'd been without for five whole days. Unless of course he'd found someone else to keep his toes warm. The image of Bobby Jo (Boom Boom) Kolwowski, the waitress at the sports bar Tim spent so much time at suddenly came to mind.

For the next half hour she sat on the receiving end of a busy signal. Finally she called the operator and asked her to interrupt, only to be told the phone was off the hook.

"He knew I'd be calling this morning, where could he be?" She asked herself as she hung up the phone.

No sooner had she replaced the receiver back on the phone than it abruptly rang. Quickly grabbing it she brought it up to her face.

"Tim?" She asked, hoping that he had realized that the phone had been off the hook and was now calling her.

"Who?" The feminine voice from the received asked. "Oh no, sugarpie, it's Evelyn."

"Oh God!" Doreen thought. Just the sound of her voice sent a tingle between her legs.

"Yes...." Doreen answered hesitantly.

"I'm going to be finished with the last panel about two and I was wondering if you'd like to get together for a late lunch? That is if you haven't already made any other plans?"

"Well, I haven't really." Doreen answered, now aware that the tingling had spread to her nipples. She hesitated for a few moments then asked "Just lunch?"

"Well, I'll leave that up to you, darling." Evelyn laughed softly.

Doreen stared at her reflection in the mirror across the room. She had already decided that the best thing to do about last night was simply forget it ever happened. She couldn't, she mustn't do anything to change that.

"Could you hold on a minute?" She asked.

"Certainly."

Lowering the phone, Doreen repeated to herself that she had made the right decision. After all, tomorrow she would be back on her way to her real life. Back to Tim and respectability. Of course there would be some perfectly good explanation as to why he had missed her call. It was only her imagination, her guilty imagination, that put him in the bed of a bimbo.

"Just say sorry, I can't make it." Doreen said to herself.

"She'll understand. And who knows, if she really wants company, I'm sure she'd have no trouble finding it."

Returning the receiver to her mouth, Doreen opened her mouth to say just that. But instead it came out.

"I'd love to."

"Wonderful!" Evelyn exclaimed. "I'll see you about 2:30 then."

"Fine, I'll be ready." Doreen heard herself say before the phone went click.

For a long minute she stood there, staring hard at the phone in her hand. How had no turned into yes? What was she thinking? Confused he hung up the phone. Just then the phone rang again. Hesitantly she picked it up and said hello.

"Hi peaches." Said the deep masculine voice on the other end. "I'm glad I caught you."

"Timmy?" She asked.

For the next few minutes she listened as her boyfriend explained that he had knocked over his phone when he came in last night after a few too many beers. Figuring that she must've been trying to call and got a busy signal, he'd called her instead.

"So how's the conference been?" He asked.

"Very educational." She replied, thinking that was definitely the truth.

"Well I can't wait for you to get home." He said. "It's been a long and lonely week."

"Don't worry, I'll be home soon." She said and gave him all the flight information.

"Great," He replied. "Well I'm going to have to run, babe. I'm playing ball with the guys down at the bar this afternoon."

"All right, I'll see you tomorrow afternoon then."

Replacing the phone for a second time, she realized that the

tingling between her legs had now given way to a soft wetness. But was it from Evelyn or Timmy? Should she call Evelyn back and cancel?

Doreen picked up the phone and asked that Evelyn be paged. A few minutes later, Evelyn came to the phone.

"Did you forget something?" She asked.

"Err....actually...yes I did..." Doreen stammered. Silence on the other end indicated Evelyn was waiting for more of a response.

"I just wanted to say....." Doreen began, stopping to take a long deep breath.

"I just wanted to say that I wish that you'd call me Dee Dee. All my friends do."

"Of course, Dee Dee, If it makes you happy." Evelyn beamed, her smile almost visible over the phone. "But I've got to get back. I'll see you later. I'm looking forward to it."

"So am I." Dee Dee said as she too broke into a wide grin.

Turning to look at herself once more in the mirror, she said out loud to her reflection.

"I guess just once more can't really hurt. After all, this conference is supposed to be educational."

Then her thoughts turned to what she could wear, wondering if she had time to stop at that really cute lingerie boutique she saw over on 4th street.

Story 03

I sat at my desk, looking at the screen of my Compaq computer. The letters of the ad, black on white, looked so artificial. I found it hard to believe that this electronic wisp would result in what I had in mind.

The letters proclaimed "I have a desire. It is to become the best at making a woman come. Orgasms traded for lessons... Your looks, age, race are all unimportant. All I ask is that you be clean and healthy. As for myself, I am 5'8", with light auburn hair, hazel eyes, 40D-35-46. Funny how sinister these ads come off, isn't it ;) On the lighter side, you will find me a very eager and apt pupil. If interested, please email me."

It did sound awfully technical. Oh well. I supposed it would do. I pondered it a bit longer, with my fingers paused over the keyboard. Then a few keystrokes, and it was busily whizzing off to machines around the world.

It was late at night. I had the window open to let in the cool Texas air of January. From nearby, I could hear cars passing by and the occasional train on the tracks next to the apartment complex. I got up briefly to get a can of soda then resumed my seat in front of the computer.

Prying the cold can open, I leaned back in my chair and perused the newsgroups. Reading alt.sex was a labor of futility these days. Out of 200 articles, after beating my killfile, I had 40 left to read. Sad. It seemed that sex was just not a cared about topic these days. However, racism, swearing, and 900 numbers were hot topics. I didn't think Western Civilization was coming to an end, but I did wish that newsgroups would return to the happy days of the late 80s or early 90s, when commercial ads and services were a rarity. The Internet was becoming the Crudenet.

Another sip of soda. Bubbles fizzed noisily as I set it back down. Hit the "n" key. More text blazed past.

Why had I posted a personal ad. Well, long, droning histories of sexual urges are never that interesting. Suffice it to say that I had been prompted by my evil subconscious ;) As I walked to my classes, or went to nightclubs with girl friends, I found myself looking at women with a smile. Their beautiful bodies, soft hair, eyes, lips, the way they moved, the way they smelled as they passed by, the silks or cottons they draped on themselves. I also felt more natural around them, more alive. Ah, well, that all sounds like women are alien to me. Nothing could be more untrue. I felt like they were part of me, in some glorious, vague sisterhood, where the lesbian culture was a welcoming haven.

At Waldenbooks, I poured over the "Social History" section, where they had the lesbo books tucked away on the bottom shelves. At Hastings, I bought _Dykes To Watch Out For_ and Pat Califia, along with a "cover" book on gardening. I stuck a rainbow flag on my bumper and surfed the Web to look at women-made jewelry, in the forms of labyrises, or goddesses, or rainbow beads. So many little hidden symbols. The black triangle. The pink triangle. Ancient fertility symbols and the axes of Amazons. It reminded me of the Masons and their crests and rings...

Some time later, not immediately, I got a reply. Where did I live? Short and to the point. No smileys. I pictured a curt mistress in black leather, standing over my pleading form, holding a crop. She didn't say what she looked like, which was fine with me. More mystery.

I cleaned my apartment, took out the trash, vacuumed, lit some subtle incense. Put my bottle of white wine into the fridge after sticking the soda cans on the bottom shelves.

I took my time in the shower, letting the hot water beat out the tension in my shoulders. I was nervous. Yes, one of those baby dykes, who had never been with a woman. But how I had thought about it. If all it took was neuron power, I'd be the womanly Don Juan by now.

I brushed my teeth, blew my hair dry. Make-up? I had quite a stash of Loreal, but decided against it. I laughed at myself as I stood naked in front of my closet. This was not a date. Well, maybe it was, in a strange kind of way. What to wear, hmmm. I pushed a gathered blouse outside, then a earth-mother cotton dress. A black velvet mini and a satin blouse, nah.

I ended up sitting oh-so-casually on the couch in Levi's and a deep blue scoopneck teeshirt, with dangly silver earrings. No shoes. I looked up at the ceiling and realized the overhead was on. I ran over and turned it over and flicked on a couple floor lamps, that threw a golden soft light upwards. Much better.

I looked at the clock on top of the TV. I felt a little light headed. There was the sound of a car in the lot. Was it her?

I heard a car door slam, and steps outside. Pause. I held my breath. A knock that made me jump up like my alarm in the morning.

I looked through the peephole briefly. It was too smudged to really see her. All I saw was long brown hair and a white shirt. I turned the locks and opened the door with a smile.

"Hi, Ruby" she said with a grin.

I was in another world. She was... ohmigod, a real live woman RIGHT IN FRONT OF ME. And we were going to...! Finally my brain took over and I shook my head and pulled the door back further.

I laughed, then said "Sheila. Won't you come in?".

She moved past me and I caught the faint scent of musk. She sat herself down on the couch and leaned back, looking totally at ease.

I crossed in front of her, very aware of how I moved, and went into the kitchen. I opened the refridgerator, and peered in.

"Would you like anything to drink? Coke? Water? Wine? Any of the three basics?" I leaned in towards her with a grin.

"Some wine sounds great," as she leaned forward to grab a book off the coffee table. As she turned the pages in a glossy tattoo book I had, I checked the glass for smudges or dust. Looked ok. I poured some of the wine in, and felt the glass turn cold.

Giving her the misty crystal, I sat beside her and tried to look casual.

Sheila looked over at me. I looked back. She had long, golden brown hair, very thick, that hung in wavy curls down past her shoulders. Rosy skin, and a very curvy body. Sage green eyes, and on her sandalled feet, deep pink toe polish. Long eyelashes. Ears that looked like fragile shells. A mole on her right cheekbone.

"Do you have a tattoo?" she asked, pointing towards the book in her lap.

"I, uh, yep." Not exactly my shining moment in verbosity.

"Oh yeah? Cool! What of?" Her eyes shined, and she sat up further.

Hmmm! This was encouraging.

"A big furry red fox", I stage whispered. I raised my eyebrows.

"Let me see..." she said, leaning in closer. I felt like the big bad Wolf, and I liked it.

I stood up, and took off my shirt. So much for that modesty hang-up! In my bra, I sat back down with my back to her.

The fox was part of a large back piece I had had done a couple years ago. Inscribed in a perfectly deep black circle, he wrapped around the inside, with his tail, whiskers, and amber eyes in fine detail. The red ink had bothered me for a while, but eventually my skin accepted it. The heavy black fill-in had taken a few workings over, which were not the most comfortable times for me, but it had been worth it. The red fur was smooth while the black was slightly raised.

Suddenly, I felt her fingers on my skin. I jumped a little and laughed.

"It's amazing, really intense colors. I bet it was painful".

"Oh, well, one must suffer to be beautiful". I turned around a little towards her with a smile.

Reaching towards me again, she unsnapped my bra, and pushed the straps off my shoulders. I lifted up my arms and she slide it off and put it beside me.

"Much better", she whispered. Her hands smoothed over my shoulders and down my back. I felt the hair on my arms stand up, and everything seemed much crisper all of a sudden.

Deciding not to play coy, I turned around, put my hands on the side of her face, and kissed her.

Warm, silky softness, mixed with the tangy acid taste of wine. She pressed up against me, and I was surprised at the feel of her breasts against mine. The feeling of velvety pressure of her breasts and the wetness of her mouth was a revelation.

When we broke apart, I could feel my heart stuttering in my chest and the slippery heat between my legs. I imagined I could smell myself. Maybe I could.

I slowly pulled her shirt off, leaning in to taste her bare breasts. Her nipples were a light coral color, almost imperceptible from the pale skin. When hard, they only stood out a little. I played with the tips with my tongue, then lightly bit them, which elicited a gasp and having my head pressed against her. I repeated my nibbling treatment while unbuttoning and unzipping her jeans. No underwear. This was a woman who dressed for speed.

I pulled away from her breasts with a grin. "Yummy." I noticed her face was flushed, along with her nipples.

She raised herself off the couch a little and pulled down her jeans, easing them down her legs, and folding them into a neat pile that she put beside the couch.

"Eat me."

I gave her my attempt at a devilish look, and proceeded to do as commanded. I moved off the couch, and knelt in front of her. She knudged herself closer to the edge and lay back.

Dark, thick fur, and that smell. Oh God. Putting my hands on her thighs, I opened them a bit more, then moved in. She was very wet. My first lick, from the bottom to the top, was rewarded with a low groan. Ruby, this is it. Your first woman. Oh, the taste... As I went on, I tried to think of analogies but nothing came close. All I knew was that I craved more of it. The saltiness made me savor the moisture, and the creamy texture stayed with me as I enthusiastically licked her. After several searching tonguings, I settled in on top of her clit, and put my lips around it in a circle, sucking, while I flicked the tip of my tongue lightly over it... as fast as I could. Sheila went into a paroxysm of twisting and bucking, whispering to me words that made my thighs even wetter.

"Ah... God, oh... Mmmmm... AH! Yes! Please....". She reached down and grabbing my hand, brought it to herself. I followed her lead and slowly inserted two fingers into her, where they were engulfed by wet heat and an indescribable silkiness.

Just when I thought she was going to come, she drew back, and put a hand on my head.

"Wait", she commanded. She got up and went to my student futon, where she lay back, and adjusted the pillow under her head.

"Have you ever 69'ed with a woman?" she asked.

Standing over her, still in my jeans, I shook my head no.

"Well, take off those Levi's, and get down here, girl."

"Yes, ma'am."

I shucked them off, and tossed them beside the futon. I climbed over her, and gently lay myself down over her face.

All I wanted was to get my mouth back on her. As I did, I felt the first tickle of her mouth. Her technique was excellent, and I found myself hard-pressed to follow suit, with my mind reeling every time her fingers pumped into me or her tongue slid over me. Trembling, I came, my face on her thigh, gasping.

Coming back down, I resumed, letting my fingers slid inside her. I removed my middle finger and pushed it gently into the slippery, puckered hole beneath. Feeling both fingers inside her, moving at the same time, coupled with my determined licking, she shivered and clamped my head between her thighs.

I heard animalistic cries and groans, cushioned by strong thighs. Then, she stiffened like a woman made of stone, and was very quiet for a second. I felt her tighten around my hand and the quick, short little tremors ran through her. Then more silence.

She let out a loud breath and laughed, pulling herself up.

"Damn, Ruby, I think I'll need to come here more often", she grinned, and ran a hand through her tousled hair. She looked pleased. I was. Oh boy, was I.

"Teach me, oh Obi Wan." I prostrated myself in front of her, and was pulled up into a spicy kiss.

Things were looking up.

Story 04

"Her name is Allison, and she has the longest legs! And not only that but she crosses them just like you taught me to cross mine, and once while she was talking to me she laid her hand on my thigh, really high up and squeezed it real sexy like, and it was all I could do to keep from falling in her arms, cause she had these big..."

"Monica!!Whoa!! Slow down! I want to hear all about it, but you're talking so fast I can't get it all!"

"I'm sorry, I guess I'm still excited....but if you had been here you would understand...Oh, I can't wait for you to get home!!!"

"What time did you tell her to come?"

"I told her you'd probably get home around 6:00 and I asked her to come for supper around 7:00. You didn't mind my inviting her to come back did you?"

I smiled warmly at the enthusiasm and excitement that I heard in Monica's voice.The Allison she was so excited about was a lady who had come to the door selling life insurance. Monica's training allowed her to let lady salesperson's in the house as long as they were attractive and not accompanied by a male. It also encouraged her to determine if possible whether or not the sales lady might have any interest in the things we were interested in, and if so to try to set up a meeting with me if possible. Thats exactly what she had done, and it pleased me to see her so excited about it.

"No dear, thats exactly what you were trained to do. You did well. Now tell me once more what this Allison looked like."

"Well, she is really tall...she must be around 5'10" or maybe even a bit taller...she had on high heels so I may be over-estimating her height just a little. She has light brown hair, not too long, and green eyes.She was dressed conservatively, very business-like in a skirt and blouse.But I could tell she didn't have on a bra under her blouse by the way her nipples pressed the front of the soft material out. When she sat on the couch she crossed her legs and then tucked the ankle of her right leg back under the ankle of her left leg...just like you showed me...and slid her supporting foot back at that angle that makes legs look so pretty...you know what I mean."

"Was she wearing stokings?..or could you tell?", I asked.

"I really tried to tell, but it was difficult. She had on either stockings or pantyhose one, but I'm not sure which." I heard a small laugh come across the phone lines. "Maybe she'll wear the same skirt and blouse tonight and you can find out for yourself."

Chuckling, I replied, "Yes, or perhaps I'll make you find out for me."

"Yesssss, MASTER!, whatever you say!", she giggled into the phone.

"Did she say anything to make you think she might be bi?"

"Well, it wasn't so much what she said as it was the flirty way she said everything she had to say.She did say that I was very attractive and that she loved petite women. Then when she rose to leave she put her hand on my thigh, very near to my crotch and squeezed it quite hard. I didn't want her to move it, but I wasn't sure whether to say anything or not."

"I think you did everything exactly right, precious little slave- slut! I can't wait to get home...in fact I may come home just a bit early to help you get ready. This could be a fun filled night."

After we hung up I made a call to the Chamber of Commerce to check on the insurance company that this lady supposedly worked for. It was a well known company and she was listed as their sales representative for our area. She worked out of Chatanooga, Tenn. and came through our area once every three months they said.

Finally around 5:00 I got caught up enough that I could leave work.When I got home I heard the shower running and slipped into the bathroom quietly to find Monica laying back in the tub with her eyes closed.She had the Shower Massage showerhead in her hand and was letting the warm water pulse against her spread open cunt. It had almost gotten to the place that there wasn't anything that Monica did anymore that she didn't do in some kind of sexually fulfilling way. I loved it.

I slipped back out just as quietly as I had entered and slipped out of my clothes and into the nice navy smoking jacket that Monica had given me for Christmas the year before.I took the white silk wrap-around gown that I had given her out of the closet and laid it on the bed.It was a very pretty gown, quite short, but still very attractive on Monica.I found the white slippers with the very high heels and laid them beside the gown.

I was in the kitchen fixing a screwdriver for her when I heard the water finally stop.I made the drink stronger than necessary, but then she expected the drinks I fixed for her to be that way. I held the drink out to her as she came through the bathroom door rubbing her still hard nipples with both hands.

"Oh!!, you scared me, you silly!When did you get home?"

I smiled at her and kissed her gently on the mouth. "I've been here for a while. I saw you were, ahem, "busy" in the bathroom and decided to give you some privacy."

With an embarrased giggle she sipped the strong drink and replied, "Yes, I was sort of "busy", wasn't I? I'm afraid I stayed in there too long, I've not even started supper yet."

"I called for some supper to be delivered when I saw that you hadn't started anything yet. It should be here shortly. In fact, I think I hear a car in the driveway now. Here...slip a towel around you and go open the door for the delivery boy."

She gave me that "You're something, aren't you?" look, but obediently wrapped the small towel around her and opened the door for the teen-age delivery boy.I didn't have to watch to know what effect she would have on him. She told him to please put it on the dining room table for her since she couldn't let go of the towel, and turned her back giving him a good view of her cheeks as she came back in to get the money to pay him.

"Is it the kid with the big one?", I teased.

"Yes, you devil, and its even bigger than usual now...must be the towel."

"Well, too bad we've other plans, he could stay awhile...maybe another night."

Grinning a big sexy grin she took the money from me and paid the boy off.I heard him whistle an appreciative whistle as he walked away from the door toward his car.

"I think he heard us talking", she said with a smile, "his face was a beet red when I walked back in and gave him the money."

Together we set the table in the dining room and no sooner had we finished than the door-bell rang once more. This time I did the honors.

"Hello...you must be Allison, the insurance lady that Monica was telling me about. Please, come in."

"And you must be Mr. Wade. Monica was so kind to invite me for supper, I really didn't expect that...she's a delightful woman."

"Yes, she is delightful in many, many ways!" I said as I ushered Allison into the dining room.Monica was certainly right about Allison looking like something we'd be interested in. She wasn't the kind of woman who struck you right away as being beautiful, but she had an air about her which told you there was alot there both to look at and to learn about. She was quite attractive.

"I hope you'll forgive the casual way we're dressed. We enjoy the privacy of our own home and usually wear something comfortable when we are here."

"Oh, no...thats just fine. I dont' blame you, I don't wear much at home either, frankly."

"Well, we certainly want you to make yourself at home while you're with us", I said with a mischievous grin as I pulled out the chair for her.

Dinner was fine under the circumstances. I knew that Monica and I were anxious for it to be over with, and I got the impression that Allison felt the same way.Finally we were all through and we retired to the living room.

Monica and I exchanged smiles as Allison seated herself in the same manner she had earlier in the day. This time I seated myself on the couch next to her and Monica sat in the straight chair opposite us.I gave Monica the code to open her legs and smiled to myself as she sat open legged in the short gown.Her pussy was plainly obvious, but the look on her face gave not the slightest hint that she was aware of it.

Allison obviously had on the same outfit which Monica had described.I could see her nipples plainly through the material of her blouse, but it was very difficult to detect any garters through the tight skirt.She began her presentation as if there was nothing at all else on her mind, although I caught her glancing up often and looking between Monica's legs.Each time she did I could detect a nervous twitch of her eyes and watched as she swallowed hard before speaking again.

Several times she laid forms in her lap and on two or three such occasions I reached to her lap and took them to look at for myself. In doing so I was soon able to brush my hand against her thigh enough to tell that she did in fact have on a garter belt under her skirt. Her nipples grew harder and harder behind the blouse until they were literally poking out through the silky fabric.

"This is an unusual question, I'm sure, Allison", I said, "but I've always wondered what the answer is.Is there a clause in insurance policies which gives the company an out in the event that the insured dies while engaged in an unusual sexual activity?"

Allison brightened and smiled warmly. "I guess that depends on what you mean by unusual...just what do you mean by that?"

"Well, you see Monica is a rather unusual woman.By that I mean that she has needs which are somewhat more....well, I mean she often has to be....I guess what I'm trying to say is that..."

"Pleassse, please, Mr. Wade...feel free to say exactly what you mean to me, I'm a big girl, and I've seen it all, I assure you!"

"Well, ok then...Monica is a slave-slut, Allison. Its not unusual at all for Monica to be involved in group sex situations with both men and women, and believe me, sometimes they can be very physically draining.I've just often wondered what would happen as far as insurance is concerned if she had a heart attack or something under such circumstances."

Recrossing her legs and sliding her skirt higher on her full thighs, Allison rubbed her hand along her calf sexily as she answered my question."Well, thats really a very good question, and its the kind of question that more people should ask. Luckily for you, I know the answer", she smiled broadly."For insurance purposes a heart attack is a heart attack unless it can be proven that the insured suffered a self-induced heart attack as a way of committing suicide.There is no case where an insurance company ever tried to prove someone attempted suicide by fucking themselves to death."

While she had been giving her explanation to me, I had given Monica the hand signal which indicated that she was to rub her legs. Ihaddisplayed the signal long enough that the signal had additionally informed her that she was to also touch her pussy. Allison saw her hand moving on her legs out of the corner of her eye as she spoke and when she had completed her answer focused her eyes directly on Monica and watched calmly as her hand moved to her pussy.

Monica had now laid her head back and closed her eyes and without any further instruction from me was now also rubbing her breast with her left hand inside the gown.

"Would you like something to drink, Allison?", I asked with a smile.

Without taking her eyes off of the busy little slut who was performing for her, Allison replied breathlessly, "Yes, that would be nice...a good cold strong drink would be very nice."

I took my time in the kitchen fixing the drink. I knew that Monica would not stop playing with herself now unless I told her to. I also knew that Allison would not stop watching her.

What I saw when I came back into the living room proved me right on both counts. Monica's robe was now completely open, revealing her small sexy body. Her left hand was pinching and pulling at the nipple on her left breast while her right hand was busy pumping two fingers in and out of her dripping wet cunt. She had slid down on the chair now until her pussy was right at the edge of the seat, and her head was still laid back and her eyes closed tightly.

Allison had pulled her dress up to her waist and was slumped down on the couch. Her eyes were fixed on Monica and both hands were playing in her shaved and naked fuck hole. She didn't even look at me as I entered the room.

Sitting beside her, I lifted the glass to her lips and watched as she sipped from it thirstily. She still made no sign whatsoever that she was aware of my presence. Moving her drink to my right hand, I began to unbutton her blouse with my left hand, not stopping until I had it completely unbuttoned and had pulled it back to the sides to reveal her hard nipples and full breasts. Having done that I began to play with her nipples with the fingers of my left hand, pinching and pulling at them, twisting and turning them like radio knobs.She had two fingers from each hand inside her cunt now and was fucking herself with the same gusto that Monica displayed across the room. I began to talk to her in a soft sexy voice.

"Youlove watching her, don't you, Allison?....You love watching the hot little bi-slut fingering her dripping wet fuck hole, dont' you?....Look at her nipples, Allison, don't you wish you were sucking on them now?....think how good her juices must taste...think how good her mouth would feel sucking on your naked fuck hole....do you want to eat her Allison?...do you?....crawl to her, you dirty little cunt sucking tramp, crawl to her and suck her juice into your mouth...do it now!!!"

She fell forward immediately to her knees, crawled across the carpeted floor, and pressed her mouth tightly against Monica's wet cunt.She slid her arms under Monica's trim thighs and pulled her pussy into her face with her hands.

Meanwhile I moved behind her and slid her tight skirt up over her ass.Slipping off my robe, I stroked my cock once or twice and then knelt behind her.I rubbed the head of my thick fuck meat in her sloppy wet slit and then began fucking her as her mouth worked noisily on the slut cunt in front of her.Monica grabbed her head in her hands and pressed her mouth even more tightly against her trembling pussy.

I began pumping my cock in and out of Allison's hot cunt, grabbing her by the hips as I stroked my meat into her. When I had established a nice comfortable rythym, I moved one hand to her ass and began pressing a finger against her asshole. Realizing that I needed lubrication, I slid my hand up Allison's back and past her head to Monica's cunt and slid my finger in between Allison's bi-slut mouth and and the juicy dirty tramp fuck hole on which it sucked.

 Coating it quickly with the juice that Allison so obviously hungered for, I moved it back to her ass and slid it quickly into her tight little shit-hole.Her hips really began moving now as she fucked herself back and forth on my thick cock and on my finger that was moving in and out of her chute.

Monica began to moan softly, and her breathing began to come in gasps.I knew her orgasm was beginning and wanted Allison to come with her.I picked up the pace of my assault on her holes and was rewarded by a continually more frenzied movement of her hips. When Monica's ass began to lift from the chair and thrust itself into Allison's face, I felt Allison's cunt and asshole both clench noticibly.The small of her back started dipping and rising in time to the fucking of my cock in and out of her hole and I heard a deep scream begin in her throat, muffled only by the jry strong crotchand moved through the juice and cunt to her own lips and escaped strongly now. Her whore hips bucked high and strong as my cock began spewing hot wet fuck into her.She jerked from the waist back and thrusted outward from the waist up, both ends fucking, one end taking, the other end giving.Suddenly her whole body locked up, tight as a drum, and then just as suddenly she went limp, falling on the floor.My now soft cock slid out of her hole and Monica was forced to release her head from her grasp.

Rolling Allison over on her back I checked her breathing to make sure she was alright. I'd seen a similar response to orgasm before with Donna, so I knew she had just momentarily passed out. She stayed out longer than Donna had, however, and it was nearly five minutes before she came to. By that time Monica had knelt beside her also, partly out of concern for her safety, and partly out of gratitude for the orgasm she had just helped her achieve.

When she did come to we all smiled at each other and hugged warmly.It had been a very pleasant and exciting introduction for us.Monica had been right about Allison, and I was proud of her for being able to tell.How right she had been we wouldn't know until later on. But we all knew then that there would be more times for us in the future, and we were glad.Boy, were we glad.

Freakish Lesbian Erotica
Sci-Fi, & Fantasy Short Stories
Sophie Poulin

All Rights Reserved. No part of this publication may be reproduced in any form or by any means, including scanning, photocopying, or otherwise without prior written permission of the copyright holder. Copyright © 2020

This book is entirely a work of fiction. The names, characters and incidents portrayed in it are the work of the author's imagination. Any resemblance to actual persons, living or dead, events or localities is entirely coincidental.

Story 01

I saw the house as I rode into town: a stately marble villa that flashed white fire from the sun. I halted my horse and stared. A fresh breeze from the sea stirred my long hair under my helmet. Though I was an Amazon I had not cut it. Nor did I cut off my breast. Those are only stories, told by jealous men discomfited by our skill as warriors.

A peasant with a donkey-cart passed me on the road, taking a load of grain to market. "Greetings, friend," I said. "Who lives in that house at the top of the hill?"

The peasant was as brown and gnarled as an ancient root, and he spat. "They call her the Gorgon," he said. "She turns men into stone!"

"Oh?" I said, amused. I had traveled the length of Hellas while this man had probably never been more than a day's journey from home, and I knew that Homer's tales of nymphs and chimaerae were patently false...though once I had seen a monster's bones preserved in layers of rock. "If that is so, why don't the people of the town rise up against her and drive her away, hiding their faces as Perseus did with his shield?"

He had no answer; just spat again and moved on.

I glanced up at the villa again. It was odd to find such a large dwelling here, as we were many miles from Corinth. There was nothing special about this area to attract the wealthy: no great natural beauty, no cave-dwelling oracles, no mineral springs. Perhaps the house belonged to an ancestral family of this land. I touched my heels to my horse and rode into town.

The town was called Agrinon, and it was a bustling place. I bought a meal from a vendor and looked over the goods, as I needed certain items: new leather sandals, metal pins, a sack to replaced the patched one that carried my belongings. The vendors had never seen an Amazon before and they were eager to serve me. I am tall and well muscled, free of scars for the most part, and my face still looked youthful. Lovers remarked on the sensual curve of my mouth, the lean lines of my hips and belly. My breasts were still as large and firm as two wineskins, visible even under the worn mail armor I wore. As I took care of my business, I asked the townspeople about the house on the hill.

"A gorgon? Ridiculous!" a tall wine merchant said. "A young girl lives there, cousin to a great family in Corinth. A fair maiden, cultured, demure; yet sharp with her business dealings. Her name is Medusina. I had dinner with her only last week, and I assure you she is no monster."

"She manages alone?"

"Her parents left her their olive groves and their vineyards, and they turn her a profit. She could marry, I suppose; but none of the young men about here have caught her fancy. I've heard she pines secretly for a youth in the city."

"I've come from Corinth," I said.

"Then she will be pleased to see you and exchange gossip. I would pay her a visit if I were you. The comforts of her house are far better than any you'd find in town."

I thanked the man and, having made my purchases, set off for the villa. The road snaked up into the hills through the vineyards the man had spoken of. The vines dangled grapes of dark amethyst that would make a rich wine. A crumbling wall of plastered brick, much mended, surrounded the house. I passed through the gate and two slaves paused to look up at me, caught in their chores. "I've come from Corinth," I said. "My name is Hippolyte, and I am an Amazon mercenary. I hear your mistress is anxious for news of the city."

"She is," one said cautiously. "Wait here. I will fetch her for you." I dismounted and let the other slave lead off my horse. The villa looked smaller than it had from the road, and though its edifice was still grand, it was in need of repair. Weeds grew between the paving stones of the courtyard, and the marble columns had been cracked and whitewashed. Butterflies flitted about the flowering vines, and the scent of sage and verbena hung heavy in the air.

The slave reappeared at the door. "I've told my mistress you are here. Come with me to the bath, where you may refresh yourself."

I followed him inside. The cool stone walls gave a delicious shelter from the sun. The bath was a small room cordoned off by curtains. A design of nereids and porpoises had been worked into the tiles of the floor. I shrugged off my mail, leg greaves, and chiton and settled into the pool. After I had soaked and scrubbed to my heart's content I put on the clean robe the slave had left me, then brushed and bound my hair. I then left the bath for the parlor of the house.

The mistress of the place, Medusina, was already there, fingers idly plucking at a cithera. I caught my breath. She was fair, and young; as fresh as the blooms in the courtyard garden. She raised her eyes to look at me as I came in, her long, thick lashes darting up. They were as black and heavy as soot, and her hair, too, was black...a full head of lush, coiled ringlets the beribboned elegance of her chignon could barely contain. Her dewy lips parted like the petals of a rose. Indeed, she was no monster. Quite the opposite.

I bowed before her to show my respect. "My name is Hippolyte. I've brought you news from Corinth, my lady, as I was told you would want to hear it."

"I do," she said, her voice firm but girlish and high. She looked about seventeen, but I could have been wrong. She set aside her musical instrument, her lithe white arms tracing a graceful motion. Underneath her chiton, her body looked slim and pliant. I smiled. I had fine appreciation of a woman's body, from the years I had spent on the isle of Lesbos. "Phaedrus, fetch the Amazon a chair."

One of the slaves brought back a chair and I sat, arranging my long robes. I was not used to woman's clothing. The other slaves brought us cool wine from the cellar. We talked. Her manner was self-assured yet elusive. I found myself becoming more and more attracted...as if she was a small, wild animal, shy yet strong, that I might capture in my hands and caress in its fierceness.

It had been afternoon when I arrived, and now the sun touched the hills in the west. Soon it would be dusk. Smells of cooking came to me--meat, cinnamon, bread. "We shall dine in the garden," Medusina said, rising from her chair. "I would like to continue this conversation into tomorrow. You may stay the night if you wish."

Through an arch we came out into a walled garden with a balcony that overlooked the sea. Dates and palms grew there, and citrus trees with yellow fruit. Flowering shrubs sent their perfume into the air. But what really drew the eye were the statues. There were about a dozen of them, all nude, and of a superb comeliness. All seemed to be caught in some sort of erotic bliss. Here was a wide-eyed young woman, her head thrown back; there a handsome man, his organ raised, his arms outstretched as if clutching an invisible lover. All details had been rendered with exquisite care: the wrinkled buds of the nipples, the curls of the loins, the parted lips with the hint of teeth and tongues.

"You must be wealthy indeed, to afford many fine statues," I said, choosing to overlook their prurient nature for the time being.

Medusina only smiled. "It was my mother who made them. She became a libertine after my father's death. Every time she left a lover, she would hire an artisan to carve them in stone. I had a strange childhood, growing up at the feet of these silent giants."

Strange indeed, and even stranger yet to eat dinner surrounded by them. Torches were lit as the twilight deepened, and the flickering shadows made the statues seem to move in the corners of my vision. I would turn my head, expecting to catch them in motion, but they remained as still and silent as before. No wonder the townspeople called her the Gorgon. How could they not, on seeing these frozen figures?

"Do you go into town much?" I asked.

"Rarely." She took a sip of wine, the quiver of her long lashes betraying her agitation. The torchlight made sketches of warmth across her flawless skin. "The people don't understand me, that I prefer to be alone, with my servants and slaves."

"They tell stories about you."

She smiled without amusement. "I know. That I am a witch, that I am deformed. As if the veil I wear is anything other than the veil a noble lady wears to protect her skin. That and my name, which can only mean *Medusa* to them..."

How wrong it was for the townspeople to shun her. She was a strong personality, independent of spirit. I could see why she would not be forced into taking a husband she did not want merely to give herself respectability. Men make the laws that give them charge of women, and they are enraged when a woman defies their expectations. Women, too, are just as cruel. They see another woman's freedom and wish to destroy it, because it only demonstrates to them their own chains.

"I too, have fought that battle," I said quietly. "I left Themiscyra at the same age as you. When I started on my career of war, rarely did I see another Amazon. Rarely did I make a friend amongst the men I fought with. They respected my sword, but they saw only my breasts. The closest companions I've had are the fey youths in the pleasure-houses. We are of little use to each other, so no rivalries or resentments can develop."

Medusina smiled at that, a true smile. My heart warmed to see it. "Perhaps you've made another friend," she said.

We retired inside, where a slave played the cithera with a plekton, striking melodious chords. The night was warm and lazy outside, the full moon a crouching beast, tawny as a lioness. A faint smell of salt came from the sea, and one of old stone that had stood for a century. It had the taste of earth, the tang of minerals. Medusina read from a scroll of poetry, one of the many she owned. How virginal she looked, how finely made.

"You die, O thrice desired And my desire has flown like a dream. Gone with you is the girdle of my beauty, But I myself must live..."

"Are you lonely, Medusina?" I said.

She stopped her recitation, looking up at me. The dim light of the torch was behind her and I saw the outline of her waist and legs through the thin linen chiton she wore. Her nipples formed two dark flowers under the pleated fabric. She opened her mouth, but no sound came out. "I--" she began, then swallowed. Her eyes were very dark, as dark as the sky with its glimmering of stars that could have been tears. "I am content."

I touched her cheek, brushing a stray tendril of hair away. Mesmerized, she did nothing to stop me; the heavy gold necklace she wore rose and fell against her chest. "You are beautiful, Medusina." I lightly traced the lines of her creamy shoulders, savoring the softness, the delicate tracery of bones beneath their surface. She was tense, coiled as a gazelle about to leap. But she did not. It betrayed her passion to me, her unspoken need. "I would lie in love with you tonight, if you would have me."

She flushed. We had both drunk much wine; that, and the intoxicating nature of the night, were working on us. "You don't know what you're asking," she said, her voice high and whispery with fear.

So my young Medusina was a virgin, or inexperienced. Well, I would soon have a remedy for that. I unclasped her heavy necklace and slid it off, baring her neck to me, and moved my lips closer to her ear, the warmth of my mouth tickling her, teasing her, as I knew it would. "I am very skilled." I planted a kiss, a small one, at the corner of her jaw. "Did I tell you I spent two years on the isle of Lesbos, with Sappho and Alcaeus? The things they taught me, my dear. You would blush just to hear the most anecdotal of them." I took her chin in my hand, and turned her head around to face me. "Kiss me, Medusina, and you will not be alone tonight."

Her lashes fluttered, dropped. Her mouth moved towards mine as if she was hypnotized. Her lips parted, closed on mine.

Kissing her was like partaking of a spring day: fresh and new and wild. Her tongue was a delicate snake, slow to rouse, but pliant and yielding to mine. I brought my hands up to feel her young breasts, kneading them through the linen. The contrast of warm flesh and the harshly pleated yet flexible fabric made me excited. I felt my sex grow moist. Her nipples were like burning coals. I felt them harden beneath my palms, and longed to quench them in my mouth.

She pressed her firm belly into mine, her mouth growing more demanding. She tasted delicious, and I was having a hard time keeping myself from pouncing. This young girl was almost half my age.

"Do you think," I said softly, "That we should retire into a more appropriate room?"

"Yes," she whispered, the tiny word hiding a universe of unexplored feelings, feelings she did not recognize even herself.

She turned away, but it was only to dismiss her slave, who, ensconced behind a curtain, had not seen what his mistress was doing. We went to her sleeping chamber. Bowls of dried herbs gave off a spicy scent like that of a woman's body. Her bed had four posts that draped curtains of gauze, which a breeze from the windows stirred into motion. In one corner of the room stood a long mirror, an unimaginable luxury. I wondered what from land it had come. I noted the position of the bed, the angle of the mirror, and smiled. This night would be very enjoyable. As Medusina turned her back to light a few candles, I undid the pins of my robe to let it fall around my ankles.

She gasped when she saw me nude. I was well aware of the effect I had on lovers. My body is athletic and powerful, a weapon of war, but I am a woman too--my hips and buttocks and breasts attest to that--and the warm glow of the candlelight traced these feminine contours, giving them coronas bright as the flash of shields and polished swords. Yet my muscles and sinews were prominent as well, standing out with sculpted hardness. I was no soft, coddled beauty like the one who awaited me. Yet I longed for her, she that was all I was not, because she would make me complete.

Medusina blushed. I pressed my palms against her shoulders and gently guided her to the soft embroidered coverlet of the bed. We sat side by side, I nude, she dressed, and her hands gripped the hard wooden edges of the frame. I touched her chin to raise it in two fingers. "Don't be afraid," I said. "I am gentle."

"I know," she said in a quiet strangled voice. "I sense goodness in you. Oh I cannot--"

"Hush, Medusina." I kissed her soft mouth, probing it gently. "Put your arms around me." I felt her hands move behind my shoulders, wrists crossed, defenseless. I brought up my own hands behind her and deftly removed the two jeweled pins at her shoulders that held the front and back of her chiton together. The garment fell open, slithered down to her waist.

"Oh--" Medusina said, making a weak start to snatch it up. I stayed her wrists.

"No. Let me see you." I held her wrists at bay in one hand, assessing her like a slave-trader. Her muscles trembled, but she was no match for my strength. Her breasts were small and high, her nipples contracting like buds about to open. Beneath them, a faint ripple of ribs shuddered with her struggles. I drew her down so we both lay on the bed, facing each other, and ran my hand down her flank. My tanned skin was a vivid contrast against her ivory flesh. My fingers paused at her waist, then swiftly pulled down the rest of her chiton.

She was lovely, slim yet strong, her skin as pale and creamy as the flowers outside. How I longed to see that naked body walking in front of me, prancing, running, leaping, exposing to me all its variations of movement and attitude, but that would come later. Still holding her captive, I untied the silk ribbons that held her chignon together. Her thick black curls burst free, coiling like serpents over her shoulders, a lush purple-black like the ripening grapes of the vineyard. At her loins was a second mound of hair which hid a greater treasure.

Her breasts swung gently as I laid her on her back. I ran my fingertips across her coral-colored nipples, and they puckered still more under my experienced pressure. "You want me to touch you, don't you Medusina?" I whispered.

"Yes..." she said in a strangled voice. Her eyes stared at me, yearning, but no longer afraid.

I began to explore her. I squeezed those young breasts, holding them like two frightened doves that beat against her ribcage. I tasted her face and neck, skimmed my callused hand over her belly. I gently parted her thighs, fingers playing with her pubic curls. I felt like a child with a doll, but no doll had ever given such sharp gasps of pleasure, such warm sighs of bliss. I bade her be still; I wanted her to be passive yet. I slipped my hand beneath her, caressing the silky mounds of her buttocks, parting them, my fingertips skimming, but not touching, the pursed bud of her anus.

Her skin grew hot, feverish. She jerked as I touched her sex, her sleeping clit brought suddenly to life, hissing like a snake...the Medusa...her almost-namesake.

I drew her hands toward my body, holding them against my breast. "Touch me now, darling. Take my nipple between your fingers; squeeze it softly, pull it towards you. Yes, that's it..."

Her slender hands kneaded my breasts like sweet-bread dough. They were much larger than her own, without the buoyancy of youth; but the contrast they made with the hard flesh of my torso seemed to fascinate her. She pinched my nipples between her thumb and forefinger, rotating the nubs between her fingertips. The treatment made them harden almost painfully, pointing like the tips of two spears.

"Suckle me, Medusina. Use your mouth..."

She attacked my nipples like a hungry lion cub would its mother. The firm wet suction of her mouth made them stiffen further, strain towards the very teeth and tongue that tormented them. "Easy, young one," I said, with a warning tap on her head.

But she only moved rapidly from one to the other, her hands attending to the unmouthed breast, squeezing its bounty, tormenting its protuberant single eye. Her head bobbed between my breasts as she suckled, the soft skin of her cheeks caressing their sides, her hair tickling my chest. Now it was my turn to gasp helplessly.

She grew rougher and I squirmed on the coverlet, my hips rising up. I thrust my hand between my legs, pumping myself on my own fingers. Medusina's eager tongue continued to swirl around my nipples, striking them back and forth, then beginning the sweet suckling anew. I was her captive now. My breathing grew rapid, and hers grew hoarse. I was going to come. I did not often come from breast stimulation alone, but Medusina was very beautiful.

Then she stopped. Lost in her own passion, she was fingering herself, squeezing her own nipples.

Oh, the innocent thing, thinking two women together each played a solo and not a duet. I quickly clamped my lips over hers, kissing her deeply.

She moaned deep in her throat as my tongue explored her mouth. Her nipples were the prisoners of my fingers now, and like any good interrogator, I made them give up all they knew. Her belly undulated against mine, and we moved as one again, sometimes face to face, sometimes belly to back, our hands moving, exploring, always on the prowl.

But as our lovemaking progressed, Medusina broke off again and again. Indeed, she seemed actually averse to stimulating me. Her passions would drive her to feast on me, then, as I was about to reach orgasm, she would leave off that part of my body to attack another or stimulate herself. I put it down to her inexperience. I did not mind that much, as I got just as much joy out of watching her young body writhe, impaled on her slim steeple of her fingers, as I would from it straining and yearning against my own, so the frustration of my own abated pleasure could be borne; but still, I found it disturbing. I would only gently guide her attention back to me, letting my fingers take the place of her own.

Our passion mounted, and the frustration of that passion, and finally sweet Medusina was on her back, her slim legs high in the air as I devoured her dripping sex. I ran my tongue down one fold, then the other, then thrust it deep inside her. She whimpered as if tortured, her clit as hard and pointed as a pomegranate seed. I sucked it harder, my nose buried in her abundant pubic hair, and her cries became louder, a rising ululation that threatened to wake the servants of the house. Her feet arched, toes pointed, her raised legs as graceful as the necks of two swans...and between them a tawny pantheress crouched lapping at a stream, long brown hair tumbled about its prey, talons scraping its straining thighs.

Medusina's body heaved. I held her hips, grounding her. Her head flew back and forth on the pillow, eyes wanton slits; her own fingers plucked at her swollen nipples. A long wordless keen rose from her throat: "Oh....oh....oh...ah...AHHH!"

She shrieked, her head rising off the pillow, her legs trembling. Her nether regions contracted hard against my tongue. Then she shrank down, silent, breathing very hard.

I rose from my crouch and curled up against her. Her eyelids flickered as she acknowledged me. "Oh, 'Lyte..." she gasped. "I did not think..."

"Your first time, my darling, is always overwhelming," I said in my wisdom. I poured her and myself another glass of wine. "Let's rest a bit, then you shall do to me what I have done to you."

I felt her muscles tense, even though we did not touch. Why was this girl so averse to giving me an orgasm? Perhaps she was afraid she was not skilled enough. I drew close and kissed each nipple, which pouted at me, pinkish-red and sleepy, from the snowy cones of her breasts. "I could have twenty orgasms just watching you, Medusina. Drink your wine quickly. Let's not delay."

She was reluctant, or perhaps just coy. But soon we were wickedly entangled again, Medusina with an even greater abandonment than before. This time, I made her give to me, and I gave back in even greater measure. We struggled like two beasts, though whether we mated or fought, I do not know. She was as wild as a Maenad, one of the fierce girls of Bacchus. I imagined her running through the forest in animal skins, tearing the creatures she met apart with her teeth. I sorely wished for one of the double-headed phalluses the Bacchantae use in their rites, but tongues would have to do. Mouth to loin we lay sealed together, she riding me, her sex split over my face as I licked her hot, tart folds. In return she hooked my clit with her tongue, and my hips use and fell in shallow motions. This time, I decided, she would give me my climax.

She squealed in surprise as I quickly scooped her up, upside-down, and placed her on her knees on the goat's hair rug before the mirror. I grabbed the wineskin and poured the remaining contents over my belly. The rich, red wine swiftly ran down into my crotch. "This time," I said, half-playfully, half-warningly, "You will scoop up every drop of that wine with your tongue, young one, until I scream in pleasure."

Medusina quickly snapped her head up. I expected her to say no, so I quickly pressed her face between my legs before she could refuse.

She did not refuse, for now she was as drunk on passion as I was. She began to lick, and this time, she did not stop. Her tongue teased me up and down, vibrating as rapidly as the wing-beats of a bird. My fingers wound in her thick, curly hair, holding her sealed to me, the dress-mirror our silent witness. In its surface I saw myself triumphant, the delicate beauty kneeling before me subjugated, obedient, yet I was also subjugated to her, and I trembled on the spike of her tongue, at once victor and vanquished. I moaned in helpless pleasure, rubbing my crotch against her face. She spread her hands over my buttocks, steadying me, pressing me firmly against her mouth. My skin tingled, my limbs trembled. I was on fire and drowning at the same time. I brought up my hands to squeeze my breasts, molding them like clay, twirling the erect nipples between my fingers. I pressed my legs against Medusina's shoulders, pinning the slim lyre of her body between my thighs. Both of us were trapped in time, in space, and all the known world was a witness...from the furnishings of the room to the marble statues, now striped by moonlight, that stood in silent watch in the garden outside.

I was going to come. My breath quickened in tiny gasps as Medusina sucked and licked. I felt my muscles slacken, tense...slacken, tense...then the pent-up tension burst forward, curling over me like a great wave. Shock after shock of pleasure ran through me. My mouth opened silently as I spasmed. The contractions seemed to come from the earth itself, surging up through the soles of my feet to exit through my head, paralyzing me, freezing me solid...

...as solid as the statues that waited outside.

I opened my eyes. Medusina thrust herself away from me, sobbing against the tiles of the floor. A strange sensation began to suffuse the soles of my feet. Looking in the mirror, I saw the tanned skin of my toes was graying and darkening, like fabric dipped in dye, and changing textureÑto the roughness of granite, dark gray stone speckled with minute flecks of white. I was turning to stone.

Sweet Artemis, no, this wasn't happening to me! I tried to move, but could not; I was frozen in the same awkward position the orgasm had left me. The grayness washed over my feet and lapped around my ankles, then slowly licked up the length of my legs. Above it, my skin felt the cool motion of air, and I registered each anxious breath I took, every heartbeat. But below the grayness, I felt nothing.

There was no pain. No pain at all...only a numbness.

A thin film of sweat broke out on my brow. It was the precursor of worse terror.

The gray shadow whispered up my calves, transmuting them, making me into a stony goddess such as I had seen in the temples of Athens and Thebes. My feet were already immobile, planted on the tiles of Medusina's bedchamber as if only the most arduous of labors would budge them. I saw my thighs solidify into two mottled columns of stone. I would have screamed if I was able, but I could force only the faintest of whimpers from between my lips. My hard, sculpted flesh would be forever hard now.

The gray numbness cupped my buttocks like a lover, lapping lasciviously between my legs. It then swirled lazily over my hips to my front, the soft flesh there receiving the undulations of stone. With horror I saw it extend a questing tendril towards my loins and enter my body. The sensation shot through me like a second orgasm, equal parts pleasure and pain, as my insides were petrified. It was a full, heavy sensation, rather like pregnancy, but there would be no child.

Tears of fear began to flow from my eyes as the grayness rose up my torso. My breasts became two pears of stone, their soft buoyancy forever fossilized, rendered hard and immobile. The process stilled my lungs, forever silenced my heart. It petrified my nipples, then ran down my arms. My hands became gesturing sculptures, never to lift or sword or caress a lover again. I felt my hair become a solid mass of stone and fuse against my back, and understood at last here would be no escape for me. The process was irreversible. I had braved mighty warriors, sorcerers, lions and other fierce beasts. Now I, Hippolyte the Amazon, had been brought down by a mere girl.

The gray film lapped my chin like the rising tide. *Why did you do this to me?* I wanted to cry. But the dark figure of Medusina only sobbed and said nothing.

The grayness swiftly flowed over my face. My nostrils were plugged, my ears sealed. My mouth was frozen open on the silent scream I gave. Mute and helpless, I felt the numbness reach the top of my skull. The transformation was complete.

Through a dim, grayish haze I saw Medusina stand. She wiped the tears from her face. She came over to me and extended a trembling hand to cup with her palms the solid globes of my breasts. She touched with her fingertip the tips of the nipples which had given her such delight. She ran her finger around and around the blunt little nubs, as if not believing what she had done. They were still erect, in the midst of arousal. But no coming orgasm would quake and then soften them.

She ran her hands down my belly. I heard the slick sound of her wet palms on the stone. She traced the curly arabesques of hair at the juncture of my thighs, perhaps grieving for the soft fleece that had grown there, and inserted her fingers between my legs. They found no entrance. The stone had sealed me down there, as I knew it had.

She went around to my rear to explore me further, and though I could not feel her, I could tell from her motions in the mirror that she was running her hands over my buttocks. I saw her rest her cheek briefly against the rounded stone, and she might have kissed me there.

Finally she stood and came around to face me. Infinite sadness was in her eyes, and infinite regret. In the old tales the Gorgon is supposed to be die when her face is reflected back at her. But in the mirror now I saw only a sorrowful girl, and the statue of an Amazon caught forever in sexual climax.

"I am sorry for doing this to you," she said. "It is a curse, you see, and one that I regret with every fiber of my being. Whoever loves me, turns to stone. I tried to tell you that, tried to leave you unsatisfied. It is the final spasms of lust, you see, that start the process. But I could not stop in time.

"For years I have lived with this curse. I do not wish to inflict it on others, so I have devised ways of satisfying myself. Usually they work. But every once in a while, the desire for a lover grows so strong I must have satisfaction, no matter what the cost. I try to exercise caution, as you have seen, but..." her eyes darted toward her garden, "I fail often."

I wondered what it was like for her, to live in such isolation, bringing such a cruel fate to the ones she loved.

"I am sorry," she said again. "But you will never age, and never sicken or die. There may be compensation in that." She clapped her hands for her servants. Two men entered with a wheeled cart as if they expected this. My vision turned perpendicular as they grasped me, then placed me on my back in the bed of the cart, grunting because of my increased weight. I realized with awful despair I was yet aliveÑand trapped in the stone. A situation that would likely exist for eternity....or until the rain and moss and scouring wind reduced me to dust.

They wheeled me out of the bedchamber. My last sight was of Medusina as she stood naked in the darkness, a tragic figure with her head bowed, her hands pressed against her face.

#

The next day, Medusina had me mounted on a marble plinth and set me in her garden. Now I knew the origin of the other statues. And I knew that they, too, were alive, and as helpless to communicate with each other as I was. Day after day, night after night, we wait here, our only stimulation the changing seasons of the garden, the play of light and shadow, and the doings of our mistress.

From time to time she entertains a guest in the garden, a wine merchant from the town, perhaps, or a passing dignitary. And every once in a while, I observe the special brightness in her eyes, and the answering response of the other, that tells me the guest will spend the evening in her bed, and perhaps join us in the morning.

I want to cry out and warn them, but my cold, stone tongue cannot.

Story 02

It was a lovely day in the woods. Sun streamed down through the vibrant yellow leaves, making the forest floor into golden lace. Red turned her face up to look at a woodpecker hammering on an old dead tree.

Almost autumn. In her basket, Red carried bread, cheese, grapes, and some cured beef for her grandmother. A white linen napkin covered the wrapped packages, tucked neatly around it all. The wicker basket hung off the muscular arm of Red, who was in a hurry to get to the cottage before dark.

Red was sixteen. And a very sweet sixteen. Long black curls, dark blue eyes, skin like cream, and a body that was born to wear Frederick's of Hollywood. Not that she was aware of her charms. No, Red was a total innocent. Keeping a girl in a forest cabin all her life, with only occasional forays to her relatives, made her naive, and vulnerable.

Mmm, vulnerable. Grey eyes tracked Red's progress along the forest path. The red silk cape billowed around the lithe figure, the hood tilting back to reveal a soft pile of curls tied at the back of Red's neck. Underneath the curls, there was a pale swatch of skin that was normally covered by Red's hair.

The wolf's mouth watered. She was very hungry.

She started to move. Quietly.

Red looked up again. The sun was starting to set. The cottage was about an hour away. Her legs felt good, warmed up from the walking. The path was well-worn, and Red could practically walk it blind-folded. But at night, the creatures of the woods came out, and she didn't want to be around to entertain them.

She snaked a hand under the napkin, and unwrapped the grapes. She was getting a bit hungry. She'd been walking for a couple hours. The purple skin of the grape popped, and the sweet juice ran over Red's tongue. She smiled, and chewed a bit. Then stopped. Yes, that had been a branch breaking.

Nonchalantly, she turned around, not expecting much. Understandably, she was startled to see a woman leaning against a thick tree by the side of the path.

"Hello", this woman said.

Red's eyes wandered over her. The stranger was wearing a man's suit, in a light grey wool. Underneath was a white oxford, with a perfectly knotted silk satin tie. Her thick dark brown hair was cut short, long on top. Her eyes were a light grey that matched the smoke rising from the slim cigarette in her fingers. Fingers with trimmed, buffed nails. Tan hard hands. Red swallowed.

The wolf smiled. It was a very nice smile, with gleaming white teeth.

"Um... hello. Who are you?" Red asked, tightening her grip in her basket, and taking a tiny step backwards.

"You can call me Diana, darling. And your name?" the wolf asked, raising the cigarette to her lips and inhaling.

With those cool grey eyes studying her, Red paused. Wait, that was a question. Oh... yeah.

"Red." Red nervously brushed a curl out of her eyes, and smiled.

The wolf came forward, and extended her right hand towards Red.

"Charmed, I'm sure." The wolf bowed, and taking Red's hand, raised it to her lips. Red watched, aghast, as the wolf kissed it delicately.

The wolf noted that Red's skin smelled quite delicious.

"So, my dear Red, where are you off to this evening?", she asked, straightening up.

"Um... just a family visit."

"Ah! And what do you have in that cute little basket of yours? It smells wonderful. Beef? Angus beef?"

"No! Well... yes! But it's for my grandmother. I'm sorry." Red smiled apologetically and turned to go. "I have to go. It's getting late."

"Oh, well, let me accompany you! This is a dangerous place at night. Besides, I love to play protector", the wolf entreated. She stood next to Red, and offered her arm with another charming grin.

"Really, my radiant Red, I am quite harmless. You have absolutely nothing to worry about! Come, and introduce me to your grandmother. We can all spend the evening together."

Red was silent, then slid her arm around the wolf's.

"All right, Diana, let's walk together... So tell me about yourself. Do you have family around these parts?" Red asked, turning them towards the cottage.

Underneath those calm grey eyes, another warm smile spread. Why if you only knew, my dear, she thought.

After a congenial walk, Red was relaxing. Diana was really nothing to be afraid of. A wonderfully dry sense of humor. And excellent taste in cologne.

It was now dusk, and the white walls of the cottage glowed dully in the soft light remaining. The wooden shutters were open. No candlelight streamed out to greet them. It was perfectly silent. No smell of roasting meat or baking bread.

"Grandmother?" Red called out, breaking free from Diana. She opened the door and looked inside.

The cottage was neat and clean, and the wide bed was made, the quilt turned up. The hearth had a few coals glowing in the ashes. Red took a candle off the mantle and lit the wick. With the candle, she turned to the table and saw the note resting on it.

Diana came up next to her, and picked it up. Red's eyes moved over it as Diana read it aloud:

"Dear Red,

There was an emergency in town. I had to go tend to Mrs. Wiggins. She has gone into the labor, and I expect to spend the night there, and perhaps tomorrow also. I am sorry I couldn't get word to you in time, but I had to leave with Mr. Wiggins this afternoon. I will see you Friday, my dear. Make yourself at home! The towels are hanging out back.

Love, Gram"

"Oh my... Gone to see Mrs. Wiggins...", Red folded the note's corner over, and looked up at the wolf.

"Well, she'll be back in a couple days, not to worry. How about if we eat a little something together before you go to bed?" Diana asked, crouching in front of the coals.

"Hmmm. I don't see why not. All right... would you like some ale?" Red asked, reaching into the cupboards to get the cups.

"I'd love some ale." The wolf carefully piled small firewood on the coals, and blew gently on the embers.

Tiny orange flames engulfed the sticks, and wisps of smoke blew up the chimney. Diana arranged a few slender logs on the flames, and in a few minutes, she had a hearty fire burning.

She sat back, watching the popping, sizzling wood. The heat warmed her face. She stood to remove her jacket and drape it around a chair, as Red handed her the ale cup.

"Thank you. It is most appreciated." Red watched as the wolf took a sip, and licked her lips.

"Wonderful." The grey eyes were on her again.

Red wasn't sure what Diana was commenting on, but the look in Diana's eyes made her jumpy.

Red took a sip of her own, then went past the wolf to light some more candles.

After placing three fat beeswax candles on the table, and sitting down, Red glanced at Diana. Diana was busy turning the logs with the poker, and grumbling to herself.

Red unpacked the basket, putting the extra food away. She took down some plates and broke the bread and cheese into chunks. As she cubed the beef, she studied the figure in front of her.

Strong shoulders like a man's, and hands like a man's. Slender waist. Shiny hair that reflected the orange firelight. Strange. Red had never seen anyone like her before.

Diana stood up gracefully, and took another swig of ale.

"Damn good ale." The wolf took a seat opposite Red, and pulled the plate of food towards her.

"This looks wonderful. Thank you again, Red. I haven't had food like this in a long time." No, most of her food had been... well, eaten in a more primitive fashion.

The wolf looked over Red as they ate. Red ate neatly, licking her fingers as she went, unconscious of the effect she was having on her dinner guest.

The candlelight made Red look ethereal. She had taken off her red cloak. Underneath was a simple flannel dress, in navy. The deep blue made her eyes look almost phosphorescent.

Red felt the steady eyes of the wolf on her and finally looked up.

The wolf bit slowly into a hunk of beef, her white canines sinking into it, and held Red's gaze.

Red watched Diana chew, then watched as the wolf caressed the pile of grapes next to her hand. Diana broke one off, and held it to her lips, neatly splitting it in half and studiously licking the second half.

Red felt too warm suddenly. She realized she was blushing. She looked down to her lap, and rearranged her napkin. Several times.

During this domestic pause, Red's ears couldn't help but pick up the soft wet sound of grapes meeting their demise between the wolf's lips.

"More ale?" Red offered, jumping up, her hand out to grab Diana's cup. At a silent nod, Red took it and turned back to the counter. Uncorking the skin, and lifting it over the cup, she was horrified to feel her dress rising around her hips, and warm hands around her waist turning her around.

"What... Just... Hey!" Red protested, and was silenced by the wolf's wet mouth on her's.

"Shhhh" the wolf whispered, her mouth on Red's neck, her hands doing wonderful things between Red's legs.

"But... I never... Oh please..." Red pushed at the wolf, pulling her hands away. Her wet fingers.

The wolf backed away, with a very tight smile. She pulled her shirt out, and slid the knot of her tie down, and slowly started to unbutton the oxford.

Red stared, unable to move, then she was bolting for the door. She had her hand on the edge as it was ripped out of her grasp and brutally slammed shut.

She whipped around, one of her hands brushing over the wolf's breasts.

"Don't make me chase you. It just makes me irritable." Red noticed Diana had very sharp canines. Her grey eyes blazed at Red.

"Please...don't..." Red whispered. She pressed her back against the door.

"Don't? Don't what?" The wolf advanced, pressing Red's hands back against the rough wood of the door.

Red could feel her body heat and smell the ale on her breath. She trembled.

"...don't... hurt me."

"Hurt you?" the wolf laughed. As she laughed, she took the hem of Red's dress and tore it upwards. The old fabric easily ripped, and Red turned to hide herself.

"Oh, stop it." The wolf slapped her hands as Red cupped them over her breasts.

The wolf tossed the remnants of Red's dress onto the table, then swiftly maneuvered Red over to the table. Bending her at the waist, she pushed her face onto the dress.

"Now hold still. Close your eyes. If I see you move or open your eyes, it'll be the last time you do either."

Red closed her eyes, and felt a tear trickle down to her old flannel. She heard the whisper of fabric then a clunk. She turned her face sideways, and saw light through her lids.

Then there was heat right under her ass. She gasped. The candle flame wavered as she jerked slightly.

A warm hand caressed her thighs, slowly sliding over the skin, sliding between them to open her up. She rapidly conceded, feeling the candle heat spreading.

"Very nice. Oh yes. And a bit wet I see." The wolf held the taper with one hand and with the other, explored Red.

The fingers withdrew and Red heard wet noises, and appreciative murmurs.

"A good year."

The candle heat disappeared and Red felt both of the wolf's hands on her thighs, running up around the curves of her ass then back around the top of her thighs. She was spread a bit wider then there was a pause.

Then Red felt the most intense pleasure she'd ever experienced in her sixteen years.

The wolf's strong tongue slid over her, while her fingers slid alternately inside Red, and then up and down... spreading the divine wetness everywhere.

Red groaned, and gripped the table edges, her body sliding on the remains of her dress.

"Am I hurting you, my dear?" the wolf paused, her fingers still working inside Red.

Red tried to vocalize, but all that came out was a wail.

"I'll take that as a 'no' then."

Red felt her knees weakening. Her hands convulsed around the edge of the table.

Her mouth opened and closed, then opened as fingers slid under her nose. The wolf annointed her upper lip with her own wetness then forced the fingers into Red's mouth.

"How do you like your taste, my dear?" she asked, as she pressed down on Red's tongue.

"Lick them."

Red complied, her tongue gliding around the fingers massaging her tongue. As she did so, the wolf continued to finger her, harder, stroking her to the same beat she was using in Red's mouth.

"Yes, it feels gooooood, doesn't it..." the wolf whispered, bending to Red's ear.

Red could only moan.

"Now be a good girl and come for me, Red... come... come..." she kissed Red's ear, and continued her chant.

Red sucked convulsively on the wet fingers and then bucked down against the fingers stroking her, her body shaking.

The fingers were removed from her mouth, and the wolf slowly slid her hand away from between Red's legs. She turned Red over and lifted one of her eyelids.

"You can open them now." She lifted Red up off the table and walked over to the bed, where she deposited her on the quilt.

Red lay totally limp, watching as the naked Diana climbed on top of her.

***

The next morning, there was no grandmother returning, or the next day. And Red's mother never heard back from her daughter. A week later, Red's parents made the trip out to the cottage. All they found was the tattered remains of Red's cloak and her navy dress, folded neatly on the bed.

Outside, there were no tracks, and the devastated parents never saw Red or the grandmother again. And the trees remained silent, growing over the cottage, as ivy grew over its windows.

Story 03

Chapter 1

A stiff morning breeze swept through the bustling crowed as they tried to move closer towards the wood platform that held upon it a variety of both young and old female slaves. The crowed cheered onwards as the trappers, pushed, prodded, and belittled their new catch from last nights hard work. Most of the crowd was of upper class, with only a few city shop keepers willing to spend the last of their cash, hoping to buy a girl for what ever their needs would require of them.

The trappers appeared fierce as they stood tall and proud on the platform. Their job was a risky one, but the rewards were worth any blood that they may have lost during battle. This group called themselves The Pest Control, there were four in all, and they were known through out the land as being one of the most violent pack of cut throats any one could ever meet. Their leader called himself Zek, he was a brutish Racoon with a leather patch that hid old torn flesh where his right eye once rested. Zek hardly ever became involved in the bidding, as it bored him senseless, he was only in it for the love of the hunt, and for the pain it caused towards those his team had enslaved.

His partners were Cal, a tall thin Fox, and Jiuana, a slinky Rabbit, she was the only female in the team. Their job was to guard the slaves, both in capturing those that tried to escape, and those that tried to steal away any of their hard fought goods. The last member of the team was named Bigaton, he only joined The Pest Control a few months ago, after their other member Chakul died in the heat of battle. Bigaton was a deer, his job was simply to be the face of the team. He dealt the rules to the buyers, and auctioned off the meat as quickly as possible, so that they could head on before any bounty hunters discovered where they were and tried to cash in on the large rewards that sat upon each of the members heads.

Todays auction was special, this was the first time in years The Pest Control dared to display their catch openly in a large city. Zek knew the risks he was taking, but they had something special in this catch, and he sure as hell wasn't going to sell it to just any small village rich prick. He wanted good money on this one, and only the big city had the kind of gold he was asking for.

One by one Cal and Jiuana dragged their screaming prizes out onto the platform. As always with the younger girls, they would strip them down to just their fur, or feathers, and force them to expose everything their body possessed in order to rise the price of the bid even if it was only by a few gold coins. Many of the girls had never experience such abuse in their entire life, and the act of being treated like a piece of meat one would buy at a market scared them so much that sometimes they fell into shock that was never awoken from. Every now and then the bidders would demand more from the youthful goods that were on display, mostly these poor creatures would have to perform sexual acts upon themselves, or sometimes with other slaves if they were to be sold as a pair.

The older slaves were rushed off quicker and never stripped, their prices were always five to six time lower than that of a young girls costs, except on rare occasions where the old slave had a special talent that may be of interest to some of the bidders.

Time passed slowly, too slowly, for Zek, but the special item was nearing, and he always liked to keep his special items last. With a motion of his right hand he signalled for Cal and Jiuana to bring forth the prize slave. The crowed gasped in delight as the slave stood before them. Her appearance was young and innocent, the soft white coat of her body glistened in the morning light as she stood eyes closed and shaking. She was not naked, but clothed in black to hide what she had on offer. Zek knew this fine piece of meat would sell for top dollar, and with the mystery about her body kept secret it would simply spice up the bids.

Bigaton stepped forward and slapped the sword heavily into the palm of his right hand. "The bid will start at one thousand gold, and no less."

Instantly the first bid was heard, but it wasn't for the asking price, but for a much larger sum of four thousand gold. Zek smiled, he knew this would end easily within the ten, to fifteen thousand gold price range, after all not everyday one gets the chance to buy a beautiful and young unicorn.

The bids battled higher and higher, as the Unicorn looked down to her hooves in sadness. She was doomed to live the rest of her life in misery, and nothing was going to change that.

Chapter 2

The bid had now reached a straight thirteen thousand, and it appeared as if the bidders were beginning to thin out. Suddenly from out of the crowed a voice yelled "Twenty five thousand, take it or leave it!"

Zek's eyes widened in shock, he never dreamt of such a bid in his life, even if it was a unicorn on sale. He moved forward and looked down into the crowed. The offer appeared to have been spoken by a creature covered in a thick brown robe, with the hood up to hide its face. Everyone fell silent, no counter offer was thrown, and after a few restless seconds Bigaton yelled "SOLD!"

The unicorn was quickly rushed back behind the tent, as the crowed began to disperse, with or without their new slave. Soon only the winning bidder was left standing, alone in front of the near empty platform with only Bigaton its only company.

Bigaton held his sword tightly, ready for anything as he spoke. "Climb up my dear fellow, your now one proud owner of a very rare unicorn."

The stranger without hesitation, leapt up onto the platform as easily as one would climb a stair case. Bigaton jumped back, sword outstretched ready to defend himself.

The stranger laughed softly before speaking. "Is this how you treat your best buyer, with sword ready for attack?"

Bigaton lowered his weapon, but as always in his training he allowed no tension to release just in case he quickly needed it again. "Follow me." He said as he directed the buyer behind the tent.

The old tent was dark and smelly, and even with the sun shining outside, it needed two candles on a table to light the small area. Bigaton joined his pack as Zek stepped forward. "I do hope you have the money my dear fellow, otherwise I will not be very happy, and when I'm not happy, I do ghastly things to animal flesh, real ghastly!" Zek laughed, with the others.

The stranger looked up and pulled the hood back. "If there's one thing I can't stand, it's being mistaken as a boy." The stranger was now visible, and it was very clear to them that it was not a man, but a young female feline.

Zek laughed once more. "It's not often I sell a costly slave to a girl, you are one of very few." Slowly Zek's grin turned sour as he leaned over the table that separated the two. "Now where is the twenty five thousand I was promised? I hate being made a fool of, especially by a girl."

The feline moved closer to the table, and placed her hands along the edge. "Yes the money, well it appears I was mistaken. Although I did bid twenty five thousand gold, I now discover that I was wrong, and all I have on me was twenty five gold pieces, silly me!" She smirked back.

"WHAT! You fool, you've just sealed your doom." Zek said as he slowly went for his sword.

"Oh, I do have one more thing. THIS!" And with that she threw the table forward hitting Zek in the stomach sending hot wax onto his dirty fur. And before anyone could even blink she had dropped her robe and was now holding two swords ready for battle.

"KILL THE FUCKIN' WHORE!" Zek screamed as he clambered up. Instantly Cal, Bigaton, and Jiuana leaped forward, swords and axes ready for the taste of fresh feline blood.

Quickly the trappers fanned out, and with each step closer they parted wider in an attempt to circle her. Instantly Cal shot forward, as his axe swung wildly at the felines neck. With the usual grace and skill of a feline, she ducked the blow and crossed her swords to slice two deep cuts into either side of his thighs. Cal fell to the dirt floor, unable to hold his own weight anymore, as the blood gushed out and covered his red fox coat.

Jiuana screamed in passion as she saw Cal wounded so badly from the girls blades. Cal was like a brother to Jiuana, and the sight was like that of seeing a love one struck down. Without thought Jiuana sprung forward wielding her large broad sword. Even though she was small, it was obvious to any opponent that her strength was more than expected from such a small figure.

Bigaton stood back as he watched the two girls circle each other, waiting for an opening in which to strike. Once he felt that the feline was concentrating more on Jiuana than on him, he rushed forward, and sliced a clean deep cut into her right ribs. The cat pounced left, fur still ruffled as she looked down to see the wound she had just received.

With eyes of hate, she hissed, and then pounced forward tackling Bigaton to the ground. With the natural skills of her race, she released her swords and ripped at Bigaton with her bare hands. Jiuana didn't dare swing her sword, with the girl moving so fast upon the floor, as she feared that she may miss her target and strike a lethal blow to Bigaton instead.

Bigaton quickly found himself in unknown territory, as he desperately tried to fight of his attacker and get loose. The claws and teeth of the cat ripped at Bigaton's hide like a knife skinning a fish. Her fury was fast and direct, and with each new tear, Bigaton felt more life drain from him.

Jiuana knew she would have to step in no matter what the consequences were. With one wild blow of the sword, the sharp blade sliced into her targets flesh. Immense pain shot through the girl, giving Bigaton enough breathing space to not only get himself free, but head butt her with his wiry horns.

Finally Zek, Bigaton, and Jiuana stood over the feline, as Cal lay unconscious on the floor.

"This bitch is going down." Zek said as he lifted his sword ready.

Suddenly Zek felt a sharp pain in his back, as one of the girls swords thrusted firmly within him. Zek fell to his knees, and bellowed in agony. Bigaton and Jiuana turned to see the frightened unicorn standing behind where Zek had stood.

Jiuana readied her sword between the palms of her hands as she stepped forward. "That was a very stupid thing to do wasn't it little girl? You may be a white unicorn, but even though I can't kill you, simply because it ain't good business, it doesn't mean that I can't teach you a lesson, you little bitch!"

The unicorn huddled into the corner of the tent terrified and shaken, as Jiuana moved closer and closer towards her. Then all of a sudden a voice yelled out behind Jiuana.

"Move one more step and your friend here dies."

Jiuana turned in response, as her eyes fell upon the girl holding Bigaton with one of his swords pressed heavily against his neck. "Bloody hell Bigaton, how the fuck could you allow the bitch to grab ya like that?"

Bigaton held his breath unable to reply, fearing that even the slightest muscle movement may cause his neck to be cut from the tightly held blade.

The feline moved closer towards Jiuana and the unicorn, as Bigaton stumbled step by step trying to match her pace. "Let the girl pass, and I won't give your friend a new nasal passage."

Jiuana stepped back and lowered her sword, while the girl looked at the unicorn and ushered her to the tent exit. Slowly the girl moved along until she was standing near the tied back flaps. With a strong shove, the girl threw Bigaton into Jiuana, as she sprinted for the exit.

"Grab my hand, I'm getting you outta here." The girl said as she held her palm out. It wasn't long before the two females were running full speed down one of the cities small alleyways that The Pest Control had parked their platform near.

Jiuana and Bigaton soon began the chase, as the four dodged and stumbled in a feverish race that left many locals slammed hard against the walls and onto the ground. The chase continued with no end in sight, until the unicorn and her rescuer turned into a dead end. With no where to go, and the wall to high to jump, they turned and stood ready for battle as Bigaton and Jiuana turned the last corner.

The four stood silent in the dim alleyway, not moving, not even a breath escaping. It felt like minutes had passed, until finally the two trappers launched forward ready to reclaim their prize.

Suddenly, the girl leapt up onto the side of one of the building walls, and swung herself onto the high back wall with the aid of a pipe that stuck out from between the bricks. "Come on, follow me!"

The unicorn copied her steps, and with a bit of help from her rescuer, she managed to climb onto the wall and join her. Just as Jiuana was about to leap up and grab the pipe, the girl swung Bigaton's sword, slicing the pipe clean off allowing the two to escape freely.

Chapter 3

Hours had now passed since they had last saw the slave traders. Their long trip without any rest had led them from the city walls and into the thick woodlands over the hilly plains. Finally, their journey ended as they sat down near a small stream that flowed gently through the woods.

The queen leaned back against one of the large twisting grey trees, as the unicorn joined her. "Well it looks like your safe now." She said in short puffs. "My names Mouse, what's yours?"

The unicorn smiled. "Cinder."

"That's nice, it suits you, not like Mouse. Mouse is a stupid name for a feline."

Cinder gently rested her head onto Mouse's shoulder for comfort as she continued the conversation. "No, I like it, I think it sound heroic, and brave. And what you did for me today was those two things." Cinder sat quietly for a few seconds before going on. "Why did you save me, and not the others?"

"Your a white unicorn, you don't deserve to be locked away as some ones possession."

"And the others do?"

"Of course not, but your special, I couldn't save you all, so I chose you."

"Thank you Mouse."

Mouse moved her left hand onto Cinder's leg and gently began to rub it. "That's okay, you were worth it."

Cinder sighed lightly as Mouse continued to rub the pain away. "We should get cleaned up, I haven't had a decent bathe for days now, and your wounds need to be washed." With that Cinder slowly stood up and walked over to the crystal clear stream.

Her white hair even though dirty, still managed to catch the streams of sunlight upon the fine fibres that covered her petite young figure, as she moved closer towards the running water and into the flickering sunlight. Mouse watched with fascination as Cinder undressed herself. The black garments were now torn and useless, as she threw them to her side. To Mouse's eyes she was a sight like no other, and as she crouched down and splashed two palm fulls of cool water onto her face, wetting her hair back, Mouse felt a stirring from deep within that she had never felt for so many years.

Mouse watched with a growing desire as Cinder splashed the water over her body. Cinder gently rubbed the cool water onto her long thin neck and soft flowing hair, her small perky breasts, her youthful waist, her long slender legs, and finally the thinly covered soft hair that nestled between her thighs. It was a sight that Mouse knew she would never forget for a long time, and one she wished would never end.

Minutes crept by, until finally Cinder ended her bathing. "Aren't you going to clean your wounds, and have a wash?" Cinder said with her head turned towards Mouse.

Mouse finally broke out of her trance as she responded. "Umm... Incase you forgot, felines Aren't to fond of water, so there's no way in hell, your getting me anywhere near that stream."

Cinder leaned over and picked up a piece of her torn top. Once she had soaked it in water, she stood up and walked over to Mouse. "Well if I can't get you to the stream, I'll bring the stream to you." She smiled.

Mouse cringed in fear as Cinder placed the wet cloth onto her fur. It wasn't the most thrilling thing she had ever experienced, but slowly the fear faded as she watched Cinder completely naked only inches in front of her rubbing her wounds and bruises with care.

Cinder laid the cloth to one side and took a hold of the strings that held her top on. "May I?"

Mouse smiled in acceptance as Cinder began to untie the strings. As her brown leather top loosened from her body she felt the cool air rush in an touch the warm skin that was held tightly beneath it. Finally the last loop was undone, and with ease Cinder pushed open the top and slid it over her shoulder and down her arms. Mouse felt Cinder eye her own small breasts, and without warning her nipples began to grow hard with desire.

Cinder's and Mouse's eyes met, as they stared lovingly at one and other. Slowly Cinder brought her head down, and with a delicate touch of the lips, both their tongues danced gracefully within each others warm mouths. The kissing continued as Cinder began to stroke and tease Mouse's hard nipples with her fingers, until finally Cinder decided to drag her lips and tongue down her new lovers neck and continue where her playful fingers had left off. Mouse began to softly purr, as Cinder sucked, nibbled, and tasted both of her hard sensitive tips. Mouse's purr grew louder and deeper, as Cinder began to journey downwards. With a slight lift of her buttocks, Cinder pulled her tight bikini bottoms off, to reveal the soft skin and fur that laid hidden beneath it. Cinder sighed to herself as the unique aroma of Mouse grew stronger from the warm fluids that were already dampening her inner thighs.

With one simple touch of the fingers, Mouse screamed with pleasure, and instantly she parted her legs wider as Cinder began to taste the juices that were already flowing. Mouse wrapped her long thick tail around her left leg, as Cinder's tongue, darted in an out of her small entrance like only a horse or in Cinder's case, a unicorn could do.

"Oh god, your fantastic Cinder, if I die right now, I'll be happy." Mouse purred softly.

"But Mouse if you die now, you won't experience it all!"

"What do you me.. UH!" Mouse's passion instantly ended the conversation, as Cinder began to slowly ease her smooth ribbed horn into her hot moist tunnel.

"OH GOD!" Mouse groaned, as Cinder gently started to thrust in and out of her pussy.

The pleasure Cinder was creating within Mouse was extraordinary, and definitely a feeling Mouse had never experienced before in her entire life. With each thrust her desire grew tenfold, and it wasn't long before Mouse felt her orgasm grow nearer.

"Please stop." Mouse whimpered. "I want you, don't let me come without giving some back."

Cinder with hesitance, withdrew her slippery horn from Mouse, before Mouse lowered Cinder onto her back. Then once in position, Mouse climbed on top of Cinder, to allow the opportunity for both of them to kiss and lick each others burning cunts.

Their tongues darted in and out, lapping at everything that was in reach. Mouse's purr increased as she slowly tickled and kissed Cinder's hard little clit. Both tongues moved back and forth from hole to hole, and it wasn't long before Cinder could feel the tension in Mouse rising again. Instantly Cinder concentrated fully on Mouse's clit, as she inserted two fingers deep into her pussy.

Within seconds Mouse began to shudder and scream as her orgasm pulsed through her time, and time again. Cinder lapped heavily at the juices that were now flowing freely from Mouse, until finally the orgasm began to ease. Once Mouse had gained control of her body, she began to work on Cinder. With tongue, lips, and fingers, Mouse explored every nook and cranny Cinder had to offer. It wasn't long before Cinder's own orgasm began to grow, until finally with one powerful explosion, waves of sheer ecstasy surged through her small body shaking it wildly across the soft grassy ground. Slowly the waves calmed, and all that could be heard was Cinder puffing heavily under Mouse's own sweaty body.

The two continued to tenderly kiss each other, as mouse moved her way backwards, until finally their tongues were united once more, in a passionate embrace. With a few more long deep kisses, Mouse and Cinder leaned back against the old tree once again.

Cinder rested her head on Mouse's shoulder as she spoke. "That was beautiful, I've never come so hard in my life. And I must say you have a delicious pussy."

Mouse moved her left arm behind Cinder's neck, and held her tight. "It comes with the territory my dear, what else can I say?" Mouse giggled back, as Cinder smiled. "I guess we had best make camp here tonight, and look for something for you to wear tomorrow, now that your clothes are destroyed."

Cinder snuggled closer against Mouse. "Thank you again Mouse, I appreciate everything you've done for me, EVERYTHING!"

Story 04

Cynthia sat in her patio, pondering her life as she put down a book by Anais Nin. The cold morning sea breeze cut through her chiffon robe and slippers, the chill went through her body, turning her milk white skin into a row of goose pimples. Her long brown curls twirled freely in the wind, reminding her how Stephen once touched her hair. They were to be married, but Stephen left her waiting at the altar. >From then on Cynthia swore that she would never be hurt again, even if it meant she would be alone forever. From her patio she looked out at the swirling ocean and the white, foaming waves crashing on shore. The waves were like his empty promises, seemingly full of promise but ending up as little more than foam. Stephen was ready to give her the universe in and its wonders, only to give her suffering and pain .

Despite it all, at least I can still laugh at the comical tragedy that is life, Cynthia though as she reached over to the small metal table to her side. Putting her black clay mug of coffee, she drank bitterly sweet coffee. At least there was one good thing about him, the sex, Cynthia thought. The absolutely divine, ecstatic, mind blowing sex. Her body shuddered even to think about it, as she closed her eyes for a moment and relived the many happy nights they spent together. In a wave all first experiences with Stephen came tumbling back: the first kiss, the first embrace, the first time they had sex, and so much more. Deeply in her heart, Cynthia felt a pang of regret and loss...letting it out with a long sigh. Will I ever again be with someone again who can make me feel as good? Do I deserve love and pleasure? Cynthia opened her eyes the early morning light flooded back into her vision, along with the tide rushing out to sea. As she stared at the ocean, Cynthia thought she saw a nude woman emerging from the foam and froth of the sea. The woman had long cherry blonde hair, that clung to her wet body, covering her breasts. She could have been Venus coming from the sea, newly born, as she walked out of the foaming water onto the dirty white sand. Her eyes popping out of her head, Cynthia dropped her coffee mug on the patio to stand up.

"Are you all right? What happened to you?" Cynthia ran out to meet the woman. Finally meeting her between the water and her patio, standing in front of the dripping woman, her face twisted in concern.

"No Cynthia, I'm fine. But, are you all right?" the strange woman smiled mysteriously back at Cynthia, batting the wet hair out of her face and away from her plump breasts.

"How did you know my name? Who are you?" Cynthia took a step back, staring cross-eyed at the woman. The woman stepped forward, closing the distance between them. "My name is Constance ... and I heard your thoughts, you're very lonely. Is there something that I could do?" Again, she smiled, her ocean green eyes sparkling.

"What do you mean by that? You heard my thoughts?" Cynthia tied to look away from Constance, but she couldn't. She had seen thousands of women, but never really looked at a woman before, for the first time she saw the gentle curve of her hips, the contradictory hardness and softness of her plump breasts, the wispy hair that that was below her taut stomach that lead...no, she turned her back on this woman, closing her eyes, ashamed of her thoughts.

"Why should you be ashamed to be attracted to me? I'm attracted to you ... you called me. You were so lonely... " Constance stepped up to Cynthia and embraced her, kissing the small of her neck.

Pulling away and then turning again to face this strange woman, Cynthia stared at her with fire in her blue eyes. "But I've always heard that it was wrong to things like that with another woman. I don't even know how to do it...What are you?"

"I'm what you've wanted for so long ... do you always question your deepest thoughts and desires? Why not just accept them." Constance again stepped forward, simply looking at Cynthia, smiling gently.

Cynthia's face was wrought with confusion, but at the same time a longing for something that she hadn't felt in a long time. Cynthia sighed, and closed her eyes, folding her arms against her chest. As she folded her chest, Constance put her arms around her, gently kissing her cheek blushed cheeks.

Cynthia opened her eyes then unfolded her arms, starting to embrace Constance returning her kiss on the lips. Constance also kissed her, locking her lips with Cynthia's with passion and love. Suddenly, she stopped, and broke away from Constance, shaking and moaning.

"No, no...I can't do it...no, I can't do it...someone may see..."she ran back to her patio, opening her siding glass door, shutting it and then running to her bedroom, slamming the door behind her. As she shut the door behind her, she turned, screaming as she put her hands out in a defensive manner, her body shaking like a fish dangling on a fisherman's line. Constance, if that really was her name, was in her bedroom, standing directly in front of her.

"How did you get in here? This can't be..."Cynthia shook even more violently, moaning in what might have been horror or delight as her hands tried to go for the doorknob. But she couldn't open the door since she felt an irresistible urge to wildly embrace this woman kiss her and make love to her. Cynthia began to lose her breath, reaching to the tie of her robe and pulling it lose throwing it down on the floor. She embraced Constance, kissing her savagely, biting her bottom lip as she threw her arms around the strange woman. Constance did the same thing exactly, matching the kiss and the embrace with the same ferocity and vigor.

Constance pulled her head back for a moment, and only held Cynthia to her, she smiled and said: "Now you can live out your fantasies and dreams that you buried and hid deep down in your mind. Love me as you have loved none other in your life, take me Cynthia. Take me now."

Cynthia smiled with wild delight as she took Constance's hand, leading her to her king size bed. Constance, then Cynthia got on the bed and lay down, to embrace one another, kissing and holding each other close. Cynthia went to Constance's ear, putting her ear to it and sucking on it. She whispered in Constance's ear: "This is just the first thing I've always wanted to do..." With her tongue in Constance's ear, Cynthia slowly moved her hands to Constance's fine hands and simply held them, grasping them tightly. Constance also moved her hands to Cynthia's breasts slowly to gently massage them.

Cynthia's tongue slowly went down her neck licking and kissing every inch of Constance's wet skin, going down Constance's arm, down to the elbow and finally to her hand. She sucked on Constance's hand, pulling it in and out of her mouth, and finally sucking on the individual fingers. Constance closed her eyes, smiling and moaning softly under her breath. Preoccupied with her own pleasure for the moment, Constance simply laid her hand on Cynthia's breast, slowly moving as she shuddered in ecstasy.

Cynthia pulled the now moist hand from her mouth, holding it in front of Constance's oval face. "Touch me with your hand." she put Constance's hand directly above her clit.

Constance did exactly as she was told, as she move her hand down then began to rub Cynthia's clit, slowly and gently. She did it with some hesitation, very deliberately and slowly, as Cynthia frowned.

"That's not how I like it...do it this way."

Cynthia put her hand on Constance's clit, and began to rub. She rubbed violently and deliberately, making Constance shriek in pleasure, arching her back slightly. Cynthia smiled as Constance cried out, which only added to her own pleasure. Finally, Constance returned her hand to Cynthia's clit, rubbing it again. This time, Cynthia screamed, still rubbing at the same time, only increasing the speed. The two of them rubbed each other, moaning and breathing simultaneously, as though they were exact duplicates. Suddenly Constance stopped, pushing Cynthia on her back, she began to rub her clit against as Cynthia rubbed against her. They began to moan and pant in unison, so enraptured by each other.

The two women rubbed against each other faster and faster, wet hair and dry hair flew in all directions as their speed only increased. Finally, the two women let out half a scream and half a moan as they orgasmed at the same time, both their bodies releasing the built tension. Constance pulled away, putting one finger in Cynthia, then another and then next, until her entire hand was inside her. Cynthia's body shook again, wincing in pain and in pleasure as Constance clinched her hand into a fist, then thrusted forward. After only a moment, Cynthia's entire body shook as she came again. Cynthia grabbed Constance, pulling her to her, to greedily kissing her. The room smelled of a combination of sweat, sea salt and vaginal tears, the two women embracing and kissing each other.

Constance moved to Cynthia's side, taking the still shaking woman into her arms and putting her head on her shoulder. "I know you enjoyed that as much as I did. We have to do that again, and we will -- soon." Constance smiled and cooed, playing with Cynthia's hair. "But, I must go now..."

Cynthia moaned, not in pleasure, but in anguish, clinging to Constance beginning to cry. "You can't leave me. You can't..." Her hands grabbed Constance's shoulders, holding them down weakly, just as a little girl would cling to her favourite doll as her younger sister might try to tear it out of her hands.

Constance brought her hands to Cynthia's head, bringing it from her breast as she leaned to kiss her passionately on her lips. "No, you'll never be alone again. Just go to the beach ... and rub this ..." A brilliant ruby cut in a heart, that was surrounded by gold and hung on a glowing silver chain suddenly appeared in Constance's hand. "If ever you feel alone, rub this and I will be there. I am yours forever."

Constance kissed Cynthia once more, her lips locking around Cynthia's, their tongues meeting and touching as they embraced as both their hands moved up and down their backs gently. Constance put the necklace over Cynthia's neck, the ruby falling to rest between her breasts, a perfect contrast between the pale white skin and the blood red ruby. Slowly and ever so gently Constance broke away from Cynthia, with a tear in her eye. "Remember, you'll never be alone again. Come and walk with me to the sea." Constance got up from the bed, taking Cynthia's hand in hers leading her to the door.

They walked out the patio and down the beach, hand in hand, still completely nude. A gentle breeze embraced the two lovers as they reached the shore. The once clear morning had become a blustery afternoon, black storm clouds still far out to sea slowly making their way over the bay to the shore. The two women walked until they reached they very edge of the sea, stopping as the waves washed against their long legs. They embraced once more, clinging and kissing each other, as if they both knew it would be the last time they would be together.

Constance's lips made their way to Cynthia's quivering ears, kissing and whispering in it.

"Remember me, Cynthia. Dream of me, my love..." They hugged each other tightly, squeezing one another in desperation. This time it was Constance who broke away, starry eyed, clearing her throat, sadly gazing on her lover. "I am yours forever..." Constance waved and slowly walked into the sea, her head turned to look at Constance tears also clouding her green eyes.

"Be well..." Cynthia grasped the ruby between her breasts with her right hand, a biting pain at her heart. She walked at Constance's side into the warm sea. They held hands as they went into the froth, tightly gripping each other's hands deeper and deeper until they no longer held hands. Cynthia winced, turning around and swimming back to the shore. The west wind bit at her, but she was not cold, she was full of warmth and love from the ruby that hung around her neck, singing a love song. Oblivious of her nudity, Cynthia smiled, wrapping her arms around her chest and walking from the sea to go home, full of relief that she would never be alone. She did wonder when she would see her lover from the ocean again and, what would happen when she would call on her...

Story 05

Gena's sister read the ad out loud;

"Applicants requested for medical experimentation. Six

months Quarantined service required for studies in viral

infection. Free room and board, plus $9,000.00 at end of

six month service. Call for interview 555-6969."

They had just been evicted, for non payment of rent, from their second apartment and six months with a cold didn't sound half bad. The $9,000 wasn't anything to sneeze at either.

"Let's see...," said Tina, her twin sister. "9,000 divided by 6 is...... Shit. I can't divide without a calculator!"

"Here!" Gena said handing her cheap plastic solar calculator to her sister. Tina pushed the buttons and came up with a figure. "That's 1,500 a month! And with BOTH of us in, we would make 18,000 dollars! That would be great! Let's check this out!"

They called the number and were directed to a drab building on the university campus. The air inside smelled of isopropyl alcohol, and reminded them of a hospital. They were put through a battery of tests that covered just about everything, including bust size and vaginal strength. This seemed strange for viral research, but doctors were that way.

The doctor, a woman in her mid fifties but still trim and bright eyed looked them over. "Twins! That is very exciting. It will be interesting to see if you are both effected the same way by the virus."

"You mean we're hired?!" Tina blurted out with obvious excitement in her voice.

"We will see what the test results yield. But yes, I do think we can use you." the doctor said with a warm smile. "What does your family think of this?"

"Oh, we aren't very close to our family...", Gena started to say when Tina broke in with "We're orphans."

"Perfect.", the doctor said, adding, "You will be notified in two days. If the tests turn out well, be prepared to move into the research facility immediately." Then she turned away.

The next two days were very long. It seemed like they would wait forever. The experiment was all that Tina could talk about. Then they got the letter. They had been accepted. They were to meet the van to the experimental center at the same building they had been tested in.

The van took them a long way into the country. At last they rounded a curve and there was an old institutional looking building looming up behind a tall chain-link fence. The place used to be an asylum, but had now been converted into an experimental center. It looked very imposing and still had bars on the lower windows. But there was now a brightly colored logo and sign on the lawn proclaiming it as a Virus Research Facility.

When they arrived, a swirl of attendants met them at the door. The staff seemed very interested in them and followed their every move with interest. Their bags were taken and they were escorted to the orientation center. There they were briefed on the policies of the facility and given swipe badges with their code numbers on them. "GEF-26A" was inscribed on Gena's and "GEF-26B" was Tina's. She wondered what GEF stood for. They were led to a concrete cell for exposure to the virus. Once in the cell, they were stripped and their wrists were securely fastened together. The wrist restraints were then attached to a strap that was attached to a motorized system in the ceiling of the chamber and they were hauled up to standing position, their arms held comfortably over their heads. The girls didn't know what to expect, but it certainly wasn't this.

Gena and her sister stood side by side. They were stark naked, their wrists tied over their heads exposing their bodies. They stood there, feeling very naked and vulnerable. They looked each other over, noticing the family resemblance. They had wide hips, but small pointed breasts. The concrete chamber was cool, and their nipples stood out. Both pubic mounds were covered by sparse blond hair that tended toward long.

The heavy steel door opened, and a naked woman entered. She was completely nude, except for a smooth round heavy silver collar around her neck. She was very curvaceous; large hips and breasts with big pink nipples that pointed straight out from her body. Her breasts were surprisingly buoyant and jiggled seductively as she walked. She had a very pronounced pubic mound that was devoid of hair, brazenly exposing her vaginal slit making it seem obscene. Gena became embarrassed by the thrill that she felt and looked up from the woman's body only to be captivated by her amazing eyes.

Her eyes were Turquoise! They had a brilliant predatory gleam in them as the strange woman looked at the two helpless girls. The woman walked right up to her and stared directly into Gena's eyes. Gena stared back, trying to see the telltale sign of colored contact lenses, but they weren't there.

"Your eyes!..."Gena said in amazement.

The woman smiled knowingly, reached out and gently took Gena's head in both hands. Her eyes came closer as the she leaned against Gena, their tits meeting, and the warmth of the stranger's large firm breasts against her own gave Gena a thrill. Then without a word, the woman kissed her.

This kiss wasn't a friendly peck, but a deep French kiss. The strange woman's tongue surged into Gena's mouth and down her throat. It felt as if it were a foot long and as it went deeper into her throat. Much deeper than any tongue had a right to be. She started to feel the panic of the gag reflex. The woman stopped her advance and explored every inch of the inside of Gena's mouth with that incredible tongue. She felt violated, and astonished!

After the kiss, the woman smiled at her and bent down taking each of Gena's nipples into her mouth. She gently sucked them until they ached for more. Gena could feel the sucking all the way down to her cunt, and the woman kept sucking until Gena's cunt was throbbing hard. Her tits had never been sucked like that before.

The woman stood up, smiled and then knelt on the floor before her. She watched as the woman pressed her lips to her still throbbing cunt. Then she felt the woman's incredible tongue. It started at the top of her slit and followed it down the center of her cunt. Then up again. She kept this up until Gena could clearly feel the woman's tongue on her engorged inner lips and she knew her cunt must be opening up like a flower to accept the woman's tongue. Her entire crotch was wet and she knew it wasn't all saliva.

Gena felt that she had never been so aroused before. Her breath rushed raggedly in and out and her heart was pounding like mad. She realized with a start that she was very close to orgasm. She had no idea that being introduced to a virus could be so much fun!

She was panting and moaning as she watched her legs involuntarily open wider to accept this strange woman. It was as if her body had taken over, despite what her mind might think. Her hips started to rock in an involuntary dance as the woman extended her wonderful tongue to caress the entire length of her vaginal slit. Then the woman pressed her upper lip against Gena's engorged clit and the tip of her long tongue hooked into the opening of her cunt at the same time. Gena came with explosive force, and the woman went lower shoving her hot wet tongue deep into Gena's cunt. The tongue felt as big as a man's cock, and her cunt contracted on it, sending waves of pleasure up her body.

"Ga...ga...ga..god!" she said as her whole abdomen contracted around the woman's long tongue. Her body convulsed and her hips thrust forward as the woman moved even lower and stuck the full length of her incredible tongue deep into Gena's cunt. It felt like it reached all the way up to her chest! She felt her body milk that tongue like it had never done before. Her cunt worked with all her strength until her knees were weak and she collapsed against her wrist restraints.

The woman licked a stripe all the way from Gena's slit to her mouth. Kissed her again, leaving the taste of her own cunt in her mouth, hugged her tight pressing her hairless mound against Gena's cunt then stepped back with a proud smile, leaving Gena quivering and spasming slightly.

Gena looked at her sister who stared in horror and disbelief at her sister. Then Tina looked at the strange woman who had so thoroughly violated her sister.

Gena's restraints slowly lowered her to the floor, and she watched dreamily as her strange woman gently held her sisters head in both hands and kissed that deep French kiss. Tina stared in amazement as the woman performed the same ritual she had just seen her sister go through. In fact, Tina came sooner than Gena had, panting and sweating, her whole body in fucking motion. Her body shuddered with orgasm as she came on the strange woman's incredible tongue. She was nearly faint when the strange woman performed that final slit to mouth lick that sent another series of shivers through Tina's body.

The stranger stepped back as Tina's restraints lowered her to the floor, and smiled knowingly at the exhausted pair. The sisters watched as the woman turned and strode provocatively away, her ass jiggling enticingly. They noticed a large tattoo on the woman's ass that resembled a scrollwork S with a bar through it and oblong dots inside each curve. They wondered what it could mean.

Gena rolled to her side facing her sister. She looked at her sister, savoring the afterglow of orgasm. She was voraciously hungry, as she always was after great sex, but she was content to lay there for a while. They stared at each other for a long time after the naked woman left. Neither saying a word, but sharing the same secret thoughts. Thoughts too embarrassing to talk about out loud.

Gena awoke to find that she had been sleeping. Her hands were free, and she was laying naked in a soft warm bed in a private room. She found that her room connected to a suite of rooms that included her sister Tina's private room. They were quite comfortable, and had TV, good meals and books to pass the time. They talked, but not about the strange woman. Most of the talk was about how they would spent the 18,000 dollars when this was all over. Gena started to wonder if the woman had been a dream.

The doctor that had examined them before came in once or twice a day to examine them. So far they had felt no symptoms, but the doctor assured them that would change.

Two days later, a rash developed on Gena's pubic mound, under her arms, on her legs, and in her mouth. Her tongue and throat seemed especially effected. She experienced severe vaginal cramping. She discovered that her sister had the same symptoms and they wondered if they had caught some terrible VD from their encounter. They talked about the encounter for the first time late that night. Gena had extremely erotic dreams that night, and in the morning, her throat was too sore to talk.

Her throat felt like it was on fire. Her nose ran. Her voice became lower and her tongue swelled up and seemed to fill her mouth. She started to lisp harshly when she did talk, but her lisp was improving as she got used to the condition. Her whole neck hurt, and she hardly talked at all.

Then Gena noticed that her breasts ached. Then they hurt! The doctor assured them that this was all part of the virus that they had been exposed to, and that they would be fine in about a month.

They started experiencing severe headaches mostly centered around the eyes and back of the head. The rash started to clear up, but they noticed that their pubic hair was thinning. Soon the rash was gone, and so was the hair. Their legs and underarms were similarly affected.

Gena's thoughts turned mostly to sex. She was having horrendous fantasies in which she was fucking everything in sight. She started spending more time in bed. Supposedly to shake the virus, but in reality it was so she could masturbate, which she did almost constantly. Since she lost her pubic hair, she couldn't keep her hands off of her newly bared pussy. It just felt so GREAT to touch it. Her orgasms were getting stronger too. Her tits still hurt, but her cunt felt great. She noticed that she got a throb of pleasure whenever she squeezed down on her cunt muscles, and especially when she had something to squeeze on, like her fingers.

She found herself constantly fantasizing about sex. Sex with men, women, Horses! She even thought her sister was starting to look really good. She hadn't been dressed in a while, so when her sister came into her room with her shirt open, she didn't know what to think. Her first thought, naturally, was that they were going to have sex. She was excited about the prospect, and sprang from her bed to meet Tina.

"Look, I can't get my shirt closed over my tits.", Tina said, trying to stretch the material over her now enormous tits.

Gena looked down at her own tits and saw that they were large and round too. their nipples were very big, and pink. She looked up at her sister. And for the first time she noticed that her sister's eyes had turned turquoise! She saw the look of astonishment in her sisters turquoise eyes and realized that her own eyes must match those of her twin sister.

"Watsh happenig to ush?" Tina lisped. "My titsh are growing. I didn't say anytshing before becaush I didn't believe it. Now I see yoursh! They're beautiful!" And she stared at her sister's large round globes, the big pink nipples pointing enticingly at her own at precisely the same angle. They were enticing, inviting.

Tina stood with her shirt open, wearing no pants or any other garment. Gena stood stark naked, staring at her sister's hairless pussy. Tina reached out and touched Gena's left tit. She squeezed it and brought the nipple between her thumb and forefinger.

That was all the invitation Gena needed. Overcome by the uncontrollable urge to suck her sisters nipples, she leaned forward saying, "I have been so horny lately..." and taking Tina's tits in her hands she opened her mouth and stuck out her tongue. It reached out a full 5 inches before she noticed it's length, and there was more inside still. The tip of her tongue touched her sister's big nipple, and she thought of her tongue. It was the first time she had seen it that far out before, and she was shocked. She stiffened, retracted her tongue and stood up straight. Her sister, a dreamy look in her eyes, hugged her, pressing her tits against her own, then kissed her. Deeply.

Her sister's long tongue snaked down her throat, and she didn't gag. That reflex had apparently been suppressed, only to be replaced by the most erotic stimulus she had ever felt above the waist. WOW! Her throat felt like the inside of her cunt, only in her neck. Her sister started slowly fucking her throat with her long tongue, moaning with pleasure, and Gena realized that her tongue must also feel pleasurable stimulus. She pushed her own tongue into Tina's mouth and felt the double stimulus of fucking/being fucked. They hugged their bodies closer as the first waves of orgasm coursed down their bodies. It felt like their heads would explode. When they pressed their hairless pussies together, they both experienced earth shattering orgasm.

Now Gena fucked her sister's throat with her tongue and came so hard she almost passed out. Her first tongue orgasm. Then a throat orgasm. Soon they started working lower, experiencing tit orgasms, and finally ending up in a 69 that yielded the most incredible orgasms of all. Tongue/vaginal orgasms that promised to blow the tops off their heads. Her sister's cunt throbbed so hard it felt like it would blow a gasket, and she knew her own was doing the same.

Each orgasm rejuvenated them for more. The 69 session lasted the rest of the afternoon and late into the night. Gena found great pleasure licking her sisters smooth mound and slit. Pleasure she had never dreamed possible. They finally collapsed or passed out around 3:00 AM, and the next day they were at it again.

They could just barely control themselves enough to stop fucking when the doctor came in. She looked at them with a proud smile. "Look at you two. Nearly a perfect match. The splicing effected you both the same way. I only wish you were past your virulent stage. The Senator's party would love to see you. In fact, I bet we can even go for an increase in funding after this." The doctor then explained that they had been enhanced by a mutant gene, introduced by a virus carried by Cara GEF-17, GEF stands for Genetically Enhanced Female and she is the seventeenth specimen to carry the strain. The twins had puzzled looks on their faces and they squirmed distractedly.When she explained that Cara was the strange naked woman they had met the first day, both girls sat up and showed acute interest.

The mention of that first encounter sent a thrill through both of them. "Is she still here?" asked Tina, a glint in her eye.

The doctor smiled, "Yes, she is still on the premises. There are also genetically enhanced males that you will want to meet. I intend to introduce you in a couple of weeks, when the virus recedes and you are fully matured. You see it gets better.", the doctor said. "You may notice that your breasts are larger and more sensitive to pleasurable stimulus than normal. Your tongues and throats have been enhanced into sexual organs. Your vaginas are stronger and more sensitive to pleasurable stimulus, as is your pubic mound and your clitoris. Your pubic hair under your arms and vaginal as well as the hair on your legs has been genetically removed. That means no more shaving for you girls.

Your eyes have changed to turquoise. Kind of a genetic trademark of mine, that allows us to recognize our enhanced specimens.

You may also have noticed your thoughts turning to sex lately. That is also caused by a genetic re balancing of your brain chemistry, resulting in insatiable desire for sex in any form, subservience, and a desire to please. These desires extend into masochism, and a strong desire to be bound and forced to perform sex acts as a total slave. You have probably experienced lesbian fantasies as well as heterosexual, another genetic signature.

So girls, you are now genetically mutated sex slaves. Does that thought appeal to you?"

The doctor looked at the sisters. Gena with her hand between her legs finger fucking herself as she stared vacantly smiling at the doctor. And Tina with her hands wrapped in her shirt behind her back, in self imposed bondage, jutting her breasts out for the doctors benefit, her legs spread wide and her mouth slightly open.

"Of course it does", the doctor smiled, "Of course it does."

Made in the USA
Monee, IL
23 March 2023

30371325R10444